THE COMPLETE
SCIENCE FICTION TREASURY
OF
H. G. Wells

WITH A PREFACE BY THE AUTHOR

THE TIME MACHINE

THE ISLAND OF DR. MOREAU

THE INVISIBLE MAN

THE WAR OF THE WORLDS

THE FIRST MEN IN THE MOON

THE FOOD OF THE GODS

IN THE DAYS OF THE COMET

AVENEL BOOKS • NEW YORK

All illustrations in this volume are
courtesy of the New York Public Library.

This edition is published by special arrangement with
Alfred A. Knopf, Inc. The original edition was entitled
Seven Famous Novels by H.G. Wells.
This edition is published by Avenel Books,
distributed by Crown Publishers, Inc.
g h
AVENEL 1978 EDITION
Manufactured in the United States of America

Library of Congress Cataloging in Publication Data
Wells, Herbert George, 1866-1946.
 The complete science fiction treasury of H. G. Wells.
 Reprint of the 1934 ed. published by Knopf, New York,
under title: Seven famous novels.
 CONTENTS: The time machine.—The island of Dr. Moreau.
—The invisible man.—The war of the worlds. [etc.]
 1. Science fiction, English. I. Title. II. Title:
Science fiction treasury.
PZ3. W465Hab 1978 [PR5771.5] 823'.9'12 78-58095
ISBN 0-517-26188-X

Contents

PREFACE

Mr. KNOPF has asked me to write a preface to this collection of my fantastic stories. They are put in chronological order, but let me say here right at the beginning of the book, that for anyone who does not as yet know anything of my work it will probably be more agreeable to begin with *The Invisible Man* or *The War of the Worlds*. *The Time Machine* is a little bit stiff about the fourth dimension and *The Island of Dr. Moreau* rather painful.

These tales have been compared with the work of Jules Verne and there was a disposition on the part of literary journalists at one time to call me the English Jules Verne. As a matter of fact there is no literary resemblance whatever between the anticipatory inventions of the great Frenchman and these fantasies. His work dealt almost always with actual possibilities of invention and discovery, and he made some remarkable forecasts. The interest he invoked was a practical one; he wrote and believed and told that this or that thing could be done, which was not at that time done. He helped his reader to imagine it done and to realise what fun, excitement or mischief would ensue. Many of his inventions have "come true." But these stories of mine collected here do not pretend to deal with possible things; they are exercises of the imagination in a quite different field. They belong to a class of writing which includes the *Golden Ass of Apuleius*, the *True Histories of Lucian*, *Peter Schlemil* and the story of *Frankenstein*. It includes too some admirable inventions by Mr. David Garnett, *Lady into Fox* for instance. They are all fantasies; they do not aim to project a serious possibility; they aim indeed only at the same amount of conviction as one gets in a good gripping dream. They have to hold the reader to the end by art and illusion and not by proof and argument, and the moment he closes the cover and reflects he wakes up to their impossibility.

In all this type of story the living interest lies in their non-fantastic elements and not in the invention itself. They are appeals for human sympathy quite as much as any "sympathetic" novel, and the fantastic element, the strange property or the strange world, is used only to throw up and intensify our natural reactions of wonder, fear or perplexity. The invention is nothing in itself and when this kind of thing is attempted by clumsy writers who do not understand this elementary principle nothing could be conceived

more silly and extravagant. Anyone can invent human beings inside out or worlds like dumbbells or a gravitation that repels. The thing that makes such imaginations interesting is their translation into commonplace terms and a rigid exclusion of other marvels from the story. Then it becomes human. "How would you feel and what might not happen to you," is the typical question, if for instance pigs could fly and one came rocketing over a hedge at you. How would you feel and what might not happen to you if suddenly you were changed into an ass and couldn't tell anyone about it? Or if you became invisible? But no one would think twice about the answer if hedges and houses also began to fly, or if people changed into lions, tigers, cats and dogs left and right, or if everyone could vanish anyhow. Nothing remains interesting where anything may happen.

For the writer of fantastic stories to help the reader to play the game properly, he must help him in every possible unobtrusive way to *domesticate* the impossible hypothesis. He must trick him into an unwary concession to some plausible assumption and get on with his story while the illusion holds. And that is where there was a certain slight novelty in my stories when first they appeared. Hitherto, except in exploration fantasies, the fantastic element was brought in by magic. Frankenstein even, used some jiggery-pokery magic to animate his artificial monster. There was trouble about the thing's soul. But by the end of last century it had become difficult to squeeze even a momentary belief out of magic any longer. It occurred to me that instead of the usual interview with the devil or a magician, an ingenious use of scientific patter might with advantage be substituted. That was no great discovery. I simply brought the fetish stuff up to date, and made it as near actual theory as possible.

As soon as the magic trick has been done the whole business of the fantasy writer is to keep everything else human and real. Touches of prosaic detail are imperative and a rigorous adherence to the hypothesis. Any *extra* fantasy outside the cardinal assumption immediately gives a touch of irresponsible silliness to the invention. So soon as the hypothesis is launched the whole interest becomes the interest of looking at human feelings and human ways, from the new angle that has been acquired. One can keep the story within the bounds of a few individual experiences as Chamisso does in *Peter Schlemil,* or one can expand it to a broad criticism of human institutions and limitations as in *Gulliver's Travels.* My early, profound and lifelong admiration for Swift, appears again and again in this collection, and it is particularly evident in a predisposition to make the stories reflect upon contemporary political and social discussions. It is an incurable habit with literary critics to lament some lost artistry and innocence in my early work and to accuse me of having become

polemical in my later years. That habit is of such old standing that the late Mr. Zangwill in a review in 1895 complained that my first book, *The Time Machine*, concerned itself with "our present discontents." *The Time Machine* is indeed quite as philosophical and polemical and critical of life and so forth, as *Men like Gods* written twenty-eight years later. No more and no less. I have never been able to get away from life in the mass and life in general as distinguished from life in the individual experience, in any book I have ever written. I differ from contemporary criticism in finding them inseparable.

For some years I produced one or more of these "scientific fantasies," as they were called, every year. In my student days we were much exercised by talk about a possible fourth dimension of space; the fairly obvious idea that events could be presented in a rigid four dimensional space time framework had occurred to me, and this is used as the magic trick for a glimpse of the future that ran counter to the placid assumption of that time that Evolution was a pro-human force making things better and better for mankind. *The Island of Dr. Moreau* is an exercise in youthful blasphemy. Now and then, though I rarely admit it, the universe projects itself towards me in a hideous grimace. It grimaced that time, and I did my best to express my vision of the aimless torture in creation. *The War of the Worlds* like *The Time Machine* was another assault on human self-satisfaction.

All these three books are consciously grim, under the influence of Swift's tradition. But I am neither a pessimist nor an optimist at bottom. This is an entirely indifferent world in which wilful wisdom seems to have a perfectly fair chance. It is after all rather cheap to get force of presentation by loading the scales on the sinister side. Horror stories are easier to write than gay and exalting stories. In *The First Men in the Moon* I tried an improvement on Jules Verne's shot, in order to look at mankind from a distance and burlesque the effects of specialisation. Verne never landed on the moon because he never knew of radio and of the possibility of sending back a message. So it was his shot that came back. But equipped with radio, which had just come out then, I was able to land and even see something of the planet.

The two later books are distinctly on the optimistic side. *The Food of the Gods* is a fantasia on the change of scale in human affairs. Everybody nowadays realises that change of scale; we see the whole world in disorder through it; but in 1904 it was not a very prevalent idea. I had hit upon it while working out the possibilities of the near future in a book of speculations called *Anticipations* (1901). The last story is Utopian. The world is gassed and cleaned up morally by the benevolent tail of a comet. *Men like Gods*, written seventeen years after *In the Days of the Comet*, and not included in this volume, was almost the

last of my scientific fantasies. It did not horrify or frighten, was not much of a success, and by that time I had tired of talking in playful parables to a world engaged in destroying itself. I was becoming too convinced of the strong probability of very strenuous and painful human experiences in the near future to play about with them much more. But I did two other sarcastic fantasies, not included here, *Mr. Blettsworthy on Rampole Island* and *The Autocracy of Mr. Parham*, in which there is I think a certain gay bitterness, before I desisted altogether.

The Autocracy of Mr. Parham is all about dictators, and dictators are all about us, but it has never struggled through to a really cheap edition. Work of this sort gets so stupidly reviewed nowadays that it has little chance of being properly read. People are simply warned that there are ideas in my books and advised not to read them, and so a fatal suspicion has wrapped about the later ones. " Ware stimulants! " It is no good my saying that they are quite as easy to read as the earlier ones and much more timely.

It becomes a bore doing imaginative books that do not touch imaginations, and at length one stops even planning them. I think I am better employed now nearer reality, trying to make a working analysis of our deepening social perplexities in such labours as *The Work, Wealth and Happiness of Mankind* and *After Democracy*. The world in the presence of cataclysmal realities has no need for fresh cataclysmal fantasies. That game is over. Who wants the invented humours of Mr. Parham in Whitehall, when day by day we can watch Mr. Hitler in Germany? What human invention can pit itself against the fantastic fun of the Fates? I am wrong in grumbling at reviewers. Reality had taken a leaf from my book and set itself to supersede me. H. G. W.

THE TIME MACHINE

§ 1

THE TIME TRAVELLER (for so it will be convenient to speak of him) was expounding a recondite matter to us. His grey eyes shone and twinkled, and his usually pale face was flushed and animated. The fire burned brightly, and the soft radiance of the incandescent lights in the lilies of silver caught the bubbles that flashed and passed in our glasses. Our chairs, being his patents, embraced and caressed us rather than submitted to be sat upon, and there was that luxurious after-dinner atmosphere, when thought runs gracefully free of the trammels of precision. And he put it to us in this way — marking the points with a lean forefinger — as we sat and lazily admired his earnestness over this new paradox (as we thought it) and his fecundity.

"You must follow me care-fully. I shall have to controvert one or two ideas that are almost universally accepted. The geometry, for instance, they taught you at school is founded on a misconception."

"Is not that rather a large thing to expect us to begin upon?" said Filby, an argumentative person with red hair.

"I do not mean to ask you to accept anything without reasonable ground for it. You will soon admit as much as I need from you. You know of course that a mathematical line, a line of thickness *nil,* has no real existence. They taught you that? Neither has a mathematical plane. These things are mere abstractions."

"That is all right," said the Psychologist.

"Nor, having only length, breadth, and thickness, can a cube have a real existence."

"There I object," said Filby. "Of course a solid body may exist. All real things — "

"So most people think. But wait a moment. Can an *instantaneous* cube exist?"

"Don't follow you," said Filby.

"Can a cube that does not last for any time at all, have a real existence?"

Filby became pensive. "Clear-

ly," the Time Traveller proceeded, "any real body must have extension in *four* directions: it must have Length, Breadth, Thickness, and — Duration. But through a natural infirmity of the flesh, which I will explain to you in a moment, we incline to overlook this fact. There are really four dimensions, three which we call the three planes of Space, and a fourth, Time. There is, however, a tendency to draw an unreal distinction between the former three dimensions and the latter, because it happens that our consciousness moves intermittently in one direction along the latter from the beginning to the end of our lives."

"That," said a very young man, making spasmodic efforts to relight his cigar over the lamp; "that . . . very clear indeed."

"Now, it is very remarkable that this is so extensively overlooked," continued the Time Traveller, with a slight accession of cheerfulness. "Really this is what is meant by the Fourth Dimension, though some people who talk about the Fourth Dimension do not know they mean it. It is only another way of looking at Time. *There is no difference between Time and any of the three dimensions of Space except that our consciousness moves along it.* But some foolish people have got hold of the wrong side of that idea. You have all heard what they have to say about this Fourth Dimension?"

"*I* have not," said the Provincial Mayor.

"It is simply this. That Space, as our mathematicians have it, is

spoken of as having three dimensions, which one may call Length, Breadth, and Thickness, and is always definable by reference to three planes, each at right angles to the others. But some philosophical people have been asking why *three* dimensions particularly — why not another direction at right angles to the other three? — and have even tried to construct a Four-Dimensional geometry. Professor Simon Newcomb was expounding this to the New York Mathematical Society only a month or so ago. You know how on a flat surface, which has only two dimensions, we can represent a figure of a three-dimensional solid, and similarly they think that by models of three dimensions they could represent one of four — if they could master the perspective of the thing. See?"

"I think so," murmured the Provincial Mayor; and, knitting his brows, he lapsed into an introspective state, his lips moving as one who repeats mystic words. "Yes, I think I see it now," he said after some time, brightening in a quite transitory manner.

"Well, I do not mind telling you I have been at work upon this geometry of Four Dimensions for some time. Some of my results are curious. For instance, here is a portrait of a man at eight years old, another at fifteen, another at seventeen, another at twenty-three, and so on. All these are evidently sections, as it were, Three-Dimensional representations of his Four-Dimensioned being, which is a fixed and unalterable thing."

"Scientific people," proceeded the Time Traveller, after the pause required for the proper assimilation of this, "know very well that Time is only a kind of Space. Here is a popular scientific diagram, a weather record. This line I trace with my finger shows the movement of the barometer. Yesterday it was so high, yesterday night it fell, then this morning it rose again, and so gently upward to here. Surely the mercury did not trace this line in any of the dimensions of Space generally recognised? But certainly it traced such a line, and that line, therefore, we must conclude was along the Time-Dimension."

"But," said the Medical Man, staring hard at a coal in the fire, "if Time is really only a fourth dimension of Space, why is it, and why has it always been, regarded as something different? And why cannot we move in Time as we move about in the other dimensions of Space?"

The Time Traveller smiled. "Are you so sure we can move freely in Space? Right and left we can go, backward and forward freely enough, and men always have done so. I admit we move freely in two dimensions. But how about up and down? Gravitation limits us there."

"Not exactly," said the Medical Man. "There are balloons."

"But before the balloons, save for spasmodic jumping and the inequalities of the surface, man had no freedom of vertical movement."

"Still, they could move a little up and down," said the Medical Man.

"Easier, far easier down than up."

"And you cannot move at all in Time, you cannot get away from the present moment."

"My dear sir, that is just where you are wrong. That is just where the whole world has gone wrong. We are always getting away from the present moment. Our mental existences, which are immaterial and have no dimensions, are passing along the Time-Dimension with a uniform velocity from the cradle to the grave. Just as we should travel *down* if we began our existence fifty miles above the earth's surface."

"But the great difficulty is this," interrupted the Psychologist. "You *can* move about in all directions of Space, but you cannot move about in Time."

"That is the germ of my great discovery. But you are wrong to say that we cannot move about in Time. For instance, if I am recalling an incident very vividly I go back to the instant of its occurrence: I become absent-minded, as you say. I jump back for a moment. Of course we have no means of staying back for any length of Time, any more than a savage or an animal has of staying six feet above the ground. But a civilised man is better off than the savage in this respect. He can go up against gravitation in a balloon, and why should he not hope that ultimately he may be able to stop or accelerate his drift along the Time-Dimension, or even turn about and travel the other way?"

"Oh, *this*," began Filby, "is all — "

"Why not?" said the Time Traveller.

"It's against reason," said Filby.

"What reason?" said the Time Traveller.

"You can show black is white by argument," said Filby, "but you will never convince me."

"Possibly not," said the Time Traveller. "But now you begin to see the object of my investigations into the geometry of Four Dimensions. Long ago I had a vague inkling of a machine — "

"To travel through Time!" exclaimed the Very Young Man.

"That shall travel indifferently in any direction of Space and Time, as the driver determines."

Filby contented himself with laughter.

"But I have experimental verification," said the Time Traveller.

"It would be remarkably convenient for the historian," the Psychologist suggested. "One might travel back and verify the accepted account of the Battle of Hastings, for instance!"

"Don't you think you would attract attention?" said the Medical Man. "Our ancestors had no great tolerance for anachronisms."

"One might get one's Greek from the very lips of Homer and Plato," the Very Young Man thought.

"In which case they would certainly plough you for the Littlego. The German scholars have improved Greek so much."

"Then there is the future," said the Very Young Man. "Just

think! One might invest all one's money, leave it to accumulate at interest, and hurry on ahead!"

"To discover a society," said I, "erected on a strictly communistic basis."

"Of all the wild extravagant theories!" began the Psychologist.

"Yes, so it seemed to me, and so I never talked of it until — "

"Experimental verification!" cried I. "You are going to verify *that*?"

"The experiment!" cried Filby, who was getting brain-weary.

"Let's see your experiment anyhow," said the Psychologist, "though it's all humbug, you know."

The Time Traveller smiled round at us. Then, still smiling faintly, and with his hands deep in his trousers pockets, he walked slowly out of the room, and we heard his slippers shuffling down the long passage to his laboratory.

The Psychologist looked at us. "I wonder what he's got?"

"Some sleight-of-hand trick or other," said the Medical Man, and Filby tried to tell us about a conjurer he had seen at Burslem, but before he had finished his preface the Time Traveller came back, and Filby's anecdote collapsed.

The thing the Time Traveller held in his hand was a glittering metallic framework, scarcely larger than a small clock, and very delicately made. There was ivory in it, and some transparent crystalline substance. And now I must be explicit, for this that follows — unless his explanation is

to be accepted — is an absolutely unaccountable thing. He took one of the small octagonal tables that were scattered about the room, and set it in front of the fire, with two legs on the hearth-rug. On this table he placed the mechanism. Then he drew up a chair, and sat down. The only other object on the table was a small shaded lamp, the bright light of which fell full upon the model. There were also perhaps a dozen candles about, two in brass candlesticks upon the mantel and several in sconces, so that the room was brilliantly illuminated. I sat in a low armchair nearest the fire, and I drew this forward so as to be almost between the Time Traveller and the fireplace. Filby sat behind him, looking over his shoulder. The Medical Man and the Provincial Mayor watched him in profile from the right, the Psychologist from the left. The Very Young Man stood behind the Psychologist. We were all on the alert. It appears incredible to me that any kind of trick, however subtly conceived and however adroitly done, could have been played upon us under these conditions.

The Time Traveller looked at us, and then at the mechanism. " Well? " said the Psychologist.

"This little affair," said the Time Traveller, resting his elbows upon the table and pressing his hands together above the apparatus, " is only a model. It is my plan for a machine to travel through time. You will notice that it looks singularly askew, and that there is an odd twin-

kling appearance about this bar, as though it was in some way unreal." He pointed to the part with his finger. " Also, here is one little white lever, and here is another."

The Medical Man got up out of his chair and peered into the thing. " It's beautifully made," he said.

" It took two years to make," retorted the Time Traveller. Then, when we had all imitated the action of the Medical Man, he said: " Now I want you clearly to understand that this lever, being pressed over, sends the machine gliding into the future, and this other reverses the motion. This saddle represents the seat of a time traveller. Presently I am going to press the lever, and off the machine will go. It will vanish, pass into future time, and disappear. Have a good look at the thing. Look at the table too, and satisfy yourselves there is no trickery. I don't want to waste this model and then be told I'm a quack."

There was a minute's pause perhaps. The Psychologist seemed about to speak to me, but changed his mind. Then the Time Traveller put forth his finger towards the lever. " No," he said suddenly. " Lend me your hand." And turning to the Psychologist, he took that individual's hand in his own and told him to put out his forefinger. So that it was the Psychologist himself who sent forth the model Time Machine on its interminable voyage. We all saw the lever turn. I am absolutely certain there was no trickery. There was

a breath of wind, and the lamp flame jumped. One of the candles on the mantel was blown out, and the little machine suddenly swung round, became indistinct, was seen as a ghost for a second perhaps, as an eddy of faintly glittering brass and ivory; and it was gone — vanished! Save for the lamp the table was bare.

Every one was silent for a minute. Then Filby said he was damned.

The Psychologist recovered from his stupor, and suddenly looked under the table. At that the Time Traveller laughed cheerfully. "Well?" he said, with a reminiscence of the Psychologist. Then, getting up, he went to the tobacco jar on the mantel, and with his back to us began to fill his pipe.

We stared at each other. "Look here," said the Medical Man, "are you in earnest about this? Do you seriously believe that that machine has travelled into time?"

"Certainly," said the Time Traveller, stooping to light a spill at the fire. Then he turned, lighting his pipe, to look at the Psychologist's face. (The Psychologist, to show that he was not unhinged, helped himself to a cigar and tried to light it uncut.) "What is more, I have a big machine nearly finished in there" — he indicated the laboratory — "and when that is put together I mean to have a journey on my own account."

"You mean to say that that machine has travelled into the future?" said Filby.

"Into the future or the past — I don't, for certain, know which."

After an interval the Psychologist had an inspiration. "It must have gone into the past if it has gone anywhere," he said.

"Why?" said the Time Traveller.

"Because I presume that it has not moved in space, and if it travelled into the future it would still be here all this time, since it must have travelled through this time."

"But," said I, "if it travelled into the past it would have been visible when we came first into this room; and last Thursday when we were here; and the Thursday before that; and so forth!"

"Serious objections," remarked the Provincial Mayor, with an air of impartiality, turning towards the Time Traveller.

"Not a bit," said the Time Traveller, and to the Psychologist: "You think. *You* can explain that. It's presentation below the threshold, you know, diluted presentation."

"Of course," said the Psychologist, and reassured us. "That's a simple point of psychology. I should have thought of it. It's plain enough, and helps the paradox delightfully. We cannot see it, nor can we appreciate this machine, any more than we can the spoke of a wheel spinning, or a bullet flying through the air. If it is travelling through time fifty times or a hundred times faster than we are, if it gets through a minute while we get through a second, the impression it creates will of course be only one-fiftieth or one-hundredth of

what it would make if it were not travelling in time. That's plain enough." He passed his hand through the space in which the machine had been. "You see?" he said, laughing.

We sat and stared at the vacant table for a minute or so. Then the Time Traveller asked us what we thought of it all.

"It sounds plausible enough to-night," said the Medical Man; "but wait until to-morrow. Wait for the common sense of the morning."

"Would you like to see the Time Machine itself?" asked the Time Traveller. And therewith, taking the lamp in his hand, he led the way down the long, draughty corridor to his laboratory. I remember vividly the flickering light, his queer broad head in silhouette, the dance of the shadows, how we all followed him, puzzled but incredulous, and how there in the laboratory we beheld a larger edition of the little mechanism which we had seen vanish from before our eyes. Parts were of nickel, parts of ivory, parts had certainly been filed or sawn out of rock crystal. The thing was generally complete, but the twisted crystalline bars lay unfinished upon the bench beside some sheets of drawings, and I took one up for a better look at it. Quartz it seemed to be.

"Look here," said the Medical Man, "are you perfectly serious? Or is this a trick — like that ghost you showed us last Christmas?"

"Upon that machine," said the Time Traveller, holding the lamp aloft, "I intend to explore time. Is that plain? I was never more serious in my life."

None of us quite knew how to take it.

I caught Filby's eye over the shoulder of the Medical Man, and he winked at me solemnly.

§2

I THINK that at that time none of us quite believed in the Time Machine. The fact is, the Time Traveller was one of those men who are too clever to be believed: you never felt that you saw all around him; you always suspected some subtle reserve, some ingenuity in ambush, behind his lucid frankness. Had Filby shown the model and explained the matter in the Time Traveller's words, we should have shown *him* far less scepticism. For we should have perceived his motives: a pork-butcher could understand Filby. But the Time Traveller had more than a touch of whim among his elements, and we distrusted him. Things that would have made the fame of a less clever man seemed tricks in his hands. It is a mistake to do things too easily. The serious people who took him seriously never felt quite sure of his deportment: they were somehow aware that trusting their reputations for judgment with him was

like furnishing a nursery with eggshell china. So I don't think any of us said very much about time travelling in the interval between that Thursday and the next, though its odd potentialities ran, no doubt, in most of our minds: its plausibility, that is, its practical incredibleness, the curious possibilities of anachronism and of utter confusion it suggested. For my own part, I was particularly preoccupied with the trick of the model. That I remember discussing with the Medical Man, whom I met on Friday at the Linnæan. He said he had seen a similar thing at Tübingen, and laid considerable stress on the blowing-out of the candle. But how the trick was done he could not explain.

The next Thursday I went again to Richmond—I suppose I was one of the Time Traveller's most constant guests—and, arriving late, found four or five men already assembled in his drawing-room. The Medical Man was standing before the fire with a sheet of paper in one hand and his watch in the other. I looked round for the Time Traveller, and—"It's half-past seven now," said the Medical Man. "I suppose we'd better have dinner?"

"Where's—?" said I, naming our host.

"You've just come? It's rather odd. He's unavoidably detained. He asks me in this note to lead off with dinner at seven if he's not back. Says he'll explain when he comes."

"It seems a pity to let the dinner spoil," said the Editor of a well-known daily paper; and thereupon the Doctor rang the bell.

The Psychologist was the only person besides the Doctor and myself who had attended the previous dinner. The other men were Blank, the Editor aforementioned, a certain journalist, and another—a quiet, shy man with a beard—whom I didn't know, and who, as far as my observation went, never opened his mouth all the evening. There was some speculation at the dinner-table about the Time Traveller's absence, and I suggested time travelling, in a half jocular spirit. The Editor wanted that explained to him, and the Psychologist volunteered a wooden account of the "ingenious paradox and trick" we had witnessed that day week. He was in the midst of his exposition when the door from the corridor opened slowly and without noise. I was facing the door, and saw it first. "Hallo!" I said. "At last!" And the door opened wider, and the Time Traveller stood before us. I gave a cry of surprise. "Good heavens! man, what's the matter?" cried the Medical Man, who saw him next. And the whole tableful turned towards the door.

He was in an amazing plight. His coat was dusty and dirty, and smeared with green down the sleeves; his hair disordered, and as it seemed to me greyer—either with dust and dirt or because its colour had actually faded. His face was ghastly pale; his chin had a brown cut on it—a cut half healed; his expression was haggard and drawn, as by intense

suffering. For a moment he hesitated in the doorway, as if he had been dazzled by the light. Then he came into the room. He walked with just such a limp as I have seen in footsore tramps. We stared at him in silence, expecting him to speak.

He said not a word, but came painfully to the table, and made a motion towards the wine. The Editor filled a glass of champagne, and pushed it towards him. He drained it, and it seemed to do him good: for he looked round the table, and the ghost of his old smile flickered across his face. "What on earth have you been up to, man?" said the Doctor. The Time Traveller did not seem to hear. "Don't let me disturb you," he said, with a certain faltering articulation. "I'm all right." He stopped, held out his glass for more, and took it off at a draught. "That's good," he said. His eyes grew brighter, and a faint colour came into his cheeks. His glance flickered over our faces with a certain dull approval, and then went round the warm and comfortable room. Then he spoke again, still as it were feeling his way among his words. "I'm going to wash and dress, and then I'll come down and explain things. . . . Save me some of that mutton. I'm starving for a bit of meat."

He looked across at the Editor, who was a rare visitor, and hoped he was all right. The Editor began a question. "Tell you presently," said the Time Traveller. "I'm—funny! Be all right in a minute."

He put down his glass, and walked towards the staircase door. Again I remarked his lameness and the soft padding sound of his footfall, and standing up in my place, I saw his feet as he went out. He had nothing on them but a pair of tattered, blood-stained socks. Then the door closed upon him. I had half a mind to follow, till I remembered how he detested any fuss about himself. For a minute, perhaps, my mind was wool gathering. Then, "Remarkable Behaviour of an Eminent Scientist," I heard the Editor say, thinking (after his wont) in headlines. And this brought my attention back to the bright dinner-table.

"What's the game?" said the Journalist. "Has he been doing the Amateur Cadger? I don't follow." I met the eye of the Psychologist, and read my own interpretation in his face. I thought of the Time Traveller limping painfully upstairs. I don't think any one else had noticed his lameness.

The first to recover completely from this surprise was the Medical Man, who rang the bell—the Time Traveller hated to have servants waiting at dinner—for a hot plate. At that the Editor turned to his knife and fork with a grunt, and the silent man followed suit. The dinner was resumed. Conversation was exclamatory for a little while, with gaps of wonderment; and then the Editor got fervent in his curiosity. "Does our friend eke out his modest income with a crossing? or has he his Nebuchadnezzar phases?" he inquired. "I feel assured it's this business of the

Time Machine," I said, and took up the Psychologist's account of our previous meeting. The new guests were frankly incredulous. The Editor raised objections. "What *was* this time travelling? A man couldn't cover himself with dust by rolling in a paradox, could he?" And then, as the idea came home to him, he resorted to caricature. Hadn't they any clothes-brushes in the Future? The Journalist, too, would not believe at any price, and joined the Editor in the easy work of heaping ridicule on the whole thing. They were both the new kind of journalist — very joyous, irreverent young men. "Our Special Correspondent in the Day after To-morrow reports," the Journalist was saying — or rather shouting — when the Time Traveller came back. He was dressed in ordinary evening clothes, and nothing save his haggard look remained of the change that had startled me.

"I say," said the Editor hilariously, "these chaps here say you have been travelling into the middle of next week!! Tell us all about little Rosebery, will you? What will you take for the lot?"

The Time Traveller came to the place reserved for him without a word. He smiled quietly, in his old way. "Where's my mutton?" he said. "What a treat it is to stick a fork into meat again!"

"Story!" cried the Editor.

"Story be damned!" said the Time Traveller. "I want something to eat. I won't say a word until I get some peptone into my arteries. Thanks. And the salt."

"One word," said I. "Have you been time travelling?"

"Yes," said the Time Traveller, with his mouth full, nodding his head.

"I'd give a shilling a line for a verbatim note," said the Editor. The Time Traveller pushed his glass towards the Silent Man and rang it with his finger nail; at which the Silent Man, who had been staring at his face, started convulsively, and poured him wine. The rest of the dinner was uncomfortable. For my own part, sudden questions kept on rising to my lips, and I dare say it was the same with the others. The Journalist tried to relieve the tension by telling anecdotes of Hettie Potter. The Time Traveller devoted his attention to his dinner, and displayed the appetite of a tramp. The Medical Man smoked a cigarette, and watched the Time Traveller through his eyelashes. The Silent Man seemed even more clumsy than usual, and drank champagne with regularity and determination out of sheer nervousness. At last the Time Traveller pushed his plate away, and looked round us. "I suppose I must apologise," he said. "I was simply starving. I've had a most amazing time." He reached out his hand for a cigar, and cut the end. "But come into the smoking-room. It's too long a story to tell over greasy plates." And ringing the bell in passing, he led the way into the adjoining room.

"You have told Blank, and Dash, and Chose about the ma-

chine?" he said to me, leaning back in his easy chair and naming the three new guests.

"But the thing's a mere paradox," said the Editor.

"I can't argue to-night. I don't mind telling you the story, but I can't argue. I will," he went on, "tell you the story of what has happened to me, if you like, but you must refrain from interruptions. I want to tell it. Badly. Most of it will sound like lying. So be it! It's true — every word of it, all the same. I was in my laboratory at four o'clock, and since then . . . I've lived eight days . . . such days as no human being ever lived before! I'm nearly worn out, but I shan't sleep till I've told this thing over to you. Then I shall go to bed. But no interruptions! Is it agreed?"

"Agreed," said the Editor, and the rest of us echoed "Agreed." And with that the Time Traveller began his story as I have set it forth. He sat back in his chair at first, and spoke like a weary man. Afterwards he got more animated. In writing it down I feel with only too much keenness the inadequacy of pen and ink — and, above all, my own inadequacy — to express its quality. You read, I will suppose, attentively enough; but you cannot see the speaker's white, sincere face in the bright circle of the little lamp, nor hear the intonation of his voice. You cannot know how his expression followed the turns of his story! Most of us hearers were in shadow, for the candles in the smoking-room had not been lighted, and only the face of the Journalist and the legs of the Silent Man from the knees downward were illuminated. At first we glanced now and again at each other. After a time we ceased to do that, and looked only at the Time Traveller's face.

§ 3

"I TOLD some of you last Thursday of the principles of the Time Machine, and showed you the actual thing itself, incomplete in the workshop. There it is now, a little travel-worn, truly; and one of the ivory bars is cracked, and a brass rail bent; but the rest of it's sound enough. I expected to finish it on Friday; but on Friday, when the putting together was nearly done, I found that one of the nickel bars was exactly one inch too short, and this I had to get re-made; so that the thing was not complete until this morning. It was at ten o'clock to-day that the first of all Time Machines began its career. I gave it a last tap, tried all the screws again, put one more drop of oil on the quartz rod, and sat myself in the saddle. I suppose a suicide who holds a pistol to his skull feels much the same wonder at what will come next as I felt

then. I took the starting lever in one hand and the stopping one in the other, pressed the first, and almost immediately the second. I seemed to reel; I felt a nightmare sensation of falling; and, looking round, I saw the laboratory exactly as before. Had anything happened? For a moment I suspected that my intellect had tricked me. Then I noted the clock. A moment before, as it seemed, it had stood at a minute or so past ten; now it was nearly half-past three!

" I drew a breath, set my teeth, gripped the starting lever with both hands, and went off with a thud. The laboratory got hazy and went dark. Mrs. Watchett came in, and walked, apparently without seeing me, towards the garden door. I suppose it took her a minute or so to traverse the place, but to me she seemed to shoot across the room like a rocket. I pressed the lever over to its extreme position. The night came like the turning out of a lamp, and in another moment came to-morrow. The laboratory grew faint and hazy, then fainter and ever fainter. To-morrow night came black, then day again, night again, day again, faster and faster still. An eddying murmur filled my ears, and a strange, dumb confusedness descended on my mind.

" I am afraid I cannot convey the peculiar sensations of time travelling. They are excessively unpleasant. There is a feeling exactly like that one has upon a switchback — of a helpless headlong motion! I felt the same horrible anticipation, too, of an im-minent smash. As I put on pace, night followed day like the flapping of a black wing. The dim suggestion of the laboratory seemed presently to fall away from me, and I saw the sun hopping swiftly across the sky, leaping it every minute, and every minute marking a day. I supposed the laboratory had been destroyed, and I had come into the open air. I had a dim impression of scaffolding, but I was already going too fast to be conscious of any moving things. The slowest snail that ever crawled dashed by too fast for me. The twinkling succession of darkness and light was excessively painful to the eye. Then, in the intermittent darknesses, I saw the moon spinning swiftly through her quarters from new to full, and had a faint glimpse of the circling stars. Presently, as I went on, still gaining velocity, the palpitation of night and day merged into one continuous greyness; the sky took on a wonderful deepness of blue, a splendid luminous colour like that of early twilight; the jerking sun became a streak of fire, a brilliant arch, in space, the moon a fainter fluctuating band; and I could see nothing of the stars, save now and then a brighter circle flickering in the blue.

" The landscape was misty and vague. I was still on the hillside upon which this house now stands, and the shoulder rose above me grey and dim. I saw trees growing and changing like puffs of vapour, now brown, now green: they grew, spread, shivered, and passed away. I saw

huge buildings rise up faint and fair, and pass like dreams. The whole surface of the earth seemed changed — melting and flowing under my eyes. The little hands upon the dials that registered my speed raced round faster and faster. Presently I noted that the sun-belt swayed up and down, from solstice to solstice, in a minute or less, and that, consequently, my pace was over a year a minute; and minute by minute the white snow flashed across the world, and vanished, and was followed by the bright, brief green of spring.

"The unpleasant sensations of the start were less poignant now. They merged at last into a kind of hysterical exhilaration. I remarked, indeed, a clumsy swaying of the machine, for which I was unable to account. But my mind was too confused to attend to it, so with a kind of madness growing upon me, I flung myself into futurity. At first I scarce thought of stopping, scarce thought of anything but these new sensations. But presently a fresh series of impressions grew up in my mind — a certain curiosity and therewith a certain dread — until at last they took complete possession of me. What strange developments of humanity, what wonderful advances upon our rudimentary civilisation, I thought, might not appear when I came to look nearly into the dim elusive world that raced and fluctuated before my eyes! I saw great and splendid architecture rising about me, more massive than any buildings of our own time, and yet, as it seemed, built of glimmer and mist. I saw a richer green flow up the hillside, and remain there without any wintry intermission. Even through the veil of my confusion the earth seemed very fair. And so my mind came round to the business of stopping.

"The peculiar risk lay in the possibility of my finding some substance in the space which I, or the machine, occupied. So long as I travelled at a high velocity through time, this scarcely mattered: I was, so to speak, attenuated — was slipping like a vapour through the interstices of intervening substances! But to come to a stop involved the jamming of myself, molecule by molecule, into whatever lay in my way: meant bringing my atoms into such intimate contact with those of the obstacle that a profound chemical reaction — possibly a far-reaching explosion — would result, and blow myself and my apparatus out of all possible dimensions — into the Unknown. This possibility had occurred to me again and again while I was making the machine; but then I had cheerfully accepted it as an unavoidable risk — one of the risks a man has got to take! Now the risk was inevitable, I no longer saw it in the same cheerful light. The fact is that, insensibly, the absolute strangeness of everything, the sickly jarring and swaying of the machine, above all, the feeling of prolonged falling, had absolutely upset my nerve. I told myself that I could never stop, and with a gust of petulance I resolved to stop forthwith. Like an impatient fool, I

lugged over the lever, and incontinently the thing went reeling over, and I was flung headlong through the air.

"There was the sound of a clap of thunder in my ears. I may have been stunned for a moment. A pitiless hail was hissing round me, and I was sitting on soft turf in front of the overset machine. Everything still seemed grey, but presently I remarked that the confusion in my ears was gone. I looked round me. I was on what seemed to be a little lawn in a garden, surrounded by rhododendron bushes, and I noticed that their mauve and purple blossoms were dropping in a shower under the beating of the hailstones. The rebounding, dancing hail hung in a cloud over the machine, and drove along the ground like smoke. In a moment I was wet to the skin. 'Fine hospitality,' said I, ' to a man who has travelled innumerable years to see you.'

"Presently I thought what a fool I was to get wet. I stood up and looked round me. A colossal figure, carved apparently in some white stone, loomed indistinctly beyond the rhododendrons through the hazy downpour. But all else of the world was invisible.

"My sensations would be hard to describe. As the columns of hail grew thinner, I saw the white figure more distinctly. It was very large, for a silver birch tree touched its shoulder. It was of white marble, in shape something like a winged sphinx, but the wings, instead of being carried vertically at the sides, were spread so that it seemed to hover. The pedestal, it appeared to me, was of bronze, and was thick with verdigris. It chanced that the face was towards me; the sightless eyes seemed to watch me; there was the faint shadow of a smile on the lips. It was greatly weatherworn, and that imparted an unpleasant suggestion of disease. I stood looking at it for a little space — half a minute, perhaps, or half an hour. It seemed to advance and to recede as the hail drove before it denser or thinner. At last I tore my eyes from it for a moment, and saw that the hail curtain had worn threadbare, and that the sky was lightening with the promise of the sun.

"I looked up again at the crouching white shape, and the full temerity of my voyage came suddenly upon me. What might appear when that hazy curtain was altogether withdrawn? What might not have happened to men? What if cruelty had grown into a common passion? What if in this interval the race had lost its manliness, and had developed into something inhuman, unsympathetic, and overwhelmingly powerful? I might seem some old-world savage animal, only the more dreadful and disgusting for our common likeness — a foul creature to be incontinently slain.

"Already I saw other vast shapes — huge buildings with intricate parapets and tall columns, with a wooded hillside dimly creeping in upon me through the lessening storm. I was seized with a panic fear. I turned frantically to the Time Machine, and strove hard to readjust it. As I did so

the shafts of the sun smote through the thunderstorm. The grey downpour was swept aside and vanished like the trailing garments of a ghost. Above me, in the intense blue of the summer sky, some faint brown shreds of cloud whirled into nothingness. The great buildings about me stood out clear and distinct, shining with the wet of the thunderstorm, and picked out in white by the unmelted hailstones piled along their courses. I felt naked in a strange world. I felt as perhaps a bird may feel in the clear air, knowing the hawk wings above and will swoop. My fear grew to frenzy. I took a breathing space, set my teeth, and again grappled fiercely, wrist and knee, with the machine. It gave under my desperate onset and turned over. It struck my chin violently. One hand on the saddle, the other on the lever, I stood panting heavily in attitude to mount again.

"But with this recovery of a prompt retreat my courage recovered. I looked more curiously and less fearfully at this world of the remote future. In a circular opening, high up in the wall of the nearer house, I saw a group of figures clad in rich soft robes. They had seen me, and their faces were directed towards me.

"Then I heard voices approaching me. Coming through the bushes by the White Sphinx were the heads and shoulders of men running. One of these, emerged in a pathway leading straight to the little lawn upon which I stood with my machine.

He was a slight creature — perhaps four feet high — clad in a purple tunic, girdled at the waist with a leather belt. Sandals or buskins — I could not clearly distinguish which — were on his feet; his legs were bare to the knees, and his head was bare. Noticing that, I noticed for the first time how warm the air was.

"He struck me as being a very beautiful and graceful creature, but indescribably frail. His flushed face reminded me of the more beautiful kind of consumptive — that hectic beauty of which we used to hear so much. At the sight of him I suddenly regained confidence. I took my hands from the machine."

§4

"In another moment we were standing face to face, I and this fragile thing out of futurity. He came straight up to me and laughed into my eyes. The absence from his bearing of any sign of fear struck me at once. Then he turned to the two others who were following him and spoke to them in a strange and very sweet and liquid tongue.

"There were others coming, and presently a little group of perhaps eight or ten of these exquisite creatures were about me. One of them addressed me. It

came into my head, oddly enough, that my voice was too harsh and deep for them. So I shook my head, and pointing to my ears, shook it again. He came a step forward, hesitated, and then touched my hand. Then I felt other soft little tentacles upon my back and shoulders. They wanted to make sure I was real. There was nothing in this at all alarming. Indeed, there was something in these pretty little people that inspired confidence—a graceful gentleness, a certain childlike ease. And besides, they looked so frail that I could fancy myself flinging the whole dozen of them about like nine-pins. But I made a sudden motion to warn them when I saw their little pink hands feeling at the Time Machine. Happily then, when it was not too late, I thought of a danger I had hitherto forgotten, and reaching over the bars of the machine, I unscrewed the little levers that would set it in motion, and put these in my pocket. Then I turned again to see what I could do in the way of communication.

"And then, looking more nearly into their features, I saw some further peculiarities in their Dresden china type of prettiness. Their hair, which was uniformly curly, came to a sharp end at the neck and cheek; there was not the faintest suggestion of it on the face, and their ears were singularly minute. The mouths were small, with bright red, rather thin lips, and the little chins ran to a point. The eyes were large and mild; and— this may seem egotism on my part—I fancied even then that there was a certain lack of the interest I might have expected in them.

"As they made no effort to communicate with me, but simply stood round me smiling and speaking in soft cooing notes to each other, I began the conversation. I pointed to the Time Machine and to myself. Then, hesitating for a moment how to express Time, I pointed to the sun. At once a quaintly pretty little figure in chequered purple and white followed my gesture, and then astonished me by imitating the sound of thunder.

"For a moment I was staggered, though the import of his gesture was plain enough. The question had come into my mind abruptly: were these creatures fools? You may hardly understand how it took me. You see I had always anticipated that the people of the year Eight Hundred and Two Thousand odd would be incredibly in front of us in knowledge, art, everything. Then one of them suddenly asked me a question that showed him to be on the intellectual level of one of our five-year-old children —asked me, in fact, if I had come from the sun in a thunderstorm! It let loose the judgment I had suspended upon their clothes, their frail light limbs and fragile features. A flow of disappointment rushed across my mind. For a moment I felt that I had built the Time Machine in vain.

"I nodded, pointed to the sun, and gave them such a vivid rendering of a thunderclap as startled them. They all withdrew a

pace or so and bowed. Then came one laughing towards me, carrying a chain of beautiful flowers altogether new to me, and put it about my neck. The idea was received with melodious applause; and presently they were all running to and fro for flowers, and laughingly flinging them upon me until I was almost smothered with blossoms. You who have never seen the like can scarcely imagine what delicate and wonderful flowers countless years of culture had created. Then someone suggested that their plaything should be exhibited in the nearest building, and so I was led past the sphinx of white marble, which had seemed to watch me all the while with a smile at my astonishment, towards a vast grey edifice of fretted stone. As I went with them the memory of my confident anticipations of a profoundly grave and intellectual posterity came, with irresistible merriment, to my mind.

"The building had a huge entry, and was altogether of colossal dimensions. I was naturally most occupied with the growing crowd of little people, and with the big open portals that yawned before me shadowy and mysterious. My general impression of the world I saw over their heads was of a tangled waste of beautiful bushes and flowers, a long neglected and yet weedless garden. I saw a number of tall spikes of strange white flowers, measuring a foot perhaps across the spread of the waxen petals. They grew scattered, as if wild, among the variegated shrubs, but, as I say, I did not examine them closely at this time. The Time Machine was left deserted on the turf among the rhododendrons.

"The arch of the doorway was richly carved, but naturally I did not observe the carving very narrowly, though I fancied I saw suggestions of old Phœnician decorations as I passed through, and it struck me that they were very badly broken and weather-worn. Several more brightly-clad people met me in the doorway, and so we entered, I, dressed in dingy nineteenth-century garments, looking grotesque enough, garlanded with flowers, and surrounded by an eddying mass of bright, soft-coloured robes and shining white limbs, in a melodious whirl of laughter and laughing speech.

"The big doorway opened into a proportionately great hall hung with brown. The roof was in shadow, and the windows, partially glazed with coloured glass and partially unglazed, admitted a tempered light. The floor was made up of huge blocks of some very hard white metal, not plates nor slabs, — blocks, and it was so much worn, as I judged by the going to and fro of past generations, as to be deeply channelled along the more frequented ways. Transverse to the length were innumerable tables made of slabs of polished stone, raised, perhaps, a foot from the floor, and upon these were heaps of fruits. Some I recognised as a kind of hypertrophied raspberry and orange, but for the most part they were strange.

" Between the tables was scattered a great number of cushions. Upon these my conductors seated themselves, signing for me to do likewise. With a pretty absence of ceremony they began to eat the fruit with their hands, flinging peel and stalks and so forth, into the round openings in the sides of the tables. I was not loth to follow their example, for I felt thirsty and hungry. As I did so I surveyed the hall at my leisure.

" And perhaps the thing that struck me most was its dilapidated look. The stained-glass windows, which displayed only a geometrical pattern, were broken in many places, and the curtains that hung across the lower end were thick with dust. And it caught my eye that the corner of the marble table near me was fractured. Nevertheless, the general effect was extremely rich and picturesque. There were, perhaps, a couple of hundred people dining in the hall, and most of them, seated as near to me as they could come, were watching me with interest, their little eyes shining over the fruit they were eating. All were clad in the same soft, and yet strong, silky material.

" Fruit, by the bye, was all their diet. These people of the remote future were strict vegetarians, and while I was with them, in spite of some carnal cravings, I had to be frugivorous also. Indeed, I found afterwards that horses, cattle, sheep, dogs, had followed the Ichthyosaurus into extinction. But the fruits were very delightful; one, in particular, that seemed to be in season all the time I was there — a floury thing in a three-sided husk — was especially good, and I made it my staple. At first I was puzzled by all these strange fruits, and by the strange flowers I saw, but later I began to perceive their import.

" However, I am telling you of my fruit dinner in the distant future now. So soon as my appetite was a little checked, I determined to make a resolute attempt to learn the speech of these new men of mine. Clearly that was the next thing to do. The fruits seemed a convenient thing to begin upon, and holding one of these up I began a series of interrogative sounds and gestures. I had some considerable difficulty in conveying my meaning. At first my efforts met with a stare of surprise or inextinguishable laughter, but presently a fair-haired little creature seemed to grasp my intention and repeated a name. They had to chatter and explain the business at great length to each other, and my first attempts to make the exquisite little sounds of their language caused an immense amount of amusement. However, I felt like a schoolmaster amidst children, and persisted, and presently I had a score of noun substantives at least at my command; and then I got to demonstrative pronouns, and even the verb " to eat." But it was slow work, and the little people soon tired and wanted to get away from my interrogations, so I determined, rather of necessity, to let them give their lessons in little doses when they felt inclined. And very

little doses I found they were before long, for I never met people more indolent or more easily fatigued.

"A queer thing I soon discovered about my little hosts, and that was their lack of interest. They would come to me with eager cries of astonishment, like children, but, like children, they would soon stop examining me, and wander away after some other toy. The dinner and my conversational beginnings ended, I noted for the first time that almost all those who had surrounded me at first were gone. It is odd, too, how speedily I came to disregard these little people. I went out through the portal into the sunlit world again so soon as my hunger was satisfied. I was continually meeting more of these men of the future, who would follow me a little distance, chatter and laugh about me, and, having smiled and gesticulated in a friendly way, leave me again to my own devices.

"The calm of evening was upon the world as I emerged from the great hall, and the scene was lit by the warm glow of the setting sun. At first things were very confusing. Everything was so entirely different from the world I had known — even the flowers. The big building I had left was situate on the slope of a broad river valley, but the Thames had shifted, perhaps, a mile from its present position. I resolved to mount to the summit of a crest, perhaps a mile and a half away, from which I could get a wider view of this our planet in the year Eight Hundred and Two Thousand Seven Hundred and One, A.D. For that, I should explain, was the date the little dials of my machine recorded.

"As I walked I was watchful for every impression that could possibly help to explain the condition of ruinous splendour in which I found the world — for ruinous it was. A little way up the hill, for instance, was a great heap of granite, bound together by masses of aluminium, a vast labyrinth of precipitous walls and crumbled heaps, amidst which were thick heaps of very beautiful pagoda-like plants — nettles possibly — but wonderfully tinted with brown about the leaves, and incapable of stinging. It was evidently the derelict remains of some vast structure, to what end built I could not determine. It was here that I was destined, at a later date, to have a very strange experience — the first intimation of a still stranger discovery — but of that I will speak in its proper place.

"Looking round, with a sudden thought, from a terrace on which I rested for a while, I realised that there were no small houses to be seen. Apparently, the single house, and possibly even the household, had vanished. Here and there among the greenery were palace-like buildings, but the house and the cottage, which form such characteristic features of our own English landscape, had disappeared.

"'Communism,' said I to myself.

"And on the heels of that came another thought. I looked at the

half-dozen little figures that were following me. Then, in a flash, I perceived that all had the same form of costume, the same soft hairless visage, and the same girlish rotundity of limb. It may seem strange, perhaps, that I had not noticed this before. But everything was so strange. Now, I saw the fact plainly enough. In costume, and in all the differences of texture and bearing that now mark off the sexes from each other, these people of the future were alike. And the children seemed to my eyes to be but the miniatures of their parents. I judged then that the children of that time were extremely precocious, physically at least, and I found afterwards abundant verification of my opinion.

" Seeing the ease and security in which these people were living, I felt that this close resemblance of the sexes was after all what one would expect; for the strength of a man and the softness of a woman, the institution of the family, and the differentiation of occupations are mere militant necessities of an age of physical force. Where population is balanced and abundant, much child-bearing becomes an evil rather than a blessing to the State: where violence comes but rarely and offspring are secure, there is less necessity — indeed there is no necessity — for an efficient family, and the specialisation of the sexes with reference to their children's needs disappears. We see some beginnings of this even in our own time, and in this future age it was complete. This, I must remind you, was my speculation at the time. Later, I was to appreciate how far it fell short of the reality.

" While I was musing upon these things, my attention was attracted by a pretty little structure, like a well under a cupola. I thought in a transitory way of the oddness of wells still existing, and then resumed the thread of my speculations. There were no large buildings towards the top of the hill, and as my walking powers were evidently miraculous, I was presently left alone for the first time. With a strange sense of freedom and adventure I pushed on up to the crest.

" There I found a seat of some yellow metal that I did not recognise, corroded in places with a kind of pinkish rust and half smothered in soft moss, the armrests cast and filed into the resemblance of griffins' heads. I sat down on it, and I surveyed the broad view of our old world under the sunset of that long day. It was as sweet and fair a view as I have ever seen. The sun had already gone below the horizon and the west was flaming gold, touched with some horizontal bars of purple and crimson. Below was the valley of the Thames, in which the river lay like a band of burnished steel. I have already spoken of the great palaces dotted about among the variegated greenery, some in ruins and some still occupied. Here and there rose a white or silvery figure in the waste garden of the earth, here and there came the sharp vertical line of some cupola or obelisk. There were no hedges, no signs of proprietary

rights, no evidences of agriculture; the whole earth had become a garden.

" So watching, I began to put my interpretation upon the things I had seen, and as it shaped itself to me that evening, my interpretation was something in this way. (Afterwards I found I had got only a half-truth — or only a glimpse of one facet of the truth.)

" It seemed to me that I had happened upon humanity upon the wane. The ruddy sunset set me thinking of the sunset of mankind. For the first time I began to realise an odd consequence of the social effort in which we are at present engaged. And yet, come to think, it is a logical consequence enough. Strength is the outcome of need: security sets a premium on feebleness. The work of ameliorating the conditions of life — the true civilising process that makes life more and more secure — had gone steadily on to a climax. One triumph of a united humanity over Nature had followed another. Things that are now mere dreams had become projects deliberately put in hand and carried forward. And the harvest was what I saw!

" After all, the sanitation and the agriculture of to-day are still in the rudimentary stage. The science of our time has attacked but a little department of the field of human disease, but, even so, it spreads its operations very steadily and persistently. Our agriculture and horticulture destroy a weed just here and there and cultivate perhaps a score or so of wholesome plants, leaving the greater number to fight out a balance as they can We improve our favourite plants and animals — and how few they are — gradually by selective breeding; now a new and better peach, now a seedless grape, now a sweeter and larger flower, now a more convenient breed of cattle. We improve them gradually, because our ideals are vague and tentative, and our knowledge is very limited; because Nature, too, is shy and slow in our clumsy hands. Some day all this will be better organised, and still better. That is the drift of the current in spite of the eddies. The whole world will be intelligent, educated, and co-operating; things will move faster and faster towards the subjugation of Nature. In the end, wisely and carefully we shall readjust the balance of animal and vegetable life to suit our human needs.

" This adjustment, I say, must have been done, and done well: done indeed for all time, in the space of Time across which my machine had leapt. The air was free from gnats, the earth from weeds or fungi; everywhere were fruits and sweet and delightful flowers; brilliant butterflies flew hither and thither. The ideal of preventive medicine was attained. Diseases had been stamped out. I saw no evidence of any contagious diseases during all my stay. And I shall have to tell you later that even the processes of putrefaction and decay had been profoundly affected by these changes.

" Social triumphs, too, had been effected. I saw mankind housed in splendid shelters, glori-

ously clothed, and as yet I had found them engaged in no toil. There were no signs of struggle, neither social nor economical struggle. The shop, the advertisement, traffic, all that commerce which constitutes the body of our world, was gone. It was natural on that golden evening that I should jump at the idea of a social paradise. The difficulty of increasing population had been met, I guessed, and population had ceased to increase.

"But with this change in condition comes inevitably adaptations to the change. What, unless biological science is a mass of errors, is the cause of human intelligence and vigour? Hardship and freedom: conditions under which the active, strong, and subtle survive and the weaker go to the wall; conditions that put a premium upon the loyal alliance of capable men, upon self-restraint, patience, and decision. And the institution of the family, and the emotions that arise therein, the fierce jealousy, the tenderness for offspring, parental self-devotion, all found their justification and support in the imminent dangers of the young. *Now,* where are these imminent dangers? There is a sentiment arising, and it will grow, against connubial jealousy, against fierce maternity, against passion of all sorts; unnecessary things now, and things that make us uncomfortable, savage survivals, discords in a refined and pleasant life.

"I thought of the physical slightness of the people, their lack of intelligence and those big abundant ruins, and it strengthened my belief in a perfect conquest of Nature. For after the battle comes Quiet. Humanity had been strong, energetic, and intelligent, and had used all its abundant vitality to alter the conditions under which it lived. And now came the reaction of the altered conditions.

"Under the new conditions of perfect comfort and security, that restless energy, that with us is strength, would become weakness. Even in our own time certain tendencies and desires, once necessary to survival, are a constant source of failure. Physical courage and the love of battle, for instance, are no great help — may even be hindrances — to a civilised man. And in a state of physical balance and security, power, intellectual as well as physical, would be out of place. For countless years I judged there had been no danger of war or solitary violence, no danger from wild beasts, no wasting disease to require strength of constitution, no need of toil. For such a life, what we should call the weak are as well equipped as the strong, are indeed no longer weak. Better equipped indeed they are, for the strong would be fretted by an energy for which there was no outlet. No doubt the exquisite beauty of the buildings I saw was the outcome of the last surgings of the now purposeless energy of mankind before it settled down into perfect harmony with the conditions under which it lived — the flourish of that triumph which began the last great peace. This has ever

been the fate of energy in security; it takes to art and to eroticism, and then come languor and decay.

"Even this artistic impetus would at last die away — had almost died in the Time I saw. To adorn themselves with flowers, to dance, to sing in the sunlight; so much was left of the artistic spirit, and no more. Even that would fade in the end into a contented inactivity. We are kept keen on the grindstone of pain and necessity, and, it seemed to me, that here was that hateful grindstone broken at last!

"As I stood there in the gathering dark I thought that in this simple explanation I had mastered the problem of the world — mastered the whole secret of these delicious people. Possibly the checks they had devised for the increase of population had succeeded too well, and their numbers had rather diminished than kept stationary. That would account for the abandoned ruins. Very simple was my explanation, and plausible enough — as most wrong theories are!"

§ 5

"As I stood there musing over this too perfect triumph of man, the full moon, yellow and gibbous, came up out of an over-flow of silver light in the north-east. The bright little figures ceased to move about below, a noiseless owl flitted by, and I shivered with the chill of the night. I determined to descend and find where I could sleep.

"I looked for the building I knew. Then my eye travelled along to the figure of the White Sphinx upon the pedestal of bronze, growing distinct as the light of the rising moon grew brighter. I could see the silver birch against it. There was the tangle of rhododendron bushes, black in the pale light, and there was the little lawn. I looked at the lawn again. A queer doubt chilled my complacency. 'No,' said I stoutly to myself, 'that was not the lawn.'

"But it *was* the lawn. For the white leprous face of the sphinx was towards it. Can you imagine what I felt as this conviction came home to me? But you cannot. The Time Machine was gone!

"At once, like a lash across the face, came the possibility of losing my own age, of being left helpless in this strange new world. The bare thought of it was an actual physical sensation. I could feel it grip me at the throat and stop my breathing. In another moment I was in a passion of fear, and running with great leaping strides down the slope. Once I fell headlong and cut my face; I lost no time in stanching the blood, but jumped up and ran on, with a warm trickle down my cheek and chin. All the time I ran I was saying to myself, 'They have moved it

a little, pushed it under the bushes out of the way.' Nevertheless, I ran with all my might. All the time, with the certainty that sometimes comes with excessive dread, I knew that such assurance was folly, knew instinctively that the machine was removed out of my reach. My breath came with pain. I suppose I covered the whole distance from the hill crest to the little lawn, two miles, perhaps, in ten minutes. And I am not a young man. I cursed aloud, as I ran, at my confident folly in leaving the machine, wasting good breath thereby. I cried aloud, and none answered. Not a creature seemed to be stirring in that moonlit world.

"When I reached the lawn my worst fears were realised. Not a trace of the thing was to be seen. I felt faint and cold when I faced the empty space, among the black tangle of bushes. I ran round it furiously, as if the thing might be hidden in a corner, and then stopped abruptly, with my hands clutching my hair. Above me towered the sphinx, upon the bronze pedestal, white, shining, leprous, in the light of the rising moon. It seemed to smile in mockery of my dismay.

"I might have consoled myself by imagining the little people had put the mechanism in some shelter for me, had I not felt assured of their physical and intellectual inadequacy. That is what dismayed me: the sense of some hitherto unsuspected power, through whose intervention my invention had vanished. Yet, of one thing I felt assured: unless some other age had produced its exact duplicate, the machine could not have moved in time. The attachment of the levers — I will show you the method later — prevented any one from tampering with it in that way when they were removed. It had moved, and was hid, only in space. But then, where could it be?

"I think I must have had a kind of frenzy. I remember running violently in and out among the moonlit bushes all round the sphinx, and startling some white animal that, in the dim light, I took for a small deer. I remember, too, late that night, beating the bushes with my clenched fists until my knuckles were gashed and bleeding from the broken twigs. Then, sobbing and raving in my anguish of mind, I went down to the great building of stone. The big hall was dark, silent, and deserted. I slipped on the uneven floor, and fell over one of the malachite tables, almost breaking my shin. I lit a match and went on past the dusty curtains, of which I have told you.

"There I found a second great hall covered with cushions, upon which, perhaps, a score or so of the little people were sleeping. I have no doubt they found my second appearance strange enough, coming suddenly out of the quiet darkness with inarticulate noises and the splutter and flare of a match. For they had forgotten about matches. 'Where is my Time Machine?' I began, bawling like an angry child, laying hands upon them and shaking them up together. It must

have been very queer to them. Some laughed, most of them looked sorely frightened. When I saw them standing round me, it came into my head that I was doing as foolish a thing as it was possible for me to do under the circumstances, in trying to revive the sensation of fear. For, reasoning from their daylight behaviour, I thought that fear must be forgotten.

"Abruptly, I dashed down the match, and knocking one of the people over in my course, went blundering across the big dining-hall again, out under the moonlight. I heard cries of terror and their little feet running and stumbling this way and that. I do not remember all I did as the moon crept up the sky. I suppose it was the unexpected nature of my loss that maddened me. I felt hopelessly cut off from my own kind —a strange animal in an unknown world. I must have raved to and fro, screaming and crying upon God and Fate. I have a memory of horrible fatigue, as the long night of despair wore away; of looking in this impossible place and that; of groping among moonlit ruins and touching strange creatures in the black shadows; at last, of lying on the ground near the sphinx, and weeping with absolute wretchedness. I had nothing left but misery. Then I slept, and when I woke again it was full day, and a couple of sparrows were hopping round me on the turf within reach of my arm.

"I sat up in the freshness of the morning, trying to remember how I had got there, and why I had such a profound sense of desertion and despair. Then things came clear in my mind. With the plain, reasonable daylight, I could look my circumstances fairly in the face. I saw the wild folly of my frenzy overnight, and I could reason with myself. 'Suppose the worst?' I said. 'Suppose the machine altogether lost— perhaps destroyed? It behoves me to be calm and patient, to learn the way of the people, to get a clear idea of the method of my loss, and the means of getting materials and tools; so that in the end, perhaps, I may make another.' That would be my only hope, a poor hope, perhaps, but better than despair. And, after all, it was a beautiful and curious world.

"But probably the machine had only been taken away. Still, I must be calm and patient, find its hiding-place, and recover it by force or cunning. And with that I scrambled to my feet and looked about me, wondering where I could bathe. I felt weary, stiff, and travel-soiled. The freshness of the morning made me desire an equal freshness. I had exhausted my emotion. Indeed, as I went about my business, I found myself wondering at my intense excitement overnight. I made a careful examination of the ground about the little lawn. I wasted some time in futile questionings, conveyed, as well as I was able, to such of the little people as came by. They all failed to understand my gestures: some were simply stolid; some thought it was a jest, and laughed at me. I had the hardest task in

the world to keep my hands off their pretty laughing faces. It was a foolish impulse, but the devil begotten of fear and blind anger was ill curbed, and still eager to take advantage of my perplexity. The turf gave better counsel. I found a groove ripped in it, about midway between the pedestal of the sphinx and the marks of my feet where, on arrival, I had struggled with the overturned machine. There were other signs of removal about, with queer narrow footprints like those I could imagine made by a sloth. This directed my closer attention to the pedestal. It was, as I think I have said, of bronze. It was not a mere block, but highly decorated with deep framed panels on either side. I went and rapped at these. The pedestal was hollow. Examining the panels with care I found them discontinuous with the frames. There were no handles or keyholes, but possibly the panels, if they were doors, as I supposed, opened from within. One thing was clear enough to my mind. It took no very great mental effort to infer that my Time Machine was inside that pedestal. But how it got there was a different problem.

" I saw the heads of two orange-clad people coming through the bushes and under some blossom-covered apple-trees towards me. I turned smiling to them, and beckoned them to me. They came, and then, pointing to the bronze pedestal, I tried to intimate my wish to open it. But at my first gesture towards this they behaved very oddly. I don't know

how to convey their expression to you. Suppose you were to use a grossly improper gesture to a delicate-minded woman — it is how she would look. They went off as if they had received the last possible insult. I tried a sweet-looking little chap in white next, with exactly the same result. Somehow, his manner made me feel ashamed of myself. But, as you know, I wanted the Time Machine, and I tried him once more. As he turned off, like the others, my temper got the better of me. In three strides I was after him, had him by the loose part of his robe round the neck, and began dragging him towards the sphinx. Then I saw the horror and repugnance of his face, and all of a sudden I let him go.

" But I was not beaten yet. I banged with my fist at the bronze panels. I thought I heard something stir inside — to be explicit, I thought I heard a sound like a chuckle — but I must have been mistaken. Then I got a big pebble from the river, and came and hammered till I had flattened a coil in the decorations, and the verdigris came off in powdery flakes. The delicate little people must have heard me hammering in gusty outbreaks a mile away on either hand, but nothing came of it. I saw a crowd of them upon the slopes, looking furtively at me. At last, hot and tired, I sat down to watch the place. But I was too restless to watch long; I am too Occidental for a long vigil. I could work at a problem for years, but to wait inactive for twenty-four hours — that is another matter.

" I got up after a time, and began walking aimlessly through the bushes towards the hill again. 'Patience,' said I to myself. 'If you want your machine again you must leave that sphinx alone. If they mean to take your machine away, it's little good your wrecking their bronze panels, and if they don't, you will get it back as soon as you can ask for it. To sit among all those unknown things before a puzzle like that is hopeless. That way lies monomania. Face this world. Learn its ways, watch it, be careful of too hasty guesses at its meaning. In the end you will find clues to it all.' Then suddenly the humour of the situation came into my mind: the thought of the years I had spent in study and toil to get into the future age, and now my passion of anxiety to get out of it. I had made myself the most complicated and the most hopeless trap that ever a man devised. Although it was at my own expense, I could not help myself. I laughed aloud.

" Going through the big palace, it seemed to me that the little people avoided me. It may have been my fancy, or it may have had something to do with my hammering at the gates of bronze. Yet I felt tolerably sure of the avoidance. I was careful, however, to show no concern, and to abstain from any pursuit of them, and in the course of a day or two things got back to the old footing. I made what progress I could in the language, and, in addition, I pushed my explorations here and there. Either I missed some subtle point, or their language was excessively simple — almost exclusively composed of concrete substantives and verbs. There seemed to be few, if any, abstract terms, or little use of figurative language. Their sentences were usually simple and of two words, and I failed to convey or understand any but the simplest propositions. I determined to put the thought of my Time Machine, and the mystery of the bronze doors under the sphinx, as much as possible in a corner of memory, until my growing knowledge would lead me back to them in a natural way. Yet a certain feeling, you may understand, tethered me in a circle of a few miles round the point of my arrival.

" So far as I could see, all the world displayed the same exuberant richness as the Thames valley. From every hill I climbed I saw the same abundance of splendid buildings, endlessly varied in material and style; the same clustering thickets of evergreens, the same blossom-laden trees and tree ferns. Here and there water shone like silver, and beyond, the land rose into blue undulating hills, and so faded into the serenity of the sky. A peculiar feature, which presently attracted my attention, was the presence of certain circular wells, several, as it seemed to me, of a very great depth. One lay by the path up the hill, which I had followed during my first walk. Like the others it was rimmed with bronze, curiously wrought, and protected by a little cupola from the rain. Sitting by the side

of these wells, and peering down into the shafted darkness, I could see no gleam of water, nor could I start any reflection with a lighted match. But in all of them I heard a certain sound: a thud — thud — thud, like the beating of some big engine; and I discovered, from the flaring of my matches, that a steady current of air set down the shafts. Further, I threw a scrap of paper into the throat of one; and, instead of fluttering slowly down, it was at once sucked swiftly out of sight.

"After a time, too, I came to connect these wells with tall towers standing here and there upon the slopes; for above them there was often just such a flicker in the air as one sees on a hot day above a sun-scorched beach. Putting things together, I reached a strong suggestion of an extensive system of subterranean ventilation, whose true import it was difficult to imagine. I was at first inclined to associate it with the sanitary apparatus of these people. It was an obvious conclusion, but it was absolutely wrong.

"And here I must admit that I learned very little of drains and bells and modes of conveyance, and the like conveniences, during my time in this real future. In some of these visions of Utopias and coming times which I have read, there is a vast amount of detail about building, and social arrangements, and so forth. But while such details are easy enough to obtain when the whole world is contained in one's imagination, they are altogether inaccessible to a real traveller amid such realities as I found here.

Conceive the tale of London which a negro, fresh from Central Africa, would take back to his tribe! What would he know of railway companies, of social movements, of telephone and telegraph wires, of the Parcels Delivery Company, and postal orders and the like? Yet we, at least, should be willing enough to explain these things to him! And even of what he knew, how much could he make his untravelled friend either apprehend or believe? Then, think how narrow the gap between a negro and a white man of our own times, and how wide the interval between myself and these of the Golden Age! I was sensible of much which was unseen, and which contributed to my comfort; but, save for a general impression of automatic organisation, I fear I can convey very little of the difference to your mind.

"In the matter of sepulture, for instance, I could see no signs of crematoria nor anything suggestive of tombs. But it occurred to me that, possibly, there might be cemeteries (or crematoria) somewhere beyond the range of my explorings. This, again, was a question I deliberately put to myself, and my curiosity was at first entirely defeated upon the point. The thing puzzled me, and I was led to make a further remark, which puzzled me still more: that aged and infirm among this people there were none.

"I must confess that my satisfaction with my first theories of an automatic civilisation and a decadent humanity did not long

endure. Yet I could think of no other. Let me put my difficulties. The several big palaces I had explored were mere living places, great dining-halls and sleeping apartments. I could find no machinery, no appliances of any kind. Yet these people were clothed in pleasant fabrics that must at times need renewal, and their sandals, though undecorated, were fairly complex specimens of metal-work. Somehow such things must be made. And the little people displayed no vestige of a creative tendency. There were no shops, no workshops, no sign of importations among them. They spent all their time in playing gently, in bathing in the river, in making love in a half-playful fashion, in eating fruit and sleeping. I could not see how things were kept going.

"Then, again, about the Time Machine: something, I knew not what, had taken it into the hollow pedestal of the White Sphinx. *Why?* For the life of me I could not imagine. Those waterless wells, too, those flickering pillars. I felt I lacked a clue. I felt — how shall I put it? Suppose you found an inscription, with sentences here and there in excellent plain English, and, interpolated therewith, others made up of words, of letters even, absolutely unknown to you? Well, on the third day of my visit, that was how the world of Eight Hundred and Two Thousand Seven Hundred and One presented itself to me!

"That day, too, I made a friend — of a sort. It happened that, as I was watching some of the little people bathing in a shallow, one of them was seized with cramp, and began drifting downstream. The main current ran rather swiftly, but not too strongly for even a moderate swimmer. It will give you an idea, therefore, of the strange deficiency in these creatures, when I tell you that none made the slightest attempt to rescue the weakly-crying little thing which was drowning before their eyes. When I realised this, I hurriedly slipped off my clothes, and, wading in at a point lower down, I caught the poor mite, and drew her safe to land. A little rubbing of the limbs soon brought her round, and I had the satisfaction of seeing she was all right before I left her. I had got to such a low estimate of her kind that I did not expect any gratitude from her. In that, however, I was wrong.

"This happened in the morning. In the afternoon I met my little woman, as I believe it was, as I was returning towards my centre from an exploration: and she received me with cries of delight, and presented me with a big garland of flowers — evidently made for me and me alone. The thing took my imagination. Very possibly I had been feeling desolate. At any rate I did my best to display my appreciation of the gift. We were soon seated together in a little stone arbour, engaged in conversation, chiefly of smiles. The creature's friendliness affected me exactly as a child's might have done. We passed each other flowers, and

she kissed my hands. I did the same to hers. Then I tried talk, and found that her name was Weena, which, though I don't know what it meant, somehow seemed appropriate enough. That was the beginning of a queer friendship which lasted a week, and ended — as I will tell you!

"She was exactly like a child. She wanted to be with me always. She tried to follow me everywhere, and on my next journey out and about it went to my heart to tire her down, and leave her at last, exhausted and calling after me rather plaintively. But the problems of the world had to be mastered. I had not, I said to myself, come into the future to carry on a miniature flirtation. Yet her distress when I left her was very great, her expostulations at the parting were sometimes frantic, and I think, altogether, I had as much trouble as comfort from her devotion. Nevertheless she was, somehow, a very great comfort. I thought it was mere childish affection that made her cling to me. Until it was too late, I did not clearly know what I had inflicted upon her when I left her. Nor until it was too late did I clearly understand what she was to me. For, by merely seeming fond of me, and showing in her weak futile way that she cared for me, the little doll of a creature presently gave my return to the neighbourhood of the White Sphinx almost the feeling of coming home; and I would watch for her tiny figure of white and gold so soon as I came over the hill.

"It was from her, too, that I learned that fear had not yet left the world. She was fearless enough in the daylight and she had the oddest confidence in me; for once, in a foolish moment, I made threatening grimaces at her, and she simply laughed at them. But she dreaded the dark, dreaded shadows, dreaded black things. Darkness to her was the one thing dreadful. It was a singularly passionate emotion, and it set me thinking and observing. I discovered then, among other things, that these little people gathered into the great houses after dark, and slept in droves. To enter upon them without a light was to put them into a tumult of apprehension. I never found one out of doors, or one sleeping alone within doors, after dark. Yet I was still such a blockhead that I missed the lesson of that fear, and, in spite of Weena's distress, I insisted upon sleeping away from these slumbering multitudes.

"It troubled her greatly, but in the end her odd affection for me triumphed, and for five of the nights of our acquaintance, including the last night of all, she slept with her head pillowed on my arm. But my story slips away from me as I speak of her. It must have been the night before her rescue that I was awakened about dawn. I had been restless, dreaming most disagreeably that I was drowned, and that sea-anemones were feeling over my face with their soft palps. I woke with a start, and with an odd fancy that some greyish animal had just rushed

out of the chamber. I tried to get to sleep again, but I felt restless and uncomfortable. It was that dim grey hour when things are just creeping out of darkness, when everything is colourless and clear cut, and yet unreal. I got up, and went down into the great hall, and so out upon the flagstones in front of the palace. I thought I would make a virtue of necessity, and see the sunrise.

" The moon was setting, and the dying moonlight and the first pallor of dawn were mingled in a ghastly half-light. The bushes were inky black, the ground a sombre grey, the sky colourless and cheerless. And up the hill I thought I could see ghosts. Three several times, as I scanned the slope, I saw white figures. Twice I fancied I saw a solitary white, ape-like creature running rather quickly up the hill, and once near the ruins I saw a leash of them carrying some dark body. They moved hastily. I did not see what became of them. It seemed that they vanished among the bushes. The dawn was still indistinct, you must understand. I was feeling that chill, uncertain, early-morning feeling you may have known. I doubted my eyes.

" As the eastern sky grew brighter, and the light of the day came on and its vivid colouring returned upon the world once more, I scanned the view keenly. But I saw no vestige of my white figures. They were mere creatures of the half-light. ' They must have been ghosts,' I said; ' I wonder whence they dated.' For a queer notion of Grant Allen's came into my head, and amused

me. If each generation die and leave ghosts, he argued, the world at last will get overcrowded with them. On that theory they would have grown innumerable some Eight Hundred Thousand Years hence, and it was no great wonder to see four at once. But the jest was unsatisfying, and I was thinking of these figures all the morning, until Weena's rescue drove them out of my head. I associated them in some indefinite way with the white animal I had startled in my first passionate search for the Time Machine. But Weena was a pleasant substitute. Yet all the same, they were soon destined to take far deadlier possession of my mind.

" I think I have said how much hotter than our own was the weather of this Golden Age. I cannot account for it. It may be that the sun was hotter, or the earth nearer the sun. It is usual to assume that the sun will go on cooling steadily in the future. But people, unfamiliar with such speculations as those of the younger Darwin, forget that the planets must ultimately fall back one by one into the parent body. As these catastrophes occur, the sun will blaze with renewed energy; and it may be that some inner planet had suffered this fate. Whatever the reason, the fact remains that the sun was very much hotter than we know it.

" Well, one very hot morning — my fourth, I think — as I was seeking shelter from the heat and glare in a colossal ruin near the great house where I slept and

fed, there happened this strange thing. Clambering among these heaps of masonry, I found a narrow gallery whose end and side windows were blocked by fallen masses of stone. By contrast with the brilliancy outside, it seemed at first impenetrably dark to me. I entered it groping, for the change from light to blackness made spots of colour swim before me. Suddenly I halted spellbound. A pair of eyes, luminous by reflection against the daylight without, was watching me out of the darkness.

" The old instinctive dread of wild beasts came upon me. I clenched my hands and steadfastly looked into the glaring eyeballs. I was afraid to turn. Then the thought of the absolute security in which humanity appeared to be living came to my mind. And then I remembered that strange terror of the dark. Overcoming my fear to some extent, I advanced a step and spoke. I will admit that my voice was harsh and ill-controlled. I put out my hand and touched something soft. At once the eyes darted sideways, and something white ran past me. I turned with my heart in my mouth, and saw a queer little ape-like figure, its head held down in a peculiar manner, running across the sunlit space behind me. It blundered against a block of granite, staggered aside, and in a moment was hidden in a black shadow beneath another pile of ruined masonry.

" My impression of it is, of course, imperfect; but I know it was a dull white, and had strange large greyish-red eyes; also that there was flaxen hair on its head and down its back. But, as I say, it went too fast for me to see distinctly. I cannot even say whether it ran on all fours, or only with its forearms held very low. After an instant's pause I followed it into the second heap of ruins. I could not find it at first; but, after a time in the profound obscurity, I came upon one of those round well-like openings of which I have told you, half closed by a fallen pillar. A sudden thought came to me. Could this Thing have vanished down the shaft? I lit a match, and, looking down, I saw a small, white, moving creature, with large bright eyes which regarded me steadfastly as it retreated. It made me shudder. It was so like a human spider! It was clambering down the wall, and now I saw for the first time a number of metal foot and hand rests forming a kind of ladder down the shaft. Then the light burned my fingers and fell out of my hand, going out as it dropped, and when I had lit another the little monster had disappeared.

" I do not know how long I sat peering down that well. It was not for some time that I could succeed in persuading myself that the thing I had seen was human. But, gradually, the truth dawned on me: that Man had not remained one species, but had differentiated into two distinct animals: that my graceful children of the Upper World were not the sole descendants of our generation, but that this bleached, obscene, nocturnal Thing, which had

flashed before me, was also heir to all the ages.

" I thought of the flickering pillars and of my theory of an underground ventilation. I began to suspect their true import. And what, I wondered, was this Lemur doing in my scheme of a perfectly balanced organisation? How was it related to the indolent serenity of the beautiful Upper-worlders? And what was hidden down there, at the foot of that shaft? I sat upon the edge of the well telling myself that, at any rate, there was nothing to fear, and that there I must descend for the solution of my difficulties. And withal I was absolutely afraid to go! As I hesitated, two of the beautiful Upper-world people came running in their amorous sport across the daylight into the shadow. The male pursued the female, flinging flowers at her as he ran.

" They seemed distressed to find me, my arm against the overturned pillar, peering down the well. Apparently it was considered bad form to remark these apertures; for when I pointed to this one, and tried to frame a question about it in their tongue, they were still more visibly distressed and turned away. But they were interested by my matches, and I struck some to amuse them. I tried them again about the well, and again I failed. So presently I left them, meaning to go back to Weena, and see what I could get from her. But my mind was already in revolution; my guesses and impressions were slipping and sliding to a new adjustment. I had now a clue to the import of these wells, to the ventilating towers, to the mystery of the ghosts: to say nothing of a hint at the meaning of the bronze gates and the fate of the Time Machine! And very vaguely there came a suggestion towards the solution of the economic problem that had puzzled me.

" Here was the new view. Plainly, this second species of Man was subterranean. There were three circumstances in particular which made me think that its rare emergence above ground was the outcome of a long-continued underground habit. In the first place, there was the bleached look common in most animals that live largely in the dark — the white fish of the Kentucky caves, for instance. Then, those large eyes, with that capacity for reflecting light, are common features of nocturnal things — witness the owl and the cat. And last of all, that evident confusion in the sunshine, that hasty yet fumbling and awkward flight towards dark shadow, and that peculiar carriage of the head while in the light — all reinforced the theory of an extreme sensitiveness of the retina.

" Beneath my feet then the earth must be tunnelled enormously, and these tunnellings were the habitat of the new race. The presence of ventilating-shafts and wells along the hill slopes — everywhere, in fact, except along the river valley — showed how universal were its ramifications. What so natural, then, as to assume that it was in this artificial underworld that such work as was necessary to the

comfort of the daylight race was done? The notion was so plausible that I at once accepted it, and went on to assume the *how* of this splitting of the human species. I dare say you will anticipate the shape of my theory, though, for myself, I very soon felt that it fell far short of the truth.

"At first, proceeding from the problems of our own age, it seemed clear as daylight to me that the gradual widening of the present merely temporary and social difference between the Capitalist and the Labourer, was the key to the whole position. No doubt it will seem grotesque enough to you — and wildly incredible! — and yet even now there are existing circumstances to point that way. There is a tendency to utilise underground space for the less ornamental purposes of civilisation; there is the Metropolitan Railway in London, for instance, there are new electric railways, there are subways, there are underground workrooms and restaurants, and they increase and multiply. Evidently, I thought, this tendency had increased till Industry had gradually lost its birthright in the sky. I mean that it had gone deeper and deeper into larger and ever larger underground factories, spending a still-increasing amount of its time therein, till, in the end —! Even now, does not an East-end worker live in such artificial conditions as practically to be cut off from the natural surface of the earth?

"Again, the exclusive tendency of richer people — due, no doubt,

to the increasing refinement of their education, and the widening gulf between them and the rude violence of the poor — is already leading to the closing, in their interest, of considerable portions of the surface of the land. About London, for instance, perhaps half the prettier country is shut in against intrusion. And this same widening gulf — which is due to the length and expense of the higher educational process and the increased facilities for and temptations towards refined habits on the part of the rich — will make that exchange between class and class, that promotion by inter-marriage which at present retards the splitting of our species along lines of social stratification, less and less frequent. So, in the end, above ground you must have the Haves, pursuing pleasure and comfort and beauty, and below ground the Havenots; the Workers getting continually adapted to the conditions of their labour. Once they were there they would, no doubt, have to pay rent, and not a little of it, for the ventilation of their caverns; and if they refused, they would starve or be suffocated for arrears. Such of them as were so constituted as to be miserable and rebellious would die; and, in the end, the balance being permanent, the survivors would become as well adapted to the conditions of underground life, and as happy in their way, as the Upper-world people were to theirs. As it seemed to me, the refined beauty and the etiolated pallor followed naturally enough.

"The great triumph of Hu-

manity I had dreamed of took a different shape in my mind. It had been no such triumph of moral education and general co-operation as I had imagined. Instead, I saw a real aristocracy, armed with a perfected science and working to a logical conclusion the industrial system of today. Its triumph had not been simply a triumph over nature, but a triumph over nature and the fellow-man. This, I must warn you, was my theory at the time. I had no convenient cicerone in the pattern of the Utopian books. My explanation may be absolutely wrong. I still think it is the most plausible one. But even on this supposition the balanced civilisation that was at last attained must have long since passed its zenith, and was now far fallen into decay. The too-perfect security of the Upper-worlders had led them to a slow movement of degeneration, to a general dwindling in size, strength, and intelligence. That I could see clearly enough already. What had happened to the Under-grounders I did not yet suspect; but, from what I had seen of the Morlocks — that, by the by, was the name by which these creatures were called — I could imagine that the modification of the human type was even far more profound than among the 'Eloi,' the beautiful race that I already knew.

"Then came troublesome doubts. Why had the Morlocks taken my Time Machine? For I felt sure it was they who had taken it. Why, too, if the Eloi were masters, could they not re-store the machine to me? And why were they so terribly afraid of the dark? I proceeded, as I have said, to question Weena about this Underworld, but here again I was disappointed. At first she would not understand my questions, and presently she refused to answer them. She shivered as though the topic was unendurable. And when I pressed her, perhaps a little harshly, she burst into tears. They were the only tears, except my own, I ever saw in that Golden Age. When I saw them I ceased abruptly to trouble about the Morlocks, and was only concerned in banishing these signs of the human inheritance from Weena's eyes. And very soon she was smiling and clapping her hands, while I solemnly burnt a match."

§6

"IT may seem odd to you, but it was two days before I could follow up the new-found clue in what was manifestly the proper way. I felt a peculiar shrinking from those pallid bodies. They were just the half-bleached colour of the worms and things one sees preserved in spirit in a zoological museum. And they were filthily cold to the touch. Probably my shrinking was largely due to the sympathetic influence

of the Eloi, whose disgust of the Morlocks I now began to appreciate.

"The next night I did not sleep well. Probably my health was a little disordered. I was oppressed with perplexity and doubt. Once or twice I had a feeling of intense fear for which I could perceive no definite reason. I remember creeping noiselessly into the great hall where the little people were sleeping in the moonlight — that night Weena was among them — and feeling reassured by their presence. It occurred to me, even then, that in the course of a few days the moon must pass through its last quarter, and the nights grow dark, when the appearances of these unpleasant creatures from below, these whitened Lemurs, this new vermin that had replaced the old, might be more abundant. And on both these days I had the restless feeling of one who shirks an inevitable duty. I felt assured that the Time Machine was only to be recovered by boldly penetrating these underground mysteries. Yet I could not face the mystery. If only I had had a companion it would have been different. But I was so horribly alone, and even to clamber down into the darkness of the well appalled me. I don't know if you will understand my feeling, but I never felt quite safe at my back.

" It was this restlessness, this insecurity, perhaps, that drove me further and further afield in my exploring expeditions. Going to the south-westward towards the rising country that is now called Combe Wood, I observed far off, in the direction of nineteenth-century Banstead, a vast green structure, different in character from any I had hitherto seen. It was larger than the largest of the palaces or ruins I knew, and the façade had an Oriental look: the face of it having the lustre, as well as the pale-green tint, a kind of bluish-green, of a certain type of Chinese porcelain. This difference in aspect suggested a difference in use, and I was minded to push on and explore. But the day was growing late, and I had come upon the sight of the place after a long and tiring circuit; so I resolved to hold over the adventure for the following day, and I returned to the welcome and the caresses of little Weena. But next morning I perceived clearly enough that my curiosity regarding the Palace of Green Porcelain was a piece of self-deception, to enable me to shirk, by another day, an experience I dreaded. I resolved I would make the descent without further waste of time, and started out in the early morning towards a well near the ruins of granite and aluminium.

" Little Weena ran with me. She danced beside me to the well, but when she saw me lean over the mouth and look downward, she seemed strangely disconcerted. ' Good-bye, little Weena,' I said, kissing her; and then, putting her down, I began to feel over the parapet for the climbing hooks. Rather hastily, I may as well confess, for I feared my courage might leak away! At first she watched me in amazement.

Then she gave a most piteous cry, and, running to me, began to pull at me with her little hands. I think her opposition nerved me rather to proceed. I shook her off, perhaps a little roughly, and in another moment I was in the throat of the well. I saw her agonised face over the parapet, and smiled to reassure her. Then I had to look down at the unstable hooks to which I clung.

"I had to clamber down a shaft of perhaps two hundred yards. The descent was effected by means of metallic bars projecting from the sides of the well, and these being adapted to the needs of a creature much smaller and lighter than myself, I was speedily cramped and fatigued by the descent. And not simply fatigued! One of the bars bent suddenly under my weight, and almost swung me off into the blackness beneath. For a moment I hung by one hand, and after that experience I did not dare to rest again. Though my arms and back were presently acutely painful, I went on clambering down the sheer descent with as quick a motion as possible. Glancing upward, I saw the aperture, a small blue disk, in which a star was visible, while little Weena's head showed as a round black projection. The thudding sound of a machine below grew louder and more oppressive. Everything save that little disk above was profoundly dark, and when I looked up again Weena had disappeared.

"I was in an agony of discomfort. I had some thought of trying to go up the shaft again, and leave the Underworld alone. But even while I turned this over in my mind I continued to descend. At last, with intense relief, I saw dimly coming up, a foot to the right of me, a slender loophole in the wall. Swinging myself in, I found it was the aperture of a narrow horizontal tunnel in which I could lie down and rest. It was not too soon. My arms ached, my back was cramped, and I was trembling with the prolonged terror of a fall. Besides this, the unbroken darkness had had a distressing effect upon my eyes. The air was full of the throb and hum of machinery pumping air down the shaft.

"I do not know how long I lay. I was roused by a soft hand touching my face. Starting up in the darkness I snatched at my matches and, hastily striking one, I saw three stooping white creatures similar to the one I had seen above ground in the ruin, hastily retreating before the light. Living, as they did, in what appeared to me impenetrable darkness, their eyes were abnormally large and sensitive, just as are the pupils of the abysmal fishes, and they reflected the light in the same way. I have no doubt they could see me in that rayless obscurity, and they did not seem to have any fear of me apart from the light. But, so soon as I struck a match in order to see them, they fled incontinently, vanishing into dark gutters and tunnels, from which their eyes glared at me in the strangest fashion.

"I tried to call to them, but the language they had was apparently different from that of the Upper-world people; so that I

was needs left to my own unaided efforts, and the thought of flight before exploration was even then in my mind. But I said to myself, 'You are in for it now,' and, feeling my way along the tunnel, I found the noise of machinery grow louder. Presently the walls fell away from me, and I came to a large open space, and, striking another match, saw that I had entered a vast arched cavern, which stretched into utter darkness beyond the range of my light. The view I had of it was as much as one could see in the burning of a match.

"Necessarily my memory is vague. Great shapes like big machines rose out of the dimness, and cast grotesque black shadows, in which dim spectral Morlocks sheltered from the glare. The place, by the bye, was very stuffy and oppressive, and the faint halitus of freshly-shed blood was in the air. Some way down the central vista was a little table of white metal, laid with what seemed a meal. The Morlocks at any rate were carnivorous! Even at the time, I remember wondering what large animal could have survived to furnish the red joint I saw. It was all very indistinct: the heavy smell, the big unmeaning shapes, the obscene figures lurking in the shadows, and only waiting for the darkness to come at me again! Then the match burned down, and stung my fingers, and fell, a wriggling red spot in the blackness.

"I have thought since how particularly ill-equipped I was for such an experience. When I had started with the Time Machine, I had started with the absurd assumption that the men of the Future would certainly be infinitely ahead of ourselves in all their appliances. I had come without arms, without medicine, without anything to smoke — at times I missed tobacco frightfully! — even without enough matches. If only I had thought of a Kodak! I could have flashed that glimpse of the Underworld in a second, and examined it at leisure. But, as it was, I stood there with only the weapons and the powers that Nature had endowed me with — hands, feet, and teeth; these, and four safety matches that still remained to me.

"I was afraid to push my way in among all this machinery in the dark, and it was only with my last glimpse of light I discovered that my store of matches had run low. It had never occurred to me until that moment that there was any need to economise them, and I had wasted almost half the box in astonishing the Upper-worlders, to whom fire was a novelty. Now, as I say, I had four left, and while I stood in the dark, a hand touched mine, lank fingers came feeling over my face, and I was sensible of a peculiar unpleasant odour. I fancied I heard the breathing of a crowd of those dreadful little beings about me. I felt the box of matches in my hand being gently disengaged, and other hands behind me plucking at my clothing. The sense of these unseen creatures examining me was indescribably unpleasant. The sudden realisation of my ignorance of their ways of thinking and doing came home to me very vividly in

the darkness. I shouted at them as loudly as I could. They started away, and then I could feel them approaching me again. They clutched at me more boldly, whispering odd sounds to each other. I shivered violently, and shouted again — rather discordantly. This time they were not so seriously alarmed, and they made a queer laughing noise as they came back at me. I will confess I was horribly frightened. I determined to strike another match and escape under the protection of its glare. I did so, and eking out the flicker with a scrap of paper from my pocket, I made good my retreat to the narrow tunnel. But I had scarce entered this when my light was blown out, and in the blackness I could hear the Morlocks rustling like wind among leaves, and pattering like the rain, as they hurried after me.

"In a moment I was clutched by several hands, and there was no mistaking that they were trying to haul me back. I struck another light, and waved it in their dazzled faces. You can scarce imagine how nauseatingly inhuman they looked — those pale, chinless faces and great, lidless, pinkish-grey eyes! — as they stared in their blindness and bewilderment. But I did not stay to look, I promise you: I retreated again, and when my second match had ended, I struck my third. It had almost burned through when I reached the opening into the shaft. I lay down on the edge, for the throb of the great pump below made me giddy. Then I felt sideways for the projecting hooks, and, as I did so, my feet were grasped from behind, and I was violently tugged backward. I lit my last match . . . and it incontinently went out. But I had my hand on the climbing bars now, and, kicking violently, I disengaged myself from the clutches of the Morlocks, and was speedily clambering up the shaft, while they stayed peering and blinking up at me: all but one little wretch who followed me for some way, and well-nigh secured my boot as a trophy.

"That climb seemed interminable to me. With the last twenty or thirty feet of it a deadly nausea came upon me. I had the greatest difficulty in keeping my hold. The last few yards was a frightful struggle against this faintness. Several times my head swam, and I felt all the sensations of falling. At last, however, I got over the well-mouth somehow, and staggered out of the ruin into the blinding sunlight. I fell upon my face. Even the soil smelt sweet and clean. Then I remember Weena kissing my hands and ears, and the voices of others among the Eloi. Then, for a time, I was insensible."

§7

"Now, indeed, I seemed in a worse case than before. Hitherto, except during my night's anguish at the loss of the Time Machine, I had felt a sustaining hope of

ultimate escape, but that hope was staggered by these new discoveries. Hitherto I had merely thought myself impeded by the childish simplicity of the little people, and by some unknown forces which I had only to understand to overcome; but there was an altogether new element in the sickening quality of the Morlocks — a something inhuman and malign. Instinctively I loathed them. Before, I had felt as a man might feel who had fallen into a pit; my concern was with the pit and how to get out of it. Now I felt like a beast in a trap, whose enemy would come upon him soon.

" The enemy I dreaded may surprise you. It was the darkness of the new moon. Weena had put this into my head by some at first incomprehensible remarks about the Dark Nights. It was not now such a very difficult problem to guess what the coming Dark Nights might mean. The moon was on the wane: each night there was a longer interval of darkness. And I now understood to some slight degree at least the reason of the fear of the little Upper-world people for the dark. I wondered vaguely what foul villainy it might be that the Morlocks did under the new moon. I felt pretty sure now that my second hypothesis was all wrong. The Upper-world people might once have been the favoured aristocracy, and the Morlocks their mechanical servants; but that had long since passed away. The two species that had resulted from the evolution of man were sliding down towards, or had already arrived at, an altogether new relationship. The Eloi, like the Carlovingian kings, had decayed to a mere beautiful futility. They still possessed the earth on sufferance: since the Morlocks, subterranean for innumerable generations, had come at last to find the daylit surface intolerable. And the Morlocks made their garments, I inferred, and maintained them in their habitual needs, perhaps through the survival of an old habit of service. They did it as a standing horse paws with his foot, or as a man enjoys killing animals in sport: because ancient and departed necessities had impressed it on the organism. But, clearly, the old order was already in part reversed. The Nemesis of the delicate ones was creeping on apace. Ages ago, thousands of generations ago, man had thrust his brother man out of the ease and the sunshine. And now that brother was coming back — changed! Already the Eloi had begun to learn one old lesson anew. They were becoming reacquainted with Fear. And suddenly there came into my head the memory of the meat I had seen in the Underworld. It seemed odd how it floated into my mind: not stirred up as it were by the current of my meditations, but coming in almost like a question from outside. I tried to recall the form of it. I had a vague sense of something familiar, but I could not tell what it was at the time.

" Still, however helpless the little people in the presence of their mysterious Fear, I was differently

constituted. I came out of this age of ours, this ripe prime of the human race, when Fear does not paralyse and mystery has lost its terrors. I at least would defend myself. Without further delay I determined to make myself arms and a fastness where I might sleep. With that refuge as a base, I could face this strange world with some of that confidence I had lost in realising to what creatures night by night I lay exposed. I felt I could never sleep again until my bed was secure from them. I shuddered with horror to think how they must already have examined me.

"I wandered during the afternoon along the valley of the Thames, but found nothing that commended itself to my mind as inaccessible. All the buildings and trees seemed easily practicable to such dexterous climbers as the Morlocks, to judge by their wells, must be. Then the tall pinnacles of the Palace of Green Porcelain and the polished gleam of its walls came back to my memory; and in the evening, taking Weena like a child upon my shoulder, I went up the hills towards the south-west. The distance, I had reckoned, was seven or eight miles, but it must have been nearer eighteen. I had first seen the place on a moist afternoon when distances are deceptively diminished. In addition, the heel of one of my shoes was loose, and a nail was working through the sole — they were comfortable old shoes I wore about indoors — so that I was lame. And it was already long past sunset when I came in sight of the palace, silhouetted black against the pale yellow of the sky.

"Weena had been hugely delighted when I began to carry her, but after a time she desired me to let her down, and ran along by the side of me, occasionally darting off on either hand to pick flowers to stick in my pockets. My pockets had always puzzled Weena, but at the last she had concluded that they were an eccentric kind of vase for floral decoration. At least she utilised them for that purpose. And that reminds me! In changing my jacket I found . . ."

The Time Traveller paused, put his hand into his pocket, and silently placed two withered flowers, not unlike very large white mallows, upon the little table. Then he resumed his narrative.

"As the hush of evening crept over the world and we proceeded over the hill crest towards Wimbledon, Weena grew tired and wanted to return to the house of grey stone. But I pointed out the distant pinnacles of the Palace of Green Porcelain to her, and contrived to make her understand that we were seeking a refuge there from her Fear. You know that great pause that comes upon things before the dusk? Even the breeze stops in the trees. To me there is always an air of expectation about that evening stillness. The sky was clear, remote, and empty save for a few horizontal bars far down in the sunset. Well, that night the expectation took the colour of my fears. In that darkling calm my senses seemed preternaturally sharpened. I fancied I could even feel the hollow-

ness of the ground beneath my feet: could, indeed, almost see through it the Morlocks on their ant-hill going hither and thither and waiting for the dark. In my excitement I fancied that they would receive my invasion of their burrows as a declaration of war. And why had they taken my Time Machine?

" So we went on in the quiet, and the twilight deepened into night. The clear blue of the distance faded, and one star after another came out. The ground grew dim and the trees black. Weena's fears and her fatigue grew upon her. I took her in my arms and talked to her and caressed her. Then, as the darkness grew deeper, she put her arms round my neck, and, closing her eyes, tightly pressed her face against my shoulder. So we went down a long slope into a valley, and there in the dimness I almost walked into a little river. This I waded, and went up the opposite side of the valley, past a number of sleeping houses, and by a statue — a Faun, or some such figure, *minus* the head. Here, too, were acacias. So far I had seen nothing of the Morlocks, but it was yet early in the night, and the darker hours before the old moon rose were still to come.

" From the brow of the next hill I saw a thick wood spreading wide and black before me. I hesitated at this. I could see no end to it, either to the right or the left. Feeling tired — my feet in particular, were very sore — I carefully lowered Weena from my shoulder as I halted, and sat down upon the turf. I could no longer see the Palace of Green Porcelain, and I was in doubt of my direction. I looked into the thickness of the wood and thought of what it might hide. Under that dense tangle of branches one would be out of sight of the stars. Even were there no other lurking danger — a danger I did not care to let my imagination loose upon — there would still be all the roots to stumble over and the tree boles to strike against. I was very tired, too, after the excitements of the day; so I decided that I would not face it, but would pass the night upon the open hill.

" Weena, I was glad to find, was fast asleep. I carefully wrapped her in my jacket, and sat down beside her to wait for the moonrise. The hillside was quiet and deserted, but from the black of the wood there came now and then a stir of living things. Above me shone the stars, for the night was very clear. I felt a certain sense of friendly comfort in their twinkling. All the old constellations had gone from the sky, however: that slow movement which is imperceptible in a hundred human lifetimes, had long since re-arranged them in unfamiliar groupings. But the Milky Way, it seemed to me, was still the same tattered streamer of star-dust as of yore. Southward (as I judged it) was a very bright red star that was new to me: it was even more splendid than our own green Sirius. And amid all these scintillating points of light one bright planet shone kindly

and steadily like the face of an old friend.

"Looking at these stars suddenly dwarfed my own troubles and all the gravities of terrestrial life. I thought of their unfathomable distance, and the slow inevitable drift of their movements out of the unknown past into the unknown future. I thought of the great precessional cycle that the pole of the earth describes. Only forty times had that silent revolution occurred during all the years that I had traversed. And during these few revolutions all the activity, all the traditions, the complex organisations, the nations, languages, literatures, aspirations, even the mere memory of Man as I knew him, had been swept out of existence. Instead were these frail creatures who had forgotten their high ancestry, and the white Things of which I went in terror. Then I thought of the Great Fear that was between the two species, and for the first time, with a sudden shiver, came the clear knowledge of what the meat I had seen might be. Yet it was too horrible! I looked at little Weena sleeping beside me, her face white and starlike under the stars, and forthwith dismissed the thought.

"Through that long night I held my mind off the Morlocks as well as I could, and whiled away the time by trying to fancy I could find signs of the old constellations in the new confusion. The sky kept very clear, except for a hazy cloud or so. No doubt I dozed at times. Then, as my vigil wore on, came a faintness in the eastward sky, like the reflection of some colourless fire, and the old moon rose, thin and peaked and white. And close behind, and overtaking it, and overflowing it, the dawn came, pale at first, and then growing pink and warm. No Morlocks had approached us. Indeed, I had seen none upon the hill that night. And in the confidence of renewed day it almost seemed to me that my fear had been unreasonable. I stood up and found my foot with the loose heel swollen at the ankle and painful under the heel; so I sat down again, took off my shoes, and flung them away.

"I awakened Weena, and we went down into the wood, now green and pleasant instead of black and forbidding. We found some fruit wherewith to break our fast. We soon met others of the dainty ones, laughing and dancing in the sunlight as though there was no such thing in nature as the night. And then I thought once more of the meat that I had seen. I felt assured now of what it was, and from the bottom of my heart I pitied this last feeble rill from the great flood of humanity. Clearly, at some time in the Long-Ago of human decay the Morlocks' food had run short. Possibly they had lived on rats and suchlike vermin. Even now man is far less discriminating and exclusive in his food than he was — far less than any monkey. His prejudice against human flesh is no deep-seated instinct. And so these inhuman sons of men — ! I tried to look at

the thing in a scientific spirit. After all, they were less human and more remote than our cannibal ancestors of three or four thousand years ago. And the intelligence that would have made this state of things a torment had gone. Why should I trouble myself? These Eloi were mere fatted cattle, which the ant-like Morlocks preserved and preyed upon — probably saw to the breeding of. And there was Weena dancing at my side!

"Then I tried to preserve myself from the horror that was coming upon me, by regarding it as a rigorous punishment of human selfishness. Man had been content to live in ease and delight upon the labours of his fellow-man, had taken Necessity as his watchword and excuse, and in the fulness of time Necessity had come home to him. I even tried a Carlyle-like scorn of this wretched aristocracy in decay. But this attitude of mind was impossible. However great their intellectual degradation, the Eloi had kept too much of the human form not to claim my sympathy, and to make me perforce a sharer in their degradation and their Fear.

"I had at that time very vague ideas as to the course I should pursue. My first was to secure some safe place of refuge, and to make myself such arms of metal or stone as I could contrive. That necessity was immediate. In the next place, I hoped to procure some means of fire, so that I should have the weapon of a torch at hand, for nothing, I knew, would be more efficient against these Morlocks. Then I wanted to arrange some contrivance to break open the doors of bronze under the White Sphinx. I had in mind a battering-ram. I had a persuasion that if I could enter these doors and carry a blaze of light before me I should discover the Time Machine and escape. I could not imagine the Morlocks were strong enough to move it far away. Weena I had resolved to bring with me to our own time. And turning such schemes over in my mind I pursued our way towards the building which my fancy had chosen as our dwelling."

§8

"I found the Palace of Green Porcelain, when we approached it about noon, deserted and falling into ruin. Only ragged vestiges of glass remained in its windows, and great sheets of the green facing had fallen away from the corroded metallic framework. It lay very high upon a turfy down, and looking northeastward before I entered it, I was surprised to see a large estuary, or even creek, where I judged Wandsworth and Battersea must once have been. I thought then — though I never followed up the thought — of what might have happened, or might be happen-

ing, to the living things in the sea.

" The material of the Palace proved on examination to be indeed porcelain, and along the face of it I saw an inscription in some unknown character. I thought, rather foolishly, that Weena might help me to interpret this, but I only learned that the bare idea of writing had never entered her head. She always seemed to me, I fancy, more human than she was, perhaps because her affection was so human.

" Within the big valves of the door — which were open and broken — we found, instead of the customary hall, a long gallery lit by many side windows. At the first glance I was reminded of a museum. The tiled floor was thick with dust, and a remarkable array of miscellaneous objects was shrouded in the same grey covering. Then I perceived, standing strange and gaunt in the centre of the hall, what was clearly the lower part of a huge skeleton. I recognised by the oblique feet that it was some extinct creature after the fashion of the Megatherium. The skull and the upper bones lay beside it in the thick dust, and in one place, where rain-water had dropped through a leak in the roof, the thing itself had been worn away. Further in the gallery was the huge skeleton barrel of a Brontosaurus. My museum hypothesis was confirmed. Going towards the side I found what appeared to be sloping shelves, and, clearing away the thick dust, I found the old familiar glass cases of our own time.

But they must have been airtight, to judge from the fair preservation of some of their contents.

" Clearly we stood among the ruins of some latter-day South Kensington! Here, apparently, was the Palæontological Section, and a very splendid array of fossils it must have been, though the inevitable process of decay that had been staved off for a time, and had, through the extinction of bacteria and fungi, lost ninety-nine hundredths of its force, was, nevertheless, with extreme sureness if with extreme slowness at work again upon all its treasures. Here and there I found traces of the little people in the shape of rare fossils broken to pieces or threaded in strings upon reeds. And the cases had in some instances been bodily removed — by the Morlocks as I judged. The place was very silent. The thick dust deadened our footsteps. Weena, who had been rolling a sea-urchin down the sloping glass of a case, presently came, as I stared about me, and very quietly took my hand and stood beside me.

" And at first I was so much surprised by this ancient monument of an intellectual age, that I gave no thought to the possibilities it presented. Even my preoccupation about the Time Machine receded a little from my mind.

" To judge from the size of the place, this Palace of Green Porcelain had a great deal more in it than a Gallery of Palæontology; possibly historical galleries; it might be, even a library! To me,

at least in my present circumstances, these would be vastly more interesting than this spectacle of old-time geology in decay. Exploring, I found another short gallery running transversely to the first. This appeared to be devoted to minerals, and the sight of a block of sulphur set my mind running on gun-powder. But I could find no saltpetre; indeed, no nitrates of any kind. Doubtless they had deliquesced ages ago. Yet the sulphur hung in my mind, and set up a train of thinking. As for the rest of the contents of that gallery, though on the whole they were the best preserved of all I saw, I had little interest. I am no specialist in mineralogy, and I went on down a very ruinous aisle running parallel to the first hall I had entered. Apparently this section had been devoted to natural history, but everything had long since passed out of recognition. A few shrivelled and blackened vestiges of what had once been stuffed animals, desiccated mummies in jars that had once held spirit, a brown dust of departed plants; that was all! I was sorry for that, because I should have been glad to trace the patient readjustments by which the conquest of animated nature had been attained. Then we came to a gallery of simply colossal proportions, but singularly ill-lit, the floor of it running downward at a slight angle from the end at which I entered. At intervals white globes hung from the ceiling — many of them cracked and smashed — which suggested that

originally the place had been artificially lit. Here I was more in my element, for rising on either side of me were the huge bulks of big machines, all greatly corroded and many broken down, but some still fairly complete. You know I have a certain weakness for mechanism, and I was inclined to linger among these: the more so as for the most part they had the interest of puzzles, and I could make only the vaguest guesses at what they were for. I fancied that if I could solve their puzzles I should find myself in possession of powers that might be of use against the Morlocks.

" Suddenly Weena came very close to my side. So suddenly that she startled me. Had it not been for her I do not think I should have noticed that the floor of the gallery sloped at all.[1] The end I had come in at was quite above ground, and was lit by rare slit-like windows. As you went down the length, the ground came up against these windows, until at last there was a pit like the 'area' of a London house before each, and only a narrow line of daylight at the top. I went slowly along, puzzling about the machines, and had been too intent upon them to notice the gradual diminution of the light, until Weena's increasing apprehensions drew my attention. Then I saw that the gallery ran down at last into a thick darkness. I hesitated, and then,

[1] It may be, of course, that the floor did not slope, but that the museum was built into the side of a hill. — ED.

as I looked round me, I saw that the dust was less abundant and its surface less even. Further away towards the dimness, it appeared to be broken by a number of small narrow footprints. My sense of the immediate presence of the Morlocks revived at that. I felt that I was wasting my time in this academic examination of machinery. I called to mind that it was already far advanced in the afternoon, and that I had still no weapon, no refuge, and no means of making a fire. And then down in the remote blackness of the gallery I heard a peculiar pattering, and the same odd noises I had heard down the well.

"I took Weena's hand. Then, struck with a sudden idea, I left her and turned to a machine from which projected a lever not unlike those in a signal-box. Clambering upon the stand, and grasping this lever in my hands, I put all my weight upon it sideways. Suddenly Weena, deserted in the central aisle, began to whimper. I had judged the strength of the lever pretty correctly, for it snapped after a minute's strain, and I rejoined her with a mace in my hand more than sufficient, I judged, for any Morlock skull I might encounter. And I longed very much to kill a Morlock or so. Very inhuman, you may think, to want to go killing one's own descendants! But it was impossible, somehow, to feel any humanity in the things. Only my disinclination to leave Weena, and a persuasion that if I began to slake my thirst for murder my Time Machine might suffer, restrained me from going straight down the gallery and killing the brutes I heard.

"Well, mace in one hand and Weena in the other, I went out of that gallery and into another and still larger one, which at the first glance reminded me of a military chapel hung with tattered flags. The brown and charred rags that hung from the sides of it, I presently recognised as the decaying vestiges of books. They had long since dropped to pieces, and every semblance of print had left them. But here and there were warped boards and cracked metallic clasps that told the tale well enough. Had I been a literary man I might, perhaps, have moralised upon the futility of all ambition. But as it was, the thing that struck me with keenest force was the enormous waste of labour to which this sombre wilderness of rotting paper testified. At the time I will confess that I thought chiefly of the *Philosophical Transactions* and my own seventeen papers upon physical optics.

"Then, going up a broad staircase, we came to what may once have been a gallery of technical chemistry. And here I had not a little hope of useful discoveries. Except at one end where the roof had collapsed, this gallery was well preserved. I went eagerly to every unbroken case. And at last, in one of the really air-tight cases, I found a box of matches. Very eagerly I tried them. They were perfectly good.

They were not even damp. I turned to Weena. 'Dance,' I cried to her in her own tongue. For now I had a weapon indeed against the horrible creatures we feared. And so, in that derelict museum, upon the thick soft carpeting of dust, to Weena's huge delight, I solemnly performed a kind of composite dance, whistling *The Land of the Leal* as cheerfully as I could. In part it was a modest *cancan,* in part a step dance, in part a skirt dance (so far as my tail-coat permitted), and in part original. For I am naturally inventive, as you know.

"Now, I still think that for this box of matches to have escaped the wear of time for immemorial years was a most strange, as for me it was a most fortunate, thing. Yet, oddly enough, I found a far unlikelier substance, and that was camphor. I found it in a sealed jar, that by chance, I suppose, had been really hermetically sealed. I fancied at first that it was paraffin wax, and smashed the glass accordingly. But the odour of camphor was unmistakable. In the universal decay this volatile substance had chanced to survive, perhaps through many thousands of centuries. It reminded me of a sepia painting I had once seen done from the ink of a fossil Belemnite that must have perished and become fossilised millions of years ago. I was about to throw it away, but I remembered that it was inflammable and burned with a good bright flame — was, in fact, an excellent candle — and I put it in my pocket. I found no explosives, however, nor any means of breaking down the bronze doors. As yet my iron crowbar was the most helpful thing I had chanced upon. Nevertheless I left that gallery greatly elated.

" I cannot tell you all the story of that long afternoon. It would require a great effort of memory to recall my explorations in at all the proper order. I remember a long gallery of rusting stands of arms, and how I hesitated between my crowbar and a hatchet or a sword. I could not carry both, however, and my bar of iron promised best against the bronze gates. There were numbers of guns, pistols, and rifles. The most were masses of rust, but many were of some new metal, and still fairly sound. But any cartridges or powder there may once have been had rotted into dust. One corner I saw was charred and shattered: perhaps, I thought, by an explosion among the specimens. In another place was a vast array of idols — Polynesian, Mexican, Grecian, Phœnician, every country on earth I should think. And here, yielding to an irresistible impulse, I wrote my name upon the nose of a steatite monster from South America that particularly took my fancy.

" As the evening drew on, my interest waned. I went through gallery after gallery, dusty, silent, often ruinous, the exhibits sometimes mere heaps of rust and lignite, sometimes fresher. In one place I suddenly found myself near the model of a tin-mine,

and then by the merest accident I discovered, in an air-tight case, two dynamite cartridges! I shouted 'Eureka,' and smashed the case with joy. Then came a doubt. I hesitated. Then, selecting a little side gallery, I made my essay. I never felt such a disappointment as I did in waiting five, ten, fifteen minutes for an explosion that never came. Of course the things were dummies, as I might have guessed from their presence. I really believe that, had they not been so, I should have rushed off incontinently and blown Sphinx, bronze doors, and (as it proved) my chances of finding the Time Machine, all together into non-existence.

"It was after that, I think, that we came to a little open court within the palace. It was turfed, and had three fruit-trees. So we rested and refreshed ourselves. Towards sunset I began to consider our position. Night was creeping upon us, and my inaccessible hiding-place had still to be found. But that troubled me very little now. I had in my possession a thing that was, perhaps, the best of all defences against the Morlocks — I had matches! I had the camphor in my pocket, too, if a blaze were needed. It seemed to me that the best thing we could do would be to pass the night in the open, protected by a fire. In the morning there was the getting of the Time Machine. Towards that, as yet, I had only my iron mace. But now, with my growing knowledge, I felt very differently towards those bronze doors. Up to this, I had refrained from forcing them, largely because of the mystery on the other side. They had never impressed me as being very strong, and I hoped to find my bar of iron not altogether inadequate for the work."

§ 9

"We emerged from the palace while the sun was still in part above the horizon. I was determined to reach the White Sphinx early the next morning, and ere the dusk I purposed pushing through the woods that had stopped me on the previous journey. My plan was to go as far as possible that night, and then, building a fire, to sleep in the protection of its glare. Accordingly, as we went along I gathered any sticks or dried grass I saw, and presently had my arms full of such litter. Thus loaded, our progress was slower than I had anticipated, and besides Weena was tired. And I began to suffer from sleepiness too; so that it was full night before we reached the wood. Upon the shrubby hill of its edge Weena would have stopped, fearing the darkness before us; but a singular sense of impending calamity, that should indeed have served me as a warning, drove me onward. I

had been without sleep for a night and two days, and I was feverish and irritable. I felt sleep coming upon me, and the Morlocks with it.

" While we hesitated, among the black bushes behind us, and dim against their blackness, I saw three crouching figures. There was scrub and long grass all about us, and I did not feel safe from their insidious approach. The forest, I calculated, was rather less than a mile across. If we could get through it to the bare hillside, there, as it seemed to me, was an altogether safer resting-place: I thought that with my matches and my camphor I could contrive to keep my path illuminated through the woods. Yet it was evident that if I was to flourish matches with my hands I should have to abandon my firewood; so, rather reluctantly, I put it down. And then it came into my head that I would amaze our friends behind by lighting it. I was to discover the atrocious folly of this proceeding, but it came to my mind as an ingenious move for covering our retreat.

" I don't know if you have ever thought what a rare thing flame must be in the absence of man and in a temperate climate. The sun's heat is rarely strong enough to burn, even when it is focussed by dew-drops, as is sometimes the case in more tropical districts. Lightning may blast and blacken, but it rarely gives rise to widespread fire. Decaying vegetation may occasionally smoulder with the heat of its fermentation, but this rarely results in flame. In this decadence, too, the art of fire-making had been forgotten on the earth. The red tongues that went licking up my heap of wood were an altogether new and strange thing to Weena.

" She wanted to run to it and play with it. I believe she would have cast herself into it had I not restrained her. But I caught her up, and, in spite of her struggles, plunged boldly before me into the wood. For a little way the glare of my fire lit the path. Looking back presently, I could see, through the crowded stems, that from my heap of sticks the blaze had spread to some bushes adjacent, and a curved line of fire was creeping up the grass of the hill. I laughed at that, and turned again to the dark trees before me. It was very black, and Weena clung to me convulsively, but there was still, as my eyes grew accustomed to the darkness, sufficient light for me to avoid the stems. Overhead it was simply black, except where a gap of remote blue sky shone down upon us here and there. I struck none of my matches because I had no hands free. Upon my left arm I carried my little one, in my right hand I had my iron bar.

" For some way I heard nothing but the crackling twigs under my feet, the faint rustle of the breeze above, and my own breathing and the throb of the blood-vessels in my ears. Then I seemed to know of a pattering about me. I pushed on grimly. The pattering grew more distinct, and then I caught the same queer sounds and voices I had heard in the Underworld. There were evidently several of the Morlocks,

and they were closing in upon me. Indeed, in another minute I felt a tug at my coat, then something at my arm. And Weena shivered violently, and became quite still.

" It was time for a match. But to get one I must put her down. I did so, and, as I fumbled with my pocket, a struggle began in the darkness about my knees, perfectly silent on her part and with the same peculiar cooing sounds from the Morlocks. Soft little hands, too, were creeping over my coat and back, touching even my neck. Then the match scratched and fizzed. I held it flaring, and saw the white backs of the Morlocks in flight amid the trees. I hastily took a lump of camphor from my pocket, and prepared to light it as soon as the match should wane. Then I looked at Weena. She was lying clutching my feet and quite motionless, with her face to the ground. With a sudden fright I stooped to her. She seemed scarcely to breathe. I lit the block of camphor and flung it to the ground, and as it split and flared up and drove back the Morlocks and the shadows, I knelt down and lifted her. The wood behind seemed full of the stir and murmur of a great company!

" She seemed to have fainted. I put her carefully upon my shoulder and rose to push on, and then there came a horrible realisation. In manœuvring with my matches and Weena, I had turned myself about several times, and now I had not the faintest idea in what direction lay my path. For all I knew, I might be facing back towards the Palace of Green Porcelain. I found myself in a cold sweat. I had to think rapidly what to do. I determined to build a fire and encamp where we were. I put Weena, still motionless, down upon a turfy bole, and very hastily, as my first lump of camphor waned, I began collecting sticks and leaves. Here and there out of the darkness round me the Morlocks' eyes shone like carbuncles.

" The camphor flickered and went out. I lit a match, and as I did so, two white forms that had been approaching Weena dashed hastily away. One was so blinded by the light that he came straight for me and I felt his bones grind under the blow of my fist. He gave a whoop of dismay, staggered a little way, and fell down. I lit another piece of camphor, and went on gathering my bonfire. Presently I noticed how dry was some of the foliage above me, for since my arrival on the Time Machine, a matter of a week, no rain had fallen. So, instead of casting about among the trees for fallen twigs, I began leaping up and dragging down branches. Very soon I had a choking smoky fire of green wood and dry sticks, and could economise my camphor. Then I turned to where Weena lay beside my iron mace. I tried what I could to revive her, but she lay like one dead. I could not even satisfy myself whether or not she breathed.

" Now, the smoke of the fire beat over towards me, and it must have made me heavy of a sudden. Moreover, the vapour of camphor was in the air. My fire

would not need replenishing for an hour or so. I felt very weary after my exertion, and sat down. The wood, too, was full of a slumbrous murmur that I did not understand. I seemed just to nod and open my eyes. But all was dark, and the Morlocks had their hands upon me. Flinging off their clinging fingers I hastily felt in my pocket for the match-box, and — it had gone! Then they gripped and closed with me again. In a moment I knew what had happened. I had slept, and my fire had gone out, and the bitterness of death came over my soul. The forest seemed full of the smell of burning wood. I was caught by the neck, by the hair, by the arms, and pulled down. It was indescribably horrible in the darkness to feel all these soft creatures heaped upon me. I felt as if I was in a monstrous spider's web. I was overpowered, and went down. I felt little teeth nipping at my neck. I rolled over, and as I did so my hand came against my iron lever. It gave me strength. I struggled up, shaking the human rats from me, and, holding the bar short, I thrust where I judged their faces might be. I could feel the succulent giving of flesh and bone under my blows, and for a moment I was free.

"The strange exultation that so often seems to accompany hard fighting came upon me. I knew that both I and Weena were lost, but I determined to make the Morlocks pay for their meat. I stood with my back to a tree, swinging the iron bar before me. The whole wood was full of the stir and cries of them. A minute passed. Their voices seemed to rise to a higher pitch of excitement, and their movements grew faster. Yet none came within reach. I stood glaring at the blackness. Then suddenly came hope. What if the Morlocks were afraid? And close on the heels of that came a strange thing. The darkness seemed to grow luminous. Very dimly I began to see the Morlocks about me — three battered at my feet — and then I recognised, with incredulous surprise, that the others were running, in an incessant stream, as it seemed, from behind me, and away through the wood in front. And their backs seemed no longer white, but reddish. As I stood agape, I saw a little red spark go drifting across a gap of starlight between the branches, and vanish. And at that I understood the smell of burning wood, the slumbrous murmur that was growing now into a gusty roar, the red glow, and the Morlocks' flight.

"Stepping out from behind my tree and looking back, I saw, through the black pillars of the nearer trees, the flames of the burning forest. It was my first fire coming after me. With that I looked for Weena, but she was gone. The hissing and crackling behind me, the explosive thud as each fresh tree burst into flame, left little time for reflection. My iron bar still gripped, I followed in the Morlocks' path. It was a close race. Once the flames crept forward so swiftly on my right as I ran, that I was outflanked, and had to strike off to the left. But at last I emerged upon a small open space, and as I did so, a Morlock

came blundering towards me, and past me, and went on straight into the fire!

" And now I was to see the most weird and horrible thing, I think, of all that I beheld in that future age. This whole space was as bright as day with·the reflection of the fire. In the centre was a hillock or tumulus, surmounted by a scorched hawthorn. Beyond this was another arm of the burning forest, with yellow tongues already writhing from it, completely encircling the space with a fence of fire. Upon the hill-side were some thirty or forty Morlocks, dazzled by the light and heat, and blundering hither and thither against each other in their bewilderment. At first I did not realise their blindness, and struck furiously at them with my bar, in a frenzy of fear, as they approached me, killing one and crippling several more. But when I had watched the gestures of one of them groping under the hawthorn against the red sky, and heard their moans, I was assured of their absolute helplessness and misery in the glare, and I struck no more of them.

" Yet every now and then one would come straight towards me, setting loose a quivering horror that made me quick to elude him. At one time the flames died down somewhat, and I feared the foul creatures would presently be able to see me. I was even thinking of beginning the fight by killing some of them before this should happen; but the fire burst out again brightly, and I stayed my hand. I walked about the hill among them and avoided them,

looking for some trace of Weena. But Weena was gone.

" At last I sat down on the summit of the hillock, and watched this strange incredible company of blind things groping to and fro, and making uncanny noises to each other, as the glare of the fire beat on them. The coiling uprush of smoke streamed across the sky, and through the rare tatters of that red canopy, remote as though they belonged to another universe, shone the little stars. Two or three Morlocks came blundering into me, and I drove them off with blows of my fists, trembling as I did so.

" For the most part of that night I was persuaded it was a nightmare. I bit myself and screamed in a passionate desire to awake. I beat the ground with my hands, and got up and sat down again, and wandered here and there, and again sat down. Then I would fall to rubbing my eyes and calling upon God to let me awake. Thrice I saw Morlocks put their heads down in a kind of agony and rush into the flames. But, at last, above the subsiding red of the fire, above the streaming masses of black smoke and the whitening and blackening tree stumps, and the diminishing numbers of these dim creatures, came the white light of the day.

" I searched again for traces of Weena, but there were none. It was plain that they had left her poor little body in the forest. I cannot describe how it relieved me to think that it had escaped the awful fate to which it seemed destined. As I thought of that, I

was almost moved to begin a massacre of the helpless abominations about me, but I contained myself. The hillock, as I have said, was a kind of island in the forest. From its summit I could now make out through a haze of smoke the Palace of Green Porcelain, and from that I could get my bearings for the White Sphinx. And so, leaving the remnant of these damned souls still going hither and thither and moaning, as the day grew clearer, I tied some grass about my feet and limped on across smoking ashes and among black stems that still pulsated internally with fire, towards the hiding place of the Time Machine. I walked slowly, for I was almost exhausted, as well as lame, and I felt the intensest wretchedness for the horrible death of little Weena. It seemed an overwhelming calamity. Now, in this old familiar room, it is more like the sorrow of a dream than an actual loss. But that morning it left me absolutely lonely again — terribly alone. I began to think of this house of mine, of this fireside, of some of you, and with such thoughts came a longing that was pain.

"But, as I walked over the smoking ashes under the bright morning sky, I made a discovery. In my trouser pocket were still some loose matches. The box must have leaked before it was lost."

§ 10

"About eight or nine in the morning I came to the same seat of yellow metal from which I had viewed the world upon the evening of my arrival. I thought of my hasty conclusions upon that evening, and could not refrain from laughing bitterly at my confidence. Here was the same beautiful scene, the same abundant foliage, the same splendid palaces and magnificent ruins, the same silver river running between its fertile banks. The gay robes of the beautiful people moved hither and thither among the trees. Some were bathing in exactly the place where I had saved Weena, and that suddenly gave me a keen stab of pain. And like blots upon the landscape rose the cupolas above the ways to the under-world. I understood now what all the beauty of the over-world people covered. Very pleasant was their day, as pleasant as the day of the cattle in the field. Like the cattle, they knew of no enemies, and provided against no needs. And their end was the same.

"I grieved to think how brief the dream of the human intellect had been. It had committed suicide. It had set itself steadfastly towards comfort and ease, a bal-

anced society with security and permanency as its watchword, it had attained its hopes — to come to this at last. Once, life and property must have reached almost absolute safety. The rich had been assured of his wealth and comfort, the toiler assured of his life and work. No doubt in that perfect world there had been no unemployed problem, no social question left unsolved. And a great quiet had followed.

"It is a law of nature we overlook, that intellectual versatility is the compensation for change, danger, and trouble. An animal perfectly in harmony with its environment is a perfect mechanism. Nature never appeals to intelligence until habit and instinct are useless. There is no intelligence where there is no change and no need of change. Only those animals partake of intelligence that have to meet a huge variety of needs and dangers.

"So, as I see it, the Upperworld man had drifted towards his feeble prettiness, and the Under-world to mere mechanical industry. But that perfect state had lacked one thing even for mechanical perfection — absolute permanency. Apparently, as time went on, the feeding of the Under-world, however it was effected, had become disjointed. Mother Necessity, who had been staved off for a few thousand years, came back again, and she began below. The Under-world being in contact with machinery, which, however perfect, still needs some little thought outside habit, had probably retained perforce rather more initiative, if less of every other human character, than the upper. And when other meat failed them, they turned to what old habit had hitherto forbidden. So I say I saw it in my last view of the world of Eight Hundred and Two Thousand Seven Hundred and One. It may be as wrong an explanation as mortal wit could invent. It is how the thing shaped itself to me, and as that I give it to you.

"After the fatigues, excitements, and terrors of the past days, and in spite of my grief, this seat and the tranquil view and the warm sunlight were very pleasant. I was very tired and sleepy, and soon my theorising passed into dosing. Catching myself at that, I took my own hint, and spreading myself out upon the turf I had a long and refreshing sleep.

"I awoke a little before sunsetting. I now felt safe against being caught napping by the Morlocks, and, stretching myself, I came on down the hill towards the White Sphinx. I had my crowbar in one hand, and the other hand played with the matches in my pocket.

"And now came a most unexpected thing. As I approached the pedestal of the sphinx I found the bronze valves were open. They had slid down into grooves.

"At that I stopped short before them, hesitating to enter.

"Within was a small apartment, and on a raised place in the corner of this was the Time Machine. I had the small levers in my pocket. So here, after all my elaborate preparations for the

siege of the White Sphinx, was a meek surrender. I threw my iron bar away, almost sorry not to use it.

"A sudden thought came into my head as I stooped towards the portal. For once, at least, I grasped the mental operations of the Morlocks. Suppressing a strong inclination to laugh, I stepped through the bronze frame and up to the Time Machine. I was surprised to find it had been carefully oiled and cleaned. I have suspected since that the Morlocks had even partially taken it to pieces while trying in their dim way to grasp its purpose.

"Now as I stood and examined it, finding a pleasure in the mere touch of the contrivance, the thing I had expected happened. The bronze panels suddenly slid up and struck the frame with a clang. I was in the dark—trapped. So the Morlocks thought. At that I chuckled gleefully.

"I could already hear their murmuring laughter as they came towards me. Very calmly I tried to strike the match. I had only to fix on the levers and depart then like a ghost. But I had overlooked one little thing. The matches were of that abominable kind that light only on the box.

"You may imagine how all my calm vanished. The little brutes were close upon me. One touched me. I made a sweeping blow in the dark at them with the levers, and began to scramble into the saddle of the machine. Then came one hand upon me and then another. Then I had simply to fight against their persistent fingers for my levers, and at the same time feel for the studs over which these fitted. One, indeed, they almost got away from me. As it slipped from my hand, I had to butt in the dark with my head—I could hear the Morlock's skull ring—to recover it. It was a nearer thing than the fight in the forest, I think, this last scramble.

"But at last the lever was fixed and pulled over. The clinging hands slipped from me. The darkness presently fell from my eyes. I found myself in the same grey light and tumult I have already described."

§ 11

"I HAVE already told you of the sickness and confusion that comes with time travelling. And this time I was not seated properly in the saddle, but sideways and in an unstable fashion. For an indefinite time I clung to the machine as it swayed and vibrated, quite unheeding how I went, and when I brought myself to look at the dials again I was amazed to find where I had arrived. One dial records days, another thousands of days, another millions of days, and another thousands of millions. Now, instead of reversing the levers I had pulled them over so as to

go forward with them, and when I came to look at these indicators I found that the thousands hand was sweeping round as fast as the seconds hand of a watch — into futurity.

"As I drove on, a peculiar change crept over the appearance of things. The palpitating greyness grew darker; then — though I was still travelling with prodigious velocity — the blinking succession of day and night, which was usually indicative of a slower pace, returned, and grew more and more marked. This puzzled me very much at first. The alternations of night and day grew slower and slower, and so did the passage of the sun across the sky, until they seemed to stretch through centuries. At last a steady twilight brooded over the earth, a twilight only broken now and then when a comet glared across the darkling sky. The band of light that had indicated the sun had long since disappeared; for the sun had ceased to set — it simply rose and fell in the west, and grew ever broader and more red. All trace of the moon had vanished. The circling of the stars, growing slower and slower, had given place to creeping points of light. At last, some time before I stopped, the sun, red and very large, halted motionless upon the horizon, a vast dome glowing with a dull heat, and now and then suffering a momentary extinction. At one time it had for a little while glowed more brilliantly again, but it speedily reverted to its sullen red-heat. I perceived by this slowing down of its rising and setting that the work of the tidal drag was done. The earth had come to rest with one face to the sun, even as in our own time the moon faces the earth. Very cautiously, for I remembered my former headlong fall, I began to reverse my motion. Slower and slower went the circling hands until the thousands one seemed motionless, and the daily one was no longer a mere mist upon its scale. Still slower, until the dim outlines of a desolate beach grew visible.

"I stopped very gently and sat upon the Time Machine, looking round. The sky was no longer blue. North-eastward it was inky black, and out of the blackness shown brightly and steadily the pale white stars. Overhead it was a deep Indian red and starless, and south-eastward it grew brighter to a glowing scarlet where, cut by the horizon, lay the huge hull of the sun, red and motionless. The rocks about me were of a harsh reddish colour, and all the trace of life that I could see at first was the intensely green vegetation that covered every projecting point on their south-eastern face. It was the same rich green that one sees on forest moss or on the lichen in caves: plants which like these grow in a perpetual twilight.

"The machine was standing on a sloping beach. The sea stretched away to the south-west, to rise into a sharp bright horizon against the wan sky. There were no breakers and no waves, for not a breath of wind was stirring. Only a slight oily swell rose and fell like a gentle breath-

ing, and showed that the eternal sea was still moving and living. And along the margin where the water sometimes broke was a thick incrustation of salt — pink under the lurid sky. There was a sense of oppression in my head, and I noticed that I was breathing very fast. The sensation reminded me of my only experience of mountaineering, and from that I judged the air to be more rarefied than it is now.

"Far away up the desolate slope I heard a harsh scream, and saw a thing like a huge white butterfly go slanting and fluttering up into the sky and, circling, disappear over some low hillocks beyond. The sound of its voice was so dismal that I shivered and seated myself more firmly upon the machine. Looking round me again, I saw that, quite near, what I had taken to be a reddish mass of rock was moving slowly towards me. Then I saw the thing was really a monstrous crab-like creature. Can you imagine a crab as large as yonder table, with its many legs moving slowly and uncertainly, its big claws swaying, its long antennæ, like carters' whips, waving and feeling, and its stalked eyes gleaming at you on either side of its metallic front? Its back was corrugated and ornamented with ungainly bosses, and a greenish incrustation blotched it here and there. I could see the many palps of its complicated mouth flickering and feeling as it moved.

"As I stared at this sinister apparition crawling towards me, I felt a tickling on my cheek as though a fly had lighted there. I tried to brush it away with my hand, but in a moment it returned, and almost immediately came another by my ear. I struck at this, and caught something threadlike. It was drawn swiftly out of my hand. With a frightful qualm, I turned, and saw that I had grasped the antenna of another monster crab that stood just behind me. Its evil eyes were wriggling on their stalks, its mouth was all alive with appetite, and its vast ungainly claws, smeared with an algal slime, were descending upon me. In a moment my hand was on the lever, and I had placed a month between myself and these monsters. But I was still on the same beach, and I saw them distinctly now as soon as I stopped. Dozens of them seemed to be crawling here and there, in the sombre light, among the foliated sheets of intense green.

"I cannot convey the sense of abominable desolation that hung over the world. The red eastern sky, the northward blackness, the salt Dead Sea, the stony beach crawling with these foul, slow-stirring monsters, the uniform poisonous-looking green of the lichenous plants, the thin air that hurt one's lungs; all contributed to an appalling effect. I moved on a hundred years, and there was the same red sun — a little larger, a little duller — the same dying sea, the same chill air, and the same crowd of earthly crustacea creeping in and out among the green weed and the red rocks. And in the westward sky I saw a curved pale line like a vast new moon.

" So I travelled, stopping ever and again, in great strides of a thousand years or more, drawn on by the mystery of the earth's fate, watching with a strange fascination the sun grow larger and duller in the westward sky, and the life of the old earth ebb away. At last, more than thirty million years hence, the huge red-hot dome of the sun had come to obscure nearly a tenth part of the darkling heavens. Then I stopped once more, for the crawling multitude of crabs had disappeared, and the red beach, save for its livid green liverworts and lichens, seemed lifeless. And now it was flecked with white. A bitter cold assailed me. Rare white flakes ever and again came eddying down. To the north-eastward, the glare of snow lay under the starlight of the sable sky, and I could see an undulating crest of hillocks pinkish-white. There were fringes of ice along the sea margin, with drifting masses further out; but the main expanse of that salt ocean, all bloody under the eternal sunset, was still unfrozen.

" I looked about me to see if any traces of animal-life remained. A certain indefinable apprehension still kept me in the saddle of the machine. But I saw nothing moving, in earth or sky or sea. The green slime on the rocks alone testified that life was not extinct. A shallow sandbank had appeared in the sea and the water had receded from the beach. I fancied I saw some black object flopping about upon this bank, but it became motionless as I looked at it, and I judged that my eye had been deceived, and that the black object was merely a rock. The stars in the sky were intensely bright and seemed to me to twinkle very little.

" Suddenly I noticed that the circular westward outline of the sun had changed; that a concavity, a bay, had appeared in the curve. I saw this grow larger. For a minute perhaps I stared aghast at this blackness that was creeping over the day, and then I realised that an eclipse was beginning. Either the moon or the planet Mercury was passing across the sun's disk. Naturally, at first I took it to be the moon, but there is much to incline me to believe that what I really saw was the transit of an inner planet passing very near to the earth.

" The darkness grew apace; a cold wind began to blow in freshening gusts from the east, and the showering white flakes in the air increased in number. From the edge of the sea came a ripple and whisper. Beyond these lifeless sounds the world was silent. Silent? It would be hard to convey the stillness of it. All the sounds of man, the bleating of sheep, the cries of birds, the hum of insects, the stir that makes the background of our lives — all that was over. As the darkness thickened, the eddying flakes grew more abundant, dancing before my eyes; and the cold of the air more intense. At last, one by one, swiftly, one after the other, the white peaks of the distant hills vanished into blackness. The breeze rose to a moaning wind. I saw the black central shadow of

the eclipse sweeping towards me. In another moment the pale stars alone were visible. All else was rayless obscurity. The sky was absolutely black.

"A horror of this great darkness came on me. The cold, that smote to my marrow, and the pain I felt in breathing overcame me. I shivered, and a deadly nausea seized me. Then like a red-hot bow in the sky appeared the edge of the sun. I got off the machine to recover myself. I felt giddy and incapable of facing the return journey. As I stood sick and confused I saw again the moving thing upon the shoal — there was no mistake now that it was a moving thing — against the red water of the sea. It was a round thing, the size of a foot-ball perhaps, or, it may be, bigger, and tentacles trailed down from it; it seemed black against the weltering blood-red water, and it was hopping fitfully about. Then I felt I was fainting. But a terrible dread of lying helpless in that remote and awful twilight sustained me while I clambered upon the saddle."

§ 12

"So I came back. For a long time I must have been insensible upon the machine. The blinking succession of the days and nights was resumed, the sun got golden again, the sky blue. I breathed with greater freedom. The fluctuating contours of the land ebbed and flowed. The hands spun backward upon the dials. At last I saw again the dim shadows of houses, the evidences of decadent humanity. These, too, changed and passed, and others came. Presently, when the million dial was at zero, I slackened speed. I began to recognise our own petty and familiar architecture, the thousands hand ran back to the starting-point, the night and day flapped slower and slower. Then the old walls of the laboratory came round me. Very gently, now, I slowed the mechanism down.

"I saw one little thing that seemed odd to me. I think I have told you that when I set out, before my velocity became very high, Mrs. Watchett had walked across the room, travelling, as it seemed to me, like a rocket. As I returned, I passed again across that minute when she traversed the laboratory. But now her every motion appeared to be the exact inversion of her previous ones. The door at the lower end opened, and she glided quietly up the laboratory, back foremost, and disappeared behind the door by which she had previously entered. Just before that I seemed to see Hillyer for a moment; but he passed like a flash.

"Then I stopped the machine, and saw about me again the old familiar laboratory, my tools, my appliances just as I had left them. I got off the thing very shakily, and sat down upon my bench.

For several minutes I trembled violently. Then I became calmer. Around me was my old workshop again, exactly as it had been. I might have slept there, and the whole thing have been a dream.

"And yet, not exactly! The thing had started from the south-east corner of the laboratory. It had come to rest again in the north-west, against the wall where you saw it. That gives you the exact distance from my little lawn to the pedestal of the White Sphinx, into which the Morlocks had carried my machine.

"For a time my brain went stagnant. Presently I got up and came through the passage here, limping, because my heel was still painful, and feeling sorely begrimed. I saw the *Pall Mall Gazette* on the table by the door. I found the date was indeed to-day, and looking at the time-piece, saw the hour was almost eight o'clock. I heard your voices and the clatter of plates. I hesitated — I felt so sick and weak. Then I sniffed good wholesome meat, and opened the door on you. You know the rest. I washed, and dined, and now I am telling you the story.

"I know," he said, after a pause, "that all this will be absolutely incredible to you, but to me the one incredible thing is that I am here to-night in this old familiar room, looking into your friendly faces, and telling you these strange adventures." He looked at the Medical Man. "No. I cannot expect you to believe it. Take it as a lie — or a prophecy. Say I dreamed it in the workshop. Consider I have been speculating upon the destinies of our race until I have hatched this fiction. Treat my assertion of its truth as a mere stroke of art to enhance its interest. And, taking it as a story, what do you think of it?"

He took up his pipe, and began, in his old accustomed manner, to tap with it nervously upon the bars of the grate. There was a momentary stillness. Then chairs began to creak and shoes to scrape upon the carpet. I took my eyes off the Time Traveller's face, and looked round at his audience. They were in the dark, and little spots of colour swam before them. The Medical Man seemed absorbed in the contemplation of our host. The Editor was looking hard at the end of his cigar — the sixth. The Journalist fumbled for his watch. The others, as far as I remember, were motionless.

The Editor stood up with a sigh. "What a pity it is you're not a writer of stories!" he said, putting his hand on the Time Traveller's shoulder.

"You don't believe it?"

"Well —"

"I thought not."

The Time Traveller turned to us. "Where are the matches?" he said. He lit one and spoke over his pipe, puffing. "To tell you the truth . . . I hardly believe it myself. . . . And yet . . ."

His eye fell with a mute inquiry upon the withered white flowers upon the little table. Then he turned over the hand holding his pipe, and I saw he was looking at some half-healed scars on his knuckles.

The Medical Man rose, came to the lamp, and examined the flowers. " The gynæceum's odd," he said. The Psychologist leant forward to see, holding out his hand for a specimen.

" I'm hanged if it isn't a quarter to one," said the Journalist. " How shall we get home? "

" Plenty of cabs at the station," said the Psychologist.

" It's a curious thing," said the Medical Man; " but I certainly don't know the natural order of these flowers. May I have them? "

The Time Traveller hesitated. Then suddenly: " Certainly not."

" Where did you really get them? " said the Medical Man.

The Time Traveller put his hand to his head. He spoke like one who was trying to keep hold of an idea that eluded him. " They were put into my pocket by Weena, when I travelled into Time." He stared round the room. " I'm damned if it isn't all going. This room and you and the atmosphere of every day is too much for my memory. Did I ever make a Time Machine, or a model of a Time Machine? Or is it all only a dream? They say life is a dream, a precious poor dream at times — but I can't stand another that won't fit. It's madness. And where did the dream come from? . . . I must look at that machine. If there *is* one! "

He caught up the lamp swiftly, and carried it, flaring red, through the door into the corridor. We followed him. There in the flickering light of the lamp was the machine sure enough,

squat, ugly, and askew, a thing of brass, ebony, ivory, and translucent glimmering quartz. Solid to the touch — for I put out my hand and felt the rail of it — and with brown spots and smears upon the ivory, and bits of grass and moss upon the lower parts, and one rail bent awry.

The Time Traveller put the lamp down on the bench, and ran his hand along the damaged rail. " It's all right now," he said. " The story I told you was true. I'm sorry to have brought you out here in the cold." He took up the lamp, and, in an absolute silence, we returned to the smoking-room.

He came into the hall with us, and helped the Editor on with his coat. The Medical Man looked into his face and, with a certain hesitation, told him he was suffering from overwork, at which he laughed hugely. I remember him standing in the open doorway, bawling good-night.

I shared a cab with the Editor. He thought the tale a " gaudy lie." For my own part I was unable to come to a conclusion. The story was so fantastic and incredible, the telling so credible and sober. I lay awake most of the night thinking about it. I determined to go next day and see the Time Traveller again. I was told he was in the laboratory, and, being on easy terms in the house, I went up to him. The laboratory however was empty. I stared for a minute at the Time Machine and put out my hand and touched the lever. At that the squat substantial-looking

mass swayed like a bough shaken by the wind. Its instability startled me extremely, and I had a queer reminiscence of the childish days when I used to be forbidden to meddle. I came back through the corridor. The Time Traveller met me in the smoking-room. He was coming from the house. He had a small camera under one arm and a knapsack under the other. He laughed when he saw me, and gave me an elbow to shake. "I'm frightfully busy," said he, "with that thing in there."

"But is it not some hoax?" I said. "Do you really travel through Time?"

"Really and truly I do." And he looked frankly into my eyes. He hesitated. His eye wandered about the room. "I only want half an hour," he said. "I know why you came, and it's awfully good of you. There's some magazines here. If you'll stop to lunch I'll prove you this time travelling up to the hilt, specimens and all. If you'll forgive my leaving you now?"

I consented, hardly comprehending then the full import of his words, and he nodded and went on down the corridor. I heard the door of the laboratory slam, seated myself in a chair, and took up a daily paper. What was he going to do before lunch-time? Then suddenly I was reminded by an advertisement that I had promised to meet Richardson, the publisher, at two. I looked at my watch, and saw that I could barely save that engagement. I got up and went down the pas-

sage to tell the Time Traveller.

As I took hold of the handle of the door I heard an exclamation, oddly truncated at the end, and a click and a thud. A gust of air whirled round me as I opened the door, and from within came the sound of broken glass falling on the floor. The Time Traveller was not there. I seemed to see a ghostly, indistinct figure sitting in a whirling mass of black and brass for a moment — a figure so transparent that the bench behind with its sheets of drawings was absolutely distinct; but this phantasm vanished as I rubbed my eyes. The Time Machine had gone. Save for a subsiding stir of dust, the further end of the laboratory was empty. A pane of the skylight had, apparently, just been blown in.

I felt an unreasonable amazement. I knew that something strange had happened, and for the moment could not distinguish what the strange thing might be. As I stood staring, the door into the garden opened, and the man-servant appeared.

We looked at each other. Then ideas began to come. "Has Mr. —— gone out that way?" said I.

"No, sir. No one has come out this way. I was expecting to find him here."

At that I understood. At the risk of disappointing Richardson I stayed on waiting for the Time Traveller: waiting for the second, perhaps still stranger story, and the specimens and photographs he would bring with him. But I am beginning now to fear that

I must wait a lifetime. The Time Traveller vanished three years ago. And, as everybody knows now, he has never returned.

EPILOGUE

ONE cannot choose but wonder. Will he ever return? It may be that he swept back into the past, and fell among the blood-drinking, hairy savages of the Age of Unpolished Stone; into the abysses of the Cretaceous Sea; or among the grotesque saurians, the huge reptilian brutes of the Jurassic times. He may even now — if I may use the phrase — be wandering on some plesiosaurus-haunted Oolitic coral reef or beside the lonely saline lakes of the Triassic Age. Or did he go forward, into one of the nearer ages, in which men are still men, but with the riddles of our own time answered and its wearisome problems solved? Into the manhood of the race: for I, for my own part, cannot think that these latter days of weak experiment, fragmentary theory, and mutual discord are indeed man's culminating time! I say, for my own part. He, I know — for the question had been discussed among us long before the Time Machine was made — thought but cheerlessly of the Advancement of Mankind, and saw in the growing pile of civilisation only a foolish heaping that must inevitably fall back upon and destroy its makers in the end. If that is so, it remains for us to live as though it were not so. But to me the future is still black and blank — is a vast ignorance, lit at a few casual places by the memory of his story. And I have by me, for my comfort, two strange white flowers — shrivelled now, and brown and flat and brittle — to witness that even when mind and strength had gone, gratitude and a mutual tenderness still lived on in the heart of man.

" 'SO FAR, NOT THE SLIGHTEST ATTEMPT HAS BEEN MADE
TO INTERFERE WITH ME.' "

Drawn by E. Hering, 1900 for THE FIRST MEN IN THE MOON.

"I . . . PERCEIVED THEY WERE THE CARCASSES OF MOON
CALVES BEING CUT UP, MUCH AS A MOORED WHALE
MIGHT BE CUT UP BY THE CREW OF A WHALER."

Drawn by E. Hering, 1901 for *THE FIRST MEN IN THE MOON.*

THE ISLAND OF DR. MOREAU

CHAPTER 1

IN THE DINGEY OF THE "LADY VAIN"

I do not propose to add anything to what has already been written concerning the loss of the *Lady Vain*. As everyone knows, she collided with a derelict when ten days out from Callao. The long-boat with seven of the crew was picked up eighteen days after by H.M. gun-boat *Myrtle*, and the story of their privations has become almost as well known as the far more terrible *Medusa* case. I have now, however, to add to the published story of the *Lady Vain* another as horrible, and certainly far stranger. It has hitherto been supposed that the four men who were in the dingey perished, but this is incorrect. I have the best evidence for this assertion — I am one of the four men.

But, in the first place, I must state that there never were four men in the dingey; the number was three. Constans, who was "seen by the captain to jump into the gig" (*Daily News*, March 17, 1887), luckily for us, and unluckily for himself, did not reach us. He came down out of the tangle of ropes under the stays of the smashed bowsprit; some small rope caught his heel as he let go and he hung for a moment head downward, and then fell and struck a block or spar floating in the water. We pulled towards him, but he never came up.

I say luckily for us he did not reach us, and I might also add luckily for himself, for there were only a small beaker of water and some soddened ship's biscuits with us — so sudden had been the alarm, so unprepared the ship for any disaster. We thought the people on the launch would be better provisioned (though it seems they were not), and we tried to hail them. They could not have heard us, and the next morning when the drizzle cleared — which was not until past mid-day — we could see nothing of them. We could not stand up to

look about us because of the pitching of the boat. The sea ran in great rollers, and we had much ado to keep the boat's head to them. The two other men who had escaped so far with me were a man named Helmar, a passenger like myself, and a seaman whose name I don't know, a short sturdy man with a stammer.

We drifted famishing, and, after our water had come to an end, tormented by an intolerable thirst, for eight days altogether. After the second day the sea subsided slowly to a glassy calm. It is quite impossible for the ordinary reader to imagine those eight days. He has not — luckily for himself — anything in his memory to imagine with. After the first day we said little to one another, and lay in our places in the boat and stared at the horizon, or watched, with eyes that grew larger and more haggard every day, the misery and weakness gaining upon our companions. The sun became pitiless. The water ended on the fourth day, and we were already thinking strange things and saying them with our eyes; but it was, I think, the sixth before Helmar gave voice to the thing we all had in mind. I remember our voices dry and thin, so that we bent towards one another and spared our words. I stood out against it with all my might, was rather for scuttling the boat and perishing together among the sharks that followed us; but when Helmar said that if his proposal was accepted we should have drink, the sailor came round to him.

I would not draw lots, however, and in the night the sailor whispered to Helmar again and again, and I sat in the bows with my clasp-knife in my hand — though I doubt if I had the stuff in me to fight. And in the morning I agreed to Helmar's proposal, and we handed halfpence to find the odd man.

The lot fell upon the sailor, but he was the strongest of us and would not abide by it, and attacked Helmar with his hands. They grappled together and almost stood up. I crawled along the boat to them, intending to help Helmar by grasping the sailor's leg, but the sailor stumbled with the swaying of the boat, and the two fell upon the gunwhale and rolled overboard together. They sank like stones. I remember laughing at that and wondering why I laughed. The laugh caught me suddenly like a thing from without.

I lay across one of the thwarts for I know not how long, thinking that if I had the strength I would drink sea-water and madden myself to die quickly. And even as I lay there I saw, with no more interest than if it had been a picture, a sail come up towards me over the skyline. My mind must have been wandering, and yet I remember all that happened quite distinctly. I remember how my head swayed with the seas, and the horizon with the sail above it danced up and down. But I also remember as distinctly that I had a persuasion that I was dead, and that I thought what a jest it was they should come too late by such a little to catch me in my body.

For an endless period, as it seemed to me, I lay with my head on the thwart watching the dancing schooner — she was a little ship, schooner-rigged fore and aft — come up out of the sea. She kept tacking to and fro in a widening compass, for she was sailing dead into the wind. It never entered my head to attempt to attract attention, and I do not remember anything distinctly after the sight of her side, until I found myself in a little cabin aft. There is a dim half memory of being lifted up to the gangway and of a big round countenance, covered with freckles and surrounded with red hair, staring at me over the bulwarks. I also had a disconnected impression of a dark face with extraordinary eyes close to mine, but that I thought was a nightmare until I met it again. I fancy I recollect some stuff being poured in between my teeth. And that is all.

CHAPTER 2

THE MAN WHO WAS
GOING NOWHERE

THE CABIN in which I found myself was small and rather untidy. A youngish man with flaxen hair, a bristly straw-coloured moustache, and a dropping nether lip was sitting and holding my wrist. For a minute we stared at one another without speaking. He had watery grey expressionless eyes.

Then just overhead came a sound like an iron bedstead being knocked about and the low angry growling of some large animal. At the same time the man spoke again.

He repeated his question: "How do you feel now?"

I think I said I felt all right. I could not recollect how I had got there. He must have seen the question in my face, for my voice was inaccessible to me.

"You were picked up in a boat — starving. The name on the boat was the *Lady Vain,* and there were queer marks on the gunwhale." At the same time my eye caught my hand, so thin that it looked like a dirty skin purse full of loose bones, and all the business of the boat came back to me.

"Have some of this," said he, and gave me a dose of some scarlet stuff, iced.

It tasted like blood, and made me feel stronger.

"You were in luck," said he, "to get picked up by a ship with a medical man aboard." He spoke with a slobbering articulation, with the ghost of a lisp.

"What ship is this?" I said slowly, hoarse from my long silence.

"It's a little trader from Arica and Callao. I never asked where she came from in the beginning. Out of the land of born fools, I guess. I'm a passenger myself

from Arica. The silly ass who owns her — he's captain too, named Davis — he's lost his certificate or something. You know the kind of man — calls the thing the *Ipecacuanha* — of all silly infernal names, though when there's much of a sea without any wind she certainly acts according."

Then the noise overhead began again, a snarling growl and the voice of a human being together. Then another voice telling some "Heaven-forsaken idiot" to desist.

"You were nearly dead," said my interlocutor. "It was a very near thing indeed. But I've put some stuff into you now. Notice your arms sore? Injections. You've been insensible for nearly thirty hours."

I thought slowly. I was distracted now by the yelping of a number of dogs. "May I have solid food?" I asked.

"Thanks to me," he said. "Even now the mutton is boiling."

"Yes," I said, with assurance; "I could eat some mutton."

"But," said he, with a momentary hesitation, "you know I'm dying to hear how you came to be alone in the boat." I thought I detected a certain suspicion in his eyes.

"*Damn that howling!*"

He suddenly left the cabin, and I heard him in violent controversy with someone who seemed to me to talk gibberish in response to him. The matter sounded as though it ended in blows, but in that I thought my ears were mistaken. Then he

shouted at the dogs and returned to the cabin.

"Well?" said he, in the doorway. "You were just beginning to tell me."

I told him my name, Edward Prendick, and how I had taken to natural history as a relief from the dulness of my comfortable independence. He seemed interested in this. "I've done some science myself — I did my Biology at University College, — getting out the ovary of the earthworm and the radula of the snail and all that. Lord! it's ten years ago. But go on, go on — tell me about the boat."

He was evidently satisfied with the frankness of my story, which I told in concise sentences enough — for I felt horribly weak, — and when it was finished he reverted presently to the topic of natural history and his own biological studies. He began to question me closely about Tottenham Court Road and Gower Street. "Is Caplatzi still flourishing? What a shop that was!" He had evidently been a very ordinary medical student, and drifted incontinently to the topic of the music-halls. He told me some anecdotes. "Left it all," he said, "ten years ago. How jolly it all used to be! But I made a young ass of myself. . . . Played myself out before I was twenty-one. I daresay it's all different now. . . . But I must look up that ass of a cook and see what he's doing to your mutton."

The growling overhead was renewed, so suddenly and with so much savage anger that it startled me. "What's that?" I called

after him, but the door had closed. He came back again with the boiled mutton, and I was so excited by the appetising smell of it, that I forgot the noise of the beast forthwith.

After a day of alternate sleep and feeding I was so far recovered as to be able to get from my bunk to the scuttle and see the green seas trying to keep pace with us. I judged the schooner was running before the wind. Montgomery — that was the name of the flaxen-haired man — came in again as I stood there, and I asked him for some clothes. He lent me some duck things of his own, for those I had worn in the boat, he said, had been thrown overboard. They were rather loose for me, for he was large and long in his limbs.

He told me casually that the captain was three parts drunk in his own cabin. As I assumed the clothes I began asking him some questions about the destination of the ship. He said the ship was bound to Hawaii, but that it had to land him first.

"Where?" said I.

"It's an island. . . . Where I live. So far as I know, it hasn't got a name."

He stared at me with his nether lip dropping, and looked so wilfully stupid of a sudden that it came into my head that he desired to avoid my questions. "I'm ready," I said. He lead the way out of the cabin.

CHAPTER 3

THE STRANGE FACE

At the companion was a man obstructing our way. He was standing on the ladder with his back to us, peering over the combing of the hatchway. He was, I could see, a misshapen man, short, broad, and clumsy, with a crooked back, a hairy neck, and a head sunk between his shoulders. He was dressed in dark blue serge, and had peculiarly thick coarse black hair. I heard the unseen dogs growl furiously, and forthwith he ducked back, coming into contact with the hand I put out to fend him off from myself. He turned with animal swiftness.

The black face thus flashed upon me startled me profoundly. It was a singularly deformed one. The facial part projected, forming something dimly suggestive of a muzzle, and the huge half-open mouth showed as big white teeth as I had ever seen in a human mouth. His eyes were bloodshot at the edges, with scarcely a rim of white round the hazel pupils. There was a curious glow of excitement in his face.

"Confound you!" said Mont-

gomery. "Why the devil don't you get out of the way?" The black-faced man started aside without a word.

I went on up the companion, still staring at him almost against my will as I did so. Montgomery stayed at the foot for a moment. "You have no business here, you know," he said, in a deliberate tone. "Your place is forward."

The black-faced man cowered. "They . . . won't have me forward." He spoke slowly, with a hoarse quality in his voice.

"Won't have you forward!" said Montgomery in a menacing voice. "But I tell you to go." He was on the brink of saying something further, then looked up at me suddenly and followed me up the ladder. I had paused half-way through the hatchway, looking back, still astonished beyond measure at the grotesque ugliness of this black-faced creature. I had never beheld such a repulsive and extraordinary face before, and yet — if the contradiction is credible — I experienced at the same time an odd feeling that in some way I *had* already encountered exactly the features and gestures that now amazed me. Afterwards it occurred to me that probably I had seen him as I was lifted aboard, and yet that scarcely satisfied my suspicion of a previous acquaintance. Yet how one could have set eyes on so singular a face and have forgotten the precise occasion passed my imagination.

Montgomery's movement to follow me released my attention, and I turned and looked about

me at the flush deck of the little schooner. I was already half prepared by the sounds I had heard for what I saw. Certainly I never beheld a deck so dirty. It was littered with scraps of carrot, shreds of green stuff, and indescribable filth. Fastened by chains to the mainmast were a number of grisly staghounds, who now began leaping and barking at me, and by the mizzen a huge puma was cramped in a little iron cage, far too small even to give it turning-room. Further under the starboard bulwark were some big hutches containing a number of rabbits, and a solitary llama was squeezed in a mere box of a cage forward. The dogs were muzzled by leather straps. The only human being on deck was a gaunt and silent sailor at the wheel.

The patched and dirty spankers were tense before the wind, and up aloft the little ship seemed carrying every sail she had. The sky was clear, the sun midway down the western sky; long waves, capped by the breeze with froth, were running with us. We went past the steersman to the taffrail and stared side by side for a space at the water foaming under the stern and the bubbles dancing and vanishing in her wake. I turned and surveyed the unsavoury length of the ship.

"Is this an ocean menagerie?" said I.

"Looks like it," said Montgomery.

"What are these beasts for? Merchandise, curios? Does the captain think he is going to sell

them somewhere in the South Seas?"

"It looks like it, doesn't it?" said Montgomery, and turned towards the wake again.

Suddenly we heard a yelp and a volley of furious blasphemy coming from the companion hatchway, and the deformed man with the black face clambered up hurriedly. He was immediately followed by a heavy red-haired man in a white cap. At the sight of the former the staghounds, who had all tired of barking at me by this time, became furiously excited, howling and leaping against their chains. The black hesitated before them, and this gave the red-haired man time to come up with him and deliver a tremendous blow between the shoulder-blades with his fist. The poor devil went down like a felled ox, and rolled in the dirt among the furiously excited dogs. It was lucky for him they were muzzled. The red-haired man gave a yawp of exultation and stood staggering and, as it seemed to me, in serious danger of either going backwards down the companion hatchway, or forwards upon his victim.

So soon as the second man had appeared, Montgomery had started violently. "Steady on there!" he cried, in a tone of remonstrance. A couple of sailors appeared on the forecastle.

The black-faced man, howling in a singular voice, rolled about under the feet of the dogs. No one attempted to help him. The brutes did their best to worry him, butting their muzzles at him. There was a quick dance of their lithe grey bodies over the clumsy prostrate figure. The sailors forward shouted to them as though it was admirable sport. Montgomery gave an angry exclamation, and went striding down the deck. I followed him.

In another second the black-faced man had scrambled up and was staggering forward. He stumbled up against the bulwark by the main shrouds, where he remained panting and glaring over his shoulder at the dogs. The red-haired man laughed a satisfied laugh.

"Look here, captain," said Montgomery, with his lisp a little accentuated, gripping the elbows of the red-haired man; "this won't do."

I stood behind Montgomery. The captain came half round and regarded him with the dull and solemn eyes of a drunken man. "Wha' won't do?" he said; and added, after looking sleepily into Montgomery's face for a minute, "Blasted Sawbones!"

With a sudden movement he shook his arms free, and after two ineffectual attempts stuck his freckled fists into his side-pockets.

"That man's a passenger," said Montgomery. "I'd advise you to keep your hands off him."

"Go to hell!" said the captain loudly. He suddenly turned and staggered towards the side. "Do what I like on my own ship," he said.

I think Montgomery might have left him then—seeing the brute was drunk. But he only turned a shade paler, and followed the captain to the bulwarks.

" Look here, captain," he said. " That man of mine is not to be ill-treated. He has been hazed ever since he came aboard."

For a minute alcoholic fumes kept the captain speechless. " Blasted Sawbones! " was all he considered necessary.

I could see that Montgomery had an ugly temper, and I saw too that this quarrel had been some time growing. " The man's drunk," said I, perhaps officiously; " you'll do no good."

Montgomery gave an ugly twist to his dropping lip. " He's always drunk. Do you think that excuses his assaulting his passengers? "

" My ship," began the captain, waving his hand unsteadily towards the cages, " was a clean ship. Look at it now." It was certainly anything but clean. " Crew," continued the captain, " clean respectable crew."

" You agreed to take the beasts."

" I wish I'd never set eyes on your infernal island. What the devil . . . want beasts for on an island like that? Then that man of yours . . . Understood he was a man. He's a lunatic. And he hadn't no business aft. Do you think the whole damned ship belongs to you? "

" Your sailors began to haze the poor devil as soon as he came aboard."

" That's just what he is — he's a devil, an ugly devil. My men can't stand him. *I* can't stand him. None of us can't stand him. Nor *you* either."

Montgomery turned away.

" *You* leave that man alone, anyhow," he said, nodding his head as he spoke.

But the captain meant to quarrel now. He raised his voice: " If he comes this end of the ship again I'll cut his insides out, I tell you. Cut out his blasted insides! Who are *you* to tell *me* what *I'm* to do. I tell you I'm captain of the ship — Captain and Owner. I'm the law here, I tell you — the law and the prophets. I bargained to take a man and his attendant to and from Arica and bring back some animals. I never bargained to carry a mad devil and a silly Sawbones, a — "

Well, never mind what he called Montgomery. I saw the latter take a step forward, and interposed. " He's drunk," said I. The captain began some abuse even fouler than the last. " Shut up," I said, turning on him sharply, for I had seen danger in Montgomery's white face. With that I brought the downpour on myself.

However, I was glad to avert what was uncommonly near a scuffle, even at the price of the captain's drunken ill-will. I do not think I have ever heard quite so much vile language come in a continuous stream from any man's lips before, though I have frequented eccentric company enough. I found some of it hard to endure — though I am a mild-tempered man. But certainly when I told the captain to shut up I had forgotten I was merely a bit of human flotsam, cut off from my resources, and with my

fare unpaid, a mere casual dependant on the bounty — or speculative enterprise — of the ship. He reminded me of it with considerable vigour. But at any rate I prevented a fight.

CHAPTER 4

AT THE SCHOONER'S RAIL

THAT night land was sighted after sundown, and the schooner hove to. Montgomery intimated that was his destination. It was too far to see any details; it seemed to me then simply a low-lying patch of dim blue in the uncertain blue-grey sea. An almost vertical streak of smoke went up from it into the sky.

The captain was not on deck when it was sighted. After he had vented his wrath on me he had staggered below, and I understand he went to sleep on the floor of his own cabin. The mate practically assumed the command. He was the gaunt, taciturn individual we had seen at the wheel. Apparently he too was in an evil temper with Montgomery. He took not the slightest notice of either of us. We dined with him in a sulky silence, after a few ineffectual efforts on my part to talk. It struck me, too, that the men regarded my companion and his animals in a singularly unfriendly manner. I found Montgomery very reticent about his purpose with these creatures and about his destination, and though I was sensible of a growing curiosity I did not press him.

We remained talking on the quarter-deck until the sky was thick with stars. Except for an occasional sound in the yellow-lit forecastle, and a movement of the animals now and then, the night was very still. The puma lay crouched together, watching us with shining eyes, a black heap in the corner of its cage. The dogs seemed to be asleep. Montgomery produced some cigars.

He talked to me of London in a tone of half-painful reminiscence, asking all kinds of questions about changes that had taken place. He spoke like a man who had loved his life there, and had been suddenly and irrevocably cut off from it. I gossiped as well as I could of this and that. All the time the strangeness of him was shaping itself in my mind, and as I talked I peered at his odd pallid face in the dim light of the binnacle lantern behind me. Then I looked out at the darkling sea, where in the dimness his little island was hidden.

This man, it seemed to me, had come out of Immensity merely to save my life. To-morrow he would drop over the side

and vanish again out of my existence. Even had it been under commonplace circumstances it would have made me a trifle thoughtful. But in the first place was the singularity of an educated man living on this unknown little island, and coupled with that, the extraordinary nature of his luggage. I found myself repeating the captain's question: What did he want with the beasts? Why, too, had he pretended they were not his when I had remarked about them at first? Then again, in his personal attendant there was a bizarre quality that had impressed me profoundly. These circumstances threw a haze of mystery round the man. They laid hold of my imagination and hampered my tongue.

Towards midnight our talk of London died away, and we stood side by side leaning over the bulwarks, and staring dreamily over the silent starlit sea, each pursuing his own thoughts. It was the atmosphere for sentiment, and I began upon my gratitude.

" If I may say it," said I, after a time, " you have saved my life."

" Chance," he answered; " just chance."

" I prefer to make my thanks to the accessible agent."

" Thank no one. You had the need, and I the knowledge, and I injected and fed you much as I might have collected a specimen. I was bored, and wanted something to do. If I'd been jaded that day, or hadn't liked your face, well —; it's a curious question where you would have been now."

This damped my mood a little. " At any rate — " I began.

" It's a chance, I tell you," he interrupted, " as everything is in a man's life. Only the asses won't see it. Why am I here now — an outcast from civilisation — instead of being a happy man enjoying all the pleasures of London? Simply because — eleven years ago — I lost my head for ten minutes on a foggy night."

He stopped. " Yes? " said I.

." That's all."

We relapsed into silence. Presently he laughed. " There's something in this starlight that loosens one's tongue. I'm an ass, and yet somehow I would like to tell you."

" Whatever you tell me, you may rely upon my keeping to myself. . . . If that's it."

He was on the point of beginning, and then shook his head doubtfully. " Don't," said I. " It is all the same to me. After all, it is better to keep your secret. There's nothing gained but a little relief, if I respect your confidence. If I don't . . . well? "

He grunted undecidedly. I felt I had him at a disadvantage, had caught him in the mood of indiscretion; and, to tell the truth, I was not curious to learn what might have driven a young medical student out of London. I have an imagination. I shrugged my shoulders, and turned away. Over the taffrail leant a silent black figure, watching the stars. It was Montgomery's strange attendant. It looked over its

shoulder quickly with my movement, then looked away again.

It may seem a little thing to you, perhaps, but it came like a sudden blow to me. The only light near us was a lantern at the wheel. The creature's face was turned for one brief instant out of the dimness of the stern towards this illumination, and I saw that the eyes that glanced at me shone with a pale green light.

I did not know then that a reddish luminosity, at least, is not uncommon in human eyes. The thing came to me as a stark inhumanity. That black figure, with its eyes of fire, struck down through all my adult thoughts and feelings, and for a moment the forgotten horrors of childhood came back to my mind. Then the effect passed as it had come. An uncouth black figure of a man, a figure of no particular import, hung over the taffrail, against the starlight, and I found Montgomery was speaking to me.

"I'm thinking of turning in, then," said he; "if you've had enough of this."

I answered him incongruously. We went below, and he wished me good-night at the door of my cabin.

That night I had some very unpleasant dreams. The waning moon rose late. Its light struck a ghostly faint white beam across my cabin, and made an ominous shape on the planking by my bunk. Then the staghounds woke and began howling and baying, so that I dreamt fitfully and scarcely slept until the approach of dawn.

CHAPTER 5

THE LANDING ON THE ISLAND

In the early morning — it was the second morning after my recovery, and I believe the fourth after I was picked up — I awoke through an avenue of tumultuous dreams, dreams of guns and howling mobs, and became sensible of a hoarse shouting above me. I rubbed my eyes, and lay listening to the noise, doubtful for a little while of my whereabouts. Then came a sudden pattering of bare feet, the sound of heavy objects being thrown about, a violent creaking and rattling of chains. I heard the swish of the water as the ship was suddenly brought round, and a foamy yellow-green wave flew across the little round window and left it streaming. I jumped into my clothes and went on deck.

As I came up the ladder I saw against the flushed sky — for the sun was just rising — the broad back and red hair of the captain, and over his shoulder the puma spinning from a tackle rigged on to the mizzen spanker boom. The poor brute seemed horribly scared, and crouched in the bot-

tom of its little cage. "Overboard with 'em!" bawled the captain. "Overboard with 'em! We'll have a clean ship soon of the whole bilin' of 'em."

He stood in my way, so that I had perforce to tap his shoulder to come on deck. He came round with a start, and staggered back a few paces to stare at me. It needed no expert eye to tell that the man was still drunk. "Hullo!" said he stupidly, and then with a light coming into his eyes, "Why, it's Mister — Mister — ?"

"Prendick," said I.

"Prendick be damned!" said he. "Shut Up — that's your name. Mister Shut Up."

It was no good answering the brute. But I certainly did not expect his next move. He held out his hand to the gangway by which Montgomery stood talking to a massive white-haired man in dirty blue flannels, who had apparently just come aboard. "That way, Mister Blasted Shut Up. That way," roared the captain.

Montgomery and his companion turned as he spoke.

"What do you mean?" said I.

"That way, Mister Blasted Shut Up — that's what I mean. Overboard, Mister Shut Up — and sharp. We're clearing the ship out, cleaning the whole blessed ship out. And overboard you go."

I stared at him dumbfounded. Then it occurred to me it was exactly the thing I wanted. The lost prospect of a journey as sole passenger with this quarrelsome sot was not one to mourn over. I turned towards Montgomery.

"Can't have you," said Montgomery's companion concisely.

"You can't have me!" said I, aghast. He had the squarest and most resolute face I ever set eyes upon.

"Look here," I began, turning to the captain.

"Overboard," said the captain. "This ship ain't for beasts and cannibals, and worse than beasts, any more. Overboard you go . . . Mister Shut Up. If they can't have you, you goes adrift. But anyhow you go! With your Friends. I've done with this blessed island for evermore amen! I've had enough of it!"

"But, Montgomery," I appealed.

He distorted his lower lip, and nodded his head hopelessly at the grey-haired man beside him, to indicate his powerlessness to help me.

"I'll see to *you* presently," said the captain.

Then began a curious three-cornered altercation. Alternately I appealed to one and another of the three men, first to the grey-haired man to let me land, and then to the drunken captain to keep me aboard. I even bawled entreaties to the sailors. Montgomery said never a word; only shook his head. "You're going overboard, I tell you," was the captain's refrain. . . . "Law be damned! I'm king here."

At last, I must confess, my voice suddenly broke in the middle of a vigorous threat. I felt a gust of hysterical petulance, and went aft, and stared dismally at nothing.

Meanwhile the sailors pro-

gressed rapidly with the task of unshipping the packages and caged animals. A large launch with two standing lugs lay under the lee of the schooner, and into this the assortment of goods was swung. I did not then see the hands from the island that were receiving the packages, for the hull of the launch was hidden from me by the side of the schooner.

Neither Montgomery nor his companion took the slightest notice of me, but busied themselves in assisting and directing the four or five sailors who were unloading the goods. The captain went forward, interfering rather than assisting. I was alternately despairful and desperate. Once or twice, as I stood waiting there for things to accomplish themselves, I could not resist an impulse to laugh at my miserable quandary. I felt all the wretcheder for the lack of a breakfast. Hunger and a lack of blood-corpuscles take all the manhood from a man. I perceived pretty clearly that I had not the stamina either to resist what the captain chose to do to expel me, or to force myself upon Montgomery and his companion. So I waited passively upon fate, and the work of transferring Montgomery's possessions to the launch went on as if I did not exist.

Presently that work was finished, and then came a struggle; I was hauled, resisting weakly enough, to the gangway. Even then I noticed the oddness of the brown faces of the men who were with Montgomery in the launch. But the launch was now fully laden, and was shoved off hastily. A broadening gap of green water appeared under me, and I pushed back with all my strength to avoid falling headlong.

The hands in the launch shouted derisively, and I heard Montgomery curse at them. And then the captain, the mate and one of the seamen helping him, ran me aft towards the stern. The dingey of the *Lady Vain* had been towing behind; it was half full of water, had no oars, and was quite unvictualled. I refused to go aboard her, and flung myself full-length on the deck. In the end they swung me into her by a rope — for they had no stern ladder — and cut me adrift.

I drifted slowly from the schooner. In a kind of stupor I watched all hands take to the rigging and slowly but surely she came round to the wind. The sails fluttered, and then bellied out as the wind came into them. I stared at her weather-beaten side heeling steeply towards me. And then she passed out of my range of view.

I did not turn my head to follow her. At first I could scarcely believe what had happened. I crouched in the bottom of the dingey, stunned, and staring blankly at the vacant oily sea. Then I realised I was in that little hell of mine again, now half-swamped. Looking back over the gunwhale I saw the schooner standing away from me, with the red-haired captain mocking at me over the taffrail; and, turning towards the island, saw the launch growing smaller as she approached the beach.

Abruptly the cruelty of this desertion became clear to me. I had no means of reaching the land unless I should chance to drift there. I was still weak, you must remember, from my exposure in the boat; I was empty and very faint, or I should have had more heart. But as it was I suddenly began to sob and weep as I had never done since I was a little child. The tears ran down my face. In a passion of despair I struck with my fists at the water in the bottom of the boat, and kicked savagely at the gunwhale. I prayed aloud to God that he would let me die.

CHAPTER 6

THE EVIL–LOOKING BOATMEN

But the islanders, seeing I was really adrift, took pity on me. I drifted very slowly to the eastward, approaching the island slantingly, and presently I saw with hysterical relief the launch come round and return towards me. She was heavily laden, and as she drew near I could make out Montgomery's white-haired broad-shouldered companion sitting cramped up with the dogs and several packing-cases in the stern sheets. This individual stared fixedly at me without moving or speaking. The black-faced cripple was glaring at me as fixedly in the bows near the puma. There were three other men besides, strange brutish-looking fellows, at whom the staghounds were snarling savagely. Montgomery, who was steering, brought the boat by me and, rising, caught and fastened my painter to the tiller to tow me — for there was no room aboard.

I had recovered from my hysterical phase by this time, and answered his hail as he approached bravely enough. I told him the dingey was nearly swamped, and he reached me a piggin. I was jerked back as the rope tightened between the boats. For some time I was busy baling.

It was not until I had got the water under — for the water in the dingey had been shipped, the boat was perfectly sound — that I had leisure to look at the people in the launch again.

The white-haired man, I found, was still regarding me steadfastly, but with an expression, as I now fancied, of some perplexity. When my eyes met his he looked down at the staghounds that sat between his knees. He was a powerfully built man, as I have said, with a fine forehead and rather heavy features; but his eyes had that odd drooping of the skin above the lids that often comes with advancing years, and the fall of his heavy mouth at the corners gave him an expression of pugnacious resolution. He talked to Montgomery in a tone too low for me to hear. From him

my eyes travelled to his three men, and a strange crew they were. I saw only their faces, yet there was something in their faces — I knew not what — that gave me a spasm of disgust. I looked steadily at them, and the impression did not pass, though I failed to see what had occasioned it. They seemed to me then to be brown men, but their limbs were oddly swathed in some thin dirty white stuff down even to the fingers and feet. I have never seen men so wrapped up before, and women so only in the East. They wore turbans, too, and thereunder peered out their elfin faces at me, faces with protruding lower jaws and bright eyes. They had lank black hair almost like horse-hair, and seemed, as they sat, to exceed in stature any race of men I have seen. The white-haired man, who I knew was a good six feet in height, sat a head below any one of the three. I found afterwards that really none were taller than myself, but their bodies were abnormally long and the thigh-part of the leg short and curiously twisted. At any rate they were an amazingly ugly gang, and over the heads of them, under the forward lug, peered the black face of the man whose eyes were luminous in the dark.

As I stared at them they met my gaze, and then first one and then another turned away from my direct stare and looked at me in an odd furtive manner. It occurred to me that I was perhaps annoying them, and I turned my attention to the island we were approaching.

It was low, and covered with thick vegetation, chiefly of the inevitable palm-trees. From one point a thin white thread of vapour rose slantingly to an immense height, and then frayed out like a down feather. We were now within the embrace of a broad bay flanked on either hand by a low promontory. The beach was of a dull grey sand, and sloped steeply up to a ridge, perhaps sixty or seventy feet above the sea-level, and irregularly set with trees and undergrowth. Half-way up was a square stone enclosure that I found subsequently was built partly of coral and partly of pumiceous lava. Two thatched roofs peeped from within this enclosure.

A man stood awaiting us at the water's edge. I fancied, while we were still far off, that I saw some other and very grotesque-looking creatures scuttle into the bushes upon the slope, but I saw nothing of these as we drew nearer. This man was of a moderate size, and with a black negroid face. He had a large, almost lipless mouth, extraordinary, lank arms, long thin feet and bow legs, and stood with his heavy face thrust forward staring at us. He was dressed like Montgomery and his white-haired companion, in jacket and trousers of blue serge.

As we came still nearer, this individual began to run to and fro on the beach, making the most grotesque movements. At a word of command from Montgomery the four men in the launch sprang up with singular awkward gestures and struck the

lugs. Montgomery steered us round and into a narrow little dock excavated in the beach. Then the man on the beach hastened towards us. This dock, as I call it, was really a mere ditch just long enough at this phase of the tide to take the long-boat.

I heard the bows ground in the sand, staved the dingey off the rudder of the big boat with my piggin, and, freeing the painter, landed. The three muffled men, with the clumsiest movements, scrambled out upon the sand, and forthwith set to landing the cargo, assisted by the man on the beach. I was struck especially with the curious movements of the legs of the three swathed and bandaged boatmen — not stiff they were, but distorted in some odd way, almost as if they were jointed in the wrong place. The dogs were still snarling, and strained at their chains after these men, as the white-haired man landed with them.

The three big fellows spoke to one another in odd guttural tones, and the man who had waited for us on the beach, began chattering to them excitedly — a foreign language, as I fancied — as they laid hands on some bales piled near the stern. Somewhere I had heard such a voice before, and I could not think where. The white-haired man stood holding in a tumult of six dogs and bawling orders over their din. Montgomery, having unshipped the rudder, landed likewise, and all set to work at unloading. I was too faint, what with my long fast and the sun beating down on my bare head, to offer any assistance.

Presently the white-haired man seemed to recollect my presence, and came up to me. " You look," said he, " as though you had not breakfasted."

His little eyes were a brilliant black under his heavy brows. " I must apologise for that. Now you are our guest, we must make you comfortable — though you are uninvited, you know."

He looked keenly into my face. " Montgomery says you are an educated man, Mr. Prendick — says you know something of science. May I ask what that signifies? "

I told him I had spent some years at the Royal College of Science, and had done some research in biology under Huxley. He raised his eyebrows slightly at that.

" That alters the case a little, Mr. Prendick," he said, with a trifle more respect in his manner. " As it happens, we are biologists here. This is a biological station — of a sort." His eye rested on the men in white, who were busily hauling the puma, on rollers, towards the walled yard. " I and Montgomery, at least," he added.

Then, " When you will be able to get away, I can't say. We're off the track to anywhere. We see a ship once in a twelvemonth or so."

He left me abruptly and went up the beach past this group, and, I think, entered the enclosure. The other two men were with Montgomery erecting a pile of smaller packages on a low-

wheeled truck. The llama was still on the launch with the rabbit-hutches; the staghounds still lashed to the thwarts. The pile of things completed, all three men laid hold of the truck, and began shoving the ton-weight or so upon it after the puma. Presently Montgomery left them, and, coming back to me, held out his hand.

"I'm glad," said he, "for my own part. That captain was a silly ass. He'd have made things lively for you."

"It was you," said I, "that saved me again."

"That depends. You'll find this island an infernally rum place, I promise you. I'd watch my goings carefully if I were you. *He* — " He hesitated, and seemed to alter his mind about what was on his lips. "I wish you'd help me with these rabbits," he said.

His procedure with the rabbits was singular. I waded in with him and helped him lug one of the hutches ashore. No sooner was that done than he opened the door of it, and tilting the thing on one end, turned its living contents out on the ground. They fell in a struggling heap one on the top of the other. He clapped his hands, and forthwith they went off with that hopping run of theirs, fifteen or twenty of them, I should think, up the beach. "Increase and multiply, my friends," said Montgomery. "Replenish the island. Hitherto we've had a certain lack of meat here."

As I watched them disappearing, the white-haired man returned with a brandy flask and some biscuits. "Something to go on with, Prendick," said he in a far more familiar tone than before.

I made no ado, but set to work on the biscuits at once, while the white-haired man helped Montgomery to release about a score more of the rabbits. Three big hutches, however, went up to the house with the puma. The brandy I did not touch, for I have been an abstainer from my birth.

CHAPTER 7

THE LOCKED DOOR

THE READER will perhaps understand that at first everything was so strange about me, and my position was the outcome of such unexpected adventures, that I had no discernment of the relative strangeness of this or that thing about me. I followed the llama up the beach, and was overtaken by Montgomery who asked me not to enter the stone enclosure. I noticed then that the puma in its cage and the pile of packages had been placed outside the entrance to this quadrangle.

I turned and saw that the launch had now been unloaded, run out again, and beached, and

the white-haired man was walking towards us. He addressed Montgomery.

" And now comes the problem of this uninvited guest. What are we to do with him? "

" He knows something of science," said Montgomery.

" I'm itching to get to work again — with this new stuff," said the grey-haired man, nodding towards the enclosure. His eyes grew brighter.

" I daresay you are," said Montgomery, in anything but a cordial tone.

" We can't send him over there, and we can't spare the time to build him a new shanty. And we certainly can't take him into our confidence just yet."

" I'm in your hands," said I. I had no idea of what he meant by " over there."

" I've been thinking of the same things," Montgomery answered. " There's my room with the outer door — "

" That's it," said the elder man promptly, looking at Montgomery, and all three of us went towards the enclosure. " I'm sorry to make a mystery, Mr. Prendick — but you'll remember you're uninvited. Our little establishment here contains a secret or so, is a kind of Bluebeard's Chamber, in fact. Nothing very dreadful really — to a sane man. But just now — as we don't know you — "

" Decidedly," said I; " I should be a fool to take offence at any want of confidence."

He twisted his heavy mouth into a faint smile — he was one of those saturnine people who smile with the corners of the mouth

down — and bowed his acknowledgment of my complaisance. The main entrance to the enclosure was passed; it was a heavy wooden gate, framed in iron and locked, with the cargo of the launch piled outside it; and at the corner we came to a small doorway I had not previously observed. The grey-haired man produced a bundle of keys from the pocket of his greasy blue jacket, opened this door, and entered. His keys and the elaborate locking up of the place, even while it was still under his eye, struck me as peculiar.

I followed him, and found myself in a small apartment, plainly but not uncomfortably furnished, and with its inner door, which was slightly ajar, opening into a paved courtyard. This inner door Montgomery at once closed. A hammock was slung across the darker corner of the room, and a small unglazed window, defended by an iron bar, looked out towards the sea.

This, the grey-haired man told me, was to be my apartment, and the inner door, which, " for fear of accidents," he said, he would lock on the other side, was my limit inward. He called my attention to a convenient deck-chair before the window, and to an array of old books, chiefly, I found, surgical works and editions of the Latin and Greek classics — languages I cannot read with any comfort — on a shelf near the hammock. He left the room by the outer door, as if to avoid opening the inner one again.

" We usually have our meals in here," said Montgomery, and

then, as if in doubt, went out after the other. "Moreau," I heard him call, and for the moment I do not think I noticed. Then as I handled the books on the shelf it came up in consciousness: where had I heard the name of Moreau before?

I sat down before the window, took out the biscuits that still remained to me, and ate them with an excellent appetite. "Moreau?"

Through the window I saw one of those unaccountable men in white lugging a packing-case along the beach. Presently the window-frame hid him. Then I heard a key inserted and turned in the lock behind me. After a little while I heard, through the locked door, the noise of the staghounds, which had now been brought up from the beach. They were not barking, but sniffing and growling in a curious fashion. I could hear the rapid patter of their feet and Montgomery's voice soothing them.

I was very much impressed by the elaborate secrecy of these two men regarding the contents of the place, and for some time I was thinking of that, and of the unaccountable familiarity of the name of Moreau. But so odd is the human memory, that I could not then recall that well-known name in its proper connection. From that my thoughts went to the indefinable queerness of the deformed and white-swathed man on the beach. I never saw such a gait, such odd motions, as he pulled at the box. I recalled that none of these men had spoken to me, though most of them I had found looking at me at one time

or another in a peculiar furtive manner, quite unlike the frank stare of your unsophisticated savage. I wondered what language they spoke. They had all seemed remarkably taciturn, and when they did speak, endowed with very uncanny voices. What was wrong with them? Then I recalled the eyes of Montgomery's ungainly attendant.

Just as I was thinking of him, he came in. He was now dressed in white, and carried a little tray with some coffee and boiled vegetables thereon. I could hardly repress a shuddering recoil as he came, bending amiably, and placed the tray before me on the table.

Then astonishment paralysed me. Under his stringy black locks I saw his ear! It jumped upon me suddenly, close to my face. The man had pointed ears, covered with a fine fur!

"Your breakfast, sair," he said. I stared at his face without attempting to answer him. He turned and went towards the door, regarding me oddly over his shoulder.

I followed him out with my eyes, and as I did so, by some trick of unconscious cerebration, there came surging into my head the phrase: "The Moreau — Hollows" was it? "The Moreau — ?" Ah! it sent my memory back ten years. "The Moreau Horrors." The phrase drifted loose in my mind for a moment, and then I saw it in red lettering on a little buff-coloured pamphlet, that to read made one shiver and creep. Then I remembered distinctly all about it. That long-forgotten

pamphlet came back with startling vividness to my mind. I had been a mere lad then, and Moreau was, I suppose, about fifty; a prominent and masterful physiologist, well known in scientific circles for his extraordinary imagination and his brutal directness in discussion. Was this the same Moreau? He had published some very astonishing facts in connection with the transfusion of blood, and, in addition, was known to be doing valuable work on morbid growths. Then suddenly his career was closed. He had to leave England. A journalist obtained access to his laboratory in the capacity of laboratory assistant, with the deliberate intention of making sensational exposures; and by the help of a shocking accident — if it was an accident — his gruesome pamphlet became notorious. On the day of its publication, a wretched dog, flayed and otherwise mutilated, escaped from Moreau's house.

It was in the silly season, and a prominent editor, a cousin of the temporary laboratory assistant, appealed to the conscience of the nation. It was not the first time that conscience has turned against the methods of research. The doctor was simply howled out of the country. It may be he deserved to be, but I still think the tepid support of his fellow-investigators and his desertion by the great body of scientific workers, was a shameful thing. Yet some of his experiments, by the journalist's account, were wantonly cruel. He might perhaps have purchased his social peace by abandoning his investigations, but he apparently preferred the latter, as most men would who have once fallen under the overmastering spell of research. He was unmarried, and had indeed nothing but his own interests to consider. . . .

I felt convinced that this must be the same man. Everything pointed to it. It dawned upon me to what end the puma and the other animals, which had now been brought with other luggage into the enclosure behind the house, were destined; and a curious faint odour, the halitus of something familiar, an odour that had been in the background of my consciousness hitherto, suddenly came forward into the forefront of my thoughts. It was the antiseptic odour of the operating-room. I heard the puma growling through the wall, and one of the dogs yelped as though it had been struck.

Yet surely, and especially to another scientific man, there was nothing so horrible in vivisection as to account for this secrecy. And by some odd leap in my thoughts the pointed ears and luminous eyes of Montgomery's attendant came back again before me with the sharpest definition. I stared before me out at the green sea, frothing under a freshening breeze, and let these and other strange memories of the last few days chase each other through my mind.

What could it mean? A locked enclosure on a lonely island, a notorious vivisector, and these crippled and distorted men? . . .

CHAPTER 8

THE CRYING OF THE
PUMA

Montgomery interrupted my tangle of mystification and suspicion about one, and his grotesque attendant followed him with a tray bearing bread, some herbs, and other eatables, a flask of whisky, a jug of water, and three glasses and knives. I glanced askance at this strange creature, and found him watching me with his queer restless eyes. Montgomery said he would lunch with me, but that Moreau was too preoccupied with some work to come.

"Moreau!" said I; "I know that name."

"The devil you do!" said he. "What an ass I was to mention it to you. I might have thought. Anyhow, it will give you an inkling of our — mysteries. Whisky?"

"No thanks — I'm an abstainer."

"I wish I'd been. But it's no use locking the door after the steed is stolen. It was that infernal stuff led to my coming here. That and a foggy night. I thought myself in luck at the time when

Moreau offered to get me off. It's queer. . . ."

"Montgomery," said I suddenly, as the outer door closed; "why has your man pointed ears?"

"Damn!" he said, over his first mouthful of food. He stared at me for a moment, and then repeated: "Pointed ears?"

"Little points to them," said I, as calmly as possible, with a catch in my breath; "and a fine brown fur at the edges."

He helped himself to whisky and water with great deliberation. "I was under the impression . . . that his hair covered his ears."

"I saw them as he stooped by me to put that coffee you sent to me on the table. And his eyes shine in the dark."

By this time Montgomery had recovered from the surprise of my question. "I always thought," he said deliberately, with a certain accentuation of his flavouring of lisp; "that there *was* something the matter with his ears. From the way he covered them. . . . What were they like?"

I was persuaded from his manner that this ignorance was a pretence. Still I could hardly tell the man I thought him a liar. "Pointed," I said; "rather small and furry — distinctly furry. But the whole man is one of the strangest beings I ever set eyes on."

A sharp, hoarse cry of animal pain came from the enclosure behind us. Its depth and volume testified to the puma. I saw Montgomery wince.

"Yes!" he said.

"Where did you pick the creature up?"

"Er — San Francisco. . . . He's an ugly brute, I admit. Half-witted, you know. Can't remember where he came from. But I'm used to him, you know. We both are. How does he strike you?"

"He's unnatural," I said. "There's something about him. . . . Don't think me fanciful, but it gives me a nasty little sensation, a tightening of my muscles, when he comes near me. It's a touch . . . of the diabolical, in fact."

Montgomery had stopped eating while I told him ' this. "Rum," he said. "*I* can't see it."

He resumed his meal. "I had no idea of it," he said, and masticated. "The crew of the schooner . . . must have felt it the same. . . . Made a dead set at the poor devil. . . . You saw the captain?"

Suddenly the puma howled again, this time more painfully. Montgomery swore under his breath. I had half a mind to attack him about the men on the beach. Then the poor brute within gave vent to a series of short, sharp screams.

"Your men on the beach," said I; "what race are they?"

"Excellent fellows, aren't they?" said he absent-mindedly, knitting his brows as the animal yelled. I said no more. There was another outcry worse than the former. He looked at me with his dull grey eyes, and then took some more whisky. He tried to draw me into a discussion about alcohol, professing to have saved my life with it. He seemed anx-ious to lay stress on the fact that I owed my life to him. I answered him distractedly. Presently our meal came to an end, the mis-shapen monster with the pointed ears cleared away, and Montgomery left me alone in the room again. All the time he was in a state of ill-concealed irritation at the noise of the vivisected puma. He spoke of his odd want of nerve, and left me to the obvious application.

I found myself that the cries were singularly irritating, and they grew in depth and intensity as the afternoon wore on. They were painful at first, but their constant resurgence at last altogether upset my balance. I flung aside a crib of Horace I had been reading, and began to clench my fists, to bite my lips, and pace the room.

Presently I got to stopping my ears with my fingers.

The emotional appeal of those yells grew upon me steadily, grew at last to such an exquisite expression of suffering that I could stand it in that confined room no longer. I stepped out of the door into the slumberous heat of the late afternoon, and walking past the main entrance — locked again I noticed — turned the corner of the wall.

The crying sounded even louder out of doors. It was as if all the pain in the world had found a voice. Yet had I known such pain was in the next room, and had it been dumb, I believe — I have thought since — I could have stood it well enough. It is when suffering finds a voice and

sets our nerves quivering that this pity comes troubling us. But in spite of the brilliant sunlight and the green fans of the trees waving in the soothing sea-breeze, the world was a confusion, blurred with drifting black and red phantasms, until I was out of earshot of the house in the stone wall.

CHAPTER 9

THE THING IN THE FOREST

I STRODE through the undergrowth that clothed the ridge behind the house, scarcely heeding whither I went, passed on through the shadow of a thick cluster of straight-stemmed trees beyond it, and so presently found myself some way on the other side of the ridge, and descending towards a streamlet that ran through a narrow valley. I paused and listened. The distance I had come, or the intervening masses of thicket, deadened any sound that might be coming from the enclosure. The air was still. Then with a rustle a rabbit emerged, and went scampering up the slope before me. I hesitated, and sat down in the edge of the shade.

The place was a pleasant one. The rivulet was hidden by the luxuriant vegetation of the banks, save at one point, where I caught a triangular patch of its glittering water. On the further side I saw through a bluish haze a tangle of trees and creepers, and above these again the luminous blue of the sky. Here and there a splash of white or crimson marked the blooming of some trailing epiphyte. I let my eyes wander over this scene for a while, and then began to turn over in my mind again the strange peculiarities of Montgomery's man. But it was too hot to think elaborately, and presently I fell into a tranquil state midway between dozing and waking.

From this I was aroused, after I know not how long, by a rustling amidst the greenery on the other side of the stream. For a moment I could see nothing but the waving summits of the ferns and reeds. Then suddenly upon the bank of the stream appeared something — at first I could not distinguish what it was. It bowed its head to the water and began to drink. Then I saw it was a man, going on all-fours like a beast!

He was clothed in bluish cloth, and was of a copper-coloured hue, with black hair. It seemed that grotesque ugliness was an invariable character of these islanders. I could hear the suck of the water at his lips as he drank.

I leant forward to see him better, and a piece of lava, detached by my hand, went pattering down the slope. He looked up guiltily,

and his eyes met mine. Forthwith he scrambled to his feet and stood wiping his clumsy hand across his mouth and regarding me. His legs were scarcely half the length of his body. So, staring one another out of countenance, we remained for perhaps the space of a minute. Then, stopping to look back once or twice, he slunk off among the bushes to the right of me, and I heard the swish of the fronds grow faint in the distance and die away. Every now and then he regarded me with a steadfast stare. Long after he had disappeared I remained sitting up staring in the direction of his retreat. My drowsy tranquillity had gone.

I was startled by a noise behind me, and, turning suddenly, saw the flapping white tail of a rabbit vanishing up the slope. I jumped to my feet.

The apparition of this grotesque half-bestial creature had suddenly populated the stillness of the afternoon for me. I looked around me rather nervously, and regretted that I was unarmed. Then I thought that the man I had just seen had been clothed in bluish cloth, had not been naked as a savage would have been, and I tried to persuade myself from that fact that he was after all probably a peaceful character, that the dull ferocity of his countenance belied him.

Yet I was greatly disturbed at the apparition. I walked to the left along the slope, turning my head about and peering this way and that among the straight stems of the trees. Why should a man go on all-fours and drink with his lips? Presently I heard an animal wailing again, and taking it to be the puma, I turned about and walked in a direction diametrically opposite to the sound. This led me down to the stream, across which I stepped and pushed my way up through the undergrowth beyond.

I was startled by a great patch of vivid scarlet on the ground, and going up to it found it to be a peculiar fungus branched and corrugated like a foliaceous lichen, but deliquescing into slime at the touch. And then in the shadow of some luxuriant ferns I came upon an unpleasant thing, the dead body of a rabbit, covered with shining flies but still warm, and with its head torn off. I stopped aghast at the sight of the scattered blood. Here at least was one visitor to the island disposed of!

There were no traces of other violence about it. It looked as though it had been suddenly snatched up and killed. And as I stared at the little furry body came the difficulty of how the thing had been done. The vague dread that had been in my mind since I had seen the inhuman face of the man at the stream grew distincter as I stood there. I began to realise the hardihood of my expedition among these unknown people. The thicket about me became altered to my imagination. Every shadow became something more than a shadow, became an ambush, every rustle became a threat. Invisible things seemed watching me.

I resolved to go back to the enclosure on the beach. I suddenly turned away and thrust myself violently — possibly even frantically — through the bushes, anxious to get a clear space about me again.

I stopped just in time to prevent myself emerging upon an open space. It was a kind of glade in the forest made by a fall; seedlings were already starting up to struggle for the vacant space, and beyond, the dense growth of stems and twining vines and splashes of fungus and flowers closed in again. Before me, squatting together upon the fungoid ruins of a huge fallen tree, and still unaware of my approach, were three grotesque human figures.

One was evidently a female. The other two were men. They were naked, save for swathings of scarlet cloth about the middles, and their skins were of a dull pinkish drab colour, such as I had seen in no savages before. They had fat heavy chinless faces, retreating foreheads, and a scant bristly hair upon their heads. Never before had I seen such bestial-looking creatures.

They were talking, or at least one of the men was talking to the other two, and all three had been too closely interested to heed the rustling of my approach. They swayed their heads and shoulders from side to side. The speaker's words came thick and sloppy, and though I could hear them distinctly I could not distinguish what he said. He seemed to me to be reciting some complicated gibberish. Presently his articulation became shriller, and spreading his hands he rose to his feet.

At that time the others began to gibber in unison, also rising to their feet, spreading their hands, and swaying their bodies in rhythm with their chant. I noticed then the abnormal shortness of their legs and their lank clumsy feet. All three began slowly to circle round, rising and stamping their feet and waving their arms; a kind of tune crept into their rhythmic recitation, and a refrain — " Aloola " or " Baloola " it sounded like. Their eyes began to sparkle and their ugly faces to brighten with an expression of strange pleasure. Saliva dropped from their lipless mouths.

Suddenly, as I watched their grotesque and unaccountable gesture, I perceived clearly for the first time what it was that had offended me, what had given me the two inconsistent and conflicting impressions of utter strangeness and yet of the strangest familiarity. The three creatures engaged in this mysterious rite were human in shape, and yet human beings with the strangest air about them of some familiar animal. Each of these creatures, despite its human form, its rag of clothing, and the rough humanity of its bodily form, had woven into it, into its movements, into the expression of its countenance, into its whole presence, some now irresistible suggestion of a hog, a swinish taint, the unmistakable mark of the beast.

I stood overcome by this realisation, and then the most horrible questionings came rushing

into my mind. They began leaping into the air, first one and then the other, whooping and grunting. Then one slipped, and for a moment was on all-fours, to recover indeed forthwith. But that transitory gleam of the true animalism of these monsters was enough.

I turned as noiselessly as possible, and becoming every now and then rigid with the fear of being discovered as a branch cracked or leaf rustled, I pushed back into the bushes. It was long before I grew bolder and dared to move freely.

My one idea for the moment was to get away from these foul beings, and I scarcely noticed that I had emerged upon a faint pathway amidst the trees. Then, suddenly traversing a little glade, I saw with an unpleasant start two clumsy legs among the trees, walking with noiseless footsteps parallel with my course, and perhaps thirty yards away from me. The head and upper part of the body were hidden by a tangle of creeper. I stopped abruptly, hoping the creature did not see me. The feet stopped as I did. So nervous was I that I controlled an impulse to headlong flight with the utmost difficulty.

Then, looking hard, I distinguished through the interlacing network the head and body of the brute I had seen drinking. He moved his head. There was an emerald flash in his eyes as he glanced at me from the shadow of the trees, a half-luminous colour, that vanished as he turned his head again. He was motionless for a moment, and then with

noiseless tread began running through the green confusion. In another moment he had vanished behind some bushes. I could not see him, but I felt that he had stopped and was watching me again.

What on earth was he — man or animal? What did he want with me? I had no weapon, not even a stick. Flight would be madness. At any rate the Thing, whatever it was, lacked the courage to attack me. Setting my teeth hard I walked straight towards him. I was anxious not to show the fear that seemed chilling my backbone. I pushed through a tangle of tall white-flowered bushes, and saw him twenty yards beyond, looking over his shoulder at me and hesitating. I advanced a step or two looking steadfastly into his eyes.

"Who are you?" said I. He tried to meet my gaze.

"No!" he said suddenly, and turning, went bounding away from me through the undergrowth. Then he turned and stared at me again. His eyes shone brightly out of the dusk under the trees.

My heart was in my mouth, but I felt my only chance was to face the danger, and walked steadily towards him. He turned again and vanished into the dusk. Once more I thought I caught the glint of his eyes, and that was all.

For the first time I realised how the lateness of the hour might affect me. The sun had set some minutes since, the swift dusk of the tropics was already fading out of the eastern sky, and

a pioneer moth fluttered silently by my head. Unless I would spend the night among the unknown dangers of the mysterious forest, I must hasten back to the enclosure.

The thought of a return to that pain-haunted refuge was extremely disagreeable, but still more so was the idea of being overtaken in the open by darkness, and all that darkness might conceal. I gave one more look into the blue shadows that had swallowed up this odd creature, and then retraced my way down the slope towards the stream, going as I judged in the direction from which I had come.

I walked eagerly, perplexed by all these things, and presently found myself in a level among scattered trees. The colourless clearness that comes after the sunset flush was darkling. The blue sky above grew momentarily deeper, and the little stars one by one pierced the attenuated light; the interspaces of the trees, the gaps in the further vegetation that had been hazy blue in the daylight, grew black and mysterious.

I pushed on. The colour vanished from the world, the treetops rose against the luminous blue sky in inky silhouette, and all below that outline melted into formless blackness. Presently the trees grew thinner, and the shrubby undergrowth more abundant. Then there was a desolate space covered with white sand, and then another expanse of tangled bushes.

I was tormented by a faint rustling upon my right hand. I thought at first it was fancy, for whenever I stopped there was silence save for the evening breeze in the tree-tops. Then when I went on again there was an echo to my footsteps.

I moved away from the thickets, keeping to the more open ground, and endeavouring by sudden turns now and then to surprise this thing, if it existed, in the act of creeping upon me. I saw nothing, and nevertheless my sense of another presence grew steadily. I increased my pace, and after some time came to a slight ridge, crossed it and turned sharply, regarding it steadfastly from the further side. It came out black and clear-cut against the darkling sky.

And presently a shapeless lump heaved up momentarily against the skyline and vanished again. I felt assured now that my tawny-faced antagonist was stalking me again. And coupled with that was another unpleasant realisation, that I had lost my way.

For a time I hurried on hopelessly perplexed, pursued by that stealthy approach. Whatever it was, the thing either lacked the courage to attack me, or it was waiting to take me at some disadvantage. I kept studiously to the open. At times I would turn and listen, and presently I half-persuaded myself that my pursuer had abandoned the chase, or was a mere creation of my disordered imagination. Then I heard the sound of the sea. I quickened my footsteps almost to a run, and immediately there was a stumble in my rear.

I turned suddenly and stared at the uncertain trees behind me. One black shadow seemed to leap into another. I listened rigid, and heard nothing but the whisper of the blood in my ears. I thought that my nerves were unstrung, and that my imagination was tricking me, and turned resolutely towards the sound of the sea again.

In a minute or so the trees grew thinner, and I emerged upon a bare low headland running out into the sombre water. The night was calm and clear, and the reflection of the growing multitude of the stars shivered in the tranquil heaving of the sea. Some way out, the wash upon an irregular band of reef shone with a pallid light of its own. Westward I saw the zodiacal light mingling with the yellow brilliance of the evening star. The coast fell away from me to the east, and westward it was hidden by the shoulder of the cape. Then I recalled the fact that Moreau's beach lay to the west.

A twig snapped behind me and there was a rustle. I turned and stood facing the dark trees. I could see nothing — or else I could see too much. Every dark form in the dimness had its ominous quality, its peculiar suggestion of alert watchfulness. So I stood for perhaps a minute, and then, with an eye to the trees still, turned westward to cross the headland. And as I moved, one among the lurking shadows moved to follow me.

My heart beat quickly. Presently the broad sweep of a bay to the westward became visible, and I halted again. The noiseless shadow halted a dozen yards from me. A little point of light shone on the further bend of the curve, and the grey sweep of the sandy beach lay faint under the starlight. Perhaps two miles away was that little point of light. To get to the beach I should have to go through the trees where the shadows lurked, and down a bushy slope.

I could see the thing rather more distinctly now. It was no animal, for it stood erect. At that I opened my mouth to speak, and found a hoarse phlegm choked my voice. I tried again, and shouted, "Who is there?" There was no answer. I advanced a step. The thing did not move; only gathered itself together. My foot struck a stone.

That gave me an idea. Without taking my eyes off the black form before me I stooped and picked up this lump of rock. But at my motion the thing turned abruptly as a dog might have done, and slunk obliquely into the further darkness. Then I recalled a schoolboy expedient against big dogs, twisted the rock into my handkerchief, and gave this a turn round my wrist. I heard a movement further off among the shadows as if the thing was in retreat. Then suddenly my tense excitement gave way; I broke into a profuse perspiration and fell a-trembling, with my adversary routed and this weapon in my hand.

It was some time before I could summon resolution to go down through the trees and bushes upon the flank of the headland

to the beach. At last I did it at a run, and as I emerged from the thicket upon the sand I heard some other body come crashing after me.

At that I completely lost my head with fear, and began running along the sand. Forthwith there came the swift patter of soft feet in pursuit. I gave a wild cry and redoubled my pace. Some dim black things about three or four times the size of rabbits went running or hopping up from the beach towards the bushes as I passed. So long as I live I shall remember the terror of that chase. I ran near the water's edge, and heard every now and then the splash of the feet that gained upon me. Far away, hopelessly far, was the yellow light. All the night about us was black and still. Splash, splash came the pursuing feet nearer and nearer. I felt my breath going, for I was quite out of training: it whooped as I drew it, and I felt a pain like a knife at my side. I perceived the thing would come up with me long before I reached the enclosure, and, desperate and sobbing for breath, I wheeled round upon it and struck at it as it came up to me — struck with all my strength. The stone came out of the sling of the handkerchief as I did so.

As I turned, the thing, which had been running on all-fours, rose to its feet, and the missile fell fair on its left temple. The skull rang loud and the animal-man blundered into me, thrust me back with its hands, and went staggering past me to fall headlong upon the sand with its face

in the water. And there it lay still.

I could not bring myself to approach that black heap. I left it there with the water rippling round it under the still stars, and giving it a wide berth, pursued my way towards the yellow glow of the house. And presently, with a positive effect of relief, came the pitiful moaning of the puma, the sound that had originally driven me out to explore this mysterious island. At that, though I was faint and horribly fatigued, I gathered together all my strength and began running again towards the light. It seemed to me a voice was calling me.

CHAPTER 10

THE CRYING OF THE MAN

As I drew near the house I saw that the light shone from the open door of my room; and then I heard, coming from out the darkness at the side of that orange oblong, the voice of Montgomery shouting "Prendick."

I continued running. Presently I heard him again. I replied by a feeble "Hullo!" and in another moment had staggered up to him.

"Where have you been?" said he, holding me at arm's-length, so that the light from the door fell on my face. "We have both been so busy that we forgot about you until about half an hour ago."

He led me into the room and sat me down in the deck chair. For a while I was blinded by the light. "We did not think you would start to explore this island of ours without telling us," he said. And then, "I was afraid! But . . . what . . . Hullo!"

For my last remaining strength slipped from me, and my head fell forward on my chest. I think he found a certain satisfaction in giving me brandy. "For God's sake," said I, "fasten that door."

"You've been meeting some of our curiosities, eh?" said he. He locked the door and turned to me again. He asked me no questions, but gave me some more brandy and water, and pressed me to eat. I was in a state of collapse. He said something vague about his forgetting to warn me, and asked me briefly when I left the house and what I had seen. I answered him as briefly in fragmentary sentences. "Tell me what it all means," said I, in a state bordering on hysterics.

"It's nothing so very dreadful," said he. "But I think you have been about enough for one day." The puma suddenly gave a sharp yell of pain. At that he swore under his breath. "I'm damned," said he, "if this place is not as bad as Gower Street — with its cats."

"Montgomery," said I, "what was that thing that came after me. Was it a beast, or was it a man?"

"If you don't sleep to-night," he said, "you'll be off your head to-morrow."

I stood up in front of him. "What was that thing that came after me?" I asked.

He looked me squarely in the eyes and twisted his mouth askew. His eyes, which had seemed animated a minute before, went dull. "From your account," said he, "I'm thinking it was a bogle."

I felt a gust of intense irritation that passed as quickly as it came. I flung myself into the chair again and pressed my hands on my forehead. The puma began again.

Montgomery came round behind me and put his hand on my shoulder. "Look here, Prendick," he said; "I had no business to let you drift out into this silly island of ours. But it's not so bad as you feel, man. Your nerves are worked to rags. Let me give you something that will make you sleep. *That* . . . will keep on for hours yet. You must simply get to sleep, or I won't answer for it."

I did not reply. I bowed forward and covered my face with my hands. Presently he returned with a small measure containing a dark liquid. This he gave me. I took it unresistingly, and he helped me into the hammock.

When I awoke it was broad day. For a little while I lay flat, staring at the roof above me. The rafters, I observed, were made out of the timbers of a ship. Then I turned my head and saw a meal prepared for me on the table. I perceived that I was hun-

gry, and prepared to clamber out of the hammock which, very politely anticipating my intention, twisted round and deposited me upon all-fours on the floor.

I got up and sat down before the food. I had a heavy feeling in my head, and only the vaguest memory at first of the things that had happened over-night. The morning breeze blew very pleasantly through the unglazed window, and that and the food contributed to the sense of animal comfort I experienced. Presently the door behind me, the door inward towards the yard of the enclosure, opened. I turned and saw Montgomery's face. " All right? " said he. " I'm frightfully busy." And he shut the door. Afterwards I discovered that he forgot to relock it.

Then I recalled the expression of his face the previous night, and with that the memory of all I had experienced reconstructed itself before me. Even as that fear returned to me came a cry from within. But this time it was not the cry of the puma.

I put down the mouthful that hesitated upon my lips, and listened. Silence, save for the whisper of the morning breeze. I began to think my ears had deceived me.

After a long pause I resumed my meal, but with my ear still vigilant. Presently I heard something else very faint and low. I sat as if frozen in my attitude. Though it was faint and low, it moved me more profoundly than all that I had hitherto heard of the abominations behind the wall. There was no mistake this time in the quality of the dim broken sounds, no doubt at all of their source; for it was groaning, broken by sobs and gasps of anguish. It was no brute this time. It was a human being in torment!

And as I realised this I rose, and in three steps had crossed the room, seized the handle of the door into the yard, and flung it open before me.

" Prendick, man! Stop! " cried Montgomery, intervening. A startled deerhound yelped and snarled. There was blood, I saw, in the sink, brown, and some scarlet, and I smelt the peculiar smell of carbolic acid. Then through an open doorway beyond in the dim light of the shadow, I saw something bound painfully upon a framework, scarred, red, and bandaged. And then blotting this out appeared the face of old Moreau, white and terrible.

In a moment he had gripped me by the shoulder with a hand that was smeared red, had twisted me off my feet, and flung me headlong · back into my own room. He lifted me as though I was a little child. I fell at full length upon the floor, and the door slammed and shut out the passionate intensity of his face. Then I heard the key turn in the lock and Montgomery's voice in expostulation.

" Ruin the work of a lifetime! " I heard Moreau say.

" He does not understand," said Montgomery, and other things that were inaudible.

" I can't spare the time yet," said Moreau.

The rest I did not hear. I picked myself up and stood trembling, my mind a chaos of the most horrible misgivings. Could the vivisection of men be possible? The question shot like lightning across a tumultuous sky. And suddenly the clouded horror of my mind condensed into a vivid realisation of my danger.

CHAPTER 11

THE HUNTING OF THE MAN

IT came before my mind with an unreasonable hope of escape, that the outer door of my room was still open to me. I was convinced now, absolutely assured, that Moreau had been vivisecting a human being. All the time since I had heard his name I had been trying to link in my mind in some way the grotesque animalism of the islanders with his abominations; and now I thought I saw it all. The memory of his works in the transfusion of blood recurred to me. These creatures I had seen were the victims of some hideous experiment!

These sickening scoundrels had merely intended to keep me back, to fool me with their display of confidence, and presently to fall upon me with a fate more horrible than death, with torture, and after torture the most hideous degradation it was possible to conceive — to send me off, a lost soul, a beast, to the rest of their Comus rout. I looked round for some weapon. Nothing. Then, with an inspiration, I turned over the deck chair, put my foot on the side of it, and tore away the side rail. It happened that a nail came away with the wood, and, projecting, gave a touch of danger to an otherwise petty weapon. I heard a step outside, incontinently flung open the door, and found Montgomery within a yard of it. He meant to lock the outer door.

I raised this nailed stick of mine and cut at his face, but he sprang back. I hesitated a moment, then turned and fled round the corner of the house. "Prendick, man!" I heard his astonished cry. "Don't be a silly ass, man!"

Another minute, thought I, and he would have had me locked in, and as ready as a hospital rabbit for my fate. He emerged behind the corner, for I heard him shout, "Prendick!" Then he began to run after me, shouting things as he ran.

This time, running blindly, I went north-eastward, in a direction at right angles to my previous expedition. Once, as I went running headlong up the beach, I glanced over my shoulder and saw his attendant with him. I ran furiously up the slope, over it, then turned eastward along a rocky valley, fringed on either

side with jungle. I ran perhaps a mile altogether, my chest straining, my heart beating in my ears, and then, hearing nothing of Montgomery or his man and feeling upon the verge of exhaustion, I doubled sharply back towards the beach, as I judged, and lay down in the shelter of a cane brake.

There I remained for a long time, too fearful to move, and indeed too fearful even to play a course of action. The wild scene about me lay sleeping silently under the sun, and the only sound near me was the thin hum of some small gnats that had discovered me. Presently I became aware of a drowsy breathing sound — the soughing of the sea upon the beach.

After about an hour I heard Montgomery shouting my name far away to the north. That set me thinking of my plan of action. As I interpreted it then, this island was inhabited only by these two vivisectors and their animalised victims. Some of these, no doubt, they could press into their service against me, if need arose. I knew both Moreau and Montgomery carried revolvers; and, save for a feeble bar of deal, spiked with a small nail, the merest mockery of a mace, I was unarmed.

So I lay still where I was until I began to think of food and drink. And at that moment the real hopelessness of my position came home to me. I knew no way of getting anything to eat; I was too ignorant of botany to discover any resort of root or fruit that might lie about me; I had no

means of trapping the few rabbits upon the island. It grew blanker the more I turned the prospect over. At last, in the desperation of my position, my mind turned to the animal-men I had encountered. I tried to find some hope in what I remembered of them. In turn I recalled each one I had seen, and tried to draw some augury of assistance from my memory.

Then suddenly I heard a staghound bay, and at that realised a new danger. I took little time to think, or they would have caught me then, but snatching up my nailed stick, rushed headlong from my hiding-place towards the sound of the sea. I remember a growth of thorny plants with spines that stabbed like penknives. I emerged, bleeding and with torn clothes, upon the lip of a long creek opening northward. I went straight into the waves without a minute's hesitation, wading up the creek, and presently finding myself knee-deep in a little stream. I scrambled out at last on the westward bank, and, with my heart beating loudly in my ears, crept into a tangle of ferns to await the issue. I heard the dog — it was only one — draw nearer, and yelp when it came to the thorns. Then I heard no more, and presently began to think I had escaped.

The minutes passed, the silence lengthened out, and at last, after an hour of security, my courage began to return to me.

By this time I was no longer very terrified or very miserable. For I had, as it were, passed the limit of terror and despair. I felt

now that my life was practically lost, and that persuasion made me capable of daring anything. I had even a certain wish to encounter Moreau face to face. And, as I had waded into the water, I remembered that if I were too hard pressed at least one path of escape from torment still lay open to me — they could not very well prevent my drowning myself. I had half a mind to drown myself then, but an odd wish to see the whole adventure out, a queer impersonal spectacular interest in myself, restrained me. I stretched my limbs, sore and painful from the pricks of the spiny plants, and stared around me at the trees; and, so suddenly that it seemed to jump out of the green tracery about it, my eyes lit upon a black face watching me.

I saw that it was the simian creature who had met the launch upon the beach. He was clinging to the oblique stem of a palm-tree. I gripped my stick, and stood up facing him. He began chattering. " You, you, you," was all I could distinguish at first. Suddenly he dropped from the tree, and in another moment was holding the fronds apart, and staring curiously at me.

I did not feel the same repugnance towards this creature that I had experienced in my encounters with the other Beast Men. "You," he said, "in the boat." He was a man, then — at least, as much of a man as Montgomery's attendant — for he could talk.

"Yes," I said, " I came in the boat. From the ship."

" Oh! " he said, and his bright restless eyes travelled over me, to my hands, to the stick I carried, to my feet, to the tattered places in my coat, and the cuts and scratches I had received from the thorns. He seemed puzzled at something. His eyes came back to my hands. He held his own hand out, and counted his digits slowly, " One, Two, Three, Four, Five — eh? "

I did not grasp his meaning then. Afterwards I was to find that a great proportion of these Beast People had malformed hands lacking sometimes even three digits. But guessing this was in some way a greeting, I did the same thing by way of reply. He grinned with immense satisfaction. Then his quick roving glance went round again. He made a swift movement, and vanished. The fern fronds he had stood between came swishing together.

I pushed out of the brake after him, and was astonished to find him swinging cheerfully by one lank arm from a rope of creepers that looped down from the foliage overhead. His back was to me.

"Hullo! " said I.

He came down with a twisting jump, and stood facing me. " I say," said I, " where can I get something to eat? "

"Eat! " he said. "Eat man's food now." And his eyes went back to the swing of ropes. "At the huts."

"But where are the huts? "

"Oh! "

" I'm new, you know."

At that he swung round, and set off at a quick walk. All his motions were curiously rapid. "Come along," said he. I went with him to see the adventure

out. I guessed the huts were some rough shelter, where he and some more of these Beast People lived. I might perhaps find them friendly, find some handle in their minds to take hold of. I did not know yet how far they were from the human heritage I ascribed to them.

My ape-like companion trotted along by my side, with his hands hanging down and his jaw thrust forward. I wondered what memory he might have in him. "How long have you been on this island?" said I.

"How long?" he asked. And, after having the question repeated, he held up three fingers. The creature was little better than an idiot. I tried to make out what he meant by that, and it seems I bored him. After another question or two, he suddenly left my side and sprang at some fruit that hung from a tree. He pulled down a handful of prickly husks, and went on eating the contents. I noted this with satisfaction, for here, at least, was a hint for feeding. I tried him with some other questions, but his chattering prompt responses were, as often as not, at cross-purposes with my question. Some few were appropriate, others quite parrot-like.

I was so intent upon these peculiarities that I scarcely noted the path we followed. Presently we came to trees, all charred and brown, and so to a bare place covered with a yellow-white incrustation, across which went a drifting smoke, pungent in whiffs to nose and eyes. On our right, over a shoulder of bare rock, I saw the level blue of the sea. The path coiled down abruptly into a narrow ravine between two tumbled and knotty masses of blackish scoriæ. Into this we plunged.

It was extremely dark, this passage, after the blinding sunlight reflected from the sulphurous ground. Its walls grew steep, and approached one another. Blotches of green and crimson drifted across my eyes. My conductor stopped suddenly. "Home," said he, and I stood in a floor of a chasm that was at first absolutely dark to me. I heard some strange noises, and thrust the knuckles of my left hand into my eyes. I became aware of a disagreeable odour like that of a monkey's cage ill-cleaned. Beyond, the rock opened again upon a gradual slope of sunlit greenery, and on either hand the light smote down through a narrow channel into the central gloom.

CHAPTER 12

THE SAYERS OF THE LAW

THEN something cold touched my hand. I started violently, and saw close to me a dim pinkish thing, looking more like a flayed child than anything else in the world. The creature had exactly

the mild but repulsive features of a sloth, the same low forehead and slow gestures. As the first shock of the change of light passed, I saw about me more distinctly. The little sloth-like creature was standing and staring at me. My conductor had vanished.

The place was a narrow passage between high walls of lava, a crack in its knotted flow and on either side interwoven heaps of sea-mat, palm fans and reeds leaning against the rock, formed rough and impenetrably dark dens. The winding way up the ravine between these was scarcely three yards wide, and was disfigured by lumps of decaying fruit pulp and other refuse which accounted for the disagreeable stench of the place.

The little pink sloth creature was still blinking at me when my Ape Man reappeared at the aperture of the nearest of these dens, and beckoned me in. As he did so a slouching monster wriggled out of one of the places further up this strange street, and stood up in featureless silhouette against the bright green beyond, staring at me. I hesitated — had half a mind to bolt the way I had come — and then, determined to go through with the adventure, gripped my nailed stick about the middle, and crawled into the little evil-smelling lean-to after my conductor.

It was a semicircular space, shaped like the half of a bee-hive, and against the rocky wall that formed the inner side of it was a pile of variegated fruits, cocoa-nuts and others. Some rough vessels of lava and wood stood about

the floor, and one on a rough stool. There was no fire. In the darkest corner of the hut sat a shapeless mass of darkness that grunted "Hey!" as I came in, and my Ape Man stood in the dim light of the doorway and held out a split cocoa-nut to me as I crawled into the other corner and squatted down. I took it and began gnawing it, as serenely as possible in spite of my tense trepidation and the nearly intolerable closeness of the den. The little pink sloth creature stood in the aperture of the hut, and something else with a drab face and bright eyes came staring over its shoulder.

"Hey," came out of the lump of mystery opposite. "It is a man! It is a man!" gabbled my conductor — "a man, a man, a live man, like me."

"Shut up!" said the voice from the dark, and grunted. I gnawed my cocoa-nut amid an impressive silence. I peered hard into the blackness, but could distinguish nothing. "It is a man," the voice repeated. "He comes to live with us?" It was a thick voice with something in it, a kind of whistling overtone, that struck me as peculiar, but the English accent was strangely good.

The Ape Man looked at me as though he expected something. I perceived the pause was interrogative.

"He comes to live with you," I said.

"It is a man. He must learn the Law."

I began to distinguish now a deeper blackness in the black, a vague outline of a hunched-up

figure. Then I noticed the opening of the place was darkened by two more heads. My hand tightened on my stick. The thing in the dark repeated in a louder tone, " Say the words." I had missed its last remark. " Not to go on all-Fours; that is the Law " — it repeated in a kind of sing-song.

I was puzzled. " Say the words," said the Ape Man, repeating, and the figures in the doorway echoed this with a threat in the tone of their voices. I realised I had to repeat this idiotic formula. And then began the insanest ceremony. The voice in the dark began intoning a mad litany, line by line, and I and the rest to repeat it. As they did so, they swayed from side to side, and beat their hands upon their knees, and I followed their example. I could have imagined I was already dead and in another world. The dark hut, these grotesque dim figures, just flecked here and there by a glimmer of light, and all of them swaying in unison and chanting:

" Not to go on all-Fours; *that* is the Law. Are we not Men? "

" Not to suck up Drink; *that* is the Law. Are we not Men? "

" Not to eat Flesh or Fish; *that* is the Law. Are we not Men? "

" Not to claw Bark of Trees; *that* is the Law. Are we not Men? "

" Not to chase other Men; *that* is the Law. Are we not Men? "

And so from the prohibition of these acts of folly, on to the prohibition of what I thought then were the maddest, most impossible and most indecent things one could well imagine. A kind of rhythmic fervour fell on all of us; we gabbled and swayed faster and faster, repeating this amazing law. Superficially the contagion of these brute men was upon me, but deep down within me laughter and disgust struggled together. We ran through a long list of prohibitions, and then the chant swung round to a new formula:

" *His* is the House of Pain.

" *His* is the Hand that makes.

" *His* is the Hand that wounds.

" *His* is the Hand that heals."

And so on for another long series, mostly quite incomprehensible gibberish to me, about *Him,* whoever he might be. I could have fancied it was a dream, but never before have I heard chanting in a dream.

" *His* is the lightning-flash," we sang. " *His* is the deep salt sea."

A horrible fancy came into my head that Moreau, after animalising these men, had infected their dwarfed brains with a kind of deification of himself. However, I was too keenly aware of white teeth and strong claws about me to stop my chanting on that account. " *His* are the stars in the sky."

At last that song ended. I saw the Ape Man's face shining with perspiration, and my eyes being now accustomed to the darkness, I saw more distinctly the figure in the corner from which the voice came. It was the size of a man, but it seemed covered with a dull grey hair almost like a Skye terrier. What was it? What were they all? Imagine yourself surrounded by all the most hor-

rible cripples and maniacs it is possible to conceive, and you may understand a little of my feelings with these grotesque caricatures of humanity about me.

"He is a five-man, a five-man, a five-man . . . like me," said the Ape Man.

I held out my hands. The grey creature in the corner leant forward. "Not to run on all-Fours; that is the Law. Are we not Men?" he said. He put out a strangely distorted talon, and gripped my fingers. The thing was almost like the hoof of a deer produced into claws. I could have yelled with surprise and pain. His face came forward and peered at my nails, came forward into the light of the opening of the hut, and I saw with a quivering disgust that it was like the face of neither man nor beast, but a mere shock of grey hair, with three shadowy over-archings to mark the eyes and mouth.

"He has little nails," said this grisly creature in his hairy beard. "It is well. Many are troubled with big nails."

He threw my hand down, and instinctively I gripped my stick. "Eat roots and herbs — it is His will," said the Ape Man.

"I am the Sayer of the Law," said the grey figure. "Here come all that be new, to learn the Law. I sit in the darkness and say the Law."

"It is even so," said one of the beasts in the doorway.

"Evil are the punishments of those who break the Law. None escape."

"None escape," said the Beast folk, glancing furtively at each other.

"None, none," said the Ape Man. "None escape. See! I did a little thing, a wrong thing once. I jabbered, jabbered, stopped talking. None could understand. I am burnt, branded in the hand. He is great, he is good!"

"None escape," said the great creature in the corner.

"None escape," said the Beast People, looking askance at one another.

"For every one the want that is bad," said the grey Sayer of the Law. "What you will want, we do not know. We shall know. Some want to follow things that move, to watch and slink and wait and spring, to kill and bite, bite deep and rich, sucking the blood. . . . It is bad. 'Not to chase other Men; that is the Law. *Are we not Men?* Not to eat Flesh nor Fish; that is the Law. *Are we not Men?*'"

"None escape," said a dappled brute standing in the doorway.

"For every one the want that is bad," said the grey Sayer of the Law. "Some want to go tearing with teeth and hands into the roots of things, snuffing into the earth. . . . It is bad."

"None escape," said the men in the door.

"Some go clawing trees, some go scratching at the graves of the dead; some go fighting with fore-heads or feet or claws; some bite suddenly, none giving occasion; some love uncleanness."

"None escape," said the Ape Man, scratching his calf.

"None escape," said the little pink sloth creature.

"Punishment is sharp and sure. Therefore learn the Law. Say the words," and incontinently he began again the strange litany of the Law, and again I and all these creatures began singing and swaying. My head reeled with this jabbering and the close stench of the place, but I kept on, trusting to find presently some chance of a new development. "Not to go on all-Fours; that is the Law. *Are we not Men?*"

We were making such a noise that I noticed nothing of a tumult outside, until someone, who, I think was one of the two Swine Men I had seen, thrust his head over the little pink sloth creature and shouted something excitedly, something that I did not catch. Incontinently those at the opening of the hut vanished, my Ape Man rushed out, the thing that had sat in the dark followed him — I only observed it was big and clumsy, and covered with silvery hair, — and I was left alone.

Then before I reached the aperture I heard the yelp of a staghound.

In another moment I was standing outside the hovel, my chair-rail in my hand, every muscle of me quivering. Before me were the clumsy backs of perhaps a score of these Beast People, their misshapen heads half-hidden by their shoulder-blades. They were gesticulating excitedly. Other half-animal faces glared interrogation out of the hovels. Looking in the direction in which they faced I saw coming through the haze under the trees beyond the end of the passage of dens the dark figure and awful white face of Moreau. He was holding the leaping staghound back, and close behind him came Montgomery, revolver in hand.

For a moment I stood horror-struck.

I turned and saw the passages behind me blocked by another heavy brute with a huge grey face and twinkling little eyes, advancing towards me. I looked round and saw to the right of me, and half a dozen yards in front of me, a narrow gap in the wall of rock through which a ray of light slanted into the shadows. "Stop!" cried Moreau, as I strode toward this, and then, "Hold him!" At that, first one face turned towards me, and then others. Their bestial minds were happily slow.

I dashed my shoulder into a clumsy monster who was turning to see what Moreau meant, and flung him forward into another. I felt his hands fly round, clutching at me and missing me. The little pink sloth creature dashed at me and I cut it over, gashed down its ugly face with the nail in my stick, and in another minute I was scrambling up a steep side pathway, a kind of sloping chimney out of the ravine. I heard a howl behind me, and cries of "Catch him!" "Hold him!" and the grey-faced creature appeared behind me and jammed his huge bulk into the cleft. "Go on, go on!" they howled. I clambered up the narrow cleft in the rock, and came out upon the sulphur on the westward side of the village of the Beast Men.

I ran over the white space and down a steep slope through a scattered growth of trees, and came to a low-lying stretch of tall reeds. Through this I pushed into a dark thick undergrowth that was black and succulent under foot. That gap was altogether fortunate for me, for the narrow way slanting obliquely upward must have impeded the nearer pursuers. As I plunged into the reeds the foremost had only just emerged from the gap. I broke my way through this undergrowth for some minutes. The air behind me and about me was soon full of threatening cries. I heard the tumult of my pursuers in the gap up the slope, then the crashing of the reeds, and every now and then the crackling of a branch. Some of the creatures roared like excited beasts of prey. The staghound yelped to the left. I heard Moreau and Montgomery shouting in the same direction. I turned sharply to the right. It seemed to me even then that I heard Montgomery shouting for me to run for my life.

Presently the ground gave, rich and oozy, under my feet; but I was desperate, and went headlong into it, struggled through knee-deep, and so came to a winding path among tall canes. The noise of my pursuers passed away to my left. In one place three strange pink hopping animals, about the size of cats, bolted before my footsteps. This pathway ran up-hill, across another open space covered with white incrustation, and plunged into a canebrake again.

Then suddenly it turned parallel with the edge of a steep walled gap which came without warning like the haha of an English park — turned with unexpected abruptness. I was still running with all my might, and I never saw this drop until I was flying headlong through the air.

I fell on my forearms and head, among thorns, and rose with a torn ear and bleeding face. I had fallen into a precipitous ravine, rocky and thorny, full of a hazy mist that drifted about me in wisps, and with a narrow streamlet, from which this mist came, meandering down the centre. I was astonished at this thin fog in the full blaze of daylight, but I had no time to stand wondering then. I turned to my right down-stream, hoping to come to the sea in that direction, and so have my way open to drown myself. It was only later I found that I had dropped my nailed stick in my fall.

Presently the ravine grew narrower for a space, and carelessly I stepped into the stream. I jumped out again pretty quickly for the water was almost boiling. I noticed, too, there was a thin sulphurous scum drifting upon its coiling water. Almost immediately came a turn in the ravine and the indistinct blue horizon. The nearer sea was flashing the sun from a myriad facets. I saw my death before me.

But I was hot and panting. I felt more than a touch of exultation, too, at having distanced my pursuers. It was not in me then to go out and drown myself. My blood was too warm.

I stared back the way I had

come. I listened. Save for the hum of the gnats and the chirp of some small insects that hopped among the thorns, the air was absolutely still.

Then came the yelp of a dog, very faint, and a chattering and gibbering, the snap of a whip and voices. They grew louder, then fainter again. The noise receded up the stream and faded away. For a while the chase was over.

But I knew now how much hope of help for me lay in the Beast People.

CHAPTER 13

A PARLEY

I TURNED again and went on down towards the sea. I found the hot stream broadened out to a shallow weedy sand, in which an abundance of crabs, and long-bodied, many-legged creatures started from my footfall. I walked to the very edge of the salt water, and then I felt I was safe. I turned and stared — arms akimbo — at the thick green behind me, into which the steamy ravine cut like a smoking gash. But as I say, I was too full of excitement, and — a true saying, though those who have never known danger may

doubt it — too desperate to die.

Then it came into my head that there was one chance before me yet. While Moreau and Montgomery and their bestial rabble chased me through the island, might I not go round the beach until I came to their enclosure? — make a flank march upon them, in fact, and then with a rock, lugged out of their loosely built wall perhaps smash in the lock of the smaller door and see what I could find — knife, pistol, or what not — to fight them with when they returned? It was at any rate a chance of getting a price for my life.

So I turned to the westward and walked along by the water's edge. The setting sun flashed his blinding heat into my eyes. The slight Pacific tide was running in with a gentle ripple.

Presently the shore fell away southward and the sun came round upon my right hand. Then suddenly, far in front of me, I saw first one and then several figures emerging from the bushes — Moreau with his grey staghound, then Montgomery, and two others. At that I stopped.

They saw me and began gesticulating and advancing. I stood watching them approach. The two Beast Men came running forward to cut me off from the undergrowth inland. Montgomery came running also, but straight towards me. Moreau followed slower with the dog.

At last I roused myself from inaction, and turning seaward walked straight into the water. The water was very shallow at first. I was thirty yards out before

the waves reached to my waist. Dimly I could see the inter-tidal creatures darting away from my feet.

"What are you doing, man?" cried Montgomery.

I turned, standing waist-deep, and stared at them.

Montgomery stood panting at the margin of the water. His face was bright red with exertion, his long flaxen hair blown about his head, and his dropping nether lip showed his irregular teeth. Moreau was just coming up, his face pale and firm, and the dog at his hand barked at me. Both men had heavy whips. Further up the beach stared the Beast Men.

"What am I doing?—I am going to drown myself," said I.

Montgomery and Moreau looked at one another. "Why?" asked Moreau.

"Because that is better than being tortured by you."

"I told you so," said Montgomery, and Moreau said something in a low tone.

"What makes you think I shall torture you?" asked Moreau.

"What I saw," I said. "And those—yonder."

"Hush!" said Moreau, and held up his hand.

"I will not," said I; "they were men: what are they now? I at least will not be like them." I looked past my interlocutors. Up the beach were M'ling, Montgomery's attendant, and one of the white swathed brutes from the boat. Further up, in the shadow of the trees, I saw my little Ape Man, and behind him some other dim figures.

"Who are these creatures?"

said I, pointing to them, and raising my voice more and more that it might reach them. "They were men—men like yourselves, whom you have infected with some bestial taint, men whom you have enslaved, and whom you still fear.—You who listen," I cried, pointing now to Moreau, and shouting past him to the Beast Man, "You who listen! Do you not see these men still fear you, go in dread of you? Why then do you fear them? You are many—"

"For God's sake," cried Montgomery, "stop that, Prendick!"

"Prendick!" cried Moreau.

They both shouted together as if to drown my voice. And behind them lowered the staring faces of the Beast Men, wondering, their deformed hands hanging down, their shoulders hunched up. They seemed, as I fancied then, to be trying to understand me, to remember something of their human past.

I went on shouting, I scarcely remember what. That Moreau and Montgomery could be killed; that they were not to be feared: that was the burthen of what I put into the heads of the Beast People to my own ultimate undoing. I saw the green-eyed man in the dark rags, who had met me on the evening of my arrival, come out from among the trees, and others followed him to hear me better.

At last for want of breath I paused.

"Listen to me for a moment," said the steady voice of Moreau, "and then say what you will."

"Well?" said I.

He coughed, thought, then shouted: "Latin, Prendick! Bad Latin! Schoolboy Latin! But try and understand. *Hi non sunt homines, sunt animalia qui nos habemus* . . . vivisected. A humanising process. I will explain. Come ashore."

I laughed. "A pretty story," said I. "They talk, build houses, cook. They were men. It's likely I'll come ashore."

"The water just beyond where you stand is deep . . . and full of sharks."

"That's my way," said I. "Short and sharp. Presently."

"Wait a minute." He took something out of his pocket that flashed back the sun, and dropped the object at his feet. "That's a loaded revolver," said he. "Montgomery here will do the same. Now we are going up the beach until you are satisfied the distance is safe. Then come and take the revolvers."

"Not I. You have a third between you."

"I want you to think over things, Prendick. In the first place, I never asked you to come upon this island. In the next, we had you drugged last night, had we wanted to work you any mischief; and in the next, now your first panic is over, and you can think a little — is Montgomery here quite up to the character you give him? We have chased you for your good. Because this island is full of . . . inimical phenomena. Why should we want to shoot you when you have just offered to drown yourself?"

"Why did you set . . . your people on to me when I was in the hut?"

"We felt sure of catching you and bringing you out of danger. Afterwards we drew away from the scent — for your good."

I mused. It seemed just possible. Then I remembered something again.

"But I saw," said I, "in the enclosure — "

"That was the puma."

"Look here, Prendick," said Montgomery. "You're a silly ass. Come out of the water and take these revolvers, and talk. We can't do anything more then than we could do now."

I will confess that then, and indeed always, I distrusted and dreaded Moreau. But Montgomery was a man I felt I understood.

"Go up the beach," said I, after thinking, and added, "holding your hands up."

"Can't do that," said Montgomery, with an explanatory nod over his shoulder. "Undignified."

"Go up to the trees, then," said I, "as you please."

"It's a damned silly ceremony," said Montgomery.

Both turned and faced the six or seven grotesque creatures, who stood there in the sunlight, solid, casting shadows, moving, and yet so incredibly unreal. Montgomery cracked his whip at them, and forthwith they all turned and fled helter-skelter into the trees. And when Montgomery and Moreau were at a distance I judged sufficient, I waded ashore, and picked up and examined the revolvers. To satisfy myself against the sublest trickery I dis-

charged one at a rounded lump of lava, and had the satisfaction of seeing the stone pulverised and the beach splashed with lead.

Still I hesitated for a moment.

"I'll take the risk," said I, at last, and with a revolver in each hand I walked up the beach towards them.

"That's better," said Moreau, without affectation. "As it is, you have wasted the best part of my day with your confounded panic."

And with a touch of contempt that humiliated me he and Montgomery turned and went on in silence before me.

The knot of Beast Men, still wondering, stood back among the trees. I passed them as serenely as possible. One started to follow me, but retreated again when Montgomery cracked his whip. The rest stood silent — watching. They may once have been animals. But I never before saw an animal trying to think.

CHAPTER 14

DOCTOR MOREAU
EXPLAINS

"And now, Prendick, I will explain," said Doctor Moreau, so soon as we had eaten and drunk. "I must confess you are the most dictatorial guest I ever entertained. I warn you that this is the last I do to oblige you. The next thing you threaten to commit suicide about I shan't do — even at some personal inconvenience."

He sat in my deck chair, a cigar half consumed in his white dexterous-looking fingers. The light of the swinging lamp fell on his white hair; he stared through the little window out at the starlight. I sat as far away from him as possible, the table between us and the revolvers to hand. Montgomery was not present. I did not care to be with the two of them in such a little room.

"You admit that vivisected human being, as you called it, is after all only the puma?" said Moreau. He had made me visit the horror in the inner room to assure myself of its inhumanity.

"It is the puma," I said, "still alive, but so cut and mutilated as I pray I may never see living flesh again. Of all vile — "

"Never mind that," said Moreau. "At least spare me those youthful horrors. Montgomery used to be just the same. You admit it is the puma. Now be quiet while I reel off my physiological lecture to you." And forthwith, beginning in the tone of a man supremely bored, but presently warming a little, he explained his work to me. He was very simple and convincing. Now and then there was a touch of sarcasm in his voice. Presently I found myself hot with shame at our mutual positions.

The creatures I had seen were not men, had never been men.

They were animals — humanised animals — triumphs of vivisection.

" You forget all that a skilled vivisector can do with living things," said Moreau. " For my own part I'm puzzled why the things I have done here have not been done before. Small efforts of course have been made — amputation, tongue-cutting, excisions. Of course you know a squint may be induced or cured by surgery? Then in the case of excisions you have all kinds of secondary changes, pigmentary disturbances, modifications of the passions, alterations in the secretion of fatty tissue. I have no doubt you have heard of these things?"

" Of course," said I. " But these foul creatures of yours —"

" All in good time," said he, waving his hand at me; " I am only beginning. Those are trivial cases of alteration. Surgery can do better things than that. There is building up as well as breaking down and changing. You have heard, perhaps, of a common surgical operation resorted to in cases where the nose has been destroyed. A flap of skin is cut from the forehead, turned down on the nose, and heals in the new position. This is a kind of grafting in a new position of part of an animal upon itself. Grafting of a freshly obtained material from another animal is also possible — the case of teeth, for example. The grafting of skin and bone is done to facilitate healing. The surgeon places in the middle of the wound pieces of skin snipped from another animal, or fragments of bone from a victim freshly killed. Hunter's cockspur — possibly you have heard of that — flourished on the bull's neck. And the rhinocerous rats of the Algerian zouaves are also to be thought of — monsters manufactured by transferring a slip from the tail of an ordinary rat to its snout, and allowing it to heal in that position."

" Monsters manufactured!" said I. " Then you mean to tell me —"

" Yes. These creatures you have seen are animals carven and wrought into new shapes. To that — to the study of the plasticity of living forms — my life has been devoted. I have studied for years, gaining in knowledge as I go. I see you look horrified, yet I am telling you nothing new. It all lay in the surface of practical anatomy years ago, but no one had the temerity to touch it. It's not simply the outward form of an animal I can change. The physiology, the chemical rhythm of the creature may also be made to undergo an enduring modification, of which vaccination and other methods of inoculation with living or dead matter are examples that will, no doubt, be familiar to you. A similar operation is the transfusion of blood, with which subject indeed I began. These are all familiar cases. Less so, and probably far more extensive, were the operations of those mediæval practitioners who made dwarfs and beggar cripples and show-monsters; some vestiges of whose art still remain in the preliminary manipulation of the young mountebank or contor-

tionist. Victor Hugo gives an account of them in *L'Homme qui Rit.* . . . But perhaps my meaning grows plain now. You began to see that it is a possible thing to transplant tissue from one part of an animal to another or from one animal to another, to alter its chemical reactions and methods of growth, to modify the articulations of its limbs, and indeed to change it in its most intimate structure?

"And yet this extraordinary branch of knowledge has never been sought as an end, and systematically, by modern investigators, until I took it up! Some such things have been hit upon in the last resort of surgery; most of the kindred evidence that will recur to your mind has been demonstrated, as it were, by accident — by tyrants, by criminals, by the breeders of horses and dogs, by all kinds of untrained clumsy-handed men working for their own immediate needs. I was the first man to take up this question armed with antiseptic surgery, and with a really scientific knowledge of the laws of growth.

"Yet one would imagine it must have been practised in secret before. Such creatures as the Siamese Twins. . . . And in the vaults of the Inquisition. No doubt their chief aim was artistic torture, but some at least of the inquisitors must have had a touch of scientific curiosity. . . ."

"But," said I. "These things — these animals *talk!*"

He said that was so, and proceeded to point out that the possibilities of vivisection do not stop at a mere physical metamorphosis. A pig may be educated. The mental structure is even less determinate than the bodily. In our growing science of hypnotism we find the promise of a possibility of replacing old inherent instincts by new suggestions, grafting upon or replacing the inherited fixed ideas. Very much indeed of what we call moral education is such an artificial modification and perversion of instinct; pugnacity is trained into courageous self-sacrifice, and suppressed sexuality into religious emotion. And the great difference between man and monkey is in the larynx, he said, in the incapacity to frame delicately different sound-symbols by which thought could be sustained. In this I failed to agree with him, but with a certain incivility he declined to notice my objection. He repeated that the thing was so, and continued his account of his work.

But I asked him why he had taken the human form as a model. There seemed to me then, and there still seems to me now, a strange wickedness in that choice.

He confessed that he had chosen that form by chance. "I might just as well have worked to form sheep into llamas, and llamas into sheep. I suppose there is something in the human form that appeals to the artistic turn of mind more powerfully than any animal shape can. But I've not confined myself to man-making. Once or twice . . ." He was silent, for a minute perhaps. "These years! How they have

slipped by! And here I have wasted a day saving your life, and am now wasting an hour explaining myself! "

" But," said I, " I still do not understand. Where is your justification for inflicting all this pain? The only thing that could excuse vivisection to me would be some application — "

" Precisely," said he. " But you see I am differently constituted. We are on different platforms. You are a materialist."

" I am *not* a materialist," I began hotly.

" In my view — in my view. For it is just this question of pain that parts us. So long as visible or audible pain turns you sick, so long as your own pains drive you, so long as pain underlies your propositions about sin, so long, I tell you, you are an animal, thinking a little less obscurely what an animal feels. This pain — "

I gave an impatient shrug at such sophistry.

" Oh! but it is such a little thing. A mind truly opened to what science has to teach must see that it is a little thing. It may be that save in this little planet, this speck of cosmic dust, invisible long before the nearest star could be attained — it may be, I say, that nowhere else does this thing called pain occur. But the laws we feel our way towards . . . Why, even on this earth, even among living things, what pain is there? "

He drew a little penknife, as he spoke, from his pocket, opened the smaller blade and moved his chair so that I could see his thigh. Then, choosing the place deliber-ately, he drove the blade into his leg and withdrew it.

" No doubt you have seen that before. It does not hurt a pin-prick. But what does it show? The capacity for pain is not needed in the muscle, and it is not placed there; it is but little needed in the skin, and only here and there over the thigh is a spot capable of feeling pain. Pain is simply our intrinsic medical adviser to warn us and stimulate us. All living flesh is not painful, nor is all nerve, nor even all sensory nerve. There's no taint of pain, real pain, in the sensations of the optic nerve. If you wound the optic nerve you merely see flashes of light, just as disease of the auditory nerve merely means a humming in our ears. Plants do not feel pain; the lower animals — it's possible that such animals as the starfish and crayfish do not feel pain. Then with men, the more intelligent they become the more intelligently they will see after their own welfare, and the less they will need the goad to keep them out of danger. I never yet heard of a useless thing that was not ground out of existence by evolution sooner or later. Did you? And pain gets needless.

" Then I am a religious man, Prendick, as every sane man must be. It may be I fancy I have seen more of the ways of this world's Maker than you — for I have sought his laws, in *my* way, all my life, while you, I understand, have been collecting butterflies. And I tell you, pleasure and pain have nothing to do with heaven and hell. Pleasure and pain — Bah! What is your theologian's

ecstasy but Mahomet's houri in the dark? This store men and women set on pleasure and pain, Prendick, is the mark of the beast upon them, the mark of the beast from which they came. Pain! Pain and pleasure — they are for us, only so long as we wriggle in the dust. . . .

"You see, I went on with this research just the way it led me. That is the only way I ever heard of research going. I asked a question, devised some method of getting an answer, and got — a fresh question. Was this possible, or that possible? You cannot imagine what this means to an investigator, what an intellectual passion grows upon him. You cannot imagine the strange colourless delight of these intellectual desires. The thing before you is no longer an animal, a fellow-creature, but a problem. Sympathetic pain — all I know of it I remember as a thing I used to suffer from years ago. I wanted — it was the only thing I wanted — to find out the extreme limit of plasticity in a living shape."

"But," said I, "the thing is an abomination — "

"To this day I have never troubled about the ethics of the matter. The study of Nature makes a man at last as remorseless as Nature. I have gone on, not heeding anything but the question I was pursuing, and the material has . . . dripped into the huts yonder. . . . It is nearly eleven years since we came here, I and Montgomery and six Kanakas. I remember the green stillness of the island and the empty ocean about us as though it was yesterday. The place seemed waiting for me.

"The stores were landed and the house was built. The Kanakas founded some huts near the ravine. I went to work here upon what I had brought with me. Some disagreeable things happened at first. I began with a sheep, and killed it after a day and a half by a slip of the scalpel; I took another sheep and made a thing of pain and fear, and left it bound up to heal. It looked quite human to me when I had finished it, but when I went to it I was discontented with it; it remembered me, and was terrified beyond imagination, and it had no more than the wits of a sheep. The more I looked at it the clumsier it seemed, until at last I put the monster out of its misery. These animals without courage, these fear-haunted pain-driven things, without a spark of pugnacious energy to face torment — they are no good for man-making.

"Then I took a gorilla I had, and upon that, working with infinite care, and mastering difficulty after difficulty, I made my first man. All the week, night and day, I moulded him. With him it was chiefly the brain that needed moulding; much had to be added, much changed. I thought him a fair specimen of the negroid type when I had done him, and he lay, bandaged, bound, and motionless before me. It was only when his life was assured that I left him, and came into the room and found Montgomery much as you are. He had heard some of the cries as the thing grew human,

cries like those that disturbed *you* so. I didn't take him completely into my confidence at first. And the Kanakas, too, had realised something of it. They were scared out of their wits by the sight of me. I got Montgomery over to me — in a way, but I and he had the hardest job to prevent the Kanakas deserting. Finally they did, and so we lost the yacht. I spent many days educating the brute — altogether I had him for three or four months. I taught him the rudiments of English, gave him ideas of counting, even made the thing read the alphabet. But at that he was slow — though I've met with idiots slower. He began with a clean sheet, mentally; had no memories left in his mind of what he had been. When his scars were quite healed, and he was no longer anything but painful and stiff, and able to converse a little, I took him yonder and introduced him to the Kanakas as an interesting stowaway.

"They were horribly afraid of him at first, somehow — which offended me rather, for I was conceited about him — but his ways seemed so mild, and he was so abject, that after a time they received him and took his education in hand. He was quick to learn, very imitative and adaptive, and built himself a hovel rather better, it seemed to me, than their own shanties. There was one among the boys, a bit of a missionary, and he taught the thing to read, or at least to pick out letters, and gave him some rudimentary ideas of morality, but it seems the beast's habits were not all that is desirable.

"I rested from work for some days, and was in a mind to write an account of the whole affair to wake up English physiology. Then I came upon the creature squatting up in a tree gibbering at two of the Kanakas who had been teasing him. I threatened him, told him the inhumanity of such a proceeding, aroused his sense of shame, and came here resolved to do better before I took my work back to England. I have been doing better; but somehow the things drift back again, the stubborn beast flash grows, day by day, back again. . . . I mean to do better things still. I mean to conquer that. This puma . . .

"But that's the story. All the Kanaka boys are dead now. One fell overboard the launch, and one died of a wounded heel that he poisoned in some way with plant-juice. Three went away in the yacht, and I suppose, and hope, were drowned. The other one . . . was killed. Well — I have replaced them. Montgomery went on much as you are disposed to do at first, and then . . ."

"What became of the other one?" said I sharply — "the other Kanaka who was killed?"

"The fact is, after I had made a number of human creatures I made a thing — " He hesitated.

"Yes?" said I.

"It was killed."

"I don't understand," said I; "do you mean to say . . ."

"It killed the Kanaka — yes. It killed several other things that it caught. We chased it for a couple of days. It only got loose by acci-

dent — I never meant it to get away. It wasn't finished. It was purely an experiment. It was a limbless thing with a horrible face that writhed along the ground in a serpentine fashion. It was immensely strong and in infuriating pain, and it travelled in a rolling way like a porpoise swimming. It lurked in the woods for some days, doing mischief to all it came across, until we hunted it, and then it wriggled into the northern part of the island, and we divided the party to close in upon it. Montgomery insisted upon coming with me. The man had a rifle, and when his body was found one of the barrels was curved into the shape of an S, and very nearly bitten through. . . . Montgomery shot the thing. . . . After that I stuck to the ideal of humanity — except for little things."

He became silent. I sat in silence watching his face.

" So for twenty years altogether — counting nine years in England — I have been going on, and there is still something in everything I do that defeats me, makes me dissatisfied, challenges me to further effort. Sometimes I rise above my level, sometimes I fall below it, but always I fall short of the things I dream. The human shape I can get now, almost with ease, so that it is lithe and graceful, or thick and strong; but often there is trouble with the hands and claws — painful things that I dare not shape too freely. But it is in the subtle grafting and re-shaping one must needs do to the brain that my trouble lies. The intelligence is often oddly low, with unaccountable blank ends, unexpected gaps. And least satisfactory of all is something that I cannot touch, somewhere — I cannot determine where — in the seat of the emotions. Cravings, instincts, desires that harm humanity, a strange hidden reservoir to burst suddenly and inundate the whole being of the creature with anger, hate, or fear. These creatures of mine seemed strange and uncanny to you as soon as you began to observe them, but to me, just after I make them, they seem to be indisputable human beings. It's afterwards as I observe them that the persuasion fades. First one animal trait, then another, creeps to the surface and stares at me. . . . But I will conquer yet. Each time I dip a living creature into the bath of burning pain, I say: this time I will burn out all the animal, this time I will make a rational creature of my own. After all, what is ten years? Man has been a hundred thousand in the making."

He thought darkly. " But I am drawing near the fastness. This puma of mine . . ."

After a silence: " And they revert. As soon as my hand is taken from them the beast begins to creep back, begins to assert itself again. . . ."

Another long silence.

" Then you take the things you make into those dens? " said I.

" They go. I turn them out when I begin to feel the beast in them, and presently they wander there. They all dread this house and me. There is a kind of travesty of humanity over there.

Montgomery knows about it, for he interferes in their affairs. He has trained one or two of them to our service. He's ashamed of it, but I believe he half likes some of these beasts. It's his business, not mine. They only sicken me with a sense of failure. I take no interest in them. I fancy they follow in the lines the Kanaka missionary marked out, and have a kind of mockery of a rational life—poor beasts! There's something they call the Law. Sing hymns about 'all thine.' They build themselves their dens, gather fruit and pull herbs—marry even. But I can see through it all, see into their very souls, and see there nothing but the souls of beasts, beasts that perish—anger, and the lusts to live and gratify themselves. . . . Yet they're odd. Complex, like everything else alive. There is a kind of upward striving in them, part vanity, part waste sexual emotion, part waste curiosity. It only mocks me. . . . I have some hope of that puma; I have worked hard at her head and brain. . . .

"And now," said he, standing up after a long gap of silence, during which we had each pursued our own thoughts; "what do you think? Are you in fear of me still?"

I looked at him, and saw but a white-faced, white-haired man, with calm eyes. Save for his serenity, the touch almost of beauty that resulted from his set tranquillity and from his magnificent build, he might have passed muster among a hundred other comfortable old gentlemen. Then I shivered. By way of answer to his second question, I handed him a revolver with either hand.

"Keep them," he said, and snatched at a yawn. He stood up, stared at me for a moment and smiled. "You have had two eventful days," said he. "I should advise some sleep. I'm glad it's all clear. Good-night."

He thought me over for a moment, then went out by the inner door. I immediately turned the key in the outer one.

I sat down again, sat for a time in a kind of stagnant mood, so weary emotionally, mentally, and physically, that I could not think beyond the point at which he left me. The black window stared at me like an eye. At last with an effort I put out the lamp and got into the hammock. Very soon I was asleep.

CHAPTER 15

CONCERNING THE BEAST FOLK

I WOKE early. Moreau's explanation stood before my mind, clear and definite, from the moment of my awakening. I got out of the hammock and went to the door to assure myself that the key was turned. Then I tried the window-bar, and found it firmly fixed.

That these man-like creatures were in truth only bestial monsters, mere grotesque travesties of men, filled me with a vague uncertainty of their possibilities that was far worse than any definite fear. A tapping came at the door, and I heard the glutinous accents of M'ling speaking. I pocketed one of the revolvers (keeping one hand upon it), and opened to him.

"Good-morning, sair," he said, bringing in addition to the customary herb breakfast, an ill-cooked rabbit. Montgomery followed him. His roving eye caught the position of my arm, and he smiled askew.

The puma was resting to heal that day; but Moreau, who was singularly solitary in his habits, did not join us. I talked with Montgomery to clear my ideas of the way in which the Beast Folk lived. In particular, I was urgent to know how these inhuman monsters were kept from falling upon Moreau and Montgomery, and from rending one another.

He explained to me that the comparative safety of Moreau and himself was due to the limited mental scope of these monsters. In spite of their increased intelligence, and the tendency of their animal instincts to reawaken, they had certain Fixed Ideas implanted by Moreau in their minds which absolutely bounded their imaginations. They were really hypnotised, had been told certain things were impossible, and certain things were not to be done, and these prohibitions were woven into the texture of their minds beyond any possibility of

disobedience or dispute. Certain matters, however, in which old instinct was at war with Moreau's convenience, were in a less stable condition. A series of propositions called the Law — I had already heard them recited — battled in their minds with the deep-seated, ever rebellious cravings of their animal natures. This Law they were perpetually repeating, I found, and — perpetually breaking. Both Montgomery and Moreau displayed particular solicitude to keep them ignorant of the taste of blood. They feared the inevitable suggestions of that flavour.

Montgomery told me that the Law, especially among the feline Beast People, became oddly weakened about nightfall; that then the animal was at its strongest; a spirit of adventure sprang up in them at the dusk, they would dare things they never seemed to dream about by day. To that I owed my stalking by the Leopard Man on the night of my arrival. But during these earlier days of my stay they broke the Law only furtively, and after dark; in the daylight there was a general atmosphere of respect for its multifarious prohibitions.

And here perhaps I may give a few general facts about the island and the Beast People. The island, which was of irregular outline and lay low upon the wide sea, had a total area, I suppose of seven or eight square miles. It was volcanic in origin, and was now fringed on three sides by coral reefs. Some fumaroles to the northward, and a hot spring, were the only vestiges of the

forces that had long since origi-
nated it. Now and then a faint
quiver of earthquake would be
sensible, and sometimes the as-
cent of the spire of smoke would
be rendered tumultuous by gusts
of steam. But that was all. The
population of the island, Mont-
gomery informed me, now num-
bered rather more than sixty of
these strange creations of Mo-
reau's art, not counting the
smaller monstrosities which lived
in the undergrowth and were
without human form. Altogether,
he had made nearly a hundred
and twenty, but many had died;
and others, like the writhing Foot-
less Thing of which he had told
me, had come by violent ends. In
answer to my question, Mont-
gomery said that they actually
bore offspring, but that these
generally died. There was no
evidence of the inheritance of
the acquired human character-
istics. When they lived, Moreau
took them and stamped the
human form upon them. The
females were less numerous
than the males, and liable to
much furtive persecution in
spite of the monogamy the Law
enjoined.

It would be impossible for me
to describe these Beast People in
detail — my eye has had no train-
ing in details — and unhappily
I cannot sketch. Most striking
perhaps in their general appear-
ance was the disproportion be-
tween the legs of these creatures
and the length of their bodies;
and yet — so relative is our idea
of grace — my eye became habitu-
ated to their forms, and at last I
even fell in with their persua-
sion that my own long thighs
were ungainly. Another point was
the forward carriage of the head,
and the clumsy and inhuman
curvature of the spine. Even the
Ape Man lacked that inward
sinuous curve of the back that
makes the human figure so grace-
ful. Most had their shoulders
hunched clumsily, and their short
forearms hung weakly at their
sides. Few of them were con-
spicuously hairy — at least, until
the end of my time upon the
island.

The next most obvious de-
formity was in their faces, al-
most all of which were prog-
nathous, malformed about the
ears, with large and protuberant
noses, very furry or very bristly
hair, and often strangely col-
oured or strangely placed eyes.
None could laugh, though the
Ape Man had a mirthless grin.
Beyond these general characters
their heads had little in common;
each preserved the quality of its
particular species: the human
mark distorted but did not hide
the leopard, the ox, or the sow,
or other animal or animals from
which the creature had been
moulded. The voices, too, varied
exceedingly. The hands were al-
ways malformed; and though
some surprised me by their un-
expected humanity, almost all
were deficient in the number of
the digits, clumsy about the
finger-nails, and lacking any tac-
tile sensibility.

The two most formidable ani-
mal-men were my Leopard Man
and a creature made of hyæna
and swine. Larger than these
were the three bull creatures who

pulled in the boat. Then came the Silvery Hairy Man, who was also the Sayer of the Law, M'ling, and a satyr-like creature of ape and goat. There were three Swine Men and a Swine Woman, a Horse-Rhinoceros creature, and several other females whose sources I did not ascertain. There were several Wolf creatures, a Bear-Bull, and a Saint Bernard Dog Man. I have already described the Ape Man, and there was a particularly hateful (and evil-smelling) old woman made of Vixen and Bear, whom I hated from the beginning. She was said to be a passionate votary of the Law. Smaller creatures were certain dappled youths and my little sloth creature.

At first I had a shivering horror of the brutes, felt all too keenly that they were still brutes, but insensibly I became a little habituated to the idea of them, and, moreover, I was affected by Montgomery's attitude towards them. He had been with them so long that he had come to regard them as almost normal human beings — his London days seemed a glorious impossible past to him. Only once in a year or so did he go to Arica to deal with Moreau's agent, a trader in animals there. He hardly met the finest type of mankind in that seafaring village of Spanish mongrels. The men aboard ship, he told me, seemed at first just as strange to him as the Beast Men seemed to me, — unnaturally long in the leg, flat in the face, prominent in the forehead, suspicious, dangerous, and cold-hearted. In fact, he did not

like men. His heart had warmed to me, he thought, because he had saved my life.

I fancied even then that he had a sneaking kindness for some of these metamorphosed brutes, a vicious sympathy with some of their ways, but that he attempted to veil from me at first.

M'ling, the black-faced man, his attendant, the first of the Beast Folk I had encountered, did not live with the others across the island, but in a small kennel at the back of the enclosure. The creature was scarcely so intelligent as the Ape Man, but far more docile, and the most human-looking of all the Beast Folk, and Montgomery had trained it to prepare food and indeed to discharge all the trivial domestic offices that were required. It was a complex trophy of Moreau's horrible skill, a bear, tainted with dog and ox, and one of the most elaborately made of all the creatures. It treated Montgomery with a strange tenderness and devotion; sometimes he would notice it, pat it, call it half-mocking, half-jocular names, and so make it caper with extraordinary delight; sometimes he would ill-treat it, especially after he had been at the whisky, kicking it, beating it, pelting it with stones or lighted fusees. But whether he treated it well or ill, it loved nothing so much as to be near him.

I say I became habituated to the Beast People, that a thousand things that had seemed unnatural and repulsive speedily became natural and ordinary to me. I suppose everything in existence

takes its colour from the average hue of our surroundings: Montgomery and Moreau were too peculiar and individual to keep my general impressions of humanity well defined. I would see one of the bovine creatures who worked the launch treading heavily through the undergrowth, and find myself trying hard to recall how he differed from some really human yokel trudging home from his mechanical labours; or I would meet the Fox-Bear Woman's vulpine shifty face, strangely human in its speculative cunning, and even imagine I had met it before in some city byway.

Yet every now and then the beast would flash out upon me beyond doubt or denial. An ugly-looking man, a hunchbacked human savage to all appearance, squatting in the aperture of one of the dens, would stretch his arms and yawn, showing with startling suddenness scissor-edged incisors and sabre-like canines, keen and brilliant as knives. Or in some narrow pathway, glancing with a transitory daring into the eyes of some lithe white-swathed female figure, I would suddenly see with a spasmodic revulsion that they had slit-like pupils, or, glancing down, note the curving nail with which she held her shapeless wrap about her. It is a curious thing, by the by, for which I am quite unable to account, that these weird creatures — the females I mean — had in the earlier days of my stay an instinctive sense of their own repulsive clumsiness, and displayed in consequence a more

than human regard for the decencies and decorum of external costume.

CHAPTER 16

HOW THE BEAST FOLK TASTED BLOOD

BUT my inexperience as a writer betrays me, and I wander from the thread of my story. After I had breakfasted with Montgomery he took me across the island to see the fumarole and the source of the hot spring, into whose scalding waters I had blundered on the previous day. Both of us carried whips and loaded revolvers. While going through a leafy jungle on our road thither we heard a rabbit squealing. We stopped and listened, but we heard no more; and presently we went on our way and the incident dropped out of our minds. Montgomery called my attention to certain little pink animals with long hind legs, that went leaping through the undergrowth. He told me they were creatures made of the offspring of the Beast People, that Moreau had invented. He had fancied they might serve for meat, but a rabbit-like habit of devouring

their young had defeated this intention. I had already encountered some of these creatures, once during my moonlight flight from the Leopard Man, and once during my pursuit by Moreau on the previous day. By chance, one hopping to avoid us leapt into the hole caused by the uprooting of a windblown tree. Before it could extricate itself we managed to catch it. It spat like a cat, scratched and kicked vigorously with its hind legs and made an attempt to bite, but its teeth were too feeble to inflict more than a painless pinch. It seemed to me rather a pretty little creature, and as Montgomery stated that it never destroyed the turf by burrowing, and was very cleanly in its habits, I should imagine it might prove a convenient substitute for the common rabbit in gentlemen's parks.

We also saw on our way the trunk of a tree barked in long strips and splintered deeply. Montgomery called my attention to this. "Not to claw Bark of Trees; *that* is the Law," he said. "Much some of them care for it!" It was after this, I think, that we met the Satyr and the Ape Man. The Satyr was a gleam of classical memory on the part of Moreau, his face ovine in expression — like the coarser Hebrew type — his voice a harsh bleat, his nether extremities Satanic. He was gnawing the husk of a pod-like fruit as he passed us. Both of them saluted Montgomery.

"Hail," said they, "to the Other with the whip!"

"There's a third with a whip now," said Montgomery. "So you'd better mind!"

"Was he not made?" said the Ape Man. "He said — he said he was made."

The Satyr Man looked curiously at me. "The Third with the whip, he that walks sweeping into the sea, has a thin white face."

"He has a thin long whip," said Montgomery.

"Yesterday he bled and wept," said the Satyr. "You never bleed nor weep. The Master does not bleed nor weep."

"Ollendorffian beggar!" said Montgomery. "You'll bleed and weep if you don't look out."

"He has five fingers; he is a five-man like me," said the Ape Man.

"Come along, Prendick," said Montgomery, taking my arm, and I went on with him.

The Satyr and the Ape Man stood watching us and making other remarks to each other.

"He says nothing," said the Satyr. "Men have voices."

"Yesterday he asked me of things to eat," said the Ape Man. "He did not know." Then they spoke inaudible things, and I heard the Satyr laughing.

It was on our way back that we came upon the dead rabbit. The red body of the wretched little beast was rent to pieces, many of the ribs stripped white, and the backbone indisputably gnawed.

At that Montgomery stopped. "Good God!" said he, stooping down and picking up some of the crushed vertebræ to examine them more closely. "Good God!"

he repeated, "what can this mean?"

"Some carnivore of yours has remembered its old habits," I said, after a pause. "This backbone has been bitten through."

He stood staring, with his face white and his lip pulled askew. "I don't like this," he said slowly.

"I saw something of the same kind," said I, "the first day I came here."

"The devil you did! What was it?"

"A rabbit with its head twisted off."

"The day you came here?"

"The day I came here. In the undergrowth, at the back of the enclosure, when I came out in the evening. The head was completely wrung off."

He gave a low whistle.

"And what is more, I have an idea which of your brutes did the thing. It's only a suspicion, you know. Before I came on the rabbit I saw one of your monsters drinking in the stream."

"Sucking his drink?"

"Yes."

"Not to suck your Drink; *that* is the Law. Much the brutes care for the Law, eh — when Moreau's not about?"

"It was the brute who chased me."

"Of course," said Montgomery; "it's just the way with carnivores. After a kill they drink. It's the taste of blood, you know."

"What was the brute like?" he asked. "Would you know him again?" He glanced about us, standing astride over the mess of dead rabbit, his eyes roving among the shadows and screens of greenery, the lurking-places and ambuscades of the forest, that bounded us in. "The taste of blood," he said again.

He took out his revolver, examined the cartridges in it, and replaced it. Then he began to pull at his dropping lip.

"I think I should know the brute again. I stunned him. He ought to have a handsome bruise on the forehead of him."

"But then we have to *prove* he killed the rabbit," said Montgomery. "I wish I'd never brought the things here."

I should have gone on, but he stayed there thinking over the mangled rabbit in a puzzleheaded way. As it was, I went to such a distance that the rabbit's remains were hidden.

"Come on!" I said.

Presently he woke up and came towards me. "You see," he said, almost in a whisper, "they are all supposed to have a fixed idea against eating anything that runs on land. If some brute has by accident tasted blood . . ."

We went on some way in silence. "I wonder what can have happened," he said to himself. Then, after a pause, again: "I did a foolish thing the other day. That servant of mine . . . I showed him how to skin and cook a rabbit. It's odd . . . I saw him licking his hands . . . It never occurred to me."

Then: "We must put a stop to this. I must tell Moreau."

He could think of nothing else on our homeward journey.

Moreau took the matter even more seriously than Montgomery, and I need scarcely say I was

infected by their evident consternation. "We must make an example," said Moreau. "I've no doubt in my own mind that the Leopard Man was the sinner. But how can we prove it? I wish, Montgomery, you had kept your taste for meat in hand, and gone without these exciting novelties. We may find ourselves in a mess yet through it."

"I was a silly ass," said Montgomery. "But the thing's done now. And you said I might have them, you know."

"We must see to the thing at once," said Moreau. "I suppose, if anything should turn up, M'ling can take care of himself?"

"I'm not so sure of M'ling," said Montgomery. "I think I ought to know him."

In the afternoon, Moreau, Montgomery, myself, and M'ling went across the island to the huts in the ravine. We three were armed. M'ling carried the little hatchet he used in chopping firewood, and some coils of wire. Moreau had a huge cowherd's horn slung over his shoulder. "You will see a gathering of the Beast People," said Montgomery. "It's a pretty sight." Moreau said not a word on the way, but his heavy white-fringed face was grimly set.

We crossed the ravine, down which smoked the stream of hot water, and followed the winding pathway through the cane brakes until we reached a wide area covered over with a thick powdery yellow substance which I believe was sulphur. Above the shoulder of a weedy bank the sea glittered. We came to a kind of shallow natural amphitheatre, and here the four of us halted. Then Moreau sounded the horn and broke the sleeping stillness of the tropical afternoon. He must have had strong lungs. The hooting note rose and rose amidst its echoes to at last an ear-penetrating intensity. "Ah!" said Moreau, letting the curved instrument fall to his side again.

Immediately there was a crashing through the yellow canes, and a sound of voices from the dense green jungle that marked the morass through which I had run on the previous day. Then at three or four points on the edge of the sulphurous area appeared the grotesque forms of the Beast People, hurrying towards us. I could not help a creeping horror as I perceived first one and then another trot out from the trees or reeds, and come shambling along over the hot dust. But Moreau and Montgomery stood calmly enough, and, perforce, I stuck beside them. First to arrive was the Satyr, strangely unreal for all that he cast a shadow, and tossed the dust with his hoofs; after him from the brake came a monstrous lout, a thing of horse and rhinoceros, chewing a straw as it came; and then appeared the Swine Woman and two Wolf Women; then the Fox-Bear Witch with her red eyes in her peaked red face, and then others — all hurrying eagerly. As they came forward they began to cringe towards Moreau and chant, quite regardless of one another, fragments of the latter half of the litany of the Law: "*His* is the Hand that wounds,

His is the Hand that heals," and so forth.

As soon as they had approached within a distance of perhaps thirty yards they halted, and bowing on knees and elbows, began flinging the white dust upon their heads. Imagine the scene if you can. We three blue-clad men, with our misshapen black-faced attendant, standing in a wide expanse of sunlit yellow dust under the blazing blue sky, and surrounded by this circle of crouching and gesticulating monstrosities, some almost human save in their subtle expression and gestures, some like cripples, some so strangely distorted as to resemble nothing but the denizens of our wildest dreams. And beyond, the reedy lines of a cane brake in one direction and a dense tangle of palm-trees on the other, separating us from the ravine with the huts, and to the north the hazy horizon of the Pacific Ocean.

"Sixty-two, sixty-three," counted Moreau. "There are four more."

"I do not see the Leopard Man," said I.

Presently Moreau sounded the great horn again, and at the sound of it all the Beast People writhed and grovelled in the dust. Then, slinking out of the cane brake, stooping near the ground, and trying to join the dust-throwing circle behind Moreau's back, came the Leopard Man. And I saw that his forehead was bruised. The last of the Beast People to arrive was the little Ape Man. The earlier animals, hot and weary with their grovel-ling, shot vicious glances at him.

"Cease," said Moreau, in his firm loud voice, and the Beast People sat back upon their hams and rested from their worshipping.

"Where is the Sayer of the Law?" said Moreau, and the hairy grey monster bowed his face in the dust.

"Say the words," said Moreau, and forthwith all in the kneeling assembly, swaying from side to side and dashing up the sulphur with their hands, first the right hand and a puff of dust, and then the left, began once more to chant their strange litany.

When they reached "Not to eat Flesh or Fish; that is the Law," Moreau held up his lank white hand. "*Stop!*" he cried, and there fell absolute silence upon them all.

I think they all knew and dreaded what was coming. I looked round at their strange faces. When I saw their wincing attitudes and the furtive dread in their bright eyes, I wondered that I had ever believed them to be men.

"That Law has been broken," said Moreau.

"None escape," from the face-less creature with the Silvery Hair. "None escape," repeated the kneeling circle of Beast People.

"Who is he?" cried Moreau, and looked round at their faces, cracking his whip. I fancied the Hyæna-Swine looked dejected, so too did the Leopard Man. Moreau stopped, facing this creature, who cringed towards him with the memory and dread of

infinite torment. "Who is he?" repeated Moreau, in a voice of thunder.

"Evil is he who breaks the Law," chanted the Sayer of the Law.

Moreau looked into the eyes of the Leopard Man, and seemed to be dragging the very soul out of the creature.

"Who breaks the Law —" said Moreau, taking his eyes off his victim and turning towards us. It seemed to me there was a touch of exultation in his voice. "— goes back to the House of Pain," they all clamoured; "goes back to the House of Pain, O Master!"

"Back to the House of Pain — back to the House of Pain," gabbled the Ape Man, as though the idea was sweet to him.

"Do you hear?" said Moreau, turning back to the criminal, "my friend . . . Hullo!"

For the Leopard Man, released from Moreau's eye, had risen straight from his knees, and now, with eyes aflame and his huge feline tusks flashing out from under his curling lips, leapt towards his tormentor. I am convinced that only the madness of unendurable fear could have prompted this attack. The whole circle of three-score monsters seemed to rise about us. I drew my revolver. The two figures collided. I saw Moreau reeling back from the Leopard Man's blow. There was a furious yelling and howling all about us. Everyone was moving rapidly. For a moment I thought it was a general revolt.

The furious face of the Leop-

ard Man flashed by mine, with M'ling close in pursuit. I saw the yellow eyes of the Hyæna-Swine blazing with excitement, his attitude as if he were half-resolved to attack me. The Satyr, too, glared at me over the Hyæna-Swine's hunched shoulders. I heard the crack of Moreau's pistol, and saw the pink flash dart across the tumult. The whole crowd seemed to swing round in the direction of the glint of fire, and I, too, was swung round by the magnetism of the movement. In another second I was running, one of a tumultuous shouting crowd, in pursuit of the escaping Leopard Man.

That is all I can tell definitely. I saw the Leopard Man strike Moreau, and then everything spun about me, until I was running headlong.

M'ling was ahead, close in pursuit of the fugitive. Behind, their tongues already lolling out, ran the Wolf-Women in great leaping strides. The Swine-Folk followed, squealing with excitement, and the two Bull Men in their swathings of white. Then came Moreau in a cluster of the Beast People, his wide-brimmed straw hat blown off, his revolver in hand, and his lank white hair streaming out. The Hyæna-Swine ran beside me, keeping pace with me, and glancing furtively at me out of his feline eyes, and the others came pattering and shouting behind us.

The Leopard Man went bursting his way through the long canes, which sprang back as he passed and rattled in M'ling's

face. We others in the rear found a trampled path for us when we reached the brake. The chase lay through the brake for perhaps a quarter of a mile, and then plunged into a dense thicket that retarded our movements exceedingly, though we went through it in a crowd together — fronds flicking into our faces, ropy creepers catching us under the chin, or gripping our ankles, thorny plants hooking into and tearing cloth and flesh together.

" He has gone on all-fours through this," panted Moreau, now just ahead of me.

" None escape," said the Wolf-Bear, laughing into my face with the exultation of hunting.

We burst out again among rocks, and saw the quarry ahead, running lightly on all-fours, and snarling at us over his shoulder. At that the Wolf-Folk howled with delight. The thing was still clothed, and, at a distance, its face still seemed human, but the carriage of its four limbs was feline, and the furtive droop of its shoulder was distinctly that of a hunted animal. It leapt over some thorny yellow-flowering bushes and was hidden. M'ling was half-way across the space.

Most of us now had lost the first speed of the chase, and had fallen into a longer and steadier stride. I saw, as we traversed the open, that the pursuit was now spreading from a column into a line. The Hyæna-Swine still ran close to me, watching me as it ran, every now and then puckering its muzzle with a snarling laugh.

At the edge of the rocks the Leopard Man, realising he was making for the projecting cape upon which he had stalked me on the night of my arrival, had doubled in the undergrowth. But Montgomery had seen the manœuvre, and turned him again.

So, panting, tumbling against rocks, torn by brambles, impeded by ferns and reeds, I helped to pursue the Leopard Man who had broken the Law, and the Hyæna-Swine ran, laughing savagely, by my side. I staggered on, my head reeling, and my heart beating against my ribs, tired almost to death, and yet not daring to lose sight of the chase, lest I should be left alone with this horrible companion. I staggered on in spite of infinite fatigue and the dense heat of the tropical afternoon.

And at last the fury of the hunt slackened. We had pinned the wretched brute into a corner of the island. Moreau, whip in hand, marshalled us all into an irregular line, and we advanced now slowly, shouting to one another as we advanced, and tightening the cordon about our victim. He lurked, noiseless and invisible, in the bushes through which I had run from him during that midnight pursuit.

" Steady! " cried Moreau; " steady! " as the ends of the line crept round the tangle of undergrowth, and hemmed the brute in.

" 'Ware a rush! " came the voice of Montgomery from beyond the thicket.

I was on the slope above the bushes. Montgomery and Moreau beat along the beach beneath.

Slowly we pushed in among the fretted network of branches and leaves. The quarry was silent.

"Back to the House of Pain, the House of Pain, the House of Pain!" yelped the voice of the Ape Man, some twenty yards to the right.

When I heard that I forgave the poor wretch all the fear he had inspired in me.

I heard the twigs snap and the boughs swish aside before the heavy tread of the Horse-Rhinoceros upon my right. Then suddenly, through a polygon of green, in the half-darkness under the luxuriant growth, I saw the creature we were hunting. I halted. He was crouched together into the smallest possible compass, his luminous green eyes turned over his shoulder regarding me.

It may seem a strange contradiction in me — I cannot explain the fact — but now, seeing the creature there in a perfectly animal attitude, with the light gleaming in its eyes, and its imperfectly human face distorted with terror, I realised again the fact of its humanity. In another moment other of its pursuers would see it, and it would be overpowered and captured, to experience once more the horrible tortures of the enclosure. Abruptly I slipped out my revolver, aimed between his terror-struck eyes and fired.

As I did so the Hyæna-Swine saw the thing, and flung itself upon it with an eager cry, thrusting thirsty teeth into its neck. All about me the green masses of the thicket were swaying and cracking as the Beast People came rushing together. One face and then another appeared.

"Don't kill it, Prendick!" cried Moreau. "Don't kill it!" And I saw him stooping as he pushed through the under fronds of the big ferns.

In another moment he had beaten off the Hyæna-Swine with the handle of his whip, and he and Montgomery were keeping away the excited carnivorous Beast People, and particularly M'ling from the still quivering body. The Hairy Grey Thing came sniffing at the corpse under my arm. The other animals, in their animal ardour, jostled me to get a nearer view.

"Confound you, Prendick!" said Moreau. "I wanted him."

"I'm sorry," said I, though I was not. "It was the impulse of the moment." I felt sick with exertion and excitement. Turning, I pushed my way out of the crowding Beast People and went on alone up the slope towards the higher part of the headland. Under the shouted instructions of Moreau, I heard the three white-swathed Bull Men begin dragging the victim down towards the water.

It was easy now for me to be alone. The Beast People manifested a quite human curiosity about the dead body, and followed it in a thick knot, sniffing and growling at it, as the Bull Men dragged it down the beach. I went to the headland, and watched the Bull Men, black against the evening sky, as they carried the weighted dead body

out to sea, and, like a wave across my mind, came the realisation of the unspeakable aimlessness of things upon the island. Upon the beach, among the rocks beneath me, were the Ape Man, the Hyæna-Swine, and several other of the Beast People, standing about Montgomery and Moreau. They were all intensely excited, and all overflowing with noisy expressions of their loyalty to the Law. Yet I felt an absolute assurance in my own mind that the Hyæna-Swine was implicated in the rabbit-killing. A strange persuasion came upon me that, save for the grossness of the line, the grotesqueness of the forms, I had here before me the whole balance of human life in miniature, the whole interplay of instinct, reason, and fate, in its simplest form. The Leopard Man had happened to go under. That was all the difference.

Poor brutes! I began to see the viler aspect of Moreau's cruelty. I had not thought before of the pain and trouble that came to these poor victims after they had passed from Moreau's hands. I had shivered only at the days of actual torment in the enclosure. But now that seemed to be the lesser part. Before they had been beasts, their instincts fitly adapted to their surroundings, and happy as living things may be. Now they stumbled in the shackles of humanity, lived in a fear that never died, fretted by a law they could not understand; their mock-human existence began in an agony, was one long internal struggle, one long dread of Moreau — and

for what? It was the wantonness that stirred me.

Had Moreau had any intelligible object I could have sympathised at least a little with him. I am not so squeamish about pain as that. I could have forgiven him a little even had his motive been hate. But he was so irresponsible, so utterly careless. His curiosity, his mad, aimless investigations, drove him on, and the things were thrown out to live a year or so, to struggle and blunder and suffer; at last to die painfully. They were wretched in themselves, the old animal hate moved them to trouble one another, the Law held them back from a brief hot struggle and a decisive end of their natural animosities.

In those days my fear of the Beast People went the way of my personal fear for Moreau. I fell indeed into the morbid state, deep and enduring, alien to fear, which has left permanent scars upon my mind. I must confess I lost faith in the sanity of the world when I saw it suffering the painful disorder of this island. A blind fate, a vast pitiless mechanism, seemed to cut and shape the fabric of existence, and I, Moreau by his passion for research, Montgomery by his passion for drink, the Beast People, with their instincts and mental restrictions, were torn and crushed, ruthlessly, inevitably, amid the infinite complexity of its incessant wheels. But this condition did not come all at once. . . . I think indeed that I anticipate a little in speaking of it now.

CHAPTER 17

A CATASTROPHE

SCARCELY six weeks passed before I had lost every feeling but dislike and abhorrence for these infamous experiments of Moreau's. My one idea was to get away from these horrible caricatures of my Maker's image, back to the sweet and wholesome intercourse of men. My fellow-creatures, from whom I was thus separated, began to assume idyllic virtue and beauty in my memory. My first friendship with Montgomery did not increase. His long separation from humanity, his secret vice of drunkenness, his evident sympathy with the Beast People, tainted him to me. Several times I let him go alone among them. I avoided intercourse with them in every possible way. I spent an increasing proportion of my time upon the beach, looking for some liberating sail that never appeared, until one day there fell upon us an appalling disaster, that put an altogether different aspect upon my strange surroundings.

It was about seven or eight weeks after my landing — rather more, I think, though I had not troubled to keep account of the time — when this catastrophe occurred. It happened in the early morning — I should think about six. I had risen and breakfasted early, having been aroused by the noise of three Beast Men carrying wood into the enclosure.

After breakfast I went to the open gateway of the enclosure and stood there smoking a cigarette and enjoying the freshness of the early morning. Moreau presently came round the corner of the enclosure and greeted me. He passed by me, and I heard him behind me unlock and enter his laboratory. So indurated was I at that time to the abomination of the place, that I heard without a touch of emotion the puma victim begin another day of torture. It met its persecutor with a shriek almost exactly like that of an angry virago.

Then something happened. I do not know what it was exactly to this day. I heard a sharp cry behind me, a fall, and turning, saw an awful face rushing upon me, not human, not animal, but hellish, brown, seamed with red branching scars, red drops starting out upon it, and the lidless eyes ablaze. I flung up my arm to defend myself from the blow that flung me headlong with a broken forearm, and the great monster, swathed in lint and with red-stained bandages fluttering about it, leaped over me and passed. I rolled over and over down the beach, tried to sit up, and collapsed upon my broken arm. Then Moreau appeared, his massive white face all the more terrible for the blood that

trickled from his forehead. He carried a revolver in one hand. He scarcely glanced at me, but rushed off at once in pursuit of the puma.

I tried the other arm and sat up. The muffled figure in front ran in great striding leaps along the beach, and Moreau followed her. She turned her head and saw him, then, doubling abruptly, made for the bushes. She gained upon him at every stride. I saw her plunge into them, and Moreau, running slantingly to intercept her, fired and missed as she disappeared. Then he too vanished in the green confusion.

I stared after them, and then the pain in my arm flamed up, and with a groan I staggered to my feet. Montgomery appeared in the doorway dressed, and with his revolver in his hand.

"Great God, Prendick!" he said, not noticing that I was hurt. "That brute's loose! Tore the fetter out of the wall. Have you seen them?" Then sharply, seeing I gripped my arm, "What's the matter?"

"I was standing in the doorway," said I.

He came forward and took my arm. "Blood on the sleeve," said he, and rolled back the flannel. He pocketed the weapon, felt my arm painfully, and let me inside. "Your arm is broken," he said; and then, "Tell me exactly how it happened — what happened."

I told him what I had seen, told him in broken sentences, with gasps of pain between them, and very dexterously and swiftly he bound my arm meanwhile. He

slung it from my shoulder, stood back, and looked at me. "You'll do," he said. "And now?" He thought. Then he went out and locked the gates of the enclosure. He was absent some time.

I was chiefly concerned about my arm. The incident seemed merely one more of many horrible things. I sat down in the deck chair and, I must admit, swore heartily at the island. The first dull feeling of injury in my arm had already given way to a burning pain when Montgomery reappeared.

His face was rather pale, and he showed more of his lower gums than ever. "I can neither see nor hear anything of him," he said. "I've been thinking he may want my help." He stared at me with his expressionless eyes. "That was a strong brute," he said. "It simply wrenched its fetter out of the wall."

He went to the window, then to the door, and there turned to me. "I shall go after him," he said. "There's another revolver I can leave with you. It's just possible you may need it."

He obtained the weapon and put it ready to my hand on the table, then went out, leaving a restless contagion in the air. I did not sit long after he left. I took the revolver in hand and went to the doorway.

The morning was as still as death. Not a whisper of wind stirred, the sea was like polished glass, the sky empty, the beach desolate. This stillness of things oppressed me.

I tried to whistle, and the tune died away. I swore again —

the second time that morning. Then I went to the corner of the enclosure and stared inland at the green bush that had swallowed up Moreau and Montgomery. When would they return. And how?

Then far away up the beach a little grey Beast Man appeared, ran down to the water's edge, and began splashing about. I strolled back to the doorway, then to the corner again, and so began pacing to and fro like a sentinel upon duty. Once I was arrested by the distant voice of Montgomery bawling, "Coo-ee . . . Mor-eau!" My arm became less painful, but very hot. I got feverish and thirsty. My shadow grew shorter. I watched the distant figure until it went away again. Would Moreau and Montgomery never return? Three sea-birds began fighting for some stranded treasure.

Then from far away behind the enclosure I heard a pistol-shot. A long silence, and then came another. Then a yelling cry nearer, and another dismal gap of silence. My unfortunate imagination set to work to torment me. Then suddenly a shot close by.

I went to the corner, startled, and saw Montgomery, his face scarlet, his hair disordered, and the knee of his trousers torn. His face expressed profound consternation. Behind him slouched the Beast Man M'ling, and round M'ling's jaws were some ominous brown stains.

"Has he come?" he said.

"Moreau?" said I. "No."

"My God!" The man was panting, almost sobbing for breath. "Go back in," he said, taking my arm. "They're mad. They're all rushing about mad. What can have happened? I don't know. I'll tell you when my breath comes. Where's some brandy?"

He limped before me into the room and sat down in the deck chair. M'ling flung himself down just outside the doorway, and began panting like a dog. I got Montgomery some brandy and water. He sat staring blankly in front of him, recovering his breath. After some minutes he began to tell me what had happened.

He had followed their track for some way. It was plain enough at first on account of the crushed and broken bushes, white rags torn from the puma's bandages, and occasional smears of blood on the leaves of the shrubs and undergrowth. He lost the track, however, on the stony ground beyond the stream where I had seen the Beast Man drinking, and went wandering aimlessly westward shouting Moreau's name. Then M'ling had come to him carrying a light hatchet. M'ling had seen nothing of the puma affair, had been felling wood and heard him calling. They went on shouting together. Two Beast Men came crouching and peering at them through the undergrowth, with gestures and a furtive carriage that alarmed Montgomery by their strangeness. He hailed them, and they fled guiltily. He stopped shouting after that, and after wandering some time fur-

ther in an undecided way, determined to visit the huts.

He found the ravine deserted. Growing more alarmed every minute, he began to retrace his steps. Then it was he encountered the two Swine Men I had seen dancing on the night of my arrival; blood-stained they were about the mouth, and intensely excited. They came crashing through the ferns, and stopped with fierce faces when they saw him. He cracked his whip in some trepidation, and forthwith they rushed at him. Never before had a Beast Man dared to do that. One he shot through the head, M'ling flung himself upon the other, and the two rolled grappling. M'ling got his brute under and with his teeth in its throat, and Montgomery shot that too as it struggled in M'ling's grip. He had some difficulty in inducing M'ling to come on with him.

Thence they had hurried back to me. On the way M'ling had suddenly rushed into a thicket and driven out an undersized Ocelot Man, also blood-stained, and lame through a wound in the foot. This brute had run a little way and then turned savagely at bay, and Montgomery — with a certain wantonness, I thought — had shot him.

"What does it all mean?" said I.

He shook his head and turned once more to the brandy.

CHAPTER 18

THE FINDING OF MOREAU

WHEN I saw Montgomery swallow a third dose of brandy I took it upon myself to interfere. He was already more than half fuddled. I told him that some serious thing must have happened to Moreau by this time, or he would have returned, and that it behoved us to ascertain what that catastrophe was. Montgomery raised some feeble objections, and at last agreed. We had some food, and then all three of us started.

It is possibly due to the tension of my mind at the time, but even now that start into the hot stillness of the hot tropical afternoon is a singularly vivid impression. M'ling went first, his shoulders hunched, his strange black head moving with quick starts as he peered first on this side of the way and then on that. He was unarmed. His axe he had dropped when he encountered the Swine Men. Teeth were *his* weapons when it came to fighting. Montgomery followed with stumbling footsteps, his hands in his pockets, his face downcast;

he was in a state of muddled sullenness with me on account of the brandy. My left arm was in a sling — it was lucky it was my left — and I carried my revolver in my right.

We took a narrow path through the wild luxuriance of the island, going northwestward. And presently M'ling stopped and became rigid with watchfulness. Montgomery almost staggered into him, and then stopped too. Then, listening intently, we heard, coming through the trees, the sound of voices and footsteps approaching us.

" He is dead," said a deep vibrating voice.

" He is not dead, he is not dead," jabbered another.

" We saw, we saw," said several voices.

" *Hul*-lo! " suddenly shouted Montgomery. " Hullo there! "

" Confound you! " said I, and gripped my pistol.

There was a silence, then a crashing among the interlacing vegetation, first here, then there, and then half a dozen faces appeared, strange faces, lit by a strange light. M'ling made a growling noise in his throat. I recognised the Ape Man — I had, indeed, already identified his voice — and two of the white-swathed brown-featured creatures I had seen in Montgomery's boat. With them were the two dappled brutes, and that grey, horrible, crooked creature who said the Law, with grey hair streaming down its cheeks, heavy grey eyebrows, and grey locks pouring off from a central parting upon its sloping forehead, a heavy face-

less thing, with strange red eyes, looking at us curiously from amidst the green.

For a space no one spoke. Then Montgomery hiccoughed, " Who . . . said he was dead? "

The Monkey Man looked guiltily at the Hairy Grey Thing. " He is dead," said this monster. " They saw."

There was nothing threatening about this detachment at any rate. They seemed awe-stricken and puzzled. " Where is he? " said Montgomery.

" Beyond," and the grey creature pointed.

" Is there a Law now? " asked the Ape Man. " Is it still to be this and that? Is he dead indeed? " " Is there a Law? " repeated the man in white. " Is there a Law, thou Other with the whip? He is dead," said the Hairy Grey Thing. And they all stood watching us.

" Prendick," said Montgomery, turning his dull eyes to me. " He's dead — evidently."

I had been standing behind him during this colloquy. I began to see how things lay with them. I suddenly stepped in front of him and lifted up my voice: " Children of the Law," I said, " he is *not* dead."

M'ling turned his sharp eyes on me. " He has changed his shape — he has changed his body," I went on. " For a time you will not see him. He is . . . there " — I pointed upward — " where he can watch you. You cannot see him. But he can see you. Fear the Law."

I looked at them squarely. They flinched. " He is great, he is

good," said the Ape Man, peering fearfully upward among the dense trees.

"And the other Thing?" I demanded.

"The Thing that bled and ran screaming and sobbing — that is dead too," said the Grey Thing, still regarding me.

"That's well," grunted Montgomery.

"The Other with the whip," began the Grey Thing.

"Well?" said I.

"Said he was dead."

But Montgomery was still sober enough to understand my motive in denying Moreau's death. "He is not dead," he said slowly. "Not dead at all. No more dead than me."

"Some," said I, "have broken the Law. They will die. Some have died. Show us now where his old body lies. The body he cast away because he had no more need of it."

"It is this way, Man who walked in the Sea," said the Grey Thing.

And with these six creatures guiding us, we went through the tumult of ferns and creepers and tree-stems towards the northwest. Then came a yelling, a crashing among the branches, and a little pink homunculus rushed by us shrieking. Immediately after appeared a feral monster in headlong pursuit, blood-bedabbled, who was amongst us almost before he could stop his career. The Grey Thing leapt aside; M'ling with a snarl flew at it, and was struck aside; Montgomery fired and missed, bowed his head, threw

up his arm, and turned to run. I fired, and the thing still came on; fired again point-blank into its ugly face. I saw its features vanish in a flash. Its face was driven in. Yet it passed me, gripped Montgomery, and holding him, fell headlong beside him, and pulled him sprawling upon itself — in its death-agony.

I found myself alone with M'ling, the dead brute, and the prostrate man. Montgomery raised himself slowly and stared in a muddled way at the shattered Beast Man beside him. It more than half sobered him. He scrambled to his feet. Then I saw the Grey Thing returning cautiously through the trees.

"See," said I, pointing to the dead brute. "Is the Law not alive? This came of breaking the Law."

He peered at the body. "He sends the Fire that kills," said he in his deep voice, repeating part of the ritual.

The others gathered round and stared for a space.

At last we drew near the westward extremity of the island. We came upon the gnawed and mutilated body of the puma, its shoulder-bone smashed by a bullet, and perhaps twenty yards further found at last what we sought. He lay face downwards in a trampled space in a cane brake. One hand was almost severed at the wrist, and his silvery hair was dabbled in blood. His head had been battered in by the fetters of the puma. The broken canes beneath him were smeared with blood. His revolver

we could not find, Montgomery turned him over.

Resting at intervals, and with the help of the seven Beast People — for he was a heavy man — we carried him back to the enclosure. The night was darkling. Twice we heard unseen creatures howling and shrieking past our little band, and once the little pink sloth creature appeared and stared at us, and vanished again. But we were not attacked again. At the gates of the enclosure our company of Beast People left us — M'ling going with the rest. We locked ourselves in, and then took Moreau's mangled body into the yard, and laid it upon a pile of brushwood.

Then we went into the laboratory and put an end to all we found living there.

CHAPTER 19

MONTGOMERY'S "BANK HOLIDAY"

WHEN this was accomplished, and we had washed and eaten, Montgomery and I went into my little room and seriously discussed our position for the first time. It was then near midnight. He was almost sober, but greatly disturbed in his mind. He had been strangely under the influence of Moreau's personality. I do not think it had ever occurred to him that Moreau could die. This disaster was the sudden collapse of the habits that had become part of his nature in the ten or more monotonous years he had spent on the island. He talked vaguely, answered my questions crookedly, wandered into general questions.

"This silly ass of a world," he said. "What a muddle it all is! I haven't had any life. I wonder when it's going to begin. Sixteen years being bullied by nurses and schoolmasters at their own sweet will, five in London grinding hard at medicine — bad food, shabby lodgings, shabby clothes, shabby vice — a blunder — *I* didn't know any better — and hustled off to this beastly island. Ten years here! What's it all for, Prendick? Are we bubbles blown by a baby?"

It was hard to deal with such ravings. "The thing we have to think of now," said I, "is how to get away from this island."

"What's the good of getting away? I'm an outcast. Where am *I* to join on? It's all very well for *you*, Prendick. Poor old Moreau! We can't leave him here to have his bones picked. As it is . . . And besides, what will become of the decent part of the Beast Folk?"

"Well," said I. "That will do to-morrow. I've been thinking we might make the brushwood into a pyre and burn his body — and those other things . . . Then what will happen with the Beast Folk?"

"*I* don't know. I suppose those

that were made of beasts of prey will make silly asses of themselves sooner or later. We can't massacre the lot,—can we? I suppose that's what *your* humanity would suggest? . . . But they'll change. They are sure to change."

He talked thus inconclusively until at last I felt my temper going. "Damnation!" he exclaimed, at some petulance of mine. "Can't you see I'm in a worse hole than you are?" And he got up and went for the brandy. "Drink," he said, returning. "You logic-chopping, chalky-faced saint of an atheist, drink."

"Not I," said I, and sat grimly watching his face under the yellow paraffin flare as he drank himself into a garrulous misery. I have a memory of infinite tedium. He wandered into a maudlin defence of the Beast People and of M'ling. M'ling, he said, was the only thing that had ever really cared for him. And suddenly an idea came to him.

"I'm damned!" said he, staggering to his feet, and clutching the brandy-bottle. By some flash of intuition I knew what it was he intended. "You don't give drink to that beast!" I said, rising and facing him.

"Beast!" said he. "You're the beast. He takes his liquor like a Christian. Come out of the way, Prendick."

"For God's sake," said I.

"*Get* . . . out of the way," he roared, and suddenly whipped out his revolver.

"Very well," said I, and stood aside, half-minded to fall upon him as he put his hand upon the latch, but deterred by the thought of my useless arm. "You've made a beast of yourself. To the beasts you may go."

He flung the doorway open and stood, half facing me, between the yellow lamp-light and the pallid glare of the moon; his eye-sockets were blotches of black under his stubbly eyebrows. "You're a solemn prig, Prendick, a silly ass! You're always fearing and fancying. We're on the edge of things. I'm bound to cut my throat to-morrow. I'm going to have a damned good bank holiday to-night."

He turned and went out into the moonlight. "M'ling," he cried; "M'ling, old friend!"

Three dim creatures in the silvery light came along the edge of the wan beach, one a white-wrapped creature, the other two blotches of blackness following it. They halted, staring. Then I saw M'ling's haunched shoulders as he came round the corner of the house.

"Drink," cried Montgomery; "drink, ye brutes! Drink, and be men. Dammy, I'm the cleverest. Moreau forgot this. This is the last touch. Drink, I tell you." And waving the bottle in his hand, he started off at a kind of quick trot to the westward, M'ling ranging himself between him and the three dim creatures who followed.

I went to the doorway. They were already indistinct in the mist of the moonlight before Montgomery halted. I saw him administer a dose of the raw brandy to M'ling, and saw the five figures melt into one vague patch. "Sing," I heard Mont-

gomery shout; "sing all together, 'Confound old Prendick.' . . . That's right. Now, again: 'Confound old Prendick.'"

The black group broke up into five separate figures and wound slowly away from me along the band of shining beach. Each went howling at his own sweet will, yelping insult at me, or giving whatever other vent this new inspiration of brandy demanded. Presently I heard Montgomery's remote voice shouting, "Right turn!" and they passed with their shouts and howls into the blackness of the landward trees. Slowly, very slowly, they receded into silence.

The peaceful splendour of the night healed again. The moon was now past the meridian and travelling down the west. It was at its full, and very bright, riding through the empty blue sky. The shadow of the wall lay, a yard wide and of inky blackness, at my feet. The eastward sea was a featureless grey, dark and mysterious, and between the sea and the shadow the grey sands (of volcanic glass and crystals), flashed and shone like a beach of diamonds. Behind me the paraffin lamp flared hot and ruddy.

Then I shut the door, locked it, and went into the enclosure where Moreau lay beside his latest victims — the staghounds and the llama, and some other wretched brutes — his massive face, calm even after his terrible death, and with the hard eyes open, staring at the dead white moon above. I sat down upon the edge of the sink, and, with my eyes upon that ghastly pile of

silvery light and ominous shadows, began to turn over plans in my mind.

In the morning I would gather some provisions in the dingey, and after setting fire to the pyre before me, push out into the desolation of the high sea once more. I felt that for Montgomery there was no help; that he was in truth half akin to these Beast Folk, unfitted for human kindred. I do not know how long I sat there scheming. It must have been an hour or so. Then my planning was interrupted by the return of Montgomery to my neighbourhood. I heard a yelling from many throats, a tumult of exultant cries, passing down towards the beach, whooping and howling and excited shrieks, that seemed to come to a stop near the water's edge. The riot rose and fell; I heard heavy blows and the splintering smash of wood, but it did not trouble me then. A discordant chanting began.

My thoughts went back to my means of escape. I got up, brought the lamp, and went into a shed to look at some kegs I had seen there. Then I became interested in the contents of some biscuit tins, and opened one. I saw something out of the tail of my eye, a red flicker, and turned sharply.

Behind me lay the yard, vividly black and white in the moonlight, and the pile of wood and faggots on which Moreau and his mutilated victims lay, one on another. They seemed to be gripping one another in one last revengeful grapple. His wounds

gaped black as night, and the blood that had dripped lay in black patches upon the sand. Then I saw, without understanding, the cause of the phantom, a ruddy glow that came and danced and went upon the wall opposite. I misinterpreted this, fancied it was a reflection of my flickering lamp, and turned again to the stores in the shed. I went on rummaging among them as well as a one-armed man could, finding this convenient thing and that, and putting them aside for to-morrow's launch. My movements were slow, and the time passed quickly. Presently the daylight crept upon me.

The chanting died down, gave place to a clamour, then began again, and suddenly broke into a tumult. I heard cries of " More, more! " a sound like quarrelling, and a sudden wild shriek. The quality of the sounds changed so greatly that it arrested my attention. I went out into the yard and listened. Then, cutting like a knife across the confusion, came the crack of a revolver.

I rushed at once through my room to the little doorway. As I did so I heard some of the packing-cases behind me go sliding down and smash together, with a clatter of glass on the floor of the shed. But I did not heed these. I flung the door open and looked out.

Up the beach by the boathouse a bonfire was burning, raining up sparks into the indistinctness of the dawn. Around this struggled a mass of black figures. I heard Montgomery call my name. I began to run at once towards this fire, revolver in hand. I saw the pink tongue of Montgomery's pistol lick out once, close to the ground. He was down. I shouted with all my strength and fired into the air.

I heard someone cry " The Master! " The knotted black struggle broke into scattering units, the fire leapt and sank down. The crowd of Beast People fled in sudden panic before me up the beach. In my excitement I fired at their retreating backs as they disappeared among the bushes. Then I turned to the black heaps upon the ground.

Montgomery lay on his back with the hairy grey Beast Man sprawling across his body. The brute was dead, but still gripping Montgomery's throat with its curving claws. Near by lay M'ling on his face, and quite still, his neck bitten open, and the upper part of the smashed brandy-bottle in his hand. Two other figures lay near the fire, the one motionless, the other groaning fitfully, every now and then raising its head slowly, then dropping it again.

I caught hold of the Grey Man and pulled him off Montgomery's body; his claws drew down the torn coat reluctantly as I dragged him away.

Montgomery was dark in the face and scarcely breathing. I splashed sea-water on his face, and pillowed his head on my rolled-up coat. M'ling was dead. The wounded creature by the fire — it was a Wolf Brute with a bearded grey face — lay, I found, with the fore part of its body upon the still glowing timber.

The wretched thing was injured so dreadfully that in mercy I blew its brains out at once. The other brute was one of the Bull Men swathed in white. He, too, was dead.

The rest of the Beast People had vanished from the beach. I went to Montgomery again and knelt beside him, cursing my ignorance of medicine.

The fire beside me had sunk down, and only charred beams of timber glowing at the central ends, and mixed with a grey ash of brushwood, remained. I wondered casually where Montgomery had got his wood. Then I saw that the dawn was upon us. The sky had grown brighter, the setting moon was growing pale and opaque in the luminous blue of the day. The sky to the eastward was rimmed with red.

Then I heard a thud and a hissing behind me, and, looking round, sprang to my feet with a cry of horror. Against the warm dawn great tumultuous masses of black smoke were boiling up out of the enclosure, and through their stormy darkness shot flickering threads of blood-red flame. Then the thatched roof caught. I saw the curving charge of the flames across the sloping straw. A spurt of fire jetted from the window of my room.

I knew at once what had happened. I remembered the crash I had heard. When I had rushed out to Montgomery's assistance I had overturned the lamp.

The hopelessness of saving any of the contents of the enclosure stared me in the face. My mind came back to my plan of flight, and turning swiftly I looked to see where the two boats lay upon the beach. They were gone! Two axes lay upon the sands beside me, chips and splinters were scattered broadcast, and the ashes of the bonfire were blackening and smoking under the dawn. He had burnt the boats to revenge himself upon me and prevent our return to mankind.

A sudden convulsion of rage shook me. I was almost moved to batter his foolish head in as he lay there helpless at my feet. Then suddenly his hand moved, so feebly, so pitifully, that my wrath vanished. He groaned and opened his eyes for a minute.

I knelt down beside him and raised his head. He opened his eyes again, staring silently at the dawn, and then they met mine. The lids fell. " Sorry," he said presently, with an effort. He seemed trying to think. " The last," he murmured, " the last of this silly universe. What a mess — "

I listened. His head fell helplessly to one side. I thought some drink might revive him, but there was neither drink nor vessel in which to bring drink at hand. He seemed suddenly heavier. My heart went cold.

I bent down to his face, put my hand through the rent in his blouse. He was dead; and even as he died a line of white heat, the limb of the sun, rose eastward beyond the projection of the bay, splashing its radiance across the sky and turning the dark sea into a weltering tumult of dazzling light. It fell like a glory upon his death-shrunken face. .

I let his head fall gently upon the rough pillow I had made for him, and stood up. Before me was the glittering desolation of the sea, the awful solitude upon which I had already suffered so much; behind me the island, hushed under the dawn, its Beast People silent and unseen. The enclosure with all its provisions and ammunition burnt noisily with sudden gusts of flame, a fitful crackling, and now and then a crash. The heavy smoke drove up the beach away from me, rolling low over the distant tree-tops towards the huts in the ravine. Beside me were the charred vestiges of the boats and these five dead bodies.

Then out of the bushes came three Beast People, with hunched shoulders, protruding heads, misshapen hands awkwardly held, and inquisitive unfriendly eyes, and advanced towards me with hesitating gestures.

CHAPTER 20

ALONE WITH THE BEAST FOLK

I FACED these people, facing my fate in them single-handed — now literally single-handed, for I had a broken arm. In my pocket was a revolver with two empty chambers. Among the chips scattered about the beach lay the two axes that had been used to chop up the boats. The tide was creeping in behind me.

There was nothing for it but courage. I looked squarely into the faces of the advancing monsters. They avoided my eyes, and their quivering nostrils investigated the bodies that lay beyond me on the beach. I took half a dozen steps, picked up the blood-stained whip that lay beneath the body of the Wolf Man, and cracked it.

They stopped and stared at me. "Salute," said I. "Bow down!"

They hesitated. One bent his knees. I repeated my command, with my heart in my mouth, and advanced upon them. One knelt, then the other two.

I turned and walked towards the dead bodies, keeping my face towards the three kneeling Beast Men, very much as an actor passing up the stage faces his audience.

"They broke the Law," said I, putting my foot on the Sayer of the Law. "They have been slain. Even the Sayer of the Law. Even the Other with the whip. Great is the Law! Come and see."

"None escape," said one of them, advancing and peering.

"None escape," said I. "Therefore hear and do as I command." They stood up, looking questioningly at one another.

"Stand there," said I.

I picked up the hatchets and swung them by their heads from the sling of my arm, turned Montgomery over, picked up his

revolver, still loaded in two chambers, and bending down to rummage, found half a dozen cartridges in his pocket.

"Take him," said I, standing up again and pointing with the whip; "take him and carry him out, and cast him into the sea."

They came forward, evidently still afraid of Montgomery, but still more afraid of my cracking red whip-lash, and, after some fumbling and hesitation, some whip-cracking and shouting, lifted him gingerly, carried him down to the beach, and went splashing into the dazzling welter of the sea. "On," said I, "on!—carry him far."

They went in up to their armpits and stood regarding me. "Let go," said I, and the body of Montgomery vanished with a splash. Something seemed to tighten across my chest. "Good!" said I, with a break in my voice, and they came back, hurrying and fearful, to the margin of the water, leaving long wakes of black in the silver. At the water's edge they stopped, turning and glaring into the sea as though they presently expected Montgomery to arise thencefrom and exact vengeance.

"Now these," said I, pointing to the other bodies.

They took care not to approach the place where they had thrown Montgomery into the water, but, instead, carried the four dead Beast People slantingly along the beach for perhaps a hundred yards before they waded out and cast them away.

As I watched them disposing of the mangled remains of M'ling

I heard a light footfall behind me, and turning quickly saw the big Hyæna-Swine perhaps a dozen yards away. His head was bent down, his bright eyes were fixed upon me, his stumpy hands clenched and held close by his side. He stopped in this crouching attitude when I turned, his eyes a little averted.

For a moment we stood eye to eye. I dropped the whip and snatched at the pistol in my pocket. For I meant to kill this brute—the most formidable of any left now upon the island—at the first excuse. It may seem treacherous, but so I was resolved. I was far more afraid of him than of any other two of the Beast Folk. His continued life was, I knew, a threat against mine.

I was perhaps a dozen seconds collecting myself. Then I cried, "Salute! Bow down!"

His teeth flashed upon me in a snarl. "Who are *you*, that I should. . . ."

Perhaps a little too spasmodically, I drew my revolver, aimed, and quickly fired. I heard him yelp, saw him run sideways and turn, knew I had missed, and clicked back the cock with my thumb for the next shot. But he was already running headlong, jumping from side to side, and I dared not risk another miss. Every now and then he looked back at me over his shoulder. He went slanting along the beach, and vanished beneath the driving masses of dense smoke that were still pouring out from the burning enclosure. For some time I stood staring after him. I turned to my three obedient Beast Folk

again, and signalled them to drop the body they still carried. Then I went back to the place by the fire where the bodies had fallen, and kicked the sand until all the brown bloodstains were absorbed and hidden.

I dismissed my three serfs with a wave of the hand, and went up the beach into the thickets. I carried my pistol in my hand, my whip thrust, with the hatchets, in the sling of my arm. I was anxious to be alone, to think out the position in which I was now placed.

A dreadful thing, that I was only beginning to realise, was that over all this island there was now no safe place where I could be alone, and secure to rest or sleep. I had recovered strength amazingly since my landing, but I was still inclined to be nervous and to break down under any great stress. I felt I ought to cross the island and establish myself with the Beast People, making myself secure in their confidence. And my heart failed me. I went back to the beach and, turning eastward past the burning enclosure, made for a point where a shallow spit of coral sand ran out towards the reef. Here I could sit down and think, my back to the sea and my face against any surprise. And there I sat, chin on knees, the sun beating down upon my head and a growing dread in my mind, plotting how I could live on against the hour of my rescue (if ever rescue came). I tried to review the whole situation as calmly as I could, but it was impossible to clear the thing of emotion.

I began turning over in my mind the reason of Montgomery's despair. " They will change," he said. " They are sure to change." And Moreau — what was it that Moreau had said? " The stubborn beast flesh grows day by day back again. . . ." Then I came round to the Hyæna-Swine. I felt assured that if I did not kill that brute he would kill me. . . . The Sayer of the Law was dead — worse luck! . . . They knew now that we of the Whips could be killed, even as they themselves were killed. . . .

Were they peering at me already out of the green masses of ferns and palms over yonder — watching until I came within their spring? Were they plotting against me? What was the Hyæna-Swine telling them? My imagination was running away with me into a morass of unsubstantial fears.

My thoughts were disturbed by a crying of sea-birds, hurrying towards some black object that had been stranded by the waves on the beach near the enclosure. I knew what that object was, but I had not the heart to go back and drive them off. I began walking along the beach in an opposite direction, designing to come round the eastward corner of the island, and so approach the ravine of the hut, without traversing the possible ambuscades of the thickets.

Perhaps half a mile along the beach I became aware of one of my three Beast Folk advancing out of the landward bushes towards me. I was now so nervous with my own imaginings that I

immediately drew my revolver. Even the propitiatory gestures of the creature failed to disarm me.

He hesitated as he approached. "Go away," cried I. There was something very suggestive of a dog in the cringing attitude of the creature. It retreated a little way, very like a dog being sent home, and stopped, looking at me imploringly with canine brown eyes. "Go away," said I. "Do not come near me."

"May I not come near you?" it said.

"No. Go away," I insisted, and snapped my whip. Then, putting my whip in my teeth, I stooped for a stone, and with that threat drove the creature away.

So, in solitude, I came round by the ravine of the Beast People, and, hiding among the weeds and reeds that separated this crevice from the sea, I watched such of them as appeared, trying to judge from their gestures and appearance how the death of Moreau and Montgomery and the destruction of the House of Pain had affected them. I know now the folly of my cowardice. Had I kept my courage up to the level of the dawn, had I not allowed it to ebb away in solitary thought, I might have grasped the vacant sceptre of Moreau, and ruled over the Beast People. As it was, I lost the opportunity, and sank to the position of a mere leader among my fellows.

Towards noon certain of them came and squatted basking in the hot sand. The imperious voices of hunger and thirst prevailed over my dread. I came out of the bushes, and, revolver in hand, walked down towards these seated figures. One, a Wolf Woman, turned her head and stared at me, and then the others. None attempted to rise or salute me. I felt too faint and weary to insist against so many, and I let the moment pass.

"I want food," said I, almost apologetically, and drawing near.

"There is food in the huts," said an Ox-Boar Man drowsily, and looking away from me.

I passed them, and went down into the shadow and odours of the almost deserted ravine. In an empty hut I feasted on some fruit, and then, after I had propped some specked and half-decayed branches and sticks about the opening, and placed myself with my face towards it, and my hand upon my revolver, the exhaustion of the last thirty hours claimed its own, and I let myself fall into a light slumber, trusting that the flimsy barricade I had erected would cause sufficient noise in its removal to save me from surprise.

CHAPTER 21

THE REVERSION OF
THE BEAST FOLK

In this way I became one among the Beast People in the Island of Doctor Moreau. When I awoke it was dark about me. My

arm ached in its bandages. I sat up, wondering at first where I might be. I heard coarse voices talking outside. Then I saw that my barricade had gone, and that the opening of the hut stood clear. My revolver was still in my hand.

I heard something breathing, saw something crouched together close beside me. I held my breath, trying to see what it was. It began to move slowly, interminably. Then something soft and warm and moist passed across my hand.

All my muscles contracted. I snatched my hand away. A cry of alarm began, and was stifled in my throat. Then I just realised what had happened sufficiently to stay my fingers on the revolver.

"Who is that?" I said in a hoarse whisper, the revolver still pointed.

"I, Master."

"Who are you?"

"They say there is no Master now. But I know, I know. I carried the bodies into the sea, O Walker in the Sea, the bodies of those you slew. I am your slave, Master."

"Are you the one I met on the beach?" I asked.

"The same, Master."

The thing was evidently faithful enough, for it might have fallen upon me as I slept. "It is well," I said, extending my hand for another licking kiss. I began to realise what its presence meant, and the tide of my courage flowed. "Where are the others?" I asked.

"They are mad. They are fools," said the Dog Man. "Even now they talk together beyond there. They say, 'The Master is dead; the Other with the Whip is dead. That Other who walked in the Sea is — as we are. We have no Master, no Whips, no House of Pain any more. There is an end. We love the Law, and will keep it; but there is no pain, no Master, no Whips for ever again.' So they say. But I know, Master, I know."

I felt in the darkness and patted the Dog Man's head. "It is well," I said again.

"Presently you will slay them all," said the Dog Man.

"Presently," I answered, "I will slay them all — after certain days and certain things have come to pass. Every one of them save those you spare, every one of them shall be slain."

"What the Master wishes to kill the Master kills," said the Dog Man with a certain satisfaction in his voice.

"And that their sins may grow," I said; "let them live in their folly until their time is ripe. Let them not know that I am the Master."

"The Master's will is sweet," said the Dog Man, with the ready tact of his canine blood.

"But one has sinned," said I. "Him I will kill, whenever I may meet him. When I say to you, '*That is he*,' see that you fall upon him. — And now I will go to the men and women who are assembled together."

For a moment the opening of the hut was blackened by the exit of the Dog Man. Then I followed and stood up, almost in the exact spot where I had been when I had heard Moreau and his staghound pursuing me. But now it was night, and all the miasmatic

ravine about me was black, and beyond, instead of a green sunlit slope, I saw a red fire before which hunched grotesque figures moved to and fro. Further were the thick trees, a bank of black fringed above with the black lace of the upper branches. The moon was just riding up on the edge of the ravine, and like a bar across its face drove the spire of vapour that was for ever streaming from the fumaroles of the island.

" Walk by me," said I, nerving myself, and side by side we walked down the narrow way, taking little heed of the dim things that peered at us out of the huts.

None about the fire attempted to salute me. Most of them disregarded me — ostentatiously. I looked round for the Hyæna-Swine, but he was not there. Altogether, perhaps, twenty of the Beast Folk squatted, staring into the fire or talking to one another.

" He is dead, he is dead, the Master is dead," said the voice of the Ape Man to the right of me. " The House of Pain — there *is* no House of Pain."

" He is not dead," said I, in a loud voice. " Even now he watches us."

This startled them. Twenty pairs of eyes regarded me.

" The House of Pain is gone," said I. " It will come again. The Master you cannot see. Yet even now he listens above you."

" True, true! " said the Dog Man.

They were staggered at my assurance. An animal may be ferocious and cunning enough, but it takes a real man to tell a lie.

" The Man with the Bandaged Arm speaks a strange thing," said one of the Beast Folk.

" I tell you it is so," I said. " The Master and the House of Pain will come again. Woe be to him who breaks the Law! "

They looked curiously at one another. With an affectation of indifference I began to chop idly at the ground in front of me with my hatchet. They looked, I noticed, at the deep cuts I made in the turf.

Then the Satyr raised a doubt; I answered him, and then one of the dappled things objected, and an animated discussion sprang up round the fire. Every moment I began to feel more convinced of my present security. I talked now without the catching in my breath, due to the intensity of my excitement, that had troubled me at first. In the course of about an hour I had really convinced several of the Beast Folk of the truth of my assertions, and talked most of the others into a dubious state. I kept a sharp eye for my enemy the Hyæna-Swine, but he never appeared. Every now and then a suspicious movement would startle me, but my confidence grew rapidly. Then as the moon crept down from the zenith, one by one the listeners began to yawn (showing the oddest teeth in the light of the sinking fire), and first one, and then another, retired towards the dens in the ravine. And I, dreading the silence and darkness, went with them, knowing I was safer with several of them than with one alone.

In this manner began the longer part of my sojourn upon

this Island of Doctor Moreau. But from that night until the end came there was but one thing happened to tell, save a series of innumerable small unpleasant details, and the fretting of an incessant uneasiness. So that I prefer to make no chronicle for that gap of time, to tell only one cardinal incident of the ten months I spent as an intimate of these half-humanised brutes. There is much that sticks in my memory that I could write, things that I would cheerfully give my right hand to forget. But they do not help the telling of the story. In the retrospect it is strange to remember how soon I fell in with these monsters' ways and gained my confidence again. I had my quarrels, of course, and could show some teethmarks still, but they soon gained a wholesome respect for my trick of throwing stones and the bite of my hatchet. And my St. Bernard Dog Man's loyalty was of infinite service to me. I found their simple scale of honour was based mainly on the capacity for inflicting trenchant wounds. Indeed I may say — without vanity, I hope — that I held something like a pre-eminence among them. One or two whom in various disputes I had scarred rather badly, bore me a grudge, but it vented itself, chiefly behind my back, and at a safe distance from my missiles, in grimaces.

The Hyæna-Swine avoided me, and I was always on the alert for him. My inseparable Dog Man hated and dreaded him intensely. I really believe that was at the root of the brute's attachment to me. It was soon evident to me that the former monster had tasted blood and gone the way of the Leopard Man. He formed a lair somewhere in the forest, and became solitary. Once I tried to induce the Beast Folk to hunt him, but I lacked the authority to make them co-operate for one end. Again and again I tried to approach his den and come upon him unawares, but always he was too acute for me, and saw or winded me and got away. He too made every forest pathway dangerous to me and my allies with his lurking ambuscades. The Dog Man scarcely dared to leave my side.

In the first month or so the Beast Folk, compared with their latter condition, were human enough, and for one or two besides my canine friend I even conceived a friendly tolerance. The little pink sloth creature displayed an odd affection for me, and took to following me about. The Monkey Man bored me however. He assumed, on the strength of his five digits, that he was my equal, and was for ever jabbering at me, jabbering the most arrant nonsense. One thing about him entertained me a little: he had a fantastic trick of coining new words. He had an idea, I believe, that to gabble about names that meant nothing was the proper use of speech. He called it " big thinks," to distinguish it from " little thinks " — the sane everyday interests of life. If ever I made a remark he did not understand, he would praise it very much, ask me to say it again, learn it by heart, and go off repeating it, with a word

wrong here or there, to all the milder of the Beast People. He thought nothing of what was plain and comprehensible. I invented some very curious " big thinks " for his especial use. I think now that he was the silliest creature I ever met; he had developed in the most wonderful way the distinctive silliness of man without losing one jot of the natural folly of a monkey.

This, I say, was in the earlier weeks of my solitude among these brutes. During that time they respected the usage established by the Law, and behaved with general decorum. Once I found another rabbit torn to pieces — by the Hyæna-Swine, I am assured — but that was all. It was about May when I first distinctly perceived a growing difference in their speech and carriage, a growing coarseness of articulation, a growing disinclination to talk. My Ape Man's jabber multiplied in volume, but grew less and less comprehensible, more and more simian. Some of the others seemed altogether slipping their hold upon speech, though they still understood what I said to them at that time. Can you imagine language, once clear-cut and exact, softening and guttering, losing shape and import, becoming mere lumps of sound again? And they walked erect with an increasing difficulty. Though they evidently felt ashamed of themselves, every now and then I would come upon one or other running on toes and finger-tips, and quite unable to recover the vertical attitude. They held things more clumsily; drinking by

suction, feeding by gnawing, grew commoner every day. I realised more keenly than ever what Moreau had told me about the "stubborn beast flesh." They were reverting, and reverting very rapidly.

Some of them — the pioneers, I noticed with some surprise, were all females — began to disregard the injunction of decency — deliberately for the most part. Others even attempted public outrages upon the institution of monogamy. The tradition of the Law was clearly losing its force. I cannot pursue this disagreeable subject. My Dog Man imperceptibly slipped back to the dog again; day by day he became dumb, quadrupedal, hairy. I scarcely noticed the transition from the companion on my right hand to the lurching dog at my side. As the carelessness and disorganisation increased from day to day, the lane of dwelling-places, at no time very sweet, became so loathsome that I left it, and going across the island made myself a hovel of boughs amid the black ruins of Moreau's enclosure. Some memory of pain, I found, still made that place the safest from the Beast Folk.

It would be impossible to detail every step of the lapsing of these monsters; to tell how, day by day, the human semblance left them; how they gave up bandagings and wrappings, abandoned at last every stitch of clothing; how the hair began to spread over the exposed limbs; how their foreheads fell away and their faces projected; how the quasi-human intimacy I had permitted

myself with some of them in the first month of my loneliness became a horror to recall.

The change was slow and inevitable. For them and for me it came without any definite shock. I still went among them in safety, because no jolt in the downward glide had released the increasing charge of explosive animalism that ousted the human day by day. But I began to fear that soon now that shock must come. My St. Bernard Brute followed me to the enclosure, and his vigilance enabled me to sleep at times in something like peace. The little pink sloth thing became shy and left me, to crawl back to its natural life once more among the tree-branches. We were in just the state of equilibrium that would remain in one of those " Happy Family " cages that animal-tamers exhibit, if the tamer were to leave it for ever.

Of course these creatures did not decline into such beasts as the reader has seen in zoological gardens — into ordinary bears, wolves, tigers, oxen, swine, and apes. There was still something strange about each; in each Moreau had blended this animal with that; one perhaps was ursine chiefly, another feline chiefly, another bovine chiefly, but each was tainted with other creatures — a kind of generalised animalism appeared through the specific dispositions. And the dwindling shreds of the humanity still startled me every now and then, a momentary recrudescence of speech perhaps, an unexpected dexterity of the forefeet, a pitiful attempt to walk erect.

I, too, must have undergone strange changes. My clothes hung about me as yellow rags, through whose rents glowed the tanned skin. My hair grew long, and became matted together. I am told that even now my eyes have a strange brightness, a swift alertness of movement.

At first I spent the daylight hours on the southward beach watching for a ship, hoping and praying for a ship. I counted on the *Ipecacuanha* returning as the year wore on, but she never came. Five times I saw sails, and thrice smoke, but nothing ever touched the island. I always had a bonfire ready, but no doubt the volcanic reputation of the island was taken to account for that.

It was only about September or October that I began to think of making a raft. By that time my arm had healed, and both my hands were at my service again. At first I found my helplessness appalling. I had never done any carpentry or suchlike work in my life, and I spent day after day in experimental chopping and binding among the trees. I had no ropes, and could hit on nothing wherewith to make ropes; none of the abundant creepers seemed limber or strong enough, and with all my litter of scientific education I could not devise any way of making them so. I spent more than a fortnight grubbing among the black ruins of the enclosure and on the beach where the boats had been burnt, looking for nails and other stray pieces of metal that might prove of service. Now and then some Beast creature would watch me,

and go leaping off when I called to it. There came a season of thunderstorms and heavy rain that greatly retarded my work, but at last the raft was completed. I was delighted with it. But with a certain lack of practical sense that has always been my bane I had made it a mile or more from the sea, and before I had dragged it down to the beach the thing had fallen to pieces. Perhaps it is as well I was saved from launching it. But at the time my misery at my failure was so acute, that for some days I simply moped on the beach and stared at the water and thought of death.

But I did not mean to die, and an incident occurred that warned me unmistakably of the folly of letting the days pass so — for each fresh day was fraught with increasing danger from the Beast Monsters. I was lying in the shade of the enclosure wall staring out to sea, when I was startled by something cold touching the skin of my heel, and starting round found the little pink sloth creature blinking into my face. He had long since lost speech and active movement, and the lank hair of the little brute grew thicker every day, and his stumpy claws more askew. He made a moaning noise when he saw he had attracted my attention, went a little way towards the bushes, and looked back at me.

At first I did not understand, but presently it occurred to me that he wished me to follow him, and this I did at last, slowly — for the day was hot. When he reached the trees he clambered into them, for he could travel better among their swinging creepers than on the ground.

And suddenly in a trampled space I came upon a ghastly group. My St. Bernard creature lay on the ground dead, and near his body crouched the Hyæna-Swine, gripping the quivering flesh with misshapen claws, gnawing at it and snarling with delight. As I approached the monster lifted its glaring eyes to mine, its lips went trembling back from its red-stained teeth, and it growled menacingly. It was not afraid and not ashamed; the last vestige of the human taint had vanished. I advanced a step further, stopped, pulled out my revolver. At last I had him face to face.

The brute made no sign of retreat. But its ears went back, its hair bristled, and its body crouched together. I aimed between the eyes and fired. As I did so the thing rose straight at me in a leap, and I was knocked over like a ninepin. It clutched at me with its crippled hand, and struck me in the face. Its spring carried it over me. I fell under the hind part of its body, but luckily I had hit as I meant, and it had died even as it leapt. I crawled out from under its unclean weight and stood up trembling, staring at its quivering body. That danger at least was over. But this, I knew, was only the first of the series of relapses that must come.

I burnt both the bodies on a pyre of brushwood. Now, indeed, I saw clearly that unless I left the island my death was only a ques-

tion of time. The Beasts by that time had, with one or two exceptions, left the ravine, and made themselves lairs according to their tastes among the thickets of the island. Few prowled by day; most of them slept, and the island might have seemed deserted to a newcomer; but at night the air was hideous with their calls and howling. I had half a mind to make a massacre of them — to build traps or fight them with my knife. Had I possessed sufficient cartridges, I should not have hesitated to begin the killing. There could now be scarcely a score left of the dangerous carnivores; the braver of these were already dead. After the death of this poor dog of mine, my last friend, I too adopted to some extent the practice of slumbering in the daytime, in order to be on my guard at night. I rebuilt my den in the walls of the enclosure with such a narrow opening that anything attempting to enter must necessarily make a considerable noise. The creatures had lost the art of fire, too, and recovered their fear of it. I turned once more, almost passionately now, to hammering together stakes and branches to form a raft for my escape.

I found a thousand difficulties. I am an extremely unhandy man — my schooling was over before the days of Slöjd — but most of the requirements of a raft I met at last in some clumsy circuitous way or other, and this time I took care of the strength. The only insurmountable obstacle was, that I had no vessel to contain the water I should need if I floated forth upon these untrav-elled seas. I would have even tried pottery, but the island contained no clay. I used to go moping about the island, trying with all my might to solve this one last difficulty. Sometimes I would give way to wild outbursts of rage, and hack and splinter some unlucky tree in my intolerable vexation. But I could think of nothing.

And then came a day, a wonderful day, that I spent in ecstasy. I saw a sail to the southwest, a small sail like that of a little schooner, and forthwith I lit a great pile of brushwood and stood by it in the heat of it and the heat of the midday sun, watching. All day I watched that sail, eating or drinking nothing, so that my head reeled; and the Beasts came and glared at me, and seemed to wonder, and went away. The boat was still distant when night came and swallowed it up, and all night I toiled to keep my blaze bright and high, and the eyes of the Beasts shone out of the darkness, marvelling. In the dawn it was nearer, and I saw it was the dirty lug-sail of a small boat. My eyes were weary with watching, and I peered and could not believe them. Two men were in the boat, sitting low down, one by the bows and the other at the rudder. But the boat sailed strangely. The head was not kept to the wind; it yawed and fell away.

As the day grew brighter I began waving the last rag of my jacket to them; but they did not notice me, and sat still facing one another. I went to the lowest point of the low headland and

gesticulated and shouted. There was no response, and the boat kept on her aimless course, making slowly, very slowly, for the bay. Suddenly a great white bird flew up out of the boat, and neither of the men stirred nor noticed it. It circled round, and then came sweeping overhead with its strong wings outspread.

Then I stopped shouting, and sat down on the headland and rested my chin on my hands and stared. Slowly, slowly, the boat drove past towards the west. I would have swum out to it, but something, a cold vague fear, kept me back. In the afternoon the tide stranded it, and left it a hundred yards or so to the westward of the ruins of the enclosure.

The men in it were dead, had been dead so long that they fell to pieces when I tilted the boat on its side and dragged them out. One had a shock of red hair like the captain of the *Ipecacuanha,* and a dirty white cap lay in the bottom of the boat. As I stood beside the boat, three of the Beasts came slinking out of the bushes and sniffing towards me. One of my spasms of disgust came upon me. I thrust the little boat down the beach and clambered on board her. Two of the brutes were Wolf Beasts, and came forward with quivering nostrils and glittering eyes; the third was the horrible nondescript of bear and bull.

When I saw them approaching those wretched remains, heard them snarling at one another, and caught the gleam of their teeth, a frantic horror succeeded

my repulsion. I turned my back upon them, struck the lug, and began paddling out to sea. I could not bring myself to look behind me.

But I lay between the reef and the island that night, and the next morning went round to the stream and filled the empty keg aboard with water. Then, with such patience as I could command, I collected a quantity of fruit, and waylaid and killed two rabbits with my last three cartridges. While I was doing this I left the boat moored to an inward projection of the reef, for fear of the Beast Monsters.

CHAPTER 22

THE MAN ALONE

IN the evening I started and drove out to sea before a gentle wind from the south-west, slowly and steadily; and the island grew smaller and smaller, and the lank spire of smoke dwindled to a finer and finer line against the hot sunset. The ocean rose up around me, hiding that low dark patch from my eyes. The daylight, the trailing glory of the sun, went streaming out of the sky, was drawn aside like some luminous curtain, and at last I looked into that blue gulf of

immensity that the sunshine hides, and saw the floating hosts of the stars. The sea was silent, the sky was silent; I was alone with the night and silence.

So I drifted for three days, eating and drinking sparingly, and meditating upon all that happened to me, nor desiring very greatly to see men again. One unclean rag was about me, my hair a black tangle. No doubt my discoverers thought me a madman. It is strange, but I felt no desire to return to mankind. I was only glad to be quit of the foulness of the Beast Monsters. And on the third day I was picked up by a brig from Apia to San Francisco. Neither the captain nor the mate would believe my story, judging that solitude and danger had made me mad. And fearing their opinion might be that of others, I refrained from telling my adventures further, and professed to recall nothing that had happened to me between the loss of the *Lady Vain* and the time when I I was picked up again — the space of a year.

I had to act with the utmost circumspection to save myself from the suspicion of insanity. My memory of the Law, of the two dead sailors, of the ambuscades of the darkness, of the body in the cane brake, haunted me. And, unnatural as it seems, with my return to mankind came, instead of that confidence and sympathy I had expected, a strange enhancement of the uncertainty and dread I had experienced during my stay upon the island. No one would believe me, I was almost as queer to men as I had been to the Beast People. I may have caught something of the natural wildness of my companions.

They say that terror is a disease, and anyhow, I can witness that for several years now, a restless fear has dwelt in my mind, such a restless fear as a half-tamed lion cub may feel. My trouble took the strangest form. I could not persuade myself that the men and women I met were not also another, still passably human, Beast People, animals half-wrought into the outward image of human souls; and that they would presently begin to revert, to show first this bestial mark and then that. But I have confided my case to a strangely able man, a man who had known Moreau, and seemed half to credit my story, a mental specialist — and he has helped me mightily.

Though I do not expect that the terror of that island will ever altogether leave me, at most times it lies far in the back of my mind, a mere distant cloud, a memory and a faint distrust; but there are times when the little cloud spreads until it obscures the whole sky. Then I look about me at my fellow men. And I go in fear. I see faces keen and bright, others dull or dangerous, others unsteady, insincere; none that have the calm authority of a reasonable soul. I feel as though the animal was surging up through them; that presently the degradation of the Islanders will be played over again on a larger scale. I know this is an illusion, that these seeming men and women about me are indeed

men and women, men and women for ever, perfectly reasonable creatures, full of human desires and tender solicitude, emancipated from instinct, and the slaves of no fantastic Law — beings altogether different from the Beast Folk. Yet I shrink from them, from their curious glances, their inquiries and assistance, and long to be away from them and alone.

For that reason I live near the broad free downland, and can escape thither when this shadow is over my soul; and very sweet is the empty downland then, under the wind-swept sky. When I lived in London the horror was well-nigh insupportable. I could not get away from men; their voices came through windows; locked doors were flimsy safeguards. I would go out into the streets to fight with my delusion, and prowling women would mew after me, furtive craving men glance jealously at me, weary pale workers go coughing by me, with tired eyes and eager paces like wounded deer dripping blood, old people, bent and dull, pass murmuring to themselves, and all unheeding a ragged tail of gibing children. Then I would turn aside into some chapel, and even there, such was my disturbance, it seemed that the preacher gibbered Big Thinks even as the Ape Man had done; or into some library, and there the intent faces over the books seemed but patient creatures waiting for prey. Particularly nauseous were the blank expressionless faces of people in trains and omnibuses; they seemed no more my fellow-creatures than dead bodies would be, so that I did not dare to travel unless I was assured of being alone. And even it seemed that I, too, was not a reasonable creature, but only an animal tormented with some strange disorder in its brain, that sent it to wander alone, like a sheep stricken with the gid.

But this is a mood that comes to me now — I thank God — more rarely. I have withdrawn myself from the confusion of cities and multitudes, and spend my days surrounded by wise books, bright windows in this life of ours lit by the shining souls of men. I see few strangers, and have but a small household. My days I devote to reading and to experiments in chemistry, and I spend many of the clear nights in the study of astronomy. There is, though I do not know how there is or why there is, a sense of infinite peace and protection in the glittering hosts of heaven. There it must be, I think, in the vast and eternal laws of matter, and not in the daily cares and sins and troubles of men, that whatever is more than animal within us must find its solace and its hope. I hope, or I could not live. And so, in hope and solitude, my story ends.

EDWARD PRENDICK.

NOTE. — The substance of the chapter entitled "Dr. Moreau explains," which contains the essential idea of the story, appeared as a middle article in the *Saturday Review* in January 1895. This is the only portion of

this story that has been previously published, and it has been entirely recast to adapt it to the narrative form. Strange as it may seem to the unscientific reader, there can be no denying that, whatever amount of credibility attaches to the detail of this story, the manufacture of monsters — and perhaps even *quasi*-human monsters — is within the possibilities of vivisection.

"WE SEEMED TO BE MARCHING DOWN THAT TUNNEL FOR
A LONG TIME."

Drawn by E. Hering, 1901 for THE FIRST MEN IN THE MOON.

"REDWOOD FELL IN LOVE WITH THAT GREAT NURSERY."

Drawn by Cyrus Cuneo, 1904 for *THE FOOD OF THE GODS.*

"I STOOD FOR A MOMENT STRUCK BY THE GROTESQUE EFFECT OF HIS SOARING FIGURE."

THE INVISIBLE MAN

CHAPTER 1

THE STRANGE MAN'S ARRIVAL

THE STRANGER came early in February one wintry day, through a biting wind and a driving snow, the last snowfall of the year, over the down, walking as it seemed from Bramblehurst railway station and carrying a little black portmanteau in his thickly gloved hand. He was wrapped up from head to foot, and the brim of his soft felt hat hid every inch of his face but the shiny tip of his nose; the snow had piled itself against his shoulders and chest, and added a white crest to the burden he carried. He staggered into the Coach and Horses, more dead than alive as it seemed, and flung his portmanteau down. "A fire," he cried, "in the name of human charity! A room and a fire!" He stamped and shook the snow from off himself in the bar, and followed Mrs. Hall into her guest parlour to strike his bargain. And with that much introduction, that and a ready acquiescence to terms and a couple of sovereigns flung upon the table, he took up his quarters in the inn.

Mrs. Hall lit the fire and left him there while she went to prepare him a meal with her own hands. A guest to stop at Iping in the winter-time was an unheard-of piece of luck, let alone a guest who was no "haggler," and she was resolved to show herself worthy of her good fortune. As soon as the bacon was well under way, and Millie, her lymphatic aid, had been brisked up a bit by a few deftly chosen expressions of contempt, she carried the cloth, plates, and glasses into the parlour and began to lay them with the utmost *éclat*. Although the fire was burning up briskly, she was surprised to see that her visitor still wore his hat and coat, standing with his back to her and staring out of the window at the falling snow in the yard. His gloved hands were clasped behind him, and he

seemed to be lost in thought. She noticed that the melted snow that still sprinkled his shoulders dripped upon her carpet. " Can I take your hat and coat, sir," she said, "and give them a good dry in the kitchen?"

" No," he said without turning.

She was not sure she had heard him, and was about to repeat her question.

He turned his head and looked at her over his shoulder. " I prefer to keep them on," he said with emphasis, and she noticed that he wore big blue spectacles with side-lights and had a bushy side-whisker over his coat-collar that completely hid his face.

" Very well, sir," she said. " *As* you like. In a bit the room will be warmer."

He made no answer and had turned his face away from her again; and Mrs. Hall, feeling that her conversational advances were ill-timed, laid the rest of the table things in a quick staccato and whisked out of the room. When she returned he was still standing there like a man of stone, his back hunched, his collar turned up, his dripping hat-brim turned down, hiding his face and ears completely. She put down the eggs and bacon with considerable emphasis, and called rather than said to him, "Your lunch is served, sir."

"Thank you," he said at the same time, and did not stir until she was closing the door. Then he swung round and approached the table.

As she went behind the bar to the kitchen she heard a sound repeated at regular intervals. Chirk, chirk, chirk, it went, the sound of a spoon being rapidly whisked round a basin. "That girl!" she said. "There! I clean forgot it. It's her being so long!" And while she herself finished mixing the mustard, she gave Millie a few verbal stabs for her excessive slowness. She had cooked the ham and eggs, laid the table, and done everything, while Millie (help indeed!) had only succeeded in delaying the mustard. And him a new guest and wanting to stay! Then she filled the mustard pot, and, putting it with a certain stateliness upon a gold and black tea-tray, carried it into the parlour.

She rapped and entered promptly. As she did so her visitor moved quickly, so that she got but a glimpse of a white object disappearing behind the table. It would seem he was picking something from the floor. She rapped down the mustard pot on the table, and then she noticed the overcoat and hat had been taken off and put over a chair in front of the fire. A pair of wet boots threatened rust to her steel fender. She went to these things resolutely. "I suppose I may have them to dry now," she said in a voice that brooked no denial.

"Leave the hat," said her visitor in a muffled voice, and turning she saw he had raised his head and was sitting looking at her.

For a moment she stood gaping at him, too surprised to speak.

He held a white cloth — it was a serviette he had brought with

him — over the lower part of his face, so that his mouth and jaws were completely hidden, and that was the reason of his muffled voice. But it was not that which startled Mrs. Hall. It was the fact that all his forehead above his blue glasses was covered by a white bandage, and that another covered his ears, leaving not a scrap of his face exposed excepting only his pink, peaked nose. It was bright pink, and shiny just as it had been at first. He wore a dark-brown velvet jacket with a high black linen lined collar turned up about his neck. The thick black hair, escaping as it could below and between the cross bandages, projected in curious tails and horns, giving him the strangest appearance conceivable. This muffled and bandaged head was so unlike what she had anticipated, that for a moment she was rigid.

He did not remove the serviette, but remained holding it, as she saw now, with a brown gloved hand, and regarding her with his inscrutable blue glasses. "Leave the hat," he said, speaking very distinctly through the white cloth.

Her nerves began to recover from the shock they had received. She placed the hat on the chair again by the fire. "I didn't know, sir," she began, "that — " and she stopped embarrassed.

"Thank you," he said drily, glancing from her to the door and then at her again.

"I'll have them nicely dried, sir, at once," she said, and carried his clothes out of the room. She glanced at his white-swathed head and blue goggles again as she was going out of the door; but his napkin was still in front of his face. She shivered a little as she closed the door behind her, and her face was eloquent of her surprise and perplexity. "I *never,*" she whispered. "There!" She went quite softly to the kitchen, and was too preoccupied to ask Millie what she was messing about with *now,* when she got there.

The visitor sat and listened to her retreating feet. He glanced inquiringly at the window before he removed his serviette and resumed his meal. He took a mouthful, glanced suspiciously at the window, took another mouthful, then rose and, taking the serviette in his hand, walked across the room and pulled the blind down to the top of the white muslin that obscured the lower panes. This left the room in twilight. This done, he returned with an easier air to the table and his meal.

"The poor soul's had an accident or an op'ration or something," said Mrs. Hall. "What a turn them bandages did give me, to be sure!"

She put on some more coal, unfolded the clothes-horse, and extended the traveller's coat upon this. "And they goggles! Why, he looked more like a divin' helmet than a human man!" She hung his muffler on a corner of the horse. "And holding that handkercher over his mouth all the time. Talkin' through it! . . . Perhaps his mouth was hurt too — maybe."

She turned round, as one who

suddenly remembers. "Bless my soul alive!" she said, going off at a tangent; "ain't you done them taters *yet*, Millie?"

When Mrs. Hall went to clear away the stranger's lunch, her idea that his mouth must also have been cut or disfigured in the accident she supposed him to have suffered, was confirmed, for he was smoking a pipe, and all the time that she was in the room he never loosened the silk muffler he had wrapped round the lower part of his face to put the mouthpiece to his lips. Yet it was not forgetfulness, for she saw he glanced at it as it smouldered out. He sat in the corner with his back to the window-blind and spoke now, having eaten and drunk and being comfortably warmed through, with less aggressive brevity than before. The reflection of the fire lent a kind of red animation to his big spectacles they had lacked hitherto.

"I have some luggage," he said, "at Bramblehurst station," and he asked her how he could have it sent. He bowed his bandaged head quite politely in acknowledgment of her explanation. "To-morrow!" he said. "There is no speedier delivery?" and seemed quite disappointed when she answered "No." Was she quite sure? No man with a trap who would go over?

Mrs. Hall, nothing loath, answered his questions and developed a conversation. "It's a steep road by the down, sir," she said in answer to the question about a trap; and then, snatching at an opening said, "It was there a carriage was upsettled, a year

ago and more. A gentleman killed, besides his coachman. Accidents, sir, happen in a moment, don't they?"

But the visitor was not to be drawn so easily. "They do," he said through his muffler, eyeing her quietly through his impenetrable glasses.

"But they take long enough to get well, sir, don't they? . . . There was my sister's son, Tom, jest cut his arm with a scythe, tumbled on it in the 'ayfield, and, bless me! he was three months tied up, sir. You'd hardly believe it. It's regular given me a dread of a scythe, sir."

"I can quite understand that," said the visitor.

"He was afraid, one time, that he'd have to have an op'ration— he was that bad, sir."

The visitor laughed abruptly, a bark of a laugh that he seemed to bite and kill in his mouth. "*Was* he?" he said.

"He was, sir. And no laughing matter to them as had the doing for him, as I had—my sister being took up with her little ones so much. There was bandages to do, sir, and bandages to undo. So that if I may make so bold as to say it, sir—"

"Will you get me some matches?" said the visitor, quite abruptly. "My pipe is out."

Mrs. Hall was pulled up suddenly. It was certainly rude of him, after telling him all she had done. She gasped at him for a moment, and remembered the two sovereigns. She went for the matches.

"Thanks," he said concisely, as she put them down, and turned

his shoulder upon her and stared out of the window again. It was altogether too discouraging. Evidently he was sensitive on the topic of operations and bandages. She did not "make so bold as to say," however, after all. But his snubbing way had irritated her, and Millie had a hot time of it that afternoon.

The visitor remained in the parlour until four o'clock, without giving the ghost of an excuse for an intrusion. For the most part he was quite still during that time; it would seem he sat in the growing darkness smoking in the firelight, perhaps dozing.

Once or twice a curious listener might have heard him at the coals, and for the space of five minutes he was audible pacing the room. He seemed to be talking to himself. Then the armchair creaked as he sat down again.

CHAPTER 2

MR. TEDDY HENFREY'S FIRST IMPRESSIONS

At four o'clock, when it was fairly dark and Mrs. Hall was screwing up her courage to go in and ask her visitor if he would take some tea, Teddy Henfrey, the clock-jobber, came into the bar. "My sakes! Mrs. Hall," said he, "but this is terrible weather for thin boots!" The snow outside was falling faster.

Mrs. Hall agreed with him, and then noticed he had his bag and hit upon a brilliant idea. "Now you're here, Mr. Teddy," said she, "I'd be glad if you'd give th' old clock in the parlour a bit of a look. 'Tis going, and it strikes well and hearty; but the hour-hand won't do nuthin' but point at six."

And leading the way, she went across to the parlour door and rapped and entered.

Her visitor, she saw as she opened the door, was seated in the armchair before the fire, dozing it would seem, with his bandaged head drooping on one side. The only light in the room was the red glow from the fire — which lit his eyes like adverse railway signals, but left his downcast face in darkness — and the scanty vestiges of the day that came in through the open door. Everything was ruddy, shadowy, and indistinct to her, the more so since she had just been lighting the bar lamp, and her eyes were dazzled. But for a second it seemed to her that the man she looked at had an enormous mouth wide open, — a vast and incredible mouth that swallowed the whole of the lower portion of his face. It was the sensation of a moment: the white-bound head, the monstrous goggle eyes, and this huge yawn below it. Then he stirred, started up in his chair, put up his hand. She opened the door wide, so that the

room was lighter, and she saw him more clearly, with the muffler held to his face just as she had seen him hold the serviette before. The shadows, she fancied, had tricked her.

"Would you mind, sir, this man a-coming to look at the clock, sir?" she said, recovering from her momentary shock.

"Look at the clock?" he said, staring round in a drowsy manner and speaking over his hand, and then getting more fully awake, "certainly."

Mrs. Hall went away to get a lamp, and he rose and stretched himself. Then came the light, and Mr. Teddy Henfrey, entering, was confronted by this bandaged person. He was, he says, "taken aback."

"Good-afternoon," said the stranger, regarding him, as Mr. Henfrey says with a vivid sense of the dark spectacles, "like a lobster."

"I hope," said Mr. Henfrey, "that it's no intrusion."

"None whatever," said the stranger. "Though I understand," he said, turning to Mrs. Hall, "that this room is really to be mine for my own private use."

"I thought, sir," said Mrs. Hall, "you'd prefer the clock—" She was going to say "mended."

"Certainly," said the stranger, "certainly—but, as a rule, I like to be alone and undisturbed.

"But I'm really glad to have the clock seen to," he said, seeing a certain hesitation in Mr. Henfrey's manner. "Very glad." Mr. Henfrey had intended to apolo-gise and withdraw, but this anticipation reassured him. The stranger stood round with his back to the fireplace and put his hands behind his back. "And presently," he said, "when the clock-mending is over, I think I should like to have some tea. But not until the clock-mending is over."

Mrs. Hall was about to leave the room,—she made no conversational advances this time, because she did not want to be snubbed in front of Mr. Henfrey, —when her visitor asked her if she had made any arrangements about his boxes at Bramblehurst. She told him she had mentioned the matter to the postman, and that the carrier could bring them over on the morrow. "You are certain that is the earliest?" he said.

She was certain, with a marked coldness.

"I should explain," he added, "what I was really too cold and fatigued to do before, that I am an experimental investigator."

"Indeed, sir," said Mrs. Hall, much impressed.

"And my baggage contains apparatus and appliances."

"Very useful things indeed they are, sir," said Mrs. Hall.

"And I'm naturally anxious to get on with my inquiries."

"Of course, sir."

"My reason for coming to Iping," he proceeded, with a certain deliberation of manner, "was—a desire for solitude. I do not wish to be disturbed in my work. In addition to my work, an accident—"

" I thought as much," said Mrs. Hall to herself.

" — necessitates a certain retirement. My eyes — are sometimes so weak and painful that I have to shut myself up in the dark for hours together. Lock myself up. Sometimes — now and then. Not at present, certainly. At such times the slightest disturbance, the entry of a stranger into the room, is a source of excruciating annoyance to me — it is well these things should be understood."

" Certainly, sir," said Mrs. Hall. " And if I might make so bold as to ask — "

" That, I think, is all," said the stranger, with that quietly irresistible air of finality he could assume at will. Mrs. Hall reserved her question and sympathy for a better occasion.

After Mrs. Hall had left the room, he remained standing in front of the fire, glaring, so Mr. Henfrey puts it, at the clock-mending. Mr. Henfrey not only took off the hands of the clock, and the face, but extracted the works; and he tried to work in as slow and quiet and unassuming a manner as possible. He worked with the lamp close to him, and the green shade threw a brilliant light upon his hands, and upon the frame and wheels, and left the rest of the room shadowy. When he looked up, coloured patches swam in his eyes. Being constitutionally of a curious nature, he had removed the works — a quite unnecessary proceeding — with the idea of delaying his departure and perhaps falling into conversation with the stranger. But the stranger stood there, perfectly silent and still. So still, it got on Henfrey's nerves. He felt alone in the room and looked up, and there, grey and dim, was the bandaged head and huge blue lenses staring fixedly, with a mist of green spots drifting in front of them. It was so uncanny-looking to Henfrey that for a minute they remained staring blankly at one another. Then Henfrey looked down again. Very uncomfortable position! One would like to say something. Should he remark that the weather was very cold for the time of year?

He looked up as if to take aim with that introductory shot. " The weather — " he began.

" Why don't you finish and go?" said the rigid figure, evidently in a state of painfully suppressed rage. " All you've got to do is to fix the hour-hand on its axle. You're simply humbugging — "

" Certainly, sir — one minute more, sir. I overlooked — " And Mr. Henfrey finished and went.

But he went off feeling excessively annoyed. " Damn it! " said Mr. Henfrey to himself, trudging down the village through the thawing snow; " a man must do a clock at times, sure-lie."

And again: " Can't a man look at you? — Ugly! "

And yet again: " Seemingly not. If the police was wanting you you couldn't be more wropped and bandaged."

At Gleeson's corner he saw Hall, who had recently married the stranger's hostess at the Coach

and Horses, and who now drove the Iping conveyance, when occasional people required it, to Sidderbridge Junction, coming towards him on his return from that place. Hall had evidently been "stopping a bit" at Sidderbridge, to judge by his driving. "'Ow do, Teddy?" he said, passing.

"You got a rum un up home!" said Teddy.

Hall very sociably pulled up. "What's that?" he asked.

"Rum-looking customer stopping at the Coach and Horses," said Teddy. "My sakes!"

And he proceeded to give Hall a vivid description of his grotesque guest. "Looks a bit like a disguise, don't it? I'd like to see a man's face if I had him stopping in *my* place," said Henfrey. "But women are that trustful,—where strangers are concerned. He's took your rooms and he ain't even given a name, Hall."

"You don't say so!" said Hall, who was a man of sluggish apprehension.

"Yes," said Teddy. "By the week. Whatever he is, you can't get rid of him under the week. And he's got a lot of luggage coming to-morrow, so he says. Let's hope it won't be stones in boxes, Hall."

He told Hall how his aunt at Hastings had been swindled by a stranger with empty portmanteaux. Altogether he left Hall vaguely suspicious. "Get up, old girl," said Hall. "I s'pose I must see 'bout this."

Teddy trudged on his way with his mind considerably relieved.

Instead of "seeing 'bout it,"

however, Hall on his return was severely rated by his wife on the length of time he had spent in Sidderbridge, and his mild inquiries were answered snappishly and in a manner not to the point. But the seed of suspicion Teddy had sown germinated in the mind of Mr. Hall in spite of these discouragements. "You wim' don't know everything," said Mr. Hall, resolved to ascertain more about the personality of his guest at the earliest possible opportunity. And after the stranger had gone to bed, which he did about half-past nine, Mr. Hall went aggressively into the parlour and looked very hard at his wife's furniture, just to show that the stranger wasn't master there, and scrutinised closely and a little contemptuously a sheet of mathematical computation the stranger had left. When retiring for the night he instructed Mrs. Hall to look very closely at the stranger's luggage when it came next day.

"You mind your own business, Hall," said Mrs. Hall, "and I'll mind mine."

She was all the more inclined to snap at Hall because the stranger was undoubtedly an unusually strange sort of stranger, and she was by no means assured about him in her own mind. In the middle of the night she woke up dreaming of huge white heads like turnips, that came trailing after her at the end of interminable necks, and with vast black eyes. But being a sensible woman, she subdued her terrors and turned over and went to sleep again.

CHAPTER 3

THE THOUSAND AND ONE BOTTLES

THUS it was that on the ninth day of February, at the beginning of the thaw, this singular person fell out of infinity into Iping Village. Next day his luggage arrived through the slush. And very remarkable luggage it was. There was a couple of trunks indeed, such as a rational man might need, but in addition there were a box of books, — big, fat books, of which some were just in an incomprehensible handwriting, — and a dozen or more crates, boxes,. and cases, containing objects packed in straw, as it seemed to Hall, tugging with a casual curiosity at the straw — glass bottles. The stranger, muffled in hat, coat, gloves, and wrapper, came out impatiently to meet Fearenside's cart, while Hall was having a word or so of gossip preparatory to helping bring them in. Out he came, not noticing Fearenside's dog, who was sniffing in a *dilettante* spirit at Hall's legs. "Come along with those boxes," he said. "I've been waiting long enough."

And he came down the steps towards the tail of the cart as if to lay hands on the smaller crate.

No sooner had Fearenside's dog caught sight of him, however, than it began to bristle and growl savagely, and when he rushed down the steps it gave an undecided hop, and then sprang straight at his hand. "Whup!" cried Hall, jumping back, for he was no hero with dogs, and Fearenside howled, "Lie down!" and snatched his whip.

They saw the dog's teeth had slipped the hand, heard a kick, saw the dog execute a flanking jump and get home on the stranger's leg, and heard the rip of his trousering. Then the finer end of Fearenside's whip reached his property, and the dog, yelping with dismay, retreated under the wheels of the waggon. It was all the business of a half-minute. No one spoke, every one shouted. The stranger glanced swiftly at his torn glove and at his leg, made as if he would stoop to the latter, then turned and rushed up the steps into the inn. They heard him go headlong across the passage and up the uncarpeted stairs to his bedroom.

"You brute, you!" said Fearenside, climbing off the waggon with his whip in his hand, while the dog watched him through the wheel. "Come here!" said Fearenside — "You'd better."

Hall had stood gaping. "He wuz bit," said Hall. "I'd better go and see to en," and he trotted after the stranger. He met Mrs. Hall in the passage. "Carrier's darg," he said, "bit en."

He went straight upstairs, and the stranger's door being ajar, he

pushed it open and was entering without any ceremony, being of a naturally sympathetic turn of mind.

The blind was down and the room dim. He caught a glimpse of a most singular thing, what seemed a handless arm waving towards him, and a face of three huge indeterminate spots on white, very like the face of a pale pansy. Then he was struck violently in the chest, hurled back, and the door slammed in his face and locked, all so rapidly that he had no time to observe. A waving of indecipherable shapes, a blow, and a concussion. There he stood on the dark little landing, wondering what it might be that he had seen.

After a couple of minutes he rejoined the little group that had formed outside the Coach and Horses. There was Fearenside telling about it all over again for the second time; there was Mrs. Hall saying his dog didn't have no business to bite her guests; there was Huxter, the general dealer from over the road, interrogative; and Sandy Wadgers from the forge, judicial; besides women and children,—all of them saying fatuities: "Wouldn't let en bite *me*, I knows"; "'Tasn't right *have* such dargs"; "Whad *'e* bite'n for then?" and so forth.

Mr. Hall, staring at them from the steps and listening, found it incredible that he had seen anything very remarkable happen upstairs. Besides, his vocabulary was altogether too limited to express his impressions.

"He don't want no help, he says," he said in answer to his wife's enquiry. "We'd better be a-takin' of his luggage in."

"He ought to have it cauterised at once," said Mr. Huxter; "especially if it's at all inflamed."

"I'd shoot en, that's what I'd do," said a lady in the group.

Suddenly the dog began growling again.

"Come along," cried an angry voice in the doorway, and there stood the muffled stranger with his collar turned up, and his hat-brim bent down. "The sooner you get those things in the better I'll be pleased." It is stated by an anonymous bystander that his trousers and gloves had been changed.

"Was you hurt, sir?" said Fearenside. "I'm rare sorry the darg—"

"Not a bit," said the stranger. "Never broke the skin. Hurry up with those things."

He then swore to himself, so Mr. Hall asserts.

Directly the first crate was carried into the parlour, in accordance with his directions, the stranger flung himself upon it with extraordinary eagerness, and began to unpack it, scattering the straw with an utter disregard of Mrs. Hall's carpet. And from it he began to produce bottles—little fat bottles containing powders, small and slender bottles containing coloured and white fluids, fluted blue bottles labelled *Poison*, bottles with round bodies and slender necks, large green-glass bottles, large white-glass bottles, bottles with glass stoppers and frosted labels, bottles with fine corks, bottles with bungs, bot-

tles with wooden caps, wine bottles, salad-oil bottles — putting them in rows on the chiffonier, on the mantel, on the table under the window, round the floor, on the book-shelf — everywhere. The chemist's shop in Bramblehurst could not boast half so many. Quite a sight it was. Crate after crate yielded bottles, until all six were empty and the table high with straw; the only things that came out of these crates besides the bottles were a number of test-tubes and a carefully packed balance.

And directly the crates were unpacked, the stranger went to the window and set to work, not troubling in the least about the litter of straw, the fire which had gone out, the box of books outside, nor for the trunks and other luggage that had gone upstairs.

When Mrs. Hall took his dinner in to him, he was already so absorbed in his work, pouring little drops out of the bottles into test-tubes, that he did not hear her until she had swept away the bulk of the straw and put the tray on the table, with some little emphasis perhaps, seeing the state that the floor was in. Then he half turned his head and immediately turned it away again. But she saw he had removed his glasses; they were beside him on the table, and it seemed to her that his eye sockets were extraordinarily hollow. He put on his spectacles again, and then turned and faced her. She was about to complain of the straw on the floor when he anticipated her.

" I wish you wouldn't come in without knocking," he said in the tone of abnormal exasperation that seemed so characteristic of him.

" I knocked, but seemingly — "

" Perhaps you did. But in my investigations — my really very urgent and necessary investigations — the slightest disturbance, the jar of a door — I must ask you — "

" Certainly, sir. You can turn the lock if you're like that, you know — any time."

" A very good idea," said the stranger.

" This stror, sir, if I might make so bold as to remark — "

" Don't. If the straw makes trouble put it down in the bill." And he mumbled at her — words suspiciously like curses.

He was so odd, standing there, so aggressive and explosive, bottle in one hand and test-tube in the other, that Mrs. Hall was quite alarmed. But she was a resolute woman. " In which case, I should like to know, sir, what you consider — "

" A shilling. Put down a shilling. Surely a shilling's enough?"

" So be it," said Mrs. Hall, taking up the tablecloth and beginning to spread it over the table. " If you're satisfied, of course — "

He turned and sat down, with his coat-collar towards her.

All the afternoon he worked with the door locked and, as Mrs. Hall testifies, for the most part in silence. But once there was a concussion and a sound of bottles ringing together as though the table had been hit, and the smash of a bottle flung violently down, and then a rapid pacing athwart the room. Fearing " something

was the matter," she went to the door and listened, not caring to knock.

"I can't go on," he was raving. "I *can't* go on. Three hundred thousand, four hundred thousand! The huge multitude! Cheated! All my life it may take me! Patience! Patience indeed! Fool and liar!"

There was a noise of hobnails on the bricks in the bar, and Mrs. Hall very reluctantly had to leave the rest of his soliloquy. When she returned the room was silent again, save for the faint crepitation of his chair and the occasional clink of a bottle. It was all over. The stranger had resumed work.

When she took in his tea she saw broken glass in the corner of the room under the concave mirror, and a golden stain that had been carelessly wiped. She called attention to it.

"Put it down in the bill," snapped her visitor. "For God's sake don't worry me. If there's damage done, put it down in the bill"; and he went on ticking a list in the exercise book before him.

"I'll tell you something," said Fearenside mysteriously. It was late in the afternoon, and they were in the little beer-shop of Iping Hanger.

"Well?" said Teddy Henfrey.

"This chap you're speaking of, what my dog bit. Well—he's black. Leastways, his legs are I seed through the tear of his trousers and the tear of his glove. You'd have expected a sort of pinky to show, wouldn't you? Well—there wasn't none. Just blackness. I tell you, he's as black as my hat."

"My sakes!" said Henfrey. "It's a rummy case altogether. Why, his nose is as pink as paint!"

"That's true," said Fearenside. "I knows that. And I tell 'ee what I'm thinking. That marn's a piebald, Teddy. Black here and white there—in patches. And he's ashamed of it. He's a kind of half-breed, and the colour's come off patchy instead of mixing. I've heard of such things before. And it's the common way with horses, as anyone can see."

CHAPTER 4

MR. CUSS INTERVIEWS THE STRANGER

I HAVE told the circumstances of the stranger's arrival in Iping with a certain fulness of detail, in order that the curious impression he created may be understood by the reader. But excepting two odd incidents, the circumstances of his stay until the extraordinary day of the Club Festival may be passed over very cursorily. There were a number of skirmishes with Mrs. Hall on matters of domestic discipline, but in every case until late in April, when the first signs

of penury began, he over-rode her by the easy expedient of an extra payment. Hall did not like him, and whenever he dared he talked of the advisability of getting rid of him; but he showed his dislike chiefly by concealing it ostentatiously, and avoiding his visitor as much as possible. "Wait till the summer," said Mrs. Hall, sagely, "when the artisks are beginning to come. Then we'll see. He may be a bit overbearing, but bills settled punctual is bills settled punctual, whatever you like to say."

The stranger did not go to church, and indeed made no difference between Sunday and the irreligious days, even in costume. He worked, as Mrs. Hall thought, very fitfully. Some days he would come down early and be continuously busy. On others he would rise late, pace his room, fretting audibly for hours together, smoke, sleep in the armchair by the fire. Communication with the world beyond the village he had none. His temper continued very uncertain; for the most part his manner was that of a man suffering under almost unendurable provocation, and once or twice things were snapped, torn, crushed, or broken in spasmodic gusts of violence. He seemed under a chronic irritation of the greatest intensity. His habit of talking to himself in a low voice grew steadily upon him, but though Mrs. Hall listened conscientiously she could make neither head nor tail of what she heard.

He rarely went abroad by daylight, but at twilight he would go out muffled up enormously, whether the weather were cold or not, and he chose the loneliest paths and those most overshadowed by trees and banks His goggling spectacles and ghastly bandaged face under the penthouse of his hat, came with a disagreeable suddenness out of the darkness upon one or two home-going labourers; and Teddy Henfrey, tumbling out of the Scarlet Coat one night at half-past nine, was scared shamefully by the stranger's skull-like head (he was walking hat in hand) lit by the sudden light of the opened door. Such children as saw him at nightfall dreamt of bogies, and it seemed doubtful whether he disliked boys more than they disliked him, or the reverse —but there was certainly a vivid enough dislike on either side.

It was inevitable that a person of so remarkable an appearance and bearing should form a frequent topic in such a village as Iping. Opinion was greatly divided about his occupation. Mrs. Hall was sensitive on the point. When questioned, she explained very carefully that he was an "experimental investigator," going gingerly over the syllables as one who dreads pitfalls. When asked what an experimental investigator was, she would say with a touch of superiority that most educated people knew that, and would then explain that he "discovered things." Her visitor had had an accident, she said, which temporarily discoloured his face and hands; and being of a sensitive disposition, he was

averse to any public notice of the fact.

Out of her hearing there was a view largely entertained that he was a criminal trying to escape from justice by wrapping himself up so as to conceal himself altogether from the eye of the police. This idea sprang from the brain of Mr. Teddy Henfrey. No crime of any magnitude dating from the middle or end of February was known to have occurred. Elaborated in the imagination of Mr. Gould, the probationary assistant in the National School, this theory took the form that the stranger was an Anarchist in disguise, preparing explosives, and he resolved to undertake such detective operations as his time permitted. These consisted for the most part in looking very hard at the stranger whenever they met, or in asking people who had never seen the stranger leading questions about him. But he detected nothing.

Another school of opinion followed Mr. Fearenside, and either accepted the piebald view or some modification of it; as, for instance, Silas Durgan, who was heard to assert that " if he choses to show enself at fairs he'd make his fortune in no time," and being a bit of a theologian, compared the stranger to the man with the one talent. Yet another view explained the entire matter by regarding the stranger as a harmless lunatic. That had the advantage of accounting for everything straight away.

Between these main groups there were waverers and compromisers. Sussex folk have few superstitions, and it was only after the events of early April that the thought of the supernatural was first whispered in the village. Even then it was only credited among the women folks.

But whatever they thought of him, people in Iping on the whole agreed in disliking him. His irritability, though it might have been comprehensible to an urban brain-worker, was an amazing thing to these quiet Sussex villagers. The frantic gesticulations they surprised now and then, the headlong pace after nightfall that swept him upon them round quiet corners, the inhuman bludgeoning of all the tentative advances of curiosity, the taste for twilight that led to the closing of doors, the pulling down of blinds, the extinction of candles and lamps — who could agree with such goings on? They drew aside as he passed down the village, and when he had gone by, young humorists would up with coat-collars and down with hat-brims, and go pacing nervously after him in imitation of his occult bearing. There was a song popular at that time called the " Bogey Man "; Miss Statchell sang it at the schoolroom concert (in aid of the church lamps), and thereafter whenever one or two of the villagers were gathered together and the stranger appeared, a bar or so of this tune, more or less sharp or flat, was whistled in the midst of them. Also belated little children would call " Bogey Man! " after him, and make off tremulously elated.

Cuss, the general practitioner, was devoured by curiosity. The

bandages excited his professional interest, the report of the thousand and one bottles aroused his jealous regard. All through April and May he coveted an opportunity of talking to the stranger; and at last, towards Whitsuntide, he could stand it no longer, and hit upon the subscription-list for a village nurse as an excuse. He was surprised to find that Mr. Hall did not know his guest's name. "He give a name," said Mrs. Hall — an assertion which was quite unfounded — "but I didn't rightly hear it." She thought it seemed so silly not to know the man's name.

Cuss rapped at the parlour door and entered. There was a fairly audible imprecation from within. "Pardon my intrusion," said Cuss, and then the door closed and cut Mrs. Hall off from the rest of the conversation.

She could hear the murmur of voices for the next ten minutes, then a cry of surprise, a stirring of feet, a chair flung aside, a bark of laughter, quick steps to the door, and Cuss appeared, his face white, his eyes staring over his shoulder. He left the door open behind him, and without looking at her strode across the hall and went down the steps, and she heard his feet hurrying along the road. He carried his hat in his hand. She stood behind the door, looking at the open door of the parlour. Then she heard the stranger laughing quietly, and then his footsteps came across the room. She could not see his face where she stood. The parlour door slammed, and the place was silent again.

Cuss went straight up the village to Bunting the vicar. "Am I mad?" Cuss began abruptly, as he entered the shabby little study. "Do I look like an insane person?"

"What's happened?" said the vicar, putting the ammonite on the loose sheets of his forthcoming sermon.

"That chap at the inn — "

"Well?"

"Give me something to drink," said Cuss, and he sat down.

When his nerves had been steadied by a glass of cheap sherry — the only drink the good vicar had available — he told him of the interview he had just had. "Went in," he gasped, "and began to demand a subscription for that Nurse Fund. He'd stuck his hands in his pockets as I came in, and he sat down lumpily in his chair. Sniffed. I told him I'd heard he took an interest in scientific things. He said yes. Sniffed again. Kept on sniffing all the time; evidently recently caught an infernal cold. No wonder, wrapped up like that! I developed the nurse idea, and all the while kept my eyes open. Bottles — chemicals — everywhere. Balance, test-tubes in stands, and a smell of — evening primrose. Would he subscribe? Said he'd consider it. Asked him, point-blank, was he researching. Said he was. A long research? Got quite cross. 'A damnable long research,' said he, blowing the cork out, so to speak. 'Oh,' said I. And out came the grievance. The man was just on the boil, and my question boiled him over. He had been given a prescrip-

tion, most valuable prescription — what for he wouldn't say. Was it medical? 'Damn you! What are you fishing after?' I apologised. Dignified sniff and cough. He resumed. He'd read it. Five ingredients. Put it down; turned his head. Draught of air from window lifted the paper. Swish, rustle. He was working in a room with an open fireplace, he said. Saw a flicker, and there was the prescription burning and lifting chimneyward. Rushed towards it just as it whisked up chimney. So! Just at that point, to illustrate his story, out came his arm."

" Well? "

" No hand — just an empty sleeve. Lord! I thought, *that's* a deformity! Got a cork arm, I suppose, and has taken it off. Then, I thought, there's something odd in that. What the devil keeps that sleeve up and open, if there's nothing in it? There was nothing in it, I tell you. Nothing down it, right down to the joint. I could see right down it to the elbow, and there was a glimmer of light shining through a tear of the cloth. ' Good God! ' I said. Then he stopped. Stared at me with those black goggles of his, and then at his sleeve."

" Well? "

" That's all. He never said a word; just glared, and put his sleeve back in his pocket quickly. ' I was saying,' said he, ' that there was the prescription burning, wasn't I?' Interrogative cough. ' How the devil,' said I, ' can you move an empty sleeve like that?' ' Empty sleeve?' ' Yes,' said I, ' an empty sleeve.'

" ' It's an empty sleeve, is it? You saw it was an empty sleeve?'

He stood up right away. I stood up too. He came towards me in three very slow steps, and stood quite close. Sniffed venomously. I didn't flinch, though I'm hanged if that bandaged knob of his, and those blinkers, aren't enough to unnerve any one, coming quietly up to you.

" ' You said it was an empty sleeve?' he said. ' Certainly,' I said. At staring and saying nothing a barefaced man, unspectacled, starts scratch. Then very quietly he pulled his sleeve out of his pocket again, and raised his arm towards me as though he would show it to me again. He did it very, very slowly. I looked at it. Seemed an age. ' Well?' said I, clearing my throat, ' there's nothing in it.' Had to say something. I was beginning to feel frightened. I could see right down it. He extended it straight towards me, slowly, slowly — just like that — until the cuff was six inches from my face. Queer thing to see an empty sleeve come at you like that! And then — "

" Well? "

" Something — exactly like a finger and thumb it felt — nipped my nose."

Bunting began to laugh.

" There wasn't anything there! " said Cuss, his voice running up into a shriek at the " there." " It's all very well for you to laugh, but I tell you I was so startled, I hit his cuff hard, and turned round, and cut out of the room — I left him — "

Cuss stopped. There was no mistaking the sincerity of his panic. He turned round in a helpless way and took a second glass of the excellent vicar's very

inferior sherry. "When I hit his cuff," said Cuss, "I tell you, it felt exactly like hitting an arm. And there wasn't an arm! There wasn't the ghost of an arm!"

Mr. Bunting thought it over. He looked suspiciously at Cuss. "It's a most remarkable story," he said. He looked very wise and grave indeed. "It's really," said Mr. Bunting with judicial emphasis, "a most remarkable story."

CHAPTER 5

THE BURGLARY AT THE VICARAGE

THE FACTS of the burglary at the vicarage came to us chiefly through the medium of the vicar and his wife. It occurred in the small hours of Whit-Monday — the day devoted in Iping to the Club festivities. Mrs. Bunting, it seems, woke up suddenly in the stillness that comes before the dawn, with the strong impression that the door of their bedroom had opened and closed. She did not arouse her husband at first, but sat up in bed listening. She then distinctly heard the pad, pad, pad of bare feet coming out of the adjoining dressing-room and walking along the passage towards the staircase. As soon as

she felt assured of this, she aroused the Rev. Mr. Bunting as quietly as possible. He did not strike a light, but putting on his spectacles, her dressing-gown, and his bath slippers, he went out on the landing to listen. He heard quite distinctly a fumbling going on at his study desk downstairs, and then a violent sneeze.

At that he returned to his bedroom, armed himself with the most obvious weapon, the poker, and descended the staircase as noiselessly as possible. Mrs. Bunting came out on the landing.

The hour was about four, and the ultimate darkness of the night was past. There was a faint shimmer of light in the hall, but the study doorway yawned impenetrably black. Everything was still except the faint creaking of the stairs under Mr. Bunting's tread, and the slight movements in the study. Then something snapped, the drawer was opened, and there was a rustle of papers. Then came an imprecation, and a match was struck and the study was flooded with yellow light. Mr. Bunting was now in the hall, and through the crack of the door he could see the desk and the open drawer and a candle burning on the desk. But the robber he could not see. He stood there in the hall undecided what to do, and Mrs. Bunting, her face white and intent, crept slowly downstairs after him. One thing kept up Mr. Bunting's courage: the persuasion that this burglar was a resident in the village.

They heard the chink of money, and realised that the robber had found the housekeeping reserve of gold — two pounds ten

in half-sovereigns altogether. At that sound Mr. Bunting was nerved to abrupt action. Gripping the poker firmly, he rushed into the room, closely followed by Mrs. Bunting. " Surrender! " cried Mr. Bunting, fiercely, and then stopped amazed. Apparently the room was perfectly empty.

Yet their conviction that they had, that very moment, heard somebody moving in the room had amounted to a certainty. For half a minute, perhaps, they stood gaping, then Mrs. Bunting went across the room and looked behind the screen, while Mr. Bunting, by a kindred impulse, peered under the desk. Then Mrs. Bunting turned back the window-curtains, and Mr. Bunting looked up the chimney and probed it with the poker. Then Mrs. Bunting scrutinised the waste-paper basket and Mr. Bunting opened the lid ofthe coal-scuttle. Then they came to a stop and stood with eyes interrogating each other.

" I could have sworn — " said Mr. Bunting.

" The candle! " said Mr. Bunting. " Who lit the candle? "

" The drawer! " said Mrs. Bunting. " And the money's gone! "

She went hastily to the doorway.

" Of all the extraordinary occurrences — "

There was a violent sneeze in the passage. They rushed out, and as they did so the kitchen door slammed. " Bring the candle," said Mr. Bunting, and led the way. They both heard a sound of bolts being hastily shot back.

As he opened the kitchen door he saw through the scullery that the back door was just opening, and the faint light of early dawn displayed the dark masses of the garden beyond. He is certain that nothing went out of the door. It opened, stood open for a moment, and then closed with a slam. As it did so, the candle Mrs. Bunting was carrying from the study flickered and flared. It was a minute or more before they entered the kitchen.

The place was empty. They re-fastened the back door, examined the kitchen, pantry, and scullery thoroughly, and at last went down into the cellar. There was not a soul to be found in the house, search as they would.

Daylight found the vicar and his wife, a quaintly-costumed little couple, still marvelling about on their own ground floor by the unnecessary light of a guttering candle.

CHAPTER 6

THE FURNITURE THAT WENT MAD

Now it happened that in the early hours of Whit-Monday, before Millie was hunted out for the day, Mr. Hall and Mrs. Hall both rose and went noiselessly

down into the cellar. Their business there was of a private nature, and had something to do with the specific gravity of their beer. They had hardly entered the cellar when Mrs. Hall found she had forgotten to bring down a bottle of sarsaparilla from their joint-room. As she was the expert and principal operator in this affair, Hall very properly went upstairs for it.

On the landing he was surprised to see that the stranger's door was ajar. He went on into his own room and found the bottle as he had been directed.

But returning with the bottle, he noticed that the bolts of the front door had been shot back, that the door was in fact simply on the latch. And with a flash of inspiration he connected this with the stranger's room upstairs and the suggestions of Mr. Teddy Henfrey. He distinctly remembered holding the candle while Mrs. Hall shot those bolts overnight. At the sight he stopped, gaping, then with the bottle still in his hand went upstairs again. He rapped at the stranger's door. There was no answer. He rapped again; then pushed the door wide open and entered.

It was as he expected. The bed, the room also, was empty. And what was stranger, even to his heavy intelligence, on the bedroom chair and along the rail of the bed were scattered the garments, the only garments so far as he knew, and the bandages of their guest. His big slouch hat even was cocked jauntily over the bed-post.

As Hall stood there he heard his wife's voice coming out of the depth of the cellar, with that rapid telescoping of the syllables and interrogative cocking up of the final words to a high note, by which the West Sussex villager is wont to indicate a brisk impatience. " George! You gart what a wand? "

At that he turned and hurried down to her. " Janny," he said, over the rail of the cellar steps, " 'tas the truth what Henfrey sez. 'E's not in uz room, 'e ent. And the front door's unbolted."

At first Mrs. Hall did not understand, and as soon as she did she resolved to see the empty room for herself. Hall, still holding the bottle, went first. " If 'e ent there," he said, " his close are. And what's 'e doin' without his close, then? 'Tas a most curious basness."

As they came up the cellar steps, they both, it was afterwards ascertained, fancied they heard the front door open and shut, but seeing it closed and nothing there, neither said a word to the other about it at the time. Mrs. Hall passed her husband in the passage and ran on first upstairs. Some one sneezed on the staircase. Hall, following six steps behind, thought that he heard her sneeze. She, going on first, was under the impression that Hall was sneezing. She flung open the door and stood regarding the room. " Of all the curious! " she said.

She heard a sniff close behind her head as it seemed, and, turning, was surprised to see Hall a dozen feet off on the topmost stair.' But in another moment he was beside her. She bent forward and put her hand on

the pillow and then under the clothes.

"Cold," she said. "He's been up this hour or more."

As she did so, a most extraordinary thing happened — the bed-clothes gathered themselves together, leapt up suddenly into a sort of peak, and then jumped headlong over the bottom rail. It was exactly as if a hand had clutched them in the centre and flung them aside. Immediately after, the stranger's hat hopped off the bed-post, describing a whirling flight in the air through the better part of a circle, and then dashed straight at Mrs. Hall's face. Then as swiftly came the sponge from the washstand; and then the chair, flinging the stranger's coat and trousers carelessly aside, and laughing dryly in a voice singularly like the stranger's, turned itself up with its four legs at Mrs. Hall, seemed to take aim at her for a moment, and charged at her. She screamed and turned, and then the chair legs came gently but firmly against her back and impelled her and Hall out of the room. The door slammed violently and was locked. The chair and bed seemed to be executing a dance of triumph for a moment, and then abruptly everything was still.

Mrs. Hall was left almost in a fainting condition in Mr. Hall's arms on the landing. It was with the greatest difficulty that Mr. Hall and Millie, who had been roused by her scream of alarm, succeeded in getting her downstairs, and applying the restoratives customary in these cases.

"'Tas sperrits," said Mrs. Hall. "I know 'tas sperrits. I've read in papers of en. Tables and chairs leaping and dancing — !"

"Take a drop more, Janny," said Hall. "'Twill steady ye."

"Lock him out," said Mrs. Hall. "Don't let him come in again. I half guessed — I might ha' known. With them goggling eyes and bandaged head, and never going to church of a Sunday. And all they bottles — more'n it's right for any one to have. He's put the sperrits into the furniture. My good old furniture! 'Twas in that very chair my poor dear mother used to sit when I was a little girl. To think it should rise up against me now!".

"Just a drop more, Janny," said Hall. "Your nerves is all upset."

They sent Millie across the street through the golden five o'clock sunshine to rouse up Mr. Sandy Wadgers, the blacksmith. Mr. Hall's compliments and the furniture upstairs was behaving most extraordinary. Would Mr. Wadgers come round? He was a knowing man, was Mr. Wadgers, and very resourceful. He took quite a grave view of the case. "Arm darmed ef thet ent witchcraft," was the view of Mr. Sandy Wadgers. "You warnt horseshoes for such gentry as he."

He came round greatly concerned. They wanted him to lead the way upstairs to the room, but he didn't seem to be in any hurry. He preferred to talk in the passage. Over the way Huxter's apprentice came out and began taking down the shutters of the

tobacco window. He was called over to join the discussion. Mr. Huxter naturally followed in the course of a few minutes. The Anglo-Saxon genius for parliamentary government asserted itself; there was a great deal of talk and no decisive action. "Let's have the facts first," insisted Mr. Sandy Wadgers. "Let's be sure we'd be acting perfectly right in bustin' that there door open. A door onbust is always open to bustin', but ye can't onbust a door once you've busted en."

And suddenly and most wonderfully the door of the room upstairs opened of its own accord, and as they looked up in amazement, they saw descending the stairs the muffled figure of the stranger staring more blackly and blankly than ever with those unreasonably large blue glass eyes of his. He came down stiffly and slowly, staring all the time; he walked across the passage staring, then stopped.

"Look there!" he said, and their eyes followed the direction of his gloved finger and saw a bottle of sarsaparilla hard by the cellar door. Then he entered the parlour, and suddenly, swiftly, viciously slammed the door in their faces.

Not a word was spoken until the last echoes of the slam had died away. They stared at one another. "Well, if that don't lick everything!" said Mr. Wadgers, and left the alternative unsaid.

"I'd go in and ask'n 'bout it," said Wadgers, to Mr. Hall. "I'd d'mand an explanation."

It took some time to bring the landlady's husband up to that pitch. At last he rapped, opened the door, and got as far as, "Excuse me — "

"Go to the devil!" said the stranger in a tremendous voice, and "Shut that door after you." So that brief interview terminated.

CHAPTER 7

THE UNVEILING OF THE STRANGER

THE STRANGER went into the little parlour of the Coach and Horses about half-past five in the morning, and there he remained until near midday, the blinds down, the door shut, and none, after Hall's repulse, venturing near him.

All that time he must have fasted. Thrice he rang his bell, the third time furiously and continuously, but no one answered him. "Him and his 'go to the devil' indeed!" said Mrs. Hall. Presently came an imperfect rumour of the burglary at the vicarage, and two and two were put together. Hall, assisted by Wadgers, went off to find Mr. Shuckleforth, the magistrate, and take his advice. No one ventured upstairs. How the stranger occupied himself is unknown. Now and

then he would stride violently up and down, and twice came an outburst of curses, a tearing of paper, and a violent smashing of bottles.

The little group of scared but curious people increased. Mrs. Huxter came over; some gay young fellows resplendent in black ready-made jackets and *piqué* paper ties, for it was Whit-Monday, joined the group with confused interrogations. Young Archie Harker distinguished himself by going up the yard and trying to peep under the window-blinds. He could see nothing, but gave reason for supposing that he did, and others of the Iping youth presently joined him.

It was the finest of all possible Whit-Mondays, and down the village street stood a row of nearly a dozen booths and a shooting gallery, and on the grass by the forge were three yellow and chocolate waggons and some picturesque strangers of both sexes putting up a cocoanut shy. The gentlemen wore blue jerseys, the ladies white aprons and quite fashionable hats with heavy plumes. Wodger of the Purple Fawn and Mr. Jaggers the cobbler, who also sold second-hand ordinary bicycles, were stretching a string of union-jacks and royal ensigns (which had originally celebrated the Jubilee) across the road. . . .

And inside, in the artificial darkness of the parlour, into which only one thin jet of sunlight penetrated, the stranger, hungry we must suppose, and fearful, hidden in his uncomfortable hot wrappings, pored

through his dark glasses upon his paper or chinked his dirty little bottles, and occasionally swore savagely at the boys, audible if invisible, outside the windows. In the corner by the fireplace lay the fragments of half a dozen smashed bottles, and a pungent tang of chlorine tainted the air. So much we know from what was heard at the time and from what was subsequently seen in the room.

About noon he suddenly opened his parlour door and stood glaring fixedly at the three or four people in the bar. " Mrs. Hall," he said. Somebody went sheepishly and called for Mrs. Hall.

Mrs. Hall appeared after an interval, a little short of breath, but all the fiercer for that. Hall was still out. She had deliberated over the scene, and she came holding a little tray with an unsettled bill upon it. " Is it your bill you're wanting, sir? " she said.

" Why wasn't my breakfast laid? Why haven't you prepared my meals and answered my bell? Do you think I live without eating? "

" Why isn't my bill paid? " said Mrs. Hall. " That's what I want to know." .

" I told you three days ago I was awaiting a remittance — "

" I told you two days ago I wasn't going to await no remittances. You can't grumble if your breakfast waits a bit, if my bill's been waiting these five days, can you? "

The stranger swore briefly but vividly

" Nar, nar! " from the bar.

" And I'd thank you kindly, sir, if you'd keep your swearing to yourself, sir," said Mrs. Hall.

The stranger stood looking more like an angry diving-helmet than ever. It was universally felt in the bar that Mrs. Hall had the better of him. His next words showed as much.

" Look here, my good woman — " he began.

" Don't good woman *me*," said Mrs. Hall.

" I've told you my remittance hasn't come — "

" Remittance indeed! " said Mrs. Hall.

"Still, I daresay in my pocket—"

" You told me two days ago that you hadn't anything but a sovereign's worth of silver upon you — "

"Well, I've found some more—"

" 'Ul-*lo!* " from the bar.

" I wonder where you found it! " said Mrs. Hall.

That seemed to annoy the stranger very much. He stamped his foot. " What do you mean? " he said.

" That I wonder where you found it," said Mrs. Hall. " And before I take any bills or get any breakfasts, or do any such things whatsoever, you got to tell me one or two things I don't understand, and what nobody don't understand, and what everybody is very anxious to understand. I want know what you been doing t' my chair upstairs, and I want know how 'tis your room was empty, and how you got in again. Them as stops in this house comes in by the doors — that's the rule of the house, and

that you *didn't* do, and what I want know is how you *did* come in. And I want know — "

Suddenly the stranger raised his gloved hands clenched, stamped his foot, and said, " Stop! " with such extraordinary violence that he silenced her instantly.

" You don't understand," he said, " who I am or what I am. I'll show you. By Heaven! I'll show you." Then he put his open palm over his face and withdrew it. The centre of his face became a black cavity. " Here," he said. He stepped forward and handed Mrs. Hall something which she, staring at his metamorphosed face, accepted automatically. Then, when she saw what it was, she screamed loudly, dropped it, and staggered back. The nose — it was the stranger's nose! pink and shining — rolled on the floor.

Then he removed his spectacles, and every one in the bar gasped. He took off his hat, and with a violent gesture tore at his whiskers and bandages. For a moment they resisted him. A flash of horrible anticipation passed through the bar. " Oh, my Gard! " said some one. Then off they came.

It was worse than anything. Mrs. Hall, standing open-mouthed and horror-struck, shrieked at what she saw, and made for the door of the house. Every one began to move. They were prepared for scars, disfigurements, tangible horrors, but *nothing!* The bandages and false hair flew across the passage into the bar, making a hobbledehoy

jump to avoid them. Every one tumbled on every one else down the steps. For the man who stood there shouting some incoherent explanation, was a solid gesticulating figure up to the coat-collar of him, and then — nothingness, no visible thing at all!

People down the village heard shouts and shrieks, and looking up the street saw the Coach and Horses violently firing out its humanity. They saw Mrs. Hall fall down and Mr. Teddy Henfrey jump to avoid tumbling over her, and then they heard the frightful screams of Millie, who, emerging suddenly from the kitchen at the noise of the tumult, had come upon the headless stranger from behind.

Forthwith every one all down the street, the sweet-stuff seller, cocoanut shy proprietor and his assistant, the swing man, little boys and girls, rustic dandies, smart wenches, smocked elders and aproned gipsies, began running towards the inn; and in a miraculously short space of time a crowd of perhaps forty people, and rapidly increasing, swayed and hooted and inquired and exclaimed and suggested, in front of Mrs. Hall's establishment. Every one seemed eager to talk at once, and the result was babel. A small group supported Mrs. Hall, who was picked up in a state of collapse. There was a conference, and the incredible evidence of a vociferous eye-witness. " O'Bogey! " " What's he been doin', then? " " Ain't hurt the girl, 'as 'e? " " Run at en with a knife, I believe." " No 'ed, I tell ye. I don't mean no manner

of speaking, I mean *marn 'ithout a' ed!* " " Narnsense! 'tas some conjuring trick." " Fetched off 'is wrappin's, 'e did — "

In its struggles to see in through the open door, the crowd formed itself into a straggling wedge, with the more adventurous apex nearest the inn. " He stood for a moment, I heerd the gal scream, and he turned. I saw her skirts whisk, and he went after her. Didn't take ten seconds. Back he comes with a knife in uz hand and a loaf; stood just as if he was staring. Not a moment ago. Went in that there door. I tell 'e, 'e ain't gart no 'ed 't all. You just missed en — "

There was a disturbance behind, and the speaker stopped to step aside for a little procession that was marching very resolutely towards the house — first Mr. Hall, very red and determined, then Mr. Bobby Jaffers, the village constable, and then the wary Mr. Wadgers. They had come now armed with a warrant.

People shouted conflicting information of the recent circumstances. " 'Ed or no 'ed," said Jaffers, " I got to 'rest en, and 'rest en I *will.*"

Mr. Hall marched up the steps, marched straight to the door of the parlour and flung it open. " Constable," he said, " do your duty."

Jaffers marched in, Hall next, Wadgers last. They saw in the dim light the headless figure facing them, with a gnawed crust of bread in one gloved hand and a chunk of cheese in the other.

" That's him! " said Hall.

" What the devil's this? " came in a tone of angry expostulation from above the collar of the figure.

" You're a damned rum customer, mister," said Mr. Jaffers. " But 'ed or no 'ed, the warrant says ' body,' and duty's duty — "

" Keep off! " said the figure, starting back.

Abruptly he whipped down the bread and cheese, and Mr. Hall just grasped the knife on the table in time to save it. Off came the stranger's left glove and was slapped in Jaffers' face. In another moment Jaffers, cutting short some statement concerning a warrant, had gripped him by the handless wrist and caught his invisible throat. He got a sounding kick on the shin that made him shout, but he kept his grip. Hall sent the knife sliding along the table to Wadgers, who acted as goal-keeper for the offensive, so to speak, and then stepped forward as Jaffers and the stranger swayed and staggered towards him, clutching and hitting in. A chair stood in the way, and went aside with a crash as they came down together.

" Get the feet," said Jaffers between his teeth.

Mr. Hall, endeavouring to act on instructions, receiving a sounding kick in the ribs that disposed of him for a moment, and Mr. Wadgers, seeing the decapitated stranger had rolled over and got the upper side of Jaffers, retreated towards the door, knife in hand, and so collided with Mr. Huxter and the Siddermorton carter coming to the rescue of law and order. At the same moment down came three or four bottles from the chiffonier and shot a web of pungency into the air of the room.

" I'll surrender," cried the stranger, though he had Jaffers down, and in another moment he stood up panting, a strange figure, headless and handless — for he had pulled off his right glove now as well as his left. " It's no good," he said, as if sobbing for breath.

It was the strangest thing in the world to hear that voice coming as if out of empty space, but the Sussex peasants are perhaps the most matter-of-fact people under the sun. Jaffers got up also and produced a pair of handcuffs. Then he started.

" I say! " said Jaffers, brought up short by a dim realisation of the incongruity of the whole business. " Darm it! Can't use 'em as I can see."

The stranger ran his arm down his waistcoat, and as if by a miracle the buttons to which his empty sleeve pointed became undone. Then he said something about his shin, and stooped down. He seemed to be fumbling with his shoes and socks.

" Why! " said Huxter, suddenly, " that's not a man at all. It's just empty clothes. Look! You can see down his collar and the linings of his clothes. I could put my arm — "

He extended his hand; it seemed to meet something in mid-air, and he drew it back with a sharp exclamation. " I wish you'd keep your fingers out of my eye," said the aerial voice, in a tone of savage expostulation.

" The fact is, I'm all here: head, hands, legs, and all the rest of it, but it happens I'm invisible. It's a confounded nuisance, but I am. That's no reason why I should be poked to pieces by every stupid bumpkin in Iping, is it? "

The suit of clothes, now all unbuttoned and hanging loosely upon its unseen supports, stood up, arms akimbo.

Several other of the men folks had now entered the room, so that it was closely crowded. " Invisible, eigh? " said Huxter, ignoring the stranger's abuse. " Who ever heard the likes of that? "

" It's strange, perhaps, but it's not a crime. Why am I assaulted by a policeman in this fashion? "

" Ah! that's a different matter," said Jaffers. " No doubt you are a bit difficult to see in this light, but I got a warrant, and it's all correct. What I'm after ain't no invisibility — it's burglary. There's a house been broken into and money took."

" Well? "

" And circumstances certainly point — "

" Stuff and nonsense! " said the Invisible Man.

" I hope so, sir; but I've got my instructions."

" Well," said the stranger, " I'll come. I'll *come*. But no handcuffs."

" It's the regular thing," said Jaffers.

" No handcuffs," stipulated the stranger.

" Pardon me," said Jaffers.

Abruptly the figure sat down, and before any one could realise what was being done, the slippers, socks, and trousers had been kicked off under the table. Then he sprang up again and flung off his coat.

" Here, stop that," said Jaffers, suddenly realising what was happening. He gripped the waistcoat; it struggled, and the shirt slipped out of it and left it limp and empty in his hand. " Hold him! " said Jaffers loudly. " Once he gets they things off — ! "

" Hold him! " cried every one, and there was a rush at the fluttering white shirt which was now all that was visible of the stranger.

The shirt-sleeve planted a shrewd blow in Hall's face that stopped his open-armed advance, and sent him backward into old Toothsome the sexton, and in another moment the garment was lifted up and became convulsed and vacantly flapping about the arms, even as a shirt that is being thrust over a man's head. Jaffers clutched at it, and only helped to pull it off; he was struck in the mouth out of the air, and incontinently drew his truncheon and smote Teddy Henfrey savagely upon the crown of his head.

" Look out! " said everybody, fencing at random and hitting at nothing. " Hold him! Shut the door! Don't let him loose! I got something! Here he is! " A perfect babel of noises they made. Everybody, it seemed, was being hit all at once, and Sandy Wadgers, knowing as ever and his wits sharpened by a frightful blow in the nose, reopened the door and led the rout. The others, following incontinently, were jammed for a moment in the corner by

the doorway. The hitting continued. Phipps, the Unitarian, had a front tooth broken, and Henfrey was injured in the cartilage of his ear. Jaffers was struck under the jaw, and, turning, caught at something that intervened between him and Huxter in the mêlée, and prevented their coming together. He felt a muscular chest, and in another moment the whole mass of struggling, excited men shot out into the crowded hall.

"I got him!" shouted Jaffers, choking and reeling through them all, and wrestling with purple face and swelling veins against his unseen enemy.

Men staggered right and left as the extraordinary conflict swayed swiftly towards the house door, and went spinning down the half-dozen steps of the inn. Jaffers cried in a strangled voice — holding tight, nevertheless, and making play with his knee — spun round, and fell heavily undermost with his head on the gravel. Only then did his fingers relax.

There were excited cries of "Hold him!" "Invisible!" and so forth, and a young fellow, a stranger in the place whose name did not come to light, rushed in at once, caught something, missed his hold, and fell over the constable's prostrate body. Halfway across the road, a woman screamed as something pushed by her; a dog, kicked apparently, yelped and ran howling into Huxter's yard, and with that the transit of the Invisible Man was accomplished. For a space people stood amazed and gesticulating, and then came Panic, and scat-

tered them abroad through the village as a gust scatters dead leaves.

But Jaffers lay quite still, face upward and knees bent.

CHAPTER 8

IN TRANSIT

THE EIGHTH chapter is exceedingly brief, and relates that Gibbins, the amateur naturalist of the district, while lying out on the spacious open downs without a soul within a couple of miles of him, as he thought, and almost dozing, heard close to him the sound as of a man coughing, sneezing, and then swearing savagely to himself; and looking, beheld nothing. Yet the voice was indisputable. It continued to swear with that breadth and variety that distinguishes the swearing of a cultivated man. It grew to a climax, diminished again, and died away in the distance, going as it seemed to him in the direction of Adderdean. It lifted to a spasmodic sneeze and ended. Gibbins had heard nothing of the morning's occurrences, but the phenomenon was so striking and disturbing that his philosophical tranquillity vanished; he got up hastily, and hurried down the

steepness of the hill towards the village, as fast as he could go.

CHAPTER 9

MR. THOMAS MARVEL

You must picture Mr. Thomas Marvel as a person of copious, flexible visage, a nose of cylindrical protrusion, a liquorish, ample, fluctuating mouth, and a beard of bristling eccentricity. His figure inclined to embonpoint; his short limbs accentuated this inclination. He wore a furry silk hat, and the frequent substitution of twine and shoe-laces for buttons, apparent at critical points of his costume, marked a man essentially bachelor.

Mr. Thomas Marvel was sitting with his feet in a ditch by the roadside over the down toward Adderdean, about a mile and a half out of Iping. His feet, save for socks of irregular openwork, were bare, his big toes were broad, and pricked like the ears of a watchful dog. In a leisurely manner — he did everything in a leisurely manner — he was contemplating trying on a pair of boots. They were the soundest boots he had come across for a long time, but too large for him; whereas the ones he had were,

in dry weather, a very comfortable fit, but too thin-soled for damp. Mr. Thomas Marvel hated roomy boots, but then he hated damp. He had never properly thought out which he hated most, and it was a pleasant day, and there was nothing better to do. So he put the four boots in a graceful group on the turf and looked at them. And seeing them there among the grass and springing agrimony, it suddenly occurred to him that both pairs were exceedingly ugly to see. He was not at all startled by a voice behind him.

"They're boots, anyhow," said the voice.

"They are — charity boots," said Mr. Thomas Marvel, with his head on one side regarding them distastefully; "and which is the ugliest pair in the whole blessed universe, I'm darned if I know!"

"H'm," said the voice.

"I've worn worse — in fact, I've worn none. But none so owdacious ugly — if you'll allow the expression. I've been cadging boots — in particular — for days. Because I was sick of *them*. They're sound enough, of course. But a gentleman on tramp sees such a thundering lot of his boots. And if you'll believe me, I've raised nothing in the whole blessed county, try as I would, but THEM. Look at 'em! And a good county for boots, too, in a general way. But it's just my promiscuous luck. I've got my boots in this county ten years or more. And then they treat you like this."

"It's a beast of a county,"

said the voice. "And pigs for people."

"Ain't it?" said Mr. Thomas Marvel. "Lord! But them boots! It beats it."

He turned his head over his shoulder to the right, to look at the boots of his interlocutor with a view to comparisons, and lo! where the boots of his interlocutor should have been were neither legs nor boots. He turned his head over his shoulder to the left, and there also were neither legs nor boots. He was irradiated by the dawn of a great amazement. "Where *are* yar?" said Mr. Thomas Marvel over his shoulder and coming round on all fours. He saw a stretch of empty downs with the wind swaying and remote green-pointed furze bushes.

"Am I drunk?" said Mr. Marvel. "Have I had visions? Was I talking to myself? What the—"

"Don't be alarmed," said a voice.

"None of your ventriloquising *me*," said Mr. Thomas Marvel, rising sharply to his feet. "Where *are* yer? Alarmed, indeed!"

"Don't be alarmed," repeated the voice.

"*You'll* be alarmed in a minute, you silly fool," said Mr. Thomas Marvel. "Where *are* yer? Lemme get my mark on yer—"

"Are you *buried*?" said Mr. Thomas Marvel, after an interval.

There was no answer. Mr. Thomas Marvel stood bootless and amazed, his jacket nearly thrown off.

"Peewit," said a peewit, very remote.

"Peewit, indeed!" said Mr. Thomas Marvel. "This ain't no time for foolery." The down was desolate, east and west, north and south; the road with its shallow ditches and white bordering stakes, ran smooth and empty north and south, and, save for that peewit, the blue sky was empty too. "So help me," said Mr. Thomas Marvel, shuffling his coat on to his shoulders again. "It's the drink! I might ha' known."

"It's not the drink," said the voice. "You keep your nerves steady."

"Ow!" said Mr. Marvel, and his face grew white amidst its patches. "It's the drink," his lips repeated noiselessly. He remained staring about him, rotating slowly backwards. "I could have *swore* I heard a voice," he whispered.

"Of course you did."

"It's there again," said Mr. Marvel, closing his eyes and clasping his hand on his brow with a tragic gesture. He was suddenly taken by the collar and shaken violently and left more dazed than ever. "Don't be a fool," said the voice.

"I'm — off — my — blooming — chump," said Mr. Marvel. "It's no good. It's fretting about them blarsted boots. I'm off my blessed blooming chump. Or it's spirits."

"Neither one thing nor the other," said the voice. "Listen!"

"Chump," said Mr. Marvel.

"One minute," said the voice penetratingly, — tremulous with self-control.

"Well?" said Mr. Thomas Marvel, with a strange feeling of having been dug in the chest by a finger.

"You think I'm just imagination? Just imagination?"

"What else *can* you be?" said Mr. Thomas Marvel, rubbing the back of his neck.

"Very well," said the voice, in a tone of relief. "Then I'm going to throw flints at you till you think differently."

"But where *are* yer?"

The voice made no answer. Whiz came a flint, apparently out of the air, and missed Mr. Marvel's shoulder by a hair's breadth. Mr. Marvel, turning, saw a flint jerk up into the air, trace a complicated path, hang for a moment, and then fling at his feet with almost invisible rapidity. He was too amazed to dodge. Whiz it came, and ricocheted from a bare toe into the ditch. Mr. Thomas Marvel jumped a foot and howled aloud. Then he started to run, tripped over an unseen obstacle, and came head over heels into a sitting position.

"*Now,*" said the voice, as a third stone curved upward and hung in the air above the tramp. "Am I imagination?"

Mr. Marvel by way of reply struggled to his feet, and was immediately rolled over again. He lay quiet for a moment. "If you struggle any more," said the voice, "I shall throw the flint at your head."

"It's a fair do," said Mr. Thomas Marvel, sitting up, taking his wounded toe in hand and fixing his eye on the third missile. "I don't understand it. Stones flinging themselves. Stones talking. Put yourself down. Rot away. I'm done."

The third flint fell.

"It's very simple," said the voice. "I'm an invisible man."

"Tell us something I don't know," said Mr. Marvel, gasping with pain. "Where you've hid — how you do it — I *don't* know, I'm beat."

"That's all," said the voice. "I'm invisible. That's what I want you to understand."

"Any one could see that. There is no need for you to be so confounded impatient, mister. *Now* then. Give us a notion. How are you hid?"

"I'm invisible. That's the great point. And what I want you to understand is this — "

"But whereabouts?" interrupted Mr. Marvel.

"Here! Six yards in front of you."

"Oh, *come!* I ain't blind. You'll be telling me next you're just thin air. I'm not one of your ignorant tramps — "

"Yes, I am — thin air. You're looking through me."

"What! Ain't there any stuff to you? *Vox et* — what is it? — jabber. Is it that?"

"I am just a human being — solid, needing food and drink, needing covering too — But I'm invisible. You see? Invisible. Simple idea. Invisible."

"What, real like?"

"Yes, real."

"Let's have a hand of you," said Marvel, "if you *are* real. It

won't be so darn out-of-the-way like, then — *Lord!*" he said, "how you made me jump! — gripping me like that!"

He felt the hand that had closed round his wrist with his disengaged fingers, and his touch went timorously up the arm, patted a muscular chest, and explored a bearded face. Marvel's face was astonishment.

"I'm dashed!" he said. "If this don't beat cock-fighting! Most remarkable! — And there I can see a rabbit clean through you, 'arf a mile away! Not a bit of you visible — except — "

He scrutinised the apparently empty space keenly. "You 'aven't been eatin' bread and cheese?" he asked, holding the invisible arm.

"You're quite right, and it's not quite assimilated into the system."

"Ah!" said Mr. Marvel. "Sort of ghostly, though."

"Of course, all this isn't so wonderful as you think."

"It's quite wonderful enough for *my* modest wants," said Mr. Thomas Marvel. "Howjer manage it? How the dooce is it done?"

"It's too long a story. And besides — "

"I tell you, the whole business fair beats me," said Mr. Marvel.

"What I want to say at present is this: I need help. I have come to that — I came upon you suddenly. I was wandering, mad with rage, naked, impotent. I could have murdered. And I saw you — "

"*Lord!*" said Mr. Marvel.

"I came up behind you — hesitated — went on — "

Mr. Marvel's expression was eloquent.

"— then stopped. 'Here,' I said, 'is an outcast like myself. This is the man for me.' So I turned back and came to you — you. And — "

"*Lord!*" said Mr. Marvel. "But I'm all in a dizzy. May I ask — How is it? And what you may be requiring in the way of help? — Invisible!"

"I want you to help me get clothes — and shelter — and then, with other things. I've left them long enough. If you won't — well! But you *will* — *must*."

"Look here," said Mr. Marvel. "I'm too flabbergasted. Don't knock me about any more. And leave me go. I must get steady a bit. And you've pretty near broken my toe. It's all so unreasonable. Empty downs, empty sky. Nothing visible for miles except the bosom of Nature. And then comes a voice. A voice out of heaven! And stones! And a fist — Lord!"

"Pull yourself together," said the voice, "for you have to do the job I've chosen for you."

Mr. Marvel blew out his cheeks, and his eyes were round.

"I've chosen you," said the voice. "You are the only man, except some of those fools down there, who knows there is such a thing as an invisible man. You have to be my helper. Help me — and I will do great things for you. An invisible man is a man of power." He stopped for a moment to sneeze violently.

"But if you betray me," he said, "if you fail to do as I direct you — "

He paused and tapped Mr. Marvel's shoulder smartly. Mr. Marvel gave a yelp of terror at the touch. "*I* don't want to betray you," said Mr. Marvel, edging away from the direction of the fingers. "Don't you go a-thinking that, whatever you do. All I want to do is to help you — just tell me what I got to do. (Lord!) Whatever you want done, that I'm most willing to do."

CHAPTER 10

MR. MARVEL'S VISIT
TO IPING

AFTER the first gusty panic had spent itself Iping became argumentative. Scepticism suddenly reared its head — rather nervous scepticism, not at all assured of its back, but scepticism nevertheless. It is so much easier not to believe in an invisible man; and those who had actually seen him dissolve into air, or felt the strength of his arm, could be counted on the fingers of two hands. And of these witnesses Mr. Wadgers was presently missing, having retired impregnably behind the bolts and bars of his own house, and Jaffers was lying stunned in the parlour of the Coach and Horses. Great and strange ideas transcending experience often have less effect upon men and women than smaller, more tangible considerations. Iping was gay with bunting, and everybody was in gala dress. Whit-Monday had been looked forward to for a month or more. By the afternoon even those who believed in the Unseen were beginning to resume their little amusements in a tentative fashion, on the supposition that he had quite gone away, and with the sceptics he was already a jest. But people, sceptics and believers alike, were remarkably sociable all that day.

Haysman's meadow was gay with a tent, in which Mrs. Bunting and other ladies were preparing tea, while, without, the Sunday-school children ran races and played games under the noisy guidance of the curate and the Misses Cuss and Sackbut. No doubt there was a slight uneasiness in the air, but people for the most part had the sense to conceal whatever imaginative qualms they experienced. On the village green an inclined string, down which, clinging the while to a pulley-swung handle, one could be hurled violently against a sack at the other end, came in for considerable favour among the adolescent. There were swings and cocoanut shies and promenading, and the steam organ attached to the swings filled the air with a pungent flavour of oil and with equally pungent music.

Members of the Club, who had attended church in the morning, were splendid in badges of pink and green, and some of the gayer-minded had also adorned their bowler hats with brilliant-coloured favours of ribbon. Old Fletcher, whose conceptions of holiday-making were severe, was visible through the jasmine about his window or through the open door (whichever way you chose to look), poised delicately on a plank supported on two chairs, and whitewashing the ceiling of his front room.

About four o'clock a stranger entered the village from the direction of the downs. He was a short, stout person in an extraordinarily shabby top hat, and he appeared to be very much out of breath. His cheeks were alternately limp and tightly puffed. His mottled face was apprehensive, and he moved with a sort of reluctant alacrity. He turned the corner by the church, and directed his way to the Coach and Horses. Among others old Fletcher remembers seeing him, and indeed the old gentleman was so struck by his peculiar agitation that he inadvertently allowed a quantity of whitewash to run down the brush into the sleeve of his coat while regarding him.

This stranger, to the perceptions of the proprietor of the cocoanut shy, appeared to be talking to himself, and Mr. Huxter remarked the same thing. He stopped at the foot of the Coach and Horses steps, and, according to Mr. Huxter, appeared to undergo a severe internal struggle before he could induce himself to enter the house. Finally he marched up the steps, and was seen by Mr. Huxter to turn to the left and open the door of the parlour. Mr. Huxter heard voices from within the room and from the bar apprising the man of his error. " That room's private!" said Hall, and the stranger shut the door clumsily and went into the bar.

In the course of a few minutes he reappeared, wiping his lips with the back of his hand with an air of quiet satisfaction that somehow impressed Mr. Huxter as assumed. He stood looking about him for some moments, and then Mr. Huxter saw him walk in an oddly furtive manner towards the gates of the yard, upon which the parlour window opened. The stranger, after some hesitation, leant against one of the gate-posts, produced a short clay pipe, and prepared to fill it. His fingers trembled while doing so. He lit it clumsily, and folding his arms began to smoke in a languid attitude, an attitude which his occasional quick glances up the yard altogether belied.

All this Mr. Huxter saw over the canisters of the tobacco window, and the singularity of the man's behaviour prompted him to maintain his observation.

Presently the stranger stood up abruptly and put his pipe in his pocket. Then he vanished into the yard. Forthwith Mr. Huxter, conceiving he was witness of some petty larceny, leapt round his counter and ran out into the road to intercept the thief. As he did so, Mr. Marvel reappeared,

his hat askew, a big bundle in a blue table-cloth in one hand, and three books tied together — as it proved afterwards with the Vicar's braces — in the other. Directly he saw Huxter he gave a sort of gasp, and turning sharply to the left, began to run. "Stop thief!" cried Huxter, and set off after him. Mr. Huxter's sensations were vivid but brief. He saw the man just before him and spurting briskly for the church corner and the hill road. He saw the village flags and festivities beyond, and a face or so turned towards him. He bawled, "Stop!" again. He had hardly gone ten strides before his shin was caught in some mysterious fashion, and he was no longer running, but flying with inconceivable rapidity through the air. He saw the ground suddenly close to his face. The world seemed to splash into a million whirling specks of light, and subsequent proceedings interested him no more.

CHAPTER 11

IN THE COACH AND HORSES

Now in order clearly to understand what had happened in the inn, it is necessary to go back to the moment when Mr. Marvel first came into view of Mr. Huxter's window. At that precise moment Mr. Cuss and Mr. Bunting were in the parlour. They were seriously investigating the strange occurrences of the morning, and were, with Mr. Hall's permission, making a thorough examination of the Invisible Man's belongings. Jaffers had partially recovered from his fall and had gone home in the charge of his sympathetic friends. The stranger's scattered garments had been removed by Mrs. Hall and the room tidied up. And on the table under the window where the stranger had been wont to work, Cuss had hit almost at once on three big books in manuscript labelled "Diary."

"Diary!" said Cuss, putting the three books on the table. "Now, at any rate, we shall learn something." The Vicar stood with his hands on the table.

"Diary," repeated Cuss, sitting down, putting two volumes to support the third, and opening it. "H'm — no name on the flyleaf. Bother! — cypher. And figures."

The Vicar came round to look over his shoulder.

Cuss turned the pages over with a face suddenly disappointed. "I'm — dear me! It's all cypher, Bunting."

"There are no diagrams?" asked Mr. Bunting. "No illustrations throwing light —"

"See for yourself," said Mr. Cuss. "Some of it's mathematical and some of it's Russian or some such language (to judge by the letters), and some of it's Greek. Now the Greek I thought *you* —"

"Of course," said Mr. Bunting,

taking out and wiping his spectacles and feeling suddenly very uncomfortable, — for he had no Greek left in his mind worth talking about; "yes — the Greek, of course, may furnish a clue."

"I'll find you a place."

"I'd rather glance through the volumes first," said Mr. Bunting, still wiping. "A general impression first, Cuss, and *then*, you know, we can go looking for clues."

He coughed, put on his glasses, arranged them fastidiously, coughed again, and wished something would happen to avert the seemingly inevitable exposure. Then he took the volume Cuss handed him in a leisurely manner. And then something did happen.

The door opened suddenly.

Both gentlemen started violently, looked round, and were relieved to see a sporadically rosy face beneath a furry silk hat. "Tap?" asked the face, and stood staring.

"No," said both gentlemen at once.

"Over the other side, my man," said Mr. Bunting. And "Please shut that door," said Mr. Cuss irritably.

"All right," said the intruder, as it seemed, in a low voice curiously different from the huskiness of its first enquiry. "Right you are," said the intruder in the former voice. "Stand clear!" and he vanished and closed the door.

"A sailor, I should judge," said Mr. Bunting. "Amusing fellows they are. Stand clear! indeed. A nautical term referring to his getting back out of the room, I suppose."

"I daresay so," said Cuss. "My nerves are all loose to-day. It quite made me jump — the door opening like that."

Mr. Bunting smiled as if he had not jumped. "And now," he said with a sigh, "these books."

"One minute," said Cuss, and went and locked the door. "Now I think we are safe from interruption."

Some one sniffed as he did so.

"One thing is indisputable," said Bunting, drawing up a chair next to that of Cuss. "There certainly have been very strange things happen in Iping during the last few days — very strange. I cannot of course believe in this absurd invisibility story — "

"It's incredible," said Cuss, " — incredible. But the fact remains that I saw — I certainly saw right down his sleeve — "

"But did you — are you sure? Suppose a mirror, for instance, — hallucinations are so easily produced. I don't know if you have ever seen a really good conjuror — "

"I won't argue again," said Cuss. "We've thrashed that out, Bunting. And just now there's these books — Ah! here's some of what I take to be Greek! Greek letters certainly."

He pointed to the middle of the page. Mr. Bunting flushed slightly and brought his face nearer, apparently finding some difficulty with his glasses. Suddenly he became aware of a strange feeling at the nape of his neck. He tried to raise his head, and encountered an immovable resistance. The feeling was a curious pressure, the grip of a heavy, firm hand, and it bore his chin

irresistibly to the table. *"Don't move, little men,"* whispered a voice, *" or I'll brain you both!"* He looked into the face of Cuss, close to his own, and each saw a horrified reflection of his own sickly astonishment.

"I'm sorry to handle you roughly," said the Voice, "but it's unavoidable.

"Since when did you learn to pry into an investigator's private memoranda?" said the Voice; and two chins struck the table simultaneously and two sets of teeth rattled.

"Since when did you learn to invade the private rooms of a man in misfortune?" and the concussion was repeated.

"Where have they put my clothes?

"Listen," said the Voice. "The windows are fastened and I've taken the key out of the door. I am a fairly strong man, and I have the poker handy — besides being invisible. There's not the slightest doubt that I could kill you both and get away quite easily if I wanted to — do you understand? Very well. If I let you go will you promise not to try any nonsense and do what I tell you?"

The Vicar and the Doctor looked at one another, and the Doctor pulled a face. "Yes," said Mr. Bunting, and the Doctor repeated it. Then the pressure on the necks relaxed, and the Doctor and the Vicar sat up, both very red in the face and wriggling their heads.

"Please keep sitting where you are," said the Invisible Man. "Here's the poker, you see.

"When I came into this room," continued the Invisible Man, after presenting the poker to the tip of the nose of each of his visitors, "I did not expect to find it occupied, and I expected to find, in addition to my books of memoranda, an outfit of clothing. Where is it? No, — don't rise. I can see it's gone. Now, just at present, though the days are quite warm enough for an invisible man to run about stark, the evenings are chilly. I want clothing — and other accommodation; and I must also have those three books."

CHAPTER 12

THE INVISIBLE MAN
LOSES HIS TEMPER

IT is unavoidable that at this point the narrative should break off again, for a certain very painful reason that will presently be apparent. While these things were going on in the parlour, and while Mr. Huxter was watching Mr. Marvel smoking his pipe against the gate, not a dozen yards away were Mr. Hall and Teddy Henfrey discussing in a state of cloudy puzzlement the one Iping topic.

Suddenly there came a violent

thud against the door of the parlour, a sharp cry, and then — silence.

"*Hul* — lo!" said Teddy Henfrey.

"Hul — *lo!*" from the Tap.

Mr. Hall took things in slowly but surely. "That ain't right," he said, and came round from behind the bar towards the parlour door.

He and Teddy approached the door together, with intent faces. Their eyes considered. "Summat wrong," said Hall, and Henfrey nodded agreement. Whiffs of an unpleasant chemical odour met them, and there was a muffled sound of conversation, very rapid and subdued.

"You all raight thur?" asked Hall, rapping.

The muttered conversation ceased abruptly, for a moment silence, then the conversation was resumed in hissing whispers, then a sharp cry of "No! no, you don't!" There came a sudden motion and the oversetting of a chair, a brief struggle. Silence again.

"What the dooce?" exclaimed Henfrey, *sotto voce.*

"You — all — raight — thur?" asked Mr. Hall sharply, again.

The Vicar's voice answered with a curious jerking intonation: "Quite ri — ight. Please don't — interrupt."

"Odd!" said Mr. Henfrey.

"Odd!" said Mr. Hall.

"Says, 'Don't interrupt,'" said Henfrey.

"I heerd'n," said Hall.

"And a sniff," said Henfrey.

They remained listening. The conversation was rapid and subdued. "I *can't,*" said Mr. Bunting, his voice rising; "I tell you, sir, I *will* not."

"What was that?" asked Henfrey.

"Says he wi' nart," said Hall. "Warn't speakin' to us, wuz he?"

"Disgraceful!" said Mr. Bunting, within.

"'Disgraceful,'" said Mr. Henfrey. "I heard it — *distinct.*"

"Who's that speaking now?" asked Henfrey.

"Mr. Cuss, I s'pose," said Hall. "Can you hear — anything?"

Silence. The sounds within indistinct and perplexing.

"Sounds like throwing the table-cloth about," said Hall.

Mrs. Hall appeared behind the bar. Hall made gestures of silence and invitation. This roused Mrs. Hall's wifely opposition. "What yer listenin' there for, Hall?" she asked. "Ain't you nothin' better to do — busy day like this?"

Hall tried to convey everything by grimaces and dumb show, but Mrs. Hall was obdurate. She raised her voice So Hall and Henfrey, rather crestfallen, tiptoed back to the bar, gesticulating to explain to her.

At first she refused to see anything in what they had heard at all. Then she insisted on Hall keeping silence, while Henfrey told her his story. She was inclined to think the whole business nonsense — perhaps they were just moving the furniture about. "I heerd'n say 'disgraceful'; *that* I did," said Hall.

"*I* heerd that, Mis' Hall," said Henfrey.

"Like as not —" began Mrs. Hall.

"Hsh!" said Mr. Teddy Henfrey. "Didn't I hear the window?"

"What window?" asked Mrs. Hall.

"Parlour window," said Henfrey.

Every one stood listening intently. Mrs. Hall's eyes, directed straight before her, saw without seeing the brilliant oblong of the inn door, the road white and vivid, and Huxter's shop-front blistering in the June sun. Abruptly Huxter's door opened and Huxter appeared, eyes staring with excitement, arms gesticulating. "*Yap!*" cried Huxter. "Stop thief!" and he ran obliquely across the oblong towards the yard gates, and vanished.

Simultaneously came a tumult from the parlour, and a sound of windows being closed.

Hall, Henfrey, and the human contents of the Tap rushed out at once pell-mell into the street. They saw some one whisk round the corner towards the down road, and Mr. Huxter executing a complicated leap in the air that ended on his face and shoulder. Down the street people were standing astonished or running towards them.

Mr. Huxter was stunned. Henfrey stopped to discover this, but Hall and the two labourers from the Tap rushed at once to the corner, shouting incoherent things, and saw Mr. Marvel vanishing by the corner of the church wall. They appear to have jumped to the impossible conclusion that this was the Invisible Man suddenly become visible, and set off at once along the lane in pursuit. But Hall had hardly run a dozen yards before he gave a loud shout of astonishment and went flying headlong sideways, clutching one of the labourers and bringing him to the ground. He had been charged just as one charges a man at football. The second labourer came round in a circle, stared, and conceiving that Hall had tumbled over of his own accord, turned to resume the pursuit, only to be tripped by the ankle just as Huxter had been. Then, as the first labourer struggled to his feet, he was kicked sideways by a blow that might have felled an ox.

As he went down, the rush from the direction of the village green came round the corner. The first to appear was the proprietor of the cocoanut shy, a burly man in a blue jersey. He was astonished to see the lane empty save for three men sprawling absurdly on the ground. And then something happened to his rear-most foot, and he went headlong and rolled sideways just in time to graze the feet of his brother and partner, following headlong. The two were then kicked, knelt on, fallen over, and cursed by quite a number of over-hasty people.

Now when Hall and Henfrey and the labourers ran out of the house, Mrs. Hall, who had been disciplined by years of experience, remained in the bar next

the till. And suddenly the parlour door was opened, and Mr. Cuss appeared, and without glancing at her rushed at once down the steps towards the corner. " Hold him! " he cried. " Don't let him drop that parcel! You can see him so long as he holds the parcel." He knew nothing of the existence of Marvel. For the Invisible Man had handed over the books and bundle in the yard. The face of Mr. Cuss was angry and resolute, but his costume was defective, a sort of limp white kilt that could only have passed muster in Greece. " Hold him! " he bawled. " He's got my trousers! And every stitch of the Vicar's clothes!

" 'Tend to him in a minute! " he cried to Henfrey as he passed the prostrate Huxter, and coming round the corner to join the tumult, was promptly knocked off his feet into an indecorous sprawl. Somebody in full flight trod heavily on his finger. He yelled, struggled to regain his feet, was knocked against and thrown on all fours again, and became aware that he was involved not in a capture, but a rout. Every one was running back to the village. He rose again and was hit severely behind the ear. He staggered and set off back to the Coach and Horses forthwith, leaping over the deserted Huxter, who was now sitting up, on his way.

Behind him as he was halfway up the inn steps he heard a sudden yell of rage, rising sharply out of the confusion of cries, and a sounding smack in some one's

face. He recognised the voice as that of the Invisible Man, and the note was that of a man suddenly infuriated by a painful blow.

In another moment Mr. Cuss was back in the parlour. " He's coming back, Bunting! " he said, rushing in. " Save yourself! He's gone mad! "

Mr. Bunting was standing in the window engaged in an attempt to clothe himself in the hearth-rug and a *West Surrey Gazette*. " Who's coming? " he said, so startled that his costume narrowly escaped disintegration.

" Invisible Man," said Cuss, and rushed to the window. " We'd better clear out from here! He's fighting mad! Mad! "

In another moment he was out in the yard.

" Good heavens! " said Mr. Bunting, hesitating between two horrible alternatives. He heard a frightful struggle in the passage of the inn, and his decision was made. He clambered out of the window, adjusted his costume hastily, and fled up the village as fast as his fat little legs would carry him.

From the moment when the Invisible Man screamed with rage and Mr. Bunting made his memorable flight up the village, it became impossible to give a consecutive account of affairs in Iping. Possibly the Invisible Man's original intention was simply to cover Marvel's retreat with the clothes and books. But his temper, at no time very good, seems to have gone completely at some chance blow, and forth-

with he set to smiting and over-throwing, for the mere satisfaction of hurting.

You must figure the street full of running figures, of doors slamming and fights for hiding-places. You must figure the tumult suddenly striking on the unstable equilibrium of old Fletcher's planks and two chairs,—with cataclysmal results. You must figure an appalled couple caught dismally in a swing. And then the whole tumultuous rush has passed and the Iping streets with its gauds and flags is deserted save for the still raging Unseen, and littered with cocoanuts, overthrown canvas screens, and the scattered stock in trade of a sweetstuff stall. Everywhere there is a sound of closing shutters and shoving bolts, and the only visible humanity is an occasional flitting eye under a raised eyebrow in the corner of a window pane.

The Invisible Man amused himself for a little while by breaking all the windows in the Coach and Horses, and then he thrust a street lamp through the parlour window of Mrs. Gribble. He it must have been who cut the telegraph wire to Adderdean just beyond Higgins' cottage on the Adderdean road. And after that, as his peculiar qualities allowed, he passed out of human perceptions altogether, and he was neither heard, seen, nor felt in Iping any more. He vanished absolutely.

But it was the best part of two hours before any human being ventured out again into the desolation of Iping Street.

CHAPTER 13

MR. MARVEL DISCUSSES HIS RESIGNATION

WHEN the dusk was gathering and Iping was just beginning to peep timorously forth again upon the shattered wreckage of its Bank Holiday, a short, thick-set man in a shabby silk hat was marching painfully through the twilight behind the beechwoods on the road to Bramblehurst. He carried three books bound together by some sort of ornamental elastic ligature, and a bundle wrapped in a blue tablecloth. His rubicund face expressed consternation and fatigue; he appeared to be in a spasmodic sort of hurry. He was accompanied by a Voice other than his own, and ever and again he winced under the touch of unseen hands.

" If you give me the slip again," said the Voice; " if you attempt to give me the slip again—"

" Lord! " said Mr. Marvel. " That shoulder's a mass of bruises as it is."

" —on my honour," said the Voice, " I will kill you."

" I didn't try to give you the

slip," said Marvel, in a voice that was not far remote from tears. "I swear I didn't. I didn't know the blessed turning, that was all! How the devil was I to know the blessed turning? As it is, I've been knocked about—"

"You'll get knocked about a great deal more if you don't mind," said the Voice, and Mr. Marvel abruptly became silent. He blew out his cheeks, and his eyes were eloquent of despair.

"It's bad enough to let these floundering yokels explode my little secret, without *your* cutting off with my books. It's lucky for some of them they cut and ran when they did! Here am I—No one knew I was invisible! And now what am I to do?"

"What am *I* to do?" asked Marvel, *sotto voce*.

"It's all about. It will be in the papers! Everybody will be looking for me; everyone on their guard—" The Voice broke off into vivid curses and ceased.

The despair of Mr. Marvel's face deepened, and his pace slacked.

"Go on!" said the Voice.

Mr. Marvel's face assumed a greyish tint between the ruddier patches.

"Don't drop those books, stupid," said the Voice, sharply—overtaking him.

"The fact is," said the Voice, "I shall have to make use of you. You're a poor tool, but I must."

"I'm a *miserable* tool," said Marvel.

"You are," said the Voice.

"I'm the worst possible tool you could have," said Marvel.

"I'm not strong," he said after a discouraging silence.

"I'm not over strong," he repeated.

"No?"

"And my heart's weak. That little business—I pulled it through, of course—but bless you! I could have dropped."

"Well?"

"I haven't the nerve and strength for the sort of thing you want."

"*I'll* stimulate you."

"I wish you wouldn't. I wouldn't like to mess up your plans, you know. But I might,—out of sheer funk and misery."

"You'd better not," said the Voice, with quiet emphasis.

"I wish I was dead," said Marvel.

"It ain't justice," he said; "you must admit—It seems to me I've a perfect right—"

"*Get* on!" said the Voice.

Mr. Marvel mended his pace, and for a time they went in silence again.

"It's devilish hard," said Mr. Marvel.

This was quite ineffectual. He tried another tack.

"What do I make by it?" he began again in a tone of unendurable wrong.

"Oh! *shut up!*" said the Voice, with sudden amazing vigour. "I'll see to you all right. You do what you're told. You'll do it all right. You're a fool and all that, but you'll do—"

"I tell you, sir, I'm not the man for it. Respectfully—but it is so—"

"If you don't shut up I shall twist your wrist again," said

the Invisible Man. "I want to think."

Presently two oblongs of yellow light appeared through the trees, and the square tower of a church loomed through the gloaming. "I shall keep my hand on your shoulder," said the Voice, "all through the village. Go straight through and try no foolery. It will be the worse for you if you do."

"I know that," sighed Mr. Marvel, "I know all that."

The unhappy-looking figure in the obsolete silk hat passed up the street of the little village with his burdens, and vanished into the gathering darkness beyond the lights of the windows.

CHAPTER 14

AT PORT STOWE

TEN o'clock the next morning found Mr. Marvel, unshaven, dirty, and travel-stained, sitting with the books beside him and his hands deep in his pockets, looking very weary, nervous, and uncomfortable, and inflating his cheeks at frequent intervals, on the bench outside a little inn on the outskirts of Port Stowe. Beside him were the books, but now they were tied with string.

The bundle had been abandoned in the pinewoods beyond Bramblehurst, in accordance with a change in the plans of the Invisible Man. Mr. Marvel sat on the bench, and although no one took the slightest notice of him, his agitation remained at fever heat. His hands would go ever and again to his various pockets with a curious nervous fumbling.

When he had been sitting for the best part of an hour, however, an elderly mariner, carrying a newspaper, came out of the inn and sat down beside him. "Pleasant day," said the mariner.

Mr. Marvel glanced about him with something very like terror. "Very," he said.

"Just seasonable weather for the time of year," said the mariner, taking no denial.

"Quite," said Mr. Marvel.

The mariner produced a toothpick, and (saving his regard) was engrossed thereby for some minutes. His eyes meanwhile were at liberty to examine Mr. Marvel's dusty figure and the books beside him. As he had approached Mr. Marvel he had heard a sound like the dropping of coins into a pocket. He was struck by the contrast of Mr. Marvel's appearance with this suggestion of opulence. Thence his mind wandered back again to a topic that had taken a curiously firm hold of his imagination.

"Books?" he said suddenly, noisily finishing with the toothpick.

Mr. Marvel started and looked at them. "Oh, yes," he said. "Yes, they're books."

"There's some extra-ordinary

things in books," said the mariner.

"I believe you," said Mr. Marvel.

"And some extra-ordinary things out of 'em," said the mariner.

"True likewise," said Mr. Marvel. He eyed his interlocutor, and then glanced about him.

"There's some extra-ordinary things in newspapers, for example," said the mariner.

"There are."

"In *this* newspaper," said the mariner.

"Ah!" said Mr. Marvel.

"There's a story," said the mariner, fixing Mr. Marvel with an eye that was firm and deliberate; "there's a story about an Invisible Man, for instance."

Mr. Marvel pulled his mouth askew and scratched his cheek and felt his ears glowing. "What will they be writing next?" he asked faintly. "Ostria, or America?"

"Neither," said the mariner. "*Here!*"

"Lord!" said Mr. Marvel, starting.

"When I say *here*," said the mariner, to Mr. Marvel's intense relief, "I don't of course mean here in this place, I mean hereabouts."

"An Invisible Man!" said Mr. Marvel. "And what's *he* been up to?"

"Everything," said the mariner, controlling Marvel with his eye, and then amplifying: "Every Blessed Thing."

"I ain't seen a paper these four days," said Marvel.

"Iping's the place he started at," said the mariner.

"In-*deed!*" said Mr. Marvel.

"He started there. And where he came from, nobody don't seem to know. Here it is: Pe Culiar Story from Iping. And it says in this paper that the evidence is extra-ordinary strong — extra-ordinary."

"Lord!" said Mr. Marvel.

"But then, it's a extra-ordinary story. There is a clergyman and a medical gent witnesses, — saw 'im all right and proper — or leastways, didn't see 'im. He was staying, it says, at the Coach an' Horses, and no one don't seem to have been aware of his misfortune, it says, aware of his misfortune, until in an Alteration in the inn, it says, his bandages on his head was torn off. It was then ob-served that his head was invisible. Attempts were At Once made to secure him, but casting off his garments, it says, he succeeded in escaping, but not until after a desperate struggle, In Which he had inflicted serious injuries, it says, on our worthy and able constable, Mr. J. A. Jaffers. Pretty straight story, eigh? Names and everything."

"Lord!" said Mr. Marvel, looking nervously about him, trying to count the money in his pockets by his unaided sense of touch, and full of a strange and novel idea. "It sounds most astonishing."

"Don't it? Extra-ordinary, *I* call it. Never heard tell of Invisible Men before, I haven't, but nowadays one hears such a lot of extra-ordinary things — that — "

"That all he did?" asked Marvel, trying to seem at his ease.

"It's enough, ain't it?" said the mariner.

"Didn't go Back by any chance?" asked Marvel. "Just escaped and that's all, eh?"

"All!" said the mariner. "Why!—ain't it enough?"

"Quite enough," said Marvel.

"I should think it was enough," said the mariner. "I should think it was enough."

"He didn't have any pals—it don't say he had any pals, does it?" asked Mr. Marvel, anxious.

"Ain't one of a sort enough for you?" asked the mariner.

"No, thank Heaven, as one might say, he didn't."

He nodded his head slowly. "It makes me regular uncomfortable, the bare thought of that chap running about the country! He is at present At Large, and from certain evidence it is supposed that he has—taken—*took*, I suppose they mean—the road to Port Stowe. You see we're right *in* it! None of your American wonders, this time. And just think of the things he might do! Where'd you be, if he took a drop over and above, and had a fancy to go for you? Suppose he wants to rob—who can prevent him? He can trespass, he can burgle, he could walk through a cordon of policemen as easy as me or you could give the slip to a blind man! Easier! For these here blind chaps hear uncommon sharp, I'm told. And wherever there was liquor he fancied—"

"He's got a tremenjous advantage, certainly," said Marvel. "And—well."

"You're right," said the mariner. "He *has*."

All this time Mr. Marvel had been glancing about him intently, listening for faint footfalls, trying to detect imperceptible movements. He seemed on the point of some great resolution. He coughed behind his hand.

He looked about him again, listened, bent towards the mariner, and lowered his voice: "The fact of it is—I happen—to know just a thing or two about this Invisible Man. From private sources."

"Oh!" said the mariner, interested. "*You?*"

"Yes," said Mr. Marvel. "Me."

"Indeed!" said the mariner. "And may I ask—"

"You'll be astonished," said Mr. Marvel behind his hand. "It's tremenjous."

"Indeed!" said the mariner.

"The fact is," began Mr. Marvel eagerly in a confidential undertone. Suddenly his expression changed marvellously. "Ow!" he said. He rose stiffly in his seat. His face was eloquent of physical suffering. "Wow!" he said.

"What's up?" said the mariner, concerned.

"Toothache," said Mr. Marvel, and put his hand to his ear. He caught hold of his books. "I must be getting on, I think," he said. He edged in a curious way along the seat away from his interlocutor. "But you was just agoing to tell me about this here Invisible Man!" protested the mariner. Mr. Marvel seemed to consult with himself. "Hoax," said a voice. "It's a hoax," said Mr. Marvel.

"But it's in the paper," said the mariner.

"Hoax all the same," said Marvel. "I know the chap that started the lie. There ain't no Invisible Man whatsoever — Blimey."

"But how 'bout this paper? D'you mean to say — ?"

"Not a word of it," said Marvel, stoutly.

The mariner stared, paper in hand. Mr. Marvel jerkily faced about. "Wait a bit," said the mariner, rising and speaking slowly. "D'you mean to say — ?"

"I do," said Mr. Marvel.

"Then why did you let me go on and tell you all this blarsted stuff, then? What d'yer mean by letting a man make a fool of himself like that for? Eigh?"

Mr. Marvel blew out his cheeks. The mariner was suddenly very red indeed; he clenched his hands. "I been talking here this ten minutes," he said; "and you, you little potbellied, leathery-faced son of an old boot, couldn't have the elementary manners — "

"Don't you come bandying words with *me*," said Mr. Marvel.

"Bandying words! I'm a jolly good mind — "

"Come up," said a voice, and Mr. Marvel was suddenly whirled about and started marching off in a curious spasmodic manner. "You'd better move on," said the mariner. "*Who's* moving on?" said Mr. Marvel. He was receding obliquely with a curious hurrying gait, with occasional violent jerks forward. Some way along the road he began a muttered monologue, protests and recriminations.

"Silly devil!" said the mariner, legs wide apart, elbows akimbo, watching the receding figure. "I'll show you, you silly ass, — hoaxing *me!* It's here — on the paper!"

Mr. Marvel retorted incoherently and, receding, was hidden by a bend in the road, but the mariner still stood magnificent in the midst of the way, until the approach of a butcher's cart dislodged him. Then he turned himself towards Port Stowe. "Full of extra-ordinary asses," he said softly to himself. "Just to take me down a bit — that was his silly game — It's on the paper!"

And there was another extraordinary thing he was presently to hear, that had happened quite close to him. And that was a vision of a "fist full of money" (no less) travelling without visible agency, along by the wall at the corner of St. Michael's Lane. A brother mariner had seen this wonderful sight that very morning. He had snatched at the money forthwith and had been knocked headlong, and when he had got to his feet the butterfly money had vanished. Our mariner was in the mood to believe anything, he declared, but that was a bit *too* stiff. Afterwards, however, he began to think things over.

The story of the flying money was true. And all about that neighbourhood, even from the august London and Country Banking Company, from the tills of shops and inns — doors standing that sunny weather entirely open — money had been quietly

and dexterously making off that day in handfuls and rouleaux, floating quietly along by walls and shady places, dodging quickly from the approaching eyes of men. And it had, though no man had traced it, invariably ended its mysterious flight in the pocket of that agitated gentleman in the obsolete silk hat, sitting outside the little inn on the outskirts of Port Stowe.

CHAPTER 15

THE MAN WHO WAS RUNNING

IN the early evening time Doctor Kemp was sitting in his study in the belvedere on the hill overlooking Burdock. It was a pleasant little room, with three windows, north, west, and south, and bookshelves crowded with books and scientific publications, and a broad writing-table, and, under the north window, a microscope, glass slips, minute instruments, some cultures, and scattered bottles of reagents. Doctor Kemp's solar lamp was lit, albeit the sky was still bright with the sunset light, and his blinds were up because there was no offence of peering outsiders to require them pulled down. Doctor Kemp was

a tall and slender young man, with flaxen hair and a moustache almost white, and the work he was upon would earn him, he hoped, the fellowship of the Royal Society, so highly did he think of it.

And his eye presently wandering from his work caught the sunset blazing at the back of the hill that is over against his own. For a minute perhaps he sat, pen in mouth, admiring the rich golden colour above the crest, and then his attention was attracted by the little figure of a man, inky black, running over the hill-brow towards him. He was a shortish little man, and he wore a high hat, and he was running so fast that his legs verily twinkled.

"Another of those fools," said Doctor Kemp. "Like that ass who ran into me this morning round a corner, with his ''Visible Man a-coming, sir!' I can't imagine what possesses people. One might think we were in the thirteenth century."

He got up, went to the window, and stared at the dusky hillside and the dark little figure tearing down it. "He seems in a confounded hurry," said Doctor Kemp, "but he doesn't seem to be getting on. If his pockets were full of lead, he couldn't run heavier.

"Spurted, sir," said Doctor Kemp.

In another moment the higher of the villas that had clambered up the hill from Burdock had occulted the running figure. He was visible again for a moment, and again, and then again, three times between the three detached

houses that came next, and then the terrace hid him.

"Asses!" said Doctor Kemp, swinging round on his heel and walking back to his writing-table.

But those who saw the fugitive nearer, and perceived the abject terror on his perspiring face, being themselves in the open roadway, did not share in the doctor's contempt. By the man pounded, and as he ran he chinked like a well-filled purse that is tossed to and fro. He looked neither to the right nor the left, but his dilated eyes stared straight downhill to where the lamps were being lit, and the people were crowded in the street. And his ill-shaped mouth fell apart, and a glairy foam lay on his lips, and his breath came hoarse and noisy. All he passed stopped and began staring up the road and down, and interrogating one another with an inkling of discomfort for the reason of his hate.

And then presently, far up the hill, a dog playing in the road yelped and ran under a gate, and as they still wondered something — a wind — a pad, pad, pad, — a sound like a panting breathing, — rushed by.

People screamed. People sprang off the pavement. It passed in shouts, it passed by instinct down the hill. They were shouting in the street before Marvel was half-way there. They were bolting into houses and slamming the doors behind them, with the news. He heard it and made one last desperate spurt. Fear came striding by, rushed ahead of him, and in a moment had seized the town.

"The Invisible Man is coming!
The Invisible Man."

CHAPTER 16

IN THE JOLLY
CRICKETERS

THE JOLLY CRICKETERS is just at the bottom of the hill, where the tram-lines begin. The barman leant his fat red arms on the counter and talked of horses with an anæmic cabman, while a black-bearded man in grey snapped up biscuit and cheese, drank Burton, and conversed in American with a policeman off duty.

"What's the shouting about?" said the anæmic cabman going off at a tangent, trying to see up the hill over the dirty yellow blind in the low window of the inn. Somebody ran by outside. "Fire, perhaps," said the barman.

Footsteps approached, running heavily, the door was pushed open violently, and Marvel, weeping and dishevelled, his hat gone, the neck of his coat torn open, rushed in, made a convulsive turn, and attempted to shut the door. It was held half open by a strap.

"Coming!" he bawled, his voice shrieking with terror. "He's coming. The 'Visible Man! After

me! For Gawd's sake! Elp! Elp! Elp! "

" Shut the doors," said the policeman. " Who's coming? What's the row? " He went to the door, released the strap, and it slammed. The American closed the other door.

" Lemme go inside," said Marvel, staggering and weeping, but still clutching the books. " Lemme go inside. Lock me in — somewhere. I tell you he's after me. I give him the slip. He said he'd kill me and he will."

" *You're* safe," said the man with the black beard. " The door's shut. What's it all about? "

" Lemme go inside," said Marvel, and shrieked aloud as a blow suddenly made the fastened door shiver and was followed by a hurried rapping and a shouting outside. " Hullo," cried the policeman, " who's there? " Mr. Marvel began to make frantic dives at panels that looked like doors. " He'll kill me — he's got a knife or something. For Gawd's sake! "

" Here you are," said the barman. " Come in here." And he held up the flap of the bar.

Mr. Marvel rushed behind the bar as the summons outside was repeated. " Don't open the door," he screamed. " *Please* don't open the door. *Where* shall I hide? "

" This, this Invisible Man, then? " asked the man with the black beard, with one hand behind him. " I guess it's about time we saw him."

The window of the inn was suddenly smashed in, and there was a screaming and running to and fro in the street. The policeman had been standing on the settee staring out, craning to see who was at the door. He got down with raised eyebrows. " It's that," he said. The barman stood in front of the bar-parlour door which was now locked on Mr. Marvel, stared at the smashed window and came round to the two other men.

Everything was suddenly quiet. " I wish I had my truncheon," said the policeman, going irresolutely to the door. " Once we open, in he comes. There's no stopping him."

" Don't you be in too much hurry about that door," said the anæmic cabman, anxiously.

" Draw the bolts," said the man with the black beard, " and if he comes — " He showed a revolver in his hand.

" That won't do," said the policeman; " that's murder."

" I know what country I'm in," said the man with the beard. " I'm going to let off at his legs. Draw the bolts."

" Not with that thing going off behind me," said the barman, craning over the blind.

" Very well," said the man with the black beard, and stooping down, revolver ready, drew them himself. Barman, cabman, and policeman faced about.

" Come in," said the bearded man in an undertone, standing back and facing the unbolted doors with his pistol behind him. No one came in, the door remained closed. Five minutes afterwards when a second cabman pushed his head in cautiously, they were still waiting, and an anxious face peered out of the bar-parlour and supplied information. " Are all the doors of the

house shut?" asked Marvel. "He's going round — prowling round. He's as artful as the devil."

"Good Lord!" said the burly barman. "There's the back! Just watch them doors! I say! — " He looked about him helplessly. The bar-parlour door slammed and they heard the key turn. "There's the yard door and the private door. The yard door — "

He rushed out of the bar.

In a minute he reappeared with a carving-knife in his hand. "The yard door was open!" he said, and his fat underlip dropped.

"He may be in the house now!" said the first cabman.

"He's not in the kitchen," said the barman. "There's two women there, and I've stabbed every inch of it with this little beef slicer. And they don't think he's come in. They haven't noticed — "

"Have you fastened it?" asked the first cabman.

"I'm out of frocks," said the barman.

The man with the beard replaced his revolver. And even as he did so the flap of the bar was shut down and the bolt clicked, and then with a tremendous thud the catch of the door snapped and the bar-parlour door burst open. They heard Marvel squeal like a caught leveret, and forthwith they were clambering over the bar to his rescue. The bearded man's revolver cracked and the looking-glass at the back of the parlour was starred brightly and came smashing and tinkling down.

As the barman entered the room he saw Marvel, curiously crumpled up and struggling against the door that led to the yard and kitchen. The door flew open while the barman hesitated, and Marvel was dragged into the kitchen. There was a scream and a clatter of pans. Marvel, head down, and lugging back obstinately, was forced to the kitchen door, and the bolts were drawn.

Then the policeman, who had been trying to pass the barman, rushed in, followed by one of the cabmen, gripped the wrist of the invisible hand that collared Marvel, was hit in the face and went reeling back. The door opened, and Marvel made a frantic effort to obtain a lodgment behind it. Then the cabman clutched something. "I got him," said the cabman. The barman's red hands came clawing at the unseen. "Here he is!" said the barman.

Mr. Marvel, released, suddenly dropped to the ground and made an attempt to crawl behind the legs of the fighting men. The struggle blundered round the edge of the door. The voice of the Invisible Man was heard for the first time, yelling out sharply, as the policeman trod on his foot. Then he cried out passionately and his fists flew round like flails. The cabman suddenly whooped and doubled up, kicked under the diaphragm. The door into the bar-parlour from the kitchen slammed and covered Mr. Marvel's retreat. The men in the kitchen found themselves clutching at and struggling with empty air.

"Where's he gone?" cried the man with the beard. "Out?"

"This way," said the police-

man, stepping into the yard and stopping.

A piece of tile whizzed by his head and smashed among the crockery on the kitchen table.

"I'll show him," shouted the man with the black beard, and suddenly a steel barrel shone over the policeman's shoulder, and five bullets had followed one another into the twilight whence the missile had come. As he fired, the man with the beard moved his hand in a horizontal curve, so that his shots radiated out into the narrow yard like spokes from a wheel.

A silence followed. "Five cartridges," said the man with the black beard. "That's the best of all. Four aces and the joker. Get a lantern, some one, and come and feel about for his body."

CHAPTER 17

DOCTOR KEMP'S VISITOR

Doctor Kemp had continued writing in his study until the shots aroused him. Crack, crack, crack, they came one after the other.

"Hello!" said Doctor Kemp, putting his pen into his mouth again and listening. "Who's let-ting off revolvers in Burdock? What are the asses at now?"

He went to the south window, threw it up, and leaning out stared down on the network of windows, beaded gas-lamps and shops with black interstices of roof and yard that made up the town at night. "Looks like a crowd down the hill," he said, "by the Cricketers," and remained watching. Thence his eyes wandered over the town to far away where the ships' lights shone, and the pier glowed, a little illuminated pavilion like a gem of yellow light. The moon in its first quarter hung over the western hill, and the stars were clear and almost tropically bright.

After five minutes, during which his mind had travelled into a remote speculation of social conditions of the future, and lost itself at last over the time dimension, Doctor Kemp roused himself with a sigh, pulled down the window again, and returned to his writing-desk.

It must have been about an hour after this that the front-door bell rang. He had been writing slackly and with intervals of abstraction, since the shots. He sat listening. He heard the servant answer the door, and waited for her feet on the staircase, but she did not come. "Wonder what that was," said Doctor Kemp.

He tried to resume his work, failed, got up, went downstairs from his study to the landing, rang, and called over the balustrade to the housemaid as she appeared in the hall below. "Was that a letter?" he asked.

" Only a runaway ring, sir," she answered.

" I'm restless to-night," he said to himself. He went back to his study, and this time attacked his work resolutely. In a little while he was hard at work again, and the only sounds in the room were the ticking of the clock and the subdued shrillness of his quill, hurrying in the very centre of the circle of light his lamp-shade threw on his table.

It was two o'clock before Doctor Kemp had finished his work for the night. He rose, yawned, and went downstairs to bed. He had already removed his coat and vest, when he noticed that he was thirsty. He took a candle and went down to the dining-room in search of a siphon and whisky.

Doctor Kemp's scientific pursuits had made him a very observant man, and as he recrossed the hall, he noticed a dark spot on the linoleum near the mat at the foot of the stairs. He went on upstairs, and then it suddenly occurred to him to ask himself what the spot on the linoleum might be. Apparently some subconscious element was at work. At any rate, he turned with his burden, went back to the hall, put down the siphon and whisky, and bending down, touched the spot. Without any great surprise he found it had the stickiness and colour of drying blood.

He took up his burden again, and returned upstairs, looking about him and trying to account for the blood-spot. On the landing he saw something and stopped astonished. The door-handle of his own room was blood-stained.

He looked at his own hand. It was quite clean, and then he remembered that the door of his room had been open when he came down from his study, and that consequently he had not touched the handle at all. He went straight into his room, his face quite calm — perhaps a trifle more resolute than usual. His glance, wandering inquisitively, fell on the bed. On the counterpane was a mess of blood, and the sheet had been torn. He had not noticed this before because he had walked straight to the dressing-table. On the further side the bed-clothes were depressed as if some one had been recently sitting there.

Then he had an odd impression that he had heard a loud voice say, " Good Heavens! — *Kemp!* " But Doctor Kemp was no believer in Voices.

He stood staring at the tumbled sheets. Was that really a voice? He looked about again, but noticed nothing further than the disordered and blood-stained bed. Then he distinctly heard a movement across the room, near the wash-hand stand. All men, however highly educated, retain some superstitious inklings. The feeling that is called " eerie " came upon him. He closed the door of the room, came forward to the dressing-table, and put down his burdens. Suddenly, with a start, he perceived a coiled and blood-stained bandage of linen rag hanging in mid-air, between him and the wash-hand stand.

He stared at this in amazement. It was an empty bandage, a bandage properly tied but quite

empty. He would have advanced to grasp it, but a touch arrested him, and a voice speaking quite close to him.

"Kemp!" said the Voice.

"Eigh?" said Kemp, with his mouth open.

"Keep your nerve," said the Voice. "I'm an Invisible Man."

Kemp made no answer for a space, simply stared at the bandage. "Invisible Man," he said.

"I'm an Invisible Man," repeated the Voice.

The story he had been active to ridicule only that morning rushed through Kemp's brain. He does not appear to have been either very much frightened or very greatly surprised at the moment. Realisation came later.

"I thought it was all a lie," he said. The thought uppermost in his mind was the reiterated arguments of the morning. "Have you a bandage on?" he asked.

"Yes," said the Invisible Man.

"Oh!" said Kemp, and then roused himself. "I say!" he said. "But this is nonsense. It's some trick." He stepped forward suddenly, and his hand, extended towards the bandage, met invisible fingers.

He recoiled at the touch and his colour changed.

"Keep steady, Kemp, for God's sake! I want help badly. Stop!"

The hand gripped his arm. He struck at it.

"Kemp!" cried the Voice. "Kemp! Keep steady!" and the grip tightened.

A frantic desire to free himself took possession of Kemp. The hand of the bandaged arm gripped his shoulder, and he was suddenly tripped and flung backwards upon the bed. He opened his mouth to shout, and the corner of the sheet was thrust between his teeth. The Invisible Man had him down grimly, but his arms were free and he struck and tried to kick savagely.

"Listen to reason, will you?" said the Invisible Man, sticking to him in spite of a pounding in the ribs. "By Heaven! you'll madden me in a minute!

"Lie still, you fool!" bawled the Invisible Man in Kemp's ear.

Kemp struggled for another moment and then lay still.

"If you shout I'll smash your face," said the Invisible Man, relieving his mouth.

"I'm an Invisible Man. It's no foolishness, and no magic. I really am an Invisible Man. And I want your help. I don't want to hurt you, but if you behave like a frantic rustic, I must. Don't you remember me, Kemp? — Griffin, of University College?"

"Let me get up," said Kemp. "I'll stop where I am. And let me sit quiet for a minute."

He sat up and felt his neck.

"I am Griffin, of University College, and I have made myself invisible. I am just an ordinary man — a man you have known — made invisible."

"Griffin?" said Kemp.

"Griffin," answered the Voice —"a younger student, almost an albino, six feet high, and broad, with a pink and white face and red eyes — who won the medal for chemistry."

"I am confused," said Kemp. "My brain is rioting. What has this to do with Griffin?"

" I *am* Griffin."

Kemp thought. " It's horrible," he said. " But what devilry must happen to make a man invisible? "

" It's no devilry. It's a process, sane and intelligible enough — "

" It's horrible! " said Kemp. " How on earth — ? "

" It's horrible enough. But I'm wounded and in pain, and tired — Great God! Kemp, you are a man. Take it steady. Give me some food and drink, and let me sit down here."

Kemp stared at the bandage as it moved across the room, then saw a basket chair dragged across the floor and come to rest near the bed. It creaked, and the seat was depressed the quarter of an inch or so. He rubbed his eyes and felt his neck again. " This beats ghosts," he said, and laughed stupidly.

" That's better. Thank Heaven, you're getting sensible! "

" Or silly," said Kemp, and knuckled his eyes.

" Give me some whisky. I'm near dead."

" It didn't feel so. Where are you? If I get up shall I run into you? *There!* all right. Whisky? Here. Where shall I give it you? "

The chair creaked and Kemp felt the glass drawn away from him. He let go by an effort; his instinct was all against it. It came to rest poised twenty inches above the front edge of the seat of the chair. He stared at it in infinite perplexity. " This is — this *must* be — hypnotism. You must have suggested you are invisible."

" Nonsense," said the Voice.

" It's frantic."

" Listen to me."

" I demonstrated conclusively this morning," began Kemp, " that invisibility — "

" Never mind what you've demonstrated! — I'm starving," said the Voice, " and the night is — chilly to a man without clothes."

" Food! " said Kemp.

The tumbler of whisky tilted itself. " Yes," said the Invisible Man, rapping it down. " Have you got a dressing-gown? "

Kemp made some exclamation in an undertone. He walked to a wardrobe and produced a robe of dingy scarlet. " This do? " he asked. It was taken from him. It hung limp for a moment in mid-air, fluttered weirdly, stood full and decorous buttoning itself, and sat down in his chair. " Drawers, socks, slippers would be a comfort," said the Unseen, curtly. " And food."

" Anything. But this is the insanest thing I ever was in, in my life! "

He turned out his drawers for the articles, and then went downstairs to ransack his larder. He came back with some cold cutlets and bread, pulled up a light table, and placed them before his guest. " Never mind knives," said his visitor, and a cutlet hung in mid-air, with a sound of gnawing.

" Invisible! " said Kemp, and sat down on a bedroom chair.

" I always like to get something about me before I eat," said the Invisible Man, with a full mouth, eating greedily. " Queer fancy! "

" I suppose that wrist is all right," said Kemp.

"Trust me," said the Invisible Man.

"Of *all* the strange and wonderful —"

"Exactly. But it's odd I should blunder into *your* house to get my bandaging. My first stroke of luck. Anyhow I meant to sleep in this house to-night. You must stand that! It's a filthy nuisance, my blood showing, isn't it? Quite a clot over there. Gets visible as it coagulates, I see. I've been in the house three hours."

"But how's it done?" began Kemp, in a tone of exasperation. "Confound it! The whole business — it's unreasonable from beginning to end."

"Quite reasonable," said the Invisible Man. "Perfectly reasonable."

He reached over and secured the whisky bottle. Kemp stared at the devouring dressing-gown. A ray of candle-light penetrating a torn patch in the right shoulder, made a triangle of light under the left ribs. "What were the shots?" he asked. "How did the shooting begin?"

"There was a fool of a man — a sort of confederate of mine — curse him! — who tried to steal my money. *Has* done so."

"Is *he* invisible too?"

"No."

"Well?"

"Can't I have some more to eat before I tell you all that? I'm hungry — in pain. And you want me to tell stories!"

Kemp got up. "*You* didn't do any shooting?" he asked.

"Not me," said his visitor.

"Some fool I'd never seen fired at random. A lot of them got scared. They all got scared at me. Curse them! — I say — I want more to eat than this, Kemp."

" I'll see what there is more to eat downstairs," said Kemp. "Not much, I'm afraid."

After he had done eating, and he made a heavy meal, the Invisible Man demanded a cigar. He bit the end savagely before Kemp could find a knife, and cursed when the outer leaf loosened. It was strange to see him smoking; his mouth and throat, pharynx and nares, became visible as a sort of whirling smoke cast.

"This blessed gift of smoking!" he said, and puffed vigorously. "I'm lucky to have fallen upon you, Kemp. You must help me. Fancy tumbling on you just now! I'm in a devilish scrape. I've been mad, I think. The things I have been through! But we will do things yet. Let me tell you —"

He helped himself to more whisky and soda. Kemp got up, looked about him, and fetched himself a glass from his spare room. "It's wild — but I suppose I may drink."

"You haven't changed much, Kemp, these dozen years. You fair men don't. Cool and methodical — after the first collapse. I must tell you. We will work together!"

"But how was it all done?" said Kemp, "and how did you get like this?"

"For God's sake, let me smoke in peace for a little while! And then I will begin to tell you."

But the story was not told that night. The Invisible Man's wrist was growing painful, he was feverish, exhausted, and his mind came round to brood upon his chase down the hill and the struggle about the inn. He spoke in fragments of Marvel, he smoked faster, his voice grew angry. Kemp tried to gather what he could.

"He was afraid of me, I could see he was afraid of me," said the Invisible Man many times over. "He meant to give me the slip —he was always casting about! What a fool I was!

"The cur!

"I should have killed him—"

"Where did you get the money?" asked Kemp, abruptly.

The Invisible Man was silent for a space. "I can't tell you to-night," he said.

He groaned suddenly and leant forward, supporting his invisible head on invisible hands. "Kemp," he said, "I've had no sleep for near three days — except a couple of dozes of an hour or so. I must sleep soon."

"Well, have my room — have this room."

"But how can I sleep? If I sleep—he will get away. Ugh! What does it matter?"

"What's the shot-wound?" asked Kemp, abruptly.

"Nothing—scratch and blood. Oh, God! How I want sleep!"

"Why not?"

The Invisible Man appeared to be regarding Kemp. "Because I've a particular objection to being caught by my fellow-men," he said slowly.

Kemp started.

"Fool that I am!" said the Invisible Man, striking the table smartly. "I've put the idea into your head."

CHAPTER 18

THE INVISIBLE MAN
SLEEPS

EXHAUSTED and wounded as the Invisible Man was, he refused to accept Kemp's word that his freedom should be respected. He examined the two windows of the bedroom, drew up the blinds, and opened the sashes to confirm Kemp's statement that a retreat by them would be possible. Outside the night was very quiet and still, and the new moon was setting over the down. Then he examined the keys of the bedroom and the two dressing-room doors, to satisfy himself that these also could be made an assurance of freedom. Finally he expressed himself satisfied. He stood on the hearth-rug and Kemp heard the sound of a yawn.

"I'm sorry," said the Invisible Man, "if I cannot tell you all that I have done to-night. But I am worn out. It's grotesque, no doubt. It's horrible! But believe me, Kemp, it is quite a possible thing. I have made a discovery.

I meant to keep it to myself. I can't. I must have a partner. And you — We can do such things — But to-morrow. Now, Kemp, I feel as though I must sleep or perish."

Kemp stood in the middle of the room staring at the headless garment. " I suppose I must leave you," he said. " It's — incredible. Three things happening like this, overturning all my preconceptions, would make me insane. But it's real! Is there anything more that I can get you? "

" Only bid me good-night," said Griffin.

" Good-night," said Kemp, and shook an invisible hand. He walked sideways to the door. Suddenly the dressing-gown walked quickly towards him. " Understand me!" said the dressing-gown. " No attempts to hamper me, or capture me! Or — "

Kemp's face changed a little. " I thought I gave you my word," he said.

Kemp closed the door softly behind him, and the key was turned upon him forthwith. Then, as he stood with an expression of passive amazement on his face, the rapid feet came to the door of the dressing-room and that too was locked. Kemp slapped his brow with his hand. " Am I dreaming? Has the world gone mad — or have I? "

He laughed, and put his hand to the locked door. " Barred out of my own bedroom, by a flagrant absurdity! " he said.

He walked to the head of the staircase, turned, and stared at the locked doors. " It's fact," he said. He put his fingers to his slightly bruised neck. " Undeniable fact!

" But — "

He shook his head hopelessly, turned, and went downstairs.

He lit the dining-room lamp, got out a cigar, and began pacing the room, ejaculating. Now and then he would argue with himself.

" Invisible! " he said.

" Is there such a thing as an invisible animal? In the sea, yes. Thousands! millions! All the larvæ, all the little nauplii and tornarias, all the microscopic things, the jelly-fish. In the sea there are more things invisible than visible! I never thought of that before. And in the ponds too! All those little pond-life things — specks of colourless translucent jelly! But in air? No!

" It can't be.

" But after all — why not?

" If a man was made of glass he would still be visible."

His meditation became profound. The bulk of three cigars had passed into the invisible or diffused as a white ash over the carpet before he spoke again. Then it was merely an exclamation. He turned aside, walked out of the room, and went into his little consulting-room and lit the gas there. It was a little room, because Dr. Kemp did not live by practice, and in it were the day's newspapers. The morning's paper lay carelessly opened and thrown aside. He caught it up, turned it over, and read the account of a " Strange Story from Iping " that the Mariner at Port Stowe had spelt over so pain-

fully to Mr. Marvel. Kemp read it swiftly.

"Wrapped up!" said Kemp. "Disguised! Hiding it! 'No one seems to have been aware of his misfortune.' What the devil *is* his game?"

He dropped the paper, and his eye went seeking. "Ah!" he said, and caught up the *St. James' Gazette,* lying folded up as it arrived. "Now we shall get at the truth," said Dr. Kemp. He rent the paper open; a couple of columns confronted him. "An Entire Village in Sussex goes Mad" was the heading.

"Good Heavens!" said Kemp, reading eagerly an incredulous account of the events in Iping the previous afternoon, that have already been described. Over the leaf the report in the morning paper had been reprinted.

He re-read it. "Ran through the streets striking right and left. Jaffers insensible. Mr. Huxter in great pain — still unable to describe what he saw. Painful humiliation — vicar. Women ill with terror! Windows smashed. This extraordinary story probably a fabrication. Too good not to print — *cum grano!*"

He dropped the paper and stared blankly in front of him. "Probably a fabrication!"

He caught up the paper again, and re-read the whole business. "But where does the Tramp come in? Why the deuce was he chasing a Tramp?"

He sat down abruptly on the surgical couch. "He's not only invisible," he said, "but he's mad! Homicidal!"

When dawn came to mingle its pallor with the lamp-light and cigar smoke of the dining-room, Kemp was still pacing up and down, trying to grasp the incredible.

He was altogether too excited to sleep. His servants, descending sleepily, discovered him, and were inclined to think that over-study had worked this ill on him. He gave them extraordinary but quite explicit instructions to lay breakfast for two in the belvedere study — and then to confine themselves to the basement and ground-floor. Then he continued to pace the dining-room until the morning's paper came. That had much to say and little to tell, beyond the confirmation of the evening before and a very baldly written account of another remarkable tale from Port Burdock. This gave Kemp the essence of the happenings at the Jolly Cricketers, and the name of Marvel. "He has made me keep with him twenty-four hours," Marvel testified. Certain minor facts were added to the Iping story, notably the cutting of the village telegraph-wire. But there was nothing to throw light on the connection between the Invisible Man and the Tramp; for Mr. Marvel had supplied no information about the three books, or the money with which he was lined. The incredulous tone had vanished and a shoal of reporters and inquirers were already at work elaborating the matter.

Kemp read every scrap of the report and sent his housemaid out to get every one of the morning papers she could. These also he devoured.

"He is invisible!" he said. "And it reads like rage growing to mania! The things he may do! The things he may do! And he's upstairs free as the air. What on earth ought I to do?

"For instance, would it be a breach of faith if — ? No."

He went to a little untidy desk in the corner, and began a note. He tore this up half written, and wrote another. He read it over and considered it. Then he took an envelope and addressed it to "Colonel Adye, Port Burdock."

The Invisible Man awoke even as Kemp was doing this. He awoke in an evil temper, and Kemp, alert for every sound, heard his pattering feet rush suddenly across the bedroom overhead. Then a chair was flung over and the wash-hand stand tumbler smashed. Kemp hurried upstairs and rapped eagerly.

CHAPTER 19

CERTAIN FIRST PRINCIPLES

"WHAT's the matter?" asked Kemp, when the Invisible Man admitted him.

"Nothing," was the answer.

"But, confound it! The smash?"

"Fit of temper," said the Invisible Man. "Forgot this arm; and it's sore."

"You're rather liable to that sort of thing."

"I am."

Kemp walked across the room and picked up the fragments of broken glass. "All the facts are out about you," said Kemp, standing up with the glass in his hand; "all that happened in Iping, and down the hill. The world has become aware of its invisible citizen. But no one knows you are here."

The Invisible Man swore.

"The secret's out. I gather it was a secret. I don't know what your plans are, but of course I'm anxious to help you."

The Invisible Man sat down on the bed.

"There's breakfast upstairs," said Kemp, speaking as easily as possible, and he was delighted to find his strange guest rose willingly. Kemp led the way up the narrow staircase to the belvedere.

"Before we can do anything else," said Kemp, "I must understand a little more about this invisibility of yours." He had sat down, after one nervous glance out of the window, with the air of a man who has talking to do. His doubts of the sanity of the entire business flashed and vanished again as he looked across to where Griffin sat at the breakfast-table, — a headless, handless dressing-gown, wiping unseen lips on a miraculously held serviette.

"It's simple enough — and credible enough," said Griffin, putting the serviette aside and

leaning the invisible head on an invisible hand.

"No doubt, to you, but—" Kemp laughed.

"Well, yes; to me it seemed wonderful at first, no doubt. But now, great God!—But we will do great things yet! I came on the stuff first at Chesilstowe."

"Chesilstowe?"

"I went there after I left London. You know I dropped medicine and took up physics? No? —well, I did. Light—fascinated me."

"Ah!"

"Optical density! The whole subject is a network of riddles— a network with solutions glimmering elusively through. And being but two-and-twenty and full of enthusiasm, I said, 'I will devote my life to this. This is worth while.' You know what fools we are at two-and-twenty?"

"Fools then or fools now," said Kemp.

"As though Knowing could be any satisfaction to a man!

"But I went to work—like a nigger. And I had hardly worked and thought about the matter six months before light came through one of the meshes suddenly—blindingly! I found a general principle of pigments and refraction,—a formula, a geometrical expression involving four dimensions. Fools, common men, even common mathematicians, do not know anything of what some general expression may mean to the student of molecular physics. In the books— the books that Tramp has hidden —there are marvels, miracles! But this was not a method, it was an idea that might lead to a method by which it would be possible, without changing any other property of matter,—except, in some instances, colours, —to lower the refractive index of a substance, solid or liquid, to that of air—so far as all practical purposes are concerned."

"Phew!" said Kemp. "That's odd! But still I don't see quite —I can understand that thereby you could spoil a valuable stone, but personal invisibility is a far cry."

"Precisely," said Griffin. "But consider: Visibility depends on the action of the visible bodies on light. Either a body absorbs light, or it reflects or refracts it, or does all these things. If it neither reflects nor refracts nor absorbs light, it cannot of itself be visible. You see an opaque red box, for instance, because the colour absorbs some of the light and reflects the rest, all the red part of the light, to you. If it did not absorb any particular part of the light, but reflected it all, then it would be a shining white box. Silver! A diamond box would neither absorb much of the light nor reflect much from the general surface, but just here and there where the surfaces were favourable the light would be reflected and refracted, so that you would get a brilliant appearance of flashing reflections and translucencies,—a sort of skeleton of light. A glass box would not be so brilliant, not so clearly visible, as a diamond box, because there would be less refraction and reflection. See that? From certain points of view you

would see quite clearly through it. Some kinds of glass would be more visible than others, a box of flint glass would be brighter than a box of ordinary window glass. A box of very thin common glass would be hard to see in a bad light, because it would absorb hardly any light and refract and reflect very little. And if you put a sheet of common white glass in water, still more if you put it in some denser liquid than water, it would vanish almost altogether, because light passing from water to glass is only slightly refracted or reflected or indeed affected in any way. It is almost as invisible as a jet of coal gas or hydrogen is in air. And for precisely the same reason!"

"Yes," said Kemp, "that is pretty plain sailing."

"And here is another fact you will know to be true. If a sheet of glass is smashed, Kemp, and beaten into a powder, it becomes much more visible while it is in the air; it becomes at last an opaque white powder. This is because the powdering multiplies the surfaces of the glass at which refraction and reflection occur. In the sheet of glass there are only two surfaces; in the powder the light is reflected or refracted by each grain it passes through, and very little gets right through the powder. But if the white powdered glass is put into water, it forthwith vanishes. The powdered glass and water have much the same refractive index; that is, the light undergoes very little refraction or reflection in passing from one to the other.

"You make the glass invisible by putting it into a liquid of nearly the same refractive index; a transparent thing becomes invisible if it is put in any medium of almost the same refractive index. And if you will consider only a second, you will see also that the powder of glass might be made to vanish in air, if its refractive index could be made the same as that of air; for then there would be no refraction or reflection as the light passed from glass to air."

"Yes, yes," said Kemp. "But a man's not powdered glass!"

"No," said Griffin. "He's more transparent!"

"Nonsense!"

"That from a doctor! How one forgets! Have you already forgotten your physics, in ten years? Just think of all the things that are transparent and seem not to be so. Paper, for instance, is made up of transparent fibres, and it is white and opaque only for the same reason that a powder of glass is white and opaque. Oil white paper, fill up the interstices between the particles with oil so that there is no longer refraction or reflection except at the surfaces, and it becomes as transparent as glass. And not only paper, but cotton fibre, linen fibre, wool fibre, woody fibre, and *bone*, Kemp, *flesh*, Kemp, *hair*, Kemp, *nails* and *nerves*, Kemp, in fact the whole fabric of a man except the red of his blood and the black pigment of hair, are all made up of transparent, colourless tissue. So little suffices to make us visible one to the other. For the most part the fibres of a living crea-

ture are no more opaque than water."

"Great Heavens!" cried Kemp. "Of course, of course! I was thinking only last night of the sea larvæ and all jelly-fish!"

"*Now* you have me! And all that I knew and had in mind a year after I left London — six years ago. But I kept it to myself. I had to do my work under frightful disadvantages. Oliver, my professor, was a scientific bounder, a journalist by instinct, a thief of ideas, — he was always prying! And you know the knavish system of the scientific world. I simply would not publish, and let him share my credit. I went on working. I got nearer and nearer making my formula into an experiment, a reality. I told no living soul, because I meant to flash my work upon the world with crushing effect, — to become famous at a blow. I took up the question of pigments to fill up certain gaps. And suddenly, not by design but by accident, I made a discovery in physiology."

"Yes?"

"You know the red colouring matter of blood; it can be made white — colourless — and remain with all the functions it has now!"

Kemp gave a cry of incredulous amazement.

The Invisible Man rose and began pacing the little study. "You may well exclaim. I remember that night. It was late at night, — in the daytime one was bothered with the gaping, silly students, — and I worked then sometimes till dawn. It came suddenly, splendid and complete into my mind. I was alone; the laboratory was still, with the tall lights burning brightly and silently. In all my great moments I have been alone. 'One could make an animal — a tissue — transparent! One could make it invisible! All except the pigments. I could be invisible!' I said, suddenly realising what it meant to be an albino with such knowledge. It was overwhelming. I left the filtering I was doing, and went and stared out of the great window at the stars. 'I could be invisible!' I repeated.

"To do such a thing would be to transcend magic. And I beheld, unclouded by doubt, a magnificent vision of all that invisibility might mean to a man, — the mystery, the power, the freedom. Drawbacks I saw none. You have only to think! And I, a shabby, poverty-struck, hemmed-in demonstrator, teaching fools in a provincial college, might suddenly become — this. I ask you, Kemp, if *you* — Any one, I tell you, would have flung himself upon that research. And I worked three years, and every mountain of difficulty I toiled over showed another from its summit. The infinite details! And the exasperation, — a professor, a provincial professor, always prying. 'When are you going to publish this work of yours?' was his everlasting question. And the students, the cramped means! Three years I had of it —

"And after three years of secrecy and exasperation, I found that to complete it was impossible, — impossible."

"How?" asked Kemp.

"Money," said the Invisible Man, and went again to stare out of the window.

He turned round abruptly. " I robbed the old man — robbed my father.

"The money was not his, and he shot himself."

CHAPTER 20

AT THE HOUSE IN GREAT PORTLAND STREET

FOR a moment Kemp sat in silence, staring at the back of the headless figure at the window. Then he started, struck by a thought, rose, took the Invisible Man's arm, and turned him away from the outlook.

"You are tired," he said, "and while I sit, you walk about. Have my chair."

He placed himself between Griffin and the nearest window.

For a space Griffin sat silent, and then he resumed abruptly:

"I had left the Chesilstowe cottage already," he said, "when that happened. It was last December. I had taken a room in London, a large unfurnished room in a big ill-managed lodging-house in a slum near Great Portland Street. The room was soon full of the appliances I had bought with his money; the work was going on steadily, successfully, drawing near an end. I was like a man emerging from a thicket, and suddenly coming on some unmeaning tragedy. I went to bury him. My mind was still on this research, and I did not lift a finger to save his character. I remember the funeral, the cheap hearse, the scant ceremony, the windy frost-bitten hillside, and the old college friend of his who read the service over him, — a shabby, black, bent old man with a snivelling cold.

"I remember walking back to the empty home, through the place that had once been a village and was now patched and tinkered by the jerry builders into the ugly likeness of a town. Every way the roads ran out at last into the desecrated fields and ended in rubble heaps and rank wet weeds. I remember myself as a gaunt black figure, going along the slippery, shiny pavement, and the strange sense of detachment I felt from the squalid respectability, the sordid commercialism of the place.

"I did not feel a bit sorry for my father. He seemed to me to be the victim of his own foolish sentimentality. The current cant required my attendance at his funeral, but it was really not my affair.

"But going along the High Street, my old life came back to me for a space, for I met the girl I had known ten years since. Our eyes met.

"Something moved me to turn

back and talk to her. She was a very ordinary person.

" It was all like a dream, that visit to the old places. I did not feel then that I was lonely, that I had come out from the world into a desolate place. I appreciated my loss of sympathy, but I put it down to the general inanity of things. Re-entering my room seemed like the recovery of reality. There were the things I knew and loved. There stood the apparatus, the experiments arranged and waiting. And now there was scarcely a difficulty left, beyond the planning of details.

" I will tell you, Kemp, sooner or later, all the complicated processes. We need not go into that now. For the most part, saving certain gaps I chose to remember, they are written in cypher in those books that tramp has hidden. We must hunt him down. We must get those books again. But the essential phase was to place the transparent object whose refractive index was to be lowered between two radiating centres of a sort of ethereal vibration, of which I will tell you more fully later. No, not these Röntgen vibrations — I don't know that these others of mine have been described. Yet they are obvious enough. I needed two little dynamos, and these I worked with a cheap gas engine. My first experiment was with a bit of white wool fabric. It was the strangest thing in the world to see it in the flicker of the flashes soft and white, and then to watch it fade like a wreath of smoke and vanish.

" I could scarcely believe I had done it. I put my hand into the emptiness, and there was the thing as solid as ever. I felt it awkwardly, and threw it on the floor. I had a little trouble finding it again.

" And then came a curious experience. I heard a miaow behind me, and turning, saw a lean white cat, very dirty, on the cistern cover outside the window. A thought came into my head. ' Everything ready for you,' I said, and went to the window, opened it, and called softly. She came in, purring, — the poor beast was starving, — and I gave her some milk. All my food was in a cupboard in the corner of the room. After that she went smelling round the room, — evidently with the idea of making herself at home. The invisible rag upset her a bit; you should have seen her spit at it! But I made her comfortable on the pillow of my truckle-bed. And I gave her butter to get her to wash."

" And you processed her? "

" I processed her. But giving drugs to a cat is no joke, Kemp! And the process failed."

" Failed! "

" In two particulars. These were the claws and the pigment stuff — what is it? — at the back of the eye in a cat. You know? "

" *Tapetum*."

" Yes, the *tapetum*. It didn't go. After I'd given the stuff to bleach the blood and done certain other things to her, I gave the beast opium, and put her and the pillow she was sleeping on, on the apparatus. And after all the rest had faded and vanished,

there remained two little ghosts of her eyes."

"Odd!"

"I can't explain it. She was bandaged and clamped, of course, — so I had her safe; but she woke while she was still misty, and miaowed dismally, and some one came knocking. It was an old woman from downstairs, who suspected me of vivisecting, — a drink-sodden old creature, with only a white cat to care for in all the world. I whipped out some chloroform, and applied it, and answered the door. 'Did I hear a cat?' she asked. 'My cat?' 'Not here,' said I, very politely. She was a little doubtful and tried to peer past me into the room; strange enough to her no doubt, — bare walls, uncurtained windows, truckle-bed, with the gas engine vibrating, and the seethe of the radiant points, and that faint ghastly stinging of chloroform in the air. She had to be satisfied at last and went away again."

"How long did it take?" asked Kemp.

"Three or four hours — the cat. The bones and sinews and the fat were the last to go, and the tips of the coloured hairs. And, as I say, the back part of the eye, tough iridescent stuff it is, wouldn't go at all.

"It was night outside long before the business was over, and nothing was to be seen but the dim eyes and the claws. I stopped the gas engine, felt for and stroked the beast, which was still insensible, and then, being tired, left it sleeping on the invisible pillow and went to bed. I found it hard to sleep. I lay awake thinking weak aimless stuff, going over the experiment over and over again, or dreaming feverishly of things growing misty and vanishing about me, until everything, the ground I stood on, vanished, and so I came to that sickly falling nightmare one gets. About two, the cat began miaowing about the room. I tried to hush it by talking to it, and then I decided to turn it out. I remember the shock I had when striking a light — there were just the round eyes shining green — and nothing round them. I would have given it milk, but I hadn't any. It wouldn't be quiet, it just sat down and miaowed at the door. I tried to catch it, with an idea of putting it out of the window, but it wouldn't be caught, it vanished. Then it began miaowing in different parts of the room. At last I opened the window and made a bustle. I suppose it went out at last. I never saw any more ·of it.

"Then — Heaven knows why — I fell thinking of my father's funeral again, and the dismal windy hillside, until the day had come. I found sleeping was hopeless, and, locking my door after me, wandered out into the morning streets."

"You don't mean to say there's an invisible cat at large!" said Kemp.

"If it hasn't been killed," said the Invisible Man. "Why not?"

"Why not?" said Kemp. "I didn't mean to interrupt."

"It's very probably been killed," said the Invisible Man. "It was alive four days after, I know, and down a grating in Great Titchfield Street; because I

saw a crowd round the place, trying to see whence the miaowing came."

He was silent for the best part of a minute. Then he resumed abruptly:

" I remember that morning before the change very vividly. I must have gone up Great Portland Street. I remember the barracks in Albany Street, and the horse soldiers coming out, and at last I found myself sitting in the sunshine and feeling very ill and strange, on the summit of Primrose Hill. It was a sunny day in January, — one of those sunny, frosty days that came before the snow this year. My weary brain tried to formulate the position, to plot out a plan of action.

" I was surprised to find, now that my prize was within my grasp, how inconclusive its attainment seemed. As a matter of fact I was worked out; the intense stress of nearly four years' continuous work left me incapable of any strength of feeling. I was apathetic, and I tried in vain to recover the enthusiasm of my first inquiries, the passion of discovery that had enabled me to compass even the downfall of my father's grey hairs. Nothing seemed to matter. I saw pretty clearly this was a transient mood, due to overwork and want of sleep, and that either by drugs or rest it would be possible to recover my energies.

" All I could think clearly was that the thing had to be carried through; the fixed idea still ruled me. And soon, for the money I had was almost exhausted. I looked about me at the hillside, with children playing and girls watching them, and tried to think of all the fantastic advantages an invisible man would have in the world. After a time I crawled home, took some food and a strong dose of strychnine, and went to sleep in my clothes on my unmade bed. Strychnine is a grand tonic, Kemp, to take the flabbiness out of a man."

" It's the devil," said Kemp. " It's the palæolithic in a bottle."

" I awoke vastly invigorated and rather irritable. You know? "

" I know the stuff."

" And there was some one rapping at the door. It was my landlord with threats and inquiries, an old Polish Jew in a long grey coat and greasy slippers. I had been tormenting a cat in the night he was sure, — the old woman's tongue had been busy. He insisted on knowing all about it. The laws of this country against vivisection were very severe, — he might be liable. I denied the cat. Then the vibration of the little gas engine could be felt all over the house, he said. That was true, certainly. He edged round me into the room, peering about over his German-silver spectacles, and a sudden dread came into my mind that he might carry away something of my secret. I tried to keep between him and the concentrating apparatus I had arranged, and that only made him more curious. What was I doing? Why was I always alone and secretive? Was it legal? Was it dangerous? I paid nothing but the usual rent. His had always been a most respectable house — in a disreputable neighbourhood. Suddenly my temper gave way. I told him to

get out. He began to protest, to jabber of his right of entry. In a moment I had him by the collar; something ripped, and he went spinning out into his own passage. I slammed and locked the door and sat down quivering.

"He made a fuss outside, which I disregarded, and after a time he went away.

"But this brought matters to a crisis. I did not know what he would do, nor even what he had power to do. To move to fresh apartments would have meant delay; altogether I had barely twenty pounds left in the world, — for the most part in the bank, — and I could not afford that. Vanish! It was irresistible. Then there would be an inquiry, the sacking of my room —

"At the thought of the possibility of my work being exposed or interrupted at its very climax, I became angry and active. I hurried out with my three books of notes, my cheque-book, — the tramp has them now, — and directed them from the nearest Post Office to a house of call for letters and parcels in Great Portland Street. I tried to go out noiselessly. Coming in, I found my landlord going quietly upstairs; he had heard the door close, I suppose. You would have laughed to see him jump aside on the landing as I came tearing after him. He glared at me as I went by him, and I made the house quiver with the slamming of my door. I heard him come shuffling up to my floor, hesitate, and go down. I set to work upon my preparations forthwith.

"It was all done that evening and night. While I was still sitting under the sickly, drowsy influence of the drugs that decolourise blood, there came a repeated knocking at the door. It ceased, footsteps went away and returned, and the knocking was resumed. There was an attempt to push something under the door — a blue paper. Then in a fit of irritation I rose and went and flung the door wide open. 'Now then?' said I.

"It was my landlord, with a notice of ejectment or something. He held it out to me, saw something odd about my hands, I expect, and lifted his eyes to my face.

"For a moment he gaped. Then he gave a sort of inarticulate cry, dropped candle and writ together, and went blundering down the dark passage to the stairs. I shut the door, locked it, and went to the looking-glass. Then I understood his terror. My face was white — like white stone.

"But it was all horrible. I had not expected the suffering. A night of racking anguish, sickness and fainting. I set my teeth, though my skin was presently afire; all my body afire; but I lay there like grim death. I understood now how it was the cat had howled until I chloroformed it. Lucky it was I lived alone and untended in my room. There were times when I sobbed and groaned and talked. But I stuck to it. I became insensible and woke languid in the darkness.

"The pain had passed. I thought I was killing myself and I did not care. I shall never forget that dawn, and the strange horror of seeing that my hands had become as clouded glass, and

watching them grow clearer and thinner as the day went by, until at last I could see the sickly disorder of my room through them, though I closed my transparent eyelids. My limbs became glassy, the bones and arteries faded, vanished, and the little white nerves went last. I ground my teeth and stayed there to the end. At last only the dead tips of the finger-nails remained, pallid and white, and the brown stain of some acid upon my fingers.

" I struggled up. At first I was as incapable as a swathed infant, — stepping with limbs I could not see. I was weak and very hungry. I went and stared at nothing in my shaving-glass, at nothing save where an attenuated pigment still remained behind the retina of my eyes, fainter than mist. I had to hang on to the table and press my forehead to the glass.

" It was only by a frantic effort of will that I dragged myself back to the apparatus and completed the process.

" I slept during the forenoon, pulling the sheet over my eyes to shut out the light, and about midday I was awakened again by a knocking. My strength had returned. I sat up and listened and heard a whispering. I sprang to my feet and as noiselessly as possible began to detach the connections of my apparatus, and to distribute it about the room, so as to destroy the suggestions of its arrangement. Presently the knocking was renewed and voices called, first my landlord's, and then two others. To gain time I answered them. The invisible rag

and pillow came to hand and I opened the window and pitched them out on to the cistern cover. As the window opened, a heavy crash came at the door. Some one had charged it with the idea of smashing the lock. But the stout bolts I had screwed up some days before stopped him. That startled me, made me angry. I began to tremble and do things hurriedly.

" I tossed together some loose paper, straw, packing paper and so forth, in the middle of the room, and turned on the gas. Heavy blows began to rain upon the door. I could not find the matches. I beat my hands on the wall with rage. I turned down the gas again, stepped out of the window on the cistern cover, very softly lowered the sash, and sat down, secure and invisible, but quivering with anger, to watch events. They split a panel, I saw, and in another moment they had broken away the staples of the bolts and stood in the open doorway. It was the landlord and his two step-sons, sturdy young men of three or four and twenty. Behind them fluttered the old hag of a woman from downstairs.

" You may imagine their astonishment on finding the room empty. One of the younger men rushed to the window at once, flung it up and stared out. His staring eyes and thick-lipped bearded face came a foot from my face. I was half minded to hit his silly countenance, but I arrested my doubled fist. He stared right through me. So did the others as they joined him. The old man went and peered under the bed, and then they all made a rush for the cupboard. They had to

argue about it at length in Yiddish and Cockney English. They concluded I had not answered them, that their imagination had deceived them. A feeling of extraordinary elation took the place of my anger as I sat outside the window and watched these four people — for the old lady came in, glancing suspiciously about her like a cat, trying to understand the riddle of my behaviour.

"The old man, so far as I could understand his *patois*, agreed with the old lady that I was a vivisectionist. The sons protested in garbled English that I was an electrician, and appealed to the dynamos and radiators. They were all nervous against my arrival, although I found subsequently that they had bolted the front door. The old lady peered into the cupboard and under the bed, and one of the young men pushed up the register and stared up the chimney. One of my fellow lodgers, a costermonger who shared the opposite room with a butcher, appeared on the landing, and he was called in and told incoherent things.

"It occurred to me that the radiators, if they fell into the hands of some acute well-educated person, would give me away too much, and watching my opportunity, I came into the room and tilted one of the little dynamos off its fellow on which it was standing, and smashed both apparatus. Then, while they were trying to explain the smash, I dodged out of the room and went softly downstairs.

"I went into one of the sitting-rooms and waited until they came down, still speculating and argumentative, all a little disappointed at finding no 'horrors,' and all a little puzzled how they stood with regard to me. Then I slipped up again with a box of matches, fired my heap of paper and rubbish, put the chairs and bedding thereby, led the gas to the affair, by means of an india-rubber tube, and waving a farewell to the room left it for the last time."

"You fired the house!" exclaimed Kemp.

"Fired the house. It was the only way to cover my trail — and no doubt it was insured. I slipped the bolts of the front door quietly and went out into the street. I was invisible, and I was only just beginning to realise the extraordinary advantage my invisibility gave me. My head was already teeming with plans of all the wild and wonderful things I had now impunity to do."

CHAPTER 21

IN OXFORD STREET

"In going downstairs the first time I found an unexpected difficulty because I could not see my feet; indeed I stumbled twice, and there was an unaccustomed

clumsiness in gripping the bolt. By not looking down, however, I managed to walk on the level passably well.

" My mood, I say, was one of exaltation. I felt as a seeing man might do, with padded feet and noiseless clothes, in a city of the blind, I experienced a wild impulse to jest, to startle people, to clap men on the back, fling people's hats astray, and generally revel in my extraordinary advantage.

" But hardly had I emerged upon Great Portland Street, however (my lodgings was close to the big draper's shop there), when I heard a clashing concussion and was hit violently behind, and turning saw a man carrying a basket of soda-water siphons, and looking in amazement at his burden. Although the blow had really hurt me, I found something so irresistible in his astonishment that I laughed aloud. ' The devil's in the basket,' I said, and suddenly twisted it out of his hand. He let go incontinently, and I swung the whole weight into the air.

" But a fool of a cabman, standing outside a public house, made a sudden rush for this, and his extending fingers took me with excruciating violence under the ear. I let the whole down with a smash on the cabman, and then, with shouts and the clatter of feet about me, people coming out of shops, vehicles pulling up, I realised what I had done for myself, and cursing my folly, backed against a shop window and prepared to dodge out of the confusion. In a moment

I should be wedged into a crowd and inevitably discovered. I pushed by the butcher boy, who luckily did not turn to see the nothingness that shoved him aside, and dodged behind the cabman's four-wheeler. I do not know how they settled the business. I hurried straight across the road, which was happily clear, and hardly heeding which way I went, in the fright of detection the incident had given, plunged into the afternoon throng of Oxford Street.

" I tried to get into the stream of people, but they were too thick for me, and in a moment my heels were being trodden upon. I took to the gutter, the roughness of which I found painful to my feet, and forthwith the shaft of a crawling hansom dug me forcibly under the shoulder blade, reminding me that I was already bruised severely. I staggered out of the way of the cab, avoided a perambulator by a convulsive movement, and found myself behind the hansom. A happy thought saved me, and as this drove slowly along I followed in its immediate wake, trembling and astonished at the turn of my adventure. And not only trembling, but shivering. It was a bright day in January and I was stark naked and the thin slime of mud that covered the road was freezing. Foolish as it seems to me now, I had not reckoned that, transparent or not, I was still amenable to the weather and all its consequences.

" Then suddenly a bright idea came into my head. I ran round and got into the cab. And so,

shivering, scared, and sniffing with the first intimations of a cold, and with the bruises in the small of my back growing upon my attention, I drove slowly along Oxford Street and past Tottenham Court Road. My mood was as different from that in which I had sallied forth ten minutes ago as it is possible to imagine. *This* invisibility indeed! The one thought that possessed me was — how was I to get out of the scrape I was in.

"We crawled past Mudie's, and there a tall woman with five or six yellow-labelled books hailed my cab, and I sprang out just in time to escape her, shaving a railway van narrowly in my flight. I made off up the roadway to Bloomsbury Square, intending to strike north past the Museum and so get into the quiet district. I was now cruelly chilled, and the strangeness of my situation so unnerved me that I whimpered as I ran. At the northward corner of the Square a little white dog ran out of the Pharmaceutical Society's offices, and incontinently made for me, nose down.

"I had never realised it before, but the nose is to the mind of a dog what the eye is to the mind of a seeing man. Dogs perceive the scent of a man moving as men perceive his vision. This brute began barking and leaping, showing, as it seemed to me, only too plainly that he was aware of me. I crossed Great Russell Street, glancing over my shoulder as I did so, and went some way along Montague Street before I realised what I was running towards.

"Then I became aware of a blare of music, and looking along the street saw a number of people advancing out of Russell Square, red shirts, and the banner of the Salvation Army to the fore. Such a crowd, chanting in the roadway and scoffing on the pavement, I could not hope to penetrate, and dreading to go back and farther from home again, and deciding on the spur of the moment, I ran up the white steps of a house facing the Museum railings, and stood there until the crowd should have passed. Happily the dog stopped at the noise of the band too, hesitated, and turned tail, running back to Bloomsbury Square again.

"On came the band, bawling with unconscious irony some hymn about 'When shall we see his Face?' and it seemed an interminable time to me before the tide of the crowd washed along the pavement by me. Thud, thud, thud, came the drum with a vibrating resonance, and for the moment I did not notice two urchins stopping at the railings by me. 'See 'em,' said one. 'See what?' said the other. 'Why — them footmarks — *bare*. Like what you makes in mud.'

"I looked down and saw the youngsters had stopped and were gaping at the muddy footmarks I had left behind me up the newly whitened steps. The passing people elbowed and jostled them, but their confounded intelligence was arrested. 'Thud, thud, thud, When, thud, shall we see, thud, his face, thud, thud.' 'There's a barefoot man gone up them steps, or I don't know nothing,' said one. 'And he ain't never come down again. And his foot was a-bleeding.'

" The thick of the crowd had already passed. 'Looky there, Ted,' quoth the younger of the detectives, with the sharpness of surprise in his voice, and pointed straight to my feet. I looked down and saw at once the dim suggestion of their outline sketched in splashes of mud. For a moment I was paralysed.

" ' Why, that's rum,' said the elder. ' Dashed rum! It's just like the ghost of a foot, ain't it? ' He hesitated and advanced with outstretched hand. A man pulled up short to see what he was catching, and then a girl. In another moment he would have touched me. Then I saw what to do. I made a step, the boy started back with an exclamation, and with a rapid movement I swung myself over into the portico of the next house. But the smaller boy was sharp-eyed enough to follow the movement, and before I was well down the steps and upon the pavement, he had recovered from his momentary astonishment and was shouting out that the feet had gone over the wall.

" They rushed round and saw my new footmarks flash into being on the lower step and upon the pavement. ' What's up? ' asked some one. ' Feet! Look! Feet running! ' Everybody in the road, except my three pursuers, was pouring along after the Salvation Army, and this not only impeded me but them. There was an eddy of surprise and interrogation. At the cost of bowling over one young fellow I got through, and in another moment I was rushing headlong round the circuit of Russell Square, with six or seven astonished people following my footmarks. There was no time for explanation, or else the whole host would have been after me.

" Twice I doubled round corners, thrice I crossed the road and came back on my tracks, and then, as my feet grew hot and dry, the damp impressions began to fade. At last I had a breathing space and rubbed my feet clean with my hands, and so got away altogether. The last I saw of the chase was a little group of a dozen people perhaps, studying with infinite perplexity a slowly drying footprint that had resulted from a puddle in Travistock Square — a footprint as isolated and incomprehensible to them as Crusoe's solitary discovery.

" This running warmed me to a certain extent, and I went on with a better courage through the maze of less frequented roads that runs hereabouts. My back had now become very stiff and sore, my tonsils were painful from the cabman's fingers, and the skin of my neck had been scratched by his nails; my feet hurt exceedingly and I was lame from a little cut on one foot. I saw in time a blind man approaching me, and fled limping, for I feared his subtle intuitions. Once or twice accidental collisions occurred and I left people amazed, with unaccountable curses ringing in their ears. Then came something silent and quiet against my face, and across the Square fell a thin veil of slowly falling flakes of snow. I had caught a cold, and do as I would I could not avoid an occasional sneeze. And every dog that came in sight, with its point-

ing nose and curious sniffing, was a terror to me.

"Then came men and boys running, first one and then others, and shouting as they ran. It was a fire. They ran in the direction of my lodging, and looking back down a street I saw a mass of black smoke streaming up above the roofs and telephone wires. It was my lodging burning; my clothes, my apparatus, all my resources indeed, except my cheque-book and the three volumes of memoranda that awaited me in Great Portland Street, were there. Burning! I had burnt my boats — if ever a man did! The place was blazing."

The Invisible Man paused and thought. Kemp glanced nervously out of the window. "Yes?" he said. "Go on."

CHAPTER 22

IN THE EMPORIUM

"So last January, with the beginning of a snowstorm in the air about me — and if it settled on me it would betray me! — weary, cold, painful, inexpressibly wretched, and still but half convinced of my invisible quality, I began this new life to which I am committed. I had no refuge, no appliances, no human being in the world in whom I could confide. To have told my secret would have given me away — made a mere show and rarity of me. Nevertheless, I was half minded to accost some passer-by and throw myself upon his mercy. But I knew too clearly the terror and brutal cruelty my advances would evoke. I made no plans in the street. My sole object was to get shelter from the snow, to get myself covered and warm; then I might hope to plan. But even to me, an Invisible Man, the rows of London houses stood latched, barred, and bolted impregnably.

"Only one thing could I see clearly before me, the cold exposure and misery of the snowstorm and the night.

"And then I had a brilliant idea. I turned down one of the roads leading from Gower Street to Tottenham Court Road, and found myself outside Omniums, the big establishment where everything is to be bought — you know the place — meat, grocery, linen, furniture, clothing, oil paintings even — a huge meandering collection of shops rather than a shop. I had thought I should find the doors open, but they were closed, and as I stood in the wide entrance a carriage stopped outside, and a man in uniform — you know the kind of personage with 'Omnium' on his cap — flung open the door. I contrived to enter, and walking down the shop — it was a department where they were selling ribbons and gloves and stockings and that kind of thing — came to a more spacious region devoted

to picnic baskets and wicker furniture.

" I did not feel safe there, however; people were going to and fro, and I prowled restlessly about until I came upon a huge section in an upper floor containing scores and hundreds of bedsteads, and beyond these I found a resting-place at last among a huge pile of folded flock mattresses. The place was already lit up and agreeably warm, and I decided to remain where I was, keeping a cautious eye on the two or three sets of shopmen and customers who were meandering through the place until closing time came. Then I should be able, I thought, to rob the place for food and clothing, and disguised, prowl through it and examine its resources, perhaps sleep on some of the bedding. That seemed an acceptable plan. My idea was to procure clothing to make myself a muffled but acceptable figure, to get money, and then to recover my books and parcels where they awaited me, take a lodging somewhere and elaborate plans for the complete realisation of the advantages my invisibility gave me (as I still imagined) over my fellow-men.

" Closing time arrived quickly enough; it could not have been more than an hour after I took up my position on the mattresses before I noticed the blinds of the windows being drawn, and customers being marched doorward. And then a number of brisk young men began with remarkable alacrity to tidy up the goods that remained disturbed. I left my lair as the crowds diminished, and prowled cautiously out into the less desolate parts of the shop. I was really surprised to observe how rapidly the young men and women whipped away the goods displayed for sale during the day. All the boxes of goods, the hanging fabrics, the festoons of lace, the boxes of sweets in the grocery section, the displays of this and that, were being whipped down, folded up, slapped into tidy receptacles, and everything that could not be taken down and put away had sheets of some coarse stuff like sacking flung over it. Finally all the chairs were turned up on to the counters, leaving the floor clear. Directly each of these young people had done, he or she made promptly for the door with such an expression of animation as I have rarely observed in a shop assistant before. Then came a lot of youngsters scattering sawdust and carrying pails and brooms. I had to dodge to get out of the way, and as it was, my ankle got stung with the sawdust. For some time, wandering through the swathed and darkened departments, I could hear the brooms at work. And at last a good hour or more after the shop had been closed, came a noise of locking doors. Silence came upon the place, and I found myself wandering through the vast and intricate shops, galleries and showrooms of the place, alone. It was very still; in one place I remember passing near one of the Tottenham Court Road entrances and listening to the tapping of bootheels of the passers-by.

" My first visit was to the place where I had seen stockings and gloves for sale. It was dark, and I had the devil of a hunt after matches, which I found at last in the drawer of the little cash desk. Then I had to get a candle. I had to tear down wrappings and ransack a number of boxes and drawers, but at last I managed to turn out what I sought; the box label called them lambs-wool pants, and lambswool vests. Then socks, a thick comforter, and then I went to the clothing place and got trousers, a lounge jacket, an overcoat and a slouch hat — a clerical sort of hat with the brim turned down. I began to feel a human being again, and my next thought was food.

" Upstairs was a refreshment department, and there I got cold meat. There was coffee still in the urn, and I lit the gas and warmed it up again, and altogether I did not do badly. Afterwards, prowling through the place in search of blankets — I had to put up at last with a heap of down quilts — I came upon a grocery section with a lot of chocolate and candied fruits, more than was good for me indeed — and some white burgundy. And near that was a toy department, and I had a brilliant idea. I found some artificial noses — dummy noses, you know, and I thought of dark spectacles. But Omniums had no optical department. My nose had been a difficulty indeed — I had thought of paint. But the discovery set my mind running on wigs and masks and the like. Finally I went to sleep on a heap of down quilts, very warm and comfortable.

" My last thoughts before sleeping were the most agreeable I had had since the change. I was in a state of physical serenity, and that was reflected in my mind. I thought that I should be able to slip out unobserved in the morning with my clothes upon me, muffling my face with a white wrapper I had taken, purchase, with the money I had taken, spectacles and so forth, and so complete my disguise. I lapsed into disorderly dreams of all the fantastic things that had happened during the last few days. I saw the ugly little Jew of a landlord vociferating in his rooms; I saw his two sons marvelling, and the wrinkled old woman's gnarled face as she asked for her cat. I experienced again the strange sensation of seeing the cloth disappear, and so I came round to the windy hillside and the sniffing old clergyman mumbling ' Dust to dust, earth to earth,' and my father's open grave.

" ' You also,' said a voice, and suddenly I was being forced towards the grave. I struggled, shouted, appealed to the mourners, but they continued stonily following the service; the old clergyman, too, never faltered droning and sniffing through the ritual. I realised I was invisible and inaudible, that overwhelming forces had their grip on me. I struggled in vain, I was forced over the brink, the coffin rang hollow as I fell upon it, and the gravel came flying after me in spadefuls. Nobody heeded

me, nobody was aware of me. I made convulsive struggles and awoke.

"The pale London dawn had come, the place was full of a chilly grey light that filtered round the edges of the window blinds. I sat up, and for a time I could not think where this ample apartment, with its counters, its piles of rolled stuff, its heap of quilts and cushions, its iron pillars, might be. Then, as recollection came back to me, I heard voices in conversation.

"Then far down the place, in the brighter light of some department which had already raised its blinds, I saw two men approaching. I scrambled to my feet, looking about me for some way of escape, and even as I did so the sound of my movement made them aware of me. I suppose they saw merely a figure moving quietly and quickly away. 'Who's that?' cried one, and 'Stop there,' shouted the other. I dashed round a corner and came full tilt — a faceless figure, mind you! — on a lanky lad of fifteen. He yelled and I bowled him over, rushed past him, turned another corner, and by a happy inspiration threw myself flat behind a counter. In another moment feet went running past and I heard voices shouting, 'All hands to the doors!' asking what was 'up,' and giving one another advice how to catch me.

"Lying on the ground, I felt scared out of my wits. But — odd as it may seem — it did not occur to me at the moment to take off my clothes as I should have done.

I had made up my mind, I suppose, to get away in them, and that ruled me. And then down the vista of the counters came a bawling of 'Here he is!'

"I sprang to my feet, whipped a chair off the counter, and sent it whirling at the fool who had shouted, turned, came into another round a corner, sent him spinning, and rushed up the stairs. He kept his footing, gave a view hallo! and came up the staircase hot after me. Up the staircase were piled a multitude of those bright-coloured pot things — what are they?"

"Art pots," suggested Kemp.

"That's it! Art pots. Well, I turned at the top step and swung round, plucked one out of a pile and smashed it on his silly head as he came at me. The whole pile of pots went headlong, and I heard shouting and footsteps running from all parts. I made a mad rush for the refreshment place, and there was a man in white like a man cook, who took up the chase. I made one last desperate turn and found myself among lamps and ironmongery. I went behind the counter of this, and waited for my cook, and as he bolted in at the head of the chase, I doubled him up with a lamp. Down he went, and I crouched behind the counter and began whipping off my clothes as fast as I could. Coat, jacket, trousers, shoes were all right, but a lambswool vest fits a man like a skin. I heard more men coming, my cook was lying quiet on the other side of the counter, stunned or scared speechless, and I had to make another

dash for it, like a rabbit hunted out of a wood-pile.

"'This way, policeman!' I heard some one shouting. I found myself in my bedstead store-room again, and at the end a wilderness of wardrobes. I rushed among them, went flat, got rid of my vest after infinite wriggling, and stood a free man again, panting and scared, as the policeman and three of the shopmen came round the corner. They made a rush for the vest and pants, and collared the trousers. 'He's dropping his plunder,' said one of the young men. 'He *must* be somewhere here.'

"But they did not find me all the same.

"I stood watching them hunt for me for a time, and cursing my ill-luck in losing the clothes. Then I went into the refreshment-room, drank a little milk I found there, and sat down by the fire to consider my position.

"In a little while two assistants came and began to talk over the business very excitedly and like the fools they were. I heard a magnified account of my depredations, and other speculations as to my whereabouts. Then I fell to scheming again. The insurmountable difficulty of the place, especially now it was alarmed, was to get any plunder out of it. I went down into the warehouse to see if there was any chance of packing and addressing a parcel, but I could not understand the system of checking. About eleven o'clock, the snow having thawed as it fell, and the day being finer and a little warmer than the previous one, I decided

that the Emporium was hopeless, and went out again, exasperated at my want of success, with only the vaguest plans of action in my mind."

CHAPTER 23

IN DRURY LANE

" But you begin to realise now," said the Invisible Man, " the full disadvantage of my condition. I had no shelter, no covering. To get clothing was to forego all my advantage, to make of myself a strange and terrible thing. I was fasting; for to eat, to fill myself with unassimilated matter, would be to become grotesquely visible again."

" I never thought of that," said Kemp.

" Nor had I. And the snow had warned me of other dangers. I could not go abroad in snow — it would settle on me and expose me. Rain, too, would make me a watery outline, a glistening surface of a man — a bubble. And fog — I should be like a fainter bubble in a fog, a surface, a greasy glimmer of humanity. Moreover, as I went abroad — in the London air — I gathered dirt about my ankles, floating smuts and dust upon my skin. I did not

know how long it would be before I should become visible from that cause also. But I saw clearly it could not be for long.

" Not in London at any rate.

" I went into the slums towards Great Portland Street, and found myself at the end of the street in which I had lodged. I did not go that way, because of the crowd halfway down it opposite to the still smoking ruins of the house I had fired. My most immediate problem was to get clothing. What to do with my face puzzled me. Then I saw in one of those little miscellaneous shops — news, sweets, toys, stationery, belated Christmas tomfoolery, and so forth — an array of masks and noses. I realised that problem was solved. In a flash I saw my course. I turned about, no longer aimless, and went — circuitously in order to avoid the busy ways, towards the back streets north of the Strand; for I remembered, though not very distinctly where, that some theatrical costumiers had shops in that district.

" The day was cold, with a nipping wind down the northward running streets. I walked fast to avoid being overtaken. Every crossing was a danger, every passenger a thing to watch alertly. One man as I was about to pass him at the top of Bedford Street, turned upon me abruptly and came into me, sending me into the road and almost under the wheel of a passing hansom. The verdict of the cab-rank was that he had had some sort of stroke. I was so unnerved by this encounter that I went into Covent Garden Market and sat down for some time in a quiet corner by a stall of violets, panting and trembling. I found I had caught a fresh cold, and had to turn out after a time lest my sneezes should attract attention.

" At last I reached the object of my quest, a dirty fly-blown little shop in a byway near Drury Lane, with a window full of tinsel robes, sham jewels, wigs, slippers, dominoes and theatrical photographs. The shop was old-fashioned and low and dark, and the house rose above it for four storeys, dark and dismal. I peered through the window and, seeing no one within, entered. The opening of the door set a clanking bell ringing. I left it open, and walked round a bare costume stand, into a corner behind a cheval glass. For a minute or so no one came. Then I heard heavy feet striding across a room, and a man appeared down the shop.

" My plans were now perfectly definite. I proposed to make my way into the house, secrete myself upstairs, watch my opportunity, and when everything was quiet, rummage out a wig, mask, spectacles, and costume, and go into the world, perhaps a grotesque but still a credible figure. And incidentally of course I could rob the house of any available money.

" The man who had entered the shop was a short, slight, hunched, beetle-browed man, with long arms and very short bandy legs. Apparently I had interrupted a meal. He stared about the shop with an expression of expectation. This gave

way to surprise, and then anger, as he saw the shop empty. 'Damn the boys!' he said. He went to stare up and down the street. He came in again in a minute, kicked the door to with his foot spitefully, and went muttering back to the house door.

"I came forward to follow him, and at the noise of my movement he stopped dead. I did so too, startled by his quickness of ear. He slammed the house door in my face.

"I stood hesitating. Suddenly I heard his quick footsteps returning, and the door reopened. He stood looking about the shop like one who was still not satisfied. Then, murmuring to himself, he examined the back of the counter and peered behind some fixtures. Then he stood doubtful. He had left the house door open and I slipped into the inner room.

"It was a queer little room, poorly furnished and with a number of big masks in the corner. On the table was his belated breakfast, and it was a confoundedly exasperating thing for me, Kemp, to have to sniff his coffee and stand watching while he came in and resumed his meal. And his table manners were irritating. Three doors opened into the little room, one going upstairs and one down, but they were all shut. I could not get out of the room while he was there, I could scarcely move because of his alertness, and there was draught down my back. Twice I strangled a sneeze just in time.

"The spectacular quality of my sensations was curious and novel, but for all that I was heartily tired and angry long before he had done his eating. But at last he made an end and putting his beggarly crockery on the black tin tray upon which he had had his teapot, and gathering all the crumbs up on the mustard-stained cloth, he took the whole lot of things after him. His burden prevented his shutting the door behind him — as he would have done; I never saw such a man for shutting doors — and I followed him into a very dirty underground kitchen and scullery. I had the pleasure of seeing him begin to wash up, and then, finding no good in keeping down there, and the brick floor being cold to my feet, I returned upstairs and sat in his chair by the fire. It was burning low, and scarcely thinking, I put on a little coal. The noise of this brought him up at once, and he stood aglare. He peered about the room and was within an ace of touching me. Even after that examination, he scarcely seemed satisfied. He stopped in the doorway and took a final inspection before he went down.

"I waited in the little parlour for an age, and at last he came up and opened the upstairs door. I just managed to get by him.

"On the staircase he stopped suddenly, so that I very nearly blundered into him. He stood looking back right into my face and listening. 'I could have sworn,' he said. His long hairy hand pulled at his lower lip. His eye went up and down the staircase. Then he grunted and went on up again.

" His hand was on the handle of a door, and then he stopped again with the same puzzled anger on his face. He was becoming aware of the faint sounds of my movements about him. The man must have had diabolically acute hearing. He suddenly flashed into rage. ' If there's any one in this house,' he cried with an oath, and left the threat unfinished. He put his hand in his pocket, failed to find what he wanted, and rushing past me went blundering noisily and pugnaciously downstairs. But I did not follow him. I sat on the head of the staircase until his return.

" Presently he came up again, still muttering. He opened the door of the room, and before I could enter, slammed it in my face.

" I resolved to explore the house, and spent some time in doing so as noiselessly as possible. The house was very old and tumbledown, damp so that the paper in the attics was peeling from the walls, and rat-infested. Some of the door handles were stiff and I was afraid to turn them. Several rooms I did inspect were unfurnished, and others were littered with theatrical lumber, bought second-hand, I judged, from its appearance. In one room next to his I found a lot of old clothes. I began routing among these, and in my eagerness forgot again the evident sharpness of his ears. I heard a stealthy footstep and, looking up just in time, saw him peering in at the tumbled heap and holding an old-fashioned revolver in his

hand. I stood perfectly still while he stared about open-mouthed and suspicious. ' It must have been her,' he said slowly. ' Damn her! '

" He shut the door quietly, and immediately I heard the key turn in the lock. Then his footsteps retreated. I realised abruptly that I was locked in. For a minute I did not know what to do. I walked from door to window and back, and stood perplexed. A gust of anger came upon me. But I decided to inspect the clothes before I did anything further, and my first attempt brought down a pile from an upper shelf. This brought him back, more sinister than ever. That time he actually touched me, jumped back with amazement and stood astonished in the middle of the room.

" Presently he calmed a little. ' Rats,' he said in an undertone, fingers on lip. He was evidently a little scared. I edged quietly out of the room, but a plank creaked. Then the infernal little brute started going all over the house, revolver in hand and locking door after door and pocketing the keys. When I realised what he was up to I had a fit of rage — I could hardly control myself sufficiently to watch my opportunity. By this time I knew he was alone in the house, and so I made no more ado, but knocked him on the head."

" Knocked him on the head! " exclaimed Kemp.

" Yes — stunned him — as he was going downstairs. Hit him from behind with a stool that stood on the landing. He went

downstairs like a bag of old boots."

"But — ! I say! The common conventions of humanity — "

"Are all very well for common people. But the point was, Kemp, that I had to get out of that house in a disguise without his seeing me. I couldn't think of any other way of doing it. And then I gagged him with a Louis Quatorze vest and tied him up in a sheet."

"Tied him up in a sheet!"

"Made a sort of bag of it. It was rather a good idea to keep the idiot scared and quiet, and a devilish hard thing to get out of — head away from the string. My dear Kemp, it's no good your sitting and glaring as though I was a murderer. It had to be done. He had his revolver. If once he saw me he would be able to describe me — "

"But still," said Kemp, "in England — to-day. And the man was in his own house, and you were — well, robbing."

"Robbing! Confound it! You'll call me a thief next! Surely, Kemp, you're not fool enough to dance on the old strings. Can't you see my position?"

"And his too," said Kemp.

The Invisible Man stood up sharply. "What do you mean to say?"

Kemp's face grew a trifle hard. He was about to speak and checked himself. "I suppose, after all," he said with a sudden change of manner, "the thing had to be done. You were in a fix. But still — "

"Of course I was in a fix — an infernal fix. And he made me wild too — hunting me about the house, fooling about with his revolver, locking and unlocking doors. He was simply exasperating. You don't blame me, do you? You don't blame me?"

"I never blame any one," said Kemp. "It's quite out of fashion. What did you do next?"

"I was hungry. Downstairs I found a loaf and some rank cheese — more than sufficient to satisfy my hunger. I took some brandy and water, and then went up past my impromptu bag — he was lying quite still — to the room containing the old clothes. This looked out upon the street, two lace curtains brown with dirt guarding the window. I went and peered out through their interstices. Outside the day was bright — by contrast with the brown shadows of the dismal house in which I found myself, dazzlingly bright. A brisk traffic was going by, fruit carts, a hansom, a four-wheeler with a pile of boxes, a fishmonger's cart. I turned with spots of colour swimming before my eyes to the shadowy fixtures behind me. My excitement was giving place to a clear apprehension of my position again. The room was full of a faint scent of benzoline, used, I suppose, in cleaning the garments.

"I began a systematic search of the place. I should judge the hunchback had been alone in the house for some time. He was a curious person. Everything that could possibly be of service to me I collected in the clothes store-room, and then I made a deliberate selection. I found a

handbag I thought a suitable possession, and some powder, rouge, and sticking-plaster.

"I had thought of painting and powdering my face and all that there was to show of me, in order to render myself visible, but the disadvantage of this lay in the fact that I should require turpentine and other appliances and a considerable amount of time before I could vanish again. Finally I chose a mask of the better type, slightly grotesque but not more so than many human beings, dark glasses, greyish whiskers, and a wig. I could find no underclothing, but that I could buy subsequently, and for the time I swathed myself in calico dominoes and some white cashmere scarfs. I could find no socks, but the hunchback's boots were rather a loose fit and sufficed. In a desk in the shop were three sovereigns and about thirty shillings' worth of silver, and in a locked cupboard I burst in the inner room were eight pounds in gold. I could go forth into the world again, equipped.

"Then came a curious hesitation. Was my appearance really — credible? I tried myself with a little bedroom looking-glass, inspecting myself from every point of view to discover any forgotten chink, but it all seemed sound. I was grotesque to the theatrical pitch, a stage miser, but I was certainly not a physical impossibility. Gathering confidence, I took my looking-glass down into the shop, pulled down the shop blinds, and surveyed myself from every point of view with the help of the cheval glass in the corner.

"I spent some minutes screwing up my courage and then unlocked the shop door and marched out into the street, leaving the little man to get out of his sheet again when he liked. In five minutes a dozen turnings intervened between me and the costumier's shop. No one appeared to notice me very pointedly. My last difficulty seemed overcome."

He stopped again.

"And you troubled no more about the hunchback?" said Kemp.

"No," said the Invisible Man. "Nor have I heard what became of him. I suppose he untied himself or kicked himself out. The knots were pretty tight."

He became silent, and went to the window and stared out.

"What happened when you went out into the Strand?"

"Oh! — disillusionment again. I thought my troubles were over. Practically I thought I had impunity to do whatever I chose, everything — save to give away my secret. So I thought. Whatever I did, whatever the consequences might be, was nothing to me. I had merely to fling aside my garments and vanish. No person could hold me. I could take my money where I found it. I decided to treat myself to a sumptuous feast, and then put up at a good hotel, and accumulate a new outfit of property. I felt amazingly confident — it's not particularly pleasant recalling that I was an ass. I went into a place and was already ordering a lunch, when it occurred to me that I could not eat unless I exposed my invisible face. I finished

ordering the lunch, told the man I should be back in ten minutes, and went out exasperated. I don't know if you have ever been disappointed in your appetite."

"Not quite so badly," said Kemp, "but I can imagine it."

"I could have smashed the silly devils. At last, faint with the desire for tasteful food, I went into another place and demanded a private room. 'I am disfigured,' I said. 'Badly.' They looked at me curiously, but of course it was not their affair — and so at last I got my lunch. It was not particularly well served, but it sufficed; and when I had had it, I sat over a cigar, trying to plan my line of action. And outside a snowstorm was beginning.

"The more I thought it over, Kemp, the more I realised what a helpless absurdity an Invisible Man was — in a cold and dirty climate and a crowded civilised city. Before I made this mad experiment I had dreamt of a thousand advantages. That afternoon it seemed all disappointment. I went over the heads of the things a man reckons desirable. No doubt invisibility made it possible to get them, but it made it impossible to enjoy them when they are got. Ambition — what is the good of pride of place when you cannot appear there? What is the good of the love of woman when her name must needs be Delilah? I have no taste for politics, for the blackguardisms of fame, for philanthropy, for sport. What was I to do? And for this I had become a wrapped-up mystery, a swathed and bandaged caricature of a man!"

He paused, and his attitude suggested a roving glance at the window.

"But how did you get to Iping?" said Kemp, anxious to keep his guest busy talking.

"I went there to work. I had one hope. It was a half idea! I have it still. It is a full blown idea now. A way of getting back! Of restoring what I have done. When I choose. When I have done all I mean to do invisibly. And that is what I chiefly want to talk to you about now."

"You went straight to Iping?"

"Yes. I had simply to get my three volumes of memoranda and my cheque-book, my luggage and underclothing, order a quantity of chemicals to work out this idea of mine — I will show you the calculations as soon as I get my books — and then I started. Jove! I remember the snowstorm now, and the accursed bother it was to keep the snow from damping my pasteboard nose."

"At the end," said Kemp, "the day before yesterday, when they found you out, you rather — to judge by the papers —"

"I did. Rather. Did I kill that fool of a constable?"

"No," said Kemp. "He's expected to recover."

"That's his luck, then. I clean lost my temper, the fools! Why couldn't they leave me alone? And that grocer lout?"

"There are no deaths expected," said Kemp.

"I don't know about that tramp of mine," said the Invisible Man, with an unpleasant laugh.

"By Heaven, Kemp, you don't

know what rage *is!* To have worked for years, to have planned and plotted, and then to get some fumbling purblind idiot messing across your course! Every conceivable sort of silly creature that has ever been created has been sent to cross me.

"If I have much more of it, I shall go wild — I shall start mowing 'em.

"As it is, they've made things a thousand times more difficult."

"No doubt it's exasperating," said Kemp, dryly.

CHAPTER 24

THE PLAN THAT FAILED

"But now," said Kemp, with a side glance out of the window, "what are we to do?"

He moved nearer his guest as he spoke in such a manner as to prevent the possibility of a glimpse of the three men who were advancing up the hill road — with an intolerable slowness, as it seemed to Kemp.

"What were you planning to do when you were heading for Port Burdock? *Had* you any plan?"

"I was going to clear out of the country. But I have altered that

plan rather since seeing you. I thought it would be wise, now the weather is hot and invisibility possible, to make for the South. Especially as my secret was known, and every one would be on the lookout for a masked and muffled man. You have a line of steamers from here to France. My idea was to get aboard one and run the risks of the passage. Thence I could go by train into Spain, or else get to Algiers. It would not be difficult. There a man might always be invisible — and yet live. And do things. I was using that tramp as a money box and luggage carrier, until I decided how to get my books and things sent over to meet me."

"That's clear."

"And then the filthy brute must needs try and rob me! He has hidden my books, Kemp. Hidden my books! If I can lay my hands on him!"

"Best plan to get the books out of him first."

"But where is he? Do you know?"

"He's in the town police station, locked up, by his own request, in the strongest cell in the place."

"Cur!" said the Invisible Man.

"But that hangs up your plans a little."

"We must get those books; those books are vital."

"Certainly," said Kemp, a little nervously, wondering if he heard footsteps outside. "Certainly we must get those books. But that won't be difficult, if he doesn't know they're for you."

"No," said the Invisible Man, and thought.

Kemp tried to think of something to keep the talk going, but the Invisible Man resumed of his own accord.

"Blundering into your house, Kemp," he said, "changes all my plans. For you are a man that can understand. In spite of all that has happened, in spite of this publicity, of the loss of my books, of what I have suffered, there still remain great possibilities, huge possibilities —

"You have told no one I am here?" he asked abruptly.

Kemp hesitated. "That was implied," he said.

"No one?" insisted Griffin.

"Not a soul."

"Ah! Now —" The Invisible Man stood up, and sticking his arms akimbo began to pace the study.

"I made a mistake, Kemp, a huge mistake, in carrying this thing through alone. I have wasted strength, time, opportunities. Alone — it is wonderful how little a man can do alone! To rob a little, to hurt a little, and there is the end.

"What I want, Kemp, is a goal-keeper, a helper, and a hiding-place, an arrangement whereby I can sleep and eat and rest in peace, and unsuspected. I must have a confederate. With a confederate, with food and rest — a thousand things are possible.

"Hitherto I have gone on vague lines. We have to consider all that invisibility means, all that it does not mean. It means little advantage for eavesdropping and so forth — one makes sounds. It's of little help, a little help perhaps — in housebreaking and

so forth. Once you've caught me you could easily imprison me. But on the other hand I am hard to catch. This invisibility, in fact, is only good in two cases: It's useful in getting away, it's useful in approaching. It's particularly useful, therefore, in killing. I can walk round a man, whatever weapon he has, choose my point, strike as I like. Dodge as I like. Escape as I like."

Kemp's hand went to his moustache. Was that a movement downstairs?

"And it is killing we must do, Kemp."

"It is killing we must do," repeated Kemp. "I'm listening to your plan, Griffin, but I'm not agreeing, mind. *Why* killing?"

"Not wanton killing, but a judicious slaying. The point is they know there is an Invisible Man — as well as we know there is an Invisible Man. And that Invisible Man, Kemp, must now establish a Reign of Terror. Yes — no doubt it's startling. But I mean it. A Reign of Terror. He must take some town like your Burdock and terrify and dominate it. He must issue his orders. He can do that in a thousand ways — scraps of paper thrust under doors would suffice. And all who disobey his orders he must kill, and kill all who would defend the disobedient."

"Humph!" said Kemp, no longer listening to Griffin but to the sound of his front door opening and closing. "It seems to me, Griffin," he said, to cover his wandering attention, "that your confederate would be in a difficult position."

"No one would know he was a confederate," said the Invisible Man, eagerly. And then suddenly, "*Hush!* What's that downstairs?"

"Nothing," said Kemp, and suddenly began to speak loud and fast. "I don't agree to this, Griffin," he said. "Understand me, I don't agree to this. Why dream of playing a game against the race? How can you hope to gain happiness? Don't be a lone wolf. Publish your results; take the world — take the nation at least — into your confidence. Think what you might do with a million helpers — "

The Invisible Man interrupted Kemp. "There are footsteps coming upstairs," he said in a low voice.

"Nonsense," said Kemp.

"Let me see," said the Invisible Man, and advanced, arm extended, to the door.

Kemp hesitated for a second and then moved to intercept him. The Invisible Man started and stood still. "Traitor!" cried the Voice, and suddenly the dressing-gown opened, and sitting down the Unseen began to disrobe. Kemp made three swift steps to the door, and forthwith the Invisible Man — his legs had vanished — sprang to his feet with a shout. Kemp flung the door open.

As it opened, there came a sound of hurrying feet downstairs and voices.

With a quick movement Kemp thrust the Invisible Man back, sprang aside, and slammed the door. The key was outside and ready. In another moment Griffin would have been alone in the belvedere study, a prisoner. Save for one little thing. The key had been slipped in hastily that morning. As Kemp slammed the door it fell noisily upon the carpet.

Kemp's face became white. He tried to grip the door handle with both hands. For a moment he stood lugging. Then the door gave six inches. But he got it closed again. The second time it was jerked a foot wide, and the dressing-gown came wedging itself into the opening. His throat was gripped by invisible fingers, and he left his hold on the handle to defend himself. He was forced back, tripped and pitched heavily into the corner of the landing. The empty dressing-gown was flung on the top of him.

Halfway up the staircase was Colonel Adye, the recipient of Kemp's letter, the chief of the Burdock police. He was staring aghast at the sudden appearance of Kemp, followed by the extraordinary sight of clothing tossing empty in the air. He saw Kemp felled, and struggling to his feet. He saw him rush forward, and go down again, felled like an ox.

Then suddenly he was struck violently. By nothing! A vast weight, it seemed, leapt upon him, and he was hurled headlong down the staircase, with a grip at his throat and a knee in his groin. An invisible foot trod on his back, a ghostly patter passed downstairs, he heard the two police officers in the hall shout and run, and the front door of the house slammed violently.

He rolled over and sat up star-

ing. He saw, staggering down the staircase, Kemp, dusty and dishevelled, one side of his face white from a blow, his lip bleeding, holding a pink dressing-gown and some underclothing in his arms.

"My God!" cried Kemp, "the game's up! He's gone!"

CHAPTER 25

THE HUNTING OF THE INVISIBLE MAN

FOR a space Kemp was too inarticulate to make Adye understand the swift things that had just happened. The two men stood on the landing, Kemp speaking swiftly, the grotesque swathings of Griffin still on his arm. But presently Adye began to grasp something of the situation.

"He's mad," said Kemp; "inhuman. He is pure selfishness. He thinks of nothing but his own advantage, his own safety. I have listened to such a story this morning of brutal self-seeking! He has wounded men. He will kill them unless we can prevent him. He will create a panic. Nothing can stop him. He is going out now — furious!"

"He must be caught," said Adye. "That is certain."

"But how?" cried Kemp, and suddenly became full of ideas. "You must begin at once. You must set every available man to work. You must prevent his leaving this district. Once he gets away he may go through the countryside as he wills, killing and maiming. He dreams of a reign of terror! A reign of terror, I tell you. You must set a watch on trains and roads and shipping. The garrison must help. You must wire for help. The only thing that may keep him here is the thought of recovering some books of notes he counts of value. I will tell you of that! There is a man in your police station — Marvel."

"I know," said Adye, "I know. Those books — yes."

"And you must prevent him from eating or sleeping; day and night the country must be astir for him. Food must be locked up and secured, all food, so that he will have to break his way to it. The houses everywhere must be barred against him. Heaven send us cold nights and rain! The whole country-side must begin hunting and keep hunting. I tell you, Adye, he is a danger, a disaster; unless he is pinned and secured, it is frightful to think of the things that may happen."

"What else can we do?" said Adye. "I must go down at once and begin organising. But why not come? Yes — you come too! Come, and we must hold a sort of council of war, — get Hopps to help — and the railway managers.

By jove! it's urgent. Come along — tell me as we go. What else is there we can do? Put that stuff down."

In another moment Adye was leading the way downstairs. They found the front door open and the policemen standing outside staring at empty air. "He's got away, sir," said one.

"We must go to the central station at once," said Adye. "One of you go on down and get a cab to come up and meet us — quickly. And now, Kemp, what else?"

"Dogs," said Kemp. "Get dogs. They don't see him, but they wind him. Get dogs."

"Good," said Adye. "It's not generally known, but the prison officials over at Halstead know a man with bloodhounds. Dogs. What else?"

"Bear in mind," said Kemp, "his food shows. After eating, his food shows until it is assimilated. So that he has to hide after eating. You must keep on beating — every thicket, every quiet corner. And put all weapons, all implements that might be weapons, away. He can't carry such things for long. And what he can snatch up and strike men with must be hidden away."

"Good again," said Adye. "We shall have him yet!"

"And on the roads," said Kemp, and hesitated.

"Yes?" said Adye.

"Powdered glass," said Kemp. "It's cruel, I know. But think of what he may do!"

Adye drew the air in between his teeth sharply. "It's unsportsmanlike. I don't know. But I'll have powdered glass got ready. If he goes too far — "

"The man's become inhuman, I tell you," said Kemp. "I am as sure he will establish a reign of terror — so soon as he has got over the emotions of this escape — as I am sure I am talking to you. Our only chance is to be ahead. He has cut himself off from his kind. His blood be upon his own head."

CHAPTER 26

THE WICKSTEED
MURDER

THE INVISIBLE MAN seems to have rushed out of Kemp's house in a state of blind fury. A little child playing near Kemp's gateway was violently caught up and thrown aside, so that its ankle was broken, and thereafter for some hours the Invisible Man passed out of human perceptions. No one knows where he went nor what he did. But one can imagine him hurrying through the hot June forenoon, up the hill and on to the open downland behind Port Burdock, raging and despairing at his intolerable fate, and sheltering at last, heated and

weary, amid the thickets of Hin-
tondean, to piece together again
his shattered schemes against his
species. That seems the most
probable refuge for him, for
there it was he re-asserted himself
in a grimly tragical manner about
two in the afternoon.

One wonders what his state of
mind may have been during that
time, and what plans he devised.
No doubt he was almost ecstati-
cally exasperated by Kemp's
treachery, and though we may
be able to understand the motives
that led to that deceit, we may
still imagine and even sympathise
a little with the fury the at-
tempted surprise must have occa-
sioned. Perhaps something of the
stunned astonishment of his Ox-
ford Street experiences may have
returned to him, for evidently
he had counted on Kemp's co-
operation in his brutal dream of
a terrorised world. At any rate he
vanished from human ken about
midday, and no living witness can
tell what he did until about half-
past two. It was a fortunate thing,
perhaps, for humanity, but for
him it was a fatal inaction.

During that time a growing
multitude of men scattered over
the countryside were busy. In the
morning he had still been simply
a legend, a terror; in the after-
noon, by virtue chiefly of Kemp's
drily worded proclamation, he
was presented as a tangible an-
tagonist, to be wounded, cap-
tured, or overcome, and the coun-
tryside began organising itself
with inconceivable rapidity. By
two o'clock even he might still
have removed himself out of the
district by getting aboard a train,
but after two that became im-
possible. Every passenger train
along the lines on a great paral-
lelogram between Southampton,
Manchester, Brighton, and Hor-
sham, travelled with locked doors,
and the goods traffic was almost
entirely suspended. And in a
great circle of twenty miles round
Port Burdock, men armed with
guns and bludgeons were pres-
ently setting out in groups of
three and four, with dogs, to beat
the roads and fields.

Mounted policemen rode along
the country lanes, stopping at
every cottage and warning the
people to lock up their houses,
and keep indoors unless they
were armed, and all the elemen-
tary schools had broken up by
three o'clock, and the children,
scared and keeping together in
groups, were hurrying home.
Kemp's proclamation — signed in-
deed by Adye — was posted over
almost the whole district by four
or five o'clock in the afternoon.
It gave briefly but clearly all the
conditions of the struggle, the
necessity of keeping the Invisible
Man from food and sleep, the
necessity for incessant watchful-
ness and for a prompt attention
to any evidence of his movements.
And so swift and decided was the
action of the authorities, so
prompt and universal was the be-
lief in this strange being, that be-
fore nightfall an area of several
hundred square miles was in a
stringent state of siege. And be-
fore nightfall, too, a thrill of hor-
ror went through the whole
watching nervous countryside.
Going from whispering mouth to
mouth, swift and certain over the

length and breadth of the county, passed the story of the murder of Mr. Wicksteed.

If our supposition that the Invisible Man's refuge was the Hintondean thickets, then we must suppose that in the early afternoon he sallied out again bent upon some project that involved the use of a weapon. We cannot know what the project was, but the evidence that he had the iron rod in hand before he met Wicksteed is to me at least overwhelming.

We can know nothing of the details of the encounter. It occurred on the edge of a gravel pit, not two hundred yards from Lord Burdock's Lodge gate. Everything points to a desperate struggle,— the trampled ground, the numerous wounds Mr. Wicksteed received, his splintered walking-stick; but why the attack was made—save in a murderous frenzy—it is impossible to imagine. Indeed the theory of madness is almost unavoidable. Mr. Wicksteed was a man of forty-five or forty-six, steward to Lord Burdock, of inoffensive habits and appearance, the very last person in the world to provoke such a terrible antagonist. Against him it would seem the Invisible Man used an iron rod dragged from a broken piece of fence. He stopped this quiet man, going quietly home to his midday meal, attacked him, beat down his feeble defences, broke his arm, felled him, and smashed his head to a jelly.

He must have dragged this rod out of the fencing before he met his victim; he must have been carrying it ready in his hand. Only two details beyond what has already been stated seem to bear on the matter. One is the circumstance that the gravel pit was not in Mr. Wicksteed's direct path home, but nearly a couple of hundred yards out of his way. The other is the assertion of a little girl to the effect that, going to her afternoon school, she saw the murdered man " *trotting* " in a peculiar manner across a field towards the gravel pit. Her pantomime of his action suggests a man pursuing something on the ground before him and striking at it ever and again with his walking-stick. She was the last person to see him alive. He passed out of her sight to his death, the struggle being hidden from her only by a clump of beech trees and a slight depression in the ground.

Now this, to the present writer's mind at least, lifts the murder out of the realm of the absolutely wanton. We may imagine that Griffin had taken the rod as a weapon indeed, but without any deliberate intention of using it in murder. Wicksteed may then have come by and noticed this rod inexplicably moving through the air. Without any thought of the Invisible Man—for Port Burdock is ten miles away—he may have pursued it. It is quite conceivable that he may not even have heard of the Invisible Man. One can then imagine the Invisible Man making off—quietly in order to avoid discovering his presence in the neighbourhood, and Wicksteed, excited and curious, pursuing this unaccountably

locomotive object — finally striking at it.

No doubt the Invisible Man could easily have distanced his middle-aged pursuer under ordinary circumstances, but the position in which Wicksteed's body was found suggests that he had the ill luck to drive his quarry into a corner between a drift of stinging nettles and the gravel pit. To those who appreciate the extraordinary irascibility of the Invisible Man, the rest of the encounter will be easy to imagine.

But this is pure hypothesis. The only undeniable facts — for stories of children are often unreliable — are the discovery of Wicksteed's body, done to death, and of the blood-stained iron rod flung among the nettles. The abandonment of the rod by Griffin, suggests that in the emotional excitement of the affair, the purpose for which he took it — if he had a purpose — was abandoned. He was certainly an intensely egotistical and unfeeling man, but the sight of his victim, his first victim, bloody and pitiful at his feet, may have released some long pent fountain of remorse to flood for a time whatever scheme of action he had contrived.

After the murder of Mr. Wicksteed, he would seem to have struck across the country towards the downland. There is a story of a voice heard about sunset by a couple of men in a field near Fern Bottom. It was wailing and laughing, sobbing and groaning, and ever and again it shouted. It must have been queer hearing. It drove up across the middle of a clover field and died away towards the hills.

That afternoon the Invisible Man must have learnt something of the rapid use Kemp had made of his confidences. He must have found houses locked and secured; he may have loitered about railway stations and prowled about inns, and no doubt he read the proclamations and realised something of the nature of the campaign against him. And as the evening advanced, the fields became dotted here and there with groups of three or four men, and noisy with the yelping of dogs. These men-hunters had particular instructions as to the way they should support one another in the case of an encounter. He avoided them all. We may understand something of his exasperation, and it could have been none the less because he himself had supplied the information that was being used so remorselessly against him. For that day at least he lost heart; for nearly twenty-four hours, save when he turned on Wicksteed, he was a hunted man. In the night, he must have eaten and slept; for in the morning he was himself again, active, powerful, angry, and malignant, prepared for his last great struggle against the world.

CHAPTER 27

THE SIEGE OF KEMP'S HOUSE

KEMP read a strange missive, written in pencil on a greasy sheet of paper.

"You have been amazingly energetic and clever," this letter ran, "though what you stand to gain by it I cannot imagine. You are against me. For a whole day you have chased me; you have tried to rob me of a night's rest. But I have had food in spite of you, I have slept in spite of you, and the game is only beginning. The game is only beginning. There is nothing for it, but to start the Terror. This announces the first day of the Terror. Port Burdock is no longer under the Queen tell your Colonel of Police, and the rest of them; it is under me — the Terror! This is day one of year one of the new epoch — the Epoch of the Invisible Man. I am Invisible Man the First. To begin with the rule will be easy. The first day there will be one execution for the sake of example — a man named Kemp. Death starts for him to-day. He may lock himself away, hide himself away, get guards about him, put on armour if he likes; Death, the unseen Death, is coming. Let him take precautions; it will impress my people. Death starts from the pillar-box by midday. The letter will fall in as the postman comes along, then off! The game begins. Death starts. Help him not, my people, lest Death fall upon you also. To-day Kemp is to die."

Kemp read this letter twice. "It's no hoax," he said. "That's his voice! And he means it."

He turned the folded sheet over and saw on the addressed side of it the postmark Hintondean, and the prosaic detail, "2d. to pay."

He got up, leaving his lunch unfinished — the letter had come by the one o'clock post — and went into his study. He rang for his housekeeper, and told her to go round the house at once, examine all the fastenings of the windows, and close all the shutters. He closed the shutters of his study himself. From a locked drawer in his bedroom he took a little revolver, examined it carefully, and put it into the pocket of his lounge jacket. He wrote a number of brief notes, one to Colonel Adye, gave them to his servant to take, with explicit instructions as to her way of leaving the house. "There is no danger," he said, and added a mental reservation, "to you." He remained meditative for a space after doing this, and then returned to his cooling lunch.

He ate with gaps of thought. Finally he struck the table sharply. "We will have him!" he said; "and I am the bait. He will come too far."

He went up to the belvedere, carefully shutting every door after him. "It's a game," he said, "an odd game — but the chances are all for me, Mr. Griffin, in spite of your invisibility. Griffin *contra mundum* — with a vengeance!"

He stood at the window staring at the hot hillside. "He must get food every day — and I don't envy him. Did he really sleep last night? Out in the open somewhere — secure from collisions. I wish we could get some good cold wet weather instead of the heat.

"He may be watching me now."

He went close to the window. Something rapped smartly against the brickwork over the frame, and made him start violently.

"I'm getting nervous," said Kemp. But it was five minutes before he went to the window again. "It must have been a sparrow," he said.

Presently he heard the front-door bell ringing, and hurried downstairs. He unbolted and unlocked the door, examined the chain, put it up, and opened cautiously without showing himself. A familiar voice hailed him. It was Adye.

"Your servant's been assaulted, Kemp," he said round the door.

"What!" exclaimed Kemp.

"Had that note of yours taken away from her. He's close about here. Let me in."

Kemp released the chain, and Adye entered through as narrow an opening as possible. He stood in the hall, looking with infinite relief at Kemp refastening the door. "Note was snatched out of her hand. Scared her horribly. She's down at the station. Hysterics. He's close here. What was it about?"

Kemp swore.

"What a fool I was," said Kemp. "I might have known. It's not an hour's walk from Hintondean. Already!"

"What's up?" said Adye.

"Look here!" said Kemp, and led the way into his study. He handed Adye the Invisible Man's letter. Adye read it and whistled softly. "And you —?" said Adye.

"Proposed a trap — like a fool," said Kemp, "and sent my proposal out by a maid servant. To him."

Adye followed Kemp's profanity.

"He'll clear out," said Adye.

"Not he," said Kemp.

A resounding smash of glass came from upstairs. Adye had a silvery glimpse of a little revolver half out of Kemp's pocket. "It's a window, upstairs!" said Kemp, and led the way up. There came a second smash while they were still on the staircase. When they reached the study they found two of the three windows smashed, half the room littered with splintered glass, and one big flint lying on the writing table. The two men stopped in the doorway, contemplating the wreckage. Kemp swore again, and as he did so the third window went with a snap like a pistol, hung starred for a moment, and collapsed in jagged, shivering triangles into the room.

"What's this for?" said Adye.

"It's a beginning," said Kemp.

"There's no way of climbing up here?"

"Not for a cat," said Kemp.

"No shutters?"

"Not here. All the downstairs rooms — Hullo!"

Smash, and then whack of boards hit hard came from downstairs. "Confound him!" said Kemp. "That must be — yes — it's one of the bedrooms. He's going to do all the house. But he's a fool. The shutters are up, and the glass will fall outside. He'll cut his feet."

Another window proclaimed its destruction. The two men stood on the landing perplexed. "I have it!" said Adye. "Let me have a stick or something, and I'll go down to the station and get the bloodhounds put on. That ought to settle him! They're hard by — not ten minutes —"

Another window went the way of its fellows.

"You haven't a revolver?" asked Adye.

Kemp's hand went to his pocket. Then he hesitated. "I haven't one — at least to spare."

"I'll bring it back," said Adye, "you'll be safe here."

Kemp handed him the weapon. "Now for the door," said Adye.

As they stood hesitating in the hall, they heard one of the first-floor bedroom windows crack and clash. Kemp went to the door and began to slip the bolts as silently as possible. His face was a little paler than usual. "You must step straight out," said Kemp. In another moment Adye was on the doorstep and the bolts were dropping back into the staples. He hesitated for a moment, feeling more comfortable with his back against the door. Then he marched, upright and square, down the steps. He crossed the lawn and approached the gate. A little breeze seemed to ripple over the grass. Something moved near him. "Stop a bit," said a Voice, and Adye stopped dead and his hand tightened on the revolver.

"Well?" said Adye, white and grim, and every nerve tense.

"Oblige me by going back to the house," said the Voice, as tense and grim as Adye's.

"Sorry," said Adye a little hoarsely, and moistened his lips with his tongue. The Voice was on his left front, he thought. Suppose he were to take his luck with a shot?

"What are you going for?" said the Voice, and there was a quick movement of the two, and a flash of sunlight from the open lip of Adye's pocket.

Adye desisted and thought. "Where I go," he said slowly, "is my own business." The words were still on his lips, when an arm came round his neck, his back felt a knee, and he was sprawling backward. He drew clumsily and fired absurdly, and in another moment he was struck in the mouth and the revolver wrested from his grip. He made a vain clutch at a slippery limb, tried to struggle up and fell back. "Damn!" said Adye. The Voice laughed. "I'd kill you now if it wasn't the waste of a bullet," it said. He saw the revolver in mid-air, six feet off, covering him.

"Well?" said Adye, sitting up.

"Get up," said the Voice.

Adye stood up.

"Attention," said the Voice, and then fiercely, "Don't try any games. Remember I can see your face if you can't see mine. You've got to go back to the house."

"He won't let me in," said Adye.

"That's a pity," said the Invisible Man. "I've got no quarrel with you."

Adye moistened his lips again. He glanced away from the barrel of the revolver and saw the sea far off very blue and dark under the midday sun, the smooth green down, the white cliff of the Head, and the multitudinous town, and suddenly he knew that life was very sweet. His eyes came back to this little metal thing hanging between heaven and earth, six yards away. "What am I to do?" he said sullenly.

"What am *I* to do?" asked the Invisible Man. "You will get help. The only thing is for you to go back."

"I will try. If he lets me in will you promise not to rush the door?"

"I've got no quarrel with you," said the Voice.

Kemp had hurried upstairs after letting Adye out, and now crouching among the broken glass and peering cautiously over the edge of the study window-sill, he saw Adye stand parleying with the Unseen. "Why doesn't he fire?" whispered Kemp to himself. Then the revolver moved a little and the glint of the sunlight flashed in Kemp's eyes. He shaded his eyes and tried to see the source of the blinding beam.

"Surely!" he said. "Adye has given up the revolver."

"Promise not to rush the door," Adye was saying. "Don't push a winning game too far. Give a man a chance."

"You go back to the house. I tell you flatly I will not promise anything."

Adye's decision seemed suddenly made. He turned towards the house, walking slowly with his hands behind him. Kemp watched him — puzzled. The revolver vanished, flashed again into sight, vanished again, and became evident on a closer scrutiny as a little dark object following Adye. Then things happened very quickly. Adye leapt backwards, swung round, clutched at this little object, missed it, threw up his hands and fell forward on his face, leaving a little puff of blue in the air. Kemp did not hear the sound of the shot. Adye writhed, raised himself on one arm, fell forward, and lay still.

For a space Kemp remained staring at the quiet carelessness of Adye's attitude. The afternoon was very hot and still, nothing seemed stirring in all the world save a couple of yellow butterflies chasing each other through the shrubbery between the house and the road gate. Adye lay on the lawn near the gate. The blinds of all the villas down the hill-road were drawn, but in one little green summer-house was a white figure, apparently an old man asleep. Kemp scrutinised the surroundings of the house for a glimpse of the re-

volver, but it had vanished. His eyes came back to Adye. The game was opening well.

Then came a ringing and knocking at the front door, that grew at last tumultuous, but pursuant to Kemp's instructions the servants had locked themselves into their rooms. This was followed by a silence. Kemp sat listening and then began peering cautiously out of the three windows, one after another. He went to the staircase head and stood listening uneasily. He armed himself with his bedroom poker, and went to examine the interior fastenings of the ground-floor windows again. Everything was safe and quiet. He returned to the belvedere. Adye lay motionless over the edge of the gravel just as he had fallen. Coming along the road by the villas were the housemaid and two policemen.

Everything was deadly still. The three people seemed very slow in approaching. He wondered what his antagonist was doing.

He started. There was a smash from below. He hesitated and went downstairs again. Suddenly the house resounded with heavy blows and the splintering of wood. He heard a smash and the destructive clang of the iron fastenings of the shutters. He turned the key and opened the kitchen door. As he did so, the shutters, split and splintering, came flying inward. He stood aghast. The window frame, save for one cross bar, was still intact, but only little teeth of glass remained in the frame. The shutters had been driven in with an axe, and now the axe was descending in sweeping blows upon the window frame and the iron bars defending it. Then suddenly it leapt aside and vanished. He saw the revolver lying on the path outside, and then the little weapon sprang into the air. He dodged back. The revolver cracked just too late, and a splinter from the edge of the closing door flashed over his head. He slammed and locked the door, and as he stood outside he heard Griffin shouting and laughing. Then the blows of the axe, with their splitting and smashing accompaniments, were resumed.

Kemp stood in the passage trying to think. In a moment the Invisible Man would be in the kitchen. This door would not keep him a moment, and then —

A ringing came at the front door again. It would be the policemen. He ran into the hall, put up the chain, and drew the bolts. He made the girl speak before he dropped the chain, and the three people blundered into the house in a heap, and Kemp slammed the door again.

"The Invisible Man!" said Kemp. "He has a revolver, with two shots — left. He's killed Adye. Shot him anyhow. Didn't you see him on the lawn? He's lying there."

"Who?" said one of the policemen.

"Adye," said Kemp.

"We came round the back way," said the girl.

"What's that smashing?" asked one of the policemen.

"He's in the kitchen — or will be. He has found an axe — "

Suddenly the house was full of the Invisible Man's resounding blows on the kitchen door. The girl stared towards the kitchen, shuddered, and retreated into the dining-room. Kemp tried to explain in broken sentences. They heard the kitchen door give.

"This way," cried Kemp, starting into activity, and bundled the policemen into the dining-room doorway.

"Poker," said Kemp, and rushed to the fender. He handed a poker to each policeman. He suddenly flung himself backward. "Whup!" said one policeman, ducked, and caught the axe on his poker. The pistol snapped its penultimate shot and ripped a valuable Sidney Cooper. The second policeman brought his poker down on the little weapon, as one might knock down a wasp, and sent it rattling to the floor.

At the first clash the girl screamed, stood screaming for a moment by the fireplace, and then ran to open the shutters — possibly with an idea of escaping by the shattered window.

The axe receded into the passage, and fell to a position about two feet from the ground. They could hear the Invisible Man breathing. "Stand away, you two," he said. "I want that man Kemp."

"We want you," said the first policeman, making a quick step forward and wiping with his poker at the Voice. The Invisible Man must have started back. He blundered into the umbrella stand. Then, as the policeman staggered with the swing of the blow he had aimed, the Invisible Man countered with the axe, the helmet crumpled like paper, and the blow sent the man spinning to the floor at the head of the kitchen stairs. But the second policeman, aiming behind the axe with his poker, hit something soft that snapped. There was a sharp exclamation of pain and the axe fell to the ground. The policeman wiped again at vacancy and hit nothing; he put his foot on the axe, and struck again. Then he stood, poker clubbed, listening intent for the slightest movement.

He heard the dining-room window open, and a quick rush of feet within. His companion rolled over and sat up with the blood running down between his eye and ear. "Where is he?" asked the man on the floor.

"Don't know. I've hit him. He's standing somewhere in the hall. Unless he's slipped past you. Doctor Kemp — sir."

Pause.

"Doctor Kemp," cried the policeman again.

The second policeman struggled to his feet. He stood up. Suddenly the faint pad of bare feet on the kitchen stairs could be heard. "Yap!" cried the first policeman and incontinently flung his poker. It smashed a little gas bracket.

He made as if he would pursue the Invisible Man downstairs. Then he thought better of it and stepped into the dining-room.

"Doctor Kemp," he began, and stopped short —

"Doctor Kemp's in here," he said, as his companion looked over his shoulder.

The dining-room window was wide open, and neither house-maid nor Kemp was to be seen.

The second policeman's opinion of Kemp was terse and vivid.

CHAPTER 28

THE HUNTER HUNTED

MR. HEELAS, Mr. Kemp's nearest neighbour among the villa holders, was asleep in his summer house when the siege of Kemp's house began. Mr. Heelas was one of the sturdy minority who refused to believe "in all this nonsense" about an Invisible Man. His wife, however, as he was to be reminded subsequently, did. He insisted upon walking about his garden just as if nothing was the matter, and he went to sleep in the afternoon in accordance with the custom of years. He slept through the smashing of the windows, and then woke up suddenly with a curious persuasion of something wrong. He looked across at Kemp's house, rubbed his eyes and looked again. Then he put his feet to the ground, and sat listening. He said he was damned, and still the strange thing was visible. The house looked as though it had been deserted for weeks — after a violent riot. Every window was broken, and every window, save those of the belvedere study, was blinded by the internal shutters.

"I could have sworn it was all right" — he looked at his watch — "twenty minutes ago."

He became aware of a measured concussion and the clash of glass, far away in the distance. And then, as he sat open-mouthed, came a still more wonderful thing. The shutters of the drawing-room window were flung open violently, and the housemaid in her outdoor hat and garments, appeared struggling in a frantic manner to throw up the sash. Suddenly a man appeared beside her, helping her — Dr. Kemp! In another moment the window was open, and the housemaid was struggling out; she pitched forward and vanished among the shrubs. Mr. Heelas stood up, exclaiming vaguely and vehemently at all these wonderful things. He saw Kemp stand on the sill, spring from the window, and reappear almost instantaneously running along a path in the shrubbery and stooping as he ran, like a man who evades observation. He vanished behind a laburnum, and appeared again clambering a fence that abutted on the open down. In a second he had tumbled over and was running at a tremendous pace down the slope towards Mr. Heelas.

"Lord!" cried Mr. Heelas,

struck with an idea; "it's that Invisible Man brute! It's right, after all!"

With Mr. Heelas to think things like that was to act, and his cook watching him from the top window was amazed to see him come pelting towards the house at a good nine miles an hour. Thought he wasn't afraid," said the cook. "Mary, just come here!" There was a slamming of doors, a ringing of bells, and the voice of Mr. Heelas bellowing like a bull. "Shut the doors, shut the windows, shut everything! the Invisible Man is coming!" Instantly the house was full of screams and directions, and scurrying feet. He ran to shut the French windows himself that opened on the veranda; as he did so Kemp's head and shoulders and knee appeared over the edge of the garden fence. In another moment Kemp had ploughed through the asparagus, and was running across the tennis lawn to the house.

"You can't come in," said Mr. Heelas, shutting the bolts. "I'm very sorry if he's after you, but you can't come in!"

Kemp appeared with a face of terror close to the glass, rapping and then shaking frantically at the French window. Then, seeing his efforts were useless, he ran along the veranda, vaulted the end, and went to hammer at the side door. Then he ran round by the side gate to the front of the house, and so into the hill-road. And Mr. Heelas staring from his window — a face of horror — had scarcely witnessed Kemp

vanish, ere the asparagus was being trampled this way and that by feet unseen. At that Mr. Heelas fled precipitately upstairs, and the rest of the chase is beyond his purview. But as he passed the staircase window, he heard the side gate slam.

Emerging into the hill-road, Kemp naturally took the downward direction, and so it was he came to run in his own person the very race he had watched with such a critical eye from the belvedere study only four days ago. He ran it well for a man out of training; and though his face was white and wet, his wits were cool to the last. He ran with wide strides, and wherever a patch of rough ground intervened, wherever there came a patch of raw flints, or a bit of broken glass shone dazzling, he crossed it and left the bare invisible feet that followed to take what line they would.

For the first time in his life Kemp discovered that the hill-road was indescribably vast and desolate, and that the beginnings of the town far below at the hill foot were strangely remote. Never had there been a slower or more painful method of progression than running. All the gaunt villas, sleeping in the afternoon sun, looked locked and barred; no doubt they were locked and barred — by his own orders. But at any rate they might have kept a lookout for an eventuality like this! The town was rising up now, the sea had dropped out of sight behind it, and people down below were stirring. A tram was

just arriving at the hill foot. Beyond that was the police station. Was that footsteps he heard behind him? Spurt.

The people below were staring at him, one or two were running, and his breath was beginning to saw in his throat. The tram was quite near now, and the Jolly Cricketers was noisily barring its doors. Beyond the tram were posts and heaps of gravel — the drainage works. He had a transitory idea of jumping into the tram and slamming the doors, and then he resolved to go to the police station. In another moment he had passed the door of the Jolly Cricketers, and was in the blistering fag end of the street, with human beings about him. The tram driver and his helper — arrested by the sight of his furious haste — stood staring with the tram horses unhitched. Further on the astonished features of navvies appeared above the mounds of gravel.

His pace broke a little, and then he heard the swift pad of his pursuer, and leapt forward again. "The Invisible Man!" he cried to the navvies, with a vague indicative gesture, and by an inspiration leapt the excavation and placed a burly group between him and the chase. Then abandoning the idea of the police station he turned into a little side street, rushed by a greengrocer's cart, hesitated for the tenth of a second at the door of a sweetstuff shop, and then made for the mouth of an alley that ran back into the main Hill Street again. Two or three little

children were playing here, and shrieked and scattered running at his apparition, and forthwith doors and windows opened and excited mothers revealed their hearts. Out he shot into Hill Street again, three hundred yards from the tramline end, and immediately he became aware of a tumultuous vociferation and running people.

He glanced up the street towards the hill. Hardly a dozen yards off ran a huge navvy, cursing in fragments and slashing viciously with a spade, and hard behind him came the tram conductor with his fists clenched. Up the street others followed these two, striking and shouting. Down towards the town, men and women were running, and he noticed clearly one man coming out of a shop-door with a stick in his hand. "Spread out! Spread out!" cried some one. Kemp suddenly grasped the altered condition of the chase. He stopped, and looked round, panting. "He's close here!" he cried. "Form a line across —"

"Aha!" shouted a voice.

He was hit hard under the ear, and went reeling, trying to face round towards his unseen antagonist. He just managed to keep his feet, and he struck a vain counter in the air. Then he was hit again under the jaw, and sprawled headlong on the ground. In another moment a knee compressed his diaphragm, and a couple of eager hands gripped his throat, but the grip of one was weaker than the other; he grasped the wrists, heard a cry

of pain from his assailant, and then the spade of the navvy came whirling through the air above him, and struck something with a dull thud. He felt a drop of moisture on his face. The grip at his throat suddenly relaxed, and with a convulsive effort Kemp loosed himself, grasped a limp shoulder, and rolled uppermost. He gripped the unseen elbows near the ground. "I've got him!" screamed Kemp. "Help! Help! hold! He's down! Hold his feet!"

In another second there was a simultaneous rush upon the struggle, and a stranger coming into the road suddenly might have thought an exceptionally savage game of Rugby football was in progress. And there was no shouting after Kemp's cry — only a sound of blows and feet and a heavy breathing.

Then came a mighty effort, and the Invisible Man threw off a couple of his antagonists and rose to his knees. Kemp clung to him in front like a hound to a stag, and a dozen hands gripped, clutched, and tore at the Unseen. The tram conductor suddenly got the neck and shoulders and lugged him back.

Down went the heap of struggling men again and rolled over. There was, I am afraid, some savage kicking. Then suddenly a wild scream of "Mercy! Mercy!" that died down swiftly to a sound like choking.

"Get back, you fools!" cried the muffled voice of Kemp, and there was a vigorous shoving back of stalwart forms. "He's hurt, I tell you. Stand back!"

There was a brief struggle to clear a space, and then the circle of eager eyes saw the doctor kneeling, as it seemed, fifteen inches in the air, and holding invisible arms to the ground. Behind him a constable gripped invisible ankles.

"Don't you leave go of en," cried the big navvy, holding a bloodstained spade; "he's shamming."

"He's not shamming," said the doctor, cautiously raising his knee; "and I'll hold him." His face was bruised and already going red; he spoke thickly because of a bleeding lip. He released one hand and seemed to be feeling at the face. "The mouth's all wet," he said. And then, "Good God!"

He stood up abruptly and then knelt down on the ground by the side of the thing unseen. There was a pushing and shuffling, a sound of heavy feet as fresh people turned up to increase the pressure of the crowd. People now were coming out of the houses. The doors of the Jolly Cricketers were suddenly wide open. Very little was said.

Kemp felt about, his hand seeming to pass through empty air. "He's not breathing," he said, and then, "I can't feel his heart. His side — ugh!"

Suddenly an old woman, peering under the arm of the big navvy, screamed sharply. "Looky there!" she said, and thrust out a wrinkled finger.

And looking where she pointed, every one saw, faint and transparent as though it was made of

glass, so that veins and arteries and bones and nerves could be distinguished, the outline of a hand, a hand limp and prone. It grew clouded and opaque even as they stared.

"Hullo!" cried the constable. "Here's his feet a-showing!"

And so, slowly, beginning at his hands and feet and creeping along his limbs to the vital centres of his body, that strange change continued. It was like the slow spreading of a poison. First came the little white nerves, a hazy grey sketch of a limb, then the glassy bones and intricate arteries, then the flesh and skin, first a faint fogginess and then growing rapidly dense and opaque. Presently they could see his crushed chest and his shoulders, and the dim outline of his drawn and battered features.

When at last the crowd made way for Kemp to stand erect, there lay, naked and pitiful on the ground, the bruised and broken body of a young man about thirty. His hair and beard were white—not grey with age but white with the whiteness of albinism, and his eyes were like garnets. His hands were clenched, his eyes wide open, and his expression was one of anger and dismay.

"Cover his face!" said a man. "For Gawd's sake, cover that face!" and three little children, pushing forward through the crowd, were suddenly twisted round and sent packing off again.

Some one brought a sheet from the Jolly Cricketers; and having covered him, they carried him into that house.

THE EPILOGUE

So ends the story of the strange and evil experiment of the Invisible Man. And if you would learn more of him you must go to a little inn near Port Stowe and talk to the landlord. The sign of the inn is an empty board save for a hat and boots, and the name is the title of this story. The landlord is a short and corpulent little man with a nose of cylindrical protrusion, wiry hair, and a sporadic rosiness of visage. Drink generously, and he will tell you generously of all the things that happened to him after that time, and of how the lawyers tried to do him out of the treasure found upon him.

"When they found they couldn't prove who's money was which, I'm blessed," he says, "if they didn't try to make me out a blooming treasure trove! Do I *look* like a Treasure Trove? And then a gentleman gave me a guinea a night to tell the story at the Empire Music 'all—just tell 'em in my own words—barring one."

And if you want to cut off the flow of his reminiscences abruptly, you can always do so by asking if there weren't three manuscript books in the story. He admits there were and proceeds to ex-

plain, with asseverations that everybody thinks *he* has 'em! But bless you! he hasn't. "The Invisible Man it was took 'em off to hide 'em when I cut and ran for Port Stowe. It's that Mr. Kemp put people on with the idea of *my* having 'em."

And then he subsides into a pensive state, watches you furtively, bustles nervously with glasses, and presently leaves the bar.

He is a bachelor man — his tastes were ever bachelor, and there are no women folk in the house. Outwardly he buttons — it is expected of him — but in his more vital privacies, in the matter of braces for example, he still turns to string. He conducts his house without enterprise, but with eminent decorum. His movements are slow, and he is a great thinker. But he has a reputation for wisdom and for a respectable parsimony in the village, and his knowledge of the roads of the South of England would beat Cobbett.

And on Sunday mornings, every Sunday morning all the year round, while he is closed to the outer world, and every night after ten, he goes into his bar parlour bearing a glass of gin faintly tinged with water; and having placed this down, he locks the door and examines the blinds, and even looks under the table. And then, being satisfied of his solitude, he unlocks the cupboard and a box in the cupboard and a

drawer in that box, and produces three volumes bound in brown leather, and places them solemnly in the middle of the table. The covers are weather-worn and tinged with an algal green — for once they sojourned in a ditch and some of the pages have been washed blank by dirty water. The landlord sits down in an armchair, fills a long clay pipe slowly, gloating over the books the while. Then he pulls one towards him and opens it, and begins to study it — turning over the leaves backwards and forwards.

His brows are knit and his lips move painfully. "Hex, little two up in the air, cross and a fiddle-de-dee. Lord! what a one he was for intellect!"

Presently he relaxes and leans back, and blinks through his smoke across the room at things invisible to other eyes. "Full of secrets," he says. "Wonderful secrets!

"Once I get the haul of them — Lord!

"I wouldn't do what *he* did; I'd just — well!" He pulls at his pipe.

So he lapses into a dream, the undying wonderful dream of his life. And though Kemp has fished unceasingly, and Adye has questioned closely, no human being save the landlord knows those books are there, with the subtle secret of invisibility and a dozen other strange secrets written therein. And none other will know of them until he dies.

"THE DESTROYING MONSTERS FROM MARS WRECK THE RAILWAYS."

Drawn by Warwick Goble, 1897 for *THE WAR OF THE WORLDS.*

"IN A GROUP ROUND THE MOUTH WERE SIXTEEN SLENDER, ALMOST WHIP-LIKE TENTACLES, ARRANGED IN TWO BUNCHES OF EIGHT EACH."

Drawn by Warwick Goble, 1897 for *THE WAR OF THE WORLDS.*

THE WAR OF THE WORLDS

But who shall dwell in these worlds if they be inhabited? ... Are we or they
Lords of the World? ... And how are all things made for man? –
 KEPLER
(quoted in *The Anatomy of Melancholy*).

Book I: *The Coming of the Martians*

CHAPTER 1

THE EVE OF THE WAR

No one would have believed in the last years of the nineteenth century that this world was being watched keenly and closely by intelligences greater than man's and yet as mortal as his own; that as men busied themselves about their various concerns they were scrutinised and studied, perhaps almost as narrowly as a man with a microscope might scrutinise the transient creatures that swarm and multiply in a drop of water. With infinite complacency men went to and fro over this globe about their little affairs, serene in their assurance of their empire over matter. It is possible that the infusoria under the microscope do the same. No one gave a thought to the older worlds of space as sources of human danger, or thought of them only to dismiss the idea of life upon them as impossible or improbable. It is curious to recall some of the mental habits of those departed days. At most, terrestrial men fancied there might be other men upon Mars, perhaps inferior to themselves and ready to welcome a missionary enterprise. Yet across the gulf of space, minds that are to our minds as ours are to those of the beasts that perish, intellects vast and cool and unsympathetic, regarded this earth with envious eyes, and slowly and surely drew their plans against us. And early in the twentieth century came the great disillusionment.

The planet Mars, I scarcely need remind the reader, revolves about the sun at a mean distance of 140,000,000 miles, and the light and heat it receives from the sun is barely half of that received by this world. It must be, if the nebular hypothesis has any truth, older than our world; and long before this earth ceased to be molten, life upon its surface must have begun its course. The fact that it is scarcely one-seventh of the volume of the earth must have accelerated its cooling to the temperature at which life could be-

gin. It has air and water and all that is necessary for the support of animated existence.

Yet so vain is man and so blinded by his vanity, that no writer, up to the very end of the nineteenth century, expressed any idea that intelligent life might have developed there far, or indeed at all, beyond its earthly level. Nor was it generally understood that since Mars is older than our earth, with scarcely a quarter of the superficial area and remoter from the sun, it necessarily follows that it is not only more distant from life's beginning but nearer its end.

The secular cooling that must some day overtake our planet has already gone far indeed with our neighbour. Its physical condition is still largely a mystery, but we know now that even in its equatorial region the mid-day temperature barely approaches that of our coldest winter. Its air is much more attenuated than ours, its oceans have shrunk until they cover but a third of its surface, and as its slow seasons change huge snow-caps gather and melt about either pole and periodically inundate its temperate zones. That last stage of exhaustion, which to us is still incredibly remote, has become a present-day problem for the inhabitants of Mars. The immediate pressure of necessity has brightened their intellects, enlarged their powers, and hardened their hearts. And looking across space with instruments, and intelligences such as we have scarcely dreamed of, they see, at its near-

est distance only 35,000,000 of miles sunward of them, a morning star of hope, our own warmer planet, green with vegetation and grey with water, with a cloudy atmosphere eloquent of fertility, with glimpses through its drifting cloud-wisps of broad stretches of populous country and narrow, navy-crowded seas.

And we men, the creatures who inhabit this earth, must be to them at least as alien and lowly as are the monkeys and lemurs to us. The intellectual side of man already admits that life is an incessant struggle for existence, and it would seem that this too is the belief of the minds upon Mars. Their world is far gone in its cooling and this world is still crowded with life, but crowded only with what they regard as inferior animals. To carry warfare sunward is, indeed, their only escape from the destruction that generation after generation creeps upon them.

And before we judge of them too harshly we must remember what ruthless and utter destruction our own species has wrought, not only upon animals, such as the vanished bison and the dodo, but upon its own inferior races. The Tasmanians, in spite of their human likeness, were entirely swept out of existence in a war of extermination waged by European immigrants, in the space of fifty years. Are we such apostles of mercy as to complain if the Martians warred in the same spirit?

The Martians seem to have calculated their descent with amaz-

ing subtlety — their mathematical learning is evidently far in excess of ours — and to have carried out their preparations with a well-nigh perfect unanimity. Had our instruments permitted it, we might have seen the gathering trouble far back in the nineteenth century. Men like Schiaparelli watched the red planet — it is odd, by-the-bye, that for countless centuries Mars has been the star of war — but failed to interpret the fluctuating appearances of the markings they mapped so well. All that time the Martians must have been getting ready.

During the opposition of 1894 a great light was seen on the illuminated part of the disk, first at the Lick Observatory, then by Perrotin of Nice, and then by other observers. English readers heard of it first in the issue of *Nature* dated August 2nd. I am inclined to think that this blaze may have been the casting of the huge gun, in the vast pit sunk into their planet, from which their shots were fired at us. Peculiar markings, as yet unexplained, were seen near the site of that outbreak during the next two oppositions.

The storm burst upon us six years ago now. As Mars approached opposition, Lavelle of Java set the wires of the astronomical exchange palpitating with the amazing intelligence of a huge outbreak of incandescent gas upon the planet. It had occurred towards midnight of the 12th; and the spectroscope, to which he had at once resorted, indicated a mass of flaming gas, chiefly hydrogen, moving with an enormous velocity towards this earth. This jet of fire had become invisible about a quarter past twelve. He compared it to a colossal puff of flame suddenly and violently squirted out of the planet, " as flaming gases rushed out of a gun."

A singularly appropriate phrase it proved. Yet the next day there was nothing of this in the papers except a little note in the *Daily Telegraph,* and the world went in ignorance of one of the gravest dangers that ever threatened the human race. I might not have heard of the eruption at all had I not met Ogilvy, the well-known astronomer, at Ottershaw. He was immensely excited at the news, and in the excess of his feelings invited me up to take a turn with him that night in a scrutiny of the red planet.

In spite of all that has happened since, I still remember that vigil very distinctly: the black and silent observatory, the shadowed lantern throwing a feeble glow upon the floor in the corner, the steady ticking of the clockwork of the telescope, the little slit in the roof — an oblong profundity with the star-dust streaked across it. Ogilvy moved about, invisible but audible. Looking through the telescope, one saw a circle of deep blue and the little round planet swimming in the field. It seemed such a little thing, so bright and small and still, faintly marked with transverse stripes, and slightly flattened from the perfect round. But so little it was, so silvery warm — a

pin's-head of light! It was as if it quivered, but really this was the telescope vibrating with the activity of the clockwork that kept the planet in view.

As I watched, the planet seemed to grow larger and smaller and to advance and recede, but that was simply that my eye was tired. Forty millions of miles it was from us — more than forty millions of miles of void. Few people realise the immensity of vacancy in which the dust of the material universe swims.

Near it in the field, I remember, were three faint points of light, three telescopic stars infinitely remote, and all around it was the unfathomable darkness of empty space. You know how that blackness looks on a frosty starlight night. In a telescope it seems far profounder. And invisible to me because it was so remote and small, flying swiftly and steadily towards me across that incredible distance, drawing nearer every minute by so many thousands of miles, came the Thing they were sending us, the Thing that was to bring so much struggle and calamity and death to the earth. I never dreamed of it then as I watched; no one on earth dreamed of that unerring missile.

That night, too, there was another jetting out of gas from the distant planet. I saw it. A reddish flash at the edge, the slightest projection of the outline just as the chronometer struck midnight; and at that I told Ogilvy and he took my place. The night was warm and I was thirsty, and I went, stretching my legs clumsily and feeling my way in the darkness, to the little table where the siphon stood, while Ogilvy exclaimed at the streamer of gas that came out towards us.

That night another invisible missile started on its way to the earth from Mars, just a second or so under twenty-four hours after the first one. I remember how I sat on the table there in the blackness, with patches of green and crimson swimming before my eyes. I wished I had a light to smoke by, little suspecting the meaning of the minute gleam I had seen and all that it would presently bring me. Ogilvy watched till one, and then gave it up; and we lit the lantern and walked over to his house. Down below in the darkness were Ottershaw and Chertsey and all their hundreds of people, sleeping in peace.

He was full of speculation that night about the condition of Mars, and scoffed at the vulgar idea of its having inhabitants who were signalling us. His idea was that meteorites might be falling in a heavy shower upon the planet, or that a huge volcanic explosion was in progress. He pointed out to me how unlikely it was that organic evolution had taken the same direction in the two adjacent planets.

"The chances against anything man-like on Mars are a million to one," he said.

Hundreds of observers saw the flame that night and the night after about midnight, and again the night after; and so for ten nights, a flame each night. Why the shots ceased after the tenth

no one on earth has attempted to explain. It may be the gases of the firing caused the Martians inconvenience. Dense clouds of smoke or dust, visible through a powerful telescope on earth as little grey, fluctuating patches, spread through the clearness of the planet's atmosphere and obscured its more familiar features.

Even the daily papers woke up to the disturbances at last, and popular notes appeared here, there, and everywhere concerning the volcanoes upon Mars. The serio-comic periodical *Punch*, I remember, made a happy use of it in the political cartoon. And, all unsuspected, those missiles the Martians had fired at us drew earthward, rushing now at a pace of many miles a second through the empty gulf of space, hour by hour and day by day, nearer and nearer. It seems to me now almost incredibly wonderful that, with that swift fate hanging over us, men could go about their petty concerns as they did. I remember how jubilant Markham was at securing a new photograph of the planet for the illustrated paper he edited in those days. People in these latter times scarcely realise the abundance and enterprise of our nineteenth-century papers. For my own part, I was much occupied in learning to ride the bicycle, and busy upon a series of papers discussing the probable developments of moral ideas as civilisation progressed.

One night (the first missile then could scarcely have been 10,000,000 miles away) I went for a walk with my wife. It was starlight, and I explained the Signs of the Zodiac to her, and pointed out Mars, a bright dot of light creeping zenithward, towards which so many telescopes were pointed. It was a warm night. Coming home, a party of excursionists from Chertsey or Isleworth passed us singing and playing music. There were lights in the upper windows of the houses as the people went to bed. From the railway station in the distance came the sound of shunting trains, ringing and rumbling, softened almost into melody by the distance. My wife pointed out to me the brightness of the red, green, and yellow signal lights hanging in a framework against the sky. It seemed so safe and tranquil.

CHAPTER 2

THE FALLING-STAR

THEN came the night of the first falling-star. It was seen early in the morning rushing over Winchester eastward, a line of flame high in the atmosphere. Hundreds must have seen it, and taken it for an ordinary falling-star. Albin described it as leaving a greenish streak behind it that glowed for some seconds. Denning, our greatest authority on

meteorites, stated that the height of its first appearance was about ninety or one hundred miles. It seemed to him that it fell to earth about one hundred miles east of him.

I was at home at that hour and writing in my study; and although my French windows face towards Ottershaw and the blind was up (for I loved in those days to look up at the night sky), I saw nothing of it. Yet this strangest of all things that ever came to earth from outer space must have fallen while I was sitting there, visible to me had I only looked up as it passed. Some of those who saw its flight say it travelled with a hissing sound. I myself heard nothing of that. Many people in Berkshire, Surrey, and Middlesex must have seen the fall of it, and, at most, have thought that another meteorite had descended. No one seems to have troubled to look for the fallen mass that night.

But very early in the morning poor Ogilvy, who had seen the shooting-star and who was persuaded that a meteorite lay somewhere on the common between Horsell, Ottershaw, and Woking, rose early with the idea of finding it. Find it he did, soon after dawn, and not far from the sand-pits. An enormous hole had been made by the impact of the projectile, and the sand and gravel had been flung violently in every direction over the heath, forming heaps visible a mile and a half away. The heather was on fire eastward, and a thin blue smoke rose against the dawn.

The Thing itself lay almost entirely buried in sand, amidst the scattered splinters of a fir-tree it had shivered to fragments in its descent. The uncovered part had the appearance of a huge cylinder, caked over and its outline softened by a thick scaly dun-coloured incrustation. It had a diameter of about thirty yards. He approached the mass, surprised at the size and more so at the shape, since most meteorites are rounded more or less completely. It was, however, still so hot from its flight through the air as to forbid his near approach. A stirring noise within its cylinder he ascribed to the unequal cooling of its surface; for at that time it had not occurred to him that it might be hollow.

He remained standing at the edge of the pit that the Thing had made for itself, staring at its strange appearance, astonished chiefly at its unusual shape and colour, and dimly perceiving even then some evidence of design in its arrival. The early morning was wonderfully still, and the sun, just clearing the pine-trees towards Weybridge, was already warm. He did not remember hearing any birds that morning, there was certainly no breeze stirring, and the only sounds were the faint movements from within the cindery cylinder. He was all alone on the common.

Then suddenly he noticed with a start that some of the grey clinker, the ashy incrustation that covered the meteorite, was falling off the circular edge of the end. It was dropping off in flakes and

raining down upon the sand. A large piece suddenly came off and fell with a sharp noise that brought his heart into his mouth.

For a minute he scarcely realised what this meant, and, although the heat was excessive, he clambered down into the pit close to the bulk to see the Thing more clearly. He fancied even then that the cooling of the body might account for this, but what disturbed that idea was the fact that the ash was falling only from the end of the cylinder.

And then he perceived that, very slowly, the circular top of the cylinder was rotating on its body. It was such a gradual movement that he discovered it only through noticing that a black mark that had been near him five minutes ago was now at the other side of the circumference. Even then he scarcely understood what this indicated, until he heard a muffled grating sound and saw the black mark jerk forward an inch or so. Then the thing came upon him in a flash. The cylinder was artificial—hollow—with an end that screwed out! Something within the cylinder was unscrewing the top!

"Good heavens!" said Ogilvy. "There's a man in it—men in it! Half roasted to death! Trying to escape!"

At once, with a quick mental leap, he linked the Thing with the flash upon Mars.

The thought of the confined creature was so dreadful to him that he forgot the heat, and went forward to the cylinder to help turn. But luckily the dull radia-tion arrested him before he could burn his hands on the still glowing metal. At that he stood irresolute for a moment, then turned, scrambled out of the pit, and set off running wildly into Woking. The time then must have been somewhere about six o'clock. He met a waggoner and tried to make him understand, but the tale he told and his appearance were so wild—his hat had fallen off in the pit—that the man simply drove on. He was equally unsuccessful with the potman who was just unlocking the doors of the public-house by Horsell Bridge. The fellow thought he was a lunatic at large and made an unsuccessful attempt to shut him into the tap-room. That sobered him a little; and when he saw Henderson, the London journalist, in his garden, he called over the palings and made himself understood.

"Henderson," he called, "you saw that shooting-star last night?"

"Well?" said Henderson.

"It's out on Horsell Common now."

"Good Lord!" said Henderson. "Fallen meteorite! That's good."

"But it's something more than a meteorite. It's a cylinder—an artificial cylinder, man! And there's something inside."

Henderson stood up with his spade in his hand.

"What's that?" he said. He was deaf in one ear.

Ogilvy told him all that he had seen. Henderson was a minute or so taking it in. Then he dropped

his spade, snatched up his jacket, and came out into the road. The two men hurried back at once to the common, and found the cylinder still lying in the same position. But now the sounds inside had ceased, and a thin circle of bright metal showed between the top and the body of the cylinder. Air was either entering or escaping at the rim with a thin, sizzling sound.

They listened, rapped on the scaly burnt metal with a stick, and, meeting with no response, they both concluded the man or men inside must be insensible or dead.

Of course the two were quite unable to do anything. They shouted consolation and promises, and went off back to the town again to get help. One can imagine them, covered with sand, excited and disordered, running up the little street in the bright sunlight just as the shop folks were taking down their shutters and people were opening their bedroom windows. Henderson went into the railway station at once, in order to telegraph the news to London. The newspaper articles had prepared men's minds for the reception of the idea.

By eight o'clock a number of boys and unemployed men had already started for the common to see the " dead men from Mars." That was the form the story took. I heard of it first from my newspaper boy about a quarter to nine when I went out to get my *Daily Chronicle*. I was naturally startled, and lost no time in going out and across the Ottershaw bridge to the sand-pits.

CHAPTER 3

ON HORSELL COMMON

I FOUND a little crowd of perhaps twenty people surrounding the huge hole in which the cylinder lay. I have already described the appearance of that colossal bulk, embedded in the ground. The turf and gravel about it seemed charred as if by a sudden explosion. No doubt its impact had caused a flash of fire. Henderson and Ogilvy were not there. I think they perceived that nothing was to be done for the present, and had gone away to breakfast at Henderson's house.

There were four or five boys sitting on the edge of the pit, with their feet dangling, and amusing themselves — until I stopped them — by throwing stones at the giant mass. After I had spoken to them about it, they began playing at " touch " in and out of the group of bystanders.

Among these were a couple of cyclists, a jobbing gardener I employed sometimes, a girl carrying a baby, Gregg the butcher and his little boy, and two or three loafers and golf caddies who were accustomed to hang about the railway station. There was very

little talking. Few of the common people in England had anything but the vaguest astronomical ideas in those days. Most of them were staring quietly at the big table-like end of the cylinder, which was still as Ogilvy and Henderson had left it. I fancy the popular expectation of a heap of charred corpses was disappointed at this inanimate bulk. Some went away while I was there, and other people came. I clambered into the pit and fancied I heard a faint movement under my feet. The top had certainly ceased to rotate.

It was only when I got thus close to it that the strangeness of this object was at all evident to me. At the first glance it was really no more exciting than an overturned carriage or a tree blown across the road. Not so much so, indeed. It looked like a rusty gas-float. It required a certain amount of scientific education to perceive that the grey scale of the Thing was no common oxide, that the yellowish-white metal that gleamed in the crack between the lid and the cylinder had an unfamiliar hue. "Extra-terrestrial" had no meaning for most of the onlookers.

At that time it was quite clear in my own mind that the Thing had come from the planet Mars, but I judged it improbable that it contained any living creature. I thought the unscrewing might be automatic. In spite of Ogilvy, I still believed that there were men in Mars. My mind ran fancifully on the possibilities of its containing manuscript, on the difficulties in translation that might arise, whether we should find coins and models in it, and so forth. Yet it was a little too large for assurance on this idea. I felt an impatience to see it opened. About eleven, as nothing seemed happening, I walked back, full of such thought, to my home in Maybury. But I found it difficult to get to work upon my abstract investigations.

In the afternoon the appearance of the common had altered very much. The early editions of the evening papers had startled London with enormous head-lines:

"A MESSAGE RECEIVED FROM MARS."
"REMARKABLE STORY FROM WOKING,"

and so forth. In addition, Ogilvy's wire to the Astronomical Exchange had roused every observatory in the three kingdoms.

There were half a dozen flys or more from the Woking station standing in the road by the sand-pits, a basket-chaise from Chobham, and a rather lordly carriage. Besides that, there was quite a heap of bicycles. In addition, a large number of people must have walked, in spite of the heat of the day, from Woking and Chertsey, so that there was altogether quite a considerable crowd — one or two gaily dressed ladies among the others.

It was glaringly hot, not a cloud in the sky nor a breath of wind, and the only shadow was that of the few scattered pine-trees. The burning heather had been extinguished, but the level

ground towards Ottershaw was blackened as far as one could see, and still giving off vertical streamers of smoke. An enterprising sweet-stuff dealer in the Chobham Road had sent up his son with a barrow-load of green apples and ginger-beer.

Going to the edge of the pit, I found it occupied by a group of about half a dozen men — Henderson, Ogilvy, and a tall, fair-haired man that I afterwards learned was Stent, the Astronomer Royal, with several workmen wielding spades and pickaxes. Stent was giving directions in a clear, high-pitched voice. He was standing on the cylinder, which was now evidently much cooler; his face was crimson and streaming with perspiration, and something seemed to have irritated him.

A large portion of the cylinder had been uncovered, though its lower end was still embedded. As soon as Ogilvy saw me among the staring crowd on the edge of the pit he called to me to come down, and asked me if I would mind going over to see Lord Hilton, the lord of the manor.

The growing crowd, he said, was becoming a serious impediment to their excavations, especially the boys. They wanted a light railing put up, and help to keep the people back. He told me that a faint stirring was occasionally still audible within the case, but that the workmen had failed to unscrew the top, as it afforded no grip to them. The case appeared to be enormously thick, and it was possible that the faint sounds we heard represented a noisy tumult in the interior.

I was very glad to do as he asked, and so become one of the privileged spectators within the contemplated enclosure. I failed to find Lord Hilton at his house, but I was told he was expected from London by the six o'clock train from Waterloo; and as it was then about a quarter past five, I went home, had some tea, and walked up to the station to waylay him.

CHAPTER 4

THE CYLINDER OPENS

When I returned to the common the sun was setting. Scattered groups were hurrying from the direction of Woking, and one or two persons were returning. The crowd about the pit had increased, and stood out black against the lemon-yellow of the sky — a couple of hundred people, perhaps. There were raised voices, and some sort of struggle appeared to be going on about the pit. Strange imaginings passed through my mind. As I drew nearer I heard Stent's voice:

" Keep back! Keep back! "

A boy came running towards me.

" It's a-movin'," he said to me as he passed — " a-screwin' and a-screwin' out. I don't like it. I'm a-goin' 'ome, I am."

I went on to the crowd. There were really, I should think, two or three hundred people elbowing and jostling one another, the one or two ladies there being by no means the least active.

" He's fallen in the pit! " cried some one.

" Keep back! " said several.

The crowd swayed a little, and I elbowed my way through. Everyone seemed greatly excited. I heard a peculiar humming sound from the pit.

" I say! " said Ogilvy; " help keep these idiots back. We don't know what's in the confounded thing, you know! "

I saw a young man, a shop assistant in Woking I believe he was, standing on the cylinder and trying to scramble out of the hole again. The crowd had pushed him in.

The end of the cylinder was being screwed out from within. Nearly two feet of shining screw projected. Somebody blundered against me, and I narrowly missed being pitched on to the top of the screw. I turned, and as I did so the screw must have come out, for the lid of the cylinder fell upon the gravel with a ringing concussion. I stuck my elbow into the person behind me, and turned my head towards the Thing again. For a moment that circular cavity seemed perfectly black. I had the sunset in my eyes.

I think every one expected to see a man emerge — possibly something a little unlike us terrestrial men, but in all essentials a man. I know I did. But, looking, I presently saw something stirring within the shadow: greyish billowy movements, one above another, and then two luminous disks — like eyes. Then something resembling a little grey snake, about the thickness of a walking-stick, coiled up out of the writhing middle, and wriggled in the air towards me — and then another.

A sudden chill came over me. There was a loud shriek from a woman behind. I half turned, keeping my eyes fixed upon the cylinder still, from which other tentacles were now projecting, and began pushing my way back from the edge of the pit. I saw astonishment giving place to horror on the faces of the people about me. I heard inarticulate exclamations on all sides. There was a general movement backwards. I saw the shopman struggling still on the edge of the pit. I found myself alone, and saw the people on the other side of the pit running off, Stent among them. I looked again at the cylinder, and ungovernable terror gripped me. I stood petrified and staring.

A big greyish rounded bulk, the size, perhaps, of a bear, was rising slowly and painfully out of the cylinder. As it bulged up and caught the light, it glistened like wet leather.

Two large dark-coloured eyes were regarding me steadfastly. The mass that framed them, the head of the thing, it was rounded, and had, one might say, a face. There was a mouth under

the eyes, the lipless brim of which quivered and panted, and dropped saliva. The whole creature heaved and pulsated convulsively. A lank tentacular appendage gripped the edge of the cylinder, another swayed in the air.

Those who have never seen a living Martian can scarcely imagine the strange horror of its appearance. The peculiar V-shaped mouth with its pointed upper lip, the absence of brow ridges, the absence of a chin beneath the wedge-like lower lip, the incessant quivering of this mouth, the Gorgon groups of tentacles, the tumultuous breathing of the lungs in a strange atmosphere, the evident heaviness and painfulness of movement due to the greater gravitational energy of the earth — above all, the extraordinary intensity of the immense eyes — were at once vital, intense, inhuman, crippled and monstrous. There was something fungoid in the oily brown skin, something in the clumsy deliberation of the tedious movements unspeakably nasty. Even at this first encounter, this first glimpse, I was overcome with disgust and dread.

Suddenly the monster vanished. It had toppled over the brim of the cylinder and fallen into the pit, with a thud like the fall of a great mass of leather. I heard it give a peculiar thick cry, and forthwith another of these creatures appeared darkly in the deep shadow of the aperture.

I turned and, running madly, made for the first group of trees, perhaps a hundred yards away; but I ran slantingly and stumbling, for I could not avert my face from these things.

There, among some young pine-trees and furze-bushes, I stopped, panting, and waited further developments. The common round the sand-pits was dotted with people, standing like myself in a half-fascinated terror, staring at these creatures, or rather at the heaped gravel at the edge of the pit in which they lay. And then, with a renewed horror, I saw a round, black object bobbing up and down on the edge of the pit. It was the head of the shopman who had fallen in, but showing as a little black object against the hot western sky. Now he got his shoulder and knee up, and again he seemed to slip back until only his head was visible. Suddenly he vanished, and I could have fancied a faint shriek had reached me. I had a momentary impulse to go back and help him that my fears overruled.

Everything was then quite invisible, hidden by the deep pit and the heap of sand that the fall of the cylinder had made. Any one coming along the road from Chobham or Woking would have been amazed at the sight — a dwindling multitude of perhaps a hundred people or more standing in a great irregular circle, in ditches, behind bushes, behind gates and hedges, saying little to one another and that in short, excited shouts, and staring, staring hard at a few heaps of sand. The barrow of ginger-beer stood, a queer derelict, black against the burning sky, and in the sand-pits

was a row of deserted vehicles with their horses feeding out of nose-bags or pawing the ground.

CHAPTER 5

THE HEAT-RAY

AFTER the glimpse I had had of the Martians emerging from the cylinder in which they had come to the earth from their planet, a kind of fascination paralysed my actions. I remained standing knee-deep in the heather, staring at the mound that hid them. I was a battle-ground of fear and curiosity.

I did not dare to go back towards the pit, but I felt a passionate longing to peer into it. I began walking, therefore, in a big curve, seeking some point of vantage and continually looking at the sandheaps that hid these newcomers to our earth. Once a leash of thin black whips, like the arms of an octopus, flashed across the sunset and was immediately withdrawn, and afterwards a thin rod rose up, joint by joint, bearing at its apex a circular disk that spun with a wobbling motion. What could be going on there?

Most of the spectators had gathered in one or two groups — one a little crowd towards Woking, the other a knot of people in the direction of Chobham. Evidently they shared my mental conflict. There were few near me. One man I approached — he was, I perceived, a neighbour of mine, though I did not know his name — and accosted. But it was scarcely a time for articulate conversation.

" What ugly *brutes*! " he said. " Good God! what ugly brutes! " He repeated this over and over again.

" Did you see a man in the pit? " I said; but he made no answer to that. We became silent, and stood watching for a time side by side, deriving, I fancy, a certain comfort in one another's company. Then I shifted my position to a little knoll that gave me the advantage of a yard or more of elevation, and when I looked for him presently he was walking towards Woking.

The sunset faded to twilight before anything further happened. The crowd far away on the left, towards Woking, seemed to grow, and I heard now a faint murmur from it. The little knot of people towards Chobham dispersed. There was scarcely an intimation of movement from the pit.

It was this, as much as anything, that gave people courage, and I suppose the new arrivals from Woking also helped to restore confidence. At any rate, as the dusk came on a slow, intermittent movement upon the sandpits began, a movement that seemed to gather force as the still-

ness of the evening about the cylinder remained unbroken. Vertical black figures in twos and threes would advance, stop, watch and advance again, spreading out as they did so in a thin irregular crescent that promised to enclose the pit in its attenuated horns. I, too, on my side began to move towards the pit.

Then I saw some cabmen and others had walked boldly into the sand-pits, and heard the clatter of hoofs and the gride of wheels. I saw a lad trundling off the barrow of apples. And then, within thirty yards of the pit, advancing from the direction of Horsell, I noted a little black knot of men, the foremost of whom was waving a white flag.

This was the Deputation. There had been a hasty consultation, and since the Martians were evidently, in spite of their repulsive forms, intelligent creatures, it had been resolved to show them, by approaching them with signals, that we too were intelligent.

Flutter, flutter, went the flag, first to the right, then to the left. It was too far for me to recognise any one there, but afterwards I learned that Ogilvy, Stent, and Henderson were with others in this attempt at communication. This little group had in its advance dragged inward, so to speak, the circumference of the now almost complete circle of people, and a number of dim black figures followed it at discreet distances.

Suddenly there was a flash of light, and a quantity of luminous greenish smoke came out of the pit in three distinct puffs, which drove up, one after the other, straight into the still air.

This smoke (or flame, perhaps, would be the better word for it) was so bright that the deep blue sky overhead and the hazy stretches of brown common towards Chertsey, set with black pine-trees, seemed to darken abruptly as these puffs arose, and to remain the darker after their dispersal. At the same time a faint hissing sound became audible.

Beyond the pit stood the little wedge of people with the white flag at its apex, arrested by these phenomena, a little knot of small vertical black shapes upon the black ground. As the green smoke arose, their faces flashed out pallid green, and faded again as it vanished. Then slowly the hissing passed into a humming, into a long, loud, droning noise. Slowly a humped shape rose out of the pit, and the ghost of a beam of light seemed to flicker out from it.

Forthwith flashes of actual flame, a bright glare leaping from one to another, sprang from the scattered group of men. It was as if some invisible jet impinged upon them and flashed into white flame. It was as if each man were suddenly and momentarily turned to fire.

Then, by the light of their own destruction, I saw them staggering and falling, and their supporters turning to run.

I stood staring, not as yet realising that this was death leaping

from man to man in that little distant crowd. All I felt was that it was something very strange. An almost noiseless and blinding flash of light, and a man fell headlong and lay still; and as the unseen shaft of heat passed over them, pine-trees burst into fire, and every dry furze-bush became with one dull thud a mass of flames. And far away towards Knaphill I saw the flashes of trees and hedges and wooden buildings suddenly set alight.

It was sweeping round swiftly and steadily, this flaming death, this invisible, inevitable sword of heat. I perceived it coming towards me by the flashing bushes it touched, and was too astounded and stupefied to stir. I heard the crackle of fire in the sand-pits and the sudden squeal of a horse that was as suddenly stilled. Then it was as if an invisible yet intensely heated finger were drawn through the heather between me and the Martians, and all along a curving line beyond the sand-pits the dark ground smoked and crackled. Something fell with a crash far away to the left where the road from Woking station opens out on the common. Forthwith the hissing and humming ceased, and the black, dome-like object sank slowly out of sight into the pit.

All this had happened with such swiftness that I had stood motionless, dumbfounded and dazzled by the flashes of light. Had that death swept through a full circle, it must inevitably have slain me in my surprise. But it passed and spared me, and left the night about me suddenly dark and unfamiliar.

The undulating common seemed now dark almost to blackness, except where its roadways lay grey and pale under the deep-blue sky of the early night. It was dark, and suddenly void of men. Overhead the stars were mustering, and in the west the sky was still a pale, bright, almost greenish blue. The tops of the pine-trees and the roofs of Horsell came out sharp and black against the western afterglow. The Martians and their appliances were altogether invisible, save for that thin mast upon which their restless mirror wobbled. Patches of bush and isolated trees here and there smoked and glowed still, and the houses towards Woking station were sending up spires of flame into the stillness of the evening air.

Nothing was changed save for that and a terrible astonishment. The little group of black specks with the flag of white had been swept out of existence, and the stillness of the evening, so it seemed to me, had scarcely been broken.

It came to me that I was upon this dark common, helpless, unprotected, and alone. Suddenly, like a thing falling upon me from without, came — fear.

With an effort I turned and began a stumbling run through the heather.

The fear I felt was no rational fear, but a panic terror not only of the Martians, but of the dusk and stillness all about me. Such an extraordinary effect in unman-

ning me it had that I ran weeping silently as a child might do. Once I had turned, I did not dare to look back.

I remember I felt an extraordinary persuasion that I was being played with, that presently, when I was upon the very verge of safety, this mysterious death — as swift as the passage of light — would leap after me from the pit about the cylinder and strike me down.

CHAPTER 6

THE HEAT–RAY IN THE CHOBHAM ROAD

It is still a matter of wonder how the Martians are able to slay men so swiftly and so silently. Many think that in some way they are able to generate an intense heat in a chamber of practically absolute non-conductivity. This intense heat they project in a parallel beam against any object they choose by means of a polished parabolic mirror of unknown composition, much as the parabolic mirror of a light-house projects a beam of light. But no one has absolutely proved these details. However it is done, it is certain that a beam of heat is the essence of the matter. Heat, and invisible, instead of visible light. Whatever is combustible flashes into flame at its touch, lead runs like water, it softens iron, cracks and melts glass, and when it falls upon water, incontinently that explodes into steam.

That night nearly forty people lay under the starlight about the pit, charred and distorted beyond recognition, and all night long the common from Horsell to Maybury was deserted and brightly ablaze.

The news of the massacre probably reached Chobham, Woking, and Ottershaw about the same time. In Woking the shops had closed when the tragedy happened, and a number of people, shop-people and so forth, attracted by the stories they had heard, were walking over the Horsell Bridge and along the road between the hedges that runs out at last upon the common. You may imagine the young people brushed up after the labours of the day, and making this novelty, as they would make any novelty, the excuse for walking together and enjoying a trivial flirtation. You may figure to yourself the hum of voices along the road in the gloaming. . . .

As yet, of course, few people in Woking even knew that the cylinder had opened, though poor Henderson had sent a messenger on a bicycle to the post-office with a special wire to an evening paper.

As these folks came out by twos and threes upon the open, they found little knots of people talk-

ing excitedly and peering at the spinning mirror over the sand-pits, and the new-comers were, no doubt, soon infected by the excitement of the occasion.

By half-past eight, when the Deputation was destroyed, there may have been a crowd of three hundred people or more at this place, besides those who had left the road to approach the Martians nearer. There were three policemen too, one of whom was mounted, doing their best, under instructions from Stent, to keep the people back and deter them from approaching the cylinder. There was some booing from those more thoughtless and excitable souls to whom a crowd is always an occasion for noise and horse-play.

Stent and Ogilvy, anticipating some possibilities of a collision, had telegraphed from Horsell to the barracks as soon as the Martians emerged, for the help of a company of soldiers to protect these strange creatures from violence. After that they returned to lead that ill-fated advance. The description of their death, as it was seen by the crowd, tallies very closely with my own impressions: the three puffs of green smoke, the deep humming note, and the flashes of flame.

But that crowd of people had a far narrower escape than mine. Only the fact that a hummock of heathery sand intercepted the lower part of the Heat-Ray saved them. Had the elevation of the parabolic mirror been a few yards higher, none could have lived to tell the tale. They saw the flashes and the men falling, and an invisible hand, as it were, lit the bushes as it hurried towards them through the twilight. Then, with a whistling note that rose above the droning of the pit, the beam swung close over their heads, lighting the tops of the beech-trees that line the road, and splitting the bricks, smashing the windows, firing the window-frames, and bringing down in crumbling ruin a portion of the gable of the house nearest the corner.

In the sudden thud, hiss, and glare of the igniting trees, the panic-stricken crowd seems to have swayed hesitatingly for some moments. Sparks and burning twigs began to fall into the road, and single leaves like puffs of flame. Hats and dresses caught fire. Then came a crying from the common. There were shrieks and shouts, and suddenly a mounted policeman came galloping through the confusion with his hands clasped over his head, screaming.

"They're coming!" a woman shrieked, and incontinently every one was turning and pushing at those behind, in order to clear their way to Woking again. They must have bolted as blindly as a flock of sheep. Where the road grows narrow and black between the high banks the crowd jammed, and a desperate struggle occurred. All that crowd did not escape; three persons at least, two women and a little boy, were crushed and trampled there, and left to die amid the terror and the darkness.

CHAPTER 7

HOW I REACHED HOME

FOR my own part, I remember
nothing of my flight except the
stress of blundering against trees
and stumbling through the
heather. All about me gathered
the invisible terrors of the Mar-
tians; that pitiless sword of heat
seemed whirling to and fro, flour-
ishing overhead before it de-
scended and smote me out of
life. I came into the road be-
tween the cross-roads and Horsell,
and ran along this to the cross-
roads.

At last I could go no further;
I was exhausted with the vio-
lence of my emotion and of my
flight, and I staggered and fell by
the wayside. That was near the
bridge that crosses the canal by
the gasworks. I fell and lay still.

I must have remained there
some time.

I sat up, strangely perplexed.
For a moment, perhaps, I could
not clearly understand how I
came there. My terror had fallen
from me like a garment. My hat
had gone, and my collar had
burst away from its fastener. A
few minutes before there had
only been three real things be-

fore me — the immensity of the
night and space and nature, my
own feebleness and anguish, and
the near approach of death. Now
it was as if something turned
over, and the point of view al-
tered abruptly. There was no
sensible transition from one state
of mind to the other. I was im-
mediately the self of every day
again — a decent, ordinary citi-
zen. The silent common, the im-
pulse of my flight, the starting
flames, were as if they had been
in a dream. I asked myself had
these latter things indeed hap-
pened? I could not credit it.

I rose and walked unsteadily
up the steep incline of the bridge.
My mind was blank wonder. My
muscles and nerves seemed
drained of their strength. I dare
say I staggered drunkenly. A
head rose over the arch, and the
figure of a workman carrying a
basket appeared. Beside him ran
a little boy. He passed me, wish-
ing me good-night. I was minded
to speak to him, but did not. I
answered his greeting with a
meaningless mumble and went
on over the bridge.

Over the Maybury arch a train,
a billowing tumult of white, fire-
lit smoke, and a long caterpillar
of lighted windows, went flying
south — clatter, clatter, clap, rap,
and it had gone. A dim group of
people talked in the gate of one
of the houses in the pretty little
row of gables that was called
Oriental Terrace. It was all so
real and so familiar. And that
behind me! It was frantic, fan-
tastic! Such things, I told myself,
could not be.

Perhaps I am a man of excep-

tional moods. I do not know how far my experience is common. At times I suffer from the strangest sense of detachment from myself and the world about me; I seem to watch it all from the outside, from somewhere inconceivably remote, out of time, out of space, out of the stress and tragedy of it all. This feeling was very strong upon me that night. Here was another side to my dream.

But the trouble was the blank incongruity of this serenity and the swift death flying yonder, not two miles away. There was a noise of business from the gasworks, and the electric-lamps were all alight. I stopped at the group of people.

"What news from the common?" said I.

There were two men and a woman at the gate.

"Eh?" said one of the men, turning.

"What news from the common?" I said.

"'Ain't yer just *been* there?" asked the men.

"People seem fair silly about the common," said the woman over the gate. "What's it all abart?"

"Haven't you heard of the men from Mars?" said I—"the creatures from Mars?"

"Quite enough," said the woman over the gate. "Thenks"; and all three of them laughed.

I felt foolish and angry. I tried and found I could not tell them what I had seen. They laughed again at my broken sentences.

"You'll hear more yet," I said, and went on to my home.

I startled my wife at the doorway, so haggard was I. I went into the dining-room, sat down, drank some wine, and so soon as I could collect myself sufficiently I told her the things I had seen. The dinner, which was a cold one, had already been served, and remained neglected on the table while I told my story.

"There is one thing," I said, to allay the fears I had aroused —"they are the most sluggish things I ever saw crawl. They may keep the pit and kill people who come near them, but they cannot get out of it. . . . But the horror of them!"

"Don't, dear!" said my wife, knitting her brows and putting her hand on mine.

"Poor Ogilvy!" I said. "To think he may be lying dead there!"

My wife at least did not find my experience incredible. When I saw how deadly white her face was, I ceased abruptly.

"They may come here," she said again and again.

I pressed her to take wine, and tried to reassure her.

"They can scarcely move," I said.

I began to comfort her and myself by repeating all that Ogilvy had told me of the impossibility of the Martians establishing themselves on the earth. In particular I laid stress on the gravitational difficulty. On the surface of the earth the force of gravity is three times what it is on the surface of Mars. A Martian, therefore, would weigh three times more than on Mars, albeit his muscular strength would be the same. His own body would

be a cope of lead to him. That, indeed, was the general opinion. Both *The Times* and the *Daily Telegraph,* for instance, insisted on it the next morning, and both overlooked, just as I did, two obvious modifying influences.

The atmosphere of the earth, we now know, contains far more oxygen or far less argon (whichever way one likes to put it) than does Mars. The invigorating influences of this excess of oxygen upon the Martians indisputably did much to counterbalance the increased weight of their bodies. And, in the second place, we all overlooked the fact that such mechanical intelligence as the Martian possessed was quite able to dispense with muscular exertion at a pinch.

But I did not consider these points at the time, and so my reasoning was dead against the chances of the invaders. With wine and food, the confidence of my own table, and the necessity of reassuring my wife, I grew by insensible degrees courageous and secure.

"They have done a foolish thing," said I, fingering my wineglass. "They are dangerous because, no doubt, they are mad with terror. Perhaps they expected to find no living things — certainly no intelligent living things.

"A shell in the pit," said I, "if the worst comes to the worst, will kill them all."

The intense excitement of the events had no doubt left my perceptive powers in a state of erethism. I remember that dinnertable with extraordinary vividness even now. My dear wife's sweet anxious face peering at me from under the pink lamp-shade, the white cloth with its silver and glass table furniture — for in those days even philosophical writers had many little luxuries — the crimson-purple wine in my glass, are photographically distinct. At the end of it I sat, tempering nuts with a cigarette, regretting Ogilvy's rashness, and denouncing the short-sighted timidity of the Martians.

So some respectable dodo in the Mauritius might have lorded it in his nest, and discussed the arrival of that shipful of pitiless sailors in want of animal food. "We will peck them to death to-morrow, my dear."

I did not know it, but that was the last civilised dinner I was to eat for very many strange and terrible days.

CHAPTER 8

FRIDAY NIGHT

THE MOST extraordinary thing to my mind, of all the strange and wonderful things that happened upon that Friday, was the dovetailing of the commonplace habits of our social order with the first beginnings of the series of events that was to topple that social order headlong. If on Fri-

day night you had taken a pair of compasses and drawn a circle with a radius of five miles round the Woking sand-pits, I doubt if you would have had one human being outside it, unless it were some relation of Stent or of the three or four cyclists or London people lying dead on the common, whose emotions or habits were at all affected by the newcomers. Many people had heard of the cylinder, of course, and talked about it in their leisure, but it certainly did not make the sensation that an ultimatum to Germany would have done.

In London that night poor Henderson's telegram describing the gradual unscrewing of the shot was judged to be a canard, and his evening paper, after wiring for authentication from him and receiving no reply — the man was killed — decided not to print a special edition.

Even within the five-mile circle the great majority of people were inert. I have already described the behaviour of the men and women to whom I spoke. All over the district people were dining and supping; working-men were gardening after the labours of the day, children were being put to bed, young people were wandering through the lanes love-making, students sat over their books.

Maybe there was a murmur in the village streets, a novel and dominant topic in the public-houses, and here and there a messenger, or even an eye-witness of the later occurrences, caused a whirl of excitement, a shouting, and a running to and fro; but for the most part the daily routine of working, eating, drinking, sleeping, went on as it had done for countless years — as though no planet Mars existed in the sky. Even at Woking station and Horsell and Chobham that was the case.

In Woking junction, until a late hour, trains were stopping and going on, others were shunting on the sidings, passengers were alighting and waiting, and everything was proceeding in the most ordinary way. A boy from the town, trenching on Smith's monopoly, was selling papers with the afternoon's news. The ringing impact of trucks, the sharp whistle of the engines from the junction, mingled with their shouts of "Men from Mars!" Excited men came into the station about nine o'clock with incredible tidings, and caused no more disturbance than drunkards might have done. People rattling Londonwards peered into the darkness outside the carriage windows, and saw only a rare, flickering, vanishing spark dance up from the direction of Horsell, a red glow and a thin veil of smoke driving across the stars, and thought that nothing more serious than a heath fire was happening. It was only round the edge of the common that any disturbance was perceptible. There were half a dozen villas burning on the Woking border. There were lights in all the houses on the common side of the three villages, and the people there kept awake till dawn.

A curious crowd lingered restlessly, people coming and going but the crowd remaining, both on the Chobham and Horsell

bridges. One or two adventurous souls, it was afterwards found, went into the darkness and crawled quite near the Martians; but they never returned, for now and again a light-ray, like the beam of a warship's searchlight, swept the common, and the Heat-Ray was ready to follow. Save for such, that big area of common was silent and desolate, and the charred bodies lay about on it all night under the stars, and all the next day. A noise of hammering from the pit was heard by many people.

So you have the state of things on Friday night. In the centre, sticking into the skin of our old planet Earth like a poisoned dart, was this cylinder. But the poison was scarcely working yet. Around it was a patch of silent common, smouldering in places, and with a few dark, dimly seen objects lying in contorted attitudes here and there. Here and there was a burning bush or tree. Beyond was a fringe of excitement, and farther than that fringe the inflammation had not crept as yet. In the rest of the world the stream of life still flowed as it had flowed for immemorial years. The fever of war that would presently clog vein and artery, deaden nerve and destroy brain, had still to develop.

All night long the Martians were hammering and stirring, sleepless, indefatigable, at work upon the machines they were making ready, and ever and again a puff of greenish-white smoke whirled up to the starlit sky.

About eleven a company of soldiers came through Horsell, and deployed along the edge of the common to form a cordon. Later a second company marched through Chobham to deploy on the north side of the common. Several officers from the Inkerman barracks had been on the common earlier in the day, and one, Major Eden, was reported to be missing. The colonel of the regiment came to the Chobham bridge and was busy questioning the crowd at midnight. The military authorities were certainly alive to the seriousness of the business. About eleven, the next morning's papers were able to say, a squadron of hussars, two Maxims, and about four hundred men of the Cardigan regiment started from Aldershot.

A few seconds after midnight the crowd in the Chertsey road, Woking, saw a star fall from heaven into the pine-woods to the north-west. It had a greenish colour, and caused a silent brightness like summer lightning. This was the second cylinder.

CHAPTER 9

THE FIGHTING BEGINS

SATURDAY lives in my memory as a day of suspense. It was a day of lassitude too, hot and close,

with, I am told, a rapidly fluctuating barometer. I had slept but little, though my wife had succeeded in sleeping, and I rose early. I went into my garden before breakfast and stood listening, but towards the common there was nothing stirring but a lark.

The milkman came as usual. I heard the rattle of his chariot, and I went round to the side-gate to ask the latest news. He told me that during the night the Martians had been surrounded by troops, and that guns were expected. Then — a familiar, reassuring note — I heard a train running towards Woking.

"They aren't to be killed," said the milkman, "if that can possibly be avoided."

I saw my neighbour gardening, chatted with him for a time, and then strolled in to breakfast. It was a most unexceptional morning. My neighbour was of opinion that the troops would be able to capture or to destroy the Martians during the day.

"It's a pity they make themselves so unapproachable," he said. "It would be curious to know how they live on another planet; we might learn a thing or two."

He came up to the fence and extended a handful of strawberries, for his gardening was as generous as it was enthusiastic. At the same time he told me of the burning of the pine-woods about the Byfleet Golf Links.

"They say," said he, "that there's another of those blessed things fallen there — number two. But one's enough, surely. This lot'll cost the insurance people a pretty penny before everything's settled." He laughed with an air of the greatest good-humour as he said this. The woods, he said, were still burning, and pointed out a haze of smoke to me. "They will be hot underfoot for days, on account of the thick soil of pine-needles and turf," he said, and then grew serious over "poor Ogilvy."

After breakfast, instead of working, I decided to walk down towards the common. Under the railway bridge I found a group of soldiers — sappers, I think, men in small round caps, dirty red jackets unbuttoned, and showing their blue shirts, dark trousers, and boots coming to the calf. They told me no one was allowed over the canal, and, looking along the road towards the bridge, I saw one of the Cardigan men standing sentinel there. I talked with these soldiers for a time; I told them of my sight of the Martians on the previous evening. None of them had seen the Martians, and they had but the vaguest ideas of them, so that they plied me with questions. They said that they did not know who had authorised the movements of the troops; their idea was that a dispute had arisen at the Horse Guards. The ordinary sapper is a great deal better educated than the common soldier, and they discussed the peculiar conditions of the possible fight with some acuteness. I described the Heat-Ray to them, and they began to argue among themselves.

"Crawl up under cover and rush 'em, say I," said one.

"Get aht!" said another. "What's cover against this 'ere 'eat? Sticks to cook yer! What we got to do is to go as near as the ground'll let us, and then drive a trench."

"Blow yer trenches! You always want trenches; you ought to ha' been born a rabbit, Snippy."

"'Ain't they got any necks, then?" said a third, abruptly — a little, contemplative, dark man, smoking a pipe.

I repeated my description.

"Octopuses," said he, "that's what I calls 'em. Talk about fishers of men — fighters of fish it is this time!"

"It ain't no murder killing beasts like that," said the first speaker.

"Why not shell the darned things strite off and finish 'em?" said the little dark man. "You carn tell what they might do."

"Where's your shells?" said the first speaker. "There ain't no time. Do it in a rush, that's my tip, and do it at once."

So they discussed it. After a while I left them, and went on to the railway station to get as many morning papers as I could.

But I will not weary the reader with a description of that long morning and of the longer afternoon. I did not succeed in getting a glimpse of the common, for even Horsell and Chobham church towers were in the hands of the military authorities. The soldiers I addressed didn't know anything; the officers were mysterious as well as busy. I found people in the town quite secure again in the presence of the military, and I heard for the first time from Marshall, the tobacconist, that his son was among the dead on the common. The soldiers had made the people on the outskirts of Horsell lock up and leave their houses.

I got back to lunch about two, very tired, for, as I have said, the day was extremely hot and dull; and in order to refresh myself I took a cold bath in the afternoon. About half-past four I went up to the railway station to get an evening paper, for the morning papers had contained only a very inaccurate description of the killing of Stent, Henderson, Ogilvy, and the others. But there was little I didn't know. The Martians did not show an inch of themselves. They seemed busy in their pit, and there was a sound of hammering and an almost continuous streamer of smoke. Apparently they were busy getting ready for a struggle. "Fresh attempts have been made to signal, but without success," was the stereotyped formula of the papers. A sapper told me it was done by a man in a ditch with a flag on a long pole. The Martians took as much notice of such advances as we should of the lowing of a cow.

I must confess the sight of all this armament, all this preparation, greatly excited me. My imagination became belligerent, and defeated the invaders in a dozen striking ways; something of my schoolboy dreams of battle and heroism came back. It hardly seemed a fair fight to me at that time. They seemed very helpless in that pit of theirs.

About three o'clock there be-

gan the thud of a gun at measured intervals from Chertsey or Addlestone. I learned that the smouldering pine-wood into which the second cylinder had fallen was being shelled, in the hope of destroying that object before it opened. It was only about five, however, that a field-gun reached Chobham for use against the first body of Martians.

About six in the evening, as I sat at tea with my wife in the summer-house talking vigorously about the battle that was lowering upon us, I heard a muffled detonation from the common, and immediately after a gust of firing. Close on the heels of that came a violent, rattling crash quite close to us, that shook the ground; and, starting out upon the lawn, I saw the tops of the trees about the Oriental College burst into smoky red flame, and the tower of the little church beside it slide down into ruin. The pinnacle of the mosque had vanished, and the roof-line of the college itself looked as if a hundred-ton gun had been at work upon it. One of our chimneys cracked as if a shot had hit it, flew, and a piece of it came clattering down the tiles and made a heap of broken red fragments upon the flower-bed by my study window.

I and my wife stood amazed. Then I realised that the crest of Maybury Hill must be within range of the Martians' Heat-Ray now that the college was cleared out of the way.

At that I gripped my wife's arm, and without ceremony ran her out into the road. Then I fetched out the servant, telling her I would go upstairs myself for the box she was clamouring for.

"We can't possibly stay here," I said; and as I spoke the firing reopened for a moment upon the common.

"But where are we to go?" said my wife in terror.

I thought, perplexed. Then I remembered her cousins at Leatherhead.

"Leatherhead!" I shouted above the sudden noise.

She looked away from me downhill. The people were coming out of their houses astonished.

"How are we to get to Leatherhead?" she said.

Down the hill I saw a bevy of hussars ride under the railway bridge; three galloped through the open gates of the Oriental College; two others dismounted, and began running from house to house. The sun, shining through the smoke that drove up from the tops of the trees, seemed blood-red, and threw an unfamiliar lurid light upon everything.

"Stop here," said I; "you are safe here;" and I started off at once for the Spotted Dog, for I knew the landlord had a horse and dog-cart. I ran, for I perceived that in a moment every one upon this side of the hill would be moving. I found him in his bar, quite unaware of what was going on behind his house. A man stood with his back to me, talking to him.

"I must have a pound," said the landlord, "and I've no one to drive it."

"I'll give you two," said I, over the stranger's shoulder.

"What for?"

"And I'll bring it back by midnight," I said.

"Lord!" said the landlord; "what's the hurry? I'm selling my bit of a pig. Two pounds, and you bring it back? What's going on now?"

I explained hastily that I had to leave my home, and so secured the dog-cart. At the time it did not seem to me nearly so urgent that the landlord should leave his. I took care to have the cart there and then, drove it off down the road, and, leaving it in charge of my wife and servant, rushed into my house and packed a few valuables, such plate as we had, and so forth. The beech-trees below the house were burning while I did this, and the palings up the road glowed red. While I was occupied in this way, one of the dismounted hussars came running up. He was going from house to house, warning people to leave. He was going on as I came out of my front-door, lugging my treasures, done up in a table-cloth. I shouted after him:

"What news?"

He turned, stared, bawled something about "crawling out in a thing like a dish cover," and ran on to the gate of the house at the crest. A sudden whirl of black smoke driving across the road hid him for a moment. I ran to my neighbour's door and rapped to satisfy myself of what I already knew, that his wife had gone to London with him and had locked up their house. I went in again, according to my promise, to get my servant's box, lugged it out, clapped it beside her on the tail of the dog-cart, and then caught the reins and jumped up into the driver's seat beside my wife. In another moment we were clear of the smoke and noise, and spanking down the opposite slope of Maybury Hill towards Old Woking.

In front was a quiet, sunny landscape, a wheatfield ahead on either side of the road, and the Maybury Inn with its swinging sign. I saw the doctor's cart ahead of me. At the bottom of the hill I turned my head to look at the hill-side I was leaving. Thick streamers of black smoke shot with threads of red fire were driving up into the still air, and throwing dark shadows upon the green tree-tops eastward. The smoke already extended far away to the east and west — to the Byfleet pine-woods eastward, and to Woking on the west. The road was dotted with people running towards us. And very faint now, but very distinct through the hot, quiet air, one heard the whirr of a machine-gun that was presently stilled, and an intermittent cracking of rifles. Apparently the Martians were setting fire to everything within range of their Heat-Ray.

I am not an expert driver, and I had immediately to turn my attention to the horse. When I looked back again the second hill had hidden the black smoke. I slashed the horse with the whip, and gave him a loose rein until

Woking and Send lay between us and that quivering tumult. I overtook and passed the doctor between Woking and Send.

CHAPTER 10

IN THE STORM

LEATHERHEAD is about twelve miles from Maybury Hill. The scent of hay was in the air through the lush meadows beyond Pyrford, and the hedges on either side were sweet and gay with multitudes of dog-roses. The heavy firing that had broken out while we were driving down Maybury Hill ceased as abruptly as it began, leaving the evening very peaceful and still. We got to Leatherhead without misadventure about nine o'clock, and the horse had an hour's rest while I took supper with my cousins and commended my wife to their care.

My wife was curiously silent throughout the drive, and seemed oppressed with forebodings of evil. I talked to her reassuringly, pointing out that the Martians were tied to the pit by sheer heaviness, and at the utmost could but crawl a little out of it; but she answered only in mono-syllables. Had it not been for my promise to the innkeeper, she would, I think, have urged me to stay in Leatherhead that night. Would that I had! Her face, I remember, was very white as we parted.

For my own part, I had been feverishly excited all day. Something very like the war-fever that occasionally runs through a civilised community had got into my blood, and in my heart I was not so very sorry that I had to return to Maybury that night. I was even afraid that that last fusillade I had heard might mean the extermination of our invaders from Mars. I can best express my state of mind by saying that I wanted to be in at the death.

It was nearly eleven when I started to return. The night was unexpectedly dark; to me, walking out of the lighted passage of my cousins' house, it seemed indeed black, and it was as hot and close as the day. Overhead the clouds were driving fast, albeit not a breath stirred the shrubs about us. My cousins' man lit both lamps. Happily, I knew the road intimately. My wife stood in the light of the doorway, and watched me until I jumped up into the dog-cart. Then abruptly she turned and went in, leaving my cousins side by side wishing me good hap.

I was a little depressed at first with the contagion of my wife's fears, but very soon my thoughts reverted to the Martians. At that time I was absolutely in the dark as to the course of the evening's fighting. I did not know even the

circumstances that had precipitated the conflict. As I came through Ockham (for that was the way I returned, and not through Send and Old Woking) I saw along the western horizon a blood-red glow, which, as I drew nearer, crept slowly up the sky. The driving clouds of the gathering thunderstorm mingled there with masses of black and red smoke.

Ripley Street was deserted, and except for a lighted window or so the village showed not a sign of life; but I narrowly escaped an accident at the corner of the road to Pyrford, where a knot of people stood with their backs to me. They said nothing to me as I passed. I do not know what they knew of the things happening beyond the hill, nor do I know if the silent houses I passed on my way were sleeping securely, or deserted and empty, or harassed and watching against the terror of the night.

From Ripley until I came through Pyrford I was in the valley of the Wey, and the red glare was hidden from me. As I ascended the little hill beyond Pyrford Church the glare came into view again, and the trees about me shivered with the first intimation of the storm that was upon me. Then I heard midnight pealing out from Pyrford Church behind me, and then came the silhouette of Maybury Hill, with its tree-tops and roofs black and sharp against the red.

Even as I beheld this a lurid green glare lit the road about me and showed the distant woods towards Addlestone. I felt a tug at the reins. I saw that the driving clouds had been pierced as it were by a thread of green fire, suddenly lighting their confusion and falling into the field to my left. It was the Third Falling-Star!

Close on its apparition, and blindingly violet by contrast, danced out the first lightning of the gathering storm, and the thunder burst like a rocket overhead. The horse took the bit between his teeth and bolted.

A moderate incline runs towards the foot of Maybury Hill, and down this we clattered. Once the lightning had begun, it went on in as rapid a succession of flashes as I have ever seen. The thunder-claps, treading one on the heels of another and with a strange crackling accompaniment, sounded more like the working of a gigantic electric machine than the usual detonating reverberations. The flickering light was blinding and confusing, and a thin hail smote gustily at my face as I drove down the slope.

At first I regarded little but the road before me, and then abruptly my attention was arrested by something that was moving rapidly down the opposite slope of Maybury Hill. At first I took it for the wet roof of a house, but one flash following another showed it to be in swift rolling movement. It was an elusive vision — a moment of bewildering darkness, and then, in a flash like daylight, the red masses of the Orphanage near the crest

of the hill, the green tops of the pine-trees, and this problematical object came out clear and sharp and bright.

And this Thing I saw! How can I describe it? A monstrous tripod, higher than many houses, striding over the young pine-trees, and smashing them aside in its career; a walking engine of glittering metal, striding now across the heather; articulate ropes of steel dangling from it, and the clattering tumult of its passage mingling with the riot of the thunder. A flash, and it came out vividly, heeling over one way with two feet in the air, to vanish and reappear almost instantly as it seemed, with the next flash, a hundred yards nearer. Can you imagine a milking-stool tilted and bowled violently along the ground? That was the impression those instant flashes gave. But instead of a milking-stool imagine it a great body of machinery on a tripod stand.

Then suddenly the trees in the pine-wood ahead of me were parted, as brittle reeds are parted by a man thrusting through them; they were snapped off and driven headlong, and a second huge tripod appeared, rushing, as it seemed, headlong towards me. And I was galloping hard to meet it! At the sight of the second monster my nerve went altogether. Not stopping to look again, I wrenched the horse's head hard round to the right, and in another moment the dog-cart had heeled over upon the horse; the shafts smashed noisily, and I was flung sideways and fell

heavily into a shallow pool of water.

I crawled out almost immediately, and crouched, my feet still in the water, under a clump of furze. The horse lay motionless (his neck was broken, poor brute!) and by the lightning flashes I saw the black bulk of the overturned dog-cart and the silhouette of the wheel still spinning slowly. In another moment the colossal mechanism went striding by me, and passed uphill towards Pyrford.

Seen nearer, the Thing was incredibly strange, for it was no mere insensate machine driving on its way. Machine it was, with a ringing metallic pace, and long, flexible, glittering tentacles (one of which gripped a young pine-tree) swinging and rattling about its strange body. It picked its road as it went striding along, and the brazen hood that surmounted it moved to and fro with the inevitable suggestion of a head looking about. Behind the main body was a huge mass of white metal like a gigantic fisherman's basket, and puffs of green smoke squirted out from the joints of the limbs as the monster swept by me. And in an instant it was gone.

So much I saw then, all vaguely for the flickering of the lightning, in blinding high lights and dense black shadows.

As it passed it set up an exultant deafening howl that drowned the thunder — "Aloo! aloo!" — and in another minute it was with its companion, half a mile away, stooping over something in

the field. I have no doubt this Thing in the field was the third of the ten cylinders they had fired at us from Mars.

For some minutes I lay there in the rain and darkness watching, by the intermittent light, these monstrous beings of metal moving about in the distance over the hedge-tops. A thin hail was now beginning, and as it came and went their figures grew misty and then flashed into clearness again. Now and then came a gap in the lightning, and the night swallowed them up.

I was soaked with hail above and puddle-water below. It was some time before my blank astonishment would let me struggle up the bank to a drier position, or think at all of my imminent peril.

Not far from me was a little one-roomed squatter's hut of wood, surrounded by a patch of potato-garden. I struggled to my feet at last, and, crouching and making use of every chance of cover, I made a run for this. I hammered at the door, but I could not make the people hear (if there were any people inside), and after a time I desisted, and, availing myself of a ditch for the greater part of the way, succeeded in crawling, unobserved by these monstrous machines, into the pine-wood towards Maybury.

Under cover of this I pushed on, wet and shivering now, towards my own house. I walked among the trees trying to find the footpath. It was very dark indeed in the wood, for the lightning was now becoming infrequent, and the hail, which was pouring down in a torrent, fell in columns through the gaps in the heavy foliage.

If I had fully realised the meaning of all the things I had seen I should have immediately worked my way round through Byfleet to Street Cobham, and so gone back to rejoin my wife at Leatherhead. But that night the strangeness of things about me, and my physical wretchedness, prevented me, for I was bruised, weary, wet to the skin, deafened and blinded by the storm.

I had a vague idea of going on to my own house, and that was as much motive as I had. I staggered through the trees, fell into a ditch and bruised my knees against a plank, and finally splashed out into the lane that ran down from the College Arms. I say splashed, for the storm water was sweeping the sand down the hill in a muddy torrent. There in the darkness a man blundered into me and sent me reeling back.

He gave a cry of terror, sprang sideways, and rushed on before I could gather my wits sufficiently to speak to him. So heavy was the stress of the storm just at this place that I had the hardest task to win my way up the hill. I went close up to the fence on the left and worked my way along its palings.

Near the top I stumbled upon something soft, and, by a flash of lightning, saw between my feet a heap of black broadcloth and a pair of boots. Before I could distinguish clearly how the man lay, the flicker of light had passed. I

stood over him waiting for the next flash. When it came, I saw that he was a sturdy man, cheaply but not shabbily dressed; his head was bent under his body, and he lay crumpled up close to the fence, as though he had been flung violently against it.

Overcoming the repugnance natural to one who had never before touched a dead body, I stooped and turned him over to feel for his heart. He was quite dead. Apparently his neck had been broken. The lightning flashed for a third time, and his face leaped upon me. I sprang to my feet. It was the landlord of the Spotted Dog, whose conveyance I had taken.

I stepped over him gingerly and pushed on up the hill. I made my way by the police-station and the College Arms towards my own house. Nothing was burning on the hill-side, though from the common there still came a red glare and a rolling tumult of ruddy smoke beating up against the drenching hail. So far as I could see by the flashes, the houses about me were mostly uninjured. By the College Arms a dark heap lay in the road.

Down the road towards Maybury Bridge there were voices and the sound of feet, but I had not the courage to shout or to go to them. I let myself in with my latch-key, closed, locked and bolted the door, staggered to the foot of the staircase, and sat down. My imagination was full of those striding metallic monsters, and of the dead body smashed against the fence.

I crouched at the foot of the staircase with my back to the wall, shivering violently.

CHAPTER 11

AT THE WINDOW

I HAVE already said that my storms of emotion have a trick of exhausting themselves. After a time I discovered that I was cold and wet, and with little pools of water about me on the stair-carpet. I got up almost mechanically, went into the dining-room and drank some whiskey, and then I was moved to change my clothes.

After I had done that I went upstairs to my study, but why I did so I do not know. The window of my study looks over the trees and the railway towards Horsell Common. In the hurry of our departure this window had been left open. The passage was dark, and, by contrast with the picture the window-frame enclosed, the side of the room seemed impenetrably dark. I stopped short in the doorway.

The thunderstorm had passed. The towers of the Oriental College and the pine-trees about it had gone, and very far away, lit by a vivid red glare, the com-

mon about the sand-pits was visible. Across the light, huge black shapes, grotesque and strange, moved busily to and fro.

It seemed indeed as if the whole country in that direction was on fire — a broad hill-side set with minute tongues of flame, swaying and writhing with the gusts of the dying storm, and throwing a red reflection upon the cloud-scud above. Every now and then a haze of smoke from some nearer conflagration drove across the window and hid the Martian shapes. I could not see what they were doing, nor the clear form of them, nor recognise the black objects they were busied upon. Neither could I see the nearer fire, though the reflections of it danced on the wall and ceiling of the study. A sharp, resinous tang of burning was in the air.

I closed the door noiselessly and crept towards the window. As I did so, the view opened out until, on the one hand, it reached to the houses about Woking station, and on the other to the charred and blackened pine-woods of Byfleet. There was a light down below the hill, on the railway, near the arch, and several of the houses along the Maybury road and the streets near the station were glowing ruins. The light upon the railway puzzled me at first; there were a black heap and a vivid glare, and to the right of that a row of yellow oblongs. Then I perceived this was a wrecked train, the fore-part smashed and on fire, the hinder carriages still upon the rails.

Between these three main centres of light, the houses, the train, and the burning country towards Chobham, stretched irregular patches of dark country, broken here and there by intervals of dimly glowing and smoking ground. It was the strangest spectacle, that black expanse set with fire. It reminded me, more than anything else, of the Potteries at night. At first I could distinguish no people at all, though I peered intently for them. Later I saw against the light of Woking station a number of black figures hurrying one after the other across the line.

And this was the little world in which I had been living securely for years, this fiery chaos! What had happened in the last seven hours I still did not know; nor did I know, though I was beginning to guess, the relation between these mechanical colossi and the sluggish lumps I had seen disgorged from the cylinder. With a queer feeling of impersonal interest I turned my desk-chair to the window, sat down, and stared at the blackened country, and particularly at the three gigantic black things that were going to and fro in the glare about the sand-pits.

They seemed amazingly busy. I began to ask myself what they could be. Were they intelligent mechanisms? Such a thing I felt was impossible. Or did a Martian sit within each, ruling, directing, using, much as a man's brain sits and rules in his body? I began to compare the things to human machines, to ask myself for the first time in my life how

an iron-clad or a steam-engine would seem to an intelligent lower animal.

The storm had left the sky clear, and over the smoke of the burning land the little fading pin-point of Mars was dropping into the west, when a soldier came into my garden. I heard a slight scraping at the fence, and rousing myself from the lethargy that had fallen upon me, I looked down and saw him dimly, clambering over the palings. At the sight of another human being my torpor passed, and I leaned out of the window eagerly.

"Hist!" said I, in a whisper.

He stopped astride of the fence in doubt. Then he came over and across the lawn to the corner of the house. He bent down and stepped softly.

"Who's there?" he said, also whispering, standing under the window and peering up.

"Where are you going?" I asked.

"God knows."

"Are you trying to hide?"

"That's it."

"Come into the house," I said.

I went down, unfastened the door, and let him in, and locked the door again. I could not see his face. He was hatless, and his coat was unbuttoned.

"My God!" he said, as I drew him in.

"What has happened?" I asked.

"What hasn't?" In the obscurity I could see he made a gesture of despair. "They wiped us out—simply wiped us out," he repeated again and again.

He followed me, almost mechanically, into the dining-room.

"Take some whiskey," I said, pouring out a stiff dose.

He drank it. Then abruptly he sat down before the table, put his head on his arms, and began to sob and weep like a little boy, in a perfect passion of emotion, while I, with a curious forgetfulness of my own recent despair, stood beside him, wondering.

It was a long time before he could steady his nerves to answer my questions, and then he answered perplexingly and brokenly. He was a driver in the artillery, and had only come into action about seven. At that time firing was going on across the common, and it was said the first party of Martians were crawling slowly towards their second cylinder under cover of a metal shield.

Later this shield staggered up on tripod legs and became the first of the fighting-machines I had seen. The gun he drove had been unlimbered near Horsell, in order to command the sand-pits, and its arrival it was that had precipitated the action. As the limber gunners went to the rear, his horse trod in a rabbit-hole and came down, throwing him into a depression of the ground. At the same moment the gun exploded behind him, the ammunition blew up, there was fire all about him, and he found himself lying under a heap of charred dead men and dead horses.

"I lay still," he said, "scared out of my wits, with the forequarter of a horse atop of me. We'd been wiped out. And the

smell — good God! Like burnt meat! I was hurt across the back by the fall of the horse, and there I had to lie until I felt better. Just like parade it had been a minute before — then stumble, bang, swish!

"Wiped out!" he said.

He had hid under the dead horse for a long time, peeping out furtively across the common. The Cardigan men had tried a rush, in skirmishing order, at the pit, simply to be swept out of existence. Then the monster had risen to its feet, and had begun to walk leisurely to and fro across the common among the few fugitives, with its headlike hood turning about exactly like the head of a cowled human being. A kind of arm carried a complicated metallic case, about which green flashes scintillated, and out of the funnel of this there smote the Heat-Ray.

In a few minutes there was, so far as the soldier could see, not a living thing left upon the common, and every bush and tree upon it that was not already a blackened skeleton was burning. The hussars had been on the road beyond the curvature of the ground, and he saw nothing of them. He heard the Maxims rattle for a time and then become still. The giant saved Woking station and its cluster of houses until the last; then in a moment the Heat-Ray was brought to bear, and the town became a heap of fiery ruins. Then the Thing shut off the Heat-Ray, and, turning its back upon the artilleryman, began to waddle away towards the smouldering pine-woods that sheltered the second cylinder. As it did so a second glittering Titan built itself up out of the pit.

The second monster followed the first, and at that the artilleryman began to crawl very cautiously across the hot heather ash towards Horsell. He managed to get alive into the ditch by the side of the road, and so escaped to Woking. There his story became ejaculatory. The place was impassable. It seems there were a few people alive there, frantic for the most part, and many burned and scalded. He was turned aside by the fire, and hid among some almost scorching heaps of broken wall as one of the Martian giants returned. He saw this one pursue a man, catch him up in one of its steely tentacles, and knock his head against the trunk of a pine-tree. At last, after nightfall, the artilleryman made a rush for it and got over the railway embankment.

Since then he had been skulking along towards Maybury, in the hope of getting out of danger Londonward. People were hiding in trenches and cellars, and many of the survivors had made off towards Woking village and Send. He had been consumed with thirst until he found one of the water mains near the railway arch smashed, and the water bubbling out like a spring upon the road.

That was the story I got from him, bit by bit. He grew calmer telling me and trying to make me see the things he had seen. He had eaten no food since mid-day, he told me early in his narrative,

and I found some mutton and bread in the pantry and brought it into the room. We lit no lamp for fear of attracting the Martians, and ever and again our hands would touch upon bread or meat. As he talked, things about us came darkly out of the darkness, and the trampled bushes and broken rose-trees outside the window grew distinct. It would seem that a number of men or animals had rushed across the lawn. I began to see his face, blackened and haggard, as no doubt mine was also.

When we had finished eating we went softly upstairs to my study, and I looked again out of the open window. In one night the valley had become a valley of ashes. The fires had dwindled now. Where flames had been there were now streamers of smoke; but the countless ruins of shattered and gutted houses and blasted and blackened trees that the night had hidden stood out now gaunt and terrible in the pitiless light of dawn. Yet here and there some object had had the luck to escape — a white railway signal here, the end of a green-house there, white and fresh amid the wreckage. Never before in the history of warfare had destruction been so indiscriminate and so universal. And shining with the growing light of the east, three of the metallic giants stood about the pit, their cowls rotating as though they were surveying the desolation they had made.

It seemed to me that the pit had been enlarged, and ever and again puffs of vivid green vapour streamed up out of it towards the brightening dawn — streamed up, whirled, broke, and vanished.

Beyond were the pillars of fire about Chobham. They became pillars of bloodshot smoke at the first touch of day.

CHAPTER 12

WHAT I SAW OF THE DESTRUCTION OF WEYBRIDGE AND SHEPPERTON

As the dawn grew brighter we withdrew from the window from which we had watched the Martians, and went very quietly downstairs.

The artilleryman agreed with me that the house was no place to stay in. He proposed, he said, to make his way Londonward, and thence rejoin his battery — No. 12, of the Horse Artillery. My plan was to return at once to Leatherhead; and so greatly had the strength of the Martians impressed me that I had determined to take my wife to Newhaven, and go with her out of the country forthwith. For I already perceived clearly that the country about London must inevitably be

the scene of a disastrous struggle before such creatures as these could be destroyed.

Between us and Leatherhead, however, lay the Third Cylinder, with its guarding giants. Had I been alone, I think I should have taken my chance and struck across country. But the artilleryman dissuaded me: "It's no kindness to the right sort of wife," he said, "to make her a widow"; and in the end I agreed to go with him, under cover of the woods, northward as far as Street Cobham before I parted with him. Thence I would make a big detour by Epsom to reach Leatherhead.

I should have started at once, but my companion had been in active service and he knew better than that. He made me ransack the house for a flask, which he filled with whiskey; and we lined every available pocket with packets of biscuits and slices of meat. Then we crept out of the house, and ran as quickly as we could down the ill-made road by which I had come overnight. The houses seemed deserted. In the road lay a group of three charred bodies close together, struck dead by the Heat-Ray; and here and there were things that people had dropped — a clock, a slipper, a silver spoon, and the like poor valuables. At the corner turning up towards the post-office a little cart, filled with boxes and furniture, and horseless, heeled over on a broken wheel. A cash-box had been hastily smashed open and thrown under the débris.

Except the lodge at the Or-phanage, which was still on fire, none of the houses had suffered very greatly here. The Heat-Ray had shaved the chimney-tops and passed. Yet, save ourselves, there did not seem to be a living soul on Maybury Hill. The majority of the inhabitants had escaped, I suppose, by way of the Old Woking road — the road I had taken when I drove to Leather-head — or they had hidden.

We went down the lane, by the body of the man in black, sodden now from the overnight hail, and broke into the woods at the foot of the hill. We pushed through these towards the rail-way without meeting a soul. The woods across the line were but the scarred and blackened ruins of woods; for the most part the trees had fallen, but a certain proportion still stood, dismal grey stems, with dark brown foliage instead of green.

On our side the fire had done no more than scorch the nearer trees; it had failed to secure its footing. In one place the wood-men had been at work on Satur-day; trees, felled and freshly trimmed, lay in a clearing, with heaps of sawdust by the sawing-machine and its engine. Hard by was a temporary hut, deserted. There was not a breath of wind this morning, and everything was strangely still. Even the birds were hushed, and as we hurried along I and the artilleryman talked in whispers and looked now and again over our shoul-ders. Once or twice we stopped to listen.

After a time we drew near the road, and as we did so we heard

the clatter of hoofs and saw through the tree-stems three cavalry soldiers riding slowly towards Woking. We hailed them, and they halted while we hurried towards them. It was a lieutenant and a couple of privates of the 8th Hussars, with a stand like a theodolite, which the artilleryman told me was a heliograph.

"You are the first men I've seen coming this way this morning," said the lieutenant. "What's brewing?"

His voice and face were eager. The men behind him stared curiously. The artilleryman jumped down the bank into the road and saluted.

"Gun destroyed last night, sir. Have been hiding. Trying to rejoin battery, sir. You'll come in sight of the Martians, I expect, about half a mile along this road."

"What the dickens are they like?" asked the lieutenant.

"Giants in armour, sir. Hundred feet high. Three legs and a body like 'luminium, with a mighty great head in a hood, sir."

"Get out!" said the lieutenant. "What confounded nonsense!"

"You'll see, sir. They carry a kind of box, sir, that shoots fire and strikes you dead."

"What d'ye mean—a gun?"

"No, sir," and the artilleryman began a vivid account of the Heat-Ray. Half-way through, the lieutenant interrupted him and looked up at me. I was still standing on the bank by the side of the road.

"It's perfectly true," I said.

"Well," said the lieutenant, "I suppose it's my business to see it too. Look here"—to the artilleryman—"we're detailed here clearing people out of their houses. You'd better go along and report yourself to Brigadier-General Marvin, and tell him all you know. He's at Weybridge. Know the way?"

"I do," I said; and he turned his horse southward again.

"Half a mile, you say?" said he.

"At most," I answered, and pointed over the tree-tops southward. He thanked me and rode on, and we saw them no more.

Farther along we came upon a group of three women and two children in the road, busy clearing out a labourer's cottage. They had got hold of a little hand-truck, and were piling it up with unclean looking bundles and shabby furniture. They were all too assiduously engaged to talk to us as we passed.

By Byfleet station we emerged from the pine-trees, and found the country calm and peaceful under the morning sunlight. We were far beyond the range of the Heat-Ray there, and had it not been for the silent desertion of some of the houses, the stirring movement of packing in others, and the knot of soldiers standing on the bridge over the railway and staring down the line towards Woking, the day would have seemed very like any other Sunday.

Several farm waggons and carts were moving creakily along the road to Addlestone, and sud-

denly through the gate of a field we saw, across a stretch of flat meadow, six twelve-pounders standing neatly at equal distances pointing towards Woking. The gunners stood by the guns waiting, and the ammunition waggons were at a business-like distance. The men stood almost as if under inspection.

"That's good!" said I. "They will get one fair shot, at any rate."

The artilleryman hesitated at the gate.

"I shall go on," he said.

Farther on towards Weybridge, just over the bridge, there were a number of men in white fatigue jackets throwing up a long rampart, and more guns behind.

"It's bows and arrows against the lightning, anyhow," said the artilleryman. "They 'aven't seen that fire-beam yet."

The officers who were not actively engaged stood and stared over the tree-tops south-westward, and the men digging would stop every now and again to stare in the same direction.

Byfleet was in a tumult; people packing, and a score of hussars, some of them dismounted, some on horseback, were hunting them about. Three or four black government waggons, with crosses in white circles, and an old omnibus, among other vehicles, were being loaded in the village street. There were scores of people, most of them sufficiently sabbatical to have assumed their best clothes. The soldiers were having the greatest difficulty in making them realise the gravity of their position. We saw one shrivelled old

fellow with a huge box and a score or more of flower-pots containing orchids, angrily expostulating with the corporal who would leave them behind. I stopped and gripped his arm.

"Do you know what's over there?" I said, pointing at the pine-tops that hid the Martians.

"Eh?" said he, turning. "I was explainin' these is vallyble."

"Death!" I shouted. "Death is coming! Death!" and leaving him to digest that if he could, I hurried on after the artilleryman. At the corner I looked back. The soldier had left him, and he was still standing by his box, with the pots of orchids on the lid of it, and staring vaguely over the trees.

No one in Weybridge could tell us where the headquarters were established; the whole place was in such confusion as I had never seen in any town before. Carts, carriages everywhere, the most astonishing miscellany of conveyances and horseflesh. The respectable inhabitants of the place, men in golf and boating costumes, wives prettily dressed, were packing, river-side loafers energetically helping, children excited, and, for the most part, highly delighted at this astonishing variation of their Sunday experiences. In the midst of it all the worthy vicar was very pluckily holding an early celebration, and his bell was jangling out above the excitement.

I and the artilleryman, seated on the step of the drinking-fountain, made a very passable meal upon what we had brought with us. Patrols of soldiers—here no

longer hussars, but grenadiers in white — were warning people to move now or to take refuge in their cellars as soon as the firing began. We saw as we crossed the railway bridge that a growing crowd of people had assembled in and about the railway station, and the swarming platform was piled with boxes and packages. The ordinary traffic had been stopped, I believe, in order to allow of the passage of troops and guns to Chertsey, and I have heard since that a savage struggle occurred for places in the special trains that were put on at a later hour.

We remained at Weybridge until mid-day, and at that hour we found ourselves at the place near Shepperton Lock where the Wey and Thames join. Part of the time we spent helping two old women to pack a little cart. The Wey has a treble mouth, and at this point boats are to be hired, and there was a ferry across the river. On the Shepperton side was an inn with a lawn, and beyond that the tower of Shepperton Church — it has been replaced by a spire — rose above the trees.

Here we found an excited and noisy crowd of fugitives. As yet the flight had not grown to a panic, but there were already far more people than all the boats going to and fro could enable to cross. People came panting along under heavy burdens; one husband and wife were even carrying a small outhouse door between them, with some of their household goods piled thereon. One man told us he meant to try to get away from Shepperton station.

There was a lot of shouting, and one man was even jesting. The idea people seemed to have here was that the Martians were simply formidable human beings, who might attack and sack the town, to be certainly destroyed in the end. Every now and then people would glance nervously across the Wey, at the meadows towards Chertsey, but everything over there was still.

Across the Thames, except just where the boats landed, everything was quiet, in vivid contrast with the Surrey side. The people who landed there from the boats went tramping off down the lane. The big ferry-boat had just made a journey. Three or four soldiers stood on the lawn of the inn, staring and jesting at the fugitives, without offering to help. The inn was closed, as it was now within prohibited hours.

"What's that?" cried a boatman, and "Shut up, you fool!" said a man near me to a yelping dog. Then the sound came again, this time from the direction of Chertsey, a muffled thud — the sound of a gun.

The fighting was beginning. Almost immediately unseen batteries across the river to our right, unseen because of the trees, took up the chorus, firing heavily one after the other. A woman screamed. Everyone stood arrested by the sudden stir of battle, near us and yet invisible to us. Nothing was to be seen save flat meadows, cows feeding unconcernedly for the most part,

and silvery pollard willows motionless in the warm sunlight.

"The sojers'll stop 'em," said a woman beside me, doubtfully. A haziness rose over the treetops.

Then suddenly we saw a rush of smoke far away up the river, a puff of smoke that jerked up into the air and hung; and forthwith the ground heaved underfoot and a heavy explosion shook the air, smashing two or three windows in the houses near, and leaving us astonished.

"Here they are!" shouted a man in a blue jersey. "Yonder! D'yer see them? Yonder!"

Quickly, one after the other, one, two, three, four of the armoured Martians appeared, far away over the little trees, across the flat meadows that stretched towards Chertsey, and striding hurriedly towards the river. Little cowled figures they seemed at first, going with a rolling motion and as fast as flying birds.

Then, advancing obliquely towards us, came a fifth. Their armoured bodies glittered in the sun as they swept swiftly forward upon the guns, growing rapidly larger as they drew nearer. One on the extreme left, the remotest that is, flourished a huge case high in the air, and the ghostly, terrible Heat-Ray I had already seen on Friday night smote towards Chertsey, and struck the town.

At sight of these strange, swift, and terrible creatures the crowd near the water's edge seemed to me to be for a moment horrorstruck. There was no screaming or shouting, but a silence. Then a hoarse murmur and a movement of feet—a splashing from the water. A man, too frightened to drop the portmanteau he carried on his shoulder, swung round and sent me staggering with a blow from the corner of his burden. A woman thrust at me with her hand and rushed past me. I turned with the rush of the people, but I was not too terrified for thought. The terrible Heat-Ray was in my mind. To get under water! That was it!

"Get under water!" I shouted, unheeded.

I faced about again, and rushed towards the approaching Martian, rushed right down the gravelly beach and headlong into the water. Others did the same. A boatload of people putting back came leaping out as I rushed past. The stones under my feet were muddy and slippery, and the river was so low that I ran perhaps twenty feet scarcely waist-deep. Then, as the Martian towered overhead scarcely a couple of hundred yards away, I flung myself forward under the surface. The splashes of the people in the boats leaping into the river sounded like thunderclaps in my ears. People were landing hastily on both sides of the river.

But the Martian machine took no more notice for the moment of the people running this way and that than a man would of the confusion of ants in a nest against which his foot has kicked. When, half suffocated, I raised my head above water, the Mar-

tian's hood pointed at the batteries that were still firing across the river, and as it advanced it swung loose what must have been the generator of the Heat-Ray.

In another moment it was on the bank, and in a stride wading half-way across. The knees of its foremost legs bent at the farther bank, and in another moment it had raised itself to its full height again, close to the village of Shepperton. Forthwith the six guns which, unknown to any one on the right bank, had been hidden behind the outskirts of that village, fired simultaneously. The sudden near concussion, the last close upon the first, made my heart jump. The monster was already raising the case generating the Heat-Ray as the first shell burst six yards above the hood.

I gave a cry of astonishment. I saw and thought nothing of the other four Martian monsters; my attention was riveted upon the nearer incident. Simultaneously two other shells burst in the air near the body as the hood twisted round in time to receive, but not in time to dodge, the fourth shell.

The shell burst clean in the face of the Thing. The hood bulged, flashed, was whirled off in a dozen tattered fragments of red flesh and glittering metal.

"Hit!" shouted I, with something between a scream and a cheer.

I heard answering shouts from the people in the water about me. I could have leaped out of the water with that momentary exultation.

The decapitated colossus reeled like a drunken giant; but it did not fall over. It recovered its balance by a miracle, and, no longer heeding its steps and with the camera that fired the Heat-Ray now rigidly upheld, it reeled swiftly upon Shepperton. The living intelligence, the Martian within the hood, was slain and splashed to the four winds of heaven, and the Thing was now but a mere intricate device of metal whirling to destruction. It drove along in a straight line, incapable of guidance. It struck the tower of Shepperton Church, smashing it down as the impact of a battering-ram might have done, swerved aside, blundered on, and collapsed with tremendous force into the river out of my sight.

A violent explosion shook the air, and a spout of water, steam, mud, and shattered metal shot far up into the sky. As the camera of the Heat-Ray hit the water, the latter had immediately flashed into steam. In another moment a huge wave, like a muddy tidal bore but almost scaldingly hot, came sweeping round the bend up-stream. I saw people struggling shorewards, and heard their screaming and shouting faintly above the seething and roar of the Martian's collapse.

For a moment I heeded nothing of the heat, forgot the patent need of self-preservation. I splashed through the tumultuous water, pushing aside a man in black to do so, until I could see round the bend. Half a dozen deserted boats pitched aimlessly

upon the confusion of the waves. The fallen Martian came into sight down-stream, lying across the river, and for the most part submerged.

Thick clouds of steam were pouring off the wreckage, and through the tumultuously whirling wisps I could see, intermittently and vaguely, the gigantic limbs churning the water and flinging a splash and spray of mud and froth into the air. The tentacles swayed and struck like living arms, and, save for the helpless purposelessness of these movements, it was as if some wounded thing were struggling for its life amid the waves. Enormous quantities of a ruddy-brown fluid were spurting up in noisy jets out of the machine.

My attention was diverted from this death flurry by a furious yelling, like that of the thing called a siren in our manufacturing towns. A man, knee-deep near the towing-path, shouted inaudibly to me and pointed. Looking back, I saw the other Martians advancing with gigantic strides down the river-bank from the direction of Chertsey. The Shepperton guns spoke this time unavailingly.

At that I ducked at once under water, and, holding my breath until movement was an agony, blundered painfully ahead under the surface as long as I could. The water was in a tumult about me, and rapidly growing hotter.

When for a moment I raised my head to take breath and throw the hair and water from my eyes, the steam was rising in a whirling white fog that at first hid the Martians altogether. The noise was deafening. Then I saw them dimly, colossal figures of grey, magnified by the mist. They had passed by me, and two were stooping over the frothing, tumultuous ruins of their comrade.

The third and fourth stood beside him in the water, one perhaps two hundred yards from me, the other towards Laleham. The generators of the Heat-Rays waved high, and the hissing beams smote down this way and that.

The air was full of sound, a deafening and confusing conflict of noises — the clangorous din of the Martians, the crash of falling houses, the thud of trees, fences. sheds flashing into flame, and the crackling and roaring of fire. Dense black smoke was leaping up to mingle with the steam from the river, and as the Heat-Ray went to and fro over Weybridge its impact was marked by flashes of incandescent white, that gave place at once to a smoky dance of lurid flames. The nearer houses still stood intact, awaiting their fate, shadowy, faint, and pallid in the steam, with the fire behind them going to and fro.

For a moment perhaps I stood there, breast-high in the almost boiling water, dumbfounded at my position, hopeless of escape. Through the reek I could see the people who had been with me in the river scrambling out of the water through the reeds, like little frogs hurrying through grass from the advance of a man, or running to and fro in utter dismay on the towing-path.

Then suddenly the white flashes of the Heat-Ray came leaping towards me. The houses caved in as they dissolved at its touch, and darted out flames; the trees changed to fire with a roar. The Ray flickered up and down the towing-path, licking off the people who ran this way and that, and came down to the water's edge not fifty yards from where I stood. It swept across the river to Shepperton, and the water in its track rose in a boiling weal crested with steam. I turned shoreward.

In another moment the huge wave, wellnigh at the boiling-point, had rushed upon me. I screamed aloud, and scalded, half blinded, agonised, I staggered through the leaping, hissing water towards the shore. Had my foot stumbled, it would have been the end. I fell helplessly, in full sight of the Martians, upon the broad, bare gravelly spit that runs down to mark the angle of the Wey and Thames. I expected nothing but death.

I have a dim memory of the foot of a Martian coming down within a score of yards of my head, driving straight into the loose gravel, whirling it this way and that, and lifting again; of a long suspense, and then of the four carrying the débris of their comrade between them, now clear and then presently faint through a veil of smoke, receding interminably, as it seemed to me, across a vast space of river and meadow. And then, very slowly, I realised that by a miracle I had escaped.

CHAPTER 13

HOW I FELL IN WITH THE CURATE

AFTER getting this sudden lesson in the power of terrestrial weapons, the Martians retreated to their original position upon Horsell Common; and in their haste, and encumbered with the débris of their smashed companion, they no doubt overlooked many such a stray and negligible victim as myself. Had they left their comrade and pushed on forthwith, there was nothing at that time between them and London but batteries of twelve-pounder guns, and they would certainly have reached the capital in advance of the tidings of their approach; as sudden, dreadful, and destructive their advent would have been as the earthquake that destroyed Lisbon a century ago.

But they were in no hurry. Cylinder followed cylinder on its interplanetary flight; every twenty-four hours brought them reinforcement. And meanwhile the military and naval authorities, now fully alive to the tremendous power of their antagonists, worked with furious energy. Every minute a fresh gun came

into position until, before twilight, every copse, every row of suburban villas on the hilly slopes about Kingston and Richmond, masked an expectant black muzzle. And through the charred and desolated area — perhaps twenty square miles altogether — that encircled the Martian encampment on Horsell Common, through charred and ruined villages among the green trees, through the blackened and smoking arcades that had been but a day ago pine spinneys, crawled the devoted scouts with the heliographs that were presently to warn the gunners of the Martian approach. But the Martians now understood our command of artillery and the danger of human proximity, and not a man ventured within a mile of either cylinder, save at the price of his life.

It would seem that these giants spent the earlier part of the afternoon in going to and fro, transferring everything from the second and third cylinders — the second in Addlestone Golf Links and the third at Pyrford — to their original pit on Horsell Common. Over that, above the blackened heather and ruined buildings that stretched far and wide, stood one as sentinel, while the rest abandoned their vast fighting-machines and descended into the pit. They were hard at work there far into the night, and the towering pillar of dense green smoke that rose therefrom could be seen from the hills about Merrow, and even, it is said, from Banstead and Epsom Downs.

And while the Martians behind me were thus preparing for their next sally, and in front of me Humanity gathered for the battle, I made my way with infinite pains and labour from the fire and smoke of burning Weybridge towards London.

I saw an abandoned boat, very small and remote, drifting downstream; and throwing off the most of my sodden clothes, I went after it, gained it, and so escaped out of that destruction. There were no oars in the boat, but I contrived to paddle, as well as my parboiled hands would allow, down the river towards Halliford and Walton, going very tediously and continually looking behind me, as you may well understand. I followed the river, because I considered that the water gave me my best chance of escape should these giants return.

The hot water from the Martian's overthrow drifted downstream with me, so that for the best part of a mile I could see little of either bank. Once, however, I made out a string of black figures hurrying across the meadows from the direction of Weybridge. Halliford, it seemed, was deserted, and several of the houses facing the river were on fire. It was strange to see the place quite tranquil, quite desolate under the hot, blue sky, with the smoke and little threads of flame going straight up into the heat of the afternoon. Never before had I seen houses burning without the accompaniment of an obstructive crowd. A little farther on the dry reeds up the bank were smoking and glowing, and a line of fire inland was marching steadily across a late field of hay.

For a long time I drifted, so

painful and weary was I after the violence I had been through, and so intense the heat upon the water. Then my fears got the better of me again, and I resumed my paddling. The sun scorched my bare back. At last, as the bridge at Walton was coming into sight round the bend, my fever and faintness overcame my fears, and I landed on the Middlesex bank and lay down, deadly sick, amid the long grass. I suppose the time was then about four or five o'clock. I got up presently, walked perhaps half a mile without meeting a soul, and then lay down again in the shadow of a hedge. I seem to remember talking, wanderingly, to myself during that last spurt. I was also very thirsty, and bitterly regretful I had drunk no more water. It is a curious thing that I felt angry with my wife; I cannot account for it, but my impotent desire to reach Leatherhead worried me excessively.

I do not clearly remember the arrival of the curate, so that probably I dozed. I became aware of him as a seated figure in soot-smudged shirt-sleeves, and with his upturned, clean-shaven face staring at a faint flickering that danced over the sky. The sky was what is called a mackerel sky — rows and rows of faint down-plumes of cloud, just tinted with the midsummer sunset.

I sat up, and at the rustle of my motion he looked at me quickly.

"Have you any water?" I asked abruptly.

He shook his head.

"You have been asking for water for the last hour," he said.

For a moment we were silent, taking stock of each other. I dare say he found me a strange enough figure, naked, save for my water-soaked trousers and socks, scalded, and my face and shoulders blackened by the smoke. His face was a fair weakness, his chin retreated, and his hair lay in crisp, almost flaxen curls on his low forehead; his eyes were rather large, pale-blue, and blankly staring. He spoke abruptly, looking vacantly away from me.

"What does it mean?" he said. "What do these things mean?"

I stared at him and made no answer.

He extended a thin white hand and spoke in almost a complaining tone.

"Why are these things permitted? What sins have we done? The morning service was over, I was walking through the roads to clear my brain for the afternoon, and then — fire, earthquake, death! As if it were Sodom and Gomorrah! All our work undone, all the work — What are these Martians?"

"What are we?" I answered, clearing my throat.

He gripped his knees and turned to look at me again. For half a minute, perhaps, he stared silently.

"I was walking through the roads to clear my brain," he said. "And suddenly — fire, earthquake, death!"

He relapsed into silence, with his chin now sunken almost to his knees.

Presently he began waving his hand.

"All the work — all the Sunday-schools — What have we done

— what has Weybridge done? Everything gone — everything destroyed. The church! We rebuilt it only three years ago. Gone! — swept out of existence! Why?"

Another pause, and he broke out again like one demented.

"The smoke of her burning goeth up for ever and ever!" he shouted.

His eyes flamed, and he pointed a lean finger in the direction of Weybridge.

By this time I was beginning to take his measure. The tremendous tragedy in which he had been involved — it was evident he was a fugitive from Weybridge — had driven him to the very verge of his reason.

"Are we far from Sunbury?" I said, in a matter-of-fact tone.

"What are we to do?" he asked. "Are these creatures everywhere? Has the earth been given over to them?"

"Are we far from Sunbury?"

"Only this morning I officiated at early celebration —"

"Things have changed," I said, quietly. "You must keep your head. There is still hope."

"Hope!"

"Yes. Plentiful hope — for all this destruction!"

I began to explain my view of our position. He listened at first, but as I went on the interest dawning in his eyes gave place to their former stare, and his regard wandered from me.

"This must be the beginning of the end," he said, interrupting me. "The end! The great and terrible day of the Lord! When men shall call upon the mountains and the rocks to fall upon them

and hide them — hide them from the face of Him that sitteth upon the throne!"

I began to understand the position. I ceased my laboured reasoning, struggled to my feet, and, standing over him, laid my hand on his shoulder.

"Be a man!" said I. "You are scared out of your wits! What good is religion if it collapses under calamity? Think of what earthquakes and floods, wars and volcanoes, have done before to men! Did you think God had exempted Weybridge? He is not an insurance agent."

For a time he sat in blank silence.

"But how can we escape?" he asked, suddenly. "They are invulnerable, they are pitiless."

"Neither the one nor, perhaps, the other," I answered. "And the mightier they are the more sane and wary should we be. One of them was killed yonder not three hours ago."

"Killed!" he said, staring about him. "How can God's ministers be killed?"

"I saw it happen." I proceeded to tell him. "We have chanced to come in for the thick of it," said I, "and that is all."

"What is that flicker in the sky?" he asked abruptly.

I told him it was the heliograph signalling — that it was the sign of human help and effort in the sky.

"We are in the midst of it," I said, "quiet as it is. That flicker in the sky tells of the gathering storm. Yonder, I take it, are the Martians, and London-ward, where those hills rise about

Richmond and Kingston and the trees give cover, earthworks are being thrown up and guns are being placed. Presently the Martians will be coming this way again."

And even as I spoke he sprang to his feet and stopped me by a gesture.

" Listen! " he said.

From beyond the low hills across the water came the dull resonance of distant guns and a remote weird crying. Then everything was still. A cockchafer came droning over the hedge and past us. High in the west the crescent moon hung faint and pale above the smoke of Weybridge and Shepperton and the hot, still splendour of the sunset.

" We had better follow this path," I said, " northward."

CHAPTER 14

IN LONDON

My younger brother was in London when the Martians fell at Woking. He was a medical student, working for an imminent examination, and he heard nothing of the arrival until Saturday morning. The morning papers on Saturday contained, in addition to lengthy special articles on the planet Mars, on life in the planets, and so forth, a brief and vaguely worded telegram, all the more striking for its brevity.

The Martians, alarmed by the approach of a crowd, had killed a number of people with a quick-firing gun, so the story ran. The telegram concluded with the words: " Formidable as they seem to be, the Martians have not moved from the pit into which they have fallen, and, indeed, seem incapable of doing so. Probably this is due to the relative strength of the earth's gravitational energy." On that last text their leader-writer expanded very comfortingly.

Of course all the students in the crammer's biology class, to which my brother went that day, were intensely interested, but there were no signs of any unusual excitement in the streets. The afternoon papers puffed scraps of news under big headlines. They had nothing to tell beyond the movements of troops about the common, and the burning of the pine-woods between Woking and Weybridge, until eight. Then the *St. James's Gazette,* in an extra special edition, announced the bare fact of the interruption of telegraphic communication. This was thought to be due to the falling of burning pine-trees across the line. Nothing more of the fighting was known that night, the night of my drive to Leatherhead and back.

My brother felt no anxiety about us, as he knew from the description in the papers that the cylinder was a good two miles from my house. He made up his

mind to run down that night to me, in order, as he says, to see the Things before they were killed. He despatched a telegram, which never reached me, about four o'clock, and spent the evening at a music-hall.

In London, also, on Saturday night there was a thunderstorm, and my brother reached Waterloo in a cab. On the platform from which the midnight train usually starts he learned, after some waiting, that an accident prevented trains from reaching Woking that night. The nature of the accident he could not ascertain; indeed, the railway authorities did not clearly know at that time. There was very little excitement in the station, as the officials, failing to realise that anything further than a breakdown between Byfleet and Woking junction had occurred, were running the theatre trains which usually passed through Woking, round by Virginia Water or Guildford. They were busy making the necessary arrangements to alter the route of the Southampton and Portsmouth Sunday League excursions. A nocturnal newspaper reporter, mistaking my brother for the traffic manager, to whom he bears a slight resemblance, waylaid and tried to interview him. Few people, excepting the railway officials, connected the breakdown with the Martians.

I have read, in another account of these events, that on Sunday morning "all London was electrified by the news from Woking." As a matter of fact, there was nothing to justify that very extravagant phrase. Plenty of Londoners did not hear of the Martians until the panic of Monday morning. Those who did took some time to realise all that the hastily worded telegrams in the Sunday papers conveyed. The majority of people in London do not read Sunday papers.

The habit of personal security, moreover, is so deeply fixed in the Londoner's mind, and startling intelligence so much a matter of course in the papers, that they could read without any personal tremors: " About seven o'clock last night the Martians came out of the cylinder, and, moving about under an armour of metallic shields, have completely wrecked Woking station with the adjacent houses, and massacred an entire battalion of the Cardigan Regiment. No details are known. Maxims have been absolutely useless against their armour; the field-guns have been disabled by them. Flying hussars have been galloping into Chertsey. The Martians appear to be moving slowly towards Chertsey or Windsor. Great anxiety prevails in West Surrey, and earthworks are being thrown up to check the advance Londonward." That was how the Sunday *Sun* put it, and a clever and remarkably prompt " hand-book " article in the *Referee* compared the affair to a menagerie suddenly let loose in a village.

No one in London knew positively of the nature of the armoured Martians, and there was still a fixed idea that these monsters must be sluggish: " crawling," " creeping painfully " — such expressions occurred in al-

most all the earlier reports. None of the telegrams could have been written by an eye-witness of their advance. The Sunday papers printed separate editions as further news came to hand, some even in default of it. But there was practically nothing more to tell people until late in the afternoon, when the authorities gave the press-agencies the news in their possession. It was stated that the people of Walton and Weybridge, and all the district, were pouring along the roads Londonward, and that was all.

My brother went to church at the Foundling Hospital in the morning, still in ignorance of what had happened on the previous night. There he heard allusions made to the invasion, and a special prayer for peace. Coming out, he bought a *Referee*. He became alarmed at the news in this, and went again to Waterloo station to find out if communication were restored. The omnibuses, carriages, cyclists, and innumerable people walking in their best clothes seemed scarcely affected by the strange intelligence that the news-venders were disseminating. People were interested, or, if alarmed, alarmed only on account of the local residents. At the station he heard for the first time that the Windsor and Chertsey lines were now interrupted. The porters told him that several remarkable telegrams had been received in the morning from Byfleet and Chertsey stations, but that these had abruptly ceased. My brother could get very little precise detail out of them. " There's fighting going on about

Weybridge" was the extent of their information.

The train service was now very much disorganised. Quite a number of people who had been expecting friends from places on the South-Western network were standing about the station. One grey-headed old gentleman came and abused the South-Western Company bitterly to my brother. " It wants showing up," he said.

One or two trains came in from Richmond, Putney, and Kingston, containing people who had gone out for a day's boating and found the locks closed and a feeling of panic in the air. A man in a blue-and-white blazer addressed my brother, full of strange tidings.

" There's hosts of people driving into Kingston in traps and carts and things, with boxes of valuables and all that," he said. " They come from Molesey and Weybridge and Walton, and they say there's been guns heard at Chertsey, heavy firing, and that mounted soldiers have told them to get off at once because the Martians are coming. *We* heard guns firing at Hampton Court station, but we thought it was thunder. What the dickens does it all mean? The Martians can't get out of their pit, can they? "

My brother could not tell him.

Afterwards he found that the vague feeling of alarm had spread to the clients of the underground railway, and that the Sunday excursionists began to return from all over the South-Western " lung " — Barnes, Wimbledon, Richmond Park, Kew, and so forth — at unnaturally

early hours; but not a soul had anything more than vague hearsay to tell of. Every one connected with the terminus seemed ill-tempered.

About five o'clock the gathering crowd in the station was immensely excited by the opening of the line of communication, which is almost invariably closed, between the South-Eastern and the South-Western stations, and the passage of carriage-trucks bearing huge guns and carriages crammed with soldiers. These were the guns that were brought up from Woolwich and Chatham to cover Kingston. There was an exchange of pleasantries: "You'll get eaten!" "We're the beast-tamers!" and so forth. A little while after that a squad of police came into the station and began to clear the public off the platforms, and my brother went out into the street again.

The church bells were ringing for evensong, and a squad of Salvation Army lassies came singing down Waterloo Road. On the bridge a number of loafers were watching a curious brown scum that came drifting down the stream in patches. The sun was just setting, and the Clock Tower and the Houses of Parliament rose against one of the most peaceful skies it is possible to imagine, a sky of gold, barred with long transverse stripes of reddish-purple cloud. There was talk of a floating body. One of the men there, a reservist he said he was, told my brother he had seen the heliograph flickering in the west.

In Wellington Street my brother met a couple of sturdy roughs who had just rushed out of Fleet Street with still wet newspapers and staring placards. "Dreadful catastrophe!" they bawled one to the other down Wellington Street. "Fighting at Weybridge! Full description! Repulse of the Martians! London in Danger!" He had to give threepence for a copy of that paper.

Then it was, and then only, that he realised something of the full power and terror of these monsters. He learned that they were not merely a handful of small sluggish creatures, but that they were minds swaying vast mechanical bodies; and that they could move swiftly and smite with such power that even the mightiest guns could not stand against them.

They were described as "vast spider-like machines, nearly a hundred feet high, capable of the speed of an express-train, and able to shoot out a beam of intense heat." Masked batteries, chiefly of field-guns, had been planted in the country about Horsell Common, and especially between the Woking district and London. Five of the machines had been seen moving towards the Thames, and one, by a happy chance, had been destroyed. In the other cases the shells had missed, and the batteries had been at once annihilated by the Heat-Rays. Heavy losses of soldiers were mentioned, but the tone of the despatch was optimistic.

The Martians had been repulsed; they were not invulner-

able. They had retreated to their triangle of cylinders again, in the circle about Woking. Signallers with heliographs were pushing forward upon them from all sides. Guns were in rapid transit from Windsor, Portsmouth, Aldershot, Woolwich — even from the north; among others, long wire-guns of ninety-five tons from Woolwich. Altogether one hundred and sixteen were in position or being hastily placed, chiefly covering London. Never before in England had there been such a vast or rapid concentration of military material.

Any further cylinders that fell, it was hoped, could be destroyed at once by high explosives, which were being rapidly manufactured and distributed. No doubt, ran the report, the situation was of the strangest and gravest description, but the public was exhorted to avoid and discourage panic. No doubt the Martians were strange and terrible in the extreme, but at the outside there could not be more than twenty of them against our millions.

The authorities had reason to suppose, from the size of the cylinders, that at the outside there could not be more than five in each cylinder — fifteen altogether. And one at least was disposed of — perhaps more. The public would be fairly warned of the approach of danger, and elaborate measures were being taken for the protection of the people in the threatened southwestern suburbs. And so, with reiterated assurances of the safety of London and the ability of the authorities to cope with the diffi-culty, this quasi-proclamation closed.

This was printed in enormous type on paper so fresh that it was still wet, and there had been no time to add a word of comment. It was curious, my brother said, to see how ruthlessly the usual contents of the paper had been hacked and taken out to give this place.

All down Wellington Street people could be seen fluttering out the pink sheets and reading, and the Strand was suddenly noisy with the voices of an army of hawkers following these pioneers. Men came scrambling off buses to secure copies. Certainly this news excited people intensely, whatever their previous apathy. The shutters of a map-shop in the Strand were being taken down, my brother said, and a man in his Sunday raiment, lemon-yellow gloves even, was visible inside the window hastily fastening maps of Surrey to the glass.

Going on along the Strand to Trafalgar Square, the paper in his hand, my brother saw some of the fugitives from West Surrey. There was a man with his wife and two boys and some articles of furniture in a cart such as green-grocers use. He was driving from the direction of Westminster Bridge; and close behind him came a hay-waggon with five or six respectable-looking people in it, and some boxes and bundles. The faces of these people were haggard, and their entire appearance contrasted conspicuously with the Sabbath-best appearance of the people on the

omnibuses. People in fashionable clothing peeped at them out of cabs. They stopped at the Square as if undecided which way to take, and finally turned eastward along the Strand. Some way behind these came a man in workday clothes, riding one of those old-fashioned tricycles with a small front-wheel. He was dirty and white in the face.

My brother turned down towards Victoria, and met a number of such people. He had a vague idea that he might see something of me. He noticed an unusual number of police regulating the traffic. Some of the refugees were exchanging news with the people on the omnibuses. One was professing to have seen the Martians. "Boilers on stilts, I tell you, striding along like men." Most of them were excited and animated by their strange experience.

Beyond Victoria the public-houses were doing a lively trade with these arrivals. At all the street corners groups of people were reading papers, talking excitedly, or staring at these unusual Sunday visitors. They seemed to increase as night drew on, until at last the roads, my brother said, were like Epsom High Street on a Derby Day. My brother addressed several of these fugitives and got unsatisfactory answers from most.

None of them could tell him any news of Woking except one man, who assured him that Woking had been entirely destroyed on the previous night. "I come from Byfleet," he said; "a man on a bicycle came through the place in the early morning, and ran from door to door warning us to come away. Then came soldiers. We went out to look, and there were clouds of smoke to the south — nothing but smoke, and not a soul coming that way. Then we heard the guns at Chertsey, and folks coming from Weybridge. So I've locked up my house and come on."

At that time there was a strong feeling in the streets that the authorities were to blame for their incapacity to dispose of the invaders without all this inconvenience.

About eight o'clock a noise of heavy firing was distinctly audible all over the south of London. My brother could not hear it for the traffic in the main thoroughfares, but by striking through the quiet back-streets to the river he was able to distinguish it quite plainly.

He walked from Westminster to his apartments near Regent's Park, about two. He was now very anxious on my account, and disturbed at the evident magnitude of the trouble. His mind was inclined to run, even as mine had run on Saturday, on military details. He thought of all those silent, expectant guns, of the suddenly nomadic countryside; he tried to imagine "boilers on stilts" a hundred feet high.

There were one or two cartloads of refugees passing along Oxford Street, and several in the Marylebone Road, but so slowly was the news spreading that Regent Street and Portland Place were full of their usual Sunday-

night promenaders, albeit they talked in groups, and along the edge of Regent's Park there were as many silent couples "walking out" together under the scattered gas-lamps as ever there had been. The night was warm and still, and a little oppressive; the sound of guns continued intermittently, and after midnight there seemed to be sheet-lightning in the south.

He read and re-read the paper, fearing the worst had happened to me. He was restless, and after supper prowled out again aimlessly. He returned and tried in vain to divert his attention to his examination notes. He went to bed a little after midnight, and was awakened from lurid dreams in the small hours of Monday by the sound of door-knockers, feet running in the street, distant drumming, and a clamour of bells. Red reflections danced on the ceiling. For a moment he lay astonished, wondering whether day had come or the world gone mad. Then he jumped out of bed and ran to the window.

His room was an attic and as he thrust his head out, up and down the street there were a dozen echoes to the noise of his window-sash, and heads in every kind of night disarray appeared. Enquiries were being shouted. "They are coming!" bawled a policeman, hammering at the door; "the Martians are coming!" and hurried to the next door.

The sound of drumming and trumpeting came from the Albany Street Barracks, and every church within earshot was hard at work killing sleep with a vehement disorderly tocsin. There was a noise of doors opening, and window after window in the houses opposite flashed from darkness into yellow illumination.

Up the street came galloping a closed carriage, bursting abruptly into noise at the corner, rising to a clattering climax under the window, and dying away slowly in the distance. Close on the rear of this came a couple of cabs, the forerunners of a long procession of flying vehicles, going for the most part to Chalk Farm station, where the North-Western special trains were loading up, instead of coming down the gradient into Euston.

For a long time my brother stared out of the window in blank astonishment, watching the policemen hammering at door after door, and delivering their incomprehensible message. Then the door behind him opened, and the man who lodged across the landing came in, dressed only in shirt, trousers, and slippers, his braces loose about his waist, his hair disordered from his pillow.

"What the devil is it?" he asked. "A fire? What a devil of a row!"

They both craned their heads out of the window, straining to hear what the policemen were shouting. People were coming out of the side-streets, and standing in groups at the corners talking.

"What the devil is it all about?" said my brother's fellow-lodger.

My brother answered him vaguely and began to dress, running with each garment to the window in order to miss nothing of the growing excitement. And presently men selling unnaturally early newspapers came bawling into the street:

"London in danger of suffocation! The Kingston and Richmond defences forced! Fearful massacres in the Thames Valley!"

And all about him — in the rooms below, in the houses on each side and across the road, and behind in the Park Terraces and in the hundred other streets of that part of Marylebone, and the Westbourne Park district and St. Pancras, and westward and northward in Kilburn and St. John's Wood and Hampstead, and eastward in Shoreditch and Highbury and Haggerston and Hoxton, and, indeed, through all the vastness of London from Ealing to East Ham — people were rubbing their eyes, and opening windows to stare out and ask aimless questions, and dressing hastily as the first breath of the coming storm of Fear blew through the streets. It was the dawn of the great panic. London, which had gone to bed on Sunday night oblivious and inert, was awakened, in the small hours of Monday morning to a vivid sense of danger.

Unable from his window to learn what was happening, my brother went down and out into the street, just as the sky between the parapets of the houses grew pink with the early dawn. The flying people on foot and in vehicles grew more numerous every moment. "Black Smoke!" he heard people crying, and again "Black Smoke!" The contagion of such a unanimous fear was inevitable. As my brother hesitated on the door-step, he saw another news-vender approaching, and got a paper forthwith. The man was running away with the rest, and selling his papers for a shilling each as he ran — a grotesque mingling of profit and panic.

And from this paper my brother read that catastrophic despatch of the Commander-in-Chief:

"The Martians are able to discharge enormous clouds of a black and poisonous vapour by means of rockets. They have smothered our batteries, destroyed Richmond, Kingston, and Wimbledon, and are advancing slowly towards London, destroying everything on the way. It is impossible to stop them. There is no safety from the Black Smoke but in instant flight."

That was all, but it was enough. The whole population of the great six-million city was stirring, slipping, running; presently it would be pouring *en masse* northward.

"Black Smoke!" the voices cried. "Fire!"

The bells of the neighboring church made a jangling tumult, a cart carelessly driven smashed, amid shrieks and curses, against the water-trough up the street. Sickly yellow lights went to and fro in the houses, and some of the passing cabs flaunted unextinguished lamps. And overhead

the dawn was growing brighter, clear and steady and calm.

He heard footsteps running to and fro in the rooms, and up and down stairs behind him. His landlady came to the door, loosely wrapped in dressing-gown and shawl; her husband followed ejaculating.

As my brother began to realise the import of all these things, he turned hastily to his own room, put all his available money — some ten pounds altogether — into his pockets, and went out again into the streets.

CHAPTER 15

WHAT HAD HAPPENED IN SURREY

It was while the curate had sat and talked so wildly to me under the hedge in the flat meadows near Halliford, and while my brother was watching the fugitives stream over Westminster Bridge, that the Martians had resumed the offensive. So far as one can ascertain from the conflicting accounts that have been put forth, the majority of them remained busied with preparations in the Horsell pit until nine that night, hurrying on some operation that disengaged huge volumes of green smoke.

But three certainly came out about eight o'clock, and, advancing slowly and cautiously, made their way through Byfleet and Pyrford towards Ripley and Weybridge, and so came in sight of the expectant batteries against the setting sun. These Martians did not advance in a body, but in a line, each perhaps a mile and a half from his nearest fellow. They communicated with one another by means of siren-like howls, running up and down the scale from one note to another.

It was this howling and firing of the guns at Ripley and St. George's Hill that we had heard at Upper Halliford. The Ripley gunners, unseasoned artillery volunteers who ought never to have been placed in such a position, fired one wild, premature, ineffectual volley, and bolted on horse and foot through the deserted village, while the Martian, without using his Heat-Ray, walked serenely over their guns, stepped gingerly among them, passed in front of them, and so came unexpectedly upon the guns in Painshill Park, which he destroyed.

The St. George's Hill men, however, were better led or of a better mettle. Hidden by a pinewood as they were, they seem to have been quite unsuspected by the Martian nearest to them. They laid their guns as deliberately as if they had been on parade, and fired at about a thousand yards range.

The shells flashed all round him, and he was seen to advance

a few paces, stagger, and go down. Everybody yelled together, and the guns were reloaded in frantic haste. The overthrown Martian set up a prolonged ululation, and immediately a second glittering giant, answering him, appeared over the trees to the south. It would seem that a leg of the tripod had been smashed by one of the shells. The whole of the second volley flew wide of the Martian on the ground, and, simultaneously, both his companions brought their Heat-Rays to bear on the battery. The ammunition blew up, the pine-trees all about the guns flashed into fire, and only one or two of the men who were already running over the crest of the hill escaped.

After this it would seem that the three took counsel together and halted, and the scouts who were watching them report that they remained absolutely stationary for the next half-hour. The Martian who had been overthrown crawled tediously out of his hood, a small brown figure, oddly suggestive from that distance of a speck of blight, and apparently engaged in the repair of his support. About nine he had finished, for his cowl was then seen above the trees again.

It was a few minutes past nine that night when these three sentinels were joined by four other Martians, each carrying a thick black tube. A similar tube was handed to each of the three, and the seven proceeded to distribute themselves at equal distances along a curved line between St. George's Hill, Weybridge, and the village of Send, southwest of Ripley.

A dozen rockets sprang out of the hills before them so soon as they begin to move, and warned the waiting batteries about Ditton and Esher. At the same time four of their fighting machines, similarly armed with tubes, crossed the river, and two of them, black against the western sky, came into sight of myself and the curate as we hurried wearily and painfully along the road that runs northward out of Halliford. They moved, as it seemed to us, upon a cloud, for a milky mist covered the fields and rose to a third of their height.

At this sight the curate cried faintly in his throat, and began running; but I knew it was no good running from a Martian, and I turned aside and crawled through dewy nettles and brambles into the broad ditch by the side of the road. He looked back, saw what I was doing, and turned to join me.

The two halted, the nearer to us standing and facing Sunbury, the remoter being a grey indistinctness towards the evening star, away towards Staines.

The occasional howling of the Martians had ceased; they took up their positions in the huge crescent about their cylinders in absolute silence. It was a crescent with twelve miles between its horns. Never since the devising of gunpowder was the beginning of a battle so still. To us and to an observer about Ripley it would have had precisely the same effect — the Martians

seemed in solitary possession of the darkling night, lit only as it was by the slender moon, the stars, the after-glow of the daylight, and the ruddy glare from St. George's Hill and the woods of Painshill.

But facing that crescent everywhere — at Staines, Hounslow, Ditton, Esher, Ockham, behind hills and woods south of the river, and across the flat grass meadows to the north of it, wherever a cluster of trees or village houses gave sufficient cover — the guns were waiting. The signal rockets burst and rained their sparks through the night and vanished, and the spirit of all those watching batteries rose to a tense expectation. The Martians had but to advance into the line of fire, and instantly those motionless black forms of men, those guns glittering so darkly in the early night, would explode into a thunderous fury of battle.

No doubt the thought that was uppermost in a thousand of those vigilant minds, even as it was uppermost in mine, was the riddle — how much they understood of us. Did they grasp that we in our millions were organised, disciplined, working together? Or did they interpret our spurts of fire, the sudden stinging of our shells, our steady investment of their encampment, as we should the furious unanimity of onslaught in a disturbed hive of bees? Did they dream they might exterminate us? (At that time no one knew what food they needed.) A hundred such questions struggled together in my mind as I watched that vast sentinel shape. And in the back of my mind was the sense of all the huge unknown and hidden forces Londonward. Had they prepared pitfalls? Were the powder-mills at Hounslow ready as a snare? Would the Londoners have the heart and courage to make a greater Moscow of their mighty province of houses?

Then, after an interminable time, as it seemed to us, crouching and peering through the hedge, came a sound like the distant concussion of a gun. Another nearer, and then another. And then the Martian beside us raised his tube on high and discharged it, gunwise, with a heavy report that made the ground heave. The one towards Staines answered him. There was no flash, no smoke, simply that loaded detonation.

I was so excited by these heavy minute-guns following one another that I so far forgot my personal safety and my scalded hands as to clamber up into the hedge and stare towards Sunbury. As I did so a second report followed, and a big projectile hurtled overhead towards Hounslow. I expected at least to see smoke or fire, or some such evidence of its work. But all I saw was the deep-blue sky above, with one solitary star, and the white mist spreading wide and low beneath. And there had been no crash, no answering explosion. The silence was restored; the minute lengthened to three.

"What has happened?" said the curate, standing up beside me.

"Heaven knows!" said I.

A bat flickered by and vanished. A distant tumult of shouting began and ceased. I looked again at the Martian, and saw he was now moving eastward along the river-bank, with a swift, rolling motion.

Every moment I expected the fire of some hidden battery to spring upon him; but the evening calm was unbroken. The figure of the Martian grew smaller as he receded, and presently the mist and the gathering night had swallowed him up. By a common impulse we clambered higher. Towards Sunbury was a dark appearance, as though a conical hill had suddenly come into being there, hiding our view of the farther country; and then, remoter across the river, over Walton, we saw another such summit. These hill-like forms grew lower and broader even as we stared.

Moved by a sudden thought, I looked northward, and there I perceived a third of these cloudy black kopjes had risen.

Everything had suddenly become very still. Far away to the south-east, marking the quiet, we heard the Martians hooting to one another, and then the air quivered again with the distant thud of their guns. But the earthly artillery made no reply.

Now at the time we could not understand these things, but later I was to learn the meaning of these ominous kopjes that gathered in the twilight. Each of the Martians, standing in the great crescent I have described, had discharged, by means of the gun-like tube he carried, a huge canister over whatever hill, copse, cluster of houses, or other possible cover for guns, chanced to be in front of him. Some fired only one of these, some two — as in the case of the one we had seen; the one at Ripley is said to have discharged no fewer than five at that time. These canisters smashed on striking the ground — they did not explode — and incontinently disengaged an enormous volume of heavy, inky vapour, coiling and pouring upward in a huge and ebony cumulus cloud, a gaseous hill that sank and spread itself slowly over the surrounding country. And the touch of that vapour, the inhaling of its pungent wisps, was death to all that breathes.

It was heavy, this vapour, heavier than the densest smoke, so that, after the first tumultuous uprush and outflow of its impact, it sank down through the air and poured over the ground in a manner rather liquid than gaseous, abandoning the hills, and streaming into the valleys and ditches and water-courses even as I have heard the carbonic-acid gas that pours from volcanic clefts is wont to do. And where it came upon water some chemical action occurred, and the surface would be instantly covered with a powdery scum that sank slowly and made way for more. The scum was absolutely insoluble, and it is a strange thing, seeing the instant effect of the gas, that one could drink without hurt the water from which it had been strained. The vapour did not diffuse as a true gas would do. It hung to-

gether in banks, flowing sluggishly down the slope of the land and driving reluctantly before the wind, and very slowly it combined with the mist and moisture of the air, and sank to the earth in the form of dust. Save that an unknown element giving a group of four lines in the blue of the spectrum is concerned, we are still entirely ignorant of the nature of this substance.

Once the tumultuous upheaval of its dispersion was over, the black smoke clung so closely to the ground, even before its precipitation, that fifty feet up in the air, on the roofs and upper stories of high houses and on great trees, there was a chance of escaping its poison altogether, as was proved even that night at Street Cobham and Ditton.

The man who escaped at the former place tells a wonderful story of the strangeness of its coiling flow, and how he looked down from the church spire and saw the houses of the village rising like ghosts out of its inky nothingness. For a day and a half he remained there, weary, starving and sun-scorched, the earth under the blue sky and against the prospect of the distant hills a velvet-black expanse, with red roofs, green trees, and, later, black-veiled shrubs and gates, barns, out-houses, and walls, rising here and there into the sunlight.

But that was at Street Cobham, where the black vapour was allowed to remain until it sank of its own accord into the ground. As a rule the Martians, when it had served its purpose, cleared the air of it again by wading into it and directing a jet of steam upon it.

This they did with the vapour-banks near us, as we saw in the starlight from the window of a deserted house at Upper Halliford, whither we had returned. From there we could see the search-lights on Richmond Hill and Kingston Hill going to and fro, and about eleven the windows rattled, and we heard the sound of the huge siege guns that had been put in position there. These continued intermittently for the space of a quarter of an hour, sending chance shots at the invisible Martians at Hampton and Ditton, and then the pale beams of the electric light vanished, and were replaced by a bright red glow.

Then the fourth cylinder fell — a brilliant green meteor — as I learned afterwards, in Bushey Park. Before the guns on the Richmond and Kingston line of hills began, there was a fitful cannonade far away in the southwest, due, I believe, to guns being fired haphazard before the black vapour could overwhelm the gunners.

So, setting about it as methodically as men might smoke out a wasps' nest, the Martians spread this strange stifling vapour over the Londonward country. The horns of the crescent slowly moved apart, until at last they formed a line from Hanwell to Coombe and Malden. All night through their destructive tubes advanced. Never once, after the Martian at St. George's Hill was

brought down, did they give the artillery the ghost of a chance against them. Wherever there was a possibility of guns being laid for them unseen, a fresh canister of the black vapour was discharged, and where the guns were openly displayed the Heat-Ray was brought to bear.

By midnight the blazing trees along the slopes of Richmond Park and the glare of Kingston Hill threw their light upon a network of black smoke, blotting out the whole Valley of the Thames and extending as far as the eye could reach. And through this two Martians slowly waded, and turned their hissing steam-jets this way and that.

They were sparing of the Heat-Ray that night, either because they had but a limited supply of material for its production or because they did not wish to destroy the country but only to crush and overawe the opposition they had aroused. In the latter aim they certainly succeeded. Sunday night was the end of the organised opposition to their movements. After that no body of men would stand against them, so hopeless was the enterprise. Even the crews of the torpedo-boats and destroyers that had brought their quick-firers up the Thames refused to stop, mutinied, and went down again. The only offensive operation men ventured upon after that night was the preparation of mines and pitfalls, and even in that their energies were frantic and spasmodic.

One has to imagine, as well as one may, the fate of those batteries towards Esher, waiting so tensely in the twilight. Survivors there were none. One may picture the orderly expectation, the officers alert and watchful, the gunners ready, the ammunition piled to hand, the limber gunners with their horses and waggons, the groups of civilian spectators standing as near as they were permitted, the evening stillness, the ambulances and hospital tents with the burned and wounded from Weybridge; then the dull resonance of the shots the Martians fired, and the clumsy projectile whirling over the trees and houses and smashing amid the neighbouring fields.

One may picture, too, the sudden shifting of the attention, the swiftly spreading coils and bellyings of that blackness advancing headlong, towering heavenward, turning the twilight to a palpable darkness, a strange and horrible antagonist of vapour striding upon its victims, men and horses near it seen dimly, running, shrieking, falling headlong, shouts of dismay, the guns suddenly abandoned, men choking and writhing on the ground, and the swift broadening-out of the opaque cone of smoke. And then night and extinction — nothing but a silent mass of impenetrable vapour hiding its dead.

Before dawn the black vapour was pouring through the streets of Richmond, and the disintegrating organism of government was, with a last expiring effort, rousing the population of London to the necessity of flight.

CHAPTER 16

THE EXODUS FROM LONDON

So you understand the roaring wave of fear that swept through the greatest city in the world just as Monday was dawning — the stream of flight rising swiftly to a torrent, lashing in a foaming tumult round the railway stations, banked up into a horrible struggle about the shipping in the Thames, and hurrying by every available channel northward and eastward. By ten o'clock the police organisation, and by mid-day even the railway organisations, were losing coherency, losing shape and efficiency, guttering, softening, running at last in that swift liquefaction of the social body.

All the railway lines north of the Thames and the South-Eastern people at Cannon Street had been warned by midnight on Sunday, and trains were being filled. People were fighting savagely for standing-room in the carriages even at two o'clock. By three, people were being trampled and crushed even in Bishopsgate Street, a couple of hundred yards or more from Liverpool Street station; revolvers were fired, people stabbed, and the policemen who had been sent to direct the traffic, exhausted and infuriated, were breaking the heads of the people they were called out to protect.

And as the day advanced and the engine-drivers and stokers refused to return to London, the pressure of the flight drove the people in an ever-thickening multitude away from the stations and along the northward-running roads. By mid-day a Martian had been seen at Barnes, and a cloud of slowly sinking black vapour drove along the Thames and across the flats of Lambeth, cutting off all escape over the bridges in its sluggish advance. Another bank drove over Ealing, and surrounded a little island of survivors on Castle Hill, alive, but unable to escape.

After a fruitless struggle to get aboard a North-Western train at Chalk Farm — the engines of the trains that had loaded in the goods yard there *ploughed* through shrieking people, and a dozen stalwart men fought to keep the crowd from crushing the driver against his furnace — my brother emerged upon the Chalk Farm road, dodged across through a hurrying swarm of vehicles, and had the luck to be foremost in the sack of a cycle shop. The front tire of the machine he got was punctured in dragging it through the window, but he got up and off, notwithstanding, with no further injury than a cut wrist. The steep foot

of Haverstock Hill was impassable owing to several overturned horses, and my brother struck into Belsize Road.

So he got out of the fury of the panic, and, skirting the Edgware Road, reached Edgware about seven, fasting and wearied, but well ahead of the crowd. Along the road people were standing in the roadway, curious, wondering. He was passed by a number of cyclists, some horsemen, and two motor-cars. A mile from Edgware the rim of the wheel broke, and the machine became unridable. He left it by the road-side and trudged through the village. There were shops half opened in the main street of the place, and people crowded on the pavement and in the doorways and windows, staring astonished at this extraordinary procession of fugitives that was beginning. He succeeded in getting some food at an inn.

For a time he remained in Edgware not knowing what next to do. The flying people increased in number. Many of them, like my brother, seemed inclined to loiter in the place. There was no fresh news of the invaders from Mars.

At that time the road was crowded, but as yet far from congested. Most of the fugitives at that hour were mounted on cycles, but there were soon motor-cars, hansom cabs, and carriages hurrying along, and the dust hung in heavy clouds along the road to St. Albans.

It was perhaps a vague idea of making his way to Chelmsford, where some friends of his lived,

that at last induced my brother to strike into a quiet lane running eastward. Presently he came upon a stile, and, crossing it, followed a foot-path north-eastward. He passed near several farmhouses and some little places whose names he did not learn. He saw few fugitives until, in a grass lane towards High Barnet, he happened upon two ladies who became his fellow-travellers. He came upon them just in time to save them.

He heard their screams, and, hurrying round the corner, saw a couple of men struggling to drag them out of the little pony-chaise in which they had been driving, while a third with difficulty held the frightened pony's head. One of the ladies, a short woman dressed in white, was simply screaming; the other, a dark, slender figure, slashed at the man who gripped her arm with a whip she held in her disengaged hand.

My brother immediately grasped the situation, shouted, and hurried towards the struggle. One of the men desisted and turned towards him, and my brother, realising from his antagonist's face that a fight was unavoidable, and being an expert boxer, went into him forthwith and sent him down against the wheel of the chaise.

It was no time for pugilistic chivalry and my brother laid him quiet with a kick, and gripped the collar of the man who pulled at the slender lady's arm. He heard the clatter of hoofs, the whip stung across his face, a third antagonist struck him between

the eyes, and the man he held wrenched himself free and made off down the lane in the direction from which he had come.

Partly stunned, he found himself facing the man who had held the horse's head, and became aware of the chaise receding from him down the lane, swaying from side to side, and with the women in it looking back. The man before him, a burly rough, tried to close, and he stopped him with a blow in the face. Then, realising that he was deserted, he dodged round and made off down the lane after the chaise, with the sturdy man close behind him, and the fugitive, who had turned now, following remotely.

Suddenly he stumbled and fell; his immediate pursuer went headlong, and he rose to his feet to find himself with a couple of antagonists again. He would have had little chance against them had not the slender lady very pluckily pulled up and returned to his help. It seems she had had a revolver all this time, but it had been under the seat when she and her companion were attacked. She fired at six yards' distance, narrowly missing my brother. The less courageous of the robbers made off, and his companion followed him, cursing his cowardice. They both stopped in sight down the lane where the third man lay insensible.

" Take this! " said the slender lady, and she gave my brother her revolver.

" Go back to the chaise," said my brother, wiping the blood from his split lip.

She turned without a word —

they were both panting — and they went back to where the lady in white struggled to hold back the frightened pony.

The robbers had evidently had enough of it. When my brother looked again they were retreating.

" I'll sit here," said my brother, " if I may "; and he got upon the empty front seat. The lady looked over her shoulder.

" Give me the reins," she said, and laid the whip along the pony's side. In another moment a bend in the road hid the three men from my brother's eyes.

So, quite unexpectedly, my brother found himself, panting, with a cut mouth, a bruised jaw, and blood-stained knuckles, driving along an unknown lane with these two women.

He learned they were the wife and the younger sister of a surgeon living at Stanmore, who had come in the small hours from a dangerous case at Pinner, and heard at some railway station on his way of the Martian advance. He had hurried home, roused the women — their servant had left them two days before — packed some provisions, put his revolver under the seat — luckily for my brother — and told them to drive on to Edgware, with the idea of getting a train there. He stopped behind to tell the neighbours. He would overtake them, he said, at about half-past four in the morning, and now it was nearly nine and they had seen nothing of him. They could not stop in Edgware because of the growing traffic through the place, and so they had come into this side lane.

That was the story they told my brother in fragments when presently they stopped again, nearer to New Barnet. He promised to stay with them, at least until they could determine what to do, or until the missing man arrived, and professed to be an expert shot with the revolver — a weapon strange to him — in order to give them confidence.

They made a sort of encampment by the wayside, and the pony became happy in the hedge. He told them of his own escape out of London, and all that he knew of these Martians and their ways. The sun crept higher in the sky, and after a time their talk died out and gave place to an uneasy state of anticipation. Several wayfarers came along the lane, and of these my brother gathered such news as he could. Every broken answer he had deepened his impression of the great disaster that had come on humanity, deepened his persuasion of the immediate necessity for prosecuting this flight. He urged the matter upon them.

" We have money," said the slender woman, and hesitated.

Her eyes met my brother's, and her hesitation ended.

" So have I," said my brother.

She explained that they had as much as thirty pounds in gold, besides a five-pound note, and suggested that with that they might get upon a train at St. Albans or New Barnet. My brother thought that was hopeless, seeing the fury of the Londoners to crowd upon the trains, and broached his own idea of striking across Essex towards Harwich and thence escaping from the country altogether.

Mrs. Elphinstone — that was the name of the woman in white — would listen to no reasoning, and kept calling upon " George "; but her sister-in-law was astonishingly quiet and deliberate, and at last agreed to my brother's suggestion. So, designing to cross the Great North Road, they went on towards Barnet, my brother leading the pony to save it as much as possible.

As the sun crept up the sky the day became excessively hot, and under foot a thick, whitish sand grew burning and blinding, so that they travelled only very slowly. The hedges were grey with dust. And as they advanced towards Barnet a tumultuous murmuring grew stronger.

They began to meet more people. For the most part these were staring before them, murmuring indistinct questions, jaded, haggard, unclean. One man in evening dress passed them on foot, his eyes on the ground. They heard his voice, and, looking back at him saw one hand clutched in his hair and the other beating invisible things. His paroxysm of rage over, he went on his way without once looking back.

As my brother's party went on towards the cross-roads to the south of Barnet they saw a woman approaching the road across some fields on their left, carrying a child and with two other children; and then passed a man in dirty black, with a thick stick in one hand and a small portmanteau in the other. Then

round the corner of the lane, from between the villas that guarded it at its confluence with the highroad, came a little cart drawn by a sweating black pony and driven by a sallow youth in a bowler hat, grey with dust. There were three girls, East End factory girls, and a couple of little children crowded in the cart.

"This'll tike us rahnd Edgware?" asked the driver, wild-eyed, white-faced; and when my brother told him it would if he turned to the left, he whipped up at once without the formality of thanks.

My brother noticed a pale grey smoke or haze rising among the houses in front of them, and veiling the white façade of a terrace beyond the road that appeared between the backs of the villas. Mrs. Elphinstone suddenly cried out at a number of tongues of smoky red flame leaping up above the houses in front of them against the hot, blue sky. The tumultuous noise resolved itself now into the disorderly mingling of many voices, the gride of many wheels, the creaking of waggons, and the staccato of hoofs. The lane came round sharply not fifty yards from the cross-roads.

"Good heavens!" cried Mrs. Elphinstone. "What is this you are driving us into?"

My brother stopped.

For the main road was a boiling stream of people, a torrent of human beings rushing northward, one pressing on another. A great bank of dust, white and luminous in the blaze of the sun, made everything within twenty feet of the ground grey and in-distinct and was perpetually re-newed by the hurrying feet of a dense crowd of horses and of men and women on foot, and by the wheels of vehicles of every de-scription.

"Way!" my brother heard voices crying. "Make way!"

It was like riding into the smoke of a fire to approach the meeting-point of the lane and road; the crowd roared like a fire, and the dust was hot and pun-gent. And, indeed, a little way up the road a villa was burning and sending rolling masses of black smoke across the road to add to the confusion.

Two men came past them. Then a dirty woman, carrying a heavy bundle and weeping. A lost retriever dog, with hanging tongue, circled dubiously round them, scared and wretched, and fled at my brother's threat.

So much as they could see of the road Londonward between the houses to the right was a tumultuous stream of dirty, hur-rying people, pent in between the villas on either side; the black heads, the crowded forms, grew into distinctness as they rushed towards the corner, hur-ried past, and merged their indi-viduality again in a receding mul-titude that was swallowed up at last in a cloud of dust.

"Go on! Go on!" cried the voices. "Way! Way!"

One man's hands pressed on the back of another. My brother stood at the pony's head. Irre-sistibly attracted, he advanced slowly, pace by pace, down the lane.

Edgware had been a scene of

confusion, Chalk Farm a riotous tumult, but this was a whole population in movement. It is hard to imagine that host. It had no character of its own. The figures poured out past the corner, and receded with their backs to the group in the lane. Along the margin came those who were on foot threatened by the wheels, stumbling in the ditches, blundering into one another.

The carts and carriages crowded close upon one another, making little way for those swifter and more impatient vehicles that darted forward every now and then when an opportunity showed itself of doing so, sending the people scattering against the fences and gates of the villas.

"Push on!" was the cry. "Push on! They are coming!"

In one cart stood a blind man in the uniform of the Salvation Army, gesticulating with his crooked fingers and bawling, "Eternity! eternity!" His voice was hoarse and very loud so that my brother could hear him long after he was lost to sight in the dust. Some of the people who crowded in the carts whipped stupidly at their horses and quarrelled with other drivers; some sat motionless, staring at nothing with miserable eyes; some gnawed their hands with thirst, or lay prostrate in the bottoms of their conveyances. The horses' bits were covered with foam, their eyes bloodshot.

There were cabs, carriages, shop-carts, waggons, beyond counting; a mail-cart, a road-cleaner's cart marked "Vestry of St. Pancras," a huge timber-waggon crowded with roughs. A brewer's dray rumbled by with its two near wheels splashed with fresh blood.

"Clear the way!" cried the voices. "Clear the way!"

"Eter-nity! eter-nity!" came echoing down the road.

There were sad, haggard women tramping by, well dressed, with children that cried and stumbled, their dainty clothes smothered in dust, their weary faces smeared with tears. With many of these came men, sometimes helpful, sometimes lowering and savage. Fighting side by side with them pushed some weary street outcast in faded black rags, wide-eyed, loud-voiced, and foul-mouthed. There were sturdy workmen thrusting their way along, wretched, unkempt men, clothed like clerks or shopmen, struggling spasmodically; a wounded soldier my brother noticed, men dressed in the clothes of railway porters, one wretched creature in a night-shirt with a coat thrown over it.

But varied as its composition was, certain things all that host had in common. There were fear and pain on their faces, and fear behind them. A tumult up the road, a quarrel for a place in a waggon, sent the whole host of them quickening their pace; even a man so scared and broken that his knees bent under him was galvanised for a moment into renewed activity. The heat and dust had already been at work upon this multitude. Their skins were dry, their lips black and cracked. They were all thirsty,

weary, and footsore. And amid the various cries one heard disputes, reproaches, groans of weariness and fatigue; the voices of most of them were hoarse and weak. Through it all ran a refrain:

"Way! way! The Martians are coming!"

Few stopped and came aside from that flood. The lane opened slantingly into the main road with a narrow opening, and had a delusive appearance of coming from the direction of London. Yet a kind of eddy of people drove into its mouth; weaklings elbowed out of the stream, who for the most part rested but a moment before plunging into it again. A little way down the lane, with two friends bending over him, lay a man with a bare leg, wrapped about with bloody rags. He was a lucky man to have friends.

A little old man, with a grey military moustache and a filthy black frock-coat, limped out and sat down beside the trap, removed his boot—his sock was blood-stained—shook out a pebble, and hobbled on again; and then a little girl of eight or nine, all alone, threw herself under the hedge close by my brother, weeping.

"I can't go on! I can't go on!"

My brother woke from his torpor of astonishment and lifted her up, speaking gently to her, and carried her to Miss Elphinstone. So soon as my brother touched her she became quite still, as if frightened.

"Ellen!" shrieked a woman in the crowd, with tears in her voice—"Ellen!" And the child suddenly darted away from my brother, crying "Mother!"

"They are coming," said a man on horseback, riding past along the lane.

"Out of the way, there!" bawled a coachman, towering high; and my brother saw a closed carriage turning into the lane.

The people crushed back on one another to avoid the horse. My brother pushed the pony and chaise back into the hedge, and the man drove by and stopped at the turn of the way. It was a carriage, with a pole for a pair of horses, but only one was in the traces. My brother saw dimly through the dust that two men lifted out something on a white stretcher and put it gently on the grass beneath the privet hedge.

One of the men came running to my brother.

"Where is there any water?" he said. "He is dying fast, and very thirsty. It is Lord Garrick."

"Lord Garrick!" said my brother—"the Chief Justice?"

"The water?" he said.

"There may be a tap," said my brother, "in some of the houses. We have no water. I dare not leave my people."

The man pushed against the crowd towards the gate of the corner house.

"Go on!" said the people, thrusting at him. "They are coming! Go on!"

Then my brother's attention was distracted by a bearded, eagle-faced man lugging a small

hand-bag, which split even as my brother's eyes rested on it and disgorged a mass of sovereigns that seemed to break up into separate coins as it struck the ground. They rolled hither and thither among the struggling feet of men and horses. The man stopped and looked stupidly at the heap, and the shaft of a cab struck his shoulder and sent him reeling. He gave a shriek and dodged back, and a cart-wheel shaved him narrowly.

"Way!" cried the men all about him. "Make way!"

So soon as the cab had passed, he flung himself, with both hands open, upon the heap of coins, and began thrusting handfuls in his pocket. A horse rose close upon him, and in another moment, half rising, he had been borne down under the horse's hoofs.

"Stop!" screamed my brother, and pushing a woman out of his way, tried to clutch the bit of the horse.

Before he could get to it, he heard a scream under the wheels, and saw through the dust the rim passing over the poor wretch's back. The driver of the cart slashed his whip at my brother, who ran round behind the cart. The multitudinous shouting confused his ears. The man was writhing in the dust among his scattered money, unable to rise, for the wheel had broken his back, and his lower limbs lay limp and dead. My brother stood up and yelled at the next driver, and a man on a black horse came to his assistance.

"Get him out of the road," said he; and, clutching the man's collar with his free hand, my brother lugged him sideways. But he still clutched after his money, and regarded my brother fiercely, hammering at his arm with a handful of gold. "Go on! Go on!" shouted angry voices behind. "Way! Way!"

There was a smash as the pole of a carriage crashed into the cart that the man on horseback stopped. My brother looked up, and the man with the gold twisted his head round and bit the wrist that held his collar. There was a concussion, and the black horse came staggering sideways, and the cart-horse pushed beside it. A hoof missed my brother's foot by a hair's breadth. He released his grip on the fallen man and jumped back. He saw anger change to terror on the face of the poor wretch on the ground, and in a moment he was hidden and my brother was borne backward and carried past the entrance of the lane, and had to fight hard in the torrent to recover it.

He saw Miss Elphinstone covering her eyes, and a little child, with all a child's want of sympathetic imagination, staring with dilated eyes at a dusty something that lay black and still, ground and crushed under the rolling wheels. "Let us go back!" he shouted, and began turning the pony round. "We cannot cross this—hell," he said; and they went back a hundred yards the way they had come, until the fighting crowd was hidden. As

they passed the bend in the lane my brother saw the face of the dying man in the ditch under the privet, deadly white and drawn, and shining with perspiration. The two women sat silent, crouching in their seat and shivering.

Then beyond the bend my brother stopped again. Miss Elphinstone was white and pale, and her sister-in-law sat weeping, too wretched even to call upon "George." My brother was horrified and perplexed. So soon as they had retreated he realised how urgent and unavoidable it was to attempt this crossing. He turned to Miss Elphinstone, suddenly resolute.

"We must go that way," he said, and led the pony round again.

For the second time that day this girl proved her quality. To force their way into the torrent of people, my brother plunged into the traffic and held back a cab-horse, while she drove the pony across its head. A waggon locked wheels for a moment and ripped a long splinter from the chaise. In another moment they were caught and swept forward by the stream. My brother, with the cabman's whip-marks red across his face and hands, scrambled into the chaise and took the reins from her.

"Point the revolver at the man behind," he said, giving it to her, "if he presses us too hard. No! — point it at his horse."

Then he began to look out for a chance of edging to the right across the road. But once in the stream he seemed to lose volition, to become a part of that dusty rout. They swept through Chipping Barnet with the torrent; they were nearly a mile beyond the centre of the town before they had fought across to the opposite side of the way. It was din and confusion indescribable; but in and beyond the town the road forks repeatedly, and this to some extent relieved the stress.

They struck eastward through Hadley, and there on either side of the road, and at another place farther on they came upon a great multitude of people drinking at the stream, some fighting to come at the water. And farther on, from a hill near East Barnet, they saw two trains running slowly one after the other without signal or order — trains swarming with people, with men even among the coals behind the engines — going northward along the Great Northern Railway. My brother supposes they must have filled outside London, for at that time the furious terror of the people had rendered the central termini impossible.

Near this place they halted for the rest of the afternoon, for the violence of the day had already utterly exhausted all three of them. They began to suffer the beginnings of hunger; the night was cold, and none of them dared to sleep. And in the evening many people came hurrying along the road near by their stopping-place, fleeing from unknown dangers before them, and going in the direction from which my brother had come.

CHAPTER 17

THE "THUNDER CHILD"

Had the Martians aimed only at destruction, they might on Monday have annihilated the entire population of London, as it spread itself slowly through the home counties. Not only along the road through Barnet, but also through Edgware and Waltham Abbey, and along the roads eastward to Southend and Shoeburyness, and south of the Thames to Deal and Broadstairs, poured the same frantic rout. If one could have hung that June morning in a balloon in the blazing blue above London every northward and eastward road running out of the tangled maze of streets would have seemed stippled black with the streaming fugitives, each dot a human agony of terror and physical distress. I have set forth at length in the last chapter my brother's account of the road through Chipping Barnet, in order that my readers may realise how that swarming of black dots appeared to one of those concerned. Never before in the history of the world had such a mass of human beings moved and suffered together.

The legendary hosts of Goths and Huns, the hugest armies Asia has ever seen, would have been but a drop in that current. And this was no disciplined march; it was a stampede — a stampede gigantic and terrible — without order and without a goal, six million people, unarmed and unprovisioned, driving headlong. It was the beginning of the rout of civilisation, of the massacre of mankind.

Directly below him the balloonist would have seen the network of streets far and wide, houses, churches, squares, crescents, gardens — already derelict — spread out like a huge map, and in the southward *blotted*. Over Ealing, Richmond, Wimbledon, it would have seemed as if some monstrous pen had flung ink upon the chart. Steadily, incessantly, each black splash grew and spread, shooting out ramifications this way and that, now banking itself against rising ground, now pouring swiftly over a crest into a new-found valley, exactly as a gout of ink would spread itself upon blotting-paper.

And beyond, over the blue hills that rise southward of the river, the glittering Martians went to and fro, calmly and methodically spreading their poison-cloud over this patch of country and then over that, laying it again with their steam jets when it had served its purpose, and taking possession of the conquered country. They do not seem to have aimed at extermination so much as at complete demoralisation and the destruction of any opposition. They ex-

ploded any stores of powder they came upon, cut every telegraph, and wrecked the railways here and there. They were hamstringing mankind. They seemed in no hurry to extend the field of their operations, and did not come beyond the central part of London all that day. It is possible that a very considerable number of people in London stuck to their houses through Monday morning. Certain it is that many died at home suffocated by the Black Smoke.

Until about mid-day the Pool of London was an astonishing scene. Steamboats and shipping of all sorts lay there, tempted by the enormous sums of money offered by fugitives, and it is said that many who swam out to these vessels were thrust off with boat-hooks and drowned. About one o'clock in the afternoon the thinning remnant of a cloud of the black vapour appeared between the arches of Blackfriars Bridge. At that the Pool became a scene of mad confusion, fighting, and collision, and for some time a multitude of boats and barges jammed in the northern arch of the Tower Bridge, and the sailors and lightermen had to fight savagely against the people who swarmed upon them from the river front. People were actually clambering down the piers of the bridge from above.

When, an hour later, a Martian appeared beyond the Clock Tower and waded down the river, nothing but wreckage floated above Limehouse.

Of the falling of the fifth cylinder I have presently to tell.

The sixth star fell at Wimbledon. My brother, keeping watch beside the women in the chaise in a meadow, saw the green flash of it far beyond the hills. On Tuesday the little party, still set upon getting across the sea, made its way through the swarming country towards Colchester. The news that the Martians were now in possession of the whole of London was confirmed. They had been seen at Highgate, and even, it was said, at Neasden. But they did not come into my brother's view until the morrow.

That day the scattered multitudes began to realise the urgent need of provisions. As they grew hungry the rights of property ceased to be regarded. Farmers were out to defend their cattle-sheds, granaries, and ripening root crops with arms in their hands. A number of people now, like my brother, had their faces eastward, and there were some desperate souls even going back towards London to get food. These were chiefly people from the northern suburbs, whose knowledge of the Black Smoke came by hearsay. He heard that about half the members of the government had gathered at Birmingham, and that enormous quantities of high explosives were being prepared to be used in automatic mines across the Midland counties.

He was also told that the Midland Railway Company had replaced the desertions of the first day's panic, had resumed traffic, and was running northward trains from St. Albans to relieve the congestion of the home coun-

ties. There was also a placard in Chipping Ongar announcing that large stores of flour were available in the northern towns and that within twenty-four hours bread would be distributed among the starving people in the neighbourhood. But this intelligence did not deter him from the plan of escape he had formed, and the three pressed eastward all day, and heard no more of the bread distribution than this promise. Nor, as a matter of fact, did anyone else hear more of it. That night fell the seventh star, falling upon Primrose Hill. It fell while Miss Elphinstone was watching, for she took that duty alternately with my brother. She saw it.

On Wednesday the three fugitives — they had passed the night in a field of unripe wheat — reached Chelmsford, and there a body of the inhabitants, calling itself the Committee of Public Supply, seized the pony as provisions, and would give nothing in exchange for it but the promise of a share in it the next day. Here there were rumours of Martians at Epping, and news of the destruction of Waltham Abbey Powder Mills in a vain attempt to blow up one of the invaders.

People were watching for Martians here from the church towers. My brother, very luckily for him as it chanced, preferred to push on at once to the coast rather than wait for food, although all three of them were very hungry. By mid-day they passed through Tillingham, which, strangely enough, seemed to be quite silent and deserted, save for a few furtive plunderers hunting for food. Near Tillingham they suddenly came in sight of the sea, and the most amazing crowd of shipping of all sorts that it is possible to imagine.

For after the sailors could no longer come up the Thames, they came on to the Essex coast, to Harwich and Walton and Clacton, and afterwards to Foulness and Shoebury, to bring off the people. They lay in a huge sickle-shaped curve that vanished into mist at last towards the Naze. Close inshore was a multitude of fishing-smacks — English, Scotch, French, Dutch, and Swedish; steam-launches from the Thames, yachts, electric boats; and beyond were ships of large burden, a multitude of filthy colliers, trim merchantmen, cattle-ships, passenger-boats, petroleum-tanks, ocean tramps, an old white transport even, neat white and grey liners from Southampton and Hamburg; and along the blue coast across the Blackwater my brother could make out dimly a dense swarm of boats chaffering with the people on the beach, a swarm which also extended up the Blackwater almost to Maldon.

About a couple of miles out lay an ironclad, very low in the water, almost, to my brother's perception, like a water-logged ship. This was the ram *Thunder Child*. It was the only war-ship in sight, but far away to the right over the smooth surface of the sea — for that day there was a dead calm — lay a serpent of black smoke to mark the next

ironclads of the Channel Fleet, which hovered in an extended line, steam up and ready for action, across the Thames estuary during the course of the Martian conquest, vigilant and yet powerless to prevent it.

At the sight of the sea, Mrs. Elphinstone, in spite of the assurances of her sister-in-law, gave way to panic. She had never been out of England before, she would rather die than trust herself friendless in a foreign country, and so forth. She seemed, poor woman, to imagine that the French and the Martians might prove very similar. She had been growing increasingly hysterical, fearful, and depressed during the two days' journeyings. Her great idea was to return to Stanmore. Things had been always well and safe at Stanmore. They would find George at Stanmore.

It was with the greatest difficulty they could get her down to the beach, where presently my brother succeeded in attracting the attention of some men on a paddle steamer from the Thames. They sent a boat and drove a bargain for thirty-six pounds for the three. The steamer was going, these men said, to Ostend.

It was about two o'clock when my brother, having paid their fares at the gangway, found himself safely aboard the steamboat with his charges. There was food aboard, albeit at exorbitant prices, and the three of them contrived to eat a meal on one of the seats forward.

There were already a couple of score of passengers aboard, some of whom had expended their last money in securing a passage, but the captain lay off the Blackwater until five in the afternoon, picking up passengers until the seated decks were even dangerously crowded. He would probably have remained longer had it not been for the sound of guns that began about that hour in the south. As if in answer, the ironclad seaward fired a small gun and hoisted a string of flags. A jet of smoke sprang out of her funnels.

Some of the passengers were of opinion that this firing came from Shoeburyness, until it was noticed that it was growing louder. At the same time, far away in the south-east the masts and upper-works of three ironclads rose one after the other out of the sea, beneath clouds of black smoke. But my brother's attention speedily reverted to the distant firing in the south. He fancied he saw a column of smoke rising out of the distant grey haze.

The little steamer was already flapping her way eastward of the big crescent of shipping, and the low Essex coast was growing blue and hazy, when a Martian appeared, small and faint in the remote distance, advancing along the muddy coast from the direction of Foulness. At that the captain on the bridge swore at the top of his voice with fear and anger at his own delay, and the paddles seemed infected with his terror. Every soul aboard stood at the bulwarks or on the seats of the steamer and stared at that distant shape, higher than the trees or church towers inland,

and advancing with a leisurely parody of a human stride.

It was the first Martian my brother had seen, and he stood, more amazed than terrified, watching this Titan advancing deliberately towards the shipping, wading farther and farther into the water as the coast fell away. Then, far away beyond the Crouch, came another, striding over some stunted trees, and then yet another, still farther off, wading deeply through a shiny mud-flat that seemed to hang half-way up between sea and sky. They were all stalking seaward, as if to intercept the escape of the multitudinous vessels that were crowded between Foulness and the Naze. In spite of the throbbing exertions of the engines of the little paddle-boat, and the pouring foam that her wheels flung behind her, she receded with terrifying slowness from this ominous advance.

Glancing north-westward, my brother saw the large crescent of shipping already writhing with the approaching terror; one ship passing behind another, another coming round from broadside to end on, steamships whistling and giving off volumes of steam, sails being let out, launches rushing hither and thither. He was so fascinated by this and by the creeping danger away to the left that he had no eyes for anything seaward. And then a swift movement of the steamboat (she had suddenly come round to avoid being run down) flung him headlong from the seat upon which he was standing. There was a shouting all about him, a tram-

pling of feet, and a cheer that seemed to be answered faintly. The steamboat lurched and rolled him over upon his hands.

He sprang to his feet and saw to starboard, and not a hundred yards from their heeling, pitching boat, a vast iron bulk like the blade of a plough tearing through the water, tossing it on either side in huge waves of foam that leaped towards the steamer, flinging her paddles helplessly in the air, and then sucking her deck down almost to the water-line.

A douche of spray blinded my brother for a moment. When his eyes were clear again he saw the monster had passed and was rushing landward. Big iron upper-works rose out of this headlong structure, and from that twin funnels projected and spat a smoking blast shot with fire. It was the torpedo-ram, *Thunder Child*, steaming headlong, coming to the rescue of the threatened shipping.

Keeping his footing on the heaving deck by clutching the bulwarks, my brother looked past this charging leviathan at the Martians again, and he saw the three of them now close together, and standing so far out to sea that their tripod supports were almost entirely submerged. Thus sunken, and seen in remote perspective, they appeared far less formidable than the huge iron bulk in whose wake the steamer was pitching so helplessly. It would seem they were regarding this new antagonist with astonishment. To their intelligence, it may be, the giant was even

such another as themselves. The *Thunder Child* fired no gun, but simply drove full speed towards them. It was probably her not firing that enabled her to get so near the enemy as she did. They did not know what to make of her. One shell, and they would have sent her to the bottom forthwith with the Heat-Ray.

She was steaming at such a pace that in a minute she seemed half-way between the steamboat and the Martians — a diminishing black bulk against the receding horizontal expanse of the Essex coast.

Suddenly the foremost Martian lowered his tube and discharged a canister of the black gas at the ironclad. It hit her larboard side and glanced off in an inky jet that rolled away to seaward, an unfolding torrent of Black Smoke, from which the ironclad drove clear. To the watchers from the steamer, low in the water and with the sun in their eyes, it seemed as though she were already among the Martians.

They saw the gaunt figures separating and rising out of the water as they retreated shoreward, and one of them raised the camera-like generator of the Heat-Ray. He held it pointing obliquely downward, and a bank of steam sprang from the water at its touch. It must have driven through the iron of the ship's side like a white-hot iron rod through paper.

A flicker of flame went up through the rising steam, and then the Martian reeled and staggered. In another moment he was cut down, and a great body of water and steam shot high in the air. The guns of the *Thunder Child* sounded through the reek, going off one after the other, and one shot splashed the water high close by the steamer, ricochetted towards the other flying ships to the north, and smashed a smack to match-wood.

But no one heeded that very much. At the sight of the Martian's collapse the captain on the bridge yelled inarticulately, and all the crowding passengers on the steamer's stern shouted together. And then they yelled again. For, surging out beyond the white tumult drove something long and black, the flames streaming from its middle parts, its ventilators and funnels spouting fire.

She was alive still; the steering-gear, it seems, was intact and her engines working. She headed straight for a second Martian, and was within a hundred yards of him when the Heat-Ray came to bear. Then with a violent thud, a blinding flash, her decks, her funnels, leaped upward. The Martian staggered with the violence of her explosion, and in another moment the flaming wreckage, still driving forward with the impetus of its pace, had struck him and crumpled him up like a thing of card-board. My brother shouted involuntarily. A boiling tumult of steam hid everything again.

"Two!" yelled the captain.

Every one was shouting. The whole steamer from end to end rang with frantic cheering that was taken up first by one and

then by all in the crowding multitude of ships and boats that was driving out to sea.

The steam hung upon the water for many minutes, hiding the third Martian and the coast altogether. And all this time the boat was paddling steadily out to sea and away from the fight; and when at last the confusion cleared, the drifting bank of black vapour intervened, and nothing of the *Thunder Child* could be made out, nor could the third Martian be seen. But the ironclads to seaward were now quite close and standing in towards shore past the steamboat.

The little vessel continued to beat its way seaward, and the ironclads receded slowly towards the coast, which was hidden still by a marbled bank of vapour, part steam, part black gas, eddying and combining in the strangest way. The fleet of refugees was scattering to the north-east; several smacks were sailing between the ironclads and the steamboat. After a time, and before they reached the sinking cloud-bank, the warships turned northward, and then abruptly went about and passed into the thickening haze of evening southward. The coast grew faint, and at last indistinguishable amid the low banks of clouds that were gathering about the sinking sun.

Then suddenly out of the golden haze of the sunset came the vibration of guns, and a form of black shadows moving. Every one struggled to the rail of the steamer and peered into the blinding furnace of the west, but nothing was to be distinguished clearly. A mass of smoke rose slanting and barred the face of the sun. The steamboat throbbed on its way through an interminable suspense.

The sun sank into grey clouds, the sky flushed and darkened, the evening star trembled into sight. It was deep twilight when the captain cried out and pointed. My brother strained his eyes. Something rushed up into the sky out of the greyness — rushed slantingly upward and very swiftly into the luminous clearness above the clouds in the western sky; something flat and broad and very large, that swept round in a vast curve, grew smaller, sank slowly, and vanished again into the grey mystery of the night. And as it flew it rained down darkness upon the land.

Book II: *The Earth Under the Martians*

CHAPTER 1

UNDER FOOT

In the first book I have wandered so much from my own adventures to tell of the experiences of my brother that all through the last two chapters I and the curate have been lurking in the empty house at Halliford whither we fled to escape the Black Smoke. There I will resume. We stopped there all Sunday night and all the next day—the day of the panic—in a little island of daylight, cut off by the Black Smoke from the rest of the world. We could do nothing but wait in aching inactivity during those two weary days.

My mind was occupied by anxiety for my wife. I figured her at Leatherhead, terrified, in danger, mourning me already as a dead man. I paced the rooms and cried aloud when I thought of how I was cut off from her, of all that might happen to her in my absence. My cousin I knew was brave enough for any emergency, but he was not the sort of man to realise danger quickly, to rise promptly. What was needed now was not bravery, but circumspection. My only consolation was to believe that the Martians were moving Londonward and away from her. Such vague anxieties keep the mind sensitive and painful. I grew very weary and irritable with the curate's perpetual ejaculations; I tired of the sight of his selfish despair. After some ineffectual remonstrance I kept away from him, staying in a room —evidently a children's schoolroom—containing globes, forms, and copy-books. When he followed me thither, I went to a box-room at the top of the house and, in order to be alone with my aching miseries, locked myself in.

We were hopelessly hemmed in by the Black Smoke all that day and the morning of the next. There were signs of people in the next house on Sunday evening —a face at a window and moving lights, and later the slamming of a door. But I do not know who these people were, nor what be-

came of them. We saw nothing of them next day. The Black Smoke drifted slowly riverward all through Monday morning, creeping nearer and nearer to us, driving at last along the roadway outside the house that hid us.

A Martian came across the fields about mid-day, laying the stuff with a jet of superheated steam that hissed against the walls, smashed all the windows it touched, and scalded the curate's hand as he fled out of the front room. When at last we crept across the sodden rooms and looked out again, the country northward was as though a black snowstorm had passed over it. Looking towards the river, we were astonished to see an unaccountable redness mingling with the black of the scorched meadows.

For a time we did not see how this change affected our position, save that we were relieved of our fear of the Black Smoke. But later I perceived that we were no longer hemmed in, that now we might get away. So soon as I realised that the way of escape was open, my dream of action returned. But the curate was lethargic, unreasonable.

"We are safe here," he repeated; "safe here."

I resolved to leave him — would that I had! Wiser now for the artilleryman's teaching, I sought out food and drink. I had found oil and rags for my burns, and I also took a hat and a flannel shirt that I found in one of the bedrooms. When it was clear to him that I meant to go alone —

had reconciled myself to going alone — he suddenly roused himself to come. And all being quiet throughout the afternoon, we started about five o'clock, as I should judge, along the blackened road to Sunbury.

In Sunbury, and at intervals along the road, were dead bodies lying in contorted attitudes, horses as well as men, overturned carts and luggage, all covered thickly with black dust. That pall of cindery powder made me think of what I had read of the destruction of Pompeii. We got to Hampton Court without misadventure, our minds full of strange and unfamiliar appearances, and at Hampton Court our eyes were relieved to find a patch of green that had escaped the suffocating drift. We went through Bushey Park, with its deer going to and fro under the chestnuts, and some men and women hurrying in the distance towards Hampton, and so we came to Twickenham. These were the first people we saw.

Away across the road the woods beyond Ham and Petersham were still afire. Twickenham was uninjured by either Heat-Ray or Black Smoke, and there were more people about here, though none could give us news. For the most part they were like ourselves, taking advantage of a lull to shift their quarters. I have an impression that many of the houses here were still occupied by scared inhabitants, too frightened even for flight. Here, too, the evidence of a hasty rout was abundant along the road. I

remember most vividly three smashed bicycles in a heap, pounded into the road by the wheels of subsequent carts. We crossed Richmond Bridge about half-past eight. We hurried across the exposed bridge, of course, but I noticed floating down the stream a number of red masses, some many feet across. I did not know what these were — there was no time for scrutiny — and I put a more horrible interpretation on them than they deserved. Here again on the Surrey side were black dust that had once been smoke, and dead bodies — a heap near the approach to the station; but we had no glimpse of the Martians until we were some way towards Barnes.

We saw in the blackened distance a group of three people running down a side street towards the river, but otherwise it seemed deserted. Up the hill Richmond town was burning briskly; outside the town of Richmond there was no trace of the Black Smoke.

Then suddenly, as we approached Kew, came a number of people running, and the upperworks of a Martian fighting-machine loomed in sight over the house-tops, not a hundred yards away from us. We stood aghast at our danger, and had the Martian looked down we must immediately have perished. We were so terrified that we dared not go on, but turned aside and hid in a shed in a garden. There the curate crouched, weeping silently, and refusing to stir again.

But my fixed idea of reaching Leatherhead would not let me rest, and in the twilight I ventured out again. I went through a shrubbery, and along a passage beside a big house standing in its own grounds, and so emerged upon the road towards Kew. The curate I left in the shed, but he came hurrying after me.

That second start was the most foolhardy thing I ever did. For it was manifest the Martians were about us. No sooner had the curate overtaken me than we saw either the fighting-machine we had seen before or another, far away across the meadows in the direction of Kew Lodge. Four or five little black figures hurried before it across the green-grey of the field, and in a moment it was evident this Martian pursued them. In three strides he was among them, and they ran radiating from his feet in all directions. He used no Heat-Ray to destroy them, but picked them up one by one. Apparently he tossed them into the great metallic carrier which projected behind him, much as a workman's basket hangs over his shoulder.

It was the first time I realised that the Martians might have any other purpose than destruction with defeated humanity. We stood for a moment petrified, then turned and fled through a gate behind us into a walled garden, fell into, rather than found, a fortunate ditch, and lay there, scarce daring to whisper to each other until the stars were out.

I suppose it was nearly eleven o'clock before we gathered courage to start again, no longer venturing into the road, but sneaking along hedge-rows and through plantations, and watching keenly through the darkness, he on the right and I on the left, for the Martians, who seemed to be all about us. In one place we blundered upon a scorched and blackened area, now cooling and ashen, and a number of scattered dead bodies of men, burned horribly about the heads and trunks but with their legs and boots mostly intact; and of dead horses, fifty feet, perhaps, behind a line of four ripped guns and smashed gun-carriages.

Sheen, it seemed, had escaped destruction, but the place was silent and deserted. Here we happened on no dead, though the night was too dark for us to see into the side roads of the place. In Sheen my companion suddenly complained of faintness and thirst, and we decided to try one of the houses.

The first house we entered, after a little difficulty with the window, was a small semi-detached villa, and I found nothing eatable left in the place but some mouldy cheese. There was, however, water to drink; and I took a hatchet, which promised to be useful in our next house-breaking.

We then crossed to a place where the road turns towards Mortlake. Here there stood a white house within a walled garden, and in the pantry of this domicile we found a store of food — two loaves of bread in a pan, an uncooked steak, and the half of a ham. I give this catalogue so precisely because, as it happened, we were destined to subsist upon this store for the next fortnight. Bottled beer stood under a shelf, and there were two bags of haricot beans and some limp lettuces. This pantry opened into a kind of wash-up kitchen, and in this was firewood; there was also a cupboard, in which we found nearly a dozen of burgundy, tinned soups and salmon, and two tins of biscuits.

We sat in the adjacent kitchen in the dark — for we dared not strike a light — and ate bread and ham, and drank beer out of the same bottle. The curate, who was still timorous and restless, was now, oddly enough, for pushing on, and I was urging him to keep up his strength by eating when the thing happened that was to imprison us.

"It can't be midnight yet," I said, and then came a blinding glare of vivid green light. Everything in the kitchen leaped out, clearly visible in green and black, and vanished again. And then followed such a concussion as I have never heard before or since. So close on the heels of this as to seem instantaneous came a thud behind me, a clash of glass, a crash and rattle of falling masonry all about us, and the plaster of the ceiling came down upon us, smashing into a multitude of fragments upon our heads. I was knocked headlong across the floor against the oven handle and stunned. I was in-

sensible for a long time, the curate told me, and when I came to we were in darkness again, and he, with a face wet, as I found afterwards, with blood from a cut forehead, was dabbing water over me.

For some time I could not recollect what had happened. Then things came to me slowly. A bruise on my temple asserted itself.

"Are you better?" asked the curate, in a whisper.

At last I answered him. I sat up.

"Don't move," he said. "The floor is covered with smashed crockery from the dresser. You can't possibly move without making a noise, and I fancy *they* are outside."

We both sat quite silent, so that we could scarcely hear each other breathing. Everything seemed deadly still, but once something near us, some plaster or broken brick-work, slid down with a rumbling sound. Outside and very near was an intermittent, metallic rattle.

"That!" said the curate, when presently it happened again.

"Yes," I said. "But what is it?"

"A Martian!" said the curate. I listened again.

"It was not like the Heat-Ray," I said, and for a time I was inclined to think one of the great fighting-machines had stumbled against the house, as I had seen one stumble against the tower of Shepperton Church.

Our situation was so strange and incomprehensible that for three or four hours, until the dawn came, we scarcely moved. And then the light filtered in, not through the window, which remained black, but through a triangular aperture between a beam and a heap of broken bricks in the wall behind us. The interior of the kitchen we now saw greyly for the first time.

The window had been burst in by a mass of garden mould, which flowed over the table upon which we had been sitting and lay about our feet. Outside, the soil was banked high against the house. At the top of the window-frame we could see an uprooted drainpipe. The floor was littered with smashed hardware; the end of the kitchen towards the house was broken into, and since the daylight shone in there, it was evident the greater part of the house had collapsed. Contrasting vividly with this ruin was the neat dresser, stained in the fashion, pale green, and with a number of copper and tin vessels below it, the wall-paper imitating blue and white tiles, and a couple of coloured supplements fluttering from the walls above the kitchen range.

As the dawn grew clearer, we saw through the gap in the wall the body of a Martian, standing sentinel, I suppose, over the still glowing cylinder. At the sight of that we crawled as circumspectly as possible out of the twilight of the kitchen into the darkness of the scullery.

Abruptly the right interpretation dawned upon my mind.

"The fifth cylinder," I whis-

pered, " the fifth shot from Mars, has struck this house and buried us under the ruins! "

For a time the curate was silent, and then he whispered:

" God have mercy upon us! "

I heard him presently whimpering to himself.

Save for that sound we lay quite still in the scullery; I for my part scarce dared breathe, and sat with my eyes fixed on the faint light of the kitchen door. I could just see the curate's face, a dim, oval shape, and his collar and cuffs. Outside there began a metallic hammering, then a violent hooting, and then again, after a quiet interval, a hissing like the hissing of an engine. These noises, for the most part problematical, continued intermittently, and seemed if anything to increase in number as time wore on. Presently a measured thudding and a vibration that made everything about us quiver and the vessels in the pantry ring and shift, began and continued. Once the light was eclipsed, and the ghostly kitchen doorway became absolutely dark. For many hours we must have crouched there, silent and shivering, until our tired attention failed. . . .

At last I found myself awake and very hungry. I am inclined to believe we must have spent the greater portion of a day before that awakening. My hunger was at a stride so insistent that it moved me to action. I told the curate I was going to seek food, and felt my way towards the pantry. He made me no answer, but so soon as I began eating the faint noise I made stirred him up and I heard him crawling after me.

CHAPTER 2

WHAT WE SAW FROM THE RUINED HOUSE

AFTER eating we crept back to the scullery, and there I must have dozed again, for when presently I looked round I was alone. The thudding vibration continued with wearisome persistence. I whispered for the curate several times, and at last felt my way to the door of the kitchen. It was still daylight, and I perceived him across the room, lying against the triangular hole that looked out upon the Martians. His shoulders were hunched, so that his head was hidden from me.

I could hear a number of noises almost like those in an engine-shed; and the place rocked with that beating thud. Through the aperture in the wall I could see the top of a tree touched with gold and the warm blue of a tranquil evening sky. For a minute or so I remained watching the curate, and then I advanced, crouching and stepping with extreme care amid the

broken crockery that littered the floor.

I touched the curate's leg, and he started so violently that a mass of plaster went sliding down outside and fell with a loud impact. I gripped his arm, fearing he might cry out, and for a long time we crouched motionless. Then I turned to see how much of our rampart remained. The detachment of the plaster had left a vertical slit open in the débris, and by raising myself cautiously across a beam I was able to see out of this gap into what had been overnight a quiet suburban roadway. Vast, indeed, was the change that we beheld.

The fifth cylinder must have fallen right into the midst of the house we had first visited. The building had vanished, completely smashed, pulverised, and dispersed by the blow. The cylinder lay now far beneath the original foundations — deep in a hole, already vastly larger than the pit I had looked into at Woking. The earth all round it had splashed under that tremendous impact — " splashed " is the only word — and lay in heaped piles that hid the masses of the adjacent houses. It had behaved exactly like mud under the violent blow of a hammer. Our house had collapsed backward; the front portion, even on the ground floor, had been destroyed completely; by a chance the kitchen and scullery had escaped, and stood buried now under soil and ruins, closed in by tons of earth on every side save towards the cylinder. Over that aspect we hung now on the very edge of the great circular pit the Martians were engaged in making. The heavy beating sound was evidently just behind us, and ever and again a bright green vapour drove up like a veil across our peep-hole.

The cylinder was already opened in the centre of the pit, and on the farther edge of the pit, amid the smashed and gravel-heaped shrubbery, one of the great fighting-machines, deserted by its occupant, stood stiff and tall against the evening sky. At first I scarcely noticed the pit and the cylinder, although it has been convenient to describe them first, on account of the extraordinary glittering mechanism I saw busy in the excavation, and on account of the strange creatures that were crawling slowly and painfully across the heaped mould near it.

The mechanism it certainly was that held my attention first. It was one of those complicated fabrics that have since been called handling-machines, and the study of which has already given such an enormous impetus to terrestrial invention. As it dawned upon me first it presented a sort of metallic spider with five jointed, agile legs, and with an extraordinary number of jointed levers, bars, and reaching and clutching tentacles about its body. Most of its arms were retracted, but with three long tentacles it was fishing out a number of rods, plates, and bars which lined the covering and apparently strengthened the walls,

of the cylinder. These, as it extracted them, were lifted out and deposited upon a level surface of earth behind it.

Its motion was so swift, complex, and perfect that at first I did not see it as a machine, in spite of its metallic glitter. The fighting-machines were co-ordinated and animated to an extraordinary pitch, but nothing to compare with this. People who have never seen these structures, and have only the ill-imagined efforts of artists or the imperfect descriptions of such eye-witnesses as myself to go upon, scarcely realise that living quality.

I recall particularly the illustration of one of the first pamphlets to give a consecutive account of the war. The artist had evidently made a hasty study of one of the fighting-machines, and there his knowledge ended. He presented them as tilted, stiff tripods, without either flexibility or subtlety, and with an altogether misleading monotony of effect. The pamphlet containing these renderings had a considerable vogue, and I mention them here simply to warn the reader against the impression they may have created. They were no more like the Martians I saw in action than a Dutch doll is like a human being. To my mind, the pamphlet would have been much better without them.

At first, I say, the handling-machine did not impress me as a machine, but as a crab-like creature with a glittering integument, the controlling Martian whose delicate tentacles actuated its movements seeming to be simply the equivalent of the crab's cerebral portion. But then I perceived the resemblance of its grey-brown, shiny, leathery integument to that of the other sprawling bodies beyond, and the true nature of this dexterous workman dawned upon me. With that realisation my interest shifted to those other creatures, the real Martians. Already I had had a transient impression of these, and the first nausea no longer obscured my observation. Moreover, I was concealed and motionless, and under no urgency of action.

They were, I now saw, the most unearthly creatures it is possible to conceive. They were huge round bodies — or, rather, heads — about four feet in diameter, each body having in front of it a face. This face had no nostrils — indeed, the Martians do not seem to have had any sense of smell, but it had a pair of very large dark-coloured eyes, and just beneath this a kind of fleshy beak. In the back of this head or body — I scarcely know how to speak of it — was the single tight tympanic surface, since known to be anatomically an ear, though it must have been almost useless in our denser air. In a group round the mouth were sixteen slender, almost whip-like tentacles, arranged in two bunches of eight each. These bunches have since been named rather aptly, by that distinguished anatomist, Professor Howes, the *hands*. Even as I saw these Martians for the first time they seemed to be endeavouring to raise themselves on these hands, but of course, with

the increased weight of terrestrial conditions, this was impossible. There is reason to suppose that on Mars they may have progressed upon them with some facility.

The internal anatomy, I may remark here, as dissection has since shown, was almost equally simple. The greater part of the structure was the brain, sending enormous nerves to the eyes, ear, and tactile tentacles. Besides this were the bulky lungs, into which the mouth opened, and the heart and its vessels. The pulmonary distress caused by the denser atmosphere and greater gravitational attraction was only too evident in the convulsive movements of the outer skin.

And this was the sum of the Martian organs. Strange as it may seem to a human being, all the complex apparatus of digestion, which makes up the bulk of our bodies, did not exist in the Martians. They were heads — merely heads. Entrails they had none. They did not eat, much less digest. Instead, they took the fresh, living blood of other creatures, and *injected* it into their own veins. I have myself seen this being done, as I shall mention in its place. But, squeamish as I may seem, I cannot bring myself to describe what I could not endure even to continue watching. Let it suffice to say, blood obtained from a still living animal, in most cases from a human being, was run directly by means of a little pipette into the recipient canal. . . .

The bare idea of this is no doubt horribly repulsive to us, but at the same time I think that we should remember how repulsive our carnivorous habits would seem to an intelligent rabbit.

The physiological advantages of the practice of injection are undeniable, if one thinks of the tremendous waste of human time and energy occasioned by eating and the digestive process. Our bodies are half made up of glands and tubes and organs, occupied in turning heterogeneous food into blood. The digestive processes and their reaction upon the nervous system sap our strength and colour our minds. Men go happy or miserable as they have healthy or unhealthy livers, or sound gastric glands. But the Martians were lifted above all these organic fluctuations of mood and emotion.

Their undeniable preference for men as their source of nourishment is partly explained by the nature of the remains of the victims they had brought with them as provisions from Mars. These creatures, to judge from the shrivelled remains that have fallen into human hands, were bipeds with flimsy, silicious skeletons (almost like those of the silicious sponges) and feeble musculature, standing about six feet high and having round, erect heads, and large eyes in flinty sockets. Two or three of these seem to have been brought in each cylinder, and all were killed before earth was reached. It was just as well for them, for the mere attempt to stand upright upon our planet would have broken every bone in their bodies.

And while I am engaged in this description, I may add in this place certain further details which, although they were not all evident to us at the time, will enable the reader who is unacquainted with them to form a clearer picture of these offensive creatures.

In three other points their physiology differed strangely from ours. Their organisms did not sleep, any more than the heart of man sleeps. Since they had no extensive muscular mechanism to recuperate, that periodical extinction was unknown to them. They had little or no sense of fatigue, it would seem. On earth they could never have moved without effort, yet even to the last they kept in action. In twenty-four hours they did twenty-four hours of work, as even on earth is perhaps the case with the ants.

In the next place, wonderful as it seems in a sexual world, the Martians were absolutely without sex, and therefore without any of the tumultuous emotions that arise from that difference among men. A young Martian, there can now be no dispute, was really born upon earth during the war, and it was found attached to its parent, partially *budded* off, just as young lily-bulbs bud off, or like the young animals in the fresh-water polyp.

In man, in all the higher terrestrial animals, such a method of increase has disappeared; but even on this earth it was certainly the primitive method. Among the lower animals, up even to those first cousins of the vertebrated animals, the Tunicates, the two processes occur side by side, but finally the sexual method superseded its competitor altogether. On Mars, however, just the reverse has apparently been the case.

It is worthy of remark that a certain speculative writer of quasi-scientific repute, writing long before the Martian invasion, did forecast for man a final structure not unlike the actual Martian condition. His prophecy, I remember, appeared in November or December, 1893, in a long defunct publication, the *Pall Mall Budget,* and I recall a caricature of it in a pre-Martian periodical called *Punch*. He pointed out — writing in a foolish, facetious tone — that the perfection of mechanical appliances must ultimately supersede limbs; the perfection of chemical devices, digestion; that such organs as hair, external nose, teeth, ears, and chin were no longer essential parts of the human being, and that the tendency of natural selection would lie in the direction of their steady diminution through the coming ages. The brain alone remained a cardinal necessity. Only one other part of the body had a strong case for survival, and that was the hand, "teacher and agent of the brain." While the rest of the body dwindled, the hands would grow larger.

There is many a true word written in jest, and here in the Martians we have beyond dispute the actual accomplishment of such a suppression of the animal side of the organism by the intelligence. To me it is quite cred-

ible that the Martians may be descended from beings not unlike ourselves, by a gradual development of brain and hands (the latter giving rise to the two bunches of delicate tentacles at last) at the expense of the rest of the body. Without the body the brain would, of course, become a mere selfish intelligence, without any of the emotional substratum of the human being.

The last salient point in which the systems of these creatures differed from ours was in what one might have thought a very trivial particular. Micro-organisms, which cause so much disease and pain on earth, have either never appeared upon Mars or Martian sanitary science eliminated them ages ago. A hundred diseases, all the fevers and contagions of human life, consumption, cancers, tumours and such morbidities, never enter the scheme of their life. And speaking of the differences between the life on Mars and terrestrial life, I may allude here to the curious suggestions of the red weed.

Apparently the vegetable kingdom in Mars, instead of having green for a dominant colour, is of a vivid blood-red tint. At any rate, the seeds which the Martians (intentionally or accidentally) brought with them gave rise in all cases to red-coloured growths. Only that known popularly as the red weed, however, gained any footing in competition with terrestrial forms. The red creeper was quite a transitory growth, and few people have seen it growing. For a time, however, the red weed grew with astonishing vigour and luxuriance. It spread up the sides of the pit by the third or fourth day of our imprisonment, and its cactus-like branches formed a carmine fringe to the edges of our triangular window. And afterwards I found it broadcast throughout the country, and especially wherever there was a stream of water.

The Martians had what appears to have been an auditory organ, a single round drum at the back of the head-body, and eyes with a visual range not very different from ours except that, according to Philips, blue and violet were as black to them. It is commonly supposed that they communicated by sounds and tentacular gesticulations; this is asserted, for instance, in the able but hastily compiled pamphlet (written evidently by some one not an eye-witness of Martian actions) to which I have already alluded, and which, so far, has been the chief source of information concerning them. Now no surviving human being saw so much of the Martians in action as I did. I take no credit to myself for an accident, but the fact is so. And I assert that I watched them closely time after time, and that I have seen four, five, and (once) six of them sluggishly performing the most elaborately complicated operations together without either sound or gesture. Their peculiar hooting invariably preceded feeding; it had no modulation, and was, I believe, in no sense a signal, but merely the expiration of air preparatory to the suctional operation. I have a certain claim to at least an elemen-

tary knowledge of psychology, and in this matter I am convinced — as firmly as I am convinced of anything — that the Martians interchanged thoughts without any physical intermediation. And I have been convinced of this in spite of strong preconceptions. Before the Martian invasion, as an occasional reader here or there may remember, I had written with some little vehemence against the telepathic theory.

The Martians wore no clothing. Their conceptions of ornament and decorum were necessarily different from ours; and not only were they evidently much less sensible of changes of temperature than we are, but changes of pressure do not seem to have affected their health at all seriously. Yet though they wore no clothing, it was in the other artificial additions to their bodily resources that their great superiority over man lay. We men, with our bicycles and road-skates, our Lilienthal soaring-machines, our guns and sticks and so forth, are just in the beginning of the evolution that the Martians have worked out. They have become practically mere brains, wearing different bodies according to their needs just as men wear suits of clothes and take a bicycle in a hurry or an umbrella in the wet. And of their appliances, perhaps nothing is more wonderful to a man than the curious fact that what is the dominant feature of almost all human devices in mechanism is absent — the *wheel* is absent; among all the things they brought to earth there is no trace or suggestion of their use of wheels. One would have at least expected it in locomotion. And in this connection it is curious to remark that even on this earth Nature has never hit upon the wheel, or has preferred other expedients to its development. And not only did the Martians either not know of (which is incredible), or abstain from, the wheel, but in their apparatus singularly little use is made of the fixed pivot, or relatively fixed pivot, with circular motions thereabout confined to one plane. Almost all the joints of the machinery present a complicated system of sliding parts moving over small but beautifully curved friction bearings. And while upon this matter of detail, it is remarkable that the long leverages of their machines are in most cases actuated by a sort of sham musculature of disks in an elastic sheath; these disks become polarised and drawn closely and powerfully together when traversed by a current of electricity. In this way the curious parallelism to animal motions, which was so striking and disturbing to the human beholder, was attained. Such quasi-muscles abounded in the crab-like handling-machine which, on my first peeping out of the slit, I watched unpacking the cylinder. It seemed infinitely more alive than the actual Martians lying beyond it in the sunset light, panting, stirring ineffectual tentacles, and moving feebly after their vast journey across space.

While I was still watching their sluggish motions in the sunlight, and noting each strange detail of their form, the curate reminded

me of his presence by pulling violently at my arm. I turned to a scowling face, and silent, eloquent lips. He wanted the slit, which permitted only one of us to peep through; and so I had to forego watching them for a time while he enjoyed that privilege.

When I looked again, the busy handling-machine had already put together several of the pieces of apparatus it had taken out of the cylinder into a shape having an unmistakable likeness to its own; and down on the left a busy little digging mechanism had come into view, emitting jets of green vapour and working its way round the pit, excavating and embanking in a methodical and discriminating manner. This it was which had caused the regular beating noise, and the rhythmic shocks that had kept our ruinous refuge quivering. It piped and whistled as it worked. So far as I could see, the thing was without a directing Martian at all.

CHAPTER 3

THE DAYS OF
IMPRISONMENT

THE ARRIVAL of a second fighting-machine drove us from our peep-hole into the scullery, for we feared that from his elevation the Martian might see down upon us behind our barrier. At a later date we began to feel less in danger of their eyes, for to an eye in the dazzle of the sunlight outside our refuge must have been blank blackness, but at first the slightest suggestion of approach drove us into the scullery in heart-throbbing retreat. Yet terrible as was the danger we incurred, the attraction of peeping was for both of us irresistible. And I recall now with a sort of wonder that, in spite of the infinite danger in which we were between starvation and a still more terrible death, we could yet struggle bitterly for that horrible privilege of sight. We would race across the kitchen in a grotesque way between eagerness and the dread of making a noise, and strike each other, and thrust and kick, within a few inches of exposure.

The fact is that we had absolutely incompatible dispositions and habits of thought and action, and our danger and isolation only accentuated the incompatibility. At Halliford I had already come to hate the curate's trick of helpless exclamation, his stupid rigidity of mind. His endless muttering monologue vitiated every effort I made to think out a line of action, and drove me at times, thus pent up and intensified, almost to the verge of craziness. He was as lacking in restraint as a silly woman. He would weep for hours together, and I verily believe that to the very end this spoiled child of life thought his weak tears in some way efficacious. And I would sit in the darkness unable to keep my mind off him

by reason of his importunities. He ate more than I did, and it was in vain I pointed out that our only chance of life was to stop in the house until the Martians had done with their pit, that in that long patience a time might presently come when we should need food. He ate and drank impulsively in heavy meals at long intervals. He slept little.

As the days wore on, his utter carelessness of any consideration so intensified our distress and danger that I had, much as I loathed doing it, to resort to threats, and at last to blows. That brought him to reason for a time. But he was one of those weak creatures, void of pride, timorous, anæmic, hateful souls, full of shifty cunning who face neither God nor man, who face not even themselves.

It is disagreeable for me to recall and write these things, but I set them down that my story may lack nothing. Those who have escaped the dark and terrible aspects of life will find my brutality, my flash of rage in our final tragedy, easy enough to blame; for they know what is wrong as well as any, but not what is possible to tortured men. But those who have been under the shadow, who have gone down at last to elemental things, will have a wider charity.

And while within we fought out our dark, dim contest of whispers, snatched food and drink, and gripping hands and blows, without, in the pitiless sunlight of that terrible June, was the strange wonder, the unfamiliar routine of the Martians in the pit. Let me return to those first new experiences of mine. After a long time I ventured back to the peep-hole, to find that the new-comers had been reinforced by the occupants of no fewer than three of the fighting-machines. These last had brought with them certain fresh appliances that stood in an orderly manner about the cylinder. The second handling-machine was now completed, and was busied in serving one of the novel contrivances the big machine had brought. This was a body resembling a milk-can in its general form, above which oscillated a pear-shaped receptacle, and from which a stream of white powder flowed into a circular basin below.

The oscillatory motion was imparted to this by one tentacle of the handling-machine. With two spatulate hands the handling-machine was digging out and flinging masses of clay into the pear-shaped receptacle above, while with another arm it periodically opened a door and removed rusty and blackened clinkers from the middle part of the machine. Another steely tentacle directed the powder from the basin along a ribbed channel towards some receiver that was hidden from me by the mound of bluish dust. From this unseen receiver a little thread of green smoke rose vertically into the quiet air. As I looked, the handling-machine, with a faint and musical clinking, extended, telescopic fashion, a tentacle that had been a moment before a mere blunt projection, until its end was hidden behind the

mound of clay. In another second it had lifted a bar of white aluminum into sight, untarnished as yet and shining dazzlingly, and deposited it in a growing stack of bars that stood at the side of the pit. Between sunset and starlight this dexterous machine must have made more than a hundred such bars out of the crude clay, and the mound of bluish dust rose steadily until it topped the side of the pit.

The contrast between the swift and complex movements of these contrivances and the inert, panting clumsiness of their masters was acute, and for days I had to tell myself repeatedly that these latter were indeed the living of the two things.

The curate had possession of the slit when the first men were brought to the pit. I was sitting below, huddled up, listening with all my ears. He made a sudden movement backward, and I, fearful that we were observed, crouched in a spasm of terror. He came sliding down the rubbish and crept beside me in the darkness, inarticulate, gesticulating, and for a moment I shared his panic. His gesture suggested a resignation of the slit, and after a little while my curiosity gave me courage, and I rose up, stepped across him, and clambered up to it. At first I could see no reason for his frantic behaviour. The twilight had now come, the stars were little and faint, but the pit was illuminated by the flickering green fire that came from the aluminium-making. The whole picture was a flickering scheme of green gleams and shifting rusty black shadows, strangely trying to the eyes. Over and through it all went the bats, heeding it not at all. The sprawling Martians were no longer to be seen, the mound of blue-green powder had risen to cover them from sight, and a fighting-machine, with its legs contracted, crumpled, and abbreviated, stood across the corner of the pit. And then, amid the clangour of the machinery, came a drifting suspicion of human voices, that I entertained at first only to dismiss.

I crouched, watching this fighting-machine closely, satisfying myself now for the first time that the hood did indeed contain a Martian. As the green flames lifted I could see the oily gleam of his integument and the brightness of his eyes. And suddenly I heard a yell, and saw a long tentacle reaching over the shoulder of the machine to the little cage that hunched upon its back. Then something — something struggling violently — was lifted high against the sky, a black, vague enigma against the starlight; and as this black object came down again, I saw by the green brightness that it was a man. For an instant he was clearly visible. He was a stout, ruddy, middle-aged man, well dressed; three days before he must have been walking the world, a man of considerable consequence. I could see his staring eyes and gleams of light on his studs and watch-chain. He vanished behind the mound, and for a moment there was silence. And

then began a shrieking and a sustained and cheerful hooting from the Martians.

I slid down the rubbish, struggled to my feet, clapped my hands over my ears, and bolted into the scullery. The curate, who had been crouching silently with his arms over his head, looked up as I passed, cried out quite loudly at my desertion of him, and came running after me.

That night, as we lurked in the scullery balanced between our horror and the terrible fascination this peeping had, although I felt an urgent need of action I tried in vain to conceive some plan of escape; but afterwards, during the second day, I was able to consider our position with great clearness. The curate, I found, was quite incapable of discussion; this new and culminating atrocity had robbed him of all vestiges of reason or forethought. Practically he had already sunk to the level of an animal. But, as the saying goes, I gripped myself with both hands. It grew upon my mind, once I could face the facts, that, terrible as our position was, there was as yet no justification for absolute despair. Our chief chance lay in the possibility of the Martians making the pit nothing more than a temporary encampment. Or even if they kept it permanently, they might not consider it necessary to guard it, and a chance of escape might be afforded us. I also weighed very carefully the possibility of our digging a way out in a direction away from the pit, but the chances of our emerging within sight of some sentinel fighting-machine seemed at first too great. And I should have had to do all the digging myself. The curate would certainly have failed me.

It was on the third day, if my memory serves me right, that I saw the lad killed. It was the only occasion on which I actually saw the Martians feed. After that experience I avoided the hole in the wall for the better part of a day. I went into the scullery, removed the door, and spent some hours digging with my hatchet as silently as possible; but when I had made a hole about a couple of feet deep the loose earth collapsed noisily, and I did not dare continue. I lost heart, and lay down on the scullery floor for a long time, having no spirit even to move. And after that I abandoned altogether the idea of escaping by excavation.

It says much for the impression the Martians had made upon me that at first I entertained little or no hope of our escape being brought about by their overthrow through any human effort. But on the fourth or fifth night I heard a sound like heavy guns.

It was very late in the night, and the moon was shining brightly. The Martians had taken away the excavating-machine, and, save for a fighting-machine that stood in the remoter bank of the pit and a handling-machine that was buried out of my sight in a corner of the pit immediately beneath my peep-hole, the place was deserted by them. Except for the pale glow from the

handling-machine and the bars and patches of white moonlight, the pit was in darkness, and, except for the clinking of the handling-machine, quite still. That night was a beautiful serenity; save for one planet, the moon seemed to have the sky to herself. I heard a dog howling, and that familiar sound it was that made me listen. Then I heard quite distinctly a booming exactly like the sound of great guns. Six distinct reports I counted, and after a long interval six again. And that was all.

CHAPTER 4

THE DEATH OF THE CURATE

IT was on the sixth day of our imprisonment that I peeped for the last time, and presently found myself alone. Instead of keeping close to me and trying to oust me from the slit, the curate had gone back into the scullery. I was struck by a sudden thought. I went back quickly and quietly into the scullery. In the darkness I heard the curate drinking. I snatched in the darkness, and my fingers caught a bottle of burgundy.

For a few minutes there was a tussle. The bottle struck the floor and broke, and I desisted and rose. We stood panting and threatening each other. In the end I planted myself between him and the food, and told him of my determination to begin a discipline. I divided the food in the pantry into rations to last us ten days. I would not let him eat any more that day. In the afternoon he made a feeble effort to get at the food. I had been dozing, but in an instant I was awake. All day and all night we sat face to face, I weary but resolute, and he weeping and complaining of his immediate hunger. It was, I know, a night and a day, but to me it seemed — it seems now — an interminable length of time.

And so our widened incompatibility ended at last in open conflict. For two vast days we struggled in undertones and wrestling contests. There were times when I beat and kicked him madly, times when I cajoled and persuaded him, and once I tried to bribe him with the last bottle of burgundy, for there was a rain-water pump from which I could get water. But neither force nor kindness availed; he was indeed beyond reason. He would neither desist from his attacks on the food nor from his noisy babbling to himself. The rudimentary precautions to keep our imprisonment endurable he would not observe. Slowly I began to realise the complete overthrow of his intelligence, to perceive that my sole companion in this

close and sickly darkness was a man insane.

From certain vague memories I am inclined to think my own mind wandered at times. I had strange and hideous dreams whenever I slept. It sounds paradoxical, but I am inclined to think that the weakness and insanity of the curate warned me, braced me, and kept me a sane man.

On the eighth day he began to talk aloud instead of whispering, and nothing I could do would moderate his speech.

" It is just, O God! " he would say, over and over again. " It is just. On me and mine be the punishment laid. We have sinned, we have fallen short. There was poverty, sorrow; the poor were trodden in the dust, and I held my peace. I preached acceptable folly — my God, what folly! — when I should have stood up, though I died for it, and called upon them to repent — repent! . . . Oppressors of the poor and needy! . . . The wine-press of God! "

Then he would suddenly revert to the matter of the food I withheld from him, praying, begging, weeping, at last threatening. He began to raise his voice — I prayed him not to. He perceived a hold on me — he threatened he would shout and bring the Martians upon us. For a time that scared me; but any concession would have shortened our chance of escape beyond estimating. I defied him, although I felt no assurance that he might not do this thing. But that day, at any rate, he did not. He talked with his voice rising slowly, through the greater part of the eighth and ninth days — threats, entreaties, mingled with a torrent of half-sane and always frothy repentance for his vacant sham of God's service, such as made me pity him. Then he slept awhile, and began again with renewed strength, so loudly that I must needs make him desist.

" Be still! " I implored.

He rose to his knees, for he had been sitting in the darkness near the copper.

" I have been still too long," he said, in a tone that must have reached the pit, " and now I must bear my witness. Woe unto this unfaithful city! Woe! woe! Woe! woe! woe! to the inhabitants of the earth by reason of the other voices of the trumpet — "

" Shut up! " I said, rising to my feet, and in a terror lest the Martians should hear us. " For God's sake — "

" Nay," shouted the curate, at the top of his voice, standing likewise and extending his arms. " Speak! The word of the Lord is upon me! "

In three strides he was at the door leading into the kitchen.

" I must bear my witness! I go! It has already been too long delayed."

I put out my hand and felt the meat-chopper hanging to the wall. In a flash I was after him. I was fierce with fear. Before he was half-way across the kitchen I had overtaken him. With one last touch of humanity I turned

the blade back and struck him with the butt. He went headlong forward and lay stretched on the ground. I stumbled over him and stood panting. He lay still.

Suddenly I heard a noise without, the run and smash of slipping plaster, and the triangular aperture in the wall was darkened. I looked up and saw the lower surface of a handling-machine coming slowly across the hole. One of its gripping limbs curled amid the débris; another limb appeared, feeling its way over the fallen beams. I stood petrified, staring. Then I saw through a sort of glass plate near the edge of the body the face, as we may call it, and the large dark eyes of a Martian, peering, and then a long metallic snake of tentacle came feeling slowly through the hole.

I turned by an effort, stumbled over the curate, and stopped at the scullery door. The tentacle was now some way, two yards or more, in the room, and twisting and turning, with queer sudden movements, this way and that. For a while I stood fascinated by that slow, fitful advance. Then, with a faint, hoarse cry, I forced myself across the scullery, I trembled violently; I could scarcely stand upright. I opened the door of the coal-cellar, and stood there in the darkness staring at the faintly lit door-way into the kitchen, and listening. Had the Martian seen me? What was it doing now?

Something was moving to and fro there, very quietly; every now and then it tapped against the wall, or started on its movements with a faint metallic ringing, like the movements of keys on a split-ring. Then a heavy body —I knew too well what—was dragged across the floor of the kitchen towards the opening. Irresistibly attracted, I crept to the door and peeped into the kitchen. In the triangle of bright outer sunlight I saw the Martian, in its Briareus of a handling-machine, scrutinising the curate's head. I thought at once that it would infer my presence from the mark of the blow I had given him.

I crept back to the coal-cellar, shut the door, and began to cover myself up as much as I could, and as noiselessly as possible in the darkness, among the firewood and coal therein. Every now and then I paused, rigid, to hear if the Martian had thrust its tentacles through the opening again.

Then the faint metallic jingle returned. I traced it slowly feeling over the kitchen. Presently I heard it nearer—in the scullery, as I judged. I thought that its length might be insufficient to reach me. I prayed copiously. It passed, scraping faintly across the cellar door. An age of almost intolerable suspense intervened; then I heard it fumbling at the latch! It had found the door! The Martians understood doors!

It worried at the catch for a minute, perhaps, and then the door opened.

In the darkness I could just see the thing—like an elephant's trunk more than anything else— waving towards me and touching

and examining the wall, coals, wood and ceiling. It was like a black worm swaying its blind head to and fro.

Once, even, it touched the heel of my boot. I was on the verge of screaming; I bit my hand. For a time the tentacle was silent. I could have have fancied it had been withdrawn. Presently, with an abrupt click, it gripped something — I thought it had me! — and seemed to go out of the cellar again. For a minute I was not sure. Apparently it had taken a lump of coal to examine.

I seized the opportunity of slightly shifting my position, which had become cramped, and then listened. I whispered passionate prayers for safety.

Then I heard the slow, deliberate sound creeping towards me again. Slowly, slowly it drew near, scratching against the walls and tapping the furniture.

While I was still doubtful, it rapped smartly against the cellar door and closed it. I heard it go into the pantry, and the biscuit-tins rattled and a bottle smashed, and then came a heavy bump against the cellar door. Then silence, that passed into an infinity of suspense.

Had it gone?

At last I decided that it had.

It came into the scullery no more; but I lay all the tenth day in the close darkness, buried among coals and firewood, not daring even to crawl out for the drink for which I craved. It was the eleventh day before I ventured so far from my security.

CHAPTER 5

THE STILLNESS

My first act before I went into the pantry was to fasten the door between the kitchen and the scullery. But the pantry was empty; every scrap of food had gone. Apparently, the Martian had taken it all on the previous day. At that discovery I despaired for the first time. I took no food, or no drink either, on the eleventh or the twelfth day.

At first my mouth and throat were parched, and my strength ebbed sensibly. I sat about in the darkness of the scullery, in a state of despondent wretchedness. My mind ran on eating. I thought I had become deaf, for the noises of movement I had been accustomed to hear from the pit had ceased absolutely. I did not feel strong enough to crawl noiselessly to the peep-hole, or I would have gone there.

On the twelfth day my throat was so painful that, taking the chance of alarming the Martians, I attacked the creaking rain-water pump that stood by the sink, and got a couple of glassfuls of blackened and tainted rain-water. I

was greatly refreshed by this, and emboldened by the fact that no enquiring tentacle followed the noise of my pumping.

During these days, in a rambling, inconclusive way, I thought much of the curate and of the manner of his death.

On the thirteenth day I drank some more water, and dozed and thought disjointedly of eating and of vague impossible plans of escape. Whenever I dozed I dreamt of horrible phantasms, of the death of the curate, or of sumptuous dinners; but, asleep or awake, I felt a keen pain that urged me to drink again and again. The light that came into the scullery was no longer grey, but red. To my disordered imagination it seemed the colour of blood.

On the fourteenth day I went into the kitchen, and I was surprised to find that the fronds of the red weed had grown right across the hole in the wall, turning the half-light of the place into a crimson-coloured obscurity.

It was early on the fifteenth day that I heard a curious, familiar sequence of sounds in the kitchen, and, listening, identified it as the snuffing and scratching of a dog. Going into the kitchen, I saw a dog's nose peering in through a break among the ruddy fronds. This greatly surprised me. At the scent of me he barked shortly.

I thought if I could induce him to come into the place quietly I should be able, perhaps, to kill and eat him; and in any case, it

would be advisable to kill him, lest his actions attracted the attention of the Martians.

I crept forward, saying "Good dog!" very softly; but he suddenly withdrew his head and disappeared.

I listened — I was not deaf — but certainly the pit was still. I heard a sound like the flutter of a bird's wings, and a hoarse croaking, but that was all.

For a long while I lay close to the peep-hole, but not daring to move aside the red plants that obscured it. Once or twice I heard a faint pitter-patter like the feet of the dog going hither and thither on the sand far below me, and there were more birdlike sounds, but that was all. At length, encouraged by the silence, I looked out.

Except in the corner, where a multitude of crows hopped and fought over the skeletons of the dead the Martians had consumed, there was not a living thing in the pit.

I stared about me, scarcely believing my eyes. All the machinery had gone. Save for the big mound of greyish-blue powder in one corner, certain bars of aluminium in another, the black birds, and the skeletons of the killed, the place was merely an empty circular pit in the sand.

Slowly I thrust myself out through the red weed, and stood upon the mound of rubble. I could see in any direction save behind me, to the north, and neither Martians nor sign of Martians were to be seen. The pit dropped sheerly from my feet,

but a little way along the rubbish afforded a practicable slope to the summit of the ruins. My chance of escape had come. I began to tremble.

I hesitated for some time, and then, in a gust of desperate resolution, and with a heart that throbbed violently, I scrambled to the top of the mound in which I had been buried so long.

I looked about again. To the northward, too, no Martian was visible.

When I had last seen this part of Sheen in the daylight it had been a straggling street of comfortable white and red houses, interspersed with abundant shady trees. Now I stood on a mound of smashed brickwork, clay, and gravel, over which spread a multitude of red cactus-shaped plants, knee-high, without a solitary terrestrial growth to dispute their footing. The trees near me were dead and brown, but further a network of red threads scaled the still living stems.

The neighbouring houses had all been wrecked, but none had been burned; their walls stood, sometimes to the second story, with smashed windows and shattered doors. The red weed grew tumultuously in their roofless rooms. Below me was the great pit, with the crows struggling for its refuse. A number of other birds hopped about among the ruins. Far away I saw a gaunt cat slink crouchingly along a wall, but traces of men there were none.

The day seemed, by contrast with my recent confinement, dazzlingly bright, the sky a glowing blue. A gentle breeze kept the red weed that covered every scrap of unoccupied ground gently swaying. And oh! the sweetness of the air!

CHAPTER 6

THE WORK OF FIFTEEN DAYS

FOR some time I stood tottering on the mound regardless of my safety. Within that noisome den from which I had emerged I had thought with a narrow intensity only of our immediate security. I had not realised what had been happening to the world, had not anticipated this startling vision of unfamiliar things. I had expected to see Sheen in ruins — I found about me the landscape, weird and lurid, of another planet.

For that moment I touched an emotion beyond the common range of men, yet one that the poor brutes we dominate know only too well. I felt as a rabbit might feel returning to his burrow and suddenly confronted by the work of a dozen busy navvies digging the foundations of a house. I felt the first inkling of a thing that presently grew quite clear in my mind, that oppressed

me for many days, a sense of dethronement, a persuasion that I was no longer a master, but an animal among the animals, under the Martian heel. With us it would be as with them, to lurk and watch, to run and hide; the fear and empire of man had passed away.

But so soon as this strangeness had been realised it passed, and my dominant motive became the hunger of my long and dismal fast. In the direction away from the pit I saw, beyond a red-covered wall, a patch of garden ground unburied. This gave me a hint, and I went knee-deep, and sometimes neck-deep, in the red weed. The density of the weed gave me a reassuring sense of hiding. The wall was some six feet high, and when I attempted to clamber it I found I could not lift my feet to the crest. So I went along by the side of it, and came to a corner and a rockwork that enabled me to get to the top, and tumble into the garden I coveted. Here I found some young onions, a couple of gladiolus bulbs, and a quantity of immature carrots, all of which I secured, and, scrambling over a ruined wall, went on my way through scarlet and crimson trees towards Kew — it was like walking through an avenue of gigantic blood-drops — possessed with two ideas: to get more food, and to limp, as soon and as far as my strength permitted, out of this accursed unearthly region of the pit.

Some way farther, in a grassy place, was a group of mushrooms which also I devoured, and then I came upon a brown sheet of flowing shallow water, where meadows used to be. These fragments of nourishment served only to whet my hunger. At first I was surprised at this flood in a hot, dry summer, but afterwards I discovered that it was caused by the tropical exuberance of the red weed. Directly this extraordinary growth encountered water it straightway became gigantic and of unparalleled fecundity. Its seeds were simply poured down into the water of the Wey and Thames, and its swiftly growing and Titanic water-fronds speedily choked both those rivers.

At Putney, as I afterwards saw, the bridge was almost lost in a tangle of this weed, and at Richmond, too, the Thames water poured in a broad and shallow stream across the meadows of Hampton and Twickerham. As the waters spread the weed followed them, until the ruined villas of the Thames valley were for a time lost in this red swamp, whose margin I explored, and much of the desolation the Martians had caused was concealed.

In the end the red weed succumbed almost as quickly as it had spread. A cankering disease, due, it is believed, to the action of certain bacteria, presently seized upon it. Now by the action of natural selection, all terrestrial plants have acquired a resisting power against bacterial diseases — they never succumb without a severe struggle, but the red weed rotted like a thing already dead. The fronds became bleached, and then shrivelled

and brittle. They broke off at the least touch, and the waters that had stimulated their early growth carried their last vestiges out to sea.

My first act on coming to this water was, of course, to slake my thirst. I drank a great deal of it and, moved by an impulse, gnawed some fronds of red weed; but they were watery, and had a sickly, metallic taste. I found the water was sufficiently shallow for me to wade securely, although the red weed impeded my feet a little; but the flood evidently got deeper towards the river, and I turned back to Mortlake. I managed to make out the road by means of occasional ruins of its villas and fences and lamps, and so presently I got out of this spate and made my way to the hill going up towards Roehampton and came out on Putney Common.

Here the scenery changed from the strange and unfamiliar to the wreckage of the familiar: patches of ground exhibited the devastation of a cyclone, and in a few score yards I would come upon perfectly undisturbed spaces, houses with their blinds trimly drawn and doors closed, as if they had been left for a day by the owners, or as if their inhabitants slept within. The red weed was less abundant; the tall trees along the lane were free from the red creeper. I hunted for food among the trees, finding nothing, and I also raided a couple of silent houses, but they had already been broken into and ransacked. I rested for the remainder of the daylight in a shrubbery, being, in my enfeebled condition, too fatigued to push on.

All this time I saw no human beings, and no signs of the Martians. I encountered a couple of hungry-looking dogs, but both hurried circuitously away from the advances I made them. Near Roehampton I had seen two human skeletons — not bodies, but skeletons, picked clean — and in the wood by me I found the crushed and scattered bones of several cats and rabbits and the skull of a sheep. But though I gnawed parts of these in my mouth, there was nothing to be got from them.

After sunset I struggled on along the road towards Putney, where I think the Heat-Ray must have been used for some reason. And in the garden beyond Roehampton I got a quantity of immature potatoes, sufficient to stay my hunger. From this garden one looked down upon Putney and the river. The aspect of the place in the dusk was singularly desolate: blackened trees, blackened, desolate ruins, and down the hill the sheets of the flooded river, red-tinged with the weed. And over all — silence. It filled me with indescribable terror to think how swiftly that desolating change had come.

For a time I believed that mankind had been swept out of existence, and that I stood there alone, the last man left alive. Hard by the top of Putney Hill I came upon another skeleton, with the arms dislocated and removed several yards from the rest of the body. As I proceeded I became more and more con-

vinced that the extermination of mankind was, save for such stragglers as myself, already accomplished in this part of the world. The Martians, I thought, had gone on and left the country desolated, seeking food elsewhere. Perhaps even now they were destroying Berlin or Paris, or it might be they had gone northward.

CHAPTER 7

THE MAN ON PUTNEY HILL

I SPENT that night in the inn that stands at the top of Putney Hill, sleeping in a made bed for the first time since my flight to Leatherhead. I will not tell the needless trouble I had breaking into that house — afterwards I found the front door was on the latch — nor how I ransacked every room for food, until, just on the verge of despair, in what seemed to me to be a servant's bedroom, I found a rat-gnawed crust and two tins of pineapple. The place had been already searched and emptied. In the bar I afterwards found some biscuits and sandwiches that had been overlooked. The latter I could not eat, they were too rotten, but the former not only stayed my hunger, but filled my pockets. I lit no lamps, fearing some Martian might come beating that part of London for food in the night. Before I went to bed I had an interval of restlessness, and prowled from window to window, peering out for some sign of these monsters. I slept little. As I lay in bed I found myself thinking consecutively — a thing I do not remember to have done since my last argument with the curate. During all the intervening time my mental condition had been a hurrying succession of vague emotional states or a sort of stupid receptivity. But in the night my brain, reinforced, I suppose, by the food I had eaten, grew clear again, and I thought.

Three things struggled for possession of my mind: the killing of the curate, the whereabouts of the Martians, and the possible fate of my wife. The former gave me no sensation of horror or remorse to recall; I saw it simply as a thing done, a memory infinitely disagreeable but quite without the quality of remorse. I saw myself then as I see myself now, driven step by step towards that hasty blow, the creature of a sequence of accidents leading inevitably to that. I felt no condemnation; yet the memory, static, unprogressive, haunted me. In the silence of the night, with that sense of the nearness of God that sometimes comes into the stillness and the darkness, I stood my trial, my only trial, for that moment of wrath and fear. I retraced every step of our conversation from the moment when I

had found him crouching beside me, heedless of my thirst, and pointing to the fire and smoke that streamed up from the ruins of Weybridge. We had been incapable of co-operation — grim chance had taken no heed of that. Had I foreseen, I should have left him at Halliford. But I did not foresee; and crime is to foresee and do. And I set this down as I have set all this story down, as it was. There were no witnesses — all these things I might have concealed. But I set it down, and the reader must form his judgment as he will.

And when, by an effort, I had set aside that picture of a prostrate body, I faced the problem of the Martians and the fate of my wife. For the former I had no data; I could imagine a hundred things, and so, unhappily, I could for the latter. And suddenly that night became terrible. I found myself sitting up in bed, staring at the dark. I found myself praying that the Heat-Ray might have suddenly and painlessly struck her out of being. Since the night of my return from Leatherhead I had not prayed. I had uttered prayers, fetish prayers, had prayed as heathens mutter charms when I was in extremity; but now I prayed indeed, pleading steadfastly and sanely, face to face with the darkness of God. Strange night! strangest in this, that so soon as dawn had come, I, who had talked with God, crept out of the house like a rat leaving its hiding-place — a creature scarcely larger, an inferior animal, a thing that for any passing whim of our masters might

be hunted and killed. Perhaps they also prayed confidently to God. Surely, if we have learned nothing else, this war has taught us pity — pity for those witless souls that suffer our dominion.

The morning was bright and fine, and the eastern sky glowed pink, and was fretted with little golden clouds. In the road that runs from the top of Putney Hill to Wimbledon was a number of poor vestiges of the panic torrent that must have poured London-ward on the Sunday night after the fighting began. There was a little two-wheeled cart inscribed with the name of Thomas Lobb, Green-grocer, New Malden, with a smashed wheel and an abandoned tin trunk; there was a straw hat trampled into the now hardened mud, and at the top of West Hill a lot of blood-stained glass about the overturned water-trough. My movements were languid, my plans of the vaguest. I had an idea of going to Leatherhead, though I knew that there I had the poorest chance of finding my wife. Certainly, unless death had overtaken them suddenly, my cousins and she would have fled thence; but it seemed to me I might find or learn there whither the Surrey people had fled. I knew I wanted to find my wife, that my heart ached for her and the world of men, but I had no clear idea how the finding might be done. I was also sharply aware now of my intense loneliness. From the corner I went, under cover of a thicket of trees and bushes, to the edge of Wimbledon Common, stretching wide and far.

That dark expanse was lit in patches by yellow gorse and broom; there was no red weed to be seen, and as I prowled, hesitating, on the verge of the open, the sun rose, flooding it all with light and vitality. I came upon a busy swarm of little frogs in a swampy place among the trees. I stopped to look at them, drawing a lesson from their stout resolve to live. And presently, turning suddenly, with an odd feeling of being watched, I beheld something crouching amid a clump of bushes. I stood regarding this. I made a step towards it, and it rose up and became a man armed with a cutlass. I approached him slowly. He stood silent and motionless, regarding me.

As I drew nearer I perceived he was dressed in clothes as dusty and filthy as my own; he looked, indeed, as though he had been dragged through a culvert. Nearer, I distinguished the green slime of ditches mixing with the pale drab of dried clay and shiny, coaly patches. His black hair fell over his eyes, and his face was dark and dirty and sunken, so that at first I did not recognise him. There was a red cut across the lower part of his face.

"Stop!" he cried, when I was within ten yards of him, and I stopped. His voice was hoarse. "Where do you come from?" he said.

I thought, surveying him.

"I come from Mortlake," I said. "I was buried near the pit the Martians made about their cylinder. I have worked my way out and escaped."

"There is no food about here," he said. "This is my country. All this hill down to the river, and back to Clapham, and up to the edge of the common There is only food for one. Which way are you going?"

I answered slowly.

"I don't know," I said. "I have been buried in the ruins of a house thirteen or fourteen days. I don't know what has happened."

He looked at me doubtfully, then started, and looked with a changed expression.

"I've no wish to stop about here," said I. "I think I shall go to Leatherhead, for my wife was there."

He shot out a pointing finger.

"It is you," said he — "the man from Woking. And you weren't killed at Weybridge?"

I recognised him at the same moment.

"You are the artilleryman who came into my garden."

"Good luck!" he said. "We are lucky ones! Fancy *you!*" He put out a hand, and I took it. "I crawled up a drain," he said. "But they didn't kill every one. And after they went away I got off towards Walton across the fields. But — It's not sixteen days altogether — and your hair is grey." He looked over his shoulder suddenly. "Only a rook," he said. "One gets to know that birds have shadows these days. This *is* a bit open. Let us crawl under those bushes and talk."

"Have you seen any Martians?" I said. "Since I crawled out — "

"They've gone away across London," he said. "I guess

they've got a bigger camp there. Of a night, all over there, Hampstead way, the sky is alive with their lights. It's like a great city, and in the glare you can just see them moving. By daylight you can't. But nearer — I haven't seen them — " (he counted on his fingers) " five days. Then I saw a couple across Hammersmith way carrying something big. And the night before last " — he stopped and spoke impressively — " it was just a matter of lights, but it was something up in the air. I believe they've built a flying-machine, and are learning to fly."

I stopped, on hands and knees, for we had come to the bushes.

" Fly! "

" Yes," he said, " fly."

I went on into a little bower, and sat down.

" It is all over with humanity," I said. " If they can do that they will simply go round the world."

He nodded.

" They will. But — It will relieve things over here a bit. And besides — " He looked at me. " Aren't you satisfied it *is* up with humanity? I am. We're down; we're beat."

I stared. Strange as it may seem, I had not arrived at this fact — a fact perfectly obvious so soon as he spoke. I had still held a vague hope; rather, I had kept a lifelong habit of mind. He repeated his words, " We're beat." They carried absolute conviction.

" It's all over," he said. " They've lost *one* — just *one*. And they've made their footing good and crippled the greatest power in the world. They've

walked over us. The death of that one at Weybridge was an accident. And these are only pioneers. They kept on coming. These green stars — I've seen none these five or six days, but I've no doubt they're falling somewhere every night. Nothing's to be done. We're under! We're beat! "

I made him no answer. I sat staring before me, trying in vain to devise some countervailing thought.

" This isn't a war," said the artilleryman. " It never was a war, any more than there's war between men and ants."

Suddenly I recalled the night in the observatory.

" After the tenth shot they fired no more — at least, until the first cylinder came."

" How do you know? " said the artilleryman. I explained. He thought. " Something wrong with the gun," he said. " But what if there is? They'll get it right again. And even if there's a delay, how can it alter the end? It's just men and ants. There's the ants builds their cities, live their lives, have wars, revolutions, until the men want them out of the way, and then they go out of the way. That's what we are now — just ants. Only — "

" Yes," I said.

" We're eatable ants."

We sat looking at each other.

" And what will they do with us? " I said.

" That's what I've been thinking," he said — " that's what I've been thinking. After Weybridge I went south — thinking. I saw what was up. Most of the people

were hard at it squealing and exciting themselves. But I'm not so fond of squealing. I've been in sight of death once or twice; I'm not an ornamental soldier, and at the best and worst, death —it's just death. And it's the man that keeps on thinking comes through. I saw every one tracking away south. Says I, 'Food won't last this way,' and I turned right back. I went for the Martians like a sparrow goes for man. All round"—he waved a hand to the horizon—"they're starving in heaps, bolting, treading on each other." . . .

He saw my face, and halted awkwardly.

"No doubt lots who had money have gone away to France," he said. He seemed to hesitate whether to apologise, met my eyes, and went on: "There's food all about here. Canned things in shops; wines, spirits, mineral waters; and the water mains and drains are empty. Well, I was telling you what I was thinking. 'Here's intelligent things,' I said, 'and it seems they want us for food. First, they'll smash us up—ships, machines, guns, cities, all the order and organisation. All that will go. If we were the size of ants we might pull through. But we're not. It's all too bulky to stop. That's the first certainty.' Eh?"

I assented.

"It is; I've thought it out. Very well, then—next; at present we're caught as we're wanted. A Martian has only to go a few miles to get a crowd on the run. And I saw one, one day, out by Wandsworth, picking houses to pieces and routing among the wreckage. But they wont keep on doing that. So soon as they've settled all our guns and ships, and smashed our railways, and done all the things they are doing over there, they will begin catching us systematic, picking the best and storing us in cages and things. That's what they will start doing in a bit. Lord! they haven't begun on us yet. Don't you see that?"

"Not begun!" I exclaimed.

"Not begun. All that's happened so far is through our not having the sense to keep quiet— worrying them with guns and such foolery. And losing our heads, and rushing off in crowds to where there wasn't any more safety than where we were. They don't want to bother us yet. They're making their things— making all the things they couldn't bring with them, getting things ready for the rest of their people. Very likely that's why the cylinders have stopped for a bit, for fear of hitting those who are here. And instead of our rushing about blind, on the howl, or getting dynamite on the chance of busting them up, we've got to fix ourselves up according to the new state of affairs. That's how I figure it out. It isn't quite according to what a man wants for his species, but it's about what the facts point to. And that's the principle I acted upon. Cities, nations, civilisation, progress—it's all over. That game's up. We're beat."

"But if that is so, what is there to live for?"

The artilleryman looked at me for a moment.

"There won't be any more blessed concerts for a million years or so; there won't be any Royal Academy of Arts, and no nice little feeds at restaurants. If it's amusement you're after, I reckon the game is up. If you've got any drawing-room manners or a dislike to eating peas with a knife or dropping 'em away. They ain't no further use."

"You mean—"

"I mean that men like me are going on living—for the sake of the breed. I tell you, I'm grim set on living. And if I'm not mistaken, you'll show what insides *you've* got, too, before long. We aren't going to be exterminated. And I don't mean to be caught either, and tamed and fattened and bred like a thundering ox. Ugh! Fancy those brown creepers!"

"You don't mean to say—"

"I do. I'm going on. Under their feet. I've got it planned; I've thought it out. We men are beat. We don't know enough. We've got to learn before we've got a chance. And we've got to live and keep independent while we learn. See! That's what has to be done."

I stared, astonished, and stirred profoundly by the man's resolution.

"Great God!" cried I. "But you are a man indeed!" And suddenly I gripped his hand.

"Eh!" he said, with his eyes shining. "I've thought it out, eh?"

"Go on," I said.

"Well, those who mean to escape their catching must get ready. I'm getting ready. Mind you, it isn't all of us that are made for wild beasts; and that's what it's got to be? That's why I watched you. I had my doubts. You're slender. I didn't know that it was you, you see, or just how you'd been buried. All these —the sort of people that lived in these houses, and all those damn little clerks that used to live down that way—they'd be no good. They haven't any spirit in them—no proud dreams and no proud lusts; and a man who hasn't one or the other—Lord! what is he but funk and precautions? They just used to skedaddle off to work—I've seen hundreds of 'em, bit of breakfast in hand, running wild and shining to catch their little season-ticket train, for fear they'd get dismissed if they didn't; working at businesses they were afraid to take the trouble to understand; skedaddling back for fear they wouldn't be in time for dinner; keeping indoors after dinner for fear of the back streets, and sleeping with the wives they married, not because they wanted them, but because they had a bit of money that would make for safety in their one little miserable skedaddle through the world. Lives insured and a bit invested for fear of accidents. And on Sundays—fear of the hereafter. As if hell was built for rabbits! Well, the Martians will just be a godsend to these. Nice roomy cages, fattening food, careful breeding, no worry. After a week or so chasing about the

fields and lands on empty stomachs, they'll come and be caught cheerful. They'll be quite glad after a bit. They'll wonder what people did before there were Martians to take care of them. And the bar-loafers, and mashers, and singers — I can imagine them. I can imagine them," he said, with a sort of sombre gratification. "There'll be any amount of sentiment and religion loose among them. There's hundreds of things I saw with my eyes that I've only begun to see clearly these last few days. There's lots will take things as they are — fat and stupid; and lots will be worried by a sort of feeling that it's all wrong, and that they ought to be doing something. Now whenever things are so that a lot of people feel they ought to be doing something, the weak, and those who go weak with a lot of complicated thinking, always make for a sort of do-nothing religion, very pious and superior, and submit to persecution and the will of the Lord. Very likely you've seen the same thing. It's energy in a gale of funk, and turned clean inside out. These cages will be full of psalms and hymns and piety. And those of a less simple sort will work in a bit of — what is it? — eroticism."

He paused.

"Very likely these Martians will make pets of some of them; train them to do tricks — who knows? — get sentimental over the pet boy who grew up and had to be killed. And some, maybe, they will train to hunt us."

"No," I cried, "that's impossible! No human being —"

"What's the good of going on with such lies?" said the artilleryman. "There's men who'd do it cheerful. What nonsense to pretend there isn't!"

And I succumbed to his conviction.

"If they come after me," he said — "Lord, if they come after me!" and subsided into a grim meditation.

I sat contemplating these things. I could find nothing to bring against this man's reasoning. In the days before the invasion no one would have questioned my intellectual superiority to his — I, a professed and recognised writer on philosophical themes, and he, a common soldier; and yet he had already formulated a situation that I had scarcely realised.

"What are you doing?" I said, presently. "What plans have you made?"

He hesitated.

"Well, it's like this," he said. "What have we to do? We have to invent a sort of life where men can live and breed, and be sufficiently secure to bring the children up. Yes — wait a bit, and I'll make it clearer what I think ought to be done. The tame ones will go like all tame beasts; in a few generations they'll be big, beautiful, rich-blooded, stupid — rubbish! The risk is that we who keep wild will go savage — degenerate into a sort of big, savage rat. . . . You see, how I mean to live is underground. I've been thinking about the drains. Of course those who don't know drains think horrible things; but under this London are miles and miles

—hundreds of miles—and a few days' rain and London empty will leave them sweet and clean. The main drains are big enough and airy enough for any one. Then there's cellars, vaults, stores, from which bolting passages may be made to the drains. And the railway tunnels and subways. Eh? You begin to see? And we form a band—able-bodied, clean-minded men. We're not going to pick up any rubbish that drifts in. Weaklings go out again."

"As you meant me to go?"

"Well—I parleyed, didn't I?"

"We won't quarrel about that. Go on."

"Those who stop obey orders. Able-bodied, clean-minded women we want also—mothers and teachers. No lackadaisical ladies—no blasted rolling eyes. We can't have any weak or silly. Life is real again, and the useless and cumbersome and mischievous have to die. They ought to die. They ought to be willing to die. It's a sort of disloyalty, after all, to live and taint the race. And they can't be happy. Moreover, dying's none so dreadful; it's the funking makes it bad. And in all those places we shall gather. Our district will be London. And we may even be able to keep a watch, and run about in the open when the Martians keep away. Play cricket, perhaps. That's how we shall save the race. Eh? It's a possible thing? But saving the race is nothing in itself. As I say, that's only being rats. It's saving our knowledge and adding to it is the thing. There men like you come in. There's books,

there's models. We must make great safe places down deep, and get all the books we can; not novels and poetry swipes, but ideas, science books. That's where men like you come in. We must go to the British Museum and pick all those books through. Especially we must keep up our science—learn more. We must watch these Martians. Some of us must go as spies. When it's all working, perhaps I will. Get caught, I mean. And the great thing is, we must leave the Martians alone. We mustn't even steal. If we get in their way, we clear out. We must show them we mean no harm. Yes, I know. But they're intelligent things, and they won't hunt us down if they have all they want, and think we're just harmless vermin."

The artilleryman paused and laid a brown hand upon my arm.

"After all, it may not be so much we may have to learn before—Just imagine this: Four or five of their fighting-machines suddenly starting off—Heat-Rays right and left, and not a Martian in 'em. Not a Martian in 'em, but men—men who have learned the way how. It may be in my time, even—those men. Fancy having one of them lovely things, with its Heat-Ray wide and free! Fancy having it in control! What would it matter if you smashed to smithereens at the end of the run, after a bust like that? I reckon the Martians'll open their beautiful eyes! Can't you see them, man? Can't you see them hurrying, hurrying—puffing and blowing and hooting to their

other mechanical affairs? Something out of gear in every case. And swish, bang, rattle, swish! just as they are fumbling over it, *swish* comes the Heat-Ray, and, behold! man has come back to his own."

For a while the imaginative daring of the artilleryman, and the tone of assurance and courage he assumed, completely dominated my mind. I believed unhesitatingly both in his forecast of human destiny and in the practicability of his astonishing scheme, and the reader who thinks me susceptible and foolish must contrast his position, reading steadily with all his thoughts about his subject, and mine, crouching fearfully in the bushes and listening, distracted by apprehension. We talked in this manner through the early morning time, and later crept out of the bushes, and, after scanning the sky for Martians, hurried precipitately to the house on Putney Hill where he had made his lair. It was the coal-cellar of the place, and when I saw the work he had spent a week upon — it was a burrow scarcely ten yards long, which he designed to reach to the main drain on Putney Hill — I had my first inkling of the gulf between his dreams and his powers. Such a hole I could have dug in a day. But I believed in him sufficiently to work with him all that morning until past mid-day at his digging. We had a garden-barrow and shot the earth we removed against the kitchen range. We refreshed ourselves with a tin of mock-turtle soup and wine from the neighbouring pantry. I

found a curious relief from the aching strangeness of the world in this steady labour. As we worked, I turned his project over in my mind, and presently objections and doubts began to arise; but I worked there all the morning, so glad was I to find myself with a purpose again. After working an hour I began to speculate on the distance one had to go before the cloaca was reached, the chances we had of missing it altogether. My immediate trouble was why we should dig this long tunnel, when it was possible to get into the drain at once down one of the manholes, and work back to the house. It seemed to me, too, that the house was inconveniently chosen, and required a needless length of tunnel. And just as I was beginning to face these things, the artilleryman stopped digging, and looked at me.

"We're working well," he said. He put down his spade. "Let us knock off a bit," he said. "I think it's time we reconnoitred from the roof of the house."

I was for going on, and after a little hesitation he resumed his spade; and then suddenly I was struck by a thought. I stopped, and so did he at once.

"Why were you walking about the Common," I said, "instead of being here?"

"Taking the air," he said. "I was coming back. It's safer by night."

"But the work?"

"Oh, one can't always work," he said, and in a flash I saw the man plain. He hesitated, holding his spade. "We ought to rec-

onnoitre now," he said, "because if any come near they may hear the spades and drop upon us unawares."

I was no longer disposed to object. We went together to the roof and stood on a ladder peeping out of the roof door. No Martians were to be seen, and we ventured out on the tiles, and slipped down under shelter of the parapet.

From this position a shrubbery hid the greater portion of Putney, but we could see the river below, a bubbly mass of red weed, and the low parts of Lambeth flooded and red. The red creeper swarmed up the trees about the old palace, and their branches stretched gaunt and dead, and set with shrivelled leaves, from amid its clusters. It was strange how entirely dependent both these things were upon flowing water for their propagation. About us neither had gained a footing; laburnums, pink mays, snowballs, and trees of arborvitæ, rose out of laurels and hydrangeas, green and brilliant into the sunlight. Beyond Kensington dense smoke was rising, and that and a blue haze hid the northward hills.

The artilleryman began to tell me of the sort of people who still remained in London.

"One night last week," he said, "some fools got the electric light in order, and there was all Regent Street and the Circus ablaze, crowded with painted and ragged drunkards, men and women, dancing and shouting till dawn. A man who was there told me. And as the day came they became aware of a fighting-machine standing near by the Langham and looking down at them. Heaven knows how long he had been there. It must have given some of them a nasty turn. He came down the road towards them, and picked up nearly a hundred too drunk or frightened to run away."

Grotesque gleam of a time no history will ever fully describe!

From that, in answer to my questions, he came round to his grandiose plans again. He grew enthusiastic. He talked so eloquently of the possibility of capturing a fighting-machine that I more than half believed in him again. But now that I was beginning to understand something of his quality, I could divine the stress he laid on doing nothing precipitately. And I noted that now there was no question that he personally was to capture and fight the great machine.

After a time we went down to the cellar. Neither of us seemed disposed to resume digging, and when he suggested a meal, I was nothing loath. He became suddenly very generous, and when we had eaten he went away and returned with some excellent cigars. We lit these, and his optimism glowed. He was inclined to regard my coming as a great occasion.

"There's some champagne in the cellar," he said.

"We can dig better on this Thames-side burgundy," said I.

"No," said he; "I am host to-day. Champagne! Great God! we've a heavy enough task before us! Let us take a rest and gather

strength while we may. Look at these blistered hands!"

And pursuant to this idea of a holiday, he insisted upon playing cards after we had eaten. He taught me euchre, and after dividing London between us, I taking the northern side and he the southern, we played for parish points. Grotesque and foolish as this will seem to the sober reader, it is absolutely true, and, what is more remarkable, I found the card game and several others we played extremely interesting.

Strange mind of man! that, with our species upon the edge of extermination or appalling degradation, with no clear prospect before us but the chance of a horrible death, we could sit following the chance of this painted pasteboard, and playing the "joker" with vivid delight. Afterwards he taught me poker, and I beat him at three tough chess games. When dark came we decided to take the risk, and lit a lamp.

After an interminable string of games, we supped, and the artilleryman finished the champagne. We went on smoking the cigars. He was no longer the energetic regenerator of his species I had encountered in the morning. He was still optimistic, but it was a less kinetic, a more thoughtful optimism. I remember he wound up with my health, proposed in a speech of small variety and considerable intermittence. I took a cigar, and went upstairs to look at the lights of which he had spoken, that blazed so greenly along the Highgate hills.

At first I stared unintelligently across the London valley. The northern hills were shrouded in darkness; the fires near Kensington glowed redly, and now and then an orange-red tongue of flame flashed up and vanished in the deep blue night. All the rest of London was black. Then, nearer, I perceived a strange light, a pale, violet-purple fluorescent glow, quivering under the night breeze. For a space I could not understand it, and then I knew that it must be the red weed from which this faint irradiation proceeded. With that realisation my dormant sense of wonder, my sense of the proportion of things, awoke again. I glanced from that to Mars, red and clear, glowing high in the west, and then gazed long and earnestly at the darkness of Hampstead and Highgate.

I remained a very long time upon the roof, wondering at the grotesque changes of the day. I recalled my mental states from the midnight prayer to the foolish card-playing. I had a violent revulsion of feeling. I remember I flung away the cigar with a certain wasteful symbolism. My folly came to me with glaring exaggeration. I seemed a traitor to my wife and to my kind; I was filled with remorse. I resolved to leave this strange undisciplined dreamer of great things to his drink and gluttony, and to go on into London. There, it seemed to me, I had the best chance of learning what the Martians and my fellowmen were doing. I was still upon the roof when the late moon rose.

CHAPTER 8

DEAD LONDON

AFTER I had parted from the artilleryman, I went down the hill, and by the High Street across the bridge to Fulham. The red weed was tumultuous at that time, and nearly choked the bridge roadway; but its fronds were already whitened in patches by the spreading disease that presently removed it so swiftly.

At the corner of the lane that runs to Putney Bridge station I found a man lying. He was as black as a sweep with the black dust, alive, but helplessly and speechlessly drunk. I could get nothing from him but curses and furious lunges at my head. I think I should have stayed by him but for the brutal expression of his face.

There was black dust along the roadway from the bridge onwards, and it grew thicker in Fulham. The streets were horribly quiet. I got food — sour, hard, and mouldy, but quite eatable — in a baker's shop here. Some way towards Walham Green the streets became clear of powder, and I passed a white terrace of houses on fire; the noise of the burning was an absolute relief. Going on towards Brompton, the streets were quiet again.

Here I came once more upon the black powder in the streets and upon dead bodies. I saw altogether about a dozen in the length of the Fulham Road. They had been dead many days, so that I hurried quickly past them. The black powder covered them over, and softened their outlines. One or two had been disturbed by dogs.

Where there was no black powder, it was curiously like a Sunday in the City, with the closed shops, the houses locked up and the blinds drawn, the desertion, and the stillness. In some places plunderers had been at work, but rarely at other than the provision and wine shops. A jeweller's window had been broken open in one place, but apparently the thief had been disturbed, and a number of gold chains and a watch lay scattered on the pavement. I did not trouble to touch them. Farther on was a tattered woman in a heap on a doorstep; the hand that hung over her knee was gashed and bled down her rusty brown dress, and a smashed magnum of champagne formed a pool across the pavement. She seemed asleep, but she was dead.

The farther I penetrated into London, the profounder grew the stillness. But it was not so much the stillness of death — it was the stillness of suspense, of expectation. At any time the destruction that had already singed the north-western borders of the

metropolis, and had annihilated Ealing and Kilburn, might strike among these houses and leave them smoking ruins. It was a city condemned and derelict. . . .

In South Kensington the streets were clear of dead and of black powder. It was near South Kensington that I first heard the howling. It crept almost imperceptibly upon my senses. It was a sobbing alternation of two notes, "Ulla, ulla, ulla, ulla," keeping on perpetually. When I passed streets that ran northward it grew in volume, and houses and buildings seemed to deaden and cut it off again. It came in a full tide down Exhibition Road. I stopped, staring towards Kensington Gardens, wondering at this strange, remote wailing. It was as if that mighty desert of houses had found a voice for its fear and solitude.

"Ulla, ulla, ulla, ulla," wailed that superhuman note — great waves of sound sweeping down the broad, sunlit roadway, between the tall buildings on each side. I turned northwards, marvelling, towards the iron gates of Hyde Park. I had half a mind to break into the Natural History Museum and find my way up to the summits of the towers, in order to see across the park. But I decided to keep to the ground, where quick hiding was possible, and so went on up the Exhibition Road. All the large mansions on each side of the road were empty and still, and my footsteps echoed against the sides of the houses. At the top, near the park gate, I came upon a strange sight — a bus overturned,

and the skeleton of a horse picked clean. I puzzled over this for a time, and then went on to the bridge over the Serpentine. The voice grew stronger and stronger, though I could see nothing above the house-tops on the north side of the park, save a haze of smoke to the northwest.

"Ulla, ulla, ulla, ulla," cried the voice, coming, as it seemed to me, from the district about Regent's Park. The desolating cry worked upon my mind. The mood that had sustained me passed. The wailing took possession of me. I found I was intensely weary, footsore, and now again hungry and thirsty.

It was already past noon. Why was I wandering alone in this city of the dead? Why was I alone when all London was lying in state, and in its black shroud? I felt intolerably lonely. My mind ran on old friends that I had forgotten for years. I thought of the poisons in the chemists' shops, of the liquors the wine-merchants stored; I recalled the two sodden creatures of despair, who so far as I knew, shared the city with myself. . . .

I came into Oxford Street by the Marble Arch, and here again were black powder and several bodies, and an evil, ominous smell from the gratings of the cellars of some of the houses. I grew very thirsty after the heat of my long walk. With infinite trouble I managed to break into a public-house and get food and drink. I was weary after eating, and went into the parlour behind the bar, and slept on a

black horsehair sofa I found there.

I awoke to find that dismal howling still in my ears, "Ulla, ulla, ulla, ulla." It was now dusk, and after I had routed out some biscuits and a cheese in the bar — there was a meat-safe, but it contained nothing but maggots — I wandered on through the silent residential squares to Baker Street — Portman Square is the only one I can name — and so came out at last upon Regent's Park. And as I emerged from the top of Baker Street, I saw far away over the trees in the clearness of the sunset the hood of the Martian giant from which this howling proceeded. I was not terrified. I came upon him as if it were a matter of course. I watched him for some time, but he did not move. He appeared to be standing and yelling, for no reason that I could discover.

I tried to formulate a plan of action. That perpetual sound of "Ulla, ulla, ulla, ulla," confused my mind. Perhaps I was too tired to be very fearful. Certainly I was more curious to know the reason of this monotonous crying than afraid. I turned back away from the park and struck into Park Road, intending to skirt the park, went along under the shelter of the terraces, and got a view of this stationary, howling Martian from the direction of St. John's Wood. A couple of hundred yards out of Baker Street I heard a yelping chorus, and saw, first a dog with a piece of putrescent red meat in his jaws coming headlong towards me, and then a pack of starving mongrels in pursuit of him. He made a wide curve to avoid me, as though he feared I might prove a fresh competitor. As the yelping died away down the silent road, the wailing sound of "Ulla, ulla, ulla, ulla," reasserted itself.

I came upon the wrecked handling-machine halfway to St. John's Wood station. At first I thought a house had fallen across the road. It was only as I clambered among the ruins that I saw, with a start, this mechanical Samson lying, with its tentacles bent and smashed and twisted, among the ruins it had made. The forepart was shattered. It seemed as if it had driven blindly straight at the house, and had been overwhelmed in its overthrow. It seemed to me then that this might have happened by a handling-machine escaping from the guidance of its Martian. I could not clamber among the ruins to see it, and the twilight was now so far advanced that the blood with which its seat was smeared, and the gnawed gristle of the Martian that the dogs had left, were invisible to me.

Wondering still more at all that I had seen, I pushed on towards Primrose Hill. Far away, through a gap in the trees, I saw a second Martian, as motionless as the first, standing in the park towards the Zoological Gardens, and silent. A little beyond the ruins about the smashed handling-machine I came upon the red weed again, and found the Regent's Canal, a spongy mass of dark-red vegetation.

As I crossed the bridge, the

sound of " Ulla, ulla, ulla, ulla," ceased. It was, as it were, cut off. The silence came like a thunder-clap.

The dusky houses about me stood faint and tall and dim; the trees towards the park were growing black. All about me the red weed clambered among the ruins, writhing to get above me in the dimness. Night, the mother of fear and mystery, was coming upon me. But while that voice sounded the solitude, the deso-lation, had been endurable; by virtue of it London had still seemed alive, and the sense of life about me had upheld me. Then suddenly a change, the passing of something — I knew not what — and then a stillness that could be felt. Nothing but this gaunt quiet.

London about me gazed at me spectrally. The windows in the white houses were like the eye-sockets of skulls. About me my imagination found a thousand noiseless enemies moving. Terror seized me, a horror of my temer-ity. In front of me the road be-came pitchy black as though it was tarred, and I saw a con-torted shape lying across the pathway. I could not bring my-self to go on. I turned down St. John's Wood Road, and ran headlong from this unendurable stillness towards Kilburn. I hid from the night and the silence, until long after midnight, in a cabmen's shelter in Harrow Road. But before the dawn my courage returned, and while the stars were still in the sky I turned once more towards Re-gent's Park. I missed my way among the streets, and presently saw down a long avenue, in the half-light of the early dawn, the curve of Primrose Hill. On the summit, towering up to the fading stars, was a third Martian, erect and motionless like the others.

An insane resolve possessed me. I would die and end it. And I would save myself even the trouble of killing myself. I marched on recklessly towards this Titan, and then, as I drew nearer and the light grew, I saw that a multitude of black birds was circling and clustering about the hood. At that my heart gave a bound, and I began running along the road.

I hurried through the red weed that choked St. Edmund's Ter-race (I waded breast-high across a torrent of water that was rush-ing down from the waterworks towards the Albert Road), and emerged upon the grass before the rising of the sun. Great mounds had been heaped about the crest of the hill, making a huge redoubt of it — it was the final and largest place the Mar-tians had made — and from be-hind these heaps there rose a thin smoke against the sky. Against the sky-line an eager dog ran and disappeared. The thought that had flashed into my mind grew real, grew credible. I felt no fear, only a wild, trembling exulta-tion, as I ran up the hill towards the motionless monster. Out of the hood hung lank shreds of brown, at which the hungry birds pecked and tore.

In another moment I had scrambled up the earthen ram-

part and stood upon its crest, and the interior of the redoubt was below me. A mighty space it was, with gigantic machines here and there within it, huge mounds of material and strange shelter-places. And scattered about it, some in their overturned war-machines, some in the now rigid handling-machines, and a dozen of them stark and silent and laid in a row, were the Martians — *dead!* — slain by the putrefactive and disease bacteria against which their systems were unprepared; slain as the red weed was being slain; slain, after all man's devices had failed, by the humblest things that God, in his wisdom, has put upon this earth.

For so it had come about, as indeed I and many men might have foreseen had not terror and disaster blinded our minds. These germs of disease have taken toll of humanity since the beginning of things — taken toll of our prehuman ancestors since life began here. But by virtue of this natural selection of our kind we have developed resisting power; to no germs do we succumb without a struggle, and to many — those that cause putrefaction in dead matter, for instance — our living frames are altogether immune. But there are no bacteria in Mars, and directly these invaders arrived, directly they drank and fed, our microscopic allies began to work their overthrow. Already when I watched them they were irrevocably doomed, dying and rotting even as they went to and fro. It was inevitable. By the

toll of a billion deaths man has bought his birthright of the earth, and it is his against all comers; it would still be his were the Martians ten times as mighty as they are. For neither do men live nor die in vain.

Here and there they were scattered, nearly fifty altogether, in that great gulf they had made, overtaken by a death that must have seemed to them as incomprehensible as any death could be. To me also at that time this death was incomprehensible. All I knew was that these things that had been alive and so terrible to men were dead. For a moment I believed that the destruction of Sennacherib had been repeated, that God had repented, that the Angel of Death had slain them in the night.

I stood staring into the pit, and my heart lightened gloriously, even as the rising sun struck the world to fire about me with his rays. The pit was still in darkness; the mighty engines, so great and wonderful in their power and complexity, so unearthly in their tortuous forms, rose weird and vague and strange out of the shadows towards the light. A multitude of dogs, I could hear, fought over the bodies that lay darkly in the depth of the pit, far below me. Across the pit on its farther lip, flat and vast and strange, lay the great flying-machine with which they had been experimenting upon our denser atmosphere when decay and death arrested them. Death had come not a day too soon. At the sound of a cawing overhead I looked up

at the huge fighting-machine that would fight no more for ever, at the tattered red shreds of flesh that dripped down upon the overturned seats on the summit of Primrose Hill.

I turned and looked down the slope of the hill to where, enhaloed now in birds, stood those other two Martians that I had seen overnight, just as death had overtaken them. The one had died, even as it had been crying to its companions; perhaps it was the last to die, and its voice had gone on perpetually until the force of its machinery was exhausted. They glittered now, harmless tripod towers of shining metal, in the brightness of the rising sun.

All about the pit, and saved as by a miracle from everlasting destruction, stretched the great Mother of Cities. Those who have only seen London veiled in her sombre robes of smoke can scarcely imagine the naked clearness and beauty of the silent wilderness of houses.

Eastward, over the blackened ruins of the Albert Terrace and the splintered spire of the church, the sun blazed dazzling in a clear sky, and here and there some facet in the great wilderness of roofs caught the light and glared with a white intensity.

Northward were Kilburn and Hampstead, blue and crowded with houses; westward the great city was dimmed; and southward, beyond the Martians, the green waves of Regent's Park, the Langham Hotel, the dome of the Albert Hall, the Imperial Institute, and the giant mansions of the Brompton Road came out clear and little in the sunrise, the jagged ruins of Westminster rising hazily beyond. Far away and blue were the Surrey hills, and the towers of the Crystal Palace glittered like two silver rods. The dome of St. Paul's was dark against the sunrise, and injured, I saw for the first time, by a huge gaping cavity on its western side.

And as I looked at this wide expanse of houses and factories and churches, silent and abandoned; as I thought of the multitudinous hopes and efforts, the innumerable hosts of lives that had gone to build this human reef, and of the swift and ruthless destruction that had hung over it all; when I realised that the shadow had been rolled back, and that men might still live in the streets, and this dear vast dead city of mine be once more alive and powerful, I felt a wave of emotion that was near akin to tears.

The torment was over. Even that day the healing would begin. The survivors of the people scattered over the country — leaderless, lawless, foodless, like sheep without a shepherd — the thousands who had fled by sea, would begin to return; the pulse of life, growing stronger and stronger, would beat again in the empty streets and pour across the vacant squares. Whatever destruction was done, the hand of the destroyer was stayed. All the gaunt wrecks, the blackened skeletons of houses that stared so dismally at the sunlit grass of the hill, would presently be

echoing with the hammers of the restorers and ringing with the tapping of their trowels. At the thought I extended my hands towards the sky and began thanking God. In a year, thought I — in a year. . . .

With overwhelming force came the thought of myself, of my wife, and the old life of hope and tender helpfulness that had ceased for ever.

CHAPTER 9

WRECKAGE

AND now comes the strangest thing in my story. Yet, perhaps, it is not altogether strange. I remember, clearly and coldly and vividly, all that I did that day until the time that I stood weeping and praising God upon the summit of Primrose Hill. And then I forget.

Of the next three days I know nothing. I have learned since that, so far from my being the first discoverer of the Martian overthrow, several such wanderers as myself had already discovered this on the previous night. One man — the first — had gone to St. Martin's-le-Grand, and, while I sheltered in the cabmen's hut, had contrived to tele-graph to Paris. Thence the joyful news had flashed all over the world; a thousand cities, chilled by ghastly apprehensions, suddenly flashed into frantic illuminations; they knew of it in Dublin, Edinburgh, Manchester, Birmingham, at the time when I stood upon the verge of the pit. Already men, weeping with joy, as I have heard, shouting and staying their work to shake hands and shout, were making up trains, even as near as Crewe, to descend upon London. The church bells that had ceased a fortnight since suddenly caught the news, until all England was bell-ringing. Men on cycles, lean-faced, unkempt, scorched along every country lane shouting of unhoped deliverance, shouting to gaunt, staring figures of despair. And for the food! Across the Channel, across the Irish Sea, across the Atlantic, corn, bread, and meat were tearing to our relief. All the shipping in the world seemed going Londonward in those days. But of all this I have no memory. I drifted — a demented man. I found myself in a house of kindly people, who had found me on the third day wandering, weeping, and raving through the streets of St. John's Wood. They have told me since that I was singing some inane doggerel about "The Last Man Left Alive! Hurrah! The Last Man Left Alive!" Troubled as they were with their own affairs, these people, whose name, much as I would like to express my gratitude to them, I may not even give here, nevertheless cumbered themselves with me, shel-

tered me, and protected me from myself. Apparently they had learned something of my story from me during the days of my lapse.

Very gently, when my mind was assured again, did they break to me what they had learned of the fate of Leatherhead. Two days after I was imprisoned it had been destroyed, with every soul in it, by a Martian. He had swept it out of existence, as it seemed, without any provocation, as a boy might crush an ant-hill, in the mere wantonness of power.

I was a lonely man, and they were very kind to me. I was a lonely man and a sad one, and they bore with me. I remained with them four days after my recovery. All that time I felt a vague, a growing craving to look once more on whatever remained of the little life that seemed so happy and bright in my past. It was a mere hopeless desire to feast upon my misery. They dissuaded me. They did all they could to divert me from this morbidity. But at last I could resist the impulse no longer, and, promising faithfully to return to them, and parting, as I will confess, from these four-day friends with tears, I went out again into the streets that had lately been so dark and strange and empty.

Already they were busy with returning people; in places even there were shops open, and I saw a drinking-fountain running water.

I remember how mockingly bright the day seemed as I went back on my melancholy pilgrimage to the little house at Woking, how busy the streets and vivid the moving life about me. So many people were abroad everywhere, busied in a thousand activities, that it seemed incredible that any great proportion of the population could have been slain. But then I noticed how yellow were the skins of the people I met, how shaggy the hair of the men, how large and bright their eyes, and that every other man still wore his dirty rags. Their faces seemed all with one of two expressions — a leaping exultation and energy or a grim resolution. Save for the expression of the faces, London seemed a city of tramps. The vestries were indiscriminately distributing bread sent us by the French government. The ribs of the few horses showed dismally. Haggard special constables with white badges stood at the corners of every street. I saw little of the mischief wrought by the Martians until I reached Wellington Street, and there I saw the red weed clambering over the buttresses of Waterloo Bridge.

At the corner of the bridge, too, I saw one of the common contrasts of that grotesque time — a sheet of paper flaunting against a thicket of the red weed, transfixed by a stick that kept it in place. It was the placard of the first newspaper to resume publication — the *Daily Mail*. I bought a copy for a blackened shilling I found in my pocket. Most of it was in blank, but the solitary compositor who did the thing had amused himself by making a grotesque scheme of advertisement stereo on the back

page. The matter he printed was emotional; the news organisation had not as yet found its way back. I learned nothing fresh except that already in one week the examination of the Martian mechanisms had yielded astonishing results. Among other things, the article assured me what I did not believe at the time, that the "Secret of Flying" was discovered. At Waterloo I found the free trains that were taking people to their homes. The first rush was already over. There were few people in the train, and I was in no mood for casual conversation. I got a compartment to myself, and sat with folded arms, looking greyly at the sunlit devastation that flowed past the windows. And just outside the terminus the train jolted over temporary rails, and on either side of the railway the houses were blackened ruins. To Clapham Junction the face of London was grimy with powder of the Black Smoke, in spite of two days of thunderstorms and rain, and at Clapham Junction the line had been wrecked again; there were hundreds of out-of-work clerks and shopmen working side by side with the customary navvies, and we were jolted over a hasty relaying.

All down the line from there the aspect of the country was gaunt and unfamiliar; Wimbledon particularly had suffered. Walton, by virtue of its unburned pine-woods, seemed the least hurt of any place along the line. The Wandle, the Mole, every little stream, was a heaped mass of red weed, in appearance between butcher's meat and pickled cabbage. The Surrey pine-woods were too dry, however, for the festoons of the red climber. Beyond Wimbledon, within sight of the line, in certain nursery grounds, were the heaped masses of earth about the sixth cylinder. A number of people were standing about it, and some sappers were busy in the midst of it. Over it flaunted a Union Jack, flapping cheerfully in the morning breeze. The nursery grounds were everywhere crimson with the weed, a wide expanse of livid colour cut with purple shadows, and very painful to the eye. One's gaze went with infinite relief from the scorched greys and sullen reds of the foreground to the blue-green softness of the eastward hills.

The line on the London side of Woking station was still undergoing repair, so I descended at Byfleet station and took the road to Maybury, past the place where I and the artilleryman had talked to the hussars, and on by the spot where the Martian had appeared to me in the thunderstorm. Here, moved by curiosity, I turned aside to find, among a tangle of red fronds, the warped and broken dog-cart with the whitened bones of the horse scattered and gnawed. For a time I stood regarding these vestiges. . . .

Then I returned through the pine-wood, neck-high with red weed here and there, to find the landlord of the Spotted Dog had already found burial, and so came home past the College Arms. A man standing at an open cottage door greeted me by name as I passed.

I looked at my house with a quick flash of hope that faded immediately. The door had been forced; it was unfastened, and was opening slowly as I approached.

It slammed again. The curtains of my study fluttered out of the open window from which I and the artilleryman had watched the dawn. No one had closed it since. The smashed bushes were just as I had left them nearly four weeks ago. I stumbled into the hall, and the house felt empty. The stair-carpet was ruffled and discoloured where I had crouched, soaked to the skin from the thunderstorm the night of the catastrophe. Our muddy footsteps I saw still went up the stairs.

I followed them to my study, and found lying on my writing-table still, with the selenite paper-weight upon it, the sheet of work I had left on the afternoon of the opening of the cylinder. For a space I stood reading over my abandoned arguments. It was a paper on the probable development of Moral Ideas with the development of the civilising process; and the last sentence was the opening of a prophecy: " In about two hundred years," I had written, " we may expect — " The sentence ended abruptly. I remembered my inability to fix my mind that morning, scarcely a month gone by, and how I had broken off to get my *Daily Chronicle* from the newsboy. I remembered how I went down to the garden gate as he came along, and how I had listened to his odd story of " Men from Mars."

I came down and went into the dining-room. There were the mutton and the bread, both far gone now in decay, and a beer bottle overturned, just as I and the artilleryman had left them. My home was desolate. I perceived the folly of the faint hope I had cherished so long. And then a strange thing occurred. " It is no use," said a voice. " The house is deserted. No one has been here these ten days. Do not stay here to torment yourself. No one escaped but you."

I was startled. Had I spoken my thought aloud? I turned, and the French window was open behind me. I made a step to it, and stood looking out.

And there, amazed and afraid, even as I stood amazed and afraid, were my cousin and my wife — my wife white and tearless. She gave a faint cry.

" I came," she said. " I knew — knew — "

She put her hand to her throat — swayed. I made a step forward, and caught her in my arms.

CHAPTER 10

THE EPILOGUE

I CANNOT but regret, now that I am concluding my story, how little I am able to contribute to the discussion of the many

debatable questions which are still unsettled. In one respect I shall certainly provoke criticism. My particular province is speculative philosophy. My knowledge of comparative physiology is confined to a book or two, but it seems to me that Carver's suggestions as to the reason of the rapid death of the Martians is so probable as to be regarded almost as a proven conclusion. I have assumed that in the body of my narrative.

At any rate, in all the bodies of the Martians that were examined after the war, no bacteria except those already known as terrestrial species were found. That they did not bury any of their dead, and the reckless slaughter they perpetrated, point also to an entire ignorance of the putrefactive process. But probable as this seems, it is by no means a proven conclusion.

Neither is the composition of the Black Smoke known, which the Martians used with such deadly effect, and the generator of the Heat-Rays remains a puzzle. The terrible disasters at the Ealing and South Kensington laboratories have disinclined analysts for further investigations upon the latter. Spectrum analysis of the black powder points unmistakably to the presence of an unknown element with a brilliant group of three lines in the green, and it is possible that it combines with argon to form a compound which acts at once with deadly effect upon some constituent in the blood. But such unproven speculations will scarcely be of interest to the general reader, to whom this story is addressed. None of the brown scum that drifted down the Thames after the destruction of Shepperton was examined at the time, and now none is forthcoming.

The results of an anatomical examination of the Martians, so far as the prowling dogs had left such an examination possible, I have already given. But everyone is familiar with the magnificent and almost complete specimen in spirits at the Natural History Museum, and the countless drawings that have been made from it; and beyond that the interest of their physiology and structure is purely scientific.

A question of graver and universal interest is the possibility of another attack from the Martians. I do not think that nearly enough attention is being given to this aspect of the matter. At present the planet Mars is in conjunction, but with every return to opposition I, for one, anticipate a renewal of their adventure. In any case, we should be prepared. It seems to me that it should be possible to define the position of the gun from which the shots are discharged, to keep a sustained watch upon this part of the planet, and to anticipate the arrival of the next attack.

In that case the cylinder might be destroyed with dynamite or artillery before it was sufficiently cool for the Martians to emerge, or they might be butchered by means of guns so soon as the screw opened. It seems to me that they have lost a vast advantage in the failure of their first surprise.

Possibly they see it in the same light.

Lessing has advanced excellent reasons for supposing that the Martians have actually succeeded in effecting a landing on the planet Venus. Seven months ago now, Venus and Mars were in alignment with the sun; that is to say, Mars was in opposition from the point of view of an observer on Venus. Subsequently a peculiar luminous and sinuous marking appeared on the unillumined half of the inner planet, and almost simultaneously a faint dark mark of a similar sinuous character was detected upon a photograph of the Martian disk. One needs to see the drawings of these appearances in order to appreciate fully their remarkable resemblance in character.

At any rate, whether we expect another invasion or not, our views of the human future must be greatly modified by these events. We have learned now that we cannot regard this planet as being fenced in and a secure abiding-place for Man; we can never anticipate the unseen good or evil that may come upon us suddenly out of space. It may be that in the larger design of the universe this invasion from Mars is not without its ultimate benefit for men; it has robbed us of that serene confidence in the future which is the most fruitful source of decadence, the gifts to human science it has brought are enormous, and it has done much to promote the conception of the commonweal of mankind. It may be that across the immensity of space the Martians have watched the fate of these pioneers of theirs and learned their lesson, and that on the planet Venus they have found a securer settlement. Be that as it may, for many years yet there will certainly be no relaxation of the eager scrutiny of the Martian disk, and those fiery darts of the sky, the shooting stars, will bring with them as they fall an unavoidable apprehension to all the sons of men.

The broadening of men's views that has resulted can scarcely be exaggerated. Before the cylinder fell there was a general persuasion that through all the deep of space no life existed beyond the petty surface of our minute sphere. Now we see further. If the Martians can reach Venus, there is no reason to suppose that the thing is impossible for men, and when the slow cooling of the sun makes this earth uninhabitable, as at last it must do, it may be that the thread of life that has begun here will have streamed out and caught our sister planet within its toils.

Dim and wonderful is the vision I have conjured up in my mind of life spreading slowly from this little seed-bed of the solar system throughout the inanimate vastness of sidereal space. But that is a remote dream. It may be, on the other hand, that the destruction of the Martians is only a reprieve. To them, and not to us, perhaps, is the future ordained.

I must confess the stress and danger of the time have left an abiding sense of doubt and insecurity in my mind. I sit in my

study writing by lamplight, and suddenly I see again the healing valley below set with writhing flames, and feel the house behind and about me empty and desolate. I go out into the Byfleet Road, and vehicles pass me, a butcher-boy in a cart, a cabful of visitors, a workman on a bicycle, children going to school, and suddenly they become vague and unreal, and I hurry again with the artilleryman through the hot, brooding silence. Of a night I see the black powder darkening the silent streets, and the contorted bodies shrouded in that layer; they rise upon me tattered and dog-bitten. They gibber and grow fiercer, paler, uglier, mad distortions of humanity at last, and I wake, cold and wretched, in the darkness of the night.

I go to London and see the busy multitudes in Fleet Street and the Strand, and it comes across my mind that they are but the ghosts of the past, haunting the streets that I have seen silent and wretched, going to and fro, phantasms in a dead city, the mockery of life in a galvanised body. And strange, too, it is to stand on Primrose Hill, as I did but a day before writing this last chapter, to see the great province of houses, dim and blue through the haze of the smoke and mist, vanishing at last into the vague lower sky, to see the people walking to and fro among the flower-beds on the hill, to see the sight-seers about the Martian machine that stands there still, to hear the tumult of playing children, and to recall the time when I saw it all bright and clear-cut, hard and silent, under the dawn of that last great day. . . .

And strangest of all is it to hold my wife's hand again, and to think that I have counted her, and that she has counted me, among the dead.

"THE WHOLE AREA WAS A MOON, A STUPENDOUS SIMITAR OF WHITE DAWN."

"'RADIANT ENERGY,' HE MADE ME UNDERSTAND, WAS ANYTHING LIKE LIGHT OR HEAT OR THOSE RÖNTGEN RAYS THERE WAS SO MUCH TALK ABOUT A YEAR OR SO AGO."

THE FIRST MEN IN THE MOON

Three thousand stadia from the earth to the moon... Marvel not, my comrade, if I appear talking to you on super-terrestrial and aerial topics. The long and the short of the matter is that I am running over the order of a Journey I have lately made.

<div align="right">LUCIEN'S Icaromenippus.</div>

CHAPTER 1

MR. BEDFORD MEETS MR. CAVOR AT LYMPNE

As I sit down to write here amidst the shadows of vine-leaves under the blue sky of southern Italy it comes to me with a certain quality of astonishment that my participation in these amazing adventures of Mr. Cavor was, after all, the outcome of the purest accident. It might have been anyone. I fell into these things at a time when I thought myself removed from the slightest possibility of disturbing experiences. I had gone to Lympne because I had imagined it the most uneventful place in the world. "Here at any rate," said I, "I shall find peace and a chance to work!"

And this book is the sequel. So utterly at variance is Destiny with all the little plans of men.

I may perhaps mention here that very recently I had come an ugly cropper in certain business enterprises. At the present moment, surrounded by all the circumstances of wealth, there is a luxury in admitting my extremity. I can even admit that to a certain extent my disasters were conceivably of my own making. It may be there are directions in which I have some capacity; the conduct of business operations is not among these. But in those days I was young, and my youth, among other objectionable forms, took that of a pride in my capacity for affairs. I am young still in years, but the things that have happened to me have rubbed something of the youth from my mind. Whether they have brought any wisdom to light below it, is a more doubtful matter.

It is scarcely necessary to go into the details of the speculations that landed me at Lympne in Kent. Nowadays even about business transactions there is a strong spice of adventure. I took risks. In these things there is invariably a certain amount to give and take, and it fell to me

finally to do the giving reluctantly enough. Even when I had got out of everything one cantankerous creditor saw fit to be malignant. Perhaps you have met that flaming sense of outraged virtue or perhaps you have only felt it. He ran me hard. It seemed to me at last that there was nothing for it but to write a play, unless I wanted to drudge for my living as a clerk. I have a certain imagination, and luxurious tastes, and I meant to make a vigorous fight for it before that fate overtook me. In addition to my belief in my powers as a business man I had always in those days had an idea that I was equal to writing a very good play. It is not, I believe, an uncommon persuasion. I knew there was nothing a man can do outside legitimate business transactions that has such opulent possibilities, and very probably that biased my opinion. I had indeed got into the habit of regarding this unwritten drama as a convenient little reserve put by for a rainy day. That rainy day had come and I set to work.

I soon discovered that writing a play was a longer business than I had supposed — at first I had reckoned ten days for it — and it was to have a *pied-à-terre* while it was in hand that I came to Lympne. I reckoned myself lucky in getting that little bungalow. I got it on a three-years' agreement. I put in a few sticks of furniture, and while the play was in hand I did my own cooking. My cooking would have shocked Mrs. Beeton. And yet, you know, it had a flavour. I had a coffee-pot, a saucepan for eggs and one for potatoes, and a frying-pan for sausages and bacon. Such was the simple apparatus of my comfort. One can't always be magnificent, but simplicity is always a possible alternative. For the rest I laid in an eighteen-gallon cask of beer on credit, and a trustful baker came each day. It was not perhaps in the style of Sybaris, but I have had worse times. I was a little sorry for the baker, who was a very decent man; but even for him I hoped.

Certainly if anyone wants solitude the place is Lympne. It is in the clay part of Kent, and my bungalow stood on the edge of an old sea cliff and stared across the flats of Romney marsh at the sea. In very wet weather the place is almost inaccessible, and I have heard that at times the postman used to traverse the more succulent portions of his route with boards upon his feet. I never saw him doing so, but I can quite imagine it. Outside the doors of the few cottages and houses that make up the present village, big birch besoms are stuck to wipe off the worst of the clay, which will give some idea of the texture of the district. I doubt if the place would be there at all if it were not a fading memory of things gone for ever. It was the big port of England in Roman times, Portus Lemanis, and now the sea is four miles away. All down the steep hill are boulders and masses of Roman brickwork, and from it old Watling Street, still paved in places, starts like an arrow to

the north. I used to stand on the hill and think of it all, the galleys and legions, the captives and officials, the women and traders, the speculators like myself, all the swarm and tumult that came clanking in and out of the harbour. And now just a few lumps of rubble on a grassy slope and a sheep or two — and I! And where the port had been were the levels of the marsh, sweeping round in a broad curve to distant Dungeness and dotted here and there with tree clumps and the church towers of old medieval towns that are following Lemanis now towards extinction.

That outlook on the marsh was indeed one of the finest views I have ever seen. I suppose Dungeness was fifteen miles away; it lay like a raft on the sea, and farther westward were the hills by Hastings under the setting sun. Sometimes they hung close and clear, sometimes they were faded and low, and often the drift of weather took them clean out of sight. And all the nearer parts of the marsh were laced and lit by ditches and canals.

The window at which I worked looked over the skyline of this crest, and it was from this window that I first set eyes on Cavor. It was just as I was struggling with my scenario, holding down my mind to the sheer hard work of it, and naturally enough he arrested my attention.

The sun had set, the sky was a vivid tranquillity of green and yellow, and against that he came out black, the oddest little figure.

He was a short, round-bodied, thin-legged little man, with a jerky quality in his motions; he had seen fit to clothe his extraordinary mind in a cricket cap, an overcoat, and cycling knickerbockers and stockings. Why he did so I do not know, for he never cycled and he never played cricket. It was a fortuitous concurrence of garments arising I know not how. He gesticulated with his hands and arms and jerked his head about and buzzed. He buzzed like something electric. You never heard such buzzing. And ever and again he cleared his throat with a most extraordinary noise.

There had been rain, and that spasmodic walk of his was enhanced by the extreme slipperiness of the footpath. Exactly as he came against the sun he stopped, pulled out a watch, hesitated. Then with a sort of convulsive gesture he turned and retreated with every manifestation of haste, no longer gesticulating, but going with ample strides that showed the relatively large size of his feet — they were I remember grotesquely exaggerated in size by adhesive clay — to the best possible advantage.

This occurred on the first day of my sojourn when my playwriting energy was at its height, and I regarded the incident simply as an annoying distraction — the waste of five minutes. I returned to my scenario. But when next evening the apparition was repeated with remarkable precision, and again the next evening, and indeed every evening when rain was not falling, concentration upon the scenario became a considerable

effort. " Confound the man," said I, " one would think he was learning to be a marionette! " and for several evenings I cursed him pretty heartily.

Then my annoyance gave way to amazement and curiosity. Why on earth should a man do this thing? On the fourteenth evening I could stand it no longer, and as soon as he appeared I opened the French window, crossed the veranda, and directed myself to the point where he invariably stopped.

He had his watch out as I came up to him. He had a chubby rubicund face, with reddish-brown eyes — previously I had seen him only against the light. " One moment, sir," said I as he turned.

He stared. " One moment," he said, " certainly. Or if you wish to speak to me for longer, and it is not asking too much — your moment is up — would it trouble you to accompany me —? "

" Not in the least," said I, placing myself beside him.

" My habits are regular. My time for intercourse — limited."

" This, I presume, is your time for exercise? "

" It is. I come here to enjoy the sunset."

" You don't."

" Sir? "

" You never look at it."

" Never look at it? "

" No. I've watched you thirteen nights and not once have you looked at the sunset. Not once."

He knitted his brows like one who encounters a problem.

" Well, I enjoy the sunlight —

the atmosphere. I go along this path, through that gate " — he jerked his head over his shoulder — " and round — "

" You don't. You never have been. It's all nonsense. There isn't a way. To-night for instance — "

" Oh! to-night! Let me see. Ah! I just glanced at my watch, saw that I had already been out just three minutes over the precise half-hour, decided there was not time to go round, turned — "

" You always do."

He looked at me, reflected. " Perhaps I do — now I come to think of it. . . . But what was it you wanted to speak to me about? "

" Why — *this*! "

" This? "

" Yes. Why do you do it? Every night you come making a noise — "

" Making a noise? "

" Like this." I imitated his buzzing noise. He looked at me and it was evident the buzzing awakened distaste. " Do I do *that*? " he asked.

" Every blessed evening."

" I had no idea."

He stopped. He regarded me gravely. " Can it be," he said, " that I have formed a habit? "

" Well, it looks like it. Doesn't it? "

He pulled down his lower lip between finger and thumb. He regarded a puddle at his feet.

" My mind is much occupied," he said. " And you want to know why! Well, sir, I can assure you that not only do I not know why I do these things, but I did not even know I did them. Come to

think, it is just as you say; I never *have* been beyond that field. . . . And these things annoy you?"

For some reason I was beginning to relent towards him. " Not annoy," I said. " But — imagine yourself writing a play! "

" I couldn't."

" Well, anything that needs concentration."

" Ah," he said, " of course," and meditated. His expression became so eloquent of distress that I relented still more. After all there is a touch of aggression in demanding, of a man you don't know, why he hums on a public footpath.

" You see," he said weakly, " it's a habit."

" Oh, I recognise that."

" I must stop it."

" But not if it puts you out. After all, I had no business — it's something of a liberty."

" Not at all, sir," he said, " not at all. I am greatly indebted to you. I should guard myself against these things. In future I will. Could I trouble you — once again? that noise? "

" Something like this," I said. " Zuzzoo, zuzzoo — But really you know — "

" I am greatly obliged to you. In fact — I know — I am getting absurdly absent-minded. You are quite justified, sir — perfectly justified. Indeed, I am indebted to you. The thing shall end. And now, sir, I have already brought you farther than I should have done."

" I do hope my impertinence — "

" Not at all, sir, not at all."

We regarded each other for a moment. I raised my hat and wished him a good evening. He responded convulsively, and so we went our ways.

At the stile I looked back at his receding figure. His bearing had changed remarkably; he seemed limp, shrunken. The contrast with his former gesticulating, zuzzooing self took me in some absurd way as pathetic. I watched him out of sight. Then, wishing very heartily I had kept to my own business, I returned to my bungalow and my play.

The next evening I saw nothing of him, nor the next. But he was very much in my mind, and it had occurred to me that as a sentimental comic character he might serve a useful purpose in the development of my plot. The third day he called upon me.

For a time I was puzzled to think what had brought him — he made indifferent conversation in the most formal way — then abruptly he came to business. He wanted to buy me out of my bungalow.

" You see," he said, " I don't blame you in the least, but you've destroyed a habit and it disorganises my day. I've walked past here for years — years. No doubt I've hummed. . . . You've made all that impossible! "

I suggested he might try some other direction.

" No. There is no other direction. This is the only one. I've inquired. And now every afternoon at four — I come to a dead wall."

"But, my dear sir, if the thing is so important to you — "

"It's vital! You see I'm — I'm an investigator — I am engaged in a scientific research. I live — " he paused and seemed to think. "Just over there," he said, and pointed suddenly dangerously near my eyes. "The house with white chimneys you see just over the trees. And my circumstances are abnormal — abnormal. I am on the point of completing one of the most important demonstrations, I can assure you, one of the most important of all the demonstrations that have ever been made. It requires constant thought, constant mental ease and activity. And the afternoon was my brightest time! — effervescing with new ideas — new points of view."

"But why not come by still?"

"It would be all different. I should be self-conscious. I should think of you at your play — watching me, irritated! Instead of thinking of my work. No! I must have the bungalow."

I meditated. Naturally I wanted to think the matter over thoroughly before anything decisive was said. I was generally ready enough for business in those days and selling always attracted me, but in the first place it was not my bungalow, and even if I sold it to him at a good price I might get inconvenienced in the delivery if the current owner got wind of the transaction, and in the second I was, well — undischarged. It was clearly a business that required delicate handling. Moreover the possibility of his being in pursuit

of some valuable invention also interested me. It occurred to me that I would like to know more of this research, not with any dishonest intention, but simply with an idea that to know what it was would be a relief from playwriting. I threw out feelers.

He was quite willing to supply information. Indeed, once he was fairly under way the conversation became a monologue. He talked like a man long pent up, who has had it over with himself again and again. He talked for nearly an hour, and I must confess I found it a pretty stiff bit of listening. But through it all there was the undertone of satisfaction one feels when one is neglecting work one has set oneself. During that first interview I gathered very little of the drift of his work. Half his words were technicalities entirely strange to me, and he illustrated one or two points with what he was pleased to call elementary mathematics, computing on an envelope with a copying ink pencil, in a manner that made it hard even to seem to understand. "Yes," I said. "Yes. Go on!" Nevertheless I made out enough to convince me that he was no mere crank playing at discoveries. In spite of his cranklike appearance there was a force about him that made that impossible. Whatever it was it was a thing with mechanical possibilities. He told me of a workshed he had and of three assistants, originally jobbing carpenters whom he had trained. Now from the workshed to the patent office is clearly only one step. He invited me to see these things. I

accepted readily and took care by a remark or so to underline that. The proposed transfer of the bungalow remained very conveniently in suspense.

At last he rose to depart with an apology for the length of his call. Talking over his work was, he said, a pleasure enjoyed only too rarely. It was not often he found such an intelligent listener as myself. He mingled very little with professional scientific men.

"So much pettiness," he explained, "so much intrigue! And really when one has an idea — a novel, fertilising idea — I don't wish to be uncharitable, but — "

I am a man who believes in impulses. I made what was perhaps a rash proposition. But you must remember that I had been alone, playwriting in Lympne for fourteen days, and my compunction for his ruined walk still hung about me. "Why not," said I, "make this your new habit? In the place of the one I spoilt. At least — until we can settle about the bungalow. What you want is to turn over your work in your mind. That you have always done during your afternoon walk. Unfortunately that's over — you can't get things back as they were. But why not come and talk about your work to me — use me as a sort of wall against which you may throw your thoughts and catch them again. It's certain I don't know enough to steal your ideas myself, and I know no scientific men. . . ."

I stopped. He was considering. Evidently the thing attracted him. "But I'm afraid I should bore you," he said.

"You think I'm too dull?"

"Oh no, but technicalities — "

"Anyhow you've interested me immensely this afternoon."

"Of course, it would be a great help to me. Nothing clears up one's ideas so much as explaining them. Hitherto — "

"My dear sir, say no more."

"But really can you spare the time?"

"There is no rest like change of occupation," I said with profound conviction.

The affair was over. On my veranda steps he turned. "I am already greatly indebted to you," he said.

I made an interrogative noise.

"You have completely cured me of that ridiculous habit of humming," he explained.

I think I said I was glad to be of any service to him, and he turned away.

Immediately the train of thought that our conversation had suggested must have resumed its sway. His arms began to wave in their former fashion. The faint echo of "*zuzzoo*" came back to me on the breeze. . . .

Well — after all that was not my affair. . . .

He came the next day and again the next day after that, and delivered two lectures on physics to our mutual satisfaction. He talked with an air of being extremely lucid about the "ether" and "tubes of force" and "gravitational potential" and such things, and I sat in my other folding-chair and said "Yes," "Go on," "I follow you," to

keep him going. It was tremendously difficult stuff, but I do not think he ever suspected how much I did not understand him. There were moments when I doubted whether I was well employed, but at any rate I was resting from that confounded play. Now and then things gleamed on me clearly for a space, only to vanish just when I thought I had hold of them. Sometimes my attention failed altogether, and I would give it up and sit and stare at him, wondering whether after all it would not be better to use him as a central figure in a good farce and let all this other stuff slide. And then perhaps I would comprehend again for a bit.

At the earliest opportunity I went to see his house. It was large and carelessly furnished; there were no servants other than his three assistants, and his dietary and private life were characterised by a philosophical simplicity. He was a water-drinker, a vegetarian, and all those logical, disciplinary things. But the sight of his equipment settled many doubts. It looked like business from cellar to attic — an amazing little place to find in an out-of-the-way village. The ground floor rooms contained benches and apparatus, the bakehouse and scullery boiler had developed into respectable furnaces, dynamos occupied the cellar, and there was a gasometer in the garden. He showed it to me with all the confiding zest of a man who has been living too much alone. His seclusion was overflowing now in an excess of confidence, and I had the good luck to be the recipient.

The three assistants were creditable specimens of the class of " handy men " from which they came. Conscientious if unintelligent, strong, civil, and willing. One, Spargus, who did the cooking and all the metal work, had been a sailor; a second, Gibbs, was a joiner, and the third was an ex-jobbing gardener and now general assistant. They were the merest labourers; all the intelligent work was done by Cavor. Theirs was the darkest ignorance compared even with my muddled impression.

And now, as to the nature of these inquiries. Here unhappily comes a grave difficulty. I am no scientific expert, and if I were to attempt to set forth in the highly scientific language of Mr. Cavor the aim to which his experiments tended, I am afraid I should confuse not only the reader but myself, and almost certainly I should make some blunder that would bring upon me the mockery of every up-to-date student of mathematical physics in the country. The best thing I can do therefore is, I think, to give my impressions in my own inexact language without any attempt to wear a garment of knowledge to which I have no claim.

The object of Mr. Cavor's search was a substance that should be " opaque " — he used some other word I have forgotten, but " opaque " conveys the idea — to " all forms of radiant en-

ergy." "Radiant energy," he made me understand, was anything like light or heat or those Röntgen rays there was so much talk about a year or so ago, or the electric waves of Marconi, or gravitation. All these things, he said, *radiate* from centres and act on bodies at a distance, whence comes the term "radiant energy." Now almost all substances are opaque to some form or other of radiant energy. Glass, for example, is transparent to light, but much less so to heat, so that it is useful as a fire-screen; and alum is transparent to light, but blocks heat completely. A solution of iodine in carbon bisulphide, on the other hand, completely blocks light but is quite transparent to heat. It will hide a fire from you but permit all its warmth to reach you. Metals are not only opaque to light and heat but also to electrical energy, which passes through both iodine solution and glass almost as though they were not interposed. And so on.

Now all known substances are "transparent" to gravitation. You can use screens of various sorts to cut off the light or heat or electrical influence of the sun, or the warmth of the earth from anything; you can screen things by sheets of metal from Marconi's rays, but nothing will cut off the gravitational attraction of the sun or the gravitational attraction of the earth. Yet why there should be nothing is hard to say. Cavor did not see why such a substance should not exist, and certainly I could not tell him. I had never thought of such a possibility before. He showed me by calculations on paper which Lord Kelvin, no doubt, or Professor Lodge or Professor Karl Pearson, or any of those great scientific people might have understood, but which simply reduced me to a hopeless muddle, that not only was such a substance possible, but that it must satisfy certain conditions. It was an amazing piece of reasoning. Much as it amazed and exercised me at the time, it would be impossible to reproduce it here. "Yes," I said to it all, "Yes. Go on!" Suffice it for this story that he believed he might be able to manufacture this possible substance opaque to gravitation out of a complicated alloy of metals and something new — a new element I fancy — called, I believe, *helium,* which was sent to him from London in sealed stone jars. Doubt has been thrown upon this detail, but I am almost certain it was *helium* he had sent him in sealed stone jars. It was certainly something very gaseous and thin.

If only I had taken notes. . . .

But then how was I to foresee the necessity of taking notes?

Anyone with the merest germ of imagination will understand the extraordinary possibilities of such a substance, and will sympathise a little with the emotion I felt as this understanding emerged from the haze of abstruse phrases in which Cavor expressed himself. Comic relief in a play indeed! It was some time before I would believe that I

had interpreted him aright, and I was very careful not to ask questions that would have enabled him to gauge the profundity of misunderstanding into which he dropped his daily exposition. But no one reading the story of it here will sympathise fully, because from my barren narrative it will be impossible to gather the strength of my conviction that this astonishing substance was positively going to be made.

I do not recall that I gave my play an hours' work at any one time after my visit to his house. My imagination had other things to do. There seemed no limit to the possibilities of the scheme; whichever way I tried, I came on miracles and revolutions. For example, if one wanted to lift a weight, however enormous, one had only to get a sheet of this substance beneath it and one might lift it with a straw. My first natural impulse was to apply this principle to guns and ironclads and all the material and methods of war and from that to shipping, locomotion, building, every conceivable form of human industry. The chance that had brought me into the very birth chamber of this new time — it was an epoch, no less — was one of those chances that come once in a thousand years. The thing unrolled, it expanded and expanded. Among other things I saw in it my redemption as a business man. I saw a parent company and daughter companies, applications to right of us, applications to left, rings and trusts, privileges and concessions spreading and spreading, until one vast stupendous Cavorite Company ran and ruled the world.

And I was in it.

I took my line straight away. I knew I was staking everything, but I jumped there and then. "We're on absolutely the biggest thing that has ever been invented," I said, and put the accent on "we." "If you want to keep me out of this, you'll have to do it with a gun. I'm coming down to be your fourth labourer to-morrow."

He seemed surprised at my enthusiasm, but not a bit suspicious or hostile. Rather he was self-depreciatory.

He looked at me doubtfully. "But do you really think — ? " he said. "And your play! How about that play? "

"It's vanished! " I cried. "My dear sir, don't you see what you've got? Don't you see what you're going to do? "

That was merely a rhetorical turn, but positively he didn't. At first I could not believe it. He had not had the beginning of the inkling of an idea! This astonishing little man had been working on purely theoretical grounds the whole time! When he said it was "the most important" research the world had ever seen he simply meant it squared up so many theories, settled so much that was in doubt; he had troubled no more about the application of the stuff he was going to turn out than if he had been a machine that makes guns. This was a possible substance, and he was going to make

it! *V'là tout,* as the Frenchman says.

Beyond that — he was childish! If he made it, it would go down to posterity as Cavorite or Cavorine and he would be made an F.R.S. and his portrait as a scientific worthy given away with *Nature,* and things like that. And that was all he saw! He would have dropped this bombshell into the world as though he had discovered a new species of gnat, if it had not happened that I had come along. And there it would have lain and fizzled, like one or two other little things these scientific people have lit and dropped about.

When I realised this, it was I did the talking and Cavor who said " Go on! " I jumped up. I paced the room, gesticulating like a boy of twenty. I tried to make him understand his duties and responsibilities in the matter — *our* duties and responsibilities in the matter. I assured him we might make wealth enough to work any sort of social revolution we fancied; we might own and order the whole world. I told him of companies and patents and the case for secret processes. All these things seemed to impress him much as his mathematics had impressed me. A look of perplexity came into his ruddy little face. He stammered something about indifference to wealth, but I brushed all that aside. He had got to be rich and it was no use stammering. I gave him to understand the sort of man I was, and that I had had very considerable business experience. I did not tell him I was an undis-

charged bankrupt at the time, because that was temporary, but I think I reconciled my evident poverty with my financial claims. And quite insensibly in the way such projects grow, the understanding of a Cavorite monopoly grew up between us. He was to make the stuff and I was to make the boom.

I stuck like a leech to the " we " — " you " and " I " didn't exist for me.

His idea was that the profits I spoke of might go to endow research, but that of course was a matter we had to settle later. " That's all right," I shouted. " That's all right." The great point, as I insisted, was to get the thing done.

" Here is a substance," I cried, " no home, no factory, no fortress, no ship can dare to be without — more universally applicable even than a patent medicine! There isn't a solitary aspect of it, not one of its ten thousand possible uses, that will not make us rich, Cavor, beyond the dreams of avarice! "

" No! " he said. " I begin to see. It's extraordinary how one gets new points of view by talking over things! "

" And as it happens you have talked to just the right man! "

" I suppose no one," he said, " is absolutely *averse* to enormous wealth. Of course there is one thing — "

He paused. I stood still.

" It is just possible, you know, that we may not be able to make it after all. It may be one of those things that are a theoretical possibility but a practical ab-

surdity. Or when we make it, there may be some little hitch — ! "

" We'll tackle the hitch when it comes," said I.

CHAPTER 2

THE FIRST MAKING
OF CAVORITE

But Cavor's fears were groundless so far as the actual making was concerned. On the fourteenth of October, 1899, this incredible substance was made.

Oddly enough it was made at last by accident when Mr. Cavor least expected it. He had fused together a number of metals and certain other things — I wish I knew the particulars now — and he intended to leave the mixture a week and then allow it to cool slowly. Unless he had miscalculated, the last stage in the combination would occur when the stuff sank to a temperature of sixty degrees Fahrenheit. But it chanced that, unknown to Cavor, dissension had arisen among the men about the furnace-tending. Gibbs, who had previously seen to this, had suddenly attempted to shift it to the man who had been a gardener, on the score that coal was soil, being dug, and

therefore could not possibly fall within the province of a joiner; the man who had been a jobbing gardener alleged, however, that coal was a metallic or ore-like substance, let alone that he was cook. But Spargus insisted on Gibbs doing the coaling, seeing that he was a joiner and that coal is notoriously fossil wood. Consequently Gibbs ceased to replenish the furnace and no one else did so, and Cavor was too much immersed in certain interesting problems concerning a Cavorite flying machine (neglecting the resistance of the air and one or two other points) to perceive that anything was wrong. And the premature birth of his invention took place just as he was coming across the field to my bungalow for our afternoon talk and tea.

I remember the occasion with extreme vividness. The water was boiling and everything was prepared and the sound of his " zuzzoo " had brought me out upon the veranda. His active little figure was black against the autumnal sunset, and to the right the chimneys of his house just rose above a gloriously tinted group of trees. Remoter rose the Wealden Hills, faint and blue, while to the left the hazy marsh spread out spacious and serene. And then — !

The chimneys jerked heavenward, smashing into a string of bricks as they rose, and the roof and a miscellany of furniture followed. Then overtaking them came a huge white flame. The trees about the building swayed and whirled and tore themselves

to pieces that sprang toward the flare. My ears were smitten with a clap of thunder that left me deaf on one side for life, and all about me windows smashed unheeded.

I took three steps from the verandah towards Cavor's house, and even as I did so came the wind.

Instantly my coat tails were over my head and I was progressing in great leaps and bounds and quite against my will, towards him. In the same moment the discoverer was seized, whirled about, and blown through the screaming air. I saw one of my chimney pots hit the ground within six yards of me, leap a score of feet, and so hurry in great strides towards the focus of the disturbance. Cavor, kicking and flapping, came down again, rolled over and over on the ground for a space, struggled up and was lifted and borne forward at an enormous velocity, vanishing at last among the labouring, lashing trees that writhed about his house.

A mass of smoke and ashes and a square bluish shining substance rushed up towards the zenith. A large fragment of fencing came sailing past me, dropped edgewise, hit the ground and fell flat, and then the worst was over. The aerial commotion fell swiftly until it was merely a strong gale, and I became once more aware that I had breath and feet. By leaning back against the wind I managed to stop, and could collect such wits as still remained to me.

In that instant the whole face of the world had changed. The tranquil sunset had vanished, the sky was dark with scurrying clouds, everything was flattened and swaying with the gale. I glanced back to see if my bungalow was still in a general way standing, then staggered forward towards the trees among which Cavor had vanished and through whose tall and leaf-denuded branches shone the flames of his burning house.

I entered the copse, dashing from one tree to another and clinging to them, and for a space I sought him in vain. Then amidst a heap of smashed branches and fencing that had banked itself against a portion of his garden wall, I perceived something stir. I made a run for this, but before I reached it a brown object separated itself, rose on two muddy legs and protruded two drooping, bleeding hands. Some tattered ends of garment fluttered out from its middle portion and streamed before the wind.

For a moment I did not recognise this earthly lump, and then I saw that it was Cavor, caked in the mud in which he had rolled. He leaned forward against the wind, rubbing the dirt from his eyes and mouth.

He extended a muddy lump of hand, and staggered a pace towards me. His face worked with emotion; little lumps of mud kept falling from it. He looked as damaged and pitiful as any living creature I have ever seen, and his remark therefore amazed me exceedingly. " Gratulate me," he gasped; " gratulate me! "

"Congratulate you!" said I. "Good heavens! What for?"

"I've done it."

"You *have*. What on earth caused that explosion?"

A gust of wind blew his words away. I understood him to say that it wasn't an explosion at all. The wind hurled me into collision with him, and we stood clinging to each other.

"Try to get back to my bungalow," I bawled in his ear. He did not hear me, and shouted something about "three martyrs — science," and also something about "not much good." At the time he laboured under the impression that his three attendants had perished in this whirlwind. Happily this was incorrect. As soon as he had left for my bungalow they had gone off to the public house in Lympne, to discuss the question of the furnaces over some trivial refreshment.

I repeated my suggestion of getting back to my bungalow, and this time he understood. We clung arm in arm and started, managing at last to reach the shelter of as much roof as was left to me. For a space we sat in armchairs and panted. All the windows were broken and the lighter articles of furniture were in great disorder, but no irrevocable damage was done. Happily the kitchen door had stood the pressure upon it, so that all my crockery and cooking materials had escaped damage. The oil-stove was still burning and I put on the water to boil again for tea. That prepared, I could turn to Cavor for his explanation.

"Quite correct," he insisted; "quite correct. I've done it, and it's all right."

"But —" I protested. "All right! Why, there can't be a rick standing, or a fence or a thatched roof undamaged for twenty miles round. . . ."

"It's all right — *really*. I didn't, of course, foresee this little upset. My mind was preoccupied with another problem, and I'm apt to disregard these practical side issues. But it's all right —"

"My dear sir," I cried, "don't you see you've done thousands of pounds' worth of damage?"

"There, I throw myself on your discretion. I'm not a practical man, of course, but don't you think they will regard it as a cyclone —"

"But the explosion —"

"It was not an explosion. It's perfectly simple. Only, as I say, I'm apt to overlook these little things. It's the zuzzoo business on a larger scale. Inadvertently I made this substance of mine, this Cavorite, in a thin wide sheet. . . ."

He paused. "You are quite clear that the stuff is opaque to gravitation, that it cuts off objects from gravitating towards each other?"

"Yes," said I. "Yes?"

"Well, so soon as it reached a temperature of sixty degrees Fahrenheit and the process of its manufacture was complete, the air above it, the portions of roof and ceiling and floor above it ceased to have weight. I suppose you know — everybody knows nowadays — that, as a usual thing, the air *has* weight, that it presses on everything at

the surface of the earth, presses in all directions, with a pressure of fourteen and a half pounds to the square inch?"

"I know that," said I. "Go on."

"I know that too," he remarked. "Only this shows you how useless knowledge is unless you apply it. You see, over our Cavorite this ceased to be the case, the air there ceased to exert any pressure, and the air round it, and not over the Cavorite, was exerting a pressure of fourteen pounds and a half to the square inch upon this suddenly weightless air. Ah! you begin to see! The air all about the Cavorite crushed in upon the air above it with irresistible force. The air above the Cavorite was forced upwards violently, the air that rushed in to replace it immediately lost weight, ceased to exert any pressure, followed suit, blew the ceiling through and the roof off. . . .

"You perceive," he said, "it formed a sort of atmospheric fountain, a kind of chimney in the atmosphere. And if the Cavorite itself hadn't been loose and so got sucked up the chimney, does it occur to you what would have happened?"

I thought, "I suppose," I said, "the air would be rushing up and up over that infernal piece of stuff now."

"Precisely," he said. "A huge fountain!"

"Spouting into space! Good heavens! Why, it would have squirted all the atmosphere of the earth away! It would have robbed the world of air! It would have been the death of all man-

kind! That little lump of stuff!"

"Not exactly into space," said Cavor, "but as bad—practically. It would have whipped the air off the world as one peels a banana, and flung it thousands of miles. It would have dropped back again of course—but on an asphyxiated world! From our point of view very little better than if it never came back!"

I stared. As yet I was too amazed to realise how all my expectations had been upset. "What do you mean to do now?" I asked.

"In the first place, if I may borrow a garden trowel I will remove some of this earth with which I am encased, and then if I may avail myself of your domestic conveniences, I will have a bath. This done, we will converse more at leisure. It will be wise, I think"—he laid a muddy hand on my arm—"if nothing were said of this affair beyond ourselves. I know I have caused great damage—probably even dwelling-houses may be ruined here and there upon the country side. But on the other hand, I cannot possibly pay for the damage I have done, and if the real cause of this is published it will lead only to heart-burning and the obstruction of my work. One cannot foresee everything, you know, and I cannot consent for one moment to add the burden of practical considerations to my theorising. Later on, when you have come in with your practical mind and Cavorite is floated—floated is the word, isn't it? and it has realised all you anticipate for it, we may set matters right with these people. But not now—not

now. If no other explanation is offered, people, in the present unsatisfactory state of meteorological science, will ascribe all this to a cyclone; there might be a public subscription, and as my house has collapsed and been burnt I should in that case receive a considerable share in the compensation which would be extremely helpful to the prosecution of our researches. But if it is known that *I* caused this, there will be no public subscription, and everybody will be put out. Practically, I shall never get a chance of working in peace again. My three assistants may or may not have perished. That is a detail. If they have it is no great loss; they were more zealous than able, and this premature event must be largely due to their joint neglect of the furnace. If they have not perished, I doubt if they have the intelligence to explain the affair. They will accept the cyclone story. And if during the temporary unfitness of my house for occupation, I may lodge in one of the untenanted rooms of this bungalow of yours — "

He paused and regarded me.

A man of such possibilities, I reflected, is no ordinary guest to entertain.

"Perhaps," said I, rising to my feet, "we had better begin by looking for a trowel," and I led the way to the scattered vestiges of the greenhouse.

While he was having his bath I considered the entire question alone. It was clear there were drawbacks to Mr. Cavor's society I had not foreseen. The absentmindedness that had just escaped depopulating the terrestrial globe might at any moment result in some other grave inconvenience. On the other hand I was young, my affairs were in a mess, and I was in just the mood for reckless adventure, with a chance of something good at the end of it. I had quite settled in my mind that I was to have half at least in that aspect of the affair. Fortunately I held my bungalow, as I have already explained, on a three years' agreement, without being responsible for repairs, and my furniture, such as there was of it, had been hastily purchased, was unpaid for, insured, and altogether devoid of associations. In the end I decided to keep on with him and see the business through.

Certainly the aspect of things had changed very greatly. I no longer doubted at all the enormous possibilities of the substance, but I began to have doubts about the gun-carriage and the patent boots.

We set to work at once to reconstruct his laboratory and to proceed with our experiments. Cavor talked more on my level than he had ever done before when it came to question of how we should make the stuff next.

"Of course we must make it again," he said, with a sort of glee I had not expected in him, "of course we must make it again. We have caught a tartar, perhaps, but we have left the theoretical behind us for good and all. If we can possibly avoid wrecking this little planet of ours we will. But — there must be risks! There must be. In experimental work there always are!

And here, as a practical man, *you* must come in. For my own part, it seems to me we might make it edgewise, perhaps, and very thin. Yet I don't know — I have a certain dim perception of another method. I can hardly explain it yet. But curiously enough it came into my mind while I was rolling over and over in the mud before the wind and very doubtful how the whole adventure was to end, as being absolutely the thing I ought to have done."

Even with my aid we found some little difficulty and meanwhile we kept at work restoring the laboratory. There was plenty to do before it was absolutely necessary to decide upon the precise form and method of our second attempt. Our only hitch was the strike of the three labourers, who objected to my activity as a foreman. But that matter we compromised after two days' delay.

CHAPTER 3

THE BUILDING OF
THE SPHERE

I REMEMBER very distinctly the occasion when Cavor told me of his idea of the sphere. He had had intimations of it before, but at the time it seemed to come to him in a rush. We were returning to the bungalow for tea, and on the way he fell humming. Suddenly he shouted: "That's it! That finishes it! A sort of roller blind."

"Finishes what?" I asked.

"Space—anywhere! The moon!"

"What do you mean?"

"Mean? Why — it must be a sphere! That's what I mean!"

I saw I was out of it, and for a time I let him talk in his own fashion. I hadn't the ghost of an idea then of his drift. But after he had taken tea he made it clear to me.

"It's like this," he said. "Last time I ran this stuff into a flat tank with an overlap that held it down. When it had cooled and the manufacture was completed, all that uproar happened; nothing above it weighed anything, the air went squirting up, the house squirted up, and if the stuff itself hadn't squirted up too, I don't know what would have happened! But suppose the substance is loose and quite free to go up?"

"It will go up at once!"

"Exactly. With no more disturbance than firing a big gun."

"But what good will that do?"

"I'm going up with it!"

I put down my teacup and stared at him.

"Imagine a sphere," he explained, "large enough to hold two people and their luggage. It will be made of steel, lined with thick glass, it will contain a proper store of solidified air, concentrated food, water, distilling apparatus and so forth, and

enamelled as it were on the outer steel — "

" Cavorite? "

" Yes."

" But how will you get inside? "

" There was a similar problem about a dumpling."

" Yes, I know. But how? "

" That's perfectly easy. An air-tight manhole is all that is needed. That of course will have to be a little complicated; there will have to be a valve, so that things may be thrown out if necessary without much loss of air."

" Like Jules Verne's apparatus in *A Trip to the Moon*? "

But Cavor was not a reader of fiction.

" I begin to see," I said, slowly. " And you could get in and screw yourself up while the Cavorite was warm, and as soon as it cooled it would become impervious to gravitation, and off you would fly — "

" At a tangent."

" You would go off in a straight line — " I stopped abruptly. " What is to prevent the thing travelling in a straight line into space for ever? " I asked. " You're not sure to get anywhere, and if you do — how will you get back? "

" I've just thought of that," said Cavor. " That's what I meant when I said the thing was finished. The inner glass sphere can be air-tight and except for the manhole, continuous, and the steel sphere can be made in sections, each section capable of rolling up after the fashion of a roller blind. These can easily be worked by springs, and released and checked by electricity conveyed by platinum wires fused through the glass. All that is merely a question of detail. So you see that except for the thickness of the blind rollers, the Cavorite exterior of the sphere will consist of windows or blinds, whichever you like to call them. Well, when all these windows or blinds are shut, no light, no heat, no gravitation, no radiant energy of any sort will get at the inside of the sphere; it will fly on through space in a straight line as you say. But open a window — imagine one of the windows open! Then at once any heavy body that chances to be in that direction will attract us — "

I sat taking it in.

" You see? " he said.

" Oh, I *see*."

" Practically we shall be able to tack about in space just as we wish. Get attracted by this and that."

" Oh yes. That's clear enough. Only — "

" Well? "

" I don't quite see what we shall do it for! It's really only jumping off the world and back again."

" Surely! For example! One might go to the moon."

" And when one got there! What would you find? "

" We should see — ! Oh! Consider the new knowledge! "

" Is there air there? "

" There may be."

I shook my head. " It's a fine idea," I said, " but it strikes me as a large order all the same. The

moon! I'd much rather try some smaller things first."

" They're out of the question — because of the air difficulty."

" Why not apply that idea of spring blinds — Cavorite blinds in strong steel cases — to lifting weights? "

" It wouldn't work," he insisted. " After all to go into outer space is not so much worse, if at all, than a polar expedition. Men go on polar expeditions."

" Not business men. Besides they get paid for polar expeditions. And if anything goes wrong there are relief parties. But this — it's just firing ourselves off the world for nothing."

" Call it prospecting."

" You'll have to call it that. . . . One might make a book of it perhaps."

" I have no doubt there will be minerals," said Cavor.

" For example? "

" Oh! sulphur, ores, gold perhaps; possibly new elements."

" Cost of carriage," I said; " you know you're not a practical man. The moon's a quarter of a million miles away."

" It seems to me it wouldn't cost much to cart any weight anywhere if you packed it in a Cavorite case."

" I had not thought of that. Delivered free on head of purchaser, eh? "

" It isn't as though you were confined to the moon."

" You mean — ? "

" There's Mars — clear atmosphere, novel surroundings, exhilarating sense of lightness. It might be pleasant to go there."

" Is there air on Mars? "

" Oh yes! "

" Seems as though you might run it as a sanatorium. By the way, how far is Mars? "

" Two hundred million miles at present," said Cavor airily; " and you go close by the sun."

My imagination was picking itself up again. " After all," I said, " there's something in these things. There's travel — "

An extraordinary possibility came rushing into my mind. Suddenly I saw as in a vision the whole solar system threaded with Cavorite liners and spheres *de luxe*. " Rights of pre-emption," came floating into my head — planetary rights of pre-emption. I recalled the old Spanish monopoly in American gold. It wasn't as if it was just this planet or that — it was all of them. I stared at Cavor's rubicund face and suddenly my imagination was leaping and dancing. I stood up, I walked up and down; my tongue was loosened.

" I'm beginning to take it in," I said. " I'm beginning to take it in." The transition from doubt to enthusiasm seemed to take scarcely any time at all. " But this is tremendous! " I cried; " this is imperial! I haven't been dreaming of this sort of thing."

Once the chill of my opposition was removed, his own pent-up excitement had play. He too got up and paced. He too gesticulated and shouted. We behaved like men inspired. We *were* men inspired.

" We'll settle all that! " he said, in answer to some incidental

difficulty that had pulled me up. "We'll soon settle all that. We'll start the drawing for mouldings this very night."

"We'll start them now," I responded, and we hurried off to the laboratory to begin upon this work forthwith.

I was like a child in wonderland all that night. The dawn found us both still at work; we kept our electric light going heedless of the day. I remember now exactly how those drawings looked — I shaded and tinted while Cavor drew — smudged and haste-marked they were in every line, but wonderfully correct. We got out the orders for the steel blinds and frames we needed from that night's work, and the glass sphere was designed within a week. We gave up our afternoon conversations and our old routine altogether. We worked, and we slept and ate when we could work no longer for hunger and fatigue. Our enthusiasm infected even our three men, though they had no idea what the sphere was for. Through those days the man Gibbs gave up walking and went everywhere, even across the room, at a sort of fussy run.

And it grew, the sphere. December passed, January — I spent a day with a broom sweeping a path through the snow from bungalow to laboratory — February, March. By the end of March the completion was in sight. In January had come a team of horses, a huge packing case; we had our thick glass sphere now ready and in position, under the crane we had rigged to sling it into the steel shell. All the bars and blinds of the steel shell — it was not really a spherical shell, but polyhedral, with a roller blind to each facet — had arrived by February, and the lower half was bolted together. The Cavorite was half made by March, the metallic paste had gone through two of the stages in its manufacture, and we had plastered quite half of it on to the steel bars and blinds. It was astonishing how closely we kept to the lines of Cavor's first inspiration in working out the scheme. When the bolting together of the sphere was finished he proposed to remove the rough roof of the temporary laboratory in which the work was done and build a furnace about it. So the last stage of Cavorite making, in which the paste is heated to a dull red glow in a stream of helium, would be accomplished when it was already on the sphere.

And then we had to discuss and decide what provisions we were to take, compressed foods, concentrated essences, steel cylinders containing reserve oxygen, an arrangement for removing carbonic acid and waste from the air and restoring oxygen by means of sodium peroxide, water condensers, and so forth. I remember the little heap they made in the corner, tins and rolls and boxes — convincingly matter-of-fact.

It was a strenuous time, with little chance of thinking. But one day, when we were drawing near the end, an odd mood came over me. I had been bricking up the furnace all the morning, and I

sat down by these possessions, tired out. Everything seemed dull and incredible.

" But look here, Cavor," I said. " After all! What's it all for? "

He smiled. " The thing now is to go."

" The moon," I reflected. " But what do you expect? I thought the moon was a dead world."

He shrugged his shoulders.

" What do you expect? "

" We're going to see."

" Are we? " I said and stared before me.

" You are tired," he remarked. " You'd better take a walk this afternoon."

" No," I said obstinately; " I'm going to finish this brickwork."

And I did, and ensured myself a night of insomnia.

I don't think I have ever had such a night. I had some bad times before my business collapse but the very worst of those was sweet slumber compared to this infinity of aching wakefulness. I was suddenly in the most enormous funk at the thing we were going to do.

I do not remember before that night thinking at all of the risks we were running. Now they came like that array of spectres that once beleaguered Prague, and camped around me. The strangeness of what we were about to do, the unearthliness of it, overwhelmed me. I was like a man awakened out of pleasant dreams to the most horrible surroundings. I lay, eyes wide open; and the sphere seemed to get more flimsy and feeble, and Cavor more unreal and fantastic and the whole enterprise madder and madder every moment.

I got out of bed and wandered about. I sat at the window and stared at the immensity of space. Between the stars was the void, the unfathomable darkness — ! I tried to recall the fragmentary knowledge of astronomy I had gained in my irregular reading, but it was all too vague to furnish any idea of the things we might expect.

At last I got back to bed and snatched some moments of sleep, moments of nightmare rather, in which I fell and fell and fell for evermore into the abyss of the sky.

I astonished Cavor at breakfast. I told him shortly: " I'm not coming with you in the sphere."

I met all his protests with a sullen persistence. " The thing's too mad," I said, " and I won't come. The thing's too mad."

I would not go with him to the laboratory. I fretted about my bungalow for a time, and then took hat and stick and set off alone, I knew not whither. It chanced to be a glorious morning; a warm wind and deep blue sky, the first green of spring abroad and multitudes of birds singing. I lunched on beef and beer in a little public-house near Elham, and startled the landlord by remarking, *à propos* of the weather: " A man who leaves the world when days of this sort are about is a fool! "

" That's what I says when I heerd on it! " said the landlord, and I found that for one poor soul at least this world had proved excessive and there had

been a throat-cutting. I went on with a new twist to my thoughts.

In the afternoon I had a pleasant sleep in a sunny place, and went my way refreshed.

I came to a comfortable-looking inn near Canterbury. It was bright with creepers, and the landlady was a clean old woman who took my eye. I found I had just enough money to pay for my lodging with her. I decided to spend the night there. She was a talkative body, and among many other particulars I learnt she had never been to London. "Canterbury's as far as ever I been," she said. "I'm not one of your gad-about sort."

"How would you like a trip to the moon?" I cried.

"I never did hold with them ballooneys," she said, evidently under the impression that this was a common excursion enough. "I wouldn't go up in one — not for ever so."

This struck me as being funny. After I had supped I sat on a bench by the door of the inn and gossiped with two labourers about brickmaking and motor cars and the cricket of last year. And in the sky a faint new crescent, blue and vague as a distant Alp, sank westward over the sun.

The next day I returned to Cavor. "I am coming," I said. "I've been a little out of order — that's all."

That was the only time I felt any serious doubt of our enterprise. Nerves purely! After that I worked a little more carefully and took a trudge for an hour

every day. And at last, save for the heating in the furnace, our labours were at an end.

CHAPTER 4

INSIDE THE SPHERE

"Go on," said Cavor as I sat across the edge of the manhole and looked down into the black interior of the sphere. We two were alone. It was evening, the sun had set and the stillness of twilight was upon everything.

I drew my other leg inside and slid down the smooth glass to the bottom of the sphere; then turned to take the cans of food and other impedimenta from Cavor. The interior was warm, the thermometer stood at eighty, and as we should lose little or none of this by radiation, we were dressed in slippers and thin flannels. We had however a bundle of thick woollen clothing and several thick blankets to guard against mischance. By Cavor's direction I placed the packages, the cylinders of oxygen and so forth, loosely about my feet; and soon we had everything in. He walked about the roofless shed for a time, seeking anything we had

overlooked, and then crawled in after me. I noted something in his hand.

" What have you there? " I asked.

" Haven't you brought anything to read? "

" Good Lord! No! "

" I forgot to tell you. There are uncertainties — The voyage may last — We may be weeks! "

" But — "

" We shall be floating in this sphere with absolutely no occupation."

" I wish I'd known — "

He peered out of the manhole. " Look! " he said. " There's something there! "

" Is there time? "

" We shall be an hour."

I looked out. It was an old number of *Tit-Bits,* that one of the men must have brought. Farther away in the corner I saw a torn *Lloyd's News.* I scrambled back into the sphere with these things.

" What have you got? " I said.

I took the book from his hand and read, " The Works of William Shakespeare."

He coloured slightly. " My education has been so purely scientific — " he said apologetically.

" Never read him? "

" Never."

" He knew a little, you know — in an irregular sort of way."

" Precisely what I am told," said Cavor.

I assisted him to screw in the glass cover of the manhole, and then he pressed a stud to close the corresponding blind in the outer case. The little oblong of twilight vanished. We were in darkness.

For a time neither of us spoke. Although our case would not be impervious to sound, everything was very still. I perceived there was nothing to grip when the shock of our start should come, and I realised that I should be uncomfortable for want of a chair.

" Why have we no chairs? " I asked.

" I've settled all that," said Cavor. " We shan't need them."

" Why not? "

" You will see," he said, in the tone of a man who refuses to talk.

I became silent. Suddenly it had come to me, clear and vivid, that I was a fool to be inside that sphere. Even now, I asked myself, is it too late to withdraw? The world outside the sphere, I knew, would be cold and inhospitable enough to me — for weeks I had been living on subsidies from Cavor — but after all, would it be as cold as the infinite zero, as inhospitable as empty space? If it had not been for the appearance of cowardice, I believe that even then I should have made him let me out. But I hesitated on that score and hesitated, and grew fretful and angry, and the time passed.

There came a little jerk, a noise like champagne being uncorked in another room, and a faint whistling sound. For just one instant I had a sense of enormous tension, a transient conviction that my feet were pressing downward with a force of count-

less tons. It lasted for an infinitesimal time.

But it stirred me to action. " Cavor! " I said in the darkness, " my nerve's in rags . . . I don't think — "

I stopped. He made no answer. " Confound it? " I cried; " I'm a fool! What business have I here? I'm not coming, Cavor. The thing's too risky. I'm getting out."

" You can't," he said.

" Can't! We'll soon see about that! "

He made no answer for ten seconds. " It's too late for us to quarrel now, Bedford," he said. " That little jerk was the start. Already we are flying as swiftly as a bullet up into the gulf of space."

" I — " I said, and then it did not seem to matter what happened. For a time I was, as it were, stunned. I had nothing to say. It was just as if I had never heard of this idea of leaving the earth before. Then I perceived an unaccountable change in my bodily sensations. It was a feeling of lightness, of unreality. Coupled with that was a queer sensation in the head, an apoplectic effect almost, and a thumping of blood-vessels in the ears. Neither of these feelings diminished as time went on, but at last I got so used to them that I experienced no inconvenience.

I heard a click, and a little glow lamp came into being.

I saw Cavor's face, as white as I felt my own to be. We regarded each other in silence. The transparent blackness of the glass behind him made him seem to be floating in a void.

" Well, we're committed," I said at last.

" Yes," he said, " we're committed."

" Don't move," he exclaimed, at some suggestion of a gesture. " Let your muscles keep quite lax — as if you were in bed. We are in a little universe of our own. Look at those things! "

He pointed to the loose cases and bundles that had been lying on the blankets in the bottom of the sphere. I was astonished to see that they were floating now nearly a foot from the spherical wall. Then I saw from his shadow that Cavor was no longer leaning against the glass. I thrust out my hand behind me and found that I too was suspended in space, clear of the glass.

I did not cry out nor gesticulate, but fear came upon me. It was like being lifted and held by something — you know not what. The mere touch of my hand against the glass moved me rapidly. I understood what had happened but that did not prevent my being afraid. We were cut off from all exterior gravitation — only the attraction of objects within our sphere had effect. Consequently everything that was not fixed to the glass was falling — slowly because of the slightness of our masses — towards the centre of gravity of our little world, which seemed to be somewhere about the middle of the sphere, but rather nearer to myself than to Cavor on account of my greater weight.

" We must turn round," said

Cavor, "and float back to back, with the things between us."

It was the strangest sensation conceivable, floating thus loosely in space, at first indeed horribly strange, and when the horror passed, not disagreeable at all, exceedingly restful! indeed the nearest thing in earthly experience to it that I know is lying on a very thick soft feather bed. But the quality of utter detachment and independence! I had not reckoned on anything like this. I had expected a violent jerk at starting, a giddy sense of speed. Instead I felt — as if I were disembodied. It was not like the beginning of a journey; it was like the beginning of a dream.

CHAPTER 5

THE JOURNEY TO
THE MOON

PRESENTLY Cavor extinguished the light. He said we had not overmuch energy stored and what we had we must economise for reading. For a time, whether it was long or short I do not know, there was nothing but blank darkness.

A question floated up out of the void. "How are we pointing," I said. "What is our direction?"

"We are flying away from the earth at a tangent, and as the moon is near her third quarter, we are going somewhere towards her. I will open a blind —"

There came a click and then a window in the outer case yawned open. The sky outside was as black as the darkness within the sphere, but the shape of the open window was marked by an infinite number of stars.

Those who have seen the starry sky only from the earth cannot imagine its appearance when the vague half-luminous veil of our air has been withdrawn. The stars we see on earth are the mere scattered survivors that penetrate our misty atmosphere. But now at last I could realise the meaning of the hosts of heaven! Stranger! things we were presently to see, but that airless, star-dusted sky! Of all things I think that will be one of the last I shall forget.

The little window vanished with a click, another beside it snapped open and instantly closed, and then a third, and for a moment I had to close my eyes because of the blinding splendour of the waning moon.

For a space I had to stare at Cavor and the whitelit things about me to season my eyes to light again, before I could turn them towards that pallid glare.

Four windows were open in order that the gravitation of the moon might act upon all the substances in our sphere. I found I was no longer floating freely in space, but that my feet were

resting on the glass in the direction of the moon. The blankets and cases of provisions were also creeping slowly down the glass, and presently came to rest so as to block out a portion of the view. It seemed to me, of course, that I looked "down" when I looked at the moon. On earth "down" means earthward, the way things fall, and "up" the reverse direction. Now the pull of gravitation was towards the moon, and for all I knew to the contrary our earth was overhead. And of course, when all the Cavorite blinds were closed, "down" was towards the centre of our sphere, and "up" towards its outer wall.

It was curiously unlike earthly experience, too, to have the light coming up. On earth light falls from above or comes slanting down sidewise, but here it came from beneath our feet, and to see our shadows we had to look up.

At first it gave me a sort of vertigo to stand only on thick glass and look down upon the moon through hundreds of thousands of miles of vacant space. But this sickness passed very speedily. And then — the splendour of the sight!

The reader may imagine it best if he will lie on the ground some warm summer's night and look between his upraised feet at the moon, but for some reason, probably because the absence of air made it so much more luminous, the moon seemed already considerably larger than it does from earth. The minutest details of its surface were acutely clear. And since we did not see it through air, its outline was bright and sharp; there was no glow or halo about it and the star-dust that covered the sky came right to its very margin and marked the outline of its illuminated part. And as I stood and stared at the moon between my feet, that perception of the impossible that had been with me off and on ever since our start returned again with tenfold conviction.

"Cavor," I said, "this takes me queerly. Those companies we were going to run and all that about minerals — "

"Well?"

"I don't see 'em here."

"No," said Cavor, "but you'll get over all that."

"I suppose I'm made to turn right side up again. Still *this* — For a moment I could half believe there never was a world."

"That copy of *Lloyd's News* might help you."

I stared at the paper for a moment, then held it above the level of my face and found I could read it quite easily. I struck a column of mean little advertisements. "A gentleman of private means is willing to lend money," I read. I knew that gentleman. Then somebody eccentric wanted to sell a Cutaway bicycle, "quite new and cost £15," for £5, and a lady in distress wished to dispose of some fish knives and forks, "a wedding present," at a great sacrifice. No doubt some simple soul was sagely examining those knives and forks, and another triumphantly riding off on that bicycle, and a third trustfully consulting that benevolent gentleman of

means, even as I read. I laughed and let the paper drift from my hand.

"Are we visible from the earth?" I asked.

"Why?"

"I knew someone — who was interested in astronomy. It occurred to me that it would be odd if — my friend — chanced to be looking through a telescope and should chance to see us."

"It would need the most powerful telescope on earth even now to see us as the minutest speck."

For a time I stared in silence at the moon.

"It's a world," I said; "one feels that infinitely more than one ever did on earth. People perhaps —"

"People!" he exclaimed. "No! Banish all that! Think yourself a sort of ultra Arctic voyager exploring the desolate places of space. Look at it!"

He waved his hand at the shining whiteness below. "It's dead — dead! Vast extinct volcanoes, lava wildernesses, tumbled wastes of snow or frozen carbonic acid or frozen air, and everywhere landslips, seams and cracks and gulfs. Nothing happens. Men have watched this planet systematically with telescopes for over two hundred years. How much change do you think they have seen?"

"None."

"They have traced two indisputable land-slips, a doubtful crack and one slight periodic change of colour. And that's all."

"I didn't know they'd traced even that."

"Oh, yes. But as for people — !"

"By the way," I asked, "how small a thing will the biggest telescopes show upon the moon?"

"One could see a fair-sized church. One could certainly see any towns or buildings or anything like the handiwork of men. There might perhaps be insects, something in the way of ants for example, something able to hide in deep burrows from the lunar night. Or some new sort of creatures having no earthly parallel. That is the most probable thing if we are to find life there at all. Think of the difference in conditions! Life must fit itself to a day as long as fourteen earthly days, a cloudless sun-blaze of fourteen days, and then a night of equal length, growing ever colder and colder under these cold, sharp stars. In that night there must be cold, the ultimate cold, absolute zero, 273 degrees Centigrade, below the earthly freezing point. Whatever life there is must hibernate through that — and rise again each day."

He mused. "One can imagine something wormlike," he said, "taking its air solid as an earthworm swallows earth, or thick-skinned monsters —"

"By the bye," I said, "why didn't we bring a gun?"

He did not answer that question. "No," he concluded, "we just have to go. We shall see when we get there."

I remembered something. "Of course, there's my minerals anyhow," I said, "whatever the conditions may be."

Presently he told me he wished

to alter our course a little by letting the earth tug at us for a moment. He was going to open one earthward blind for thirty seconds. He warned me that it would make my head swim, and advised me to extend my hands against the glass to break my fall. I did as he directed, and thrust my feet against the bales of food cases and air cylinders to prevent their falling upon me. Then with a click the window flew open. I fell clumsily upon hands and face and saw for a moment between my black extended fingers, our mother earth — a planet in a downward sky.

We were still very near — Cavor told me the distance was, perhaps, eight hundred miles — and the huge terrestrial disc filled all heaven. But already it was plain to see that the world was a globe. The land below us was in twilight and vague, but westward the vast grey stretches of the Atlantic shone like molten silver under the receding day. I think I recognised the cloud-dimmed coastlines of France and Spain and the south of England, and then with a click the shutter closed again and I found myself in a state of extraordinary confusion, sliding slowly over the smooth glass.

When at last matters settled themselves in my mind again, it seemed quite beyond question that the moon was "down" under my feet, and that the earth was somewhere away on the level of the horizon, the earth that had been "down" to me and my kindred since the beginning of things.

So slight were the exertions required of us, so easy did the practical annihilation of our weight make all we had to do, that the necessity for taking refreshment did not occur to us for nearly six hours (by Cavor's chronometer) after our start. I was amazed at that lapse of time. Even then I was satisfied with very little. Cavor examined the apparatus for absorbing carbonic acid and water, and pronounced it to be in satisfactory order, our consumption of oxygen having been extraordinarily slight; our talk being exhausted for the time, and there being nothing further for us to do, we gave way to a curious drowsiness that had come upon us, and spreading our blankets on the bottom of the sphere in such a manner as to shut out most of the moonlight, wished each other good night, and almost immediately fell asleep.

And so sleeping, and sometimes talking and reading a little, at times eating, though without any keenness of appetite,[1] but for the most part in a sort of quiescence that was neither waking nor slumber, we fell through a space of time that had neither night nor day in it, silently, softly, and swiftly down towards the moon.

[1] It is a curious thing that while we were in the sphere we felt not the slightest desire for food nor did we feel the want of it when we abstained. At first we forced our appetite but afterwards we fasted completely. Altogether we did not consume one-twentieth part of the compressed provision we had brought with us. The amount of carbonic acid we exhaled was also unnaturally low, but why this was so I am quite unable to explain.

CHAPTER 6

THE LANDING ON
THE MOON

I REMEMBER how one day Cavor suddenly opened six of our shutters and blinded me so that I cried aloud at him. The whole area was moon, a stupendous scimitar of white dawn with its edge hacked out by notches of darkness, the crescent shore of an ebbing tide of darkness, out of which peaks and pinnacles came climbing into the blaze of the sun. I take it the reader has seen pictures or photographs of the moon, so that I need not describe the broader features of that landscape, those spacious, ringlike ranges vaster than any terrestrial mountains, their summits shining in the day, their shadows harsh and deep; the grey disordered plains, the ridges, hills, and craterlets all passing at last from a blazing illumination into a common mystery of black. Athwart this world we were flying scarcely a hundred miles above its crests and pinnacles. And now we could see, what no human eye had ever seen before, that under the blaze of the day the harsh outlines of

the rocks and ravines of the plains and crater floor grew grey and indistinct under a thickening haze, that the white of their lit surfaces broke into lumps and patches and broke again and shrank and vanished, and that here and there strange tints of brown and olive grew and spread.

But little time we had for watching them. For now we had come to the real danger of our journey. We had to drop ever closer to the moon as we spun about it, to slacken our pace and watch our chance until at last we could dare to drop upon its surface.

For Cavor that was a time of intense exertion; for me it was an anxious inactivity. I seemed perpetually to be getting out of his way. He leaped about the sphere from point to point with an agility that would have been impossible on earth. He was perpetually opening and closing the Cavorite windows, making calculations, consulting his chronometer by means of the glow-lamp during those last eventful hours. For a long time we had all our windows closed, and hung silently in darkness, hurtling through space.

Then he was feeling for the shutter studs, and suddenly four windows were open. I staggered and covered my eyes, drenched and scorched and blinded by the unaccustomed splendour of the sun beneath my feet. Then again the shutters snapped, leaving my brain spinning in a darkness that pressed against the eyes. And after that I floated in another vast black silence.

Then Cavor switched on the electric light, and told me he proposed to bind all our luggage together with blankets about it, against the concussion of our descent. We did this with our windows closed, because in that way our goods arranged themselves naturally at the centre of the sphere. That too was a strange business; we two men floating loose in that spherical space and packing and pulling ropes. Imagine it if you can! No up nor down, and every effort resulting in unexpected movements. Now I would be pressed against the glass with the full force of Cavor's thrust; again I would be kicking helplessly in a void. Now the star of the electric light would be overhead, now under foot. Now Cavor's feet would float up before my eyes, and now we would be crosswise to each other. But at last our goods were safely bound together in a big soft bale, all except two blankets with head holes that we were to wrap about ourselves.

Then for a flash Cavor opened a window moonward, and we saw that we were dropping towards a huge central crater, with a number of minor craters grouped in a cross about it. And then again Cavor flung our little sphere open to the scorching, blinding sun. I think he was using the sun's attraction as a brake. "Cover yourself with a blanket," he cried, thrusting himself from me, and for a moment I did not understand.

Then I hauled the blanket from beneath my feet and got it about me and over my head and

eyes. Abruptly he closed the shutters, snapped one open again and closed it; then suddenly began snapping them all open, each safely into its steel roller. There came a jar and then we were rolling over and over, bumping against the glass and against the big bale of our luggage, and clutching at each other, and outside some white substance splashed as if we were rolling down a slope of snow. . . .

Over, clutch, bump, clutch, bump, over. . . .

Came a thud, and I was half buried under the bale of our possessions, and for a space everything was still. Then I could hear Cavor puffing and grunting and the snapping of a shutter in its sash. I made an effort, thrust back our blanket-wrapped luggage, and emerged from beneath it. Our open windows were just visible as a deeper black set with stars.

We were still alive, and we were lying in the darkness of the shadow of the wall of the great crater into which we had fallen.

We sat getting our breath again and feeling the bruises on our limbs. I think neither of us had had a very clear expectation of such rough handling as we had received. I struggled painfully to my feet. "And now," said I, "to look at the landscape of the moon! But! — It's tremendously dark, Cavor!"

The glass was dewy, and as I spoke I wiped at it with my blanket. "We're half an hour or so beyond the day," he said. "We must wait."

It was impossible to distinguish

anything. We might have been in a sphere of steel for all that we could see. My rubbing with the blanket simply smeared the glass, and as fast as I wiped it, it became opaque again with freshly-condensed moisture, mixed with an increasing quantity of blanket hairs. Of course I ought not to have used the blanket. In my efforts to clear the glass I slipped upon the damp surface and hurt my shin against one of the oxygen cylinders that protruded from our bale.

The thing was exasperating — it was absurd. Here we were just arrived upon the moon, amidst we knew not what wonders, and all we could see was the grey and streaming wall of the bubble in which we had come.

"Confound it," I said, "but at this rate we might have stopped at home!" and I squatted on the bale and shivered and drew my blanket closer about me.

Abruptly the moisture turned to spangles and fronds of frost. "Can you reach the electric heater?" said Cavor. "Yes — that black knob. Or we shall freeze."

I did not wait to be told twice. "And now," said I, "what are we to do?"

"Wait," he said.

"Wait?"

"Of course. We shall have to wait until our air gets warm again, and then this glass will clear. We can't do anything till then. It's night here yet — we must wait for the day to overtake us. Meanwhile, don't you feel hungry?"

For a space I did not answer him, but sat fretting. I turned reluctantly from the crater wall. These hummocks looked like snow. At the time I thought they were snow. But they were not — they were mounds and masses of frozen air!

So it was at first; and then, sudden, swift, and amazing, came the lunar day.

The sunlight had crept down the cliff, it touched the drifted masses at its base, and incontinently came striding with seven-leagued boots towards us. The distant cliff seemed to shift and quiver, and at the touch of the sun a reek of grey vapour poured upwards from the crater floor, whirls and puffs and drifting wraiths of grey, thicker and broader and denser, until at last the whole westward plain was steaming like a wet handkerchief held before the fire, and the westward cliffs were no more than a refracted glare beyond.

"It is air," said Cavor, "It must be air — or it would not rise like this — at this mere touch of a sunbeam. And at this pace. . . ."

He peered upwards. "Look!" he said.

"What?" I asked.

"In the sky. Already. On the blackness — a little touch of blue. See! The stars seem larger; the little ones and all those dim nebulosities we saw in empty space — they are hidden!"

Swiftly, steadily the day approached us. Grey summit after grey summit was overtaken by the blaze, and turned to a smoking white intensity. At last there

was nothing to the west of us but a bank of surging fog, the tumultuous advance and ascent of cloudy haze. The distant cliff had receded farther and farther, had loomed and changed through the whirl, had foundered and vanished at last in its confusion.

Nearer came that steaming advance, nearer and nearer, coming as fast as the shadow of a cloud before the south-west wind. About us rose a thin, anticipatory haze.

Cavor gripped my arms. "What?" I said.

"Look! The sunrise! The sun!"

He turned me about and pointed to the brow of the eastward cliff, looming above the haze about us, scarcely lighter than the darkness of the sky. But now its line was marked by strange reddish shapes—tongues of vermilion flame that writhed and danced. I fancied it must be spirals of vapour that had caught the light and made this crest of fiery tongues against the sky, but indeed it was the solar prominences I saw, a crown of fire about the sun that is for ever hidden from earthly eyes by our atmospheric veil.

And then—the sun!

Steadily, inevitably, came a brilliant line—came a thin edge of intolerable effulgence that took a circular shape, became a bow, became a blazing sceptre, and hurled a shaft of heat at us as though it were a spear.

It seemed verily to stab my eyes! I cried aloud and turned about blinded, groping for my blanket beneath the bale.

And with that incandescence came a sound, the first sound that had reached us from without since we left the earth, a hissing and rustling, the stormy trailing of the aerial garment of the advancing day. And with the coming of the sound and the light the sphere lurched, and, blinded and dazzled, we staggered helplessly against each other. It lurched again, and the hissing grew louder. I had shut my eyes perforce; I was making clumsy efforts to cover my head with my blanket, and this second lurch sent me helplessly off my feet. I fell against the bale, and, opening my eyes, had a momentary glimpse of the air just outside our glass. It was running—it was boiling—like snow into which a white-hot rod is thrust. What had been solid air had suddenly, at the touch of the sun, become a paste, a mud, a slushy liquefaction that hissed and bubbled into gas.

There came a still more violent whirl of the sphere, and we had clutched each other. In another moment we were spun about again. Round we went and over, and then I was on all fours. The lunar dawn had hold of us. It meant to show us little men what the moon could do with us.

I caught a second glimpse of things without, puffs of vapour, half-liquid slush, excavated, sliding, falling, sliding. We dropped into darkness. I went down with Cavor's knees in my chest. Then he seemed to fly away from me, and for a moment I lay, with all the breath out of my body, staring upwards. A huge landslip, as

it were, of melting stuff had splashed over us, buried us, and now it thinned and boiled away from us. I saw the bubbles dancing on the glass above. I heard Cavor exclaiming feebly.

Then some huge landslip in the thawing air had caught us and, spluttering expostulation, we began to roll down a slope, rolling faster and faster, leaping crevasses and rebounding from banks, faster and faster, westward into the white-hot boiling tumult of the lunar day.

Clutching at each other we spun about, pitched this way and that, our bale of packages leaping at us, pounding at us. We collided, we gripped, we were torn asunder—our heads met, and the whole universe burst into fiery darts and stars! On the earth we should have smashed each other a dozen times, but on the moon luckily for us our weight was only one-sixth of what it is terrestrially, and we fell very mercifully. I recall a sensation of utter sickness, a feeling as if my brain were upside down within my skull, and then—

Something was at work upon my face; some thin feelers worried my ears. Then I discovered the brilliance of the landscape around was mitigated by blue spectacles. Cavor bent over me, and I saw his face upside down, his eyes also protected by tinted goggles. His breath came regularly, and his lip was bleeding from a bruise. "Better?" he said, wiping the blood with the back of his hand.

Everything seemed swaying for a space, but that was simply my giddiness. I perceived that he had closed some of the shutters in the outer sphere to save me from the direct blaze of the sun. I was aware that everything about us was very brilliant.

"Lord!" I gasped. "But this—"

I craned my neck to see. I perceived there was a blinding glare outside, an utter change from the gloomy darkness of our first impressions. "Have I been insensible long?" I asked.

"I don't know—the chronometer is broken. Some little time. . . . My dear chap! I have been afraid. . . ."

I lay for a space taking this in. I saw his face still bore evidences of emotion. For a while I said nothing. I passed an inquisitive hand over my contusions, and surveyed his face for similar damages. The back of my right hand had suffered most, and was skinless and raw. My forehead was bruised and had bled. He handed me a measure with some of the restorative—I forget the name of it—he had brought with us. After a time I felt a little better. I began to stretch my limbs carefully. Soon I could talk.

"It wouldn't have done," I said, as though there had been no interval.

"No, it *wouldn't!*"

He thought, his hands hanging over his knees. He peered through the glass and then stared at me. "Good Lord!" he said. "No!"

"What has happened?" I asked after a pause; "have we jumped to the tropics?"

"It was as I expected. This air

has evaporated. If it is air. At any rate it has evaporated, and the surface of the moon is showing. We are lying on a bank of earthy rock. Here and there bare soil is exposed; a queer sort of soil."

It occurred to him that it was unnecessary to explain. He assisted me into a sitting position, and I could see with my own eyes.

CHAPTER 7

A LUNAR MORNING

THE HARSH emphasis, the pitiless black and white of the scenery had altogether disappeared. The glare of the sun had taken upon itself a faint tinge of amber; the shadows upon the cliff of the crater wall were deeply purple. To the eastward a dark bank of fog still crouched and sheltered from the sunrise, but to the westward the sky was blue and clear. I began to realise the length of my insensibility.

We were no longer in a void. An atmosphere had risen about us. The outline of things had gained in character, had grown acute and varied; save for a shadowed space of white substance here and there, white substance that was no longer air but snow,

the Arctic appearance had gone altogether. Everywhere broad, rusty-brown spaces of bare and tumbled earth spread to the blaze of the sun. Here and there at the edge of the snowdrifts were transient little pools and eddies of water, the only things stirring in that expanse of barrenness. The sunlight inundated the upper two-thirds of our sphere and turned our climate to high summer, but our feet were still in shadow and the sphere was lying upon a drift of snow.

And scattered here and there upon the slope, and emphasised by little white threads of unthawed snow upon their shady sides, were shapes like sticks — dry, twisted sticks of the same rusty hue as the rock upon which they lay. That caught one's thoughts sharply. Sticks! On a lifeless world? Then as my eye grew more accustomed to the texture of their substance I perceived that almost all this surface had a fibrous texture, like the carpet of brown needles one finds beneath the shade of pine trees.

"Cavor!" I said.

"Yes?"

"It may be a dead world now — but once —"

Something arrested my attention. I had discovered among these needles a number of little round objects. It seemed to me that one of these had moved.

"Cavor," I whispered.

"What?"

But I did not answer at once. I stared incredulous. For an instant I could not believe my eyes. I gave an inarticulate cry.

I gripped his arm. I pointed. "Look!" I cried, finding my tongue. "There! Yes! And there!"

His eyes followed my pointing finger. "Eh?" he said.

How can I describe the thing I saw? It is so petty a thing to state, and yet it seemed so wonderful, so pregnant with emotion. I have said that amidst the stick-like litter were these round bodies, these little oval bodies that might have passed as very small pebbles. And now first one and then another had stirred, had rolled over and cracked, and down the crack of each of them showed a minute line of yellowish green, thrusting outward to meet the hot encouragement of the newly risen sun. For a moment that was all, and then there stirred and burst a third!

"It is a seed," said Cavor. And then I heard him whisper, very softly: "*Life!*"

"Life!" and immediately it poured upon us that our vast journey had not been made in vain, that we had come to no arid waste of minerals, but to a world that lived and moved! We watched intensely. I remember I kept rubbing the glass before me with my sleeve, jealous of the faintest suspicion of mist.

The picture was clear and vivid only in the middle of the field. All about that centre the dead fibres and seeds were magnified and distorted by the curvature of the glass. But we could see enough! One after another all down the sunlit slope these miraculous little brown bodies burst and gaped apart, like seed-pods, like the husks of fruits; opened eager mouths that drank in the heat and light pouring in a cascade from the newly risen sun.

Every moment more of these seed-coats ruptured, and even as they did so the swelling pioneers overflowed their rent distended seed-cases and passed into the second stage of growth. With a steady assurance, a swift deliberation, these amazing seeds thrust a rootlet downward to the earth and a queer bundle-like bud into the air. In a little while the whole slope was dotted with minute plantlets standing at attention in the blaze of the sun.

They did not stand for long. The bundle-like buds swelled and strained and opened with a jerk, thrusting out a coronet of red sharp tips, spreading a whorl of tiny, spiky, brownish leaves, that lengthened rapidly, lengthened visibly even as we watched. The movement was slower than any animal's, swifter than any plant's I have ever seen before. How can I suggest it to you — the way that growth went on? The leaf tips grew so that they moved onward even while we looked at them. The brown seed-case shrivelled and was absorbed with an equal rapidity. Have you ever on a cold day taken a thermometer into your warm hand and watched the little thread of mercury creep up the tube? These moon-plants grew like that.

In a few minutes, as it seemed, the buds of the more forward of these plants had lengthened into a stem, and were even putting forth a second whorl of leaves, and all the slope that had

seemed so recently a lifeless stretch of litter was now dark with the stunted, olive-green herbage of bristling spikes that swayed with the vigour of their growing.

I turned about, and behold! along the upper edge of a rock to the eastward a similar fringe, in a scarcely less forward condition, swayed and bent, dark against the blinding glare of the sun. And beyond this fringe was the silhouette of a plant mass, branching clumsily like a cactus and swelling visibly, swelling like a bladder that fills with air.

Then to the westward also I discovered another such distended form was rising over the scrub. But here the light fell upon its sleek sides, and I could see that its colour was a vivid orange. It rose as one watched it; if one looked away from it for a minute and then back, its outline had changed: it thrust out blunt, congested branches, until in a little time it rose a coralline shape of many feet in height. Compared with such a growth the terrestrial puff-ball which will sometimes swell a foot in diameter in a single night, would be a hopeless laggard. But then the puff-ball grows against a gravitational pull of six times that of the moon. Beyond, out of gullies and flats that had been hidden from us but not from the quickening sun, over reefs and banks of shining rock, a bristling beard of spiky and fleshy vegetation was straining into view, hurrying tumultuously to take advantage of the brief day in which it must flower and fruit and seed

again and die. It was like a miracle, that growth. So, one must imagine, the trees and plants arose at the Creation, and covered the desolation of the new-made earth.

Imagine it! Imagine that dawn! The resurrection of the frozen air, the stirring and quickening of the soil, and then this silent uprising of vegetation, this unearthly ascent of fleshliness and spikes. Conceive it all lit by a blaze that would make the intensest sunlight of earth seem watery and weak. And still amidst this stirring jungle wherever there was shadow lingered banks of bluish snow. And to have the picture of our impression complete you must bear in mind that we saw it all through a thick bent glass, distorting it as things are distorted by a lens, acute only in the centre of the picture and very bright there, and towards the edges magnified and unreal.

CHAPTER 8

PROSPECTING BEGINS

WE ceased to gaze. We turned to each other, the same thought, the same question in our eyes. For these plants to grow there must

be some air, however attenuated — air that we also should be able to breathe.

" The manhole? " I said.

" Yes," said Cavor; " if it is air we see!"

" In a little while," I said, " these plants will be as high as we are. Suppose — suppose, after all — Is it certain? How do you know that stuff *is* air? It may be nitrogen; it may be carbonic acid even!"

" That is easy," he said, and set about proving it. He produced a big piece of crumpled paper from the bale, lit it, and thrust it hastily through the manhole valve. I bent forward and peered down through the thick glass for its appearance outside, that little flame on whose evidence depended so much!

I saw the paper drop out and lie lightly upon the snow. The pink flame of its burning vanished. For an instant it seemed to be extinguished. . . . And then I saw a little blue tongue upon the edge of it that trembled and crept and spread!

Quietly the whole sheet, save where it lay in immediate contact with the snow, charred and shrivelled and sent up a quivering thread of smoke. There was no doubt left to me: the atmosphere of the moon was either pure oxygen or air, and capable therefore, unless its tenuity were excessive, of supporting our alien life. We might emerge — and live!

I sat down with my legs on either side of the manhole and prepared to unscrew it, but Cavor stopped me. " There is first a little precaution," he said. He pointed out that, although it was certainly an oxygenated atmosphere outside, it might still be so rarefied as to cause us grave injury. He reminded me of mountain sickness and of the bleeding that often afflicts aeronauts who have ascended too swiftly, and he spent some time in the preparation of a sickly tasting drink which he insisted on my sharing. It made me feel a little numb, but otherwise had no effect on me. Then he permitted me to begin unscrewing.

Presently the glass stopper of the manhole was so far undone that the denser air within our sphere began to escape along the thread of the screw, singing as a kettle sings before it boils. Thereupon he made me desist. It speedily became evident that the pressure outside was very much less than it was within. How much less it was we had no means of telling.

I sat grasping the stopper with both hands, ready to close it again if, in spite of our intense hope, the lunar atmosphere should after all prove too rarefied for us, and Cavor sat with a cylinder of compressed oxygen at hand to restore our pressure. We looked at each other in silence, and then at the fantastic vegetation that swayed and grew visibly and noiselessly without. And ever that shrill piping continued.

The blood-vessels began to throb in my ears, and the sound of Cavor's movements diminished. I noted how still everything had become because of the thinning of the air.

As our air sizzled out from the

screw the moisture of it condensed in little puffs.

Presently I experienced a peculiar shortness of breath — that lasted, indeed, during the whole of the time of our exposure to the moon's exterior atmosphere, and a rather unpleasant sensation about the ears and fingernails and the back of the throat grew on my attention, and presently passed off again.

But then came vertigo and nausea that abruptly changed the quality of my courage. I gave the lid of the manhole half a turn and made a hasty explanation to Cavor, but now he was the more sanguine. He answered me in a voice that seemed extraordinarily small and remote because of the thinness of the air that carried the sound. He recommended a nip of brandy, and set me the example, and presently I felt better. I turned the manhole stopper back again. The throbbing in my ears grew louder, and then I remarked that the piping note of the outrush had ceased. For a time I could not be sure that it had ceased.

" Well? " said Cavor, in the ghost of a voice.

" Well? " said I.

" Shall we go on? "

I thought. " Is this all? "

" If you can stand it."

By way of answer I went on unscrewing. I lifted the circular operculum from its place and laid it carefully on the bale. A flake or so of snow whirled and vanished as that thin and unfamiliar air took possession of our sphere. I knelt and then seated myself at the edge of the manhole, peering over it. Beneath, within a yard of my face, lay the untrodden snow of the moon.

There came a little pause. Our eyes met.

" It doesn't distress your lungs too much? " said Cavor.

" No," I said. " I can stand this."

He stretched out his hand for his blanket, thrust his head through its central hole, and wrapped it about him. He sat down on the edge of the manhole; he let his feet drop until they were within six inches of the lunar snow. He hesitated for a moment, then thrust himself forwards, dropped these intervening inches, and stood upon the untrodden soil of the moon.

As he stepped forwards he was refracted grotesquely by the edge of the glass. He stood for a moment looking this way and that. Then he drew himself together and leaped.

The glass distorted everything, but it seemed to me even then to be an extremely big leap. He had at one bound become remote. He seemed twenty or thirty feet off. He was standing high upon a rocky mass and gesticulating back to me. Perhaps he was shouting — but the sound did not reach me. But how the deuce had he done this? I felt like a man who has just seen a new conjuring trick.

Still in a puzzled state of mind, I too dropped through the manhole. I stood up. Just in front of me the snow-drift had fallen away and made a sort of ditch. I made a step and jumped.

I found myself flying through the air, saw the rock on which he stood coming to meet me, clutched it, and clung in a state of infinite amazement. I gasped a painful laugh. I was tremendously confused. Cavor bent down and shouted in piping tones for me to be careful. I had forgotten that on the moon, with only an eighth part of the earth's mass and a quarter of its diameter, my weight was barely a sixth what it was on earth. But now that fact insisted on being remembered.

"We are out of Mother Earth's leading-strings now," he said.

With a guarded effort I raised myself to the top and, moving as cautiously as a rheumatic patient, stood up beside him under the blaze of the sun. The sphere lay behind us on its dwindling snow-drift thirty feet away.

As far as the eye could see over the enormous disorder of rocks that formed the crater floor the same bristling scrub that surrounded us was starting into life, diversified here and there by bulging masses of a cactus form, and scarlet and purple lichens that grew so fast they seemed to crawl over the rocks. The whole area of the crater seemed to me then to be one similar wilderness up to the very foot of the surrounding cliff.

This cliff was apparently bare of vegetation save at its base, and with buttresses and terraces and platforms that did not very greatly attract our attention at the time. It was many miles away from us in every direction; we seemed to be almost at the centre of the crater, and we saw it through a certain haziness that drove before the wind. For there was even a wind now in the thin air — a swift yet weak wind that chilled exceedingly, but exerted little pressure. It was blowing round the crater, as it seemed, to the hot, illuminated side from the foggy darkness under the sunward wall. It was difficult to look into this eastward fog; we had to peer with half-closed eyes beneath the shade of our hands, because of the fierce intensity of the motionless sun.

"It seems to be deserted," said Cavor, "absolutely desolate."

I looked about me again. I retained even then a clinging hope of some quasi-human evidence, some pinnacle of building, some house or engine; but everywhere spread the tumbled rocks in peaks and crests, and the darting scrub and those bulging cacti that swelled and swelled, a flat negation as it seemed of all such hope.

"It looks as though these plants had it to themselves," I said. "I see no trace of any other creature."

"No insects — no birds — no! Not a trace, not a scrap or particle of animal life. If there was — what would they do in the night? . . . No; there's just these plants alone."

I shaded my eyes with my hand. "It's like the landscape of a dream. These things are less like earthly land plants than the things one imagines among the rocks at the bottom of the sea. Look at that, yonder! One might imagine it a lizard changed into a plant. And the glare!"

"This is only the fresh morning," said Cavor.

He sighed and looked about him. "This is no world for men," he said. "And yet in a way . . . it appeals."

He became silent for a time, then commenced his meditative humming. I started at a gentle touch, and found a thin sheet of livid lichen lapping over my shoe. I kicked at it; it fell to powder, and each speck began to grow. I heard Cavor exclaim sharply, and perceived that one of the fixed bayonets of the scrub had pricked him.

He hesitated, his eyes sought among the rocks about us. A sudden blaze of pink had crept up a ragged pillar of crag. It was a most extraordinary pink, a livid magenta.

"Look!" said I, turning, and behold Cavor had vanished.

For an instant I stood transfixed. Then I made a hasty step to look over the verge of the rock. But, in my surprise at his disappearance, I forgot once more that we were on the moon. The thrust of my foot that I made in striding would have carried me a yard on earth; on the moon it carried me six — a good five yards over the edge. For the moment the thing had something of the effect of one of those nightmares when one falls and falls. For while one falls sixteen feet in the first second of a fall on earth, on the moon one falls two, and with only a sixth of one's weight. I fell, or rather I jumped down, about ten yards I supposed. It seemed to take a long time — five or six seconds, I should think. I floated through the air and fell like a feather, knee-deep in a snow-drift in the bottom of a gully of blue-grey, white-veined rock.

I looked about me. "Cavor!" I cried, but no Cavor was visible.

"Cavor!" I cried louder, and the rocks echoed me.

I turned fiercely to the rocks and clambered to the summit of them. "Cavor," I cried. My voice sounded like the voice of a lost lamb.

The sphere too was not in sight, and for a moment a horrible feeling of desolation pinched my heart.

Then I saw him. He was laughing and gesticulating to attract my attention. He was on a bare patch of rock twenty or thirty yards away. I could not hear his voice, but "Jump!" said his gestures. I hesitated, the distance seemed enormous. Yet I reflected that surely I must be able to clear a greater distance than Cavor.

I made a step back, gathered myself together, and leaped with all my might. I seemed to shoot up in the air as if I should never come down.

It was horrible and delightful, and as wild as a nightmare to go flying off in this fashion. I realised my leap had been altogether too violent. I flew clean over Cavor's head, and beheld a spiky confusion in a gully spreading to meet my fall. I gave a yelp of alarm. I put out my hands and straightened my legs.

I hit a huge fungoid bulk that burst all about me, scattering a mass of orange spores in every direction, and covering me with orange powder. I rolled over

spluttering, and came to rest convulsed with breathless laughter.

I became aware of Cavor's little round face peering over a bristling hedge. He shouted some faded inquiry. "Eh?" I tried to shout, but could not do so for want of breath. He made his way towards me, coming gingerly among the bushes. "We've got to be careful!" he said. "This moon has no discipline. She'll let us smash ourselves."

He helped me to my feet. "You exerted yourself too much," he said, dabbing at the yellow stuff with his hand to remove it from my garments.

I stood passive and panting, allowing him to beat off the jelly from my knees and elbows and lecture me upon my misfortunes. "We don't quite allow for the gravitation. Our muscles are scarcely educated yet. We must practice a little. When you have got your breath."

I pulled two or three little thorns out of my hand, and sat for a time on a boulder of rock. My muscles were quivering, and I had that feeling of personal disillusionment that comes to the learner of cycling on earth at his first fall.

It suddenly occurred to Cavor that the cold air in the gully after the brightness of the sun might give me a fever. So we clambered back into the sunlight. We found that beyond a few abrasions I had received no serious injuries from my tumble, and at Cavor's suggestion we were presently looking round for some safe and easy landing-place for my next leap. We chose a rocky slab some ten yards off, separated from us by a little thicket of olive-green spikes.

"Imagine it there!" said Cavor, who was assuming airs of a trainer, and he pointed to a spot about four feet from my toes. This leap I managed without difficulty, and I must confess I found a certain satisfaction in Cavor's falling short by a foot or so and tasting the spikes of the scrub. "One has to be careful, you see," he said, pulling out his thorns, and with that he ceased to be my mentor and became my fellow-learner in the art of lunar locomotion.

We chose a still easier jump and did it without difficulty, and then leaped back again and to and fro several times, accustoming our muscles to the new standard. I could never have believed, had I not experienced it, how rapid that adaptation would be. In a very little time indeed, certainly after fewer than thirty leaps, we could judge the effort necessary for a distance with almost terrestrial assurance.

And all this time the lunar plants were growing around us, higher and denser and more entangled, every moment thicker and taller, spiked plants, green cactus masses, fungi, fleshy and lichenous things, strange radiate and sinuous shapes. But we were so intent upon our leaping that for a time we gave no heed to their unfaltering expansion.

An extraordinary elation had taken possession of us. Partly I think it was our sense of release from the confinement of the sphere. Mainly, however, the thin

sweetness of the air, which I am certain contained a much larger proportion of oxygen than our terrestrial atmosphere. In spite of the strange quality of all about us, I felt as adventurous and experimental as a Cockney placed for the first time among mountains; and I do not think it occurred to either of us, face to face though we were with the Unknown, to be very greatly afraid.

We were bitten by a spirit of enterprise. We selected a lichenous kopje, perhaps fifteen yards away, and landed neatly on its summit one after the other. "Good!" we cried to each other, "good"; and Cavor made three steps and went off to a tempting slope of snow a good twenty yards and more beyond. I stood for a moment struck by the grotesque effect of his soaring figure, his dirty cricket cap and spiky hair, his little round body, his arms and his knickerbockered legs tucked up tightly against the weird spaciousness of the lunar scene. A gust of laughter seized me, and then I stepped off to follow. Plump! I dropped beside him.

We made a few Gargantuan strides, leaped three or four times more, and sat down at last in a lichenous hollow. Our lungs were painful. We sat holding our sides and recovering our breath, looking appreciation at each other. Cavor panted something about "amazing sensations." And then came a thought into my head. For the moment it did not seem a particularly appalling thought, simply a natural question arising out of the situation.

"By the way," I said, "Where exactly is the sphere?"

Cavor looked at me. "Eh?"

The full meaning of what we were saying struck me sharply.

"Cavor!" I cried, laying a hand on his arm. "Where is the sphere?"

CHAPTER 9

LOST MEN IN THE MOON

His face caught something of my dismay. He stood up and stared about him at the scrub that fenced us in and rose about us, straining upwards in a passion of growth. He put a dubious hand to his lips. He spoke with a sudden lack of assurance. "I think," he said, slowly, "we left it . . . somewhere . . . about *there*."

He pointed a hesitating finger that wavered in an arc.

"I'm not sure." His look of consternation deepened. "Anyhow," he said, with his eyes on me, "it can't be far."

We had both stood up. We made unmeaning ejaculations.

All about us on the sunlit slopes frothed and swayed the

darting shrubs, the swelling cactus, the creeping lichens, and wherever the shade remained the snow-drifts lingered. North, south, east and west spread an identical monotony of unfamiliar forms. And somewhere, buried already among this tangled confusion, was our sphere, our home, our only provision, our only hope of escape from this fantastic wilderness of ephemeral growths into which we had come.

"I think, after all," he said, pointing suddenly, "it might be over there."

"No," I said. "We have turned in a curve. See! here is the mark of my heels. It's clear the thing must be more to the eastward, much more. No! the sphere must be over there."

"I *think*," said Cavor, "I kept the sun upon my right all the time."

"Every leap, it seems to me," I said, "my shadow flew before me."

We stared into each other's eyes. The area of the crater had become enormously vast to our imaginations, the growing thickets already impenetrably dense.

"Good heavens! What fools we have been!"

"It's evident that we must find it again," said Cavor, "and that soon. The sun grows stronger. We should be fainting with the heat already if it wasn't so dry. And . . . I'm hungry."

I stared at him. I had not suspected this aspect of the matter before. But it came to me at once —a positive craving. "Yes," I said with emphasis, "I am hungry, too."

He stood up with a look of active resolution. "Certainly we must find the sphere."

As calmly as possible we surveyed the interminable reefs and thickets that formed the floor of the crater, each of us weighing in silence the chances of our finding the sphere before we were overtaken by heat and hunger.

"It can't be fifty yards from here," said Cavor, with indecisive gestures. "The only thing is to beat round about until we come upon it."

"That is all we can do," I said, without any alacrity to begin our hunt. "I wish this confounded spike bush did not grow so fast!"

"That's just it," said Cavor. "But it was lying on a bank of snow."

I stared about me in the vain hope of recognising some knoll or shrub that had been near the sphere. But everywhere was a confusing sameness, everywhere the aspiring bushes, the distending fungi, the dwindling snowbanks, steadily and inevitably changed. The sun scorched and stung; the faintness of an unaccountable hunger mingled with our infinite perplexity. And even as we stood there, confused and lost amidst unprecedented things, we became aware for the first time of a sound upon the moon other than the stir of the growing plants, the faint sighing of the wind, or those that we ourselves had made.

Boom . . . Boom . . . Boom . . .
It came from beneath our feet,

a sound in the ground. We seemed to hear it with our feet as much as with our ears. Its dull resonance was muffled by distance, thick with the quality of intervening substance. No sound that I can imagine could have astonished us more, nor have changed more completely the quality of things about us. For this sound, rich, slow, and deliberate, seemed to us like the striking of some gigantic buried clock.

Boom . . . Boom . . . Boom . . .

Sound suggestive of still cloisters, of sleepless nights in crowded cities, of vigils and the awaited hour, of all that is orderly and methodical in life, booming out pregnant and mysterious in this fantastic desert! To the eye everything was unchanged; the desolation of bushes and cacti waving silently in the wind, stretched unbroken to the distant cliffs; the still, dark sky was empty overhead, and the hot sun hung and burned. And through it all, a warning, a threat, throbbed this enigma of sound.

Boom . . . Boom . . . Boom . . .

We questioned each other in faint and faded voices. " A clock? "

"Like a clock! "

"What is it? "

"What can it be? "

"Count," was Cavor's belated suggestion, and at that word the striking ceased.

The silence, the rhythmic disappointment of the silence, came as a fresh shock. For a moment one could doubt whether one had ever heard a sound. Or whether it might not still be going on! Had I indeed heard a sound?

I felt the pressure of Cavor's hand upon my arm. He spoke in an undertone as if he feared to wake some sleeping thing. " Let us keep together," he whispered, " and look for the sphere. We must get back to the sphere. This is beyond understanding."

" Which way shall we go? "

He hesitated. An intense persuasion of presences, of unseen things about us and near us, dominated our minds. What could they be? Where could they be? Was this arid desolation, alternately frozen and scorched, only the outer rind and mask of some subterranean world? And if so, what sort of world? What sort of inhabitants might it not presently disgorge upon us?

And then stabbing the aching stillness, as vivid and sudden as an unexpected thunder-clap, came a clang and rattle as though great gates of metal had suddenly been flung apart.

It arrested our steps. We stood gaping helplessly. Then Cavor stole towards me.

"I do not understand! " he whispered, close to my face. He waved his hand vaguely skywards, the vague suggestions of still vaguer thoughts.

" A hiding-place! If anything came — "

I looked about us. I nodded my head in assent to him.

We started off, moving stealthily, with the most exaggerated precautions against noise. We went towards a thicket of scrub. A clangour as of hammers flung

about a boiler hastened our steps. "We must crawl," whispered Cavor.

The lower leaves of the bayonet plants, already overshadowed by the newer ones above, were beginning to wilt and shrivel so that we could thrust our way among the thickening stems without any serious injury. A stab in the face or arm we did not heed. At the heart of the thicket I stopped and stared panting into Cavor's face.

"Subterranean," he whispered. "Below."

"They may come out."

"We must find the sphere!"

"Yes," I said, "but how?"

"Crawl till we come to it."

"But if we don't?"

"Keep hidden. See what they are like."

"We will keep together," said I.

He thought. "Which way shall we go?"

"We must take our chance."

We peered this way and that. Then very circumspectly we began to crawl through the lower jungle, making so far as we could judge a circuit, halting now at every waving fungus, at every sound, intent only on the sphere from which we had so foolishly emerged. Ever and again from out of the ground beneath us came concussions, beatings, strange, inexplicable, mechanical sounds, and once and then again we thought we heard something, a faint rattle and tumult, borne to us through the air. But fearful as we were we dared attempt no vantage-point to survey the crater. For long we saw nothing of the beings whose sounds were so abundant and insistent. But for the faintness of our hunger and the drying of our throats that crawling would have had the quality of a very vivid dream. It was so absolutely unreal. The only element with any touch of reality was these sounds.

Picture it to yourself. About us the dreamlike jungle, with the silent bayonet leaves darting overhead, and the silent, vivid, sunsplashed lichens under our hands and knees, waving with the vigour of their growth as a carpet waves when the wind gets beneath it. Ever and again one of the bladder fungi, bulging and distending under the sun, loomed upon us. Ever and again in vivid colour some novel shape obtruded. The very cells that built up these plants were as large as my thumb, like beads of coloured glass. And all these things were saturated in the unmitigated glare of the sun, were seen against a sky that was bluishblack and spangled still, in spite of the sunlight, with a few surviving stars. Strange! the very forms and texture of the stones were strange. It was all strange: the feeling of one's body was unprecedented, every other movement ended in a surprise. The breath sucked thin in one's throat, the blood flowed through one's ears in a throbbing tide, thud, thud, thud . . .

And ever and again came gusts of turmoil, hammering, the clanging and throb of machinery, and presently — the bellowing of great beasts!

CHAPTER 10

THE MOONCALF
PASTURES

So we two poor terrestrial casta-
ways, lost in that wild-growing
moon jungle, crawled in terror
before the sounds that had come
upon us. We crawled as it seemed
a long time before we saw either
Selenite or mooncalf, though we
heard the bellowing and gruntu-
lous noises of these latter con-
tinually drawing nearer to us. We
crawled through stony ravines,
over snow slopes, amidst fungi
that ripped like thin bladders at
our thrust, emitting a watery hu-
mour over a perfect pavement of
things like puff-balls and beneath
interminable thickets of scrub.
And ever more hopelessly our
eyes sought for our abandoned
sphere. The noise of the moon-
calves would at times be a vast,
flat, calf-like sound, at times it
rose to an amazed and wrathy
bellowing, and again it would
become a clogged, bestial sound
as though these unseen creatures
had sought to eat and bellow at
the same time.

Our first view was but an in-
adequate, transitory glimpse, yet
none the less disturbing because

it was incomplete. Cavor was
crawling in front at the time, and
he first was aware of their prox-
imity. He stopped, arresting me
with a single gesture.

A crackling and smashing of
the scrub appeared to be advanc-
ing directly upon us, and then, as
we squatted close and endeav-
oured to judge of the nearness
and direction of this noise, there
came a terrific bellow behind us,
so close and vehement that the
tops of the bayonet scrub bent
before it, and one felt the breath
of it hot and moist. Turning
about we saw indistinctly through
a crowd of swaying stems the
mooncalf's shining sides and the
long line of its back looming
against the sky.

Of course it is hard for me now
to say how much I saw at that
time, because my impressions
were corrected by subsequent ob-
servation. First of all was its enor-
mous size: the girth of its body
was some fourscore feet, its length
perhaps two hundred. Its sides
rose and fell with its laboured
breathing. I perceived that its
gigantic flabby body lay along
the ground and that its skin was
of corrugated white, dappling
into blackness along the back-
bone. But of its feet we saw noth-
ing. I think also that we saw then
the profile at least of the almost
brainless head, with its fat-en-
cumbered neck, its slobbering,
omnivorous mouth, its little nos-
trils, and tight shut eyes. (For the
mooncalf invariably shuts its eyes
in the presence of the sun.) We
had a glimpse of a vast red pit
as it opened its mouth to bleat
and bellow again, we had a

breath from the pit, and then the monster heeled over like a ship, dragged forward along the ground, creasing all his leathery skin, rolled again, and so wallowed past us, smashing a path amidst the scrub, and was speedily hidden from our eyes by the dense interlacing beyond. Another appeared more distantly, and then another, and then, as though he was driving these animated lumps of provender to their pasture, a Selenite came momentarily into view. My grip upon Cavor's foot became convulsive at the sight of him, and we remained motionless and peering long after he had passed out of our range.

By contrast with the mooncalves he seemed a trivial being, a mere ant, scarcely five feet high. He was wearing garments of some leathery substance so that no portion of his actual body appeared —but of this of course we were entirely ignorant. He presented himself, therefore, as a compact bristling creature, having much of the quality of a complicated insect, with whip-like tentacles, and a clanging arm projecting from his shining cylindrical body-case. The form of his head was hidden by his enormous, many-spiked helmet—we discovered afterwards that he used the spikes for prodding refractory mooncalves—and a pair of goggles of darkened glass set very much at the side gave a bud-like quality to the metallic apparatus that covered his face. His arms did not project beyond his body-case, and he carried himself upon short legs that, wrapped though

they were in warm coverings, seemed to our terrestrial eyes inordinately flimsy. They had very short thighs, very long shanks, and little feet.

In spite of his heavy-looking clothing he was progressing with what would be from the terrestrial point of view very considerable strides, and his clanging arm was busy. The quality of his motion during the instant of his passing suggested haste and a certain anger, and soon after we had lost sight of him we heard the bellow of a mooncalf change abruptly into a short, sharp squeal, followed by the scuffle of its acceleration. And gradually that bellowing receded, and then came to an end, as if the pastures sought had been reached.

We listened. For a space the moon world was still. But it was some time before we resumed our crawling search for the vanished sphere.

When next we saw mooncalves they were some little distance away from us, in a place of tumbled rocks. The sloping surfaces of the rocks were thick with a speckled green plant, growing in dense, mossy clumps, upon which these creatures were browsing. At the sight of them we stopped on the margin of the reeds amidst which we were crawling, peering through at them and looking round for a second glimpse of a Selenite. They lay against their food like stupendous slugs, huge, greasy hulls, eating greedily and noisily, with a sort of sobbing avidity. They seemed monsters of mere fatness, clumsy and overwhelmed to a degree that would

make a Smithfield ox seem a model of agility. Their busy, writhing, chewing mouths, their closed eyes, together with the appetising sound of their munching, made up an effect of animal enjoyment that was singularly stimulating to our empty frames.

"Hogs!" said Cavor, with unusual passion. "Disgusting hogs!" and after one glare of angry envy crawled off through the bushes to our right. I stayed long enough to see that the speckled plant was quite hopeless for human nourishment, then crawled after him, nibbling a quill of it between my teeth.

Presently we were arrested again by the proximity of a Selenite, and this time we were able to observe him more exactly. Now we could see that the Selenite covering was indeed clothing, and not a sort of crustacean integument. He was similar in costume to the former one we had glimpsed, except that ends of something like wadding were protruding from his neck, and he stood on a promontory of rock and moved his head this way and that as though he was surveying the crater. We lay quite still, fearing to attract his attention if we moved, and after a time he turned about and disappeared.

We came upon another drove of mooncalves bellowing up a ravine, and then we passed over a place of sounds, sounds of beating machinery, as if some huge hall of industry came near the surface there. And while these sounds were still about us we came to the edge of a great open space, perhaps two hundred yards

in diameter, and perfectly level. Save for a few lichens that advanced from its margin, this space was bare, and presented a powdery surface of a dusty yellow colour. We were afraid to strike out across this space, but as it presented less obstruction to our crawling than the scrub, we went down upon it and began very circumspectly to skirt its edge.

For a little while the noises below ceased, and everything, save for the faint stir of the growing vegetation, was very still. Then abruptly there began an uproar, louder, more vehement, and nearer than any we had so far heard. Of a certainty it came from below. Instinctively we crouched as flat as we could, ready for a prompt plunge into the thicket beside us. Each knock and throb seemed to vibrate through our bodies. Louder grew this throbbing and beating, and that irregular vibration increased until the whole moon world seemed to be jerking and pulsing.

"Cover," whispered Cavor, and I turned towards the bushes.

At that instant came a thud like the thud of a gun, and then a thing happened—it still haunts me in my dreams. I had turned my head to look at Cavor's face, and thrust out my hand in front of me as I did so. My hand met nothing! I plunged suddenly into a bottomless hole!

My chest hit something hard, and I found myself with my chin on the edge of an unfathomable abyss that had suddenly opened beneath me, my hand extended stiffly into the void. The whole of

that flat circular area was no more than a gigantic lid, that was now sliding sideways from off the pit it had covered into a slot prepared for it.

Had it not been for Cavor I think I should have remained rigid, hanging over this margin and staring into the enormous gulf below until at last the edges of the slot scraped me off and hurled me into its depths. But Cavor had not received the shock that had paralysed me. He had been a little distance from the edge when the lid had first opened, and, perceiving the peril that held me helpless, gripped my legs and pulled me backward. I came into a sitting position, crawled away from the edge for a space on all fours, then staggered up and ran after him across the thundering, quivering sheet of metal. It seemed to be swinging open with a steadily-accelerated velocity, and the bushes in front of me shifted sideways as I ran.

I was none too soon. Cavor's back vanished amidst the bristling thicket, and as I scrambled up after him the monstrous valve came into its position with a clang. For a long time we lay panting, not daring to approach the pit.

But at last, very cautiously, and bit by bit, we crept into a position from which we could peer down. The bushes about us creaked and waved with the force of a breeze that was blowing down the shaft. We could see nothing at first except smooth, vertical walls descending at last into an impenetrable black. And then gradually we became aware of a number of very faint and little lights going to and fro.

For a time that stupendous gulf of mystery held us so that we forgot even our sphere. In time as we grew more accustomed to the darkness we could make out very small dim illusive shapes moving about among those needle-point illuminations. We peered, amazed and incredulous, understanding so little that we could find no words to speak. We could distinguish nothing that would give us a clue to the meaning of the faint shapes we saw.

"What can it be?" I asked; "what can it be?"

"The engineering! . . . They must live in these caverns during the night and come out during the day."

"Cavor!" I said. "Can they be—*that*—it was something like—men?"

"*That* was not a man."

"No."

"We dare risk nothing!"

"We dare do nothing until we find the sphere," he assented with a groan, and stirred himself to move. He stared about him for a space, sighed, and indicated a direction. We struck out through the jungle. For a time we crawled resolutely, then with diminishing vigour. Presently among great shapes of flabby purple there came a noise of trampling and of cries about us. We lay close, and for a long time the sounds went to and fro and very near. But this time we saw nothing. I tried to whisper to Cavor that I could

hardly go without food much longer, but my mouth had become too dry for whispering.

"Cavor," I said, "I must have food."

He turned a face full of dismay towards me. "It's a case for holding out," he said.

"But I *must*," I said; "and look at my lips!"

"I've been thirsty some time."

"If only some of the snow had remained!"

"It's clean gone! We're driving from Arctic to tropical at the rate of a degree a minute. . . ."

I gnawed my hand.

"The sphere!" he said. "There is nothing for it but the sphere." We roused ourselves to another spurt of crawling. My mind ran entirely on edible things, on the hissing profundity of summer drinks; more particularly I craved for beer. I was haunted by the memory of the eighteen-gallon cask that had swaggered in my Lympne cellar. I thought of the adjacent larder, and especially of steak and kidney pie — tender steak and plenty of kidney, and rich, thick gravy between. Ever and again I was seized with fits of hungry yawning. We came to flat places overgrown with fleshy red things, monstrous coralline growths; as we pushed against them they snapped and broke. I noted the quality of the broken surfaces. The confounded stuff certainly looked of a biteable texture.

I picked up a fragment and sniffed at it.

"Cavor," I said, in a hoarse undertone.

He glanced at me with his

face screwed up. "Don't," he said. I put down the fragment, and we crawled on through this tempting fleshiness for a space.

"Cavor," I asked, "why not?"

"Poison," I heard him say, but he did not look round.

We crawled some way before I decided.

"I'll chance it," said I.

He made a belated gesture to prevent me. I stuffed my mouth full. He crouched, watching my face, his own twisted into the oddest expression. "It's good," I said.

"Oh, Lord!" he cried.

He watched me munch, his face wrinkled between desire and disapproval, then suddenly succumbed to appetite, and began to tear off huge mouthfuls. For a time we did nothing but eat.

The stuff was not unlike a terrestrial mushroom, only it was much laxer in texture, and as one swallowed it, it warmed the throat. At first we experienced a mere mechanical satisfaction in eating. Then our blood began to run warmer, and we tingled at the lips and fingers, and then new and slightly irrelevant ideas came bubbling up in our minds.

"It's good," said I. "Infernally good! What a home for our surplus population! Our poor surplus population," and I broke off another large portion.

It filled me with a curiously benevolent satisfaction that there was such good food on the moon. The depression of my hunger gave way to an irrational exhilaration. The dread and discomfort in which I had been living vanished entirely. I perceived the

moon no longer as a planet from which I most earnestly desired the means of escape, but as a possible refuge for human destitution. I think I forgot the Selenites, the mooncalves, the lid, and the noises completely as soon as I had eaten that fungus.

Cavor replied to my third repetition of my "surplus population" remark with similar words of approval. I felt that my head swam, but I put this down to the stimulating effect of food after a long fast. "Ess'lent discov'ry, yours, Cavor," said I. "S'end on'y to the 'tato."

"Whajer mean?" asked Cavor. "'Scovery of the moon — se'nd on'y to the 'tato?"

I looked at him, shocked at his suddenly hoarse voice and by the badness of his articulation. It occurred to me in a flash that he was intoxicated, possibly by the fungus. It also occurred to me that he erred in imagining that he had discovered the moon — he had not discovered it, he had only reached it. I tried to lay my hand on his arm and explain this to him, but the issue was too subtle for his brain. It was also unexpectedly difficult to express. After a momentary attempt to understand me — I remember wondering if the fungus had made my eyes as fishy as his — he set off upon some observations on his own account.

"We are," he announced, with a solemn hiccup, "the creashurs o' what we eat and drink."

He repeated this, and as I was now in one of my subtle moods I determined to dispute it. Possibly I wandered a little from

the point. But Cavor certainly did not attend at all properly. He stood up as well as he could, putting a hand on my head to steady himself, which was disrespectful, and stood staring about him, quite devoid now of any fear of the moon beings.

I tried to point out that this was dangerous, for some reason that was not perfectly clear to me; but the word "dangerous" had somehow got mixed with "indiscreet," and come out rather more like "injurious" than either, and after an attempt to disentangle them I resumed my argument, addressing myself principally to the unfamiliar but attentive coralline growths on either side. I felt that it was necessary to clear up this confusion between the moon and a potato at once — I wandered into a long parenthesis on the importance of precision of definition in argument. I did my best to ignore the fact that my bodily sensations were no longer agreeable.

In some way that I have now forgotten my mind was led back to projects of colonisation. "We must annex this moon," I said. "There must be no shilly-shally. This is part of the White Man's Burden. Cavor — we are — *hic* — Satap — mean Satraps! Nempire Cæsar never dreamt. B'in all the newspapers. Cavorecia. Bedfordecia. Bedfordecia. Hic — Limited. Mean — unlimited! Practically."

Certainly I was intoxicated. I embarked upon an argument to show the infinite benefits our arrival would confer upon the moon. I involved myself in a rather difficult proof that the ar-

rival of Columbus was, after all, beneficial to America. I found I had forgotten the line of argument I had intended to pursue, and continued to repeat "sim'lar to C'lumbus" to fill up time.

From that point my memory of the action of that abominable fungus becomes confused. I remember vaguely that we declared our intention of standing no nonsense from any confounded insects, that we decided it ill became men to hide shamefully upon a mere satellite, that we equipped ourselves with huge armfuls of the fungi — whether for missile purposes or not I do not know — and, heedless of the stabs of the bayonet shrub, we started forth into the sunshine.

Almost immediately we must have come upon the Selenites. There were six of them, and they were marching in single file over a rocky place, making the most remarkable piping and whining sounds. They all seemed to become aware of us at once, all instantly became silent and motionless like animals, with their faces turned towards us.

For a moment I was sobered.

"Insects," murmured Cavor, "insects! — and they think I'm going to crawl about on my stomach — on my vertebrated stomach!

"Stomach," he repeated, slowly, as though he chewed the indignity.

Then suddenly, with a sort of fury, he made three vast strides and leaped towards them. He leaped badly; he made a series of somersaults in the air, whirled right over them, and vanished with an enormous splash amidst the cactus bladders. What the Selenites made of this amazing, and to my mind undignified, irruption from another planet, I have no means of guessing. I seem to remember the sight of their backs as they ran in all directions — but I am not sure. All these last incidents before oblivion came are vague and faint in my mind. I know I made a step to follow Cavor, and tripped and fell headlong among the rocks. I was, I am certain, suddenly and vehemently ill. I seem to remember a violent struggle, and being gripped by metallic clasps. . . .

My next clear recollection is that we were prisoners at we knew not what depth beneath the moon's surface; we were in darkness and amidst strange, distracting noises; our bodies covered with scratches and bruises, and our heads racked with pain.

CHAPTER 11

THE SELENITE'S FACE

I FOUND myself sitting crouched together in a tumultuous darkness. For a long time I could not understand where I was nor how I had come to this perplexity. I

thought of the cupboard into which I had been thrust at times when I was a child, and then of a very dark and noisy bedroom in which I had slept during an illness. But these sounds about me were not noises I had known, and there was a thin flavour in the air like the wind of a stable. Then I supposed we must still be at work on the sphere, and that somehow I had got into the cellar of Cavor's house. I remembered we had finished the sphere, and fancied I must still be in it and travelling through space.

"Cavor," I said, "cannot we have some light?"

There came no answer.

"Cavor!" I insisted.

I was answered by a groan. "My head!" I heard him say, "my head!"

I attempted to press my hands to my brow, which ached, and discovered they were tied together. This startled me very much. I brought them up to my mouth and felt the cold smoothness of metal. They were chained together. I tried to separate my legs and made out they were similarly fastened, and also I was fastened to the ground by a much thicker chain about the middle of my body.

I was more frightened than I had yet been by anything in all our strange experiences. For a time I tugged silently at my bonds. "Cavor!" I cried out, sharply, "why am I tied? Why have you tied me hand and foot?"

"I haven't tied you," he answered. "It's the Selenites."

The Selenites! My mind hung on that for a space. Then my memories came back to me; the snowy desolation, the thawing of the air, the growth of the plants, our strange hopping and crawling among the rocks and vegetation of the crater. All the distress of our frantic search for the sphere returned to me. . . . Finally the opening of the great lid that covered the pit!

Then as I strained to trace our later movements down to our present plight the pain in my head became intolerable. I came to an insurmountable barrier, an obstinate blank.

"Cavor!"

"Yes."

"Where are we?"

"How should I know?"

"Are we dead?"

"What nonsense!"

"They've got us, then!"

He made no answer but a grunt. The lingering traces of the poison seemed to make him oddly irritable.

"What do you mean to do?"

"How should I know what to do?"

"Oh, very well," said I, and became silent. Presently, I was roused from a stupor. "Oh, Lord!" I cried, "I wish you'd stop that buzzing."

We lapsed into silence again, listening to the dull confusion of noises, like the muffled sounds of a street or factory, that filled our ears. I could make nothing of it; my mind pursued first one rhythm and then another, and questioned it in vain. But after a long time I became aware of a new and sharper element, not mingling with the rest, but stand-

ing out, as it were, against that cloudy background of sound. It was a series of little definite sounds, tappings and rubbings like a loose spray of ivy against a window or a bird moving about upon a box. We listened and peered about us, but the darkness was a velvet pall. There followed a noise like the subtle movement of the wards of a well-oiled lock. And then there appeared before me, hanging as it seemed in an immensity of black, a thin bright line.

"Look!" whispered Cavor, very softly.

"What is it?"

"I don't know."

We stared.

The thin bright line became a band, broader and paler. It took upon itself the quality of a bluish light falling upon a whitewashed wall. It ceased to be parallel sided; it developed a deep indentation on one side. I turned to remark this to Cavor, and was amazed to see his ear in a brilliant illumination — all the rest of him in shadow. I twisted my head round as well as my bonds would permit. "Cavor!" I said, "it's behind!"

His ear vanished — gave place to an eye!

Suddenly the crack that had been admitting the light broadened out and revealed itself as the space of an opening door. Beyond was a sapphire vista, and in the doorway stood a grotesque outline silhouetted against the glare.

We both made convulsive efforts to turn, and, failing, sat staring over our shoulders at

this. My first impression was of some clumsy quadruped with lowered head. Then I perceived it was the slender, pinched body and short and extremely attenuated bandy legs of a Selenite, with his head depressed between his shoulders. He was without the helmet and body-covering they wear upon the exterior.

He was a blank black figure to us, but instinctively our imaginations supplied features to his very human outline. I at least took it instantly that he was somewhat hunchbacked, with a high forehead and long features.

He came forward three steps and paused for a time. His movements seemed absolutely noiseless. Then he came forward again. He walked like a bird — his feet fell one in front of the other. He stepped out of the ray of light that came through the doorway and it seemed that he vanished altogether in the shadow.

For a moment my eyes sought him in the wrong place, and then I perceived him standing facing us both in the full light. Only the human features I had attributed to him were not there at all!

Of course I ought to have expected that, only I did not. It came to me as an absolute, for a moment an overwhelming, shock. It seemed as though it wasn't a face; as though it must needs be a mask, a horror, a deformity that would presently be disavowed or explained. There was no nose, and the thing had bulging eyes at the side — in the silhouette I had supposed they were

ears . . . I have tried to draw one of these heads, but I cannot.

There was a mouth, downwardly curved, like a human mouth in a face that stared ferociously.

The neck on which the head was poised was jointed in three places, almost like the short joints in the leg of a crab. The joints of the limbs I could not see because of the puttee-like straps in which they were swathed, and which formed the only clothing this being wore.

At the time my mind was taken up by the mad impossibility of the creature. I suppose he also was amazed — and with more reason, perhaps, for amazement than we. Only, confound him, he did not show it. We did at least know what had brought about this meeting of incompatible creatures. But conceive how it would seem to decent Londoners, for example, to come upon a couple of living things, as big as men and absolutely unlike any other earthly animals, careering about among the sheep in Hyde Park!

It must have taken him like that.

Imagine us! We were bound hand and foot, fagged and filthy, our beards two inches long, our faces scratched and bloody. Cavor you must imagine in his knickerbockers (torn in several places by the bayonet scrub), his Jæger shirt and old cricket cap, his wiry hair wildly disordered, a tail to every quarter of the heavens. In that blue light his face did not look red, but very dark; his lips and the drying blood upon his hands seemed black. If possible I was in a worse plight than he, on account of the yellow fungus into which I had jumped. Our jackets were unbuttoned, and our shoes had been taken off and lay at our feet. We were sitting with our backs to the queer, bluish light peering at such a monster as Dürer might have invented.

Cavor broke the silence, started to speak, went hoarse, and cleared his throat. Outside began a terrific bellowing, as of a mooncalf in trouble. It ended in a shriek, and everything was still again.

Presently the Selenite turned about, flickered into the shadow, stood for a moment retrospective at the door, and then closed it on us, and once more we were in that murmurous mystery of darkness into which we had awakened.

CHAPTER 12

MR. CAVOR MAKES
SOME SUGGESTIONS

For a time neither of us spoke. To focus all the things we had brought upon ourselves seemed beyond my mental powers.

"They've got us," I said at last.

"It was that fungus."

"Well, if I hadn't taken it·we should have fainted and starved."

"We might have found the sphere."

I lost my temper at his persistence and swore to myself. For a time we hated each other in silence. I drummed with my finger on the floor between my knees and ground the links of my fetters together. Presently I was forced to talk again.

"What do you make of it, anyhow?" I asked humbly.

"They are reasonable creatures — they can make things and do things. Those lights we saw. . . ."

He stopped. It was clear he could make nothing of it.

When he spoke again it was to confess. "After all, they are more human than we had a right to expect. I suppose —"

He stopped irritatingly.

"Yes?"

"I suppose anyhow — on any planet, where there is an intelligent animal, it will carry its brain case upward, and have hands and walk erect. . . ."

Presently he broke away in another direction.

"We are some way in," he said. "I mean — perhaps a couple of thousand feet or more."

"Why?"

"It's cooler. And our voices are so much louder. That faded quality — it has altogether gone. And the feeling in one's ears and throat."

I had not noted that, but I did now.

The air is denser. We must be some depth — a mile even we may be — inside the moon."

"We never thought of a world inside the moon."

"No."

"How could we?"

"We might have done. Only — one gets into habits of mind."

He thought for a time.

"Now," he said, "it seems such an obvious thing. Of course! The moon must be enormously cavernous with an atmosphere within, and at the centre of its caverns a sea. One knew that the moon had a lower specific gravity than the earth; one knew that it had little air or water outside; one knew, too, that it was sister planet to the earth and that it was unaccountable that it should be different in composition. The inference that it was hollowed out was as clear as day. And yet one never saw it as a fact. Kepler, of course —"

His voice had the interest now of a man who has discovered a pretty sequence of reasoning.

"Yes," he said, "Kepler, with his *subvolvani*, was right after all."

"I wish you had taken the trouble to find that out before we came," I said.

He answered nothing, buzzing to himself softly as he pursued his thoughts. My temper was going. "What do you think has become of the sphere, anyhow?" I asked.

"Lost," he said, like a man who answers an uninteresting question.

"Among those plants?"

"Unless they find it."

"And then?"

"How can I tell?"

"Cavor," I said, with a sort of

hysterical bitterness, " things look bright for my Company."

He made no answer.

" Good Lord! " I exclaimed. " Just think of all the trouble we took to get into this pickle! What did we come for? What are we after? What was the moon to us, or we to the moon? We wanted too much, we tried too much. We ought to have started the little things first. It was you proposed the moon! Those Cavorite spring blinds! I am certain we could have worked them for terrestrial purposes. Certain! Did you really understand what I proposed? A steel cylinder — "

" Rubbish! " said Cavor.

We ceased to converse.

For a time Cavor kept up a broken monologue without much help to me.

" If they find it," he began; " if they find it . . . what will they do with it? Well, that's the question! It may be that's *the* question. They won't understand it, anyhow. If they understood that sort of thing they would have come long since to the earth. Would they? Why shouldn't they? But they would have sent something — They couldn't keep their hands off such a possibility. No! But they will examine it. Clearly they are intelligent and inquisitive. They will examine it — get inside it — trifle with the studs. Off! . . . That would mean the moon for us for all the rest of our lives. Strange creatures, strange knowledge. . . ."

" As for strange knowledge — ! " said I, and language failed me.

" Look here, Bedford," said Cavor. " You came on this ex-pedition of your own free will."

" You said to me — ' call it prospecting.' "

" There are always risks in prospecting."

" Especially when you do it un-armed and without thinking out every possibility."

" I was so taken up with the sphere. The thing rushed on us and carried us away."

" Rushed on *me,* you mean."

" Rushed on me just as much. How was I to know when I set to work on molecular physics that the business would bring me here — of all places? "

" It's this accursed Science," I cried. " It's the very Devil. The medieval priests and persecutors were right, and the moderns are all wrong. You tamper with it and it offers you gifts. And directly you take them it knocks you to pieces in some unexpected way. Old passions and new weap-ons — now it upsets your reli-gion, now it upsets your social ideas, now it whirls you off to desolation and misery! "

" Anyhow, it's no use your quarrelling with me now. These creatures — the Selenites — or whatever we choose to call them, have got us tied hand and foot. Whatever temper you choose to go through with it in, you will have to go through with it. . . . We have experiences before us that will need all our coolness."

He paused as if he required my assent. But I sat sulking. " Confound your science! " I said.

" The problem is communica-tion. Gestures, I fear, will be dif-ferent. Pointing, for example. No

creatures but men and monkeys point."

That was too obviously wrong for me. " Pretty nearly every animal," I cried, " points with its eyes or nose."

Cavor meditated over that. " Yes," he said at last, " and we don't. There are such differences! Such differences!

" One might. . . . But how can I tell? There is speech. The sounds they make, a sort of fluting and piping. I don't see how we are to imitate that. Is it their speech, that sort of thing? They may have different senses, different means of communication. Of course they are minds and we are minds — there must be something in common. Who knows how far we may not get to an understanding? "

" The things are outside us," I said. " They're more different from us than the strangest animals on earth. They are a different clay. What is the good of talking like this? "

Cavor thought. " I don't see that. Where there are minds, they will have something similar — even though they have been evolved on different planets. Of course, if it was a question of instinct — if we or they were no more than animals — "

" Well, are they? They're much more like ants on their hind legs than human beings, and who ever got to any sort of understanding with ants? "

" But these machines and clothing! No, I don't hold with you, Bedford. The difference is wide — "

" It's insurmountable."

" The resemblance must bridge it. I remember reading once a paper by the late Professor Galton on the possibility of communication between the planets. Unhappily at that time it did not seem probable that it would be of any material benefit to me, and I fear I did not give it the attention I should have done, in view of this state of affairs. Yet. . . . Now, let, me see!

" His idea was to begin with those broad truths that must underlie all conceivable mental existences and establish a basis on those. The great principles of geometry, to begin with. He proposed to take some leading proposition of Euclid's, and show by construction that its truth was known to us; to demonstrate, for example, that the angles at the base of an isosceles triangle are equal, and that if the equal sides be produced the angles on the other side of the base are equal also; or that the square on the hypotenuse of a right-triangle is equal to the sum of the squares on the two other sides. By demonstrating our knowledge of these things we should demonstrate our possession of a reasonable intelligence. . . . Now, suppose I . . . I might draw the geometrical figure with a wet finger or even trace it in the air. . . ."

He fell silent. I sat meditating his words. For a time his wild hope of communication, of interpretation with these weird beings, held me. Then that angry despair that was a part of my exhaustion and physical misery resumed its sway. I perceived with a sudden novel vividness the ex-

traordinary folly of everything I had ever done. "Ass!" I said, "oh, ass, unutterable ass . . . I seem to exist only to go about doing preposterous things. . . . Why did we ever leave the sphere? . . . Hopping about looking for patents and concessions in the craters of the moon! . . . If only we had had the sense to fasten a handkerchief to a stick to show where we had left the sphere!"

I subsided fuming.

"It is clear," meditated Cavor, "they are intelligent. One can hypothecate certain things. As they have not killed us at once they must have ideas of mercy. Mercy! At any rate of restraint. Possibly of intercourse. They may meet us. And this apartment and the glimpses we had of its guardian! These fetters! A high degree of intelligence. . . ."

"I wish to Heaven," cried I, "I'd thought even twice. Plunge after plunge. First one fluky start and then another. It was my confidence in you. Why didn't I stick to my play? That was what I was equal to. That was my world and the life I was made for. I could have finished that play. I'm certain . . . it was a good play. I had the scenario as good as done. Then. . . . Conceive it! Leaping to the moon! Practically — I've thrown my life away! That old woman in the inn near Canterbury had better sense."

I looked up, and stopped in mid-sentence. The darkness had given place to that bluish light again. The door was opening, and several noiseless Selenites were coming into the chamber. I became quite still staring at their grotesque faces.

Then suddenly my sense of disagreeable strangeness changed to interest. I perceived that the foremost and second carried bowls. One elemental need at least our minds could understand in common. They were bowls of some metal that, like our fetters, looked dark in that bluish light; and each contained a number of whitish fragments. All the cloudy pain and misery that oppressed me rushed together and took the shape of hunger. I eyed these bowls wolfishly. It seemed that at the end of the arms that lowered one towards me were not hands, but a sort of flap and thumb, like the end of an elephant's trunk.

The stuff in the bowl was loose in texture and whitish-brown in colour — rather like lumps of some cold soufflé, and it smelt faintly like mushrooms. From a partly-divided carcass of a mooncalf that we presently saw I am inclined to believe it must have been mooncalf flesh.

My hands were so tightly chained that I could barely contrive to reach the bowl, but when they saw the effort I made two of them dexterously released one of the turns about my wrist. Their tentacle hands were soft and cold to my skin. I immediately seized a mouthful of the food. It had the same laxness in texture that all organic structures seem to have upon the moon; it tasted rather like a *gauffre,* or a damp meringue, but in no way was it disagreeable. I took two other mouthfuls. "I wanted — food!" said I, tearing off a still larger piece. . . .

For a time we ate with an utter absence of self-consciousness. We ate and presently drank like tramps in a soup kitchen. Never before, nor since, have I been hungry to the ravenous pitch, and save that I have had this very experience I could never have believed that a quarter of a million of miles out of our proper world, in utter perplexity of soul, surrounded, watched, touched by beings more grotesque and inhuman than the worst creatures of a nightmare, it would be possible for me to eat in utter forgetfulness of all these things. They stood about us, watching us, and ever and again making a slight elusive twittering that stood them, I suppose, in the stead of speech. I did not even shiver at their touch. And when the first zeal of my feeding was over I could note that Cavor too had been eating with the same shameless abandon.

CHAPTER 13

EXPERIMENTS IN INTERCOURSE

WHEN at last we had made an end of eating, the Selenites linked our hands closely together again, and then untwisted the chains about our feet and rebound them, so as to give us a limited freedom of movement. Then they unfastened the chains about our waists. To do all this they had to handle us freely, and ever and again one of their queer heads came down close to my face, or a soft tentacle-hand touched my head or neck. I do not remember that I was afraid then or repelled by their proximity. I think that our incurable anthropomorphism made us imagine there were human heads inside their masks. The skin, like everything else, looked bluish, but that was on account of the light, and it was hard and shiny quite in the beetle-wing fashion, not soft or moist or hairy as a vertebrated animal's would be. Along the crest of the head was a low ridge of whitish spines running from back to front, and a much larger ridge curved on each side over the eyes. The Selenite who untied me used his mouth to help his hands.

"They seem to be releasing us," said Cavor. "Remember, we are on the moon! Make no sudden movements!"

"Are you going to try that geometry?"

"If I get a chance. But, of course, they may make an advance first."

We remained passive, and the Selenites, having finished their arrangements stood back from us, and seemed to be looking at us. I say seemed to be because as their eyes were at the sides and not in front one had the same difficulty in determining the direction in which they were look-

ing as one has in the case of a hen or a fish. They conversed with one another in their reedy tones, that seemed to me impossible to imitate or define. The door behind us opened wider, and glancing over my shoulder I saw a vague large space beyond in which a little crowd of Selenites were standing. They seemed a curiously miscellaneous rabble.

" Do they want us to imitate those sounds? " I asked Cavor.

" I don't think so," he said.

" It seems to me that they are trying to make us understand something."

" I can't make anything of their gestures. Do you notice this one, who is worrying with his head like a man with an uncomfortable collar? "

" Let us shake our heads at him."

We did that, and finding it ineffectual, attempted an imitation of the Selenite's movements. That seemed to interest them. At any rate, they all set up the same movement. But as that seemed to lead to nothing we desisted at last, and so did they, and fell into a piping argument among themselves. Then one of them, shorter and very much thicker than the other, and with a particularly wide mouth, squatted down suddenly beside Cavor, and put his hands and feet in the same posture as Cavor's were bound, and then by a dexterous movement stood up.

" Cavor," I shouted, " they want us to get up! "

He stared open-mouthed. " That's it! " he said.

And with much heaving and grunting, because our hands were tied together, we contrived to struggle to our feet. The Selenites made way for our elephantine heavings, and seemed to twitter more volubly. As soon as we were on our feet the thick-set Selenite came and patted each of our faces with his tentacles, and walked towards the open doorway. That also was plain enough and we followed him. We saw that four of the Selenites standing in the doorway were much taller than the others, and clothed in the same manner as those we had seen in the crater, namely, with spiked, round helmets and cylindrical body-cases, and that each of the four carried a goad, with spike and guard made of that same dull-looking metal as the bowls. These four closed about us, one on either side of each of us, as we emerged from our chamber into the cavern from which the light had come.

We did not get our impression of that cavern all at once. Our attention was taken up by the movements and attitudes of the Selenites immediately about us, and by the necessity of controlling our motion, lest we should startle and alarm them and ourselves by some excessive stride. In front of us was the short, thick-set being who had solved the problem of asking us to get up, moving with gestures that seemed, almost all of them, intelligible to us, inviting us to follow him. His spout-like face turned from one of us to the other with a quickness that was clearly interrogative. For a time,

I say, we were taken up with these things.

But at last the great place that formed a background to our movements asserted itself. It became apparent that the source of much at least of the tumult of sounds which had filled our ears ever since we had recovered from the stupefaction of the fungus was a vast mass of machinery in active movement, whose flying and whirling parts were visible indistinctly over the heads and between the bodies of the Selenites who walked about us. And not only did the web of sounds that filled the air proceed from this mechanism, but also the peculiar blue light that irradiated the whole place. We had taken it as a natural thing that a subterranean cavern should be artificially lit, and even now, though the fact was patent to my eyes, I did not really grasp its import until presently the darkness came. The meaning and structure of this huge apparatus I cannot explain, because we neither of us learnt what it was for or how it worked. One after another, big shafts of metal flung out and up from its centre, their heads travelling in what seemed to me to be a parabolic path; each dropped a sort of dangling arm as it rose towards the apex of its flight and plunged down into a vertical cylinder, forcing this down before it. About it moved the shapes of tenders, little figures that seemed vaguely different from the beings about us. As each of the three dangling arms of the machine plunged down there was

a clank and then a roaring, and out of the top of the vertical cylinder came pouring this incandescent substance, that lit the place and ran over as milk runs over a boiling pot and dripped luminously into a tank of light below. It was a cold blue light, a sort of phosphorescent glow, but infinitely brighter, and from the tanks into which it fell it ran in conduits athwart the cavern.

Thud, thud, thud, thud, came the sweeping arms of this unintelligible apparatus, and the light substance hissed and poured. At first the thing seemed only reasonably large and near to us; and then I saw how exceedingly little the Selenites upon it seemed, and I realised the full immensity of cavern and machine. I looked from this tremendous affair to the faces of the Selenites with a new respect. I stopped, and Cavor stopped, and stared at this thunderous engine.

"But this is stupendous!" I said. "What can it be for?"

Cavor's blue-lit face was full of an intelligent respect. "I can't dream! Surely these beings — Men could not make a thing like that! Look at those arms: are they on connecting rods?"

The thick-set Selenite had gone some paces unheeded. He came back and stood between us and the great machine. I avoided seeing him, because I guessed somehow that his idea was to beckon us onward. He walked away in the direction he wished us to go, and turned and came back, and

flicked our faces to attract our attention.

Cavor and I looked at each other.

" Cannot we show him we are interested in the machine? " I said.

"Yes," said Cavor. "We'll try that." He turned to our guide, and smiled, and pointed to the machine, and pointed again, and then to his head, and then to the machine. By some defect of reasoning he seemed to imagine that broken English might help these gestures. "Me look 'im," he said; "me think 'im very much. Yes."

His behaviour seemed to check the Selenites in their desire for our progress for a moment. They faced one another, their queer heads moved, the twittering voices came quick and liquid. Then one of them, a lean, tall creature, with a sort of mantle added to the puttee in which the others were dressed, twisted his elephant trunk of a hand about Cavor's waist, and pulled him gently to follow our guide, who again went on ahead.

Cavor resisted. "We may just as well begin explaining ourselves now! They may think we are new animals, a new sort of mooncalf, perhaps! It is most important that we should show an intelligent interest from the outset."

He began to shake his head violently. "No, no," he said; " me not come on one minute. Me look at 'im."

" Isn't there some geometrical point you might bring in apropos of that affair? " I suggested, as the Selenites conferred again.

" Possibly a parabolic — " he began.

He yelled loudly and leaped six feet or more!

One of the four armed moonmen had pricked him with a goad!

I turned on the goad-bearer behind me with a swift, threatening gesture and he started back. This and Cavor's sudden shout and leap clearly astonished all the Selenites. They receded hastily, facing us. For one of those movements that seem to last for ever we stood in angry protest, with a scattered semicircle of these inhuman beings about us.

" He pricked me! " said Cavor, with a catching of the voice.

" I saw him," I answered.

"Confound it! " I said to the Selenites; "we're not going to stand that! What on earth do you take us for? "

I glanced quickly right and left. Far away across the blue wilderness of cavern I saw a number of other Selenites running towards us; broad and slender they were and one with a larger head than the others. The cavern spread wide and low, and receded in every direction into darkness. Its roof, I remember, seemed to bulge down as if with the weight of the vast thickness of rocks that prisoned us. There was no way out of it — no way out of it. Above, below, in every direction, was the unknown, and these inhuman creatures with goads and gestures confronting us, and we two unsupported men!

CHAPTER 14

THE GIDDY BRIDGE

JUST for a moment that hostile pause endured. I suppose that both we and the Selenites did some very rapid thinking. My clearest impression was that there was nothing to put my back against and that we were bound to be surrounded and killed. The overwhelming folly of our presence there loomed over me in black, enormous reproach. Why had I ever launched myself on this mad, inhuman expedition?

Cavor came to my side and laid his hand on my arm. His pale and terrified face was ghastly in the blue light.

"We can't do anything," he said. "It's a mistake. They don't understand. We must go — as they want us to go."

I looked down at him, and then at the fresh Selenites who were coming to help their fellows. "If I had my hands free —"

"It's no use," he panted.

"No."

"We'll go."

And he turned about and led the way in the direction that had been indicated for us.

I followed, trying to look as subdued as possible, and feeling at the chains about my wrists. My blood was boiling. I noted nothing more of that cavern, though it seemed to take a long time before we had marched across it, or if I noted anything I forgot it as I saw it. My thoughts were concentrated, I think, upon my chains and the Selenites, and particularly upon the helmeted ones with the goads. At first they marched parallel with us, and at a respectable distance, but presently they were overtaken by three others, and then they drew nearer until they were within arms' length again. I winced like a spurred horse as they came near to us. The shorter, thicker Selenite marched at first on our right flank, but presently came in front of us again.

How well the picture of that grouping has bitten into my brain: the back of Cavor's downcast head just in front of me, and the dejected droop of his shoulders, and our guide's gaping visage, perpetually jerking about him, and the goad-bearers on each side, watchful yet open-mouthed — a blue monochrome. And after all, I do remember one other thing besides the purely personal affair, which is that a sort of gutter came presently across the floor of the cavern and then ran along by the side of the path of rock we followed. It was full of that same bright blue luminous stuff that flowed out of the great machine. I walked close beside it, and I can testify it radiated not a particle of heat. It was brightly shining,

and yet it was neither warmer nor colder than anything else in the cavern.

Clang, clang, clang, we passed under the thumping levers of another vast machine, and so came at last to a wide tunnel, in which we could even hear the pad, pad of our shoeless feet, and which, save for the trickling thread of blue to the right of us, was quite unlit. The shadows made gigantic travesties of our shapes and those of the Selenites on the irregular wall and roof of the tunnel. Ever and again crystals in the walls scintillated like gems, ever and again the passage expanded into a stalactitic cavern, or gave off branches that vanished into darkness.

We seemed to be marching down that tunnel for a long time. "Trickle, trickle," went the flowing light very softly, and our footfalls, and their echoes made an irregular paddle, paddle. My mind settled down to the question of my chains. If I were to slip off one turn, *so,* and then to twist it *so* . . .

If I tried to do it very gradually, would they see I was slipping my wrist out of the looser turn? If they did, what would they do?

"Bedford," said Cavor, "it goes down. It keeps on going down."

His remark roused me from my sullen preoccupation. "If they wanted to kill us," he said, dropping back to come level with me, "there is no reason why they should not have done it."

"No," I admitted; "that's true."

"They don't understand us," he said; "they think we are merely strange animals, some wild sort of mooncalf birth, perhaps. It will be only when they observe us better that they will begin to think we have minds —"

"When you trace those geometrical problems?" said I.

"It may be that."

We tramped on for a space.

"You see," said Cavor, "these may be Selenites of a lower class."

"The infernal fools," said I, viciously, glancing at their exasperating faces.

"If we endure what they do to us —"

"We've got to endure it," said I.

"There may be others less stupid. This is the mere outer fringe of their world. It must go down and down, cavern, passage, tunnel, down at last to the sea, hundreds of miles below."

His words made me think of the mile or so of rock and tunnel that might be over our heads already. It was like a weight dropping on my shoulders. "Away from the sun and air," I said. "Even a mine half a mile deep is stuffy."

"This is not — anyhow. It's probable — Ventilation! The air would blow from the dark side of the moon to the sunlit, and all the carbonic acid would well out there and feed those plants. Up this tunnel, for example — there is quite a breeze. And what a world it must be! The earnest we have in that shaft, and those machines —"

"And the goad," I said. "Don't forget the goad!"

He walked a little in front of me for a time.

"Even that goad —" he said.

"Well?"

"I was angry at the time. But — it was perhaps necessary we should get on. They have different skins and probably different nerves. They may not understand our objection — just as a being from Mars might not like our earthly habit of nudging."

"They'd better be careful how they nudge me."

"And about that geometry. After all, their way is a way of understanding too. They begin with the elements of life and not of thought. Food. Compulsion. Pain. They strike at fundamentals."

"There's no doubt about that," I said.

He went on to talk of the enormous and wonderful world into which we were being taken. I realised slowly from his tone that even now he was not absolutely in despair at the prospect of going ever deeper into this inhuman planet burrow. His mind ran on machines and invention to the exclusion of a thousand dark things that beset me. It wasn't that he intended to make any use of these things: he simply wanted to know them.

"After all," he said, "this is a tremendous occasion. It is the meeting of two worlds. What are we going to see? Think of what is below us here."

"We shan't see much if the light isn't better," I remarked.

"This is only the outer crust. Down below — On this scale — There will be everything. Do you notice how different they seem one from another? The story we shall take back!"

"Some rare sort of animal," I said, "might comfort himself in that way while they were bringing him to the Zoo. . . . It doesn't follow that we are going to be shown all these things."

"When they find we have reasonable minds," said Cavor, "they will want to learn about the earth. Even if they have no generous emotions they will teach in order to learn. . . . And the things they must know! The unanticipated things!"

He went on to speculate on the possibility of their knowing things he had never hoped to learn on earth, speculating in that way, with a raw wound from that goad already in his skin! Much that he said I forgot, for my attention was drawn to the fact that the tunnel along which we had been marching was opening out wider and wider. We seemed from the feeling of the air to be going out into a huge space. But how big the space might really be we could not tell, because it was unlit. Our little stream of light ran in a dwindling thread and vanished far ahead. Presently the rocky walls had disappeared altogether on either hand. There was nothing to be seen but the path in front of us and the trickling, hurrying rivulet of blue phosphorescence. The figures of Cavor and the guiding Selenite marched before me; the sides of their legs and heads that were towards the rivulet were clear and bright blue; their darkened sides, now that the reflection of the tunnel wall no longer lit them, merged indis-

tinguishably in the darkness beyond.

And soon I perceived that we were approaching a declivity of some sort, because the little blue stream dipped suddenly out of sight.

In another moment, as it seemed, we had reached the edge. The shining stream gave one meander of hesitation and then rushed over. It fell to a depth at which the sound of its descent was absolutely lost to us. Far below was a bluish glow, a sort of blue mist. And the darkness the stream dropped out of became utterly void and black, save that a thing like a plank projected from the edge of the cliff and stretched out and faded and vanished altogether. There was a warm air blowing up out of the gulf.

For a moment Cavor and I stood as near the edge as we dared peering into a blue tinged profundity. And then our guide was pulling at my arm.

He left me and walked to the end of that plank and stepped upon it, looking back. When he perceived we watched him, he turned about and went on over it, walking as surely as though he was on firm earth. For a moment his form was distinct, then he became a blue blur, and vanished into the obscurity. I was aware of some vague shape looming darkly out of the black.

There was a pause. " Surely —!" said Cavor.

One of the other Selenites walked a few paces out upon the plank and turned and looked back at us unconcernedly. The others stood ready to follow us.

Our guide's expectant figure reappeared. He was returning to see why we had not advanced.

" What is that beyond there?" I asked.

" I can't see."

" We can't cross this at any price," said I.

" I could not go three steps on it," said Cavor, " even with my hands free."

We looked at each other's drawn faces in blank consternation.

" They can't know what it is to be giddy," said Cavor.

" It's quite impossible for us to walk that plank."

" I don't believe they see as we do. I've been watching them. I wonder if they know this is simply blackness for us. How can we make them understand?"

" Anyhow, we must make them understand."

I think we said these things with a vague half hope the Selenites might somehow understand. I knew quite clearly that all that was needed was an explanation. Then, as I saw their faces, I realised that an explanation was impossible. Just here it was that our resemblances were not going to bridge our differences. Well, I wasn't going to walk the plank anyhow. I slipped one wrist very quickly out of the coil of chain that was loose, and then began to twist both in opposite directions. I was standing nearest to the bridge, and as I did this two of the Selenites laid hold of me and pulled me gently towards it.

I shook my head violently. " No go," I said, " no use. You don't understand."

Another Selenite added his

compulsion. I was forced to step forward.

" I've got an idea," said Cavor, but I knew his ideas.

" Look here! " I exclaimed to the Selenites. " Steady on! It's all very well for you — "

I swung round upon my heel; I burst out into curses. For one of the armed Selenites had stabbed me behind with his goad.

I wrenched my wrist free from the little tentacles that held them. I turned on the goad-bearer. " Confound you! " I cried. " I've warned you of that. What on earth do you think I'm made of, to stick that into me? If you touch me again — ! "

By way of answer he pricked me forthwith.

I heard Cavor's voice in alarm and entreaty. Even then I think he wanted to compromise with these creatures. " I say, Bedford," he cried, " I know a way! " But the sting of that second stab seemed to set free some pent-up reserve of energy in my being. Instantly a link of the wrist-chain snapped, and with it snapped all considerations that had held us unresisting in the hands of these moon-creatures. For that second, at least, I was mad with fear and anger. I took no thought of consequences. I hit straight out at the face of the thing with the goad. The chain was twisted round my fist. . . .

There came another of those beastly surprises of which the moon world is full.

My mailed hand seemed to go clean through him. He smashed like some sort of sweetmeat with liquid in it. He broke right in. He squelched and splashed. It was like hitting a damp toadstool. The flimsy body went spinning a dozen yards and fell with a flabby impact. I was astonished. I was incredulous that any living thing could be so flimsy. For an instant I could have believed the whole thing a dream.

Then it had become real and imminent again. Neither Cavor nor the other Selenites seemed to have done anything from the time when I had turned about to the time when the dead Selenite hit the ground. Everyone stood back from us two, everyone alert. That arrest seemed to last at least a second after the Selenite was down. Everyone must have been taking the thing in. I seem to remember myself standing with my arm half retracted, trying also to take it in. " What next? " clamoured my brain; " what next? " Then in a moment everyone was moving!

I perceived we must get our chains loose, and that before we could do this these Selenites had to be beaten off. I faced towards the group of the three goad-bearers. Instantly one threw his goad at me. It swished over my head, and I suppose went flying into the abyss behind.

I leaped right at him with all my might as the goad flew over me. He turned to run as I jumped, and I bore him to the ground, came down right upon him, and slipped upon his smashed body and fell. He seemed to wriggle under my feet.

I came into a sitting position, and on every hand the blue backs of the Selenites were receding into the darkness. I bent a link by main force and untwisted the

chain that had hampered me about the ankles, and sprang to my feet, with the chain in my hand. Another goad, flung javelin-wise, whistled by me, and I made a rush towards the darkness out of which it had come. Then I turned back towards Cavor, who was still standing in the light of the rivulet near the gulf, convulsively busy with his wrists, and at the same time jabbering nonsense about his idea.

"Come on!" I cried.

"My hands!" he answered.

Then, realising that I dared not run back to him because my ill-calculated steps might carry me over the edge, he came shuffling towards me, with his hands held out before him.

I gripped his chains at once to unfasten them.

"Where are they?" he panted.

"Run away. They'll come back. They're throwing things! Which way shall we go?"

"By the light. To that tunnel. Eh?"

"Yes," said I, and his hands were free.

I dropped on my knees and fell to work on his ankle bonds. Whack came something — I know not what — and splashed the livid streamlet into drops about us. Far away on our right a piping and whistling began.

I whipped the chain off his feet, and put it in his hand. "Hit with that!" I said, and without waiting for an answer set off in big bounds along the path by which we had come. I had a nasty feeling that these things could jump out of the darkness on to my back. I heard the impact of Cavor's leaps come following after me.

We ran in vast strides. But that running, you must understand, was an altogether different thing from any running on earth. On earth one leaps and almost instantly hits the ground again; but on the moon, because of its weaker pull, one shot through the air for several seconds before one came to earth. In spite of our violent hurry this gave an effect of long pauses, pauses in which one might have counted seven or eight. Step, and one soared off. All sorts of questions ran through my mind: "Where are the Selenites? What will they do? Shall we ever get to that tunnel? Is Cavor far behind? Are they likely to cut him off?" Then, whack, stride, and off again for another step.

I saw a Selenite running in front of me, his legs going exactly as a man's would go on earth, saw him glance over his shoulder, and heard him shriek as he ran aside out of my way into the darkness. He was, I think, our guide, but I am not sure. Then in another vast stride the walls of rock had come into view on either hand, and in two more strides I was in the tunnel, and tempering my pace to its low roof. I went on to a bend, then stopped and turned back, and plug, plug, plug, Cavor came into view, splashing into the stream of blue light at every stride, and grew larger and blundered into me. We stood clutching each other. For a moment, at least, we had shaken off our captors and were alone.

We were both very much out

of breath. We spoke in panting, broken sentences.

"You spoiled it all!" panted Cavor.

"Nonsense," I cried. "It was that or death."

"What are we to do?"

"Hide."

"How can we?"

"It's dark enough."

"But where?"

"Up one of these side caverns."

"And then?"

"Think."

"Right — come on."

We strode on, and presently came to a radiating, dark cavern. Cavor was in front. He hesitated, and chose a black mouth that seemed to promise good hiding. He went towards it and turned.

"It's dark," he said.

"Your legs and feet will light us. You're wet with that luminous stuff."

"But —"

A tumult of sounds, and in particular a sound like a clanging gong became audible advancing up the main tunnel. It was horribly suggestive of a tumultuous pursuit. We made a bolt for the unlit cavern forthwith. As we ran our way was lit by the irradiation of Cavor's legs. "It's lucky," I panted, "they took off our boots, or we should fill this place with clatter." On we rushed, taking the smallest steps we could to avoid striking the roof of the cavern. After a time we seemed to be gaining on the uproar. It became muffled, it dwindled, it died away.

I stopped and looked back and I heard the pad, pad of Cavor's feet receding. Then he stopped also. "Bedford," he whispered, "there's a sort of light in front of us."

I looked, and at first could see nothing. Then I perceived his head and shoulders dimly outlined against a fainter darkness. I saw also that this mitigation of the darkness was not blue as all the other light within the moon had been, but a pallid grey, a very vague faint white, the daylight colour. Cavor noted this difference as soon or sooner than I did, and I think, too, that it filled him with much the same wild hope.

"Bedford," he whispered, and his voice trembled, "that light — it is possible —"

He did not dare to say the thing he hoped. There came a pause. Suddenly I knew by the sound of his feet that he was striding towards that pallor. I followed him with a beating heart.

CHAPTER 15

POINTS OF VIEW

THE LIGHT grew stronger as we advanced. In a little time it was nearly as strong as the phosphorescence on Cavor's legs. Our tun-

nel was expanding into a cavern and this new light was at the farther end of it. I perceived something that set my hopes leaping and bounding.

"Cavor," I said, "it comes from above! I am certain it comes from above!"

He made no answer, but hurried on.

Indisputably it was a grey light, a silver light.

In another moment we were beneath it. It filtered down through a chink in the walls of the cavern, and as I stared up, drip, came a huge drop of water upon my face. I started, and stood aside; drip, fell another drop quite audibly on the rocky floor.

"Cavor," I said, "if one of us lifts the other, he can reach that crack!"

"I'll lift you," he said, and incontinently hoisted me as though I were a baby.

I thrust an arm into the crack, and just at my finger-tips found a little ledge by which I could hold. The white light was very much brighter now. I pulled myself up by two fingers with scarcely an effort, though on earth I weigh twelve stone, reached to a still higher corner of rock, and so got my feet on the narrow ledge. I stood up and searched up the rocks with my fingers; the cleft broadened out upwardly. "It's climbable," I said to Cavor. "Can you jump up to my hand if I hold it down to you?"

I wedged myself between the sides of the cleft, rested knee and foot on the ledge, and extended a hand. I could not see Cavor, but I could hear the rustle of his movements as he crouched to spring. Then whack, and he was hanging to my arm — and no heavier than a kitten! I lugged him up until he had a hand on my ledge and could release me.

"Confound it!" I said, "anyone could be a mountaineer on the moon," and so set myself in earnest to climbing. For a few minutes I clambered steadily, and then I looked up again. The cleft opened out gradually, and the light was brighter. Only —

It was not daylight after all!

In another moment I could see what it was, and at the sight I could have beaten my head against the rocks with disappointment. For I beheld simply an irregularly sloping open space, and all over its slanting floor stood a forest of little club-shaped fungi, each shining gloriously with that pinkish, silvery light. For a moment I stared at their soft radiance, then sprang forward and upward among them. I plucked up half a dozen and flung them against the rocks, and then sat down, laughing bitterly, as Cavor's ruddy face came into view.

"It's phosphorescence again," I said. "No need to hurry. Sit down and make yourself at home." And as he spluttered over our disappointment I began to fling more of these growths into the cleft.

"I thought it was daylight," he said.

"Daylight!" I cried. "Day-break, sunset, clouds, and windy

skies! Shall we ever see such things again?"

As I spoke a little picture of our world seemed to rise before me, bright and dainty and clear, like the background of some old Italian picture. "The sky that changes, and the sea that changes, and the hills and the green trees, and the towns and cities shining in the sun. Think of a wet roof at sunset, Cavor! Think of the windows of a westward house!"

He made no answer.

"Here we are burrowing in this beastly world that isn't a world, with its inky ocean hidden in some abominable blackness below, and outside that torrid day and that death stillness of night. And all those things that are chasing us now, beastly men of leather—insect men, that come out of a nightmare! After all, they're right! What business have we here, smashing them and disturbing their world? For all we know the whole planet is up and after us already. In a minute we may hear them whimpering and their gongs going. What are we to do? Where are we to go? Here we are as comfortable as snakes from Jamrach's loose in a Surbiton villa!"

"It was your fault," said Cavor.

"My fault!" I shouted. "Good Lord!"

"I had an idea."

"Curse your ideas!"

"If we had refused to budge—"

"Under those goads?"

"Yes. They would have carried us."

"Over that bridge?"

"Yes. They must have carried us from outside."

"I'd rather be carried by a fly across a ceiling. Good Heavens!"

I resumed my destruction of the fungi. Then suddenly I saw something that struck me even then.

"Cavor," I said, "these chains are of gold!"

He was thinking intently, with his hands gripping his cheeks. He turned his head slowly and stared at me and, when I had repeated my words, at the twisted chain about his right hand. "So they are," he said, "so they are." His face lost its transitory interest even as he looked. He hesitated for a moment, then went on with his interrupted meditation. I sat for a space puzzling over the fact that I had only just observed this, until I considered the blue light in which we had been and which had taken all the colour out of the metal. And from that discovery I started upon a train of thought that carried me wide and far. I forgot that I had just been asking what business we had in the moon. Gold. . . .

It was Cavor who spoke first. "It seems to me that there are two courses open to us."

"Well?"

"Either we can attempt to make our way—fight our way if necessary—out to the exterior and then hunt for our sphere until either we find it or the cold of the night comes to kill us, or else—"

He paused. "Yes," I said, though I knew what was coming.

" We might attempt once more to establish some sort of understanding with the minds of the people in the moon."

" So far as I'm concerned — it's the first."

" I doubt."

" I don't."

" You see," said Cavor, " I do not think we can judge the Selenites by what we have seen of them. Their central world, their civilised world, will be far below in the profounder caverns about their sea. This region of the crust in which we are is an outlying district, a pastoral region. At least, that is my interpretation. These Selenites we have seen may be only the equivalent of cowboys and engine-tenders. Their use of goads — in all probability mooncalf goads — the lack of imagination they show in expecting us to be able to do just what they can do, their indisputable brutality, all seem to point to something of that sort. But if we endured — "

" Neither of us could endure a six-inch plank across the bottomless pit for very long."

" No," said Cavor, " but then — "

" I *won't*," I said.

He discovered a new line of possibilities. " Well, suppose we got ourselves into some corner, where we could defend ourselves against these hinds and labourers. If, for example, we could hold out for a week or so, it is probable that the news of our appearance would filter down to the more intelligent and populous parts — "

" If they exist."

" They must exist, or whence come those tremendous machines? "

" That's possible, but it's the worst of the two chances."

" We might write up inscriptions on walls — "

" How do we know their eyes could see the marks we made?"

" If we cut them — "

" That's possible of course."

I took up a new thread of thought. " After all," I said, " I suppose you don't think these Selenites so infinitely wiser than men? "

" They must know a lot more — or at least a lot of different things."

" Yes, but — " I hesitated. " I think you'll admit, Cavor, that you're rather an exceptional man."

" How? "

" Well, you — you're a rather lonely man; have been, that is. You haven't married."

" Never wanted to. But why? "

" And you never grew richer than you happened to be? "

" Never wanted that either."

" You've just rooted after knowledge."

" Well, a certain curiosity is natural — "

" You think so. That's just it. You think every other mind wants to know. I remember once, when I asked you why you conducted all these researches, you said you wanted your F.R.S., and to have the stuff called Cavorite, and things like that. You know perfectly well you didn't do it for that; but at the time my

question took you by surprise, and you felt you ought to have something to look like a motive. Really, you conducted researches because you had to. It's your twist."

"Perhaps it is — "

"It isn't one man in a million has that twist. Most men want — well, various things, but very few want knowledge for its own sake. I don't. I know perfectly well. Now these Selenites seem to be a driving, busy sort of people, but how do you know that even the most intelligent will take an interest in us or our world? I don't believe they'll even know we have a world. They never come out at night — they'd freeze if they did. They've probably never seen any heavenly body at all except that blazing sun. How are they to know there is another world? What does it matter to them if they do? Well, even if they have had a glimpse of a few stars or even of the earth crescent, what of that? Why should people living inside a planet trouble to observe that sort of thing? Men wouldn't have done it except for the seasons and sailing; why should the moon people? . . .

"Well, suppose there are a few philosophers like yourself. They are just the very Selenites who'll never hear of our existence. Suppose a Selenite had dropped on the earth when you were at Lympne; you'd have been the last man in the world to hear he had come. You never read a newspaper. You see the chances against you. Well, it's for these chances we're sitting here doing

nothing while precious time is flying. I tell you we've got into a fix. We've come unarmed, we've lost our sphere, we've got no food, we've shown ourselves to the Selenites and made them think we're strange, strong, dangerous animals, and unless these Selenites are perfect fools they'll set about now and hunt us till they find us, and when they find us they'll take us if they can and kill us if they can't, and that's the end of the matter. After they take us they'll probably kill us through some misunderstanding. After we're done for they may discuss us, perhaps, but we sha'n't get much fun out of that."

"Go on."

"On the other hand, here's gold knocking about like cast-iron at home. If only we can get some of it back, if only we can find our sphere again before they do and get back, then — "

"Yes?"

"We might put the thing on a sounder footing. Come back in a bigger sphere with guns."

"Good Lord!" cried Cavor, as though the idea was horrible.

I shied another luminous fungus down the cleft.

"Look here, Cavor," I said, "I've half the voting power anyhow in this affair, and this is a case for a practical man. I'm a practical man, and you are not. I'm not going to trust to Selenites and geometrical diagrams again if I can help it. . . . That's all. Get back. Drop all this secrecy — or most of it. And come again."

He reflected. "When I came

to the moon," he said, "I ought to have come alone."

"The question before the meeting," I said, "is how to get back to the sphere."

For a time we nursed our knees in silence. Then he seemed to decide to accept my reasons.

"I think," he said, "one can get data. It is clear that, while the sun is on this side of the moon, the air will be blowing through this planet sponge from the dark side hither. On this side, at any rate, the air will be expanding and flowing out of the moon caverns into the crater. . . . Very well, there's a draught here."

"So there is."

"And that means that this is not a dead end, somewhere behind us this cleft goes on and up. The draught is blowing up, and that is the way we have to go. If we try to get up any sort of chimney or gully there is, we shall not only get out of these passages where they are hunting for us—"

"But suppose the gully is too narrow."

"We'll come down again."

"Ssh!" I said, suddenly; "what's that?"

We listened. At first it was an indistinct murmur, and then one picked out the clang of a gong. "They must think we are mooncalves," said I, "to be frightened at that."

"They're coming along that passage," said Cavor. "They must be."

"They'll not think of the cleft. They'll go past."

I listened again for a space. "This time," I whispered, "they're likely to have some sort of weapon."

Then suddenly I sprang to my feet. "Good heavens, Cavor!" I cried. "But they *will*. They'll see the fungi I have been pitching down. They'll—"

I didn't finish my sentence. I turned about and made a leap over the fungus-tops towards the upper end of the cavity. I saw that the space turned upwards and became a draughty cleft again, ascending to impenetrable darkness. I was about to clamber up into this, and then with a happy inspiration turned back.

"What are you doing?" asked Cavor.

"Go on!" said I, and went back and got two of the shining fungi, and putting one into the breast pocket of my flannel jacket so that it stuck out to light our climbing, went back with the other for Cavor. The noise of the Selenites was now so loud that it seemed they must be already beneath the cleft. But it might be they would have difficulty in clambering into it, or might hesitate to ascend it against our possible resistance. At any rate we had now the comforting knowledge of the enormous muscular superiority that was the gift of our birth on another planet. The next moment I was clambering with gigantic vigour after Cavor's blue-lit heels.

CHAPTER 16

THE FIGHT IN THE CAVE OF THE MOON BUTCHERS

I DO not know how far we clambered before we came to the grating. It may be we ascended only a few hundred feet, but at the time it seemed to me we might have hauled and jammed and hopped and wedged ourselves through a mile or more of vertical ascent. Whenever I recall that time there comes into my head the heavy clank of our golden chains that followed every movement. Very soon my knuckles and knees were raw, and I had a bruise on one cheek. After a time the first violence of our efforts diminished, and our movements became more deliberate and less painful.

The noise of the pursuing Selenites had died away altogether. It seemed almost as if they had not traced us up the crack after all, in spite of the tell-tale heap of broken fungi that must have lain beneath it. At times the cleft narrowed so much that we could scarce squeeze into it, at others it expanded into great drusy cavities studded with prickly crystals, or thickly beset with dull, shining fungoid pimples. Sometimes it twisted spirally and at other times slanted down nearly to the horizontal direction. Ever and again there was the intermittent drip and trickle of water by us. Once or twice it seemed to us that small living things had rustled out of our reach, but what they were we never saw. They may have been venomous beasts for all I know, but they did us no harm, and we were now tuned to a pitch when a weird creeping thing more or less mattered little. And at last, far above came the familiar bluish light again, and then we saw that it filtered through a grating that barred our way.

We whispered as we pointed this out to each other and became more and more cautious in our ascent. Presently we were close under the grating, and by pressing my face against its bars I could see a limited portion of the cavern beyond. It was clearly a large space, and lit no doubt by some rivulet of the same blue light that we had seen flow from the beating machinery. An intermittent trickle of water dropped ever and again between the bars near my face.

My first endeavour was naturally to see what might be upon the floor of the cavern, but our grating lay in a depression whose rim hid all this from our eyes. Our foiled attention then fell back upon the suggestion of the various sounds we heard, and presently my eye caught a number of faint shadows that played

across the dim roof, far over-
head.

Indisputably there were sev-
eral Selenites, perhaps a consider-
able number in this space, for
we could hear the noises of their
intercourse and faint sounds that
I identified as their footfalls.
There was also a succession of
regularly repeated sounds, chid,
chid, chid, which began and
ceased, suggestive of a knife or
spade hacking at some soft sub-
stance. Then came a clank as of
chains, a whistle and a rumble
as of a truck running over a
hollowed place, and then again
that chid, chid, chid, resumed.
The shadows told of shapes that
moved quickly and rhythmically
in agreement with that regu-
lar sound, and rested when it
ceased.

We put our heads close to-
gether and began to discuss these
things in noiseless whispers.

"They are occupied," I said;
"they are occupied in some way."

"Yes."

"They're not seeking us or
thinking of us."

"Perhaps they have not heard
of us."

"Those others are hunting
about below. If suddenly we
appeared here—"

We looked at each other.

"There might be a chance to
parley," said Cavor.

"No," I said, "not as we are."

For a space we remained, each
occupied with his own thoughts.

Chid, chid, chid went the chip-
ping, and the shadows moved
to and fro.

I looked at the grating. "It's
flimsy," I said. "We might bend

two of the bars and crawl
through."

We wasted a little time in
vague discussion. Then I took
one of the bars in both hands,
and got my feet up against the
rock until they were almost on a
level with my head, and so thrust
against the bar. It bent so sud-
denly that I almost slipped. I
clambered about and bent the
adjacent bar in the opposite di-
rection, and then took the lumi-
nous fungus from my pocket and
dropped it down the fissure.

"Don't do anything hastily,"
whispered Cavor, as I twisted
myself up through the opening
I had enlarged. I had a glimpse
of busy figures as I came through
the grating, and immediately
bent down, so that the rim of
the depression in which the grat-
ing lay hid me from their eyes,
and so lay flat, signalling advice
to Cavor as he also prepared to
come through. Presently we were
side by side in the depression,
peering over the edge at the
cavern and its occupants.

It was a much larger cavern
than we had supposed from our
first glimpse of it, and we looked
up from the lowest portion of its
sloping floor. It widened out as
it receded from us, and its roof
came down and hid the remoter
portion altogether. Lying in a
line along its length, vanishing
at last far away in that tremen-
dous perspective, were a number
of huge shapes, huge pallid hulls,
upon which the Selenites were
busy. At first they seemed big
white cylinders of vague import.
Then I noted the heads upon
them lying towards us, eyeless

and skinless like the heads of
sheep at a butcher's, and per-
ceived they were the carcasses
of mooncalves being cut up,
much as the crew of a whaler
might cut up a moored whale.
They were cutting off the flesh
in strips, and on some of the
farther trunks the white ribs
were showing. It was the sound
of their hatchets that made that
chid, chid, chid. Some distance
away a thing like a trolley, cable-
drawn and loaded with chunks
of lax meat, was running up
the slope of the cavern floor.
That enormous busy avenue of
hulls that were destined to be
food gave us a sense of the vast
populousness of the moon world
second only to the effect of our
first glimpse down the shaft.

It seemed to me at first that
the Selenites must be standing on
trestle-supported planks,[1] and
then I saw that the planks and
supports and the hatchets were
really of the same leaden hue
as my fetters had seemed before
white light came to bear on
them. A number of very thick-
looking crowbars lay about the
floor and had apparently assisted
to turn the dead mooncalf over
on its side. They were perhaps
six feet long, with shaped han-
dles; very tempting looking weap-
ons. The whole place was lit by

[1] I do not remember seeing any
wooden things on the moon; doors,
tables, everything corresponding to our
terrestrial joinery was made of metal,
and I believe for the most part of gold,
which as a metal would, of course, natu-
rally recommend itself — other things
being equal — on account of the ease
in working it and its toughness and
durability.

three transverse streams of the
blue fluid.

We lay for a long time not-
ing all these things in silence.
"Well?" said Cavor at last.

I crouched lower and turned
to him. I had come upon a bril-
liant idea. "Unless they lowered
those bodies by a crane," I said,
"we must be nearer the surface
than I thought."

"Why?"

"The mooncalf doesn't hop
and it hasn't got wings."

He peered over the edge of
the hollow again. "I wonder,
now —" he began. "After all
we have never gone far from the
surface."

I stopped him by a grip on his
arm. I had heard a noise from
the cleft below us!

We twisted ourselves about
and lay as still as death, with
every sense alert. In a little while
I did not doubt that something
was quietly ascending the cleft.
Very slowly and quite noiselessly
I assured myself of a good grip
on my chain, and waited for that
something to appear.

"Just look at those chaps with
the hatchets again," I said.

"They're all right," said
Cavor.

I took a quick provisional aim
at the gap in the grating. I
could hear now quite distinctly
the soft twittering of the ascend-
ing Selenites, the dab of their
hands against the rock, and the
falling of dust from their grips
as they clambered.

Then I could see that there
was something moving dimly in
the blackness below the grating,
but what it might be I could not

distinguish. The whole thing seemed to hang fire just for a moment; then, smash! I had sprung to my feet, struck savagely at something that had flashed out at me. It was the keen point of a spear. I have thought since that its length in the narrowness of the cleft must have prevented its being sloped to reach me. Anyhow, it shot out from the grating like the tongue of a snake and missed, and flew back and flashed again. But the second time I snatched and caught it, and wrenched it away, but not before another had darted ineffectually at me.

I shouted with triumph as I felt the hold of the Selenite resist my pull for a moment and give, and then I was jabbing down through the bars, amidst squeals from the darkness, and Cavor had snapped off the other spear, and was leaping and flourishing it beside me and making inefficient jabs. "Clang, clang," came up through the grating, and then an axe hurtled through the air and whacked against the rocks beyond to remind me of the fleshers at the carcasses up the cavern.

I turned, and they were all coming towards us in open order, waving their axes. They were short thick little beggars with long arms, strikingly different from the ones we had seen before. If they had not heard of us before they must have realised the situation with incredible swiftness. I stared at them for a moment, spear in hand. "Guard the grating Cavor," I cried, and howling to intimidate them, I rushed to meet them. Two of them missed with their hatchets, and the rest fled incontinently. Then the two also were sprinting away up the cavern, with hands clenched and heads down. I never saw men run like them.

I knew the spear I had was useless for me. It was thin and flimsy, only effectual for a thrust, and too long for a quick recovery. So I only chased the Selenites as far as the first carcass, and stopped there and picked up one of the crowbars that were lying about. It felt comfortably heavy and equal to smashing any number of Selenites. I threw away my spear, and picked up a second crowbar for the other hand. I felt five times better than I had with the spear. I shook the two threateningly at the Selenites, who had come to a halt in a little crowd far away up the cavern, and then turned about to look at Cavor.

He was leaping from side to side of the grating making threatening jabs with his broken spear. That was all right. It would keep the Selenites down — for a time at least. I looked up the cavern again. What on earth were we going to do now?

We were cornered already. But these butchers up the cavern had been surprised; they were probably scared, and they had no special weapons, only those little hatchets of theirs. And that way lay escape. Their sturdy little forms — ever so much shorter and thicker than the mooncalf herders — were scattered up the slope in a way that was eloquent of indecision. I had

the moral advantage of a mad bull in a street. But for all that there seemed a tremendous crowd of them. Very probably there was. Those Selenites down the cleft had certainly some infernally long spears. It might be they had other surprises for us. . . . But, confound it! if we charged up the cave we should let them up behind us; and if we didn't, those little brutes up the cave would probably be reinforced. Heaven alone knew what tremendous engines of warfare — guns, bombs, terrestrial torpedoes — this unknown world below our feet, this vaster world of which we had only picked the outer cuticle, might not presently send up to our destruction. It became clear the only thing to do was to charge! It became clearer as the legs of a number of fresh Selenites appeared running down the cavern towards us.

"Bedford!" cried Cavor, and behold! he was halfway between me and the grating.

"Go back!" I cried. "What are you doing—"

"They've got—it's like a gun!"

And struggling in the grating between those defensive spears appeared the head and shoulders of a singularly lean and angular Selenite bearing some complicated apparatus.

I realised Cavor's utter incapacity for the fight we had in hand. For a moment I hesitated. Then I rushed past him whirling my crowbars, and shouting to confound the aim of the Selenite. He was aiming in the queerest way with the thing against his stomach. "*Chuzz!*" The thing wasn't a gun; it went off more like a crossbow, and dropped me in the middle of a leap.

I didn't fall down — I simply came down a little shorter than I should have done if I hadn't been hit, and from the feel of my shoulder the thing might have tapped me and glanced off. Then my left hand hit against the shaft, and I perceived there was a sort of spear sticking half through my shoulder. The moment after, I got home with the crowbar in my right hand, and hit the Selenite fair and square. He collapsed — crushed and crumpled — his head smashed like an egg.

I dropped a crowbar, pulled the spear out of my shoulder, and began to jab it down the grating into the darkness. At each jab came a shriek and twitter. Finally I hurled the spear down upon them with all my strength, leaped up, picked up the crowbar again, and started for the multitude up the cavern.

"Bedford!" cried Cavor, "Bedford!" as I flew past him.

I seem to remember his footsteps coming on behind me.

Step, leap . . . whack, step, leap. . . . Each leap seemed to last ages. With each, the cave opened out and the number of visible Selenites increased. At first they seemed all running about like ants in a disturbed ant-hill, one or two waving hatchets and coming to meet me, more running away, some bolting sidewise into the avenue of carcasses; then presently others came in sight carrying spears,

and then others. I saw a most extraordinary thing, all hands and feet, bolting for cover. The cavern grew darker farther up. Flick! something flew over my head. Flick! As I soared in mid-stride I saw a spear hit and quiver in one of the carcasses to my left. Then as I came down one hit the ground before me and I heard the remote chuzz! with which their things were fired. Flick! Flick! for a moment it was a shower. They were volleying!

I stopped dead.

I don't think I thought clearly then. I seem to remember a stereotyped phrase running through my mind: "Zone of fire, seek cover!" I know I made a dash for the space between two of the carcasses, and stood there, panting and feeling very wicked.

I looked round for Cavor, and for a moment it seemed as if he had vanished from the world. Then he came out of the darkness between the row of the carcasses and the rocky wall of the cavern. I saw his little face, dark and blue, and shining with perspiration and emotion.

He was saying something, but what it was I did not heed. I had realised that we might work from mooncalf to mooncalf up the cave until we were near enough to charge home. It was charge or nothing. "Come on!" I said, and led the way.

"Bedford!" he cried, unavailingly.

My mind was busy as we went up that narrow alley between the dead bodies and the wall of the cavern. The rocks curved about

— they could not enfilade us. Though in that narrow space we could not leap, yet with our earth-born strength we were still able to go very much faster than the Selenites. I reckoned we should presently come among them. Once we were on them they would be hardly as formidable as black-beetles. Only there would first of all be a volley. I thought of a stratagem. I whipped off my flannel jacket as I ran.

"Bedford!" panted Cavor, behind me.

I glanced back. "What?" said I.

He was pointing upward over the carcasses. "White light!" he said. "White light again!"

I looked, and it was even so; a faint white ghost of twilight in the remoter cavern roof. That seemed to give me double strength.

"Keep close," I said. A flat long Selenite dashed out of the darkness and squealed and fled. I halted and stopped Cavor with my hand. I hung my jacket over my crowbar, ducked round the next carcass, dropped jacket and crowbar, showed myself, and darted back.

"Chuzz—flick," just one arrow came. We were close on the Selenites, and they were standing in a crowd, broad, short and tall together, with a little battery of their shooting implements pointing down the cave. Three or four other arrows followed the first, and then their fire ceased.

I stuck out my head, and escaped by a hair's breadth. This time I drew a dozen shots or more, and heard the Selenites

shouting and twittering as if with excitement as they shot. I picked up jacket and crowbar again.

"Now!" said I, and thrust out the jacket.

"Chuzz-zz-zz-zz! Chuzz!" In an instant my jacket had grown a thick beard of arrows, and they were quivering all over the carcass behind us. Instantly I slipped the crowbar out of the jacket, dropped the jacket — for all I know to the contrary it is lying up there in the moon now — and rushed out upon them.

For a minute perhaps it was massacre. I was too fierce to discriminate, and the Selenites were probably too scared to fight. At any rate they made no sort of fight against me. I saw scarlet, as the saying is. I remember I seemed to be wading among these leathery thin things as a man wades through tall grass, mowing and hitting, first right then left — smash, smash! Little drops of moisture flew about. I trod on things that crushed and piped and went slippery. The crowd seemed to open and close and flow like water. They seemed to have no combined plan whatever. There were spears flying about me; I was grazed over the ear by one. I was stabbed once in the arm and once in the cheek, but I only found that out afterwards when the blood had had time to run and cool and feel wet.

What Cavor did I do not know. For a space it seemed that this fighting had lasted for an age and must needs go on for ever. Then suddenly it was all over, and there was nothing to be seen but the backs of heads bobbing up and down as their owners ran in all directions. . . . I seemed altogether unhurt. I ran forward some paces, shouting, then turned about. I was amazed.

I had come through them in vast flying strides. They were all behind me, and running hither and thither to hide.

I felt an enormous astonishment at the evaporation of the great fight into which I had hurled myself, and not a little exultation. It did not seem to me that the Selenites were unexpectedly flimsy, but that I was unexpectedly strong. I laughed stupidly. This fantastic moon!

I glanced for a moment at the smashed and writhing bodies that were scattered over the cavern floor with a vague idea of further violence, then hurried on after Cavor.

CHAPTER 17

IN THE SUNLIGHT

PRESENTLY we saw that the cavern before us opened on a hazy void. In another moment we had emerged upon a slanting gallery that projected into a vast circular space, a huge cylindrical

pit running vertically up and down. Round this pit the slanting gallery ran without any parapet or protection for a turn and a half, and then plunged high above into the rock again. Somehow it reminded me then of one of those spiral turns of the railway through the Saint Gothard. It was all tremendously huge. I can scarcely hope to convey to you the Titanic proportion of all that place — the Titanic effect of it. Our eyes followed up the vast declivity of the pit wall, and overhead and far about ‎we beheld a round opening set with faint stars, and half of the lip above it well-nigh blinding with the white light of the sun. At that we cried aloud simultaneously.

"Come on!" I said, leading the way.

"But there?" said Cavor, and very carefully stepped nearer the edge of the gallery. I followed his example, craned forward and looked down, but I was dazzled by that gleam of light above, and I could see only a bottomless darkness with spectral patches of crimson and purple floating therein. Yet if I could not see I could hear. Out of this darkness came a sound — a sound like the angry hum one can hear outside a hive of bees, a sound out of that enormous hollow, it may be, for miles beneath our feet. . . .

For a moment I listened, then tightened my grip on my crowbar and led the way up the gallery.

"This must be the shaft we looked down upon," said Cavor. "Under that lid."

"And below there is where we saw the lights."

"The lights!" said he. "Yes — the lights of the world that now we shall never see."

"We'll come back," I said, for now we had escaped so much I was rashly sanguine that we should recover the sphere.

His answer I did not catch.

"Eh?" I asked.

"I doesn't matter," he answered, and we hurried on in silence.

I suppose that slanting lateral way was four or five miles long, allowing for its curvature, and it ascended at a slope that would have made it almost impossibly steep on earth, but which we strode up easily. We saw only two Selenites during all that portion of our flight, and as soon as they became aware of us they ran headlong. It was clear that the knowledge of our strength and violence had reached them. Our way to the exterior was unexpectedly plain. The spiral gallery straightened into a steeply ascendent tunnel, its floor bearing abundant traces of the mooncalves, and so straight and short in proportion to its vast arch that no part of it was absolutely dark. Almost immediately it began to lighten, and then far off and high up, and quite blindly brilliant, appeared its opening on the exterior, a slope of Alpine steepness surmounted by a crest of bayonet shrub, tall but broken down now and dry and dead, in spiky silhouette against the sun.

And it is strange that we men, to whom this very vegetation had seemed so weird and horrible a

little time ago, should now behold it with the emotion a home-coming exile might feel at sight of his native land. We welcomed even the rareness of the air that made us pant as we ran and which rendered speaking no longer the easy thing it had been. Larger grew the sunlit circle above us and larger, and all the nearer tunnel sank into a rim of indistinguishable black. We saw the dead bayonet shrub no longer with any touch of green in it, but brown and dry and thick, and the shadow of its upper branches high out of sight made a densely interlaced pattern upon the tumbled rocks. And at the immediate mouth of the tunnel was a wide trampled space where the mooncalves had come and gone.

We came out upon this space at last into a light and heat that hit and pressed upon us. We traversed the exposed area painfully, and clambered up a slope among the scrub-stems, and sat down at last panting in a high place beneath the shadow of a mass of twisted lava. Even in the shade the rock felt hot.

The air was intensely hot, and we were in great physical discomfort, but for all that we were no longer in a nightmare. We seemed to have come to our own province again, beneath the stars. All the fear and stress of our flight through the dim passages and fissures below had fallen from us. That last fight had filled us with an enormous confidence in ourselves so far as the Selenites were concerned. We looked back almost incredulously at the black opening from which we

had just emerged. Down there, in a blue glow that now in our memories seemed the next thing to absolute darkness, we had met with things like mad mockeries of men, helmet-headed creatures, and had walked in fear before them, and had submitted to them until we could submit no longer. And behold, they had smashed like wax and scattered like chaff, and fled and vanished like the creatures of a dream!

I rubbed my eyes, doubting whether we had not slept and dreamt these things by reason of the fungus we had eaten, and suddenly discovered the blood upon my face, and then that my shirt was sticking painfully to my shoulder and arm.

"Confound it!" I said, gauging my injuries with an investigatory hand, and suddenly that distant tunnel-mouth became, as it were, a watching eye.

"Cavor!" I said, "what are they going to do now? And what are we going to do?"

He shook his head, with his eyes fixed upon the tunnel. "How can one tell what they will do?"

"It depends on what they think of us, and I don't see how we can begin to guess that. And it depends upon what they have in reserve. It's as you say, Cavor: we have touched the merest outside of this world. They may have all sorts of things inside here. Even with those shooting things they might make it bad for us. . . .

"Yet, after all," I said, "even if we don't find the sphere at once, there is a chance for us. We might hold out. Even through

the night. We might go down there again and make a fight for it."

I stared about me with speculative eyes. The character of the scenery had altered altogether by reason of the enormous growth and subsequent drying of the scrub. The crest on which we sat was high and commanded a wide prospect of the crater and landscape and we saw it now all sere and dry in the late autumn of the lunar afternoon. Rising one behind the other were long slopes and fields of trampled brown where the mooncalves had pastured, and far away in the full blaze of the sun a drove of them basked slumberously, scattered shapes, each with a blot of shadow against it like sheep on the side of a down. But not a sign of Selenite was to be seen. Whether they had fled on our emergence from the interior passages or whether they were accustomed to retire after driving out the mooncalves I cannot guess. At the time I believed the former was the case.

"If we were to set fire to all this stuff," I said, "we might find the sphere among the ashes."

Cavor did not seem to hear me. He was peering under his hand at the stars, that still, in spite of the intense sunlight, were abundantly visible in the sky. "How long do you think we have been here?" he asked at last.

"Been where?"

"On the moon."

"Two earthly days, perhaps."

"More nearly ten. Do you know, the sun is past its zenith, and sinking in the west? In four days' time or less it will be night."

"But — we've only eaten once!"

"I know that. And — but there are the stars!"

"But why should time seem different because we are on a smaller planet?"

"I don't know. There it is!"

"How does one tell time?"

"Hunger — fatigue —all those things are different. Everything is different. Everything. To me it seems that since first we came out of the sphere it has been only a question of hours — long hours. At most."

"Ten days," I said; "that leaves —" I looked up at the sun for a moment and then saw that it was halfway from the zenith to the western edge. "Four days! . . . Cavor, we mustn't sit here and dream. How do you think we can begin?"

I stood up. "We must get a fixed point which we can recognise. We might hoist a flag, or a handkerchief or something — and quarter the ground and work round that."

He stood up beside me.

"Yes," he said, "there is nothing for it but to hunt for the sphere. Nothing. We may find it — certainly we may find it. And if not —"

"We must keep on looking."

He looked this way and that, glanced up at the sky and down at the tunnel and astonished me by a sudden gesture of impatience. "Oh! but we have done foolishly! To have come to this pass! Think how it might have been and the things we might have done!"

"We may do something yet."

"Never the thing we might have done. Here below our feet is a world. Think of what that world must be! Think of that machine we saw and the lid and the shaft! They were just remote outlying suggestions, and those creatures we have seen and fought with, no more than ignorant peasants, dwellers in the outskirts, yokels and labourers half akin to brutes. Down below! Caverns beneath caverns, tunnels, structures, ways. . . . It must open out and be greater and wider and more populous as one descends. Assuredly. Right down at last to the central sea that washes round the core of the moon. Think of its inky waters under the spare lights! If indeed their eyes need lights! Think of the cascading tributaries pouring down their channels to feed it. Think of the tides upon its surface and the rush and swirl of its ebb and flow. Perhaps they have ships that go upon it, perhaps down there are mighty cities and swarming ways and wisdom and order passing the wit of man. And we may die here upon it and never see the masters who must be — ruling over these things! We may freeze and die here and the air will freeze and thaw upon us, and then — ! They will come upon us, come on our stiff and silent bodies and find the sphere we cannot find and they will understand at last, too late, all the thought and effort that ended here in vain!" His voice through all that speech sounded like the voice of someone heard in a telephone, weak and far away.

"But the darkness," I said.

"One might get over that."

"How?"

"I don't know. How am I to know? One might carry a torch, one might have a lamp — The others — might understand."

He stood for a moment with his hands held down and a rueful face, staring out over the waste that defied him. Then with a gesture of renunciation he turned towards me with proposals for the systematic hunting of the sphere.

"We can return," I said.

He looked about him. "First of all we shall have to get to earth."

"We could bring back lamps to carry and climbing irons and a hundred necessary things."

"Yes," he said.

"We can take back an earnest of success in this gold."

He looked at my golden crowbars and said nothing for a space. He stood with his hands clasped behind his back staring across the crater. At last he sighed and spoke. "It was I found the way here, but to find a way isn't always to be master of a way. If I take my secret back to earth what will happen? I do not see how I can keep my secret for a year, for even a part of a year. Sooner or later it must come out, even if other men rediscover it. And then . . . Governments and powers will struggle to get hither, they will fight against one another and against these moon people. It will only spread warfare and multiply the occasions of war. In a little while, in a very little while if I tell my secret, this planet to its deepest galleries will be strewn with

human dead. Other things are doubtful, but that is certain. . . . It is not as though man had any use for the moon. What good would the moon be to men? Even of their own planet what have they made but a battle ground and theatre of infinite folly? Small as his world is, and short as his time, he has still in his little life down there far more than he can do. No! Science has toiled too long forging weapons for fools to use. It is time she held her hand. Let him find it out for himself again — in a thousand years' time."

"There are methods of secrecy," I said.

He looked up at me and smiled. "After all," he said, "why should one worry? There is little chance of our finding the sphere and down below trouble is brewing for us. It's simply the human habit of hoping till we die, that makes us think of return. Our troubles are only beginning. We have shown these moonfolk violence, we have given them a taste of our quality and our chances are about as good as a tiger's that has got loose and killed a man in Hyde Park. The news of us must be running down from gallery to gallery, down towards the central parts. . . . No sane beings will ever let us take that sphere back to earth, after so much as they have seen of us."

"We aren't improving our chances," said I, "by sitting here."

We stood up side by side.

"After all," he said, "we must separate. We must fasten up a handkerchief on these tall spikes

here and stick it firmly and from this as a centre we must work over the crater. You must go westward, moving out in semicircles to and from the setting sun. You must move first with your shadow on your right until it is at right angles with the direction of your handkerchief and then with your shadow on your left. And I will do the same to the east. We will look into every gully, examine every skerry of rocks, we will do all we can to find my sphere. If we see Selenites we will hide from them as well as we can. For drink we must take snow, and if we feel the need of food we must kill a mooncalf, if we can, and eat such flesh as it has — raw, and so each will go his own way."

"And if one of us comes upon the sphere?"

"He must come back to the white handkerchief and stand by it and signal to the other."

"And if neither —"

Cavor glanced up at the sun. "We go on seeking until the night and cold overtake us."

"Suppose the Selenites have found the sphere and hidden it?"

He shrugged his shoulders.

"Or presently they come hunting us?"

He made no answer.

"You had better take a club," I said.

He shook his head and stared away from me across the waste.

But for a moment he did not start. He looked round at me shyly, hesitated. "*Au revoir,*" he said.

I felt an odd stab of emotion. A sense of how we had galled each other and particularly how I must have galled him came to

me. "Confound it!" thought I, "we might have done better!" I was on the point of asking him to shake hands — for that was how I felt just then — when he put his feet together and leaped away from me towards the north. He drifted through the air as a dead leaf would do, fell lightly and leaped again. I stood for a moment watching him, then faced westward reluctantly, pulled myself together, and, with something of the feeling of a man who leaps into icy water, selected a point and plunged forward to explore my solitary half of the moon world. I dropped rather clumsily among rocks, stood up and looked about me, clambered to a rocky slab and leaped again. . . . When presently I looked for Cavor he was hidden from my eyes, but the handkerchief showed out bravely on its headland, white in the blaze of the sun.

I determined not to lose sight of that handkerchief whatever might betide.

CHAPTER 18

MR. BEDFORD ALONE

In a little while it seemed to me as if I had always been alone on the moon. I hunted for a time with a certain intentness, but the heat was still very great and the thinness of the air felt like a hoop about one's chest. I came presently into a hollow basin bristling with tall brown dry fronds about its edge and I sat down under these to rest and cool. I intended to stay for only a little while. I put down my club beside me and sat resting my chin on my hands. I saw with a colourless interest that the rocks of the basin, where here and there the crackling dry lichens had shrunk away to show them, were all veined and splattered with gold, that here and there bosses of rounded and wrinkled gold projected from among the litter. What did that matter now? A sort of languor had possession of my limbs and mind, I did not believe for a moment that we should ever find the sphere in that vast desiccated wilderness. I seemed to lack a motive for effort until the Selenites should come. Then I supposed I should exert myself, obeying that unreasonable imperative that urges a man before all things to preserve and defend his life, albeit he may preserve it only to die more painfully in a little while.

Why had we come to the moon?

The thing presented itself to me as a perplexing problem. What is this spirit in man that urges him for ever to depart from happiness and security, to toil, to place himself in danger, even to risk a reasonable certainty of death? It dawned upon me up there in the moon as a thing I ought always to have known, that man is not made

simply to go about being safe and comfortable and well fed and amused. Against his interest, against his happiness he is constantly being driven to do unreasonable things. Some force not himself impels him and go he must. But why? Why? Sitting there in the midst of that useless moon gold, amidst the things of another world, I took count of all my life. Assuming I was to die a castaway upon the moon, I failed altogether to see what purpose I had served; I got no light on that point, but it was clearer to me than it had ever been in my life before that I was not serving my own purpose; that all my life I had in truth never served the purposes of my private life. Whose purpose was I serving? . . . I ceased to speculate on why we had come to the moon and took a wider sweep. Why had I come to the earth? Why had I a private life at all? . . . I lost myself at last in bottomless speculation.

My thoughts became vague and cloudy, no longer leading in definite directions. I had not felt heavy or weary — I cannot imagine one doing so upon the moon — but I suppose I was greatly fatigued. At any rate I slept.

Slumbering there rested me greatly, and the sun was setting and the violence of the heat abating through all the time I slumbered. When at last I was roused from my slumbers by a remote clamour, I felt active and capable again. I rubbed my eyes and stretched my arms. I rose to my feet — I was a little stiff — and at once prepared to resume my search. I shouldered my golden clubs one on each shoulder and went on out of the ravine of the gold-veined rocks.

The sun was certainly lower, much lower than it had been, the air was very much cooler, I perceived I must have slept some time. It seemed to me that a faint touch of misty blueness hung about the western cliff. I leaped to a little boss of rock, and surveyed the crater. I could see no signs of mooncalves or Selenites, nor could I see Cavor, but I could see my handkerchief afar off spread out on its thicket of thorns. I looked about me, and then sprang forward to the next convenient viewpoint.

I beat my way round in a semicircle and back again in a still remoter crescent. It was very fatiguing and hopeless. The air was really very much cooler and it seemed to me that the shadow under the westward cliff was growing broad. Ever and again I stopped and reconnoitred, but there was no sign of Cavor, no sign of Selenites, and it seemed to me the mooncalves must have been driven in to the interior again — I could see none of them. I became more and more desirous of seeing Cavor. The winged outline of the sun had sunk now until it was scarcely the distance of its diameter from the rim of the sky. I was oppressed by the idea that the Selenites would presently close their lids and valves and shut us out under the inexorable onrush of the lunar night. It seemed to me high time that he abandoned his search and that we took counsel together. I

felt how urgent it was that we should decide soon as to our course. We had failed to find the sphere, we no longer had time to seek it. Once these valves were closed, with us outside, we were lost men. The great night of space would descend upon us, that blackness of the void which is the only absolute death. All my being shrank from that approach. We must get into the moon again, though we were slain in doing it. I was haunted by a vision of our freezing to death, of our hammering with our last strength on the valve of the great pit.

I took no thought any more of the sphere. I thought only of finding Cavor again. I was half inclined to go back into the moon without him rather than seek him until it was too late. I was already halfway towards our handkerchief, when suddenly—

I saw the sphere!

I did not find it so much as it found me. It was lying much farther to the westward than I had gone and the sloping rays of the sinking sun reflected from its glass had suddenly proclaimed its presence in a dazzling beam. For an instant I thought this was some new device of the Selenites against us, and then I understood.

I threw up my arms, shouted a ghostly shout and set off in vast leaps towards it. I missed one of my leaps and dropped into a deep ravine and twisted my ankle and after that I stumbled at almost every leap. I was in a state of hysterical agitation, trembling violently and quite breathless long before I got to it. Three times at least I had to stop with my hands resting on my sides, and in spite of the thin dryness of the air the perspiration was wet upon my face.

I thought of nothing but the sphere until I reached it. I forgot even my trouble of Cavor's whereabouts. My last leap flung me with my hands hard against its glass; then I lay against it panting and trying to shout, "Cavor! Here is the sphere!" When I recovered a little I peered through the thick glass and the things inside seemed tumbled. I stooped to peer closer. Then I attempted to get in. I had to hoist it over a little to get my head through the manhole. The screw stopper was inside and I could see now that nothing had been touched, nothing had suffered. It lay there as we had left it when we had dropped out amidst the snow. For a time I was wholly occupied in making· and remaking this inventory. I found I was trembling violently. It was good to see that familiar dark interior again! I cannot tell you how good. Presently I crept inside and sat down among the things. I looked through the glass at the moon world and shivered. I placed up my gold clubs upon the bale and sought out and took a little food, not so much because I wanted it but because it was there. Then it occurred to me that it was time to go out and signal for Cavor. But I did not go out and signal for Cavor forthwith. Something held me to the sphere.

After all, everything was coming right. There would still be time for us to get more of the magic stone that gives one mastery over men. There was gold for the picking up, and the sphere would travel as well half full of gold as though it were empty. We could go back now masters of ourselves and our world, and then —

I roused myself at last and with an effort got myself out of the sphere. I shivered as I emerged, for the evening air was growing very cold. I stood in the hollow, staring about me. I scrutinised the bushes round me very carefully before I leaped to the rocky shelf hard by and took once more what had been my first leap in the moon. But this time I made it with no effort whatever.

The growth and decay of the vegetation had gone on apace and the whole aspect of the rocks had changed, but still it was possible to make out the slope on which the seeds had germinated and the rocky mass from which we had taken our first view of the crater. But the spiky shrub on the slope stood brown and sere now and thirty feet high, and cast long shadows that stretched out of sight; and the little seeds that clustered in its upper branches were brown and ripe. Its work was done, it was brittle and ready to fall and crumple under the freezing air, so soon as the nightfall came. And the huge cacti that had swollen as we watched them had long since burst and scattered their spores to the four quarters of the moon.

Amazing little corner in the universe — the landing place of men!

Some day, thought I, I will have an inscription standing there right in the midst of the hollow. It came to me if only this teeming world within could know of the full import of that moment how curious its tumult would become!

But as yet it could scarcely be dreaming of the significance of our coming. For if it did the crater would surely be an uproar of pursuit. I looked about for some place from which I might signal to Cavor, and saw that same patch of rock to which he had leaped from my present standpoint still bare and barren in the sun. For a moment I hesitated at going so far from the sphere. Then with a pang of shame at that hesitation I leaped. . . .

From this vantage point I surveyed the crater again. Far away at the top of the enormous shadow I cast was the little white handkerchief fluttering on the bushes. It was very little and very far. Cavor was not in sight. It seemed to me that by this time he ought to be looking for me. That was the agreement. But he was nowhere to be seen.

I stood waiting and watching, hands shading my eyes, expecting every moment to distinguish him. Very probably I stood there for a long time. I tried to shout and was reminded of the thinness of the air. I made an undecided step back towards the sphere. But a lurking dread of the Selenites made me hesitate to signal my whereabouts by hoisting one of

our sleeping blankets on to the adjacent scrub. My eyes searched the crater again.

It had an effect of emptiness that chilled me. All sound of the Selenites in the world beneath had died away. It was as still as death. Save for the faint stir of the shrub about me in the little breeze that was rising, there was no sound, no shadow of a sound. And the breeze blew chill.

Confound Cavor!

I took a deep breath. I put my hands to the sides of my mouth. "Cavor!" I bawled and the sound was like some mannikin shouting far away.

I looked at the handkerchief, I looked behind me at the broadening shadows of the westward cliff, I looked under my hand at the sun. It seemed to me that almost visibly it was creeping down the sky.

I felt I must act instantly if I was to save Cavor. I whipped off my vest and flung it as a mark on the sere bayonets of the shrubs behind me, and then set off in a straight line towards the handkerchief. Perhaps it was a couple of miles away — a matter of a few hundred leaps and strides. I have already told how one seemed to hang through those lunar leaps. In each suspense I sought Cavor and marvelled why he should be hidden. In each leap I could feel the sun setting behind me. Each time I touched the ground I was tempted to go back.

A last leap and I was in the depression below our handkerchief, a stride and I stood on our former vantage point within arm's reach of it. I stood up straight and scanned the world about me, between its lengthening bars of shadow. Far away, down a long declivity, was the opening of the tunnel up which we had fled, and my shadow reached towards it, reached towards it and touched it like a finger of the night.

Not a sign of Cavor, not a sound in all the stillness, only that the stir and waving of the scrub and of the shadows increased. And suddenly and violently I shivered. "Cav'—" I began and realised once more the uselessness of the human voice in that thin air.

Silence. The silence of death.

Then it was my eye caught something — a little thing, lying perhaps fifty yards away down the slope, amidst a litter of bent and broken branches. What was it? I knew, and yet for some reason I would not know.

I went nearer to it. It was the little cricket cap Cavor had worn. I did not touch it. I stood looking at it.

I saw then that the scattered branches about it had been forcibly smashed and trampled. I hesitated, stepped forward and picked it up.

I stood with Cavor's cap in my hand, staring at the trampled reeds and thorns about me. On some of them were little smears of something dark, something that I dared not touch. A dozen yards away, perhaps, the rising breeze dragged something into view, something small and vividly white.

It was a little piece of paper crumpled as though it had been

clutched tightly. I picked it up, and on it were smears of red. My eye caught faint pencil marks. I smoothed it out and saw uneven and broken writing ending at last in a crooked streak upon the paper.

I set myself to decipher this.

"I have been injured about the knee, I think my kneecap is hurt, and I cannot run or crawl," it began — pretty distinctly written.

Then less legibly: "They have been chasing me for some time and it is only a question of" — the word "time" seemed to have been written here and erased in favour of something illegible — "before they get me. They are beating all about me."

Then the writing became convulsive. "I can hear them," I guessed the tracing meant; and then it was quite unreadable for a space. Then came a little string of words that were quite distinct, "a different sort of Selenite altogether, who appear to be directing the —" The writing became a mere hasty confusion again.

"They have larger brain cases — much larger, and slender bodies and very short legs. They make gentle noises and move with organised deliberation. . . .

"And though I am wounded and helpless here, their appearance still gives me hope." That was like Cavor. "They have not shot at me or attempted — injury. I intend —"

Then came the sudden streak of the pencil across the paper, and on the back and edges — blood!

And as I stood there, stupid and perplexed, with this dumbfounding relic in my hand, something very, very soft and light and chill touched my hand for a moment and ceased to be, and then a thing, a little white speck drifted athwart a shadow. It was a tiny snowflake, the first snowflake, the herald of the night.

I looked up with a start and the sky had darkened now almost to blackness and was thick with a gathering multitude of coldly watchful stars. I looked eastward, and the light of that shrivelled world was touched with a sombre bronze, westward, and the sun — robbed now by a thickening white mist of half its heat and splendour — was touching the crater rim, was sinking out of sight and all the shrubs and jagged and tumbled rocks stood out against it in a bristling disorder of black shapes. Into the great lake of darkness westward, a vast wreath of mist was sinking. A cold wind set all the crater shivering. Suddenly for a moment I was in a puff of falling snow and all the world about me grey and dim.

And then it was I heard, not loud and penetrating as at first, but faint and dim like a dying voice, that tolling, that same tolling that had welcomed the coming of the day: Boom. . . . Boom. . . . Boom. . . .

It went about the crater; it seemed to throb with the throbbing of the greater stars: the blood-red crescent of the sun's disc sank as it tolled out: Boom. . . . Boom. . . . Boom. . . .

What had happened to Cavor? All through that tolling I stood

there stupidly, and at last the tolling ceased. And suddenly the open mouth of the tunnel down below there shut like an eye and vanished out of sight.

Then indeed was I alone.

Over me, about me, closing in on me, embracing me ever nearer, was the Eternal, that which was before the beginning and that which triumphs over the end; that enormous void in which all light and life and being is but the thin and vanishing splendour of a falling star, the cold, the stillness, the silence — the infinite and final Night of space.

The sense of solitude and desolation became the sense of an overwhelming Presence, that stooped towards me, that almost touched me.

"No," I cried, "no! Not yet! not yet! Wait. Wait! Oh wait!" My voice went up to a faint shriek. I flung the crumpled paper from me, scrambled back to the crest to take my bearings, and then, with all the will that was in me, leaped out towards the mark I had left, dim and distant now in the very margin of the shadow.

Leap, leap, leap, and each leap was seven ages.

Before me the pale serpent-girdled sector of the sun sank and sank and the advancing shadow swept to seize the sphere before I could reach it. I was two miles away — a hundred leaps or more — and the air about me was thinning out as it thins under an air pump, and the cold was gripping at my joints. But had I died, I should have died leaping. Once, and then again my foot slipped on the gathering snow and short-

ened my leap; once I fell short into bushes that crashed and smashed into dusty chips and nothingness, and once I stumbled as I dropped and rolled head over heels into a gully and rose bruised and bleeding and confused as to my direction.

But such incidents were as nothing to the intervals, those awful pauses when one drifted through the air towards that pouring tide of night. My breathing made a piping noise, and it was as though knives were whirling in my lungs. My heart seemed to beat against the top of my brain. "Shall I reach it? Oh Heaven! shall I reach it?"

My whole being became anguish.

"Lie down," screamed my pain and despair, "lie down."

The nearer I struggled, the more impossibly remote it seemed. I was numb, I stumbled, I bruised and cut myself and did not bleed.

It was in sight.

I fell on all fours and my lungs whooped.

I crawled. The frost gathered on my lips, icicles hung from my moustache and beard, I was white with the freezing atmosphere.

I was a dozen yards from it. My eyes had become dim. "Lie down," screamed despair, "lie down!"

I touched it and halted. "Too late!" screamed despair, "lie down!"

I fought stiffly with it. I was on the manhole lip, a stupefied, half dead being. The snow was all about me. I pulled myself in. There lurked within a little warmer air. The snowflakes — the airflakes — danced in about me,

as I tried with chilling hands to thrust the valve in and spin it tight and hard. I sobbed, "I *will*." I chattered on my teeth. And then with fingers that quivered and felt brittle I turned to the shutter studs.

As I fumbled with the switches — for I had never controlled them before — I could see dimly through the steaming glass, the blazing red streamers of the sinking sun, dancing and flickering through the snowstorm and the black forms of the scrub thickening and bending and breaking beneath the accumulating snow. Thicker whirled the snow and thicker, black against the light. What if even now the switches overcame me?

Then something clicked under my hands and in an instant that last vision of the moon world was hidden from my eyes. I was in the silence and darkness of the inter-planetary sphere.

CHAPTER 19

MR. BEDFORD IN
INFINITE SPACE

It was almost as though I had been killed. Indeed I could imagine a man suddenly and violently killed would feel very much as I did. One moment, a passion of agonising existence and fear; the next, darkness and stillness, neither light nor life nor sun, moon nor stars, the black Infinite. Although the thing was done by my own act, although I had already tasted this very effect in Cavor's company, I felt astonished, dumbfounded and overwhelmed. I seemed to be borne upwards into an enormous darkness. My fingers floated off the studs, I hung as if I were annihilated, and at last very softly and gently I came against the bale and the golden chain and the crowbars that had drifted to the middle of the sphere.

I do not know how long that drifting took. In the sphere, of course, even more than on the moon one's earthly time-sense was ineffectual. At the touch of the bale it was as if I had awakened from a dreamless sleep. I immediately perceived that if I wanted to keep awake and alive I must get a light or open a window so as to get a grip of something with my eyes. And besides I was cold. I kicked off from the bale therefore, clawed on to the thin cords within the glass, crawled along until I got to the manhole rim, and so got my bearings for the light and blind studs, took a shove off, and flying once round the bale and getting a scare from something big and flimsy that was drifting loose, I got my hand on the cord quite close to the studs and reached them. I lit the little lamp first of all to see what it was I had collided with, and discovered that old copy of *Lloyd's News* had slipped its moorings, and was adrift in the void. That brought

me out of the Infinite to my own proper dimensions again. It made me laugh and pant for a time and suggested the idea of a little oxygen from one of the cylinders. After that I lit the heater until I felt warm and then I took food. Finally I set to work in a very gingerly fashion on the Cavorite blinds to see if I could guess by any means how the sphere was travelling.

The first blind I opened I shut at once, and hung for a time flattened and blinded by the sunlight that had hit me. After thinking a little I started upon the windows at right angles to this one, and got the huge crescent moon and the second time the little crescent earth behind it. I was amazed to find how far I was from the moon. I had reckoned that not only should I have little or none of the "kick-off" that the earth's atmosphere had given us at our start, but that the tangential "fly-off" of the moon's spin would be at least twenty-eight times less than the earth's. I had expected to discover myself hanging over our crater and on the edge of the night, but all that was now only a part of the outline of the white crescent that filled the sky. And Cavor—?

He was already infinitesimal.

I tried to imagine what could have happened to him. But at that time I could think of nothing but death. I seemed to see him bent and smashed at the foot of some interminably high cascade of blue. And all about him the stupid insects stared. . . .

Under the inspiring touch of the drifting newspaper I became very practical again for a while.

It was quite clear to me that what I had to do was to get back to earth, but as far as I could see I was drifting away from it. Whatever had happened to Cavor, even if he was still alive, which seemed to me incredible after that bloodstained scrap, I was powerless to help him. There he was, living or dead behind the mantle of that rayless night, and there he must remain at least until I could summon our fellow-men to his assistance. Should I do that? Something of the sort I had in my mind; to come back to earth, if it were possible, and then as maturer consideration might determine, either to show and explain the sphere to a few discreet persons and act with them, or else to keep my secret, sell my gold, obtain weapons, provisions and an assistant, and return with these advantages to deal on equal terms with the flimsy people of the moon; to rescue Cavor if that were still possible, and at any rate to procure a sufficient supply of gold to place my subsequent proceedings on a firmer basis.

But that was hoping far; I had first to get back. I set myself to decide just exactly how the return to earth could be contrived. As I struggled with that problem I ceased to worry about what I should do when I got there. My only care was to get back.

I puzzled out at last that my best chance would be to drop back towards the moon as near as I dared in order to gather velocity, then to shut my windows and fly behind it, and when I was past to open my earthward windows and so get off at a good pace

homeward. But whether I should ever reach the earth by that device or whether I might simply find myself spinning about it in some hyperbolic or parabolic curve or other, I could not tell. Later I had a happy inspiration, and by opening certain windows to the moon, which had appeared in the sky in front of the earth, I turned my course aside so as to head off the earth, behind which without some such expedient it had become evident to me I must pass. I did a very great deal of complicated thinking over these problems — for I am no mathematician — and in the end I am certain it was much more my good luck than my reasoning that enabled me to hit the earth. Had I known then, as I know now, the mathematical chances that were against me, I doubt if I should have troubled even to touch the studs to make any attempt. And having puzzled out what I considered the thing to do, I opened all my moonward windows, and squatted down — the effort lifted me for a time some foot or so into the air and I hung there in the oddest way — and waited for the crescent to get bigger and bigger until I felt I was near enough for safety. Then I would shut the windows, fly past the moon with the velocity I had got from it — if I did not smash upon it — and so go on towards the earth.

And that is what I did.

At last I felt my moonward start was sufficient. I shut out the sight of the moon from my eyes, and in a state of mind that was, I now recall, incredibly free from anxiety or any distressful quality, I sat down to begin a vigil in that little speck of matter in infinite space that would last until I should strike the earth. The heater had made the sphere tolerably warm, the air had been refreshed by the oxygen, and except for that faint congestion of the head that was always with me while I was away from earth, I felt entire physical comfort. I had extinguished the light again lest it should fail me in the end; I was in darkness save for the earthshine and the glitter of the stars below me. Everything was so absolutely silent and still that I might indeed have been the only being in the universe, and yet, strangely enough, I had no more feeling of loneliness or fear than if I had been lying in bed on earth. Now this seems all the stranger to me since during my last hours in the crater of the moon the sense of my utter loneliness had been an agony. . . .

Incredible as it will seem, this interval of time that I spent in space has no sort of proportion to any other interval of time in my life. Sometimes it seemed as though I sat through immeasurable eternities like some god upon a lotus leaf, and again as though there was a momentary pause as I journeyed from moon to earth. In truth, it was altogether some weeks of earthly time. But I had done with care and anxiety, hunger or fear, for that space. I floated, thinking with a strange breadth and freedom of all that we had undergone and of all my life and motives and the secret issues of my being. I seemed to myself to have grown greater and greater, to have lost all sense of movement,

to be floating amidst the stars; and always the sense of earth's littleness and the infinite littleness of my life upon it, was in my thoughts.

I can't profess to explain what happened in my mind. No doubt it could all be traced directly or indirectly to the curious physical conditions under which I was living. I set it down here just for what it is worth and without any comment. The most prominent quality of it was a pervading doubt of my own identity. I became, if I may so express it, dissociate from Bedford, I looked down on Bedford as a trivial incidental thing with which I chanced to be connected, I saw Bedford in many relations — as an ass or as a poor beast where I had hitherto been inclined to regard him with a quiet pride as a very spirited and rather forcible person. I saw him not only as an ass, but as the son of many generations of asses. I reviewed his schooldays and his early manhood and his first encounter with love very much as one might review the proceedings of an ant in the sand. . . . I regret that something of that period of lucidity still hangs about me, and I doubt if I shall ever recover the full-blooded self-satisfaction of my early days. But at the time, the thing was not in the least painful, because I had that extraordinary persuasion that as a matter of fact I was no more Bedford than I was anyone else, but only a mind floating in the still serenity of space. Why should I be disturbed about this Bedford's shortcomings? I was not responsible for him or them.

For a time I struggled against this really very grotesque delusion. I tried to summon the memory of vivid moments, of tender or intense emotions to my assistance; I felt that if I could recall one genuine twinge of feeling the growing rupture would be stopped. But I could not do it. I saw Bedford rushing down Chancery Lane, hat on the back of his head, coat tails flying out, *en route* for his public examination. I saw him dodging and bumping against and even saluting other similar little creatures in that swarming gutter of people. Me? I saw Bedford that same evening in the sitting-room of a certain lady, and his hat was on the table beside him and it badly wanted brushing and he was in tears. Me? I saw him with that lady in various attitudes and emotions — I never felt so detached before. . . . I saw him hurrying off to Lympne to write a play, and accosting Cavor, and in his shirt sleeves working at the sphere, and walking out to Canterbury because he was afraid to come. Me? I did not believe it.

I still reasoned that all this was hallucination due to my solitude and the fact that I had lost all weight and sense of resistance. I had endeavoured to recover that sense by hanging myself about the sphere, by pinching my hands and clasping them together. Among other things I lit the light, captured that torn copy of *Lloyd's* and read those convincingly realistic advertisements again, about the Cutaway bicycle, and the gentleman of private means and the lady in distress who was selling those

"forks and spoons." There was no doubt *they* existed surely enough, and, said I: "This is your world, and you are Bedford and you are going back to live among things like that for all the rest of your life." But the doubts within me could still argue: "It is not you that is reading, it is Bedford — but *you are not Bedford,* you know. That's just where the mistake comes in."

"Confound it!" I cried, "and if I am not Bedford, what *am* I?"

But in that direction no light was forthcoming, though the strangest fancies came drifting into my brain, queer remote suspicions like shadows seen from far away. . . . Do you know I had an idea that really I was something quite outside not only the world, but all worlds, and out of space and time, and that this poor Bedford was just a peephole through which I looked at life. . . .

Bedford! However I disavowed him, there I was most certainly bound up with him, and I knew that wherever and whatever I might be I must needs feel the stress of his desires and sympathise with all his joys and sorrows until his life should end. And with the dying of Bedford — what then? . . .

Enough of this remarkable phase of my experiences. I tell it here simply to show how one's isolation and departure from this planet touched not only the functions and feeling of every organ of the body but indeed also the very fabric of the mind with strange and unanticipated disturbances. All through the major portion of that vast space-journey I hung thinking of such immaterial things, hung dissociated and apathetic, a cloudy megalomaniac as it were, amidst the stars and planets in the void of space, and not only the world to which I was returning, but the blue-lit caverns of the Selenites, their helmet faces, their gigantic and wonderful machines, and the fate of Cavor, dragged helpless into that world, were facts infinitely minute and altogether trivial.

Until at last I began to feel the pull of the earth upon my being, drawing me back again to the life that is real for men. And then indeed it grew clearer and clearer to me that I was quite certainly Bedford after all, and returning after amazing adventures to this world of ours, and with a life that I was very likely to lose in this return. I set myself to puzzle out the conditions under which I must fall to earth.

CHAPTER 20

MR. BEDFORD AT LITTLESTONE

My line of flight was about parallel with the surface as I came into the upper air. The temperature of the sphere began to rise forthwith. I knew it behoved me to

drop at once. Far below me in a darkling twilight stretched a great expanse of sea. I opened every window I could and fell — out of sunshine into evening and out of evening into night. Vaster grew the earth and vaster, swallowing up the stars, and the silvery translucent starlit veil of cloud it wore spread out to catch me. At last the world seemed no longer a sphere, but flat, and then concave. It was no longer a planet in the sky, but the world of Man. I shut all but an inch or so of earthward window and dropped with a slackening velocity. The broadening water, now so near that I could see the dark glitter of the waves, rushed up to meet me. I snapped the last strip of window and sat scowling and biting my knuckles waiting for the impact. . . .

The sphere hit the water with a huge splash: it must have sent it fathoms high. At the splash I flung the Cavorite shutters open. Down I went, but slower and slower, and then I felt the sphere pressing against my feet and so drove up again as a bubble drives. And at the last I was floating and rocking upon the surface of the sea and my journey in space was at an end.

The night was dark and overcast. Two yellow pin-points far away showed the passing of a ship, and nearer was a red glare that came and went. Had not the electricity of my glow lamp exhausted itself, I could have got picked up that night. In spite of the inordinate fatigue I was beginning to feel, I was excited now and for a time hopeful in a feverish, impatient way that so my travelling might end.

But at last I ceased to move about, and sat, wrists on knees, staring at a distant red light. It swayed up and down, rocking, rocking. My excitement passed. I realised I had yet to spend at least another night in the sphere. I perceived myself infinitely heavy and fatigued. And so I fell asleep.

A change in my rhythmic motion awakened me. I peered through the refracting glass and saw that I had come aground upon a huge shallow of sand. Far away I saw houses and trees, and seaward a curved vague distortion of a ship hung between sea and sky.

I stood up and staggered. My one desire was to emerge. The manhole was upward and I wrestled with the screw. Slowly I opened the manhole. At last the air was singing in again as once it had sung out. But this time I did not wait until the pressure was adjusted. In another moment I had the weight of the window on my hands and it was open, wide open, to the old familiar sky of earth.

The air hit me on the chest so that I gasped. I dropped the glass screw. I cried out, put my hands to my chest and sat down. For a time I was in pain. Then I took deep breaths. At last I could rise and move about again.

I tried to thrust my head through the manhole, and the sphere rolled over. It was as though something had lugged my head down as it emerged. I ducked back sharply or I should

have been pinned face under water. After some wriggling and shoving I managed to crawl out upon sand, over which the retreating waves still came and went.

I did not attempt to stand up. It seemed to me that my body must be suddenly changed to lead. Mother Earth had her grip on me now — no Cavorite intervening. I sat down heedless of the water that came over my feet.

It was dawn, a grey dawn, rather overcast but showing here and there a long patch of greenish grey. Some way out a ship was lying at anchor, a pale silhouette of a ship with one yellow light. The water came rippling in in long shallow waves. Away to the right curved the land, a shingle bank with little hovels, and at last a lighthouse, a sailing mark and a point. Inland stretched a space of level sand, broken here and there by pools of water and ending a mile away perhaps in a low shore of scrub. To the north-east some isolated watering-place was visible; a row of gaunt lodging houses, the tallest objects that I could see on earth, dull dabs against the brightening sky. What strange men can have reared these vertical piles in such an amplitude of space I do not know. There they are like pieces of Brighton lost in the waste.

For a long time I sat there, yawning and rubbing my face. At last I struggled to rise. It made me feel that I was lifting a weight. I stood up.

I stared at the distant houses. For the first time since our starvation in the crater I thought of earthly food. " Bacon," I whispered, " eggs. Good toast and good coffee. . . . And how the devil am I going to get all this stuff to Lympne? " I wondered where I was. It was an east shore, anyhow, and I had seen Europe before I dropped.

I heard footsteps crunching in the sand and a little round-faced friendly looking man in flannels, with a bathing towel wrapped about his shoulders and his bathing dress over his arm, appeared up the beach. I knew instantly that I must be in England. He was staring most intently at the sphere and me. He advanced, staring. I dare say I looked a ferocious savage enough — dirty, unkempt to an indescribable degree, but it did not occur to me at the time. He stopped at a distance of twenty yards. " Hul-lo, my man! " he said doubtfully.

" Hullo yourself! " said I.

He advanced reassured by that. " What on earth is that thing? " he asked.

" Can you tell me where I am? " I asked.

" That's Littlestone," he said, pointing to the houses; " and that's Dungeness! Have you just landed? What's that thing you've got? Some sort of machine? "

" Yes."

" Have you floated ashore? Have you been wrecked or something? What is it? "

I meditated swiftly. I made an estimate of the little man's appearance as he drew nearer. " By Jove! " he said, " you've had a time of it! I thought you — Well — Where were you cast away? Is

that a sort of floating thing for saving life?"

I decided to take that line for the present. I made a few vague affirmatives. "I want help," I said hoarsely. "I want to get some stuff up the beach — stuff I can't very well leave about." I became aware of three other pleasant looking young men with towels, blazers and straw hats coming down the sand towards me. Evidently the early bathing section of this Littlestone.

"Help!" said the young man; "rather!" He became vaguely active. "What particularly do you want done?" He turned round and gesticulated. The three young men accelerated their pace. In a minute they were about me plying me with questions I was disinclined to answer. "I'll tell all that later," I said. "I'm dead beat. I'm a rag."

"Come up to the hotel," said the foremost little man. "We'll look after that thing there."

I hesitated. "I can't," I said. "In that sphere there's two big bars of gold."

They looked incredulously at one another, then at me with a new inquiry. I went to the sphere, stooped, crept in and presently they had the Selenites' crowbars and the broken chain before them. If I had not been so horribly fagged I could have laughed at them. It was like kittens round a beetle. They didn't know what to do with the stuff. The fat little man stooped and lifted the end of one of the bars and then dropped it with a grunt. Then they all did.

"It's lead or gold!" said one.

"Oh, it's gold!" said another.
"Gold right enough," said the third.

Then they all stared at me and then they all stared at the ship lying at anchor.

"I say!" cried the little man. "But where did you get that?"

I was too tired to keep up a lie. "I got it in the moon."

I saw them stare at one another.

"Look here!" said I, "I'm not going to argue now. Help me carry these lumps of gold up to the hotel — I guess with rests two of you can manage one and I'll trail this chain thing — and I'll tell you more when I've had some food."

"And how about that thing?"

"It won't hurt there," I said. "Anyhow — confound it! — it must stop there now. If the tide comes up, it will float all right."

And in a state of enormous wonderment these young men most obediently hoisted my treasures on their shoulders, and with limbs that felt like lead I headed a procession towards that distant fragment of "sea-front." Halfway there we were reinforced by two awe-stricken little girls with spades, and later appeared a lean little boy with a penetrating sniff. He was, I remember, wheeling a bicycle and he accompanied us at a distance of about a hundred yards on our right flank and then I suppose gave us up as uninteresting, mounted his bicycle and rode off over the level sands in the direction of the sphere.

I glanced back after him.

"He won't touch it," said the stout young man reassuringly,

and I was only too willing to be reassured.

At first something of the grey of the morning was in my mind, but presently the sun disengaged itself from the level clouds of the horizon and lit the world and turned the leaden sea to glittering waters. My spirits rose. A sense of the vast importance of the things I had done and had yet to do came with the sunlight into my mind. I laughed aloud as the foremost man staggered under my gold. When indeed I took my place in the world, how amazed the world would be!

If it had not been for my inordinate fatigue the landlord of the Littlestone hotel would have been amusing as he hesitated between my gold and my respectable company on one hand and my filthy appearance on the other. But at last I found myself in a terrestrial bathroom once more; had warm water to wash myself with and a change of raiment, preposterously small indeed, but clean, that the genial little man had lent me. He lent me a razor, too, but I could not screw up my resolution to attack even the outposts of the bristling beard that covered my face.

I sat down to an English breakfast and ate with a sort of languid appetite, an appetite many weeks old and very decrepit, and stirred myself to answer the questions of the four young men. And I told them the truth.

" Well," said I, " as you press me — I got it in the moon."

" The moon? "

" Yes, the moon in the sky."

" But how do you mean? "

" What I say, confound it! "

" That you have just come from the moon? "

" Exactly! through space — in that ball." And I took a delicious mouthful of egg. I made a private note that when I went back to the moon I would take a box of eggs.

I could see clearly that they did not believe one word of what I told them, but evidently they considered me the most respectable liar they had ever met. They glanced at one another and then concentrated the fire of their eyes on me. I fancy they expected a clue to me in the way I helped myself to salt. They seemed to find something significant in my peppering my egg. Those strangely shaped masses of gold they had staggered under held their minds. There the lumps lay in front of me, each worth thousands of pounds and as impossible for anyone to steal as a house or a piece of land. As I looked at their curious faces over my coffee cup I realised something of the enormous wilderness of explanations into which I should have to wander to render myself comprehensible again.

" You don't really mean," began the youngest young man in the tone of one who speaks to an obstinate child.

" Just pass me that toast rack," I said, and shut him up completely.

" But look here, I say," began one of the others. " We're not going to believe that, you know."

" Ah, well," said I, and shrugged my shoulders.

" He doesn't want to tell us,"

said the youngest young man in a stage voice aside, and then with an appearance of great *sang-froid:* "You don't mind if I have a cigarette?"

I waved him a cordial assent, and proceeded with my breakfast. Two of the others went and looked out of the farther window and talked audibly. I was struck by a thought. "The tide," I said, "is running out?"

There was a pause as to who should answer me. "It's near the ebb," said the fat little man.

"Well, anyhow," I said, "it won't float far."

I decapitated my third egg and began a little speech. "Look here," I said. "Please don't imagine I'm surly or telling you uncivil lies or anything of that sort. I'm forced almost to be a little short and mysterious. I can quite understand this is as queer as it can be and that your imaginations must be going it. I can assure you, you're in at a memorable time. But I can't make it clear to you now — it's impossible. I give you my word of honour I've come from the moon, and that's all I can tell you. . . . All the same I'm tremendously obliged to you, you know, tremendously. I hope that my manner hasn't in any way given you offence."

"Oh no, not in the least!" said the youngest young man affably. "We can quite understand," and staring hard at me all the time he heeled his chair back until it very nearly upset, and recovered with some exertion. "Not a bit of it," said the fat young man. "Don't you imagine that!" and they all got up and dispersed and walked about and lit cigarettes and generally tried to show they were perfectly amiable and disengaged and entirely free from the slightest curiosity about me and the sphere. "I'm going to keep an eye on that ship out there all the same," I heard one of them remarking in an undertone. If only they could have forced themselves to it they would, I believe, even have gone out and left me. I went on with my third egg.

"The weather," the fat little man remarked presently, "has been immense, has it not? I don't know when we have had such a summer. . . ."

Phoo-whizz! Like a tremendous rocket!

And somewhere a window was broken. . . .

"What's that?" said I.

"It isn't — ?" cried the little man and rushed to the corner window.

All the others rushed to the window likewise. I sat staring at them.

Suddenly I leaped up, knocked over my third egg, and rushed for the window also. I had just thought of something. "Nothing to be seen there," cried the little man, rushing for the door.

"It's that boy!" I cried, bawling in hoarse fury; "it's that accursed boy!" and turning about I pushed the waiter aside — he was just bringing me some more toast — and rushed violently out of the room and down and out upon the queer little esplanade in front of the hotel.

The sea, which had been smooth, was rough now with hurrying cats'-paws, and all about where the sphere had been was tumbled water like the wake of a ship. Above, a little puff of cloud whirled like dispersing smoke, and the three or four people on the beach were staring up with interrogative faces towards the point of that unexpected report. And that was all! Boots and waiter and the four young men in blazers came rushing out behind me. Shouts came from windows and doors and all sorts of worrying people came into sight — agape.

For a time I stood there too overwhelmed by this new development to think of the people. At first I was too stunned to see the thing as any definite disaster — I was just stunned as a man is by some accidental violent blow. It is only afterwards he begins to appreciate his specific injury.

" Good Lord! "

I felt as though somebody was pouring funk out of a can down the back of my neck. My legs became feeble. I had got the first intimation of what the disaster meant for me. There was that confounded boy — sky high! I was utterly " left." There was the gold in the coffee room, my only possession on earth. How would it all work out? The general effect was of a gigantic unmanageable confusion.

" I say," said the voice of the little man behind, " I say, you know."

I wheeled about and there were twenty or thirty people all bombarding me with dumb interrogation, with infinite doubt and suspicion. I felt the compulsion of their eyes intolerably. I groaned aloud.

" I *can't*," I shouted, " I tell you I can't! I'm not equal to it! You must puzzle and — and be damned to you! "

I gesticulated convulsively. He receded a step as though I had threatened him. I made a bolt through them into the hotel. I charged back into the coffee-room, rang the bell furiously. I gripped the waiter as he entered. " D'y hear? " I shouted. " Get help and carry these bars up to my room right away."

He failed to understand me and I shouted and raved at him. A scared looking little old man in a green apron appeared and two of the young men in flannels. I made a dash at them and commandeered their services. As soon as the gold was in my room I felt free to quarrel. " Now get out," I shouted; " all o' you get out if you don't want to see a man go mad before your eyes! " And I helped the waiter by the shoulder as he hesitated in the doorway. And then as soon as I had the door locked on them all I tore off the little man's clothes again, shied them right and left, and got into bed forthwith. And there I lay swearing and panting and cooling for a long time.

At last I was calm enough to get out of bed and ring up the round-eyed waiter for a flannel night-shirt, a soda and whisky and some good cigars. And these things being procured after an exasperating delay that drove me several times to the bell, I locked

the door again and proceeded very deliberately to look the entire situation in the face.

The net result of the great experiment presented itself as an absolute failure. It was a rout and I was the sole survivor. It was an absolute collapse and this was the final disaster. There was nothing for it but to save myself, and as much as I could in the way of prospects from our *débacle*. At one fatal crowning blow all my vague resolutions of return and recovery had vanished. My intention of going back to the moon, of getting a sphereful of gold and afterwards of having a fragment of Cavorite analysed and so recovering the great secret, perhaps finally even of recovering Cavor's body, all these ideas vanished altogether.

I was the sole survivor, and that was all.

I think that going to bed was one of the luckiest ideas I have ever had in an emergency. I really believe I should either have got looseheaded or done some fatal, indiscreet thing. But there, locked in and secure from all interruption I could think out the position in all its bearings and make my arrangements at leisure.

Of course what had happened to the boy was quite clear to me. He had crawled into the sphere, meddled with the studs, shut the Cavorite windows and gone up. It was highly improbable he had screwed in the manhole stopper, and even if he had the chances were a thousand to one against his getting back. It was fairly evi-dent that he would gravitate with my bales to somewhere near the middle of the sphere and remain there and so cease to be a legitimate terrestrial interest, however remarkable he might seem to the inhabitants of some remote quarter of space. I very speedily convinced myself on that point. And as for any responsibility I might have in the matter, the more I reflected the clearer it became that if only I kept quiet, I need not trouble myself about that. If I was faced by sorrowing parents demanding their lost boy, I had merely to demand my lost sphere — or ask them what they meant. At first I had had a vision of weeping parents and guardians and all sorts of complications, but now I saw that I simply had to keep my mouth shut and nothing in that way could arise. And indeed the more I lay and smoked and thought the more evident became the wisdom of impenetrability.

It is within the right of every British citizen, provided he does not commit damage nor indecorum, to appear suddenly wherever he pleases and as ragged and filthy as he pleases, and with whatever amount of virgin gold he sees fit to encumber himself, and no one has any right at all to hinder and detain him in this procedure. I formulated that at last to myself and repeated it over as a sort of private Magna Charta of my liberty.

Once I had put that issue on one side I could take up and consider in an equable manner certain considerations I had scarcely dared think of before, namely,

those arising out of the circumstances of my bankruptcy. But now looking at this matter calmly and at leisure, I could see that if only I suppressed my identity by a temporary assumption of some less well-known name, and retained my two months' beard, the risks of any annoyance from the spiteful creditors to whom I have already alluded became very small indeed. From that to a definite course of rational worldly action was plain sailing. It was all amazingly petty, no doubt, but what was there remaining for me to do? Whatever I did I was resolved that I would keep myself level and right side up.

I ordered up writing materials and addressed a letter to the new Romney bank — the nearest, the waiter informed me — telling the manager I wished to open an account with him and requesting him to send two trustworthy persons properly authenticated in a cab with a good horse to fetch some hundredweight of gold with which I happened to be encumbered. I signed the letter " Wells," which seemed to me to be a thoroughly respectable sort of name. This done, I got a Folkstone blue book, chose an outfitter, and asked him to send a cutter to measure me for a drab tweed suit, ordering at the same time a valise, dressing bag, brown boots, shirt, hats (to fit), and so forth, and from a watchmaker I also ordered a watch. And these letters being despatched, I had up as good a lunch as the hotel could give, and then lay smoking a cigar, as calm as possible until

in accordance with my instructions two duly authenticated clerks came from the bank and weighed and took away my gold. After that I pulled the clothes over my ears in order to drown any knocking and went very comfortably to sleep.

I went to sleep. No doubt it was a prosaic thing for the first man back from the moon to do, and I can imagine that the young and imaginative reader will find my behaviour disappointing. But I was horribly fatigued and bothered, and, confound it! what else was there to do? There certainly was not the remotest chance of my being believed, if I had told my story then, and it would certainly have subjected me to intolerable annoyances. I went to sleep. When at last I awoke I was ready to face the world, as I have always been accustomed to face 'it since I came to years of discretion. And so I got away to Italy and there it is I am writing this story. If the world will not have it as a fact, then the world may take it as fiction. It is no concern of mine.

And now that the account is finished, I am amazed to think how completely this adventure is gone and done with. Everybody believes that Cavor was a not very brilliant scientific experimenter who blew up his house and himself at Lympne, and they explain the bang that followed my arrival at Littlestone by a reference to the experiments with explosives that are going on continually at the government establishment of Lydd, two miles away. I must confess that hitherto

I have not acknowledged my share in the disappearance of Master Tommy Simmons, which was that little boy's name. That perhaps may prove a difficult bit of corroboration to explain away. They account for my appearance in rags with two bars of indisputable gold upon the Littlestone beach in various ingenious ways — it doesn't worry me what they think of me. They say I have strung all these things together to avoid being questioned too closely as to the source of my wealth. I would like to see the man who could invent a story that would hold together like this one. Well, they must take it as fiction — there it is.

I have told my story — and now I suppose I have to take up the worries of this terrestrial life again. Even if one has been to the moon, one has still to earn a living. So I am working here at Amalfi on the scenario of that play I sketched before Cavor came walking into my world, and I am trying to piece my life together as it was before ever I saw him. I must confess that I find it hard to keep my mind on the play when the moonshine comes into my room. It is full moon here, and last night I was out on the pergola for hours staring away at that shining blankness that hides so much. Imagine it! tables and chairs and trestles and bars of gold! Confound it! — if only one could hit on that Cavorite again! But such a thing as that doesn't come twice in a life. Here I am, a little better off than I was at Lympne, and that is all. And

Cavor has sought death in a more elaborate way than any human being ever did before. So the story closes as finally and completely as a dream. It fits in so little with all the other things of life, so much of it is so utterly remote from all human experience, the leaping, the queer eating, the hard breathing of those weightless times, that indeed there are moments when, in spite of my moon gold, I do more than half believe myself that the whole thing was a dream.

CHAPTER 21

THE ASTONISHING COMMUNICATION OF MR. JULIUS WENDIGEE

When I had finished the account of my return to the earth at Littlestone I wrote "The End," made a flourish and threw my pen aside, fully believing that the whole story of the First Men in the Moon was told. Not only had I done this, but I had placed my manuscript in the hands of a literary agent, had permitted it to be sold, had seen the greater portion of it appear in *The Strand Magazine,* and was setting to work again upon the scenario

of the play I had commenced at Lympne before I realised that the end was not yet. Following me from Amalfi to Algiers, there reached me (it is now about six weeks ago) one of the most astounding communications I have ever been fated to receive. Briefly, it informed me that Mr. Julius Wendigee, a Dutch electrician, who has been experimenting with certain apparatus akin to the apparatus used by Mr. Tesla in America, in the hope of discovering some method of communication with Mars, was receiving day by day a curiously fragmentary message in English which was indisputably emanating from Mr. Cavor in the moon.

At first I thought the thing was an elaborate practical joke by someone who had seen the manuscript of my narrative. I answered Mr. Wendigee jestingly, but he replied in a manner that put such suspicion altogether aside, and in a state of inconceivable excitement I hurried from Algiers to the little observatory upon the Monte Rosa in which he was working. In the presence of his record and his appliances — and above all of the messages from Mr. Cavor that were coming to hand — my lingering doubts vanished. I decided at once to accept his proposal to remain with him, assisting him to take down the record from day to day, and endeavouring with him to send a message back to the moon. Cavor, we learnt, was not only alive but free in the midst of an almost inconceivable community of these ant-like beings, these antmen, in the blue darkness of the lunar caves. He was lamed, it seemed, but otherwise in quite good health — in better health, he distinctly said, than he usually enjoyed on earth. He had had a fever, but it had left no bad effects. And naturally enough he seemed to be labouring under a conviction that I was either dead in the moon crater or lost in the deep of space.

Mr. Wendigee was engaged in quite a different investigation when he received the first message from the moon. The reader will no doubt recall the little excitement that began the century, arising out of an announcement by Mr. Nikola Tesla, the American electrical celebrity, that he had received a message from Mars. His announcement recalled attention to a fact that had long been familiar to scientific people, namely: that from some unknown source in space, waves of electro-magnetic disturbance, entirely similar to those used by Signor Marconi for his wireless telegraphy, are constantly reaching the earth. Besides Mr. Tesla several other observers have been engaged in perfecting apparatus for receiving and recording these vibrations, though few would go so far as to consider them actual messages from some extra-terrestrial sender. Among those few however we must certainly count Mr. Wendigee. Ever since 1898 he had devoted himself almost entirely to this subject, and being a man of ample means he had erected an observatory on the flanks of Monte Rosa, in a position adapted in every way for such observations.

My scientific attainments, I must admit, are not great, but so far as they enable me to judge, Mr. Wendigee's contrivances for detecting and recording any disturbances in the electro-magnetic conditions of space are eminently original and ingenious. And by a happy combination of circumstances, they were set up and in operation about two months before Cavor made his first attempt to call up the earth. Consequently we have fragments of his communications even from the beginning. Unhappily, they are only fragments, and the most momentous of all the things that he had to tell humanity, the instructions, that is, for the making of Cavorite, if indeed he ever transmitted them, have throbbed themselves away, unrecorded into space. We never succeeded in getting a response back to Cavor. He did not know therefore what we had received or what we had missed; nor indeed did he certainly know that anyone on earth was really aware of his efforts to reach us. And the persistence he displayed in sending eighteen long descriptions of lunar affairs — as they would be if we had them complete — shows how much his mind must have turned back towards his native planet since he left it two years ago.

You can imagine how amazed Mr. Wendigee must have been when he discovered his record of electro-magnetic disturbances interlaced by Cavor's straightforward English. Mr. Wendigee knew nothing of our wild journey moonward, and suddenly — this English out of the void!

It is well the reader should understand the conditions under which these messages were sent. Somewhere within the moon Cavor certainly had access for a time to a considerable amount of electrical apparatus, and it would seem he rigged up — perhaps furtively — a transmitting arrangement of the Marconi type. This he was able to operate at irregular intervals: sometimes for only half an hour or so, sometimes for three or four hours at a stretch. At these times he transmitted his earthward message, regardless of the fact that the relative position of the moon and points upon the earth's surface is constantly altering. As a consequence of this and of the necessary imperfections of our recording instruments his communication comes and goes in our records in an extremely fitful manner; it becomes blurred; it "fades out" in a mysterious and altogether exasperating way. And added to this is the fact that he was not an expert operator; he had partly forgotten, or never completely mastered, the code in general use, and as he became fatigued he dropped words and misspelt in a curious manner.

Altogether we have probably missed quite half of the communications he made, and much we have is damaged, broken, and partly effaced. In the abstract that follows the reader must be prepared therefore for a considerable amount of break, hiatus, and change of topic. Mr. Wendigee and I are collaborating in a complete and annotated edition

of the Cavor record, which we hope to publish, together with a detailed account of the instruments employed, beginning with the first volume in January next. That will be the full and scientific report, of which this is only the popular first transcript. But here we give at least sufficient to complete the story I have told, and to give the broad outlines of the state of that kindred world so near, and yet so dissimilar to our own.

CHAPTER 22

AN ABSTRACT OF THE SIX MESSAGES FIRST RECEIVED FROM MR. CAVOR

THE TWO earlier messages of Mr. Cavor may very well be reserved for that larger volume. They simply tell with greater brevity and with a difference in several details that is interesting, but not of any vital importance, the bare facts of the making of the sphere and our departure from the world. Throughout, Cavor speaks of me as a man who is dead, but with a curious change of temper as he approaches our landing on the moon. " Poor Bedford," he says of me, and " this poor young man," and he blames himself for inducing a young man, " by no means well equipped for such adventures," to leave a planet " on which he was indisputably fitted to succeed" on so precarious a mission. I think he underrates the part my energy and practical capacity played in bringing about the realisation of his theoretical sphere. " We arrived," he says, with no more account of our passage through space than if we had made a journey in a railway train.

And then he becomes increasingly unfair to me. Unfair, indeed, to an extent I should not have expected in a man trained in the search for truth. Looking back over my previously written account of these things I must insist that I have been altogether juster to Cavor than he has been to me. I have extenuated little and suppressed nothing. But his account is:

" It speedily became apparent that the entire strangeness of our circumstances and surroundings — great loss of weight, attenuated but highly oxygenated air, consequent exaggeration of the results of muscular effort, rapid development of weird plants from obscure spores, lurid sky — was exciting my companion unduly. On the moon his character seemed to deteriorate. He became impulsive, rash, and quarrelsome. In a little while his folly in devouring some gigantic vesicles and his consequent intoxication led to our capture by the Selenites — before we had had the slightest

opportunity of properly observing their ways. . . ."

(He says, you observe, nothing of his own concession to these same "vesicles.")

And he goes on from that point to say: "We came to a difficult passage with them, and Bedford, mistaking certain gestures of theirs" — pretty gestures they were! — "gave way to a panic violence. He ran amuck, killed three, and perforce I had to flee with him after the outrage. Subsequently we fought with a number who endeavoured to bar our way, and slew seven or eight more. It says much for the tolerance of these beings that on my recapture I was not instantly slain. We made our way to the exterior and to increase our chances of recovering our sphere separated in the crater of our arrival. But presently I came upon a body of Selenites led by two who were curiously different, even in form, from any of those we had seen hitherto, with larger heads and smaller bodies and much more elaborately wrapped about. After evading them for some time I fell into a crevasse, cut my head rather badly and displaced my patella, and, finding crawling very painful, decided to surrender — if they would still permit me to do so. This they did, and perceiving my helpless condition carried me with them again into the moon. And of Bedford I have heard or seen nothing more nor, so far as I can gather, has any Selenite. Either the night overtook him in the crater, or else, which is more probable, he found the sphere,

and desiring to steal a march upon me made off with it — only, I fear, to find it uncontrollable, and to a more lingering fate in outer space."

And with that Cavor dismisses me and goes on to more interesting topics. I dislike the idea of seeming to use my position as his editor to deflect his story in my own interest, but I am obliged to protest here against the turn he gives these occurrences. He says nothing about that gasping message on the blood-stained paper in which he told, or attempted to tell, a very different story. The dignified self-surrender is an altogether new view of the affair that has come to him, I must insist, since he began to feel secure among the lunar people; and as for the "stealing a march" conception, I am quite willing to let the reader decide between us on what he has before him. I know I am not a model man — I have made no pretence to be. But am I *that*?

However, that is the sum of my wrongs. From this point I can edit Cavor with an untroubled mind, for he mentions me no more.

It would seem that the Selenites who came upon him carried him to some point in the interior down "a great shaft" by means of what he describes as "a sort of balloon." We gather from the rather confused passage in which he describes this, and from a number of chance allusions and hints in other and subsequent messages, that this "great shaft" is one of an enormous system of artificial shafts

that run, each from what is called a lunar "crater" downwards for very nearly a hundred miles towards the central portion of our satellite. These shafts communicate by transverse tunnels, they throw out abysmal caverns and expand into great globular places; the whole of the moon's substance for a hundred miles inward, indeed, is a mere sponge of rock. "Partly," says Cavor, "this sponginess is natural, but very largely it is due to the enormous industry of the Selenites in the past. The great circular mounds of the excavated rock and earth that form these great circles about the tunnels are known to earthly astronomers (misled by a false analogy) as volcanoes."

It was down this shaft they took him, in this "sort of balloon" he speaks of, at first into an inky blackness and then into a region of continually increasing phosphorescence. Cavor's despatches show him to be, for a scientific man, curiously regardless of detail, but we gather that this light was due to the streams and cascades of water —"no doubt containing some phosphorescent organism"—that flowed ever more abundantly downward towards the Central Sea. And as he descended, he says: "The Selenites also became luminous." And at last far below him he saw as it were a lake of heatless fire, the waters of the Central Sea, glowing and eddying in strange perturbation, "like luminous blue milk that is about to boil."

"This Lunar Sea," says Cavor, in a later passage, "is not a stagnant ocean; a solar tide sends it in a perpetual flow around the lunar axis, and strange storms and boilings and rushings of its waters occur, and at times cold winds and thunderings that ascend out of it into the busy ways of the great ant-hill above. It is only when the water is in motion that it gives out light; in its rare seasons of calm it is black. Commonly, when one sees it, its waters rise and fall in an oily swell, and flakes and big rafts of shining, bubbly foam drift with the sluggish, faintly-glowing current. The Selenites navigate its cavernous straits and lagoons in little shallow boats of a canoe-like shape; and even before my journey to the galleries about the Grand Lunar, who is Master of the Moon, I was permitted to make a brief excursion on its waters.

"The caverns and passages are naturally very tortuous. A large proportion of these ways are known only to expert pilots among the fishermen, and not infrequently Selenites are lost for ever in their labyrinths. In their remoter recesses, I am told, strange creatures lurk, some of them so terrible and dangerous that all the science of the moon has been unable to exterminate them. There is particularly the Rapha, an inextricable mass of clutching tentacles that one hacks to pieces only to multiply; and the Tzee, a darting creature that is never seen, so subtly and suddenly does it slay. . . ."

He gives us a gleam of description.

" I was reminded on this excursion of what I have read of the Mammoth Caves; if only I had a yellow flambeau instead of the pervading blue light, and a solid-looking boatman with an oar instead of a scuttle-faced Selenite working an engine at the back of the canoe, I could have imagined I had suddenly got back to earth. The rocks about us varied, sometimes black, sometimes pale blue and veined, and once they flashed and glittered as though we had come into a mine of sapphires. And below one saw the ghostly phosphorescent fishes flash and vanish in the hardly less phosphorescent deep. Then presently a long ultramarine vista down the turgid stream of one of the channels of traffic, and a landing-stage, and then perhaps a glimpse up the enormous crowded shaft of one of the vertical ways.

" In one great place heavy with glistening stalactites a number of boats was anchored. We went alongside one of these and watched the long-armed fishing Selenites winding in a net. They were little, hunch-backed insects with very strong arms, short, bandy legs, and crinkled face-masks. As they pulled, the net seemed the heaviest thing I had come upon in the moon; it was loaded with weights — no doubt of gold — and it took a long time to draw, for in those waters the larger and more edible fish lurk deep. The fish in the net came up like a blue moonrise — a blaze of darting, tossing blue.

" Among their catch was a many-tentaculate evil-eyed black thing, ferociously active, whose appearance they greeted with shrieks and twitters, and which they hacked to pieces with quick, nervous movements. All its dissevered limbs continued to lash and writhe in a vicious manner. Afterwards when fever had hold of me I dreamt again and again of that bitter, furious creature rising so vigorous and active out of the unknown sea. It was the most active and malignant thing of all the living creatures I have yet seen in this world inside the moon. . . .

" The surface of this sea must be very nearly two hundred miles (if not more) below the level of the moon's exterior; all the cities of the moon lie, I learned, immediately above this Central Sea, in such cavernous spaces and artificial galleries as I have described, and they communicate with the exterior by enormous vertical shafts which open invariably in what are called by earthly astronomers the ' craters ' of the moon. The lid covering one such aperture I had already seen during the wanderings that had preceded my capture.

" Upon the condition of the less central portion of the moon I have not yet arrived at very precise knowledge. There is an enormous system of caverns in which the mooncalves shelter during the night; and there are abattoirs and the like — in one of these it was that Bedford and I fought with the Selenite butchers — and I have seen since balloons laden with meat descending out of the upper dark. I have

as yet scarcely learnt as much of these things as a Zulu in London will learn about the British corn supplies in the same time. It is clear, however, that these vertical shafts and the vegetation of the surface must play an essential *rôle* in ventilating and keeping fresh the atmosphere of the moon. At one time, and particularly on my first emergence from my prison, there was certainly a cold wind blowing *down* the shaft, and later there was a kind of sirocco upwards that corresponded with my fever. For at the end of about three weeks I fell ill of an indefinable fever, and in spite of sleep and the quinine tabloids that very fortunately I had brought in my pocket, I remained ill and fretting miserably, almost to the time when I was taken into the palace of the Grand Lunar, who is Master of the Moon.

"I will not dilate on the wretchedness of my condition," he remarks, "during those days of ill-health." Nevertheless he goes on with great amplitude with details I omit here. "My temperature," he concludes, "kept abnormally high for a long time, and I lost all desire for food. I had stagnant waking intervals and sleep tormented by dreams, and at one phase I was, I remember, so weak as to be earth-sick and almost hysterical. I longed almost intolerably for colour to break the everlasting blue. . . ."

He reverts again presently to the topic of this sponge-caught lunar atmosphere. I am told by astronomers and physicists that all he tells is in absolute accordance with what was already known of the moon's condition. Had earthly astronomers had the courage and imagination to push home a bold induction, says Mr. Wendigee, they might have foretold almost everything that Cavor has to say of the general structure of the moon. They know now pretty certainly that moon and earth are not so much satellite and primary as smaller and greater sisters, made out of one mass, and consequently made of the same material. And since the density of the moon is only three-fifths that of the earth, there can be nothing for it but that she is hollowed out by a great system of caverns. There was no necessity, said Sir Jabez Flap, F.R.S., that most entertaining exponent of the facetious side of the stars, that we should ever have gone to the moon to find out such easy inferences, and points the pun with an allusion to Gruyère; but he certainly might have announced his knowledge of the hollowness of the moon before. And if the moon is hollow, then the apparent absence of air and water is, of course, quite easily explained. The sea lies within at the bottom of the caverns, and the air travels through the great sponge of galleries, in accordance with simple physical laws. The caverns of the moon, on the whole, are very windy places. As the sunlight comes round the moon, the air in the outer galleries on that side is heated, its pressure increases, some flows out on the exterior and mingles with the

evaporating air of the craters
(where the plants remove its car-
bonic acid), while the greater
portion flows round through the
galleries to replace the shrinking
air of the cooling side that the
sunlight had left. There is, there-
fore, a constant eastward breeze
in the air of the outer galleries,
and an up-flow during the lunar
days up the shafts, complicated,
of course, very greatly by the
varying shape of the galleries and
the ingenious contrivances of the
Selenite mind. . . .

CHAPTER 23

THE NATURAL HIS-
TORY OF THE
SELENITES

THE MESSAGES of Cavor from the
sixth up to the sixteenth are for
the most part so much broken,
and so abounding in repetitions,
that they scarcely form a con-
secutive narrative. They will be
given in full, of course, in the
scientific report, but here it will
be far more convenient to con-
tinue simply to abstract and
quote as in the former chapter.
We have subjected every word to
a keen critical scrutiny, and my
own brief memories and impres-

sions of lunar things have been
of inestimable help in interpret-
ing what would otherwise have
been impenetrably dark. And,
naturally, as living beings, our in-
terest centres far more upon the
strange community of lunar in-
sects in which he is living, it
would seem as an honoured
guest, than upon the mere physi-
cal condition of their world.

I have already made it clear,
I think, that the Selenites I saw
resembled man in maintaining
the erect attitude and in having
four limbs, and I have compared
the general appearance of their
heads and the jointing of their
limbs to that of insects. I have
mentioned too the peculiar con-
sequence of the smaller gravita-
tion of the moon on their fragile
slightness. Cavor confirms me
upon all these points. He calls
them "animals," though of
course they fall under no divi-
sion of the classification of earth-
ly creatures, and he points out
"the insect type of anatomy had,
fortunately for men, never ex-
ceeded a relatively very small
size on earth." The largest ter-
restrial insects, living or extinct,
do not as a matter of fact meas-
ure six inches in length; "but
here, against the lesser gravita-
tion of the moon, a creature cer-
tainly as much insect as verte-
brate seems to have been able to
attain to human and ultra-hu-
man dimensions."

He does not mention the ant,
but throughout his allusions the
ant is continually brought before
my mind, in its sleepless activity,
its intelligence, its social organi-
sation, and, more particularly,

the fact that it displays, in addition to the two forms, the male and the female, produced by almost all other animals, a great variety of sexless creatures, workers, soldiers and the like, differing from one another in structure, character, power and use and yet all members of the same species. And these Selenites are of course, if only by reason of this widely extended adaptation, incomparably greater than ants. And in place of the existing four or five different forms of ant there are almost innumerably different forms of Selenites. I have endeavoured to indicate the very considerable difference observable in such Selenites of the outer crust as I happened to encounter; the differences in size, hue, and shape were certainly as wide as the difference between the most widely separated races of men. But such differences as I saw fade absolutely to nothing in comparison with the huge distinctions of which Cavor tells. It would seem the exterior Selenites I saw were, indeed, mostly of one colour and occupation — mooncalf hinds, butchers, fleshers, and the like. But within the moon practically unsuspected by me, there are, it seems, a host of variations. The moon is indeed a kind of superanthill. But in place of the five distinctive types, the worker, soldier, winged male, queen and slave of the ant-world, there are amongst the moon-folk not only hundreds of differentiations, but, within each, and linking one to the other, a whole series of fine gradations. And these Selenites are not merely colossally superior to ants, but, according to Cavor, colossally, in intelligence, morality and social wisdom, higher than man.

It would seem the discovery came upon Cavor very speedily. I infer rather than learn from his narrative that he was captured by the mooncalf hinds under the direction of those other Selenites who " have larger braincases (heads?) and very much shorter legs." Finding he would not walk even under the goad, they carried him into darkness, crossed a narrow, plank-like bridge that may have been the very bridge I had refused, and put him down in something that must have seemed at first to be some sort of lift. This was the balloon — it had certainly been absolutely invisible to us in the darkness — and what had seemed to me a mere plank-walking into the void was really, no doubt, the passage of the gangway. In this he descended towards constantly more luminous strata of the moon. At first they descended in silence — save for the twitterings of the Selenites — and then into a stir of windy movement. In a little while the profound blackness had made his eyes so sensitive that he began to see more and more of the things about him, and at last the vague took shape.

" Conceive an enormous cylindrical space," says Cavor in his seventh message, " a quarter of a mile across, perhaps; very dimly lit at first and then bright, with big platforms twisting down its sides in a spiral that vanishes at last below in a blue profundity;

and lit ever more brightly — one could not tell how or why. Think of the well of the very largest spiral staircase or lift-shaft that you have ever looked down, and magnify that by a hundred. Imagine it at twilight seen through blue glass. Imagine yourself looking down that; only imagine also that you feel extraordinarily light and have got rid of any giddy feeling you might have on earth, and you will have the first conditions of my impression. Round this enormous shaft imagine a broad gallery running in a much steeper spiral than would be credible on earth, and forming a steep road protected from the gulf only by a little parapet that vanishes at last in perspective a couple of miles below.

"Looking up I saw the very fellow of the downward vision; it had of course the effect of looking into a very steep cone. A wind was blowing down the shaft, and far above I fancied I heard, growing fainter and fainter, the bellowing of the mooncalves that were being driven down again from their evening pasturage on the exterior. And up and down the spiral galleries were scattered numerous moon people, pallid, faintly self-luminous insects, regarding our appearance or busied on unknown errands.

" Either I fancied it or a flake of snow came drifting swiftly down on the icy breeze. And then, falling like a snowflake, a little figure, a little man-insect clinging to a parachute, drove down very swiftly towards the central places of the moon.

"The big-headed Selenite sitting beside me, seeing me move my head with the gesture of one who saw, pointed with his trunk-like ' hand ' and indicated a sort of jetty coming into sight very far below: a little landing-stage, as it were, hanging into the void. As it swept up towards us our pace diminished very rapidly, and in a few moments as it seemed we were abreast of it and at rest. A mooring-place was flung and grasped and I found myself pulled down to a level with a great crowd of Selenites, who jostled to see me.

" It was an incredible crowd. Suddenly and violently there was forced upon my attention the vast amount of difference there is amongst these beings of the moon.

" Indeed, there seemed not two alike in all that jostling multitude. They differed in shape, they differed in size! Some bulged and overhung, some ran about among the feet of their fellows, some twined and interlaced like snakes. All of them had the grotesque and disquieting suggestion of an insect that has somehow contrived to burlesque humanity; all seemed to present an incredible exaggeration of some particular feature; one had a vast right forelimb, an enormous antennal arm, as it were; one seemed all leg, poised, as it were, on stilts; another protruded an enormous nose-like organ beside a sharply speculative eye that made him startlingly human until one saw his expressionless mouth. One has seen punchinellos made of lobster claws — he was like that.

The strange and (except for the want of mandibles and palps) most insectlike head of the moon-calf-minders underwent astounding transformations; here it was broad and low, here high and narrow, here its vacuous brow was drawn out into horns and strange features, here it was whiskered and divided, and there with a grotesquely human profile. There were several brain-cases distended like bladders to a huge size. The eyes, too, were strangely varied, some quite elephantine in their small alertness, some huge pits of darkness. There were amazing forms with heads reduced to microscopic proportions and blobby bodies; and fantastic, flimsy things that existed it would seem only as a basis for vast, white-rimmed, glaring eyes. And oddest of all, two or three of these weird inhabitants of a subterranean world, a world sheltered by innumerable miles of rock from sun or rain, *carried umbrellas* in their tentaculate hands! — real terrestrial-looking umbrellas! And then I thought of the parachutist.

"These moon people behaved exactly as a human crowd might have done in similar circumstances: they jostled and thrust one another, they shoved one another aside, they even clambered upon one another to get a glimpse of me. Every moment they increased in numbers, and pressed more urgently upon the discs of my ushers" — Cavor does not explain what he means by this — "every moment fresh shapes forced themselves upon my astounded attention. And

presently I was signed and helped into a sort of litter, and lifted up on the shoulders of strong-armed bearers and so borne over this seething nightmare towards the apartments that were provided for me in the moon. All about me were eyes, faces, masks, tentacles, a leathery noise like the rustling of beetle wings, and a great bleating and twittering of Selenite voices."

We gather he was taken to a "hexagonal apartment," and there for a space he was confined. Afterwards he was given a much more considerable liberty; indeed, almost as much freedom as one has in a civilised town on earth. And it would appear that the mysterious being who is the ruler and master of the moon appointed two Selenites "with large heads" to guard and study him, and to establish whatever mental communications were possible with him. Amazing and incredible as it may seem, these two creatures, these fantastic men-insects, these beings of another world, were presently communicating with Cavor by means of terrestrial speech.

Cavor speaks of them as Phi-oo and Tsi-puff. Phi-oo, he says, was about five feet high; he had small, slender legs about eighteen inches long, and slight feet of the common lunar pattern. On these balanced a little body, throbbing with the pulsations of his heart. He had long, soft, many-jointed arms ending in a tentacled grip, and his neck was many-jointed in the usual way, but exceptionally short and thick. "His head," says Cavor — apparently alluding

to some previous description that has gone astray in space — "is of the common lunar type, but strangely modified. The mouth has the usual expressionless gape, but it is unusually small and pointing downwards, and the mask is reduced to the size of a large flat nose-flap. On either side are the little hen-like eyes. The rest of the head is distended into a huge globe, and the chitinous leathery cuticle of the mooncalf hinds thins out to a mere membrane, through which the pulsating brain movements are distinctly visible. He is a creature, indeed, with a tremendously hypertrophied brain, and with the rest of his organism both relatively and absolutely dwarfed." In another passage Cavor compares the back view of him to Atlas supporting the world. Tsi-puff, it seems, was a similar insect, but his "face" was drawn out to a considerable length, and the brain hypertrophy being in different regions, his head was not round but pear-shaped, with the stalk downward. There were also in Cavor's retinue litter-carriers, lop-sided beings with enormous shoulders, very spidery ushers, and a squat foot-attendant.

The manner in which Phi-oo and Tsi-puff attacked the problem of speech was fairly obvious. They came into this "hexagonal cell" in which Cavor was confined, and began imitating every sound he made, beginning with a cough. He seems to have grasped their intention with great quickness, and to have begun repeating words to them and pointing to indicate the application. The procedure was probably always the same. Phi-oo would attend to Cavor for a space, then point also and say the word he had heard. The first word he mastered was "man," and the second "mooney"—which Cavor on the spur of the moment seems to have used instead of "Selenite" for the moon race. As soon as Phi-oo was assured of the meaning of a word he repeated it to Tsi-puff, who remembered it infallibly. They mastered over one hundred English nouns at their first session.

Subsequently it seems they brought an artist with them to assist the work of explanation with sketches and diagrams — Cavor's drawings being rather crude. "He was," says Cavor, "a being with an active arm and an arresting eye," and he seemed to draw with incredible swiftness.

The eleventh message is undoubtedly only a fragment of a longer communication. After some broken sentences, the record of which is unintelligible, it goes on:

"But it will interest only linguists, and delay me too long, to give the details of the series of intent parleys of which these were the beginning, and, indeed, I very much doubt if I could give in anything like the proper order all the twistings and turnings that we made in our pursuit of mutual comprehension. Verbs were soon plain sailing — at least, such active verbs as I could express by drawings; some adjectives were easy, but when it came to abstract nouns, to prepositions,

and the sort of hackneyed figures of speech by means of which so much is expressed on earth, it was like diving in cork jackets. Indeed, these difficulties were insurmountable until to the sixth lesson came a fourth assistant, a being with a huge, football-shaped head, whose *forte* was clearly the pursuit of intricate analogy. He entered in a preoccupied manner, stumbling against a stool, and the difficulties that arose had to be presented to him with a certain amount of clamour and hitting and pricking before they reached his apprehension. But once he was involved his penetration was amazing. Whenever there came a need of thinking beyond Phi-oo's by no means limited scope, this prolate-headed person was in request, but he invariably told the conclusion to Tsi-puff, in order that it might be remembered; Tsi-puff was ever the arsenal for facts. And so we advanced again.

"It seemed long and yet brief — a matter of days before I was positively talking with these insects of the moon. Of course, at first it was an intercourse infinitely tedious and exasperating, but imperceptibly it has grown to comprehension. And my patience has grown to meet its limitations. Phi-oo it is who does all the talking. He does it with a vast amount of meditative provisional 'M'm — M'm,' and he has caught up one or two phrases. 'If I may say,' 'If you understand,' and adorns all his speech with them.

"Thus he would discourse. Imagine him explaining his artist.

"'M'm — M'm — he — if I may say — draw. Eat little — drink little — draw. Love draw. No other thing. Hate all who not draw like him. Angry. Hate all who draw like him better. Hate most people. Hate all who not think all world for to draw. Angry. M'm. All things mean nothing to him — only draw. He like you . . . if you understand. . . . New thing to draw. Ugly — striking. Eh?'

"'He' — turning to Tsi-puff — 'love remember words. Remember wonderful more than any. Think no, draw no — remember. Say' — here he referred to his gifted assistant for a word — 'histories — all things. He hear once — say ever.'

"It is more wonderful to me than the most wonderful dream to hear these extraordinary creatures — for even familiarity fails to weaken the inhuman effect of their appearance — continually piping a nearer approach to coherent earthly speech, asking questions, giving answers. I feel that I am casting back to the fable-hearing period of childhood again when the ant and the grasshopper talked together and the bee judged between them. . . ."

And while these linguistic exercises were going on Cavor seems to have experienced a considerable relaxation of his confinement. The first dread and distrust our unfortunate conflict aroused was being, he says, "continually effaced by the deliberate rationality of all I do. . . . I am now able to come and go as I please, or I am restricted only for

my own good. So it is I have been able to get at this apparatus, and, assisted by a happy find among the material that is littered in this enormous store-cave, I have contrived to despatch these messages. So far not the slightest attempt has been made to interfere with me in this, though I have made it quite clear to Phi-oo that I am signalling to the earth.

"'You talk to other?' he asked, watching me.

"'Others,' said I.

"'Others,' he said. 'Oh, yes. Men?'

"And I went on transmitting."

Cavor was continually making corrections in his previous accounts of the Selenites, as fresh facts flowed in upon him to modify his conclusions, and accordingly one gives the quotations that follow with a certain amount of reservation. They are quoted from the ninth, thirteenth and sixteenth messages, and, altogether vague and fragmentary as they are, they probably give as complete a picture of the social life of this strange community as mankind can now hope to have for some generations.

"In the moon," says Cavor, "every citizen knows his place. He is born to that place, and the elaborate discipline of training and education and surgery he undergoes fits him at last so completely to it that he has neither ideas nor organs for any purpose beyond it. 'Why should he?' Phi-oo would ask. If, for example, a Selenite is destined to be a mathematician, his teachers and trainers set out at once to that end. They check any incipient disposition to other pursuits, they encourage his mathematical bias with a perfect psychological skill. His brain grows, or at least the mathematical faculties of his brain grow, and the rest of him only so much as is necessary to sustain this essential part of him. At last, save for rest and food, his one delight lies in the exercise and display of his faculty, his one interest in its application, his sole society the other specialists in his own line. His brain grows continually larger, at least so far as the portions engaging in mathematics are concerned; they bulge ever larger and seem to suck all life and vigour from the rest of his frame. His limbs shrivel, his heart and digestive organs diminish, his insect face is hidden under its bulging contours. His voice becomes a mere squeak for the stating of formulæ; he seems deaf to all but properly enunciated problems. The faculty of laughter, save for the sudden discovery of some paradox, is lost to him; his deepest emotion is the evolution of a novel computation. And so he attains his end.

"Or again, a Selenite appointed to be a minder of mooncalves is from his earliest years induced to think and live mooncalf, to find his pleasure in mooncalf lore, his exercise in their tending and pursuit. He is trained to become wiry and active, his eye is indurated to the tight wrappings, the angular contours that constitute a 'smart mooncalfishness.' He takes at

last no interest in the deeper part of the moon; he regards all Selenites not equally versed in mooncalves with indifference, derision, or hostility. His thoughts are of mooncalf pastures, and his dialect an accomplished mooncalf technique. So also he loves his work, and discharges in perfect happiness the duty that justifies his being. And so it is with all sorts and conditions of Selenites — each is a perfect unit in a world machine. . . .

"These beings with big heads to whom the intellectual labours fall, form a sort of aristocracy in this strange society, and at the head of them, quintessential of the moon, is that marvellous gigantic ganglion the Grand Lunar, into whose presence I am finally to come. The unlimited development of the minds of the intellectual class is rendered possible by the absence in the lunar anatomy of bony skull, that strange box of bone that clamps about the developing brain of man, imperiously insisting 'thus far and no farther' to all his possibilities. They fall into three main classes differing greatly in influence and respect. These are the administrators, of whom Phi-oo was one, Selenites of considerable initiative and versatility, responsible each for a certain cubic content of the moon's bulk; the experts, like the football-headed thinkers who are trained to perform certain special operations; and the erudite, who are repositories of all knowledge. To this latter class belongs, Tsi-puff, the first lunar professor of terrestrial languages. With regard to these latter it is

a curious little thing to note that the unlimited growth of the lunar brain has rendered unnecessary the invention of all those mechanical aids to brain work which have distinguished the career of man. There are no books, no records of any sort, no libraries, nor inscriptions. All knowledge is stored in distended brains much as the honey-ants of Texas store honey in their distended abdomens. The lunar Somerset House and the lunar British Museum Library are collections of living brains. . . .

The less specialised administrators, I note, do for the most part take a very lively interest in me whenever they encounter me. They will come out of their way and stare at me and ask questions to which Phi-oo will reply. I see them going hither and thither with a retinue of bearers, attendants, shouters, parachute-carriers, and so forth — queer groups to see. The experts for the most part ignore me completely, even as they ignore each other, or notice me only to begin a clamorous exhibition of their distinctive skill. The erudite with very few exceptions are rapt in an impervious and apoplectic complacency from which only a denial of their erudition can rouse them. Usually they are led about by little watchers and attendants, and often there are small and active-looking creatures, small females usually, that I am inclined to think are a sort of wife to them; but some of the profounder scholars are altogether too great for locomotion, and are carried from place to

place in a kind of sedan tub, wabbling jellies of knowledge that enlist my respectful astonishment. I have just passed one in coming to this place where I am permitted to amuse myself with these electrical toys, a vast, shaven, shaky head, bald and thin-skinned, carried on his grotesque stretcher. In front and behind came his bearers, and curious almost trumpet-faced, news disseminators shrieked his fame.

"I have already mentioned the retinues that accompanied most of the intellectuals: ushers, bearers, valets, extraneous tentacles and muscles as it were, to replace the abortive physical powers of these hypertrophied minds. Porters almost invariably accompany them. There are also extremely swift messengers with spider-like legs, and 'hands' for grasping parachutes, and attendants with vocal organs that could well nigh wake the dead. Apart from their controlling intelligence, these subordinates are as inert and helpless as umbrellas in a stand. They exist only in relation to the orders they have to obey, the duties they have to perform.

"The bulk of these insects, however, who go to and fro upon the spiral ways, who fill the ascending balloons and drop past me clinging to flimsy parachutes, are, I gather, of the operative class. 'Machine hands,' indeed some of these are in actual fact — it is no figure of speech; the single tentacle of the mooncalf hind is replaced by huge single or paired bunches of three, or five, or seven digits for clawing, lifting, guiding, the rest of them

no more than subordinate appendages to these important parts. Some, who I suppose deal with bell-striking mechanism, have enormous rabbit-like ears just behind the eyes; some whose work lies in delicate chemical operations project a vast olfactory organ; others again have flat feet for treadles with anchylosed joints; and others — who I have been told are glass-blowers — seem mere lung-bellows. But every one of these common Selenites is exquisitely adapted to the social need it meets. Fine work is done by fined-down workers amazingly dwarfed and neat. Some I could hold on the palm of my hand. There is even a sort of turnspit Selenite, very common, whose duty and only delight it is to supply the motive power for various small appliances. And to rule over these things and order any erring tendency there might be in some aberrant natures are the finest muscular beings I have seen in the moon, a sort of lunar police, who must have been trained from their earliest years to give a perfect respect and obedience to the swollen heads.

"The making of these various sorts of operative must be a very curious and interesting process. I am still much in the dark about it, but quite recently I came upon a number of young Selenites, confined in jars from which only the fore limbs protruded, who were being compressed to become machine-minders of a special sort. The extended 'hand' in this highly developed system of technical education is stimu-

lated by irritants and nourished by injection while the rest of the body is starved. Phi-oo, unless I misunderstood him, explained that in the earlier stages these queer little creatures are apt to display signs of suffering in their various cramped situations, but they easily become indurated to their lot; and he took me on to where a number of flexible-limbed messengers were being drawn out and broken in. It is quite unreasonable, I know, but these glimpses of the educational methods of these beings have affected me disagreeably. I hope, however, that may pass off and I may be able to see more of this aspect of this wonderful social order. That wretched-looking hand sticking out of its jar seemed to appeal for lost possibilities; it haunts me still, although, of course, it is really in the end a far more humane proceeding than our earthly method of leaving children to grow into human beings, and then making machines of them.

"Quite recently, too—I think it was on the eleventh or twelfth visit I made to this apparatus—I had a curious light upon the lives of these operatives. I was being guided through a short cut hither instead of going down the spiral and by the quays of the Central Sea. From the devious windings of a long, dark gallery we emerged into a vast, low cavern, pervaded by an earthly smell and rather brightly lit. The light came from a tumultuous growth of livid fungoid shapes—some indeed singularly like our terrestrial mushrooms, but stand-ing as high or higher than a man.

"'Mooneys eat these?' said I to Phi-oo.

"'Yes, food.'

"'Goodness me!' I cried, 'what's that?'

"My eye had just caught the figure of an exceptionally big and ungainly Selenite lying motionless among the stems, face downwards. We stopped.

"'Dead?' I asked. For as yet I have seen no dead in the moon, and I have grown curious.

"'No!' exclaimed Phi-oo. 'Him—worker—no work to do. Get little drink then—make sleep—till we him want. What good him wake, eh? No want him walking about.'

"'There's another!' cried I.

"And indeed all that huge extent of mushroom ground was, I found, peppered with these prostrate figures sleeping under an opiate until the moon had need of them. There were scores of them of all sorts, and we were able to turn some of them over and examine them more precisely than I had been able to do previously. When disturbed they breathed noisily, but did not wake. One I remember very distinctly; he left a strong impression, I think, because some trick of the light and of his attitude was strongly suggestive of a drawn-up human figure. His fore-limbs were long, delicate tentacles—he was some kind of refined manipulator—and the pose of his slumber suggested a submissive suffering. No doubt it was quite a mistake for me to interpret his expression in that way,

but I did. And as Phi-oo rolled him over into the darkness among the livid fleshiness again, I felt a distinctly unpleasant sensation, although as he rolled the insect in him was confessed.

"It simply illustrates the unthinking way in which one acquires habits of thought and feeling. To drug the worker one does not want and toss him aside is surely far better than to expel him from his factory to wander starving in the streets. In every complicated social community there is necessarily a certain intermittency in the occupation of all specialised labour, and in this way the trouble of an unemployed problem is altogether anticipated. And yet, so unreasonable are even scientifically trained minds, I still do not like the memory of those prostrate forms amidst those quiet, luminous arcades of fleshy growth, and I avoid that short cut in spite of the inconveniences of its longer, more noisy, and more crowded alternative.

"My alternative route takes me round by a huge, shadowy cavern, very crowded and clamorous, and here it is I see peering out of the hexagonal openings of a sort of honeycomb wall, or parading a large open space behind, or selecting the toys and amulets made to please them by the acephalic dainty-fingered jewellers who work in kennels below, the mothers of the moon-world — the queen bees, as it were, of the hive. They are noble-looking beings, fantastically and sometimes quite beautifully adorned, with a proud carriage and, save for

their mouths, almost microscopic heads. . . .

"Of the condition of the moon sexes, marrying and giving in marriage, and of birth and so forth among the Selenites, I have as yet been able to learn very little. With the steady progress of Phi-oo in English, however, my ignorance will no doubt as steadily disappear. I am of opinion that, as with the ants and bees, there is in this community a large majority of the members of the neuter sex. Of course on earth in our cities there are now many who never live that life of parentage which is the natural life of man. Here, as with the ants, this thing has become a normal condition of the race; and the whole of such replacement as is necessary falls upon this special and by no means numerous class of matrons, the mothers of the moon-world, large and stately beings beautifully fitted to bear the larval Selenite. Unless I misunderstand an explanation of Phi-oo's, they are absolutely incapable of cherishing the young they bring into the moon; periods of foolish indulgence alternate with moods of aggressive violence; and as soon as possible the little creatures, who are quite soft and flabby and pale coloured, are transferred to the charge of a variety of celibate females, women 'workers,' as it were, who in some cases possess brains of almost masculine dimensions."

Just at this point, unhappily, this message broke off. Fragmentary and tantalising as the matter constituting this chapter is, it

does nevertheless give a vague, broad impression of an altogether strange and wonderful world — a world with which our own must now prepare to reckon sooner or later. This intermittent trickle of messages, this whispering of a record needle in the darkness of the mountain slopes, is the first warning of such a change in human conditions as mankind has scarcely imagined heretofore. In that planet there are new elements, new appliances, new traditions, an overwhelming avalanche of new ideas, a strange race with whom we must inevitably struggle for mastery — gold as common as iron or wood. . . .

CHAPTER 24

THE GRAND LUNAR

THE PENULTIMATE message describes, occasionally even with elaborate detail, the encounter between Cavor and the Grand Lunar, who is the ruler or Master of the Moon. Cavor seems to have sent most of it without interference, but to have been interrupted in the concluding portion. The second came after an interval of a week.

The first message begins: "At last I am able to resume this — "; it then becomes illegible for a space, and after a time resumes in mid-sentence.

The missing words of the following sentence are probably "The crowd." There follows quite clearly: "grew even denser as we drew near the palace of the Grand Lunar — if I may call a series of excavations a palace. Everywhere faces stared at me — blank, chitinous gapes and masks, big eyes peering over tremendous nose tentacles, and little eyes beneath monstrous forehead plates; below, an undergrowth of smaller creatures dodged and yelped; and grotesque heads poised on sinuous, swanlike, long-jointed necks appeared craning over shoulders and beneath armpits. Keeping a welcome space about me marched a cordon of stolid, scuttle-headed guards who had joined us on our leaving the boat in which we had come along the channels of the Central Sea. The flea-like artist with the little brain joined us also, and a thick bunch of lean porter-ants swayed and struggled under the multitude of conveniences that were considered essential to my state. I was carried in a litter during the final stage of our journey. It was made of some very ductile metal that looked dark to me, meshed and woven and with bars of paler metal, and about me as I advanced there grouped itself a long and complicated procession.

"In front, after the manner of heralds, marched four trumpet-faced creatures making a devastating bray; and then came squat, almost beetle-like ushers before

and behind, and on either hand a galaxy of learned heads, a sort of animated encyclopædia, who were, Phi-oo explained, to stand about the Grand Lunar for purposes of reference. Not a thing in lunar science, not a point of view or method of thinking, that these wonderful beings did not carry in their heads. Followed guards and porters, and then Phi-oo's shivering brain borne also on a litter. Then came Tsi-puff in a slightly less important litter; then myself on a litter of greater elegance than any other and surrounded by my food and drink attendants. More trumpeters came next, splitting the ear with vehement outcries, and then several big brains, special correspondents one might well call them or historiographers, charged with the task of observing and remembering every detail of this epoch-making interview. A company of attendants, bearing and dragging banners and masses of scented fungi and curious symbols, completed the procession. The way was lined by ushers and officers in caparisons that gleamed like steel, and beyond their line the heads and tentacles of that enormous crowd surged on either hand.

"I will own that I am still by no means indurated to the peculiar effect of the Selenite appearance, and to find myself as it were adrift on this broad sea of excited entomology was by no means agreeable. Just for a space I had something like the 'horrors.' It had come to me before in these lunar caverns, when on occasion I have found myself weaponless and with an undefended back amidst a crowd of these Selenites, but never quite so vividly. It is, of course, as absolutely irrational a feeling as one could well have, and I hope gradually to subdue it. But just for a moment, as I swept forward into the welter of the vast crowd, it was only by gripping my litter tightly and summoning all my will-power that I succeeded in stifling an outcry or some such manifestation. It lasted perhaps three minutes; then I had myself in hand again.

"We ascended the spiral of a vertical way for some time and then passed through a series of huge halls, dome-roofed, and gloriously decorated. The approach to the Grand Lunar was certainly contrived to give one a vivid impression of his greatness. The halls — all happily sufficiently luminous for my terrestrial eye — were a cunning and elaborate crescendo of space and decoration. The effect of their progressive size was enhanced by the steady diminution in the lighting, and by a thin haze of incense that thickened as one advanced. In the earlier ones the vivid, clear light made everything finite and concrete to me. I seemed to advance continually to something larger, dimmer, and less material.

"I must confess that all this splendour made me feel extremely shabby and unworthy. I was unshaven and unkempt; I had brought no razor; I had a coarse beard over my mouth. On earth I have always been inclined to despise any attention to

my person beyond a proper care for cleanliness; but under the exceptional circumstances in which I found myself, representing, as I did, my planet and my kind, and depending very largely upon the attractiveness of my appearance for a proper reception, I would have given much for something a little more artistic and dignified than the husks I wore. I had been so serene in the belief that the moon was uninhabited as to overlook such precautions altogether. As it was I was dressed in a flannel jacket, knickerbockers, and golfing stockings, stained with every sort of dirt the moon offered; slippers (of which the left heel was wanting), and a blanket, through a hole in which I thrust my head. (These clothes, indeed, I still wear.) Sharp bristles are anything but an improvement to my cast of features, and there was an unmended tear at the knee of my knickerbocker that showed conspicuously as I squatted in my litter; my right stocking, too, persisted in getting about my ankle. I am fully alive to the injustice my appearance did humanity, and if by any expedient I could have improvised something a little out of the way and imposing I would have done so. But I could hit upon nothing. I did what I could with my blanket — folding it somewhat after the fashion of a toga, and for the rest I sat as upright as the swaying of my litter permitted.

"Imagine the largest hall you have ever been in, elaborately decorated with blue and whitish-blue majolica, lit by blue light, you know not how, and surging with metallic or livid-white creatures of such a mad diversity as I have hinted. Imagine this hall to end in an open archway beyond which is a still larger hall, and beyond this yet another and still larger one, and so on. At the end of the vista a flight of steps, like the steps of Ara Cœli at Rome, ascends out of sight. Higher and higher these steps appear to go as one draws nearer their base. But at last I came under a huge archway and beheld the summit of these steps, and upon it the Grand Lunar exalted on his throne.

"He was seated in a blaze of incandescent blue. A hazy atmosphere filled the place so that its walls seemed invisibly remote. This gave him an effect of floating in a blue-black void. He seemed at first a small, self-luminous cloud, brooding on his glaucous throne; his brain-case must have measured many yards in diameter. For some reason that I cannot fathom a number of blue search-lights coming from behind the throne gave a starlike radiance to the halo immediately surrounding him. About him, and little and indistinct in this glow, a number of body-servants sustained and supported him, and overshadowed and standing in a huge semicircle beneath him were his intellectual subordinates, his remembrancers and computators and searchers, his flatterers and servants, and all the distinguished insects of the court of the moon. Still lower stood ushers and messengers, and then all down the countless steps of the

throne were guards, and at the base, enormous, various, indistinct, a vast swaying multitude of the minor dignitaries of the moon. Their feet made a perpetual scraping whisper on the rocky floor, their limbs moved with a rustling murmur.

"As I entered the penultimate hall the music rose and expanded into an imperial magnificence of sound, and the shrieks of the news-bearers died away. . . .

"I entered the last and greatest hall. . . .

"My procession opened out like a fan. My ushers and guards went right and left, and the three litters bearing myself and Phi-oo and Tsi-puff marched across a shiny waste of floor to the foot of the giant stairs. Then began a vast throbbing hum that mingled with the music. The two Selenites dismounted, but I was bidden remain seated — I imagine as a special honour. The music ceased, but not that humming, and by a simultaneous movement of ten thousand respectful eyes, my attention was directed to the enhaloed supreme intelligence that hovered above us.

"At first as I peered into the radiating blaze, this quintessential brain looked very much like a thin, featureless bladder with dim, undulating ghosts of convolutions writhing visibly within. Then beneath its enormity and just above the edge of the throne one saw with a start minute elfin eyes peering out of the blaze. No face, but eyes, as if they peered through holes. At first I could see no more than these two staring little eyes, and then below I distinguished the little dwarfed body and its insect-jointed limbs, shrivelled and white. The eyes stared down at me with a strange intensity, and the lower part of the swollen globe was wrinkled. Ineffectual-looking little hand-tentacles steadied this shape on the throne. . . .

"It was great. It was pitiful. One forgot the hall and the crowd.

"I ascended the staircase by jerks. It seemed to me that the purple glowing brain-case above us spread over me, and took more and more of the whole effect into itself as I drew nearer. The tiers of attendants and helpers grouped about their master seemed to dwindle and fade into the glare. I saw that the shadowy attendants were busy spraying that great brain with a cooling spray, and patting and sustaining it. For my own part I sat gripping my swaying litter and staring at the Grand Lunar, unable to turn my gaze aside. And at last, as I reached a little landing that was separated only by ten steps or so from the supreme seat, the woven splendour of the music reached a climax and ceased, and I was left naked, as it were, in that vastness, beneath the still scrutiny of the Grand Lunar's eyes.

"He was scrutinising the first man he had ever seen. . . .

"My eyes dropped at last from his greatness to the faint figures in the blue mist about him, and then down the steps to the massed Selenites, still and expectant in their thousands, packed on the floor below. Once again an un-

reasonable horror reached out towards me . . . and passed.

"After the pause came the salutation. I was assisted from my litter, and stood awkwardly while a number of curious and no doubt deeply symbolical gestures were vicariously performed for me by two slender officials. The encyclopædic galaxy of the learned that had accompanied me to the entrance of the last hall appeared two steps above me and left and right of me, in readiness for the Grand Lunar's need, and Phi-oo's white brain placed itself about halfway up to the throne in such a position as to communicate easily between us without turning his back on either the Grand Lunar or myself. Tsi-puff took up a position behind him. Dexterous ushers sidled sidewise towards me, keeping a full face to the Presence. I seated myself Turkish fashion, and Phi-oo and Tsi-puff also knelt down above me. There came a pause. The eyes of the nearer court went from me to the Grand Lunar and came back to me, and a hissing and piping of expectation passed across the hidden multitudes below and ceased.

"That humming ceased.

"For the first and last time in my experience the moon was silent.

"I became aware of a faint wheezy noise. The Grand Lunar was addressing me. It was like the rubbing of a finger upon a pane of glass.

"I watched him attentively for a time and then glanced at the alert Phi-oo. I felt amidst those filmy beings ridiculously thick and fleshy and solid; my head all jaw and black hair. My eyes went back to the Grand Lunar. He had ceased; his attendants were busy, and his shining superficies was glistening and running with cooling spray.

"Phi-oo meditated through an interval. He consulted Tsi-puff. Then he began piping his recognisable English — at first a little nervously, so that he was not very clear.

"'M'm — the Grand Lunar — wished to say — wishes to say — he gathers you are — m'm — men — that you are a man from the planet earth. He wishes to say that he welcomes you — welcomes you — and wishes to learn — learn, if I may use the word — the state of your world, and the reason why you came to this.'

"He paused. I was about to reply when he resumed. He proceeded to remarks of which the drift was not very clear, though I am inclined to think they were intended to be complimentary. He told me that the earth was to the moon what the sun is to the earth, and that the Selenites desired very greatly to learn about the earth and men. He then told me, no doubt in compliment also, the relative magnitude and diameter of earth and moon, and the perpetual wonder and speculation with which the Selenites had regarded our planet. I meditated with downcast eyes and decided to reply that men too had wondered what might lie in the moon, and had judged it dead, little recking on such magnificence as I had seen that day. The Grand Lunar, in token of

recognition, caused his blue search-light to rotate in a very confusing manner, and all about the great hall ran the pipings and whisperings and rustlings of the report of what I had said. He then proceeded to put to Phi-oo a number of inquiries which were easier to answer.

"He understood, he explained, that we lived on the surface of the earth, that our air and sea were outside the globe; the latter part, indeed, he already knew from his astronomical specialists. He was very anxious to have more detailed information of what he called this extraordinary state of affairs, for from the solidity of the earth there had always been a disposition to regard it as uninhabitable. He endeavoured first to ascertain the extremes of temperature to which we earth beings were exposed, and he was deeply interested by my descriptive treatment of clouds and rain. His imagination was assisted by the fact that the lunar atmosphere in the outer galleries of the night side is not infrequently very foggy. He seemed inclined to marvel that we did not find the sunlight too intense for our eyes, and was interested in my attempt to explain that the sky was tempered to a bluish colour through the refraction of the air, though I doubt if he clearly understood that. I explained how the iris of the human eyes can contract the pupil and save the delicate internal structure from the excess of sunlight, and was allowed to approach within a few feet of the Presence in order that this structure might be seen. This led to a comparison of the lunar and terrestrial eyes. The former is not only excessively sensitive to such light as men can see, but it can also *see* heat, and every difference in temperature within the moon renders objects visible to it.

"The iris was quite a new organ to the Grand Lunar. For a time he amused himself by flashing his rays into my face and watching my pupils contract. As a consequence, I was dazzled and blinded for some little time. . . .

"But in spite of that discomfort, I found something reassuring by insensible degrees in the rationality of this business of question and answer. I could shut my eyes, think of my answer, and almost forget that the Grand Lunar has no face. . . .

"When I had descended again to my proper place the Grand Lunar asked how we sheltered ourselves from heat and storms, and I expounded to him the arts of building and furnishing. Here we wandered into misunderstandings and cross-purposes, due largely, I must admit, to the looseness of my expressions. For a long time I had great difficulty in making him understand the nature of a house. To him and his attendant Selenites it seemed no doubt the most whimsical thing in the world that men should build houses when they might descend into excavations, and an additional complication was introduced by the attempt I made to explain that men had originally begun their homes in caves, and that they were now

taking their railways and many establishments beneath the surface. Here I think a desire for intellectual completeness betrayed me. There was also a considerable tangle due to an equally unwise attempt on my part to explain about mines. Dismissing this topic at last in an incomplete state, the Grand Lunar inquired what we did with the interior of our globe.

"A tide of twittering and piping swept into the remotest corners of that great assembly when it was at last made clear that we men know absolutely nothing of the contents of the world upon which the immemorial generations of our ancestors have been evolved. Three times had I to repeat that of all the 4,000 miles of substance between the earth and its centre men knew only to the depth of a mile, and that very vaguely. I understood the Grand Lunar to ask why I had come to the moon seeing we had scarcely touched our own planet yet, but he did not trouble me at that time to proceed to an explanation, being too anxious to pursue the details of this mad inversion of all his ideas.

"He reverted to the question of weather, and I tried to describe the perpetually changing sky, and snow, and frost and hurricanes. 'But when the night comes,' he asked, 'is it not cold?'

"I told him it was colder than by day.

"'And does not your atmosphere freeze?'

"I told him not; that it was never cold enough for that, because our nights were so short.

"'Not even liquefy?'

"I was about to say 'No,' but then it occurred to me that one part at least of our atmosphere, the water vapour of it, does sometimes liquefy and form dew and sometimes freeze and form frost — a process perfectly analogous to the freezing of all the external atmosphere of the moon during its longer night. I made myself clear on this point, and from that the Grand Lunar went on to speak with me of sleep. For the need of sleep that comes so regularly every twenty-four hours to all things is part also of our earthly inheritance. On the moon they rest only at rare intervals and after exceptional exertions. Then I tried to describe to him the soft splendours of a summer night, and from that I passed to a description of those animals that prowl by night and sleep by day. I told him of lions and tigers, and here it seemed that we had come to a deadlock. For, save in their waters, there are no creatures in the moon not absolutely domestic and subject to his will, and so it has been for immemorial years. They have monstrous water creatures, but no evil beasts, and the idea of anything strong and large existing 'outside' in the night is very difficult for them."

[*The record is here too broken to transcribe for the space of perhaps twenty words or more.*]

"He talked with his attendants, as I suppose, upon the strange superficiality and unrea-

sonableness of (man), who lives on the mere surface of a world, a creature of waves and winds and all the chances of space, who cannot even unite to overcome the beasts that prey upon his kind, and yet who dares to invade another planet. During this aside I sat thinking, and then at his desire I told him of the different sorts of men. He searched me with questions. 'And for all sorts of work you have the same sort of men. But who thinks? Who governs?'

"I gave him an outline of the democratic method.

"When I had done he ordered cooling sprays upon his brow, and then requested me to repeat my explanation conceiving something had miscarried.

"'Do they not do different things then?' said Phi-oo.

"Some I admitted were thinkers and some officials; some hunted, some were mechanics, some artists, some toilers. 'But *all* rule,' I said.

"'And have they not different shapes to fit them to their different duties?'

"'None that you can see,' I said, 'except perhaps their clothes. Their minds perhaps differ a little,' I reflected.

"'Their minds must differ a great deal,' said the Grand Lunar, 'or they would all want to do the same things.'

"In order to bring myself into a closer harmony with his preconceptions, I said that his surmise was right. 'It was all hidden in the brain,' I said; 'but the difference was there. Perhaps if one could see the minds and

souls of men they would be as varied and unequal as the Selenites. There were great men and small men, men who could reach out far and wide, and men who could go swiftly; noisy, trumpet-minded men, and men who could remember without thinking. . . .'"

[*The record is indistinct for three words.*]

"He interrupted me to recall me to my previous statement. 'But you said all men rule?' he pressed.

"'To a certain extent,' I said, and made, I fear, a denser fog with my explanation.

"He reached out to a salient fact. 'Do you mean,' he asked, 'that there is no Grand Earthly?'

"I thought of several people, but assured him finally there was none. I explained that such autocrats and emperors as we had tried upon earth had usually ended in drink, or vice, or violence, and that the large and influential section of the people of the earth to which I belonged, the Anglo-Saxons, did not mean to try that sort of thing again. At which the Grand Lunar was even more amazed.

"'But how do you keep even such wisdom as you have?' he asked; and I explained to him the way we helped our limited"

[*A word omitted here, probably "brains."*]

"with libraries of books. I explained to him how our science was growing by the united labours of innumerable little men, and on that he made no com-

ment save that it was evident we had mastered much in spite of our social savagery, or we could not have come to the moon. Yet the contrast was very marked. With knowledge the Selenites grew and changed; mankind stored their knowledge about them and remained brutes — equipped. He said this. . . ."

[*Here there is a short piece of the record indistinct.*]

"He then caused me to describe how we went about this earth of ours, and I described to him our railways and ships. For a time he could not understand that we had had the use of steam only one hundred years, but when he did he was clearly amazed. I may mention as a singular thing that the Selenites use years to count by, just as we do on earth, though I can make nothing of their numeral system. That, however, does not matter, because Phi-oo understands ours. From that I went on to tell him that mankind had dwelt in cities only for nine or ten thousand years, and that we were still not united in one brotherhood, but under many different forms of government. This astonished the Grand Lunar very much, when it was made clear to him. At first he thought we referred merely to administrative areas.

"'Our States and Empires are still the rawest sketches of what order will some day be,' I said, and so I came to tell him. . . ."

[*At this point a length of record that probably represents thirty or forty words is totally illegible.*]

"The Grand Lunar was greatly impressed by the folly of men in clinging to the inconvenience of diverse tongues. 'They want to communicate and yet not to communicate,' he said, and then for a long time he questioned me closely concerning war.

"He was at first perplexed and incredulous. 'You mean to say,' he asked, seeking confirmation, 'that you run about over the surface of your world — this world, whose riches you have scarcely begun to scrape — killing one another for beasts to eat?'

"I told him that was perfectly correct.

"He asked for particulars to assist his imagination. 'But do not your ships and your poor little cities get injured?' he asked and I found the waste of property and conveniences seemed to impress upon him almost as much as the killing. 'Tell me more,' said the Grand Lunar; 'make me see pictures. I cannot conceive these things.'

"And so, for a space, though something loth, I told him the story of earthly War.

"I told him of the first orders and ceremonies of war, of warnings and ultimatums, and the marshalling and marching of troops. I gave him an idea of manœuvres and positions and battle joined. I told him of sieges and assaults, of starvation and hardship in trenches, and of sentinels freezing in the snow. I told him of routs and surprises, and desperate last stands and faint hopes, and the pitiless pursuit of fugitives and the dead

upon the field. I told, too, of the past, of invasions and massacres, of the Huns and Tartars, and the wars of Mahomet and the Caliphs and the Crusades. And as I went on, and Phi-oo translated, the Selenites cooed and murmured in a steadily intensified emotion.

"I told them an ironclad could fire a shot of a ton twelve miles, and go through twenty feet of iron — and how we could steer torpedoes under water. I went on to describe a Maxim gun in action and what I could imagine of the Battle of Colenso. The Grand Lunar was so incredulous that he interrupted the translation of what I had said in order to have my verification of my account. They particularly doubted my description of the men cheering and rejoicing as they went into battle.

"'But surely they do not like it!' translated Phi-oo.

"I assured them men of my race considered battle the most glorious experience of life, at which the whole assembly was stricken with amazement.

"'But what good is this war?' asked the Grand Lunar, sticking to his theme.

"'Oh! as for *good*!' said I, 'it thins the population!'

"'But why should there be a need — ?'

"There came a pause, the cooling sprays impinged upon his brow, and then he spoke again."

At this point there suddenly becomes predominant in the record a series of undulations that have been apparent as a per-plexing complication as far back as Cavor's description of the silence that fell before the first speaking of the Grand Lunar. These undulations are evidently the result of radiations proceeding from the lunar source, and their persistent approximation to the alternating signals of Cavor is curiously suggestive of some operator deliberately seeking to mix them in with his message and render it illegible. At first they are small and regular, so that with a little care and the loss of very few words we have been able to disentangle Cavor's message; then they become broad and larger, then suddenly they are irregular, with an irregularity that gives the effect at last of someone scribbling through a line of writing. For a long time nothing can be made of this madly zigzagging trace; then quite abruptly the interruption ceases, leaves a few words clear, and then resumes and continues for all the rest of the message, completely obliterating whatever Cavor was attempting to transmit. Why, if this is indeed a deliberate intervention, the Selenites should have preferred to let Cavor go on transmitting his message in happy ignorance of their obliteration of its record, when it was clearly quite in their power and much more easy and convenient for them to stop his proceedings at any time, is a problem to which I can contribute nothing. The thing seems to have happened so, and that is all I can say. This last rag of his description of the Grand Lunar begins, in mid-sentence:

"interrogated me very closely upon my secret. I was able in a little while to get to an understanding with them, and at last to elucidate what has been a puzzle to me ever since I realised the vastness of their science, namely, how it is they themselves have never discovered 'Cavorite.' I find they know of it as a theoretical substance, but they have always regarded it as a practical impossibility, because for some reason there is no helium in the moon, and helium —"

[*Across the last letters of helium slashes the resumption of that obliterating trace. Note that word "secret," for on that, and that alone, I base my interpretation of the last message, as both Mr. Wendigee and myself now believe it to be, that he is ever likely to send us.*]

CHAPTER 25

THE LAST MESSAGE CAVOR SENT TO THE EARTH

IN this unsatisfactory manner the penultimate message of Cavor dies out. One seems to see him away there amidst his blue-lit apparatus intently signalling us to the last, all unaware of the curtain of confusion that drops between us; all unaware, too, of the final dangers that even then must have been creeping upon him. His disastrous want of vulgar common sense had utterly betrayed him. He had talked of war, he had talked of all the strength and irrational violence of men, of their insatiable aggressions, their tireless futility of conflict. He had filled the whole moon-world with this impression of our race, and then I think it is plain he admitted that upon himself alone hung the possibility—at least for a long time—of any other men reaching the moon. The line the cold, inhuman reason of the moon would take seems plain enough to me, and a suspicion of it, and then perhaps some sudden sharp realisation of it, must have come to him. One imagines him going about the moon with the remorse of this fatal indiscretion growing in his mind. During a certain time most assuredly the Grand Lunar was deliberating the new situation, and for all that time Cavor went as free as ever he had gone. We imagine that obstacles of some sort prevented his getting to his electro-magnetic apparatus again after that last message I have given. For some days we received nothing. Perhaps he was having fresh audiences, and trying to evade his previous admissions. Who can hope to guess?

And then suddenly, like a cry in the night, like a cry that is followed by a stillness, came the

last message. It is the briefest fragment, the broken beginnings of two sentences.

The first was:

"I was mad to lct the Grand Lunar know—"

There was an interval of perhaps a minute. One imagines some interruption from without. A departure from the instrument —a dreadful hesitation among the looming masses of apparatus in that dim, blue-lit cavern—a sudden rush back to it, full of a resolve that came too late. Then, as if it were hastily transmitted, came:

"Cavorite made as follows: take—"

There followed one word, a quite unmeaning word as it stands—

"uless."

And that is all.

It may be he made a hasty attempt to spell "useless" when his fate was close upon him. Whatever it was that was happening about that apparatus, we cannot tell. Whatever it was we shall never, I know, receive another message from the moon. For my own part a vivid dream has come to my help, and I see, almost as plainly as though I had seen it in actual fact, a blue-lit dishevelled Cavor struggling in the grip of a great multitude of those insect Selenites, struggling ever more desperately and hopelessly as they swarm upon him, shouting, expostulating, perhaps even at last fighting, and being forced backward step by step out of all speech or sign of his fellows, for evermore into the Unknown—into the dark, into that silence that has no end.

"HIS GREAT HAND WOULD COME OVER THE GARDEN
WALLS, HE WOULD COVET THE VERY BREAD
IN THE BAKER'S CART."

Drawn by Cyrus Cuneo, 1904 for *THE FOOD OF THE GODS.*

"A MUSCULAR YOUNG PERSON...USED TO TAKE HIM FOR
HIS AIRINGS IN AN EIGHT-HORSE-POWER
HILL-CLIMBING PERAMBULATOR."

Drawn by Cyrus Cuneo, 1904 for *THE FOOD OF THE GODS.*

THE FOOD OF THE GODS AND HOW IT CAME TO EARTH

Book I: *The Dawn of the Food*

CHAPTER 1

THE DISCOVERY OF THE FOOD

§ 1

IN the middle years of the nineteenth century there first became abundant in this strange world of ours a class of men, men tending for the most part to become elderly, who are called, and who, though they dislike it extremely, are very properly called "Scientists." They dislike that word so much that from the columns of *Nature,* which was from the first their distinctive and characteristic paper, it is as carefully excluded as if it were — that other word which is the basis of all really bad language in this country. But the Great Public and its Press know better, and "Scientists" they are, and when they emerge to any sort of publicity, "distinguished scientists" and "eminent scientists" and "well-known scientists" is the very least we call them.

Certainly both Mr. Bensington and Professor Redwood quite merited any of these terms long before they came upon the marvellous discovery of which this story tells. Mr. Bensington was a Fellow of the Royal Society and a former president of the Chemical Society, and Professor Redwood was Professor of Physiology in the Bond Street College of the London University and had been grossly libelled by the anti-vivisectionists time after time. And both had led lives of academic distinction from their very earliest youth.

They were of course quite undistinguished-looking men, as indeed all true Scientists are. There is more personal distinction about the mildest-mannered actor alive than there is about the entire Royal Society. Mr. Bensington was short and very, very bald, and he stooped slightly; he wore gold-rimmed spectacles and

cloth boots that were abundantly cut open because of his numerous corns, and Professor Redwood was entirely ordinary in his appearance. Until they happened upon the Food of the Gods (as I must insist upon calling it) they led lives of such eminent and studious obscurity that it is hard to find anything whatever to tell the reader about them.

Mr. Bensington won his spurs (if one may use such an expression of a gentleman in boots of slashed cloth) by his splendid researches upon the More Toxic Alkaloids, and Professor Redwood rose to eminence — I do not clearly remember how he rose to eminence. I know he was very eminent, and that's all. But I fancy it was a voluminous work on Reaction Times with numerous plates of sphygmograph tracings (I write subject to correction) and an admirable new terminology that did the thing for him.

The general public saw little or nothing of either of these gentlemen. Sometimes at such places as the Royal Institution and the Society of Arts it did in a sort of way see Mr. Bensington, or at least his blushing baldness and something of his collar and coat, and hear fragments of a lecture or paper that he imagined himself to be reading audibly; and once I remember — one midday in the vanished past — when the British Association was at Dover, coming on Section C. or D. or some such letter, which had taken up its quarters in a public-house, and following out of mere curiosity, two serious-looking la-dies with paper parcels through a door labelled "Billiards" and "Pool" into a scandalous darkness, broken only by a magic-lantern circle of Redwood's tracings.

I watched the lantern slides come and go, and listened to a voice (I forget what it was saying) which I believe was the voice of Professor Redwood, and there was a sizzling from the lantern and another sound that kept me there, still out of curiosity, until the lights were unexpectedly turned up. And then I perceived that this sound was the sound of the munching of buns and sandwiches and things that the assembled British Associates had come there to eat under cover of the magic-lantern darkness.

And Redwood I remember went on talking all the time the lights were up and dabbing at the place where his diagram ought to have been visible on the screen — and so it was again so soon as the darkness was restored. I remember him then as a most ordinary, slightly nervous-looking dark man, with an air of being preoccupied with something else and doing what he was doing just then under an unaccountable sense of duty.

I heard Bensington also once — in the old days — at an educational conference in Bloomsbury. Like most eminent chemists and botanists, Mr. Bensington was very authoritative upon teaching — though I am certain he would have been scared out of his wits by an average Board School class in half-an-hour — and so far as I

can remember now, he was propounding an improvement of Professor Armstrong's Heuristic method, whereby at the cost of three or four hundred pounds' worth of apparatus, a total neglect of all other studies and the undivided attention of a teacher of exceptional gifts, an average child might with a peculiar sort of thumby thoroughness acquire in the course of ten or twelve years almost as much chemistry as one could learn from one of those objectionable shilling textbooks that were then so common at that date. . . .

Quite ordinary persons you perceive, both of them, outside their science. Or if anything on the unpractical side of ordinary. And that you will find is the case with "scientists" as a class all the world over. What there is great about them is an annoyance to their fellow scientists and a mystery to the general public, and what is not is evident.

There is no doubt about what is not great, no race of men have such obvious littlenesses. They live so far as their human intercourse goes, in a narrow world; their researches involve infinite attention and an almost monastic seclusion; and what is left over is not very much. To witness some queer, shy, misshapen, greyheaded, self-important little discoverer of great discoveries, ridiculously adorned with the wide ribbon of an order of chivalry and holding a reception of his fellow men, or to read the anguish of *Nature* at the "neglect of science" when the angel of the birthday honours passes the Royal Society by, or to listen to one indefatigable lichenologist commenting on the work of another indefatigable lichenologist, such things force one to realise the unfaltering littleness of men.

And withal the reef of science that these little "scientists" built and are yet building is so wonderful, so portentous, so full of mysterious half-shapen promises for the mighty future of man! They do not seem to realise the things they are doing. No doubt long ago even Mr. Bensington, when he chose this calling, when he consecrated his life to the alkaloids and their kindred compounds had some inkling of the vision — more than an inkling. Without some great inspiration, for such glories and positions only as a "scientist" may expect, what young man would have given his life to this work, as young men do? No, they *must* have seen the glory, they must have had the vision, but so near that it has blinded them. The splendour has blinded them, mercifully, so that for the rest of their lives they can hold the light of knowledge in comfort — that we may see.

And perhaps it accounts for Redwood's touch of preoccupation, that — there can be no doubt of it now — he among his fellows was different; he was different inasmuch as something of the vision still lingered in his eyes.

§ 2

THE FOOD of the Gods I call it, this substance that Mr. Bensington and Professor Redwood made between them; and having regard

now to what it has already done
and all that it is certainly going
to do, there is surely no exag-
geration in the name. But Mr.
Bensington would no more have
called it by that name in cold
blood than he would have gone
out from his flat in Sloane Street
clad in regal scarlet and a wreath
of laurel. The phrase was a mere
first cry of astonishment from
him. He called it the Food of
the Gods in his enthusiasm, and
for an hour or so at the most
altogether. After that he decided
he was being absurd. When he
first thought of the thing he saw,
as it were, a vista of enormous
possibilities — literally enormous
possibilities, but upon this daz-
zling vista, after one stare of
amazement, he resolutely shut his
eyes even as a conscientious "sci-
entist" should. After that, the
Food of the Gods sounded bla-
tant to the pitch of indecency. He
was surprised he had used the
expression. Yet for all that some-
thing of that clear-eyed moment
hung about him and broke out
ever and again. . . .

"Really, you know," he said,
rubbing his hands together and
laughing nervously, "it has more
than a theoretical interest.

"For example," he confided,
bringing his face close to the Pro-
fessor's and dropping to an un-
dertone, "it would perhaps, if
suitably handled, sell. . . .

"Precisely," he said, walking
away — "as a Food. Or at least a
food ingredient.

"Assuming of course that it is
palatable. A thing we cannot
know till we have prepared it."

He turned upon the hearthrug,

and studied the carefully de-
signed slits upon his cloth shoes.

"Name?" he said, looking up
in response to an inquiry. "For
my part I incline to the good old
classical allusion. It — it makes
Science res— Gives it a touch of
old-fashioned dignity. I have been
thinking. . . . I don't know if
you will think it absurd of me.
. . . A little fancy is surely occa-
sionally permissible. . . . Herak-
leophorbia. Eh? The nutrition of
a possible Hercules? You know
it *might*. . . .

"Of course if you think *not* —"
Redwood reflected with his eyes
on the fire and made no objec-
tion.

"You think it would do?"
Redwood moved his head
gravely.

"It might be Titanophorbia,
you know. Food of Titans. . . .
You prefer the former?

"You're quite sure you don't
think it a little *too* —"
"No."
"Ah! I'm glad."
And so they called it Herakleo-
phorbia throughout their investi-
gations, and in their report — the
report that was never published,
because of the unexpected devel-
opments that upset all their ar-
rangements, it is invariably writ-
ten in that way. There were three
kindred substances prepared be-
fore they hit on the one their
speculations had foretold, and
these they spoke of as Herakleo-
phorbia I., Herakleophorbia II.,
and Herakleophorbia III. It is
Herakleophorbia IV. which I —
insisting upon Bensington's origi-
nal name — call here the Food of
the Gods.

§3

THE IDEA was Mr. Bensington's. But as it was suggested to him by one of Professor Redwood's contributions to the Philosophical Transactions, he very properly consulted that gentleman before he carried it further. Besides which it was, as a research, a physiological quite as much as a chemical inquiry.

Professor Redwood was one of those scientific men who are addicted to tracings and curves. You are familiar — if you are at all the sort of reader I like — with the sort of scientific paper I mean. It is a paper you cannot make head nor tail of, and at the end come five or six long folded diagrams that open out and show peculiar zigzag tracings, flashes of lightning overdone, or sinuous inexplicable things called " smoothed curves " set up on ordinates and rooting in abscissæ — and things like that. You puzzle over the thing for a long time and end with the suspicion that not only do you not understand it but that the author does not understand it either. But really you know many of these scientific people understand the meaning of their own papers quite well, it is simply a defect of expression that raises the obstacle between us.

I am inclined to think that Redwood thought in tracings and curves. And after his monumental work upon Reaction Times (the unscientific reader is exhorted to stick to it for a little bit longer and everything will be as clear as daylight) Redwood began to turn out smoothed curves and sphygmographeries upon Growth, and it was one of his papers upon Growth that really gave Mr. Bensington his idea.

Redwood, you know, had been measuring growing things of all sorts, kittens, puppies, sunflowers, mushrooms, bean plants and (until his wife put a stop to it) his baby, and he showed that growth went on, not at a regular pace, or, as he put it, so

but with bursts and intermissions of this sort,

and that apparently nothing grew regularly and steadily, and so far as he could make out nothing could grow regularly and steadily; it was as if every living thing had first to accumulate force to grow, grew with vigour only for a time and then had to wait for a space before it could go on growing again. And in the muffled and highly technical language of the really careful " scientist," Redwood suggested that the process of growth probably demanded the presence of a considerable quantity of some necessary substance in the blood that was only formed very slowly, and that when this substance was used up by growth, it was only very slowly replaced, and that mean-

while the organism had to mark time. He compared his unknown substance to oil in machinery. A growing animal was rather like an engine, he suggested, that can move a certain distance and must then be oiled before it can run again. ("But why shouldn't one oil the engine from without?" said Mr. Bensington, when he read the paper.) And all this, said Redwood, with the delightful nervous inconsecutiveness of his class, might very probably be found to throw a light upon the mystery of certain of the ductless glands. As though they had anything to do with it at all!

In a subsequent communication Redwood went further. He gave a perfect Brock's benefit of diagrams—exactly like rocket trajectories they were, and the gist of it—so far as it had any gist—was the blood of puppies and kittens and the sap of sunflowers and the juice of mushrooms in what he called the "growing phase" differed as to the proportions of certain elements from their blood and sap on the days when they were not particularly growing.

And when Mr. Bensington, after holding the diagrams sideways and upside down, began to see what this difference was, a great amazement came upon him. Because, you see, the difference might probably be due to the presence of just the very substance he had recently been trying to isolate in his researches upon such alkaloids as are most stimulating to the nervous system. He put down Redwood's paper on the patent reading-desk

that swung inconveniently from his armchair, took off his gold-rimmed spectacles, breathed on them and wiped them very carefully.

"By Jove!" said Mr. Bensington.

Then replacing his spectacles again he turned to the patent reading-desk, which immediately, as his elbow came against its arm, gave a coquettish squeak and deposited the paper, with all its diagrams in a dispersed and crumpled state, on the floor. "By Jove!" said Mr. Bensington, straining his stomach over the armchair with a patient disregard of the habits of this convenience, and then, finding the pamphlet still out of reach, he went down on all fours in pursuit. It was on the floor that the idea of calling it the Food of the Gods came to him. . . .

For you see, if he was right and Redwood was right, then by injecting or administering this new substance of his in food, he would do away with the "resting phase," and instead of growth going on in this fashion

it would (if you follow me) go thus

§ 4

THE NIGHT after his conversation with Redwood Mr. Bensington could sleep scarcely a wink. He

did seem once to get into a sort of doze, but it was only for a moment, and then he dreamt he had dug a deep hole into the earth and poured in tons and tons of the Food of the Gods and the earth was swelling and swelling, and all the boundaries of the countries were bursting, and the Royal Geographical Society was all at work like one mighty guild of tailors letting out the equator.

That of course was a ridiculous dream; but it shows the state of mental excitement into which Mr. Bensington got and the real value he attached to his idea, much better than any of the things he said or did when he was awake and on his guard. Or I should not have mentioned it, because as a general rule it is not I think at all interesting for people to tell each other about their dreams.

By a singular coincidence Redwood also had a dream that night, and his dream was this:

It was a diagram done in fire upon a long scroll of the abyss. And he (Redwood) was standing on a planet before a sort of black platform, lecturing about the new sort of growth that was now possible, to the More than Royal Institution of Primordial Forces, forces which had always previously, even in the growth of races, empires, planetary systems and worlds, gone so:

And even in some cases so:

And he was explaining to them quite lucidly and convincingly that these slow, these even retrogressive methods would be very speedily quite put out of fashion by his discovery.

Ridiculous of course! But that too shows—

That either dream is to be regarded as in any way significant or prophetic beyond what I have categorically said, I do not for one moment suggest.

CHAPTER 2

THE EXPERIMENTAL FARM

§ 1

MR. BENSINGTON proposed originally to try this stuff, so soon as he was really able to prepare it, upon tadpoles. One always does try this sort of thing upon tadpoles to begin with; that being what tadpoles are for. And it was agreed that he should conduct the experiments and not Red-

wood, because Redwood's laboratory was occupied with the ballistic apparatus and animals necessary for an investigation into the Diurnal Variation in the Butting Frequency of the Young Bull Calf, an investigation that was yielding curves of an abnormal and very perplexing sort, and the presence of glass globes of tadpoles was extremely undesirable while this particular research was in progress.

But when Mr. Bensington conveyed to his cousin Jane something of what he had in mind, she put a prompt veto upon the importation of any considerable number of tadpoles, or any such experimental creatures, into their flat. She had no objection whatever to his use of one of the rooms of the flat for the purposes of a non-explosive chemistry that so far as she was concerned came to nothing; and she let him have a gas furnace and a sink and a dust-tight cupboard of refuge from the weekly storm of cleaning she would not forgo. And having known people addicted to drink, she regarded his solicitude for distinction in learned societies as an excellent substitute for the coarser form of depravity. But any sort of living things in quantity, "wriggly" as they were bound to be alive, and "smelly" dead, she could not and would not abide. She said these things were certain to be unhealthy, and Bensington was notoriously a delicate man — it was nonsense to say he wasn't. And when Bensington tried to make the enormous importance of this possible discovery clear, she said that it was all very well, but if she consented to his making everything nasty and unwholesome in the place (and that was what it all came to) then she was certain he would be the first to complain.

And Mr. Bensington went up and down the room, regardless of his corns, and spoke to her quite firmly and angrily without the slightest effect. He said that nothing ought to stand in the way of the Advancement of Science, and she said that the Advancement of Science was one thing and having a lot of tadpoles in a flat was another; he said that in Germany it was an ascertained fact that a man with an idea like his would at once have twenty thousand properly-fitted cubic feet of laboratory placed at his disposal, and she said she was glad and always had been glad that she was not a German; he said that it would make him famous for ever, and she said it was much more likely to make him ill to have a lot of tadpoles in a flat like theirs; he said he was master in his own house, and she said that rather than wait on a lot of tadpoles she'd go as matron to a school; and then he asked her to be reasonable, and she asked *him* to be reasonable then and give up all this about tadpoles; and he said she might respect his ideas, and she said not if they were smelly she wouldn't; and then he gave way completely and said — in spite of the classical remarks of Huxley upon the subject — a bad word. Not a very bad word it was, but bad enough.

And after that she was greatly

offended and had to be apologised to, and the prospect of ever trying the Food of the Gods upon tadpoles in their flat at any rate vanished completely in the apology.

So Bensington had to consider some other way of carrying out these experiments in feeding that would be necessary to demonstrate his discovery, so soon as he had his substance isolated and prepared. For some days he meditated upon the possibility of boarding out his tadpoles with some trustworthy person, and then the chance sight of the phrase in a newspaper turned his thoughts to an Experimental Farm.

And chicks. Directly he thought of it, he thought of it as a poultry farm. He was suddenly taken with a vision of wildly growing chicks. He conceived a picture of coops and runs, outsize and still more outsize coops, and runs progressively larger. Chicks are so accessible, so easily fed and observed, so much drier to handle and measure, that for his purpose tadpoles seemed to him now, in comparison with them, quite wild and uncontrollable beasts. He was quite puzzled to understand why he had not thought of chicks instead of tadpoles from the beginning. Among other things it would have saved all this trouble with his cousin Jane. And when he suggested this to Redwood, Redwood quite agreed with him.

Redwood said he was convinced that in working so much upon needlessly small animals experimental physiologists made a great mistake. It is exactly like making experiments in chemistry with an insufficient quantity of material; errors of observation and manipulation become disproportionately large. It was of extreme importance just at present that scientific men should assert their right to have their material *big*. That was why he was doing his present series of experiments at the Bond Street College upon Bull Calves, in spite of a certain amount of inconvenience to the students and professors of other subjects caused by their incidental levity in the corridors. But the curves he was getting were quite exceptionally interesting, and would, when published, amply justify his choice. For his own part, were it not for the inadequate endowment of science in this country, he would never, if he could avoid it, work on anything smaller than a whale. But a Public Vivarium on a scale sufficient to render this possible was, he feared, at present, in this country at any rate, a Utopian demand. In Germany — Etc.

As Redwood's bull calves needed his daily attention, the selection and equipment of the Experimental Farm fell largely on Bensington. The entire cost also, it was understood, was to be defrayed by Bensington, at least until a grant could be obtained. Accordingly he alternated his work in the laboratory of his flat with farm-hunting up and down the lines that run southward out of London, and his peering spectacles, his simple baldness, and his lacerated cloth shoes filled the owners of numerous undesirable properties with

vain hopes. And he advertised
in several daily papers, and *Na-
ture* for a responsible couple
(married), punctual, active, and
used to poultry, to take entire
charge of an Experimental Farm
of three acres.

He found the place he seemed
in need of at Hickleybrow, near
Urshot in Kent. It was a queer
little isolated place, in a dell sur-
rounded by old pine woods that
were black and forbidding at
night. A humped shoulder of
down cut it off from the sunset,
and a gaunt well with a shattered
penthouse dwarfed the dwelling.
The little house was creeperless,
several windows were broken,
and the cart shed had a black
shadow at midday. It was a mile
and half from the end house of
the village, and its loneliness was
very doubtfully relieved by an
ambiguous family of echoes.

The place impressed Bensing-
ton as being eminently adapted
to the requirements of scientific
research. He walked over the
premises sketching out coops and
runs with a sweeping arm, and
he found the kitchen capable of
accommodating a series of incu-
bators and foster mothers with
the very minimum of alteration.
He took the place then and
there; on his way back to London
he stopped at Dunton Green and
closed with an eligible couple
that had answered his advertise-
ments, and that same evening he
succeeded in isolating a sufficient
quantity of Herakleophorbia I.
to more than justify these engage-
ments.

The eligible couple who were
destined under Mr. Bensington

to be the first almoners on earth
of the Food of the Gods, were not
only very perceptibly aged, but
also extremely dirty. This latter
point Mr. Bensington did not
observe, because nothing destroys
the powers of general observation
quite so much as a life of experi-
mental science. They were named
Skinner, Mr. and Mrs. Skinner,
and Mr. Bensington interviewed
them in a small room with her-
metically sealed windows, a
spotted overmantel looking-glass,
and some ailing calceolarias.

Mrs. Skinner was a very little
old woman, capless, with dirty
white hair drawn back very very
tightly from a face that had
begun by being chiefly, and was
now through the loss of teeth and
chin and the wrinkling up of
everything else, ending by being
almost exclusively—nose. She
was dressed in slate colour (so
far as her dress had any colour)
slashed in one place with red
flannel. She let him in and talked
to him guardedly and peered at
him round and over her nose,
while Mr. Skinner she alleged
made some alteration in his
toilette. She had one tooth that
got into her articulation, and
she held her two long wrinkled
hands nervously together. She
told Mr. Bensington that she had
managed fowls for years, and
knew all about incubators; in
fact, they themselves had run a
Poultry Farm at one time, and
it had only failed at last through
the want of pupils. "It's the
pupils as pay," said Mrs. Skinner.

Mr. Skinner, when he appeared,
was a large-faced man with a
lisp, and a squint that made him

look over the top of your head, slashed slippers that appealed to Mr. Bensington's sympathies, and a manifest shortness of buttons. He held his coat and shirt together with one hand and traced patterns on the black and gold tablecloth with the index finger of the other, while his disengaged eye watched Mr. Bensington's sword of Damocles, so to speak, with an expression of sad detachment. "You don't want to run thith Farm for profit. No, Thir. Ith all the thame, Thir. Ekthperimenth! Prethithely."

He said they could go to the farm at once. He was doing nothing at Dunton Green except a little tailoring. "It ithn't the thmart plathe I thought it wath, and what I get ithent thkarthely worth having," he said, "tho that if it ith any convenienth to you for uth to come. . . ."

And in a week Mr. and Mrs. Skinner were installed in the farm, and the jobbing carpenter from Hickleybrow was diversifying the task of erecting runs and henhouses with a systematic discussion of Mr. Bensington.

"I haven't theen much of 'im yet," said Mr. Skinner. "But ath far ath I can make 'im out 'e theemth to be a thtewpid o' fool."

"*I* thought 'e seemed a bit dotty," said the carpenter from Hickleybrow.

"'E fanthieth 'imthelf about poultry," said Mr. Skinner. "O my goodneth! You'd think nobody knew nothin' about poultry thept 'im."

"'E *looks* like a 'en," said the carpenter from Hickleybrow;

"what with them spectacles of 'is."

Mr. Skinner came closer to the carpenter from Hickleybrow and spoke in a confidential manner, and one sad eye regarded the distant village and one was bright and wicked. "Got to be meathured every blethed day—every blethed 'en, 'e thayth. Tho' ath to thee they grow properly. What oh . . . eh? Every blethed 'en—every blethed day."

And Mr. Skinner put up his hand to laugh behind it in a refined and contagious manner, and humped his shoulders very much —and only the other eye of him failed to participate in his laughter. Then doubting if the carpenter had quite got the point of it, he repeated in a penetrating whisper:"*Meathured!*"

"'E's worse than our old guvnor; I'm dratted if 'e ain't," said the carpenter from Hickleybrow.

§2

EXPERIMENTAL work is the most tedious thing in the world (unless it be the reports of it in the *Philosophical Transactions*), and it seemed a long time to Mr. Bensington before his first dream of enormous possibilities was replaced by a crumb of realisation. He had taken the Experimental Farm in October, and it was May before the first inklings of success began. Herakleophorbia I. and II. and III. had to be tried, and failed; there was trouble with the rats of the Experimental Farm, and there was trouble with the Skinners. The only way to get Skinner to do anything he was told to do was to dismiss him.

Then he would rub his unshaven chin — he was always unshaven most miraculously and yet never bearded — with a flattened hand, and look at Mr. Bensington with one eye, and over him with the other, and say, "Oo, of courthe, Thir — if you're *theriouth.* . . !"

But at last success dawned. And its herald was a letter in the long slender handwriting of Mr. Skinner.

"The new Brood are out," wrote Mr. Skinner, "and don't quite like the look of them. Growing very rank — quite unlike what the similar lot was before your last directions was given. The last before the cat got them was a very nice stocky chick, but these are Growing like thistles. I never saw. They peck so hard, striking above boot top, that am unable to give exact Measures as requested. They are regular Giants and eating as such. We shall want more corn very soon, for you never saw such chicks to eat. Bigger than Bantams. Going on at this rate they ought to be a bird for show, rank as they are. Plymouth Rocks won't be in it. Had a scare last night thinking that cat was at them, and when I looked out at the window could have sworn I see her getting in under the wire. The chicks was all awake and pecking about hungry when I went out, but could not see anything of the cat. So gave them a peck of corn, and fastened up safe. Shall be glad to know if the Feeding to be continued as directed. Food you mixed is pretty near all gone, and do not like to mix any more myself on account of the accident with the pudding. With best wishes from us both, and soliciting continuance of esteemed favours,

"Respectfully yours,
"ALFRED NEWTON SKINNER."

The allusion towards the end referred to a milk pudding with which some Herakleophorbia II. had got itself mixed, with painful and very nearly fatal results to the Skinners.

But Mr. Bensington, reading between the lines, saw in this rankness of growth the attainment of his long-sought goal. The next morning he alighted at Urshot station, and in the bag in his hand he carried, sealed in three tins, a supply of the Food of the Gods sufficient for all the chicks in Kent.

It was a bright and beautiful morning late in May, and his corns were so much better that he resolved to walk through Hickleybrow to his farm. It was three miles and a half altogether, through the park and village and then along the green glades of the Hickleybrow preserves. The trees were all dusted with the green spangles of high spring, the hedges were full of stitchwort and campion and the woods of blue hyacinths and purple orchid, and everywhere there was a great noise of birds, thrushes, blackbirds, robins, finches, and many more; and in one warm corner of the park some bracken was unrolling, and there was a leaping and rushing of fallow deer.

These things brought back to

Mr. Bensington his early and forgotten delight in life; before him the promise of his discovery grew bright and joyful, and it seemed to him that indeed he must have come upon the happiest day in his life. And when in the sunlit run by the sandy bank under the shadow of the pine trees he saw the chicks that had eaten the food he had mixed for them, gigantic and gawky, bigger already than many a hen that is married and settled; and still growing, still in their first soft yellow plumage (just faintly marked with brown along the back), he knew indeed that his happiest day had come.

At Mr. Skinner's urgency he went into the run; but after he had been pecked through the cracks in his shoes once or twice he got out again, and watched these monsters through the wire netting. He peered close to the netting, and followed their movements as though he had never seen a chick before in his life.

"Whath they'll be when they're grown up ith impothible to think," said Mr. Skinner.

"Big as a horse," said Mr. Bensington.

"Pretty near," said Mr. Skinner.

"Several people could dine off a wing!" said Mr. Bensington. "They'd cut up into joints like butcher's meat."

"They won't go on growing at thith pathe though," said Mr. Skinner.

"No?" said Mr. Bensington.

"No," said Mr. Skinner. "I know thith thort. They begin rank, but they don't go on, bleth you! No."

There was a pause.

"It'th management," said Mr. Skinner modestly.

Mr. Bensington turned his glasses on him suddenly.

"We got 'em almoth ath big at the other plathe," said Mr. Skinner, with his better eye piously uplifted and letting himself go a little; "me and the mithith."

Mr. Bensington made his usual general inspection of the premises, but he speedily returned to the new run. It was, you know, in truth ever so much more than he had dared to expect. The course of science is so tortuous and so slow; after the clear promises and before the practical realisation arrives there comes almost always year after year of intricate contrivance, and here—here was the Food of the Gods arriving after less than a year of testing! It seemed too good—too good. That Hope Deferred which is the daily food of the scientific imagination was to be his no more! So at least it seemed to him then. He came back and stared at these stupendous chicks of his time after time.

"Let me see," he said. "They're ten days old. And by the side of an ordinary chick I should fancy—about six or seven times as big. . . ."

"It'th about time we artht for a rithe in thkrew," said Mr. Skinner to his wife. "He'th ath pleathed ath Punth about the way we got thoth chickth on in the further run—pleathed ath Punth he ith."

He bent confidentially towards her. "Thinkth it'th that old food of hith," he said behind his hand, and made a noise of suppressed laughter in his pharyngeal cavity. . . .

Mr. Bensington was indeed a happy man that day. He was in no mood to find fault with details of management. The sunshine certainly brought out the accumulating slovenliness of the Skinner couple more vividly than he had ever seen it before. But his comments were of the gentlest. The fencing of many of the runs was out of order, but he seemed to consider it quite satisfactory when Mr. Skinner explained that it was a "fokth or a dog or thomething" did it. He pointed out that the incubator had not been cleaned.

"That it *asn't*, Sir," said Mrs. Skinner with her arms folded, smiling coyly behind her nose. "We don't seem to have had time to clean it not since we been 'ere. . . ."

He went upstairs to see some ratholes that Skinner said would justify a trap—they certainly were enormous—and discovered that the room in which the Food of the Gods was mixed with meal and bran was in a quite disgraceful disorder. The Skinners were the sort of people who find a use for cracked saucers and old cans and pickle jars and mustard boxes, and the place was littered with these. In one corner a great pile of apples that Skinner had saved was decaying and from a nail in the sloping part of the ceiling hung several rabbit skins upon which he proposed to test his gift

as a furrier. ("There ithn't mutth about furth and thingth that *I* don't know," said Skinner.)

Mr. Bensington certainly sniffed critically at this disorder, but he made no unnecessary fuss, and even when he found a wasp regaling itself in a gallipot half full of Herakleophorbia IV., he simply remarked mildly that his substance was better sealed from the damp than exposed to the air in that manner.

And he turned from these things at once to remark—what had been for some time in his mind—"I *think*, you know, Skinner—I shall kill one of these chicks—as a specimen. I think we will kill it this afternoon, and I will take it back with me to London."

He pretended to peer into another gallipot and then took off his spectacles to wipe them.

"I should like," he said, "I should like very much to have some relic—some memento—of this particular brood at this particular day.

"By-the-by," he said, "you don't give those little chicks meat?"

"Oh! *no*, Thir," said Skinner, "I can athure you, Thir, we know far too much about the management of fowlth of all dethcriptionth to do anything of that thort."

"Quite sure you don't throw your dinner refuse—I thought I noticed the bones of a rabbit scattered about the far corner of the run—"

But when they came to look at them they found they were the

larger bones of a cat picked very clean and dry.

§ 3

"*That's* no chick," said Mr. Bensington's cousin Jane.

"Well, I should *think* I knew a chick when I saw it," said Mr. Bensington's cousin Jane hotly.

"It's too big for a chick, for one thing, and besides you can *see* perfectly well it isn't a chick.

"It's more like a bustard than a chick."

"For my part," said Redwood, reluctantly allowing Bensington to drag him into the argument, "I must confess that, considering all the evidence—"

"Oh! if you do *that*," said Mr. Bensington's cousin Jane, "instead of using your eyes like a sensible person—"

"Well, but really, Miss Bensington—!"

"Oh! Go *on!*" said Cousin Jane. "You men are all alike."

"Considering all the evidence, this certainly falls within the definition—no doubt it's abnormal and hypertrophied, but still—especially since it was hatched from the egg of a normal hen—Yes, I think, Miss Bensington, I must admit—this, so far as one can call it anything, is a sort of chick."

"You mean it's a chick?" said Cousin Jane.

"I *think* it's a chick," said Redwood.

"What NONSENSE!" said Mr. Bensington's cousin Jane, and "Oh!" directed at Redwood's head, "I haven't patience with you," and then suddenly she turned about and went out of the room with a slam.

"And it's a very great relief for me to see it, too, Bensington," said Redwood, when the reverberation of the slam had died away. "In spite of its being so big."

Without any urgency from Mr. Bensington he sat down in the low armchair by the fire and confessed to proceedings that even in an unscientific man would have been indiscreet. "You will think it very rash of me, Bensington, I know," he said, "but the fact is I put a little—not very much of it—but some—into Baby's bottle very nearly a week ago!"

"But suppose—!" cried Mr. Bensington.

"I know," said Redwood, and glanced at the giant chick upon the plate on the table.

"It's turned out all right, thank goodness," and he felt in his pocket for his cigarettes.

He gave fragmentary details. "Poor little chap wasn't putting on weight . . . desperately anxious. Winkles, a frightful duffer . . . former pupil of mine . . . no good. . . . Mrs. Redwood—unmitigated confidence in Winkles. . . . *You* know, man with a manner like a cliff—towering. . . . No confidence in *me*, of course. . . . Taught Winkles. . . . Scarcely allowed in the nursery. . . . Something had to be done. . . . Slipped in while the nurse was at breakfast . . . got at the bottle."

"But he'll grow," said Mr. Bensington.

"He's growing. Twenty-seven

ounces last week. . . . You should hear Winkles. It's management, he said."

"Dear me! That's what Skinner says! "

Redwood looked at the chick again. "The bother is to keep it up," he said. "They won't trust me in the nursery alone, because I tried to get a growth curve out of Georgina Phyllis — you know — and how I'm to give him a second dose — "

"Need you? "

"He's been crying two days — can't get on with his ordinary food again, anyhow. He wants some more now."

"Tell Winkles."

"Hang Winkles!" said Redwood.

"You might get at Winkles and give him powders to give the child — "

"That's about what I shall have to do," said Redwood, resting his chin on his fist and staring into the fire.

Bensington stood for a space smoothing the down on the breast of the giant chick. "They will be monstrous fowls," he said.

"They will," said Redwood, still with his eyes on the glow.

"Big as horses," said Bensington.

"Bigger," said Redwood. "That's just it! "

Bensington turned away from the specimen. "Redwood," he said, "these fowls are going to create a sensation."

Redwood nodded his head at the fire.

"And by Jove!" said Bensington, coming round suddenly with a flash in his spectacles, "so will your little boy! "

"That's just what I'm thinking of," said Redwood.

He sat back, sighed, threw his unconsumed cigarette into the fire and thrust his hands deep into his trouser pockets. "That's precisely what I'm thinking of. This Herakleophorbia is going to be queer stuff to handle. The pace that chick must have grown at — ! "

"A little boy growing at that pace," said Mr. Bensington slowly, and stared at the chick as he spoke.

"I *say!* " said Bensington, "he'll be Big."

"I shall give him diminishing doses," said Redwood. "Or at any rate Winkles will."

"It's rather too much of an experiment."

"Much."

"Yet still, you know, I must confess — . . . Some baby will sooner or later have to try it."

"Oh, we'll try it on *some* baby — certainly."

"Exactly so," said Bensington, and came and stood on the hearthrug and took off his spectacles to wipe them.

"Until I saw these chicks, Redwood, I don't think I *began* to realise — anything — of the possibilities of what we were making. It's only beginning to dawn upon me . . . the possible consequences. . . ."

And even then, you know, Mr. Bensington was far from any conception of the mine that little train would fire.

§4

THAT happened early in June. For some weeks Bensington was kept from revisiting the Experi-

mental Farm by a severe imaginary catarrh, and one necessary flying visit was made by Redwood. He returned an even more anxious-looking parent than he had gone. Altogether there were seven weeks of steady, uninterrupted growth. . . .

And then the Wasps began their career.

It was late in July and nearly a week before the hens escaped from Hickleybrow that the first of the big wasps was killed. The report of it appeared in several papers, but I do not know whether the news reached Mr. Bensington, much less whether he connected it with the general laxity of method that prevailed at the Experimental Farm.

There can be but little doubt now, that while Mr. Skinner was plying Mr. Bensington's chicks with Herakleophorbia IV., a number of wasps were just as industriously — perhaps more industriously — carrying quantities of the same paste to their early summer broods in the sand banks beyond the adjacent pine woods. And there can be no dispute whatever that these early broods found just as much growth and benefit in the substance as Mr. Bensington's hens. It is in the nature of the wasp to attain to effective maturity before the domestic fowl and of all the creatures that through the generous carelessness of the Skinners were partaking of the benefits Mr. Bensington heaped upon his hens, the wasps were the first to make any sort of figure in the world.

It was a keeper named Godfrey on the estate of Lieutenant-Colonel Rupert Hick, near Maidstone, who encountered and had the luck to kill the first of these monsters of whom history has any record. He was walking knee-high in bracken across an open space in the beech woods that diversify Lieutenant-Colonel Hick's park, and he was carrying his gun — very fortunately for him a double-barrelled gun — over his shoulder, when he first caught sight of the thing. It was, he says, coming down against the light so that he could not see it very distinctly, and as it came it made a drone "like a motor car." He admits he was frightened. It was evidently as big or bigger than a barn owl, and to his practised eye its flight, and particularly the misty whirl of its wings, must have seemed weirdly unbird-like. The instinct of self-defence, I fancy, mingled with long habit when, as he says, he "let fly, right away."

The queerness of the experience probably affected his aim; at any rate most of his shot missed, and the thing merely dropped for a moment with an angry "Wuzzzz" that revealed the wasp at once, and then rose again with all its stripes shining against the light. He says it turned on him. At any rate, he fired his second barrel at less than twenty yards and threw down his gun, ran a pace or so, and ducked to avoid it.

It flew, he is convinced, within a yard of him; struck the ground, rose again, came down again perhaps thirty yards away, and rolled over with its body wriggling and its sting stabbing out and back in its last agony. He

emptied both barrels into it again before he ventured to go near.

When he came to measure the thing, he found it was twenty-seven and a half inches across its open wings, and its sting was three inches long. The abdomen was blown clean off from its body, but he estimated the length of the creature from head to sting as eighteen inches — which is very nearly correct. Its compound eyes were the size of penny pieces.

That is the first authenticated appearance of the giant wasps. The day after, a cyclist riding feet up down the hill between Sevenoaks and Tonbridge, very narrowly missed running over a second of these giants that was crawling across the roadway. His passage seemed to alarm it, and it rose with a noise like a sawmill. His bicycle jumped the footpath in the emotion of the moment, and when he could look back the wasp was soaring away above the woods towards Westerham.

After riding unsteadily for a little time, he put on his brake, dismounted — he was trembling so violently that he fell over his machine in doing so — and sat down by the roadside to recover. He had intended to ride to Ashford, but he did not get beyond Tonbridge that day. . . .

After that, curiously enough, there is no record of any big wasps being seen for three days. I find on consulting the meteorological record of those days that they were overcast and chilly with local showers, which may perhaps account for this inter-mission. Then on the fourth day came blue sky and brilliant sunshine, and such an outburst of wasps as the world had surely never seen before.

How many big wasps came out that day it is impossible to guess. There are at least fifty accounts of their apparition. There was one victim, a grocer, who discovered one of these monsters in a sugar-cask and very rashly attacked it with a spade as it rose. He struck it to the ground for a moment, and it stung him through the boot as he struck at it again and cut its body in halves. He was first dead of the two. . . .

The most dramatic of the fifty appearances was certainly that of the wasp that visited the British Museum about midday, dropping out of the blue serene upon one of the innumerable pigeons that feed in the courtyard of that building, and flying up to the cornice to devour its victim at leisure. After that it crawled for a time over the museum roof, entered the dome of the reading-room by a skylight, buzzed about inside it for some little time — there was a stampede among the readers — and at last found another window and vanished again with a sudden silence from human observation.

Most of the other reports were of mere passings or descents. A picnic party was dispersed at Aldington Knoll and all its sweets and jam consumed, and a puppy was killed and torn to pieces near Whitstable under the very eyes of its mistress. . . .

The streets that evening re-

sounded with the cry, the newspaper placards gave themselves up exclusively in the biggest of letters to the " Gigantic Wasps in Kent." Agitated editors and assistant editors ran up and down tortuous staircases bawling things about wasps. And Professor Redwood, emerging from his college in Bond Street at five, flushed from a heated discussion with his committee about the price of bull calves, bought an evening paper, opened it, changed colour, forgot about bull calves and committee forthwith, and took a hansom headlong for Bensington's flat.

§ 5

THE FLAT was occupied, it seemed to him, to the exclusion of all other sensible objects by Mr. Skinner and his voice, if indeed you can call either him or it a sensible object!

The voice was up very high slopping about among the notes of anguish. " It'th impothible for uth to thtop, Thir. We've thtopped on hoping thingth would get better and they've only got worth, Thir. It ithn't on'y the waptheth, Thir — there'th big earwigth, Thir — big ath that, Thir." (He indicated all his hand, and about three inches of fat dirty wrist.) " They pretty near give Mithith Thkinner fitth, Thir. And the thtinging nettleth by the runth, Thir, *they're* growing, Thir, and the canary creeper, Thir, what we thowed near the think, Thir — it put itth tendril through the window in the night, Thir, and very nearly caught Mithith Thkinner by the legth,

Thir. It'th that food of yourth, Thir. Wherever we thplathed it about, Thir, a bit, it'th thet everything growing ranker, Thir, than I ever thought anything could grow. It'th impothible to thtop a month, Thir. It'th more than our liveth are worth, Thir. Even if the waptheth don't thting uth, we thall be thuffocated by the creeper, Thir. You can't imagine, Thir — unleth you come down to thee, Thir — "

He turned his superior eye to the cornice above Redwood's head. " 'Ow do we know the ratth 'aven't got it, Thir! That 'th what I think of motht, Thir. I 'aven't theen any big ratth, Thir, but 'ow do I know, Thir. We been frightened for dayth becauth of the earwigth we've theen — like lobthterth they wath — two of 'em, Thir — and the frightful way the canary creeper wath growing, and directly I heard the waptheth — directly I 'eard 'em, Thir, I underthood. I didn't wait for nothing exthept to thow on a button I'd lortht, and then I came on up. Even now, Thir, I'm arf wild with angthiety, Thir. 'Ow do *I* know wat'th happenin' to Mithith Thkinner, Thir! There'th the creeper growing all over the plathe like a thnake, Thir — thwelp me but you 'ave to watch it, Thir, and jump out of itth way! — and the earwigth gettin' bigger and bigger, and the waptheth — she 'athen't even got a Blue Bag, Thir — if anything thould happen, Thir! "

" But the hens," said Mr. Bensington; " how are the hens? "

" We fed 'em up to yethterday, thwelp me," said Mr. Skinner.

"But thith morning we didn't *dare*, Thir. The noithe of the waptheth wath — thomething awful, Thir. They wath coming out — dothenth. Ath big ath 'enth. I thayth to 'er, I thayth you juth thow me on a button or two, I thath, for I can't go to London like thith, I thayth, and I'll go up to Mither Benthington, I thayth, and ekthplain thingth to 'im. And you thtop in thith room till I come back to you, I thayth, and keep the windowth thhut jutht ath tight ath ever you can, I thayth."

"If you hadn't been so confoundedly untidy —" began Redwood.

"Oh! don't thay *that*, Thir," said Skinner. "Not now, Thir. Not with me tho diththrethed, Thir, about Mithith Thkinner, Thir! Oh, *don't*, Thir! I 'aven't the 'eart to argue with you. Thwelp me, Thir, I 'aven't! It'th the ratth I keep a thinking of — 'Ow do I know they 'aven't got at Mithith Thkinner while I been up 'ere?"

"And you haven't got a solitary measurement of all these beautiful growth curves!" said Redwood.

"I been too upthet, Thir," said Mr. Skinner. "If you knew what we been through — me and the mithith! All thith latht month. We 'aven't known what to make of it, Thir. What with the henth gettin' tho rank, and the earwigth, and the canary creeper. I dunno if I told you, Thir — the canary creeper . . ."

"You've told us all that," said Redwood. "The thing is, Bensington, what are we to do?"

"What are *we* to do?" said Mr. Skinner.

"You'll have to go back to Mrs. Skinner," said Redwood. "You can't leave her there alone all night."

"Not alone, Thir, I don't. Not if there wath a dothen Mithith Thkinnerth. Itth Mithter Benthington —"

"Nonsense," said Redwood. "The wasps will be all right at night. And the earwigs will get out of your way —"

"But about the ratth?"

"There aren't any rats," said Redwood.

§6

MR. SKINNER might have forgone his chief anxiety. Mrs. Skinner did not stop out her day.

About eleven the canary creeper, which had been quietly active all the morning, began to clamber over the window and darken it, and the darker it got the more and more clearly Mrs. Skinner perceived her position would speedily become untenable. And also that she had lived many ages since Skinner went. She peered out of the darkling window through the stirring tendrils for some time, and then went very cautiously and opened the bedroom door and listened . . .

Everything seemed quiet; and so, tucking her skirts high about her, Mrs. Skinner made a bolt for the bedroom, and having first looked under the bed and locked herself in, proceeded with the methodical rapidity of an experienced woman to pack for departure. The bed had not been made,

and the room was littered with pieces of the creeper that Skinner had hacked off in order to close the window overnight, but these disorders she did not heed. She packed in a decent sheet. She packed all her own wardrobe and a velveteen jacket that Skinner wore in his finer moments, and she packed a jar of pickles that had not been opened, and so far she was justified in her packing. But she also packed two of the hermetically closed tins containing Herakleophorbia IV. that Mr. Bensington had brought on his last visit. (She was honest, good woman — but she was a grandmother, and her heart had burned within her to see such good growth lavished on a lot of dratted chicks.)

And having packed all these things, she put on her bonnet, took off her apron, tied a new bootlace round her umbrella, and after listening for a long time at door and window, opened the door and sallied out into a perilous world. The umbrella was under her arm and she clutched the bundle with two gnarled and resolute hands. It was her best Sunday bonnet she wore, and the two poppies that reared their heads amidst its splendours of band and bead seemed instinct with the same tremulous courage that possessed her.

The features about the roots of her nose wrinkled with determination. She had had enough of it! All alone there! Skinner might come back there if he liked.

She went out by the front door, going that way not because she wanted to go to Hickleybrow (her goal was Cheasing Eyebright where her married daughter resided), but because the back door was impassable on account of the canary creeper that had been growing so furiously ever since she upset the can of food near its roots. She listened for a space and closed the front door very carefully behind her. At the corner of the house she paused and reconnoitred. . . .

An extensive sandy scar upon the hillside beyond the pine woods marked the nest of the giant wasps, and this she studied very earnestly. The coming and going of the morning was over, not a wasp chanced to be in sight then, and except for a sound scarcely more perceptible than a steam wood-saw at work amidst the pines would have been, everything was still. As for earwigs, she could see not one. Down among the cabbages indeed something was stirring, but it might just as probably be a cat stalking birds. She watched this for a time.

She went a few paces past the corner, came in sight of the run containing the giant chicks and stopped again. "Ah!" she said, and shook her head slowly at the sight of them. They were at that time about the height of emus, but of course much thicker in the body — a larger thing altogether. They were all hens and five all told, now that the two cockerels had killed each other. She hesitated at their drooping attitudes. "Poor dears!" she said, and put down her bundle; "they've got no water. And they've 'ad no

food these twenty-four hours! And such appetites, too, as they 'ave!" She put a lean finger to her lips and communed with herself.

Then this dirty old woman did what seems to me a quite heroic deed of mercy. She left her bundle and umbrella in the middle of the brick path, and went to the well and drew no fewer than three pailfuls of water for the chickens' empty trough, and then while they were all crowding about that, she undid the door of the run very softly, after which she became extremely active, resumed her package, got over the hedge at the bottom of the garden, crossed the rank meadows (in order to avoid the wasps' nest) and toiled up the winding path towards Cheasing Eyebright.

She panted up the hill; and as she went she paused ever and again to rest her bundle and get her breath and stare back at the little cottage beside the pine wood below. And when at last, as she was nearing the crest of the hill, she saw afar off three several wasps dropping heavily westward, it helped her greatly on her way.

She soon got out of the open and into the high banked lane beyond (which seemed a safer place to her) and so up by Hickleybrow Coombe to the downs. There at the foot of the downs where a big tree gave an air of shelter she rested for a space on a stile.

Then on again very resolutely. . . .

You figure her, I hope, with her white bundle, a sort of erect black ant, hurrying along the little white path-thread athwart the downland slopes under the hot sun of the summer afternoon. On she struggled after her resolute indefatigable nose, and the poppies in her bonnet quivered perpetually and her spring side boots grew whiter and whiter with the downland dust. Flip, flap, flip, flap went her footfalls through the still heat of the day, and persistently, incurably, her umbrella sought to slip from under the elbow that retained it. The mouth wrinkle under her nose was pursed to an extreme resolution, and ever and again she told her umbrella to come up or gave her tightly clutched bundle a vindictive jerk. And at times her lips mumbled with fragments of some foreseen argument between herself and Skinner.

And far away, miles and miles away, a steeple and a hanger grew insensibly out of the vague blue to mark more and more distinctly the quiet corner where Cheasing Eyebright sheltered from the tumult of the world, recking little or nothing of the Herakleophorbia concealed in that white bundle that struggled so persistently towards its orderly retirement.

§ 7

So far as I can gather, the pullets came into Hickleybrow about three o'clock in the afternoon. Their coming must have been a brisk affair, though nobody was out in the street to see it. The violent bellowing of little Skelmersdale seems to have been the first announcement of anything out of the way. Miss Durgan of

the Post Office was at the window as usual, and saw the hen that had caught the unhappy child, in violent flight up the street with its victim, closely pursued by two others. You know that swinging stride of the emancipated athletic latter-day pullet! You know the keen insistence of the hungry hen! There was Plymouth Rock in these birds, I am told, and even without Herakleophorbia that is a gaunt and striding strain.

Probably Miss Durgan was not altogether taken by surprise. In spite of Mr. Bensington's insistence upon secrecy, rumours of the great chicken Mr. Skinner was producing had been about the village for some weeks. "Lor'!" she cried, "it's what I expected."

She seems to have behaved with great presence of mind. She snatched up the sealed bag of letters that was waiting to go on to Urshot, and rushed out of the door at once. Almost simultaneously Mr. Skelmersdale himself appeared down the village, gripping a watering-pot by the spout and very white in the face. And of course in a moment or so everyone in the village was rushing to the door or window.

The spectacle of Miss Durgan all across the road, with the entire day's correspondence of Hickleybrow in her hand, gave pause to the pullet in possession of Master Skelmersdale. She halted through one instant's indecision and then turned for the open gates of Fulcher's yard. That instant was fatal. The second pullet ran in neatly, captured the child by a well-directed peck, and went over the wall into the vicarage garden.

"Charawk, chawk, chawk, chawk, chawk, chawk!" shrieked the hindmost hen, hit smartly by the watering-can Mr. Skelmersdale had thrown, and fluttered wildly over Mrs. Glue's cottage and so into the doctor's field, while the rest of those Gargantuan birds pursued the pullet in possession of the child across the vicarage lawn.

"Good heavens!" cried the curate, or (as some say) something much more manly, and ran, whirling his croquet mallet and shouting, to head off the chase.

"Stop, you wretch!" cried the curate, as though giant hens were the commonest facts in life.

And then, finding he could not possibly intercept her, he hurled his mallet with all his might and main, and out it shot in a gracious curve within a foot or so of Master Skelmersdale's head and through the glass lantern of the conservatory. Smash! The new conservatory! The vicar's wife's beautiful new conservatory!

It frightened the hen. It might have frightened anyone. She dropped her victim into a Portugal laurel (from which he was presently extracted, disordered but, save for his less delicate garments, uninjured), made a flapping leap for the roof of Fulcher's stables, put her foot through a weak place in the tiles, and descended, so to speak, out of the infinite into the contemplative quiet of Mr. Bumps the

paralytic — who, it is now proved beyond all cavil, did, on this one occasion in his life, get down the entire length of his garden and indoors without any assistance whatever, bolt the door after him, and immediately relapse again into Christian resignation and helpless dependence upon his wife. . . .

The rest of the pullets were headed off by the other croquet players, and went through the vicar's kitchen garden into the doctor's field, to which rendezvous the fifth also came at last, clucking disconsolately after an unsuccessful attempt to walk on the cucumber frames at Mr. Witherspoon's.

They seem to have stood about in a hen-like manner for a time, and scratched a little and chirrawked meditatively, and then one pecked at and pecked over a hive of the doctor's bees, and after that they set off in a gawky jerky feathery fitful sort of way across the fields towards Urshot, and Hickleybrow street saw them no more. Near Urshot they really came upon commensurate food in a field of sweeds, and pecked for a space with gusto, until their fame overtook them.

The chief immediate reaction of this astonishing irruption of gigantic poultry upon the human mind was to arouse an extraordinary passion to whoop and run and throw things, and in quite a little time almost all the available manhood of Hickleybrow, and several ladies, were out with a remarkable assortment of flappish and whangable articles in hand — to begin the scooting of the giant hens. They drove them into Urshot, where there was a Rural Fête, and Urshot took them as the crowning glory of a happy day. They began to be shot at near Findon Beeches, but at first only with a rook rifle. Of course birds of that size could absorb an unlimited quantity of small shot without inconvenience. They scattered somewhere near Sevenoaks, and near Tonbridge one of them fled clucking for a time in excessive agitation, somewhat ahead of and parallel with the afternoon boat express — to the great astonishment of everyone therein.

And about half-past five two of them were caught very cleverly by a circus proprietor at Tunbridge Wells, who lured them into a cage rendered vacant through the death of a widowed dromedary, by scattering cakes and bread. . . .

§ 8

WHEN the unfortunate Skinner got out of the South-Eastern train at Urshot that evening it was already nearly dusk. The train was late, but not inordinately late — and Mr. Skinner remarked as much to the stationmaster. Perhaps he saw a certain pregnancy in the station-master's eye. After the briefest hesitation and with a confidential movement of his hand to the side of his mouth he asked if " anything " had happened that day.

" How d'yer *mean?* " said the station-master, a man with a hard emphatic voice.

" Thethe 'ere waptheth and thingth."

" We 'aven't 'ad much time to think of waptheth," said the station-master agreeably. "We've been too busy with your brasted 'ens," and he broke the news of the pullets to Mr. Skinner as one might break the window of an adverse politician.

" You ain't 'eard anything of Mithith Thkinner?" asked Skinner, amidst that missile shower of pithy information and comment.

" No fear!" said the station-master — as though even he drew the line somewhere in the matter of knowledge.

" I mutht make inquirieth 'bout thith," said Mr. Skinner, edging out of reach of the station-master's concluding generalisations about the responsibility attaching to the excessive nurture of hens. . . .

Going through Urshot Mr. Skinner was hailed by a lime-burner from the pits over by Hankey and asked if he was looking for his hens.

" You ain't 'eard anything of Mithith Thkinner?" he asked.

The lime-burner — his exact phrases need not concern us — expressed his superior interest in hens. . . .

It was already dark — as dark at least as a clear night in the English June can be — when Skinner — or his head at any rate — came into the bar of the Jolly Drovers and said: " 'Ello! You 'aven't 'eard anything of thith 'ere thtory 'bout my 'enth, 'ave you?"

" Oh, *'aven't* we!" said Mr. Fulcher. "Why, part of the story's been and bust into my stable roof and one chapter smashed a 'ole in Missis Vicar's green'ouse — I beg 'er pardon — Conservarratory."

Skinner came in. "I'd like thomething a little comforting," he said, " 'ot gin and water'th about my figure," and everybody began to tell him things about the pullets.

" *Grathuth* me!" said Skinner.

" You 'aven't 'eard anything about Mithith Thkinner, 'ave you?" he asked in a pause.

" That we 'aven't!" said Mr. Witherspoon. "We 'aven't thought of 'er. We ain't thought nothing of either of you."

" Ain't you been 'ome to-day?" asked Fulcher over a tankard.

" If one of those brasted birds 'ave pecked 'er," began Mr. Witherspoon, and left the full horror to their unaided imaginations. . . .

It appeared to the meeting at the time that it would be an interesting end to an eventful day to go on with Skinner and see if anything *had* happened to Mrs. Skinner. One never knows what luck one may have when accidents are at large. But Skinner, standing at the bar and drinking his hot gin and water, with one eye roving over the things at the back of the bar and the other fixed on the Absolute, missed the psychological moment.

" I thuppothe there 'athen't been any trouble with any of thethe big waptheth to-day anywhere?" he asked, with an elaborate detachment of manner.

" Been too busy with your 'ens," said Fulcher.

" I thuppothe they've all gone in now anyhow," said Skinner.

" What — the 'ens? "

" I wath thinking of the waptheth more particularly," said Skinner.

And then with an air of circumspection that would have awakened suspicion in a week-old baby, and laying the accent heavily on most of the words he chose, he asked, " I *thuppothe nobody* 'athen't *'eard* of any other *big* thingth about, 'ave they? Big *dogth* or *catth* or anything of *that* thort? Theemth to me if thereth big henth and big waptheth comin' on — "

He laughed with a fine pretence of talking idly.

But a brooding expression came upon the faces of the Hickleybrow men. Fulcher was the first to give their condensing thought the concrete shape of words.

" A cat to match them 'ens — " said Fulcher.

" Ay! " said Witherspoon, " a cat to match they 'ens."

" 'Twould be a tiger," said Fulcher.

" More'n a tiger," said Witherspoon. . . .

When at last Skinner followed the lonely footpath over the swelling field that separated Hickleybrow from the sombre pine-shaded hollow in whose black shadows the gigantic canary creeper grappled silently with the Experimental Farm, he followed it alone.

He was distinctly seen to rise against the skyline, against the warm clear immensity of the northern sky — for so far public interest followed him — and to descend again into the night, into

an obscurity from which it would seem he will nevermore emerge. He passed — into a mystery. No one knows to this day what happened to him after he crossed the brow. When later on the two Fulchers and Witherspoon, moved by their own imaginations, came up the hill and stared after him, the night had swallowed him up altogether.

The three men stood close. There was not a sound out of the wooded blackness that hid the Farm from their eyes.

" It's all right," said young Fulcher, ending a silence.

" Don't see any lights," said Witherspoon.

" You wouldn't from here."

" It's misty," said the elder Fulcher.

They meditated for a space.

" 'E'd 'ave come back if anything was wrong," said young Fulcher, and this seemed so obvious and conclusive that presently old Fulcher said " Well," and the three went home to bed — thoughtfully, I will admit. . . .

A shepherd out by Huckster's Farm heard a squealing in the night that he thought was foxes, and in the morning one of his lambs had been killed, dragged half-way towards Hickleybrow and partially devoured. . . .

The inexplicable part of it all is the absence of any indisputable remains of Skinner!

Many weeks after, amidst the charred ruins of the Experimental Farm, there was found something which may or may not have been a human shoulder-blade, and in another part of the ruins a long bone greatly gnawed and

equally doubtful. Near the stile going up towards Eyebright there was found a glass eye, and many people discovered thereupon that Skinner owed much of his personal charm to such a possession. It stared out upon the world with that same inevitable effect of detachment, that same severe melancholy that had been the redemption of his else worldly countenance.

And about the ruins industrious research discovered the metal rings and charred coverings of two linen buttons, three shanked buttons entire, and one of that metallic sort which is used in the less conspicuous sutures of the human Œconomy. These remains have been accepted by persons in authority as conclusive of a destroyed and scattered Skinner, but for my own entire conviction, and in view of his distinctive idiosyncrasy, I must confess I should prefer fewer buttons and more bones.

The glass eye of course has an air of extreme conviction, but if it really *is* Skinner's — and even Mrs. Skinner did not certainly know if that immobile eye of his was glass — something has changed it from a liquid brown to a serene and confident blue. That shoulder-blade is an extremely doubtful document, and I would like to put it side by side with the gnawed scapulæ of a few of the commoner domestic animals before I admitted its humanity.

And where were Skinner's boots, for example? Perverted and strange as a rat's appetite must be, is it conceivable that the same creatures that could leave a lamb only half eaten, would finish up Skinner, hair, bones, teeth, and boots?

I have closely questioned as many as I could of those who knew Skinner at all intimately, and they one and all agreed that they cannot imagine *anything* eating him. He was the sort of man, as a retired seafaring person living in one of Mr. W. W. Jacobs' cottages at Dunton Green told me, with a guarded significance of manner not uncommon in these parts, who would "get washed up anyhow," and as regards *the* devouring element was "fit to put a fire out." He considered that Skinner would be as safe on a raft as anywhere. The retired seafaring man added that he wished to say nothing whatever against Skinner; facts were facts. And rather than have his clothes made by Skinner, the retired seafaring man remarked he would take his chance of being locked up. These observations certainly do not present Skinner in the light of an appetising object.

To be perfectly frank with the reader, I do not believe he ever went back to the Experimental Farm. I believe he hovered through long hesitations about the fields of the Hickleybrow glebe and finally, when that squeal began, took the line of least resistance out of his perplexities into the Incognito.

And in the Incognito, whether of this or of some other world unknown to us, he obstinately and quite indisputably has remained to this day. . . .

CHAPTER 3

THE GIANT RATS

§1

It was two nights after the disappearance of Mr. Skinner that the Podbourne doctor was out late near Hankey, driving in his buggy. He had been up all night assisting another undistinguished citizen into this curious world of ours; and his task accomplished, he was driving homeward in a drowsy mood enough. It was about two o'clock in the morning, and the waning moon was rising. The summer night had gone cold, and there was a low-lying whitish mist that made things indistinct. He was quite alone — for his coachman was ill in bed — and there was nothing to be seen on either hand but a drifting mystery of hedge running athwart the yellow glare of his lamps, and nothing to hear but the clitter clatter of his horse and the gride and hedge echo of his wheels. His horse was as trustworthy as himself, and one does not wonder that he dozed. . . .

You know that intermittent drowsing as one sits, the drooping of the head, the nodding to the rhythm of the wheels, then

chin upon breast, and at once the sudden start up again.

Pitter, litter, patter.

"What was that?"

It seemed to the doctor he had heard a thin shrill squeal close at hand. For a moment he was quite awake. He said a word or two of undeserved rebuke to his horse, and looked about him. He tried to persuade himself that he had heard the distant squeal of a fox — or perhaps a young rabbit gripped by a ferret.

Swish, swish, swish, pitter, patter, swish — . . .

"What was that?"

He felt he was getting fanciful. He shook his shoulders and told his horse to get on. He listened and heard nothing.

Or was it nothing?

He had the queerest impression that something had just peeped over the hedge at him, a queer big head. With round ears! He peered hard, but he could see nothing.

"Nonsense," said he.

He sat up with an idea that he had dropped into a nightmare, gave his horse the slightest touch of the whip, spoke to it and peered again over the hedge. The glare of his lamp, however, together with the mist, rendered things indistinct, and he could distinguish nothing. It came into his head, he says, that there could be nothing there, because if there was his horse would have shied at it. Yet for all that his senses remained nervously awake.

Then he heard quite distinctly a soft pattering of feet in pursuit along the road.

He would not believe his ears

about that. He could not look round, for the road just there had a sinuous curve. He whipped up his horse and glanced sideways again. And then he saw quite distinctly where a ray from his lamp leapt a low stretch of hedge, the curved back of — some big animal, he couldn't tell what, going along in quick convulsive leaps.

He says he thought of the old tales of witchcraft — the thing was so utterly unlike any animal he knew, and he tightened his hold on the reins for fear of the fear of his horse. Educated man as he was, he admits he asked himself if this could be something that his horse could not see.

Ahead, and drawing near in silhouette against the rising moon, was the outline of the little hamlet of Hankey, comforting, though it showed never a light, and he cracked his whip and spoke again and then in a flash the rats were at him!

He had passed a gate, and as he did so, the foremost rat came leaping over into the road. The thing sprang upon him out of vagueness into the utmost clearness, the sharp, eager, round-eared face, the long body exaggerated by its movement; and what particularly struck him, the pink webbed forefeet of the beast. What must have made it more horrible to him at the time, was that he had no idea the thing was any created beast he knew. He did not recognize it as a rat, because of its size. His horse gave a bound as the thing dropped into the road beside it.

The little lane woke into tumult at the report of the whip and the doctor's shout. The whole thing suddenly went fast.

Rattle-clatter, clash, clatter.

The doctor, one gathers, stood up, shouted to his horse, and slashed with all his strength. The rat winced and swerved most reassuringly at his blow — in the glare of his lamp he could see the fur furrow under the lash — and he slashed again and again, heedless and unaware of the second pursuer that gained upon his offside.

He let the reins go, and glanced back to discover the third rat in pursuit behind. . . .

His horse bounded forward. The buggy leapt high at a rut. For a frantic minute perhaps everything seemed to be going in leaps and bounds. . . .

It was sheer good luck the horse came down in Hankey and not either before or after the houses had been passed.

No one knew how the horse came down, whether it stumbled or whether the rat on the offside really got home with one of those slashing down strokes of the incisors (given with the full weight of the body) ; and the doctor never discovered that he himself was bitten until he was inside the brickmaker's house, much less did he discover when the bite occurred, though bitten he was and badly — a long slash like the slash of a double tomahawk that had cut two parallel ribbons of flesh from his left shoulder.

He was standing up in his buggy at one moment, and in the next he had leapt to the ground.

and with his ankle, though he did not know it, badly sprained, he was cutting furiously at a third rat that was flying directly at him. He scarcely remembers the leap he must have made over the top of the wheel as the buggy came over, so obliteratingly hot and swift did his impressions rush upon him. I think myself the horse reared up with the rat biting again at his throat, and fell sideways, and carried the whole affair over; and that the doctor sprang, as it were, instinctively. As the buggy came down, the receiver of the lamp smashed, and suddenly poured a flare of blazing oil, a thud of white flame into the struggle.

That was the first thing the brickmaker saw.

He had heard the clatter of the doctor's approach and — though the doctor's memory has nothing of this — wild shouting. He had got out of bed hastily, and as he did so came the terrific smash, and up shot the glare outside the rising blind. "It was brighter than day," he says. He stood, blind cord in hand, and stared out of the window at a nightmare transformation of the familiar road before him. The black figure of the doctor with its whirling whip danced out against the flame. The horse kicked indistinctly, half hidden by the blaze, with a rat at its throat. In the obscurity against the churchyard wall, the eyes of a second monster shone wickedly. Another — a mere dreadful blackness with red-lit eyes and flesh-coloured hands — clutched unsteadily on

the wall coping to which it had leapt at the flash of the exploding lamp.

You know the keen face of a rat, those two sharp teeth, those pitiless eyes. Seen magnified to near six times its linear dimensions, and still more magnified by darkness and amazement and the leaping fancies of a fitful blaze, it must have been an ill sight for the brickmaker — still more than half asleep.

Then the doctor had grasped the opportunity, that momentary respite the flare afforded, and was out of the brickmaker's sight below battering the door with the butt of his whip.

The brickmaker would not let him in until he had got a light.

There are those who have blamed the man for that, but until I know my own courage better, I hesitate to join their number.

The doctor yelled and hammered. . . .

The brickmaker says he was weeping with terror when at last the door was opened.

"Bolt," gasped the doctor, "bolt," and could say no more. He tried to move to the door to help and sank down on the chair beside the clock while the brickmaker fastened the door.

"I don't know what they *are*!" he repeated several times. "I don't know what they *are*" — with a high note on the "*are*."

The brickmaker would have got him whisky, but the doctor would not be left alone with nothing but a flickering light just then.

It was long before the brick-maker could get him to go up-stairs. . . .

And when the fire was out the giant rats came back, took the dead horse, dragged it across the churchyard into the brickfield and ate it until it was dawn, none even then daring to disturb them. . . .

§ 2

REDWOOD went round to Bensington about eleven the next morning with the " second edition " of three evening papers in his hand.

Bensington looked up from a despondent meditation over the forgotten pages of the most distracting novel the Brompton Road librarian had been able to find him. " Anything fresh? " he asked.

" Two men stung near Chartham."

" They ought to let us smoke out that nest. They really did. It's their own fault."

" It's their own fault, certainly," said Redwood.

" Have you heard anything about buying the farm? "

" The House Agent," said Redwood, " is a thing with a big mouth and made of dense wood. It pretends someone else is after the house — it always does, you know — and won't understand there's a hurry. ' This is a matter of life and death,' I said, ' don't you understand? ' It drooped its eyes half shut and said, ' Then why don't you go the other two hundred pounds? ' I'd rather live in a world of solid wasps than

give in to the stonewalling stupidity of that offensive creature. I — "

He paused, feeling that a sentence like that might very easily be spoiled by its context.

" It's too much to hope," said Bensington, " that one of the wasps — "

" The wasp has no more idea of public utility than a — than a House Agent," said Redwood.

He talked for a little while about house agents and solicitors and people of that sort, in the unjust unreasonable way that so many people do somehow get to talk of these business calculi (" Of all the cranky things in this cranky world, the most cranky of all, to my mind, is that while we expect honour, courage, efficiency, from a doctor or a soldier as a matter of course, a solicitor or a house agent is not only permitted but expected to display nothing but a sort of greedy, greasy, obstructive, over-reaching imbecility — " etc.) — and then, greatly relieved, he went to the window and stared out at the Sloane Street traffic.

Bensington had put the most exciting novel conceivable on the little table that carried his electric standard. He joined the fingers of his opposed hands very carefully and regarded them. " Redwood," he said. " Do they say much about *Us*? "

" Not so much as I should expect."

" They don't denounce us at all? "

" Not a bit. But, on the other hand, they don't back up what I

point out must be done. I've written to *The Times,* you know, explaining the whole thing—"

"We take the *Daily Chronicle,*" said Bensington.

"And *The Times* has a long leader on the subject—a very high-class, well-written leader—with three pieces of *Times* Latin—*status quo* is one—and it reads like the voice of Somebody Impersonal of the Greatest Importance suffering from Influenza Headache and talking through sheets and sheets of felt without getting any relief from it whatever. Reading between the lines, you know, it's pretty clear that *The Times* considers it is useless to mince matters and that something (indefinite of course) has to be done at once. Otherwise still more undesirable consequences—*Times* English, you know, for more wasps and stings. Thoroughly statesmanlike article!"

"And meanwhile this Bigness is spreading in all sorts of ugly ways."

"Precisely."

"I wonder if Skinner was right about those big rats—"

"Oh no! That would be too much," said Redwood.

He came and stood by Bensington's chair.

"By-the-by," he said, with a slightly lowered voice, "how does *she*—?"

He indicated the closed door.

"Cousin Jane? She simply knows nothing about it. Doesn't connect us with it and won't read the articles. 'Gigantic wasps!' she says, 'I haven't patience to read the papers.'"

"That's very fortunate," said Redwood.

"I suppose—Mrs. Redwood—?"

"No," said Redwood, "just at present it happens—she's terribly worried about the child. You know, he keeps on."

"Growing?"

"Yes. Put on forty-one ounces in ten days. Weighs nearly four stone. And only six months old! Naturally rather alarming."

"Healthy?"

"Vigorous. His nurse is leaving because he kicks so forcibly. And everything, of course, shockingly outgrown. Everything, you know, has had to be made fresh, clothes and everything. Perambulator—light affair—broke one wheel, and the youngster had to be brought home on the milkman's hand-truck. Yes. Quite a crowd. . . . And we've put Georgina Phyllis back into his cot and put him into the bed of Georgina Phyllis. His mother—naturally alarmed. Proud at first and inclined to praise Winkles. Not now. Feels the thing *can't* be wholesome. *You* know."

"I imagined you were going to put him on diminishing doses."

"I tried it."

"Didn't it work?"

"Howls. In the ordinary way the cry of a child is loud and distressing; it is for the good of the species that this should be so—but since he has been on the Herakleophorbia treatment—"

"Mm," said Bensington, regarding his fingers with more resignation than he had hitherto displayed.

"Practically the thing *must* come out. People will hear of this child, connect it up with our hens, and the whole thing will come round to my wife. . . . How she will take it I haven't the remotest idea."

"It *is* difficult," said Mr. Bensington, "to form any plan — certainly."

He removed his glasses and wiped them carefully.

"It is another instance," he generalised, "of the thing that is continually happening. We — if indeed I may presume to the adjective — *scientific* men — we work of course always for a theoretical result — a purely theoretical result. But incidentally we do set forces in operation — *new* forces. We mustn't control them and nobody else *can*. Practically, Redwood, the thing is out of our hands. *We* supply the material —"

"And they," said Redwood, turning to the window, "get the experience."

"So far as this trouble down in Kent goes I am not disposed to worry further."

"Unless they worry us."

"Exactly. And if they like to muddle about with solicitors and pettifoggers and legal obstructions and weighty considerations of the tomfool order, until they have got a number of new gigantic species of vermin well established — Things always *have* been in a muddle, Redwood."

Redwood traced a twisted, tangled line in the air.

"And our real interest lies at present with your boy."

Redwood turned about and came and stared at his collaborator.

"What do you think of him, Bensington? You can look at this business with a greater detachment than I can. What am I to do about him?"

"Go on feeding him."

"On Herakleophorbia?"

"On Herakleophorbia."

"And then he'll grow."

"He'll grow, as far as I can calculate from the hens and the wasps, to the height of about five and thirty feet — with everything in proportion —"

"And then what'll he do?"

"That," said Mr. Bensington, "is just what makes the whole thing so interesting."

"Confound it, man! Think of his clothes. And when he's grown up," said Redwood, "he'll only be one solitary Gulliver in a pigmy world."

Mr. Bensington's eye over his gold rim was pregnant.

"Why solitary?" he said, and repeated still more darkly, "*Why* solitary?"

"But you don't propose —?"

"I said," said Bensington, with the self-complacency of a man who has produced a good significant saying, "Why solitary?"

"Meaning that one might bring up other children —?"

"Meaning nothing beyond my inquiry."

Redwood began to walk about the room. "Of course," he said, "one might — But still! What are we coming to?"

Bensington evidently enjoyed his line of high intellectual detachment. "The thing that interests me most, Redwood, of all

this, is to think that his brain at the top of him will also, so far as my reasoning goes, be five and thirty feet or so above our level. . . . What's the matter?"

Redwood stood at the window and stared at a news placard on a paper-cart that rattled up the street.

"What's the matter?" repeated Bensington, rising.

Redwood exclaimed violently.

"What is it?" said Bensington.

"Get a paper," said Redwood, moving doorward.

"Why?"

"Get a paper. Something — I didn't quite catch — Gigantic rats — !"

"Rats?"

"Yes, rats. Skinner was right after all!"

"What do you mean?"

"How the Deuce am *I* to know till I see a paper? Great Rats! Good Lord! I wonder if he's been eaten!" He glanced for his hat, and decided to go hatless.

As he rushed downstairs two steps at a time, he could hear along the street the mighty howlings to and fro of the Hooligan papersellers making a Boom.

"'Orrible affair in Kent — 'orrible affair in Kent. Doctor . . . eaten by rats. 'Orrible affair — 'orrible affair — rats — eaten by Stchewpendous rats. Full perticulers — 'orrible affair."

§ 3

Cossar, the well-known civil engineer, found them in the great doorway of the flat mansions, Redwood holding out the damp pink paper and Bensington, on tiptoe, reading over his arm.

Cossar was a large-bodied man with gaunt inelegant limbs placed casually at convenient corners of his body, and a face like a carving abandoned at an early stage as altogether too unpromising for completion. His nose had been left square, and his lower jaw projected beyond his upper. He breathed audibly. Few people considered him handsome. His hair was entirely tangential, and his voice, which he used sparingly, was pitched high, and had commonly a quality of bitter protest. He wore a grey cloth jacket suit and a silk hat on all occasions. He plumped an abysmal trouser pocket with a vast red hand, paid his cabman, and came panting resolutely up the steps, a copy of the pink paper clutched about the middle like Jove's thunderbolt in his hand.

"Skinner?" Bensington was saying, regardless of his approach.

"Nothing about him," said Redwood. "Bound to be eaten. Both of them. It's too horrible. . . . Hullo! Cossar!"

"This your stuff?" asked Cossar, waving the paper.

"Well, why don't you stop it?" he demanded.

"*Can't* be Jiggered!" said Cossar.

"*Buy the place?*" he cried. "What nonsense! Burn it. I knew you chaps would fumble this. *What are you to do?* Why — what I tell you!"

"*You?* Do? Why! Go up the street to the gunsmith's, of course. *Why?* For guns! Yes — there's only one shop. Get eight guns! Rifles. Not elephant guns

— no! Too big. Not army rifles — too small. Say it's to kill — kill a bull. Say it's to shoot buffalo! See? Eh? Rats? No! How the deuce are they to understand that? . . . Because we *want* eight. Get a lot of ammunition. Don't get guns without ammunition — No! Take the lot in a cab to — where's the place? *Urshot?* Charing Cross, then. There's a train — Well, the first train that starts after two. Think you can do it! All right. Licence? Get eight at a post-office, of course. Gun licences, you know. Not game. Why? It's rats, man. You — Bensington. Got a telephone? Yes. I'll ring up five of my chaps from Ealing. *Why* five? Because it's the right number!

"Where you going, Redwood? Get a hat! *Nonsense.* Have mine. You want guns, man — not hats. Got money? Enough? All right. So long.

"Where's the telephone, Bensington?"

Bensington wheeled about obediently and led the way.

Cossar used and replaced the instrument. "Then there's the wasps," he said. "Sulphur and nitre'll do that. Obviously. Plaster of Paris. You're a chemist. Where can I get sulphur by the ton in portable sacks? *What* for? Why, Lord *bless* my heart and soul! — to smoke out the nest, of course! I suppose it must be sulphur, eh? You're a chemist. Sulphur best, eh?"

"Yes, I should *think* sulphur."

"Nothing better?"

"Right. That's your job. That's all right. Get as much sulphur as you can — saltpetre to make it

burn. Sent? Charing Cross. Right away. See they do it. Follow it up. Anything?"

He thought a moment.

"Plaster of Paris — any sort of plaster — bung up nest — holes — you know. That *I'd* better get."

"How much?"

"How much what?"

"Sulphur."

"Ton. See?"

Bensington tightened his glasses with a hand tremulous with determination. "Right," he said, very curtly.

"Money in your pocket?" asked Cossar.

"Hang cheques. They may not know you. Pay cash. Obviously. Where's your bank? All right. Stop on the way and get forty pounds — notes and gold."

Another meditation. "If we leave this job for public officials we shall have all Kent in tatters," said Cossar. "Now is there — anything? *No! HI!*"

He stretched a vast hand towards a cab that became convulsively eager to serve him ("Cab, Sir?" said the cabman. "Obviously," said Cossar); and Bensington, still hatless, paddled down the steps and prepared to mount.

"I *think*," he said with his hand on the cab apron, and a sudden glance up at the windows of his flat, "I *ought* to tell my cousin Jane —"

"More time to tell her when you come back," said Cossar, thrusting him in with a vast hand expanded over his back. . . .

"Clever chaps," remarked Cossar, "but no initiative whatever. Cousin Jane indeed! I know her.

Rot, these cousin Janes! Country infested with 'em. I suppose I shall have to spend the whole blessed night seeing they do what they know perfectly well they ought to have done all along. I wonder if it's Research makes 'em like that or Cousin Jane or what?"

He dismissed this obscure problem, meditated for a space upon his watch, and decided there would be just time to drop into a restaurant and get some lunch before he hunted up the plaster of Paris and took it to Charing Cross.

The train started at five minutes past three, and he arrived at Charing Cross at a quarter to three, to find Bensington in heated argument between two policemen and his van-driver outside, and Redwood in the luggage office involved in some technical obscurity about his ammunition. Everybody was pretending, neither to know anything nor to have any authority, in the way dear to South-Eastern officials when they catch you in a hurry.

Pity they can't shoot all these officials and get a new lot," remarked Cossar with a sigh. But the time was too limited for anything fundamental, and so he swept through these minor controversies, disinterred what may or may not have been the station-master from some obscure hiding-place, walked about the premises holding him and giving orders in his name, and was out of the station with everybody and everything aboard before that official was fully awake to the breaches in the most sacred routines and regulations that were being committed.

"Who *was* he?" said the high official, caressing the arm Cossar had gripped, and smiling with knit brows.

"'E was a gentleman, Sir," said a porter, "anyhow. 'Im and all 'is party travelled first class."

"Well, we got him and his stuff off pretty sharp — whoever he was," said the high official, rubbing his arm with something approaching satisfaction.

And as he walked slowly back, blinking in the unaccustomed daylight, towards that dignified retirement in which the higher officials at Charing Cross shelter from the importunity of the vulgar, he still smiled at his unaccustomed energy. It was a very gratifying revelation of his own possibilities, in spite of the stiffness of his arm. He wished some of those confounded armchair critics of railway management could have seen it.

§ 4

By five o'clock that evening this amazing Cossar, with no appearance of hurry at all, had got all the stuff for his fight with insurgent Bigness out of Urshot and on the road to Hickleybrow. Two barrels of paraffin and a load of dry brushwood he had bought in Urshot; plentiful sacks of sulphur, eight big game guns and ammunition, three light breech-loaders, with small-shot ammunition for the wasps, a hatchet, two billhooks, a pick and three spades, two coils of rope, some

bottled beer, soda and whisky. One gross of packets of rat poison and cold provisions for three days had come down from London. All these things he had sent on in a coal trolley and a hay waggon in the most businesslike way, except the guns and ammunition, which were stuck under the seat of the Red Lion waggonette appointed to bring on Redwood and the five picked men who had come up from Ealing at Cossar's summons.

Cossar conducted all these transactions with an invincible air of commonplace, in spite of the fact that Urshot was in a panic about the rats, and all the drivers had to be specially paid. All the shops were shut in the place, and scarcely a soul abroad in the street, and when he banged at a door a window was apt to open. He seemed to consider that the conduct of business from open windows was an entirely legitimate and obvious method. Finally he and Bensington got the Red Lion dog-cart and set off with the waggonette, to overtake the baggage. They did this a little beyond the crossroads, and so reached Hickleybrow first.

Bensington, with a gun between his knees, sitting beside Cossar in the dog-cart, developed a long-germinated amazement. All they were doing was, no doubt, as Cossar insisted, quite the obvious thing to do, only —! In England one so rarely does the obvious thing. He glanced from his neighbour's feet to the boldly sketched hands upon the reins. Cossar had apparently never

driven before, and he was keeping the lines of least resistance down the middle of the road by some no doubt obvious but certainly unusual light of his own.

"Why don't we all do the obvious?" thought Bensington. "How the world would travel if one did! I wonder for instance why I don't do such a lot of things I know would be all right to do — things I *want* to do. Is everybody like that, or is it peculiar to me?" He plunged into obscure speculation about the Will. He thought of the complex organised futilities of the daily life, and in contrast with them the plain and manifest things to do, the sweet and splendid things to do, that some incredible influences will never permit us to do. Cousin Jane? Cousin Jane he perceived was important in the question, in some subtle and difficult way. Why should we after all eat, drink, and sleep, remain unmarried, go here, abstain from going there, all out of deference to Cousin Jane? She became symbolical without ceasing to be incomprehensible. . . .

A stile and a path across the fields caught his eye and reminded him of that other bright day, so recent in time, so remote in its emotions, when he had walked from Urshot to the Experimental Farm to see the giant chicks. . . .

Fate plays with us.

"Tcheck, Tcheck," said Cossar. "Get up."

It was a hot midday afternoon, not a breath of wind, and the dust

was thick on the roads. Few people were about, but the deer beyond the park palings browsed in profound tranquillity. They saw a couple of big wasps stripping a gooseberry bush just outside Hickleybrow, and another was crawling up and down the front of the little grocer's shop in the village street trying to find an entry. The grocer was dimly visible within, with an ancient fowling-piece in hand, watching its endeavours. The driver of the waggonette pulled up outside the Jolly Drovers and informed Redwood that his part of the bargain was done. In this contention he was presently joined by the drivers of the waggon and the trolley. Not only did they maintain this, but they refused to let the horses be taken further.

"Them big rats is nuts on 'orses," the trolley driver kept on repeating.

Cossar surveyed the controversy for a moment.

"Get the things out of that waggonette," he said, and one of his men, a tall fair dirty engineer, obeyed.

"Gimme that shotgun," said Cossar.

He placed himself between the drivers. "We don't want *you* to drive," he said.

"You can say what you like," he conceded, "but we want these horses."

They began to argue, but he continued speaking.

"If you try and assault us I shall, in self-defence, let fly at your legs. The horses are going on."

He treated the incident as

closed. "Get up on the waggon, Flack," he said to a thickset, wiry little man. "Boon, take the trolley."

The two drivers blustered.

"You've done your duty to your employers," said Redwood. "You stop in this village until we come back. No one will blame you, seeing we've got guns. We've no wish to do anything unjust or violent, but this business is pressing. I'll pay if anything happens to the horses, never fear."

"*That's* all right," said Cossar, who rarely promised.

They left the waggonette behind, and the men who were not driving went afoot. Over each shoulder sloped a gun. It was the oddest little expedition for an English country road, more like a Yankee party trekking west in the good old Indian days.

They went up the road until at the crest by the stile they came into sight of the Experimental Farm. They found a little group of men there with a gun or so — the two Fulchers were among them — and one man, a stranger from Maidstone, stood out before the others and watched the place through an opera-glass.

These men turned about and stared at Redwood's party.

"Anything fresh?" said Cossar.

"The waspses keep a comin' and a goin'," said old Fulcher. "Can't see as they bring anything."

"The Canary Creeper's got in among the pine trees now," said a man with the lorgnette. "It wasn't there this morning. You can see it grow while you watch it."

He took out a handkerchief and wiped his object-glasses with careful deliberation.

"I reckon you're going down there," ventured Skelmersdale.

"Will you come?" said Cossar.

Skelmersdale seemed to hesitate.

"It's an all-night job."

Skelmersdale decided that he wouldn't.

"Rats about?" asked Cossar.

"One was up in the pines this morning — rabbiting, we reckon."

Cossar slouched on to overtake his party.

Bensington, regarding the Experimental Farm under his hand, was able to gauge now the vigour of the Food. His first impression was that the house was smaller than he had thought, very much smaller; his second was to perceive that all the vegetation between the house and the pine wood had become extremely large. The roof over the well peeped amidst tussocks of grass a good eight feet high, and the Canary Creeper wrapped about the chimney stack and gesticulated with stiff tendrils towards the heavens. Its flowers were vivid yellow splashes, distinctly visible as separate specks this mile away. A great green cable had writhed across the big wire enclosures of the giant hens' run, and flung twining leaf stems about two outstanding pines. Fully half as tall as these was the grove of nettles running round behind the cart-shed. The whole prospect, as they drew nearer, became more and more suggestive of a raid of pigmies upon a doll's house that has been left in a neglected corner of some great garden.

There was a busy coming and going from the wasps' nest, they saw. A swarm of black shapes interlaced in the air above the rusty hill-front beyond the pine cluster, and ever and again one of these would dart up into the sky with incredible swiftness and soar off upon some distant quest. Their humming became audible at more than half a mile's distance from the Experimental Farm. Once a yellow-striped monster dropped towards them and hung for a space watching them with its great compound eyes, but at an ineffectual shot from Cossar it darted off again. Down in a corner of the field, away to the right, several were crawling about over some ragged bones that were probably the remains of the lamb the rats had brought from Huxter's Farm. The horses became very restless as they drew near these creatures. None of the party was an expert driver, and they had to put a man to lead each horse and encourage it with the voice.

They could see nothing of the rats as they came up to the house, and everything seemed perfectly still except for the rising and falling "whoozzzzzzZZZ, whoooo-zoo-oo" of the wasps' nest.

They led the horses into the yard, and one of Cossar's men, seeing the door open — the whole of the middle portion of the door had been gnawed out — walked into the house. Nobody missed him for the time, the rest being occupied with the barrels of paraffin, and the first intimation they

had of his separation from them was the report of his gun and the whiz of his bullet. "Bang, bang," both barrels, and his first bullet it seems went through the cask of sulphur, smashed out a stave from the further side, and filled the air with yellow dust. Redwood had kept his gun in hand and let fly at something grey that leapt past him. He had a vision of a broad hind quarters, the long scaly tail and long soles of the hind feet of a rat, and fired his second barrel. He saw Bensington drop as the beast vanished round the corner.

Then for a time everybody was busy with a gun. For three minutes lives were cheap at the Experimental Farm, and the banging of guns filled the air. Redwood, careless of Bensington in his excitement, rushed in pursuit, and was knocked headlong by a mass of brick fragments, mortar, plaster, and rotten lath splinters that came flying out at him as a bullet whacked through the wall.

He found himself sitting on the ground with blood on his hands and lips, and a great stillness brooded over all about him.

Then a fattish voice from within the house remarked: "Gee-whiz!"

"Hullo!" said Redwood.

"Hullo there!" answered the voice.

And then: "Did you chaps get 'im?"

A sense of the duties of friendship returned to Redwood. "Is Mr. Bensington hurt?" he said.

The man inside heard imperfectly. "No one ain't to blame if I ain't," said the voice inside.

It became clearer to Redwood that he must have shot Bensington. He forgot the cuts upon his face, arose and came back to find Bensington seated on the ground and rubbing his shoulder. Bensington looked over his glasses. "We peppered him, Redwood," he said, and then; "He tried to jump over me, and knocked me down. But I let him have it with both barrels, and my! how it has hurt my shoulder to be sure!"

A man appeared in the doorway. "I got him once in the chest and once in the side," he said.

"Where's the waggons?" said Cossar, appearing amidst a thicket of gigantic canary-creeper leaves.

It became evident, to Redwood's amazement, first, that no one had been shot, and secondly, that the trolley and waggon had shifted fifty yards, and were now standing with interlocked wheels amidst the tangled distortions of Skinner's kitchen garden. The horses had stopped their plunging. Halfway towards them, the burst barrel of sulphur lay in the path with a cloud of sulphur dust above it. He indicated this to Cossar and walked towards it. "Has anyone seen that rat?" shouted Cossar, following. "I got him in between the ribs once, and once in the face as he turned on me."

They were joined by two men, as they worried at the locked wheels.

"I killed that rat," said one of the men.

"Have they got him?" asked Cossar.

" Jim Bates has found him, beyond the hedge. I got him jest as he came round the corner. . . . Whack behind the shoulder. . . ."

When things were a little shipshape again Redwood went and stared at the huge misshapen corpse. The brute lay on its side, with its body slightly bent. Its rodent teeth overhanging its receding lower jaw gave its face a look of colossal feebleness, of weak avidity. It seemed not in the least ferocious or terrible. Its fore paws reminded him of lank emaciated hands. Except for one neat round hole with a scorched rim on either ride of its neck, the creature was absolutely intact. He meditated over this fact for some time. " There must have been two rats," he said at last, turning away.

" Yes. And the one that everybody hit — got away."

" I am certain that my own shot — "

A canary-creeper leaf tendril, engaged in that mysterious search for a holdfast which constitutes a tendril's search, bent itself engagingly towards his neck and made him step aside hastily.

" Whoo-z-z-z-z-z-Z-Z-Z," from the distant wasps' nest, " whoo-oo-zoo-oo."

§ 5

THE INCIDENT left the party alert but not unstrung.

They got their stores into the house, which had evidently been ransacked by the rats after the flight of Mrs. Skinner, and four of the men took the two horses back to Hickleybrow. They dragged the dead rat through the hedge and into a position commanded by the windows of the house, and incidentally came upon a cluster of giant earwigs in the ditch. These creatures dispersed hastily, but Cossar reached out incalculable limbs and managed to kill several with his boots and gun-butt. Then two of the men hacked through several of the main stems of the canary-creeper — huge cylinders they were, a couple of feet in diameter, that came out by the sink at the back; and while Cossar set the house in order for the night, Bensington, Redwood, and one of the assistant electricians went cautiously round by the fowl-runs in search of the rat-holes.

They skirted the giant nettles widely, for these huge weeds threatened them with poison-thorns a good inch long. Then round beyond the gnawed dismantled stile they came abruptly on the huge cavernous throat of the most westerly of the giant rat-holes, an evil-smelling profundity that drew them up into a line together.

" I *hope* they'll come out," said Redwood, with a glance at the penthouse of the well.

" If they don't — " reflected Bensington.

" They will," said Redwood.

They meditated.

" We shall have to rig up some sort of flare if we *do* go in," said Redwood.

They went up a little path of white sand through the pine wood and halted presently within sight of the wasp-holes.

The sun was setting now, and

the wasps were coming home for good; their wings in the golden light made twirling haloes about them. The three men peered out from under the trees — they did not care to go right to the edge of the wood — and watched these tremendous insects drop and crawl for a little and enter and disappear. "They will be still in a couple of hours from now," said Redwood. . . . "This is like being a boy again."

"We can't miss those holes," said Bensington, "even if the night is dark. By-the-by — about the light —"

"Full moon," said the electrician. "I looked it up."

They went back and consulted with Cossar.

He said that "obviously" they must get the sulphur, nitre, and plaster of Paris through the wood before twilight, and for that they broke bulk and carried the sacks. After the necessary shouting of the preliminary directions, never a word was spoken, and as the buzzing of the wasps' nest died away there was scarcely a sound in the world but the noise of footsteps, the heavy breathing of burthened men, and the thud of the sacks. They all took turns at that labour except Mr. Bensington, who was manifestly unfit. He took post in the Skinners' bedroom with a rifle to watch the carcass of the dead rat; and of the others, they took turns to rest from sack-carrying and to keep watch two at a time upon the ratholes behind the nettle grove. The pollen sacs of the nettles were ripe, and every now and then their vigil would be en-

livened by the dehiscence of these, the bursting of the sacs sounding exactly like the crack of a pistol, and pollen grains as big as buckshot pattered all about them.

Mr. Bensington sat at his window on a hard horsehair-stuffed armchair, covered by a grubby anti-macassar that had given a touch of social distinction to the Skinners' sitting-room for many years. His unaccustomed rifle rested on the sill, and his spectacles anon watched the dark bulk of the dead rat in the thickening twilight, anon wandered about him in curious meditation. There was a faint smell of paraffin without, for one of the casks leaked, and it mingled with a less unpleasant odour arising from the hacked and crushed creeper.

Within, when he turned his head, a blend of faint domestic scents, beer, cheese, rotten apples, and old boots as the leading *motifs*, was full of reminiscences of the vanished Skinners. He regarded the dim room for a space. The furniture had been greatly disordered — perhaps by some inquisitive rat — but a coat upon a clothes-peg on the door, a razor and some dirty scraps of paper, and a piece of soap that had hardened through years of disuse into a horny cube, were redolent of Skinner's distinctive personality. It came to Bensington's mind with a complete novelty of realisation that in all probability the man had been killed and eaten, at least in part, by the monster that now lay dead there in the darkling.

To think of all that a harmless-looking discovery in chemistry may lead to!

Here he was in homely England and yet in infinite danger, sitting out alone with a gun in a twilit, ruined house, remote from every comfort, his shoulder dreadfully bruised from a gun-kick, and—by Jove!

He grasped now how profoundly the order of the universe had changed for him. He had come right away to this amazing experience, *without even saying a word to his cousin Jane!*

What must she be thinking of him?

He tried to imagine it and he could not. He had an extraordinary feeling that she and he were parted for ever and would never meet again. He felt he had taken a step and come into a world of new immensities. What other monsters might not those deepening shadows hide? . . . The tips of the giant nettles came out sharp and black against the pale green and amber of the western sky. Everything was very still, very still indeed. He wondered why he could not hear the others away there round the corner of the house. The shadow in the cart-shed was now an abysmal black.

Bang . . . Bang . . . Bang.

A sequence of echoes and a shout.

A long silence.

Bang and a diminuendo of echoes.

Stillness.

Then, thank goodness! Redwood and Cossar were coming out of the inaudible darknesses, and Redwood was calling "Bensington!"

"Bensington! We've bagged another of the rats!"

"Cossar's bagged another of the rats!"

§ 6

WHEN the Expedition had finished refreshment, the night had fully come. The stars were at their brightest, and a growing pallor towards Hankey heralded the moon. The watch on the rat-holes had been maintained, but the watchers had shifted to the hill slope above the holes, feeling this a safer firing-point. They squatted there in a rather abundant dew, fighting the damp with whisky. The others rested in the house, and the three leaders discussed the night's work with the men. The moon rose towards midnight, and as soon as it was clear of the downs, everyone except the rat-hole sentinels started off in single file, led by Cossar, towards the wasps' nest.

So far as the wasps' nest went, they found their task exceptionally easy, astonishingly easy. Except that it was a longer labour, it was no graver affair than any common wasps' nest might have been. Danger there was, no doubt, danger to life, but it never so much as thrust its head out of that portentous hillside. They stuffed in the sulphur and nitre, they bunged the holes soundly, and fired their trains. Then with a common impulse all the party but Cossar turned and ran athwart the long shadows of the pines, and, finding Cossar had stayed behind, came to a halt to-

gether in a knot, a hundred yards away, convenient to a ditch that offered cover. Just for a minute or two the moonlit night, all black and white, was heavy with a suffocated buzz, that rose and mingled to a roar, a deep abundant note, and culminated and died, and then almost incredibly the night was still.

"By Jove!" said Bensington, almost in a whisper, "*it's done!*"

All stood intent. The hillside above the black point-lace of the pine shadows seemed as bright as day and as colourless as snow. The setting plaster in the holes positively shone. Cossar's loose framework moved toward them.

"So far—" said Cossar.

"Crack—bang!"

A shot from near the house and then—stillness.

"What's *that*?" said Bensington.

"One of the rats put its head out," suggested one of the men.

"By-the-by, we left our guns up there," said Redwood.

"By the sacks."

Everyone began to walk towards the hill again.

"That must be the rats," said Bensington.

"Obviously," said Cossar, gnawing his finger nails.

"*Bang!*"

"Hullo?" said one of the men.

Then abruptly came a shout, two shots, a loud shout that was almost a scream, three shots in rapid succession and a splintering of wood. All these sounds were very clear and very small in the immense stillness of the night. Then for some moments nothing but a minute muffled confusion from the direction of the rat-holes, and then again a wild yell. . . . Each man found himself running hard for the guns.

Two shots.

Bensington found himself, gun in hand, going hard through the pine-trees after a number of receding backs. It is curious that the thought uppermost in his mind at that moment was the wish that his cousin Jane could see him. His bulbous slashed boots flew out in wild strides and his face was distorted into a permanent grin, because that wrinkled his nose and kept his glasses in place. Also he held the muzzle of his gun projecting straight before him as he flew through the chequered moonlight. The man who had run away met them full tilt—he had dropped his gun.

"Hullo," said Cossar, and caught him in his arms. "What's this?"

"They came out together," said the man.

"The rats?"

"Yes, six of them."

"Where's Flack?"

"Down."

"What's he say?" panted Bensington, coming up, unheeded.

"Flack's down?"

"He fell down."

"They came out one after the other."

"What?"

"Made a rush. I fired both barrels first."

"You left Flack?"

"They were on to us."

"Come on," said Cossar. "You come with us. Where's Flack? Show us."

The whole party moved forward. Further details of the engagement dropped from the man who had run away. The others clustered about him, except Cossar, who led.

"Where are they?"

"Back in their holes, perhaps. I cleared. They made a rush for their holes."

"What do you mean? Did you get behind them?"

"We got down by their holes. Saw 'em come out, you know, and tried to cut 'em off. They lolloped out—like rabbits. We ran down and let fly. They ran about wild after our first shot and suddenly came at us. *Went* for us."

"How many?"

"Six or seven."

Cossar led the way to the edge of the pine wood and halted.

"D'yer mean they *got* Flack?" asked someone.

"One of 'em was on to him."

"Didn't you shoot?"

"How *could* I?"

"Everyone loaded?" said Cossar over his shoulder. There was a confirmatory movement.

"But Flack—" said one.

"D'yer mean—Flack—" said another.

"There's no time to lose," said Cossar, and shouted "Flack!" as he led the way. The whole force advanced towards the rat-holes, the man who had run away a little to the rear. They went forward through the rank exaggerated weeds and skirted the body of the second dead rat. They were extended in a bunchy line, each man with his gun pointing forward, and they peered about them in the clear moonlight for some crumpled ominous shape, some crouching form. They found the gun of the man who had run away very speedily.

"Flack!" cried Cossar. "Flack!"

"He ran past the nettles and fell down," volunteered the man who ran away.

"Where?"

"Round about there."

"Where did he fall?"

He hesitated and led them athwart the long black shadows for a space and turned judicially. "About here, I think."

"Well, he's not here now."

"But his gun—?"

"Confound it!" swore Cossar, "where's everything got to?" He strode a step towards the black shadows on the hillside that masked the holes and stood staring. Then he swore again. "If they *have* dragged him in—!"

So they hung for a space tossing each other the fragments of thoughts. Bensington's glasses flashed like diamonds as he looked from one to the other. The men's faces changed from cold clearness to mysterious obscurity as they turned them to or from the moon. Everyone spoke, no one completed a sentence. Then abruptly Cossar chose his line. He flapped limbs this way and that and expelled orders in pellets. It was obvious he wanted lamps. Everyone except Cossar was moving towards the house.

"You're going into the holes?" asked Redwood.

"Obviously," said Cossar.

He made it clear once more that the lamps of the cart and

trolley were to be got and brought to him.

Bensington, grasping this, started off along the path by the well. He glanced over his shoulder and saw Cossar's gigantic figure standing out as if he were regarding the holes pensively. At the sight Bensington halted for a moment and half turned. They were all leaving Cossar—!

Cossar was able to take care of himself, of course!

Suddenly Bensington saw something that made him shout a windless " HI! " In a second three rats had projected themselves from the dark tangle of the creeper towards Cossar. For three seconds Cossar stood unaware of them, and then he had become the most active thing in the world. He didn't fire his gun. Apparently he had no time to aim, or to think of aiming; he ducked a leaping rat, Bensington saw, and then smashed at the back of its head with the butt of his gun. The monster gave one leap and fell over itself.

Cossar's form went right down out of sight among the reedy grass, and then he rose again, running towards another of the rats and whirling his gun overhead. A faint shout came to Bensington's ears, and then he perceived the remaining two rats bolting divergently, and Cossar in pursuit towards the holes.

The whole thing was an affair of misty shadows; all three fighting monsters were exaggerated and made unreal by the delusive clearness of the light. At moments Cossar was colossal, at moments invisible. The rats flashed athwart the eye in sudden unexpected leaps, or ran with a movement of the feet so swift, they seemed to run on wheels. It was all over in half a minute. No one saw it but Bensington. He could hear the others behind him still receding towards the house. He shouted something inarticulate and then ran back towards Cossar, while the rats vanished.

He came up to him outside the holes. In the moonlight the distribution of shadows that constituted Cossar's visage intimated calm. " Hullo," said Cossar, " back already? Where's the lamps? They're all back now in their holes. One I broke the neck of as it ran past me. . . . See? There! " And he pointed a gaunt finger.

Bensington was too astonished for conversation. . . .

The lamps seemed an interminable time in coming. At last they appeared, first one unwinking luminous eye, preceded by a swaying yellow glare, and then, winking now and then, and then shining out again, two others. About them came little figures with little voices, and then enormous shadows. This group made as it were a spot of inflammation upon the gigantic dreamland of moonshine.

" Flack," said the voices. " Flack."

An illuminating sentence floated up. " Locked himself in the attic."

Cossar was continually more wonderful. He produced great lumps of cotton wool and stuffed them in his ears—Bensington wondered why. Then he loaded

his gun with a quarter charge of powder. Who else could have thought of that? Wonderland culminated with the disappearance of Cossar's twin realms of boot sole up the central hole.

Cossar was on all fours with two guns, one trailing on each side from a string under his chin, and his most trusted assistant, a little dark man with a grave face, was to go in stooping behind him, holding a lantern over his head. Everything had been made as sane and obvious and proper as a lunatic's dream. The wool, it seemed, was on account of the concussion of the rifle; the man had some, too. Obviously! So long as the rats turned tail on Cossar no harm could come to him, and directly they headed for him he would see their eyes and fire between them. Since they would have to come down the cylinder of the hole, Cossar could hardly fail to hit them. It was, Cossar insisted, the obvious method, a little tedious perhaps, but absolutely certain. As the assistant stooped to enter, Bensington saw that the end of a ball of twine had been tied to the tail of his coat. By this he was to draw in the rope if it should be needed to drag out the bodies of the rats.

Bensington perceived that the object he held in his hand was Cossar's silk hat.

How had it got there? . . .

It would be something to remember him by, anyhow.

At each of the adjacent holes stood a little group with a lantern on the ground shining up the hole, and with one man kneeling and aiming at the round void before him, waiting for anything that might emerge.

There was an interminable suspense.

Then they heard Cossar's first shot, like an explosion in a mine. . . .

Everyone's nerves and muscles tightened at that, and bang! bang! bang! the rats had tried a bolt, and two more were dead. Then the man who held the ball of twine reported a twitching. "He's killed one in there," said Bensington, "and he wants the rope."

He watched the rope creep into the hole, and it seemed as though it had become animated by a serpentine intelligence — for the darkness made the twine invisible. At last it stopped crawling, and there was a long pause. Then what seemed to Bensington the queerest monster of all crept slowly from the hole, and resolved itself into the little engineer emerging backwards. After him, and ploughing deep furrows, Cossar's boots thrust out, and then came his lantern-illuminated back. . . .

Only one rat was left alive now, and this poor, doomed wretch cowered in the inmost recesses until Cossar and the lantern went in again and slew it, and finally Cossar, that human ferret, went through all the runs to make sure.

"We got 'em," he said to his nearly awe-stricken company at last. "And if I hadn't been a mud-headed mucker I should have stripped to the waist. Obviously. Feel my sleeves, Bensing-

ton! I'm wet through with per-
spiration. Jolly hard to think of
everything. Only a halfway-up of
whisky can save me from a cold."

§ 7

THERE were moments during that
wonderful night when it seemed
to Bensington that he was
planned by nature for a life of
fantastic adventure. This was par-
ticularly the case for an hour or
so after he had taken a stiff
whisky. "Shan't go back to
Sloane Street," he confided to the
tall, fair, dirty engineer.

"You won't, eh?"

"No fear," said Bensington,
nodding darkly.

The exertion of dragging the
seven dead rats to the funeral
pyre by the nettle grove left him
bathed in perspiration, and Cos-
sar pointed out the obvious
physical reaction of whisky to
save him from the otherwise in-
evitable chill. There was a sort
of brigand's supper in the old
bricked kitchen, with the row of
dead rats lying in the moonlight
against the hen-runs outside, and
after thirty minutes or so of rest
Cossar roused them all to the
labours that were still to do.
"Obviously," as he said, they
had to "wipe the place out. No
litter — no scandal. See?" He
stirred them up to the idea of
making destruction complete.
They smashed and splintered
every fragment of wood in the
house; they built trails of
chopped wood wherever big
vegetation was springing; they
made a pyre for the rat bodies
and soaked them in paraffin.

Bensington worked like a con-
scientious navvy. He had a sort of
climax of exhilaration and en-
ergy towards two o'clock. When
in the work of destruction he
wielded an axe the bravest fled
his neighbourhood. Afterwards
he was a little sobered by the
temporary loss of his spectacles,
which were found for him at last
in his side coat-pocket.

Men went to and fro about
him — grimy, energetic men. Cos-
sar moved amongst them like a
god.

Bensington drank that delight
of human fellowship that comes
to happy armies, to sturdy ex-
peditions — never to those who
live the life of the sober citizens
in cities. After Cossar had taken
his axe away and set him to carry
wood he went to and fro, saying
they were all "good fellows."
He kept on — long after he was
aware of fatigue.

At last all was ready and the
broaching of the paraffin began.
The moon, robbed now of all its
meagre night retinue of stars,
shone high above the dawn.

"Burn everything," said Cos-
sar, going to and fro, "burn the
ground and make a clean sweep
of it. See?"

Bensington became aware of
him, looking now very gaunt and
horrible in the pale beginnings
of the daylight, hurrying past
with his lower jaw projected and
a flaring torch of touchwood in
his hand.

"Come away!" said someone,
pulling Bensington's arm.

The still dawn — no birds were
singing there — was suddenly full

of a tumultuous crackling; a little dull red flame ran about the base of the pyre, changed to blue upon the ground, and set out to clamber, leaf by leaf, up the stem of a giant nettle. A singing sound mingled with the crackling. . . .

They snatched their guns from the corner of the Skinners' living-room, and then everyone was running. Cossar came after them with heavy strides. . . .

Then they were standing looking back at the Experimental Farm. It was boiling up; the smoke and flames poured out like a crowd in a panic, from doors and windows and from a thousand cracks and crevices in the roof. Trust Cossar to build a fire! A great column of smoke, shot with blood-red tongues and darting flashes, rushed up into the sky. It was like some huge giant suddenly standing up, straining upward and abruptly spreading his great arms out across the sky. It cast the night back upon them, utterly hiding and obliterating the incandescence of the sun that rose behind it. All Hickleybrow was soon aware of that stupendous pillar of smoke, and came out upon the crest, in various deshabille, to watch them coming.

Behind, like some fantastic fungus, this smoke pillar swayed and fluctuated, up, up, into the sky—making the Downs seem low and all other objects petty, and in the foreground, led by Cossar, the makers of this mischief followed the path, eight little black figures coming wearily, guns shouldered, across the meadow.

As Bensington looked back there came into his jaded brain, and echoed there, a familiar formula. What was it? "You have lit to-day —?" "You have lit to-day —?"

Then he remembered Latimer's words: "We have lit this day such a Candle in England as no man may ever put out again —"

What a man Cossar was, to be sure! He admired his back view for a space and was proud to have held that hat. Proud! Although he was an eminent investigator and Cossar only engaged in applied science.

Suddenly he fell shivering and yawning enormously and wishing he was warmly tucked away in bed in his little flat that looked out upon Sloane Street. (It didn't do even to think of Cousin Jane.) His legs became cotton strands, his feet lead. He wondered if anyone would get them coffee in Hickleybrow. He had not been up all night for three and thirty years.

§ 8

AND while these eight adventurers fought with rats about the Experimental Farm, nine miles away in the village of Cheasing Eyebright, an old lady with an excessive nose struggled with great difficulties by the light of a flickering candle. She gripped a sardine tin opener in one gnarled hand, and in the other she held a tin of Herakleophorbia, which she had resolved to open or

die. She struggled indefatigably, grunting at each fresh effort, while through the flimsy partition the voice of the Caddles infant wailed.

"Bless 'is poor 'art," said Mrs. Skinner; and then, with her solitary tooth biting her lip in an ecstasy of determination, "Come up!"

And presently, "*Jab!*" a fresh supply of the Food of the Gods was let loose to wreak its powers of giantry upon the world.

CHAPTER 4

THE GIANT CHILDREN

§ 1

FOR a time at least the spreading circle of residual consequences about the Experimental Farm must pass out of the focus of our narrative, how for a long time a power of bigness, in fungus and toadstool, in grass and weed, radiated from that charred but not absolutely obliterated centre. Nor can we tell here at any length how those mournful spinsters, the two surviving hens, made a wonder of and a show, spent their remaining years in eggless celebrity. The reader who is hungry for fuller details in these matters is referred to the newspapers of the period, to the voluminous indiscriminate files of the modern Recording Angel. Our business lies with Mr. Bensington at the focus of the disturbance.

He had come back to London to find himself a quite terribly famous man. In a night the whole world had changed with respect to him. Everybody understood. Cousin Jane, it seemed, knew all about it; the people in the streets knew all about it; the newspapers all and more. To meet Cousin Jane was terrible, of course, but when it was over not so terrible after all. The good woman had limits even to her power over facts; it was clear that she had communed with herself and accepted the Food as something in the nature of things.

She took the line of huffy dutifulness. She disapproved highly, it was evident, but she did not prohibit. The flight of Bensington, as she must have considered it, may have shaken her, and her worst was to treat him with bitter persistence for a cold he had not caught and fatigue he had long since forgotten, and to buy him a new sort of hygienic all-wool combination underwear that was as apt to get involved and turned partially inside out and partially not, and as difficult to get into for an absent-minded man, as — Society. And so for a space, and as far as this convenience left him leisure, he still continued to participate in the development of this new element in human history, the Food of the Gods.

The public mind, following its own mysterious laws of selection,

had chosen him as the one and only responsible Inventor and Promoter of this new wonder; it would hear nothing of Redwood, and without a protest it allowed Cossar to follow his natural impulse into a terribly prolific obscurity. Before he was aware of the drift of these things, Mr. Bensington was, so to speak, stark and dissected upon the hoardings. His baldness, his curious general pinkness, and his golden spectacles had become a national possession. Resolute young men with large expensive-looking cameras and a general air of complete authorisation took possession of the flat for brief but fruitful periods, let off flashlights in it that filled it for hours with dense, intolerable vapour, and retired to fill the pages of the syndicated magazines with their admirable photographs of Mr. Bensington complete and at home in his second best jacket and his slashed shoes. Other resolute-mannered persons of various ages and sexes dropped in and told him things about Boomfood — it was *Punch* first called the stuff "Boomfood"— and afterwards reproduced what they had said as his own original contribution to the Interview. The thing became quite an obsession with Broadbeam, the Popular Humorist. He scented another confounded thing he could not understand, and he fretted dreadfully in his efforts to "laugh the thing down." One saw him in clubs, a great clumsy presence with the evidences of his midnight oil-burning manifest upon his large unwholesome face, ex-

plaining to everyone he could buttonhole: "These Scientific chaps, you know, haven't a Sense of Humour, you know. That's what it is. This Science — kills it." His jests at Bensington became malignant libels. . . .

An enterprising press-cutting agency sent Bensington a long article about himself from a sixpenny weekly, entitled "A New Terror," and offered to supply one hundred such disturbances for a guinea; and two extremely charming young ladies, totally unknown to him, called and, to the speechless indignation of Cousin Jane, had tea with him and afterwards sent him their birthday books for his signature. He was speedily quite hardened to seeing his name associated with the most incongruous ideas in the public press, and to discover in the reviews articles written about Boomfood and himself in a tone of the utmost intimacy by people he had never heard of. And whatever delusions he may have cherished in the days of his obscurity about the pleasantness of Fame were dispelled utterly and for ever.

At first — except for Broadbeam — the tone of the public mind was quite free from any touch of hostility. It did not seem to occur to the public mind as anything but a mere playful supposition that any more Herakleophorbia was going to escape again. And it did not seem to occur to the public mind that the growing little band of babies now being fed on the food would presently be growing more "up" than most of us ever grow. The sort of

thing that pleased the public mind was caricatures of eminent politicians after a course of Boomfeeding, uses of the idea on hoardings, and such edifying exhibitions as the dead wasps that had escaped the fire and the remaining hens.

Beyond that the public did not care to look, until very strenuous efforts were made to turn its eyes to the remoter consequences; and even then for a while its enthusiasm for action was partial. "There's always somethin' New," said the public — a public so glutted with novelty that it would hear of the earth being split as one splits an apple without surprise, and, "I wonder what they'll do next."

But there were one or two people outside the public, as it were, who did already take that further glance, and some it seems were frightened by what they saw there. There was young Caterham, for example, cousin of the Earl of Pewterstone, and one of the most promising of English politicians, who, taking the risk of being thought a faddist, wrote a long article in the *Nineteenth Century and After* to suggest the total suppression of the food. And — in certain of his moods, there was Bensington.

"They don't seem to realise —" he said to Cossar.

"No, they don't."

"And do we? Sometimes, when I think of what it means — This poor child of Redwood's — and, of course, your three . . . forty feet high, perhaps! . . . After all, *ought* we to go on with it?"

"Go on with it!" cried Cossar, convulsed with inelegant astonishment and pitching his note higher than ever. "Of *course* you'll go on with it! What d'you think you were made for? Just to loaf about between meal-times?

"Serious consequences," he screamed, "of course! Enormous. Obviously. Ob-viously. Why, man, it's the only chance you'll ever get of a serious consequence! And you want to shirk it!" For a moment his indignation was speechless. "It's downright Wicked!" he said at last, and repeated explosively, "Wicked!"

But Bensington worked in his laboratory now with more emotion than zest. He couldn't tell whether he wanted serious consequences to his life or not; he was a man of quiet tastes. It was a marvellous discovery, of course, quite marvellous, but — He had already become the proprietor of several acres of scorched, discredited property near Hickleybrow, at a price of nearly £90 an acre; and at times he was disposed to think this as serious a consequence of speculative chemistry as any unambitious man could wish. Of course he was Famous — terribly Famous. More than satisfying, altogether more than satisfying, was the Fame he had attained.

But the habit of Research was strong in him. . . .

And at moments, rare moments in the laboratory chiefly, he would find something else than habit and Cossar's arguments to urge him to his work. This little spectacled man, poised perhaps with his slashed shoes wrapped about the legs of his high stool

and his hand upon the tweezer of his balance weights, would have again a flash of that adolescent vision, would have a momentary perception of the eternal unfolding of the seed that had been sown in his brain, would see as it were in the sky, behind the grotesque shapes and accidents of the present, the coming world of giants and all the mighty things the future has in store — vague and splendid, like some glittering palace seen suddenly in the passing of a sunbeam far away. . . . And presently it would be with him as though that distant splendour had never shone upon his brain, and he would perceive nothing ahead but sinister shadows, vast declivities and darknesses, inhospitable immensities, cold, wild, and terrible things.

§ 2

AMIDST the complex and confused happenings, the impacts from the great outer world that constituted Mr. Bensington's fame, a shining and active figure presently became conspicuous, became almost, as it were, a leader and marshal of these externalities in Mr. Bensington's eyes. This was Doctor Winkles, that convincing young practitioner, who has already appeared in this story as the means whereby Redwood was able to convey the Food to his son. Even before the great outbreak, it was evident that the mysterious powders Redwood had given him had awakened this gentleman's interest immensely, and so soon as the first wasps came he was putting two and two together.

He was the sort of doctor that is in manners, in morals, in methods and appearance, most succinctly and finally expressed by the word "rising." He was large and fair, with a hard, alert, superficial, aluminium-coloured eye and hair like chalk mud, even-featured and muscular about the clean-shaven mouth, erect in figure and energetic in movement, quick and spinning on the heel; and he wore long frock coats, black silk ties and plain gold studs and chains, and his silk hats had a special shape and brim that made him look wiser and better than anybody. He looked as young or old as anybody grown up. And after that first wonderful outbreak he took to Bensington and Redwood and the Food of the Gods with such a convincing air of proprietorship, that at times, in spite of the testimony of the Press to the contrary, Bensington was disposed to regard him as the original inventor of the whole affair.

"These accidents," said Winkles, when Bensington hinted at the dangers of further escapes, "are nothing. Nothing. The discovery is everything. Properly developed, suitably handled, sanely controlled, we have — we have something very portentous indeed in this food of ours. . . . We must keep our eye on it. . . . We mustn't let it out of control again, and — we mustn't let it rest."

He certainly did not mean to do that. He was at Bensington's now almost every day. Bensington, glancing from the window, would see the faultless equipage

come spanking up Sloane Street, and after an incredibly brief interval Winkles would enter the room with a light, strong motion, and pervade it, and protrude some newspaper and supply information and make remarks.

"Well," he would say, rubbing his hands, "how are we getting on?" and so pass to the current discussion.

"Do you see," he would say for example, "that Caterham has been talking about our stuff at the Church Association?"

"Dear me!" said Bensington, "that's a cousin of the Prime Minister, isn't it?"

"Yes," said Winkles, "a very able young man — very able. Quite wrong-headed, you know, violently reactionary — but thoroughly able. And he's evidently disposed to make capital out of this stuff of ours. Takes a very emphatic line. Talks of our proposal to use it in the elementary schools — "

"Our proposal to use it in the elementary schools!"

"*I* said something about that the other day — quite in passing — little affair at a Polytechnic. Trying to make it clear the stuff was really highly beneficial. Not in the slightest degree dangerous, in spite of those first little accidents. Which cannot possibly occur again. . . . You know it *would* be rather good stuff — But he's taken it up."

"What did you say?"

"Mere obvious nothings. But as you see — ! Takes it up with perfect gravity. Treats the thing as an attack. Says there is already

a sufficient waste of public money in elementary schools without this. Tells the old stories about piano lessons again — *you* know. No one, he says, wishes to prevent the children of the lower classes obtaining an education suited to their condition, but to give them a food of this sort will be to destroy their sense of proportion utterly. Expands the topic. What Good will it do, he asks, to make poor people six-and-thirty feet high? He really believes, you know, that they *will* be thirty-six feet high."

"So they would be," said Bensington, "if you gave them our food at all regularly. But nobody said anything — "

"*I* said something."

"But, my dear Winkles — !"

"They'll be Bigger, of course," interrupted Winkles, with an air of knowing all about it, and discouraging the crude ideas of Bensington. "Bigger indisputably. But listen to what he says! Will it make them happier? That's his point. Curious, isn't it? Will it make them better? Will they be more respectful to properly constituted authority? Is it fair to the children themselves? Curious how anxious his sort are for justice — so far as any future arrangements go. Even nowadays, he says, the cost of feeding and clothing children is more than many of their parents can contrive, and if this sort of thing is to be permitted — ! Eh?

"You see he makes my mere passing suggestion into a positive proposal. And then he calculates how much a pair of breeches for a growing lad of twenty feet high

or so will cost. Just as though he really believed — Ten pounds, he reckons, for the merest decency. Curious man, this Caterham! So concrete! The honest and struggling ratepayer will have to contribute to that, he says. He says we have to consider the Rights of the Parent. It's all here. Two columns. Every Parent has a right to have his children brought up in his own Size. . . .

"Then comes the question of school accommodation, cost of enlarged desks and forms for our already too greatly burthened National Schools. And to get what? — a proletariat of hungry giants. Winds up with a very serious passage, says even if this wild suggestion — mere passing fancy of mine, you know, and misinterpreted at that — this wild suggestion about the schools comes to nothing, that doesn't end the matter. This is a strange food, so strange as to seem to him almost wicked. It has been scattered recklessly — so he says — and it may be scattered again. Once you've taken it, it's poison unless you go on with it. ("So it is," said Bensington.) And in short he proposes the formation of a National Society for the Preservation of the Proper Proportion of Things. Odd? Eh? People are hanging on to the idea like anything."

"But what do they propose to do?"

Winkles shrugged his shoulders and threw out his hands. "Form a Society," he said, "and fuss. They want to make it illegal to manufacture this Herakleophorbia — or at any rate to circulate the knowledge of it. I've written about it a bit to show that Caterham's idea of the stuff is very much exaggerated, very much exaggerated indeed, but that doesn't seem to check it. Curious how people are turning against it. And the National Temperance Association, by-the-by, has founded a branch for Temperance in Growth."

"Hm," said Bensington, and stroked his nose.

"After all that has happened there's bound to be this uproar. On the face of it the thing's — *startling*."

Winkles walked about the room for a time, hesitated, and departed.

It became evident there was something at the back of his mind, some aspect of crucial importance to him, that he waited to display. One day, when Redwood and Bensington were at the flat together, he gave them a glimpse of this something in reserve.

"How's it all going?" he said, rubbing his hands together.

"We're getting together a sort of report."

"For the Royal Society?"

"Yes."

"Hm," said Winkles, very profoundly, and walked to the hearthrug. "Hm. But — Here's the point. *Ought* you?"

"Ought we — what?"

"Ought you to publish?"

"We're not in the Middle Ages," said Redwood.

"I know."

"As Cossar says, swapping wisdom — that's the true scientific method."

" In most cases, certainly. But — This is exceptional."

" We shall put the whole thing before the Royal Society in the proper way," said Redwood.

Winkles returned to that on a later occasion.

" It's in many ways an Exceptional Discovery."

" That doesn't matter," said Redwood.

" It's the sort of knowledge that could easily be subject to grave abuse — grave dangers, as Caterham puts it."

Redwood said nothing.

" Even carelessness, you know —

" If we were to form a committee of trustworthy people to control the manufacture of Boomfood — Herakleophorbia, I *should* say — we might —"

He paused, and Redwood, with a certain private discomfort, pretended that he did not see any sort of interrogation. . . .

Outside the apartments of Redwood and Bensington, Winkles, in spite of the incompleteness of his instructions, became a leading authority upon Boomfood. He wrote letters defending its use; he made notes and articles explaining its possibilities; he jumped up irrelevantly at the meetings of the scientific and medical associations to talk about it; he identified himself with it. He published a pamphlet called " The Truth about Boomfood," in which he minimised the whole of the Hickleybrow affair almost to nothing. He said that it was absurd to say Boomfood would make people thirty-seven feet high. That was " obviously exaggerated." It would make them Bigger, of course, but that was all. . . .

Within that intimate circle of two it was chiefly evident that Winkles was extremely anxious to help in the making of Herakleophorbia, help in correcting any proofs there might be of any paper there might be in preparation upon the subject, do anything indeed that might lead up to his participation in the details of the making of Herakleophorbia. He was continually telling them both that he felt it was a Big Thing, that it had big possibilities. If only they were — " safeguarded in some way." And at last one day he asked outright to be told just how it was made.

" I've been thinking over what you said," said Redwood.

" Well? " said Winkles, brightly.

" It's the sort of knowledge that could easily be subject to grave abuse," said Redwood.

" But I don't see how that applies," said Winkles.

" It does," said Redwood.

Winkles thought it over for a day or so. Then he came to Redwood and said that he doubted if he ought to give powders about which he knew nothing to Redwood's little boy; it seemed to him it was uncommonly like taking responsibility in the dark. That made Redwood thoughtful.

" You've seen that the Society for the Total Suppression of Boomfood claims to have several thousand members," said Winkles, changing the subject.

" They've drafted a bill," said Winkles. " They've got young

Caterham to take it up — readily enough. They're in earnest. They're forming local committees to influence candidates. They want to make it penal to prepare and store Herakleophorbia without special licence, and felony — matter of imprisonment without option — to administer Boomfood — that's what they call it, you know — to any person under one-and-twenty. But there's collateral societies, you know. All sorts of people. The Society for the Preservation of Ancient Statures is going to have Mr. Frederick Harrison on the council, they say. You know he's written an essay about it; says it is vulgar, and entirely inharmonious with that Revelation of Humanity that is found in the teachings of Comte. It is the sort of thing the Eighteenth Century *couldn't* have produced even in its worst moments. The idea of the Food never entered the head of Comte — which shows how wicked it really is. No one, he says, who really understood Comte. . . ."

"But you don't mean to say —" said Redwood, alarmed out of his disdain for Winkles.

"They'll not do all that," said Winkles. "But public opinion is public opinion, and votes are votes. Everybody can see you are up to a disturbing thing. And the human instinct is all against disturbance, you know. Nobody seems to believe Caterham's idea of people thirty-seven feet high, who won't be able to get inside a church, or a meeting-house, or any social or human institution. But for all that they're not so easy in their minds about it.

They see there's something, something more than a common discovery —"

"There is," said Redwood, "in every discovery."

"Anyhow, they're getting restive. Caterham keeps harping on what may happen if it gets loose again. I say over and over again it won't and it can't. But — there it is!"

And he bounced about the room for a little while as if he meant to reopen the topic of the secret, and then thought better of it and went.

The two scientific men looked at one another. For a space only their eyes spoke.

"If the worst comes to the worst," said Redwood at last, in a strenuously calm voice, "I shall give the Food to my little Teddy with my own hands."

§ 3

IT was only a few days after this that Redwood opened his paper to find that the Prime Minister had promised a Royal Commission on Boomfood. This sent him, newspaper in hand, round to Bensington's flat.

"Winkles, I believe, is making mischief for the stuff. He plays into the hands of Caterham. He keeps on talking about it, and what it is going to do, and alarming people. If he goes on, I really believe he'll hamper our inquiries. Even as it is — with this trouble about my little boy —"

Bensington wished Winkles wouldn't.

"Do you notice how he has dropped into the way of calling it Boomfood?"

"I don't like that name," said Bensington, with a glance over his glasses.

"It is just so exactly what it is — to Winkles."

"Why does he keep on about it? It isn't his!"

"It's something called Booming," said Redwood. "*I* don't understand. If it isn't his, everybody is getting to think it is. Not that *that* matters."

"In the event of this ignorant, this ridiculous agitation becoming — Serious," began Bensington.

"My little boy can't get on without the stuff," said Redwood. "I don't see how I can help myself now. If the worst comes to the worst —"

A slight bouncing noise proclaimed the presence of Winkles. He became visible in the middle of the room rubbing his hands together.

"I wish you'd knock," said Bensington, looking vicious over the gold rims.

Winkles was apologetic. Then he turned to Redwood. "I'm glad to find you here," he began; "the fact is —"

"Have you seen about this Royal Commission?" interrupted Redwood.

"Yes," said Winkles, thrown out. "Yes."

"What do you think of it?"

"Excellent thing," said Winkles. "Bound to stop most of this clamour. Ventilate the whole affair. Shut up Caterham. But that's not what I came round for, Redwood. The fact is —"

"I don't like this Royal Commission," said Bensington.

"I can assure you it will be all right. I may say — I don't think it's a breach of confidence — that very possibly *I* may have a place on the commission —"

"Oom," said Redwood, looking into the fire.

"I can put the whole thing right. I can make it perfectly clear, first, that the stuff is controllable, and, secondly, that nothing short of a miracle is needed before anything like that catastrophe at Hickleybrow can possibly happen again. That is just what is wanted, an authoritative assurance. Of course, I could speak with more confidence if I knew — But that's quite by the way. And just at present there's something else, another little matter, upon which I'm wanting to consult you. Ahem. The fact is — Well — I happen to be in a slight difficulty, and you can help me out."

Redwood raised his eyebrows and was secretly glad.

"The matter is — highly confidential."

"Go on," said Redwood. "Don't worry about that."

"I have recently been entrusted with a child — the child of — of an Exalted Personage."

Winkles coughed.

"You're getting on," said Redwood.

"I must confess it's largely your powders — and the reputation of my success with your little boy — There is, I cannot disguise, a strong feeling against its use. And yet I find that among the more intelligent — One must go quietly in these things, you know — little by little. Still, in the case of Her Serene High — I mean this

new little patient of mine. As a matter of fact — the suggestion came from the parent. Or I should never — "

He struck Redwood as being embarrassed.

"I thought you had a doubt of the advisability of using these powders," said Redwood.

"Merely a passing doubt."

"You don't propose to discontinue — "

"In the case of your little boy? Certainly not! "

"So far as I can see, it would be murder."

"I wouldn't do it for the world."

"You shall have the powders," said Redwood.

"I suppose you couldn't — "

"No fear," said Redwood. "There isn't a recipe. It's no good, Winkles, if you'll pardon my frankness. I'll make you the powders myself."

"Just as well, perhaps," said Winkles, after a momentary hard stare at Redwood, "just as well." And then: "I can assure you I really don't mind in the least."

§ 4

WHEN Winkles had gone Bensington came and stood on the hearthrug and looked down at Redwood.

"Her Serene Highness! " he remarked.

"Her Serene Highness! " said Redwood.

"It's the Princess of Weser Dreiburg! "

"No further than a third cousin."

"Redwood," said Bensington; "it's a curious thing to say, I know, but — do you think Winkles understands? "

"What? "

"Just what it is we have made. "Does he really understand," said Bensington, dropping his voice and keeping his eye doorward, "that in the Family — the Family of his new patient — ".

"Go on," said Redwood.

"Who have always been if anything a little *under — under —* "

"The Average? "

"Yes. And so *very* tactfully undistinguished in *any* way, he is going to produce a royal personage — an outside royal personage — of *that* size. You know, Redwood, I'm not sure whether there is not something almost — *treasonable. . . .*"

He transferred his eyes from the door to Redwood.

Redwood flung a momentary gesture — index finger erect — at the fire. "By Jove! " he said, "he *doesn't* know!

"That man," said Redwood, "doesn't know anything. That was his most exasperating quality as a student. Nothing. He passed all his examinations, he had all his facts — and he had just as much knowledge — as a rotating bookshelf containing the *Times Encyclopædia*. And he doesn't know anything *now*. He's Winkles and incapable of really assimilating anything not immediately and directly related to his superficial self. He is utterly void of imagination and, as a consequence, incapable of knowledge. No one could possibly pass so many examinations and be so well dressed, so well done, and so successful as a doctor without

that precise incapacity. That's it. And in spite of all he's seen and heard and been told, there he is — he has no idea whatever of what he has set going. He has got a Boom on, he's working it well on Boomfood, and someone has let him in to this new Royal Baby — and that's Boomier than ever! And the fact that Weser Dreiburg will presently have to face the gigantic problem of a thirty-odd-foot Princess not only hasn't entered his head, but couldn't — it couldn't!"

"There'll be a fearful row," said Bensington.

"In a year or so."

"So soon as they really see she is going on growing."

"Unless after their fashion — they hush it up."

"It's a lot to hush up."

"Rather!"

"I wonder what they'll do?"

"They never do anything — Royal tact."

"They're bound to do something."

"Perhaps *she* will."

"O Lord! Yes."

"They'll suppress her. Such things have been known."

Redwood burst into desperate laughter. "The redundant royalty — the bouncing babe in the Iron Mask!" he said. "They'll have to put her in the tallest tower of the old Weser Dreiburg castle and make holes in the ceilings as she grows from floor to floor! . . . Well, I'm in the very same pickle. And Cossar and his three boys. And — Well, well."

"There'll be a fearful row," Bensington repeated, not joining in the laughter. "A *fearful* row."

"I suppose," he argued, "you've really thought it out thoroughly, Redwood. You're quite sure it wouldn't be wiser to warn Winkles, wean your little boy gradually and — rely upon the Theoretical Triumph?"

"I wish to goodness you'd spend half an hour in my nursery when the Food's a little late," said Redwood, with a note of exasperation in his voice, "then you wouldn't talk like that, Bensington. Besides — Fancy warning Winkles! . . . No! The tide of this thing has caught us unawares, and whether we're frightened or whether we're not — *we've got to swim!*"

"I suppose we have," said Bensington, staring at his toes. "Yes. We've got to swim. And your boy will have to swim, and Cossar's boys — he's given it to all three of them. Nothing partial about Cossar — all or nothing! And Her Serene Highness. And everything. We are going on making the Food. Cossar also. We're only just in the dawn of the beginning, Redwood. It's evident all sorts of things are to follow. Monstrous great things. But I can't imagine them, Redwood. Except —"

He scanned his finger nails. He looked up at Redwood with eyes bland through his glasses.

"I've half a mind," he adventured, "that Caterham is right. At times. It's going to destroy the Proportions of Things. It's going to dislocate — What isn't it going to dislocate?"

"Whatever it dislocates," said Redwood, "my little boy must have the Food."

They heard someone falling rapidly upstairs. Then Cossar put his head into the flat. "Hullo!" he said at their expressions, and entering, "Well?"

They told him about the Princess.

"*Difficult question!*" he remarked. "Not a bit of it. *She'll* grow. Your boy'll grow. All the others you give it to 'll grow. Everything. Like anything. What's difficult about that? That's all right. A child could tell you that. What's the bother?"

They tried to make it clear to him.

"*Not go on with it!*" he shrieked. "But—! You can't help yourselves now. It's what you're for. It's what Winkles is for. It's all right. Often wondered what Winkles was for. *Now* it's obvious. What's the trouble?

"*Disturbance?* Obviously. *Upset things?* Upset everything. Finally—upset every human concern. Plain as a pikestaff. They're going to try and stop it, but they're too late. It's their way to be too late. You go on and start as much of it as you can. Thank God he has a use for you!"

"But the conflict!" said Bensington, "the stress! I don't know if you have imagined—"

"You ought to have been some sort of little vegetable, Bensington," said Cossar, "that's what you ought to have been. Something growing over a rockery. Here you are, fearfully and wonderfully made, and all you think you're made for is just to sit about and take your vittles. D'you think this world was made for old women to mop about in?

Well, anyhow, you can't help yourselves now, you've *got* to go on."

"I suppose we must," said Redwood. "Slowly—"

"No!" said Cossar, in a huge shout. "No! Make as much as you can and as soon as you can. Spread it about!"

He was inspired to a stroke of wit. He parodied one of Redwood's curves with a vast upward sweep of his arm.

"Redwood!" he said, to point the allusion, "make it SO!"

§ 5

THERE is, it seems, an upward limit to the pride of maternity, and this in the case of Mrs. Redwood was reached when her offspring completed his sixth month of terrestrial existence, broke down his high-class bassinet-perambulator and was brought home, bawling, in the milk-truck. Young Redwood at that time weighed fifty-nine and a half pounds, measured forty-eight inches in height, and gripped about sixty pounds. He was carried upstairs to the nursery by the cook and housemaid. After that, discovery was only a question of days. One afternoon Redwood came home from his laboratory to find his unfortunate wife deep in the fascinating pages of *The Mighty Atom*, and at the sight of him, she put the book aside and ran violently forward and burst into tears on his shoulder.

"Tell me what you have *done* to him," she wailed. "Tell me what you have done."

Redwood took her hand and

led her to the sofa, while he tried to think of a satisfactory line of defence.

"It's all right, my dear," he said; "it's all right. You're only a little overwrought. It's that cheap perambulator. I've arranged for a bath-chair man to come round with something stouter to-morrow—"

Mrs. Redwood looked at him tearfully over the top of her handkerchief.

"A baby in a bath-chair?" she sobbed.

"Well, why not?"

"It's like a cripple."

"It's like a young giant, my dear, and you've no cause to be ashamed of him."

"You've done something to him, Dandy," she said. "I can see it in your face."

"Well, it hasn't stopped his growth, anyhow," said Redwood heartlessly.

"I *knew*," said Mrs. Redwood, and clenched her pocket-handkerchief ball fashion in one hand. She looked at him with a sudden change to severity. "What have you done to our child, Dandy?"

"What's wrong with him?"

"He's so big. He's a monster."

"Nonsense. He's as straight and clean a baby as ever a woman bore. What's wrong with him?"

"Look at his size."

"That's all right. Look at the puny little brutes about us! He's the finest baby—"

"He's *too* fine," said Mrs. Redwood.

"It won't go on," said Redwood reassuringly; "it's just a start he's taken."

But he knew perfectly well it would go on. And it did. By the time this baby was twelve months old he measured just one inch under five feet high and scaled eight stone three; he was as big in fact as a *San Pietro in Vaticano* cherub, and his affectionate clutch at the hair and features of visitors became the talk of West Kensington. They had an invalid's chair to carry him up and down to his nursery, and his special nurse, a muscular young person just out of training, used to take him for his airings in a Panhard 8 h.p. hill-climbing-perambulator specially made to meet his requirements. It was lucky in every way that Redwood had his expert-witness connection in addition to his professorship.

When one got over the shock of little Redwood's enormous size, he was, I am told by people who used to see him almost daily teufteufing slowly about Hyde Park, a singularly bright and pretty baby. He rarely cried or needed a comforter. Commonly he clutched a big rattle, and sometimes he went along hailing the bus-drivers and policemen along the road outside the railings as "Dadda!" and "Babba!" in a sociable democratic way.

"There goes that there great Boomfood baby," the bus-driver used to say.

"Looks 'ealthy," the forward passenger would remark.

"Bottle fed," the bus-driver would explain. "They say it 'olds a gallon and 'ad to be specially made for 'im."

"Very 'ealthy child anyhow," the forward passenger would conclude.

When Mrs. Redwood realised that his growth was indeed going on indefinitely and logically — and this she really did for the first time when the motor-perambulator arrived — she gave way to a passion of grief. She declared she never wished to enter her nursery again, wished she was dead, wished the child was dead, wished everybody was dead, wished she had never married Redwood, wished no one ever married anybody, Ajaxed a little, and retired to her own room, where she lived almost exclusively on chicken broth for three days. When Redwood came to remonstrate with her, she banged pillows about and wept and tangled her hair.

"*He's* all right," said Redwood. "He's all the better for being big. You wouldn't like him smaller than other people's children."

"I want him to be *like* other children, neither smaller nor bigger. I wanted him to be a nice little boy, just as Georgina Phyllis is a nice little girl, and I wanted to bring him up nicely in a nice way, and here he is" — and the unfortunate woman's voice broke — "wearing number four grown-up shoes and being wheeled about by — booboo! — Petroleum!

"I can never love him," she wailed, "never! He's too much for me! I can never be a mother to him, such as I meant to be!"

But at last they contrived to get her into the nursery, and there was Edward Monson Redwood ("Pantagruel" was only a later nickname) swinging in a specially strengthened rocking-chair and smiling and talking "goo" and "wow." And the heart of Mrs. Redwood warmed again to her child, and she went and held him in her arms and wept.

"They've done something to you," she sobbed, "and you'll grow and grow, dear, but whatever I can do to bring you up nice I'll do for you whatever your father may say."

And Redwood, who had helped bring her to the door, went down the passage much relieved.

(Eh! but it's a base job this being a man — with women as they are!)

§ 6

BEFORE the year was out there were, in addition to Redwood's pioneer vehicle, quite a number of motor-perambulators to be seen in the west of London. I am told there were as many as eleven; but the most careful inquiries yield trustworthy evidence of only six within the Metropolitan area at that time. It would seem the stuff acted differently upon different types of constitution. At first Herakleophorbia was not adapted to injection, and there can be no doubt that quite a considerable proportion of human beings are incapable of absorbing this substance in the normal course of digestion. It was given, for example, to Winkles' youngest boy; but he seems to have been as incapable of growth as, if Redwood was right, his father was incapable of knowledge. Others again, according to the Society for the Total Suppression of Boomfood, became in some in-

explicable way corrupted by it, and perished at the onset of infantile disorders. The Cossar boys took to it with amazing avidity.

Of course a thing of this kind never comes with absolute simplicity of application into the life of man; growth in particular is a complex thing, and all generalisations must needs be a little inaccurate. But the general law of the Food would seem to be this, that when it could be taken into the system in any way it stimulated it in very nearly to the same degree in all cases. It increased the amount of growth from six to seven times, and it did not go beyond that whatever amount of the Food was taken in excess. Excess of Herakleophorbia indeed beyond the necessary minimum led, it was found, to morbid disturbances of nutrition, to cancer and tumours, ossifications and the like. And once growth upon the large scale had begun it was soon evident that it could only continue upon that scale, and that the continuous administration of Herakleophorbia in small but sufficient doses was imperative.

If it was discontinued while growth was still going on, there was first a vague restlessness and distress, then a period of voracity — as in the case of the young rats at Hankey — and then the growing creature had a sort of exaggerated anæmia and sickened and died. Plants suffered in a similar way. This, however, applied only to the growth period. So soon as adolescence was attained — in plants this was represented by

the formation of the first flower-buds — the need and appetite for Herakleophorbia diminished, and so soon as the plant or animal was fully adult, it became altogether independent of any further supply of the food. It was, as it were, completely established on the new scale. It was so completely established on the new scale that, as the thistles about Hickleybrow and the grass of the down side already demonstrated, its seed produced giant offspring after its kind.

And presently little Redwood, pioneer of the new race, first child of all who ate the food, was crawling about his nursery, smashing furniture, biting like a horse, pinching like a vice, and bawling gigantic baby talk at his "Nanny" and "Mammy" and the rather scared and awe-stricken "Daddy," who had set this mischief going.

The child was born with good intentions. "Padda be good, be good," he used to say as the breakables flew before him. "Padda" was his rendering of Pantagruel, the nickname Redwood imposed upon him. And Cossar, disregarding certain Ancient Lights that presently led to trouble, did, after a conflict with the local building regulations, get building on a vacant piece of ground adjacent to Redwood's home, a comfortable well-lit playroom, schoolroom, and nursery for their four boys; sixty feet square about this room was, and forty feet high.

Redwood fell in love with that great nursery as he and Cossar built it, and his interest in curves

faded, as he had never dreamt it could fade, before the pressing needs of his son. "There is much," he said, "in fitting a nursery. Much.

"The walls, the things in it, they will all speak to this new mind of ours, a little more, a little less eloquently, and teach it or fail to teach it a thousand things."

"Obviously," said Cossar, reaching hastily for his hat.

They worked together harmoniously, but Redwood supplied most of the educational theory required. . . .

They had the walls and woodwork painted with a cheerful vigour; for the most part a slightly warmed white prevailed, but there were bands of bright clean colour to enforce the simple lines of construction. "Clean colours we *must* have," said Redwood, and in one place had a neat horizontal band of squares, in which crimson and purple, orange and lemon, blues and greens, in many hues and many shades, did themselves honour. These squares the giant children should arrange and rearrange to their pleasure. "Decorations must follow," said Redwood; "let them first get the range of all the tints and then this may go away. There is no reason why one should bias them in favour of any particular colour or design."

Then, "The place must be full of interest," said Redwood. "Interest is food for a child and blankness torture and starvation. He must have pictures galore." There were no pictures hung about the room for any permanent service, however, but blank frames were provided into which new pictures would come and pass thence into a portfolio as soon as their fresh interest had passed. There was one window that looked down the length of a street, and in addition, for an added interest, Redwood had contrived above the roof of the nursery a camera obscura that watched the Kensington High School and not a little of the Gardens.

In one corner that most worthy implement, an Abacus, four feet square, a specially strengthened piece of ironmongery with rounded corners, awaited the young giants' incipient computations. There were few woolly lambs and such-like idols, but instead Cossar, without explanation, had brought one day in three four-wheelers a great number of toys (all just too big for the coming children to swallow) that could be piled up, arranged in rows, rolled about, bitten, made to flap and rattle, smacked together, felt over, pulled out, opened, closed and mauled and experimented with to an interminable extent. There were many bricks of wood in diverse colours, oblong and cuboid, bricks of polished china, bricks of transparent glass and bricks of india-rubber; there were slabs and slates; there were cones, truncated cones and cylinders; there were oblate and prolate spheroids, balls of varied substances, solid and hollow, many boxes of diverse size and shape, with hinged lids and screw lids and fitting lids, and one or two to catch and lock; there were

bands of elastic and leather, and a number of rough and sturdy little objects of a size together that could stand up steadily and suggest the shape of a man. "Give 'em these," said Cossar. "One at a time."

These things Redwood arranged in a locker in one corner. Along one side of the room, at a convenient height for a six or eight foot child, there was a blackboard on which the youngsters might flourish in white and coloured chalk; and near by a sort of drawing block from which sheet after sheet might be torn, and on which they could draw in charcoal; and a little desk there was, furnished with great carpenter's pencils of varying hardness and a copious supply of paper, on which the boys might first scribble and then draw more neatly. And moreover Redwood gave orders, so far ahead did his imagination go, for specially large tubes of liquid paint and boxes of pastels against the time when they should be needed. He laid in a cask or so of plasticine and modelling clay. "At first he and his tutor shall model together," he said, "and when he is more skilful he shall copy casts and perhaps animals. And that reminds me, I must also have made for him a box of tools!

"Then books. I shall have to look out a lot of books to put in his way, and they'll have to be big type. Now what sort of books will he need? There is his imagination to be fed. That, after all, is the crown of every education. The crown — as sound habits of mind and conduct are the

throne. No imagination at all is brutality; a base imagination is lust and cowardice; but a noble imagination is God walking the earth again. He must dream, too, of a dainty fairy-land and of all the quaint little things of life, in due time. But he must feed chiefly on the splendid real; he shall have stories of travel through all the world, travels and adventures and how the world was won; he shall have stories of beasts, great books splendidly and clearly done of animals and birds and plants and creeping things, great books about the deeps of the sky and the mystery of the sea; he shall have histories and maps of all the empires the world has seen, pictures and stories of all the tribes and habits and customs of men. And he must have books and pictures to quicken his sense of beauty, subtle Japanese pictures to make him love the subtler beauties of bird and tendril and falling flower; and western pictures too, pictures of gracious men and women, sweet groupings, and broad views of land and sea. He shall have books on the building of houses and palaces; he shall plan rooms and invent cities —

"I think I must give him a little theatre.

"Then there is music!"

Redwood thought that over and decided that his son might best begin with a very pure-sounding harmonicon of one octave, to which afterwards there could be an extension. "He shall play with this first, sing to it and give names to the notes," said Redwood, "and afterwards — ?"

He stared up at the window-sill overhead and measured the size of the room with his eye.

"They'll have to build his piano in here," he said. "Bring it in in pieces."

He hovered about amidst his preparations, a pensive dark little figure. If you could have seen him there he would have looked to you like a ten-inch man amidst common nursery things. A great rug — indeed it was a Turkey carpet — four hundred square feet of it, upon which young Redwood was soon to crawl, stretched to the grill-guarded electric radiator that was to warm the whole place. A man from Cossar's hung amidst scaffolding overhead, fixing the great frame that was to hold the transitory pictures. A blotting paper book for plant specimens as big as a house door leant against the wall, and from it projected a gigantic stalk, a leaf edge or so and one flower of chickweed, all of that gigantic size that was soon to make Urshot famous throughout the botanical world. . . .

A sort of incredulity came to Redwood as he stood among these things.

"If it really *is* going on — " said Redwood, staring up to the remote ceiling.

From far away came a sound like the bellowing of a Mafficking bull, almost as if in answer.

"It's going on all right," said Redwood. "Evidently."

There followed resounding blows upon a table, followed by a vast crowing shout, "Gooloo! Boozoo! Bzz . . ."

"The best thing I can do,"

said Redwood, following out some divergent line of thought, "is to teach him myself."

That beating became more insistent. For a moment it seemed to Redwood that it caught the rhythm of an engine's throbbing, the engine he could have imagined of some great train of events that bore down upon him. Then a descendant flight of sharper beats broke up that effect, and were repeated.

"Come in," he cried, perceiving that someone rapped, and the door that was big enough for a cathedral opened slowly a little way. The new winch ceased to creak, and Bensington appeared in the crack, gleaming benevolently under his protruded baldness and over his glasses.

"I've ventured round to *see*," he whispered in a confidentially furtive manner.

"Come in," said Redwood, and he did, shutting the door behind him.

He walked forward, hands behind his back, advanced a few steps, and peered up with a bird-like movement at the dimensions about him. He rubbed his chin thoughtfully.

"Every time I come in," he said, with a subdued note in his voice, "it strikes me as — '*Big.*'"

"Yes," said Redwood, surveying it all again also, as if in an endeavour to keep hold of the visible impression. "Yes. They're going to be big, too, you know."

"I know," said Bensington, with a note that was nearly awe. "*Very* big."

They looked at one another,

almost, as it were, apprehensively.

"Very big indeed," said Bensington, stroking the bridge of his nose, and with one eye that watched Redwood doubtfully for a confirmatory expression. "All of them, you know — fearfully Big. I don't seem able to imagine — even with this — just how big they're all going to be."

CHAPTER 5

THE MINIMIFICENCE OF MR. BENSINGTON

§ 1

IT was while the Royal Commission on Boomfood was preparing its report that Herakleophorbia really began to demonstrate its capacity for leakage. And the earliness of this second outbreak was the more unfortunate, from the point of view of Cossar at any rate, since the draft report still in existence shows that the Commission had, under the tutelage of that most able member, Doctor Stephen Winkles (F.R.S., M.D., F.R.C.P., D.Sc., J.P., D.L., etc.), already quite made up its mind that accidental leakages were impossible, and was prepared to recommend that to en-

trust the preparation of Boomfood to a qualified committee (Winkles chiefly), with an entire control over its sale, was quite enough to satisfy all reasonable objections to its free diffusion. This committee was to have an absolute monopoly. And it is, no doubt, to be considered as a part of the irony of life that the first and most alarming of this second series of leakages occurred within fifty yards of a little cottage at Keston occupied during the summer months by Doctor Winkles.

There can be little doubt now that Redwood's refusal to acquaint Winkles with the composition of Herakleophorbia IV. had aroused in that gentleman a novel and intense desire towards analytical chemistry. He was not an expert manipulator, and for that reason probably he saw fit to do his work not in the excellently equipped laboratories that were at his disposal in London, but without consulting anyone, and almost with an air of secrecy, in a rough little garden laboratory at the Keston establishment. He does not seem to have shown either great energy or great ability in this quest; indeed one gathers he dropped the inquiry after working at it intermittently for about a month.

This garden laboratory, in which the work was done, was very roughly equipped, supplied by a stand-pipe tap with water, and draining into a pipe that ran down into a swampy rush-bordered pool under an alder tree in a secluded corner of the common just outside the garden hedge. The pipe was cracked,

and the residuum of the Food of the Gods escaped through the crack into a little puddle amidst clumps of rushes, just in time for the spring awakening.

Everything was astir with life in that scummy little corner. There was frog spawn adrift, tremulous with tadpoles just bursting their gelatinous envelopes; there were little pond snails creeping out into life, and under the green skin of the rush stems the larvæ of a big Water Beetle were struggling out of their egg cases. I doubt if the reader knows the larva of the beetle called (I know not why) Dytıscus. It is a jointed, queer-looking thing, very muscular and sudden in its movements, and given to swimming head downwards with its tail out of water; the length of a man's top thumb joint it is, and more — two inches, that is, for those who have not eaten the Food — and it has two sharp jaws that meet in front of its head, tubular jaws with sharp points, through which its habit is to suck its victim's blood.

The first things to get at the drifting grains of the Food were the tadpoles and the water snails; the little wriggling tadpoles in particular, once they had the taste of it, took to it with zest. But scarcely did one of them begin to grow into a conspicuous position in that tadpole world and try a smaller brother or so as an aid to a vegetarian dietary, when nip! one of the Beetle larvæ had its curved bloodsucking prongs gripping into his heart, and with that red stream went Herakleophorbia IV., in a state of solution, into the being of a new client. The only thing that had a chance with these monsters to get any share of the Food were the rushes and slimy green scum in the water and the seedling weeds in the mud at the bottom. A clean-up of the study presently washed a fresh spate of the Food into the puddle, overflowed it, and carried all this sinister expansion of the struggle for life into the adjacent pool under the roots of the alder. . . .

The first person to discover what was going on was a Mr. Lukey Carrington, a special science teacher under the London Education Board, and, in his leisure, a specialist in fresh-water algæ, and he is certainly not to be envied his discovery. He had come down to Keston Common for the day to fill a number of specimen tubes for subsequent examination, and he came, with a dozen or so of corked tubes clanking faintly in his pocket, over the sandy crest and down towards the pool, spiked walking stick in hand. A garden lad standing on the top of the kitchen steps clipping Doctor Winkles' hedge saw him in this unfrequented corner, and found him and his occupation sufficiently inexplicable and interesting to watch him pretty closely.

He saw Mr. Carrington stoop down by the side of the pool, with his hand against the old alder stem, and peer into the water, but of course he could not appreciate the surprise and pleasure with which Mr. Carrington beheld the big unfamiliar-look-

ing blobs and threads of the algal scum at the bottom. There were no tadpoles visible — they had all been killed by that time — and it would seem Mr. Carrington saw nothing at all unusual except the excessive vegetation. He bared his arm to the elbow, leant forward, and dipped deep in pursuit of a specimen. His seeking hand went down. Instantly there flashed out of the cool shadow under the tree roots something —

Flash! It had buried its fangs deep into his arm — a bizarre shape it was, a foot long and more, brown and jointed like a scorpion.

Its ugly apparition, and the sharp amazing painfulness of its bite, was too much for Mr. Carrington's equilibrium. He felt himself going and yelled aloud. Over he toppled, face foremost, splash! into the pool.

The boy saw him vanish, and heard the splashing of his struggle in the water. The unfortunate man emerged again into the boy's field of vision, hatless and streaming with water, and screaming!

Never before had the boy heard screams from a man.

This astonishing stranger appeared to be tearing at something on the side of his face. There appeared streaks of blood there. He flung out his arms as if in despair, leapt in the air like a frantic creature, ran violently ten or twelve yards and then fell and rolled on the ground and over and out of sight of the boy.

The lad was down the steps and through the hedge in a trice — happily with the garden shears still in hand. As he came crashing through the gorse bushes, he says he was half minded to turn back, fearing he had to deal with a lunatic, but the possession of the shears reassured him: "I could 'ave jabbed his eyes," he explained, "anyhow." Directly Mr. Carrington caught sight of him, his demeanour became at once that of a sane but desperate man. He struggled to his feet, stumbled, stood up and came to meet the boy.

"Look!" he cried, "I can't get 'em off!"

And with a qualm of horror the boy saw that attached to Mr. Carrington's cheek, to his bare arm, and to his thigh, and lashing furiously with their lithe brown muscular bodies, were three of these horrible larvæ, their great jaws buried deep in his flesh and sucking for dear life. They had the grip of bulldogs, and Mr. Carrington's efforts to detach the monster from his face had only served to lacerate the flesh to which it had attached itself, and streak face and neck and coat with living scarlet.

"I'll cut 'im," cried the boy; "'old on, Sir."

And with the zest of his age in such proceedings, he severed one by one the heads from the bodies of Mr. Carrington's assailants. "Yup," said the boy with a wincing face as each one fell before him. Even then, so tough and determined was their grip that the severed heads remained for a space, still fiercely biting home and still sucking, with the blood streaming out of their necks behind. But the boy stopped that

with a few more slashes of his scissors — in one of which Mr. Carrington was implicated.

"I couldn't get 'em off!" repeated Carrington, and stood for a space, swaying and bleeding profusely. He dabbed feeble hands at his injuries and examined the result upon his palms. Then he gave way at the knees and fell headlong in a dead faint at the boy's feet, between the still leaping bodies of his defeated foes. Very luckily it didn't occur to the boy to splash water on his face — for there were still more of these horrors under the alder roots — and instead he passed back by the pond and went into the garden with the intention of calling assistance. And there he met the gardener-coachman and told him of the whole affair.

When they got back to Mr. Carrington he was sitting up, dazed and weak, but able to warn them against the danger in the pool.

§ 2

SUCH were the circumstances by which the world had its first notification that the Food was loose again. In another week Keston Common was in full operation as what naturalists call a centre of distribution. This time there were no wasps or rats, no earwigs and no nettles, but there were at least three water-spiders, several dragon-fly larvæ which presently became dragon-flies, dazzling all Kent with their hovering sapphire bodies, and a nasty gelatinous, scummy growth that swelled over the pond margin, and sent its slimy green masses surging halfway up the garden path to Doctor Winkles' house. And there began a growth of rushes and equisetum and potamogeton that ended only with the drying of the pond.

It speedily became evident to the public mind that this time there was not simply one centre of distribution, but quite a number of centres. There was one at Ealing, there can be no doubt now, and from that came the plague of flies and red spiders; there was one at Sunbury, productive of ferocious great eels, that could come ashore and kill sheep; and there was one in Bloomsbury that gave the world a new strain of cockroaches of a quite terrible sort — an old house it was in Bloomsbury, and much inhabited by undesirable things. Abruptly the world found itself confronted with the Hickleybrow experiences all over again, with all sorts of queer exaggerations of familiar monsters in the place of the giant hens and rats and wasps. Each centre burst out with its own characteristic local fauna and flora. . . .

We know now that everyone of these centres corresponded to one of the patients of Doctor Winkles, but that was by no means apparent at the time. Doctor Winkles was the last person to incur any odium in the matter. There was a panic quite naturally, a passionate indignation; but it was indignation not against Doctor Winkles but against the Food, and not so much against the Food as against the unfortunate Bensington, whom from the very first the

popular imagination had insisted upon regarding as the sole and only person responsible for this new thing.

The attempt to lynch him that followed is just one of those explosive events that bulk largely in history and are in reality the least significant of occurrences.

The history of the outbreak is a mystery. The nucleus of the crowd certainly came from an Anti-Boomfood meeting in Hyde Park organised by extremists of the Caterham party, but there seems no one in the world who actually first proposed, no one who ever first hinted a suggestion of the outrage at which so many people assisted. It is a problem for M. Gustave le Bon, a mystery in the psychology of crowds. The fact emerges that about three o'clock on Sunday afternoon a remarkably big and ugly London crowd, entirely out of hand, came rolling down Thursday Street intent on Bensington's exemplary death as a warning to all scientific investigators, and that it came nearer accomplishing its object than any London crowd has ever come since the Hyde Park railings came down in remote middle Victorian times. This crowd came so close to its object indeed, that for the space of an hour or more a word would have settled the unfortunate gentleman's fate.

The first intimation he had of the thing was the noise of the people outside. He went to the window and peered, realising nothing of what impended. For a minute perhaps he watched them seething about the entrance,

disposing of an ineffectual dozen policemen who barred their way, before he fully realised his own importance in the affair. It came upon him in a flash — that that roaring, swaying multitude was after him. He was all alone in the flat — fortunately perhaps — his cousin Jane having gone down to Ealing to have tea with a relation on her mother's side, and he had no more idea of how to behave under such circumstances than he had of the etiquette of the Day of Judgment. He was still dashing about the flat asking his furniture what he should do, turning keys in locks and then unlocking them again, making darts at door and window and bedroom — when the floor clerk came to him.

"There isn't a moment, Sir," he said. "They've got your number from the board in the hall! They're coming straight up!"

He ran Mr. Bensington out into the passage, already echoing with the approaching tumult from the great staircase, locked the door behind them, and led the way into the opposite flat by means of his duplicate key.

"It's our only chance now," he said.

He flung up a window which opened on a ventilating shaft, and showed that the wall was set with iron staples that made the rudest and most perilous of wall ladders to serve as a fire escape from the upper flats. He shoved Mr. Bensington out of the window, showed him how to cling on, and pursued him up the ladder, goading and jabbing his legs with a bunch of keys whenever

he desisted from climbing. It seemed to Bensington at times that he must climb that vertical ladder for evermore. Above, the parapet was inaccessibly remote, a mile perhaps, below — He did not care to think of things below.

"Steady on!" cried the clerk, and gripped his ankle. It was quite horrible having his ankle gripped like that, and Mr. Bensington tightened his hold on the iron staple above to a drowning clutch and gave a faint squeal of terror.

It became evident that the clerk had broken a window, and then it seemed he had leapt a vast distance sideways, and there came the noise of a window-frame sliding in its sash. He was bawling things.

Mr. Bensington moved his head round cautiously until he could see the clerk. "Come down six steps," the clerk commanded.

All this moving about seemed very foolish, but very, very cautiously Mr. Bensington lowered a foot.

"Don't pull me!" he cried, as the clerk made to help him from the open window.

It seemed to him that to reach the window from the ladder would be a very respectable feat for a flying fox, and it was rather with the idea of decent suicide than in any hope of accomplishing it that he made the step at last, and quite ruthlessly the clerk pulled him in. "You'll have to stop here," said the clerk: "my keys are no good here. It's an American lock. I'll get out and slam the door behind me and see

if I can find the man of this floor. You'll be locked in. Don't go to the window, that's all. It's the ugliest crowd I've ever seen. If only they think you're out they'll probably content themselves by breaking up your stuff —"

"The indicator said In," said Bensington.

"The devil it did! Well, anyhow, I'd better not be found —"

He vanished with a slam of the door.

Bensington was left to his own initiative again.

It took him under the bed.

There presently he was found by Cossar.

Bensington was almost comatose with terror when he was found, for Cossar had burst the door in with his shoulder by jumping at it across the breadth of the passage.

"Come out of it, Bensington," he said. "It's all right. It's me. We've got to get out of this. They're setting the place on fire. The porters are all clearing out. The servants are gone. It's lucky I caught the man who knew.

"Look here!"

Bensington, peering from under the bed, became aware of some unaccountable garments on Cossar's arm, and, of all things, a black bonnet in his hand!

"They're having a clear-out," said Cossar. "If they don't set the place on fire they'll come here. Troops may not be here for an hour yet. Fifty per cent. hooligans in the crowd, and the more furnished flats they go into the better they'll like it. Obviously. . . . They mean a clear-out. You put this skirt and bonnet on,

Bensington, and clear out with me."

"D'you *mean* — ?" began Bensington, protruding a head, tortoise fashion.

"I mean, put 'em on and come! Obviously." And with a sudden vehemence he dragged Bensington from under the bed, and began to dress him for his new impersonation of an elderly woman of the people.

He rolled up his trousers and made him kick off his slippers, took off his collar and tie and coat and vest, slipped a black skirt over his head, and put on a red flannel bodice and a body over the same. He made him take off his all too characteristic spectacles, and clapped the bonnet on his head. "You might have been born an old woman," he said as he tied the strings. Then came the spring-side boots — a terrible wrench for corns — and the shawl, and the disguise was complete. "Up and down," said Cossar, and Bensington obeyed.

"You'll do," said Cossar.

And in this guise it was, stumbling awkwardly over his unaccustomed skirts, shouting womanly imprecations upon his own head in a weird falsetto to sustain his part, and to the roaring note of a crowd bent upon lynching him, that the original discoverer of Herakleophorbia IV. proceeded down the corridor of Chesterfield Mansions, mingled with that inflamed disorderly multitude, and passed out altogether from the thread of events that constitutes our story.

Never once after that escape did he meddle again with the stu-

pendous development of the Food of the Gods, he of all men had done most to begin.

THIS little man who started the whole thing passes out of the story, and after a time he passed altogether out of the world of significant activities. But because he started the whole thing it is seemly to give his exit an intercalary page of attention. One may picture him in his later days as Tunbridge Wells came to know him. For it was at Tunbridge Wells he reappeared after a temporary obscurity, so soon as he fully realised how transitory, how quite exceptional and unmeaning that fury of rioting was. He reappeared under the wing of Cousin Jane, treating himself for nervous shock to the exclusion of all other interests, and totally indifferent, as it seemed, to the battles that were raging then about those new centres of distribution, and about the baby Children of the Food.

He took up his quarters at the Mount Glory Hydrotherapeutic Hotel, where there are quite extraordinary facilities for baths; Carbonated Baths, Creosote Baths, Galvanic and Faradic Treatment, Massage, Pine Baths, Starch and Hemlock Baths, Radium Baths, Light Baths, Heat Baths, Bran and Needle Baths, Tar and Birdsdown Baths, all sorts of baths; and he devoted his mind to the development of that system of curative treatment that was still imperfect when he died. And sometimes he would go out in a hired vehicle and a sealskin-

trimmed coat, and sometimes, when his feet permitted, he would walk to the Pantiles, and there he would sip chalybeate water under the eye of his cousin Jane.

His stooping shoulders, his pink appearance, his beaming glasses, became a "feature" of Tunbridge Wells. No one was the least bit unkind to him, and indeed the place and the Hotel seemed very glad to have the distinction of his presence. Nothing could rob him of that distinction now. And though he preferred not to follow the development of his great invention in the daily papers, yet when he crossed the Lounge of the Hotel or walked down the Pantiles and heard the whisper "There he is! That's him!" it was not dissatisfaction that softened his mouth and gleamed for a moment in his eye.

This little figure, this minute little figure, launched the Food of the Gods upon the world! One does not know which is the most amazing, the greatness or the littleness of these scientific and philosophical men. There you have him on the Pantiles, in the overcoat trimmed with fur. He stands under that chinaware window where the spring spouts, and holds and sips the glass of chalybeate water in his hand. One bright eye over the gilt rim is fixed, with an expression of inscrutable severity, on Cousin Jane. "M," he says, and sips.

So we make our souvenir, so we focus and photograph this discoverer of ours for the last time, and leave him, a mere dot in our foreground, and pass to the greater picture that has developed about him, to the story of his Food, how the scattered Giant Children grew up day by day into a world that was all too small for them, and how the net of Boomfood Laws and Boomfood Conventions, which the Boomfood Commission was weaving even then, drew closer and closer upon them with every year of their growth. Until—

"IT WAS EVIDENTLY AS BIG AS A BARN-OWL. ITS FLIGHT
SEEMED WEIRDLY UNBIRDLIKE."

Drawn by Cyrus Cuneo, 1903 for *THE FOOD OF THE GODS.*

Book II: *The Food in the Village*

CHAPTER 1

THE COMING OF THE FOOD

§ 1

OUR theme, which began so compactly in Mr. Bensington's study, has already spread and branched until it points this way and that, and henceforth our whole story is one of dissemination. To follow the Food of the Gods further is to trace the ramifications of a perpetually branching tree; in a little while, in the quarter of a lifetime, the Food had trickled and increased from its first spring in the little farm near Hickleybrow until it had spread, it and the report and shadow of its power, throughout the world. It spread beyond England very speedily. Soon in America, all over the continent of Europe, in Japan, in Australia, at last all over the world, the thing was working towards its appointed end. Always it worked slowly, by indirect courses and against resistance. It was bigness insurgent. In spite of prejudice, in spite of law and regulation, in spite of all that obstinate conservatism that lies at the base of the formal order of mankind, the Food of the Gods, once it had been set going, pursued its subtle and invincible progress.

The Children of the Food grew steadily through all these years; that was the cardinal fact of the time. But it is the leakages make history. The children who had eaten grew, and soon there were other children growing; and all the best intentions in the world could not stop further leakages and still further leakages. The Food insisted on escaping with the pertinacity of a thing alive. Flour treated with the stuff crumbled in dry weather almost as if by intention into an impalpable powder, and would lift and travel before the lightest breeze. Now it would be some fresh insect won its way to a temporary fatal new development, now some fresh outbreak from the sewers of rats and such-like vermin. For

some days the village of Pangbourne in Berkshire fought with giant ants. Three men were bitten and died. There would be a panic, there would be a struggle, and the salient evil would be fought down again, leaving always something behind, in the obscurer things of life — changed for ever. Then again another acute and startling outbreak, a swift upgrowth of monstrous weedy thickets, a drifting dissemination about the world of inhumanly growing thistles, of cockroaches men fought with shotguns, or a plague of mighty flies.

There were some strange and desperate struggles in obscure places. The Food begot heroes in the cause of littleness. . . .

And men took such happenings into their lives, and met them by the expedients of the moment, and told one another there was "no change in the essential order of things." After the first great panic, Caterham, in spite of his power of eloquence, became a secondary figure in the political world, remained in men's minds as the exponent of an extreme view.

Only slowly did he win a way towards a central position in affairs. "There was no change in the essential order of things " — that eminent leader of modern thought, Doctor Winkles, was very clear upon this — and the exponents of what was called in those days Progressive Liberalism grew quite sentimental upon the essential insincerity of their progress. Their dreams, it would appear, ran wholly on little na-

tions, little languages, little households, each self-supported on its little farm. A fashion for the small and neat set in. To be big was to be "vulgar," and dainty, neat, mignon, miniature, "minutely perfect," became the key words of critical approval. . . .

Meanwhile, quietly, taking their time as children must, the Children of the Food, growing into a world that changed to receive them, gathered strength and stature and knowledge, became individual and purposeful, rose slowly towards the dimensions of their destiny. Presently they seemed a natural part of the world; all these stirrings of bigness seemed a natural part of the world, and men wondered how things had been before their time. There came to men's ears stories of things the giant boys could do, and they said "Wonderful! " — without a spark of wonder. The popular papers would tell of the three sons of Cossar, and how these amazing children would lift great cannons, hurl masses of iron for hundreds of yards, and leap two hundred feet. They were said to be digging a well, deeper than any well or mine that man had ever made, seeking, it was said, for treasures hidden in the earth since ever the earth began.

These Children, said the popular magazines, will level mountains, bridge seas, tunnel your earth to a honeycomb. "Wonderful! " said the little folks, "isn't it? What a lot of conveniences we shall have! " and went about their business as though there was no such thing as the Food of

the Gods on earth. And indeed these things were no more than the first hints and promises of the powers of the Children of the Food. It was still no more than child's play with them, no more than the first use of a strength in which no purpose had arisen. They did not know themselves for what they were. They were children, slow-growing children of a new race. The giant strength grew day by day—the giant will had still to grow into purpose and an aim.

Looking at it in a shortened perspective of time, those years of transition have the quality of a single consecutive occurrence; but indeed no one saw the coming of Bigness in the world, as no one in all the world till centuries had passed saw, as one happening, the Decline and Fall of Rome. They who lived in those days were too much among these developments to see them together as a single thing. It seemed even to wise men that the Food was giving the world nothing but a crop of unmanageable, disconnected irrelevancies, that might shake and trouble indeed, but could do no more to the established order and fabric of mankind.

To one observer at least the most wonderful thing throughout that period of accumulating stress is the invincible inertia of the great mass of people, their quiet persistence in all that ignored the enormous presences, the promises of still more enormous things, that grew among them. Just as many a stream will be at its smoothest, will look most tranquil, running deep and strong, at the very verge of a cataract, so all that is most conservative in man seemed settling quietly into a serene ascendency during these latter days. Reaction became popular, there was talk of the bankruptcy of science, of the dying of Progress, of the advent of the Mandarins, talk of such things amidst the echoing footsteps of the Children of the Food. The fussy pointless Revolutions of the old time, a vast crowd of silly little people chasing some silly little monarch and the like, had indeed died out and passed away; but Change had not died out. It was only Change that had changed. The New was coming in its own fashion and beyond the common understanding of the world.

To tell fully of its coming would be to write a great history, but everywhere there was a parallel chain of happenings. To tell therefore of the manner of its coming in one place is to tell something of the whole. It chanced one stray seed of Immensity fell into the pretty petty village of Cheasing Eyebright in Kent, and the story of its queer germination there and of the tragic futility that ensued, one may attempt—following one thread, as it were, to show the direction in which the whole great interwoven fabric rolled off the loom of Time.

§2

CHEASING EYEBRIGHT had of course a Vicar. There are vicars and vicars, and of all sorts I love an innovating vicar, a piebald

progressive professional reactionary, the least. But the Vicar of Cheasing Eyebright was one of the least innovating of vicars, a most worthy, plump, ripe, and conservative-minded little man. It is becoming to go back a little in our story to tell of him. He matched his village, and one may figure them best together as they used to be, on the sunset evening when Mrs. Skinner — you will remember her flight! — brought the Food with her all unsuspected into these rustic serenities.

The village was looking its very best just then, under that western light. It lay down along the valley beneath the beech woods of the Hanger, a beading of thatched and red-tiled cottages, cottages with trellised porches and pyracanthus-lined faces, that clustered closer and closer as the road dropped from the yew trees by the church towards the bridge. The vicarage peeped not too ostentatiously between the trees beyond the inn, an early Georgian front ripened by time, and the spire of the church rose happily in the depression made by the valley in the outline of the hills. A winding stream, a thin intermittency of sky blue and foam, glittered amidst a thick margin of reeds and loose-strife and overhanging willows, along the centre of a sinuous pennant of meadow. The whole prospect had that curiously English quality of ripened cultivation, that look of still completeness that apes perfection, under the sunset warmth.

And the Vicar, too, looked mellow. He looked habitually and essentially mellow, as though he had been a mellow baby born into a mellow class, a ripe and juicy little boy. One could see, even before he mentioned it, that he had gone to an ivy-clad public school in its anecdotage, with magnificent traditions, aristocratic associations and no chemical laboratories, and proceeded thence to a venerable college in the very ripest Gothic. Few books he had younger than a thousand years; of these, Yarrow and Ellis and good pre-Methodist sermons made the bulk. He was a man of moderate height, a little shortened in appearance by his equatorial dimensions, and a face that had been mellow from the first was now climacterically ripe. The beard of a David hid his redundancy of chin; he wore no watch chain out of refinement, and his modest clerical garments were made by a West End tailor. . . . And he sat with a hand on either shin, blinking at his village in beatific approval. He waved a plump palm towards it. His burthen sang out again. What more could anyone desire?

"We are fortunately situated," he said, putting the thing tamely.

"We are in a fastness of the hills," he expanded.

He explained himself at length. "We are out of it all."

For they had been talking, he and his friend, of the Horrors of the Age, of Democracy, and Secular Education, and Sky Scrapers, and Motor Cars, and the American Invasion, the Scrappy Reading of the Public, and the disappearance of any Taste at all.

"We are out of it all," he repeated, and even as he spoke, the

footsteps of someone coming smote upon his ear and he rolled over and regarded her.

You figure the old woman's steadfastly tremulous advance, the bundle clutched in her gnarled lank hand, her nose (which was her countenance) wrinkled with breathless resolution. You see the poppies nodding fatefully on her bonnet, and the dust-white spring-sided boots beneath her skimpy skirts, pointing with an irrevocable slow alternation east and west. Beneath her arm, a restive captive, waggled and slipped a scarcely valuable umbrella. What was there to tell the Vicar that this grotesque old figure was—so far as his village was concerned at any rate—no less than Fruitful Chance and the Unforeseen, the Hag weak men call Fate. But for us, you understand, no more than Mrs. Skinner.

As she was too much encumbered for a curtsey, she pretended not to see him and his friend at all, and so passed flip, flop, within three yards of them, onward down towards the village. The Vicar watched her slow transit in silence, and ripened a remark the while. . . .

The incident seemed to him of no importance whatever. Old womankind, *ære perennius,* has carried bundles since the world began. What difference has it made?

"We are out of it all," said the Vicar. "We live in an atmosphere of simple and permanent things, Birth and Toil, simple seed-time and simple harvest. The Uproar passes us by." He

was always very great upon what he called the permanent things. "Things change," he would say, "but Humanity—*ære perennius.*"

Thus the Vicar. He loved a classical quotation subtly misapplied. Below, Mrs. Skinner, inelegant but resolute, had involved herself curiously with Wilmerding's stile.

§ 3

No one knows what the Vicar made of the Giant Puff-Balls.

No doubt he was among the first to discover them. They were scattered at intervals up and down the path between the near down and the village end, a path he frequented daily in his constitutional round. Altogether, of these abnormal fungi there were, from first to last, quite thirty. The Vicar seems to have stared at each severally and to have prodded most of them with his stick once or twice. One he attempted to measure with his arms, but it burst at his Ixion embrace.

He spoke to several people about them and said they were "marvellous!" and he related to at least seven different persons the well-known story of the flag-stone that was lifted from the cellar floor by a growth of fungi beneath. He looked up his Sowerby to see if it was *Lycoperdon cœlatum* or *giganteum*—like all his kind since Gilbert White became famous, he Gilbert-Whited. He cherished a theory that *giganteum* is unfairly named.

One does not know if he observed that those white spheres

lay in the very track that old woman of yesterday had followed, or if he noted that the last of the series swelled not a score of yards from the gate of the Caddles' cottage. If he observed these things, he made no attempt to place his observation on record. His observation in matters botanical was what the inferior sort of scientific people call a "trained observation" — you look for certain definite things and neglect everything else. And he did nothing to link this phenomenon with the remarkable expansion of the Caddles' baby that had been going on now for some weeks, indeed ever since Caddles walked over one Sunday afternoon a month or more ago to see his mother-in-law and hear Mr. Skinner (since defunct) brag about his management of hens.

§ 4

THE GROWTH of the puff-balls following on the expansion of the Caddles' baby really ought to have opened the Vicar's eyes. The latter fact had already come right into his arms at the christening — almost overpoweringly. . . .

The youngster bawled with deafening violence when the cold water that sealed its divine inheritance and its right to the name of "Albert Edward Caddles" fell upon its brow. It was already beyond maternal porterage, and Caddles, staggering indeed, but grinning triumphantly at quantitatively inferior parents, bore it back to the free-sitting occupied by his party.

"I never saw such a child!" said the Vicar.

This was the first public intimation that the Caddles' baby, which had begun its earthly career a little under seven pounds, did after all intend to be a credit to its parents. Very soon it was clear it meant to be not only a credit but a glory. And within a month their glory shone so brightly as to be in connection with people in the Caddles' position, improper.

The butcher weighed the infant eleven times. He was a man of few words, and he soon got through with them. The first time he said, "'E's a good 'un"; the next time he said, "My word!" the third time he said, "*Well*, mum," and after that he simply blew enormously each time, scratched his head, and looked at his scales with an unprecedented mistrust. Everyone came to see the Big Baby — so it was called by universal consent — and most of them said, "E's a Bouncer," and almost all remarked to him, "*Did* they?" Miss Fletcher came and said she "never *did*," which was perfectly true.

Lady Wondershoot, the village tyrant, arrived the day after the third weighing, and inspected the phenomenon narrowly through glasses that filled it with howling terror. "It's an unusually Big child," she told its mother, in a loud instructive voice. "You ought to take unusual care of it, Caddles. Of course it won't go on like this, being bottle fed, but we must do what we can for it. I'll send you down some more flannel."

The doctor came and measured

the child with a tape, and put the figures in a notebook, and old Mr. Drifthassock, who farmed by Up Marden, brought a manure traveller two miles out of his way to look at it. The traveller asked the child's age three times over, and said finally that he was blowed. He left it to be inferred how and why he was blowed; apparently it was the child's size blowed him. He also said it ought to be put into a baby show. And all day long, out of school hours, little children kept coming and saying, "Please, Mrs. Caddles, mum, may we have a look at your baby, please, mum?" until Mrs. Caddles had to put a stop to it. And amidst all these scenes of amazement came Mrs. Skinner, and stood and smiled, standing somewhat in the background, with each elbow in a lank gnarled hand, and smiling, smiling under and about her nose, with a smile of infinite profundity.

"It makes even that old wretch of a grandmother look quite pleasant," said Lady Wondershoot. "Though I'm sorry she's come back to the village."

Of course, as with almost all cottagers' babies, the eleemosynary element had already come in, but the child soon made it clear by colossal bawling, that so far as the filling of its bottle went, it hadn't come in yet nearly enough.

The baby was entitled to a nine days' wonder, and everyone wondered happily over its amazing growth for twice that time and more. And then you know, instead of its dropping into the background and giving place to other marvels, it went on growing more than ever!

Lady Wondershoot heard Mrs. Greenfield, her housekeeper, with infinite amazement.

"Caddles downstairs again. No food for the child! My dear Greenfield, it's impossible. The creature eats like a hippopotamus! I'm sure it can't be true."

"I'm sure I hope you're not being imposed upon, my lady," said Mrs. Greenfield.

"It's so difficult to tell with these people," said Lady Wondershoot. "Now I do wish, my good Greenfield, that you'd just go down there yourself this afternoon and *see* — see it have its bottle. Big as it is, I cannot imagine that it needs more than six pints a day."

"It hasn't no business to, my lady," said Mrs. Greenfield.

The hand of Lady Wondershoot quivered, with that C.O.S. sort of emotion, that suspicious rage that stirs in all true aristocrats, at the thought that possibly the meaner classes are after all — as mean as their betters, and — where the sting lies — scoring points in the game.

But Mrs. Greenfield could observe no evidence of peculation, and the order for an increasing daily supply to the Caddles' nursery was issued. Scarcely had the first instalment gone, when Caddles was back again at the great house in a state abjectly apologetic.

"We took the grates' care of 'em, Mrs. Greenfield, I do assure you, mum, but he's regular bust 'em! They flew with such vilence,

mum, that one button broke a pane of the window, mum, and one hit me a regular stinger jest 'ere, mum."

Lady Wondershoot, when she heard that this amazing child had positively burst out of its beautiful charity clothes, decided that she must speak to Caddles herself. He appeared in her presence with his hair hastily wetted and smoothed by hand, breathless, and clinging to his hat brim as though it was a life-belt, and he stumbled at the carpet edge out of sheer distress of mind.

Lady Wondershoot liked bullying Caddles. Caddles was her ideal lower-class person, dishonest, faithful, abject, industrious, and inconceivably incapable of responsibility. She told him it was a serious matter, the way his child was going on.

"It's 'is appetite, my ladyship," said Caddles, with a rising note.

"Check 'im, my ladyship, you can't," said Caddles. "There e' lies, my ladyship, and kicks out 'e does, and 'owls, that distressin'. We 'aven't the 'eart, my ladyship. If we 'ad — the neighbours would interfere. . . ."

Lady Wondershoot consulted the parish doctor.

"What I want to know," said Lady Wondershoot, "is it *right* this child should have such an extraordinary quantity of milk?"

"The proper allowance for a child of that age," said the parish doctor, "is a pint and a half to two pints in the twenty-four hours. I don't see that you are called upon to provide more. If you do, it is your own generosity. Of course we might try the legiti-

mate quantity for a few days. But the child, I must admit, seems for some reason to be physiologically different. Possibly what is called a Sport. A case of General Hypertrophy."

"It isn't fair to the other parish children," said Lady Wondershoot. "I am certain we shall have complaints if this goes on."

"I don't see that anyone can be expected to give more than the recognised allowance. We might insist on its doing with that or, if it wouldn't, send it as a case into the Infirmary."

"I suppose," said Lady Wondershoot, reflecting, "that apart from the size and the appetite, you don't find anything else abnormal — nothing monstrous?"

"No. No, I don't. But no doubt if this growth goes on, we shall find grave moral and intellectual deficiencies. One might almost prophesy' that from Max Nordau's law. A most gifted and celebrated philosopher, Lady Wondershoot. He discovered that the abnormal is — abnormal, a most valuable discovery, and well worth bearing in mind. I find it of the utmost help in practice. When I come upon anything abnormal, I say at once. "This is abnormal." His eyes became profound, his voice dropped, his manner verged upon the intimately confidential. He raised one hand stiffly. "And I treat it in that spirit," he said.

§ 5

"Tut, tut!" said the Vicar to his breakfast things — the day after the coming of Mrs. Skinner.

"Tut, tut! what's this?" and poised his glasses at his paper with a general air of remonstrance.

"Giant wasps! What's the world coming to? . . . American journalists, I suppose! Hang these Novelties! Giant gooseberries are good enough for me.

"Nonsense!" said the Vicar, and drank off his coffee at a gulp, eyes steadfast on the paper, and smacked his lips incredulously.

"Bosh!" said the Vicar, rejecting the hint altogether.

But the next day there was more of it, and the light came.

Not all at once, however. When he went for his constitutional that day he was still chuckling at the absurd story his paper would have had him believe. Wasps indeed — killing a dog! Incidentally as he passed by the site of that first crop of puffballs he remarked that the grass was growing very rank there, but he did not connect that in any way with the matter of his amusement. "We should certainly have heard something of it," he said; "Whitstable can't be twenty miles from here."

Beyond he found another puffball, one of the second crop, rising like a roc's egg out of the abnormally coarsened turf.

The thing came upon him in a flash.

He did not take his usual round that morning. Instead he turned aside by the second stile and came round to the Caddles' cottage. "Where's that baby?" he demanded, and at the sight of it, "Goodness me!"

He went up the village blessing his heart and met the doctor full tilt coming down. He grasped his arm. "What does this *mean*?" he said. "Have you seen the paper these last few days?"

The doctor said he had.

"Well, what's the matter with that child? What's the matter with everything, wasps, puff-balls, babies, eh? What's making them grow so big? This is most unexpected. In Kent too! If it was America now —"

"It's a little difficult to say just what it is," said the doctor. "So far as I can grasp the symptoms —"

"Yes?"

"It's Hypertrophy — General Hypertrophy."

"Hypertrophy?"

"Yes. General — affecting all the bodily structures — all the organism. I may say that in my own mind, between ourselves, I'm very nearly convinced it's that. . . . But one has to be careful."

"Ah," said the Vicar, a good deal relieved to find the doctor equal to the situation. "But how is it it's breaking out in this fashion, all over the place?"

"That again," said the doctor, "is difficult to say."

"Urshot. Here. It's a pretty clear case of spreading."

"Yes," said the doctor. "Yes. I think so. It has a strong resemblance at any rate to some sort of epidemic. Probably Epidemic Hypertrophy will meet the case."

"Epidemic!" said the Vicar. "You don't mean it's contagious?"

The doctor smiled gently and rubbed one hand against the

other. "That I couldn't say," he said.

"But—!" cried the Vicar, round-eyed. "If it's *catching*—it—affects *us*!"

He made a stride up the road and turned about.

"I've just been there," he cried. "Hadn't I better—? I'll go home at once and have a bath and fumigate my clothes."

The doctor regarded his retreating back for a moment and then turned about and went towards his own house. . . .

But on the way he reflected that one case had been in the village a month without anyone catching the disease, and after a pause of hesitation decided to be as brave as a doctor should be and take the risks like a man.

And indeed he was well advised by his second thoughts. Growth was the last thing that could ever happen to him again. He could have eaten—and the Vicar could have eaten—Herakleophorbia by the truckful. For growth had done with them. Growth had done with these two gentlemen for evermore.

§ 6

IT was a day or so after this conversation, a day or so that is after the burning of the Experimental Farm, that Winkles came to Redwood and showed him an insulting letter. It was an anonymous letter, and an author should respect his character's secrets. "You are only taking credit for a natural phenomenon," said the letter, "and trying to advertise yourself by your letter to *The Times*. You and your Boomfood! Let me tell

you, this absurdly named food of yours has only the most accidental connection with those big wasps and rats. The plain fact is there is an epidemic of Hypertrophy—Contagious Hypertrophy —which you have about as much claim to control as you have to control the solar system. The thing is as old as the hills. There was Hypertrophy in the family of Anak. Quite outside your range, at Cheasing Eyebright, at the present time there is a baby—"

"Shaky up and down writing. Old gentleman apparently," said Redwood. "But it's odd a baby—"

He read a few lines further and had an inspiration.

"By Jove!" said he. "That's my missing Mrs. Skinner!"

He descended upon her suddenly in the afternoon of the following day.

She was engaged in pulling onions in the little garden before her daughter's cottage when she saw him coming through the garden gate. She stood for a moment "consternated," as the country folks say, and then folded her arms, and with the little bunch of onions held defensively under her left elbow, awaited his approach. Her mouth opened and shut several times; she mumbled her remaining tooth, and once quite suddenly she curtsied, like the blink of an arc-light.

"I thought I should find you," said Redwood.

"I thought you might, Sir," she said, without joy.

"Where's Skinner?"

"'E ain't never written to me,

Sir, not once, nor come nigh of me since I came here, Sir."

"Don't you know what's become of him?"

"Him not having written, no, Sir," and she edged a step towards the left with an imperfect idea of cutting off Redwood from the barn door.

"No one knows what has become of him," said Redwood.

"I dessay 'e knows," said Mrs. Skinner.

"He doesn't tell."

"He was always a great one for looking after 'imself and leaving them that was near and dear to 'im in trouble, was Skinner. Though clever as could be," said Mrs. Skinner. . . .

"Where's this child?" asked Redwood abruptly.

She begged his pardon.

"This child I hear about, the child you've been giving our stuff to—the child that weighs two stone."

Mrs. Skinner's hands worked and she dropped the onions. "Reely, Sir," she protested, "I don't hardly know, Sir, what you mean. My daughter, Sir, Mrs. Caddles, 'as a baby, Sir." And she made an agitated curtsey and tried to look innocently inquiring by tilting her nose to one side.

"You'd better let me see that baby, Mrs. Skinner," said Redwood.

Mrs. Skinner unmasked an eye at him as she led the way towards the barn. "Of course, Sir, there may 'ave been a *little,* in a little can of Nicey I give his father to bring over from the farm, or a little perhaps what I happened to bring about with me, so to speak. Me packing in a hurry and all . . ."

"Um!" said Redwood, after he had cluckered to the infant for a space. "Oom!"

He told Mrs. Caddles the baby was a very fine child indeed, a thing that was getting well home to her intelligence—and he ignored her altogether after that. Presently she left the barn—through sheer insignificance.

"Now you've started him, you'll have to keep on with him, you know," he said to Mrs. Skinner.

He turned on her abruptly. "Don't splash it about *this* time," he said.

"Splash it about, Sir?"

"Oh! *you* know."

She indicated knowledge by convulsive gestures.

"You haven't told these people here? The parents, the squire and so on at the big house, the doctor, no one?"

Mrs. Skinner shook her head.

"I wouldn't," said Redwood. . . .

He went to the door of the barn and surveyed the world about him. The door of the barn looked between the end of the cottage and some disused piggeries through a five-barred gate upon the high road. Beyond was a high red brick wall rich with ivy and wallflower and pennywort and set along the top with broken glass. Beyond the corner of the wall, a sunlit notice board amidst green and yellow branches reared itself above the rich tones of the first fallen leaves and announced that "Trespassers in

these Woods will be Prosecuted."
The dark shadow of a gap in the
hedge threw a stretch of barbed
wire into relief.

"Um," said Redwood, then in
a deeper note, "Oom!"

There came a clatter of horses
and the sound of wheels and
Lady Wondershoot's greys came
into view. He marked the faces
of coachman and footman as the
equipage approached. The coach-
man was a very fine specimen, full
and fruity, and he drove with a
sort of sacramental dignity. Others
might doubt their calling and
position in the world, he at any
rate was sure — he drove her lady-
ship. The footman sat beside him
with folded arms and a face of
inflexible certainties. Then the
great lady herself became visible,
in a hat and mantle disdainfully
inelegant, peering through her
glasses. Two young ladies pro-
truded necks and peered also.

The Vicar passing on the other
side swept off the hat from his
David's brow unheeded. . . .

Redwood remained standing in
the doorway for a long time after
the carriage had passed, his hands
folded behind him. His eyes went
to the green-grey upland of down,
and into the cloud-curdled sky,
and came back to the glass-set
wall. He turned upon the cool
shadows within and amidst spots
and blurs of colour regarded the
giant child amidst that Rem-
brandtesque gloom, naked except
for a swathing of flannel, seated
upon a huge truss of straw and
playing with its toes.

"I begin to see what we have
done," he said.

He mused, and young Caddles

and his own child and Cossar's
brood mingled in his musing.

He laughed abruptly. "Good
Lord!" he said at some passing
thought.

He roused himself presently
and addressed Mrs. Skinner.
"Anyhow he mustn't be tortured
by a break in his food. That
at least we can prevent. I shall
send you a can every six months.
That ought to do for him all
right."

Mrs. Skinner mumbled some-
thing about "if you think so,
Sir," and "probably got packed
by mistake. . . . Thought no
harm in giving him a little," and
so by the aid of various aspen
gestures indicated that she under-
stood.

So the child went on growing.
And growing.

"Practically," said Lady Won-
dershoot, "he's eaten up every
calf in the place. If I have any
more of this sort of thing from
that man Caddles — "

§ 7

BUT even so secluded a place as
Cheasing Eyebright could not rest
for long in the theory of Hyper-
trophy — Contagious or not — in
view of the growing hubbub
about the Food. In a little while
there were painful explanations
for Mrs. Skinner — explanations
that reduced her to speechless
mumblings of her remaining
tooth — explanations that probed
her and ransacked her and ex-
posed her — until at last she was
driven to take refuge from a uni-
versal convergence of blame in
the dignity of inconsolable
widowhood. She turned her eye

—which she constrained to be watery—upon the angry Lady of the Manor, and wiped suds from her hands.

"You forget, my lady, what I'm bearing up under."

And she followed up this warning note with a slightly defiant:

"It's 'IM I think of, my lady, night *and* day."

She compressed her lips and her voice flattened and faltered: "Bein' et, my lady."

And having established herself on these grounds, she repeated the affirmation her ladyship had refused before. "I 'ad no more idea what I was giving the child, my lady, than anyone *could* 'ave. . . ."

Her ladyship turned her mind in more hopeful directions, wigging Caddles of course tremendously by the way. Emissaries, full of diplomatic threatenings, entered the whirling lives of Bensington and Redwood. They presented themselves as Parish Councillors, stolid and clinging phonographically to prearranged statements. "We hold you responsible, Mr. Bensington, for the injury inflicted upon our parish, Sir. We hold you responsible."

A firm of solicitors, with a snake of a style—Banghurst, Brown, Flapp, Codlin, Brown, Tedder, and Snoxton, they called themselves, and appeared invariably in the form of a small rufous cunning-looking gentleman with a pointed nose—said vague things about damages, and there was a polished personage, her ladyship's agent, who came in suddenly upon Redwood one day

and asked, "Well, Sir, and what do you propose to do?"

To which Redwood answered that he proposed to discontinue supplying the food for the child, if he or Bensington were bothered any further about the matter. "I give it for nothing as it is," he said, "and the child will yell your village to ruins before it dies if you don't let it have the stuff. The child's on your hands and you have to keep it. Lady Wondershoot can't always be Lady Bountiful and Earthly Providence of her parish without sometimes meeting a responsibility, you know."

"The mischief's done," Lady Wondershoot decided when they told her—with expurgations—what Redwood had said.

"The mischief's done," echoed the Vicar.

Though indeed as a matter of fact the mischief was only beginning.

CHAPTER 2

THE BRAT GIGANTIC

§1

THE GIANT child was ugly—the Vicar would insist. "He always had been ugly—as all excessive things must be." The Vicar's

views had carried him out of sight of just judgment in this matter. The child was much subjected to snapshots even in that rustic retirement, and their net testimony is against the Vicar, testifying that the young monster was at first almost pretty, with a copious curl of hair reaching to his brow and a great readiness to smile. Usually Caddles, who was slightly built, stands smiling behind the baby, perspective emphasising his relative smallness.

After the second year the good looks of the child became more subtle and more contestable. He began to grow, as his unfortunate grandfather would no doubt have put it, "rank." He lost colour and developed an increasing effect of being somehow, albeit colossal, yet slight. He was vastly delicate. His eyes and something about his face grew finer, grew, as people say, "interesting." His hair, after one cutting, began to tangle into a mat. "It's the degenerate strain coming out in him," said the parish doctor, marking these things, but just how far he was right in that, and just how far the youngster's lapse from ideal healthfulness was the result of living entirely in a white-washed barn upon Lady Wondershoot's sense of charity tempered by justice, is open to question.

The photographs of him that present him from three to six show him developing into a round-eyed, flaxen-haired youngster with a truncated nose and a friendly stare. There lurks about his lips that never very remote promise of a smile that all the photographs of the early giant children display. In summer he wears loose garments of ticking tacked together with string; there is usually one of those straw baskets upon his head that workmen use for their tools, and he is barefooted. In one picture he grins broadly and holds a bitten melon in his hand.

The winter pictures are less numerous and satisfactory. He wears huge sabots, no doubt of beechwood, and (as fragments of the inscription "John Stickells, Iping" show) sacks for socks, and his trousers and jacket are unmistakably cut from the remains of a gaily patterned carpet. Underneath that there were rude swathings of flannel; five or six yards of flannel are tied comforter fashion about his neck. The thing on his head is probably another sack. He stares, sometimes smiling, sometimes a little ruefully, at the camera. Even when he was only five years old, one sees that half whimsical wrinkling over his soft brown eyes that characterised his face.

He was from the first, the Vicar always declared, a terrible nuisance about the village. He seems to have had a proportionate impulse to play, much curiosity and sociability, and in addition there was a certain craving within him — I grieve to say — for more to eat. In spite of what Mrs. Greenfield called an "*excessively* generous" allowance of food from Lady Wondershoot, he displayed what the doctor perceived at once was the "Criminal Appetite." It carries out only too completely Lady Wondershoot's ₁ worst ex-

periences of the lower classes, that in spite of an allowance of nourishment inordinately beyond what is known to be the maximum necessity even of an adult human being, the creature was found to steal. And what he stole he ate with an inelegant voracity. His great hand would come over garden walls; he would covet the very bread in the baker's carts. Cheeses went from Marlow's store loft, and never a pig trough was safe from him. Some farmer walking over his field of swedes would find the great spoor of his feet and the evidence of his nibbling hunger, a root picked here, a root picked there, and the holes, with childish cunning, heavily erased. He ate a swede as one devours a radish. He would stand and eat apples from a tree, if no one was about, as normal children eat blackberries from a bush. In one way at any rate this shortness of provisions was good for the peace of Cheasing Eyebright — for many years he ate up every grain very nearly of the Food of the Gods that was given him. . . .

Indisputably the child was troublesome and out of place. "He was always about," the Vicar used to say. He could not go to school; he could not go to church by virtue of the obvious limitations of its cubical content. There was some attempt to satisfy the spirit of that "most foolish and destructive law" — I quote the Vicar — the Elementary Education Act of 1870, by getting him to sit outside the open window while instruction was going on within. But his presence there

destroyed the discipline of the other children. They were always popping up and peering at him, and every time he spoke they laughed together. His voice was so odd! So they let him stay away.

Nor did they persist in pressing him to come to church, for his vast proportions were of little help to devotion. Yet there they might have had an easier task; there are good reasons for guessing there were the germs of religious feeling somewhere in that big carcass. The music perhaps drew him. He was often in the churchyard on a Sunday morning, picking his way softly among the graves after the congregation had gone in, and he would sit the whole service out beside the porch, listening as one listens outside a hive of bees.

At first he showed a certain want of tact; the people inside would hear his great feet crunch restlessly round their place of worship, or become aware of his dim face peering in through the stained glass, half curious, half envious, and at times some simple hymn would catch him unawares and he would howl lugubriously in a gigantic attempt at unison. Whereupon little Sloppet, who was organ-blower and verger and beadle and sexton and bell-ringer on Sundays, besides being postman and chimney-sweep all the week, would go out very briskly and valiantly and send him mournfully away. Sloppet, I am glad to say, felt it — in his more thoughtful moments at any rate. It was like sending a dog home when you start out for a walk, he told me.

But the intellectual and moral training of young Caddles, though fragmentary, was explicit. From the first, Vicar, mother and all the world, combined to make it clear to him that his giant strength was not for use. It was a misfortune that he had to make the best of. He had to mind what was told him, do what was set him, be careful never to break anything nor hurt anything. Particularly he must not go treading on things or jostling against things or jumping about. He had to salute the gentlefolks respectfully and be grateful for the food and clothing they spared him out of their riches. And he learnt all these things submissively, being by nature and habit a teachable creature and only by food and accident gigantic.

For Lady Wondershoot, in these early days, he displayed the profoundest awe. She found she could talk to him best when she was in short skirts and had her dog-whip, and she gesticulated with that and was always a little contemptuous and shrill. But sometimes the Vicar played master, a minute, middle-aged, rather breathless David pelting a childish Goliath with reproof and reproach and dictatorial command. The monster was now so big that it seems it was impossible for anyone to remember he was after all only a child of seven, with all a child's desire for notice and amusement and fresh experience, with all a child's craving for response, attention and affection, and all a child's capacity for dependence and unrestricted dulness and misery.

The Vicar, walking down the village road some sunlit morning, would encounter an ungainly eighteen feet of the Inexplicable, as fantastic and unpleasant to him as some new form of Dissent, as it padded fitfully along with craning neck, seeking, always seeking the two primary needs of childhood, something to eat and something with which to play.

There would come a look of furtive respect into the creature's eyes and an attempt to touch the matted forelock.

In a limited way the Vicar had an imagination — at any rate, the remains of one — and with young Caddles it took the line of developing the huge possibilities of personal injury such vast muscles must possess. Suppose a sudden madness — ! Suppose a mere lapse into disrespect — ! However, the truly brave man is not the man who does not feel fear but the man who overcomes it. Every time and always the Vicar got his imagination under. And he used always to address young Caddles stoutly in a good clear service tenor.

" Being a good boy, Albert Edward? "

And the young giant, edging closer to the wall and blushing deeply, would answer, " Yessir — trying."

" Mind you do," said the Vicar and would go past him with at most a slight acceleration of his breathing. And out of respect for his manhood he made it a rule, whatever he might fancy, never to look back at the danger, when once it was passed.

In a fitful manner the Vicar would give young Caddles private

tuition. He never taught the monster to read — it was not needed — but he taught him the more important points of the Catechism, his duty to his neighbour for example, and of that Deity who would punish Caddles with extreme vindictiveness if ever he ventured to disobey the Vicar and Lady Wondershoot. The lessons would go on in the Vicar's yard, and passers-by would hear that great cranky childish voice droning out the essential teachings of the Established Church.

"To onner 'n 'bey the King and allooer put 'nthority under 'm. To s'bmit meself t'all my gov'ners, teachers, spir'shall pastors an' masters. To order myself lowly n' rev'rently t'all my betters —"

Presently it became evident that the effect of the growing giant on unaccustomed horses was like that of a camel, and he was told to keep off the high road, not only near the shrubbery (where the oafish smile over the wall had exasperated her ladyship extremely), but altogether. That law he never completely obeyed, because of the vast interest the high road had for him. But it turned what had been his constant resort into a stolen pleasure. He was limited at last almost entirely to old pasture and the Downs.

I do not know what he would have done if it had not been for the Downs. There there were spaces where he might wander for miles, and over these spaces he wandered. He would pick branches from trees and make

insane vast nosegays there until he was forbidden, take up sheep and put them in neat rows from which they immediately wandered (at this he invariably laughed very heartily) until he was forbidden, dig away the turf, great wanton holes, until he was forbidden. . . .

He would wander over the Downs as far as the hill above Wreckstone, but not further, because there he came upon cultivated land, and the people by reason of his depredations upon their root crops, and inspired moreover by a sort of hostile timidity his big unkempt appearance frequently evoked, always came out against him with yapping dogs to drive him away. They would threaten him and lash at him with cart whips. I have heard that they would sometimes fire at him with shotguns. And in the other direction he ranged within sight of Hickleybrow. From above Thursley Hanger he could get a glimpse of the London, Chatham, and Dover railway, but ploughed fields and a suspicious hamlet prevented his nearer access.

And after a time there came boards, great boards with red letters that debarred him every direction. He could not read what the letters said: "Out of Bounds," but in a little while he understood. He was often to be seen in those days, by the railway passengers, sitting, chin on knees, perched up on the Down hard by the Thursley chalk pits, where afterwards he was set working. The train seemed to inspire a dim emotion of friendli-

ness in him, and sometimes he would wave an enormous hand at it, and sometimes give it a rustic incoherent hail.

"Big," the peering passenger would say. "One of these Boom children. They say, Sir, quite unable to do anything for itself — little better than an idiot in fact, and a great burden on the locality."

"Parents quite poor, I'm told."

"Lives on the charity of the local gentry."

Everyone would stare intelligently at that distant squatting monstrous figure for a space.

"Good thing that was put a stop to," some spacious thinking mind would suggest. "Nice to 'ave a few thousand of *them* on the rates, eh?"

And usually there was someone wise enough to tell this philosopher: "You're about Right there, Sir," in hearty tones.

§ 2

HE had his bad days.

There was, for example, that trouble with the river.

He made little boats out of whole newspapers, an art he learnt by watching the Spender boy, and he set them sailing down the stream, great paper cocked hats. When they vanished under the bridge which marks the boundary of the strictly private grounds about Eyebright House, he would give a great shout and run round and across Tormat's new field — Lord! how Tormat's pigs did scamper to be sure, and turn their good fat into lean muscle! — and so to meet his boats by the ford. Right across the nearer lawns these paper boats of his used to go, right in front of Eyebright House, right under Lady Wondershoot's eyes! Disorganising folded newspapers! A pretty thing!

Gathering enterprise from impunity he began babyish hydraulic engineering. He delved a huge port for his paper fleets with an old shed door that served him as a spade, and, no one chancing to observe his operations just then, he devised an ingenious canal that incidentally flooded Lady Wondershoot's icehouse, and finally he dammed the river. He dammed it right across with a few vigorous doorfuls of earth — he must have worked like an avalanche — and down came a most amazing spate through the shrubbery and washed away Miss Spinks and her easel and the most promising water-colour sketch she had ever begun, or, at any rate, it washed away her easel and left her wet to the knees and dismally tucked up in flight to the house, and thence the waters rushed through the kitchen garden and so by the green door into the lane and down into the river bed again by Short's ditch.

Meanwhile, the Vicar, interrupted in conversation with the blacksmith, was amazed to see distressful stranded fish leaping out of a few residual pools, and heaped green weed in the bed of the stream where ten minutes before there had been eight feet and more of clear cool water.

After that, horrified at his own consequences, young Caddles fled his home for two days and nights.

He returned only at the insistent call of hunger, to bear with stoical calm an amount of violent scolding that was more in proportion to his size than anything else that had ever before fallen to his lot in the Happy Village.

§ 3

IMMEDIATELY after that affair Lady Wondershoot, casting about for exemplary additions to the abuse and fastings she had inflicted, issued a Ukase. She issued it first to her butler and very suddenly, so that she made him jump. He was clearing away the breakfast things and she was staring out of the tall window on the terrace where the fawns would come to be fed. " Jobbet," she said, in her most imperial voice, " Jobbet, this Thing must work for its living."

And she made it quite clear not only to Jobbet (which was easy), but to everyone else in the village, including young Caddles, that in this matter, as in all things, she meant what she said.

" Keep him employed," said Lady Wondershoot. " That's the tip for Master Caddles."

" It's the Tip, I fancy, for all Humanity," said the Vicar. " The simple duties, the modest round, seed-time and harvest — "

" Exactly," said Lady Wondershoot. " What *I* always say. Satan finds some mischief still for idle hands to do. At any rate among the labouring classes. We bring up our under-housemaids on that principle, always. What shall we set him to do? "

That was a little difficult. They thought of many things, and meanwhile they broke him into labour a bit by using him instead of a horse messenger to carry telegrams and notes when extra speed was needed, and he also carried luggage and packing-cases and things of that sort very conveniently in a big net they found for him. He seemed to like employment, regarding it as a sort of game, and Kinkle, Lady Wondershoot's agent, seeing him shift a rockery for her one day, was struck by the brilliant idea of putting him into her chalk quarry at Thursley Hanger hard by Hickleybrow. This idea was carried out, and it seemed they had settled his problem.

He worked in the chalk pit, at first with the zest of a playing child, and afterwards with an effect of habit, delving, loading, doing all the haulage of the trucks, running the full ones down the lines towards the siding, and hauling the empty ones up by the wire of a great windlass: working the entire quarry at last single-handed.

I am told that Kinkle made a very good thing indeed out of him for Lady Wondershoot, consuming as he did scarcely anything but his food, though that never restrained her denunciation of " the Creature " as a gigantic parasite upon her charity. . . .

At that time he used to wear a sort of smock of sacking, trousers of patched leather, and iron-shod sabots. Over his head was sometimes a queer thing, a worn-out beehive straw chair it was, but usually he went bareheaded.

He would be moving about the pit with a powerful deliberation, and the Vicar on his constitutional round would get there about midday to find him shamefully eating his vast need of food with his back to all the world.

His food was brought to him every day, a mess of grain in the husk, in a truck, a small railway truck, like one of the trucks he was perpetually filling with chalk, and this load he used to char in an old lime kiln and then devour. Sometimes he would mix with it a bag of sugar. Sometimes he would sit licking a lump of such salt as is given to cows, or eating a huge lump of dates, stones and all, such as one sees in London on barrows. For drink he walked to the rivulet beyond the burnt-out site of the Experimental Farm at Hickleybrow and put down his face to the stream. It was from his drinking in that way after eating that the Food of the Gods did at last get loose, spreading first of all in huge weeds from the river-side, then in big frogs, bigger trout and stranding carp, and at last in a fantastic exuberance of vegetation all over the little valley.

And after a year or so the queer monstrous grub things in the field before the blacksmith's grew so big and developed into such frightful skipjacks and cockchafers — motor cockchafers the boys called them — that they drove Lady Wondershoot abroad.

§ 4

But soon the Food was to enter upon a new phase of its work in him. In spite of the simple instructions of the Vicar, instructions intended to round off the modest natural life befitting a giant peasant, in the most complete and final manner, he began to ask questions, to inquire into things, to *think*. As he grew from boyhood to adolescence it became increasingly evident that his mind had processes of its own — out of the Vicar's control. The Vicar did his best to ignore this distressing phenomenon, but still — he could feel it there.

The young giant's material for thought lay about him. Quite involuntarily, with his spacious views, his constant overlooking of things, he must have seen a good deal of human life, and as it grew clearer to him that he too, save for this clumsy greatness of his, was also human, he must have come to realise more and more just how much was shut against him by his melancholy distinction. The social hum of the school, the mystery of religion that was partaken in such finery, and which exhaled so sweet a strain of melody, the jovial chorusing from the Inn, the warmly glowing rooms, candle-lit and fire-lit, into which he peered out of the darkness, or again the shouting excitement, the vigour of flannelled exercise upon some imperfectly understood issue that centred about the cricket-field, all these things must have cried aloud to his companionable heart. It would seem that as his adolescence crept upon him, he began to take a very considerable interest in the proceed-

ings of lovers, in those preferences and pairings, those close intimacies that are so cardinal in life.

One Sunday, just about that hour when the stars and the bats and the passions of rural life come out, there chanced to be a young couple " kissing each other a bit " in Love Lane, the deep hedged lane that runs out back towards the Upper Lodge. They were giving their little emotions play, as secure in the warm still twilight as any lovers could be. The only conceivable interruption they thought possible must come pacing visibly up the lane; the twelve-foot hedge towards the silent Downs seemed to them an absolute guarantee.

Then suddenly — incredibly — they were lifted and drawn apart.

They discovered themselves held up, each with a finger and thumb under the armpits, and with the perplexed brown eyes of young Caddles scanning their warm flushed faces. They were naturally dumb with the emotions of their situation.

" *Why* do you like doing that? " asked young Caddles.

I gather the embarrassment continued until the swain, remembering his manhood, vehemently, with loud shouts, threats, and virile blasphemies, such as became the occasion, bade young Caddles under penalties put them down. Whereupon young Caddles, remembering his manners, did put them down politely and very carefully, and conveniently near for a resumption of their embraces, and having hesi-

tated above them for a while, vanished again into the twilight. . . .

" But I felt precious silly," the swain confided to me. " We couldn't 'ardly look at one another. Bein' caught like that.

" Kissing we was — *you* know.

" And the cur'ous thing is, she blamed it all on to me," said the swain.

" Flew out something outrageous, and wouldn't 'ardly speak to me all the way 'ome. . . ."

The giant was embarking upon investigations, there could be no doubt. His mind, it became manifest, was throwing up questions. He put them to few people as yet, but they troubled him. His mother, one gathers, sometimes came in for cross-examination.

He used to come into the yard behind his mother's cottage, and, after a careful inspection of the ground for hens and chicks, he would sit down slowly with his back against the barn. In a minute the chicks, who liked him, would be pecking all over him at the mossy chalk mud in the seams of his clothing, and if it was blowing up for wet, Mrs. Caddles' kitten, who never lost her confidence in him, would assume a sinuous form and start scampering in to the cottage, up to the kitchen fender, round, out, up his leg, up his body, right up to his shoulder, meditative moment, then scat! back again, and so on. Sometimes she would stick her claws in his face out of sheer gaiety of heart, but he never dared to touch her because of the

uncertain weight of his hand upon a creature so frail. Besides, he rather liked to be tickled. And after a time he would put some clumsy question to his mother.

"Mother," he would say, "if it's good to work, why doesn't everyone work?"

His mother would look up at him and answer, "It's good for the likes of us."

He would meditate, "*Why?*"

And going unanswered, "What's work *for*, mother? Why do I cut chalk and you wash clothes, day after day, while Lady Wondershoot goes about in her carriage, mother, and travels off to those beautiful foreign countries you and I mustn't see, mother?"

"She's a lady," said Mrs. Caddles.

"Oh," said young Caddles, and meditated profoundly.

"If there wasn't gentlefolks to make work for us to do," said Mrs. Caddles, "how should we poor people get a living?"

This had to be digested.

"Mother," he tried again; "if there wasn't any gentlefolks, wouldn't things belong to people like me and you, and if they did—"

"Lord sakes and *drat* the Boy!" Mrs. Caddles would say—she had with the help of a good memory become quite a florid and vigorous individuality since Mrs. Skinner died. "Since your poor dear grandma was took, there's no abiding you. Don't you arst no questions and you won't be told no lies. If once I was to start out answerin' you *serious* y'r father'd ave to go and arst someone else for 'is supper—let alone finishin' the washin'."

"All right, mother," he would say, after a wondering stare at her. "I didn't mean to worry."

And he would go on thinking.

§ 5

HE was thinking too four years after, when the Vicar, now no longer ripe but over-ripe, saw him for the last time of all. You figure the old gentleman visibly a little older now, slacker in his girth, a little coarsened and a little weakened in his thought and speech, with a quivering shakiness in his hand and a quivering shakiness in his convictions, but his eye still bright and merry for all the trouble the Food had caused his village and himself. He had been frightened at times and disturbed, but was he not alive still and the same still?— and fifteen long years, a fair sample of eternity—had turned the trouble into use and wont.

"It was a disturbance, I admit," he would say, "and things are different. Different in many ways. There was a time when a boy could weed, but now a man must go out with axe and crowbar—in some places down by the thickets at least. And it's a little strange still to us old-fashioned people for all this valley, even what used to be the river bed before they irrigated, to be under wheat—as it is this year—twenty-five feet high. They used the old-fashioned scythe here twenty years ago, and they would bring home the harvest on a wain—rejoicing in a simple honest fashion. A little simple

drunkenness, a little innocent dalliance perhaps, to conclude. . . . Poor dear Lady Wonder-shoot — she didn't like these innovations. Very conservative, poor dear lady! A touch of the eighteenth century about her, I always said. Her language for example. . . . Bluff vigour. . . .

" She died comparatively poor. These big weeds got into her garden. She was not one of these gardening women, but she liked her garden in order — things growing where they were planted and as they were planted — under control. . . . The way things grew was unexpected — upset her ideas. . . . She didn't like the perpetual invasion of this young monster — at least she began to fancy he was always gaping at her over her wall. . . . She didn't like his being nearly as high as her house. . . . Jarred with her sense of proportion. Poor dear lady! I had hoped she would last my time. It was the big cockchafers we had for a year or so that decided her. They came from the giant larvæ — nasty things as big as rats — in the valley turf. . . .

" And the ants no doubt weighed with her also.

" Since everything was upset and there was no peace and quietness anywhere now, she said she thought she might just as well be at Monte Carlo as anywhere else. And she went.

" She played pretty boldly, I'm told. Died in an hotel there. Very sad end. . . . Exile. . . . Not — not what one considers meet. . . . A natural leader of our English people. . . . Uprooted. So! . . .

" Yet after all," harped the Vicar, " it comes to very little. A nuisance of course. Children cannot run about so freely as they used to do, what with ant bites and so forth. Perhaps it's as well. . . . There used to be talk — as though this stuff would revolutionise everything. . . . But there is something that defies all these forces of the New. . . . I don't know of course. I'm not one of your modern philosophers — explain everything with ether and atoms. Evolution. Rubbish like that. What I mean is something the 'Ologies don't include. Matter of reason — not understanding. Ripe wisdom. Human nature. *Ære perennius*. . . . Call it what you will."

And so at last it came to the last time.

The Vicar had no intimation of what lay so close upon him. He did his customary walk, over by Farthing Down, as he had done it for more than a score of years, and so to the place whence he would watch young Caddles. He did the rise over by the chalk pit crest a little puffily — he had long since lost the Muscular Christian stride of early days — but Caddles was not at his work, and then, as he skirted the thicket of giant bracken that was beginning to obscure and overshadow the Hanger, he came upon the monster's huge form seated on the hill — brooding as it were upon the world. Caddles' knees were drawn up, his cheek was on his hand, his head a little aslant. He sat with his shoulder towards the Vicar, so that those perplexed eyes could not be seen.

He must have been thinking very intently, at any rate he was sitting very still. . . .

He never turned round. He never knew that the Vicar, who had played so large a part in shaping his life, looked then at him for the very last of innumerable times — did not know even that he was there. (So it is so many partings happen.) The Vicar was struck at the time by the fact that, after all, no one on earth had the slightest idea of what this great monster thought about when he saw fit to rest from his labours. But he was too indolent to follow up that new theme that day; he fell back from its suggestion into his older grooves of thought.

"*Ære perennius,*" he whispered, walking slowly homeward by a path that no longer ran straight athwart the turf after its former fashion, but wound circuitously to avoid new sprung tussocks of giant grass. "No! nothing is changed. Dimensions are nothing. The simple round, the common task —"

And that night, quite painlessly, and all unknowing, he himself went the common way — out of this Mystery of Change he had spent his life in denying.

They buried him in the churchyard of Cheasing Eyebright, near to the largest yew, and the modest tombstone bearing his epitaph — it ended with: *Ut in Principio, nunc est et semper* — was almost immediately hidden from the eye of man by a spread of giant grey tasseled grass too stout for scythe or sheep, that came sweeping like a fog over the village out of the germinating moisture of the valley meadows in which the Food of the Gods had been working.

Book III: *The Harvest of the Food*

CHAPTER 1

THE ALTERED WORLD

§1

CHANGE played in its new fashion with the world for twenty years. To most men the new things came little by little and day by day, remarkably enough, but not so abruptly as to overwhelm. But to one man at least the full accumulation of those two decades of the Food's work was to be revealed suddenly and amazingly in one day. For our purpose it is convenient to take him for that one day and to tell something of the things he saw.

This man was a convict, a prisoner for life — his crime is no concern of ours — whom the law saw fit to pardon after twenty years. One summer morning this poor wretch, who had left the world a young man of three and twenty, found himself thrust out again from the grey simplicity of toil and discipline that had become his life, into a dazzling freedom. They had put unaccustomed clothes upon him; his hair had been growing for some weeks, and he had parted it now for some days, and there he stood, in a sort of shabby and clumsy newness of body and mind, blinking with his eyes and blinking indeed with his soul, *outside* again, trying to realise one incredible thing, that after all he was again for a little while in the world of life, and for all other incredible things, totally unprepared. He was so fortunate as to have a brother who cared enough for their distant common memories to come and meet him and clasp his hand, a brother he had left a little lad and who was now a bearded prosperous man — whose very eyes were unfamiliar. and together he and this stranger from his kindred came down into the town of Dover saying little to one another and feeling many things.

They sat for a space in a public-house, the one answering the questions of the other about this person and that, reviving queer old points of view, brush-

ing aside endless new aspects and new perspectives, and then it was time to go to the station and take the London train. Their names and the personal things they had to talk of do not matter to our story, but only the changes and all the strangeness that this poor returning soul found in the once familiar world.

In Dover itself he remarked little except the goodness of beer from pewter — never before had there been such a draught of beer, and it brought tears of gratitude to his eyes. " Beer's as good as ever," said he, believing it infinitely better. . . .

It was only as the train rattled them past Folkstone that he could look out beyond his more immediate emotions, to see what had happened to the world. He peered out of the window. " It's sunny," he said for the twelfth time. " I couldn't a' had better weather." And then for the first time it dawned upon him that there were novel disproportions in the world. " Lord sakes," he cried, sitting up and looking animated for the first time, " but them's mortal great thissels growing out there on the bank by that broom. If so be they *be* thissels? Or 'ave I been forgetting? "

But they were thistles, and what he took for tall bushes of broom was the new grass, and amidst these things a company of British soldiers — red-coated as ever — was skirmishing in accordance with the directions of the drill book that had been partially revised after the Boer War. Then whack! into a tunnel and,

then into Sandling Junction, which was now embedded and dark — its lamps were all alight — in a great thicket of rhododendron that had crept out of some adjacent gardens and grown enormously up the valley. There was a train of trucks on the Sandgate siding piled high with rhododendron logs, and here it was the returning citizen heard first of Boomfood.

As they sped out again into a country that seemed absolutely unchanged, the two brothers were hard at their explanations. The one was full of eager, dull questions, the other had never thought, had never troubled to see the thing as a single fact, and he was allusive and difficult to follow. " It's this here Boomfood stuff," he said, touching his bottom rock of knowledge. " Don't you know? 'Aven't they told you, any of 'em? Boomfood! You know — Boomfood. What all the election's about. Scientific sort of stuff. 'Asn't no one ever told you? "

He thought prison had made his brother a fearful duffer not to know that.

They made wide shots at each other by way of question and answer. Between these scraps of talk were intervals of window gazing. At first the man's interest in things was vague and general. His imagination had been busy with what old so and so would say, how so and so would look, how he would say to all and sundry certain things that would present his " putting away " in a mitigated light. This Boomfood came in at first as it were a thing

in an odd paragraph of the news-paper, then as a source of intel-lectual difficulty with his brother. But it came to him presently that Boomfood was persistently com-ing in upon any topic he began.

In those days the world was a patchwork of transition, so that this great new fact came to him in a series of shocks of contrast. The process of change had not been uniform; it had spread from one centre of distribution here and another centre there. The country was in patches: great areas where the Food was still to come, and areas where it was al-ready in the soil and in the air, sporadic and contagious. It was a bold new motif creeping in among ancient and venerable airs.

The contrast was very vivid in-deed along the line from Dover to London at that time. For a space they traversed just such a countryside as he had known since his childhood, the small ob-longs of field, hedge-lined, of a size for pigmy horses to plough, the little roads three cart-widths wide, the elms and oaks and poplars dotting these fields about, little thickets of willow beside the streams, ricks of hay no higher than a giant's knees, dolls' cottages with diamond panes, brickfields and straggling village streets, the larger houses of the petty great, flower-grown railway banks, garden-set stations, and all the little things of the van-ished nineteenth century still holding out against Immensity. Here and there would be a patch of wind-sown, wind-tattered giant thistle defying the axe; here and there a ten-foot puff-ball or the ashen stems of some burnt-out patch of monster grass; but that was all there was to hint at the coming of the Food.

For a couple of score of miles there was nothing else to fore-shadow in any way the strange bigness of the wheat and of the weeds that were hidden from him not a dozen miles from his route just over the hills in the Cheasing Eyebright valley. And then presently, the traces of the Food would begin. The first strik-ing thing was the great new via-duct at Tonbridge, where the swamp of the choked Medway (due to a giant variety of *Chara*) began in those days. Then again the little country, and then, as the petty multitudinous im-mensity of London spread out under its haze, the traces of man's fight to keep out greatness be-came abundant and incessant.

In that south-eastern region of London at that time, and all about where Cossar and his chil-dren lived, the Food had become mysteriously insurgent at a hun-dred points; the little life went on amidst daily portents that only the deliberation of their in-crease, the slow parallel growth of usage to their presence, had robbed of their warning. But this returning citizen peered out to see for the first time the facts of the Food strange and predomi-nant, scarred and blackened areas, big unsightly defences and preparations, barracks and ar-senals that this subtle persistent influence had forced into the life of men.

Here on an ampler scale the

experience of the first Experimental Farm had been repeated time and again. It had been in the inferior and accidental things of life — under foot and in waste places, irregularly and irrelevantly — that the coming of a new force and new issues had first declared itself. There were great evil-smelling yards and enclosures where some invincible jungle of weed furnished fuel for gigantic machinery (little cockneys came to stare at its clangorous oiliness and tip the men a sixpence); there were roads and tracks for big motors and vehicles, roads made of the interwoven fibres of hypertrophied hemp; there were towers containing steam sirens that could yell at once and warn the world against any new insurgence of vermin, or, what was queerer, venerable church towers conspicuously fitted with a mechanical scream. There were little red painted refuge huts and garrison shelters, each with its 300-yard rifle range, where the riflemen practised daily with soft-nosed ammunition at targets in the shape of monstrous rats.

Six times since the day of the Skinners there had been outbreaks of giant rats — each time from the south-west London sewers, and now they were as much an accepted fact there as tigers in the delta by Calcutta. . . .

His brother had bought a paper in a heedless sort of way at Sandling, and at last this chanced to catch the eye of the released man. He opened the unfamiliar sheets — they seemed to him to be smaller, more numerous, and different in type from the papers of the times before — and he found himself confronted with innumerable pictures about things so strange as to be uninteresting, and with tall columns of printed matter whose headings, for the most part, were as unmeaning as though they had been written in a foreign tongue — " Great Speech by Mr. Caterham"; "The Boom-food Laws."

"Who's this here Caterham?" he asked, in an attempt to make conversation.

"*He's* all right," said his brother.

"Ah! Sort of politician, eh?"

"Goin' to turn out the Government. Jolly well time he did."

"Ah!" He reflected. "I suppose all the lot *I* used to know, Chamberlain, Rosebery, all that lot — *What?*"

His brother had grasped his wrist and pointed out of the window.

"That's the Cossars!" The eyes of the released prisoner followed the finger's direction and saw —

"My Gawd!" he cried, for the first time really overcome with amazement. The paper dropped into final forgottenness between his feet. Through the trees he could see very distinctly, standing in an easy attitude, the legs wide apart and the hand grasping a ball as if about to throw it, a gigantic human figure a good forty feet high. The figure glittered in the sunlight, clad in a suit of woven white metal and belted with a broad belt of steel. For a moment it focussed all attention, and then the eye was wrested to another more distant Giant who stood prepared to

catch, and it became apparent that the whole area of that great bay in the hills just north of Sevenoaks had been scarred to gigantic ends.

A hugely banked entrenchment overhung the chalk pit, in which stood the house, a monstrous squat Egyptian shape that Cossar had built for his sons when the Giant Nursery had served its turn, and behind was a great dark shed that might have covered a cathedral, in which a spluttering incandescence came and went, and from out of which came a Titanic hammering to beat upon the ear. Then the attention leapt back to the giant as the great ball of iron-bound timber soared up out of his hand.

The two men stood up and stared. The ball seemed as big as a cask.

"Caught!" cried the man from prison, as a tree blotted out the thrower.

The train looked on these things only for the fraction of a minute and then passed behind trees into the Chislehurst tunnel. "My Gawd!" said the man from prison again as the darkness closed about them. "Why! that chap was as 'igh as a 'ouse."

"That's them young Cossars," said his brother, jerking his head allusively, "what all this trouble's about. . . ."

They emerged again to discover more siren surmounted towers, more red huts, and then the clustering villas of the outer suburbs. The art of bill-sticking had lost nothing in the interval, and from countless tall hoardings, from house ends, from palings, and a hundred such points of vantage came the polychromatic appeals of the great Boomfood election. "Caterham," "Boomfood," and "Jack the Giant-killer" again and again and again, and monstrous caricatures and distortions, a hundred varieties of misrepresentations of those great and shining figures they had passed so nearly only a few minutes before. . . .

§2

IT had been the purpose of the younger brother to do a very magnificent thing, to celebrate this return to life by a dinner at some restaurant of indisputable quality, a dinner that should be followed by all that glittering succession of impressions the Music Halls of those days were so capable of giving. It was a worthy plan to wipe off the more superficial stains of the prison house by this display of free indulgence; but so far as the second item went the plan was changed. The dinner stood, but there was a desire already more powerful than the appetite for shows, already more efficient in turning the man's mind away from his grim prepossession with his past than any theatre could be, and that was an enormous curiosity and perplexity about this Boomfood and these Boom children, this new portentous giantry that seemed to dominate the world. "I 'aven't the 'ang of 'em," he said. "They disturve me."

His brother had that fineness of mind that can even set aside a contemplated hospitality. "It's *your* evening, dear old boy," he

said. "We'll try to get into the mass meeting at the People's Palace."

And at last the man from prison had the luck to find himself wedged into a packed multitude and staring from afar at a little brightly lit platform under an organ and a gallery. The organ had been playing something that had set boots tramping as the people swarmed in; but that was over now.

Hardly had the man from prison settled into place and done his quarrel with an importunate stranger who elbowed, before Caterham came. He walked out of a shadow towards the middle of the platform, the most insignificant little pigmy, away there in the distance, a little black figure with a pink dab for a face — in profile one saw his quite distinctive aquiline nose — a little figure that trailed after it, most inexplicably, a cheer. A cheer it was that began away there and grew and spread. A little spluttering of voices about the platform at first that suddenly leapt up into a flame of sound and swept athwart the whole mass of humanity within the building and without. How they cheered! Hooray! Hoo-ray!

No one in all those myriads cheered like the man from prison. The tears poured down his face, and he only stopped cheering at last because the thing had choked him. You must have been in prison as long as he before you can understand, or even begin to understand, what it means to a man to let his lungs go in a crowd. (But for all that he did not even pretend to himself that he knew what all this emotion was about.) Hooray! O God! — Hoo-ray!

And then a sort of silence. Caterham had subsided to a conspicuous patience and subordinate and inaudible persons were saying and doing formal and insignificant things. It was like hearing voices through the noise of leaves in spring. "Wawawawa — " What did it matter? People in the audience talked to one another. "Wawawawawa — " the thing went on. Would that grey-headed duffer never have done? Interrupting? Of course they were interrupting. "Wa, wa, wa, wa — " But shall we hear Caterham any better?

Meanwhile at any rate there was Caterham to stare at, and one could stand and study the distant prospect of the great man's features. He was easy to draw was this man, and already the world had him to study at leisure on lamp chimneys and children's plates, on Anti-Boomfood medals and Anti-Boomfood flags, on the selvedges of Caterham silks and cottons and in the linings of Good Old English Caterham hats. He pervades all the caricature of that time. One sees him as a sailor standing to an old-fashioned gun, a port-fire labelled "New Boomfood Laws" in his hand; while in the sea wallows that huge ugly threatening monster, "Boomfood"; or he is cap-à-pie in armour, St. George's cross on shield and helm, and a cowardly titanic Caliban sitting amidst desecrations of the "New Boomfood

Regulations"; or he comes flying down as Perseus and rescues a chained and beautiful Andromeda (labelled distinctly about her belt as "Civilisation") from a wallowing waste of sea monster bearing upon its various necks and claws "Irreligion," "Trampling Egotism," "Mechanism," "Monstrosity," and the like. But it was as "Jack the Giant-killer" that the popular imagination considered Caterham most correctly cast, and it was in the vein of a Jack the Giant-killer poster that the man from prison enlarged that distant miniature.

The "Wawawawa" came abruptly to an end.

He's done. He's sitting down. Yes! No! Yes! It's Caterham! "Caterham!" "Caterham!" And then came the cheers.

It takes a multitude to make such a stillness as followed that disorder of cheering. A man alone in a wilderness — it's stillness of a sort of doubt, but he hears himself breathe, he hears himself move, he hears all sorts of things. Here the voice of Caterham was the one single thing heard, a thing very bright and clear, like a little light burning in a black velvet recess. Hear indeed! One heard him as though he spoke at one's elbow.

It was stupendously effective to the man from prison, that gesticulating little figure in a halo of light, in a halo of rich and swaying sounds; behind it, partially effaced as it were, sat its supporters on the platform, and in the foreground was a wide perspective of innumerable backs and profiles, a vast multitudinous attention. That little figure seemed to have absorbed the substance from them all.

Caterham spoke of our ancient institutions, "Earearear," roared the crowd. "Ear! ear!" said the man from prison. He spoke of our ancient spirit of order and justice. "Earearear!" roared the crowd. "Ear! Ear!" cried the man from prison, deeply moved. He spoke of the wisdom of our forefathers, of the slow growth of venerable institutions, of moral and social traditions that fitted our English national characteristics as the skin fits the hand. "Ear! Ear!" groaned the man from prison, with tears of excitement on his cheeks. And now all these things were to go into the melting pot. Yes, into the melting pot! Because three men in London twenty years ago had seen fit to mix something indescribable in a bottle, all the order and sanctity of things — Cries of "No! No!" — Well, if it was not to be so, they must exert themselves, they must say good-bye to hesitation — Here there came a gust of cheering. They must say good-bye to hesitation and half measures.

"We have heard, gentlemen," cried Caterham, "of nettles that become giant nettles. At first they are no more than other nettles, little plants that a firm hand may grasp and wrench away; but if you leave them — if you leave them, they grow with such a power of poisonous expansion that at last you must needs have axe and rope, you must needs have danger to life and limb, you must needs have toil and distress

—men may be killed in their felling, man may be killed in their felling—"

There came a stir and interruption and then the man from prison heard Caterham's voice again, ringing clear and strong: "Learn about Boomfood from Boomfood itself and—" He paused—"*Grasp your nettle before it is too late!*"

He stopped and stood wiping his lips. "A crystal," cried someone, "a crystal," and then came that same strange swift growth to thunderous tumult, until the whole world seemed cheering. . . .

The man from prison came out of the hall at last, marvellously stirred, and with that in his face that marks those who have seen a vision. He knew, everyone knew; his ideas were no longer vague. He had come back to a world in crisis, to the immediate decision of a stupendous issue. He must play his part in the great conflict like a man—like a free responsible man. The antagonism presented itself as a picture. On the one hand those easy gigantic mail-clad figures of the morning—one saw them now in a different light—on the other this little black-clad gesticulating creature under the limelight, that pigmy thing with its ordered flow of melodious persuasion, its little marvellously penetrating voice, John Caterham—"Jack the Giant-killer." They must all unite to "grasp the nettle" before it was "too late."

§ 3

THE TALLEST and strongest and most regarded of all the children of the Food were the three sons of Cossar. The mile or so of land near Sevenoaks in which their boyhood passed became so trenched, so dug out and twisted about, so covered with sheds and huge working models and all the play of their developing powers, it was like no other place on earth. And long since it had become too little for the things they sought to do. The eldest son was a mighty schemer of wheeled engines; he had made himself a sort of giant bicycle that no road in the world had room for, no bridge could bear. There it stood, a great thing of wheels and engines, capable of two hundred and fifty miles an hour, useless save that now and then he would mount it and fling himself backwards and forwards across that cumbered work yard. He had meant to go around the little world with it; he had made it with that intention, while he was still no more than a dreaming boy. Now its spokes were rusted deep red like wounds, wherever the enamel had been chipped away.

"You must make a road for it first, Sonnie," Cossar had said, "before you can do that."

So one morning about dawn the young giant and his brothers had set to work to make a road about the world. They seem to have had an inkling of opposition impending, and they had worked with remarkable vigour. The world had discovered them soon enough, driving that road as straight as a flight of a bullet towards the English Channel, already some miles of it levelled

and made and stamped hard. They had been stopped before midday by a vast crowd of excited people, owners of land, land agents, local authorities; lawyers, policemen, soldiers even.

"We're making a road," the biggest boy had explained.

"Make a road by all means," said the leading lawyer on the ground, "but please respect the rights of other people. You have already infringed the private rights of twenty-seven private proprietors; let alone the special privileges and property of an urban district board, nine parish councils, a county council, two gas works, and a railway company. . . ."

"Goodney!" said the elder boy Cossar.

"You will have to stop it."

"But don't you want a nice straight road in the place of all these rotten rutty little lanes?"

"I won't say it wouldn't be advantageous, but—"

"It isn't to be done," said the eldest Cossar boy, picking up his tools.

"Not in this way," said the lawyer, "certainly."

"How is it to be done?"

The leading lawyer's answer had been complicated and vague.

Cossar had come down to see the mischief his children had done, and reproved them severely and laughed enormously and seemed to be extremely happy over the affair. "You boys must wait a bit," he shouted up to them, "before you can do things like that."

"The lawyer told us we must begin by preparing a scheme, and getting special powers and all sorts of rot. Said it would take us years."

"*We'll* have a scheme before long, little boy," cried Cossar, hands to his mouth as he shouted, "never fear. For a bit you'd better play about and make models of the things you want to do."

They did as he told them like obedient sons.

But for all that the Cossar lads brooded a little.

"It's all very well," said the second to the first, "but I don't always want just to play about and plan. I want to do something *real*, you know. We didn't come into this world so strong as we are, just to play about in this messy little bit of ground, you know, and take little walks and keep out of the towns"—for by that time they were forbidden all boroughs and urban districts. "Doing nothing's just wicked. Can't we find out something the little people *want* done and do it for them—just for the fun of doing it?

"Lots of them haven't houses fit to live in," said the second boy. "Let's go and build 'em a house close up to London that will hold heaps and heaps of them and be ever so comfortable and nice, and let's make 'em a nice little road to where they all go and do business—a nice straight little road, and make it all as nice as nice. We'll make it all so clean and pretty that they won't any of them be able to live grubby and beastly like most of them do now. Water enough for them to wash with, we'll have— you know they're so dirty now

that nine out of ten of their houses haven't even baths in them, the filthy little skunks! You know, the ones that have baths spit insults at the ones that haven't, instead of helping them to get them — and call 'em the Great Unwashed. *You* know. We'll alter all that. And we'll make electricity light and cook and clean up for them, and all. Fancy! They make their women — women who are going to be mothers — crawl about and scrub floors!

"We could make it all beautifully. We could bank up a valley in that range of hills over there and make a nice reservoir, and we could make a big place here to generate our electricity and have it all simply lovely. Couldn't we? . . . And then perhaps they'd let us do some other things."

"Yes," said the elder brother, "we could do it *very* nice for them."

"Then *let's*," said the second brother.

"*I* don't mind," said the elder brother, and looked about for a handy tool.

And that led to another dreadful bother.

Agitated multitudes were at them in no time, telling them for a thousand reasons to stop, telling them to stop for no reason at all — babbling, confused, and varied multitudes. The place they were building was too high — it couldn't possibly be safe. It was ugly; it interfered with the letting of proper-sized houses in the neighbourhood; it ruined the tone of the neighbourhood; it was unneighbourly; it was contrary

to the Local Building Regulations; it infringed the right of the local authority to muddle about with a minute expensive electric supply of its own; it interfered with the concerns of the local water company.

Local Government Board clerks roused themselves to judicial obstruction. The little lawyer turned up again to represent about a dozen threatened interests; local landowners appeared in opposition; people with mysterious claims claimed to be bought off at exorbitant rates; the Trades Unions of all the building trades lifted up collective voices; and a ring of dealers in all sorts of building material became a bar. Extraordinary associations of people with prophetic visions of æsthetic horrors rallied to protect the scenery of the place where they would build the great house, of the valley where they would bank up the water. These last people were absolutely the worst asses of the lot, the Cossar boys considered. In no time that beautiful house of the Cossar boys was just like a walking stick thrust into a wasp's nest.

"I never did!" said the elder boy.

"We can't go on," said the second brother.

"Rotten little beasts they are," said the third of the brothers; "we can't do *anything*!"

"Even when it's for their own comfort. Such a *nice* place we'd have made for them too."

"They seem to spend their silly little lives getting in each other's way," said the eldest boy. "Rights and laws and regula-

tions and rascalities: it's like a game of spellicans. . . . Well, anyhow, they'll have to live in their grubby dirty silly little houses for a bit longer. It's very evident *we* can't go on with this."

And the Cossar children left that great house unfinished, a mere hole of foundations and the beginning of a wall, and sulked back to their big enclosure. After a time the hole was filled with water and with stagnation, and weeds and vermin; and the Food, either dropped there by the sons of Cossar or blowing thither as dust, set growth going in its usual fashion. Water voles came out over the country and did infinite havoc, and one day a farmer caught his pigs drinking there, and instantly and with great presence of mind — for he knew of the great hog of Oakham — slew them all. And from that deep pool it was the mosquitoes came, quite terrible mosquitoes, whose only virtue was that the sons of Cossar, after being bitten for a little, could stand it no longer, and chose a moonlight night when law and order were abed, and drained the water clean away into the river by Brook.

But they left the big weeds and the big water voles and all sorts of big undesirable things still living and breeding on the site they had chosen, the site on which the fair great house of the little people might have towered to heaven. . . .

§ 4

THAT had been in the boyhood of the Sons, but now they were nearly men. And the chains had been tightening upon them and tightening with every year of growth. Each year they grew and the Food spread and great things multiplied, each year the stress and tension rose. The Food had been at first for the great mass of mankind a distant marvel, and now it was coming home to every threshold and threatening, pressing against and distorting the whole order of life. It blocked this, it overturned that, it changed natural products, and by changing natural products it stopped employments and threw men out of work by the hundred thousand; it swept over boundaries and turned the world of trade into a world of cataclysms; no wonder mankind hated it.

And since it is easier to hate animate than inanimate things, animals more than plants, and one's fellow men more completely than any animals, the fear and trouble engendered by giant nettles and six-foot grass blades, awful insects and tiger-like vermin, grew all into one great power of detestation that aimed itself with a simple directness at that scattered band of great human beings, the Children of the Food. That hatred had become the central force in political affairs. The old party lines had been traversed and effaced altogether under the insistence of these newer issues, and the conflict lay now between the party of the temporisers, who were for setting little political men to control and regulate the Food, and the party of reaction, for whom Caterham spoke, speaking always with a more sinister ambiguity, crystal-

lising his intention first in one threatening phrase and then another, now that men must "prune the bramble growth," now that they must find a "cure for elephantiasis," and at last upon the eve of the election that they must "Grasp the nettle."

One day the three sons of Cossar, who were now no longer boys but men, sat among the masses of their futile work and talked together after their fashion of all these things. They had been working all day at one of a series of great and complicated trenches their father had bid them make, and now it was sunset and they sat in the little garden space before the great house and looked at the world and rested, until the little servants within should say their food was ready.

You must figure these mighty forms, forty feet high the least of them was, reclining on a patch of turf that would have seemed a stubble of reeds to a common man. One sat up and chipped earth from his huge boots with an iron girder he grasped in his hand; the second rested on his elbow; the third whittled a pine-tree into shape, making the air aromatic with resin. They were clothed not in cloth but in undergarments of woven rope and outer clothes of felted aluminium wire; they were shod with timber and iron and the links and buttons and belts of their clothing were all of plated steel. The great single-storeyed house they lived in, Egyptian in its massiveness, half built of monstrous blocks of chalk and half excavated from the living rock of the hill, had

a front a full hundred feet in height, and beyond, the chimneys and wheels, the cranes and covers of their work sheds rose marvellously against the sky. Through a circular window in the house there was visible a spout from which some white-hot metal dripped and dripped in measured drops into a receptacle out of sight. The place was enclosed and rudely fortified by monstrous banks of earth backed with steel both over the crests of the Downs above, and across the dip of the valley. It needed something of common size to mark the nature of the scale. The train that came rattling from Sevenoaks athwart their vision, and presently plunged into the tunnel out of their sight, looked by contrast with them like a small automatic toy.

"They have made all the woods this side of Ightham out of bounds," said one, "and moved the board that was out by Knockholt two miles and more this way."

"It is the least they could do," said the youngest, after a pause. "They are trying to take the wind out of Caterham's sails."

"It's not enough for that and —it is almost too much for us," said the third.

"They are cutting us off from Brother Redwood. Last time I went to him the red notices had crept a mile in, either way. The road to him along the Downs is no more than a narrow lane."

The speaker thought. "What has come to our Brother Redwood?"

"Why?" said the eldest brother.

The speaker hacked a bough from his pine. "He was like—as though he wasn't awake. He didn't seem to listen to what I had to say. And he said something of—love."

The youngest tapped his girder on the edge of his iron sole and laughed. "Brother Redwood," he said, "has dreams."

Neither spoke for a space. Then the eldest brother said, "This cooping up and cooping up grows more than I can bear. At last, I believe, they will draw a line round our boots and tell us to live on that."

The middle brother swept aside a heap of pine boughs with one hand and shifted his attitude. "What they do now is nothing to what they will do when Caterham has power."

"If he gets power," said the youngest brother, smiting the ground with his girder.

"As he will," said the eldest, staring at his feet.

The middle brother ceased his lopping and his eye went to the great banks that sheltered them about. "Then, brothers," he said, "our youth will be over and as Father Redwood said to us long ago, we must quit ourselves like men."

"Yes," said the eldest; "but what exactly does that mean? Just what does it mean—when that day of trouble comes?"

He too glanced at those rude vast suggestions of entrenchment about them, looking not so much at them as through them and over the hills to the innumerable

multitudes beyond. Something of the same sort came into all their minds, a vision, of little people coming out to war, in a flood, the little people inexhaustible, incessant, malignant. . . .

"They are little," said the youngest brother; "but they have numbers beyond counting, like the sands of the sea."

"They have arms—they have weapons even, that our brothers in Sunderland have made."

"Besides, Brothers, except for vermin, except for little accidents with evil things, what have we seen of killing?"

"I know," said the eldest brother. "For all that—we are what we are. When the day of trouble comes we must do the thing we have to do."

He closed his knife with a snap —the blade was the length of a man—and used his new pine staff to help himself rise. He stood up and turned towards the squat grey immensity of the house. The crimson of the sunset caught him as he rose, caught the mail and clasps about his neck and the woven metal of his arms, and to the eyes of his brother it seemed as though he was suddenly suffused with blood. . . .

As the young giant rose a little black figure became visible to him against that western incandescence on the top of the embankment that towered above the summit of the down. The black limbs waved in ungainly gestures. Something in the fling of the limbs suggested haste to the young giant's mind. He waved his pine mast in reply, filled the whole valley with his

vast Hallo! threw a "Something's up" to his brothers, and set off in twenty-foot strides to meet and help his father.

§ 5

IT chanced too that a young man who was not a giant was delivering his soul about these sons of Cossar just at that same time. He had come over the hills beyond Sevenoaks, he and his friend, and he it was did the talking. In the hedge as they came along they had heard a pitiful squealing and had intervened to rescue three nestling tits from the attack of a couple of giant ants. That adventure it was had set him talking.

"Reactionary!" he was saying, as they came within sight of the Cossar encampment. "Who wouldn't be reactionary? Look at that square of ground, that space of God's earth that was once sweet and fair, torn, desecrated, disembowelled! Those sheds! That great wind-wheel! That monstrous wheeled machine! Those dykes! Look at those three monsters squatting there, plotting some ugly devilment or other! Look — look at all the land!"

His friend glanced at his face. "You have been listening to Caterham," he said.

"Using my eyes. Looking a little into the peace and order of the past we leave behind. This foul Food is the last shape of the Devil, still set as ever upon the ruin of our world. Think what the world must have been before our days, what it was still when our mothers bore us, and see it

now! Think how these slopes once smiled under the golden harvest, how the hedges, full of sweet little flowers, parted the modest portion of this man from that, how the ruddy farm-houses dotted the land and the voice of the church bells from yonder tower stilled the whole world each Sabbath into Sabbath prayer. And now, every year, still more and more of monstrous weeds, of monstrous vermin, and these giants growing all about us, straddling over us, blundering against all that is subtle and sacred in our world. Why here — Look!"

He pointed, and his friend's eyes followed the line of his white finger.

"One of their footmarks. See! It has smashed itself three feet deep and more, a pitfall for horses and rider, a trap to the unwary. There is a briar rose smashed to death; there is grass uprooted and a teazle crushed aside, a farmer's drain pipe snapped and the edge of the pathway broken down. Destruction! So they are doing all over the world, all over the order and decency the world of men has made. Trampling on all things. Reaction! What else?"

"But — reaction. What do you hope to do?"

"Stop it!" cried the young man from Oxford. "Before it is too late."

"But —"

"It's *not* impossible," cried the young man from Oxford, with a jump in his voice. "We want the firm hand; we want the subtle plan, the resolute mind. We have

been mealy-mouthed and weak-handed; we have trifled and temporised, and the Food has grown and grown. Yet even now — "

He stopped for a moment. "This is the echo of Caterham," said his friend.

"Even now. Even now there is hope — abundant hope, if only we make sure of what we want and what we mean to destroy. The mass of people are with us, much more with us than they were a few years ago; the law is with us, the constitution and order of society, the spirit of the established religions, the customs and habits of mankind are with us — and against the Food. Why should we temporise? Why should we lie? We hate it, we don't want it; why then should we have it? Do you mean to just grizzle and obstruct passively and do nothing — till the sands are out?"

He stopped short and turned about. "Look at that grove of nettles there. In the midst of them are homes — deserted — where once families of simple men played out their honest lives!

"And there!" he swung round to where the young Cossars muttered to one another of their wrongs.

"Look at them! And I know their father, a brute, a sort of brute beast with an intolerant loud voice, a creature who has run amuck in our all too merciful world for the last thirty years and more. An engineer! To him all that we hold dear and sacred is nothing. Nothing. The splendid traditions of our race and land, the noble institutions, the

venerable order, the broad slow march from precedent to precedent that has made our English people great and this sunny island free — it is all an idle tale, told and done with. Some claptrap about the Future is worth all these sacred things. . . . This sort of man who would run a tramway over his mother's grave if he thought that was the cheapest line the tramway could take. . . . And you think to temporise, to make some scheme of compromise, that will enable you to live in your way while that — that machinery — lives in its. I tell you it is hopeless — hopeless. As well make treaties with a tiger! They want things monstrous — we want them sane and sweet. It is one thing or the other."

"But what can you do?"

"Much! All! Stop the Food! They are still scattered, these giants, still immature and disunited. Chain them, gag them, muzzle them. At any cost stop them. It is their world or ours! Stop the Food. Shut up these men who make it. Do anything to stop Cossar! You don't seem to remember — one generation — only one generation needs holding down and then — Then we could level those mounds there, fill up their footsteps, take the ugly sirens from our church towers, smash all our elephant guns, and turn our faces again to the old order, the ripe old civilisation for which the soul of man is fitted."

"It's a mighty effort."

"For a mighty end. And if we don't? Don't you see the prospect before us clear as day? Everywhere the giants will increase

and multiply; everywhere they will make and scatter the Food. The grass will grow gigantic in our fields, the weeds in our hedges, the vermin in the thickets, the rats in the drains. More and more and more. This is only a beginning. The insect world will rise on us, the plant world, the very fishes in the sea will swamp and drown our ships. Tremendous growths will obscure and hide our houses, smother our churches, smash and destroy all the order of our cities, and we shall become no more than a feeble vermin under the heels of the new race. Mankind will be swamped and drowned in things of its own begetting! And all for nothing! Size! Mere size! Enlargement and *da capo*. Already we go picking our way among the first beginnings of the coming time. And all we do is say 'How convenient!' To grumble and do nothing. *No!*"

He raised his hand.

"Let them do the thing they have to do! So also will I. I am for Reaction—unstinted and fearless Reaction. Unless you mean to take this Food also, what else is there to do in all the world? We have trifled in the middle ways too long. You! Trifling in the middle ways is your habit, your circle of existence, your space and time. So, not I. I am against the Food, with all my strength and purpose against the Food."

He turned on his companion's grunt of dissent. "Where are you?"

"It's a complicated business—"

"Oh!—Driftwood!" said the young man from Oxford, very bitterly, with a fling of all his limbs. "The middle way is nothingness. It is one thing or the other. Eat or destroy. Eat or destroy! What else is there to do?"

CHAPTER 2

THE GIANT LOVERS

§1

Now it chanced in the days when Caterham was campaigning against the Boom-children before the General Election that was— amidst the most tragic and terrible circumstances—to bring him into power, that the giant Princess, that Serene Highness whose early nutrition had played so great a part in the brilliant career of Doctor Winkles, had come from the kingdom of her father to England, on an occasion that was deemed important. She was affianced for reasons of state to a certain Prince—and the wedding was to be made an event of international significance. There had arisen mysterious delays. Rumour and Imagination collaborated in the story and many things were said. There were suggestions of a recalcitrant Prince who declared he would not be

made to look like a fool — at
least to this extent. People sym-
pathised with him. That is the
most significant aspect of the
affair.

Now it may seem a strange
thing, but it is a fact that the
giant Princess, when she came to
England, knew of no other giants
whatever. She had lived in a
world where tact is almost a pas-
sion and reservations the air of
one's life. They had kept the
thing from her; they had hedged
her about from sight or suspicion
of any gigantic form, until her
appointed coming to England
was due. Until she met young
Redwood she had no inkling that
there was such a thing as another
giant in the world.

In the kingdom of the father
of the Princess there were wild
wastes of upland and mountains
where she had been accustomed
to roam freely. She loved the sun-
rise and the sunset and all the
great drama of the open heavens
more than anything else in the
world, but among a people at
once so democratic and so ve-
hemently loyal as the English her
freedom was much restricted.
People came in brakes, in excur-
sion trains, in organised multi-
tudes to see her; they would cycle
long distances to stare at her, and
it was necessary to rise betimes
if she would walk in peace. It
was still near the dawn that
morning when young Redwood
came upon her.

The Great Park near the Pal-
ace where she lodged stretched,
for a score of miles or more, west
and south of the western palace
gates. The chestnut trees of its

avenues reached high above her
head. Each one as she passed it
seemed to proffer a more abun-
dant wealth of blossom. For a
time she was content with sight
and scent, but at last she was won
over by these offers, and set her-
self so busily to choose and pick
that she did not perceive young
Redwood until he was close upon
her.

She moved among the chest-
nut trees, with the destined lover
drawing near to her, unantici-
pated, unsuspected. She thrust
her hands in among the branches,
breaking them and gathering
them. She was alone in the world.
Then —

She looked up, and in that mo-
ment she was mated.

We must needs put our imagi-
nations to his stature to see the
beauty he saw. That unapproach-
able greatness that prevents our
immediate sympathy with her did
not exist for him. There she
stood, a gracious girl, the first
created being that had ever
seemed a mate for him, light and
slender, lightly clad, the fresh
breeze of the dawn moulding the
subtly folding robe upon her
against the soft strong lines of
her form, and with a great mass
of blossoming chestnut branches
in her hands. The collar of her
robe opened to show the white-
ness of her neck and a soft shad-
owed roundness that passed out
of sight towards her shoulders.
The breeze had stolen a strand
or so of her hair, too, and
strained its red-tipped brown
across her cheek. Her eyes were
open blue, and her lips rested
always in the promise of a

smile as she reached among the branches.

She turned upon him with a start, saw him and for a space they regarded one another. For her, the sight of him was so amazing, so incredible, as to be, for some moments at least, terrible. He came to her with the shock of a supernatural apparition; he broke all the established law of her world. He was a youth of one and twenty then, slenderly built, with his father's darkness and his father's gravity. He was clad in a sober soft brown leather, close-fitting easy garments, and in brown hose that shaped him bravely. His head went uncovered in all weathers. They stood regarding one another—she incredulously amazed, and he with his heart beating fast. It was a moment without a prelude, the cardinal meeting of their lives.

For him there was less surprise. He had been seeking her, and yet his heart beat fast. He came towards her, slowly, with his eyes upon her face.

"You are the Princess," he said. "My father has told me. You are the Princess who was given the Food of the Gods."

"I am the Princess—yes," she said, with eyes of wonder. "But —what are you?"

"I am the son of the man who made the Food of the Gods."

"The Food of the Gods!"

"Yes, the Food of the Gods."

"But—"

Her face expressed infinite perplexity.

"What? I don't understand. The Food of the Gods?"

"You have not heard?"

"The Food of the Gods! *No!*"

She found herself trembling violently. The colour left her face. "I did not know," she said. "Do you mean—?"

He waited for her.

"Do you mean there are other —giants?"

He repeated. "Did you not know?"

And she answered with the growing amazement of realisation "*No!*"

The whole world and all the meaning of the world was changing for her. A branch of chestnut slipped from her hand. "Do you mean to say," she repeated stupidly, "that there are other giants in the world? That some food—?"

He caught her amazement.

"You know nothing?" he cried. "You have never heard of us? You, whom the Food has made akin to us!"

There was terror still in the eyes that stared at him. Her hand rose towards her throat and fell again. She whispered "*No.*"

It seemed to her that she must weep or faint. Then in a moment she had rule over herself and she was speaking and thinking clearly. "All this has been kept from me," she said. "It is like a dream. I have dreamt—I have dreamt such things. But waking —No. Tell me! Tell me! What are you? What is this Food of the Gods? Tell me slowly—and clearly. Why have they kept it from me, that I am not alone?"

§ 2

"Tell me," she said, and young Redwood, tremulous and excited,

set himself to tell her — it was poor and broken telling for a time — of the Food of the Gods and the giant children who were scattered over the world.

You must figure them both, flushed and startled in their bearing, getting at one another's meaning through endless half-heard, half-spoken phrases, repeating, making perplexing breaks and new departures — a wonderful talk, in which she awakened from the ignorance of all her life. And very slowly it became clear to her that she was no exception to the order of mankind, but one of a scattered brotherhood, who had all eaten the Food and grown for ever out of the little limits of the folk beneath their feet. Young Redwood spoke of his father, of Cossar, of the Brothers scattered throughout the country, of the great dawn of wider meaning that had come at last into the history of the world. "We are in the beginning of a beginning," he said; "this world of theirs is only the prelude to the world the Food will make.

"My father believes — and I also believe — that a time will come when littleness will have passed altogether out of the world of man. When giants shall go freely about this earth — their earth — doing continually greater and more splendid things. But that — that is to come. We are not even the first generation of that — we are the first experiments."

"And of these things," she said, "I knew nothing!"

"There are times when it seems to me almost as if we had come too soon. Someone, I suppose, had to come first. But the world was unprepared for our coming and for the coming of all the lesser great things that drew their greatness from the Food. There have been blunders; there have been conflicts. The little people hate our kind. . . .

"They are hard towards us because they are so little. . . . And because our feet are heavy on the things that make their lives. But at any rate they hate us now; they will have none of us — only if we could shrink back to the common size of them would they begin to forgive. . . .

"They are happy in houses that are prison cells to us; their cities are too small for us; we go in misery along their narrow ways; we cannot worship in their churches. . . .

"We see over their walls' and over their protections; we look inadvertently into their upper windows; we look over their customs; their laws are no more than a net about our feet. . . .

"Every time we stumble we hear them shouting; every time we blunder against their limits or stretch out to any spacious act. . . .

"Our easy paces are wild flights to them, and all they deem great and wonderful no more than doll's pyramids to us. Their pettiness of method and appliance and imagination hampers and defeats our powers. There are no machines to the power of our hands, no helps to fit our needs. They hold our greatness in servitude by a thousand invisible bands. We are stronger, man for man, a hundred times, but we are

disarmed; our very greatness makes us debtors; they claim the land we stand upon; they tax our ampler need of food and shelter, and for all these things we must toil with the tools these dwarfs can make us — and to satisfy their dwarfish fancies. . . .

"They pen us in, in every way. Even to live one must cross their boundaries. Even to meet you here to-day I have passed a limit. All that is reasonable and desirable in life they make out of bounds for us. We may not go into the towns; we may not cross the bridges; we may not step on their ploughed fields or into the harbours of the game they kill. I am cut off now from all our Brethren except the three sons of Cossar, and even that way the passage narrows day by day. One could think they sought occasion against us to do some more evil thing. . . ."

"But we are strong," she said.

"We should be strong — yes. We feel, all of us — you too I know must feel — that we have power, power to do great things, power insurgent in us. But before we can do anything — "

He flung out a hand that seemed to sweep away a world.

"Though I thought I was alone in the world," she said, after a pause, "I have thought of these things. They have taught me always that strength was almost a sin, that it was better to be little than great, that all true religion was to shelter the weak and little, encourage the weak and little, help them to multiply and multiply until at last they crawled over one another, to sac-

rifice all our strength in their cause. But . . . always I have doubted the things they taught."

"This life," he said, "these bodies of ours, are not for dying."

"No."

"Nor to live in futility. But if we would not do that, it is already plain to all our Brethren a conflict must come. I know not what bitterness of conflict must presently come, before the little folks will suffer us to live as we need to live. All the Brethren have thought of that. Cossar, of whom I told you; he too has thought of that."

"They are very little and weak."

"In their way. But you know all the means of death are in their hands, and made for their hands. For hundreds of thousands of years, these little people, whose world we invade, have been learning how to kill one another. They are very able at that. They are able in many ways. And besides, they can deceive and change suddenly. . . . I do not know. . . . There comes a conflict. You — you perhaps are different from us. For us, assuredly, the conflict comes. . . . The thing they call War. We know it. In a way we prepare for it. But you know — those little people! — we do not know how to kill, at least we do not want to kill — "

"Look," she interrupted, and he heard a yelping horn.

He turned at the direction of her eyes, and found a bright yellow motor car, with dark goggled driver and fur-clad passengers, whopping, throbbing, and buzz-

ing resentfully at his heel. He moved his foot, and the mechanism, with three angry snorts, resumed its fussy way towards the town. "Filling up the roadway!" floated up to him.

Then someone said, "Look! Did you see? There is the monster Princess over beyond the trees!" and all their goggled faces came round to stare.

"I say," said another. "*That* won't do. . . ."

"All this," she said, "is more amazing than I can tell."

"That they should not have told you," he said, and left his sentence incomplete.

"Until you came upon me, I had lived in a world where I was great—alone. I had made myself a life—for that. I had thought I was the victim of some strange freak of nature. And now my world has crumbled down, in half an hour, and I see another world, other conditions, wider possibilities—fellowship—"

"Fellowship," he answered.

"I want you to tell me more yet, and much more," she said. "You know this passes through my mind like a tale that is told. You even. . . . In a day perhaps, or after several days, I shall believe in you. Now—Now I am dreaming. . . . Listen!"

The first stroke of a clock above the palace offices far away had penetrated to them. Each counted mechanically "Seven."

"This," she said, "should be the hour of my return. They will be taking my bowl of coffee into the hall where I sleep. The little officials and servants—you cannot dream how grave they are—

will be stirring about their little duties.

"They will wonder. . . . But I want to talk to you."

She thought. "But I want to think too. I want now to think alone, and think out this change in things, think away the old solitude, and think you and those others into my world. . . . I shall go. I shall go back to-day to my place in the castle, and to-morrow, as the dawn comes, I shall come again—here."

"I shall be here waiting for you."

"All day I shall dream and dream of this new world you have given me. Even now, I can scarcely believe—"

She took a step back and surveyed him from the feet to the face. Their eyes met and locked for a moment.

"Yes," she said, with a little laugh that was half a sob. "You are real. But it is very wonderful! Do you think—indeed—? Suppose to-morrow I come and find you—a pigmy like the others! . . . Yes, I must think. And so for to-day—as the little people do—"

She held out her hand, and for the first time they touched one another. Their hands clasped firmly and their eyes met again.

"Good-bye," she said, "for to-day. Good-bye! Good-bye, Brother Giant!"

He hesitated with some unspoken thing, and at last he answered her simply, "Good-bye."

For a space they held each other's hands, studying each the other's face. And many times after they had parted, she looked

back half doubtfully at him, standing still in the place where they had met. . . .

She walked into her apartments across the great yard of the Palace like one who walks in a dream, with a vast branch of chestnut trailing from her hand.

§ 3

THESE two met altogether fourteen times before the beginning of the end. They met in the Great Park, or on the heights and among the gorges of the rusty-roaded, heathery moorland, set with dusky pine woods, that stretched to the south-west. Twice they met in the great avenue of chestnuts, and five times near the broad ornamental water the king, her great-grandfather, had made. There was a place where a great trim lawn, set with tall conifers, sloped graciously to the water's edge, and there she would sit, and he would lie at her knees and look up in her face and talk, telling of all the things that had been, and of the work his father had set before him, and of the great and spacious dream of what the giant people should one day be. Commonly they met in the early dawn, but once they met there in the afternoon, and found presently a multitude of peering eavesdroppers about them, cyclists, pedestrians, peeping from the bushes, rustling (as sparrows will rustle about one in the London parks) amidst the dead leaves in the woods behind, gliding down the lake in boats towards a point of view, trying to get nearer to them and hear.

It was the first hint that offered of the enormous interest the countryside was taking in their meetings. And once — it was the seventh time, and it precipitated the scandal — they met out upon the breezy moorland under a clear moonlight, and talked in whispers there, for the night was warm and still.

Very soon they had passed from the realisation that in them and through them a new world of giantry shaped itself in the earth, from the contemplation of the great struggle between big and little, in which they were clearly destined to participate, to interests at once more personal and more spacious. Each time they met and talked and looked on one another, it crept a little more out of their subconscious being towards recognition, that something more dear and wonderful than friendship was between them, and walked between them and drew their hands together. And in a little while they came to the word itself and found themselves lovers, the Adam and Eve of a new race in the world.

They set foot side by side into the wonderful valley of love, with its deep and quiet places. The world changed about them with their changing mood, until presently it had become, as it were, a tabernacular beauty about their meetings, and the stars were no more than flowers of light beneath the feet of their love, and the dawn and sunset the coloured hangings by the way. They ceased to be beings of flesh and blood to one another and themselves; they passed into a bodily texture of tenderness and desire. They

gave it first whispers and then silence, and drew close and looked into one another's moonlit and shadowy faces under the infinite arch of the sky. And the still black pine trees stood about them like sentinels.

The beating steps of time were hushed into silence, and it seemed to them the universe hung still. Only their hearts were audible, beating. They seemed to be living together in a world where there is no death, and indeed so it was with them then. It seemed to them that they sounded, and indeed they sounded, such hidden splendours in the very heart of things as none have ever reached before. Even for mean and little souls, love is the revelation of splendours. And these were giant lovers who had eaten the Food of the Gods. . . .

You may imagine the spreading consternation in this ordered world when it became known that the Princess who was affianced to the Prince, the Princess, Her Serene Highness! with royal blood in her veins! met — frequently met — the hypertrophied offspring of a common professor of chemistry, a creature of no rank, no position, no wealth, and talked to him as though there were no Kings and Princes, no order, no reverence — nothing but Giants and Pigmies in the world, talked to him and, it was only too certain, held him as her lover.

" If those newspaper fellows get hold of it! " gasped Sir Arthur Poodle Bootlik. . . .

" I am told — " whispered the old Bishop of Frumps. . . .

" New story upstairs," said the first footman, as he nibbled among the dessert things. " So far as I can make out this here giant Princess — "

" They say — " said the lady who kept the stationer's shop by the main entrance to the Palace, where the little Americans get their tickets for the State Apartments. . . .

And then:

" We are authorised to deny — " said " Picaroon " in *Gossip*.

And so the whole trouble came out.

§ 4

" THEY say that we must part," the Princess said to her lover.

" But why? " he cried. " What new folly have these people got into their heads? "

" Do you know," she asked, " that to love me — is high treason? "

" My dear," he cried; " but does it matter? What is their right — right without a shadow of reason — and their treason and their loyalty to us? "

" You shall hear," she said, and told him of the things that had been told to her.

" It was the queerest little man who came to me — with a soft beautifully modulated voice, a softly moving little gentleman who sidled into the room like a cat and put his pretty white hand up so, whenever he had anything significant to say. He is bald, but not of course nakedly bald, and his nose and face are chubby rosy little things and his beard is trimmed to a point in quite the loveliest way. He pretended to

have emotions several times and made his eyes shine. You know he is quite a friend of the real royal family here, and he called me his dear young lady and was perfectly sympathetic even from the beginning. 'My dear young lady,' he said, 'you know—*you mustn't*,' several times, and then, 'you owe a duty.'"

"Where do they make such men?"

"He likes it," she said.

"But I don't see—"

"He told me serious things."

"You don't think," he said, turning on her abruptly, "that there's anything in the sort of thing he said?"

"There's something in it quite certainly," said she.

"You mean—?"

"I mean that without knowing it we have been trampling on the most sacred conceptions of the little folks. We who are royal are a class apart. We are worshipped prisoners, processional toys. We pay for worship by losing—our elementary freedom. And I was to have married that Prince— You know nothing of him though. Well, a pigmy Prince. He doesn't matter. . . . It seems it would have strengthened the bonds between my country and another. And this country also— was to profit. Imagine it!— strengthening the bonds!"

"And now?"

"They want me to go on with it—as though there was nothing between us two."

"Nothing!"

"Yes. But that isn't all. He said—"

"Your specialist in Tact?"

"Yes. He said, it would be better for you, better for all the giants, if we two—abstained from conversation. That was how he put it."

"But what can they do if we don't?"

"He said you might have your freedom."

"*I!*"

"He said, with a stress, 'My dear young lady, it would be better, it would be more dignified, if you parted, willingly.' That was all he said. With a stress on willingly."

"But—! What business is it of these little wretches, where we love, how we love? What have they and their world to do with us?"

"They do not think that."

"Of course," he said, "you disregard all this."

"It seems utterly foolish to me."

"That their laws should fetter us! That we, at the first spring of life, should be tripped by their old engagements, their aimless institutions! Oh—! We disregard it."

"I am yours. So far—yes."

"So far? Isn't that all?"

"But they—If they want to part us—"

"What can they do?"

"I don't know. What *can* they do?"

"Who cares what they can do, or what they will do? I am yours and you are mine. What is there more than that? I am yours and you are mine—for ever. Do you think I will stop for their little

rules, for their little prohibitions, their scarlet boards indeed! — and keep from *you?* "

"Yes. But still, what can they do? "

"You mean," he said, "what are we to do? "

"Yes."

"We? We can go on."

"But if they seek to prevent us? "

He clenched his hands. He looked round as if the little people were already coming to prevent them. Then turned away from her and looked about the world. "Yes," he said. "Your question was the right one. What can they do? "

"Here in this little land," she said and stopped.

He seemed to survey it all. "They are everywhere."

"But we might —"

"Whither? "

"We could go. We could swim the seas together. Beyond the seas —"

"I have never been beyond the seas."

"There are great and desolate mountains amidst which we should seem no more than little people, there are remote and deserted valleys, there are hidden lakes and snow-girdled uplands untrodden by the feet of men. *There —* "

"But to get there we must fight our way day after day through millions and millions of mankind."

"It is our only hope. In this crowded land there is no fastness, no shelter. What place is there for us among these multitudes?

They who are little can hide from one another, but where are we to hide? There is no place where we could eat, no place where we could sleep. If we fled — night and day they would pursue our footsteps."

A thought came to him.

"There is one place," he said, "even in this island."

"Where? "

"The place our Brothers have made over beyond there. They have made great banks about their house, north and south and east and west; they have made deep pits and hidden places and even now — one came over to me quite recently. He said — I did not altogether heed what he said then. But he spoke of arms. It may be — there — we should find shelter. . . .

"For many days," he said, after a pause, "I have not seen our Brothers. . . . Dear! I have been dreaming, I have been forgetting! The days have passed and I have done nothing but look to see you again. . . . I must go to them and talk to them and tell them of you and of all the things that hang over us. If they will help us, they can help us. Then indeed we might hope. I do not know how strong their place is, but certainly Cossar will have made it strong. Before all this — before you came to me, I remember now — there was trouble brewing. There was an election — when all the little people settle things by counting heads. It must be over now. There were threats against all our race, against all our race, that is, but you. I must

see our Brothers. I must tell them all that has happened between us and all that threatens now."

§ 5

HE did not come to their next meeting until she had waited some time. They were to meet that day about midday in a great space of park that fitted into a bend of the river, and as she waited, looking ever southward under her hand, it came to her that the world was very still, that indeed it was broodingly still. And then she perceived that, spite of the lateness of the hour, her customary retinue of voluntary spies had failed her. Left and right, when she came to look, there was no one in sight, and there was never a boat upon the silver curve of the Thames. She tried to find a reason for this strange stillness in the world. . . .

Then, a grateful sight for her, she saw young Redwood far away over a gap in the tree masses that bounded her view.

Immediately the trees hid him and presently he was thrusting through them and in sight again. She could see there was something different, and then she saw that he was hurrying unusually and then that he limped. He gestured to her and she walked towards him. His face became clearer, and she saw with infinite concern that he winced at every stride. She was running now, towards him, her mind full of questions and vague fear. He drew near to her and spoke without a greeting.

"Are we to part?" he panted.

"No," she answered. "Why? What is the matter?"

"But if we do not part—! It is *now*."

"What is the matter?"

"I do not want to part," he said. "Only—"

He broke off abruptly to ask, "You will not part from me?"

She met his eyes with a steadfast look. "What has happened?" she pressed.

"Not for a time?"

"What time?"

"Years perhaps."

"Part! No!"

"You have thought?" he insisted.

"I will not part." She took his hand. "If this meant death, *now*, I would not let you go."

"If it meant death," he said, and she felt his grip upon her fingers.

He looked about him as if he feared to see the little people coming as he spoke. And then: "It may mean death."

"Now tell me," she said.

"They tried to stop my coming."

"How?"

"And as I came out of my workshop where I make the Food of the Gods for the Cossars to store in their camp, I found a little officer of police—a man in blue with white clean gloves—who beckoned me to stop. 'This way is closed!' said he. I thought little of that; I went round my workshop to where another road runs west, and there was another officer. 'This road is closed!' he said, and added: 'all the roads are closed!'"

"And then?"

"I argued with him a little. 'They are public roads!' I said.

"'That's it,' said he. 'You spoil them for the public.'

"'Very well,' said I, 'I'll take the fields,' and then up leapt others from behind a hedge and said, 'These fields are private.'

"'Curse your public and private,' I said, 'I'm going to my Princess,' and I stooped down and picked him up very gently — kicking and shouting — and put him out of my way. In a minute all the fields about me seemed alive with running men. I saw one on horseback galloping beside me and reading something as he rode — shouting it. He finished and turned and galloped away from me — head down. I couldn't make it out. And then behind me I heard the crack of guns."

"Guns!"

"Guns — just as they shoot at the rats. The bullets came through the air with a sound like things tearing: one stung me in the leg."

"And you?"

"Came on to you here and left them shouting and running and shooting behind me. And now —"

"Now?"

"It is only the beginning. They mean that we shall part. Even now they are coming after me."

"We will not."

"No. But if we are not to part — then you must come with me to our Brothers."

"Which way?" she said.

"To the east. Yonder is the way my pursuers will be coming. This then is the way we must go. Along this avenue of trees. Let me go first, so that if they are waiting —"

He made a stride, but she had seized his arm.

"No," cried she. "I come close to you, holding you. Perhaps I am royal, perhaps I am sacred. If I hold you — Would God we could fly with my arms about you! — it may be, they will not shoot at you —"

She clasped his shoulder and seized his hand as she spoke; she pressed herself nearer to him. "It may be they will not shoot you," she repeated, and with a sudden passion of tenderness he took her into his arms and kissed her cheek. For a space he held her.

"Even if it is death," she whispered.

She put her arms about his neck and lifted her face to his.

"Dearest, kiss me once more."

He drew her to him. Silently they kissed one another on the lips, and for another moment clung to one another. Then hand in hand, and she striving always to keep her body near to his, they set forward if haply they might reach the camp of refuge the sons of Cossar had made, before the pursuit of the little people overtook them.

And as they crossed the great spaces of the park behind the castle there came horsemen galloping out from among the trees and vainly seeking to keep pace with their giant strides. And presently ahead of them were houses and men with guns running out of the houses. At the sight of that, though he sought

to go on and was even disposed to fight and push through, she made him turn aside towards the south.

As they fled a bullet whipped by them overhead.

CHAPTER 3

YOUNG CADDLES IN LONDON

§ 1

ALL unaware of the trend of events, unaware of the laws that were closing in upon all the Brethren, unaware indeed that there lived a Brother for him on the earth, young Caddles chose this time to come out of his chalk pit and see the world. His brooding came at last to that. There was no answer to all his questions in Cheasing Eyebright; the new Vicar was less luminous even than the old, and the riddle of his pointless labour grew at last to the dimensions of exasperation. " Why should I work in this pit day after day? " he asked. " Why should I walk within bounds and be refused all the wonders of the world beyond there? What have I done, to be condemned to this? "

And one day he stood up, straightened his back, and said in a loud voice, " No! "

" I won't," he said, and then with great vigour cursed the pit.

Then having few words he sought to express his thought in acts. He took a truck half filled with chalk, lifted it and flung it, smashed, against another. Then he grasped a whole row of empty trucks and spun them down a bank. He sent a huge boulder of chalk bursting among them, and then ripped up a dozen yards of rail with a mighty plunge of his foot. So he began the conscientious wrecking of the pit.

" Work all my days," he said, " at this! "

It was an astonishing five minutes for the little geologist he had, in his preoccupation, overlooked. This poor little creature having dodged two boulders by a hairbreadth, got out by the westward corner and fled athwart the hill, with flapping rucksack and twinkling knickerbockered legs, leaving a trail of Cretaceous echinoderms behind him, while young Caddles, satisfied with the destruction he had achieved, came striding out to fulfil his purpose in the world.

" Work in that old pit, until I die and rot and stink! . . . What worm did they think was living in my giant body? Dig chalk for God knows what foolish purpose! Not *I*! "

The trend of road and railway perhaps, or mere chance it was, turned his face to London; and thither he came striding, over the Downs and athwart the meadows, through the hot afternoon, to the

infinite amazement of the world. It signified nothing to him that torn posters in red and white bearing various names flapped from every wall and barn; he knew nothing of the electoral revolution that had flung Caterham, "Jack the Giant-killer," into power. It signified nothing to him that every police station along his route had what was known as Caterham's ukase upon its notice board that afternoon, proclaiming that no giant, no person whatever over eight feet in height, should go more than five miles from his "place of location" without a special permission. It signified nothing to him that on his wake belated police officers, not a little relieved to find themselves belated, shook warning handbills at his retreating back. He was going to see what the world had to show him, poor incredulous blockhead, and he did not mean that occasional spirited persons shouting "Hi!" at him should stay his course. He came on down by Rochester and Greenwich towards an ever thickening aggregation of houses, walking rather slowly now, staring about him and swinging his huge chopper.

People in London had heard something of him before, how that he was idiotic but gentle, and wonderfully managed by Lady Wondershoot's agent and the Vicar; how in his dull way he revered these authorities and was grateful to them for their care of him, and so forth. So that when they learnt from the newspaper placards that afternoon that he also was "on strike," the thing appeared to many of them as a deliberate concerted act.

"They mean to try our strength," said the men in the trains going home from business.

"Lucky we have Caterham."

"It's in answer to his proclamation."

The men in the clubs were better informed. They clustered round the tape or talked in groups in their smoking rooms.

"He has no weapons. He would have gone to Sevenoaks if he had been put up to it."

"Caterham will handle him. . . ."

The shopmen told their customers. The waiters in restaurants snatched a moment for an evening paper between the courses. The cabman read it immediately after the betting news. . . .

The placards of the chief government evening paper were conspicuous with "Grasping the Nettle." Others relied for effect on: "Giant Redwood continues to meet the Princess." The *Echo* struck a line of its own with: "Rumoured Revolt of Giants in the North of England. The Sunderland Giants start for Scotland." The *Westminster Gazette* sounded its usual warning note. "Giants Beware," said the *Westminster Gazette,* and tried to make a point out of it that might perhaps serve towards uniting the Liberal party—at that time greatly torn between seven intensely egotistical leaders. The later newspaper dropped into uniformity. "The Giant in the New Kent Road," they proclaimed.

"What I want to know," said

the pale young man in the tea shop, "is why we aren't getting any news of the young Cossars. You'd think they'd be in it most of all. . . ."

"They tell me there's another of them young giants got loose," said the barmaid, wiping out a glass. "I've always said they was dangerous things to 'ave about. Right away from the beginning. . . . It ought to be put a stop to. Any'ow, I 'ope 'e won't come along 'ere."

"I'd like to 'ave a look at 'im," said the young man at the bar recklessly, and added, "I *seen* the Princess."

"D'you think they'll 'urt 'im?" said the barmaid.

"May 'ave to," said the young man at the bar, finishing his glass.

Amidst a hum of ten million such sayings young Caddles came to London. . . .

§ 2

I THINK of young Caddles always as he was seen in the New Kent Road, the sunset warm upon his perplexed and staring face. The road was thick with its varied traffic, omnibuses, trams, vans, carts, trolleys, cyclists, motors and a marvelling crowd — loafers, women, nursemaids, shopping women, children, venturesome hobbledehoys — gathered behind his gingerly moving feet. The hoardings were untidy everywhere with the tattered election paper. A babblement of voices surged about him. One sees the customers and shopmen, crowding in the doorways of the shops, the faces that came and went at the windows, the little street boys running and shouting, the policeman taking it all quite stiffly and calmly, the workmen knocking off upon scaffoldings, the seething miscellany of the little folks. They shouted to him, vague encouragement, vague insults, the imbecile catch words of the day, and he stared down at them, at such a multitude of living creatures as he had never before imagined in the world.

Now that he had fairly entered London he had had to slacken his pace more and more, the little folks crowded so mightily upon him. The crowd grew denser at every step, and at last, at a corner where two great ways converged, he came to a stop and the multitude flowed about him and closed him in.

There he stood with his feet a little apart, his back to a big corner gin palace that towered twice his height and ended in a sky sign, staring down at the pigmies and wondering, trying, I doubt not, to collate it all with the other things of his life, with the valley among the downlands, the nocturnal lovers, the singing in the church, the chalk he hammered daily, and with instinct and death and the sky, trying to get it all together coherent and significant. His brows were knit. He put up his huge paw to scratch his coarse hair, and groaned aloud.

"I don't see it," he said.

His accent was unfamiliar. A great babblement went across the open space, a babblement amidst which the gongs of the trams, ploughing their obstinate way

through the mass, rose like red poppies amidst corn. "What did he say?" "Said he didn't see." "Said, where is the sea?" "Said, where is a seat?" "He wants a seat." "Can't the brasted fool sit on a 'ouse or somethin'?"

"What are ye for, ye swarming little people? What are ye all doing — what are ye all for?"

"What are ye doing up here, ye swarming little people, while I'm a-cutting chalk for ye, down in the chalk pits there?"

His queer voice, the voice that had been so bad for school discipline at Cheasing Eyebright, smote the multitude to silence while it sounded and splashed them all to tumult at the end. Some wit was audible screaming "Speech, speech!" "What's he saying?" was the burthen of the public mind, and an opinion was abroad that he was drunk. "Hi, hi, hi," bawled the omnibus drivers, threading a dangerous way. A drunken American sailor wandered about tearfully inquiring, "What's he want anyhow?" A leathery-faced rag-dealer upon a little pony-drawn cart soared up over the tumult by virtue of his voice. "Garn 'ome, you Brasted Giant!" he brawled. "Garn 'Ome! You Brasted Great Dangerous Thing! Can't you see you're a-frightening the 'orses? Go 'ome with you! 'Asn't anyone 'ad the sense to tell you the law?" And over all this uproar young Caddles stared, perplexed, expectant, saying no more.

Down a side road came a little string of solemn policemen, and threaded itself ingeniously into the traffic. "Stand back," said the

little voices; "keep moving, please."

Young Caddles became aware of a little dark blue figure thumping at his shin.

He looked down. "*What?*" he said, bending forward.

"Can't stand about here," shouted the inspector.

"No! You can't stand about here," he repeated.

"But where am I to go?"

"Back to your village. Place of location. Anyhow, now — you've got to move on. You're obstructing the traffic."

"What traffic?"

"Along the road."

"But where is it going? Where does it come from? What does it mean? They're all around me. What do they want. What are they doin'? I want to understand. I'm tired of cuttin' chalk and bein' all alone. What are they doin' for me while I'm a-cuttin' chalk? I may just as well understand here and now, as anywhere."

"Sorry. But we aren't here to explain things of that sort. I must arst you to move on."

"Don't you know?"

"I must arst you to move on — *if* you please. . . . I'd strongly advise you to get off 'ome. We've 'ad no special instructions yet — but it's against the law. . . . Clear away there. Clear a-way."

The pavement to his left became invitingly bare, and young Caddles went slowly on his way. But now his tongue was loosened.

"I don't understand," he muttered. "I don't understand." He would appeal brokenly to the

changing crowd that ever trailed beside him and behind. " I didn't know there were such places as this. What are all you people doing with yourselves? What's it all for? What is it all for and where do I come in?"

He had already begotten a new catch word. Young men of wit and spirit addressed each other in this manner, "Ullo Arry O'Cock. Wat's it all *for*? Eh? Wat's it all bloomin' well *for*?"

To which there sprang up a competing variety of repartees, for the most part impolite. The most popular and best adapted for general use appears to have been " *Shut* it," or, in a voice of scornful detachment —

" *Garn!* "

§ 3

WHAT was he seeking? He wanted something the pigmy world did not give, some end which the pigmy world prevented his attaining, prevented even his seeing clearly, which he was never to see clearly. It was the gigantic social side of this lonely dumb monster crying out for his race, for the things akin to him, for something he might love and something he might serve, for a purpose he might comprehend and a command he could obey. And you know, all this was *dumb,* raged dumbly within him, could not even had he met a fellow giant have found outlet and expression in speech. All the life he knew was the dull round of the village, all the speech he knew was the talk of the cottage, that failed and collapsed at the bare outline of his least gigantic need. He knew nothing of money, this monstrous simpleton, nothing of trade, nothing of the complex pretences upon which the social fabric of the little folks was built. He needed, he needed — Whatever he needed, he never found his need.

All through the day and the summer night he wandered, growing hungry but as yet untired, marking the varied traffic of the different streets, the inexplicable businesses of all these infinitesimal beings. In the aggregate it had no other colour than confusion for him. . . .

He is said to have plucked a lady from her carriage in Kensington, a lady in evening dress of the smartest sort, to have scrutinised her closely, train and shoulder blades, and to have replaced her — a little carelessly — with the profoundest sigh. For that I cannot vouch. For an hour or so he watched people fighting for places in the omnibuses at the end of Piccadilly. He was seen looming over Kennington Oval for some moments in the afternoon, but when he saw these dense thousands were engaged with the mystery of cricket and quite regardless of him he went his way with a groan.

He came back to Piccadilly Circus between eleven and twelve at night and found a new sort of multitude. Clearly they were very intent: full of things they, for inconceivable reasons, might do, and of others they might not do. They stared at him and jeered at him and went their way. The

cabmen, vulture-eyed, followed one another continually along the edge of the swarming pavement. People emerged from the restaurants or entered them, grave, intent, dignified, or gently and agreeably excited, or keen and vigilant — beyond the cheating of the sharpest waiter born. The great giant, standing at his corner, peered at them all. "What is it all for?" he murmured in a mournful vast undertone, "What is it all for? They are all so earnest. What is it I do not understand?"

And none of them seemed to see, as he could do, the drink-sodden wretchedness of the painted women at the corner, the ragged misery that sneaked along the gutters, the infinite futility of all this employment. The infinite futility! None of them seemed to feel the shadow of that giant's need, that shadow of the future, that lay athwart their paths. . . .

Across the road high up mysterious letters flamed and went, that might, could he have read them, have measured for him the dimensions of human interest, have told him of the fundamental needs and features of life as the little folks conceived it. First would come a flaming

T;
Then U would follow.
T U;
Then P,
T U P;

Until at last there stood complete, across the sky, this cheerful message to all who felt the burthen of life's earnestness:

TUPPER'S TONIC WINE FOR VIGOUR.

Snap! and it had vanished into night, to be followed in the same slow development by a second universal solicitude:

BEAUTY SOAP.

Not, you remark, mere cleansing chemicals, but something, as they say, "ideal"; and then, completing the tripod of the little life:

YANKER'S YELLOW PILLS.

After that there was nothing for it but Tupper again, in flaming crimson letters, snap, snap, across the void.

T U P P : : : :

Early in the small hours it would seem that young Caddles came to the shadowy quiet of Regent's Park, stepped over the railings and lay down on a grassy slope near where the people skate in winter time, and there he slept an hour or so. And about six o'clock in the morning he was talking to a draggled woman he had found sleeping in a ditch near Hampstead Heath, asking her very earnestly what she thought she was for. . . .

§ 4

THE WANDERING of Caddles about London came to a head on the second day in the morning. For then his hunger overcame him. He hesitated where the hot-smelling loaves were being tossed into a cart, and then very quietly knelt down and commenced robbery. He emptied the cart while

the baker's man fled for the police, and then his great hand came into the shop and cleared counter and cases. Then with an armful, still eating, he went his way looking for another shop to go on with his meal. It happened to be one of those seasons when work is scarce and food dear, and the crowd in that quarter was sympathetic even with a giant who took the food they all desired. They applauded the second phase of his meal, and laughed at his stupid grimace at the policeman.

"I woff hungry," he said, with his mouth full.

"Brayvo!" cried the crowd. "Brayvo!"

Then when he was beginning his third baker's shop, he was stopped by half a dozen policemen hammering with truncheons at his shins. "Look here, my fine giant, you come along o' me," said the officer in charge. "You ain't allowed away from home like this. You come off home with me."

They did their best to arrest him. There was a trolley, I am told, chasing up and down the streets at that time, bearing rolls of chain and ships' cable to play the part of handcuffs in that great arrest. There was no intention then of killing him. "He is no party to the plot," Caterham had said. "I will not have innocent blood upon my hands."

At first Caddles did not understand the import of these attentions. When he did, he told the policemen not to be fools and set off in great strides that left them all behind. The bakers' shops

had been in the Harrow Road, and he went through canal London to St. John's Wood and sat down in a private garden there to pick his teeth and be speedily assailed by another posse of constables.

"You lea' me alone," he growled, and slouched through the gardens — spoiling several lawns and kicking down a fence or so, while the energetic little policemen followed him up, some through the gardens, some along the road in front of the houses. Here there were one or two with guns, but they made no use of them. When he came out into the Edgware Road there was a new note and a new movement in the crowd, and a mounted policeman rode over his foot and got upset for his pains.

"You lea' me alone," said Caddles, facing the breathless crowd. "I've done nothing to you."

At that time he was unarmed, for he had left his chalk chopper in Regent's Park. But now, poor wretch, he seems to have felt the need of some weapon. He turned back towards the goods yard of the Great Western Railway, wrenched up the standard of a tall arc light, a formidable mace for him, and flung it over his shoulder. And finding the police still turning up to pester him, he went back along the Edgware Road, towards Cricklewood, and struck off sullenly to the north.

He wandered as far as Waltham, and then turned back westward and then again towards London, and came by the cemeteries and over the crest of Highgate about midday into view of

the greatness of the city again. He turned aside, and sat down in a garden with his back to a house that overlooked all London. He was breathless, and his face was lowering, and now the people no longer crowded upon him as they had done when first he came to London, but lurked in the adjacent garden, and peeped from cautious securities. They knew by now the thing was grimmer than they had thought. "Why can't they lea' me alone?" growled young Caddles. "I *mus'* eat. Why can't they lea' me alone?"

He sat with a darkling face, gnawing at his knuckles and looking down over London. All the fatigue, worry, perplexity, and impotent wrath of his wanderings was coming to a head in him. "They mean nothing," he whispered. "They mean nothing. And they *won't* let me alone, and they *will* get in my way." And again, over and over to himself, "meanin' nothing.

"Ugh! the little people!"

He bit harder at his knuckles and his scowl deepened. "Cuttin' chalk for 'em," he whispered. "And all the world is theirs! *I* don't come in — anywhere."

Presently with a spasm of sick anger he saw the now familiar form of a policeman astride the garden wall.

"Lea' me alone," grunted the giant. "Lea' me alone."

"I got to do my duty," said the little policeman, with a face that was white and resolute.

"You lea' me alone. I got to live as well as you. I got to think. I got to eat. You lea' me alone."

"It's the Law," said the little policeman, coming no further. "We never made the Law."

"Nor me," said young Caddles. "Your little people made all that before I was born. You and your law! What I must and what I mustn't. No food for me to eat unless I work a slave, no rest, no shelter, nothin', and you tell me —"

"I ain't got no business with that," said the policeman. "I'm not one to argue. All I got to do is to carry out the law," and he brought his second leg over the wall and seemed disposed to get down. Other policemen appeared behind him.

"I got no quarrel with *you* — mind," said young Caddles, with his grip tight upon his huge mace of iron, his face pale, and a lank explanatory great finger to the policeman. "I got no quarrel with you. But — *You lea' me alone.*"

The policeman tried to be calm and commonplace, with a monstrous tragedy clear before his eyes. "Give me the proclamation," he said to some unseen follower, and a little white paper was handed to him.

"Lea' me alone," said Caddles, scowling, tense, and drawn together.

"This means," said the policeman before he read, "go 'ome. Go 'ome to your chalk pit. If not, you'll be hurt."

Caddles gave an inarticulate growl.

Then when the proclamation had been read, the officer made a sign. Four men with rifles came into view and took up positions of affected ease along the wall.

They wore the uniforms of the rat police. At the sight of the guns, young Caddles blazed into anger. He remembered the sting of the Wreckstone farmers' shotguns. "You going to shoot off those at me?" he said, pointing, and it seemed to the officer he must be afraid.

"If you don't march back to your pit —"

Then in an instant the officer had slung himself back over the wall, and sixty feet above him the great electric standard whirled down to his death. Bang, bang, bang, went the heavy guns, and smash! the shattered wall, the soil and sub-soil of the garden flew. Something flew with it, that left red drops on one of the shooter's hands. The riflemen dodged this way and that and turned valiantly to fire again. But young Caddles, already shot twice through the body, had spun about to find who it was had hit him so heavily in the back. Bang! Bang! He had a vision of houses and green-houses and gardens, of people dodging at windows, the whole swaying fearfully and mysteriously. He seems to have made three stumbling strides, to have raised and dropped his huge mace, and to have clutched his chest. He was stung and wrenched by pain.

What was this, warm and wet, on his hand? . . .

One man peering from a bedroom window saw his face, saw him staring, with a grimace of weeping dismay, at the blood upon his hand, and then his knees bent under him, and he came crashing to the earth, the first of the giant nettles to fall to Caterham's resolute clutch, the very last that he had reckoned would come into his hand.

CHAPTER 4

REDWOOD'S TWO DAYS

§ 1

So soon as Caterham knew the moment for grasping his nettle had come, he took the law into his own hands and sent to arrest Cossar and Redwood.

Redwood was there for the taking. He had been undergoing an operation in the side, and the doctors had kept all disturbing things from him until his convalescence was assured. Now they had released him. He was just out of bed, sitting in a fire-warmed room with a heap of newspapers about him, reading for the first time of the agitation that had swept the country into the hands of Caterham, and of the trouble that was darkening over the Princess and his son. It was in the morning of the day when young Caddles died, and when the policeman tried to stop young Redwood on his way to the Princess. The latest newspapers Redwood had did but vaguely prefigure these imminent things. He was.

re-reading these first adumbrations of disaster with a sinking heart, reading the shadow of death more and more perceptibly into them, reading to occupy his mind until further news should come. When the officers followed the servant into his room, he looked up eagerly.

" I thought it was an early evening paper," he said. Then standing up, and with a swift change of manner: "What's this? . . ."

After that Redwood had no news of anything for two days.

They had come with a vehicle to take him away, but when it became evident that he was ill, it was decided to leave him for a day or so until he could be safely removed, and his house was taken over by the police and converted into a temporary prison. It was the same house in which Giant Redwood had been born and in which Herakleophorbia had for the first time been given to a human being, and Redwood had now been a widower and had lived alone in it eight years.

He had become an iron-grey man, with a little pointed grey beard and still active brown eyes. He was slender and soft-voiced, as he had ever been, but his features had now that indefinable quality that comes of brooding over mighty things. To the arresting officer his appearance was in impressive contrast to the enormity of his offences. "Here's this feller," said the officer in command, to his next subordinate, "has done his level best to bust up everything, and 'e's got a face like a quiet country gentleman; and here's Judge Hangbrow keep-

in' everything nice and in order for everyone, and 'e's got a 'ead like a 'og. Then their manners! One all consideration and the other snort and grunt. Which just shows you, doesn't it, that appearances aren't to be gone upon, whatever else you do."

But his praise of Redwood's consideration was presently dashed. The officers found him troublesome at first until they had made it clear that it was useless for him to ask questions or beg for papers. They made a sort of inspection of his study indeed, and cleared away even the papers he had. Redwood's voice was high and expostulatory. "But don't you see," he said over and over again, "it's my son, my only son, that is in this trouble. It isn't the Food I care for, but my son."

" I wish indeed I could tell you, Sir," said the officer. "But our orders are strict."

"Who gave the orders?" cried Redwood.

"Ah, *that,* Sir —" said the officer, and moved towards the door.

" 'E's going up and down 'is room," said the second officer, when his superior came down. "That's all right. He'll walk it off a bit."

" I hope 'e will," said the chief officer. "The fact is I didn't see it in that light before, but this here Giant what's been going on with the Princess, you know, is this man's son."

The two regarded one another and the third policeman for a space.

"Then it is a bit rough on him," the third policeman said.

It became evident that Redwood had still imperfectly apprehended the fact that an iron curtain had dropped between him and the outer world. They heard him go to the door, try the handle and rattle the lock, and then the voice of the officer who was stationed on the landing telling him it was no good to do that. Then afterwards they heard him at the windows and saw the men outside looking up. " It's no good that way," said the second officer. Then Redwood began upon the bell. The senior officer went up and explained very patiently that it could do no good to ring the bell like that, and if it was rung for nothing now it might have to be disregarded presently when he had need of something. " Any reasonable attendance, Sir," the officer said. " But if you ring it just by way of protest we shall be obliged, Sir, to disconnect."

The last word the officer heard was Redwood's high-pitched, " But at least you might tell me if my son —"

§ 2

AFTER that Redwood spent most of his time at the windows.

But the windows offered him little of the march of events outside. It was a quiet street at all times, and that day it was unusually quiet. Scarcely a cab, scarcely a tradesman's cart passed all that morning. Now and then men went by — without any distinctive air of events — now and then a little group of children, a nursemaid and a woman going shopping, and so forth. They came on to the stage right or left, up or down the street, with an exasperating suggestion of indifference to any concerns more spacious than their own; they would discover the police-guarded house with amazement and exit in the opposite direction, where the great trusses of a giant hydrangea hung across the pavement, staring back or pointing. Now and then a man would come and ask one of the policeman a question and get a curt reply. . . .

Opposite the houses seemed dead. A housemaid appeared once at a bedroom window and stared for a space, and it occurred to Redwood to signal to her. For a time she watched his gestures as if with interest and made a vague response to them, then looked over her shoulder suddenly and turned and went away. An old man hobbled out of Number 37 and came down the steps and went off to the right, altogether without looking up. For ten minutes the only occupant of the road was a cat. . . .

With such events that interminable momentous morning lengthened out.

About twelve there came a bawling of news-vendors from the adjacent road; but it passed. Contrary to their wont they left Redwood's street alone, and a suspicion dawned upon him that the police were guarding the end of the street. He tried to open the window, but this brought a policeman into the room forthwith. . . .

The clock of the parish church struck twelve, and after an abyss of time — one.

They mocked him with lunch.

He ate a mouthful and tumbled the food about a little in order to get it taken away, drank freely of whisky, and then took a chair and went back to the window. The minutes expanded into grey immensities, and for a time perhaps he slept. . . .

He awoke with a vague impression of remote concussions. He perceived a rattling of the windows like the quiver of an earthquake, that lasted for a minute or so and died away. Then after a silence it returned. . . . Then it died away again. He fancied it might be merely the passage of some heavy vehicle along the main road. What else could it be? . . .

After a time he began to doubt whether he had heard this sound.

He began to reason interminably with himself. Why after all was he seized? Caterham had been in office two days — just long enough — to grasp his Nettle! Grasp his Nettle! Grasp his Giant Nettle! The refrain once started, sang through his mind and would not be dismissed.

What after all could Caterham do? He was a religious man. He was bound in a sort of way by that not to do violence without a cause.

Grasp his Nettle! Perhaps for example the Princess was to be seized and sent abroad. There might be trouble with his son. In which case — ! But why had he been arrested? Why was it necessary to keep him in ignorance of a thing like that? The thing suggested — something more extensive.

Perhaps, for example — they meant to lay all the giants by the heels. They were all to be arrested together. There had been hints of that in the election speeches. And then?

No doubt they had got Cossar also?

Caterham was a religious man. Redwood clung to that. The back of his mind was a black curtain, and on that curtain there came and went a word — a word written in letters of fire. He struggled perpetually against that word. It was always as it were beginning to get written on the curtain and never getting completed.

He faced it at last. "Massacre!" There was the word in its full brutality.

No! No! No! It was impossible! Caterham was a religious man, a civilised man. And besides after all these years, after all these hopes!

Redwood sprang up; he paced the room. He spoke to himself; he shouted.

"*No!*"

Mankind was surely not so mad as that — surely not! It was impossible, it was incredible, it could not be. What good would it do, to kill the giant human when the gigantic in all the lower things had now inevitably come? They could not be so mad as that!

"I must dismiss such an idea," he said aloud; "dismiss such an idea! Absolutely!"

He pulled up short. What was that?

Certainly the windows had rattled. He went to look out into the street. Opposite he saw the

instant confirmation of his ears. At a bedroom at Number 35 was a woman, towel in hand, and at the dining-room of Number 37 a man was visible behind a great vase of hypertrophied maiden-hair fern, both staring out and up, both disquieted and curious. He could see now too quite clearly that the policeman on the pavement had heard it also. The thing was not his imagination.

He turned to the darkling room.

"Guns," he said.

He brooded.

"Guns?"

They brought him in strong tea, such as he was accustomed to have. It was evident his housekeeper had been taken into consultation. After drinking it, he was too restless to sit any longer at the window and he paced the room. His mind became more capable of consecutive thought.

The room had been his study for four and twenty years. It had been furnished at his marriage, and all the essential equipment dated from then, the large complex writing desk, the rotating chair, the easy chair at the fire, the rotating bookcase, the fixture of indexed pigeon-holes that filled the further recess. The vivid Turkey carpet, the later Victorian rugs and curtains had mellowed now to a rich dignity of effect, and copper and brass shone warm about the open fire. Electric lights had replaced the lamp of former days; that was the chief alteration in the original equipment. But among these things his connection with the Food had left abundant traces.

Along one wall, above the dado, ran a crowded array of black-framed photographs and photogravures, showing his son and Cossar's sons and others of the Boom-children at various ages and amidst various surroundings. Even young Caddles' vacant visage had its place in that collection. In the corner stood a sheaf of the tassels of gigantic meadow grass from Cheasing Eyebright, and on the desk there lay three empty poppy heads as big as hats. The curtain rods were grass stems. And the tremendous skull of the great hog of Oakham hung, a portentous ivory overmantle, with a Chinese jar in either eye socket, snout down above the fire. . . .

It was to the photographs that Redwood went, and in particular to the photographs of his son.

They brought back countless memories of things that had passed out of his mind, of the early days of the Food, of Bensington's timid presence, of his cousin Jane, of Cossar and the night work at the Experimental Farm. These things came to him now very little and bright and distinct, like things seen through a telescope on a sunny day. And then there was the giant nursery, the giant childhood, the young giant's first efforts to speak, his first clear signs of affection.

Guns?

It flowed in on him, irresistibly, overwhelmingly, that outside there, outside this accursed silence and mystery, his son and Cossar's sons and all these glorious first fruits of a greater age were even now — fighting. Fighting for life! Even now his son

might be in some dismal quandary, cornered, wounded, overcome. . . .

He swung away from the pictures and went up and down the room gesticulating. "It cannot be," he cried, "it cannot be! It cannot end like that!

"What was that?"

He stopped, stricken rigid.

The trembling of the windows had begun again, and then had come a thud — a vast concussion that shook the house. The concussion seemed to last for an age. It must have been very near. For a moment it seemed that something had struck the house above him — an enormous impact that broke into a tinkle of falling glass and then a stillness that ended at last with a minute clear sound of running feet in the street below.

Those feet released him from his rigor. He turned towards the window and saw it starred and broken.

His heart beat high with a sense of crisis, of conclusive occurrence, of release. And then again, his realisation of impotent confinement fell about him like a curtain!

He could see nothing outside except that the small electric lamp opposite was not lighted; he could hear nothing after the first suggestion of a wide alarm. He could add nothing to interpret or enlarge that mystery except that presently there came a reddish fluctuating brightness in the sky towards the south-east.

This light waxed and waned. When it waned he doubted if it had ever waxed. It had crept upon him very gradually with the darkling. It became the predominant fact in his long night of suspense. Sometimes it seemed to him it had the quiver one associates with dancing flames; at others he fancied it was no more than the normal reflection of the evening lights. It waxed and waned through the long hours and only vanished at last when it was submerged altogether under the rising tide of dawn. Did it mean — ? What could it mean? Almost certainly it was some sort of fire, near or remote, but he could not even tell whether it was smoke or cloud drift that streamed across the sky. But about one o'clock there began a flickering of searchlights athwart that ruddy tumult, a flickering that continued for the rest of the night. That too might mean many things? What could it mean? What did it mean? Just this stained unrestful sky he had and the suggestion of a huge explosion to occupy his mind. There came no further sounds, no further running, nothing but a shouting that might have been only the efforts of distant drunken men. . . .

He did not turn up his lights! He stood at his draughty broken window a distressful, slight black outline to the officer who looked ever and again into the room and exhorted him to rest.

All night Redwood remained at his window peering up at the ambiguous drift of the sky, and only with the coming of the dawn did he obey his fatigue and lie down upon the little bed they had prepared for him between

his writing desk and the sinking fire in the fireplace under the great hog's skull.

§3

FOR thirty-six long hours did Redwood remain imprisoned, closed in and shut off from the great drama of the Two Days, while the little people in the dawn of greatness fought against the Children of the Food. Then abruptly the iron curtain rose again and he found himself near the very centre of the struggle. That curtain rose as unexpectedly as it had fallen. In the late afternoon he was called to the window by the clatter of a cab, that stopped without. A young man descended and in another minute stood before him in the room, a slightly built young man of thirty perhaps, clean shaven, well dressed, well mannered.

"Mr. Redwood, Sir," he began, "would you be willing to come to Mr. Caterham? He needs your presence very urgently."

"Needs my presence! . . . " There leapt a question into Redwood's mind, that for a moment he could not put. He hesitated. Then in a voice that broke he asked: "What has he done to my Son?" and stood breathless for the reply.

"Your son, Sir? Your son is doing well. So at least we gather."

"Doing well?"

"He was wounded, Sir, yesterday. Have you not heard?"

Redwood smote these pretences aside. His voice was no longer coloured by fear, but by anger. "You know I have not heard. You know I have heard nothing."

"Mr. Caterham feared, Sir — It was a time of upheaval. Everyone — taken by surprise. He arrested you to save you, Sir, from any misadventure — "

"He arrested me to prevent my giving any warning or advice to my son. Go on. Tell me what has happened. Have you succeeded? Have you killed them all?"

The young man made a pace or so towards the window, and turned.

"No, Sir," he said concisely.

"What have you to tell me?"

"It's our proof, Sir, that this fighting was not planned by us. They found us . . . totally unprepared."

"You mean?"

"I mean, Sir, the giants have — to a certain extent — held their own."

The world changed for Redwood. For a moment something like hysteria had the muscles of his face and throat. Then he gave vent to a profound "Ah!" His heart bounded towards exultation. "The giants have held their own!"

"There has been terrible fighting — terrible destruction. It is all a most hideous misunderstanding. . . . In the north and midlands giants have been killed. . . . Everywhere."

"They are fighting now?"

"No, Sir. There was a flag of truce."

"From them?"

"No, Sir. Mr. Caterham sent a flag of truce. The whole thing is a hideous misunderstanding. That is why he wants to talk to you, and put his case before you.

They insist, Sir, that you should intervene—"

Redwood interrupted. "Do you know what happened to my son?" he asked.

"He was wounded."

"Tell me! Tell me!"

"He and the Princess came— before the—the movement to surround the Cossar camp was complete—the Cossar pit at Chislehurst. They came suddenly, Sir, crashing through a dense thicket of giant oats, near River, upon a column of infantry. . . . Soldiers had been very nervous all day, and this produced a panic."

"They shot him?"

"No, Sir. They ran away. Some shot at him—wildly—against orders."

Redwood gave a note of denial.

"It's true, Sir. Not on account of your son, I won't pretend, but on account of the Princess."

"Yes. That's true."

"The two giants ran shouting towards the encampment. The soldiers ran this way and that, and then some began firing. They say they saw him stagger—"

"Ugh!"

"Yes, Sir. But we know he is not badly hurt."

"How?"

"He sent the message, Sir, that he was doing well!"

"To me?"

"Who else, Sir?"

Redwood stood for nearly a minute with his arms tightly folded, taking this in. Then his indignation found a voice.

"Because you were fools in doing the thing, because you miscalculated and blundered, you would like me to think you are not murderers in intention. And besides—The rest?"

The young man looked interrogation.

"The other giants?"

The young man made no further pretence of misunderstanding. His tone fell. "Thirteen, Sir, are dead."

"And others wounded?"

"Yes, Sir."

"And Caterham," he gasped, "wants to meet me! . . . Where are the others?"

"Some got to the encampment during the fighting, Sir. . . . They seem to have known—"

"Well, of course they did. If it hadn't been for Cossar—Cossar is there?"

"Yes, Sir. And all the surviving giants are there—the ones who didn't get to the camp in the fighting have gone, or are going now under the flag of truce."

"That means," said Redwood, "that you are beaten."

"We are not beaten. No, Sir. You cannot say we are beaten. But your sons have broken the rules of war. Once last night, and now again. After our attack had been withdrawn. This afternoon they began to bombard London—"

"That's legitimate!"

"They have been firing shells filled with—poison."

"Poison?"

"Yes. Poison. The Food—"

"Herakleophorbia?"

"Yes, Sir. Mr. Caterham, Sir—"

"You are beaten! Of course that beats you. It's Cossar! What

can you hope to do now? What good is it to do anything now? You will breathe it in the dust of every street. What is there to fight for more? Rules of War, indeed! and now Caterham wants to humbug me to help him bargain. Good heavens, man! Why should I come to your exploded windbag? He has played his game . . . murdered and muddled. Why should I?"

The young man stood with an air of vigilant respect.

"It is a fact, Sir," he interrupted, "that the giants insist that they shall see you. They will have no ambassador but you. Unless you come to them, I am afraid, Sir, there will be more bloodshed."

"On *your* side, perhaps."

"No, Sir — on both sides. The world is resolved the thing must end."

Redwood looked about the study. His eyes rested for a moment on the photograph of his boy. He turned and met the expectation of the young man.

"Yes," he said at last, "I will come."

§4

His encounter with Caterham was entirely different from his anticipation. He had seen the man only twice in his life, once at dinner and once in the lobby of the House, and his imagination had been active not with the man but with the creation of the newspapers and caricaturists, the legendary Caterham, Jack the Giant-killer, Perseus, and all the rest of it. The element of a human personality came in to disorder all that.

Here was not the face of the caricatures and portraits, but the face of a worn and sleepless man, lined and drawn, yellow in the whites of the eyes, a little weakened about the mouth. Here, indeed, were the red-brown eyes, the black hair, the distinctive aquiline profile of the great demagogue, but here was also something else that smote any premeditated scorn and rhetoric aside. This man was suffering; he was suffering acutely; he was under enormous stress. From the beginning he had an air of impersonating himself. Presently, with a single gesture, the slightest movement, he revealed to Redwood that he was keeping himself up with drugs. He moved a thumb to his waistcoat pocket, and then, after a few sentences more, threw concealment aside, and slipped the little tabloid to his lips.

Moreover, in spite of the stresses upon him, in spite of the fact that he was in the wrong, and Redwood's junior by a dozen years, that strange quality in him, the something — personal magnetism one may call it for want of a better name — that had won his way for him to this eminence of disaster was with him still. On that also Redwood had failed to reckon. From the first, so far as the course and conduct of their speech went, Caterham prevailed over Redwood. All the quality of the first phase of their meeting was determined by him, all the tone and procedure was his. That happened as if it was a matter of course. All Redwood's expectations vanished at his presence. He shook hands before Redwood re-

membered that he meant to parry that familiarity; he pitched the note of their conference from the outset, sure and clear, as a search for expedients under a common catastrophe.

If he made any mistake it was when ever and again his fatigue got the better of his immediate attention, and the habit of the public meeting carried him away. Then he drew himself up — through all their interview both men stood — and looked away from Redwood, and began to fence and justify. Once even he said " Gentlemen! "

Quietly, expandingly, he began to talk. . . .

There were moments when Redwood ceased even to feel himself an interlocutor, when he became the mere auditor of a monologue. He became the privileged spectator of an extraordinary phenomenon. He perceived something almost like a specific difference between himself and this being whose beautiful voice enveloped him, who was talking, talking. This mind before him was so powerful and so limited. From its driving energy, its personal weight, its invincible oblivion to certain things, there sprang up in Redwood's mind the most grotesque and strange of images. Instead of an antagonist who was a fellow creature, a man one could hold morally responsible, and to whom one could address reasonable appeals, he saw Caterham as something, something like a monstrous rhinoceros, as it were, a civilised rhinoceros begotten of the jungle of democratic affairs, a monster of irresistible onset and invincible resistance. In all the crashing conflicts of that tangle he was supreme. And beyond? This man was a being supremely adapted to make his way through multitudes of men. For him there was no fault so important as self-contradiction, no science so significant as the reconciliation of "interests." Economic realities, topographical necessities, the barely touched mines of scientific expedients existed for him no more than railways or rifled guns or geographical literature exist for his animal prototype. What did exist were gatherings, and caucuses, and votes — above all votes. He was votes incarnate — millions of votes.

And now in the great crisis, with the giants broken but not beaten, this vote-monster talked.

It was so evident that even now he had everything to learn. He did not know there were physical laws and economic laws, quantities and reactions that all humanity voting *nemine contradicente* cannot vote away, and that are disobeyed only at the price of destruction. He did not know there are moral laws that cannot be bent by any force of glamour, or are bent only to fly back with vindictive violence. In the face of shrapnel or the Judgment Day, it was evident to Redwood that this man would have sheltered behind some curiously dodged vote of the House of Commons.

What most concerned his mind now was not the powers that held the fastness away there to the south, not defeat and death, but the effect of these things upon his Majority, the cardinal reality in

his life. He had to defeat the giants or go under. He was by no means absolutely despairful. In this hour of his utmost failure, with blood and disaster upon his hands, and the rich promise of still more horrible disaster, with the gigantic destinies of the world towering and toppling over him, he was capable of a belief that by sheer exertion of his voice, by explaining and qualifying and restating, he might yet reconstitute his power. He was puzzled and distressed no doubt, fatigued and suffering, but if only he could keep up, if only he could keep talking—

As he talked he seemed to Redwood to advance and recede, to dilate and contract. Redwood's share of the talk was of the most subsidiary sort, wedges, as it were suddenly thrust in. "That's all nonsense." "No." "It's no use suggesting that." "Then why did you begin?"

It is doubtful if Caterham really heard him at all. Round such interpolations Caterham's speech flowed indeed like some swift stream about a rock. There this incredible man stood, on his official hearthrug, talking, talking with enormous power and skill, talking as though a pause in his talk, his explanations, his presentation of standpoints and lights, of considerations and expedients, would permit some antagonistic influence to leap into being — into vocal being, the only being he could comprehend. There he stood amidst the slightly faded splendours of that official room in which one man after another had succumbed to

the belief that a certain power of intervention was the creative control of an empire. . . .

The more he talked the more certain Redwood's sense of stupendous futility grew. Did this man realise that while he stood and talked there, the whole great world was moving, that the invincible tide of growth flowed and flowed, that there were any hours but parliamentary hours, or any weapons in the hands of the Avengers of Blood? Outside, darkling the whole room, a single leaf of giant Virginian creeper tapped unheeded on the pane.

Redwood became anxious to end this amazing monologue, to escape to sanity and judgment, to that beleaguered camp, the fastness of the future, where, at the very nucleus of greatness, the Sons were gathered together. For that this talking was endured. He had a curious impression that unless this monologue ended he would presently find himself carried away by it, that he must fight against Caterham's voice as one fights against a drug. Facts had altered and were altering beneath that spell.

What was the man saying?

Since Redwood had to report it to the Children of the Food, in a sort of way he perceived it did matter. He would have to listen and guard his sense of realities as well as he could.

Much about bloodguiltiness. That was eloquence. That didn't matter. Next?

He was suggesting a convention!

He was suggesting that the surviving Children of the Food

should capitulate and go apart and form a community of their own. There were precedents, he said, for this. "We would assign them territory—"

"Where?" interjected Redwood, stooping to argue.

Caterham snatched at that concession. He turned his face to Redwood's, and his voice fell to a persuasive reasonableness. That could be determined. That he contended was a quite subsidiary question. Then he went on to stipulate: "And except for them and where they are we must have absolute control, the Food and all the Fruits of the Food must be stamped out—"

Redwood found himself bargaining: "The Princess?"

"She stands apart."

"No," said Redwood, struggling to get back to the old footing. "That's absurd."

"That afterwards. At any rate we are agreed that the making of the Food must stop—"

"I have agreed to nothing. I have said nothing—"

"But on one planet, to have two races of men, one great, one small! Consider what has happened! Consider that it is but a little foretaste of what might presently happen if this Food has its way! Consider all you have already brought upon this world! If there is to be a race of giants, increasing and multiplying—"

"It is not for me to argue," said Redwood. "I must go to our sons. I want to go to my son. That is why I have come to you. Tell me exactly what you offer."

Caterham made a speech upon his terms.

The Children of the Food were to be given a great reservation — in North America perhaps or Africa — in which they might live out their lives in their own fashion.

"But it's nonsense," said Redwood. "There are other giants now abroad. All over Europe — here and there!"

"There could be an international convention. It's *not* impossible. Something of the sort indeed has already been spoken of. . . . But in this reservation they can live out their own lives in their own way. They may do what they like; they may make what they like. We shall be glad if they will make us things. They may be happy. Think!"

"Provided there are no more children."

"Precisely. The children are for us. And so, Sir, we shall save the world, we shall save it absolutely from the fruits of your terrible discovery. It is not too late for us. Only we are eager to temper expediency with mercy. Even now we are burning and searing the places their shells hit yesterday. We can get it under. Trust me we shall get it under. But in that way, without cruelty, without injustice—"

"And suppose the Children do not agree?"

For the first time Caterham looked Redwood fully in the face.

"They must!"

"I don't think they will."

"Why should they not agree?" he asked, in richly toned amazement.

"Suppose they don't?"

"What can it be but war? We cannot have the thing go on. We cannot, Sir. Have you scientific men *no* imagination? Have you no mercy? We cannot have our world trampled under a growing herd of such monsters and monstrous growths as your Food has made. We cannot and we cannot! I ask you, Sir, what can it be but war? And remember — this that has happened is only a beginning! *This* was a skirmish. A mere affair of police. Believe me, a mere affair of police. Do not be cheated by perspective, by the immediate bigness of these newer things. Behind us is the nation — is humanity. Behind the thousands who have died there are millions. Were it not for the fear of bloodshed, Sir, behind our first attacks there would be forming other attacks, even now. Whether we can kill this Food or not, most assuredly we can kill your sons! You reckon too much on the things of yesterday, on the happenings of a mere score of years, on one battle. You have no sense of the slow course of history. I offer this convention for the sake of lives, not because it can change the inevitable end. If you think that your poor two dozen of giants can resist all the forces of our people and of all the alien peoples who will come to our aid; if you think you can change Humanity at a blow, in a single generation, and alter the nature and stature of Man —"

He flung out an arm. "Go to them now, Sir! See them, for all the evil they have done, crouching among their wounded —"

He stopped, as though he had glanced at Redwood's son by chance.

There came a pause.

"Go to them," he said.

"That is what I want to do."

"Then go now. . . ."

He turned and pressed the button of a bell; without, in immediate response, came a sound of opening doors and hastening feet.

The talk was at an end. The display was over. Abruptly Caterham seemed to contract, to shrivel up into a yellow-faced, fagged-out, middle-sized, middle-aged man. He stepped forward, as if he were stepping out of a picture, and with a complete assumption of that friendliness that lies behind all the public conflicts of our race, he held out his hand to Redwood.

As if it were a matter of course, Redwood shook hands with him for the second time.

CHAPTER 5

THE GIANT LEAGUER

§1

PRESENTLY Redwood found himself in a train going south over the Thames. He had a brief vision of the river shining under its lights, and of the smoke still going up from the place where

the shell had fallen on the north bank, and where a vast multitude of men had been organised to burn the Herakleophorbia out of the ground. The southern bank was dark, for some reason even the streets were not lit; all that was clearly visible were the outlines of the tall alarm-towers and the dark bulks of flats and schools, and after a minute of peering scrutiny he turned his back on the window and sank into thought. There was nothing more to see or do until he saw the Sons. . . .

He was fatigued by the stresses of that last two days; it seemed to him that his emotions must needs be exhausted, but he had fortified himself with strong coffee before starting, and his thoughts ran thin and clear. His mind touched many things. He reviewed again, but now in the enlightenment of accomplished events, the manner in which the Food had entered and unfolded itself in the world.

"Bensington thought it might be an excellent food for infants," he whispered to himself, with a faint smile. Then there came into his mind as vivid as if they were still unsettled his own horrible doubts after he had committed himself by giving it to his own son. From that, with a steady unfaltering expansion, in spite of every effort of men, to help and hinder, the Food had spread through the whole world of man. And now?

"Even if they kill them all," Redwood whispered, "the thing is done."

The secret of its making was known far and wide. That had been his own work. Plants, animals, a multitude of distressful growing children would conspire irresistibly to force the world to revert again to the Food, whatever happened in the present struggle. "The thing is done," he said, with his mind swinging round beyond all his controlling to rest upon the present fate of the Children and his son. Would he find them exhausted by the efforts of the battle, wounded, starving, on the verge of defeat, or would he find them still stout and hopeful, ready for the still grimmer conflict of the morrow? . . . His son was wounded! But he had sent a message!

His mind came back to his interview with Caterham.

He was roused from his thoughts by the stopping of his train in Chislehurst station. He recognised the place by the huge rat-alarm tower that crested Camden Hill, and the row of blossoming giant hemlocks that lined the road. . . .

Caterham's private secretary came to him from the other carriage and told him that half a mile further the line had been wrecked and that the rest of the journey was to be made in a motor car. Redwood descended upon a platform lit only by a hand lantern and swept by the cool night breeze. The quiet of that derelict, wood-set, weed-embedded suburb — for all the inhabitants had taken refuge in London at the outbreak of yesterday's conflict — became instantly impressive. His conductor took him down the steps to

where a motor car was waiting with blazing lights — the only lights to be seen — handed him over to the care of the driver and bade him farewell.

"You will do your best for us," he said, with an imitation of his master's manner, as he held Redwood's hand.

So soon as Redwood could be wrapped about, they started out into the night. At one moment they stood still, and then the motor car was rushing softly and swiftly down the station incline. They turned one corner and another, followed the windings of a lane of villas, and then before them stretched the road. The motor droned up to its topmost speed, and the black night swept past them. Everything was very dark under the starlight, and the whole world crouched mysteriously and was gone without a sound. Not a breath stirred the flying things by the wayside; the deserted, pallid white villas on either hand with their black unlit windows reminded him of a noiseless procession of skulls. The driver beside him was a silent man, or stricken into silence by the conditions of his journey. He answered Redwood's brief questions in monosyllables, and gruffly. Athwart the southern sky the beams of searchlights waved noiseless passes; the sole strange evidences of life they seemed in all that derelict world about the hurrying machine.

The road was presently bordered on either side by gigantic blackthorn shoots that made it very dark, and by tall grass and big campions, huge giant dead-nettles as high as trees, flickering past darkly in silhouette overhead. Beyond Keston they came to a rising hill, and the driver went slow. At the crest he stopped. The engine throbbed and became still. "There," he said, and his big gloved finger pointed, a black misshapen thing, before Redwood's eyes.

Far away as it seemed the great embankment, crested by the blaze from which the searchlights sprang, rose up against the sky. Those beams went and came among the clouds and the hilly land about them as if they traced mysterious incantations.

"I don't know," said the driver at last, and it was clear he was afraid to go on.

Presently a searchlight swept down the sky to them, stopped as it were with a start, scrutinised them, a blinding stare confused rather than mitigated by an intervening monstrous weed stem or so. They sat with their gloves held over their eyes, trying to look under them and meet that light.

"Go on," said Redwood after a while.

The driver still had his doubts; he tried to express them and died down to "I don't know" again.

At last he ventured on. "Here goes," he said, and roused his machinery to motion again, followed intently by that great white eye.

To Redwood it seemed for a long time they were no longer on earth, but passing in a state of palpitating hurry through a luminous cloud. Teuf, teuf, teuf, teuf, went the machine, and ever

and again—obeying I know not what nervous impulse—the driver sounded his horn.

They passed into the welcome darkness of a high-fenced lane, and down into a hollow and past some houses into that blinding stare again. Then for a space the road ran naked across a down, and they seemed to hang throbbing in immensity. Once more giant weeds rose about them and whirled past. Then quite abruptly close upon them loomed the figure of a giant, shining brightly where the searchlight caught him below and black against the sky above. "Hullo there!" he cried, and "Stop! There's no more road beyond. . . . Is that Father Redwood?"

Redwood stood up and gave a vague shout by way of answer, and then Cossar was in the road beside him, gripping both hands with both of his and pulling him out of the car.

"What of my son?" asked Redwood.

"He's all right," said Cossar. "They've hurt nothing serious in *him*."

"And your lads?"

"Well. All of them, well. But we've had to make a fight for it."

The giant was saying something to the motor driver. Redwood stood aside as the machine wheeled round, and then suddenly Cossar vanished, everything vanished, and he was in absolute darkness for a space. The glare was following the motor back to the crest of the Keston hill. He watched the little conveyance receding in that white

halo. It had a curious effect, as though it was not moving at all and the halo was. A group of war-blasted giant elder trees flashed into gaunt scarred gesticulations and were swallowed again by the night. . . . Redwood turned to Cossar's dim outline again and clasped his hand. "I have been shut up and kept in ignorance," he said, "for two whole days."

"We fired the Food at them," said Cossar. "Obviously! Thirty shots. Eh!"

"I come from Caterham."

"I know you do." He laughed with a note of bitterness. "I suppose he's wiping it up."

§ 2

"Where is my son?" said Redwood.

"He is all right. The giants are waiting for your message."

"Yes, but my son—"

He passed with Cossar down a long slanting tunnel that was lit red for a moment and then became dark again, and came out presently into the great pit of shelter the giants had made.

Redwood's first impression was of an enormous arena bounded by very high cliffs and with its floor greatly encumbered. It was in darkness save for the passing reflections of the watchman's searchlights that whirled perpetually high overhead, and for a red glow that came and went from a distant corner where two giants worked together amidst a metallic clangour. Against the sky, as the glare came about, his eye caught the familiar outlines of the old work-

sheds and playsheds that were made for the Cossar boys. They were hanging now, as it were, at a cliff brow, and strangely twisted and distorted with the guns of Caterham's bombardment. There were suggestions of huge gun emplacements above there, and nearer were piles of mighty cylinders that were perhaps ammunition. All about the wide space below, the forms of great engines and incomprehensible bulks were scattered in vague disorder. The giants appeared and vanished among these masses and in the uncertain light; great shapes they were, not disproportionate to the things amidst which they moved. Some were actively employed, some sitting and lying as if they courted sleep, and one near at hand, whose body was bandaged, lay on a rough litter of pine boughs and was certainly asleep. Redwood peered at these dim forms; his eyes went from one stirring outline to another.

"Where is my son, Cossar?"

Then he saw him.

His son was sitting under the shadow of a great wall of steel. He presented himself as a black shape recognisable only by his pose—his features were invisible. He sat chin upon hand, as though weary or lost in thought. Beside him Redwood discovered the figure of the Princess, the dark suggestion of her merely, and then, as the glow from the distant iron returned, he saw for an instant, red-lit and tender, the infinite kindliness of her shadowed face. She stood looking down upon her lover with her hand resting against the steel. It seemed that she whispered to him.

Redwood would have gone towards them.

"Presently," said Cossar. "First there is your message."

"Yes," said Redwood, "but—"

He stopped. His son was now looking up and speaking to the Princess, but in too low a tone for them to hear. Young Redwood raised his face and she bent down towards him, and glanced aside before she spoke.

"But if we are beaten," they heard the whispered voice of young Redwood.

She paused, and the red blaze showed her eyes bright with unshed tears. She bent nearer him and spoke still lower. There was something so intimate and private in their bearing, in their soft tones, that Redwood, Redwood who had thought for two whole days of nothing but his son, felt himself intrusive there. Abruptly he was checked. For the first time in his life perhaps he realised how much more a son may be to his father than a father can ever be to a son; he realised the full predominance of the future over the past. Here between these two he had no part. His part was played. He turned to Cossar, in the instant realisation. Their eyes met. His voice was changed to the tone of a grey resolve.

"I will deliver my message now," he said. "Afterwards—... It will be soon enough then."

The pit was so enormous and so encumbered that it was a long and tortuous route to the place

from which Redwood could speak to them all.

He and Cossar followed a steeply descending way that passed beneath an arch of interlocking machinery, and so came into a vast deep gangway that ran athwart the bottom of the pit. This gangway, wide and vacant, and yet relatively narrow, conspired with everything about it to enhance Redwood's sense of his own littleness. It became as it were an excavated gorge. High overhead, separated from him by cliffs of darkness, the searchlights wheeled and blazed, and the shining shapes went to and fro. Giant voices called to one another above there, calling the giants together to the Council of War, to hear the terms that Caterham had sent. The gangway still inclined downward towards black vastnesses, towards shadows and mysteries and inconceivable things, into which Redwood went slowly with reluctant footsteps and Cossar with a confident stride. . . .

Redwood's thoughts were busy. The two men passed into the completest darkness, and Cossar took his companion's wrist. They went now slowly perforce.

Redwood was moved to speak. "All this," he said, "is strange."

"Big," said Cossar.

"Strange. And strange that it should be strange to me — I who am, in a sense, the beginning of it all. It's —"

He stopped, wrestling with his elusive meaning, and threw an unseen gesture at the cliff.

"I have not thought of it before. I have been busy, and the years have passed. But here I see — It is a new generation, Cossar, and new emotions and new needs. All this, Cossar —"

Cossar saw now his dim gesture to the things about them.

"All this is Youth."

Cossar made no answer, and his irregular footfalls went striding on.

"It isn't *our* youth, Cossar. They are taking things over. They are beginning upon their own emotions, their own experiences, their own way. We have made a new world, and it isn't ours. This great place —"

"I planned it," said Cossar, his face close.

"But now?"

"Ah! I have given it to my sons."

Redwood could feel the loose wave of the arm that he could not see.

"That is it. We are over — or almost over."

"Your message!"

"Yes. And then —"

"We're over."

"Well — ?"

"Of course we are out of it, we two old men," said Cossar, with his familiar note of sudden anger. "Of course we are. Obviously. Each man for his own time. And now — it's *their* time beginning. That's all right. Excavator's gang. We do our job and go. See? That is what Death is for. We work out all our little brains and all our little emotions, and then this lot begins afresh. Fresh and fresh! Perfectly simple. What's the trouble?"

He paused to guide Redwood to some steps.

"Yes," said Redwood, "but one feels —"

He left his sentence incompleted.

"That is what Death is for." He heard Cossar insisting below him, "How else could the thing be done? That is what Death is for."

§ 3

AFTER devious windings and ascents they came out upon a projecting ledge from which it was possible to see over the greater extent of the giants' pit, and from which Redwood might make himself heard by the whole of their assembly. The giants were already gathered below and about him at different levels, to hear the message he had to deliver. The eldest son of Cossar stood on the bank overhead watching the revelations of the searchlights, for they feared a breach of the truce. The workers at the great apparatus in the corner stood out clear in their own light; they were near stripped; they turned their faces towards Redwood, but with a watchful reference ever and again to the castings that they could not leave. He saw these nearer figures with a fluctuating indistinctness, by lights that came and went, and the remoter ones still less distinctly. They came from and vanished again into the depths of great obscurities. For these giants had no more light than they could help in the pit, that their eyes might be ready to see effectually any attacking force that might spring upon them out of the darkness around.

Ever and again some chance glare would pick out and display this group or that of tall and powerful forms, the giants from Sunderland clothed in overlapping metal plates, and the others clad in leather, in woven rope or in woven metal, as their conditions had determined. They sat amidst or rested their hands upon, or stood erect among machines and weapons as mighty as themselves, and all their faces, as they came and went from visible to invisible, had steadfast eyes.

He made an effort to begin and did not do so. Then for a moment his son's face glowed out in a hot insurgence of the fire, his son's face looking up to him, tender as well as strong; and at that he found a voice to reach them all, speaking across a gulf as it were to his son.

"I come from Caterham," he said. "He sent me to you, to tell you the terms he offers."

He paused. "They are impossible terms I know, now that I see you here all together; they are impossible terms, but I brought them to you, because I wanted to see you all — and my son. Once more. . . . I wanted to see my son. . . ."

"Tell them the terms," said Cossar.

"This is what Caterham offers. He wants you to go apart and leave his world!"

"Where?"

"He does not know. Vaguely somewhere in the world a great region is to be set apart. . . . And you are to make no more of the Food, to have no children of your own, to live in your own

way for your own time, and then to end for ever."

He stopped.

"And that is all?"

"That is all."

There followed a great stillness. The darkness that veiled the giants seemed to look thoughtfully at him.

He felt a touch at his elbow, and Cossar was holding a chair for him—a queer fragment of doll's furniture amidst these piled immensities. He sat down and crossed his legs, and then put one across the knee of the other, and clutched his boot nervously, and felt small and self-conscious and acutely visible and absurdly placed.

Then at the sound of a voice he forgot himself again.

"You have heard, Brothers," said this voice out of the shadows.

And another answered, "We have heard."

"And the answer, Brothers?"

"To Caterham?"

"Is No!"

"And then?"

There was a silence for the space of some seconds.

Then a voice said: "These people are right. After their lights, that is. They have been right in killing all that grew larger than its kind, beast and plant and all manner of great things that arose. They were right in trying to massacre us. They are right now in saying we must not marry our kind. According to their lights they are right. They know—it is time that we also knew—that you cannot have pigmies and giants in one world together. Caterham has said that again and

again—clearly—their world or ours."

"We are not half a hundred now," said another, "and they are endless millions."

"So it may be. But the thing is as I have said."

Then another long silence.

"And are we to die then?"

"God forbid!"

"Are they?"

"No."

"But that is what Caterham says! He would have us live out our lives, die one by one, till only one remains, and that one at last would die also, and they would cut down all the giant plants and weeds, kill all the giant underlife, burn out the traces of the Food—make an end to us and to the Food for ever. Then the little pigmy world would be safe. They would go on—safe for ever, living their little pigmy lives, doing pigmy kindnesses and pigmy cruelties each to the other; they might even perhaps attain a sort of pigmy millennium, make an end to war, make an end to overpopulation, sit down in a worldwide city to practise pigmy arts, worshipping one another till the world begins to freeze. . . ."

In the corner a sheet of iron fell in thunder to the ground.

"Brothers, we know what we mean to do."

In a spluttering of light from the searchlights Redwood saw earnest youthful faces turning to his son.

"It is easy now to make the Food. It would be easy for us to make Food for all the world."

"You mean, Brother Redwood," said a voice out of the

darkness, "that it is for the little people to eat the Food."

"What else is there to do?"

"We are not half a hundred and they are many millions."

"But we held our own."

"So far."

"If it is God's will, we may still hold our own."

"Yes. But think of the dead!" Another voice took up the strain. "The dead," it said. "Think of the unborn. . . ."

"Brothers," came the voice of young Redwood, "what can we do but fight them, and if we beat them, make them take the Food? They cannot help but take the Food now. Suppose we were to resign our heritage and do this folly that Caterham suggests! Suppose we could! Suppose we give up this great thing that stirs within us, repudiate this thing our fathers did for us, that *you,* Father, did for us, and pass, when our time has come, into decay and nothingness! What then? Will this little world of theirs be as it was before? They may fight against greatness in us who are the children of men, but can they conquer? Even if they should destroy us every one, what then? Would it save them? No! For greatness is abroad, not only in us, not only in the Food, but in the purpose of all things! It is in the nature of all things, it is part of space and time. To grow and still to grow, from first to last that is Being, that is the law of life. What other law can there be?"

"To help others?"

"To grow. It is still, to grow. Unless we help them to fail. . . ."

"They will fight hard to overcome us," said a voice.

And another, "What of that?"

"They will fight," said young Redwood. "If we refuse these terms, I doubt not they will fight. Indeed I hope they will be open and fight. If after all they offer peace, it will be only the better to catch us unawares. Make no mistake, Brothers; in some way or other they will fight. The war has begun, and we must fight to the end. Unless we are wise, we may find presently we have lived only to make them better weapons against our children and our kind. This, so far, has been only the dawn of battle. All our lives will be a battle. Some of us will be killed in battle, some of us will be waylaid. There is no easy victory, no victory whatever that is not more than half defeat for us. Be sure of that. What of that? If only we keep a foothold, if only we leave behind us a growing host to fight when we are gone!"

"And to-morrow?"

"We will scatter the Food; we will saturate the world with the Food."

"Suppose they come to terms?"

"Our terms are the Food. It is not as though little and great could live together in any perfection of compromise. It is one thing or the other. What right have parents to say, my child shall have no light but the light I have had, shall grow no greater than the greatness to which I have grown? Do I speak for you, Brothers?"

Assenting murmurs answered him.

"And to the children who will be women as well as to the children who will be men," said a voice from the darkness.

"Even more so — to be mothers of a new race. . . ."

"But for the next generation there must be great and little," said Redwood, with his eyes on his son's face.

"For many generations. And the little will hamper the great and the great press upon the little. So it must needs be, Father."

"There will be conflict."

"Endless conflict. Endless misunderstanding. All life is that. Great and little cannot understand one another. But in every child born of man, Father Redwood, lurks some seed of greatness — waiting for the Food."

"Then I am to go to Caterham again and tell him — "

"You will stay with us, Father Redwood. Our answer goes to Caterham at dawn."

"He says that he will fight. . . ."

"So be it," said young Redwood, and his brethren murmured assent.

"*The iron waits,*" cried a voice, and the two giants who were working in the corner began a rhythmic hammering that made a mighty music to the scene. The metal glowed out far more brightly than it had done before, and gave Redwood a clearer view of the encampment than had yet come to him. He saw the oblong space of its full extent, with the great engines of warfare ranged ready to hand. Beyond, and at a higher level, the house of the Cossars stood. About him were the young giants, huge and beautiful, glittering in their mail, amidst the preparations for the morrow. The sight of them lifted his heart. They were so easily powerful! They were so tall and gracious! They were so steadfast in their movements! There was his son amongst them, and the first of all giant women, the Princess. . . .

There leapt into his mind the oddest contrast, a memory of Bensington, very bright and little — Bensington with his hand amidst the soft breast feathers of that first great chick, standing in that conventionally furnished room of his, peering over his spectacles dubiously as Cousin Jane banged the door. . . .

It had all happened in a yesterday of one and twenty years.

Then suddenly a strange doubt took hold of him, that this place and present greatness were but the texture of a dream; that he was dreaming and would in an instant wake to find himself in his study again, the giants slaughtered, the Food suppressed, and himself a prisoner locked in. What else indeed was life but that — always to be a prisoner locked in! This was the culmination and end of his dream. He would wake through bloodshed and battle, to find his Food the most foolish of fancies, and his hopes and faith of a greater world to come no more than the coloured film upon a pool of bottomless decay. Littleness invincible! . . .

So strong and deep was this wave of despondency, this suggestion of impending disillusion-

ment, that he started to his feet. He stood and pressed his clenched fists into his eyes, and so for a moment remained, fearing to open them again and see, lest the dream should already have passed away. . . .

The voice of the giant children spoke to one another, an undertone to that clangorous melody of the smiths. His tide of doubt ebbed. He heard the giant voices; he heard their movements about him still. It was real, surely it was real — as real as spiteful acts! More real, for these great things, it may be, are coming things, and the littleness, bestiality, and infirmity of men are the things that go. He opened his eyes.

"Done," cried one of the two ironworkers, and they flung their hammers down.

A voice sounded above. The son of Cossar standing on the great embankment had turned and was now speaking to them all.

"It is not that we would oust the little people from the world," he said, "in order that we, who are no more than one step upwards from their littleness, may hold their world for ever. It is the step we fight for and not ourselves. . . . We are here, Brothers, to what end? To serve the spirit of the purpose that has been breathed into our lives. We fight not for ourselves — for we are but the momentary hands and eyes of the Life of the World. So you, Father Redwood, taught us. Through us and through the little folk the Spirit looks and learns. From us by word and birth and act it must pass — to

still greater lives. This earth is no resting place; this earth is no playing place, else indeed we might put our throats to the little people's knife, having no greater right to live than they. And they in turn might yield to the ants and vermin. We fight not for ourselves but for growth, growth that goes on for ever. To-morrow, whether we live or die, growth will conquer through us. That is the law of the spirit for evermore. To grow according to the will of God! To grow out of these cracks and crannies, out of these shadows and darknesses, into greatness and the light! Greater," he said, speaking with slow deliberation, "greater, my Brothers! And then — still greater. To grow and again — to grow. To grow at last into the fellowship and understanding of God. Growing. . . . Till the earth is no more than a footstool. . . . Till the spirit shall have driven fear into nothingness, and spread. . . ." He swung his arms heavenward — "*There!*"

His voice ceased. The white glare of one of the searchlights wheeled about, and for a moment fell upon him, standing out gigantic with hand upraised against the sky.

For one instant he shone, looking up fearlessly into the starry deeps, mail-clad, young and strong, resolute and still. Then the light had passed and he was no more than a great black outline against the starry sky, a great black outline that threatened with one mighty gesture the firmament of heaven and all its multitude of stars.

Drawn by Cyrus Cuneo.

" 'MOTHER,' HE WOULD SAY, 'IF IT'S GOOD TO WORK, WHY DOESN'T EVERYONE WORK?' "

Drawn by Cyrus Cuneo, 1904 for THE FOOD OF THE GODS.

"BROUGHT HOME ON THE MILKMAN'S HAND-TRUCK."

Drawn by Cyrus Cuneo, 1903 for *THE FOOD OF THE GODS.*

IN THE DAYS OF THE COMET

PROLOGUE

THE MAN WHO WROTE IN THE TOWER

I SAW a grey-haired man, a figure of hale age, sitting at a desk and writing.

He seemed to be in a room in a tower, very high, so that through the tall window on his left one perceived only distances, a remote horizon of sea, a headland, and that vague haze and glitter in the sunset that many miles away marks a city. All the appointments of this room were orderly and beautiful, and in some subtle quality, in this small difference and that, new to me and strange. They were in no fashion I could name, and the simple costume the man wore suggested neither period nor country. It might, I thought, be the Happy Future, or Utopia; an errant mote of memory, Henry James's phrase and story of " The Great Good Place," twinkled across my mind, and passed and left no light.

The man I saw wrote with a thing like a fountain pen, a modern touch that prohibited any historical reference, and as he finished each sheet, writing in an easy flowing hand, he added it to a growing pile upon a graceful little table under the win-

dow. His last done sheets lay loose, partly covering others that were clipped together into fascicles.

Clearly he was unaware of my presence, and I stood waiting until his pen should come to a pause. Old as he certainly was he wrote with a steady hand. . . .

I discovered that a concave speculum hung slantingly high over his head; a movement in this caught my attention sharply, and I looked up to see, distorted and made fantastic but bright and beautifully coloured, the magnified, reflected, evasive rendering of a palace, of a terrace, of the vista of a great roadway with many people, people exaggerated, impossible-looking because of the curvature of the mirror, going to and fro. I turned my head quickly that I might see more clearly through the window behind me, but it was too high for me to survey this nearer scene directly, and after a momentary pause I came back to that distorting mirror again.

But now the writer was leaning back in his chair. He put down his pen and sighed the half resentful sigh — " ah! you work, you! how you gratify and tire me! " — of a man who has been writing to his satisfaction.

" What is this place," I asked, " and who are you? "

He looked around with the quick movement of surprise.

" *What is this place?* " *I repeated,* " *and where am I?* "

He regarded me steadfastly for a moment under his wrinkled brows, and then his expression softened to a smile. He pointed to a chair beside the table. " *I am writing,*" *he said.*

" *About this?* "

" *About the Change.*"

I sat down. It was a very comfortable chair, and well placed under the light.

" *If you would like to read —* " *he said.*

I indicated the manuscript. " *This explains?* " *I asked.*

" *That explains,*" *he answered.*

He drew a fresh sheet of paper towards him as he looked at me.

I glanced from him about his apartment and back to the little table. A fascicle marked very distinctly " *1* " *caught my attention, and I took it up. I smiled in his friendly eyes.* " *Very well,*" *said I, suddenly at my ease, and he nodded and went on writing. And in a mood between confidence and curiosity, I began to read.*

This is the story that happy, active-looking old man in that pleasant place had written.

The World's Great Age begins anew,
The Golden Years return,
The Earth doth like a Snake renew
Her Winter Skin outworn:
Heaven smiles, and Faiths and Empires gleam
Like Wrecks of a Dissolving Dream.

IN THE DAYS OF THE COMET

Book I: *The Comet*

CHAPTER 1

DUST IN THE SHADOWS

§ 1

I HAVE set myself to write the story of the Great Change, so far as it has affected my own life and the lives of one or two people closely connected with me, primarily to please myself.

Long ago, in my crude unhappy youth, I conceived a desire to write a book. To scribble secretly and dream of authorship was one of my chief alleviations, and I read with a sympathetic envy every scrap I could get about the world of literature and the lives of literary people. It is something even amidst this present happiness, to find leisure and opportunity to take up and partially realise these old and hopeless dreams. But that alone, in a world where so much of vivid and increasing interest presents itself to be done, even by an old man, would not, I think, suffice to set me at this desk. I find some such recapitulation of my past as this will involve, is becoming necessary to my own secure mental continuity. The passage of years brings a man at last to retrospection; at seventy-two one's youth is far more important that it was at forty. And I am out of touch with my youth. The old life seems so cut off from the new, so alien and so unreasonable, that at times I find it bordering upon the incredible. The data have gone, the buildings and places. I stopped dead the other afternoon in my walk across the moor, where once the dismal outskirts of Swathinglea straggled towards Leet, and asked, "Was it here indeed that I crouched among the weeds and refuse and broken crockery and loaded my revolver ready for murder? Did ever such a thing happen in my life? Was such a mood and thought and intention ever possible to me? Rather, has not some queer nightmare spirit out of dreamland slipped a pseudo-memory into the records of my vanished life?" There must be many alive still

who have the same perplexities. And I think too that those who are now growing up to take our places in the great enterprise of mankind, will need many such narratives as mine for even the most partial conception of the old world shadows that came before our day. It chances too that my case is fairly typical of the Change; I was caught midway in a gust of passion; and a curious accident put me for a time in the very nucleus of the new order. . . .

My memory takes me back across the interval of fifty years to a little ill-lit room with a sash window open to a starry sky, and instantly there returns to me the characteristic smell of that room, the penetrating odour of an ill-trimmed lamp, burning cheap paraffin. Lighting by electricity had then been perfected for fifteen years, but still the larger portion of the world used these lamps. All this first scene will go, in my mind at least, to that olfactory accompaniment. That was the evening smell of the room. By day it had a more subtle aroma, a closeness, a peculiar sort of faint pungency that I associate — I know not why — with dust.

Let me describe this room to you in detail. It was perhaps eight feet by seven in area and rather higher than either of these dimensions; the ceiling was of plaster, cracked and bulging in places, grey with the soot of the lamp, and in one place discoloured by a system of yellow and olive-green stains caused by the percolation of damp from above. The walls were covered with dun-coloured paper, upon which had

been printed in oblique reiteration a crimson shape, something of the nature of a curly ostrich feather, or an acanthus flower, that had in its less faded moments a sort of dingy gaiety. There were several big plaster-rimmed wounds in this, caused by Parload's ineffectual attempts to get nails into the wall, whereby there might hang pictures. One nail had hit between two bricks and got home, and from this depended, sustained a little insecurely by frayed and knotted blind-cord, Parload's hanging bookshelves, planks painted over with a treacly blue enamel and further decorated by a fringe of pinked American cloth insecurely fixed by tacks. Below this was a little table that behaved with a mulish vindictiveness to any knee that was thrust beneath it suddenly; it was covered with a cloth whose pattern of red and black had been rendered less monotonous by the accidents of Parload's versatile ink bottle, and on it, *leit motif* of the whole, stood and stank the lamp. This lamp, you must understand, was of some whitish translucent substance that was neither china nor glass, it had a shade of the same substance, a shade that did not protect the eyes of a reader in any measure, and it seemed admirably adapted to bring into pitiless prominence the fact that, after the lamp's trimming, dust and paraffin had been smeared over its exterior with reckless generosity.

The uneven floor boards of this apartment were covered with scratched enamel of chocolate hue, on which a small island of

frayed carpet dimly blossomed in the dust and shadows.

There was a very small grate, made of cast-iron in one piece and painted buff, and a still smaller misfit of a cast-iron fender that confessed the grey stone of the hearth. No fire was laid, only a few scraps of torn paper and the bowl of a broken corn-cob pipe were visible behind the bars, and in the corner and rather thrust away was an angular japanned coal-box with a damaged hinge. It was the custom in those days to warm every room separately from a separate fireplace, more prolific of dirt than heat, and the rickety sash window, the small chimney, and the loose-fitting door were expected to organise the ventilation of the room among themselves without any further direction.

Parload's truckle bed hid its grey sheets beneath an old patchwork counterpane on one side of the room, and veiled his boxes and such-like oddments, and invading the two corners of the window were an old whatnot and the washhandstand, on which were distributed the simple appliances of his toilet.

This washhandstand had been made of deal by someone with an excess of turnery appliances in a hurry, who had tried to distract attention from the rough economics of his workmanship by an arresting ornamentation of blobs and bulbs upon the joints and legs. Apparently the piece had then been placed in the hands of some person of infinite leisure equipped with a pot of ochreous paint, varnish, and a set of flexible combs. This person had first painted the article, then, I fancy, smeared it with varnish, and then sat down to work with the combs to streak and comb the varnish into a weird imitation of the grain of some nightmare timber. The washhandstand so made had evidently had a prolonged career of violent use, had been chipped, kicked, splintered, punched, stained, scorched, hammered, dessicated, damped, and defiled, had met indeed with almost every possible adventure except a conflagration or a scrubbing, until at last it had come to this high refuge of Parload's attic to sustain the simple requirements of Parload's personal cleanliness. There were, in chief, a basin and a jug of water and a slop-pail of tin, and, further, a piece of yellow soap in a tray, a tooth-brush, a rat-tailed shaving brush, one huckaback towel, and one or two other minor articles. In those days only very prosperous people had more than such an equipage, and it is to be remarked that every drop of water Parload used had to be carried by an unfortunate servant girl — the "slavey," Parload called her — up from the basement to the top of the house and subsequently down again. Already we begin to forget how modern an invention is personal cleanliness. It is a fact that Parload had never stripped for a swim in his life; never had a simultaneous bath all over his body since his childhood. Not one in fifty of us did in the days of which I am telling you.

A chest, also singularly grained and streaked, of two large and two small drawers, held Parload's

reserve of garments, and pegs on the door carried his two hats and completed this inventory of a "bed-sitting-room" as I knew it before the Change. But I had forgotten—there was also a chair with a "squab" that apologised inadequately for the defects of its cane seat. I forgot that for the moment because I was sitting on the chair on the occasion that best begins this story.

I have described Parload's room with such particularity because it will help you to understand the key in which my earlier chapters are written, but you must not imagine that this singular equipment or the smell of the lamp engaged my attention at that time to the slightest degree. I took all this grimy unpleasantness as if it were the most natural and proper setting for existence imaginable. It was the world as I knew it. My mind was entirely occupied then by graver and intenser matters, and it is only now in the distant retrospect that I see these details of environment as being remarkable, as significant, as indeed obviously the outward visible manifestations of the old world disorder in our hearts.

§ 2

PARLOAD stood at the open window, opera-glass in hand, and sought and found and was uncertain about and lost again, the new comet.

I thought the comet no more than a nuisance then because I wanted to talk of other matters. But Parload was full of it. My head was hot, I was feverish with

interlacing annoyances and bitterness, I wanted to open my heart to him—at least I wanted to relieve my heart by some romantic rendering of my troubles—and I gave but little heed to the things he told me. It was the first time I had heard of this new speck among the countless specks of heaven, and I did not care if I never heard of the thing again.

We were two youths much of an age together; Parload was two and twenty, and eight months older than I. He was—I think his proper definition was "engrossing clerk" to a little solicitor in Overcastle, while I was third in the office staff of Rawdon's pot-bank in Clayton. We had met first in the "Parliament" of the Young Men's Christian Association of Swathinglea; we had found we attended simultaneous classes in Overcastle, he in science and I in shorthand, and had started a practice of walking home together, and so our friendship came into being. (Swathinglea, Clayton, and Overcastle were contiguous towns, I should mention, in the great industrial area of the Midlands.) We had shared each other's secret of religious doubt, we had confided to one another a common interest in Socialism, he had come twice to supper at my mother's on a Sunday night, and I was free of his apartment. He was then a tall, flaxen-haired, gawky youth, with a disproportionate development of neck and wrist, and capable of vast enthusiasm; he gave two evenings a week to the evening classes of the organised science school in Overcastle,

physiography was his favourite "subject," and through this insidious opening of his mind the wonder of outer space had come to take possession of his soul. He had commandeered an old opera-glass from his uncle who farmed at Leet over the moors, he had bought a cheap paper planisphere and *Whitaker's Almanack,* and for a time day and moonlight were mere blank interruptions to the one satisfactory reality in his life — star-gazing. It was the deeps that had seized him, the immensities, and the mysterious possibilities that might float unlit in that unplumbed abyss. With infinite labour and the help of a very precise article in *The Heavens,* a little monthly magazine that catered for those who were under this obsession, he had at last got his opera-glass upon the new visitor to our system from outer space. He gazed in a sort of rapture upon that quivering little smudge of light among the shining pin-points — and gazed. My troubles had to wait for him.

"Wonderful," he sighed, and then as though his first emphasis did not satisfy him, "wonderful!"

He turned to me. "Wouldn't you like to see?"

I had to look, and then I had to listen, how that this scarce-visible intruder was to be, was presently to be, one of the largest comets this world has ever seen, how that its course must bring it within at most — so many score of millions of miles from the earth, a mere step, Parload seemed to think that; how that the spectroscope was already sounding its chemical secrets, perplexed by the unprecedented band in the green, how it was even now being photographed in the very act of unwinding — in an unusual direction — a sunward tail (which presently it wound up again), and all the while in a sort of undertow I was thinking first of Nettie Stuart and the letter she had just written me, and then of old Rawdon's detestable face as I had seen it that afternoon. Now I planned answers to Nettie and now belated repartees to my employer, and then again "Nettie" was blazing all across the background of my thoughts. . . .

Nettie Stuart was daughter of the head gardener of the rich Mr. Verrall's widow, and she and I had kissed and become sweethearts before we were eighteen years old. My mother and hers were second cousins and old schoolfellows, and though my mother had been widowed untimely by a train accident, and had been reduced to letting lodgings (she was the Clayton curate's landlady), a position esteemed much lower than that of Mrs. Stuart, a kindly custom of occasional visits to the gardener's cottage at Checkshill Towers still kept the friends in touch. Commonly I went with her. And I remember it was in the dusk of one bright evening in July, one of those long golden evenings that do not so much give way to night as admit at last, upon courtesy, the moon and a choice retinue of stars, that Nettie and I, at the pond of goldfish where the yew-bordered walks

converged, made our shy beginners' vow. I remember still — something will always stir in me at that memory — the tremulous emotion of that adventure. Nettie was dressed in white, her hair went off in waves of soft darkness from above her dark shining eyes; there was a little necklace of pearls about her sweetly modelled neck, and a little coin of gold that nestled in her throat. I kissed her half-reluctant lips, and for three years of my life thereafter — nay! I almost think for all the rest of her life and mine — I could have died for her sake.

You must understand — and every year it becomes increasingly difficult to understand — how entirely different the world was then from what it is now. It was a dark world; it was full of preventable disorder, preventable diseases, and preventable pain, of harshness and stupid unpremeditated cruelties; but yet, it may be even by virtue of the general darkness, there were moments of a rare and evanescent beauty that seem no longer possible in my experience. The great Change has come for evermore, happiness and beauty are our atmosphere, there is peace on earth and good will to all men. None would dare to dream of returning to the sorrows of the former time, and yet that misery was pierced, ever and again its grey curtain was stabbed through and through by joys of an intensity, by perceptions of a keenness that it seems to me are now altogether gone out of life. Is it the Change, I wonder, that has robbed life of its extremes, or is it perhaps only this, that youth has left me — even the strength of middle years leaves me now — and taken its despairs and raptures, leaving me judgment perhaps, sympathy, memories?

I cannot tell. One would need to be young now and to have been young then as well, to decide that impossible problem.

Perhaps a cool observer even in the old days would have found little beauty in our grouping. I have our two photographs at hand in this bureau as I write, and they show me a gawky youth in ill-fitting ready-made clothing, and Nettie — indeed Nettie is badly dressed, and her attitude is more than a little stiff; but I can see her through the picture, and her living brightness and something of that mystery of charm she had for me, comes back again to my mind. Her face had triumphed over the photographer — or I would long ago have cast this picture away.

The reality of beauty yields itself to no words. I wish that I had the sister art and could draw in my margin something that escapes description. There was a sort of gravity in her eyes. There was something, a matter of the minutest difference, about her upper lip so that her mouth closed sweetly and broke very sweetly to a smile. That grave, sweet smile!

After we had kissed and decided not to tell our parents for a while of the irrevocable choice we had made, the time came for us to part, shyly and before others, and I and my mother went off back across the moonlit park — the bracken thickets rus-

tling with startled deer — to the railway station at Checkshill and so to our dingy basement in Clayton, and I saw no more of Nettie — except that I saw her in my thoughts — for nearly a year. But at our next meeting it was decided that we must correspond, and this we did with much elaboration of secrecy, for Nettie would have no one at home, not even her only sister, know of her attachment. So I had to send my precious documents sealed and under cover by way of a confidential schoolfellow of hers who lived near London. . . . I could write that address down now, though house and street and suburb have gone beyond any man's tracing.

Our correspondence began our estrangement, because for the first time we came into more than sensuous contact and our minds sought expression.

Now you must understand that the world of thought in those days was in the strangest condition, it was choked with obsolete inadequate formulæ, it was tortuous to a maze-like degree with secondary contrivances and adaptations, suppressions, conventions, and subterfuges. Base immediacies fouled the truth on every man's lips. I was brought up by my mother in a quaint old-fashioned narrow faith in certain religious formulæ, certain rules of conduct, certain conceptions of social and political order, that had no more relevance to the realities and needs of everyday contemporary life than if they were clean linen that had been put away with lavender in a drawer. Indeed, her religion did actually smell of lavender; on Sundays she put away all the things of reality, the garments and even the furnishings of everyday, hid her hands, that were gnarled and sometimes chapped with scrubbing, in black, carefully mended gloves, assumed her old black silk dress and bonnet and took me, unnaturally clean and sweet also, to church. There we sang and bowed and heard sonorous prayers and joined in sonorous responses, and rose with a congregational sigh refreshed and relieved when the doxology, with its opening "Now to God the Father, God the Son," bowed out the tame, brief sermon. There was a hell in that religion of my mother's, a red-haired hell of curly flames that had once been very terrible; there was a devil, who was also *ex officio* the British King's enemy, and much denunciation of the wicked lusts of the flesh; we were expected to believe that most of our poor unhappy world was to atone for its muddle and trouble here by suffering exquisite torments for ever after, world without end, Amen. But indeed those curly flames looked rather jolly. The whole thing had been mellowed and faded into a gentle unreality long before my time; if it had much terror even in my childhood I have forgotten it, it was not so terrible as the giant who was killed by the Beanstalk, and I see it all now as a setting for my poor old mother's worn and grimy face, and almost lovingly as a part of her. And Mr. Gabbitas, our plump little lodger, strangely

transformed in his vestments and lifting his voice manfully to the quality of those Elizabethan prayers, seemed, I think, to give her a special and peculiar interest with God. She radiated her own tremulous gentleness upon Him, and redeemed Him from all the implications of vindictive theologians; she was in truth, had I but perceived it, the effectual answer to all she would have taught me.

So I see it now, but there is something harsh in the earnest intensity of youth; and having at first taken all these things quite seriously, the fiery hell and God's vindictiveness at any neglect, as though they were as much a matter of fact as Bladden's ironworks and Rawdon's pot-bank, I presently with an equal seriousness flung them out of my mind again.

Mr. Gabbitas, you see, did sometimes, as the phrase went, "take notice" of me, he had induced me to go on reading after I left school, and with the best intentions in the world and to anticipate the poison of the times, he had lent me Burble's "Scepticism Answered," and drawn my attention to the library of the Institute in Clayton.

The excellent Burble was a great shock to me. It seemed clear from his answers to the sceptic that the case for doctrinal orthodoxy and all that faded and by no means awful hereafter, which I had hitherto accepted as I accepted the sun, was an extremely poor one, and to hammer home that idea the first book I got from the Institute happened to be an American edition of the collected works of Shelley, his

gassy prose as well as his atmospheric verse. I was soon ripe for blatant unbelief. And at the Young Men's Christian Association I presently made the acquaintance of Parload, who told me, under promises of the most sinister secrecy, that he was "a Socialist out and out." He lent me several copies of a periodical with the clamant title of *The Clarion,* which was just taking up a crusade against the accepted religion. The adolescent years of any fairly intelligent youth lie open, and will always lie healthily open, to the contagion of philosophical doubts, of scorns and new ideas, and I will confess I had the fever of that phase badly. Doubt, I say, but it was not so much doubt — which is a complex thing — as startled emphatic denial. "Have I believed *this!*" And I was also, you must remember, just beginning love-letters to Nettie.

We live now in these days, when the Great Change has been in most things accomplished, in a time when everyone is being educated to a sort of intellectual gentleness, a gentleness that abates nothing from our vigour, and it is hard to understand the stifled and struggling manner in which my generation of common young men did its thinking. To think at all about certain questions was an act of rebellion that set one oscillating between the furtive and the defiant. People begin to find Shelley — for all his melody — noisy and ill-conditioned now because his Anarchs have vanished, yet there was a time when novel thought *had* to

go to that tune of breaking glass. It becomes a little difficult to imagine the yeasty state of mind, the disposition to shout and say, "Yah!" at constituted authority, to sustain a persistent note of provocation such as we raw youngsters displayed. I began to read with avidity such writing as Carlyle, Browning, and Heine have left for the perplexity of posterity, and not only to read and admire but to imitate. My letters to Nettie, after one or two genuinely intended displays of perfervid tenderness, broke out towards theology, sociology, and the cosmos in turgid and startling expressions. No doubt they puzzled her extremely.

I retain the keenest sympathy and something inexplicably near to envy for my own departed youth, but I should find it difficult to maintain my case against anyone who would condemn me altogether as having been a very silly, posturing, emotional hobbledehoy indeed and quite like my faded photograph. And when I try to recall what exactly must have been the quality and tenor of my more sustained efforts to write memorably to my sweetheart, I confess I shiver. . . . Yet I wish they were not all destroyed.

Her letters to me were simple enough, written in a roundish, unformed hand and badly phrased. Her first two or three showed a shy pleasure in the use of the word "dear," and I remember being first puzzled and then, when I understood, delighted, because she had written "Willie *asthore*" under my name. "Asthore," I gathered, meant "darling." But when the evidences of my fermentation began, her answers were less happy.

I will not weary you with the story of how we quarrelled in our silly youthful way, and how I went the next Sunday, all uninvited, to Checkshill, and made it worse, and how afterwards I wrote a letter that she thought was "lovely," and mended the matter. Nor will I tell of all our subsequent fluctuations of misunderstanding. Always I was the offender and the final penitent until this last trouble that was now beginning; and in between we had some tender near moments, and I loved her very greatly. There was this misfortune in the business, that in the darkness, and alone, I thought with great intensity of her, of her eyes, of her touch, of her sweet and delightful presence, but when I sat down to write I thought of Shelley and Burns and myself, and other such irrelevant matters. When one is in love in this fermenting way, it is harder to make love than it is when one does not love at all. And as for Nettie, she loved, I know, not me but those gentle mysteries. It was not my voice should rouse her dreams to passion. . . . So our letters continued to jar. Then suddenly she wrote me one doubting whether she could ever care for anyone who was a Socialist and did not believe in Church, and then hard upon it came another note with unexpected novelties of phrasing. She thought we were not suited to each other, we differed so in tastes and ideas, she

had long thought of releasing me from our engagement. In fact, though I really did not apprehend it fully at the first shock, I was dismissed. Her letter had reached me when I came home after old Rawdon's none too civil refusal to raise my wages. On this particular evening of which I write, therefore, I was in a state of feverish adjustment to two new and amazing, two nearly overwhelming facts, that I was neither indispensable to Nettie nor at Rawdon's. And to talk of comets!

Where did I stand!

I had grown so accustomed to think of Nettie as inseparably mine — the whole tradition of "true love" pointed me to that — that for her to face about with these precise small phrases towards abandonment, after we had kissed and whispered and come so close in the little adventurous familiarities of the young, shocked me profoundly. I! I! And Rawdon didn't find me indispensable either. I felt I was suddenly repudiated by the universe and threatened with effacement, that in some positive and emphatic way I must at once assert myself. There was no balm of the religion I had learned, or in the irreligion I had adopted, for wounded self-love.

Should I fling up Rawdon's place at once and then in some extraordinary, swift manner make the fortune of Frobisher's adjacent and closely competitive pot-bank?

The first part of that programme at any rate would be easy of accomplishment, to go to Rawdon and say, "You will hear from me again," but for the rest, Frobisher might fail me. That, however, was a secondary issue. The predominant affair was with Nettie. I found my mind thick-shot with flying fragments of rhetoric that might be of service in the letter I would write her. Scorn, irony, tenderness — what was it to be? . . .

"Bother!" said Parload suddenly.

"What?" said I.

"They're firing up at Bladden's iron-works, and the smoke comes right across my bit of sky."

The interruption came just as I was ripe to discharge my thoughts upon him.

"Parload," said I, "very likely I shall have to leave all this. Old Rawdon won't give me a rise in my wages, and after having asked I don't think I can stand going on upon the old terms any more. See? So I may have to clear out of Clayton for good and all."

§ 3

THAT made Parload put down the opera-glass and look at me.

"It's a bad time to change just now," he said after a little pause.

Rawdon had said as much, in a less agreeable tone.

But with Parload I felt always a disposition to the heroic note. "I'm tired," I said, "of humdrum drudgery for other men. One may as well starve one's body out of a place as starve one's soul in one."

"I don't know about that altogether," began Parload, slowly. . . .

And with that we began one of our interminable conversa-

tions, one of those long, wandering, intensely generalising, diffusely personal talks that will be dear to the hearts of intelligent youths until the world comes to an end. The Change has not abolished that, anyhow.

It would be an incredible feat of memory for me now to recall all that meandering haze of words, indeed I recall scarcely any of it, though its circumstances and atmosphere stand out, a sharp, clear picture in my mind. I posed after my manner and behaved very foolishly no doubt, a wounded, smarting egotist, and Parload played his part of the philosopher preoccupied with the deeps.

We were presently abroad, walking through the warm summer's night and talking all the more freely for that. But one thing that I said I can remember. "I wish at times," said I, with a gesture at the heavens, "that comet of yours or some such thing would indeed strike this world — and wipe us all away, strikes, wars, tumults, loves, jealousies, and all the wretchedness of life!"

"Ah!" said Parload, and the thought seemed to hang about him.

"It could only add to the miseries of life," he said irrelevantly when presently I was discoursing of other things.

"What would?"

"Collision with a comet. It would only throw things back. It would only make what was left of life more savage than it is at present."

"But why should *anything* be left of life?" said I. . . .

That was our style, you know, and meanwhile we walked together up the narrow street outside his lodging, up the stepway and the lanes towards Clayton Crest and the high road.

But my memories carry me back so effactually to those days before the Change that I forget that now all these places have been altered beyond recognition, that the narrow street and the stepway and the view from Clayton Crest, and indeed all the world in which I was born and bred and made, has vanished clean away, out of space and out of time, and well-nigh out of the imagination of all those who are younger by a generation than I. You cannot see, as I can see, the dark empty way between the mean houses, the dark empty way lit by a bleary gas-lamp at the corner, you cannot feel the hard checkered pavement under your boots, you cannot mark the dimly lit windows here and there, and the shadows upon the ugly and often patched and crooked blinds of the people cooped within. Nor can you presently pass the beerhouse with its brighter gas and its queer, screening windows, nor get a whiff of foul air and foul language from its door, nor see the crumpled furtive figure — some rascal child — that slinks past us down the steps.

We crossed the longer street, up which a clumsy steam tram, vomiting smoke and sparks, made its clangorous way, and adown which one saw the greasy brilliance of shop fronts and the naphtha flares of hawkers' barrows dripping fire into the night.

A hazy movement of people swayed along that road, and we heard the voice of an itinerant preacher from a waste place between the houses. You cannot see these things as I can see them, nor can you figure — unless you know the pictures that great artist Hyde has left the world — the effect of the hoarding by which we passed, lit below by a gas-lamp and towering up to a sudden sharp black edge against the pallid sky.

Those hoardings! They were the brightest coloured things in all that vanished world. Upon them, in successive layers of paste and paper, all the rough enterprises of that time joined in chromatic discord; pill vendors and preachers, theatres and charities, marvellous soaps and astonishing pickles, typewriting machines and sewing machines, mingled in a sort of visualised clamour. And passing that there was a muddy lane of cinders, a lane without a light, that used its many puddles to borrow a star or so from the sky. We splashed along unheeding as we talked.

Then across the allotments, a wilderness of cabbages and evil-looking sheds, past a gaunt abandoned factory, and so to the high-road. The high road ascended in a curve past a few houses and a beerhouse or so, and round until all the valley in which four industrial towns lay crowded and confluent was overlooked.

I will admit that with the twilight there came a spell of weird magnificence over all that land and brooded on it until dawn. The horrible meanness of its details was veiled, the hutches that were homes, the bristling multitudes of chimneys, the ugly patches of unwilling vegetation amidst the makeshift fences of barrel-stave and wire. The rusty scars that framed the opposite ridges where the iron ore was taken and the barren mountains of slag from the blast furnaces were veiled; the reek and boiling smoke and dust from foundry, pot-bank, and furnace, transfigured and assimilated by the night. The dust-laden atmosphere that was grey oppression through the day became at sundown a mystery of deep translucent colours of blues and purples, of sombre and vivid reds, of strange bright clearnesses of green and yellow athwart the darkling sky. Each upstart furnace, when its monarch sun had gone, crowned itself with flames, the dark cinder heaps began to glow with quivering fires, and each pot-bank squatted rebellious in a volcanic coronet of light. The empire of the day broke into a thousand feudal baronies of burning coal. The minor streets across the valley picked themselves out with gas-lamps of faint yellow, that brightened and mingled at all the principal squares and crossings with the greenish pallor of incandescent mantles and the high cold glare of the electric arc. The interlacing railways lifted bright signal-boxes over their intersections, and signal stars of red and green in rectangular constellations. The trains became articulated black serpents breathing fire. . . .

Moreover, high overhead, like

a thing put out of reach and near forgotten, Parload had rediscovered a realm that was ruled by neither sun nor furnace, the universe of stars.

This was the scene of many a talk we two had held together. And if in the day time we went right over the crest and looked westward there was farmland, there were parks and great mansions, the spire of a distant cathedral, and sometimes when the weather was near raining, the crests of remote mountains hung clearly in the sky. Beyond the range of sight indeed, out beyond, there was Checkshill; I felt it there always, and in the darkness more than I did by day. Checkshill, and Nettie!

And to us two youngsters, as we walked along the cinder path beside the rutted road and argued out our perplexities, it seemed that this ridge gave us compendiously a view of our whole world.

There on the one hand in a crowded darkness, about the ugly factories and work-places, the workers herded together, ill clothed, ill nourished, ill taught, badly and expensively served at every occasion in life, uncertain even of their insufficient livelihood from day to day, the chapels and churches and publichouses swelling up amidst their wretched homes like saprophytes amidst a general corruption, and on the other, in space, freedom, and dignity, scarce heeding the few cottages, as over-crowded as they were picturesque, in which the labourers festered, lived the landlords and masters who owned pot-banks and forge and farm and mine. Far away, distant, beautiful, irrelevant, from out of a little cluster of second-hand bookshops, ecclesiastical residences, and the inns and incidentals of a decaying market town, the cathedral of Lowchester pointed a beautiful, unemphatic spire to vague incredible skies. So it seemed to us that the whole world was planned in those youthful first impressions.

We saw everything simple, as young men will. We had our angry, confident solutions, and whosoever would criticise them was a friend of the robbers. It was a clear case of robbery, we held, visibly so; there in those great houses lurked the Landlord and the Capitalist, with his scoundrel the Lawyer, with his cheat the Priest, and we others were all the victims of their deliberate villainies. No doubt they winked and chuckled over their rare wines, amidst their dazzling, wickedly dressed women, and plotted further grinding for the faces of the poor. And amidst all the squalor on the other hand, amidst brutalities, ignorance, and drunkenness, suffered multitudinously their blameless victim, the Working Man. And we, almost at the first glance, had found all this out, it had merely to be asserted now with sufficient rhetoric and vehemence to change the face of the whole world. The Working Man would arise — in the form of a Labour Party, and with young men like Parload and myself to represent him — and come to his own, and then — ?

Then the robbers would get it

hot, and everything would be extremely satisfactory.

Unless my memory plays me strange tricks, that does no injustice to the creed of thought and action that Parload and I held as the final result of human wisdom. We believed it with heat, and rejected with heat the most obvious qualification of its harshness. At times in our great talks we were full of heady hopes for the near triumph of our doctrine, more often our mood was hot resentment at the wickedness and stupidity that delayed so plain and simple a reconstruction of the order of the world. Then we grew malignant, and thought of barricades and significant violence. I was very bitter, I know, upon this night of which I am now particularly telling; and the only face upon the hydra of capitalism and Monopoly that I could see at all clearly, smiled exactly as old Rawdon had smiled when he refused to give me more than a paltry twenty shillings a week.

I wanted intensely to salve my self-respect by some revenge upon him, and I felt that if that could be done by slaying the hydra, I might drag its carcass to the feet of Nettie, and settle my other trouble as well. "What do you think of me *now*, Nettie?"

That at any rate comes near enough to the quality of my thinking then, for you to imagine how I gesticulated and spouted to Parload that night. You see us as little black figures, unprepossessing in outline, set in the midst of that desolating night of flaming industrialism, and my little

voice with a rhetorical twang protesting, denouncing. . . .'.

You will consider those notions of my youth poor silly violent stuff; particularly if you are of the younger generation born since the Change you will be of that opinion. Nowadays the whole world thinks clearly, thinks with deliberation, pellucid certainties; you find it impossible to imagine how any other thinking could have been possible. Let me tell you then how you can bring yourself to something like the condition of our former state. In the first place you must get yourself out of health by unwise drinking and eating, and out of condition by neglecting your exercise; then you must contrive to be worried very much and made very anxious and uncomfortable, and then you must work very hard for four or five days and for long hours every day at something too petty to be interesting, too complex to be mechanical, and without any personal significance to you whatever. This done, get straightway into a room that is not ventilated at all, and that is already full of foul air, and there set yourself to think out some very complicated problem. In a little while you will find yourself in a state of intellectual muddle, annoyed, impatient, snatching at the obvious, presently choosing and rejecting conclusions haphazard. Try to play chess under such conditions and you will play stupidly and lose your temper. Try to do anything that taxes the brain or temper and you will fail.

Now the whole world before

the Change was as sick and fever-
ish as that; it was worried and
overworked and perplexed by
problems that would not get
stated simply, that changed and
evaded solution, it was in an at-
mosphere that had corrupted and
thickened past breathing; there
was no thorough cool thinking
in the world at all. There was
nothing in the mind of the world
anywhere but half-truths, hasty
assumptions, hallucinations, and
emotions. Nothing. . . .

I know it seems incredible, that
already some of the younger men
are beginning to doubt the great-
ness of the Change our world has
undergone, but read — read the
newspapers of that time. Every
age becomes mitigated and a lit-
tle ennobled in our minds as it
recedes into the past. It is the
part of those who like myself
have stories of that time to tell,
to supply, by a scrupulous spir-
itual realism, some antidote to
that glamour.

§ 4

ALWAYS with Parload I was chief
talker.

I can look back upon myself
with, I believe, an almost per-
fect detachment, things have so
changed that indeed now I am
another being, with scarce any-
thing in common with that boast-
ful foolish youngster whose trou-
bles I recall. I see him vulgarly
theatrical, egotistical, insincere;
indeed I do not like him save
with that instinctive material
sympathy that is the fruit of in-
cessant intimacy. Because he was
myself I may be able to feel and
write understandingly about mo-
tives that will put him out of
sympathy with nearly every
reader, but why should I palliate
or defend his quality?

Always, I say, I did the talk-
ing, and it would have amazed
me beyond measure if anyone
had told me that mine was not
the greater intelligence in these
wordy encounters. Parload was a
quiet youth, and stiff and re-
strained in all things, while I had
that supreme gift for young men
and democracies, the gift of copi-
ous expression. Parload I diag-
nosed in my secret heart as a
trifle dull; he posed as pregnant
quiet, I thought, and was ob-
sessed by the congenial notion of
" scientific caution." I did not
remark that while my hands were
chiefly useful for gesticulation or
holding a pen, Parload's hands
could do all sorts of things; and
I did not think therefore that
fibres must run from those fin-
gers to something in his brain.
Nor, though I bragged perpetu-
ally of my shorthand, of my liter-
ature, of my indispensable share
in Rawdon's business, did Par-
load lay stress on the conics and
calculus he " mugged " in the or-
ganised science school. Parload
is a famous man now, a great
figure in a great time, his work
upon intersecting radiations has
broadened the intellectual hori-
zon of mankind for ever; and I,
who am at best a hewer of intel-
lectual wood, a drawer of living
water, can smile, and he can
smile, to think how I patronised
and posed and jabbered over
him in the darkness of those early
days.

That night I was shrill and

eloquent beyond measure. Rawdon was, of course, the hub upon which I went round—Rawdon and the Rawdonesque employer and the injustice of "wages slavery" and all the immediate conditions of that industrial blind alley up which it seemed our lives were thrust. But ever and again I glanced at other things. Nettie was always there in the background of my mind, regarding me enigmatically. It was part of my pose to Parload that I had a romantic love-affair somewhere away beyond the sphere of our intercourse, and that note gave a Byronic resonance to many of the nonsensical things I produced for his astonishment.

I will not weary you with too detailed an account of the talk of a foolish youth who was also distressed and unhappy, and whose voice was balm for the humiliations that smarted in his eyes. Indeed now in many particulars I cannot disentangle this harangue of which I tell from many of the things I may have said in other talks to Parload. For example I forget if it was then or before or afterwards that, as it were by accident, I let out what might be taken as an admission that I was addicted to drugs.

"You shouldn't do that," said Parload, suddenly. "It won't do to poison your brains with that."

My brains, my eloquence, were to be very important assets to our party in the coming revolution. . . .

But one thing does clearly belong to this particular conversation I am recalling. When I started out it was quite settled in the back of my mind that I must not leave Rawdon's. I simply wanted to abuse my employer to Parload. But I talked myself quite out of touch with all the cogent reasons there were for sticking to my place, and I got home that night irrevocably committed to a spirited—not to say a defiant—policy with my employer.

"I can't stand Rawdon's much longer," I said to Parload by way of a flourish.

"There's hard times coming," said Parload.

"Next winter."

"Sooner. The Americans have been overproducing, and they mean to dump. The iron trade is going to have convulsions."

"I don't care. Pot-banks are steady."

"With a corner in borax? No. I've heard—"

"What have you heard?"

"Office secrets. But it's no secret there's trouble coming to potters. There's been borrowing and speculation. The masters don't stick to one business as they used to do. I can tell that much. Half the valley may be 'playing' before two months are out." Parload delivered himself of this unusually long speech in his most pithy and weighty manner.

"Playing" was our local euphemism for a time when there was no work and no money for a man, a time of stagnation and dreary hungry loafing day after day. Such interludes seemed in those days a necessary consequence of industrial organisation.

"You'd better stick to Rawdon's," said Parload.

"Ugh," said I, affecting a noble disgust.

"There'll be trouble," said Parload.

"Who cares?" said I. "Let there be trouble—the more the better. This system has got to end, sooner or later. These capitalists with their speculation and corners and trusts make things go from bad to worse. Why should I cower in Rawdon's office, like a frightened dog, while hunger walks the streets? Hunger is the master revolutionary. When he comes we ought to turn out and salute him. Anyway, *I'm* going to do so now."

"That's all very well," began Parload.

"I'm tired of it," I said. "I want to come to grips with all these Rawdons. I think perhaps if I was hungry and savage I could talk to hungry men—"

"There's your mother," said Parload, in his slow judicial way.

That *was* a difficulty.

I got over it by a rhetorical turn. "Why should one sacrifice the future of the world—why should one even sacrifice one's own future—because one's mother is totally destitute of imagination?"

§5

IT was late when I parted from Parload and came back to my own home.

Our house stood in a highly respectable little square near the Clayton parish church. Mr. Gabbitas, the curate of all work, lodged on our ground floor, and

upstairs there was an old lady, Miss Holroyd, who painted flowers on china and maintained her blind sister in an adjacent room; my mother and I lived in the basement and slept in the attics. The front of the house was veiled by a Virginian creeper that defined the Clayton air and clustered in untidy dependent masses over the wooden porch.

As I came up the steps I had a glimpse of Mr. Gabbitas printing photographs by candle light in his room. It was the chief delight of his little life to spend his holiday abroad in the company of a queer little snapshot camera, and to return with a great multitude of foggy and sinister negatives that he had made in beautiful and interesting places. These the camera company would develop for him on advantageous terms, and he would spend his evenings the year through in printing from them in order to inflict copies upon his undeserving friends. There was a long frameful of his work in the Clayton National School, for example, inscribed in old English lettering, "Italian Travel Pictures, by the Rev. E. B. Gabbitas." For this it seemed he lived and travelled and had his being. It was his only real joy. By his shaded light I could see his sharp little nose, his little pale eyes behind his glasses, his mouth pursed up with the endeavour of his employment. . . .

"Hireling Liar," I muttered, for was not he also part of the system, part of the scheme of robbery that made wages serfs of Parload and me?—though his

share in the proceedings was certainly small.

"Hireling Liar," said I, standing in the darkness, outside even his faint glow of travelled culture. . . .

My mother let me in.

She looked at me, mutely, because she knew there was something wrong and that it was no use for her to ask what.

"Good night, mummy," said I, and kissed her a little roughly, and lit and took my candle and went off at once up the staircase to bed, not looking at her.

"I've kept some supper for you, dear."

"Don't want any supper."

"But, dearie—"

"Good night, mother," and I went up and slammed my door upon her, blew out my candle, and lay down at once upon my bed, lay there a long time before I got up to undress.

There were times when that dumb beseeching of my mother's face irritated me unspeakably. It did so that night. I felt I had to struggle against it, that I could not exist if I gave way to its pleadings, and it hurt me and divided me to resist it, almost beyond endurance. It was clear to me that I had to think out for myself religious problems, social problems, questions of conduct, questions of expediency, that her poor dear simple beliefs could not help me at all—and she did not understand! Hers was the accepted religion, her only social ideas were blind submissions to the accepted order—to laws, to doctors, to clergymen, lawyers, masters, and all respectable persons in' authority over us, and

with her to believe was to fear. She knew from a thousand little signs—though still at times I went to church with her—that I was passing out of touch of all these things that ruled her life, into some terrible unknown. From things I said she could infer such clumsy concealments as I made. She felt my socialism, felt my spirit in revolt against the accepted order, felt the impotent resentments 'that filled me with bitterness against all she held sacred. Yet, you know, it was not her dear gods she sought to defend so much as me! She seemed always to be wanting to say to me, "Dear, I know it's hard—but revolt is harder. Don't make war on it, dear—don't! Don't do anything to offend it. I'm sure it will hurt you if you do—it will hurt you if you do."

She had been cowed into submission, as so many women of that time had been, by the sheer brutality of the accepted thing. The existing order dominated her into a worship of abject observances. It had bent her, aged her, robbed her of eyesight so that at fifty-five she peered through cheap spectacles at my face and saw it only dimly, filled her with a habit of anxiety, made her hands—Her poor dear hands! Not in the whole world now could you find a woman with hands so grimy, so needle-worn, so misshapen by toil, so chapped and coarsened, so evilly entreated. . . . At any rate, there is this I can say for myself, that my bitterness against the world and fortune was for her sake as well as for my own.

Yet that night I pushed by her

harshly. I answered her curtly, left her concerned and perplexed in the passage, and slammed my door upon her.

And for a long time I lay raging at the hardship and evil of life, at the contempt of Rawdon and the loveless coolness of Nettie's letter, at my weakness and insignificance, at the things I found intolerable, and the things I could not mend. Over and over went my poor little brain, tired out and unable to stop on my treadmill of troubles. Nettie. Rawdon. My mother. Gabbitas. Nettie. . . .

Suddenly I came upon emotional exhaustion. Some clock was striking midnight. After all, I was young; I had these quick transitions. I remember quite distinctly, I stood up abruptly, undressed very quickly in the dark, and had hardly touched my pillow again before I was asleep.

But how my mother slept that night I do not know.

Oddly enough, I do not blame myself for behaving like this to my mother, though my conscience blames me acutely for my arrogance to Parload. I regret my behaviour to my mother before the days of the Change, it is a scar among my memories that will always be a little painful to the end of my days, but I do not see how something of the sort was to be escaped under those former conditions. In that time of muddle and obscurity people were overtaken by needs and toil and hot passions before they had the chance of even a year or so of clear thinking; they settled down to an intense and strenuous application to some partial but immediate duty, and the growth of thought ceased in them. They set and hardened into narrow ways. Few women remained capable of a new idea after five and twenty, few men after thirty-one or two. Discontent with the thing that existed was regarded as immoral, it was certainly an annoyance, and the only protest against it, the only effort against that universal tendency in all human institutions to thicken and clog, to work loosely and badly, to rust and weaken towards catastrophes, came from the young — the crude unmerciful young. It seemed in those days to thoughtful men the harsh law of being — that either we must submit to our elders and be stifled, or disregard them, disobey them, thrust them aside, and make our little step of progress before we too ossified and became obstructive in our turn.

My pushing past my mother, my irresponsive departure to my own silent meditations, was, I now perceive, a figure of the whole hard relationship between parents and son in those days. There appeared no other way; that perpetually recurring tragedy was, it seemed, part of the very nature of the progress of the world. We did not think then that minds might grow ripe without growing rigid, or children honour their parents and still think for themselves. We were angry and hasty because we stifled in the darkness, in a poisoned and vitiated air. That deliberate animation of the intelligence which is now the universal quality, that vigour with consideration, that judgment with confident enterprise which shine

through all our world, were things disintegrated and unknown in the corrupting atmosphere of our former state.

(So the first fascicle ended. I put it aside and looked for the second.

"Well?" said the man who wrote.

"This is fiction?"

"It's my story."

"But you—Amidst this beauty —You are not this ill-conditioned, squalidly bred lad of whom I have been reading?"

He smiled. "There intervenes a certain Change," he said. "Have I not hinted at that?"

I hesitated upon a question, then saw the second fascicle at hand, and picked it up.)

CHAPTER 2

NETTIE

§ 1

I CANNOT now remember *(the story resumed)* what interval separated that evening on which Parload first showed me the comet—I think I only pretended to see it then—and the Sunday afternoon I spent at Checkshill.

Between the two there was time enough for me to give no-tice and leave Rawdon's, to seek for some other situation very strenuously in vain, to think and say many hard and violent things to my mother and to Parload, and to pass through some phases of very profound wretchedness. There must have been a passionate correspondence with Nettie, but all the froth and fury of that has faded now out of my memory. All I have clear now is that I wrote one magnificent farewell to her, casting her off for ever, and that I got in reply a prim little note to say that even if there was to be an end to everything, that was no excuse for writing such things as I had done, and then I think I wrote again in a vein I considered satirical. To that she did not reply. That interval was at least three weeks, and probably four, because the comet which had been on the first occasion only a dubious speck in the sky, certainly visible only when it was magnified, was now a great white presence, brighter than Jupiter, and casting a shadow on its own account. It was now actively present in the world of human thought, everyone was talking about it, everyone was looking for its waxing splendour as the sun went down—the papers, the music-halls, the hoardings, echoed it.

Yes; the comet was already dominant before I went over to make everything clear to Nettie. And Parload had spent two hoarded pounds in buying himself a spectroscope, so that he could see for himself, night after night, that mysterious, that stim-

ulating line—the unknown line in the green. How many times I wonder did I look at the smudgy, quivering symbol of the unknown things that were rushing upon us out of the inhuman void before I rebelled? But at last I could stand it no longer, and I reproached Parload very bitterly for wasting his time in "astronomical dilettantism."

"Here," said I, "we're on the verge of the biggest lockout in the history of this countryside; here's distress and hunger coming, here's all the capitalistic competitive system like a wound inflamed, and you spend your time gaping at that damned silly streak of nothing in the sky!"

Parload stared at me. "Yes, I do," he said slowly, as though it was a new idea. "Don't I? . . . I wonder why."

"*I* want to start meetings of an evening on Howden's Waste."

"You think they'd listen?"

"They'd listen fast enough now."

"They didn't before," said Parload, looking at his pet instrument.

"There was a demonstration of unemployed at Swathinglea on Sunday. They got to stone throwing."

Parload said nothing for a little while and I said several things. He seemed to be considering something.

"But, after all," he said at last, with an awkward movement towards his spectroscope, "that does signify something."

"The comet?"

"Yes."

"What can it signify? You

don't want me to believe in astrology. What does it matter what flames in the heavens—when men are starving on earth?"

"It's—it's science."

"Science! What we want now is socialism—not science."

He still seemed reluctant to give up his comet.

"Socialism's all right," he said, "but if that thing up there *was* to hit the earth it might matter."

"Nothing matters but human beings."

"Suppose it killed them all."

"Oh," said I, "that's Rot."

"I wonder," said Parload, dreadfully divided in his allegiance.

He looked at the comet. He seemed on the verge of repeating his growing information about the nearness of the paths of the earth and comet, and all that might ensue from that. So I cut in with something I had got out of a now forgotten writer called Ruskin, a volcano of beautiful language and nonsensical suggestions, who prevailed very greatly with eloquent excitable young men in those days. Something it was about the insignificance of science and the supreme importance of Life. Parload stood listening, half turned towards the sky with the tips of his fingers on his spectroscope. He seemed to come to a sudden decision.

"No. I don't agree with you, Leadford," he said. "You don't understand about science."

Parload rarely argued with that bluntness of opposition. I was so used to entire possession of our talk that his brief contradiction

struck me like a blow. "Don't agree with me!" I repeated.

"No," said Parload.

"But how?"

"I believe science is of more importance than socialism," he said. "Socialism's a theory. Science — science is something more."

And that was really all he seemed to be able to say.

We embarked upon one of those queer arguments illiterate young men used always to find so heating. Science or Socialism? It was, of course, like arguing which is right, left-handedness or a taste for onions, it was altogether impossible opposition. But the range of my rhetoric enabled me at last to exasperate Parload, and his mere repudiation of my conclusions sufficed to exasperate me, and we ended in the key of a positive quarrel. "Oh, very well!" said I. "So long as I know where we are!"

I slammed his door as though I dynamited his house, and went raging down the street but I felt that he was already back at the window worshipping his blessed line in the green, before I got round the corner.

I had to walk for an hour or so, before I was cool enough to go home.

And it was Parload who had first introduced me to socialism! Recreant!

The most extraordinary things used to run through my head in those days. I will confess that my mind ran persistently that evening upon revolutions after the best French pattern, and I sat on a Committee of Safety and tried backsliders. Parload was there, among the prisoners, backsliderissimus, aware too late of the error of his ways. His hands were tied behind his back ready for the shambles; through the open door one heard the voice of justice, the rude justice of the people. I was sorry, but I had to do my duty.

"If we punish those who would betray us to Kings," said I, with a sorrowful deliberation, "how much the more must we punish those who would give over the State to the pursuit of useless knowledge"; and so with a gloomy satisfaction sent him off to the guillotine.

"Ah, Parload! Parload! If only you'd listened to me earlier, Parload! . . ."

None the less that quarrel made me extremely unhappy. Parload was my only gossip, and it cost me much to keep away from him and think evil of him with no one to listen to me, evening after evening.

That was a very miserable time for me, even before my last visit to Checkshill. My long unemployed hours hung heavily on my hands. I kept away from home all day, partly to support a fiction that I was sedulously seeking another situation, and partly to escape the persistent question in my mother's eyes. "Why did you quarrel with Mr. Rawdon? Why *did* you? Why do you keep on going about with a sullen face and risk offending *it* more?" I spent most of the morning in the newspaper-room of the public library, writing impossible applications for impossible posts — I re-

member that among other things of the sort I offered my services to a firm of private detectives, a sinister breed of traders upon base jealousies now happily vanished from the world, and wrote apropos of an advertisement for "stevedores" that I did not know what the duties of a stevedore might be, but that I was apt and willing to learn — and in the afternoons and evenings I wandered through the strange lights and shadows of my native valley and hated all created things. Until my wanderings were checked by the discovery that I was wearing out my boots.

The stagnant inconclusive malaria of that time!

I perceive that I was an evil-tempered, ill-disposed youth with a great capacity for hatred, *but* —

There was an excuse for hate.

It was wrong of me to hate individuals, to be rude, harsh, and vindictive to this person or that, but indeed it would have been equally wrong to have taken the manifest offer life made me, without resentment. I see now clearly and calmly, what I then felt obscurely and with an unbalanced intensity, that my conditions were intolerable. My work was tedious and laborious and it took up an unreasonable proportion of my time; I was ill clothed, ill fed, ill housed, ill educated and ill trained; my will was suppressed and cramped to the pitch of torture; I had no reasonable pride in myself and no reasonable chance of putting anything right. It was a life hardly worth living. That a large proportion of the people about me had no

better a lot, that many had a worse, does not affect these facts. It was a life in which contentment would have been disgraceful. If some of them were contented or resigned, so much the worse for everyone. No doubt it was hasty and foolish of me to throw up my situation, but everything was so obviously aimless and foolish in our social organisation that I do not feel disposed to blame myself even for that, except in so far as it pained my mother and caused her anxiety.

Think of the one comprehensive fact of the lock-out!

That year was a bad year, a year of world-wide economic disorganisation. Through their want of intelligent direction the great "Trust" of American ironmasters, a gang of energetic, narrow-minded furnace owners, had smelted far more iron than the whole world had any demand for. (In those days there existed no means of estimating any need of that sort beforehand.) They had done this without even consulting the ironmasters of any other country. During their period of activity they had drawn into their employment a great number of workers, and had erected a huge productive plant. It is manifestly just that people who do headlong stupid things of this sort should suffer, but in the old days it was quite possible, it was customary, for the real blunderers in such disasters to shift nearly all the consequences of their incapacity. No one thought it wrong for a light-witted "captain of industry" who had led his work-people into overproduction, into the dis-

proportionate manufacture, that is to say, of some particular article, to abandon and dismiss them, nor was there anything to prevent the sudden frantic underselling of some trade rival in order to surprise and destroy his trade, secure his customers for one's own destined needs, and shift a portion of one's punishment upon him. This operation of spasmodic underselling was known as "dumping." The American ironmasters were now dumping on the British market. The British employers were, of course, taking their loss out of their work-people as much as possible, but in addition they were agitating for some legislation that would prevent—not stupid relative excess in production, but "dumping"—not the disease, but the consequences of the disease. The necessary knowledge to prevent either dumping or its cause, the uncorrelated production of commodities, did not exist, but this hardly weighed with them at all; and in answer to their demands there had arisen a curious party of retaliatory-protectionists who combined vague proposals for spasmodic responses to these convulsive attacks from foreign manufacturers, with the very evident intention of achieving financial adventures. The dishonest and reckless elements were indeed so evident in this movement as to add very greatly to the general atmosphere of distrust and insecurity, and in the recoil from the prospect of fiscal power in the hands of the class of men known as the "New Financiers," one heard frightened old-fashioned statesmen asserting with passion that "dumping" didn't occur, or that it was a very charming sort of thing to happen. Nobody would face and handle the rather intricate truth of the business. The whole effect upon the mind of a cool observer was of a covey of unsubstantial jabbering minds drifting over a series of irrational economic cataclysms, prices and employment tumbled about like towers in an earthquake, and amidst the shifting masses were the common work-people going on with their lives as well as they could, suffering, perplexed, unorganised, and for anything but violent, fruitless protests, impotent. You cannot hope now to understand the infinite want of adjustment in the old order of things. At one time there were people dying of actual starvation in India, while men were burning unsaleable wheat in America. It sounds like the account of a particularly mad dream, does it not? It was a dream, a dream from which no one on earth expected an awakening.

To us youngsters with the positiveness, the rationalism of youth, it seemed that the strikes and lockouts, the overproduction and misery could not possibly result simply from ignorance and want of thought and feeling. We needed more dramatic factors than these mental fogs, these mere atmospheric devils. We fled therefore to that common refuge of the unhappy ignorant, a belief in callous insensate plots —we called them "plots"— against the poor.

You can still see how we figured it in any museum by looking up the caricatures of capital and labour that adorned the German and American socialistic papers of the old time.

§ 2

I HAD cast Nettie off in an eloquent epistle, had really imagined the affair was over for ever — "I've done with women," I said to Parload — and then there was silence for more than a week.

Before that week was over I was wondering with a growing emotion what next would happen between us.

I found myself thinking constantly of Nettie, picturing her — sometimes with stern satisfaction, sometimes with sympathetic remorse — mourning, regretting, realising the absolute end that had come between us. At the bottom of my heart I no more believed that there was an end between us, than that an end would come to the world. Had we not kissed one another, had we not achieved an atmosphere of whispering nearness, breached our virgin shyness with one another? Of course she was mine, of course I was hers, and separations and final quarrels and harshness and distance were no more than flourishes upon that eternal fact. So at least I felt the thing, however I shaped my thoughts.

Whenever my imagination got to work as that week drew to its close, she came in as a matter of course, I thought of her recurrently all day and dreamt of her at night. On Saturday night I dreamt of her very vividly. Her face was flushed and wet with tears, her hair a little disordered, and when I spoke to her she turned away. In some manner this dream left in my mind a feeling of distress and anxiety. In the morning I had a raging thirst to see her.

That Sunday my mother wanted me to go to church very particularly. She had a double reason for that; she thought that it would certainly exercise a favourable influence upon my search for a situation throughout the next week, and in addition Mr. Gabbitas, with a certain mystery behind his glasses, had promised to see what he could do for me, and she wanted to keep him up to that promise. I half consented, and then my desire for Nettie took hold of me. I told my mother I wasn't going to church, and set off about eleven to walk the seventeen miles to Checkshill.

It greatly intensified the fatigue of that long tramp that the sole of my boot presently split at the toe, and after I had cut the flapping portion off, a nail worked through and began to torment me. However, the boot looked all right after that operation and gave no audible hint of my discomfort. I got some bread and cheese at a little inn on the way, and was in Checkshill park about four. I did not go by the road past the house and so round to the gardens, but cut over the crest beyond the second keeper's cottage, along a path Nettie used to call her own. It was a mere

deer track. It led up a miniature valley and through a pretty dell in which we had been accustomed to meet, and so through the hollies and along a narrow path close by the wall of the shrubbery to the gardens.

In my memory that walk through the park before I came upon Nettie stands out very vividly. The long tramp before it is foreshortened to a mere effect of dusty road and painful boot, but the bracken valley and sudden tumult of doubts and unwonted expectations that came to me, stands out now as something significant, as something unforgettable, something essential to the meaning of all that followed. Where should I meet her? What would she say? I had asked these questions before and found an answer. Now they came again with a trail of fresh implications and I had no answer for them at all. As I approached Nettie she ceased to be the mere butt of my egotistical self-projection, the custodian of my sexual pride, and drew together and became over and above this a personality of her own, a personality and a mystery, a sphinx I had evaded only to meet again.

I find a little difficulty in describing the quality of the old-world love-making so that it may be understandable now.

We young people had practically no preparation at all for the stir and emotions of adolescence. Toward the young the world maintained a conspiracy of stimulating silences. There came no initiation. There were books, stories of a curiously conventional kind that insisted on certain qualities in every love-affair and greatly intensified one's natural desire for them, perfect trust, perfect loyalty, lifelong devotion. Much of the complex essentials of love were altogether hidden. One read these things, got accidental glimpses of this and that, wondered and forgot, and so one grew. Then strange emotions, novel alarming desires, dreams strangely charged with feeling; an inexplicable impulse of self-abandonment began to trickle queerly amongst the familiar purely egotistical and materialistic things of boyhood and girlhood. We were like misguided travellers who had camped in the dry bed of a tropical river. Presently we were knee deep and neck deep in the flood. Our beings were suddenly going out from ourselves seeking other beings — we knew not why. This novel craving for abandonment to some one of the other sex, bore us away. We were ashamed and full of desire. We kept the thing a guilty secret, and were resolved to satisfy it against all the world. In this state it was we drifted in the most accidental way against some other blindly seeking creature, and linked like nascent atoms.

We were obsessed by the books we read, by all the talk about us that once we had linked ourselves we were linked for life. Then afterwards we discovered that other was also an egotism, a thing of ideas and impulses, that failed to correspond with ours.

So it was, I say, with the young of my class and most of the young people in our world. So it came about that I sought Nettie on the Sunday afternoon and suddenly came upon her, light bodied, slenderly feminine, hazel eyed, with her soft sweet young face under the shady brim of her hat of straw, the pretty Venus I had resolved should be wholly and exclusively mine.

There, all unaware of me still, she stood, my essential feminine, the embodiment of the inner thing in life for me — and moreover an unknown other, a person like myself.

She held a little book in her hand, open as if she were walking along and reading it. That chanced to be her pose, but indeed she was standing quite still, looking away towards the grey and lichenous shrubbery wall and, as I think now, listening. Her lips were a little apart, curved to that faint, sweet shadow of a smile.

§ 3

I RECALL with a vivid precision her queer start when she heard the rustle of my approaching feet, her surprise, her eyes almost of dismay for me. I could recollect, I believe, every significant word she spoke during our meeting, and most of what I said to her. At least, it seems I could, though indeed I may deceive myself. But I will not make the attempt. We were both too ill educated to speak our full meanings, we stamped out our feelings with clumsy stereotyped phrases; you who are better taught would fail to catch our intention. The effect would be inanity. But our first words I may give you, because though they conveyed nothing to me at the time, afterwards they meant much.

"*You,* Willie!" she said.

"I have come," I said — forgetting in the instant all the elaborate things I had intended to say. "I thought I would surprise you —"

"Surprise me?"

"Yes."

She stared at me for a moment. I can see her pretty face now as it looked at me — her impenetrable dear face. She laughed a queer little laugh and her colour went for a moment, and then so soon as she had spoken, came back again.

"Surprise me at what?" she said with a rising note.

I was too intent to explain myself to think of what might lie in that.

"I wanted to tell you," I said, "that I didn't mean quite . . . the things I put in my letter."

§ 4

WHEN I and Nettie had been sixteen we had been just of an age and contemporaries altogether. Now we were a year and three-quarters older, and she — her metamorphosis was almost complete, and I was still only at the beginning of a man's long adolescence.

In an instant she grasped the situation. The hidden motives of her quick-ripened little mind flashed out their intuitive scheme of action. She treated me with that neat perfection of under-

standing a young woman has for a boy.

"But how did you come?" she asked.

I told her I had walked.

"Walked!" In an instant she was leading me towards the gardens. I *must* be tired. I must come home with her at once and sit down. Indeed it was near tea-time (the Stuarts had tea at the old-fashioned hour of five). Everyone would be *so* surprised to see me. Fancy walking! Fancy! But she supposed a man thought nothing of seventeen miles. When *could* I have started!

All the while, keeping me at a distance, without even the touch of her hand.

"But, Nettie! I came over to talk to you!"

"My dear boy! Tea first, if you please! And besides — aren't we talking?"

The "dear boy" was a new note, that sounded oddly to me.

She quickened her pace a little.

"I wanted to explain—" I began.

Whatever I wanted to explain I had no chance to do so. I said a few discrepant things that she answered rather by her intonation than her words.

When we were well past the shrubbery, she slackened a little in her urgency, and so we came along the slope under the beeches to the garden. She kept her bright, straightforward-looking girlish eyes on me as we went; it seemed she did so all the time, but now I know, better than I did then, that every now and then she glanced over me and behind me towards the shrub-

bery. And all the while, behind her quick breathless, inconsecutive talk, she was thinking.

Her dress marked the end of her transition.

Can I recall it?

Not, I am afraid, in the terms a woman would use. But her bright brown hair, which had once flowed down her back in a jolly pig-tail tied with a bit of scarlet ribbon, was now caught up into an intricacy of pretty curves above her little ear and cheek, and the soft long lines of her neck; her white dress had descended to her feet; her slender waist, which had once been a mere geographical expression, an imaginary line like the equator, was now a thing of flexible beauty. A year ago she had been a pretty girl's face sticking out from a little unimportant frock that was carried upon an extremely active and efficient pair of brown-stockinged legs. Now there was coming a strange new body that flowed beneath her clothes with a sinuous insistence. Every movement, and particularly the novel droop of her hand and arm to the unaccustomed skirts she gathered about her, and a graceful forward inclination that had come to her, called softly to my eyes. A very fine scarf — I suppose you would call it a scarf — of green gossamer, that some new-wakened instinct had told her to fling about her shoulders, clung now closely to the young undulations of her body, and now streamed fluttering out for a moment in a breath of wind, and like some shy independent tentacle with a

secret to impart, came into momentary contact with my arm.

She caught it back and reproved it.

We went through the green gate in the high garden wall. I held it open for her to pass through, for this was one of my restricted stock of stiff politenesses, and then for a second she was near touching me. So we came to the trim array of flowerbeds near the head gardener's cottage and the vistas of "glass" on our left. We walked between the box edgings and beds of begonias, and into the shadow of a yew hedge within twenty yards of that very pond with the goldfish at whose brim we had plighted our vows, and so we came to the wistaria-smothered porch.

The door was wide open, and she walked in before me. "Guess who has come to see us!" she cried.

Her father answered indistinctly from the parlour, and a chair creaked. I judged he was disturbed in his nap.

"Mother!" she called in her clear young voice. "Puss!"

Puss was her sister.

She told them in a marvelling key that I had walked all the way from Clayton, and they gathered about me and echoed her notes of surprise.

"You'd better sit down, Willie," said her father; "now you have got here. How's your mother?"

He looked at me curiously as he spoke.

He was dressed in his Sunday clothes, a sort of brownish tweeds, but the waistcoat was unbuttoned for greater comfort in his slumbers. He was a brown-eyed ruddy man, and I still have now in my mind the bright effect of the red-golden hairs that started out from his cheek to flow down into his beard. He was short but strongly built, and his beard and moustache were the biggest things about him. She had taken all the possibility of beauty he possessed, his clear skin, his bright hazel-brown eyes, and wedded them to a certain quickness she got from her mother. Her mother I remember as a sharp-eyed woman of great activity; she seems to me now to have been perpetually bringing in or taking out meals or doing some such service, and to me – for my mother's sake and my own – she was always welcoming and kind. Puss was a youngster of fourteen perhaps, of whom a hard bright stare, and a pale skin like her mother's, are the chief traces on my memory. All these people were very kind to me, and among them there was a common recognition, sometimes very agreeably finding expression, that I was – "clever." They all stood about me as if they were a little at a loss.

"Sit down!" said her father. "Give him a chair, Puss."

We talked a little stiffly – they were evidently surprised by my sudden apparition, dusty, fatigued, and white-faced; but Nettie did not remain to keep the conversation going.

"There!" she cried suddenly, as if she were vexed. "I declare!" and she darted out of the room.

"Lord! what a girl it is!" said Mrs. Stuart. "I don't know what's come to her."

It was half an hour before Nettie came back. It seemed a long time to me, and yet she had been running, for when she came in again she was out of breath. In the meantime, I had thrown out casually that I had given up my place at Rawdon's. "I can do better than that," I said.

"I left my book in the dell," she said, panting. "Is tea ready?" and that was her apology. . . .

We didn't shake down into comfort even with the coming of the tea-things. Tea at the gardener's cottage was a serious meal, with a big cake and little cakes, and preserves and fruit, a fine spread upon a table. You must imagine me, sullen, awkward, and preoccupied, perplexed by the something that was inexplicably unexpected in Nettie, saying little, and glowering across the cake at her, and all the eloquence I had been concentrating for the previous twenty-four hours, miserably lost somewhere in the back of my mind. Nettie's father tried to set me talking; he had a liking for my gift of ready speech, for his own ideas came with difficulty, and it pleased and astonished him to hear me pouring out my views. Indeed, over there I was, I think, even more talkative than with Parload, though to the world at large I was a shy young lout. "You ought to write it out for the newspapers," he used to say. "That's what you ought to do. *I* never heard such nonsense."

Or, "You've got the gift of the gab, young man. We ought to ha' made a lawyer of you."

But that afternoon, even in his eyes, I didn't shine. Failing any other stimulus, he reverted to my search for a situation, but even that did not engage me.

§5

For a long time I feared I should have to go back to Clayton without another word to Nettie, she seemed insensible to the need I felt for a talk with her, and I was thinking even of a sudden demand for that before them all. It was a transparent manœuvre of her mother's, who had been watching my face, that sent us out at last together to do something — I forget now what — in one of the greenhouses. Whatever that little mission may have been it was the merest, most barefaced excuse, a door to shut, or a window to close, and I don't think it got done.

Nettie hesitated and obeyed. She led the way through one of the hot-houses. It was a low, steamy, brick-floored alley between staging that bore a close crowd of pots and ferns, and behind big branching plants that were spread and nailed overhead so as to make an impervious cover of leaves, and in that close green privacy she stopped and turned on me suddenly like a creature at bay.

"Isn't the maidenhair fern lovely?" she said, and looked at me with eyes that said, "*Now.*"

"Nettie," I began, "I was a fool to write to you as I did."

She startled me by the assent that flashed out upon her face.

But she said nothing, and stood waiting.

" Nettie," I plunged, " I can't do without you. I — I love you."

" If you loved me," she said trimly, watching the white fingers she plunged among the green branches of a selaginella, " could you write the things you do to me? "

" I don't mean them," I said. " At least not always."

I thought really they were very good letters, and that Nettie was stupid to think otherwise, but I was for the moment clearly aware of the impossibility of conveying that to her.

" You wrote them."

" But then I tramp seventeen miles to say I don't mean them."

" Yes. But perhaps you do."

I think I was at a loss; then I said, not very clearly, " I don't."

" You think you — you love me, Willie. But you don't."

" I do, Nettie! You know I do."

For answer she shook her head.

I made what I thought was a most heroic plunge. " Nettie," I said, " I'd rather have you than — than my own opinions."

The selaginella still engaged her. " You think so now," she said.

I broke out into protestations.

" No," she said shortly. " It's different now."

" But why should two letters make so much difference? " I said.

" It isn't only the letters. But it is different. It's different for good."

She halted a little with that sentence, seeking expression. She looked up abruptly into my eyes

and moved, indeed slightly, but with the intimation that she thought our talk might end.

But I did not mean it to end like that.

" For good? " said I. " No! . . . Nettie! Nettie! You don't mean that! "

" I do," she said deliberately, still looking at me, and with all her pose conveying her finality. She seemed to brace herself for the outbreak that must follow.

Of course I became wordy. But I did not submerge her. She stood intrenched, firing her contradictions like guns into my scattered discursive attack. I remember that our talk took the absurd form of disputing whether I could be in love with her or not. And there was I, present in evidence, in a deepening and widening distress of soul because she could stand there, defensive, brighter and prettier than ever, and in some inexplicable way cut off from me and inaccessible.

You know, we had never been together before without little enterprises of endearment, without a faintly guilty, quite delightful excitement.

I pleaded, I argued. I tried to show that even my harsh and difficult letters came from my desire to come wholly into contact with her. I made exaggerated fine statements of the longing I felt for her when I was away, of the shock and misery of finding her estranged and cool. She looked at me, feeling the emotion of my speech and impervious to its ideas. I had no doubt — whatever poverty in my words, coolly written down now, might convey —

that I was eloquent then. I meant most intensely what I said, indeed I was wholly concentrated upon it. I was set upon conveying to her with absolute sincerity my sense of distance, and the greatness of my desire. I toiled towards her painfully and obstinately through a jungle of words.

Her face changed very slowly — by such imperceptible degrees as when at dawn light comes into a clear sky. I could feel that I touched her, that her hardness was in some manner melting, her determination softening towards hesitation. The habit of an old familiarity lurked somewhere within her. But she would not let me reach her.

" No," she cried abruptly, starting into motion.

She laid a hand on my arm. A wonderful new friendliness came into her voice. " It's impossible, Willie. Everything is different now — everything. We made a mistake. We two young sillies made a mistake and everything is different for ever. Yes, yes."

She turned about.

"Nettie! " cried I, and, still protesting, pursued her along the narrow alley between the staging toward the hot-house door. I pursued her like an accusation, and she went before me like one who is guilty and ashamed. So I recall it now.

She would not let me talk to her again.

Yet I could see that my talk to her had altogether abolished the clear-cut distance of our meeting in the park. Ever and again I found her hazel eyes upon me. They expressed something novel — a surprise, as though she realised an unwonted relationship, and a sympathetic pity. And still — something defensive.

When we got back to the cottage, I fell talking rather more freely with her father about the nationalisation of railways, and my spirits and temper had so far mended at the realisation that I could still produce an effect upon Nettie, that I was even playful with Puss. Mrs. Stuart judged from that that things were better with me than they were, and began to beam mightily.

But Nettie remained thoughtful and said very little. She was lost in perplexities I could not fathom, and presently she slipped away from us and went upstairs.

§ 6

I WAS, of course, too footsore to walk back to Clayton, but I had a shilling and a penny in my pocket for the train between Checkshill and Two-Mile Stone, and that much of the distance I proposed to do in the train. And when I got ready to go, Nettie amazed me by waking up to the most remarkable solicitude for me. I must, she said, go by the road. It was altogether too dark for the short way to the lodge gates.

I pointed out that it was moonlight. " With the comet thrown in," said old Stuart.

" No," she insisted, " you *must* go by the road."

I still disputed.

She was standing near me. " To please *me*," she urged, in a quick undertone, and with a persuasive look that puzzled me. Even in

the moment I asked myself why should this please her.

I might have agreed had she not followed that up with, "The hollies by the shrubbery are as dark as pitch. And there's the deer-hounds."

"I'm not afraid of the dark," said I. "Nor of the deer-hounds, either."

"But those dogs! Supposing one was loose!"

That was a girl's argument, a girl who still had to understand that fear is an overt argument only for her own sex. I thought too of those grisly lank brutes straining at their chains and the chorus they could make of a night when they heard belated footsteps along the edge of the Killing Wood, and the thought banished my wish to please her. Like most imaginative natures I was acutely capable of dreads and retreats, and constantly occupied with their suppression and concealment, and to refuse the short cut when it might appear that I did it on account of half a dozen almost certainly chained dogs was impossible.

So I set off in spite of her, feeling valiant and glad to be so easily brave, but a little sorry that she should think herself crossed by me.

A thin cloud veiled the moon, and the way under the beeches was dark and indistinct. I was not so preoccupied with my love-affairs as to neglect what I will confess was always my custom at night across that wild and lonely park. I made myself a club by fastening a big flint to one end of my twisted handkerchief and

tying the other about my wrist, and with this in my pocket, went on comforted.

And it chanced that as I emerged from the hollies by the corner of the shrubbery I was startled to come unexpectedly upon a young man in evening dress smoking a cigar.

I was walking on turf, so that the sound I made was slight. He stood clear in the moonlight, his cigar glowed like a blood-red star, and it did not occur to me at the time that I advanced towards him almost invisibly in an impenetrable shadow.

"Hullo," he cried, with a sort of amiable challenge. "I'm here first!"

I came out into the light. "Who cares if you are?" said I.

I had jumped at once to an interpretation of his words. I knew that there was an intermittent dispute between the House people and the villager public about the use of this track, and it is needless to say where my sympathies fell in that dispute.

"Eh!" he cried in surprise.

"Thought I would run away, I suppose," said I, and came close up to him.

All my enormous hatred of his class had flared up at the sight of his costume, at the fancied challenge of his words. I knew him. He was Edward Verrall, son of the man who owned not only this great estate but more than half of Rawdon's pot-bank, and who had interests and possessions, collieries and rents, all over the district of the Four Towns. He was a gallant youngster, people said, and very clever. Young as he was

there was talk of parliament for him; he had been a great success at the university, and he was being sedulously popularised among us. He took with a light confidence, as a matter of course, advantages that I would have faced the rack to get, and I firmly believed myself a better man than he. He was, as he stood there, a concentrated figure of all that filled me with bitterness. One day he had stopped in a motor outside our house, and I remember the thrill of rage with which I had noted the dutiful admiration in my mother's eyes as she peered through her blind at him. "That's young Mr. Verrall," she said. "They say he's very clever."

"They would," I answered. "Damn them and him!"

But that is by the way.

He was clearly astonished to find himself face to face with a man. His note changed.

"Who the devil are *you?*" he asked.

My retort was the cheap expedient of re-echoing, "Who the devil are you?"

"*Well,*" he said.

"I'm coming along this path if I like," I said. "See? It's a public path — just as this used to be public land. You've stolen the land — you and yours, and now you want to steal the right of way. You'll ask us to get off the face of the earth next. I shan't oblige. See?"

I was shorter and I suppose a couple of years younger than he, but I had the improvised club in my pocket gripped ready, and I would have fought with him very

cheerfully. But he fell a step backward as I came towards him.

"Socialist, I presume?" he said, alert and quiet and with the faintest note of badinage.

"One of many."

"We're all socialists nowadays," he remarked philosophically, "and I haven't the faintest intention of disputing your right of way."

"You'd better not," I said.

"No!"

"No."

He replaced his cigar, and there was a brief pause. "Catching a train?" he threw out.

It seemed absurd not to answer. "Yes," I said shortly.

He said it was a pleasant evening for a walk.

I hovered for a moment and there was my path before me, and he stood aside. There seemed nothing to do but go on. "Good night," said he, as that intention took effect.

I growled a surly good night.

I felt like a bombshell of swearing that must presently burst with some violence as I went on my silent way. He had so completely got the best in our encounter.

§ 7

THERE comes a memory, an odd intermixture of two entirely divergent things, that stands out with the intensest vividness.

As I went across the last open meadow, following the short cut to Checkshill station, I perceived I had two shadows.

The thing jumped into my mind and stopped its tumid flow for a moment. I remember the

intelligent detachment of my sudden interest. I turned sharply, and stood looking at the moon and the great white comet, that the drift of the clouds had now rather suddenly unveiled.

The comet was perhaps twenty degrees from the moon. What a wonderful thing it looked floating there, a greenish-white apparition in the dark blue deeps! It looked brighter than the moon because it was smaller, but the shadow it cast, though clearer cut, was much fainter than the moon's shadow. . . . I went on noting these facts, watching my two shadows precede me.

I am totally unable to account for the sequence of my thoughts on this occasion. But suddenly, as if I had come on this new fact round a corner, the comet was out of my mind again, and I was face to face with an absolutely new idea. I wonder sometimes if the two shadows I cast, one with a sort of feminine faintness with regard to the other and not quite so tall, may not have suggested the word or the thought of an assignation to my mind. All that I have clear is that with the certitude of intuition I knew what it was that had brought the youth in evening dress outside the shrubbery. Of course! He had come to meet Nettie!

Once the mental process was started it took no time at all. The day which had been full of perplexities for me, the mysterious invisible thing that had held Nettie and myself apart, the unaccountable strange something in her manner, was revealed and explained.

I knew now why she had looked guilty at my appearance, what had brought her out that afternoon, why she had hurried me in, the nature of the "book" she had run back to fetch, the reason why she had wanted me to go back by the high-road, and why she had pitied me. It was all in the instant clear to me.

You must imagine me a black little creature, suddenly stricken still — for a moment standing rigid — and then again suddenly becoming active with an impotent gesture, becoming audible with an inarticulate cry, with two little shadows mocking my dismay, and about this figure you must conceive a great wide space of moonlit grass, rimmed by the looming suggestion of distant trees — trees very low and faint and dim, and over it all the domed serenity of that wonderful luminous night.

For a little while this realisation stunned my mind. My thoughts came to a pause, staring at my discovery. Meanwhile my feet and my previous direction carried me through the warm darkness to Checkshill station with its little lights, to the ticket-office window, and so to the train.

I remember myself as it were waking up to the thing — I was alone in one of the dingy "third-class" compartments of that time — and the sudden nearly frantic insurgence of my rage. I stood up with the cry of an angry animal, and smote my fist with all my strength against the panel of wood before me. . . .

Curiously enough I have com-

pletely forgotten my mood after
that for a little while, but I
know that later, for a minute per-
haps, I hung for a time out of
the carriage with the door open,
contemplating a leap from the
train. It was to be a dramatic
leap, and then I would go storm-
ing back to her, denounce her,
overwhelm her; and I hung, urg-
ing myself to do it. I don't re-
member how it was I decided not
to do this, at last, but in the end
I didn't.

When the train stopped at the
next station I had given up all
thoughts of going back. I was
sitting in the corner of the car-
riage with my bruised and
wounded hand pressed under my
arm, and still insensible to its
pain, trying to think out clearly
a scheme of action — action that
should express the monstrous in-
dignation that possessed me.

CHAPTER 3

THE REVOLVER

§1

" THAT comet is going to hit the
earth! "

So said one of the two men
who got into the train and set-
tled down.

" Ah! " said the other man.

" They do say that it is made
of gas, that comet. We shan't
blow up, shall us? . . ."

What did it matter to me?

I was thinking of revenge —
revenge against the primary con-
ditions of my being. I was think-
ing of Nettie and her lover. I
was firmly resolved he should not
have her — though I had to kill
them both to prevent it. I did not
care what else might happen, if
only that end was insured. All
my thwarted passions had turned
to rage. I would have accepted
eternal torment that night with-
out a second thought, to be cer-
tain of revenge. A hundred possi-
bilities of action, a hundred
stormy situations, a whirl of vio-
lent schemes, chased one another
through my shamed, exasperated
mind. The sole prospect I could
endure was of some gigantic, in-
exorably cruel vindication of my
humiliated self.

And Nettie? I loved Nettie
still, but now with the intensest
jealousy, with the keen, unmeas-
uring hatred of wounded pride,
and baffled, passionate desire.

§2

As I came down the hill from
Clayton Crest — for my shilling
and a penny only permitted my
travelling by train as far as Two-
Mile Stone, and thence I had to
walk over the hill — I remember
very vividly a little man with a
shrill voice who was preaching
under a gas-lamp against a hoard-
ing to a thin crowd of Sunday
evening loafers. He was a short
man, bald, with a little fair curly
beard and hair, and watery blue
eyes, and he was preaching that

the end of the world drew near.

I think that is the first time I heard anyone link the comet with the end of the world. He had got that jumbled up with international politics and prophecies from the Book of Daniel.

I stopped to hear him only for a moment or so. I do not think I should have halted at all but his crowd blocked my path, and the sight of his queer wild expression, the gesture of his upward-pointing finger, held me.

"There is the end of all your Sins and Follies," he bawled. "There! There is the Star of Judgments, the Judgments of the most High God! It is appointed unto all men to die — unto all men to die" — his voice changed to a curious flat chant — "and after death, the Judgment! The Judgment!"

I pushed and threaded my way through the bystanders and went on, and his curious harsh flat voice pursued me. I went on with the thoughts that had occupied me before — where I could buy a revolver, and how I might master its use — and probably I should have forgotten all about him had he not taken a part in the hideous dream that ended the little sleep I had that night. For the most part I lay awake thinking of Nettie and her lover.

Then came three strange days — three days that seem now to have been wholly concentrated upon one business.

This dominant business was the purchase of my revolver. I held myself resolutely to the idea that I must either restore myself by some extraordinary act of vigour and violence in Nettie's eyes or I must kill her. I would not let myself fall away from that. I felt that if I let this matter pass, my last shred of pride and honour would pass with it, that for the rest of my life I should never deserve the slightest respect or any woman's love. Pride kept me to my purpose between my gusts of passion.

Yet it was not easy to buy that revolver.

I had a kind of shyness of the moment when I should have to face the shopman, and I was particularly anxious to have a story ready if he should see fit to ask questions why I bought such a thing. I determined to say I was going to Texas, and I thought it might prove useful there. Texas in those days had the reputation of a wild lawless land. As I knew nothing of calibre or impact, I wanted also to be able to ask with a steady face at what distance a man or woman could be killed by the weapon that might be offered me. I was pretty cool-headed in relation to such practical aspects of my affair. I had some little difficulty in finding a gunsmith. In Clayton there were some rook-rifles and so forth in a cycle shop, but the only revolvers these people had impressed me as being too small and toylike for my purpose. It was in a pawn-shop window in the narrow High Street of Swathinglea that I found my choice, a reasonably clumsy and serious-looking implement ticketed "As used in the American army."

I had drawn out my balance

from the savings bank, a matter of two pounds and more, to make this purchase, and I found it at last a very easy transaction. The pawnbroker told me where I could get ammunition, and I went home that night with bulging pockets, an armed man.

The purchase of my revolver was, I say, the chief business of those days, but you must not think I was so intent upon it as to be insensible to the stirring things that were happening in the streets through which I went seeking the means to effect my purpose. They were full of murmurings: the whole region of the Four Towns scowled lowering from its narrow doors. The ordinary healthy flow of people going to work, people going about their business, was chilled and checked. Numbers of men stood about the streets in knots and groups, as corpuscles gather and catch in the blood-vessels in the opening stages of inflammation. The women looked haggard and worried. The iron-workers had refused the proposed reduction of their wages, and the lockout had begun. They were already at " play." The Conciliation Board was doing its best to keep the coal-miners and masters from a breach, but young Lord Redcar, the greatest of our coal-owners and landlord of all Swathinglea and half Clayton, was taking a fine upstanding attitude that made the breach inevitable. He was a handsome young man, a gallant young man; his pride revolted at the idea of being dictated to by a " lot of bally miners," and he meant, he said,

to make a fight for it. The world had treated him sumptuously from his earliest years; the shares in the common stock of five thousand people had gone to pay for his handsome upbringing, and large, romantic, expensive ambitions filled his generously nurtured mind. He had early distinguished himself at Oxford by his scornful attitude towards democracy. There was something that appealed to the imagination in his fine antagonism to the crowd — on the one hand, was the brilliant young nobleman, picturesquely alone; on the other, the ugly, inexpressive multitude, dressed inelegantly in shop-clothes, under-educated, under-fed, envious, base, and with a wicked disinclination for work and a wicked appetite for the good things it could so rarely get. For common imaginative purposes one left out the policeman from the design, the stalwart policeman protecting his lordship, and ignored the fact that while Lord Redcar had his hands immediately and legally on the workman's shelter and bread, they could touch him to the skin only by some violent breach of the law.

He lived at Lowchester House, five miles or so beyond Checkshill; but partly to show how little he cared for his antagonists, and partly no doubt to keep himself in touch with the negotiations that were still going on, he was visible almost every day in and about the Four Towns, driving that big motor-car of his that could take him sixty miles an hour. The English passion for

fair play one might have thought
sufficient to rob this bold pro-
cedure of any dangerous possi-
bilities, but he did not go alto-
gether free from insult, and on
one occasion at least an intoxi-
cated Irish woman shook her fist
at him. . . .

A dark, quiet crowd, that was
greater each day, a crowd more
than half women, brooded as a
cloud will sometimes brood per-
manently upon a mountain crest,
in the market-place outside the
Clayton Town Hall, where the
conference was held. . . .

I considered myself justified in
regarding Lord Redcar's passing
automobile with a special ani-
mosity because of the leaks in our
roof.

We held our little house on
lease; the owner was a mean, sav-
ing old man named Pettigrew,
who lived in a villa adorned with
plaster images of dogs and goats,
at Overcastle, and in spite of our
specific agreement, he would do
no repairs for us at all. He rested
secure in my mother's timidity.
Once, long ago, she had been
behind-hand with her rent, with
half of her quarter's rent, and he
had extended the days of grace
a month; her sense that some day
she might need the same mercy
again made her his abject slave.
She was afraid even to ask that
he should cause the roof to be
mended for fear he might take
offence. But one night the rain
poured in on her bed and gave
her a cold, and stained and
soaked her poor old patchwork
counterpane. Then she got me to
compose an excessively polite
letter to old Pettigrew, begging

him as a favour to perform his
legal obligations. It is part of the
general imbecility of those days
that such one-sided law as existed
was a profound mystery to the
common people, its provisions im-
possible to ascertain, its machin-
ery impossible to set in motion.
Instead of the clearly written
code, the lucid statements of
rules and principles that are now
at the service of everyone, the law
was the muddled secret of the
legal profession. Poor people,
overworked people, had con-
stantly to submit to petty wrongs
because of the intolerable uncer-
tainty not only of law but of cost,
and of the demands upon time
and energy proceedings might
make. There was indeed no jus-
tice for anyone too poor to com-
mand a good solicitor's deference
and loyalty; there was nothing
but rough police protection and
the magistrate's grudging or ec-
centric advice for the mass of the
population. The civil law, in par-
ticular, was a mysterious upper-
class weapon, and I can imagine
no injustice that would have been
sufficient to induce my poor old
mother to appeal to it.

All this begins to sound in-
credible. I can only assure you
that it was so.

But I, when I learned that old
Pettigrew had been down to tell
my mother all about his rheuma-
tism, to inspect the roof, and to
allege that nothing was needed,
gave way to my most frequent
emotion in those days, a burning
indignation, and took the matter
into my own hands. I wrote and
asked him, with a withering air
of technicality, to have the roof

repaired " as per agreement," and added, " if not done in one week from now we shall be obliged to take proceedings." I had not mentioned this high line of conduct to my mother at first, and so when old Pettigrew came down in a state of great agitation with my letter in his hand, she was almost equally agitated.

" How could you write to old Mr. Pettigrew like that? " she asked me.

I said that old Pettigrew was a shameful old rascal, or words to that effect, and I am afraid I behaved in a very undutiful way to her when she said that she had settled everything with him — she wouldn't say how, but I could guess well enough — and that I was to promise her, promise her faithfully, to do nothing more in the matter. I wouldn't promise her.

And — having nothing better to employ me then — I presently went raging to old Pettigrew in order to put the whole thing before him in what I considered the proper light. Old Pettigrew evaded my illumination; he saw me coming up his front steps — I can still see his queer old nose and the crinkled brow over his eye and the little wisp of grey hair that showed over the corner of his window-blind — and he instructed his servant to put up the chain when she answered the door, and to tell me that he would not see me. So I had to fall back upon my pen.

Then it was, as I had no idea what were the proper " proceedings " to take, the brilliant idea occurred to me of appealing to

Lord Redcar as the ground landlord, and, as it were, our feudal chief, and pointing out to him that his security for his rent was depreciating in old Pettigrew's hands. I added some general observations on leaseholds, the taxation of ground rents, and the private ownership of the soil. And Lord Redcar, whose spirit revolted at democracy and who cultivated a pert humiliating manner with his inferiors to show as much, earned my distinguished hatred for ever by causing his secretary to present his compliments to me, and his request that I would mind my own business and leave him to manage his. At which I was so greatly enraged that I first tore this note into minute innumerable pieces, and then dashed it dramatically all over the floor of my room — from which, to keep my mother from the job, I afterwards had to pick it up laboriously on all-fours.

I was still meditating a tremendous retort, an indictment of all Lord Redcar's class, their manners, morals, economic and political crimes, when my trouble with Nettie arose to swamp all minor troubles. Yet not so completely but that I snarled aloud when his lordship's motor-car whizzed by me, as I went about upon my long meandering quest for a weapon. And I discovered after a time that my mother had bruised her knee and was lame. Fearing to irritate me by bringing the thing before me again, she had set herself to move her bed out of the way of the drip without my help, and she had knocked her knee. All her poor

furnishings, I discovered, were cowering now close to the peeling bedroom walls; there had come a vast discoloration of the ceiling, and a washing-tub was in occupation of the middle of her chamber. . . .

It is necessary that I should set these things before you, should give the key of inconvenience and uneasiness in which all things were arranged, should suggest the breath of trouble that stirred along the hot summer streets, the anxiety about the strike, the rumours and indignations, the gatherings and meetings, the increasing gravity of the policemen's faces, the combative headlines of the local papers, the knots of picketers who scrutinised anyone who passed near the silent, smokeless forges, but in my mind, you must understand, such impressions came and went irregularly; they made a moving background, changing undertones, to my pre-occupation by that darkly shaping purpose to which a revolver was so imperative an essential.

Along the darkling streets, amidst the sullen crowds, the thought of Nettie, my Nettie, and her gentleman lover made ever a vivid inflammatory spot of purpose in my brain.

§ 3

It was three days after this — on Wednesday, that is to say — that the first of those sinister outbreaks occurred that ended in the bloody affair of Peacock Grove and the flooding out of the entire line of the Swathinglea collieries. It was the only one of these disturbances I was destined to see, and at most a mere trivial preliminary of that struggle.

The accounts that have been written of this affair vary very widely. To read them is to realise the extraordinary carelessness of the truth that dishonoured the press of those latter days. In my bureau I have several files of the daily papers of the old time — I collected them, as a matter of fact — and three or four of about that date I have just this moment taken out and looked through to refresh my impression of what I saw. They lie before me — queer, shrivelled, incredible things; the cheap paper has already become brittle and brown and split along the creases, the ink faded or smeared, and I have to handle them with the utmost care when I glance among their raging headlines. As I sit here in this serene place, their quality throughout, their arrangement, their tone, their arguments and exhortations, read as though they came from drugged and drunken men. They give one the effect of faded bawling, of screams and shouts heard faintly in a little gramophone. . . . It is only on Monday I find, and buried deep below the war news, that these publications contain any intimation that unusual happenings were forwarded in Clayton and Swathinglea.

What I saw was towards evening. I had been learning to shoot with my new possession. I had walked out with it four or five miles across a patch of moorland and down to a secluded little coppice full of blue-bells, half-

way along the high-road between Leet and Stafford. Here I had spent the afternoon, experimenting and practising with careful deliberation and grim persistence. I had brought an old kite-frame of cane with me, that folded and unfolded, and each shot-hole I made I marked and numbered to compare with my other endeavours. At last I was satisfied that I could hit a playing-card at thirty paces nine times out of ten; the light was getting too bad for me to see my pencilled bull's-eye, and in that state of quiet moodiness that sometimes comes with hunger to passionate men, I returned by the way of Swathinglea towards my home.

The road I followed came down between banks of wretched-looking working-men's houses, in close-packed rows on either side, and took upon itself the rôle of Swathinglea High Street, where, at a lamp and a pillar-box, the steam-trams began. So far that dirty hot way had been unusually quiet and empty, but beyond the corner, where the first group of beershops clustered, it became populous. It was very quiet still, even the children were a little inactive, but there were a lot of people standing dispersedly in little groups, and with a general direction towards the gates of the Bantock Burden coal-pit.

The place was being picketed, although at that time the miners were still nominally at work and the conferences between masters and men still in session at Clayton Town Hall. But one of the men employed at the Bantock Burden pit, Jack Briscoe, was a socialist, and he had distinguished himself by a violent letter upon the crisis to the leading socialistic paper in England, *The Clarion,* in which he had adventured among the motives of Lord Redcar. The publication of this had been followed by instant dismissal. As Lord Redcar wrote a day or so later to *The Times* — I have that *Times,* I have all the London papers of the last month before the Change —

" The man was paid off and kicked out. Any self-respecting employer would do the same." The thing had happened overnight, and the men did not at once take a clear line upon what was, after all, a very intricate and debatable occasion. But they came out in a sort of semi-official strike from all Lord Redcar's collieries beyond the canal that besets Swathinglea. They did so without formal notice, committing a breach of contract by this sudden cessation. But in the long labour struggles of the old days the workers were constantly putting themselves in the wrong and committing illegalities through that overpowering craving for dramatic promptness natural to uneducated minds.

All the men had not come out of the Bantock Burden pit. Something was wrong there, an indecision if nothing else; the mine was still working, and there was a rumour that men from Durham had been held in readiness by Lord Redcar, and were already in the mine. Now it is absolutely impossible to ascertain certainly how things stood at that time. The newspapers say this

and that, but nothing trustworthy remains.

I believe I should have gone striding athwart the dark stage of that stagnant industrial drama without asking a question, if Lord Redcar had not chanced to come upon the scene about the same time as myself and incontinently end its stagnation.

He had promised that if the men wanted a struggle he would put up the best fight they had ever had, and he had been active all the afternoon in meeting the quarrel half-way, and preparing as conspicuously as possible for the scratch force of "blacklegs" — as we called them — who were, he said and we believed, to replace the strikers in his pits.

I was an eye-witness of the whole of the affair outside the Bantock Burden pit, and — I do not know what happened.

Picture to yourself how the thing came to me.

I was descending a steep, cobbled, excavated road between banked-up footways, perhaps six feet high, upon which, in a monotonous series, opened the living-room doors of rows of dark, low cottages. The perspective of squat blue slate roofs and clustering chimneys drifted downward towards the irregular open space before the colliery — a space covered with coaly, wheel-scarred mud, with a patch of weedy dump to the left and the colliery gates to the right. Beyond, the High Street with shops resumed again in good earnest and went on, and the lines of the steam-tramway that started out from before my feet, and were

here shining and acutely visible with reflected skylight and here lost in a shadow, took up for one acute moment the greasy yellow irradiation of a newly lit gas-lamp as they vanished round the bend. To the left spread a darkling marsh of homes, an infinitude of little smoking hovels, meagre churches, public-houses, Board schools, and other buildings out of which the prevailing chimneys of Swathinglea rose detachedly. To the right, very clear and relatively high, the Bantock Burden pit-mouth was marked by a gaunt lattice bearing a great black wheel, sharp and distinct in the twilight, and beyond, in an irregular perspective, were others following the lie of the seams. The general effect, as one came down the hill, was of a dark compressed life beneath a very high and wide and luminous evening sky, against which these pit-wheels rose. And ruling the calm spaciousness of that heaven was the great comet, now green-white, and wonderful for all who had eyes to see.

The fading afterglow of the sunset threw up all the contours and skyline to the west, and the comet rose eastward out of the pouring tumult of smoke from Bladden's forges. The moon had still to rise.

By this time the comet had begun to assume the cloudlike form still familiar through the medium of a thousand photographs and sketches. At first it had been an almost telescopic speck; it had brightened to the dimensions of the greatest star in the heavens; it had still grown, hour by hour,

in its incredibly swift, noiseless and inevitable rush upon our earth, until it had equalled and surpassed the moon. Now it was the most splendid thing this sky of earth has ever held. I have never seen a photograph that gave a proper idea of it. Never at any time did it assume the conventional tailed outline comets are supposed to have. Astronomers talked of its double tail, one preceding it and one trailing behind it, but these were foreshortened to nothing, so that it had rather the form of a bellying puff of luminous smoke with an intenser, brighter heart. It rose a hot yellow colour, and only began to show its distinctive greenness when it was clear of the mists of the evening.

It compelled attention for a space. For all my earthly concentration of mind, I could but stare at it for a moment with a vague anticipation that, after all, in some way so strange and glorious an object must have significance, could not possibly be a matter of absolute indifference to the scheme and values of my life.

But how?

I thought of Parload. I thought of the panic and uneasiness that was spreading in this very matter, and the assurances of scientific men that the thing weighed so little — at the utmost a few hundred tons of thinly diffused gas and dust — that even were it to smite this earth fully, nothing could possibly ensue. And after all, said I, what earthly significance has anyone found in the stars?

Then, as one still descended, the houses and buildings rose up, the presence of those watching groups of people, the tension of the situation; and one forgot the sky.

Preoccupied with myself and with my dark dream about Nettie and my honour, I threaded my course through the stagnating threat of this gathering, and was caught unawares when suddenly the whole scene flashed into drama. . . .

The attention of everyone swung round with an irresistible magnetism towards the High Street, and caught me as a rush of waters might catch a wisp of hay. Abruptly the whole crowd was sounding one note. It was not a word, it was a sound that mingled threat and protest, something between a prolonged "Ah!" and "Ugh!" Then with a hoarse intensity of anger came a low heavy booing, "Boo! boo — oo!" a note stupidly expressive of animal savagery. "Toot, toot!" said Lord Redcar's automobile in ridiculous repartee. "Toot, toot!" One heard it whizzing and throbbing as the crowd obliged it to slow down.

Everybody seemed in motion towards the colliery gates; I, too, with the others.

I heard a shout. Through the dark figures about me I saw the motor-car stop and move forward again, and had a glimpse of something writing on the ground. . . .

It was alleged afterwards that Lord Redcar was driving, and that he quite deliberately knocked down a little boy who would not get out of his way. It

is asserted with equal confidence that the boy was a man who tried to pass across the front of the motor-car as it came slowly through the crowd, who escaped by a hair's breath, and then slipped on the tram-rail and fell down. I have both accounts set forth, under screaming headlines, in two of these sere newspapers upon my desk. No one could ever ascertain the truth. Indeed, in such a blind tumult of passion, could there be any truth?

There was a rush forward, the horn of the car sounded, everything swayed violently to the right for perhaps ten yards or so, and there was a report like a pistol-shot.

For a moment everyone seemed running away. A woman, carrying a shawl-wrapped child, blundered into me, and sent me reeling back. Everyone thought of fire arms, but as a matter of fact something had gone wrong with the motor, what in those old-fashioned contrivances was called a backfire. A thin puff of bluish smoke hung in the air behind the thing. The majority of the people scattered back in a disorderly fashion, and left a clear space about the struggle that centred upon the motor-car.

The man or boy who had fallen was lying on the ground with no one near him, a black lump, an extended arm and two sprawling feet. The motor-car had stopped, and its three occupants were standing up. Six or seven black figures surrounded the car, and appeared to be holding on to it as if to prevent it from starting again; one — it was Mitchell, a

well-known labour leader — argued in fierce low tones with Lord Redcar. I could not hear anything they said, I was not near enough. Behind me the colliery gates were open, and there was a sense of help coming to the motor-car from that direction. There was an unoccupied muddy space for fifty yards, perhaps, between car and gate, and then the wheels and head of the pit rose black against the sky. I was one of a rude semicircle of people that hung as yet indeterminate in action about this dispute.

It was natural, I suppose, that my fingers should close upon the revolver in my pocket.

I advanced with the vaguest intentions in the world, and not so quickly but that several men hurried past me to join the little knot holding up the car.

Lord Redcar, in his big furry overcoat, towered up over the group about him; his gestures were free and threatening, and his voice loud. He made a fine figure there, I must admit; he was a big, fair, handsome young man with a fine tenor voice and an instinct for gallant effect. My eyes were drawn to him at first wholly. He seemed a symbol, a triumphant symbol, of all that the theory of aristocracy claims, of all that filled my soul with resentment. His chauffeur sat crouched together, peering at the crowd under his lordship's arm. But Mitchell showed as a sturdy figure also, and his voice was firm and loud.

"You've hurt that lad," said Mitchell, over and over again.

"You'll wait here till you see if he's hurt."

"I'll wait here or not as I please," said Redcar; and to the chauffeur, "Here! get down and look at it!"

"You'd better not get down," said Mitchell; and the chauffeur stood bent and hesitating on the step.

The man on the back seat stood up, leant forward, and spoke to Lord Redcar, and for the first time my attention was drawn to him. It was young Verrall! His handsome face shone clear and fine in the green pallor of the comet.

I ceased to hear the quarrel that was raising the voice of Mitchell and Lord Redcar. This new fact sent them spinning into the background. Young Verrall!

It was my own purpose coming to meet me half-way.

There was to be a fight here, it seemed certain to come to a scuffle, and here we were —

What was I to do? I thought very swiftly. Unless my memory cheats me, I acted with prompt decision. My hand tightened on my revolver, and then I remembered it was unloaded. I had thought my course out in an instant. I turned round and pushed my way out of the angry crowd that was now surging back towards the motor-car.

It would be quiet and out of sight, I thought, among the dump heaps across the road, and there I might load unobserved. . . .

A big young man striding forward with his fists clenched, halted for one second at the sight of me.

"What!" said he. "Ain't afraid of them, are you?"

I glanced over my shoulder and back at him, was near showing him my pistol, and the expression changed in his eyes. He hung perplexed at me. Then with a grunt he went on.

I heard the voices growing loud and sharp behind me.

I hesitated, half turned towards the dispute, then set off running towards the heaps. Some instinct told me not to be detected loading. I was cool enough therefore to think of the aftermath of the thing I meant to do.

I looked back once again towards the swaying discussion — or was it a fight now? and then I dropped into the hollow, knelt among the weeds, and loaded with eager trembling fingers. I loaded one chamber, got up and went back a dozen paces, thought of possibilities, vacillated, returned and loaded all the others. I did it slowly because I felt a little clumsy, and at the end came a moment of inspection — had I forgotten anything? And then for a few seconds I crouched before I rose, resisting the first gust of reaction against my impulse. I took thought, and for a moment that great green-white meteor overhead swam back into my conscious mind. For the first time then I linked it clearly with all the fierce violence that had crept into human life. I joined up that with what I meant to do. I was going to shoot young Verrall under the benediction of that green glare.

But about Nettie?

I found it impossible to

think out that obvious complication.

I came up over the heap again, and walked slowly back towards the wrangle.

Of course I had to kill him. . . .

Now I would have you believe I did not want to murder young Verrall at all at that particular time. I had not pictured such circumstances as these, I had never thought of him in connection with Lord Redcar and our black industrial world. He was in that distant other world of Checkshill, the world of parks and gardens, the world of sunlit emotions and Nettie. His appearance here was disconcerting. I was taken by surprise. I was too tired and hungry to think clearly, and the hard implication of our antagonism prevailed with me. In the tumult of my past emotions I had thought constantly of conflicts, confrontations, deeds of violence; and now the memory of these things took possession of me as though they were irrevocable resolutions.

There was a sharp exclamation, the shriek of a woman, and the crowd came surging back. The fight had begun.

Lord Redcar, I believe, had jumped down from his car and felled Mitchell, and men were already running out to his assistance from the colliery gates.

I had some difficulty in shoving through the crowd; I can still remember very vividly being jammed at one time between two big men so that my arms were pinned to my sides, but all the other details are gone out of my mind until I found myself almost violently projected forward into the " scrap."

I blundered against the corner of the motor-car, and came round it face to face with young Verrall, who was descending from the back compartment. His face was touched with orange from the automobile's big lamps, which conflicted with the shadows of the comet light, and distorted him oddly. That effect lasted but an instant, but it put me out. Then he came a step forward, and the ruddy lights and queerness vanished.

I don't think he recognised me, but he perceived immediately I meant attacking. He struck out at once at me a haphazard blow, and touched me on the cheek.

Instinctively I let go of the pistol, snatched my right hand out of my pocket and brought it up in a belated parry, and then let out with my left full in his chest.

It sent him staggering, and as he went back I saw recognition mingle with astonishment in his face.

" You know me, you swine," I cried and hit again.

Then I was spinning sideways, half-stunned, with a huge lump of a fist under my jaw. I had an impression of Lord Redcar as a great furry bulk, towering like some Homeric hero above the fray. I went down before him — it made him seem to rush up — and he ignored me further. His big flat voice counselled young Verrall:

" Cut, Teddy! It won't do. The picketa's got i'on bahs. . . ."

Feet swayed about me, and some hobnailed miner kicked my ankle and went stumbling. There were shouts and curses, and then everything had swept past me. I rolled over on my face and beheld the chauffeur, young Verrall, and Lord Redcar — the latter holding up his long skirts of fur, and making a grotesque figure — one behind the other, in full bolt across a coldly comet-lit interval, towards the open gates of the colliery.

I raised myself up on my hands.

Young Verrall!

I had not even drawn my revolver — I had forgotten it. I was covered with coaly mud — knees, elbows, shoulders, back. I had not even drawn my revolver! . . .

A feeling of ridiculous impotence overwhelmed me. I struggled painfully to my feet.

I hesitated for a moment towards the gates of the colliery, and then went limping homeward, thwarted, painful, confused and ashamed. I had not the heart nor desire to help in the wrecking and burning of Lord Redcar's motor.

§ 4

In the night, fever, pain, fatigue — it may be the indigestion of my supper of bread and cheese — roused me at last out of a haggrid sleep to face despair. I was a soul lost amidst desolations and shame, dishonoured, evilly treated, hopeless. I raged against the God I denied, and cursed him as I lay.

And it was in the nature of my fever, which was indeed only half fatigue and illness, and the rest the disorder of passionate youth, that Nettie, a strangely distorted Nettie, should come through the brief dreams that marked the exhaustions of that vigil, to dominate my misery. I was sensible, with an exaggerated distinctness, of the intensity of her physical charm for me, of her every grace and beauty; she took to herself the whole gamut of desire in me and the whole gamut of pride. She, bodily, was my lost honour. It was not only loss but disgrace to lose her. She stood for life and all that was denied; she mocked me as a creature of failure and defeat. My spirit raised itself towards her, and then the bruise upon my jaw glowed with a dull heat, and I rolled in the mud again before my rivals.

There were times when something near madness took me, and I gnashed my teeth and dug my nails into my hands and ceased to curse and cry out only by reason of the insufficiency of words. And once towards dawn I got out of bed, and sat by my looking-glass with my revolver loaded in my hand. I stood up at last and put it carefully in my drawer and locked it — out of reach of any gusty impulse. After that I slept for a little while.

Such nights were nothing rare and strange in that old order of the world. Never a city, never a night the whole year round, but amidst those who slept were those who waked, plumbing the deeps of wrath and misery. Countless thousands there were so ill, so troubled, they agonised near to

the very border-line of madness, each one the centre of a universe darkened and lost. . . .

The next day I spent in gloomy lethargy.

I had intended to go to Checkshill that day, but my bruised ankle was too swollen for that to be possible. I sat indoors in the ill-lit downstairs kitchen, with my foot bandaged, and mused darkly and read. My dear old mother waited on me, and her brown eyes watched me and wondered at my black silences, my frowning preoccupations. I had not told her how it was my ankle came to be bruised and my clothes muddy. She had brushed my clothes in the morning before I got up.

Ah well! Mothers are not treated in that way now. That I suppose must console me. I wonder how far you will be able to picture that dark, grimy, untidy room, with its bare deal table, its tattered wall-paper, the saucepans and kettle on the narrow, cheap, but by no means economical range, the ashes under the fireplace, the rust-spotted steel fender on which my bandaged foot rested; I wonder how near you can come to seeing the scowling pale-faced hobbledehoy I was, unshaven and collarless, in the Windsor chair, and the little timid, dirty, devoted old woman who hovered about me with love peering out from her puckered eyelids. . . .

When she went to buy some vegetables in the middle of the morning she got me a halfpenny journal. It was just such a one as these upon my desk, only that the copy I read was damp from the press, and these are so dry and brittle they crack if I touch them. I have a copy of the actual issue I read that morning; it was a paper called emphatically the *New Paper,* but everybody bought it and everybody called it the " yell." It was full that morning of stupendous news and still more stupendous headlines, so stupendous that for a little while I was roused from my egotistical broodings to wider interests. For it seemed that Germany and England were on the brink of war.

Of all the monstrous irrational phenomena of the former time, war was certainly the most strikingly insane. In reality it was probably far less mischievous than such quieter evils as, for example, the general acquiescence in the private ownership of land, but its evil consequences showed so plainly that even in those days of stifling confusion one marvelled at it. On no conceivable grounds was there any sense in modern war. Save for the slaughter and mangling of a multitude of people, the destruction of vast quantities of material, and the waste of innumerable units of energy, it effected nothing. The old war of savage and barbaric nations did at least change humanity, you assumed yourselves to be a superior tribe in physique and discipline, you demonstrated this upon your neighbours, and if successful you took their land and their women and perpetuated and enlarged your superiority. The new war changed nothing but the colour of maps, the design of postage

stamps, and the relationship of a few accidentally conspicuous individuals. In one of the last of these international epileptic fits, for example, the English, with much dysentery and bad poetry and a few hundred deaths in battle, conquered the South African Boers at a gross cost of about three thousand pounds per head — they could have bought the whole of that preposterous imitation of a nation for a tenth of that sum — and except for a few substitutions of personalities, this group of partially corrupt officials in the place of that, and so forth, the permanent change was altogether insignificant. (But an excitable young man in Austria committed suicide when at length the Transvaal ceased to be a "nation.") Men went through the seat of that war after it was all over, and found humanity unchanged except for a general impoverishment and the convenience of an unlimited supply of empty ration tins and barbed wire and cartridge cases — unchanged and resuming with a slight perplexity all its old habits and misunderstandings, the nigger still in his slum-like kraal, the white in his ugly ill-managed shanty. . . .

But we in England saw all these things, or did not see them, through the mirage of the *New Paper,* in a light of mania. All my adolescence from fourteen to seventeen went to the music of that monstrous resonating futility, the cheering, the anxieties, the songs and the waving of flags, the wrongs of generous Buller and the glorious heroism of De

Wet — who *always* got away; that was the great point about the heroic De Wet — and it never occurred to us that the total population we fought against was less than half the number of those who lived cramped ignoble lives within the compass of the Four Towns.

But before and after that stupid conflict of stupidities, a greater antagonism was coming into being, was slowly and quietly defining itself as a thing inevitable, sinking now a little out of attention only to resume more emphatically, now flashing into some acute definitive expression and now percolating and pervading some new region of thought, and that was the antagonism of Germany and Great Britain.

When I think of that growing proportion of readers who belong entirely to the new order, who are growing up with only the vaguest early memories of the old world, I find the greatest difficulty in writing down the unintelligible confusions that were matter of fact to their fathers.

Here were we British, forty-one millions of people, in a state of almost indescribably aimless economic and moral muddle that we had neither the courage, the energy, nor the intelligence to improve, that most of us had hardly the courage to think about, and with our affairs hopelessly entangled with the entirely different confusions of three hundred and fifty million other persons scattered about the globe, and here were the Germans over against us, fifty-six millions, in a state of confusion no whit better

than our own; and the noisy little creatures who directed papers and wrote books and gave lectures, and generally in that time of world-dementia pretended to be the national mind, were busy in both countries, with a sort of infernal unanimity, exhorting — and not only exhorting but successfully persuading — the two peoples to divert such small common store of material, moral and intellectual energy as either possessed, into the purely destructive and wasteful business of war. And — I have to tell you these things even if you do not believe them, because they are vital to my story — there was not a man alive who could have told you of any real permanent benefit, of anything whatever to counterbalance the obvious waste and evil, that would result from a war between England and Germany, whether England shattered Germany or was smashed and overwhelmed, or whatever the end might be.

The thing was, in fact, an enormous irrational obsession; it was, in the microcosm of our nation, curiously parallel to the egotistical wrath and jealousy that swayed my individual microcosm. It measured the excess of common emotion over the common intelligence, the legacy of inordinate passion we have received from the brute from which we came. Just as I had become the slave of my own surprise and anger and went hither and thither with a loaded revolver, seeking and intending vague fluctuating crimes, so these two nations went about the earth, hot eared and muddle headed, with loaded navies and armies terribly ready at hand. Only there was not even a Nettie to justify their stupidity. There was nothing but quiet imaginary thwarting on either side.

And the press was the chief instrument that kept these two huge multitudes of people directed against one another.

The press — those newspapers that are now so strange to us — like the "Empires," the "Nations," the Trusts, and all the other great monstrous shapes of that extraordinary time — was in the nature of an unanticipated accident. It had happened, as weeds happen in abandoned gardens, just as all our world has happened — because there was no clear Will in the world to bring about anything better. Towards the end this "press" was almost entirely under the direction of youngish men of that eager, rather unintelligent type that is never able to detect itself aimless, that pursues nothing with incredible pride and zeal; and if you would really understand this mad era the comet brought to an end, you must keep in mind that every phase in the production of these queer old things was pervaded by a strong aimless energy and happened in a concentrated rush.

Let me describe to you, very briefly, a newspaper day.

Figure first, then, a hastily erected and still more hastily designed building in a dirty, paper-littered back street of old London, and a number of shabbily dressed men coming and going in this with projectile swiftness,

and within this factory companies of printers, tensely active with nimble fingers — they were always speeding up the printers — ply their type-setting machines, and cast and arrange masses of metal in a sort of kitchen inferno, above which, in a beehive of little brightly lit rooms, dishevelled men sit and scribble. There is a throbbing of telephones and a clicking of telegraph needles, a rushing of messengers, a running to and fro of heated men, clutching proofs and copy. Then begins a clatter roar of machinery catching the infection, going faster and faster, and whizzing and banging — engineers, who have never had time to wash since their birth, flying about with oil-cans, while paper runs off its rolls with a shudder of haste. The proprietor you must suppose arriving explosively on a swift motor-car, leaping out before the thing is at a standstill, with letters and documents clutched in his hand, rushing in, resolute to "hustle," getting wonderfully in everybody's way. At the sight of him even the messenger boys who are waiting, get up and scamper to and fro. Sprinkle your vision with collisions, curses, incoherencies. You imagine all the parts of this complex lunatic machine working hysterically towards a crescendo of haste and excitement as the night wears on. At last the only things that seem to travel deliberately in all those tearing vibrating premises are the hands of the clock.

Slowly things draw on towards publication, the consummation of all those stresses. Then in the small hours, into the now dark and deserted streets comes a wild whirl of carts and men, the place spurts papers at every door, bales, heaps, torrents of papers, that are snatched and flung about in what looks like a free fight, and off with a rush and clatter east, west, north, and south. The interest passes outwardly; the men from the little rooms are going homeward, the printers disperse yawning, the roaring presses slackened. The paper exists. Distribution follows manufacture, and we follow the bundles.

Our vision becomes a vision of dispersal. You see those bundles hurling into stations, catching trains by a hair's breadth, speeding on their way, breaking up, smaller bundles of them hurled with a fierce accuracy out upon the platforms that rush by, and then everywhere a division of these smaller bundles into still smaller bundles, into dispersing parcels, into separate papers, and the dawn happens unnoticed amidst a great running and shouting of boys, a shoving through letter slots, openings of windows, spreading out upon book-stalls. For the space of a few hours you must figure the whole country dotted white with rustling papers — placards everywhere vociferating the hurried lie for the day; men and women in trains, men and women eating and reading, men by study-fenders, people sitting up in bed, mothers and sons and daughters waiting for father to finish — a million scattered people reading — reading headlong — or feverishly ready to read. It is just as if some vehement jet

had sprayed that white foam of papers over the surface of the land. . . .

And then you know, wonderfully gone—gone utterly, vanished as foam might vanish upon the sand.

Nonsense! The whole affair a noisy paroxysm of nonsense, unreasonable excitement, witless mischief and waste of strength—signifying nothing. . . .

And one of those white particles was the paper I held in my hands as I sat with a bandaged foot on the steel fender in that dark underground kitchen of my mother's, clean roused from my personal troubles by the yelp of the headlines. She sat, sleeves tucked up from her ropy arms, peeling potatoes as I read.

It was like one of a flood of disease germs that have invaded a body, that paper. There I was, one corpuscle in the big amorphous body of the English community, one of forty-one million such corpuscles; and, for all my preoccupations, these potent headlines, this paper ferment, caught me and swung me about. And all over the country that day, millions read as I read, and came round into line with me, under the same magnetic spell, came round—how did we say it?—Ah—"to face the foe."

The comet had been driven into obscurity overleaf. The column headed "Distinguished Scientist says Comet will Strike our Earth. Does it Matter?" went unread. "Germany"—I usually figured this mythical malignant creature as a corseted stiff-moustached Emperor enhanced by heraldic black wings and a large sword—had insulted our flag. That was the message of the *New Paper,* and the monster towered over me, threatening fresh outrages, visibly spitting upon my faultless country's colours. Somebody had hoisted a British flag on the right bank of some tropical river I had never heard of before, and a drunken German officer under ambiguous instructions had torn it down. Then one of the convenient abundant natives of the country, a British subject indisputably, had been shot in the leg. But the facts were by no means clear. Nothing was clear except that we were not going to stand any nonsense from Germany. Whatever had or had not happened we meant to have an apology for, and apparently they did not mean apologising.

"HAS WAR COME AT LAST?"

That was the headline. One's heart leaped to assent. . . .

There were hours that day when I clean forgot Nettie, in dreaming of battles and victories by land and sea, of shell fire, and entrenchments, and the heaped slaughter of many thousands of men.

But the next morning I started for Checkshill, started, I remember, in a curiously hopeful state of mind, oblivious of comets, strikes, and wars.

§ 5

You must understand that I had no set plan of murder when I walked over to Checkshill. I had

no set plan of any sort. There was a great confusion of dramatically conceived intentions in my head, scenes of threatening and denunciation and terror, but I did not mean to kill. The revolver was to turn upon my rival my disadvantage in age and physique. . . . But that was not it really! The revolver! — I took the revolver because I had the revolver and was a foolish young lout. It was a dramatic sort of thing to take. I had, I say, no plan at all.

Ever and again during that second trudge to Checkshill I was irradiated with a novel unreasonable hope. I had awakened in the morning with the hope, it may have been the last unfaded train of some obliterated dream, that after all Nettie might relent towards me, that her heart was kind towards me in spite of all that I imagined had happened. I even thought it possible that I might have misinterpreted what I had seen. Perhaps she would explain everything. My revolver was in my pocket for all that.

I limped at the outset, but after the second mile my ankle warmed to forgetfulness, and the rest of the way I walked well. Suppose, after all, I was wrong?

I was still debating that, as I came through the park. By the corner of the paddock near the keeper's cottage, I was reminded by some belated blue hyacinths of a time when I and Nettie had gathered them together. It seemed impossible that we could really have parted for good and all. A wave of tenderness flowed over me, and still flooded me as I came through the little dell and drew towards the hollies. But there the sweet Nettie of my boy's love faded, and I thought of the new Nettie of desire and the man I had come upon in the moonlight, I thought of the narrow, hot purpose that had grown so strongly out of my springtime's freshness, and my mood darkened to night.

I crossed the beech wood and came towards the gardens with a resolute and sorrowful heart. When I reached the green door in the garden wall I was seized for a space with so violent a trembling that I could not grip the latch to lift it, for I no longer had any doubt how this would end. That trembling was succeeded by a feeling of cold and whiteness and self-pity. I was astonished to find myself grimacing, to feel my cheeks wet, and thereupon I gave way completely to a wild passion of weeping. I must take just a little time before the thing was done. . . . I turned away from the door and stumbled for a short distance, sobbing loudly, and lay down out of sight among the bracken, and so presently became calm again. I lay there some time. I had half a mind to desist, and then my emotion passed like the shadow of a cloud, and I walked very coolly into the gardens.

Through the open door of one of the glasshouses I saw old Stuart. He was leaning against the staging, his hands in his pockets, and so deep in thought he gave no heed to me. . . .

I hesitated and went on towards the cottage, slowly.

Something struck me as unusual about the place, but I could not tell at first what it was. One of the bedroom windows was open, and the customary short blind, with its brass upper rail partly unfastened, drooped obliquely across the vacant space. It looked negligent and odd, for usually everything about the cottage was conspicuously trim.

The door was standing wide open, and everything was still. But giving that usually orderly hall an odd look — it was about half-past two in the afternoon — was a pile of three dirty plates, with used knives and forks upon them, on one of the hall chairs.

I went into the hall, looked into either room, and hesitated.

Then I fell to upon the doorknocker and gave a loud rat-tat-too, and followed this up with an amiable " Hel-lo! "

For a time no one answered me, and I stood listening and expectant, with my fingers about my weapon. Someone moved about upstairs presently, and was still again. The tension of waiting seemed to brace my nerves.

I had my hand on the knocker for the second time, when Puss appeared in the doorway.

For a moment we remained staring at one another without speaking. Her hair was dishevelled, her face dirty, tear-stained, and irregularly red. Her expression at the sight of me was pure astonishment. I thought she was about to say something, and then she had darted away out of the house again.

" I say, Puss! " I said. " Puss! "

I followed her out of the door. " Puss! What's the matter? Where's Nettie? "

She vanished round the corner of the house.

I hesitated, perplexed whether I should pursue her. What did it all mean? Then I heard someone upstairs.

" Willie! " cried the voice of Mrs. Stuart. " Is that you? "

" Yes," I answered. " Where's everyone? Where's Nettie? I want to have a talk with her."

She did not answer, but I heard her dress rustle as she moved. I judged she was upon the landing overhead.

I paused at the foot of the stairs, expecting her to appear and come down.

Suddenly came a strange sound, a rush of sounds, words jumbled and hurrying, confused and shapeless, borne along upon a note of throaty distress that at last submerged the words altogether and ended in a wail. Except that it came from a woman's throat it was exactly the babbling sound of a weeping child with a grievance. " I can't," she said, " I can't," and that was all I could distinguish. It was to my young ears the strangest sound conceivable from a kindly motherly little woman, whom I had always thought of chiefly as an unparalleled maker of cakes. It frightened me. I went upstairs at once in a state of infinite alarm, and there she was upon the landing, leaning forward over the top of the chest of drawers beside her open bedroom door, and weeping. I never saw such weeping. One thick strand of black hair had escaped, and hung with a

spiral twist down her back; never before had I noticed that she had grey hairs.

As I came upon the landing her voice rose again. "Oh that I should have to tell you, Willie! Oh that I should have to tell you!" She dropped her head again, and a fresh gust of tears swept all further words away.

I said nothing, I was too astonished; but I drew nearer to her, and waited. . . .

I never saw such weeping; the extraordinary wetness of her dripping handkerchief abides with me to this day.

"That I should have lived to see this day!" she wailed. "I had rather a thousand times she was struck dead at my feet."

I began to understand.

"Mrs. Stuart," I said, clearing my throat; "what has become of Nettie?"

"That I should have lived to see this day!" she said by way of reply.

I waited till her passion abated.

There came a lull. I forgot the weapon in my pocket. I said nothing, and suddenly she stood erect before me, wiping her swollen eyes. "Willie," she gulped, "she's gone!"

"Nettie?"

"Gone! . . . Run away. . . . Run away from her home. Oh, Willie, Willie! The shame of it! The sin and shame of it!"

She flung herself upon my shoulder, and clung to me, and began again to wish her daughter lying dead at our feet.

"There, there," said I, and all my being was a-tremble. "Where has she gone?" I said as softly as I could.

But for the time she was preoccupied with her own sorrow, and I had to hold her there and comfort her with the blackness of finality spreading over my soul.

"Where has she gone?" I asked for the fourth time.

"I don't know—we don't know. And oh, Willie, she went out yesterday morning! I said to her, 'Nettie,' I said to her, 'you're mighty fine for a morning call.' 'Fine clo's for a fine day,' she said, and that was her last words to me!—Willie!—the child I suckled at my breast!"

"Yes, yes. But where has she gone?" I said.

She went on with sobs, and now telling her story with a sort of fragmentary hurry: "She went out bright and shining, out of this house for ever. She was smiling, Willie—as if she was glad to be going. ('Glad to be going,' I echoed with soundless lips.) 'You're mighty fine for the morning,' I says; 'mighty fine.' 'Let the girl be pretty,' says her father, 'while she's young!' And somewhere she'd got a parcel of her things hidden to pick up, and she was going off—out of this house for ever!"

She became quiet.

"Let the girl be pretty," she repeated; "let the girl be pretty while she's young. . . . Oh! how can we go on *living*, Willie? . . . He doesn't show it, but he's like a stricken beast. He's wounded to the heart. She was always his favourite. He never seemed to care for Puss like he did for her. And she's wounded him—"

"Where has she gone?" I reverted at last to that.

"We don't know. She leaves her own blood, she trusts herself—Oh, Willie, it'll kill me! I wish she and me together were lying in our graves."

"But"—I moistened my lips and spoke slowly—"she may have gone to marry."

"If that was so! I've prayed to God it might be so, Willie. I've prayed that he'd take pity on her—him, I mean, she's with."

I jerked out: "Who's that?"

"In her letter, she said he was a gentleman. She did say he was a gentleman."

"In her letter. Has she written? Can I see her letter?"

"Her father took it."

"But if she writes—When did she write?"

"It came this morning."

"But where did it come from? You can tell—"

"She didn't say. She said she was happy. She said love took one like a storm—"

"Curse that! Where is her letter? Let me see it. And as for this gentleman—"

She stared at me.

"You know who it is."

"Willie!" she protested.

"You know who it is, whether she said or not?" Her eyes made a mute unconfident denial.

"Young Verrall?"

She made no answer. "All I could do for you, Willie," she began presently.

"Was it young Verrall?" I insisted.

For a second, perhaps, we faced one another in stark understanding. . . . Then she plumped back to the chest of drawers, and her wet pocket-handkerchief, and I knew she sought refuge from my relentless eyes.

My pity for her vanished. She knew it was her mistress's son as well as I! And for some time she had known, she had felt.

I hovered over her for a moment, sick with amazed disgust. I suddenly bethought me of old Stuart, out in the greenhouse, and turned and went downstairs. As I did so I looked up to see Mrs. Stuart moving droopingly and lamely back into her own room.

§6

OLD Stuart was pitiful.

I found him still inert in the greenhouse where I had first seen him. He did not move as I drew near him; he glanced at me, and then stared hard again at the flowerpots before him.

"Eh, Willie," he said, "this is a black day for all of us."

"What are you going to do?" I asked.

"The missus takes on so," he said. "I came out here."

"What do you mean to do?"

"What *is* a man to do in such a case?"

"Do!" I cried, "why—Do!"

"He ought to marry her," he said.

"By God, yes!" I cried. "He must do that anyhow."

"He ought to. It's—it's cruel. But what am *I* to do? Suppose he won't? Likely he won't. What then?"

He drooped with an intensified despair.

"Here's this cottage," he said,

pursuing some contracted argument. "We've lived here all our lives, you might say. . . . Clear out. At my age. . . . One can't die in a slum."

I stood before him for a space, speculating what thoughts might fill the gaps between these broken words. I found his lethargy, and the dimly shaped mental attitudes his words indicated, abominable. I said abruptly, "You have her letter?"

He dived into his breast-pocket, became motionless for ten seconds, then woke up again and produced her letter. He drew it clumsily from its envelope, and handed it to me silently.

"Why!" he cried, looking at me for the first time, "What's come to your chin, Willie?"

"It's nothing," I said. "It's a bruise;" and I opened the letter.

It was written on greenish-tinted fancy note-paper, and with all and more than Nettie's usual triteness and inadequacy of expression. Her handwriting bore no traces of emotion; it was round and upright and clear as though it had been done in a writing lesson. Always her letters were like masks upon her image; they fell like curtains before the changing charm of her face; one altogether forgot the sound of her light clear voice, confronted by a perplexing stereotyped thing that had mysteriously got a hold upon one's heart and pride. How did that letter run? —

"My dear Mother,

"Do not be distressed at my going away. I have gone some-

where safe, and with someone who cares for me very much. I am sorry for your sakes, but it seems that it had to be. Love is a very difficult thing, and takes hold of one in ways one does not expect. Do not think I am ashamed about this, I glory in my love, and you must not trouble too much about me. I am very, very happy (deeply underlined).

"Fondest love to Father and Puss.

> "Your loving
> "Nettie."

That queer little document! I can see it now for the childish simple thing it was, but at the time I read it in a suppressed anguish of rage. It plunged me into a pit of hopeless shame; there seemed to remain no pride for me in life until I had revenge. I stood staring at those rounded upstanding letters, not trusting myself to speak or move. At last I stole a glance at Stuart.

He held the envelope in his hand, and stared down at the postmark between his horny thumbnails.

"You can't even tell where she is," he said, turning the thing round in a hopeless manner, and then desisting. "It's hard on us, Willie. Here she is; she hadn't anything to complain of; a sort of pet for all of us. Not even made to do her share of the 'ousework. And she goes off and leaves us like a bird that's learnt to fly. Can't *trust* us, that's what takes me. Puts 'erself — But there! What's to happen to her?"

"What's to happen to him?"

He shook his head to show that problem was beyond him.

"You'll go after her," I said in an even voice; "you'll make him marry her?"

"Where am I to go?" he asked helplessly, and held out the envelope with a gesture; "and what could I do? Even if I knew — How could I leave the gardens?"

"Great God!" I cried, "not leave these gardens! It's your Honour, man! If she was my daughter — if she was my daughter — I'd tear the world to pieces! . . ." I choked. "You mean to stand it?"

"What can I do?"

"Make him marry her! Horsewhip him! Horsewhip him, I say! — I'd strangle him!"

He scratched slowly at his hairy cheek, opened his mouth, and shook his head. Then, with an intolerable note of sluggish gentle wisdom, he said, "People of our sort, Willie, can't do things like that."

I came near to raving. I had a wild impulse to strike him in the face. Once in my boyhood I happened upon a bird terribly mangled by some cat, and killed it in a frenzy of horror and pity. I had a gust of that same emotion now, as this shameful mutilated soul fluttered in the dust before me. Then, you know, I dismissed him from the case.

"May I look?" I asked.

He held out the envelope reluctantly.

"There it is," he said, and pointing with his garden-rough forefinger. "I.A.P.A.M.P. What can you make of that?"

I took the thing in my hands.

The adhesive stamp customary in those days was defaced by a circular postmark, which bore the name of the office of departure and the date. The impact in this particular case had been light or made without sufficient ink, and half the letters of the name had left no impression. I could distinguish —

IAP AMP

and very faintly below D.S.O.

I guessed the name in an instant flash of intuition. It was Shaphambury. The very gaps shaped that to my mind. Perhaps in a sort of semi-visibility other letters were there, at least hinting themselves. It was a place somewhere on the east coast, I knew, either in Norfolk or Suffolk.

"Why!" cried I — and stopped. What was the good of telling him?

Old Stuart had glanced up sharply, I am inclined to think almost fearfully, into my face. "You — you haven't got it?" he said.

Shaphambury — I should remember that.

"You don't think you got it?" he said.

I handed the envelope back to him.

"For a moment I thought it might be Hampton," I said.

"Hampton," he repeated. "Hampton. How could you make Hampton?" He turned the envelope about. "H.A.M. — why, Willie, you're a worse hand at the job than me!"

He replaced the letter in the

envelope and stood erect to put it back in his breast pocket.

I did not mean to take any risks in this affair. I drew a stump of pencil from my waistcoat pocket, turned a little away from him and wrote "Shaphambury" very quickly on my frayed and rather grimy shirt cuff.

"Well," said I, with an air of having done nothing remarkable.

I turned to him with some unimportant observation — I have forgotten what.

I never finished whatever vague remark I commenced.

I looked up to see a third person waiting at the greenhouse door.

§ 7

IT was old Mrs. Verrall.

I wonder if I can convey the effect of her to you. She was a little old lady with extraordinary flaxen hair, her weak aquiline features were pursed up into an assumption of dignity, and she was richly dressed. I would like to underline that "richly dressed," or have the words printed in florid old English or Gothic lettering. No one on earth is now quite so richly dressed as she was, no one old or young indulges in so quiet and yet so profound a sumptuosity. But you must not imagine any extravagance of outline or any beauty or richness of colour. The predominant colours were black and fur browns, and the effect of richness was due entirely to the extreme costliness of the materials employed. She affected silk brocades with rich and elaborate patterns, priceless black

lace over creamy or purple satin, intricate trimmings through which threads and bands of velvet wriggled, and in the winter rare furs. Her gloves fitted exquisitely, and ostentatiously simple chains of fine gold and pearls and a great number of bracelets laced about her little person. One was forced to feel that the slightest article she wore cost more than all the wardrobe of a dozen girls like Nettie; her bonnet affected the simplicity that is beyond rubies. Richness, that is the first quality about this old lady that I would like to convey to you, and the second was cleanliness. You felt that old Mrs. Verrall was exquisitely clean. If you had boiled my poor dear old mother in soda for a month you couldn't have got her so clean as Mrs. Verrall constantly and manifestly was. And pervading all her presence shone her third great quality, her manifest confidence in the respectful subordination of the world.

She was pale and a little out of breath that day, but without any loss of her ultimate confidence; and it was clear to me that she had come to interview Stuart upon the outbreak of passion that had bridged the gulf between their families.

And here again I find myself writing in an unknown language, so far as my younger readers are concerned. You who know only the world that followed the Great Change will find much that I am telling inconceivable. Upon these points I cannot appeal, as I have appealed for other confirmations, to the old newspapers;

these were the things that no one wrote about because everyone understood and everyone had taken up an attitude. There were in England and America, and indeed throughout the world, two great informal divisions of human beings — the Secure and the Insecure. There was not and never had been in either country a nobility — it was and remains a common error that the British peers were noble — neither in law nor custom were there noble families, and we altogether lacked the edification one found in Russia, for example, of a poor nobility. A peerage was an hereditary possession that, like the family land, concerned only the eldest sons of the house; it radiated no lustre of *noblesse oblige*. The rest of the world was in law and practice common — and all America was common. But through the private ownership of land that had resulted from the neglect of feudal obligations in Britain and the utter want of political foresight in the Americas, large masses of property had become artificially stable in the hands of a small minority, to whom it was necessary to mortgage all new public and private enterprises, and who were held together not by any tradition of service and nobility but by the natural sympathy of common interests and a common large scale of living. It was a class without any very definite boundaries; vigorous individualities, by methods for the most part violent and questionable, were constantly thrusting themselves from insecurity to security, and the

sons and daughters of secure people, by marrying insecurity or by wild extravagance or flagrant vice, would sink into the life of anxiety and insufficiency which was the ordinary life of man. The rest of the population was landless and, except by working directly or indirectly for the Secure, had no legal right to exist. And such was the shallowness and insufficiency of our thought, such the stifled egotism of all our feelings before the Last Days, that very few indeed of the Secure could be found to doubt that this was the natural and only conceivable order of the world.

It is the life of the Insecure under the old order that I am displaying, and I hope that I am conveying something of its hopeless bitterness to you; but you must not imagine that the Secure lived lives of paradisiacal happiness. The pit of insecurity below them made itself felt, even though it was not comprehended. Life about them was ugly; the sight of ugly and mean houses, of ill-dressed people, the vulgar appeals of the dealers in popular commodities, were not to be escaped. There was below the threshold of their minds an uneasiness; they not only did not think clearly about social economy but they displayed an instinctive disinclination to think. Their security was not so perfect that they had not a dread of falling towards the pit, they were always lashing themselves by new ropes, their cultivation of " connections," of interests, their desire to confirm and im-

prove their positions, was a constant ignoble preoccupation. You must read Thackeray to get the full flavour of their lives. Then the bacterium was apt to disregard class distinctions, and they were never really happy in their servants. Read their surviving books. Each generation bewails the decay of that "fidelity" of servants no generation ever saw. A world that is squalid in one corner is squalid altogether, but that they never understood. They believed there was not enough of anything to go round, they believed that this was the intention of God and an incurable condition of life, and they held passionately and with a sense of right to their disproportionate share. They maintained a common intercourse as "Society" of all who were practically secure, and their choice of that word is exhaustively eloquent of the quality of their philosophy. But, if you can master these alien ideas upon which the old system rested, just in the same measure will you understand the horror these people had for marriages with the Insecure. In the case of their girls and women it was extraordinarily rare, and in the case of either sex it was regarded as a disastrous social crime. Anything was better than that.

You are probably aware of the hideous fate that was only too probably the lot, during those last dark days, of every girl of the insecure classes who loved and gave way to the impulse of self-abandonment without marriage, and so you will understand the peculiar situation of Nettie with young Verrall. One or other had to suffer. And as they were both in a state of great emotional exaltation and capable of strange generosities towards each other, it was an open question and naturally a source of great anxiety to a mother in Mrs. Verrall's position, whether the sufferer might not be her son — whether, as the outcome of that glowing irresponsible commerce, Nettie might not return prospective mistress of Checkshill Towers. The chances were greatly against that conclusion, but such things did occur.

These laws and customs sound, I know, like a record of some nasty-minded lunatic's inventions. They were invincible facts in that vanished world into which, by some accident, I had been born, and it was the dream of any better state of things that was scouted as lunacy. Just think of it! This girl I loved with all my soul, for whom I was ready to sacrifice my life, was not good enough to marry young Verrall. And I had only to look at his even, handsome, characterless face to perceive a creature weaker and no better than myself. She was to be his pleasure until he chose to cast her aside, and the poison of our social system had so saturated her nature — his evening dress, his freedom and his money had seemed so fine to her and I so clothed in squalor — that to this prospect she had consented. And to resent the social conventions that created their situation, was called "class envy"; and gently born preachers reproached us for the mildest

resentment against an injustice no living man would now either endure or consent to profit by.

What was the sense of saying "peace" when there was no peace? If there was one hope in the disorders of that old world it lay in revolt and conflict to the death.

But if you can really grasp the shameful grotesqueness of the old life, you will begin to appreciate the interpretation of old Mrs. Verrall's appearance that leaped up at once in my mind.

She had come to compromise the disaster!

And the Stuarts *would* compromise! I saw that only too well.

An enormous disgust at the prospect of the imminent encounter between Stuart and his mistress made me behave in a violent and irrational way. I wanted to escape seeing that, seeing even Stuart's first gesture in that, at any cost.

"I'm off," said I, and turned my back on him without any further farewell.

My line of retreat lay by the old lady, and so I advanced towards her.

I saw her expression change, her mouth fell a little way open, her forehead wrinkled, and her eyes grew round. She found me a queer customer even at the first sight, and there was something in the manner of my advance that took away her breath.

She stood at the top of the three or four steps that descended to the level of the hothouse floor. She receded a pace or two, with a certain offended dignity at the determination of my rush.

I gave her no sort of salutation.

Well, as a matter of fact, I did give her a sort of salutation. There is no occasion for me to begin apologising now for the thing I said to her — if only I can get them stark enough you will understand and forgive. I was filled with a brutal and over-powering desire to insult her.

And so I addressed this poor little expensive old woman in the following terms, converting her by a violent metonymy into a comprehensive plural. "You infernal land thieves!" I said point-blank into her face. "*Have you come to offer them money?*"

And without waiting to test her powers of repartee, passed rudely beyond her and vanished, striding, with my fists clenched, out of her world again. . . .

I have tried since to imagine how the thing must have looked to her. So far as her particular universe went I had not existed at all, or I had existed only as a dim black thing, an insignificant speck, far away across her park in irrelevant, unimportant transit, until this moment when she came, sedately troubled, into her own secure gardens and sought for Stuart among the greenhouses. Then abruptly I flashed into being down that green-walled, brick-floored vista as a black-avised, ill-clad young man, who first stared and then advanced scowling towards her. Once in existence I developed rapidly. I grew larger in perspective and became more and more important and sinister every moment. I came up the

steps with inconceivable hostility and disrespect in my bearing, towered over her, becoming for an instant at least a sort of second French Revolution, and delivered myself with the intensest concentration of those wicked and incomprehensible words. Just for a second I threatened annihilation. Happily that was my climax.

And then I had gone by, and the Universe was very much as it had always been except for the wild swirl in it, and the faint sense of insecurity my episode left in its wake.

The thing that never entered my head in those days was that a large proportion of the rich were rich in absolute good faith. I thought they saw things exactly as I saw them, and wickedly denied. But indeed old Mrs. Verrall was no more capable of doubting the perfection of her family's right to dominate a wide country side, than she was of examining the Thirty-nine Articles or dealing with any other of the adamantine pillars upon which her universe rested in security.

No doubt I startled and frightened her tremendously. But she could not understand.

None of her sort of people ever did seem to understand such livid flashes of hate, as ever and again lit the crowded darkness below their feet. The thing leaped out of the black for a moment and vanished, like a threatening figure by a desolate roadside lit for a moment by one's belated carriage-lamp and then swallowed up by the night. They counted it with nightmares, and did their best to forget what was evidently as insignificant as it was disturbing.

CHAPTER 4

WAR

§ 1

FROM that moment when I insulted old Mrs. Verrall I became representative, I was a man who stood for all the disinherited of the world. I had no hope of pride or pleasure left in me, I was raging rebellion against God and mankind. There were no more vague intentions swaying me this way and that; I was perfectly clear now upon what I meant to do. I would make my protest and die.

I would make my protest and die. I was going to kill Nettie — Nettie, who had smiled and promised and given herself to another, and who stood now for all the conceivable delightfulnesses, the lost imaginations of the youthful heart, the unattainable joys in life; and Verrall, who stood for all who profited by the incurable injustice of our social order. I would kill them both. And that being done I would blow my brains out and see what vengeance followed my blank refusal to live.

So indeed I was resolved. I raged monstrously. And above me, abolishing the stars, triumphant over the yellow waning moon that followed it below, the giant meteor towered up towards the zenith.

"Let me only kill!" I cried. "Let me only kill!"

So I shouted in my frenzy. I was in a fever that defied hunger and fatigue: for a long time I had prowled over the heath towards Lowchester talking to myself, and now that night had fully come I was tramping homeward, walking the long seventeen miles without a thought of rest. And I had eaten nothing since the morning.

I suppose I must count myself mad, but I can recall my ravings.

There were times when I walked weeping through that brightness that was neither night nor day. There were times when I reasoned in a topsy-turvy fashion with what I called the Spirit of All Things. But always I spoke to that white glory in the sky.

"Why am I here only to suffer ignominies?" I asked. "Why have you made me with pride that cannot be satisfied, with desires that turn and rend me? Is it a jest, this world — a joke you play on your guests? I — even I — have a better humour than that!

"Why not learn from me a certain decency of mercy? Why not undo? Have I ever tormented — day by day, some wretched worm — making filth for it to trail through, filth that disgusts it, starving it, bruising it, mocking it? Why should you? Your

jokes are clumsy. Try — try some milder fun up there; do you hear? Something that doesn't hurt so infernally.

"You say this is your purpose — your purpose with me. You are making something with me — birth pangs of a soul. Ah! How can I believe you? You forget I have eyes for other things. Let my own case go, but what of that frog beneath the cart-wheel, God? — and the bird the cat had torn?"

And after such blasphemies I would fling out a ridiculous little debating society hand. "Answer me that!"

A week ago it had been moonlight, white and black and hard across the spaces of the park, but now the light was livid and full of the quality of haze. An extraordinary low white mist, not three feet above the ground, drifted broodingly across the grass, and the trees rose ghostly out of that phantom sea. Great and shadowy and strange was the world that night, no one seemed abroad; I and my little cracked voice drifted solitary through the silent mysteries. Sometimes I argued as I have told, sometimes I stumbled along in moody vacuity, sometimes my torment was vivid and acute.

Abruptly out of apathy would come a boiling paroxysm of fury, when I thought of Nettie mocking me and laughing, and of her and Verrall clasped in one another's arms.

"I will not have it so!" I screamed. "I will not have it so!"

And in one of these raving fits

I drew my revolver from my pocket and fired into the quiet night. Three times I fired it.

The bullets tore through the air, the startled trees told one another in diminishing echoes the thing I had done, and then, with a slow finality, the vast and patient night healed again to calm. My shots, my curses and blasphemies, my prayers — for anon I prayed — that Silence took them all.

It was — how can I express it? — a stifled outcry tranquillised, lost, amid the serene assumptions, the overwhelming empire of that brightness. The noise of my shots, the impact upon things, had for the instant been enormous; then it had passed away. I found myself standing with the revolver held up, astonished, my emotions penetrated by something I could not understand. Then I looked up over my shoulder at the great star, and remained staring at it.

"Who are *you*?" I said at last.

I was like a man in a solitary desert who has suddenly heard a voice. . . .

That, too, passed.

As I came over Clayton Crest I recalled that I missed the multitude that now night after night walked out to stare at the comet; and the little preacher in the waste beyond the hoardings, who warned sinners to repent before the Judgment, was not in his usual place.

It was long past midnight, and everyone had gone home. But I did not think of this at first, and the solitude perplexed me and left a memory behind. The gas-lamps were all extinguished because of the brightness of the comet, and that too was unfamiliar. The little news-agent in the still High Street had shut up and gone to bed, but one belated board had been put out late and forgotten, and it still bore its placard.

The word upon it — there was but one word upon it in staring letters — was: "WAR."

You figure that empty mean street, emptily echoing to my footsteps — no soul awake and audible but me. Then my halt at the placard. And amidst that sleeping stillness, smeared hastily upon the board, a little askew and crumpled but quite distinct beneath that cool meteoric glare, preposterous and appalling, the measureless evil of that word —

"WAR!"

§ 2

I AWOKE in that state of equanimity that so often follows an emotional drenching.

It was late, and my mother was beside my bed. She had some breakfast for me on a battered tray.

"Don't get up yet, dear," she said. "You've been sleeping. It was three o'clock when you got home last night. You must have been tired out.

"Your poor face," she went on, "was as white as a sheet and your eyes shining. . . . It frightened me to let you in. And you stumbled on the stairs."

My eyes went quietly to my coat pocket, where something still bulged. She probably had not noticed. "I went to Checks-

hill," I said. "You know — perhaps — ?"

"I got a letter last evening, dear," and as she bent near me to put the tray upon my knees, she kissed my hair softly. For a moment we both remained still, resting on that, her cheek just touching my head.

I took the tray from her to end the pause.

"Don't touch my clothes, mummy," I said sharply, as she moved towards them. "I'm still equal to a clothes-brush."

And then, as she turned away, I astonished her by saying. "You dear mother, you! A little — I understand. Only — now — dear mother, oh! let me be! Let me be!"

And with the docility of a good servant, she went from me. Dear heart of submission that the world and I had used so ill!

It seemed to me that morning that I could never give way to a gust of passion again. A sorrowful firmness of the mind possessed me. My purpose seemed now as inflexible as iron; there was neither love nor hate nor fear left in me — only I pitied my mother greatly for all that was still to come. I ate my breakfast slowly, and thought where I could find out about Shaphambury, and how I might hope to get there. I had not five shillings in the world.

I dressed methodically, choosing the least frayed of my collars, and shaving much more carefully than was my wont; then I went down to the Public Library to consult a map.

Shaphambury was on the coast of Essex, a long and complicated journey from Clayton. I went to the railway-station and made some memoranda from the time-tables. The porters I asked were not very clear about Shaphambury, but the booking-office clerk was helpful, and we puzzled out all I wanted to know. Then I came out into the coaly street again. At the least I ought to have two pounds.

I went back to the Public Library and into the newspaper room to think over this problem.

A fact intruded itself upon me. People seemed in an altogether exceptional stir about the morning journals, there was something unusual in the air of the room, more people and more talking than usual, and for a moment I was puzzled. Then I bethought me: "This war with Germany, of course!" A naval battle was supposed to be in progress in the North Sea. Let them! I returned to the consideration of my own affairs.

Parload?

Could I go and make it up with him, and then borrow? I weighed the chances of that. Then I thought of selling or pawning something, but that seemed difficult. My winter overcoat had not cost a pound when it was new, my watch was not likely to fetch many shillings. Still, both these things might be factors. I thought with a certain repugnance of the little store my mother was probably making for the rent. She was very secretive about that, and it was locked in an old tea-caddy in her bedroom. I knew it would be almost im-

possible to get any of that money from her willingly, and though I told myself that in this issue of passion and death no detail mattered, I could not get rid of tormenting scruples whenever I thought of that tea-caddy. Was there no other course? Perhaps after every other source had been tapped I might supplement with a few shillings frankly begged from her. "These others," I said to myself, thinking without passion for once of the sons of the Secure, "would find it difficult to run their romances on a pawn-shop basis. However, we must manage it."

I felt the day was passing on, but I did not get excited about that. "Slow is swiftest," Parload used to say, and I meant to get everything thought out completely, to take a long aim and then to act as a bullet flies.

I hesitated at a pawnshop on my way home to my midday meal, but I determined not to pledge my watch until I could bring my overcoat also.

I ate silently, revolving plans.

§ 3

AFTER our midday dinner — it was a potato-pie, mostly potato with some scraps of cabbage and bacon — I put on my overcoat and got it out of the house while my mother was in the scullery at the back.

A scullery in the old world was, in the case of such houses as ours, a damp, unsavoury, mainly subterranean region behind the dark living-room kitchen, that was rendered more than typically dirty in our case by the fact that

into it the coal-cellar, a yawning pit of black uncleanness, opened, and diffused small crunchable particles about the uneven brick floor. It was the region of "washing-up," that greasy, damp function that followed every meal; its atmosphere had ever a cooling steaminess and the memory of boiled cabbage, and the sooty black stains where saucepan or kettle had been put down for a minute, scraps of potato-peel caught by the strainer of the escape-pipe, and rags of a quite indescribable horribleness of acquisition, called "dish-clouts," rise in my memory at the name. The altar of this place was the "sink," a tank of stone, revolting to a refined touch, grease-filmed and unpleasant to see, and above this was a tap for cold water, so arranged that when the water descended it splashed and wetted whoever had turned it on. This tap was our water supply. And in such a place you must fancy a little old woman, rather incompetent and very gentle, a soul of unselfishness and sacrifice, in dirty clothes, all come from their original colours to a common dusty dark grey, in worn, ill-fitting boots, with hands distorted by ill use, and untidy greying hair — my mother. In the winter her hands would be "chapped," and she would have a cough. And while she washes up I go out, to sell my overcoat and watch in order that I may desert her.

I gave way to queer hesitations in pawning my two negotiable articles. A weakly indisposition to pawn in Clayton, where the

pawnbroker knew me, carried me to the door of the place in Lynch Street, Swathinglea, where I had bought my revolver. Then came an idea that I was giving too many facts about myself to one man, and I came back to Clayton after all I forget how much money I got, but I remember that it was rather less than the sum I had made out to be the single fare to Shaphambury. Still deliberate, I went back to the Public Library to find out whether it was possible, by walking for ten or twelve miles anywhere, to shorten the journey. My boots were in a dreadful state, the sole of the left one also was now peeling off, and I could not help perceiving that all my plans might be wrecked if at this crisis I went on shoe leather in which I could only shuffle. So long as I went softly they would serve, but not for hard walking. I went to the shoemaker in Hacker Street, but he would not promise any repairs for me under forty-eight hours.

I got back home about five minutes to three, resolved to start by the five train for Birmingham in any case, but still dissatisfied about my money. I thought of pawning a book or something of that sort, but I could think of nothing of obvious value in the house. My mother's silver — two gravy-spoons and a salt-cellar — had been pawned for some weeks, since, in fact, the June quarter-day. But my mind was full of hypothetical opportunities.

As I came up the steps to our door, I remarked that Mr. Gabbitas looked at me suddenly round his dull red curtains with a sort of alarmed resolution in his eye and vanished, and as I walked along the passage he opened his door upon me and intercepted me.

You are figuring me, I hope, as a dark and sullen lout in shabby, cheap, old-world clothes that are shiny at all the wearing surfaces, and with a discoloured red tie and frayed linen. My left hand keeps in my pocket as though there is something it prefers to keep a grip upon there. Mr. Gabbitas was shorter than I, and the first note he struck in the impression he made upon anyone was of something bright and bird-like. I think he wanted to be birdlike, he possessed the possibility of an avian charm, but, as a matter of fact, there was nothing of the glowing vitality of the bird in his being. And a bird is never out of breath and with an open mouth. He was in the clerical dress of that time, that costume that seems now almost the strangest of all our old-world clothing, and he presented it in its cheapest form — black of a poor texture, ill-fitting, strangely cut. Its long skirts accentuated the tubbiness of his body, the shortness of his legs. The white tie below his all-round collar, beneath his innocent large-spectacled face, was a little grubby, and between his not very clean teeth he held a briar pipe. His complexion was whitish, and although he was only thirty-three or four perhaps, his sandy hair was already thinning from the top of his head.

To your eye, now, he would

seem the strangest figure, in the utter disregard of all physical beauty or dignity about him. You would find him extraordinarily odd, but in the old days he met not only with acceptance but respect. He was alive until within a year or so ago, but his later appearance changed. As I saw him that afternoon he was a very slovenly, ungainly little human being indeed; not only was his clothing altogether ugly and queer, but had you stripped the man stark, you would certainly have seen in the bulging paunch that comes from flabby muscles and flabbily controlled appetites, and in the rounded shoulders and flawed and yellowish skin, the same failure of any effort towards clean beauty. You had an instinctive sense that so he had been from the beginning. You felt he was not only drifting through life, eating what came in his way, believing what came in his way, doing without any vigour what came in his way, but that *into* life also he had drifted. You could not believe him the child of pride and high resolve, or of any splendid passion of love. He had just *happened*. . . . But we all happened then. Why am I taking this tone over this poor little curate in particular?

"Hello!" he said, with an assumption of friendly ease. "Haven't seen you for weeks! Come in and have a gossip."

An invitation from the drawing-room lodger was in the nature of a command. I would have liked very greatly to have refused it, never was invitation more inopportune, but I had not the wit to think of an excuse. "All right," I said awkwardly, and he held the door open for me.

"I'd be very glad if you would," he amplified. "One doesn't get much opportunity of intelligent talk in this parish."

What the devil was he up to, was my secret preoccupation. He fussed about me with a nervous hospitality, talking in jumpy fragments, rubbing his hands together, and taking peeps at me over and round his glasses. As I sat down in his leather-covered armchair, I had an odd memory of the one in the Clayton's dentist's operating room—I know not why.

"They're going to give us trouble in the North Sea, it seems," he remarked with a sort of innocent zest. "I'm glad they mean fighting."

There was an air of culture about his room that always cowed me, and that made me constrained even on this occasion. The table under the window was littered with photographic material and the later albums of his continental souvenirs, and on the American cloth trimmed shelves that filled the recesses on either side of the fireplace were what I used to think in those days a quite incredible number of books—perhaps eight hundred altogether, including the reverend gentleman's photograph albums and college and school text-books. This suggestion of learning was enforced by the little wooden shield bearing a college coat-of-arms that hung over the looking-

glass, and by a photograph of Mr. Gabbitas in cap and gown in an Oxford frame that adorned the opposite wall. And in the middle of that wall stood his writing-desk, which I knew to have pigeon-holes when it was open, and which made him seem not merely cultured but literary. At that he wrote sermons, composing them himself!

"Yes," he said, taking possession of the hearthrug, "the war had to come sooner or later. If we smash their fleet for them now — well, there's an end to the matter!"

He stood on his toes and then bumped down on his heels, and looked blandly through his spectacles at a water-colour by his sister — the subject was a bunch of violets — above the sideboard which was his pantry and tea-chest and cellar. "Yes," he said as he did so.

I coughed, and wondered how I might presently get away.

He invited me to smoke — that queer old practice! — and then when I declined, began talking in a confidential tone of this "dreadful business" of the strikes. "The war won't improve *that* outlook," he said, and was very grave for a moment.

He spoke of the want of thought for their wives and children shown by the colliers in striking merely for the sake of the union, and this stirred me to controversy, and distracted me a little from my resolution to escape.

"I don't quite agree with that," I said, clearing my throat. "If the men didn't strike for the union now, if they let that be broken up, where would they be when the pinch of reductions did come?"

To which he replied that they couldn't expect to get top-price wages when the masters were selling bottom-price coal. I replied, "That isn't it. The masters don't treat them fairly. They have to protect themselves."

To which Mr. Gabbitas answered, "Well, I don't know. I've been in the Four Towns some time, and I must say I don't think the balance of injustice falls on the masters' side."

"It falls on the men," I agreed, wilfully misunderstanding him.

And so we worked our way towards an argument. "Confound this argument!" I thought; but I had no skill in self-extraction, and my irritation crept into my voice. Three little spots of colour came into the cheeks and nose of Mr. Gabbitas, but his voice showed nothing of his ruffled temper.

"You see." I said, "I'm a socialist. I don't think this world was made for a small minority to dance on the faces of everyone else."

"My dear fellow," said the Rev. Gabbitas, "*I'm* a socialist too. Who isn't? But that doesn't lead me to class hatred."

"You haven't felt the heel of this confounded system. *I* have."

"Ah!" said he; and catching him on that note came a rap at the front door, and, as he hung suspended, the sound of my mother letting someone in and a timid rap.

"*Now,*" thought I, and stood up resolutely, but he would not let me. "No, no, no!" said he. "It's only for the Dorcas money."

He put his hand against my chest with an effect of physical compulsion, and cried, "Come in!"

"Our talk's just getting interesting," he protested; and there entered Miss Ramell, an elderly little young lady who was mighty in Church help in Clayton.

He greeted her — she took no notice of me — and went to his bureau, and I remember standing by my chair but unable to get out of the room. "I'm not interrupting?" asked Miss Ramell.

"Not in the least," he said; drew out the carriers and opened his desk. I could not help seeing what he did.

I was so fretted by my impotence to leave him that at the moment it did not connect at all with the research of the morning that he was taking out money. I listened sullenly to his talk with Miss Ramell, and saw only, as they say in Wales, with the front of my eyes, the small flat drawer that had, it seemed, quite a number of sovereigns scattered over its floor. "They're so unreasonable," complained Miss Ramell. Who could be otherwise in a social organisation that bordered on insanity?

I turned away from them, put my foot on the fender, stuck my elbow on the plush-fringed mantel-board, and studied the photographs, pipes, and ashtrays that adorned it. What was it I

had to think out before I went to the station?

Of course! My mind made a queer little reluctant leap — it felt like being forced to leap over a bottomless chasm — and alighted upon the sovereigns that were just disappearing again as Mr. Gabbitas shut his drawer.

"I won't interrupt your talk further," said Miss Ramell, receding doorward.

Mr. Gabbitas played round her politely, and opened the door for her and conducted her into the passage, and for a moment or so I had the fullest sense of proximity to those — it seemed to me there must be ten or twelve — sovereigns. . . .

The front door closed and he returned. My chance of escape had gone.

§ 4

"*I must* be going," I said, with a curiously reinforced desire to get away out of that room.

"My dear chap!" he insisted, "I can't think of it. Surely — there's nothing to call you away." Then with an evident desire to shift the venue of our talk, he asked, "You never told me what you thought of Burble's little book."

I was now, beneath my dull display of submission, furiously angry with him. It occurred to me to ask myself why I should defer and qualify my opinions to him. Why should I pretend a feeling of intellectual and social inferiority towards him. He asked what I thought of Burble. I resolved to tell him — if necessary with arrogance. Then perhaps he

would release me. I did not sit down again, but stood by the corner of the fireplace.

"That was the little book you lent me last summer?" I said.

"He reasons closely, eh?" ·he said, and indicated the armchair with a flat hand, and beamed persuasively.

I remained standing. "I didn't think much of his reasoning powers," I said.

"He was one of the cleverest bishops London ever had."

"That may be. But he was dodging about in a jolly feeble case," said I.

"You mean?"

"That he's wrong. I. don't think he proves his case. I don't think Christianity is true. He knows himself for the pretender he is. His reasoning's — Rot."

Mr. Gabbitas went, I think, a shade paler than his wont, and propitiation vanished from his manner. His eyes and mouth were round, his face seemed to get round, his eyebrows curved at my remarks.

"I'm sorry you think that," he said at last, with a catch in his breath.

He did not repeat his suggestion that I should sit. He made a step or two towards the window and turned. "I suppose you will admit — " he began, with a faintly irritating note of intellectual condescension. . . .

I will not tell you of his arguments or mine. You will find if you care to look for them, in out-of-the-way corners of our book museums, the shrivelled cheap publications — the publications of the Rationalist Press Association,

for example — on which my arguments were based. Lying in that curious limbo with them, mixed up with them and indistinguishable, are the endless "Replies" of orthodoxy, like the mixed dead in some hard-fought trench. All those disputes of our fathers, and they were sometimes furious disputes, have gone now beyond the range of comprehension. You younger people, I know, read them with impatient perplexity. You cannot understand how sane creatures could imagine they had joined issue at all in most of these controversies. All the old methods of systematic thinking, the queer absurdities of the Aristotelian logic, have followed magic numbers and mystical numbers, and the Rumpelstiltskin magic names now into the blackness of the unthinkable. You can no more understand our theological passions than you can understand the fancies that made all ancient peoples speak of their gods only. by circumlocutions, that made savages pine away and die because they had been photographed, or an Elizabethan farmer turn back from a day's expedition because he had met three crows. Even I, who have been through it all, recall our controversies now with something near incredulity.

Faith we can understand to-day, all men live by faith; but in the old time everyone confused quite hopelessly Faith and a forced, incredible Belief in certain pseudo-concrete statements. I am inclined to say that neither believers nor unbelievers had faith as we understand it — they

had insufficient intellectual power. They could not trust unless they had something to see and touch and say, like their barbarous ancestors who could not make a bargain without exchange of tokens. If they no longer worshipped stocks and stones, or eked out their needs with pilgrimages and images, they still held fiercely to audible images, to printed words and formulæ.

But why revive the echoes of the ancient logomachies?

Suffice it that we lost our tempers very readily in pursuit of God and Truth, and said exquisitely foolish things on either side. And on the whole — from the impartial perspective of my three and seventy years — I adjudicate that if my dialectic was bad, that of the Rev. Gabbitas was altogether worse.

Little pink spots came into his cheeks, a squealing note into his voice. We interrupted each other more and more rudely. We invented facts and appealed to authorities whose names I mispronounced; and, finding Gabbitas shy of the higher criticism and the Germans, I used the names of Karl Marx and Engels as Bible exegetes with no little effect. A silly wrangle! a preposterous wrangle! — you must imagine our talk becoming louder, with a developing quarrelsome note — my mother no doubt hovering on the staircase and listening in alarm as who should say, "My dear, don't offend it! Oh, don't offend it! Mr. Gabbitas enjoys its friendship. Try to think whatever Mr. Gabbitas says" — though we still kept in touch with a pre-

tence of mutual deference. The ethical superiority of Christianity to all other religions came to the fore — I know not how. We dealt with the matter in bold, imaginative generalisations, because of the insufficiency of our historical knowledge. I was moved to denounce Christianity as the ethic of slaves, and declare myself a disciple of a German writer of no little vogue in those days, named Nietzsche.

For a disciple I must confess I was particularly ill acquainted with the works of the master. Indeed, all I knew of him had come to me through a two-column article in *The Clarion* for the previous week. . . . But the Rev. Gabbitas did not read *The Clarion*.

I am, I know, putting a strain upon your credulity when I tell you that I now have little doubt that the Rev. Gabbitas was absolutely ignorant even of the name of Nietzsche, although that writer presented a separate and distinct attitude of attack upon the faith that was in the reverend gentleman's keeping.

"I'm a disciple of Nietzsche," said I, with an air of extensive explanation.

He shied away so awkwardly at the name that I repeated it at once.

"But do you know what Nietzsche says?" I pressed him viciously.

"He has certainly been adequately answered," he said, still trying to carry it off.

"Who by?" I rapped out hotly. "Tell me that!" and became mercilessly expectant.

§ 5

A HAPPY accident relieved Mr. Gabbitas from the embarrassment of that challenge, and carried me another step along my course of personal disaster.

It came on the heels of my question in the form of a clatter of horses without, and the gride and cessation of wheels. I glimpsed a straw-hatted coachman and a pair of greys. It seemed an incredibly magnificent carriage for Clayton.

" Eh! " said the Rev. Gabbitas, going to the window. " Why, it's old Mrs. Verrall! It's old Mrs. Verrall. Really! What *can* she want with me? "

He turned to me, and the flush of controversy had passed and his face shone like the sun. It was not every day, I perceived, that Mrs. Verrall came to see him.

" I get so many interruptions," he said, almost grinning. " You must excuse me a minute! Then — then I'll tell you about that fellow. But don't go. I pray you don't go. I can assure you . . . *most* interesting."

He went out of the room waving vague prohibitory gestures.

" I *must* go," I cried after him. " No, no, no! " in the passage. " I've got your answer," I think it was he added, and " quite mistaken"; and I saw him running down the steps to talk to the old lady.

I swore. I made three steps to the window, and this brought me within a yard of that accursed drawer.

I glanced at it, and then at that old woman who was so absolutely powerful, and instantly her son and Nettie's face were flaming in my brain. The Stuarts had, no doubt, already accepted accomplished facts. And I too — "

What was I doing here?

What was I doing here while judgment escaped me?

I woke up. I was injected with energy. I took one reassuring look at the curate's obsequious back, at the old lady's projected nose and quivering hand, and then with swift, clean movements I had the little drawer open, four sovereigns in my pocket, and the drawer shut again. Then again at the window — they were still talking.

That was all right. He might not look in that drawer for hours. I glanced at his clock. Twenty minutes still before the Birmingham train. Time to buy a pair of boots and get away. But how was I to get to the station?

I went out boldly into the passage, and took my hat and stick. . . . Walk past him?

Yes. That was all right! He could not argue with me while so important a person engaged him. . . . I came boldly down the steps.

" I want a list made, Mr. Gabbitas, of all the really *deserving* cases," old Mrs. Verrall was saying.

It is curious, but it did not occur to me that here was a mother whose son I was going to kill. I did not see her in that aspect at all. Instead, I was possessed by a realisation of the blazing imbecility of a social system that gave this palsied old woman

the power to give or withhold the urgent necessities of life from hundreds of her fellow-creatures just according to her poor, foolish old fancies of desert.

"We could make a *provisional* list of that sort," he was saying, and glanced round with a pre-occupied expression at me.

"I *must* go," I said at his flash of inquiry, and added, "I'll be back in twenty minutes," and went on my way. He turned again to his patroness as though he forgot me on the instant. Perhaps after all he was not sorry.

I felt extraordinarily cool and capable, exhilarated, if anything, by this prompt, effectual theft. After all, my great determination would achieve itself. I was no longer oppressed by a sense of obstacles. I felt I could grasp accidents and turn them to my advantage. I would go now down Hacker Street to the little shoemaker's — get a sound, good pair of boots — ten minutes — and then to the railway-station — five minutes more — and off! I felt as efficient and non-moral as if I was Nietzsche's Over-man already come. It did not occur to me that the curate's clock might have a considerable margin of error.

§ 6

I MISSED the train.

Partly that was because the curate's clock was slow, and partly it was due to the commercial obstinacy of the shoemaker, who would try on another pair after I had declared my time was up. I bought the final pair however, gave him a wrong address for the return of the old ones, and only ceased to feel like the Nietzschean Over-man when I saw the train running out of the station.

Even then I did not lose my head. It occurred to me almost at once that in the event of a prompt pursuit there would be a great advantage in not taking a train from Clayton; that, indeed, to have done so would have been an error from which only luck had saved me. As it was, I had already been very indiscreet in my inquiries about Shapham-bury, for once on the scent the clerk could not fail to remember me. Now the chances were against his coming into the case. I did not go into the station therefore at all, I made no demonstration of having missed the train, but walked quietly past, down the road, crossed the iron footbridge, and took the way back circuitously by White's brickfields and the allotments to the way over Clayton Crest to Two-Mile Stone, where I calculated I should have an ample margin for the 6.13 train.

I was not very greatly excited or alarmed then. Suppose, I reasoned, that by some accident the curate goes to that drawer at once: will he be certain to miss four out of ten or eleven sovereigns? If he does, will he at once think I have taken them? If he does, will he act at once or wait for my return? If he acts at once, will be talk to my mother or call in the police? Then there are a dozen roads and even railways out of the Clayton region; how is he to know which I have taken? Suppose he goes straight

at once to the right station, they will not remember my departure for the simple reason that I didn't depart. But they may remember about Shaphambury? It was unlikely.

I resolved not to go directly to Shaphambury from Birmingham, but to go thence to Monkshampton, thence to Wyvern, and then come down on Shaphambury from the north. That might involve a night at some intermediate stopping-place, but it would effectually conceal me from any but the most persistent pursuit. And this was not a case of murder yet, but only the theft of four sovereigns.

I had argued away all anxiety before I reached Clayton Crest.

At the Crest I looked back. What a world it was! And suddenly it came to me that I was looking at it for the last time. If I overtook the fugitives and succeeded, I should die with them — or hang. I stopped and looked back more attentively at that wide ugly valley.

It was my native valley, and I was going out of it, I thought, never to return; and yet in that last prospect the group of towns that had borne me and dwarfed and crippled and made me, seemed in some indefinable manner strange. I was, perhaps, more used to seeing it from this comprehensive viewpoint when it was veiled and softened by night; now it came out in all its weekday reek, under a clear afternoon sun. That may account a little for its unfamiliarity. And perhaps, too, there was something in the emotions through which I

had been passing for a week and more, to intensify my insight, to enable me to pierce the unusual, to question the accepted. But it came to me then, I am sure, for the first time how promiscuous, how higgledy-piggledy was the whole of that jumble of mines and homes, collieries and pot-banks, railway yards, canals, schools, forges and blast furnaces, churches, chapels, allotment hovels, a vast irregular agglomeration of ugly smoking accidents in which men lived as happy as frogs in a dustbin. Each thing jostled and damaged the other things about it, each thing ignored the other things about it; the smoke of the furnace defiled the pot-bank clay, the clatter of the railway deafened the worshippers in church, the public-house thrust corruption at the school doors, the dismal homes squeezed miserably amidst the monstrosities of industrialism, with an effect of groping imbecility. Humanity choked amidst its products, and all its energy went in increasing its disorder, like a blind stricken thing that struggles and sinks in a morass.

I did not think these things clearly that afternoon. Much less did I ask how I, with my murderous purpose, stood to them all. I write down that realisation of disorder and suffocation here and now as though I had thought it, but indeed then I only felt it, felt it transitorily as I looked back, and then stood with the thing escaping from my mind.

I should never see that countryside again.

I came back to that. At any

rate I wasn't sorry. The chances were I should die in sweet air, under a clean sky.

From distant Swathinglea came a little sound, the minute ululation of a remote crowd, and then rapidly three shots.

That held me perplexed for a space. . . . Well, anyhow I was leaving it all! Thank God I was leaving it all! Then, as I turned to go on, I thought of my mother.

It seemed an evil world in which to leave one's mother. My thoughts focussed upon her very vividly for a moment. Down there, under that afternoon light, she was going to and fro, unaware as yet that she had lost me, bent and poking about in the darkling underground kitchen, perhaps carrying a lamp into the scullery to trim, or sitting patiently, staring into the fire, waiting tea for me. A great pity for her, a great remorse at the blacker troubles that lowered over her innocent head, came to me. Why, after all, was I doing this thing?

Why?

I stopped again dead, with the hill crest rising between me and home. I had more than half a mind to return to her.

Then I thought of the curate's sovereigns. If he had missed them already, what should I return to? And even if I returned, how could I put them back?

And what of the night after I renounced my revenge? What of the time when young Verrall came back? And Nettie?

No! The thing had to be done.

But at least I might have kissed my mother before I came away,

left her some message, reassured her at least for a little while. All night she would listen and wait for me. . . .

Should I send her a telegram from Two-Mile Stone?

It was no good now; too late, too late. To do that would be to tell the course I had taken, to bring pursuit upon me swift and sure, if pursuit there was to be. No. My mother must suffer!

I went on grimly towards Two-Mile Stone, but now as if some greater will than mine directed my footsteps thither.

I reached Birmingham before darkness came, and just caught the last train for Monkshampton, where I had planned to pass the night.

CHAPTER 5

THE PURSUIT OF THE TWO LOVERS

§ 1

As the train carried me on from Birmingham to Monkshampton, it carried me not only into a country where I had never been before, but out of the commonplace daylight and the touch and quality of ordinary things, into the strange unprecedented night

that was ruled by the giant meteor of the last days.

There was at that time a curious accentuation of the common alternation of night and day. They became separated with a widening difference of value in regard to all mundane affairs. During the day, the comet was an item in the newspapers, it was jostled by a thousand more living interests, it was as nothing in the skirts of the war storm that was now upon us. It was an astronomical phenomenon somewhere away over China, millions of miles away in the deeps. We forgot it. But directly the sun sank one turned ever and again towards the east, and the meteor resumed its sway over us.

One waited for its rising, and yet each night it came as a surprise. Always it rose brighter than one had dared to think, always larger and with some wonderful change in its outline, and now with a strange, less luminous, greener disc upon it that grew with its growth, the umbra of the earth. It shone also with its own light, so that this shadow was not hard or black but it shone phosphorescently and with a diminishing intensity where the stimulus of the sun's rays was withdrawn. As it ascended towards the zenith, as the last trailing daylight went after the abdicating sun, its greenish white illumination banished the realities of day, diffused a bright ghostliness over all things. It changed the starless sky about it to an extraordinary deep blue, the profoundest colour in the world, such as I have never seen

before or since. I remember, too, that as I peered from the train that was rattling me along to Monkshampton, I perceived and was puzzled by a coppery red light that mingled with all the shadows that were cast by it.

It turned our ugly English industrial towns to phantom cities. Everywhere the local authorities discontinued street lighting — one could read small print in the glare — and so at Monkshampton I went about through pale, white, unfamiliar streets, whose electric globes had shadows on the path. Lit windows here and there burnt ruddy orange, like holes cut in some dream curtain that hung before a furnace. A policeman with noiseless feet showed me an inn woven of moonshine, a green-faced man opened to us, and there I abode the night. And the next morning it opened with a mighty clatter, and was a dirty little beerhouse that stank of beer, and there was a fat and grimy landlord with red spots upon his neck, and much noisy traffic going by on the cobbles outside.

I came out, after I had paid my bill, into a street that echoed to the bawlings of two newsvendors and to the noisy yappings of a dog they had raised to emulation. They were shouting: "Great British disaster in the North Sea. A battleship lost with all hands!"

I bought a paper, went on to the railway station reading such details as were given of this triumph of the old civilisation, of the blowing up of this great iron ship, full of guns and explosives

and the most costly and beautiful machinery of which that time was capable, together with nine hundred able-bodied men, all of them above the average, by a contact mine towed by a German submarine. I read myself into a fever of warlike emotion. Not only did I forget the meteor, but for a time I forgot even the purpose that took me on to the railway station, bought my ticket, and was now carrying me outward to Shaphambury.

So the hot day came to its own again, and people forgot the night.

Each night there shone upon us more and more insistently, beauty, wonder, the promise of the deeps; and we were hushed, and marvelled for a space. And at the first grey sounds of dawn again, at the shooting of bolts and the noise of milk-carts, we forgot, and the dusty habitual day came yawning and stretching back again. The stains of coal smoke crept across the heavens, and we rose to the soiled disorderly routine of life.

"Thus life has always been," we said; "thus it will always be."

The glory of those nights was almost universally regarded as spectacular merely. It signified nothing to us. So far as western Europe went, it was only a small and ignorant section of the lower classes who regarded the comet as a portent of the end of the world. Abroad, where there were peasantries, it was different, but in England the peasantry had already disappeared. Everyone read. The newspaper, in the quiet days before our swift quarrel with Germany rushed to its climax, had absolutely dispelled all possibilities of a panic in this matter. The very tramps upon the high-roads, the children in the nursery, had learned that at the utmost the whole of that shining cloud could weigh but a few score tons. This fact had been shown quite conclusively by the enormous deflections that had at last swung it round squarely at our world. It had passed near three of the smallest asteroids without producing the minutest perceptible deflection in their course; while, on its own part, it had described a course through nearly three degrees. When it struck our earth there was to be a magnificent spectacle, no doubt, for those who were on the right side of our planet to see; but beyond that nothing. It was doubtful whether we were on the right side. The meteor would loom larger and larger in the sky, but with the umbra of our earth eating its heart of brightness out, and at last it would be the whole sky, a sky of luminous green clouds, with a white brightness about the horizon west and east. Then a pause — a pause of not very exactly definite duration — and then, no doubt, a great blaze of shooting stars. They might be of some unwonted colour because of the unknown element that line in the green revealed. For a little while the zenith would spout shooting stars. Some, it was hoped, would reach the earth and be available for analysis.

That, science said, would be all. The green clouds would

whirl and vanish, and there might be thunderstorms. But through the attenuated wisps of comet shine, the old sky, the old stars, would reappear, and all would be as it had been before. And since this was to happen between one and eleven in the morning of the approaching Tuesday — I slept at Monkshampton on Saturday night — it would be only partially visible, if visible at all, on our side of the earth. Perhaps, if it came late, one would see no more than a shooting star low down in the sky. All this we had with the utmost assurances of science. Still it did not prevent the last nights being the most beautiful and memorable of human experiences.

The nights had become very warm, and when next day I had ranged Shaphambury in vain, I was greatly tormented, as that unparalleled glory of the night returned, to think that under its splendid benediction young Verrall and Nettie made love to one another.

I walked backward and forward, backward and forward, along the seafront, peering into the faces of the young couples who promenaded, with my hand in my pocket ready and a curious ache in my heart that had no kindred with rage. Until at last all the promenaders had gone home to bed, and I was alone with the star.

My train from Wyvern to Shaphambury that morning was a whole hour late; they said it was on account of the movement of troops to meet a possible raid from the Elbe.

§ 2

SHAPHAMBURY seemed an odd place to me even then. But something was quickening in me at that time to feel the oddness of many accepted things. Now in the retrospect I see it as intensely queer. The whole place was strange to my untravelled eyes; the sea even was strange. Only twice in my life had I been at the seaside before, and then I had gone by excursion to places on the Welsh coast whose great cliffs of rock and mountain backgrounds made the effect of the horizon very different from what it is upon the East Anglian seaboard. Here what they call a cliff was a crumbling bank of whitey-brown earth not fifty feet high.

So soon as I arrived I made a systematic exploration of Shaphambury. To this day I retain the clearest memories of the plan I shaped out then, and how my inquiries were incommoded by the overpowering desire of everyone to talk of the chances of a German raid, before the Channel Fleet got round to us. I slept at a small public-house in a Shaphambury back street on Sunday night. I did not get on to Shaphambury from Wyvern until two in the afternoon, because of the infrequency of Sunday trains, and I got no clue whatever until late in the afternoon of Monday. As the little local train bumped into sight of the place round the curve of a swelling hill, one saw a series of undulating grassy spaces, amidst which a number of conspicuous notice-boards appealed to the eye and cut up the distant

sea horizon. Most of these referred to comestibles or to remedies to follow the comestibles; and they were coloured with a view to the memorable rather than beautiful, to "stand out" amidst the gentle greyish tones of the east-coast scenery. The greater number, I may remark, of the advertisements that were so conspicuous a factor in the life of those days, and which rendered our vast tree-pulp newspapers possible, referred to foods, drinks, tobacco, and the drugs that promised a restoration of the equanimity these other articles had destroyed. Wherever one went one was reminded in glaring letters that, after all, man was little better than a worm, that eyeless, earless thing that burrows and lives uncomplainingly amidst nutritious dirt, "an alimentary canal with the subservient appendages thereto." But in addition to such boards there were also the big black-and-white boards of various grandiloquently named "estates." The individualistic enterprise of that time had led to the plotting out of nearly all the country round the seaside towns into roads and building-plots — all but a small portion of the south and east coast was in this condition, and had the promises of those schemes been realised the entire population of the island might have been accommodated upon the sea frontiers. nothing of the sort happened, of course; the whole of this uglification of the coast-line was done to stimulate a little foolish gambling in plots, and one saw everywhere agents' boards in every

state of freshness and decay, ill-made exploitation roads overgrown with grass, and here and there at a corner, a label, "Trafalgar Avenue," or "Sea View Road." Here and there, too, some small investor, some shopman with "savings," had delivered his soul to the local builders and built himself a house; and there it stood, ill-designed, mean-looking, isolated, ill-placed on a cheaply fenced plot, athwart which his domestic washing fluttered in the breeze amidst a bleak desolation of enterprise. Then presently our railway crossed a high road, and a row of mean yellow-brick houses — workmen's cottages, and the filthy black sheds that made the "allotments" of that time a universal eyesore, marked our approach to the more central areas of — I quote the local guidebook — "one of the most delightful resorts in the East Anglian poppy land." Then more mean houses, the gaunt ungainliness of the electric force station — it had a huge chimney, because no one understood how to make combustion of coal complete — and then we were in the railway station, and barely three-quarters of a mile from the centre of this haunt of health and pleasure.

I inspected the town thoroughly before I made my inquiries. The road began badly with a row of cheap, pretentious, insolvent-looking shops, a public-house, and a cab-stand, but, after an interval of little red villas that were partly hidden amidst shrubbery gardens, broke into a confusedly bright but not unpleas-

ing High Street, shuttered that afternoon and sabbatically still. Somewhere in the background a church bell jangled, and children in bright new-looking clothes were going to Sunday-school. Thence through a square of stuccoed lodging-houses that seemed a finer and cleaner version of my native square, I came to a garden of asphalt and euonymus — the Sea Front. I sat down on a cast-iron seat, and surveyed first of all the broad stretches of muddy, sandy beach, with its queer wheeled bathing machines painted with the advertisements of somebody's pills, and then at the house fronts that stared out upon these visceral counsels. Boarding-houses, private hotels, and lodging-houses in terraces clustered closely right and left of me, and then came to an end; in one direction scaffolding marked a building enterprise in progress, in the other, after a waste interval, rose a monstrous bulging red shape, a huge hotel, that dwarfed all other things. Northward were low pale cliffs with white denticulations of tents, where the local volunteers, all under arms, lay encamped; and southward, a spreading waste of sandy dunes, with occasional bushes and clumps of stunted pine and an advertisement board or so. A hard blue sky hung over all this prospect, the sunshine cast inky shadows, and eastward was a whitish sea. It was Sunday, and the midday meal still held people indoors. . . .

A queer world! thought I even then — to you now it must seem impossibly queer — and after an interval I forced myself back to my own affair.

How was I to ask? What was I to ask for?

I puzzled for a long time over that — at first I was a little tired and indolent — and then presently I had a flow of ideas.

My solution was fairly ingenious. I invented the following story. I happened to be taking a holiday in Shaphambury, and I was making use of the opportunity to seek the owner of a valuable feather boa, which had been left behind in the hotel of my uncle at Wyvern by a young lady, travelling with a young gentleman — no doubt, a youthful married couple. They had reached Shaphambury somewhen on Thursday. I went over the story many times, and gave my imaginary uncle and his hotel plausible names. At any rate this yarn would serve as a complete justification for all the questions I might wish to ask.

I settled that, but I still sat for a time, wanting the energy to begin. Then I turned towards the big hotel. Its gorgeous magnificence seemed to my inexpert judgment to indicate the very place a rich young man of good family would select.

Huge draught-proof doors were swung round for me by an ironically polite under-porter in a magnificent green uniform, who looked at my clothes as he listened to my question and then with a German accent referred me to a gorgeous head porter, who directed me to a princely young man behind a counter of brass and polish, like a bank —

like several banks. This young man, while he answered me, kept his eye on my collar and tie — and I knew that they were abominable.

"I want to find a lady and gentleman who came to Shaphambury on Tuesday," I said.

"Friends of yours?" he asked with a terrible fineness of irony.

I made out at last that here at any rate the young people had not been. They might have lunched there, but they had had no room. But I went out — door opened again for me obsequiously — in a state of social discomfiture, and did not attack any other establishment that afternoon.

My resolution had come to a sort of ebb. More people were promenading, and their Sunday smartness abashed me. I forgot my purpose in an acute sense of myself. I felt that the bulge of my pocket caused by the revolver was conspicuous, and I was ashamed. I went along the sea front away from the town, and presently lay down among pebbles and sea poppies. This mood of reaction prevailed with me all that afternoon. In the evening, about sundown, I went to the station and asked questions of the outporters there. But outporters, I found, were a class of men who remembered luggage rather than people, and I had no sort of idea what luggage young Verrall and Nettie were likely to have with them.

Then I fell into conversation with a salacious wooden-legged old man with a silver ring, who swept the steps that went down to the beach from the parade. He knew much about young couples, but only in general terms, and nothing of the particular young couple I sought. He reminded me in the most disagreeable way of the sensuous aspects of life, and I was not sorry when presently a gunboat appeared in the offing signalling the coastguard and the camp, and cut short his observations upon holidays, beaches, and morals.

I went — and now I was past my ebb — and sat in a seat upon the parade, and watched the brightening of those rising clouds of chilly fire that made the ruddy west seem tame. My midday lassitude was going, my blood was running warmer again. And as the twilight and that filmy brightness replaced the dusty sunlight and robbed this unfamiliar place of all its matter-of-fact queerness, its sense of aimless materialism, romance returned to me, and passion, and my thoughts of honour and revenge. I remember that change of mood as occurring very vividly on this occasion, but I fancy that less distinctly I had felt this before many times. In the old times, night and the starlight had an effect of intimate reality the daytime did not possess. The daytime — as one saw it in towns and populous places — had hold of one, no doubt, but only as an uproar might, it was distracting, conflicting, insistent. Darkness veiled the more salient aspects of those agglomerations of human absurdity, and one could exist — one could imagine.

I had a queer illusion that

night, that Nettie and her lover were close at hand, that suddenly I should come on them. I have already told how I went through the dusk seeking them in every couple that drew near. And I dropped asleep at last in an unfamiliar bedroom hung with gaudily decorated texts, cursing myself for having wasted a day.

§ 3

I SOUGHT them in vain the next morning, but after midday I came in quick succession on a perplexing multitude of clues. After failing to find any young couple that corresponded to young Verrall and Nettie, I presently discovered an unsatisfactory quartette of couples.

Any of these four couples might have been the one I sought; with regard to none of them was there conviction. They had all arrived either on Wednesday or Thursday. Two couples were still in occupation of their rooms, but neither of these were at home. Late in the afternoon I reduced my list by eliminating a young man in drab, with side whiskers and long cuffs, accompanied by a lady of thirty or more, of consciously ladylike type. I was disgusted at the sight of them; the other two young people had gone for a long walk, and though I watched their boarding-house until the fiery cloud shone out above, sharing and mingling in an unusually splendid sunset, I missed them. Then I discovered them dining at a separate table in the bow window, with red-shaded candles between them, peering out ever and again at this splendour that was neither night nor day. The girl in her pink evening dress looked very light and pretty to me — pretty enough to enrage me — she had well-shaped arms and white, well-modelled shoulders, and the turn of her cheek and the fair hair about her ears was full of subtle delights; but she was not Nettie, and the happy man with her was that degenerate type our old aristocracy produced with such odd frequency, chinless, large bony nose, small fair head, languid expression, and a neck that had demanded and received a veritable sleeve of collar. I stood outside in the meteor's livid light, hating them and cursing them for having delayed me so long. I stood until it was evident they remarked me, a black shape of envy, silhouetted against the glare.

That finished Shaphambury. The question I now had to debate was which of the remaining couple I had to pursue.

I walked back to the parade trying to reason my next step out, and muttering to myself, because there was something in that luminous wonderfulness that touched one's brain and made one feel a little light-headed.

One couple had gone to London; the other had gone to the Bungalow village at Bone Cliff. Where, I wondered, was Bone Cliff?

I came upon my wooden-legged man at the top of his steps. "Hullo," said I.

He pointed seaward with his pipe, the silver ring shone in the sky light.

"Rum," he said.

"What is?" I asked.

"Searchlights! Smoke! Ships going north! If it wasn't for this blasted Milky Way gone green up there, we might see."

He was too intent to heed my questions for a time. Then he vouchsafed over his shoulder —

"Know Bungalow village? — rather. Artis' and such. Nice goings on! Mixed bathing — something scandalous. Yes."

"But where is it?" I said, suddenly exasperated.

"There!" he said. "What's that flicker? A gunflash — or I'm a lost soul!"

"You'd hear," I said, "long before it was near enough to see a flash."

He didn't answer. Only by making it clear I would distract him until he told me what I wanted to know could I get him to turn from his absorbed contemplation of that phantom dance between the sea rim and the shine. Indeed I gripped his arm and shook him. Then he turned upon me cursing.

"Seven miles," he said, "along this road. And now go to 'ell with yer!"

I answered with some foul insult by way of thanks, and so we parted; and I set off towards the bungalow village.

I found a policeman, standing star-gazing, a little way beyond the end of the parade, and verified the wooden-legged man's directions.

"It's a lonely road, you know," he called after me. . . .

I had an odd intuition that now at last I was on the right track. I left the dark masses of Shaphambury behind me, and pushed out into the dim pallor of that night with the quiet assurance of a traveller who nears his end.

The incidents of that long tramp I do not recall in any orderly succession, the one progressive thing is my memory of a growing fatigue. The sea was for the most part smooth and shining like a mirror, a great expanse of reflecting silver barred by slow broad undulations, but at one time a little breeze breathed like a faint sigh and ruffled their long bodies into faint scaly ripples that never completely died out again. The way was sometimes sandy, thick with silvery colourless sand, and sometimes chalky and lumpy, with lumps that had shining facets; a black scrub was scattered, sometimes in thickets, sometimes in single bunches, among the somnolent hummocks of sand. At one place came grass, and ghostly great sheep looming up among the grey. After a time black pinewoods intervened, and made sustained darknesses along the road, woods that frayed out at the edges to weirdly warped and stunted trees. Then isolated pine witches would appear, and make their rigid gestures at me as I passed. Grotesquely incongruous amidst these forms, I presently came on estate boards, appealing, "Houses can be built to suit purchaser," to the silence, to the shadows, and to the glare.

Once I remember the persistent barking of a dog from somewhere inland of me, and several times I

took out and examined my revolver very carefully. I must, of course, have been full of my intention when I did that, I must have been thinking of Nettie and revenge, but I cannot now recall these emotions at all. Only I see again very distinctly the greenish gleams that ran over lock and barrel as I turned the weapon in my hand.

Then there was the sky, the wonderful, luminous, starless, moonless sky, and the empty blue deeps of the edge of it, between the meteor and the sea. And once — strange phantoms! — I saw far out upon the shine, and very small and distant, three long black warships, without masts, or sails, or smoke, or any lights, dark, deadly, furtive things, travelling very swiftly and keeping an equal distance. And when I looked again they were very small, and then the shine had swallowed them up.

Then once a flash and what I thought was a gun, until I looked up and saw a fading trail of greenish light still hanging in the sky. And after that there was a shiver and whispering in the air, a stronger throbbing in one's arteries, a sense of refreshment, a renewal of purpose. . . .

Somewhere upon my way the road forked, but I do not remember whether that was near Shaphambury or near the end of my walk. The hesitation between two rutted unmade roads alone remains clear in my mind.

At last I grew weary. I came to piled heaps of decaying seaweed and cart tracks running this way and that, and then I had missed the road and was stumbling among sand hummocks quite close to the sea. I came out on the edge of the dimly glittering sandy beach, and something phosphorescent drew me to the water's edge. I bent down and peered at the little luminous specks that floated in the ripples.

Presently with a sigh I stood erect, and contemplated the lonely peace of that last wonderful night. The meteor had now trailed its shining nets across the whole space of the sky and was beginning to set; in the east the blue was coming to its own again; the sea was an intense edge of blackness, and now, escaped from that great shine, and faint and still tremulously valiant, one weak elusive star could just be seen, hovering on the verge of the invisible.

How beautiful it was! how still and beautiful! Peace! peace! — the peace that passeth understanding, robed in light descending! . . .

My heart swelled, and suddenly I was weeping.

There was something new and strange in my blood. It came to me that indeed I did not want to kill.

I did not want to kill. I did not want to be the servant of my passions any more. A great desire had come to me to escape from life, from the daylight which is heat and conflict and desire, into that cool night of eternity — and rest. I had played — I had done.

I stood upon the edge of the great ocean, and I was filled with an inarticulate spirit of prayer,

and I desired greatly — peace from myself.

And presently, there in the east, would come again the red discolouring curtain over these mysteries, the finite world again, the grey and growing harsh certainties of dawn. My resolve I knew would take up with me again. This was a rest for me, an interlude; but to-morrow I should be William Leadford once more, ill-nourished, ill-dressed, ill-equipped and clumsy, a thief and shamed, a wound upon the face of life, a source of trouble and sorrow even to the mother I loved; no hope in life left for me now but revenge before my death.

Why this paltry thing, revenge? It entered into my thoughts that I might end the matter now and let these others go.

To wade out into the sea, into this warm lapping that mingled the natures of water and light, to stand there breast-high, to thrust my revolver barrel into my mouth — ?

Why not?

I swung about with an effort. I walked slowly up the beach thinking. . . .

I turned and looked back at the sea. No! Something within me said, " No! "

I must think.

It was troublesome to go further because the hummocks and the tangled bushes began. I sat down amidst a black cluster of shrubs, and rested, chin on hand. I drew my revolver from my pocket and looked at it, and held it in my hand. Life? Or Death? . . .

I seemed to be probing the very deeps of being, but indeed imperceptibly I fell asleep, and sat dreaming.

§ 4

Two people were bathing in the sea.

I had awakened. It was still that white and wonderful night, and the blue band of clear sky was no wider than before. These people must have come into sight as I fell asleep, and awakened me almost at once. They waded breast-deep in the water, emerging, coming shoreward, a woman, with her hair coiled about her head, and in pursuit of her a man, graceful figures of black and silver with a bright green surge flowing off from them, a pattering of flashing wavelets about them. He smote the water and splashed it towards her, she retaliated, and then they were knee-deep, and then for an instant their feet broke the long silver margin of the sea.

Each wore a tightly fitting bathing dress that hid nothing of the shining, dripping beauty of their youthful forms.

She glanced over her shoulder and found him nearer than she thought, started, gesticulated, gave a little cry that pierced me to the heart, and fled up the beach obliquely towards me, running like the wind, and passed me, vanished amidst the black distorted bushes, and was gone — she and her pursuer, in a moment, over the ridge of sand.

I heard him shout between exhaustion and laughter. . . .

And suddenly I was a thing of

bestial fury, standing with hands held up and clenched, rigid in gesture of impotent threatening, against the sky. . . .

For this striving, swift thing of light and beauty was Nettie — and this was the man for whom I had been betrayed!

And, it blazed upon me, I might have died there by the sheer ebbing of my will — unavenged!

In another moment I was running and stumbling, revolver in hand, in quite unsuspected pursuit of them, through the soft and noiseless sand.

§ 5

I CAME up over the little ridge and discovered the bungalow village I had been seeking, nestling in a crescent lap of dunes. A door slammed, and two runners had vanished, and I halted staring.

There was a group of three bungalows nearer to me than the others. Into one of these three they had gone, and I was too late to see which. All had doors and windows carelessly open, and none showed a light.

This place, upon which I had at last happened, was a fruit of the reaction of artistic-minded and carelessly living people against the costly and uncomfortable social stiffness of the more formal seaside resorts of that time. It was, you must understand, the custom of the steam-railway companies to sell their carriages after they had been obsolete for a sufficient length of years, and some genius had hit upon the possibility of turning these into habitable cabins for the summer holiday. The thing had become a fashion with a certain Bohemian-spirited class; they added cabin to cabin, and these little improvised homes, gaily painted and with broad verandahs and supplementary lean-tos added to their accommodation, made the brightest contrast conceivable to the dull rigidities of the decorous resorts. Of course there were many discomforts in such camping that had to be faced cheerfully, and so this broad sandy beach was sacred to high spirits and the young. Art muslin and banjoes, Chinese lanterns and frying, are leading "notes," I find, in the impression of those who once knew such places well. But so far as I was concerned this odd settlement of pleasure-squatters was a mystery as well as a surprise, enhanced rather than mitigated by an imaginative suggestion or so I had received from the wooden-legged man at Shaphambury. I saw the thing as no gathering of light hearts and gay idleness, but grimly — after the manner of poor men poisoned by the suppression of all their cravings after joy. To the poor man, to the grimy workers, beauty and cleanness were absolutely denied; out of a life of greasy dirt, of muddied desires, they watched their happier fellows with a bitter envy and foul, tormenting suspicions. Fancy a world in which the common people held love to be a sort of beastliness, own sister to being drunk! . . .

There was in the old time always something cruel at the bot-

tom of this business of sexual love. At least that is the impression I have brought with me across the gulf of the great Change. To succeed in love seemed such triumph as no other success could give, but to fail was as if one was tainted. . . .

I felt no sense of singularity that this thread of savagery should run through these emotions of mine and become now the whole strand of these emotions. I believed, and I think I was right in believing, that the love of all true lovers was a sort of defiance then, that they closed a system in each other's arms and mocked the world without. You loved against the world, and these two loved *at* me. They had their business with one another, under the threat of a watchful fierceness. A sword, a sharp sword, the keenest edge in life, lay among their roses.

Whatever may be true of this for others, for me and my imagination, at any rate, it was altogether true. I was never for dalliance, I was never a jesting lover. I wanted fiercely; I made love impatiently. Perhaps I had written irrelevant love-letters for that very reason; because with this stark theme I could not play. . . .

The thought of Nettie's shining form, of her shrinking bold abandon to her easy conqueror, gave me now a body of rage that was nearly too strong for my heart and nerves and the tense powers of my merely physical being. I came down among the pale sand-heaps slowly towards that queer village of careless sensuality, and now within my puny body I was

coldly sharpset for pain and death, a darkly gleaming hate, a sword of evil, drawn.

§ 6

I HALTED, and stood planning what I had to do.

Should I go to bungalow after bungalow until one of the two I sought answered to my rap? But suppose some servant intervened!

Should I wait where I was — perhaps until morning — watching? And meanwhile —

All the nearer bungalows were very still now. If I walked softly to them, from open windows, from something seen or overheard, I might get a clue to guide me. Should I advance circuitously, creeping upon them, or should I walk straight to the door? It was bright enough for her to recognise me clearly at a distance of many paces.

The difficulty to my mind lay in this, that if I involved other people by questions, I might at last confront my betrayers with these others close about me, ready to snatch my weapon and seize my hands. Besides, what names might they bear here?

" Boom! " the sound crept upon my senses, and then again it came.

I turned impatiently as one turns upon an impertinence, and beheld a great ironclad not four miles out, steaming fast across the dappled silver, and from its funnels sparks, intensely red, poured out into the night. As I turned, came the hot flash of its guns, firing seaward, and answering this, red flashes and a streaming smoke in the line between

sea and sky. So I remembered it, and I remember myself staring at it — in a state of stupid arrest. It was an irrelevance. What had these things to do with me?

With a shuddering hiss, a rocket from a headland beyond the village leaped up and burst hot gold against the glare, and the sound of the third and fourth guns reached me.

The windows of the dark bungalows, one after another, leaped out, squares of ruddy brightness that flared and flickered and became steadily bright. Dark heads appeared looking seaward, a door opened, and sent out a brief lane of yellow to mingle and be lost in the comet's brightness. That brought me back to the business in hand.

"Boom! boom!" and when I looked again at the great iron-clad, a little torchlike spurt of flame wavered behind her funnels. I could hear the throb and clangour of her straining engines. . . .

I became aware of the voices of people calling to one another in the village. A white-robed, hooded figure, some man in a bathing wrap, absurdly suggestive of an Arab in his burnous, came out from one of the nearer bungalows, and stood clear and still and shadowless in the glare.

He put his hands to shade his seaward eyes, and shouted to people within.

The people within — *my* people! My fingers tightened on my revolver. What was this war nonsense to me? I would go round among the hummocks with the idea of approaching the three

bungalows inconspicuously from the flank. This fight at sea might serve my purpose — except for that, it had no interest for me at all. Boom! boom! The huge voluminous concussions rushed past me, beat at my heart and passed. In a moment Nettie would come out to see.

First one and then two other wrappered figures came out of the bungalows to join the first. His arm pointed seaward, and his voice, a full tenor, rose in explanation. I could hear some of the words. "It's a German!" he said. "She's caught."

Someone disputed that, and there followed a little indistinct babble of argument. I went on slowly in the circuit I had marked out, watching these people as I went.

They shouted together with such a common intensity of direction that I halted and looked seaward. I saw the tall fountain flung by a shot that had just missed the great warship. A second rose still nearer us, a third and a fourth, and then a great uprush of dust, a whirling cloud, leaped out of the headland whence the rocket had come, and spread with slow deliberation right and left. Hard on that an enormous crash, and the man with the full voice leaped and cried, "Hit!"

Let me see! Of course, I had to go round beyond the bungalows, and then come up towards the group from behind.

A high-pitched woman's voice called, "Honeymooners! honeymooners! Come out and see!"

Something gleamed in the

shadow of the nearer bungalow, and a man's voice answered from within. What he said I did not catch, but suddenly I heard Nettie calling very distinctly, " We've been bathing."

The man who had first come out shouted, " Don't you hear the guns? They're fighting — not five miles from shore."

" Eh? " answered the bungalow, and a window opened.

" Out there! "

I did not hear the reply, because of the faint rustle of my own movements. Clearly these people were all too much occupied by the battle to look in my direction, and so I walked now straight towards the darkness that held Nettie and the black desire of my heart.

" Look! " cried someone, and pointed skyward.

I glanced up, and behold! The sky was streaked with bright green trails. They radiated from a point halfway between the western horizon and the zenith, and within the shining clouds of the meteor a streaming movement had begun, so that it seemed to be pouring both westwardly and back towards the east, with a crackling sound, as though the whole heaven was stippled over with phantom pistol-shots. It seemed to me then as if the meteor was coming to help me, descending with those thousand pistols like a curtain to fend off this unmeaning foolishness of the sea.

" Boom! " went a gun on the big ironclad, and " boom! " and the guns of the pursuing cruisers flashed in reply.

To glance up at that streaky, stirring light scum of the sky made one's head swim. I stood for a moment dazed, and more than a little giddy. I had a curious instant of purely speculative thought. Suppose, after all, the fanatics were right, and the world *was* coming to an end! what a score that would be for Parload!

Then it came into my head that all these things were happening to consecrate my revenge! The war below, the heavens above, were the thunderous garment of my deed. I heard Nettie's voice cry out not fifty yards away, and my passion surged again. I was to return to her amid these terrors bearing unanticipated death. I was to possess her, with a bullet, amidst thunderings and fear. At the thought I lifted up my voice to a shout that went unheard, and advanced now recklessly, revolver displayed in my hand.

It was fifty yards, forty yards, thirty yards — the little group of people, still heedless of me, was larger and more important now, the green-shot sky and the fighting ships remoter. Someone darted out from the bungalow, with an interrupted question, and stopped, suddenly aware of me. It was Nettie, with some coquettish dark wrap about her, and the green glare shining on her sweet face and white throat. I could see her expression, stricken with dismay and terror at my advance, as though something had seized her by the heart and held her still — a target for my shots.

"Boom!" came the ironclad's gunshot like a command. "Bang!" the bullet leaped from my hand. Do you know, I did not want to shoot her then. Indeed I did not want to shoot her then! Bang! and I had fired again, still striding on, and — each time it seemed I had missed.

She moved a step or so towards me, still staring, and then someone intervened, and near beside her I saw young Verrall.

A heavy stranger, the man in the hooded bathgown, a fat, foreign-looking man, came out of nowhere like a shield before them. He seemed a preposterous interruption. His face was full of astonishment and terror. He rushed across my path with arms extended and open hands, as one might try to stop a runaway horse. He shouted some nonsense. He seemed to want to dissuade me, as though dissuasion had anything to do with it now.

"Not you, you fool!" I said hoarsely. "Not you!" But he hid Nettie nevertheless.

By an enormous effort I resisted a mechanical impulse to shoot through his fat body. Anyhow, I knew I mustn't shoot him. For a moment I was in doubt, then I became very active, turned aside abruptly and dodged his pawing arm to the left, and so found two others irresolutely in my way. I fired a third shot in the air, just over their heads, and ran at them. They hastened left and right; I pulled up and faced about within a yard of a foxy-faced young man coming sideways, who seemed about to grapple me. At my resolute halt he fell back a pace, ducked, and threw up a defensive arm, and then I perceived the course was clear, and ahead of me, young Verrall and Nettie — he was holding her arm to help her — running away. "Of course!" said I.

I fired a fourth ineffectual shot, and then in an access of fury at my misses, started out to run them down and shoot them barrel to backbone. "These people!" I said, dismissing all these interferences. . . . "A yard," I panted, speaking aloud to myself, "a yard! Till then, take care, you mustn't — mustn't shoot again."

Someone pursued me, perhaps several people — I do not know, we left them all behind. . . .

We ran. For a space I was altogether intent upon the swift monotony of flight and pursuit. The sands were changed to a whirl of green moonshine, the air was thunder. A luminous green haze rolled about us. What did such things matter? We ran. Did I gain or lose? that was the question. They ran through a gap in a broken fence that sprang up abruptly out of nothingness, and turned to the right. I noted we were on a road. But this green mist! One seemed to plough through it. They were fading into it, and at that thought I made a spurt that won a dozen feet or more.

She staggered. He gripped her arm, and dragged her forward. They doubled to the left. We were off the road again and on turf. It felt like turf. I tripped and fell at a ditch that was somehow full of smoke, and was up

again, but now they were phantoms half gone into the livid swirls about me. . . .

Still I ran.

On, on! I groaned with the violence of my effort. I staggered again and swore. I felt the concussions of great guns tear past me through the murk.

They were gone! Everything was going, but I kept on running. Once more I stumbled. There was something about my feet that impeded me, tall grass or heather, but I could not see what it was, only this smoke that eddied about my knees. There was a noise and spinning in my brain, a vain resistance to a dark green curtain that was falling, falling, falling, fold upon fold. Everything grew darker and darker.

I made one last frantic effort, and raised my revolver, fired my penultimate shot at a venture, and fell headlong to the ground. And behold! the green curtain was a black one, and the earth and I and all things ceased to be.

IN THE DAYS OF THE COMET

Book II: *The Green Vapours*

CHAPTER 1

THE CHANGE

§ 1

I seemed to awaken out of a refreshing sleep.

I did not awaken with a start, but opened my eyes, and lay very comfortably looking at a line of extraordinarily scarlet poppies that glowed against a glowing sky. It was the sky of a magnificent sunrise, and an archipelago of gold-beached purple islands floated in a sea of golden green. The poppies too, swan-necked buds, blazing corollas, translucent stout seed-vessels, stoutly upheld, had a luminous quality, seemed wrought only from some more solid kind of light.

I stared unwonderingly at these things for a time, and then there rose upon my consciousness, intermingling with these, the bristling golden green heads of growing barley.

A remote faint question, where I might be, drifted and vanished again in my mind. Everything was very still.

Everything was as still as death.

I felt very light, full of the sense of physical well-being. I perceived I was lying on my side in a little trampled space in a weedy, flowering barley field, that was in some inexplicable way saturated with light and beauty. I sat up, and remained for a long time filled with the delight and charm of the delicate little convolvulus that twined among the barley stems, the pimpernel that laced the ground below.

Then that question returned. What was this place? How had I come to be sleeping here?

I could not remember.

It perplexed me that somehow my body felt strange to me. It was unfamiliar — I could not tell how — and the barley, and the beautiful weeds, and the slowly developing glory of the dawn behind; all those things partook of the same unfamiliarity. I felt as though I was a thing in some very luminous painted window, as though this dawn broke through

me. I felt I was part of some exquisite picture painted in light and joy.

A faint breeze bent and rustled the barley-heads and jogged my mind forward.

Who was I? That was a good way of beginning.

I held up my left hand and arm before me, a grubby hand, a frayed cuff; but with a quality of painted unreality, transfigured as a beggar might have been by Botticelli. I looked for a time steadfastly at a beautiful pearl sleeve-link.

I remembered Willie Leadford, who had owned that arm and hand, as though he had been someone else.

Of course! My history — its rough outline rather than the immediate past — began to shape itself in my memory, very small, very bright and inaccessible, like a thing watched through a microscope. Clayton and Swathinglea returned to my mind; the slums and darkness, Düreresque, minute and in their rich dark colours pleasing, and through them I went towards my destiny. I sat hands on knees recalling that queer passionate career that had ended with my futile shot into the growing darkness of the End. The thought of that shot awoke my emotions again.

There was something in it now, something absurd, that made me smile pityingly.

Poor little angry, miserable creature! Poor little angry, miserable world!

I sighed for pity, not only pity for myself, but for all the hot hearts, the tormented brains, the straining, striving things of hope and pain, who had found their peace at last beneath the pouring mist and suffocation of the comet. Because certainly that world was over and done. They were all so weak and unhappy, and I was now so strong and so serene. For I felt sure I was dead; no one living could have this perfect assurance of good, this strong and confident peace. I had made an end of the fever called living. I was dead, and it was all right, and these — ?

I felt an inconsistency.

These, then, must be the barley fields of God! — the still and silent barley fields of God, full of unfading poppy flowers whose seeds bear peace.

§ 2

It was queer to find barley fields in heaven, but no doubt there were many surprises in store for me.

How still everything was! Peace! The peace that passeth understanding. After all it had come to me! But, indeed, everything was very still! No bird sang. Surely I was alone in the world! No birds sang. Yes, and all the distant sounds of life had ceased, the lowing of cattle, the barking of dogs. . . .

Something that was like fear beatified came into my heart. It was all right, I knew; but to be alone! I stood up and met the hot summons of the rising sun, hurrying towards me, as it were, with glad tidings, over the spikes of the barley. . . .

Blinded, I made a step. My foot struck something hard, and

I looked down to discover my revolver, a blue-black thing, like a dead snake at my feet.

For a moment that puzzled me. Then I clean forgot about it. The wonder of the quiet took possession of my soul. Dawn, and no birds singing!

How beautiful was the world! How beautiful, but how still! I walked slowly through the barley towards a line of elder bushes, wayfaring tree and bramble that made the hedge of the field. I noted as I passed along a dead shrew mouse, as it seemed to me, among the halms; then a still toad. I was surprised that this did not leap aside from my footfalls, and I stooped and picked it up. Its body was limp like life, but it made no struggle, the brightness of its eye was veiled, it did not move in my hand.

It seems to me now that I stood holding that lifeless little creature for some time. Then very softly I stooped down and replaced it. I was trembling—trembling with a nameless emotion. I looked with quickened eyes closely among the barley stems, and behold, now everywhere I saw beetles, flies, and little creatures that did not move, lying as they fell when the vapours overcame them; they seemed no more than painted things. Some were novel creatures to me. I was very unfamiliar with natural things. "My God!" I cried; "but is it only I—?"

And then at my next movement something squealed sharply. I turned about, but I could not see it, only I saw a little stir in a rut and heard the diminishing rustle of the unseen creature's flight. And at that I turned to my toad again; and its eyes moved and it stirred. And presently, with infirm and hesitating gestures, it stretched its limbs and began to crawl away from me.

But wonder, that gentle sister of fear, had me now. I saw a little way ahead a brown and crimson butterfly perched upon a cornflower. I thought at first it was the breeze that stirred it, and then I saw its wings were quivering. And even as I watched it, it started into life, and spread itself, and fluttered into the air.

I watched it fly, a turn this way, a turn that, until suddenly it seemed to vanish. And now, life was returning to this thing and that on every side of me, with slow stretchings and bendings, with twitterings, with a little start and stir. . . .

I came slowly, stepping very carefully because of these drugged, feebly awakening things, through the barley to the hedge. It was a very glorious hedge, so that it held my eyes. It flowed along and interlaced like splendid music. It was rich with lupin, honeysuckle, campions, and ragged-robin; bed straw, hops, and wild clematis twined and hung among its branches, and all along its ditch border the starry stitchwort lifted its childish faces, and chorused in lines and masses. Never had I seen such a symphony of note-like flowers and tendrils and leaves. And suddenly in its depths, I heard a chirrup and the whir of startled wings.

Nothing was dead, but everything had changed to beauty!

And I stood for a time with clean and happy eyes looking at the intricate delicacy before me and marvelling how richly God has made his worlds. . . .

"Tweedle-Tweezle," a lark had shot the stillness with his shining thread of song; one lark, and then presently another, invisibly in the air, making out of that blue quiet a woven cloth of gold. . . .

The earth recreated — only by the reiteration of such phrases may I hope to give the intense freshness of that dawn. For a time I was altogether taken up with the beautiful details of being, as regardless of my old life of jealous passion and impatient sorrow as though I was Adam new made. I could tell you now with infinite particularity of the shut flowers that opened as I looked, of tendrils and grass blades, of a blue-tit I picked up very tenderly — never before had I remarked the great delicacy of feathers — that presently disclosed its bright black eye and judged me, and perched, swaying fearlessly, upon my finger, and spread unhurried wings and flew away, and of a great ebullition of tadpoles in the ditch; like all the things that lived beneath the water they had passed unaltered through the Change. Amid such incidents, I lived those first great moments, losing for a time in the wonder of each little part the mighty wonder of the whole.

A path ran between hedge and barley, and along this, leisurely and content and glad, looking at this beautiful thing and that, moving a step and stopping, then moving on again, I came presently to a stile and deep below it, and overgrown, was a lane.

And on the worn oak of the stile was a round label, and on the label these words, " Swindells' G 90 Pills."

I sat myself astraddle on the stile, not fully grasping all the implications of these words. But they perplexed me even more than the revolver and my dirty cuff.

About me now the birds lifted up their little hearts and sang, ever more birds and more.

I read the label over and over again, and joined it to the fact that I still wore my former clothes, and that my revolver had been lying at my feet. One conclusion stared out at me. This was no new planet, no glorious hereafter such as I had supposed. This beautiful wonderland was the world, the same old world of my rage and death! But at least it was like meeting a familiar house-slut, washed and dignified, dressed in a queen's robes, worshipful and fine. . . .

It might be the old world indeed, but something new lay upon all things, a glowing certitude of health and happiness. It might be the old world, but the dust and fury of the old life was certainly done. At least I had no doubt of that.

I recalled the last phases of my former life, that darkling climax of pursuit and anger and universal darkness and the whirling green vapours of extinction. The comet had struck the earth and made an end to all things; of that too I was assured.

But afterwards? . . .

And now?

The imaginations of my boyhood came back as speculative possibilities. In those days I had believed firmly in the necessary advent of a last day, a great coming out of the sky, trumpetings and fear, the Resurrection, and the Judgment. My roving fancy now suggested to me that this Judgment must have come and passed. That it had passed and in some manner missed me. I was left alone here, in a swept and garnished world (except, of course, for this label of Swindells') to begin again perhaps. . . .

No doubt Swindells had got his deserts.

My mind ran for a time on Swindells, on the imbecile pushfulness of that extinct creature, dealing in rubbish, covering the countryside with lies in order to get — what had he sought? — a silly, ugly, great house, a temper-destroying motor-car, a number of disrespectful, abject servants; thwarted intrigues for a party-fund baronetcy as the crest of his life, perhaps. You cannot imagine the littleness of those former times; their naïve, queer absurdities! And for the first time in my existence I thought of these things without bitterness. In the former days I had seen wickedness, I had seen tragedy, but now I saw only the extraordinary foolishness of the old life. The ludicrous side of human wealth and importance turned itself upon me, a shining novelty, poured down upon me like the sunrise, and engulfed me in laughter.

Swindells! Swindells, damned! My vision of Judgment became a delightful burlesque. I saw the chuckling Angel sayer with his face veiled, and the corporeal presence of Swindells upheld amidst the laughter of the spheres. "Here's a thing, and a very pretty thing, and what's to be done with this very pretty thing?" I saw a soul being drawn from a rotund, substantial-looking body like a whelk from its shell. . . .

I laughed loudly and long. And behold! even as I laughed the keen point of things accomplished stabbed my mirth, and I was weeping, weeping aloud, convulsed with weeping, and the tears were pouring down my face.

§ 3

EVERYWHERE the awakening came with the sunrise. We awakened to the gladness of the morning; we walked dazzled in a light that was joy. Everywhere that was so. It was always morning. It was morning because, until the direct rays of the sun touched it, the changing nitrogen of our atmosphere did not pass into its permanent phase, and the sleepers lay as they had fallen. In its intermediate state the air hung inert, incapable of producing either revival or stupefaction, no longer green, but not yet changed to the gas that now lives in us. . . .

To everyone, I think, came some parallel to the mental states I have already sought to describe — a wonder, an impression of joyful novelty. There was also very commonly a certain confusion of the intelligence, a difficulty in

self-recognition. I remember clearly as I sat on my stile that presently I had the clearest doubts of my own identity and fell into the oddest metaphysical questionings. "If this be I," I said, "then how is it I am no longer madly seeking Nettie? Nettie is now the remotest thing —and all my wrongs. Why have I suddenly passed out of all that passion? Why does not the thought of Verrall quicken my pulses? . . ."

I was only one of many millions who that morning had the same doubts. I suppose one knows one's self for one's self when one returns from sleep or insensibility by the familiarity of one's bodily sensations, and that morning all our most intimate bodily sensations were changed. The intimate chemical processes of life were changed, its nervous metaboly. For the fluctuating, uncertain, passion-darkened thought and feeling of the old time came steady, full-bodied, wholesome processes. Touch was different, sight was different, sound and all the senses were subtler; had it not been that our thought was steadier and fuller, I believe great multitudes of men would have gone mad. But, as it was, we understood. The dominant impression I would convey in this account of the Change is one of enormous release, of a vast substantial exaltation. There was an effect, as it were, of light-headedness that was also clear-headedness, and the alteration in one's bodily sensations, instead of producing the mental obfuscation, the loss of identity that was

a common mental trouble under former conditions, gave simply a new detachment from the tumid passions and entanglements of the personal life.

In this story of my bitter, restricted youth that I have been telling you, I have sought constantly to convey the narrowness, the intensity, the confusion, muddle, and dusty heat of the old world. It was quite clear to me, within an hour of my awakening, that all that was, in some mysterious way, over and done. That, too, was the common experience. Men stood up; they took the new air into their lungs —a deep long breath, and the past fell from them; they could forgive, they could disregard, they could attempt. . . . And it was no new thing, no miracle that sets aside the former order of the world. It was a change in material conditions, a change in the atmosphere, that at one bound had released them. Some of them it had released to death. . . . Indeed, man himself had changed not at all. We knew before the Change, the meanest knew, by glowing moments in ourselves and others, by histories and music and beautiful things, by heroic instances and splendid stories, how fine mankind could be, how fine almost any human being could upon occasion be; but the poison in the air, its poverty in all the nobler elements which made such moments rare and remarkable—all that has changed. The air was changed, and the Spirit of Man that had drowsed and slumbered and dreamt dull and evil things,

awakened, and stood with wonder-clean eyes, refreshed, looking again on life.

§4

THE MIRACLE of the awakening came to me in solitude, the laughter, and then the tears. Only after some time did I come upon another man. Until I heard his voice calling I did not seem to feel there were any other people in the world. All that seemed past, with all the stresses that were past. I had come out of the individual pit in which my shy egotism had lurked. I had overflowed to all humanity, I had seemed to be all humanity; I had laughed at Swindells as I could have laughed at myself, and this shout that came to me seemed like the coming of an unexpected thought in my own mind. But when it was repeated I answered.

"I am hurt," said the voice, and I descended into the lane forthwith, and so came upon Melmount sitting near the ditch with his back to me.

Some of the incidental sensory impressions of that morning bit so deeply into my mind that I verily believe, when at last I face the greater mysteries that lie beyond this life, when the things of this life fade from me as the mists of the morning fade before the sun, these irrelevant petty details will be the last to leave me, will be the last wisps visible of that attenuating veil. I believe, for instance, I could match the fur upon the collar of his great motoring coat now, could paint the dull red tinge of his big cheek with his fair eyelashes just catching the light and showing beyond. His hat was off, his dome-shaped head, with its smooth hair between red and extreme fairness, was bent forward in scrutiny of his twisted foot. His back seemed enormous. And there was something about the mere massive sight of him that filled me with liking.

"What's wrong?" said I.

"I say," he said, in his full deliberate tones, straining round to see me and showing a profile, a well-modelled nose, a sensitive, clumsy, big lip, known to every caricaturist in the world, "I'm in a fix. I fell and wrenched my ankle. Where are you?"

I walked round him and stood looking at his face. I perceived he had his gaiter and sock and boot off, the motor gauntlets had been cast aside, and he was kneading the injured part in an exploratory manner with his thick thumbs.

"By Jove!" I said, "you're Melmount!"

"Melmount!" He thought. "That's my name," he said, without looking up. . . . "But it doesn't affect my ankle."

We remained silent for a few moments except for a grunt of pain from him.

"Do you know?" I asked, "what has happened to things?"

He seemed to complete his diagnosis. "It's not broken," he said.

"Do you know," I repeated, "what has happened to everything?"

"No," he said, looking up at me incuriously for the first time. "There's some difference —"

"There's a difference." He smiled, a smile of unexpected pleasantness, and an interest was coming into his eyes. "I've been a little preoccupied with my own internal sensations. I remark an extraordinary brightness about things. Is that it?"

"That's part of it. And a queer feeling, a clear-headedness —"

He surveyed me and meditated gravely. "I woke up," he said, feeling his way in his memory.

"And I."

"I lost my way — I forget quite how. There was a curious green fog." He stared at his foot, remembering. "Something to do with a comet. I was by a hedge in the darkness. Tried to run. . . . Then I must have pitched forward into this lane. Look!" He pointed with his head. "There's a wooden rail new broken there. I must have stumbled over that out of the field above." He scrutinised this and concluded: "Yes. . . ."

"It was dark," I said, "and a sort of green gas came out of nothing everywhere. That is the last *I* remember."

"And then you woke up? So did I. . . . In a state of great bewilderment. Certainly there's something odd in the air. I was — I was rushing along a road in a motor-car, very much excited and preoccupied. I got down —" He held out a triumphant finger. "Ironclads!

"*Now* I've got it! We'd strung our fleet from her to Texel. We'd got right across them, and the Elbe mined. We'd lost the *Lord Warden*. By Jove, yes. The *Lord Warden*! A battleship that cost two million pounds — and that fool Rigby said it didn't matter! Eleven hundred men went down. . . . I remember now. We were sweeping up the North Sea like a net, with the North Atlantic fleet waiting at the Faroes for 'em — and not one of 'em had three days' coal! Now, was that a dream? No! I told a lot of people as much — a meeting was it? — to reassure them. They were warlike but extremely frightened. Queer people — paunchy and bald like gnomes, most of them. Where? Of course! We had it all over — a big dinner — oysters! — Colchester. I'd been there, just to show all this raid scare was nonsense. And I was coming back here. . . . But it doesn't seem as though that was — recent. I suppose it was. Yes, of course! — it was. I got out of my car at the bottom of the rise with the idea of walking along the cliff path, because everyone said one of their battleships was being chased along the shore. That's clear! I heard their guns —"

He reflected. "Queer I should have forgotten! Did *you* hear any guns?"

I said I had heard them.

"Was it last night?"

"Late last night. One or two in the morning."

He leaned back on his hand and looked at me, smiling frankly. "Even now," he said, "it's odd, but the whole of that seems like a silly dream. Do you think there *was* a Lord Warden. Do you really believe we sank all that machinery — for fun? It

was a dream. And yet—it happened."

By all the standards of the former time it would have been remarkable that I talked quite easily and freely with so great a man. "Yes," I said; "that's it. One feels one has awakened—from something more than that green gas. As though the other things also—weren't quite real."

He knitted his brows and felt the calf of his leg thoughtfully. "I made a speech at Colchester," he said.

I thought he was going to add something more about that, but there lingered a habit of reticence in the man that held him for the moment. "It is a very curious thing," he broke away; "that this pain should be, on the whole, more interesting than disagreeable."

"You are in pain?"

"My ankle is! It's either broken or badly sprained—I think sprained; it's very painful to move, but personally I'm not in pain. That sort of general sickness that comes with local injury—not a trace of it! . . ." He mused and remarked, "I was speaking at Colchester, and saying things about the war. I begin to see it better. The reporters—scribble, scribble. Max Sutaine, 1885. Hubbub. Compliments about the oysters. Mm—mm. . . . What was it? About the war? A war that must needs be long and bloody, taking toll from castle and cottage, taking toll! . . . Rhetorical gusto! Was I drunk last night?"

His eyebrows puckered. He had drawn up his right knee, his elbow rested thereon and his chin on his fist. The deep-set grey eyes beneath his thatch of eyebrow stared at unknown things. "My God!" he murmured, "My God!" with a note of disgust. He made a big brooding figure in the sunlight, he had an effect of more than physical largeness; he made me feel that it became me to wait upon his thinking. I had never met a man of this sort before; I did not know such men existed. . . .

It is a curious thing, that I cannot now recall any ideas whatever that I had before the Change about the personalities of statesmen, but I doubt if ever in those days I thought of them at all as tangible individual human beings, conceivably of some intellectual complexity. I believe that my impression was a straightforward blend of caricature and newspaper leader. I certainly had no respect for them. And now without servility or any insincerity whatever, as if it were a first-fruit of the Change, I found myself in the presence of a human being towards whom I perceived myself inferior and subordinate; before whom I stood without servility or any insincerity whatever, in an attitude of respect and attention. My inflamed, my rancid egotism—or was it after all only the chances of life?—had never once permitted that before the Change.

He emerged from his thoughts, still with a faint perplexity in his manner. "That speech I made last night," he said, "was damned

mischievous nonsense, you know. Nothing can alter that. Nothing. . . . No! . . . Little fat gnomes in evening dress — gobbling oysters. Gulp!"

It was a most natural part of the wonder of that morning that he should adopt this incredible note of frankness, and that it should abate nothing from my respect for him.

"Yes," he said, "you are right. It's all indisputable fact, and I can't believe it was anything but a dream."

§5

THAT memory stands out against the dark past of the world with extraordinary clearness and brightness. The air, I remember, was full of the calling and piping and singing of birds. I have a curious persuasion too that there was a distant happy clamour of pealing bells, but that I am half convinced is a mistake. Nevertheless, there was something in the fresh bite of things, in the dewy newness of sensation that set bells rejoicing in one's brain. And that big, fair, pensive man sitting on the ground had beauty even in his clumsy pose, as though indeed some Great Master of strength and humour had made him.

And — it is so hard now to convey these things — he spoke to me, a stranger, without reservations, carelessly, as men now speak to men. Before those days, not only did we think badly, but what we thought, a thousand short-sighted considerations, dignity, objective discipline, discretion, a hundred

kindred aspects of shabbiness of soul, made us muffle before we told it to our fellow-men.

"It's all returning now," he said, and told me half soliloquisingly what was in his mind.

I wish I could give every word he said to me; he struck out image after image to my nascent intelligence, with swift broken fragments of speech. If I had a precise full memory of that morning I should give it you, verbatim, minutely. But here, save for the little sharp things that stand out, I find only blurred general impressions. Throughout I have to make up again his half-forgotten sentences and speeches, and be content with giving you the general effect. But I can see and hear him now as he said, "The dream got worst at the end. The war — a perfectly horrible business! Horrible! And it was just like a nightmare, you couldn't do anything to escape from it — every one was driven!"

His sense of indiscretion was gone.

He opened the war out to me — as everyone sees it now. Only that morning it was astonishing. He sat there on the ground, absurdly forgetful of his bare and swollen foot, treating me as the humblest accessory and as altogether an equal, talking out to himself the great obsessions of his mind. "We could have prevented it! Any of us who chose to speak out could have prevented it. A little decent frankness. What was there to prevent us being frank with one another? Their emperor — his position was a pile of ri-

diculous assumptions, no doubt, but at bottom — he was a sane man." He touched off the emperor in a few pithy words, the German press, the German people, and our own. He put it as we should put it all now, but with a certain heat as of a man half guilty and wholly resentful. "Their damned little buttoned-up professors!" he cried, incidentally. "Were there ever such men? And ours! Some of us might have taken a firmer line. . . . If a lot of us had taken a firmer line and squashed that nonsense early. . . ."

He lapsed into inaudible whisperings, into silence. . . .

I stood regarding him, understanding him, learning marvellously from him. It is a fact that for the best part of the morning of the Change I forgot Nettie and Verrall as completely as though they were no more than characters in some novel that I had put aside to finish at my leisure, in order that I might talk to this man.

"Eh, well," he said waking startlingly from his thoughts. "Here we are awakened! The thing can't go on now; all this must end. How it ever began—! My dear boy, how did all those things ever begin? I feel like a new Adam. . . . Do you think this has happened — generally? Or shall we find all these gnomes and things? . . . who cares?"

He made as if to rise, and remembered his ankle. He suggested I should help him as far as his bungalow. There seemed nothing strange to either of us

that he should requisition my services or that I should cheerfully obey. I helped him bandage his ankle, and we set out, I his crutch, the two of us making up a sort of limping quadruped, along the winding lane towards the cliffs and the sea.

§ 6

His bungalow beyond the golf links was, perhaps, a mile and a quarter from the lane. We went down to the beach margin and along the pallid wave-smoothed sands, and we got along by making a swaying, hopping, tripod dance forward until I began to give under him, and then, as soon as we could, sitting down. His ankle was, in fact, broken, and he could not put it to the ground without exquisite pain. So that it took us nearly two hours to get to the house, and it would have taken longer if his butler-valet had not come out to assist me. They had found motor-car and chauffeur smashed and still at the bend of the road near the house, and had been on that side looking for Melmount, or they would have seen us before.

For most of that time we were sitting now on turf, now on a chalk boulder, now on a timber groin, and talking one to the other with the frankness proper to the intercourse of men of good intent, without reservations or aggressions, in the common, open fashion of contemporary intercourse to-day, but which then, nevertheless, was the rarest and strangest thing in the world. He for the most part talked, but at

some shape of a question I told him — as plainly as I could tell of passions that had for a time become incomprehensible to me — of my murderous pursuit of Nettie and her lover, and how the green vapours overcame me. He watched me with grave eyes and nodded understandingly, and afterwards he asked me brief penetrating questions about my education, my upbringing, my work. There was a deliberation in his manner, brief full pauses, that had in them no element of delay.

"Yes," he said, "yes — of course. What a fool I have been!" and said no more until we had made another of our tripod struggles along the beach. At first I did not see the connection of my story with that self-accusation.

"Suppose," he said, panting on the groin, "there had been such a thing as a statesman! . . ."

He turned to me. "If one had decided all this muddle shall end! If one had taken it, as an artist takes his clay, as a man who builds takes site and stone, and made — " He flung out his big broad hand at the glories of sky and sea, and drew a deep breath, "something to fit that setting."

He added in explanation, "Then there wouldn't have been such stories as yours at all, you know. . . .

"Tell me more about it," he said, "tell me all about yourself. I feel all these things have passed away, all these things are to be changed for ever. . . . You won't be what you have been from this time forth. All the things you have done — don't matter now. To us, at any rate, they don't matter at all. We have met, who were separated in that darkness behind us. Tell me.

"Yes," he said; and I told my story straight and as frankly as I have told it to you. "And there, where those little skerries of weed rock run out to the ebb, beyond the headland, is Bungalow village. What did you do with your pistol?"

"I left it lying there — among the barley."

He glanced at me from under his light eyelashes. "If others feel as you and I do," he said, "there'll be a lot of pistols left among the barley to-day. . . ."

So we talked, I and that great, strong man, with the love of brothers so plain between us it needed not a word. Our souls went out to one another in stark good faith; never before had I had anything but a guarded watchfulness for any fellow-man. Still I see him upon that wild desolate beach of the ebb tide. I see him leaning against the shelly buttress of a groin, looking down at the poor drowned sailor whose body we presently found. For we found a newly drowned man who had just chanced to miss this great dawn in which we rejoiced. We found him lying in a pool of water, among brown weeds in the dark shadow of the timberings. You must not overrate the horrors of the former days; in those days it was scarcely more common to see death in England than it would

be to-day. This dead man was a sailor from the *Rother Adler,* the great German battleship that — had we but known it — lay not four miles away along the coast amidst ploughed-up mountains of chalk ooze, a torn and battered mass of machinery, wholly submerged at high water, and holding in its interstices nine hundred drowned brave men, all strong and skilful, all once capable of doing fine things. . . .

I remember that poor boy very vividly. He had been drowned during the anæsthesia of the green gas, his fair young face was quiet and calm, but the skin of his chest had been crinkled by scalding water and his right arm was bent queerly back. Even to this needless death and all its tale of cruelty, beauty and dignity had come. Everything flowed together to significance as we stood there, I, the ill-clad, cheaply equipped proletarian, and Melmount in his great fur-trimmed coat — he was hot with walking but he had not thought to remove it — leaning upon the clumsy groins and pitying this poor victim of the war he had helped to make. "Poor lad!" he said, "poor lad! a child we blunderers sent to death! Do look at the quiet beauty of that face, that body — to be flung aside like this!"

(I remember that near this dead man's hand a stranded starfish writhed its slowly feeling limbs, struggling back toward the sea. It left grooved traces in the sand.)

"There must be no more of this," panted Melmount, leaning on my shoulder, "no more of this. . . ."

But most I recall Melmount as he talked a little later, sitting upon a great chalk boulder with the sunlight on his big, perspiration-dewed face. He made his resolves. "We must end war," he said, in that full whisper of his; "it is stupidity. With so many people able to read and think — even as it is — there is no need of anything of the sort. Gods! What have we rulers been at? . . . Drowsing like people in a stifling room, too dull and sleepy and too base towards each other for anyone to get up and open the window. What haven't we been at?"

A great powerful figure he sits there still in my memory, perplexed and astonished at himself and all things. "We must change all this," he repeated, and threw out his broad hands in a comprehensive gesture. "We have done so weakly — Heaven alone knows why!" I can see him now, queer giant that he looked on that dawnlit beach of splendour, the sea birds flying about us and that crumpled death hard by, no bad symbol in his clumsiness and needless heat of the unawakened powers of the former time. I remember it as an integral part of that picture that far away across the sandy stretches one of those white estate boards I have described, stuck up a little askew amidst the yellow-green turf upon the crest of the low cliffs.

He talked with a sort of won-

der of the former things. "Has it ever dawned upon you to imagine the pettiness — the pettiness! — of every soul concerned in a declaration of war?" he asked. He went on, as though speech was necessary to make it credible, to describe Laycock, who first gave the horror words at the cabinet council, "an undersized Oxford prig with a tenoring voice and a garbage of Greek — the sort of fool who is brought up on the admiration of his elder sisters. . . .

"All the time almost," he said, "I was watching him — thinking what an ass he was to be trusted with men's lives. . . . I might have done better to have thought that of myself. I was doing nothing to prevent it all! The damned imbecile was up to his neck in the drama of the thing, he liked to trumpet it out, he goggled round at us. 'Then it is war!' he said. Richover shrugged his shoulders. I made some slight protest and gave in. . . . Afterwards I dreamt of him.

"What a lot we were! All a little scared at ourselves — all, as it were, instrumental. . . .

"And it's fools like that lead to things like this!" He jerked his head at that dead man near by us.

"It will be interesting to know what has happened to the world. . . . This green vapour — queer stuff. But I know what has happened to me. It's Conversion. I've always known. . . . But this is being a fool. Talk! I'm going to stop it."

He motioned to rise with his clumsy outstretched hands.

"Stop what?" said I, stepping forward instinctively to help him.

"War," he said in his great whisper, putting his big hand on my shoulder and making no further attempt to rise, "I'm going to put an end to war — to any sort of war! And all these things that must end. The world is beautiful, life is great and splendid, we had only to lift up our eyes and see. Think of the glories through which we have been driving, like a herd of swine in a garden place. The colour in life — the sounds — the shapes! We have had our jealousies, our quarrels, our ticklish rights, our invincible prejudices, our vulgar enterprise and sluggish timidities, we have chattered and pecked one another and fouled the world — like daws in the temple, like unclean birds in the holy place of God. All my life has been foolishness and pettiness, gross pleasures and mean discretions — all. I am a meagre dark thing in this morning's glow, a penitence, a shame! And, but for God's mercy, I might have died this night — like that poor lad there — amidst the squalor of my sins! No more of this! No more of this! — whether the whole world has changed or no, matters nothing. *We two have seen this dawn!* . . ."

He paused.

"I will arise and go unto my Father," he began presently, "and will say unto Him —"

His voice died away in an inaudible whisper. His hand tightened painfully on my shoulder and he rose. . . .

CHAPTER 2

THE AWAKENING

§ 1

So the great Day came to me.

And even as I had awakened so in that same dawn the whole world awoke.

For the whole world of living things had been overtaken by the same tide of insensibility; in an hour, at the touch of this new gas in the comet, the shiver of catalytic change had passed about the globe. They say it was the nitrogen of the air, the old *azote*, that in the twinkling of an eye was changed out of itself, and in an hour or so became a respirable gas, differing indeed from oxygen, but helping and sustaining its action, a bath of strength and healing for nerve and brain. I do not know the precise changes that occurred, nor the names our chemists give them; my work has carried me away from such things; only this I know — I and all men were renewed.

I picture to myself this thing happening in space, a planetary moment, the faint smudge, the slender whirl of meteor, drawing nearer to this planet — this planet like a ball, like a shaded rounded ball, floating in the void, with its little, nearly impalpable coat of cloud and air, with its dark pools of ocean, its gleaming ridges of land. And as that midge from the void touches it, the transparent gaseous outer shell clouds in an instant green and then slowly clears again. . . .

Thereafter, for three hours or more — we know the minimum time for the Change was almost exactly three hours because all the clocks and watches kept going — everywhere, no man nor beast nor bird nor any living thing that breathes the air stirred at all but lay still. . . .

Everywhere on earth that day, in the ears of everyone who breathed, there had been the same humming in the air, the same rush of green vapours, the crepitation, the streaming down of shooting stars. The Hindoo had stayed his morning's work in the fields to stare and marvel and fall, the blue-clothed Chinaman fell head foremost athwart his midday bowl of rice, the Japanese merchant came out from some chaffering in his office amazed and presently lay there before his door, the evening gazers by the Golden Gates were overtaken as they waited for the rising of the great star. This had happened in every city of the world, in every lonely valley, in every home and house and shelter and every open place. On the high seas, the crowding steamship passengers, eager for any wonder, gaped and marvelled, and were suddenly terror-stricken, and struggled for the gangways and were overcome; the captain staggered on

the bridge and fell, the stoker fell headlong among his coals, the engines throbbed upon their way untended, the fishing craft drove by without a hail, with swaying rudder, heeling and dipping. . . .

The great voice of material Fate cried Halt! And in the midst of the play the actors staggered, dropped, and were still. The figure runs from my pen. In New York that very thing occurred. Most of the theatrical audiences dispersed, but in two crowded houses the company, fearing a panic, went on playing amidst the gloom, and the people, trained by many a previous disaster, stuck to their seats. There they sat, the back rows only moving a little, and there, in disciplined lines, they drooped and failed, nodded, and fell forward or slid down upon the floor. I am told by Parload — though indeed I know nothing of the reasoning on which his inference rests — that within an hour of the great moment of impact the first green modification of nitrogen had dissolved and passed away, leaving the air as translucent as ever. The rest of that wonderful interlude was clear, had any had eyes to see its clearness. In London it was night; but in New York, for example, people were in full bustle of the evening's enjoyment, in Chicago they were sitting down to dinner, the whole world was abroad. The moonlight must have illuminated streets and squares littered with crumpled figures, through which such electric cars as had no automatic brakes had ploughed on their way until they were stopped by the fallen bodies. People lay in their dress clothes, in dining-rooms, restaurants, on staircases, in halls, everywhere just as they had been overcome. Men gambling, men drinking, thieves lurking in hidden places, sinful couples, were caught, to arise with awakened mind and conscience amidst the disorder of their sin. America the comet reached in the full tide of evening life, but Britain lay asleep. But as I have told, Britain did not slumber so deeply but that she was in the full tide of what may have been battle and a great victory. Up and down the North Sea her warships swept together like a net about their foes. On land, too, that night was to have decided great issues. The German camps were under arms from Redingen to Markirch, their infantry columns were lying in swathes like mown hay, in arrested night march on every track between Longnyon and Thiancourt, and between Avricourt and Donen. The hills beyond Spincourt were dusted thick with hidden French riflemen; the thin lash of the French skirmishers sprawled out amidst spades and unfinished rifle-pits in coils that wrapped about the heads of the German columns, thence along the Vosges watershed and out across the frontier near Belfort nearly to the Rhine. . . .

The Hungarian, the Italian peasant, yawned and thought the morning dark, and turned over to fall into a dreamless sleep; the Mohometan world spread its carpet and was taken in prayer. And in Sydney, in Melbourne, in New

Zealand, the thing was a fog in the afternoon, that scattered the crowd in racecourses and cricket-fields, and stopped the unloading of shipping and brought men out from their afternoon rest to stagger and litter the streets. . . .

§ 2

MY thoughts go into the woods and wildernesses and jungles of the world, to the wild life that shared man's suspension, and I think of a thousand feral acts interrupted and truncated — as it were frozen, like the frozen words Pantagruel met at sea. Not only men it was that were quieted, all living creatures that breathe the air became insensible, impassive things. Motionless brutes and birds lay amidst the drooping trees and herbage in the universal twilight, the tiger sprawled beside his fresh-struck victim, who bled to death in a dreamless sleep. The very flies came sailing down the air with wings outspread; the spider hung crumpled in his loaded net; like some gaily painted snowflake the butterfly drifted to earth and grounded, and was still. And as a queer contrast one gathers that the fishes in the sea suffered not at all. . . .

Speaking of the fishes reminds me of a queer little inset upon that great world-dreaming. The odd fate of the crew of the submarine vessel B 94 has always seemed memorable to me. So far as I know, they were the only men alive who never saw that veil of green drawn across the world. All the while that the stillness held above, they were working into the mouth of the Elbe,

past the booms and the mines, very slowly and carefully, a sinister crustacean of steel, explosive crammed, along the muddy bottom. They trailed a long clue that was to guide their fellows from the mother ship floating awash outside. Then in the long channel beyond the forts they came up at last to mark down their victims and get air. That must have been before the twilight of dawn, for they tell of the brightness of the stars. They were amazed to find themselves not three hundred yards from an ironclad that had run ashore in the mud, and heeled over with the falling tide. It was afire amidships, but no one heeded that — no one in all that strange clear silence heeded that — and not only this wrecked vessel, but all the dark ships lying about them, it seemed to their perplexed and startled minds, must be full of dead men!

Theirs I think must have been one of the strangest of all experiences; they were never insensible; at once, and, I am told, with a sudden catch of laughter, they began to breathe the new air. None of them has proved a writer; we have no picture of their wonder, no descripton of what was said. But we know these men were active and awake for an hour and a half at least before the general awakening came, and when at last the Germans stirred and sat up they found these strangers in possession of their battleship, the submarine carelessly adrift, and the Englishmen begrimed and weary, but with a sort of furious exultation, still

busy in the bright dawn, rescuing insensible enemies from the sinking conflagration. . . .

But the thought of certain stokers the sailors of the submarine failed altogether to save brings me back to the thread of grotesque horror that runs through all this event, the thread I cannot overlook for all the splendours of human well-being that have come from it. I cannot forget the unguided ships that drove ashore, that went down in disaster with all their sleeping hands, nor how, inland, motorcars rushed to destruction upon the roads, and trains upon the railways kept on in spite of signals, to be found at last by their amazed, reviving drivers standing on unfamiliar lines, their fires exhausted, or, less lucky, to be discovered by astonished peasants or awakening porters smashed and crumpled up into heaps of smoking, crackling ruin. The foundry fires of the Four Towns still blazed, the smoke of our burning still defiled the sky. Fires burned indeed the brighter for the Change — and spread. . . .

§ 3

PICTURE to yourself what happened between the printing and composing of the copy of the *New Paper* that lies before me now. It was the first newspaper that was printed upon earth after the Great Change. It is pocket-worn and browned, made of a paper no man ever intended for preservation. I found it on the arbour table in the inn garden while I was waiting for Nettie and Verrall, before that last conversation of which I have presently to tell. As I look at it all that scene comes back to me, and Nettie stands in her white raiment against a blue-green background of sunlit garden, scrutinising my face as I read. . . .

It is so frayed that the sheet cracks along the folds and comes to pieces in my hands. It lies upon my desk, a dead souvenir of the dead ages of the world, of the ancient passions of my heart. I know we discussed its news, but for the life of me I cannot recall what we said, only I remember that Nettie said very little, and that Verrall for a time read it over my shoulder, and I did not like him to read over my shoulder. . . .

The document before me must have helped us through the first awkwardness of that meeting.

But of all that we said and did then I must tell in a later chapter. . . .

It is easy to see the *New Paper* had been set up overnight, and then large pieces of the stereo plates replaced subsequently. I do not know enough of the old methods of printing to know precisely what happened. The thing gives one an impression of large pieces of type having been cut away and replaced by fresh blocks. There is something very rough and ready about it all, and the new portions print darker and more smudgily than the old, except towards the left, where they have missed ink and indented. A friend of mine, who knows something of the old typography, has suggested to me that the machinery actually in use for

the *New Paper* was damaged that night, and that on the morning of the Change Banghurst borrowed a neighbouring office — perhaps in financial dependence upon him — to print in.

The outer pages belong entirely to the old period, the only parts of the paper that had undergone alteration are the two middle leaves. Here we found set forth in a curious little four-column oblong of print, WHAT HAS HAPPENED. This cut across a column with scare headlines beginning, "Great Naval Battle Now in Progress. The Fate of Two Empires in the Balance. Reported Loss of Two More—"

These things, one gathered, were beneath notice now. Probably it was guesswork, and fabricated news in the first instance.

It is curious to piece together the worn and frayed fragments, and reread this discoloured first intelligence of the new epoch.

The simple clear statements in the replaced portion of the paper impressed me at the time, I remember, as bald and strange, in that framework of shouting bad English. Now they seem like the voice of a sane man amidst a vast faded violence. But they witness to the prompt recovery of London from the gas; the new, swift energy of rebound in that huge population. I am surprised now, as I reread, to note how much research, experiment, and induction must have been accomplished in the day that elapsed before the paper was printed. . . . But that is by the way. As I sit and muse over this partly carbonised sheet, that same curious

remote vision comes again to me that quickened in my mind that morning, a vision of those newspaper offices I have already described to you through the crisis.

The catalytic wave must have caught the place in full swing, in its nocturnal high fever; indeed in a quite exceptional state of fever, what with the comet and the war, and more particularly with the war. Very probably the Change crept into the office imperceptibly, amidst the noise and shouting, and the glare of electric light that made the night atmosphere in that place; even the green flashes may have passed unobserved there, the preliminary descending trails of green vapour seemed no more than unseasonable drifting wisps of London fog. (In those days London even in summer was not safe against dark fogs.) And then at the last the Change poured in and overtook them.

If there was any warning at all for them, it must have been a sudden universal tumult in the street, and then a much more universal quiet. They could have had no other intimation.

There was no time to stop the presses before the main development of green vapour had overwhelmed everyone. It must have folded about them, tumbled them to the earth, masked and stilled them. My imagination is always curiously stirred by the thought of that, because I suppose it is the first picture I succeeded in making for myself of what had happened in the towns. It has never quite lost its strange-

ness for me that when the Change came, machinery went on working. I don't precisely know why that should have seemed so strange to me, but it did, and still to a certain extent does. One is so accustomed, I suppose, to regard machinery as an extension of human personality that the extent of its autonomy the Change displayed came as a shock to me. The electric lights, for example, hazy, green-haloed nebulæ, must have gone on burning at least for a time; amidst the thickening darkness the huge presses must have roared on, printing, folding, throwing aside copy after copy of that fabricated battle report with its quarter column of scare headlines, and all the place must have still quivered and throbbed with the familar roar of the engines. And this though no men ruled there at all any more! Here and there beneath that thickening fog the crumpled or outstretched forms of men lay still. A wonderful thing that would have seemed, had any man been able to resist the vapour, and could he have walked amidst it.

And soon the machines must have exhausted their feed of ink and paper, and thumped and banged and rattled emptily amidst the general quiet. Then, I suppose, the furnaces failed for want of stoking, the steam pressure fell in the pistons, the machinery slackened, the lights burned dim, and came and went with the ebb of energy from the power-station. Who can tell precisely the sequence of these things now?

And then, you know, amidst the weakening and terminating noises of men, the green vapour cleared and vanished, in an hour indeed it had gone, and it may be a breeze stirred and blew and went about the earth.

The noises of life were all dying away, but some there were that abated nothing, that sounded triumphantly amidst the universal ebb. To a heedless world the church towers tolled out two and then three. Clocks ticked and chimed everywhere about the earth to deafened ears. . . .

And then came the first flush of morning, the first rustlings of the revival. Perhaps in that office the filaments of the lamps were still glowing, the machinery was still pulsing weakly, when the crumpled, booted heaps of cloth became men again and began to stir and stare. The chapel of the printers was, no doubt, shocked to find itself asleep. Amidst that dazzling dawn the *New Paper* woke to wonder, stood up and blinked at its amazing self. . . .

The clocks of the city churches, one pursuing another, struck four. The staffs, crumpled and dishevelled, but with a strange refreshment in their veins, stood about the damaged machinery, marvelling and questioning; the editor read his overnight headlines with incredulous laughter. There was much involuntary laughter that morning. Outside, the mail men patted the necks and rubbed the knees of their awakening horses. . . .

Then, you know, slowly and with much conversation and

doubt, they set about to produce the paper.

Imagine those bemused, perplexed people, carried on by the inertia of their old occupations and doing their best with an enterprise that had suddenly become altogether extraordinary and irrational. They worked amidst questionings, and yet light-heartedly. At every stage there must have been interruptions for discussion. The paper only got down to Menton five days late.

§ 4

THEN let me give you a vivid little impression I received of a certain prosaic person, a grocer named Wiggins, and how he passed through the Change. I heard this man's story in the post-office at Menton, when, in the afternoon of the First Day, I bethought me to telegraph to my mother. The place was also a grocer's shop, and I found him and the proprietor talking as I went in. They were trade competitors, and Wiggins had just come across the street to break the hostile silence of a score of years. The sparkle of the Change was in their eyes, their slightly flushed cheeks, their more elastic gestures, spoke of new physical influences that had invaded their beings.

"It did us no good, all our hatred," Mr. Wiggins said to me, explaining the emotion of their encounter; "it did our customers no good. I've come to tell him that. You bear that in mind, young man, if ever you come to have a shop of your own. It was

a sort of stupid bitterness possessed us, and I can't make out we didn't see it before in that light. Not so much downright wickedness it wasn't as stupidity. A stupid jealousy! Think of it! —two human beings within a stone's throw, who have not spoken for twenty years, hardening our hearts against each other!"

"I can't think how we came to such a state, Mr. Wiggins," said the other, packing tea into pound packets out of mere habit as he spoke. "It was wicked pride and obstinacy. We *knew* it was foolish all the time."

I stood affixing the adhesive stamp to my telegram.

"Only the other morning," he went on to me, "I was cutting French eggs. Selling at a loss to do it. He'd marked down with a great staring ticket to ninepence a dozen—I saw it as I went past. Here's my answer!" He indicated a ticket. "'Eightpence a dozen—same as sold elsewhere for ninepence.' A whole penny down, bang off! Just a touch above cost —if that—and even then—" He leaned over the counter to say impressively, *"Not the same eggs!"*

"Now, what people in their senses would do things like that?" said Mr. Wiggins.

I sent my telegram; the proprietor despatched it for me, and while he did so I fell exchanging experiences with Mr. Wiggins. He knew no more than I did then the nature of the Change that had come over things. He had been alarmed by the green flashes, he said, so much so that

after watching for a time from behind his bedroom window blind, he had got up and hastily dressed and made his family get up also, so that they might be ready for the end. He made them put on their Sunday clothes. They all went out into the garden together, their minds divided between admiration at the gloriousness of the spectacle and a great and growing awe. They were Dissenters, and very religious people out of business hours, and it seemed to them in those last magnificent moments that, after all, science must be wrong and the fanatics right. With the green vapours came conviction, and they prepared to meet their God. . . .

This man, you must understand, was a common-looking man, in his shirt-sleeves and with an apron about his paunch, and he told his story in an Anglian accent that sounded mean and clipped to my Staffordshire ears; he told his story without a thought of pride, and as it were incidentally, and yet he gave me a vision of something heroic.

These people did not run hither and thither as many others did. The four of them stood beyond their back door in their garden pathway between the gooseberry bushes, with the terrors of their God and His Judgments closing in upon them, swiftly and wonderfully — and there they began to sing. There they stood, father and mother and two daughters, chanting out stoutly, but no doubt a little flatly after the manner of their kind —

" In Zion's Hope abiding,
My soul in Triumph sings —"

until one by one they fell, and lay still.

The postmaster had heard them in the gathering darkness, " In Zion's Hope abiding. . . ."

It was the most extraordinary thing in the world to hear this flushed and happy-eyed man telling that story of his recent death. It was like a scene shown to me, very small and very distinctly painted, in a locket.

But that effect was not confined to this particular incident. A vast number of things that had happened before the coming of the comet had undergone the same transfiguring reduction. Other people, too, I have learned since, had the same illusion, a sense of enlargement. It seems to me even now that the little dark creature who had stormed across England in pursuit of Nettie and her lover must have been about an inch high, that all that previous life of ours had been an ill-lit marionette show, acted in the twilight. . . .

§ 5

THE FIGURE of my mother comes always into my conception of the Change.

I remember how one day she confessed herself.

She had been very sleepless that night, she said, and took the reports of the falling stars for shooting; there had been rioting in Clayton and through Swathinglea all day, and so she got out of bed to look. She had a dim sense that I must certainly be mixed up in that trouble.

But she was not looking when the Change came.

"When I saw the stars a-raining down, dear," she said, "and thought of you out in it, I thought there'd be no harm in saying a prayer for you, dear? I thought you wouldn't mind that."

And so I got another of my pictures—the green vapours come and go, and there by her patched coverlet that dear old woman kneels and droops, still clasping her poor gnarled hands in the attitude of prayer—prayer to IT—for me!

Through the meagre curtains and blinds of the flawed refracting window I see the stars above the chimneys fade, the pale light of dawn creeps into the sky, and her candle flares and dies. . . .

That also went with me through the stillness—that silent kneeling figure, that frozen prayer to God to shield me, silent in a silent world, rushing through the emptiness of space. . . .

§ 6

WITH the dawn that awakening went about the earth. I have told how it came to me, and how I walked in wonder through the transfigured cornfields of Shaphambury. It came to everyone. Near me, and for the time clean forgotten by me, Verrall and Nettie woke—woke near one another; each heard before all other sounds the other's voice amidst the stillness and the light. And the scattered people who had run to and fro, and fallen on the beach of Bungalow village, awoke; the sleeping villagers of Menton started, and sat up in that unwonted freshness and newness; the contorted figures in the garden, with the hymn still upon their lips, stirred amidst the flowers, and touched each other timidly, and thought of Paradise. My mother found herself crouched against the bed, and rose—rose with a glad invisible conviction of accepted prayer. . . .

Already, when it came to us, the soldiers, crowded between the lines of dusty poplars along the road to Allarmont, were chatting and sharing coffee with the French riflemen, who had hailed them from their carefully hidden pits among the vineyards up the slopes of Beauville. A certain perplexity had come to these marksmen, who had dropped asleep tensely ready for the rocket that should wake the whir and rattle of their magazines. At the sight and sound of the stir and human confusion in the roadway below, it had come to each man individually that he could not shoot. One conscript, at least, has told his story of his awakening, and how curious he thought the rifle there beside him in his pit, how he took it on his knees to examine. Then, as his memory of its purpose grew clearer, he dropped the thing, and stood up with a kind of joyful horror at the crime escape, to look more closely at the men he was to have assassinated. "*Brave types,*" he thought, they looked for such a fate. The summoning rocket never flew. Below, the men did not fall into ranks again, but sat by the road-side, or stood in groups talking, discussing with a novel incredulity the ostensible causes of the war.

"The Emperor!" said they; and "Oh, nonsense! We're civilised men. Get someone else for this job! . . . Where's the coffee?"

The officers held their own horses and talked to the men frankly, regardless of discipline. Some Frenchmen out of the rifle-pits came sauntering down the hill. Others stood doubtfully, rifles still in hand. Curious faces scanned these latter. Little arguments sprang as: "Shoot at us! Nonsense! They're respectable French citzens." There is a picture of it all, very bright and detailed in the morning light, in the battle gallery amidst the ruins at old Nancy, and one sees the old-world uniform of the "soldier," the odd caps and belts and boots, the ammunition-belt, the water-bottle, the sort of tourist's pack the men carried, a queer elaborate equipment. The soldiers had awakened one by one, first one and then another. I wonder sometimes whether, perhaps, if the two armies had come awake in an instant, the battle, by mere habit and inertia, might not have begun. But the men who waked first, sat up, looked about them in astonishment, had time to think a little. . . .

§7

EVERYWHERE there was laughter, everywhere tears.

Men and women in the common life, finding themselves suddenly lit and exalted, capable of doing what had hitherto been impossible, incapable of doing what had hitherto been irresistible, happy, hopeful, unselfishly ener-getic, rejected altogether the supposition that this was merely a change in the blood and material texture of life. They denied the bodies God had given them, as once the Upper Nile savages struck out their canine teeth because these made them like the beasts. They declared that this was the coming of a spirit, and nothing else would satisfy their need for explanations. And in a sense the Spirit came. The Great Revival sprang directly from the Change—the last, the deepest, widest, and most enduring of all the vast inundations of religious emotion that go by that name.

But indeed it differed essentially from its innumerable predecessors. The former revivals were a phase of fever, this was the first movement of health, it was altogether quieter, more intellectual, more private, more religious than any of those others. In the old time, and more especially in the Protestant countries where the things of religion were outspoken, and the absence of confession and well-trained priests made religious states of emotion explosive and contagious, revivalism upon various scales was a normal phase in the religious life, revivals were always going on—now a little disturbance of consciences in a village, now an evening of emotion in a Mission Room, now a great storm that swept a continent, and now an organised effort that came to town with bands and banners and handbills and motor-cars for the saving of souls. Never at any time did I take part in nor was I attracted by any of these movements. My

nature, although passionate, was too critical (or sceptical if you like, for it amounts to the same thing) and shy to be drawn into these whirls; but on several occasions Parload and I sat, scoffing, but nevertheless disturbed, in the back seats of revivalist meetings.

I saw enough of them to understand their nature, and I am not surprised to learn now that before the comet came, all about the world, even among savages, even among cannibals, these same, or at any rate closely similar, periodic upheavals went on. The world was stifling; it was in a fever, and these phenomena were neither more nor less than the instinctive struggle of the organism against the ebb of its powers, the clogging of its veins, the limitation of its life. Invariably these revivals followed periods of sordid and restricted living. Men obeyed their base immediate motives until the world grew unendurably bitter. Some disappointment, some thwarting, lit up for them — darkly indeed, but yet enough for indistinct vision — the crowded squalor, the dark enclosure of life. A sudden disgust with the insensate smallness of the old-world way of living, a realisation of sin, a sense of the unworthiness of all individual things, a desire for something comprehensive, sustaining, something greater, for wider communions and less habitual things, filled them. Their souls, which were shaped for wider issues, cried out suddenly amidst the petty interests, the narrow prohibitions, of life, " Not this! not

this! " A great passion to escape from the jealous prison of themselves, an inarticulate, stammering, weeping passion shook them. . . .

I have seen — I remember how once in Clayton Calvinistic Methodist chapel I saw — his spotty fat face strangely distorted under the flickering gas-flares — old Pallet the ironmonger repent. He went to the form of repentance, a bench reserved for such exhibitions, and slobbered out his sorrow and disgust for some sexual indelicacy — he was a widower — and I can see now how his loose fat body quivered and swayed with his grief. He poured it out to five hundred people, from whom in common times he hid his every thought and purpose. And it is a fact, it shows where reality lay, that we two youngsters laughed not at all at that blubbering grotesque, we did not even think the distant shadow of a smile. We two sat grave and intent — perhaps wondering.

Only afterwards and with an effort did we scoff. . . .

Those old-time revivals were, I say, the convulsive movements of a body that suffocates. They are the clearest manifestations from before the Change of a sense in all men that things were not right. But they were too often but momentary illuminations. Their force spent itself in incoordinated shouting, gesticulations, tears. They were but flashes of outlook. Disgust of the narrow life, of all baseness, took shape in narrowness and baseness. The quickened soul ended the

night a hypocrite; prophets disputed for precedence; seductions, it is altogether indisputable, were frequent among penitents! and Ananias went home converted and returned with a falsified gift. And it was almost universal that the converted should be impatient and immoderate, scornful of reason and any choice of expedients, opposed to balance, skill, and knowledge. Incontinently full of grace, like thin old wine-skins over-filled, they felt they must burst if once they came into contact with hard fact and sane direction.

So the former revivals spent themselves; but the Great Revival did not spend itself, but grew to be, for the majority of Christendom at least, the permanent expression of the Change. For many it has taken the shape of an outright declaration that this was the Second Advent — it is not for me to discuss the validity of that suggestion, for nearly all it has amounted to an enduring broadening of the issues of life. . . .

§ 8

ONE irrelevant memory comes back to me, irrelevant, and yet by some subtle trick of quality it summarises the Change for me. It is the memory of a woman's very beautiful face, a woman with a flushed face and tear-bright eyes who went by me without speaking, rapt in some secret purpose. I passed her when in the afternoon of the first day, struck by a sudden remorse, I went down to Menton to send a telegram to my mother telling her

all was well with me. Whither this woman went I do not know, nor whence she came; I never saw her again, and only her face, glowing with that new and luminous resolve, stands out for me. . . .

But that expression was the world's.

CHAPTER 3

THE CABINET COUNCIL

§ 1

AND what a strange unprecedented thing was that cabinet council at which I was present, the council that was held two days later in Melmount's bungalow, and which convened the conference to frame the constitution of the World State. I was there because it was convenient for me to stay with Melmount. I had nowhere to go particularly, and there was no one at his bungalow, to which his broken ankle confined him, but a secretary and a valet to help him to begin his share of the enormous labours that evidently lay before the rulers of the world. I wrote shorthand, and as there was not even a phonograph available, I went in so soon as his ankle had been dressed, and sat

at his desk to write at his dictation. It is characteristic of the odd slackness that went with the spasmodic violence of the old epoch, that the secretary could not use shorthand and that there was no telephone whatever in the place. Every message had to be taken to the village post-office in that grocer's shop at Menton, half a mile away. . . . So I sat in the back of Melmount's room, his desk had been thrust aside, and made such memoranda as were needed. At that time his room seemed to me the most beautifully furnished in the world, and I could identify now the vivid cheerfulness of the chintz of the sofa on which the great statesman lay just in front of me, the fine rich paper, the red sealing-wax, the silver equipage of the desk I used. I know now that my presence in that room was a strange and remarkable thing, the open door, even the coming and going of Parker the secretary, innovations. In the old days a cabinet council was a secret conclave, secrecy and furtiveness were in the texture of all public life. In the old days everybody was always keeping something back from somebody, being wary and cunning, prevaricating, misleading — for the most part for no reason at all. Almost unnoticed, that secrecy had dropped out of life.

I close my eyes and see those men again, hear their deliberating voices. First I see them a little diffusely in the cold explicitness of daylight, and then concentrated and drawn together amidst the shadow and mystery about shaded lamps. Integral to this

and very clear is the memory of biscuit crumbs and a drop of spilt water, that at first stood shining upon and then sank into the green table-cloth. . . .

I remember particularly the figure of Lord Adisham. He came to the bungalow a day before the others, because he was Melmount's personal friend. Let me describe this statesman to you, this one of the fifteen men who made the last war. He was the youngest member of the Government, and an altogether pleasant and sunny man of forty. He had a clear profile to his clean grey face, a smiling eye, a friendly, careful voice upon his thin, cleanshaven lips, an easy disabusing manner. He had the perfect quality of a man who had fallen easily into a place prepared for him. He had the temperament of what we used to call a philosopher — an indifferent, that is to say. The Change had caught him at his week-end recreation, flyfishing; and, indeed, he said, I remember, that he recovered to find himself with his head within a yard of the water's brim. In times of crisis Lord Adisham invariably went fly-fishing at the week-end to keep his mind in tone, and when there was no crisis then there was nothing he liked so much to do as fly-fishing, and so, of course, as there was nothing to prevent it, he fished. He arrived resolved, among other things, to give up fly-fishing altogether. I was present when he came to Melmount, and heard him say as much; and by a more naïve route it was evident that he had arrived at the same

scheme of intention as my master. I left them to talk, but afterwards I came back to take down their long telegrams to their coming colleagues. He was, no doubt, as profoundly affected as Melmount by the Change, but his tricks of civility and irony and acceptable humour had survived the Change, and he expressed his altered attitude, his expanded emotions, in a quaint modification of the old-time man-of-the-world style, with excessive moderation, with a trained horror of the enthusiasm that swayed him.

These fifteen men who ruled the British Empire were curiously unlike anything I had expected, and I watched them intently whenever my services were not in request. They made a peculiar class at that time, these English politicians and statesmen, a class that has now completely passed away. In some respects they were unlike the statesmen of any other region of the world, and I do not find that any really adequate account remains of them. . . . Perhaps you are a reader of the old books. If so, you will find them rendered with a note of hostile exaggeration by Dickens in "Bleak House," with a mingling of gross flattery and keen ridicule by Disraeli, who ruled among them accidentally by misunderstanding them and pleasing the court; and all their assumptions are set forth, portentously perhaps, but truthfully so far as people of the "permanent official" class saw them, in the novels of Mrs. Humphry Ward. All these books are still in this world and at the disposal of the

curious, and in addition the philosopher Bagehot and the picturesque historian Macaulay give something of their method of thinking, the novelist Thackeray skirts the seamy side of their social life, and there are some good passages of irony, personal descriptions, and reminiscence to be found in the "Twentieth Century Garner" from the pens of such writers, for example, as Sidney Low. But a picture of them as a whole is wanting. Then they were too near and too great; now, very rapidly, they have become incomprehensible.

We common people of the old time based our conception of our statesmen almost entirely on the caricatures that formed the most powerful weapon in political controversy. Like almost every main feature of the old condition of things these caricatures were an unanticipated development, they were a sort of parasitic outgrowth from, which had finally altogether replaced, the thin and vague aspirations of the original democratic ideals. They presented not only the personalities who led our public life, but the most sacred structural conceptions of that time, in ludicrous, vulgar, and dishonourable aspects that in the end came near to destroying entirely all grave and honourable emotion or motive toward the State. The state of Britain was represented nearly always by a red-faced, purse-proud farmer with an enormous belly; that fine dream of freedom, the United States, by a cunning, lean-faced rascal in striped trousers and a blue coat. The chief

ministers of state were pick pockets, washerwomen, clowns, whales, asses, elephants, and what not; and issues that affected the welfare of millions of men were dressed and judged like a rally in some idiotic pantomime. A tragic war in South Africa, that wrecked many thousand homes, impoverished two whole lands, and brought death and disablement to fifty thousand men, was presented as a quite comical quarrel between a violent queer being named Chamberlain, with an eyeglass, an orchid, and a short temper, and "old Kroojer," an obstinate and very cunning old man in a shocking bad hat. The conflict was carried through in a mood sometimes of brutish irritability and sometimes of lax slovenliness, the merry peculator plied his trade congenially in that asinine squabble, and behind these fooleries and masked by them, marched Fate — until at last behind the clowning, the curtains of the booth opened and revealed — hunger and suffering, brands burning and swords and shame. . . . These men had come to fame and power in that atmosphere, and to me that day there was the oddest suggestion in them of actors who have suddenly laid aside grotesque and foolish parts; the paint was washed from their faces, the posing put aside.

Even when the presentation was not frankly grotesque and degrading it was entirely misleading. When I read of Laycock, for example, there arises a picture of a large, active, if a little wrong-headed, intelligence

in a compact heroic body, emitting that "Goliath" speech of his that did so much to precipitate hostilities; it tallies not at all with the stammering, high-pitched, slightly bald, and very conscience-stricken personage I saw, nor with Melmount's contemptuous first description of him. I doubt if the world at large will ever get a proper vision of those men as they were before the Change. Each year they pass more and more incredibly beyond our intellectual sympathy. Our estrangement cannot, indeed, rob them of their portion in the past, but it will rob them of any effect of reality. The whole of their history becomes more and more foreign, more and more like some queer barbaric drama played in a forgotten tongue. There they strut through their weird metamorphoses of caricature, those premiers and presidents, their height preposterously exaggerated by political buskins, their faces covered by great resonant inhuman masks, their voices couched in the foolish idiom of public utterance, disguised beyond any semblance to sane humanity, roaring and squeaking through the public press. There it stands, this incomprehensible faded show, a thing left on one side, and now still and deserted by any interest, its many emptinesses as inexplicable now as the cruelties of medieval Venice, the theology of old Byzantium. And they ruled and influenced the lives of nearly a quarter of mankind, these politicians, their clownish conflicts swayed the world, made mirth

perhaps, made excitement, and permitted — infinite misery.

I saw these men quickened indeed by the Change, but still wearing the queer clothing of the old time, the manners and conventions of the old time; if they had disengaged themselves from the outlook of the old time they still had to refer back to it constantly as a common starting-point. My refreshed intelligence was equal to that, so that I think I did indeed see them. There was Gorrell-Browning, the Chancellor of the Duchy; I remember him as a big round-faced man, the essential vanity and foolishness of whose expression, whose habit of voluminous platitudinous speech, triumphed absurdly once or twice over the roused spirit within. He struggled with it, he burlesqued himself, and laughed. Suddenly he said simply, intensely — it was a movement for everyone of clean, clear pain, " I have been a vain and self-indulgent and presumptuous old man. I am of little use here. I have given myself to politics and intrigues, and life is gone from me." Then for a long time he sat still. There was Carton, the Lord Chancellor, a white-faced man with understanding; he had a heavy, shaven face that might have stood among the busts of the Cæsars, a slow, elaborating voice, with self-indulgent, slightly oblique, and triumphant lips, and a momentary, voluntary, humorous twinkle. " We have to forgive," he said. " We have to forgive — even ourselves."

These two were at the top corner of the table, so that I saw their faces well. Madgett, the Home Secretary, a smaller man with wrinkled eyebrows, and a frozen smile on his thin wry mouth, came next to Carton; he contributed little to the discussion save intelligent comments, and when the electric lights above glowed out, the shadows deepened queerly in his eye-sockets and gave him the quizzical expression of an ironical goblin. Next him was that great peer, the Earl of Richover, whose self-indulgent indolence had accepted the rôle of a twentieth-century British-Roman patrician of culture, who had divided his time almost equally between his jockeys, politics, and the composition of literary studies in the key of his rôle. " We have done nothing worth doing," he said. " As for me, I have cut a figure! " He reflected — no doubt on his ample patrician years, on the fine great houses that had been his setting, the teeming racecourses that had roared his name, the enthusiastic meetings he had fed with fine hopes, the futile Olympian beginnings. . . . " I have been a fool," he said compactly. They heard him in a sympathetic and respectful silence.

Gurker, the Chancellor of the Exchequer, was partially occulted, so far as I was concerned, by the back of Lord Adisham. Ever and again Gurker protruded into the discussion, swaying forward, a deep throaty voice, a big nose, a coarse mouth with a drooping everted lower lip, eyes peering amidst folds and wrinkes. He made his confession for his race. " We Jews," he said, " have gone

through the system of this world, creating nothing, consolidating many things, destroying much. Our racial self-conceit has been monstrous. We seem to have used our ample coarse intellectuality for no other purpose than to develop and master and maintain the convention of property, to turn life into a sort of mercantile chess and spend our winnings grossly. . . . We have had no sense of service to mankind. Beauty which is godhead — we made it a possession."

These men and these sayings particularly remain in my memory. Perhaps, indeed, I wrote them down at the time, but that I do not now remember. How Sir Digby Privet, Revel, Markheimer, and the others sat I do not now recall; they came in as voices, interruptions, imperfectly assigned comments. . . .

One got a queer impression that except perhaps for Gurker or Revel these men had not particularly wanted the power they held; had desired to do nothing very much in the positions they had secured. They had found themselves in the cabinet, and until this moment of illumination they had not been ashamed; but they had made no ungentlemanly fuss about the matter. Eight of that fifteen came from the same school, had gone through an entirely parallel education; some Greek linguistics, some elementary mathematics, some emasculated "science," a little history, a little reading in the silent or timidly orthodox English literature of the seventeenth, eighteenth, and nineteenth centuries, all eight had imbibed the same dull gentlemanly tradition of behaviour; essentially boyish, unimaginative — with neither keen swords nor art in it, a tradition apt to slobber into sentiment at a crisis and make a great virtue of a simple duty rather clumsily done. None of these eight had made any real experiments with life, they had lived in blinkers, they had been passed from nurse to governess, from governess to preparatory school, from Eton to Oxford, home governess to preparatory social routine. Even their vices and lapses had been according to certain conceptions of good form. They had all gone to the races surreptitiously from Eton, had all cut up to town from Oxford to see life — music-hall life — had all come to heel again. Now suddenly they discovered their limitations. . . .

"What are we to do?" asked Melmount. "We have awakened; this empire in our hands. . . ." I know this will seem the most fabulous of all the things I have to tell of the old order, but, indeed, I saw it with my eyes, I heard it with my ears. It is a fact that this group of men who constituted the Government of one-fifth of the habitable land of the earth, who ruled over a million of armed men, who had such navies as mankind had never seen before, whose empire of nations, tongues, peoples still dazzles in these greater days, had no common idea whatever of what they meant to do with the world. They had been a Government for three long years, and before

the Change came to them it had never even occurred to them that it was necessary to have a common idea. There was no common idea at all. That great empire was no more than a thing adrift, an aimless thing that ate and drank and slept and bore arms, and was inordinately proud of itself because it had chanced to happen. It had no plan, no intention; it meant nothing at all. And the other great empires adrift, perilously adrift like marine mines, were in the self-same case. Absurd as a British cabinet council must seem to you now, it was no whit more absurd than the controlling ganglion, autocratic council, president's committee, or what not of each of its blind rivals. . . .

§2

I REMEMBER as one thing that struck me very forcibly at the time, the absence of any discussion, any difference of opinion, about the broad principles of our present state. These men had lived hitherto in a system of conventions and acquired motives, loyalty to a party, loyalty to various agreements and understandings, loyalty to the Crown; they had all been capable of the keenest attention to precedence, all capable of the most complete suppression of subversive doubts and inquiries, all had their religious emotions under perfect control. They had seemed protected by invisible but impenetrable barriers from all the heady and destructive speculations, the socialistic, republican, and communistic theories that one may

still trace through the literature of the last days of the comet. But now it was as if at the very moment of the awakening those barriers and defences had vanished, as if the green vapours had washed through their minds and dissolved and swept away a hundred once rigid boundaries and obstacles. They had admitted and assimilated at once all that was good in the ill-dressed propagandas that had clamoured so vehemently and vainly at the doors of their minds in the former days. It was exactly like the awakening from an absurd and limiting dream. They had come out together naturally and inevitably upon the broad daylight platform of obvious and reasonable agreement upon which we and all the order of our world now stand.

Let me try to give the chief things that had vanished from their minds. There was, first, the ancient system of "ownership" that made such an extraordinary tangle of our administration of the land upon which we lived. In the old time no one believed in that as either just or ideally convenient, but everyone accepted it. The community which lived upon the land was supposed to have waived its necessary connection with the land, except in certain limited instances of highway and common. All the rest of the land was cut up in the maddest way into patches and oblongs and triangles of various sizes between a hundred square miles and a few acres, and placed under the nearly absolute government of a series of administrators

called landowners. They owned the land almost as a man now owns his hat; they bought it and sold it, and cut it up like cheese or ham; they were free to ruin it, or leave it waste, or erect upon it horrible and devastating eyesores. If the community needed a road or a tramway, if it wanted a town or a village in any position, nay, even if it wanted to go to and fro, it had to do so by exorbitant treaties with each of the monarchs whose territory was involved. No man could find foothold on the face of the earth until he had paid toll and homage to one of them. They had practically no relations and no duties to the nominal, municipal, or national Government amidst whose larger areas their own dominions lay. . . . This sounds, I know, like a lunatic's dream, but mankind was that lunatic; and not only in the old countries of Europe and Asia, where this system had arisen out of the delegation of local control to territorial magnates did it obtain, but the "new countries," as we called them then— the United States of America, Cape Colony, Australia, and New Zealand—spent much of the nineteenth century in the frantic giving away of land for ever to any casual person who would take it. Was there coal, was there petroleum or gold, was there rich soil or harbourage, or the site for a fine city, these obsessed and witless Governments cried out for scramblers, and a stream of shabby, tricky, and violent adventurers set out to found a new section of the landed aristocracy

of the world. After a brief century of hope and pride, the great republic of the United States of America, the hope as it was deemed of mankind, became for the most part a drifting crowd of landless men; landlords and railway lords, food lords (for the land is food) and mineral lords ruled its life, gave it Universities as one gave coins to a mendicant, and spent its resources upon such vain, tawdry, and foolish luxuries as the world had never seen before. Here was a thing none of these statesmen before the Change would have regarded as anything but the natural order of the world, which not one of them now regarded as anything but the mad and vanished illusion of a period of dementia.

And as it was with the question of the land, so was it also with a hundred other systems and institutions and complicated and disingenuous factors in the life of man. They spoke of trade, and I realised for the first time there could be buying and selling that was no loss to any man; they spoke of industrial organisation, and one saw it under captains who sought no base advantages. The haze of old associations, of personal entanglements and habitual recognitions had been dispelled from every stage and process of the social training of men. Things long hidden appeared discovered with an amazing clearness and nakedness. These men who had awakened, laughed dissolvent laughs, and the old muddle of schools and colleges, books and traditions, the old fumbling,

half-figurative, half-formal teach-
ing of the Churches, the complex
of weakening and confusing sug-
gestions and hints, amidst which
the pride and honour of adoles-
cence doubted and stumbled and
fell, became nothing but a curi-
ous and pleasantly faded mem-
ory. " There must be a common
training of the young," said
Richover; " a frank initiation.
We have not so much educated
them as hidden things from
them, and set traps. And it might
have been so easy — it can all be
done so easily."

That hangs in my memory as
the refrain of that council, " It
can all be done so easily," but
when they said it then, it came
to my ears with a quality of enor-
mous refreshment and power. It
can all be done so easily, given
frankness, given courage. Time
was when these platitudes had
the freshness and wonder of a
gospel.

In this enlarged outlook the
war with the Germans — that
mythical, heroic, armed female,
Germany, had vanished from
men's imaginations — was a mere
exhausted episode. A truce had
already been arranged by Mel-
mount, and these ministers, after
some marvelling reminiscences,
set aside the matter of peace as
a mere question of particular
arrangements. . . . The whole
scheme of the world's govern-
ment had become fluid and pro-
visional in their minds, in small
details as in great, the unanalys-
able tangle of wards and vestries,
districts and municipalities, coun-
ties, states, boards, and nations,
the interlacing, overlapping, and
conflicting authorities, the felt of
little interests and claims, in
which an innumerable and in-
satiable multitude of lawyers,
agents, managers, bosses, organ-
isers lived like fleas in a dirty old
coat, the web of the conflicts,
jealousies, heated patchings up
and jobbings apart, of the old or-
der — they flung it all on one side.
" What are the new needs? "
said Melmount. " This muddle is
too rotten to handle. We're be-
ginning again. Well, let us begin
afresh."

§ 3

" Let us begin afresh! " This
piece of obvious common sense
seemed then to me instinct with
courage, the noblest of words.
My heart went out to him as he
spoke. It was, indeed, that day
as vague as it was valiant; we did
not at all see the forms of what
we were thus beginning. All that
we saw was the clear inevitable-
ness that the old order should
end. . . .

And then in a little space of
time mankind in halting but ef-
fectual brotherhood was moving
out to make its world anew.
Those early years, those first and
second decades of the new epoch,
were in their daily detail a time
of rejoicing toil; one saw chiefly
one's own share in that, and lit-
tle of the whole. It is only now
that I look back at it all from
these ripe years, from this high
tower, that I see the dramatic
sequence of its changes, see the
cruel old confusions of the an-
cient time become clarified, sim-
plified, and dissolve and vanish
away. Where is that old world

now? Where is London, that sombre city of smoke and drifting darkness, full of the deep roar and haunting music of disorder, with its oily, shining, mud-rimmed, barge-crowded river, its black pinnacles and blackened dome, its sad wildernesses of smut-greyed houses, its myriads of draggled prostitutes, its millions of hurrying clerks? The very leaves upon its trees were foul with greasy black defilements. Where is lime-white Paris, with its green and disciplined foliage, its hard unflinching tastefulness, its smartly organised viciousness, and the myriads of workers, noisily shod, streaming over the bridges in the grey cold light of dawn? Where is New York, the high city of clangour and infuriated energy, wind swept and competition swept, its huge buildings jostling one another and straining ever upward for a place in the sky, the fallen pitilessly overshadowed? Where are its lurking corners of heavy and costly luxury, the shameful bludgeoning bribing vice of its ill-ruled underways, and all the gaunt extravagant ugliness of its strenuous life? And where now is Philadelphia, with its innumerable small and isolated homes, and Chicago with its interminable bloodstained stockyards, its polyglot underworld of furious discontent?

All these vast cities have given way and gone, even as my native Potteries and the Black Country have gone, and the lives that were caught, crippled, starved, and maimed amidst their labyrinths, their forgotten and neglected maladjustments, and their vast, inhuman, ill-conceived industrial machinery have escaped — to life. Those cities of growth and accident are altogether gone, never a chimney smokes about our world to-day, and the sound of the weeping of children who toiled and hungered, the dull despair of overburdened women, the noise of brute quarrels in alleys, all shameful pleasures and all the ugly grossness of wealthy pride have gone with them, with the utter change in our lives. As I look back into the past I see a vast exultant dust of house-breaking and removal rise up into the clear air that followed the hour of the green vapours, I live again the Year of Tents, the Year of Scaffolding, and like the triumph of a new theme in a piece of music — the great cities of our new days arise. Come Caerlyon and Armedon, the twin cities of lower England, with the winding summer city of the Thames between, and I see the gaunt dirt of old Edinburgh die to rise again white and tall beneath the shadow of her ancient hill; and Dublin too, reshaped, returning enriched, fair, spacious, the city of rich laughter and warm hearts, gleaming gaily in a shaft of sunlight through the soft warm rain. I see the great cities America has planned and made; the Golden City, with ever-ripening fruit along its broad warm ways, and the bell-glad City of a Thousand Spires. I see again as I have seen, the city of theatres and meeting-places, the City of the Sunlight Bight, and the new city that is still called Utah; and dominated by its observatory dome and the

plain and dignified lines of the university façade upon the cliff, Martenãbar the great white winter city of the upland snows. And the lesser places, too, the townships, the quiet resting-places, villages half forest with a brawl of streams down their streets, villages, laced with avenues of cedar, villages of garden, of roses and wonderful flowers and the perpetual humming of bees. And through all the world go our children, our sons the old world would have made into servile clerks and shopmen, plough drudges and servants; our daughters who were erst anæmic drudges, prostitutes, sluts, anxiety-racked mothers or sere, repining failures; they go about this world glad and brave, learning, living, doing, happy and rejoicing, brave and free. I think of them wandering in the clear quiet of the ruins of Rome, among the tombs of Egypt or the temples of Athens, of their coming to Mainington and its strange happiness, to Orba and the wonder of its white and slender tower. . . . But who can tell of the fulness and pleasure of life, who can number all our new cities in the world? — cities made by the loving hands of men for living men, cities men weep to enter, so fair they are, so gracious and so kind. . . .

Some vision surely of these things must have been vouchsafed me as I sat there behind Melmount's couch, but now my knowledge of accomplished things has mingled with and effaced my expectations. Something indeed I must have foreseen — or else why was my heart so glad?

IN THE DAYS OF THE COMET

Book III: *The New World*

CHAPTER 1

LOVE AFTER THE
CHANGE

§ 1

So far I have said nothing of Nettie. I have departed widely from my individual story. I have tried to give you the effect of the change in relation to the general framework of human life, its effect of swift, magnificent dawn, of an overpowering letting in and inundation of light, and the spirit of living. In my memory all my life before the Change has the quality of a dark passage, with the dimmest side gleams of beauty that come and go. The rest is dull pain and darkness. Then suddenly the walls, the bitter confines, are smitten and vanish, and I walk, blinded, perplexed, and yet rejoicing, in this sweet, beautiful world, in its fair incessant variety, its satisfaction, its opportunities, exultant in this glorious gift of life. Had I the power of music I would make a world-wide *motif* swell and amplify, gather to itself this theme and that, and rise at last to sheer ecstasy of triumph and rejoicing. It should be all sound, all pride, all the hope of outsetting in the morning brightness, all the glee of unexpected happenings, all the gladness of painful effort suddenly come to its reward; it should be like blossoms new opened and the happy play of children, like tearful, happy mothers holding their first-born, like cities building to the sound of music, and great ships, all hung with flags and wine-bespattered, gliding down through cheering multitudes to their first meeting with the sea. Through it all should march Hope, confident Hope, radiant and invincible, until at last it would be the triumph march of Hope the conqueror, coming with trumpetings and banners through the wide-flung gates of the world.

And then out of that luminous haze of gladness comes Nettie, transfigured.

So she came again to me — amazing, a thing incredibly forgotten.

She comes back, and Verrall is in her company. She comes back into my memories now, just as she came back then, rather quaintly at first — at first not seen very clearly, a little distorted by intervening things, seen with a doubt, as I saw her through the slightly discoloured panes of crinkled glass in the window of the Menton post-office and grocer's shop. It was on the second day after the Change, and I had been sending telegrams for Melmount, who was making arrangements for his departure for Downing Street. I saw the two of them at first as small, flawed figures. The glass made them seem curved, and it enhanced and altered their gestures and paces. I felt it became me to say "Peace" to them, and I went out, to the jangling of the door-bell. At the sight of me they stopped short, and Verrall cried with the note of one who has sought, "Here he is!" and Nettie cried, "Willie!"

I went towards them, and all the perspectives of my reconstructed universe altered as I did so.

I seemed to see these two for the first time; how fine they were, how graceful and human. It was as though I had never really looked at them before, and, indeed, always before I had beheld them through a mist of selfish passion. They had shared the universal darkness and dwarfing of the former time; they shared the universal exaltation of the new. Now suddenly Nettie, and the love of Nettie, a great passion for Nettie, lived again in me. This change which had enlarged men's hearts had made no end to love. Indeed, it had enormously enlarged and glorified love. She stepped into the centre of that dream of world reconstruction that filled my mind and took possession of it all. A little wisp of hair had blown across her cheek, her lips fell apart in that sweet smile of hers; her eyes were full of wonder, of a welcoming scrutiny, of an infinitely courageous friendliness.

I took her outstretched hand, and wonder overwhelmed me. "I wanted to kill you," I said simply, trying to grasp that idea. It seemed now like stabbing the stars, or murdering the sunlight.

"Afterwards we looked for you," said Verrall; "and we could not find you. . . . We heard another shot."

I turned my eyes to him, and Nettie's hand fell from me. It was then I thought of how they had fallen together, and what it must have been to have awakened in that dawn with Nettie by one's side. I had a vision of them as I glimpsed them last amidst the thickening vapours, close together, hand in hand. The green hawks of the Change spread their darkling wings above their last stumbling paces. So they fell. And awoke — lovers together in a morning of Paradise. Who can tell how bright the sunshine was to them, how fair the flowers, how sweet the singing of the birds? . . .

This was the thought of my heart. But my lips were saying,

"When I awoke I threw my pistol away." Sheer blankness kept my thoughts silent for a little while; I said empty things. "I am very glad I did not kill you—that you are here, so fair and well. . . .

"I am going back to Clayton on the day after to-morrow," I said, breaking away to explanations. "I have been writing shorthand here for Melmount, but that is almost over now. . . ."

Neither of them said a word, and though all facts had suddenly ceased to matter anything, I went on informatively, "He is to be taken to Downing Street, where there is a proper staff, so that there will be no need of me. . . . Of course, you're a little perplexed at my being with Melmount. You see I met him—by accident—directly I recovered. I found him with a broken ankle—in that lane. . . . I am to go now to the Four Towns to help prepare a report. So that I am glad to see you both again"—I found a catch in my voice—"to say good-bye to you, and wish you well."

This was after the quality of what had come into my mind when first I saw them through the grocer's window, but it was not what I felt and thought as I said it. I went on saying it because otherwise there would have been a gap. It had come to me that it was going to be hard to part from Nettie. My words sounded with an effect of unreality. I stopped, and we stood for a moment in silence looking at one another.

It was I, I think, who was discovering most. I was realising for the first time how little the Change had altered in my essential nature. I had forgotten this bitterness of love for a time in a world of wonder. That was all. Nothing was lost from my nature, nothing had gone, only the power of thought and restraint had been wonderfully increased, and new interests had been forced upon me. The Green Vapours had passed, our minds were swept ånd garnished, but we were ourselves still, though living in a new and finer air. My affinities were unchanged; Nettie's personal charm for me was only quickened by the enhancement of my perceptions. In her presence, meeting her eyes, instantly my desire, no longer frantic but sane, was awake again.

It was just like going to Checkshill in the old time, after writing about socialism. . . .

I relinquished her hand. It was absurd to part in these terms.

So we all felt it. We hung awkwardly over our sense of that. It was Verrall, I think, who shaped the thought for me, and said that to-morrow then we must meet and say good-bye, and so turned our encounter into a transitory making of arrangements. We settled we would come to the inn at Menton, all three of us, and take our midday meal together. . . .

Yes, it was clear that was all we had to say . . . now.

We parted a little awkwardly. I went on down the village street, not looking back, surprised at myself, and infinitely perplexed. It was as if I had discovered

something overlooked that disarranged all my plans, something entirely disconcerting. For the first time I went back preoccupied and without eagerness to Melmount's work. I wanted to go on thinking about Nettie; my mind had suddenly become voluminously productive concerning her and Verrall.

§ 2

THE TALK we three had together in the dawn of the new time is very strongly impressed upon my memory. There was something fresh and simple about it, something young and flushed and exalted. We took up, we handled with a certain naïve timidity, the most difficult questions the Change had raised for men to answer. I recall we made little of them. All the old scheme of human life had dissolved and passed away, the narrow competitiveness, the greed and base aggression, the jealous aloofness of soul from soul. Where had it left us? That was what we and a thousand million others were discussing. . . .

It chances that this last meeting with Nettie is inseparably associated — I don't know why — with the landlady of the Menton inn.

The Menton inn was one of the rare pleasant corners of the old order; it was an inn of an unusual prosperity, much frequented by visitors from Shaphambury, and given to the serving of lunches and teas. It had a broad mossy bowling-green, and round about it were creeper-covered arbours amidst beds of snap-dragons, and hollyhock, and blue delphinium, and many such tall familiar summer flowers. These stood out against a background of laurels and holly, and above these again rose the gables of the inn and its signpost — a white-horsed George slaying the dragon — against copper beeches under the sky.

While I waited for Nettie and Verrall in this agreeable trysting-place, I talked to the landlady — a broad-shouldered, smiling, freckled woman — about the morning of the Change. That motherly, abundant, red-haired figure of health was buoyantly sure that everything in the world was now to be changed for the better. That confidence, and something in her voice, made me love her as I talked to her. "Now we're awake," she said, "all sorts of things will be put right that hadn't any sense in them. Why? Oh! I'm sure of it."

Her kind blue eyes met mine in an infinitude of friendliness. Her lips in her pauses shaped in a pretty faint smile.

Old tradition was strong in us; all English inns in those days charged the unexpected, and I asked what our lunch was to cost.

"Pay or not," she said, "and what you like. It's holiday these days. I suppose we'll still have paying and charging, however we manage it, but it won't be the worry it has been — that I feel sure. It's the part I never had no fancy for. Many a time I peeped through the bushes worrying to think what was just and

right to me and mine, and what would send 'em away satisfied. It isn't the money I care for. There'll be mighty changes, be sure of that; but here I'll stay, and make people happy—them that go by on the roads. It's a pleasant place here when people are merry; it's only when they're jealous or mean, or tired, or eat up beyond any stomach's digesting, or when they got the drink in 'em that Satan comes into this garden. Many's the happy face I've seen here, and many that come again like friends, but nothing to equal what's going to be, now things are being set right."

She smiled, that bounteous woman, with the joy of life and hope. "You shall have an omelette," she said, "you and your friends; such an omelette—like they'll have 'em in heaven! I feel there's cooking in me these days like I've never cooked before. I'm rejoiced to have it to do. . . ."

It was just then that Nettie and Verrall appeared under a rustic archway of crimson roses that led out from the inn. Nettie wore white and a sun-hat, and Verrall was a figure of grey. "Here are my friends," I said; but for all the magic of the Change, something passed athwart the sunlight in my soul like the passing of the shadow of a cloud. "A pretty couple," said the landlady, as they crossed the velvet green towards us. . . .

They were indeed a pretty couple, but that did not greatly gladden me. No—I winced a little at that.

§ 3

THIS old newspaper, this first re-issue of the *New Paper* desiccated last relic of a vanished age, is like the little piece of identification the superstitious of the old days—those queer religionists who brought a certain black-clad Mrs. Piper to the help of Christ—used to put into the hand of a clairvoyant. At the crisp touch of it I look across a gulf of fifty years and see again the three of us sitting about that table in the arbour, and I smell again the smell of the sweet-brier that filled the air about us, and hear in our long pauses the abundant murmuring of bees among the heliotrope of the borders.

It is the dawn of the new time, but we still bear the marks and liveries of the old.

I see myself, a dark, ill-dressed youth, with the bruise Lord Redcar gave me still blue and yellow beneath my jaw; and young Verrall sits cornerwise to me, better grown, better dressed, fair and quiet, two years my senior indeed, but looking no older than I because of his light complexion; and opposite me is Nettie, with dark eyes upon my face, graver and more beautiful than I had ever seen her in the former time. Her dress is still that white one she had worn when I came upon her in the park, and still about her dainty neck she wears her string of pearls and that little coin of gold. She is so much the same, she is so changed; a girl then and now a woman—and all

my agony and all the marvel of the Change between! Over the end of the green table about which we sit, a spotless cloth is spread, it bears a pleasant lunch spread out with a simple equipage. Behind me is the liberal sunshine of the green and various garden. I see it all. Again I sit there, eating awkwardly, this paper lies upon the table and Verrall talks of the Change.

"You can't imagine," he says in his sure, fine accents, "how much the Change has destroyed of me. I still don't feel awake. Men of my sort are so tremendously *made*; I never suspected it before."

He leans over the table towards me with an evident desire to make himself perfectly understood. "I find myself like some creature that is taken out of its shell — soft and new. I was trained to dress in a certain way, to behave in a certain way, to think in a certain way; I see now it's all wrong and narrow — most of it anyhow — a system of class shibboleths. We were decent to each other in order to be a gang to the rest of the world. Gentlemen indeed! But it's perplexing —"

I can hear his voice saying that now, and see the lift of his eyebrows and his pleasant smile.

He paused. He had wanted to say that, but it was not the thing we had to say.

I leaned forward a little and took hold of my glass very tightly. "You two," I said, "will marry?"

They looked at one another.

Nettie spoke very softly. "I did not mean to marry when I came away," she said.

"I know," I answered. I looked up with a sense of effort and met Verrall's eyes.

He answered me. "I think we two have joined our lives. . . . But the thing that took us was a sort of madness."

I nodded. "All passion," I said, "is madness." Then I fell into a doubting of those words.

"Why did we do these things?" he said, turning to her suddenly.

Her hands were clasped under her chin, her eyes downcast.

"We *had* to," she said, with her old trick of inadequate expression.

Then she seemed to open out suddenly.

"Willie," she cried with a sudden directness, with her eyes appealing to me, "I didn't mean to treat you badly — indeed I didn't. I kept thinking of you — and of father and mother, all the time. Only it didn't seem to move me. It didn't move me not one bit from the way I had chosen."

"Chosen!" I said.

"Something seemed to have hold of me," she admitted. "It's all so unaccountable. . . ."

She gave a little gesture of despair.

Verrall's fingers played on the cloth for a space. Then he turned his face to me again.

"Something said 'Take her.' Everything. It was a raging desire — for her. I don't know. Everything contributed to that — or counted for nothing. You —"

"Go on," said I.

"When I knew of you —"

I looked at Nettie. "You never told him about me?" I said, feeling, as it were, a sting out of the old time.

Verrall answered for her. "No. But things dropped; I saw you that night, my instincts were all awake. I knew it was you."

"You triumphed over me? . . . If I could I would have triumphed over you," I said. "But go on!"

"Everything conspired to make it the finest thing in life. It had an air of generous recklessness. It meant mischief, it might mean failure in that life of politics and affairs for which I was trained, which it was my honour to follow. That made it all the finer. It meant ruin or misery for Nettie. That made it all the finer. No sane or decent man would have approved of what we did. That made it more splendid than ever. I had all the advantages of position and used them basely. That mattered not at all."

"Yes," I said; "it is true. And the same dark wave that lifted you, swept me on to follow. With that revolver — and blubbering with hate. And the word to you, Nettie, what was it? 'Give?' Hurl yourself down the steep?"

Nettie's hands fell upon the table. "I can't tell what it was," she said, speaking barehearted straight to me. "Girls aren't trained as men are trained to look into their minds. I can't see it yet. All sorts of mean little motives were there — over and above the 'must.' Mean motives. I kept thinking of his clothes."

She smiled — a flash of brightness at Verrall. "I kept thinking of being like a lady and sitting in an hotel — with men like butlers waiting. It's the dreadful truth, Willie. Things as mean as that! Things meaner than that!"

I can see her now pleading with me, speaking with a frankness as bright and amazing as the dawn of the first great morning.

"It wasn't all mean," I said slowly, after a pause.

"No!" They spoke together.

"But a woman chooses more than a man does," Nettie added. "I saw it all in little bright pictures. Do you know — that jacket — there's something — You won't mind my telling you? But you won't now!"

I nodded, "No."

She spoke as if she spoke to my soul, very quietly and very earnestly, seeking to give the truth. "Something cottony in that cloth of yours," she said. "I know there's something horrible in being swung round by things like that, but they did swing me round. In the old time — to have confessed that! And I hated Clayton — and the grime of it. That kitchen! Your mother's dreadful kitchen! And besides, Willie, I was afraid of you. I didn't understand you and I did him. It's different now — but then I knew what he meant. And there was his voice."

"Yes," I said to Verrall, making these discoveries quietly, "yes, Verrall, you have a good voice. Queer I never thought of that before!"

We sat silently for a time before our vivisected passions.

"Gods!" I cried, "and there was our poor little top-hamper of intelligence on all these waves of instinct and wordless desire, the foaming things of touch and sight and feeling, like—like a coop of hens washed overboard and clucking amidst the seas."

Verrall laughed approval of the image I had struck out. "A week ago," he said, trying it further, "we were clinging to our chicken coops and going with the heave and pour. That was true enough a week ago. But to-day—"

"To-day," I said, "the wind has fallen. The world storm is over. And each chicken coop has changed by a miracle to a vessel that makes head against the sea."

§4

"WHAT are we to do?" asked Verrall.

Nettie drew a deep crimson carnation from the bowl before us, and began very neatly and deliberately to turn down the sepals of its calyx and remove, one by one, its petals. I remember that went on through all our talk. She put those ragged crimson shreds in a long row and adjusted them and readjusted them. When at last I was alone with these vestiges the pattern was still incomplete.

"Well," said I, "the matter seems fairly simple. You two"— I swallowed it—"love one another."

I paused. They answered me by silence, by a thoughtful silence.

"You belong to each other. I have thought it over and looked at it from many points of view. I happened to want—impossible things. . . . I behaved badly. I had no right to pursue you." I turned to Verrall. "You hold yourself bound to her?"

He nodded assent.

"No social influence, no fading out of all this generous clearness in the air—for that might happen—will change you back? . . ."

He answered me with honest eyes meeting mine, "No, Leadford, no!"

"I did not know you," I said. "I thought of you as something very different from this."

"I was," he interpolated.

"Now," I said, "it is all changed."

Then I halted—for my thread had slipped away from me.

"As for me," I went on, and glanced at Nettie's downcast face, and then sat forward with my eyes upon the flowers between us, "since I am swayed and shall be swayed by an affection for Nettie, since that affection is rich with the seeds of desire, since to see her yours and wholly yours is not to be endured by me—I must turn about and go from you; you must avoid me and I you. . . . We must divide the world like Jacob and Esau. . . . I must direct myself with all the will I have to other things. After all—this passion is not life! It is perhaps for brutes and savages, but for men—no! We must part and I must forget. What else is there but that?"

I did not look up, I sat very tense with the red petals printing

an indelible memory in my brain, but I felt the assent of Verrall's pose. There were some moments of silence. Then Nettie spoke. "But—" she said, and ceased.

I waited for a little while. I sighed and leaned back in my chair. "It is perfectly simple," I smiled, "now that we have cool heads."

"But *is* it simple?" asked Nettie, and slashed my discourse out of being.

I looked up and found her with her eyes on Verrall. "You see," she said, "I like Willie. It's hard to say what one feels—but I don't want him to go away like that."

"But then," objected Verrall, "how—?"

"No," said Nettie, and swept her half-arranged carnation petals back into a heap of confusion. She began to arrange them very quickly into one long straight line.

"It's so difficult—I've never before in all my life tried to get to the bottom of my mind. For one thing I've not treated Willie properly. He—he counted on me. I know he did. I was his hope. I was a promised delight —something, something to crown life—better than anything he had ever had. And a secret pride. . . . He lived upon me. I knew—when we two began to meet together, you and I—It was a sort of treachery to him—"

"Treachery!" I said. "You were only feeling your way through all these perplexities."

"You thought it treachery."

"I don't know."

"I did. In a sense I think so still. For you had need of me."

I made a slight protest at this doctrine and fell thinking.

"And even when he was trying to kill us," she said to her lover, "I felt for him down in the bottom of my mind. I can understand all the horrible things, the humiliation—the humiliation! he went through."

"Yes," I said, "but I don't see—"

"*I* don't see. I'm only trying to see. But you know, Willie, you are a part of my life. I have known you longer than I have known Edward. I know you better. Indeed I know you with all my heart. You think all your talk was thrown away upon me, that I never understood that side of you, or your ambitions or anything. I did. More than I thought at the time. Now—now it is all clear to me. What I had to understand in you was something deeper than Edward brought me. I have it now. . . . You are a part of my life, and I don't want to cut all that off from me now I have comprehended it, and thrown it away."

"But you love Verrall."

"Love is such a queer thing! . . . Is there one love? I mean, only one love?" She turned to Verrall. "I know I love you. I can speak out about that now. Before this morning I couldn't have done. It's just as though my mind had got out of a scented prison. But what is it, this love for you? It's a mass of fancies— things about you—ways you look, ways you have. It's the senses—and the senses of certain

beauties. Flattery too, things you said, hopes and deceptions for myself. And all that had rolled up together and taken to itself the wild help of those deep emotions that slumbered in my body; it seemed everything. But it wasn't. How can I describe it? It was like having a very bright lamp with a thick shade — everything else in the room was hidden. But you take the shade off and there they are — it is the same light — still there! Only it lights everyone! "

Her voice ceased. For awhile no one spoke, and Nettie, with a quick movement, swept the petals into the shape of a pyramid.

Figures of speech always distract me, and it ran through my mind like some puzzling refrain, " It is still the same light. . . ."

" No woman believes these things," she asserted abruptly.

" What things? "

" No woman ever has believed them."

" You have to choose a man," said Verrall, apprehending her before I did.

" We're brought up to that. We're told — it's in books, in stories, in the way people look, in the way they behave — one day there will come a man. He will be everything, no one else will be anything. Leave everything else; live in him."

" And a man, too, is taught that of some woman," said Verrall.

" Only men don't believe it! They have more obstinate minds. . . . Men have never behaved as though they believed it. One

need not be old to know that. By nature they don't believe it. But a woman believes nothing by nature. She goes into a mould hiding her secret thoughts almost from herself."

" She used to," I said.

" You haven't," said Verrall, " anyhow."

" I've come out. It's this comet. And Willie. And because I never really believed in the mould at all — even if I thought I did. It's stupid to send Willie off — shamed, cast out, never to see him again — when I like him as much as I do. It is cruel, it is wicked and ugly, to prance over him as if he was a defeated enemy, and pretend I'm going to be happy just the same. There's no sense in a rule of life that prescribes that: It's selfish. It's brutish. It's like something that has no sense. I — " there was a sob in her voice. " Willie! I *won't*."

I sat lowering, I mused with my eyes upon her quick fingers.

" It *is* brutish," I said at last, with a careful unemotional deliberation. " Nevertheless — it is in the nature of things. . . . No! . . . You see, after all, we are still half brutes, Nettie. And men, as you say, are more obstinate than women. The comet hasn't altered that; it's only made it clearer. We have come into being through a tumult of blind forces. . . . I come back to what I said just now! we have found our poor reasonable minds, our wills to live well, ourselves, adrift on a wash of instincts, passions, instinctive prejudices, half animal stupidities. . . . Here we are like people clinging to some-

thing—like people awakening—upon a raft."

"We come back at last to my question," said Verrall, softly; "what are we to do?"

"Part," I said. "You see, Nettie, these bodies of ours are not the bodies of angels. They are the same bodies—I have read somewhere that in our bodies you can find evidence of the lowliest ancestry; that about our inward ears—I think it is—and about our teeth, there remains still something of the fish, that there are bones that recall little—what is it?—marsupial forbears—and a hundred traces of the ape. Even your beautiful body, Nettie, carries this taint. No! Hear me out." I leaned forward earnestly. "Our emotions, our passions, our desires, the substance of them, like the substance of our bodies, is an animal, a competing thing, as well as a desiring thing. You speak to us now a mind to minds —one can do that when one has had exercise and when one has eaten, when one is not doing anything—but when one turns to live, one turns again to matter."

"Yes," said Nettie, slowly following me, "but you control it."

"Only through a measure of obedience. There is no magic in the business—to conquer matter, we must divide the enemy, and take matter as an ally. Nowadays it is indeed true, by faith a man can remove mountains; he can say to a mountain, Be thou removed and be thou cast into the sea; but he does it because he helps and trusts his brother men, because he has the wit and patience and courage to win over to his side iron, steel, obedience, dynamite, cranes, trucks, the money of other people. . . . To conquer my desire for you, I must not perpetually thwart it by your presence; I must go away so that I may not see you, I must take up other interests, thrust myself into struggles and discussions—"

"And forget?" said Nettie.

"Not forget," I said; "but anyhow—cease to brood upon you."

She hung on that for some moments.

"No," she said, demolished her last pattern and looked up at Verrall as he stirred.

Verrall leaned forward on the table, elbows upon it, and the fingers of his two hands intertwined.

"You know," he said, "I haven't thought much of these things. At school and the University, one doesn't. . . . It was part of the system to prevent it. They'll alter all that, no doubt. We seem"—he thought—"to be skating about over questions that one came to at last in Greek —with variorum readings—in Plato, but which it never occurred to any one to translate out of a dead language into living realities. . . ." He halted and answered some unspoken question from his own mind with, "No. I think with Leadford, Nettie, that, as he put it, it is in the nature of things for men to be exclusive. . . . Minds are free things and go about the world, but only one man can possess a woman. You must dismiss rivals.

We are made for the struggle for existence—we *are* the struggle for existence; the things that live are the struggle for existence incarnate—and that works out that the men struggle for their mates; for each woman one prevails. The others go away."

"Like animals," said Nettie.

"Yes. . . ."

"There are many things in life," I said, "but that is the rough universal truth."

"But," said Nettie, "you don't struggle. That has been altered because men have minds."

"You choose," I said.

"If I don't choose to choose?"

"You have chosen."

She gave a little impatient "Oh! Why are women always the slaves of sex? Is this great age of Reason and Light that has come to alter nothing of that? And men too! I think it is all—stupid! I do not believe this is the right solution of the thing, or anything but the bad habits of the time that was. . . . Instinct! You don't let your instincts rule you in a lot of other things. Here am I between you. Here is Edward. I—love him because he is gay and pleasant, and because—because I *like* him! Here is Willie—a part of me—my first secret, my oldest friend! Why must I not have both? Am I not a mind that you must think of me as nothing but a woman? imagine me always as a thing to struggle for?" She paused; then she made her distressful proposition to me. "Let us three keep together," she said. "Let us not part. To part is hate, Willie.

Why should we not anyhow keep friends? Meet and talk?"

"Talk?" I said. "About this sort of thing?"

I looked across at Verrall and met his eyes, and we studied one another. It was the clean, straight scrutiny of honest antagonism. "No," I decided. "Between us, nothing of that sort can be."

"Ever?" said Nettie.

"Never," I said, convinced.

I made an effort within myself. "We cannot tamper with the law and customs of these things," I said; "these passions are too close to one's essential self. Better surgery than a lingering disease! From Nettie my love—asks all. A man's love is not devotion—it is a demand, a challenge. And besides"—and here I forced my theme—"I have given myself now to a new mistress—and it is I, Nettie, who am unfaithful. Behind you and above you rises the coming City of the World, and I am in that building. Dear heart! you are only happiness—and that—Indeed that calls! If it is only that my life blood shall christen the foundation stones—I could almost hope that should be my part, Nettie—I will join myself in that." I threw all the conviction I could into these words. . . . "No conflict of passion," I added a little lamely, "must distract me."

There was a pause.

"Then we must part," said Nettie, with the eyes of a woman one strikes in the face.

I nodded assent. . . .

There was a little pause, and then I stood up. We stood up,

all three. We parted almost sullenly, with no more memorable words, and I was left presently in the arbour alone.

I do not think I watched them go. I only remember myself left there somehow — horribly empty and alone. I sat down again and fell into a deep shapeless musing.

§ 5

SUDDENLY I looked up. Nettie had come back and stood looking down at me.

"Since we talked I have been thinking," she said. "Edward has let me come to you alone. And I feel perhaps I can talk better to you alone."

I said nothing and that embarrassed her.

"I don't think we ought to part," she said.

"No — I don't think we ought to part," she repeated.

"One lives," she said, "in different ways. I wonder if you will understand what I am saying, Willie. It is hard to say what I feel. But I want it said. If we are to part for ever I want it said — very plainly. Always before I have had the woman's instinct and the woman's training which makes one hide. But — Edward is not all of me. Think of what I am saying — Edward is not all of me. . . . I wish I could tell you better how I see it. I am not all of myself. You, at any rate, are a part of me and I cannot bear to leave you. And I cannot see why I should leave you. There is a sort of blood link between us, Willie. We grew together. We are in one another's bones. I understand you. Now indeed I understand. In some way I have come to an understanding at a stride. Indeed I understand you and your dream. I want to help you. Edward — Edward has no dreams. . . . It is dreadful to me, Willie, to think we two are to part."

"But we have settled that — part we must."

"But *why?*"

"I love you."

"Well, and why should I hide it, Willie? — I love you. . . ." Our eyes met. She flushed, she went on resolutely: "You are stupid. The whole thing is stupid. I love you both."

I said, "You do not understand what you say. No!"

"You mean that I must go."

"Yes, yes. Go!"

For a moment we looked at one another, mute, as though deep down in the unfathomable darkness below the surface and present reality of things dumb meanings strove to be. She made to speak and desisted.

"But *must* I go?" she said at last, with quivering lips, and the tears in her eyes were stars. Then she began, "Willie —"

"Go!" I interrupted her. . . . "Yes."

Then again we were still.

She stood there, a tearful figure of pity, longing for me, pitying me. Something of that wider love that will carry our descendants at last out of all the limits, the hard, clear obligations of our personal life, moved us, like the first breath of a coming wind out of heaven that stirs and passes away. I had an impulse to take her hand and kiss it, and then a

trembling came to me, and I knew that if I touched her, my strength would all pass from me. . . .

And so, standing at a distance one from the other, we parted, and Nettie went, reluctant and looking back, with the man she had chosen, to the lot she had chosen, out of my life — like the sunlight out of my life. . . .

Then, you know, I suppose I folded up this newspaper and put it in my pocket. But my memory of that meeting ends with the face of Nettie turning to go.

§ 6

I REMEMBER all that very distinctly to this day. I could almost vouch for the words I have put into our several mouths. Then comes a blank. I have a dim memory of being back in the house near the Links and the bustle of Melmount's departure, of finding Parker's energy distasteful, and of going away down the road with a strong desire to say good-bye to Melmount alone.

Perhaps I was already doubting my decision to part for ever from Nettie, for I think I had it in mind to tell him all that had been said and done. . . .

I don't think I had a word with him or anything but a hurried hand clasp. I am not sure. It has gone out of my mind. But I have a very clear and certain memory of my phase of bleak desolation as I watched his car recede and climb and vanish over Maple-borough Hill, and that I got there my first full and definite intimation that, after all, this great Change and my new wide aims in life, were not to mean in-

discriminate happiness for me. I had a sense of protest, as against extreme unfairness, as I saw him go. "It is too soon," I said to myself, "to leave me alone."

I felt I had sacrificed too much, that after I had said good-bye to the hot immediate life of passion, to Nettie and desire, to physical and personal rivalry, to all that was most intensely myself, it was wrong to leave me alone and sore-hearted, to go on at once with these steely cold duties of the wider life. I felt new-born, and naked, and at a loss.

"Work!" I said with an effort at the heroic, and turned about with a sigh, and I was glad that the way I had to go would at least take me to my mother. . . .

But, curiously enough, I remember myself as being fairly cheerful in the town of Birmingham that night; I recall an active and interested mood. I spent the night in Birmingham because the train service was disarranged, and I could not go farther. I went to listen to a band that was playing its brassy old-world music in the public park, and I fell into conversation with a man who said he had been a reporter upon one of their minor local papers. He was full and keen upon all the plans of reconstruction that were now shaping over the lives of humanity, and I know that something of that noble dream came back to me with his words and phrases. We walked up to a place called Bournville by moonlight, and talked of the new social groupings that must replace the old isolated homes, and how the people would be housed.

This Bournville was germane

to that matter. It had been an attempt on the part of a private firm of manufacturers to improve the housing of their workers. To our ideas to-day it would seem the feeblest of benevolent efforts, but at the time it was extraordinary and famous, and people came long journeys to see its trim cottages with baths sunk under the kitchen floors (of all conceivable places), and other brilliant inventions. No one seemed to see the danger to liberty in that aggressive age, that might arise through making workpeople tenants and debtors of their employer, though an Act called the Truck Act had long ago intervened to prevent minor developments in the same direction. . . . But I and my chance acquaintance seemed that night always to have been aware of that possibility, and we had no doubt in our minds of the public nature of the housing duty. Our interest lay rather in the possibility of common nurseries and kitchens and public rooms that should economise toil and give people space and freedom.

It was very interesting, but still a little cheerless; and when I lay in bed that night I thought of Nettie and the queer modifications of preference she had made, and among other things and in a way I prayed. I prayed that night, let me confess it, to an image I had set up in my heart, an image that still serves with me as a symbol for things inconceivable, to a Master Artificer, the unseen captain of all who go about the building of the world, the making of mankind.

But before and after I prayed I imagined I was talking and reasoning and meeting again with Nettie. . . . She never came into the temple of that worshipping with me.

CHAPTER 2

MY MOTHER'S LAST DAYS

§ 1

NEXT day I came home to Clayton.

The new strange brightness of the world was all the brighter there, for the host of dark distressful memories, of darkened childhood, toilsome youth, embittered adolescence that wove about the place for me. It seemed to me that I saw morning there for the first time. No chimneys smoked that day, no furnaces were burning, the people were busy with other things. The clear strong sun, the sparkle in the dustless air, made a strange gaiety in the narrow streets. I passed a number of smiling people coming home from the public breakfasts that were given in the Town Hall until better things could be arranged, and happened on Parload among them. "You were right about that comet," I sang out at the sight of him; and he

came towards me and clasped my hand.

"What are people doing here?" said I.

"They're sending us food from outside," he said, "and we're going to level all these slums — and shift into tents on to the moors"; and he began to tell me of many things that were being arranged; the Midland land committees had got to work with remarkable celerity and directness of purpose, and the redistribution of population was already in its broad outlines planned. He was working at an improved college of engineering. Until schemes of work were made out, almost everyone was going to school again to get as much technical training as possible against the demands of the huge enterprise of reconstruction that was now beginning.

He walked with me to my door, and there I met old Pettigrew coming down the steps. He looked dusty and tired, but his eye was brighter than it used to be, and he carried in a rather unaccustomed manner a workman's tool basket.

"How's the rheumatism, Mr. Pettigrew?" I asked.

"Dietary," said old Pettigrew, "can work wonders. . . ." He looked me in the eye. "These houses," he said, "will have to come down, I suppose, and our notions of property must undergo very considerable revision — in the light of reason; but meanwhile I've been doing something to patch that disgraceful roof of mine! To think that I could have dodged and evaded —"

He raised a deprecatory hand, drew down the loose corners of his ample mouth, and shook his old head.

"The past is past, Mr. Pettigrew."

"Your poor dear mother! So good and honest a woman! So simple and kind and forgiving! To think of it! My dear young man!" — he said it manfully — "I'm ashamed."

"The whole world blushed at dawn the other day, Mr. Pettigrew," I said, "and did it very prettily. That's over now. God knows, who is *not* ashamed of all that came before last Tuesday."

I held out a forgiving hand, naïvely forgetful that in this place I was a thief, and he took it and went his way, shaking his head and repeating he was ashamed, but I think a little comforted.

The door opened and my poor old mother's face, marvellously cleaned, appeared. "Ah, Willie, boy! *You*. You!"

I ran up the steps to her, for I feared she might fall.

How she clung to me in the passage, the dear woman! . . .

But first she shut the front door. The old habit of respect for my unaccountable temper still swayed her. "Ah deary!" she said, "ah deary! But you were sorely tried," and kept her face close to my shoulder, lest she should offend me by the sight of the tears that welled within her.

She made a sort of gulping noise and was quiet for a while, holding me very tightly to her heart with her worn, long hands. . . .

She thanked me presently for my telegram, and I put my arm about her and drew her into the living room.

" It's all well with me, mother dear," I said, " and the dark times are over — are done with for ever, mother."

Whereupon she had courage and gave way and sobbed aloud, none chiding her.

She had not let me know she could still weep for five grimy years. . . .

§ 2

DEAR heart! There remained for her but a very brief while in this world that had been renewed. I did not know how short that time would be, but the little I could do — perhaps after all it was not little to her — to atone for the harshness of my days of wrath and rebellion, I did. I took care to be constantly with her, for I perceived now her curious need of me. It was not that we had ideas to exchange or pleasures to share, but she liked to see me at table, to watch me working, to have me go to and fro. There was no toil for her any more in the world, but only such light services as are easy and pleasant for a worn and weary old woman to do, and I think she was happy even at her end.

She kept to her queer old eighteenth-century version of religion, too, without a change. She had worn this particular amulet so long it was a part of her. Yet the Change was evident even in that persistence. I said to her one day, " But do you still believe in that hell of flame, dear mother? You — with your tender heart! " She vowed she did.

Some theological intricacy made it necessary to her, but still —

She looked thoughtfully at a bank of primulas before her for a time, and then laid her tremulous hand impressively on my arm. " You know, Willie dear," she said, as though she was clearing up a childish misunderstanding of mine, " I don't think anyone will *go* there. I never *did* think that. . . ."

§ 3

THAT talk stands out in my memory because of that agreeable theological decision of hers, but it was only one of a great number of talks. It used to be pleasant in the afternoon, after the day's work was done and before one went on with the evening's study — how odd it would have seemed in the old time for a young man of the industrial class to be doing post-graduate work in sociology, and how much a matter of course it seems now! — to walk out into the gardens of Lowchester House, and smoke a cigarette or so and let her talk ramblingly of the things that interested her. . . . Physically the Great Change did not do so very much to reinvigorate her — she had lived in that dismal underground kitchen in Clayton too long for any material rejuvenescence — she glowed out indeed as a dying spark among the ashes might glow under a draught of fresh air — and assuredly it hastened her end. But those closing days were very tranquil, full of

an effortless contentment. With her, life was like a rainy, windy day that clears only to show the sunset afterglow. The light has passed. She acquired no new habits amid the comforts of the new life, did no new things, but only found a happier light upon the old.

She lived with a number of other old ladies belonging to our commune in the upper rooms of Lowchester House. Those upper apartments were simple and ample, fine and well done in the Georgian style, and they had been organised to give the maximum of comfort and convenience and to economise the need of skilled attendance. We had taken over the various " great houses," as they used to be called, to make communal dining-rooms and so forth — their kitchens were conveniently large — and pleasant places for the old people of over sixty whose time of ease had come, and for suchlike public uses. We had done this not only with Lord Redcar's house, but also with Checkshill House — where old Mrs. Verrall made a dignified and capable hostess — and indeed with most of the fine residences in the beautiful wide country between the Four Towns district and the Welsh mountains. About these great houses there had usually been good out-buildings, laundries, married servants' quarters, stabling, dairies, and the like, suitably masked by trees; we turned these into homes, and to them we added first tents and wood châlets and afterwards quadrangular residential buildings. In order to be near my

mother I had two small rooms in the new collegiate buildings which our commune was almost the first to possess, and they were very convenient for the station of the high-speed electric railway that took me down to our daily conferences and my secretarial and statistical work in Clayton.

Ours had been one of the first modern communes to get in order; we were greatly helped by the energy of Lord Redcar, who had a fine feeling for the picturesque associations of his ancestral home — the detour that took our line through the beeches and bracken and bluebells of the West Wood and saved the open wildness of the park was one of his suggestions; and we had many reasons to be proud of our surroundings. Nearly all the other communes that sprang up all over the pleasant parkland round the industrial valley of the Four Towns, as the workers moved out, came to us to study the architecture of the residential squares and quadrangles with which we had replaced the back streets between the great houses and the ecclesiastical residences about the cathedral, and the way in which we had adapted all those buildings to our new social needs. Some claimed to have improved on us. But they could not emulate the rhododendron garden out beyond our shrubberies; that was a thing altogether our own in our part of England, because of its ripeness and of the rarity of good peat free from lime.

These gardens had been planned under the third Lord

Redcar, fifty years ago and more; they abounded in rhododendra and azaleas, and were in places so well sheltered and sunny that great magnolias flourished and flowered. There were tall trees smothered in crimson and yellow climbing roses, and an endless variety of flowering shrubs and fine conifers, and such pampas grass as no other garden can show. And barred by the broad shadows of these, were glades and broad spaces of emerald turf, and here and there banks of pegged roses and flower-beds, and banks given over some to spring bulbs and some to primroses and primulas and polyanthuses. My mother loved these latter banks and the little round staring eyes of their innumerable yellow, ruddy brown, and purple corollas, more than anything else in the gardens could show and in the spring of the Year so Scaffolding she would go with me day after day to the seat that showed them in the greatest multitude.

It gave her, I think, among other agreeable impressions, a sense of gentle opulence. In the old time she had never known what it was to have more than enough of anything agreeable in the world at all.

We would sit and think, or talk — there was a curious effect of complete understanding between us whether we talked or were still.

"Heaven," she said to me one day, "Heaven is a garden."

I was moved to tease her a little. "There's jewels, you know, walls and gates of jewels — and singing."

"For such as like them," said my mother firmly, and thought for a while. "There'll be things for all of us, o' course. But for me it couldn't be Heaven, dear, unless it was a garden — a nice sunny garden. . . . And feeling such as we're fond of, are close and handy by."

You of your happier generation cannot realise the wonderfulness of those early days in the new epoch, the sense of security, the extraordinary effects of contrast. In the morning, except in high summer, I was up before dawn, and breakfasted upon the swift, smooth train, and perhaps saw the sunrise as I rushed out of the little tunnel that pierced Clayton Crest, and so to work like a man. Now that we had got all the homes and schools and all the softness of life away from our coal and iron ore and clay, now that a thousand obstructive "rights" and timidities had been swept aside, we could let ourselves go, we merged this enterprise with that, cut across this or that anciently obstructive piece of private land, joined and separated, effected gigantic consolidations and gigantic economies, and the valley, no longer a pit of squalid human tragedies and meanly conflicting industries, grew into a sort of beauty of its own, a savage inhuman beauty of force and machinery and flames. One was a Titan in that Etna. Then back one came at midday to bathe and change in the train, and so to the leisurely gossiping lunch in the club dining-room in Lowchester House, and the refreshment of these

green and sunlit afternoon tranquillities.

Sometimes in her profounder moments my mother doubted whether all this last phase of her life was not a dream.

"A dream," I used to say, "a dream indeed — but a dream that is one step nearer awakening than that nightmare of the former days."

She found great comfort and assurance in my altered clothes — she liked the new fashions of dress, she alleged. It was not simply altered clothes. I did grow two inches, broaden some inches round my chest, and increase in weight three stones before I was twenty-three. I wore a soft brown cloth and she would caress my sleeve and admire it greatly — she had the woman's sense of texture very strong in her.

Sometimes she would muse upon the past, rubbing together her poor rough hands — they never got softened — one over the other. She told me much I had not heard before about my father, and her own early life. It was like finding flat and faded flowers in a book still faintly sweet, to realise that once my mother had been loved with passion; that my remote father had once shed hot tears of tenderness in her arms. And she would sometimes even speak tentatively in those narrow, old-world phrases that her lips could rob of all their bitter narrowness, of Nettie.

"She wasn't worthy of you, dear," she would say abruptly, leaving me to guess the person she intended.

"No man is worthy of a woman's love," I answered. " No woman is worthy of a man's. I love her, dear mother, and that you cannot alter."

"There's others," she would muse.

"Not for me," I said. " No! I didn't fire a shot that time; I burnt my magazine. I can't begin again, mother, not from the beginning."

She sighed and said no more then.

At another time she said — I think her words were: "You'll be lonely when I'm gone, dear."

"You'll not think of going, then," I said.

"Eh, dear! but man and maid should come together."

I said nothing to that.

"You brood overmuch on Nettie, dear. If I could see you married to some sweet girl of a woman, some good, *kind* girl — "

"Dear mother, I'm married enough. Perhaps some day — Who knows? I can wait."

"But to have nothing to do with women! "

"I have my friends. Don't you trouble, mother. There's plentiful work for a man in this world though the heart of love is cast out from him. Nettie was life and beauty for me — is — will be. Don't think I've lost too much, mother."

(Because in my heart I told myself the end had still to come.)

And once she sprang a question on me suddenly that surprised me.

"Where are they now?" she asked.

"Who? "

"Nettie and — him."

She had pierced to the marrow of my thoughts. " I don't know." I said shortly.

Her shrivelled hand just fluttered into touch of mine.

" It's better so," she said, as if pleading. " Indeed . . . it is better so."

There was something in her quivering old voice that for a moment took me back across an epoch, to the protests of the former time, to those counsels of submission, those appeals not to offend It, that had always stirred an angry spirit of rebellion within me.

" That is the thing I doubt," I said, and abruptly I felt I could talk no more to her of Nettie. I got up and walked away from her, and came back after a while, to speak of other things, with a bunch of daffodils for her in my hand.

But I did not always spend my afternoons with her. There were days when my crushed hunger for Nettie rose again, and then I had to be alone; I walked or bicycled, and presently I found a new interest and relief in learning to ride. For the horse was already very swiftly reaping the benefit of the Change. Hardly anywhere was the inhumanity of horse traction to be found after the first year of the new epoch, everywhere lugging and dragging and straining was done by machines, and the horse had become a beautiful instrument for the pleasure and carriage of youth. I rode both in the saddle and, what is finer, naked and barebacked. I found violent exercises were good for the states of enormous melancholy that came upon me, and when at last horse riding palled, I went and joined the aviators who practised soaring upon aeroplanes beyond Horsemarden Hill. . . . But at least every alternate day I spent with my mother, and altogether I think I gave her two-thirds of my afternoons.

§ 4

WHEN presently that illness, that fading weakness that made an euthanasia for so many of the older people in the beginning of the new time, took hold upon my mother, there came Anna Reeves to daughter her — after our new custom. She chose to come. She was already known to us a little from chance meetings and chance services she had done my mother in the garden; she sought to give her help. She seemed then just one of those plainly good girls the world at its worst has never failed to produce, who were indeed in the dark old times the hidden antiseptic of all our hustling, hating, faithless lives. They made their secret voiceless worship, they did their steadfast, uninspired unthanked, unselfish work as helpful daughters, as nurses, as faithful servants, as the humble providences of homes. She was almost exactly three years older than I. At first I found no beauty in her, she was short but rather sturdy and ruddy, with red-tinged hair, and fair hairy brows and red-brown eyes. But her freckled hands, I found, were full of apt help, her voice carried good cheer. . . .

At first she was no more than a blue-clad, white-aproned benevolence, that moved in the shadows behind the bed on which my old mother lay and sank restfully to death. She would come forward to anticipate some need, to proffer some simple comfort, and always then my mother smiled on her. In a little while I discovered the beauty of that helpful poise of her woman's body, I discovered the grace of untiring goodness, the sweetness of a tender pity, and the great riches of her voice, of her few reassuring words and phrases. I noted and remembered very clearly how once my mother's lean old hand patted the firm gold-flecked strength of hers, as it went by upon its duties with the coverlet.

"She is a good girl to me," said my mother one day. "A good girl. Like a daughter should be. . . . I never had a daughter—really." She mused peacefully for a space. "Your little sister died," she said.

I had never heard of that little sister.

"November the tenth," said my mother. "Twenty-nine months and three days. . . . I cried. I cried. That was before you came, dear. So long ago—and I can see it now. I was a young wife then, and your father was very kind. But I can see its hands, its dear little quiet hands. . . . Dear, they say, that now—now they will not let the little children die."

"No, dear mother," I said. "We shall do better now."

"The club doctor could not come. Your father went twice. There was someone else, someone who paid. So your father went on into Swathinglea, and that man wouldn't come unless he had his fee. And your father had changed his clothes to look more respectful and he hadn't any money, not even his tram fare home. It seemed cruel to be waiting there with my baby thing in pain. . . . And I can't help thinking perhaps we might have saved her. . . . But it was like that with the poor always in the bad old times—always. When the doctor came at last he was angry. 'Why wasn't I called before?' he said, and he took no pains. He was angry because someone hadn't explained. I begged him—but it was too late."

She said these things very quietly with drooping eyelids, like one who describes a dream. "We are going to manage all these things better now," I said, feeling a strange resentment at this pitiful story her faded, matter-of-fact voice was telling me.

"She talked," my mother went on. "She talked for her age wonderfully. . . . Hippopotamus."

"Eh?" I said.

"Hippopotamus, dear—quite plainly one day, when her father was showing her pictures. . . . And her little prayers. 'Now I lay me . . . down to sleep.' . . . I made her little socks. Knitted they was, dear, and the heel most difficult."

Her eyes were closed now. She spoke no longer to me but to herself. She whispered other vague things, ghosts of long-dead mo-

ments. . . . Her words grew less distinct.

Soon she was asleep and I got up and went out of the room, but my mind was queerly obsessed by the thought of that small life that had been glad and hopeful only to pass so inexplicably out of hope again into nonentity, this sister of whom I had never heard before. . . .

And presently I was in a black rage at all the irrecoverable sorrows of the past, of that great ocean of avoidable suffering of which this was but one luminous and quivering red drop. I walked in the garden and the garden was too small for me; I went out to wander on the moors. "The past is past," I cried, and all the while across the gulf of five and twenty years I could hear my poor mother's heart-wrung weeping for that daughter baby who had suffered and died. Indeed that old spirit of rebellion has not altogether died in me, for all the transformation of the new time. . . . I quieted down at last to a thin and austere comfort in thinking that the whole is not told to us, that it cannot perhaps be told to such minds as ours; and anyhow, and what was far more sustaining, that now we have strength and courage and this new gift of wise love, whatever cruel and sad things marred the past, none of these sorrowful things that made the very warp and woof of the old life need now go on happening. We could foresee, we could prevent and save. "The past is past," I said, between sighing and resolve, as I came into view again on my homeward way of the hundred sunset-lit windows of old Lowchester House. "Those sorrows are sorrows no more."

But I could not altogether cheat that common sadness of the new time, that memory and insoluble riddle of the countless lives that had stumbled and failed in pain and darkness before our air grew clear. . . .

CHAPTER 3

BELTANE AND NEW YEAR'S EVE

§ 1

In the end my mother died rather suddenly, and her death came as a shock to me. Diagnosis was still very inadequate at that time. The doctors were, of course, fully alive to the incredible defects of their common training and were doing all they could to supply its deficiencies, but they were still extraordinarily ignorant. Some unintelligently observed factor of her illness came into play with her, and she became feverish and sank and died very quickly. I do not know what remedial measures were attempted. I hardly knew what was happening until the whole thing was over.

At that time my attention was much engaged by the stir of the great Beltane festival that was held on Mayday in the Year of Scaffolding. It was the first of the ten great rubbish burnings that opened the new age. Young people nowadays can scarcely hope to imagine the enormous quantities of pure litter and useless accumulation with which we had to deal; had we not set aside a special day and season, the whole world would have been an incessant reek of small fires; and it was, I think, a happy idea to revive this ancient festival of the May and November burnings. It was inevitable that the old idea of purification should revive with the name, it was felt to be a burning of other than material encumbrances, innumerable quasi-spiritual things, deeds, documents, debts, vindictive records, went up on those great flares. People passed praying between the fires, and it was a fine symbol of the new and wiser tolerance that had come to me, that those who still found their comfort in the orthodox faiths came hither unpersuaded, to pray that all hate might be burned out of their professions. For even in the fires of Baal, now that men have done with base hatred, one may find the living God.

Endless were the things we had to destroy in those great purgings. First, there were nearly all the houses and buildings of the old time. In the end we did not save in England one building in five thousand that were standing when the comet came. Year by year, as we made our homes afresh in accordance with the saner needs of our new social families, we swept away more and more of those horrible structures, the ancient residential houses, hastily built, without imagination, without beauty, without common honesty, without even comfort or convenience, in which the early twentieth century had sheltered until scarcely one remained; we saved nothing but what was beautiful or interesting out of all their gaunt and melancholy abundance. The actual houses, of course, we could not drag to our fires, but we brought all their ill-fitting deal doors, their dreadful window sashes, their servant-tormenting staircases, their dank, dark cupboards, the verminous papers from their scaly walls, their dust and dirt-sodden carpets, their ill-designed and yet pretentious tables and chairs, sideboards and chests of drawers, the old dirt-saturated books, their ornaments — their dirty, decayed, and altogether painful ornaments—amidst which I remember there were sometimes even *stuffed dead birds!* — we burned them all. The paint-plastered woodwork, with coat above coat of nasty paint, that in particular blazed finely. I have already tried to give you an impression of old-world furniture, of Parload's bedroom, my mother's room, Mr. Gabbitas's sitting-room; but, thank Heaven! there is nothing in life now to convey the peculiar dinginess of it all. For one thing, there is no more imperfect combustion of coal going on everywhere, and no roadways like grassless open

scars along the earth from which dust pours out perpetually. We burned and destroyed most of our private buildings and all the woodwork, all our furniture, except a few score thousand pieces of distinct and intentional beauty from which our present forms have developed, nearly all our hangings and carpets, and also we destroyed almost every scrap of old-world clothing. Only a few carefully disinfected types and vestiges of that remain now in our museums.

One writes now with a peculiar horror of the dress of the old world. The men's clothes were worn without any cleansing process at all, except an occasional superficial brushing, for periods of a year or so; they were made of dark obscurely mixed patterns to conceal the stage of defilement they had reached, and they were of a felted and porous texture admirably calculated to accumulate drifting matter. Many women wore skirts of similar substances, and of so long and inconvenient a form that they inevitably trailed among all the abomination of our horse-frequented roads. It was our boast in England that the whole of our population was booted — their feet were for the most part ugly enough to need it — but it becomes now inconceivable how they could have imprisoned their feet in the amazing cases of leather and imitations of leather they used. I have heard it said that a large part of the physical decline that was apparent in our people during the closing years of the nineteenth century, though no doubt due in part to the miscellaneous badness of the food they ate, was in the main attributable to the vileness of the common footwear. They shirked open-air exercise altogether because their boots wore out ruinously and pinched and hurt them if they took it. I have mentioned, I think, the part my own boots played in the squalid drama of my adolescence. I had a sense of unholy triumph over a fallen enemy when at last I found myself steering truck after truck of cheap boots and shoes (unsold stock from Swathinglea) to the run-off by the top of the Glanville blast furnaces.

"Plup!" they would drop into the cone when Beltane came, and the roar of their burning would fill the air. Never a cold would come from the saturation of their brown-paper soles, never a corn from their foolish shapes, never a nail in them get home at last in suffering flesh. . . .

Most of our public buildings we destroyed and burned as we reshaped our plan of habitation, our theatre sheds, our banks, and inconvenient business warrens, our factories, and all the unmeaning repetition of silly little sham Gothic churches and meeting-houses, mean looking shells of stone and mortar without love, invention, or any beauty at all in them, that men had thrust into the face of their sweated God even as they thrust cheap food into the mouths of their sweated workers; all these we also swept away in the course of that first decade. Then we had the whole of the superseded steam-railway system

to scrap and get rid of, stations, signals, fences, rolling-stock; a plant of ill-planned, smoke-distributing nuisance apparatus, that would, under former conditions, have maintained an offensive dwindling obstructive life for perhaps half a century. Then also there was a great harvest of fences, notice boards, hoardings, ugly sheds, all the corrugated iron in the world, and everything that was smeared with tar, all our gas works and petroleum stores, all our horse vehicles and vans and lorries had to be erased. . . . But I have said enough now perhaps to give some idea of the bulk and quality of our great bonfires, our burnings up, our meltings down, our toil of sheer wreckage, over and above the constructive effort, in those early years.

But these were the coarse material bases of the Phœnix fires of the world. These were but the outward and visible signs of the innumerable claims, rights, adhesions, debts, bills, deeds, and charters that were cast upon the fires; a vast accumulation of insignia and uniforms neither curious enough nor beautiful enough to preserve, went to swell the blaze, and all (saving a few truly glorious trophies and memories) of our symbols, our apparatus and material of war. Then innumerable triumphs of our old, bastard, half-commercial, fine-art were presently condemned, great oil-paintings, done to please the half-educated middle-class, glared for a moment and were gone. Academy marbles crumbled to useful lime, a gross multitude of silly statuettes and decorative crockery, and hangings, and embroideries, and bad music, and musical instruments shared this fate. And books, countless books, too, and bales of newspapers went also to these pyres. From the private houses in Swathinglea alone — which I had deemed, perhaps not unjustly, altogether illiterate — we gathered a whole dust-cart full of cheap ill-printed editions of the minor English classics — for the most part very dull stuff indeed and still clean — and about a truckload of thumbed and dog-eared penny fiction, watery base stuff, the dropsy of our nation's mind. . . . And it seemed to me that when we gathered those books and papers together, we gathered together something more than print and paper, we gathered warped and crippled ideas and contagious base suggestions, the formulæ of dull tolerances and stupid impatiences, the mean defensive ingenuities of sluggish habits of thinking and timid and indolent evasions. There was more than a touch of malignant satisfaction for me in helping gather it all together.

I was so busy, I say, with my share in this dustman's work that I did not notice, as I should otherwise have done, the little indications of change in my mother's state. Indeed, I thought her stronger; she was slightly flushed, slightly more talkative. . . .

On Beltane Eve, and our Lowchester rummage being finished, I went along the valley to the far end of Swathinglea to help sort the stock of the detached

group of pot banks there — their chief output had been mantel ornaments in imitation of marble, and there was very little sorting, I found, to be done — and there it was nurse Anna found me at last by telephone, and told me my mother had died in the morning suddenly and very shortly after my departure.

For a while I did not seem to believe it: this obviously imminent event stunned me when it came, as though I had never had an anticipatory moment. For a while I went on working, and then almost apathetically, in a mood of half-reluctant curiosity, I started for Lowchester.

When I got there the last offices were over, and I was shown my old mother's peaceful white face, very still, but a little cold and stern to me, a little unfamiliar, lying among white flowers.

I went in alone to her, into that quiet room, and stood for a long time by her bedside. I sat down then and thought. . . .

Then at last, strangely hushed, and with the deeps of my loneliness opening beneath me, I came out of that room and down into the world again, a bright-eyed, active world, very noisy, happy, and busy with its last preparations for the mighty cremation of past and superseded things.

§ 2

I REMEMBER that first Beltane festival as the most terribly lonely night in my life. It stands in my mind in fragments, fragments of intense feeling with forgotten gaps between.

I recall very distinctly being upon the great staircase of Lowchester House (though I don't remember getting there from the room in which my mother lay), and how upon the landing I met Anna ascending as I came down. She had but just heard of my return, and she was hurrying upstairs to me. She stopped and so did I, and we stood and clasped hands, and she scrutinised my face in the way women sometimes do. So we remained for a second or so. I could say nothing to her at all, but I could feel the wave of her emotion. I halted, answered the earnest pressure of her hand, relinquished it, and after a queer second of hesitation went on down, returning to my own preoccupations. It did not occur to me at all then to ask myself what she might be thinking or feeling.

I remember the corridor full of mellow evening light, and how I went mechanically some paces towards the dining-room. Then at the sight of the little tables, and a gusty outburst of talking voices as someone in front of me swung the door open and to, I remembered that I did not want to eat. . . . After that comes an impression of myself walking across the open grass in front of the house, and the purpose I had of getting alone upon the moors, and how somebody passing me said something about a hat. I had come out without my hat.

A fragment of thought has linked itself with an effect of long shadows upon turf golden with the light of the sinking sun. The world was singularly empty, I thought, without either Nettie or

my mother. There wasn't any sense in it any more. Nettie was already back in my mind then. . . .

Then I was out on the moors. I avoided the crests where the bonfires were being piled, and sought the lonely places. . . .

I remember very clearly sitting on a gate beyond the park, in a fold just below the crest that hid the Beacon Hill bonfire and its crowd, and I was looking at and admiring the sunset. The golden earth and sky seemed like a bubble that floated in the globe of human futility. . . . Then in the twilight I walked along an unknown, bat-haunted road between high hedges.

I did not sleep under a roof that night. But I hungered and ate. I ate near midnight at an inn over towards Birmingham, and miles away from my home. Instinctively I had avoided the crests where the bonfire crowds gathered, but here there were many people, and I had to share a table with a man who had some useless mortgage deeds to burn. I talked to him about them — but my soul stood at a great distance behind my lips.

Soon each hilltop bore a tulip-shaped flame flower. Little black figures clustered round and dotted the base of its petals, and as for the rest of the multitude abroad, the kindly night swallowed them up. By leaving the roads and clear paths and wandering in the fields I contrived to keep alone, though the confused noise of voices and the roaring and crackling of great fires was always near me.

I wandered into a lonely meadow, and presently in a hollow of deep shadows I lay down to stare at the stars. I lay hidden in the darkness, and ever and again the sough and uproar of the Beltane fires that were burning up the sere follies of a vanished age, and the shouting of the people passing through the fires and praying to be delivered from the prison of themselves, reached my ears. . . .

And I thought of my mother, and then of my new loneliness and the hunger of my heart for Nettie.

I thought of many things that night, but chiefly of the overflowing personal love and tenderness that had come to me in the wake of the Change, of the greater need, the unsatisfied need in which I stood, for this one person who could fulfil all my desires. So long as my mother had lived, she had in a measure held my heart, given me a food these emotions could live upon, and mitigated that emptiness of spirit; but now suddenly that one possible comfort had left me. There had been many at the season of the Change who had thought that this great enlargement of mankind would abolish personal love; but indeed it had only made it finer, fuller, more vitally necessary. They had thought that, seeing men now were all full of the joyful passion to make and do, and glad and loving and of willing service to all their fellows, there would be no need of the one intimate trusting communion that had been the finest thing of the former life. And indeed, so

far as this was a matter of advantage and the struggle for existence, they were right. But so far as it was a matter of the spirit and the fine perceptions of life, it was altogether wrong.

We had indeed not eliminated personal love, we had but stripped it of its base wrappings, of its pride, its suspicions, its mercenary and competitive elements, until at last it stood up in our minds stark, shining and invincible. Through all the fine, divaricating ways of the new life, it grew ever more evident, there were for everyone certain persons, mysteriously and indescribably in the key of one's self, whose mere presence gave pleasure, whose mere existence was interest, whose idiosyncrasy blended with accident to make a completing and predominant harmony for their predestined lovers. They were the essential thing in life. Without them the fine brave show of the rejuvenated world was a caparisoned steed without a rider, a bowl without a flower, a theatre without a play. . . . And to me that night of Beltane, it was as clear as white flames that Nettie, and Nettie alone, roused those harmonies in me. And she had gone! I had sent her from me; I knew not whither she had gone. I had in my first virtuous foolishness cut her out of my life for ever!

So I saw it then, and I lay unseen in the darkness and called upon Nettie and wept for her, lay upon my face and wept for her, while the glad people went to and fro and the smoke streamed thick across the distant stars, and the red reflections, the shadows and the fluctuating glares, danced over the face of the world.

No! the Change had freed us from our baser passions indeed, from habitual and mechanical concupiscence and mean issues and coarse imaginings, but from the passions of love it had not freed us. It had but brought the lord of life, Eros, to his own. All through the long sorrow of that night I, who had rejected him, confessed his sway with tears and inappeasable regrets. . . .

I cannot give the remotest guess of when I rose up, nor of my tortuous wanderings in the valleys between the midnight fires, nor how I evaded the laughing and rejoicing multitudes who went streaming home between three and four to resume their lives, swept and garnished, stripped and clean. But at dawn, when the ashes of the world's gladness were ceasing to glow — it was a bleak dawn that made me shiver in my thin summer clothes — I came across a field to a little copse full of dim blue hyacinths. A queer sense of familiarity arrested my steps, and I stood puzzled. Then I was moved to go a dozen paces from the path, and at once a singularly misshapen tree hitched itself into a notch in my memory. This was the place! Here I had stood, there I had placed my old kite, and shot with my revolver, learning to use it, against the day when I should encounter Verrall.

Kite and revolver had gone now, and all my hot and narrow past; its last vestiges had shriv-

elled and vanished in the whirling gusts of the Beltane fires. So I walked through a world of grey ashes at last, back to the great house in which the dead, deserted image of my dear lost mother lay.

§3

I CAME back to Lowchester House very tired, very wretched; exhausted by my fruitless longing for Nettie. I had no thought of what lay before me.

A miserable attraction drew me into the great house to look again on the stillness that had been my mother's face, and as I came into that room, Anna, who had been sitting by the open window, rose to meet me. She had the air of one who waits. She, too, was pale with watching; all night she had watched between the dead within and the Beltane fires abroad, and longed for my coming. I stood mute between her and the bedside. . . .

"Willie," she whispered, and eyes and body seemed incarnate pity.

An unseen presence drew us together. My mother's face became resolute, commanding. I turned to Anna as a child may turn to its nurse. I put my hands about her strong shoulders, she folded me to her, and my heart gave way. I buried my face in her breast and clung to her weakly, and burst into a passion of weeping. . . .

She held me with hungry arms. She whispered to me, "There, there!" as one whispers comfort to a child. . . . Suddenly she was kissing me. She kissed me with a hungry intensity of passion, on my cheeks, on my lips. She kissed me on my lips with lips that were salt with tears. And I returned her kisses. . . .

Then abruptly we desisted and stood apart—looking at one another.

§4

IT seems to me as if the intense memory of Nettie vanished utterly out of my mind at the touch of Anna's lips. I loved Anna.

We went to the council of our group—commune it was then called—and she was given me in marriage, and within a year she had borne me a son. We saw much of one another, and talked ourselves very close together. My faithful friend she became and has been always, and for a time we were passionate lovers. Always she has loved me and kept my soul full of tender gratitude and love for her; always when we met our hands and eyes clasped in friendly greeting, all through our lives from that hour we have been each other's secure help and refuge, each other's ungrudging fastness of help and sweetly frank and open speech. . . . And after a little while my love and desire for Nettie returned as though it had never faded away.

No one will have a difficulty now in understanding how that could be, but in the evil days of the world malaria, that would have been held to be the most impossible thing. I should have had to crush that second love out of my thoughts, to have kept it secret from Anna, to have lied

about it to all the world. The old-world theory was there was only one love — we who float upon a sea of love find that hard to understand. The whole nature of a man was supposed to go out to the one girl or woman who possessed him, her whole nature to go out to him. Nothing was left over — it was a discreditable thing to have any overplus at all. They formed a secret secluded system of two, two and such children as she bore him. All other women he was held bound to find no beauty in, no sweetness, no interest; and she likewise, in no other man. The old-time men and women went apart in couples, into defensive little houses, like beasts into little pits, and in these "homes" they sat down purposing to love, but really coming very soon to jealous watching of this extravagant mutual proprietorship. All freshness passed very speedily out of their love, out of their conversation, all pride out of their common life. To permit each other freedom was blank dishonour. That I and Anna should love, and after our love-journey together, go about our separate lives and dine at the public tables, until the advent of her motherhood, would have seemed a terrible strain upon our unmitigable loyalty. And that I should have it in me to go on loving Nettie — who loved in different manner both Verrall and me — would have outraged the very quintessence of the old convention.

In the old days love was a cruel proprietary thing. But now Anna could let Nettie live in the world of my mind, as freely as a rose will suffer the presence of white lilies. If I could hear notes that were not in her compass, she was glad, because she loved me, that I should listen to other music than hers. And she, too, could see the beauty of Nettie. Life is so rich and generous now, giving friendship, and a thousand tender interests and helps and comforts, that no one stints another of the full realisation of all possibilities of beauty. For me from the beginning Nettie was the figure of beauty, the shape and colour of the divine principle that lights the world. For everyone there are certain types, certain faces and forms, gestures, voices and intonations that have that inexplicable unanalysable quality. These come through the crowd of kindly friendly fellow-men and women — one's own. These touch one mysteriously, stir deeps that must otherwise slumber, pierce and interpret the world. To refuse this interpretation is to refuse the sun, to darken and deaden all life. . . . I loved Nettie, I loved all who were like her, in the measure that they were like her, in voice, or eyes, or form, or smile. And between my wife and me there was no bitterness that the great goddess, the life-giver, Aphrodite, Queen of the living Seas, came to my imagination so. It qualified our mutual love not at all, since now in our changed world love is unstinted; it is a golden net about our globe that nets all humanity together.

I thought of Nettie much, and always movingly beautiful things

restored me to her; all fine music, all pure deep colour, all tender and solemn things. The stars were hers, and the mystery of moonlight; the sun she wore in her hair, powdered finely, beaten into gleams and threads of sunlight in the wisps and strands of her hair. . . . Then suddenly one day a letter came to me from her, in her unaltered clear handwriting, but in a new language of expression, telling me many things. She had learned of my mother's death, and the thought of me had grown so strong as to pierce the silence I had imposed on her. We wrote to one another —like ordinary friends with a certain restraint between us at first, and with a great longing to see her once more arising in my heart. For a time I left that hunger unexpressed, and then I was moved to tell it to her. And so on New Year's Day in the Year Four, she came to Lowchester and me. How I remember that coming, across the gulf of fifty years! I went out across the park to meet her, so that we might meet alone. The windless morning was clear and cold, the ground new carpeted with snow, and all the trees motionless lace and glitter of frosty crystals. The rising sun had touched the white with a spirit of gold, and my heart beat and sang within me. I remember now the snowy shoulder of the down, sunlit against the bright blue sky. And presently I saw the woman I loved coming through the white still trees. . . .

I had made a goddess of Nettie, and behold she was a fellow-creature! She came, warm-wrapped and tremulous, to me, with the tender promise of tears in her eyes, with her hands outstretched and that dear smile quivering upon her lips. She stepped out of the dream I had made of her, a thing of needs and regrets and human kindliness. Her hands as I took them were a little cold. The goddess shone through her indeed, glowed in all her body, she was a worshipful temple of love for me— yes. But I could feel, like a thing new discovered, the texture and sinews of her living, her dear personal and mortal hands. . . .

THE EPILOGUE
THE WINDOW OF THE TOWER

THIS was as much as this pleasant-looking grey-haired man had written. I had been lost in his story throughout the earlier portions of it, forgetful of the writer and his gracious room, and the high tower in which he was sitting. But gradually, as I drew near the end, the sense of strangeness returned to me. It was more and more evident to me that this was a different humanity from any I had known, unreal, having different customs, different beliefs, different interpretations, different emotions. It was no mere change in conditions and institutions the comet had wrought. It had made a change of heart and mind. In a manner it had dehumanised the world, robbed it of its spites, its intense jealousies, its inconsistencies, its humour. At the end, and particularly after the death of his mother, I felt his story had slipped away from my sympathies altogether. Those Beltane fires had burned something in him that worked living still and unsubdued in me, that rebelled in particular at that return of Nettie. I became inattentive. I no longer felt with him, nor gathered a sense

of complete understanding from his phrases. His Lord Eros indeed! He and these transfigured people — they were beautiful and noble people, like the people one sees in great pictures, like the gods of noble sculpture, but they had no nearer fellowship than these to competitive men. As the Change was realised, with every stage of realisation the gulf widened and it was harder to follow his word.

I put down the last fascicle of all, and met his friendly eyes. It was hard to dislike him.

I felt a subtle embarrassment in putting the question that perplexed me. And yet it seemed so material to me I had to put it. " And did you — ? " I asked. " Were you — lovers? "

His eyebrows rose. " Of course."

" But your wife — ? "

It was manifest he did not understand me.

I hesitated still more. I was perplexed by a conviction of baseness. " But — " I began. " You remained lovers? "

" Yes." I had grave doubts if I understood him. Or he me.

I made a still more courageous attempt. " And had Nettie no other lovers? "

" A beautiful woman like that! I know not how many loved beauty in her, nor what she found in others. But we four from

*that time were very close, you understand, we were friends,
helpers, personal lovers in a world of lovers."*

"Four?"

"There was Verrall."

*Then suddenly it came to me that the thoughts that stirred in
my mind were sinister and base, that the queer suspicions, the
coarseness and coarse jealousies of my old world were over and
done for these more finely living souls. "You made," I said, try-
ing to be liberal minded, "a home together."*

*"A home!" He looked at me, and, I know not why, I
glanced down at my feet. What a clumsy, ill-made thing a boot
is, and how hard and colourless seemed my clothing! How
harshly I stood out amidst these perfected things. I had a mo-
ment of rebellious detestation. I wanted to get out of all this.
After all, it wasn't my style. I wanted intensely to say some-
thing that would bring him down a peg, make sure, as it were,
of my suspicions by launching an offensive accusation. I looked
up and he was standing.*

*"I forgot," he said. "You are pretending the old world is still
going on. A home!"*

*He put out his hand, and quite noiselessly the great window
widened down to us, and the splendid nearer prospect of that*

dreamland city was before me. There for one clear moment I saw it; its galleries and open spaces, its trees of golden fruit and crystal waters, its music and rejoicing, love and beauty without ceasing flowing through its varied and intricate streets. And the nearer people I saw now directly and plainly, and no longer in the distorted mirror that hung overhead. They really did not justify my suspicions, and yet — ! They were such people as one sees on earth — save that they were changed. How can I express that change. As a woman is changed in the eyes of her lover, as a woman is changed by the love of a lover. They were exalted. . . .

I stood up beside him and looked out. I was a little flushed, my ears a little reddened, by the inconvenience of my curiosities, and by my uneasy sense of profound moral differences. He was taller than I. . . .

"This is our home," he said smiling, and with thoughtful eyes on me.